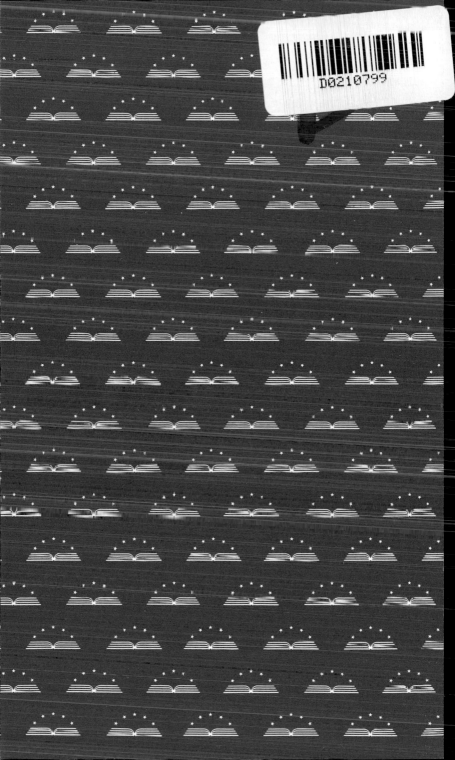

WILLIAM DEAN HOWELLS

WILLIAM DEAN HOWELLS

NOVELS 1875–1886
A Foregone Conclusion
A Modern Instance
Indian Summer
The Rise Of Silas Lapham

THE LIBRARY OF AMERICA

Library of Congress Catalog Card Number: 82–112
For Cataloging in PublicationData, see end of *Notes* section.
ISBN: 0-940450-04-6

Third Printing

Manufactured in the United States of America

EDWIN H. CADY
WROTE THE NOTES AND CHRONOLOGY
AND SELECTED THE TEXTS
FOR THIS VOLUME

The texts in this volume are reprinted from A Selected Edition of W.D. Howells, published by the Indiana University Press and the Howells Edition Editorial Board, and bear the emblem of the Modern Language Association. The texts of A Foregone Conclusion and A Modern Instance were edited by David J. Nordloh and David Kleinman, the text of Indian Summer was edited by Scott Bennett and David J. Nordloh, and the text of The Rise of Silas Lapham was edited by Walter J. Meserve and David J. Nordloh. These texts are reprinted here without change.

Grateful acknowledgement is made to the National Endowment for the Humanities and the Ford Foundation for their generous financial support of this series.

Contents

A FOREGONE CONCLUSION

I

As Don Ippolito passed down the long narrow *calle* or footway leading from the Campo San Stefano to the Grand Canal in Venice, he peered anxiously about him: now turning for a backward look up the calle where there was no living thing in sight but a cat on a garden gate, now running a quick eye along the palace walls that rose vast on either hand, and notched the slender strip of blue sky visible overhead with the lines of their jutting balconies, chimneys and cornices, and now glancing towards the canal where he could see the noiseless black boats meeting and passing. There was no sound in the calle save his own footfalls, and the harsh scream of a parrot that hung in the sunshine at one of the loftiest windows; but the note of a peasant crying pots of pinks and roses in the campo came softened to Don Ippolito's sense, and he heard the gondoliers as they hoarsely jested together, and gossipped with the canal between them at the next gondola station.

The first tenderness of spring was in the air, though down in that calle there was yet enough of the wintry rawness to chill the tip of Don Ippolito's sensitive nose, which he rubbed for comfort with a handkerchief of dark blue calico and polished for ornament with a handkerchief of white linen. He restored each to a different pocket in the sides of the ecclesiastical *talare*, or gown, reaching almost to his ancles, and then clutched the pocket in which he had replaced the linen handkerchief as if to make sure that something he prized was safe within. He paused abruptly, and looking at the doors he had passed, went back a few paces and stood before one over which hung, slightly tilted forward, an oval sign painted with the effigy of an eagle, a bundle of arrows and certain thunderbolts, and bearing the legend, CONSULATE OF THE UNITED STATES in neat characters. Don Ippolito gave a quick sigh, hesitated a moment, and then seized the bell-pull and jerked it so sharply that it seemed to thrust out, like a part of the mechanism, the head of an old serving-woman at the window above him.

3

"Who is there?" demanded this head.

"Friends," answered Don Ippolito in a rich, sad voice.

"And what do you command?" further asked the old woman.

Don Ippolito paused apparently searching for his voice, before he inquired "Is it here that the Consul of America lives?"

"Precisely."

"Is he perhaps at home?"

"I don't know. I will go ask him."

"Do me that pleasure, dear," said Don Ippolito, and remained knotting his fingers before the closed door. Presently the old woman returned, and looking out long enough to say "The consul is at home," drew some inner bolt by a wire running to the lock, that let the door start open; then, waiting to hear Don Ippolito close it again she called out from her height, "Favor me above." He climbed the dim stairway to the point where she stood, and followed her to the door which she flung open into an apartment so brightly lit by a window looking on the sunny canal, that he blinked as he entered. "Signor Console," said the old woman, "behold the gentleman who desired to see you," and at the same time Don Ippolito, having removed his broad, stiff three cornered hat, came forward, and made a beautiful bow. He had lost for the moment the trepidation which had marked his approach to the consulate, and bore himself with graceful dignity.

It was in the first year of the war, and from a motive of patriotism common at that time, Mr. Ferris (one of my many predecessors in office at Venice,) had just been crossing his two silken gondola flags above the consular book-case, where with their gilt, lance-headed staves, and their vivid stars and stripes, they made a very pretty effect. He fillipped a little dust from his coat, and begged Don Ippolito to be seated, with the air of putting even a Venetian priest on a footing of equality with other men under the folds of the national banner. Mr. Ferris had the prejudice of all Italian sympathizers against the priests; but for this he could hardly have found anything in Don Ippolito to alarm dislike. His face was a little thin, and the chin was delicate; the nose had a fine, Dantesque curve, but its final droop gave a melancholy cast to a countenance expressive of a gentle and kindly spirit; the eyes were large and dark and full of a dreamy warmth. Don Ippolito's prevailing tint was that transparent blueishness which comes from much shaving of a heavy black beard; his forehead and temples were marble white; he had a tonsure the size of a dollar. He sat silent for a little space, and softly questioned the consul's face with his dreamy eyes. Apparently he could not gather courage to speak of his business at once, for he turned his gaze upon the window, and said, "A beautiful position, Signor Console."

"Yes, it's a pretty place," answered Mr. Ferris, warily.

"So much pleasanter here on the Canalazzo than on the campos or the little canals."

"O without doubt."

"Here there must be constant amusement in watching the boats: great stir, great variety, great life. And now the fine season commences, and the Signor Console's countrymen will be coming to Venice. Perhaps," added Don Ippolito, with a polite dismay, and an air of sudden anxiety to escape from his own purpose, "I may be disturbing or detaining the Signor Console?"

"No," said Mr. Ferris, "I am quite at leisure for the present. In what can I have the honor of serving you?"

Don Ippolito heaved a long, ineffectual sigh, and taking his linen handkerchief from his pocket, wiped his forehead with it, and rolled it upon his knee. He looked at the door, and all round the room, and then rose and drew near the consul, who had officially seated himself at his desk.

"I suppose that the Signor Console gives passports?" he asked.

"Sometimes," replied Mr. Ferris with a clouding face.

Don Ippolito seemed to note the gathering distrust and to be helpless against it. He continued hastily: "Could the Signor Console give a passport for America . . . to me?"

"Are you an American citizen?" demanded the consul in the voice of a man whose suspicions are fully roused.

"American citizen?"

"Yes: subject of the American republic."

"No, surely; I have not that happiness. I am an Austrian subject," returned Don Ippolito a little bitterly, as if the last words were an unpleasant morsel in the mouth.

"Then I can't give you a passport," said Mr. Ferris, somewhat more gently. "You know," he explained, "that no government can give passports to foreign subjects. That would
be an unheard-of thing."

"But I thought that to go to America an American passport
would be needed."

"In America," returned the consul with proud compassion,
"they don't care a fig for passports. You go and you come,
and nobody meddles. To be sure," he faltered, "just now on
account of the Secessionists, they *do* require you to show a
passport at New York; but," he continued more boldly,
"American passports are usually for Europe; and besides, all
the American passports in the world wouldn't get *you* over
the frontier at Peschiera. *You* must have a passport from the
Austrian Lieutenancy of Venice."

Don Ippolito nodded his head softly several times, and said
"Precisely," and then added with an indescribable weariness,
"Patience! Signor Console, I ask your pardon for the trouble
I have given," and he made the consul another low bow.

Whether Mr. Ferris's curiosity was piqued, and feeling
himself on the safe side of his visitor, he meant to know why
he had come on such an errand, or whether he had some
kindlier motive, he could hardly have told himself, but he
said, "I'm very sorry. Perhaps there is something else in which
I could be of use to you."

"Ah, I hardly know!" cried Don Ippolito. "I really had a
kind of hope in coming to your excellency"—

"I am not an excellency," interrupted Mr. Ferris, conscientiously.

"Many excuses!— But now it seems a mere bestiality. I was
so ignorant about the other matter that doubtless I am also
quite deluded in this."

"As to that, of course I can't say," answered Mr. Ferris,
"but I hope not."

"Why listen, signore!" said Don Ippolito, placing his hand
over that pocket in which he kept his linen handkerchief. "I
had something that it had come into my head to offer your
honored government for its advantage in this deplorable rebellion."

"O," responded Mr. Ferris with a falling countenance. He had received so many offers of help for his honored government from sympathizing foreigners. Hardly a week passed but a sabre came clanking up his dim staircase with a Herr Graf or a Herr Baron attached, who appeared in the spotless panoply of his Austrian captaincy or lieutenancy to accept from the consul a brigadier-generalship in the Federal armies on condition that the consul would pay his expenses to Washington, or at least assure him of an exalted post, and reimbursement of all outlays from President Lincoln as soon as he arrived. They were beautiful men, with the complexion of blonde girls; their uniforms fitted like kid gloves; the pale blue, or pure white, or hussar black of their coats was ravishingly set off by their red or gold trimmings; and they were hard to make understand that brigadiers of American birth swarmed at Washington, and that if they went thither they must go as soldiers of fortune at their own risk. But they were very polite, they begged pardon when they knocked their scabbards against the consul's furniture, at the door they each made him a magnificent obeisance, said "Servus!" in their great voices, and were shown out by the old Marina abhorrent of their uniforms and doubtful of the Consul's political sympathies. Only yesterday she had called him up at an unwonted hour to receive the visit of a courtly gentleman who addressed him as Monsieur le Ministre, and offered him at a bargain ten thousand stand of probably obsolescent muskets belonging to the late Duke of Parma. Shabby, hungry, incapable exiles of all nations, religions and politics beset him for places of honor and emolument in the service of the Union, revolutionists out of business and the minions of banished despots were alike willing to be fed, clothed, and dispatched to Washington with swords consecrated to the perpetuity of the Republic.

"I have here," said Don Ippolito, too intent upon showing whatever it was he had to note the change in the consul's mood, "the model of a weapon of my contrivance, which I thought the government of the North could employ successfully in cases where its batteries were in danger of capture by the Spaniards."

"Spaniards? Spaniards? We have no war with Spain!" cried
the consul.

"Yes, yes, I know," Don Ippolito made haste to explain,
"but those of South America being Spanish by descent"—

"But we are not fighting the South Americans. We are
fighting our own Southern States, I am sorry to say."

"Oh! Many excuses. I am afraid I don't understand," said
Don Ippolito meekly; whereupon Mr. Ferris enlightened him
in a formula, (of which he was beginning to be weary,)
against European misconception of the American situation.
Don Ippolito nodded his head contritely, and when Mr. Ferris had ended, he was so much abashed that he made no motion to show his invention till the other added, "But no matter; I suppose the contrivance would work as well against the
Southerners as the South Americans. Let me see it, please,"
and then Don Ippolito with a gratified smile, drew from his
pocket the neatly-finished model of a breech-loading cannon.

"You perceive, Signor Console," he said with new dignity,
"that this is nothing very new as a breech-loader, though I
ask you to observe this little improvement for restoring the
breech to its place, which is original. The grand feature of my
invention, however, is this secret chamber in the breech,
which is intended to hold an explosive of high potency, with
a fuse coming out below. The gunner, finding his piece in
danger, ignites this fuse, and takes refuge in flight. At the
moment the enemy seizes the gun the contents of the secret
chamber explode, demolishing the piece, and destroying its
captors."

The dreamy warmth in Don Ippolito's deep eyes kindled to
a flame; a dark red glowed in his thin cheeks; he drew a box
from the folds of his drapery and took snuff in a great whiff
as if inhaling the sulphurous fumes of battle, or titillating his
nostrils with grains of gunpowder. He was at least in full enjoyment of the poetic power of his invention, and no doubt
had before his eyes a vivid picture of a score of secessionists
surprised and blown to atoms in the very moment of
triumph. "Behold, Signor Console!" he said.

"It's certainly very curious," said Mr. Ferris, turning the
fearful toy over in his hand, and admiring the neat workman-
ship of it. "Did you make this model yourself?"

"Surely," answered the priest with a joyous pride, "I have no money to spend upon artizans; and besides, as you might infer, signore, I am not very well seen by my superiors and associates on account of these little amusements of mine; so I keep them as much as I can to myself." Don Ippolito laughed nervously, and then fell silent with his eyes intent upon the consul's face. "What do you think, signore?" he presently resumed. "If this invention were brought to the notice of your generous government would it not patronize my labors? I have read that America is the land of enterprizes. Who knows but your government might invite me to take service under it in some capacity in which I could employ those little gifts that heaven"— He paused again, apparently puzzled by the compassionate smile on the consul's lips. "But tell me, signore, how this invention appears to you."

"Have you had any practical experience in gunnery?" asked Mr. Ferris.

"Why certainly not."

"Neither have I," continued Mr. Ferris, "but I was wondering whether the explosive in this secret chamber would not become so heated by the frequent discharges of the piece as to go off prematurely sometimes, and kill our own artillerymen instead of waiting for the secessionists?"

Don Ippolito's countenance fell, and a dull shame displaced the exultation that had glowed in it. His head sunk on his breast, and he made no attempt at reply, so that it was again Mr. Ferris who spoke. "You see, I don't really know anything more of the matter than you do, and I don't undertake to say whether your invention is disabled by the possibility I suggest or not. Haven't you any acquaintances among the military to whom you could show your model?"

"No," answered Don Ippolito, coldly, "I don't consort with the military. Besides, what would be thought of a *priest*," he asked with a bitter stress on the word, "who exhibited such an invention as that to an officer of our paternal government?"

"I suppose it would certainly surprise the Lieutenant-Governor somewhat," said Mr. Ferris with a laugh. "May I ask," he pursued after an interval, "whether you have occupied yourself with other inventions?"

"I have attempted a great many," replied Don Ippolito in a tone of dejection.

"Are they all of this warlike temper?" pursued the consul.

"No," said Don Ippolito, blushing a little, "they are nearly all of peaceful intention. It was the wish to produce something of utility which set me about this cannon. Those good friends of mine who have done me the honor of looking at my attempts, had blamed me for the uselessness of my inventions; they allowed that they were ingenious, but they said that even if they could be put in operation they would not be what the world cared for. Perhaps they were right. I know very little of the world," concluded the priest, sadly. He had risen to go, yet seemed not quite able to do so; there was no more to say, but if he had come to the consul with high hopes, it might well have unnerved him to have all end so blankly. He drew a long sibilant breath between his shut teeth, nodded to himself thrice, and turning to Mr. Ferris with a melancholy bow, said, "Signor Console, I thank you infinitely for your kindness; I beg your pardon for the disturbance, and I take my leave."

"I am sorry," said Mr. Ferris. "Let us see each other again. In regard to the inventions,—well, you must have patience." He dropped into some proverbial phrases which the obliging Latin tongues supply so abundantly for the races who must often talk when they do not feel like thinking; and he gave a start when Don Ippolito replied in English, "Yes, but hope deferred maketh the heart sick."

It was not that it was so uncommon to have Italians innocently come out with their whole slender stock of English to him, for the sake of practice, as they told him; but there were peculiarities in Don Ippolito's accent for which he could not account. "What!" he exclaimed, "do you know English?"

"I have studied it a little, by myself," answered Don Ippolito, pleased to have his English recognized, and then lapsing into the safety of Italian, he added, "And I had also the help of an English ecclesiastic who sojourned some months in Venice, last year, for his health and who used to read with me and teach me the pronunciation. He was from Dublin, this ecclesiastic."

"Oh-h!" said Mr. Ferris, with relief, "I see," and he perceived that what had puzzled him in Don Ippolito's English was a fine brogue superimposed upon his Italian accent.

"For some time I have had this idea of going to America, and I thought that the first thing to do was to equip myself with the language."

"Um!" said Mr. Ferris, "that was practical, at any rate," and he mused awhile. By and by he continued more kindly than he had yet spoken, "I wish I could ask you to sit down again; but I have an engagement which I must make haste to keep. Are you going out through the campo? Pray wait a minute, and I will walk with you."

Mr. Ferris went into another room, through the open door of which Don Ippolito saw the paraphernalia of a painter's studio: an easel with a half-finished picture on it; a chair with a palette and brushes, and crushed and twisted tubes of colors; a lay figure in one corner; on the walls scraps of stamped leather, rags of tapestry, desultory sketches on paper.

Mr. Ferris came out again brushing his hat.

"The Signor Console amuses himself with painting, I see," said Don Ippolito courteously.

"Not at all," replied Mr. Ferris, putting on his gloves; "I am a painter by profession, and I amuse myself with consulting,"* and as so open a matter needed no explanation, he said no more about it. Nor is it quite necessary to tell how as he was one day painting in New York, it occurred to him to make use of a Congressional friend, and ask for some Italian consulate, he did not care which. That of Venice happened to be vacant; the income was a few hundred dollars; as no one else wanted it, no question was made of Mr. Ferris's fitness for the post, and he presently found himself possessed of a commission requesting the Emperor of Austria to permit him to enjoy and exercise the office of Consul of the ports of the Lombardo-Venetian kingdom, to which the President of the

*Since these words of Mr. Ferris were first printed, I have been told that a more eminent painter, namely Rubens, made very much the same reply to very much the same remark, when Spanish Ambassador in England. "The Ambassador of His Catholic Majesty, I see, amuses himself by painting sometimes," said a visitor who found him at his easel. "I amuse myself by playing the ambassador sometimes," answered Rubens. In spite of the similarity of the speeches, I let that of Mr. Ferris stand, for I am satisfied that he did not know how unhandsomely Rubens had taken the words out of his mouth.

United States appointed him from a special trust in his abilities and integrity. He proceeded at once to his post of duty, called upon the ship's chandler with whom they had been left, for the consular archives, and began to paint some Venetian subjects.

He and Don Ippolito quitted the Consulate together, leaving Marina to digest with her noonday porridge the wonder that he should be walking amicably forth with a priest. The same spectacle was presented to the gaze of the campo, where they paused in friendly converse, and were seen to part with many politenesses by the doctors of the neighborhood, lounging away their leisure, as the Venetian fashion is, at the local pharmacy.

The apothecary craned forward over his counter, and peered through the open door. "What is that blessed Consul of America doing with a priest?"

"The Consul of America with a priest?" demanded a grave old man, a physician with a beautiful silvery beard, and a most reverend and senatorial presence, but one of the worst tongues in Venice. "Oh!" he added, with a laugh, after scrutiny of the two through his glasses, "it's that crack-brain Don Ippolito Rondinelli. He isn't priest enough to hurt the consul. Perhaps he's been selling him a perpetual motion for the use of his government, which needs something of the kind just now. Or maybe he's been posing to him for a picture. He would make a very pretty Joseph, give him Potiphar's wife in the background," said the Doctor, who if not maligned would have needed much more to make a Joseph of him.

II

Mr. Ferris took his way through the devious footways where the shadow was chill, and through the broad campos where the sun was tenderly warm, and the towers of the church rose against the speckless azure of the vernal heaven. As he went along, he frowned in a helpless perplexity with the case of Don Ippolito, whom he had begun by doubting for a spy with some incomprehensible motive, and had ended by pitying with a certain degree of amusement and a deep sense of the futility of his compassion. He presently began to think of him with a little disgust, as people commonly think of one whom they pity and yet cannot help, and he made haste to cast off the hopeless burden. He shrugged his shoulders, struck his stick on the smooth paving-stones, and let his eye rove up and down the fronts of the houses, for the sake of the pretty faces that glanced out of the casements. He was a young man, and it was spring, and this was Venice. He made himself joyfully part of the city and the season; he was glad of the narrowness of the streets, of the good-humored jostling and pushing; he crouched into an arched doorway to let a water carrier pass with her copper buckets dripping at the end of the yoke balanced on her shoulder, and he returned her smiles and excuses with others as broad and gay; he brushed by the swelling hoops of ladies, and stopped before the unwieldy burdens of porters, who as they staggered through the crowd with a thrust here and a shove there forgave themselves, laughing, with "We are in Venice, si gnori;" and he stood aside for the files of soldiers clanking heavily over the pavement, their muskets kindling to a blaze in the sunlit campos and quenched again in the damp shadows of the calles. His ear was taken by the vibrant jargoning of the boatmen as they pushed their craft under the bridges he crossed; and the keen notes of the canaries and the songs of the golden-billed blackbirds whose cages hung at lattices far overhead. Heaps of oranges topped by the fairest cut in halves, gave their color, at frequent intervals to the dusky corners and recesses, and the long drawn cry of the venders,

"Oranges of Palermo!" rose above the clatter of feet and the clamor of other voices. At a little shop where butter and eggs and milk abounded, together with early flowers of various sorts, he bought a bunch of hyacinths, blue and white and yellow, and he presently stood smelling these while he waited in the hotel parlor for the ladies to whom he had sent his card. He turned at the sound of drifting drapery, and could not forbear placing the hyacinths in the hand of Miss Florida Vervain, who had come into the room to receive him.

She was a girl of about seventeen years, who looked older; she was tall rather than short, and rather full,—though it could not be said that she erred in point of solidity. In the attitudes of shy hauteur into which she constantly fell, there was a touch of defiant awkwardness which had a certain fascination. She was blonde, with a throat and hands of milky whiteness; there was a suggestion of freckles on her regular face where a quick color came and went, though her cheeks were habitually somewhat pale; her eyes were very blue, under their level brows, and the lashes were even lighter in color than the masses of her fair gold hair; the edges of the lids were touched with the faintest red. The late Colonel Vervain of the United States Army, whose complexion his daughter had inherited, was an officer whom it would not have been peaceable to cross in any purpose or pleasure, and Miss Vervain seemed sometimes a little burdened by the passionate nature which he had left her together with the tropical name he had bestowed in honor of the State where he had fought the Seminoles in his youth, and where he chanced still to be stationed when she was born; she had the air of being embarrassed in presence of herself, and of having an anxious watch upon her impulses. I do not know how otherwise to describe the effect of proud, helpless femininity, which would have struck the close observer in Miss Vervain.

"Delicious!" she said, in a deep voice, which conveyed something of this anxiety in its guarded tones, and yet was not wanting in a kind of frankness. "Did you mean them for me, Mr. Ferris?"

"I didn't, but I do," answered Mr. Ferris. "I bought them in ignorance, but I understand now what they were meant for by nature," and in fact the hyacinths with their smooth textures and their pure colors, harmonized well with Miss Vervain, as she bent her face over them and inhaled their full, rich perfume.

"I will put them in water," she said, "if you'll excuse me a moment. Mother will be down directly."

Before she could return her mother rustled into the parlor.

Mrs. Vervain was gracefully, fragilely unlike her daughter. She entered with a gentle and gliding step, peering nearsightedly about through her glasses, and laughing triumphantly when she had determined Mr. Ferris's exact position where he stood, with a smile shaping his full brown beard and glancing from his hazel eyes. She was dressed in perfect taste with reference to her matronly years, and the lingering evidences of her widowhood, and she had an unaffected naturalness of manner which even at her age of forty-eight could not be called less than charming. She spoke in a trusting, caressing tone to which no man at least could respond unkindly.

"So very good of you, to take all this trouble, Mr. Ferris," she said giving him a friendly hand, "and I suppose you are letting us encroach upon very valuable time. I'm quite ashamed to take it. But isn't it a heavenly day? What *I* call a perfect day, just right every way; none of those disagreeable extremes. It's so unpleasant to have it too hot, for instance. I'm the greatest person for moderation, Mr. Ferris, and I carry the principle into everything; but I do think the breakfasts at these Italian hotels are too light altogether. I like our American breakfasts, don't you? I've been telling Florida I can't stand it; we really must make some arrangement. To be sure, you oughtn't to think of such a thing as eating in a place like Venice, all poetry; but a sound mind in a sound body, *I* say. We're perfectly wild over it. Don't you think it's a place that grows upon you very much, Mr. Ferris? All those associations, it does seem too much; and the gondolas every where. But I'm always afraid the gondoliers cheat us; and in the stores I never feel safe a moment—not a moment. I do think the Venetians are lacking in truthfulness, a little. I don't believe they understand our American fairdealing and sincerity. I shouldn't want to do them injustice; but I really think they take advantages in bargaining. Now such a thing even as corals. Florida is extremely fond of them, and we bought a set yesterday in the Piazza, and I *know* we paid too much for them. Florida," said Mrs. Vervain, for her daughter had re-entered the room, and stood with some shawls and wraps upon her arm patiently waiting for the conclusion of the elder lady's speech, "I wish you would bring down that set of corals. I'd like Mr. Ferris to give an unbiassed opinion. I'm sure we were cheated."

"I don't know anything about corals, Mrs. Vervain," interposed Mr. Ferris.

"Well, but you ought to see this set for the beauty of the color; they're really exquisite. I'm sure it will gratify your artistic taste."

Miss Vervain hesitated with a look of desire to obey, and of doubt whether to force the pleasure upon Mr. Ferris. "Wont it do another time, mother?" she asked, finally, "the gondola is waiting for us."

Mrs. Vervain gave a frailish start from the chair, into which she had sunk. "O do let us be off at once, then," she said, and when they stood on the landing-stairs of the hotel, "What gloomy things these gondolas are," she added, while the gondolier with one foot on the gunwale of the boat received the ladies' shawls, and then crooked his arm for them to rest a hand on in stepping aboard, "I wonder they don't paint them some cheerful color."

"Blue, or pink, Mrs. Vervain?" asked Mr. Ferris. "I knew you were coming to that question; they all do. But we needn't have the top on at all, if it depresses your spirits. We shall be just warm enough in the open sunlight."

"Well, have it off, then. It sends the cold chills over me to look at it. What *did* Byron call it?"

"Yes, it's time for Byron, now. It was very good of you not to mention him before, Mrs. Vervain. But I knew he had to come. He called it a coffin clapped in a canoe."

"Exactly," said Mrs. Vervain. "I always feel as if I were going to my own funeral when I get into it, and I've certainly had enough of funerals never to want to have anything to do with another, as long as I live."

She settled herself luxuriously upon the feather-stuffed leathern cushions when the cabin was removed. Death had indeed been near her very often: father and mother had been early lost to her, and the brothers and sisters orphaned with her had faded and perished one after another as they ripened to men and women; she had seen four of her own children die; her husband had been dead six years. All these bereavements had left her what they had found her. She had truly grieved, and as she said she had hardly ever been out of black since she could remember.

"I *never* was in colors when I was a girl," she went on, indulging many obituary memories as the gondola dipped and darted down the canal, "and I was married in my mourning for my last sister. It did seem a little too much when *she* went, Mr. Ferris. I was too young to feel it so much about the others, but *we* were nearly of the same age, and that makes a difference, don't you know. First a brother and then a sister; it was very strange how they kept going that way. I seemed to break the charm when I got married; though, to be sure, there was no brother left after Marian."

Miss Vervain heard her mother's mortuary prattle with a face, from which no impatience of it could be inferred, and Mr. Ferris made no comment on what was oddly various in character and manner, for Mrs. Vervain touched upon all the gloomiest facts of her history with a certain impersonal, statistical interest. They were rowing across the lagoon to the Island of San Lazzaro, where for reasons of her own she intended to venerate the convent in which Byron studied the Armenian language preparatory to writing his great poem in it; if her pilgrimage had no very earnest motive, it was worthy of the fact which it was designed to honor. The lagoon was of a perfect, shining smoothness, broken by the shallows over which the ebbing tide had left the seaweed trailed like long dishevelled hair. The fishermen as they waded about staking their nets, or stooped to gather the small shell-fish of the shallows showed legs as brown and tough as those of the apostles in Titian's Assumption. Here and there was a boat, with a boy or an old man asleep in the bottom of it. The gulls sailed high, white flakes against the illimitable blue of the heavens; the air, though it was of early spring, and in the shade had a salty pungency, was here almost languorously warm; in the motionless splendors and rich colors of the scene there was a

melancholy before which Mrs. Vervain fell fitfully silent. Now
and then Ferris briefly spoke, calling Miss Vervain's notice to
this or that, and she briefly responded. As they passed the
madhouse of San Servolo, a maniac standing at an open window took his black velvet skull-cap from his white hair,
bowed low three times, and kissed his hand to the ladies. The
Lido in front of them stretched a brown strip of sand with
white villages shining out of it; on their left the Public Gardens showed a mass of hovering green; far beyond and above,
the ghostlike snows of the Alpine heights haunted the misty
horizon.

It was chill in the shadow of the convent when they landed
at San Lazzaro, and it was cool in the parlor where they
waited for the monk who was to show them through the
place; but it was still and warm in the gardened court, where
the bees murmured among the crocuses and hyacinths under
the noonday sun. Miss Vervain stood looking out of the window upon the lagoon, while her mother drifted about the
room peering at the objects on the wall through her eyeglasses. She was praising a Chinese painting of fish on rice
paper when a young monk entered with a cordial greeting in
English for Mr. Ferris. She turned and saw them shaking
hands, but at the same moment her eyeglasses abandoned her
nose with a vigorous leap; she gave an amiable laugh, and
groping for them over her dress bowed at random as Mr.
Ferris presented Padre Girolamo.

"I've been admiring this painting *so* much, Padre Girolamo," she said with instant goodwill, and taking the monk
into the easy familiarity of her friendship by the tone with
which she spoke his name. "Some of the brothers did it, I
suppose."

"O no," said the monk, "it's a Chinese painting. We hung
it up there because it was given to us, and was curious."

"Well now, do you know," returned Mrs. Vervain, "I
thought it was Chinese? Their things *are* so odd. But really, in
an Armenian convent it's very misleading. I don't think you
ought to leave it there; it certainly does throw people off the
track," she added subduing the expression to something very
lady-like by the winning appeal with which she used it.

"O, but if they put up Armenian paintings in Chinese Convents?" said Mr. Ferris.

"You're joking!" cried Mrs. Vervain, looking at him with a graciously amused air. "There *are* no Chinese Convents. To be sure those rebels are a kind of Christians," she added thoughtfully, "but there can't be many of them left, poor things, hundreds of them executed at a time, that way. It's perfectly sickening to read of it; and you can't help it, you know. But they say they haven't really so much feeling as we have—not so nervous."

She walked by the side of the young friar as he led the way to such parts of the Convent as are open to visitors and Mr. Ferris came after with her daughter who, he fancied, met his attempts at talk with sudden and more than usual hauteur. "What a fool!" he said to himself. "Is she afraid I shall be wanting to make love to her?" and he followed in rather a sulky silence the course of Mrs. Vervain and her guide. The library, the chapel and the museum, called out her friendliest praises, and in the last she praised the mummy on show there at the expense of one she had seen in New York, but when Padre Girolamo pointed out the desk in the refectory from which one of the brothers read while the rest were eating, she took him to task. "O but I can't think that's at all good for the digestion, you know,—using the brain that way whilst you're at table. I really hope you don't listen too attentively; it would be better for you in the long run, even in a religious point of view. But now—Byron! You *must* show me his cell!" The monk deprecated the non-existence of such a cell, and glanced in perplexity at Mr. Ferris, who came to his relief. "You couldn't have seen his cell, if he'd had one, Mrs. Vervain. They don't admit ladies to the cloister."

"What nonsense!" answered Mrs. Vervain, apparently regarding this as another of Mr. Ferris's pleasantries; but Padre Girolamo silently confirmed his statement, and she briskly assailed the rule as a disrespect to the sex which reflected even upon the Virgin, the object, as he was forced to allow, of their high veneration. He smiled patiently, and confessed that Mrs. Vervain had all the reasons on her side. At the polyglot printing-office where she handsomely bought every kind of

Armenian book and pamphlet, and thus repaid in the only way possible the trouble their visit had given, he did not offer to take leave of them, but after speaking with Ferris, of whom he seemed an old friend, he led them through the garden environing the Convent to a little pavilion perched on the wall that defends the island from the tides of the lagoon. A lay-brother presently followed them bearing a tray with coffee, toasted rusk, and a jar of that conserve of rose-leaves which is the convent's delicate hospitality to favored guests. Mrs. Vervain cried out over the poetic confection when Padre Girolamo told her what it was, and her daughter suffered herself to express a guarded pleasure. The amiable matron brushed the crumbs of the *baicolo* from her lap when the lunch was ended, and fitting on her glasses leaned forward for a better look at the monk's black-bearded face. "I'm perfectly delighted," she said. "You must be very happy here. I suppose you are."

"Yes," answered the monk rapturously, "so happy that I should be content never to leave San Lazzaro. I came here when I was very young, and the greater part of my life has been passed on this little island. It is my home—my country."

"Do you never go away?"

"O yes; sometimes to Constantinople, sometimes to London and Paris."

"And you've never been to America, yet? Well now, I'll tell you: you ought to go. You would like it, I know, and our people would give you a very cordial reception."

"Reception?" The monk appealed once more to Ferris with a look.

Ferris broke into a laugh. "I don't believe Padre Girolamo would come in quality of distinguished foreigner, Mrs. Vervain, and I don't think he'd know what to do with one of our cordial receptions."

"Well, he ought to go to America, any way. He can't really know anything about us till he's been there. Just think how ignorant the English are of our country! You *will* come, wont you? I should be delighted to welcome you at my house in Providence. Rhode Island is a small State, but there's a great deal of wealth, there, and very good society in Providence.

It's quite New-Yorky, you know," said Mrs. Vervain expressively. She rose as she spoke, and led the way back to the
gondola. She told Padre Girolamo that they were to be some
weeks in Venice, and made him promise to breakfast with
them at their hotel. She smiled and nodded to him after the
boat had pushed off, and kept him bowing on the landing-
stairs.

"What a lovely place, and what a perfectly heavenly morning you *have* given us, Mr. Ferris! We never can thank you
enough for it. And now do you know what I'm thinking of?
Perhaps you can help me. It was Byron's studying there put
me in mind of it. How soon do the mosquitoes come?"

"About the end of June," responded Ferris mechanically,
staring with helpless mystification at Mrs. Vervain.

"Very well, then there's no reason why we shouldn't stay in
Venice till that time. We are both very fond of the place, and
we'd quite concluded, this morning, to stop here till the mosquitoes came. You know, Mr. Ferris, my daughter had to
leave school much earlier than she ought, for my health has
obliged me to travel a great deal since I lost my husband; and
I must have her with me, for we're all that there is of us; we
haven't a chick or a child that's related to us, anywhere. But
wherever we stop, even for a few weeks, I contrive to get her
some kind of instruction. I feel the need of it so much in my
own case; for to tell you the truth, Mr. Ferris, I married too
young. I suppose I should do the same thing over again if it
was to be done over; but don't you see, my mind wasn't properly formed, and then following my husband about from pillar to post, and my first baby born when I was nineteen—
well it wasn't education, at any rate whatever else it was; and
I've determined that Florida, though we *are* such a pair of
wanderers, shall not have my regrets. I got teachers for her in
England,—the English are not anything like so disagreeable
at home as they are in travelling, and we staid there two
years,—and I did in France, and I did in Germany. And now,
Italian. Here we are in Italy, and I think we ought to improve
the time. Florida knows a good deal of Italian already, for her
music teacher in France was an Italian and he taught her the
language as well as music. What she wants now, I should say,
is to perfect her accent and get facility. I think she ought to

have some one come everyday and read and converse an hour
or two with her."

Mrs. Vervain leaned back in her seat, and looked at Ferris,
who said, feeling that the matter was referred to him, "I
think—without presuming to say what Miss Vervain's need
of instruction is—that your idea is a very good one." He
mused in silence his wonder that so much addlepatedness as
was at once observable in Mrs. Vervain should exist along
with so much common sense. "It's certainly very good in the
abstract," he added with a glance at the daughter as if the
sense must be hers. She did not meet his glance at once, but
with an impatient recognition of the heat that was now great
for the warmth with which she was dressed, she pushed her
sleeve from her wrist, showing its delicious whiteness, and
letting her fingers trail through the cool water; she dried
them on her handkerchief, and then bent her eyes full upon
him as if challenging him to think this unladylike.

"No; clearly the sense does not come from her," said Ferris
to himself; it is impossible to think well of the mind of a girl
who treats one with tacit contempt.

"Yes," resumed Mrs. Vervain, "it's certainly very good in
the abstract. But O, dear me! you've no idea of the difficulties
in the way. I may speak frankly with you, Mr. Ferris, for you
are here as the representative of the country, and you naturally sympathize with the difficulties of Americans abroad: the
teachers *will* fall in love with their pupils."

"Mother!" began Miss Vervain; and then she checked herself.

Ferris gave a vengeful laugh. "Really, Mrs. Vervain, though
I sympathize with you in my official capacity, I must own
that as a man and a brother, I can't help feeling a little sorry
for those poor fellows too."

"To be sure, they are to be pitied, of course; and *I* feel for
them. I did when I was a girl; for the same thing used to
happen then. I don't know why Florida should be subjected
to such embarrassments, too. It does seem sometimes as if it
were something in the blood. They all get the idea that you
have money, you know."

"Then I should say that it might be something in the
pocket," suggested Ferris with a look at Miss Vervain, in

whose silent suffering, as he imagined it, he found a malicious
consolation for her scorn.

"Well, whatever it is," replied Mrs. Vervain, "it's too vex-
atious. Of course, going to new places, that way, as we're
always doing, and only going to stay for a limited time, perhaps, you can't pick and choose. And even when you *do* get
an elderly teacher, they're as bad as any. It really is too trying.
Now when I was talking with that nice monk of yours at the
Convent, there, I couldn't help thinking how perfectly delightful it would be if Florida could have *him* for a teacher.
Why couldn't she? He told me that he could come to take
breakfast or lunch with us, but not dinner, for he always had
to be at the convent before nightfall. Well, he might come to
give the lessons some time in the middle of the day."

"You couldn't manage it, Mrs. Vervain, I know you
couldn't," answered Ferris earnestly. "I'm sure the Armenians
never do anything of the kind. They're all very busy men engaged in ecclesiastical or literary work, and they couldn't give
the time."

"Why not? There was Byron."

"But Byron went to them, and he studied Armenian, not
Italian, with them. Padre Girolamo speaks perfect Italian, for
all that I can see, but I doubt if he'd undertake to impart the
native accent—which is what you want. In fact the scheme is
altogether impracticable."

"Well," said Mrs. Vervain, "I'm exceedingly sorry. I had
quite set my heart on it. I never took such a fancy to any one
in such a short time before."

"It seemed to be a case of love at first sight on both sides,"
said Ferris. "Padre Girolamo doesn't shower those syruped
rose-leaves indiscriminately upon visitors."

"Thanks," returned Mrs. Vervain, "it's very good of you to
say so, Mr. Ferris, and it's very gratifying, all round; but
don't you see, it doesn't serve the present purpose. What
teachers do you know of?"

She had been by marriage so long in the service of the
United States that she still regarded its agents as part of her
own domestic economy. Consuls she everywhere employed as
functionaries specially appointed to look after the interests of
American ladies travelling without protection. In the week

which had passed since her arrival in Venice, there had been no day on which she did not appeal to Ferris for help or sympathy or advice. She took amiable possession of him at once, and she had established an amusing sort of intimacy with him, to which the haughty trepidations of her daughter set certain bounds, but in which the demand that he should find her a suitable Italian teacher seemed trivially matter of course.

"Yes, I know several teachers," he said, after thinking, a while; "but they're all open to the objection of being human; and besides, they all do things in a set kind of way, and I'm afraid they wouldn't enter into the spirit of any scheme of instruction that departed very widely from Ollendorff." He paused, and Mrs. Vervain gave a sketch of the different professional masters whom she had employed in the various countries of her sojourn, and a disquisition upon their several lives and characters, fortifying her statements by reference of doubtful points to her daughter. This occupied some time, and Ferris listened to it all with an abstracted air. At last he said, with a smile, "There was an Italian priest came to see me this morning, who astonished me by knowing English— with a brogue that he'd learnt from an English priest straight from Dublin; perhaps he might do, Mrs. Vervain? He's professionally pledged, you know, not to give the kind of annoyance you've suffered from in teachers. He would do as well as Padre Girolamo, I suppose."

"Do you really? Are you in earnest?"

"Well no, I believe I'm not. I haven't the least idea he would do. He belongs to the church militant. He came to me with the model of a breech-loading cannon he's invented, and he wanted a passport to go to America, so that he might offer his cannon to our government."

"How curious!" said Mrs. Vervain, and her daughter looked frankly into Ferris's face. "But I know: it's one of your jokes."

"You overpraise me, Mrs. Vervain. If I could make such jokes as that priest was, I should set up for a humorist at once. He had the touch of pathos that they say all true pieces of humor ought to have," he went on, instinctively addressing himself to Miss Vervain, who did not repulse him. "He made me melancholy; and his face haunts me. I should like to paint him. Priests are generally such a snuffy, common lot. And I dare say," he concluded, "he's sufficiently commonplace too, though he didn't look it. Spare your romance, Miss Vervain."

The young lady blushed resentfully. "I see as little romance as joke in it," she said.

"It was a cannon," returned Ferris, without taking any notice of her, and with a sort of absent laugh, "that would make it very lively for the Southerners—if they had it. Poor fellow! I suppose he came with high hopes of me and expected me to receive his invention with eloquent praises. I've no doubt he figured himself furnished not only with a passport, but a letter from me to President Lincoln, and foresaw his own triumphal entry into Washington, and his honorable interviews with the admiring generals of the Union forces to whom he should display his wonderful cannon. Too bad; isn't it?"

"And why didn't you give him the passport and the letter?" asked Mrs. Vervain.

"O, that's a state secret," returned Ferris.

"And you think he wont do for our purpose?"

"I don't, indeed."

"Well, I'm not so sure of it. Tell me something more about him."

"I don't know anything more about him. Besides, there isn't time."

The gondola had already entered the canal, and was swiftly approaching the hotel.

"O yes, there is," pleaded Mrs. Vervain, laying her hand on his arm. "I want you to come in and dine with us. We dine early."

"Thank you, I can't. Affairs of the nation, you know. Rebel privateer on the canal of the Brenta."

"Really?" Mrs. Vervain leaned towards Ferris for sharper scrutiny of his face. Her glasses sprang from her nose, and precipitated themselves into his bosom.

"Allow me," he said, with burlesque politeness, withdrawing them from the recesses of his waistcoat and gravely presenting them. Miss Vervain burst into a helpless laugh; then she turned toward her mother with a kind of indignant tenderness, and gently arranged her shawl so that it should not drop off when she rose to leave the gondola. She did not look again at Ferris, who resisted Mrs. Vervain's entreaties to remain, and took leave as soon as the gondola landed.

The ladies went to their room where Florida lifted from the table a vase of divers-colored hyacinths, and stepping out upon the balcony flung the flowers into the canal. As she put down the empty vase, the lingering perfume of the banished flowers haunted the air of the room.

"Why, Florida," said her mother, "those were the flowers that Mr. Ferris gave you. Did you fancy they had begun to decay? The smell of hyacinths when they're a little old is dreadful. But I can't imagine a gentleman's giving you flowers that were at all old."

"O mother, don't speak to me!" cried Miss Vervain, passionately, clasping her hands to her face.

"Now I see that I've been saying something to vex you, my darling," and seating herself beside the young girl on the sofa, she fondly took down her hands. "Do tell me what it was. Was it about your teachers falling in love with you? You know they did, Florida: Pestachiavi and Schulze, both; and that horrid old Fleuron."

"Did you think I liked any better on that account to have you talk it over with a stranger?" asked Florida, still angrily.

"That's true, my dear," said Mrs. Vervain, penitently. "But if it worried you, why didn't you do something to stop me? Give me a hint, or just a little knock, somewhere?"

"No, mother, I'd rather not. Then you'd have come out with the whole thing to prove that you were right. It's better to let it go," said Florida with a fierce laugh, half sob. "But it's strange that you can't remember how such things torment me."

"I suppose it's my weak health, dear," answered the mother. "I didn't use to be so. But now I don't really seem to have the strength to be sensible. I know it's silly as well as you. The talk just seems to keep going on of itself,—slipping out, slipping out. But you needn't mind. Mr. Ferris wont think you could ever have done anything out of the way. I'm sure you don't act with *him* as if you'd ever encouraged anybody. I think you're too haughty with him, Florida. And now, his flowers."

"He's detestable. He's conceited and presuming beyond all endurance. I don't care what he thinks of me. But it's his manner towards you that I can't tolerate."

"I suppose it's rather free," said Mrs. Vervain. "But then you know, my dear, I shall be soon getting to be an old lady; and besides, I always feel as if consuls were a kind of one of the family. He's been very obliging since we came; I don't know what we should have done without him. And I don't object to a little ease of manner in the gentlemen; I never did."

"He makes fun of you," cried Florida, "and there at the convent," she said, bursting into angry tears, "he kept exchanging glances with that monk, as if he . . . He's insulting, and I hate him!"

"Do you mean that he thought your mother ridiculous, Florida?" asked Mrs. Vervain gravely. "You must have misunderstood his looks, indeed you must. I can't imagine why he should. I remember that I talked particularly well during our whole visit; my mind was active, for I felt unusually strong, and I was interested in everything. It's nothing but a fancy of yours; or your prejudice, Florida. But it's odd, now, I've sat down for a moment, how worn out I feel. And thirsty."

Mrs. Vervain fitted on her glasses, but even then felt uncertainly about for the empty vase on the table before her.

"It isn't a goblet mother," said Florida; "I'll get you some water."

"Do; and then throw a shawl over me. I'm sleepy, and a nap before dinner will do me good. I don't see why I'm so drowsy, of late. I suppose it's getting into the sea-air here at Venice; though it's mountain air that makes you drowsy. But you're quite mistaken about Mr. Ferris. He isn't capable of anything really rude. Besides there wouldn't have been any sense in it."

The young girl brought the water and then knelt beside the sofa on which she arranged the pillows under her mother, and covered her with soft wraps. She laid her cheek against the thinner face. "Don't mind anything I've said, mother; let's talk of something else."

The mother drew some loose threads of the daughter's hair through her slender fingers, but said little more, and presently fell into a deep slumber. Florida gently lifted her head away, and remained kneeling before the sofa, looking into the sleeping face with an expression of strenuous, compassionate devotion, mixed with a vague alarm and self-pity, and a certain wondering anxiety.

III

DON IPPOLITO had slept upon his interview with Ferris, and now sat in his laboratory, amidst the many witnesses of his inventive industry, with the model of the breech-loading cannon on the work-bench before him. He had neatly mounted it on wheels that its completeness might do him the greater credit with the consul when he should show it him, but the carriage had been broken in his pocket, on the way home, by an unlucky thrust from the burden of a porter, and the poor toy lay there disabled, as if to dramatize that premature explosion in the secret chamber.

His heart was in these inventions of his, which had as yet so grudgingly repaid his affection. For their sake he had stinted himself of many needful things. The meagre stipend which he received from the patrimony of his church, eked out with the money paid him for baptisms, funerals and marriages, and for masses by people who had friends to be prayed out of purgatory, would at best have barely sufficed to support him; but he denied himself everything save the necessary decorums of dress and lodging; he fasted like a saint, and slept hard as a hermit that he might spend upon these ungrateful creatures of his brain. They were the work of his own hands, and so he saved the expense of their construction, but there were many little outlays for materials and for tools, which he could not avoid, and with him a little was all. They not only famished him; they isolated him. His superiors in the church and his brother priests looked with doubt or ridicule upon the labors for which he shunned their company, while he gave up the other social joys, few and small, which a priest might know in the Venice of that day, when all generous spirits regarded him with suspicion for his cloth's sake, and church and state were alert to detect disaffection or indifference in him. But bearing these things willingly, and living as frugally as he might, he had still not enough, and he had been fain to assume the instruction of a young girl of old and noble family in certain branches of polite learning which a young lady of that sort might fitly know. The family was not so rich as it was old and noble, and Don Ippolito was paid from its purse rather than its pride. But the slender salary was a help; these patricians were very good to him; many a time he dined with them, and so spared the cost of his own pottage at home; they always gave him coffee when he came, and that was a saving; at the proper seasons little presents from them were not wanting. In a word, his condition was not privation. He did his duty as a teacher faithfully, and the only trouble with it was that the young girl was growing into a young woman, and that he could not go on teaching her forever. In an evil hour, as it seemed to Don Ippolito, that made the years she had been his pupil shrivel to a mere pinch of time, there came from a young count of the Friuli, visiting Venice, an offer of marriage; and Don Ippolito lost his place. It was hard, but he bade himself have patience; and he composed an ode for the nuptials of his late pupil, which, together with a brief sketch of her ancestral history, he had elegantly printed, according to the Italian usage, and distributed among the family friends; he also made a sonnet to the bridegroom and these literary tributes were handsomely acknowledged.

He managed a whole year upon the proceeds, and kept a cheerful spirit till the last soldo was spent, inventing one thing after another, and giving much time and money to a new principle of steam propulsion, which, as applied without steam to a small boat on the canal before his door, failed to work, though it had no logical excuse for its delinquency. He tried to get other pupils, but he got none, and he began to dream of going to America. He pinned his faith in all sorts of magnificent possibilities to the names of Franklin, Fulton and Morse; he was so ignorant of our politics and geography as to suppose us at war with the South American Spaniards, yet he knew that English was the language of the North, and he applied himself to the study of it. Heaven only knows what kind of inventor's Utopia our poor, patent-ridden country appeared to him in these dreams of his, and I can but dimly figure it to myself. But he might very naturally desire to come to a land where the spirit of invention is recognized and fostered, and where he could hope to find that comfort of incentive and companionship which our artists find in Italy.

The idea of the breech-loading cannon had occurred to him suddenly one day, in one of his New-World-ward reveries and he had made haste to realize it, carefully studying the form and general effect of the Austrian cannon under the gallery of the Ducal Palace, to the high embarrassment of the Croat sentry who paced up and down there, and who did not feel free to order off a priest as he would a civilian. Don Ippolito's model was of admirable finish; he even painted the carriage yellow and black because that of the original was so, and colored the piece to look like brass; and he lost a day while the paint was drying, after he was otherwise ready to show it to the consul.

He had parted from Ferris with some gleams of comfort, caught chiefly from his kindly manner, but they had died away before nightfall, and this morning he could not rekindle them.

He had had his coffee served to him on the bench, as his frequent custom was, but it stood untasted in the little copper pot beside the dismounted cannon, though it was now ten o'clock, and it was full time he had breakfasted, for he had risen early to perform the matin service for three peasant women, two beggars, a cat, and a paralytic nobleman, in the ancient and beautiful church to which he was attached. He had tried to go about his wonted occupations, but he was still sitting idle before his bench, while his servant gossiped from her balcony to the mistress of the next house, across a calle so deep and narrow that it opened like a mountain chasm beneath them, "it were well if the master read his breviary a little more, instead of always maddening himself with those blessed inventions, that eat more soldi than a Christian, and never come to anything. There he sits before his table, as if he were nailed to his chair, and lets his coffee cool—and God knows I was ready to drink it warm two hours ago—and never looks at me if I open the door twenty times to see whether he has finished. Holy patience! You have not even the advantage of fasting to the glory of God in this house, though you keep Lent the year round. It's the Devil's Lent, I say. Eh, Diana! There goes the bell. Who now? Adieu, Lusetta. To meet again, dear. Farewell!"

She ran to another window, and admitted the visitor. It

was Ferris, and she went to announce him to her master by
the title he had given, while he amused his leisure in the darkness below by falling over a cistern-top, with a loud clattering
of his cane on the copper lid, after which he heard the voice
of the priest begging him to remain at his convenience a moment till he could descend and show him the way up stairs.
His eyes were not yet used to the obscurity of the narrow
entry in which he stood, when he felt a cold hand laid on his,
and passively yielded himself to its guidance. He tried to excuse himself for intruding upon Don Ippolito so soon but the
priest in far suppler Italian overwhelmed him with lamentations that he should be so unworthy the honor done him, and
ushered his guest into his apartment. He plainly took it for
granted that Ferris had come to see his inventions, in compliance with the invitation he had given him the day before, and
he made no affectation of delay, though after the excitement
of the greetings was past, it was with a quiet dejection that
he rose and offered to lead his visitor to his laboratory. The
whole place was an outgrowth of himself, it was his history
as well as his character. It recorded his quaint and childish
tastes, his restless endeavors, his partial and halting successes.
The ante-room in which he had paused with Ferris, was
painted to look like a grape-arbor, where the vines sprang
from the floor, and flourishing up the trellised walls, with
many a wanton tendril and flaunting leaf, displayed their lavish clusters of white and purple all over the ceiling. It touched
Ferris, when Don Ippolito confessed that this decoration had
been the distraction of his own vacant moments, to find that
it was like certain grape-arbors he had seen in remote corners
of Venice before the doors of degenerate palaces, or forming
the entrances of open-air restaurants, and did not seem at all
to have been studied from grape-arbors in the country. He
perceived the archaic striving for exact truth, and he successfully praised the mechanical skill and love of reality with
which it was done; but he was silenced by a collection of
paintings in Don Ippolito's parlor, where he had been made
to sit down a moment. Hard they were in line, fixed in
expression, and opaque in color, these copies of famous master pieces,—saints of either sex, ascensions, assumptions,
martyrdoms and what not—and they were not quite compre-

hensible till Don Ippolito explained that he had made them from such prints of the subjects as he could get, and had colored them after his own fancy. All this, in a city whose art had been the glory of the world for nigh half a thousand years, struck Ferris as yet more comically pathetic than the frescoed grape-arbor; he stared about him for some sort of escape from the pictures; and his eye fell upon a piano and a melodeon placed end to end in a right angle. Don Ippolito, seeing his look of inquiry sat down and briefly played the same air with a hand upon each instrument.

Ferris smiled. "Don Ippolito, you are another Da Vinci, a universal genius."

"Bagatelles, bagatelles," said the priest pensively; but he rose with greater spirit than he had yet shown, and preceded the consul into the little room that served him for a smithy. It seemed from some peculiarities of shape to have once been an oratory, but it was now begrimed with smoke and dust from the forge which Don Ippolito had set up in it; the embers of a recent fire, the bellows, the pincers, the hammers and the other implements of the trade gave it a sinister effect as if the place of prayer had been invaded by mocking imps, or as if some hapless mortal in contract with the evil powers were here searching by the help of the adversary, for the forbidden secrets of the metals and of fire. In those days, Ferris was an uncompromising enemy of the theatricalization of Italy, or indeed of anything; but the fancy of the black-robed young priest at work in this place, appealed to him all the more potently because of the sort of tragic innocence which seemed to characterize Don Ippolito's expression. He longed intensely to sketch the picture then and there, but he had strength to rebuke the fancy as something that could not make itself intelligible without the help of such accessories as he despised, and he victoriously followed the priest into his larger workshop, where his inventions, complete and incomplete were stored, and where he had been seated when his visitor arrived. The high windows and the frescoed ceiling were festooned with dusty cobwebs; litter of shavings and whittlings strewed the floor; mechanical implements and contrivances were everywhere, and Don Ippolito's listlessness seemed to return upon him again at the sight of the familiar disorder. Conspicuous among other objects lay the illogically unsuccessful model of the new principle of steam propulsion, untouched since the day when he had lifted it out of the canal and carried it indoors through the ranks of grinning spectators. From a shelf above it he took down models of a flying-machine and a perpetual motion. "Fantastic researches in the impossible. I never expected results from these experiments, with which I nevertheless once pleased myself," he said, and turned impatiently to various pieces of portable furniture, chairs, tables, bedsteads, which by folding up their legs and tops condensed themselves into flat boxes developing handles at the side for convenience in carrying. They were painted and varnished and were in all respects complete; they had indeed won favorable mention at an exposition of the Provincial Society of Arts and Industries, and Ferris could applaud their ingenuity sincerely, though he had his tacit doubts of their usefulness. He fell silent again when Don Ippolito called his notice to a photographic camera so contrived with traps and springs that you could snatch by its help whatever joy there might be in taking your own photograph; and he did not know what to say of a submarine boat, a four-wheeled water-velocipede, a movable bridge, or the very many other principles and ideas to which Don Ippolito's cunning hand had given shape, more or less imperfect. It seemed to him that they all, however perfect or imperfect, had some fatal defect: they were aspirations toward the impossible, or realizations of the trivial and superfluous. Yet, for all this, they strongly appealed to the painter as the stunted fruit of a talent denied opportunity, instruction and sympathy. As he looked from them at last to the questioning face of the priest, and considered out of what disheartened and solitary patience they must have come in this city,—dead hundreds of years to all such endeavor,—he could not utter some glib phrases of compliment that he had on his tongue. If Don Ippolito had been taken young, he might perhaps have amounted to something though this was questionable; but at thirty—as he looked, now—with his undisciplined purposes, and his head full of vagaries of which these things were the tangible witness. . . . Ferris let his eyes drop again. They fell upon the ruin of the breech-loading cannon, and he said, "Don Ippolito it's very good of you to take the trouble of showing me these matters, and I hope you'll pardon the ungrateful return, if I cannot offer any definite opinion of them now. They are rather out of my way, I confess. I wish with all my heart I could order an experimental, life-size copy of your breech-loading cannon here, for trial by my government, but I can't; and to tell you the truth, it was not altogether the wish to see these inventions of yours that brought me here to-day."

"O," said Don Ippolito, with a mortified air, "I am afraid that I have wearied the signor console."

"Not at all, not at all," Ferris made haste to answer, with a frown at his own awkwardness. "But your speaking English yesterday. . . . Perhaps what I was thinking of is quite foreign to your tastes and possibilities" . . . He hesitated with a look of perplexity, while Don Ippolito stood before him in an attitude of expectation, pressing the points of his fingers together, and looking curiously into his face. "The case is this," resumed Ferris desperately. "There are two American ladies, friends of mine, sojourning in Venice, who expect to be here till midsummer. They are mother and daughter, and the young lady wants to read and speak Italian with some-body a few hours each day. The question is whether it is quite out of your way or not to give her lessons of this kind. I ask it quite at a venture. I suppose no harm is done at any rate," and he looked at Don Ippolito with apologetic perturbation.

"No," said the priest, "there is no harm. On the contrary, I am at this moment in a position to consider it a great favor that you do me in offering me this employment. I accept it with the greatest pleasure. O!" he cried, breaking by a sudden impulse, from the composure with which he had begun to speak, "you don't know what you do for me; you lift me out of despair. Before you came, I had reached one of those passes that seem the last bound of endeavor. But you give me new life. *Now* I can go on with my experiment. I can attest my gratitude by possessing your native country of the weapon I had designed for it—I am sure of the principle: some slight improvement; perhaps the use of some different explosive, would get over that difficulty you suggested," he said eagerly. "Yes, something can be done. God bless you, my dear little son—I mean—perdoni!—my dear sir" . . .

"Wait—not so fast," said Ferris with a laugh, yet a little annoyed that a question so purely tentative as his should have met at once such a definitive response. "Are you quite sure you can do what they want?" He unfolded to him as fully as he understood it, Mrs. Vervain's scheme.

Don Ippolito entered into it with perfect intelligence. He said that he had already had charge of the education of a young girl of noble family, and he could therefore the more confidently hope to be useful to this American lady. A light of joyful hope shone in his dreamy eyes, the whole man changed, he assumed the hospitable and caressing host. He conducted Ferris back to his parlor, and making him sit upon the hard sofa that was his hard bed by night, he summoned his servant, and bade her serve them coffee. She closed her lips firmly, and waved her finger before her face, to signify that there was no more coffee. Then he bade her fetch it from the caffè; and he listened with a sort of rapt inattention while Ferris again returned to the subject and explained that he had approached him without first informing the ladies, and that he must regard nothing as final. It was at this point that Don Ippolito, who had understood so clearly what Mrs. Vervain wanted, appeared a little slow to understand; and Ferris had a doubt whether it was from subtlety or from simplicity that the priest seemed not to comprehend the impulse on which he had acted. He finished his coffee in this perplexity, and when he rose to go, Don Ippolito followed him down to the street-door, and preserved him from a second encounter with the cistern-top.

"But Don Ippolito—remember! I make no engagement for the ladies, whom you must see before anything is settled," said Ferris.

"Surely, surely!" answered the priest, and he remained smiling at the door till the American turned the next corner. Then he went back to his workroom, and took up the broken model from the bench. But he could not work at it now; he could not work at anything; he began to walk up and down the floor.

"Could he really have been so stupid because his mind was on his ridiculous cannon?" wondered Ferris as he sauntered frowning away; and he tried to prepare his own mind for his meeting with the Vervains to whom he must now go at once. He felt abused and victimized. Yet it was an amusing experience, and he found himself able to interest both of the ladies in it. The younger had received him as coldly as the forms of greeting would allow; but as he talked she drew nearer him with a reluctant haughtiness which he noted. He turned the more conspicuously towards Mrs. Vervain. "Well, to make a long story short," he said, "I couldn't discourage Don Ippolito. He refused to be dismayed—as I should have been at the notion of teaching Miss Vervain. I didn't arrange with him not to fall in love with her as his secular predecessors have done—it seemed superfluous. But you can mention it to him if you like. In fact," said Ferris, suddenly addressing the daughter, "you might make the stipulation yourself, Miss Vervain." She looked at him a moment with a sort of defenseless pain that made him ashamed; and then walked away from him towards the window, with a frank resentment that made him smile, as he continued. "But I suppose you would like to have some explanation of my motive in precipitating Don Ippolito upon you in this way, when I told you only yesterday that he wouldn't do at all; in fact I think myself that I've behaved rather fickle-mindedly—for a representative of the country. But I'll tell you; and you wont be surprised to learn that I acted from mixed motives. I'm not at all sure that he'll do; I've had awful misgivings about it since I left him, and I'm glad of the chance to make a clean breast of it. When I came to think the matter over last night, the fact that he had taught himself English,—with the help of an Irishman for the pronunciation,—seemed to promise that he'd have the right sort of sympathy with your scheme, and it showed that he must have something practical about him, too. And here's where the selfish admixture comes in. I didn't have your interests solely in mind when I went to see Don Ippolito. I hadn't been able to get rid of him; he stuck in my thought. I fancied he might be glad of the pay of a teacher, and—I had half a notion to ask him to let me paint him. It was an even chance whether I should try to secure him for Miss Vervain, or for Art—as they call it. Miss Vervain won because she could pay him, and I didn't see how Art could. I can bring him round any time; and that's the whole inconsequent business. My consolation is that I've left you perfectly free. There's nothing decided."

"Thanks," said Mrs. Vervain, "then it's all settled. You can bring him round as soon as you like to our new place. We've taken that apartment we looked at the other day, and we're going into it this afternoon. Here's the landlord's letter," she added, drawing a paper out of her pocket. "If he's cheated us, I suppose you can see justice done. I didn't want to trouble you before."

"You're a woman of business, Mrs. Vervain," said Ferris. "The man's a perfect Jew—or a perfect Christian, one ought to say in Venice: we true believers do gouge so much more infamously here—and you let him get you in black and white before you come to me. Well," he continued, as he glanced at the paper, "you've done it! He makes you pay one half too much. However, it's cheap enough; twice as cheap as your hotel."

"But I don't care for cheapness. I hate to be imposed upon. What's to be done about it?"

"Nothing: if he has your letter as you have his. It's a bargain, and you must stand to it."

"A bargain? O nonsense, now, Mr. Ferris. This is merely a note of mutual understanding."

"Yes, that's one way of looking at it. The Civil Tribunal would call it a binding agreement of the closest tenure,—if you want to go to law about it."

"I *will* go to law about it."

"O no, you wont,—unless you mean to spend your remaining days and all your substance in Venice. Come, you haven't done so badly, Mrs. Vervain. I don't call four rooms, completely furnished for housekeeping, with that lovely garden, at all dear at eleven francs a day. Besides, the landlord is a man of excellent feeling, sympathetic and obliging, and a perfect gentleman, though he *is* such an outrageous scoundrel. He'll cheat you, of course, in whatever he can; you must look out for that; but he'll do you any sort of little neighborly kindness. Good-bye," said Ferris, getting to the door, before Mrs. Vervain could intercept him. "I'll come to your new place this evening to see how you are pleased."

"Florida," said Mrs. Vervain, "this is outrageous."

"I wouldn't mind it mother. We pay very little, after all."

"Yes, but we pay too much. That's what I can't bear. And as you said yesterday, I don't think Mr. Ferris's manners are quite respectful to me."

"He only told you the truth; I think he advised you for the best. The matter couldn't be helped now."

"But I call it a want of feeling to speak the truth so bluntly."

"We wont have to complain of that in our landlord it seems," said Florida. "Perhaps not in our priest, either," she added.

"Yes, that *was* kind of Mr. Ferris," said Mrs. Vervain. "It was thoroughly thoughtful and considerate—what I call an instance of true delicacy. I'm really quite curious to see him. Don Ippolito! How very odd to call a priest *Don*! I should have said Padre. Don always makes you think of a Spanish cavalier. Don Rodrigo: something like that."

They went on to talk, desultorily, of Don Ippolito, and what he might be like. In speaking of him the day before Ferris had hinted at some mysterious sadness in him; and to hint of sadness in a man always interests women in him, whether they are old or young: the old have suffered, the young forebode suffering. Their interest in Don Ippolito had not been diminished by what Ferris had told them of his visit to the priest's house and of the things he had seen there; for there had always been the same strain of pity in his laughing account, and he had imparted none of his doubts to them. They did not talk as if it were strange that Ferris should do to-day what he had yesterday said he would not do; perhaps as women they could not find such a thing strange; but it vexed him more and more as he went about all afternoon thinking of his inconsistency, and wondering whether he had not acted rashly.

IV

THE PALACE in which Mrs. Vervain had taken an apartment fronted on a broad campo, and hung its empty
marble balconies from gothic windows above a silence
scarcely to be matched elsewhere in Venice. The local pharmacy, the caffè, the grocery, the fruiterer's, the other shops
with which every Venetian campo is furnished, had each a
certain life about it, but it was a silent life, and at midday, a
frowsy-headed woman clacking across the flags in her
wooden-heeled shoes made echoes whose garrulity was interrupted by no other sound. In the early morning when the lid
of the public cistern in the centre of the campo was unlocked,
there was a clamor of voices and a clangor of copper vessels,
as the housewives of the neighborhood, and the local force of
strong-backed Friulan water-girls drew their day's supply of
water, and on that sort of special parochial holiday, called a
sagra, the campo hummed and clattered and shrieked with a
multitude celebrating the day around the stands where pump-
kin-seeds and roast pumpkin and anisette-water were sold,
and before the movable kitchen where cakes were fried in
caldrons of oil, and uproariously offered to the crowd by the
cook, who did not suffer himself to be embarrassed by the
rival drama of adjacent puppet-shows, but continued to bellow forth his bargains all day long and far into the night,
when the flames under his kettles painted his visage a fine
crimson. The sagra once over, however, the campo relapsed
into its habitual silence, and no one looking at the front of
the palace would have thought of it as a place for distraction-
seeking foreign sojourners. But it was not on this side that
the landlord tempted his tenants; his principal notice of lodgings to let was affixed to the water-gate of the palace which
opened on a smaller channel so near the Grand Canal, that
no wandering eye could fail to see it. The portal was a tall
arch of Venetian gothic tipped with a carven flame; steps of
white Istrian stone descended to the level of the lowest ebb,
irregularly embossed with barnacles, and dabbling long
fringes of soft green sea-mosses in the rising and falling tide.

Swarms of water-bugs and beetles played over the edges of
the steps, and crabs scuttled sidewise into deeper water at the
approach of a gondola. A length of stone-capped brick wall,
to which patches of stucco still clung, stretched from the gate
on either hand, under cover of an ivy that flung its mesh of
shining green from within, where there lurked a lovely garden, stately, spacious for Venice, and full of a delicious, half
sad surprise for whoso opened upon it. In the midst it had a
broken fountain, with a marble naiad standing on a shell, and
looking saucier than the sculptor meant from having lost the
point of her nose; nymphs and fauns, and shepherds and
shepherdesses, her kinsfolk, coquetted in and out among the
greenery in flirtation not to be embarrassed by the fracture of
an arm, or the casting of a leg, or so; one lady had no head,
but she was the boldest of all. In this garden there were some
mulberry and pomegranate trees, several of which hung about
the fountain, with seats in their shade, and for the rest there
seemed to be mostly roses and oleanders, with other shrubs
of a kind that made the greatest show of blossom and cost
the least for tendance. A wide terrace stretched across the rear
of the palace, dropping to the garden path by a flight of bal-
ustraded steps, and upon this terrace opened the long windows of Mrs. Vervain's parlor and dining-room. Her landlord
owned only the first story and the basement of the palace, in
some corner of which he cowered with his servants, his taste
for pictures and *bric à-brac*, and his little branch of inquiry
into Venetian history, whatever it was, ready to let himself or
anything he had for hire at a moment's notice, but very pleasant, gentle and unobtrusive; a cheat and a liar but of a kind
heart, and sympathetic manners. Under his protection Mrs.
Vervain set up her impermanent household gods. The apartment was taken only from week to week, and as she freely
explained to the *padrone* hovering about with offers of service,
she knew herself too well ever to unpack anything that would
not spoil by remaining packed. She made her trunks yield all
the appliances necessary for an invalid's comfort, and then left
them in a state to be strapped and transported to the station
within half a day after the desire of change or the exigencies
of her feeble health caused her going. Everything for housekeeping was furnished with the rooms. There was a gondolier

and a sort of house-servant in the employ of the landlord, of whom Mrs. Vervain hired them, and she caressingly dismissed the padrone at an early moment after her arrival, with the charge to find a maid for herself and daughter. As if she had been waiting at the next door this maid appeared promptly, and being Venetian and in domestic service her name was of course Nina. Mrs. Vervain now said to Florida that everything was perfect, and contentedly began her life in Venice by telling Mr. Ferris when he came in the evening that he could bring Don Ippolito the day after the morrow, if he liked.

She and Florida sat on the terrace waiting for them on the morning named, when Ferris with the priest in his clerical best, came up the garden path in the sunny light. Don Ippolito's best was a little poverty-stricken; he had faltered a while, before leaving home, over the sad choice between a shabby cylinder hat of obsolete fashion and his well-worn three cornered priestly beaver, and had at last put on the latter with a sigh. He had made his servant polish the buckles of his shoes, and instead of a band of linen round his throat, he wore a strip of cloth covered with small white beads, edged above and below, with a single row of pale blue ones.

As he mounted the steps with Ferris Mrs. Vervain came forward a little to meet them, while Florida rose and stood beside her chair in a sort of proud suspense and timidity. The elder lady was in that black from which she had so seldom been able to escape; but the daughter wore a dress of delicate green, in which she seemed a part of the young season that everywhere clothed itself in the same tint. The sunlight fell upon her blonde hair, melting into its light gold; her level brows frowned somewhat with the glance of scrutiny which she gave the dark young priest, who was making his stately bow to her mother, and trying to answer her English greetings in the same tongue.

"My daughter," said Mrs. Vervain, and Don Ippolito made another low bow, and then looked at the girl with a sort of frank and melancholy wonder, as she turned and exchanged a few words with Ferris, who was assaulting her seriousness and hauteur with unabashed levity of compliment. A quick light flashed and fled in her cheek as she talked, and the fringes of her serious, asking eyes swept slowly up and down as she bent them upon him a moment before she broke abruptly, not coquettishly, away from him, and moved towards her mother, while Ferris walked off to the other end of the terrace with a laugh. Mrs. Vervain and the priest were trying each other in French, and not making great advance; he explained to Florida in Italian, and she answered him hesitatingly; whereupon he praised her Italian in set phrase.

"Thank you," said the girl sincerely, "I have tried hard to learn. I hope," she added as before, "you can make me see how little I know." The deprecating wave of the hand with which Don Ippolito appealed to her from herself, seemed arrested midway by his perception of some novel quality in her. He said gravely that he should try to be of use, and then the two stood silent.

"Come, Mr. Ferris," called out Mrs. Vervain, "breakfast is ready, and I want you to take me in."

"Too much honor," said the painter coming forward and offering his arm, and Mrs. Vervain led the way indoors.

"I suppose I ought to have taken Don Ippolito's arm," she confided in undertone, "but the fact is our French is so unlike that we don't understand each other *very* well."

"O," returned Ferris, "I've known Italians and Americans whom Frenchmen themselves couldn't understand."

"You see it's an American breakfast," said Mrs. Vervain with a critical glance at the table before she sat down. "All but hot bread; *that* you *can't* have," and Don Ippolito was for the first time in his life confronted by a breakfast of beefsteak, eggs and toast, fried potatoes, and coffee with milk, with a choice of tea. He subdued all signs of the wonder he must have felt, and beyond cutting his meat into little bits before eating it, did nothing to betray his strangeness to the feast.

The breakfast had passed off very pleasantly, with occasional lapses. "We break down under the burden of so many languages," said Ferris. "It is an *embarras des richesses*. Let us fix upon a common maccheronic. May I trouble you for a poco più di sugar dans mon café, Mrs. Vervain. What do you think of the bellezza de ce weather magnifique, Don Ippolito?"

"How ridiculous!" said Mrs. Vervain in a tone of fond admiration aside to Don Ippolito, who smiled, but shrank from contributing to the new tongue.

"Very well, then," said the painter. "I shall stick to my native Bergamask, for the future; and Don Ippolito may translate for the foreign ladies."

He ended by speaking English with everybody; Don Ippolito eked out his speeches to Mrs. Vervain in that tongue with a little French; Florida, conscious of Ferris's ironical observance, used an embarrassed but defiant Italian with the priest.

"I'm *so* pleased," said Mrs. Vervain rising when Ferris said that he must go, and Florida shook hands with both guests.

"Thank you, Mrs. Vervain. I could have gone before, if I'd thought you'd have liked it," answered the painter.

"O nonsense, now," returned the lady. "You know what I mean. I'm perfectly delighted with him," she continued, getting Ferris to one side, "and I *know* he must have a good accent. So very kind of you. Will you arrange with him about the pay?—such a *shame*! Thanks. Then I needn't say anything to him about that. I'm so glad I had him to breakfast the first day; though Florida thought not. Of course, one needn't keep it up. But seriously, it isn't an ordinary case, you know."

Ferris laughed at her with a sort of affectionate disrespect, and said good-by. Don Ippolito lingered for a while to talk over the proposed lessons, and then went, after more elaborate adieux. Mrs. Vervain remained thoughtful a moment before she said:

"That was rather droll, Florida."

"What, mother."

"His cutting his meat into small bites, before he began to eat. But perhaps it's the Venetian custom. At any rate, my dear, he's a gentleman in virtue of his profession, and I couldn't do less than ask him to breakfast. He has beautiful manners; and if he must take snuff, I suppose it's neater to carry two handkerchiefs, though it does look odd. I wish he wouldn't take snuff."

"I don't see why we need care, mother. At any rate, we cannot help it."

"That's true, my dear. And his nails. Now, when they're

spread out on a book, you know, to keep it open, wont it be unpleasant?"

"They seem to have just such finger-nails all over Europe—except in England."

"O yes, I know it. I dare say we shouldn't care for it in him, if he didn't seem so very nice otherwise. How handsome he is!"

V

I<small>T WAS</small> understood that Don Ippolito should come every morning at ten o'clock, and read and talk with Miss Vervain for an hour or two; but Mrs. Vervain's hospitality was too aggressive for the letter of the agreement. She oftener had him to breakfast at nine, for as she explained to Ferris, she could not endure to have him feel that it was a mere mercenary transaction, and there was no limit fixed for the lessons on these days. When she could, she had Ferris come, too, and she missed him when he did not come. "I like that bluntness of his," she professed to her daughter, "and I don't mind his making light of me. You *are* so apt to be heavy if you're not made light of, occasionally. I certainly shouldn't want a *son* to be so respectful and obedient as you are, my dear."

The painter honestly returned her fondness, and with not much greater reason. He saw that she took pleasure in his talk, and enjoyed it even when she did not understand it; and this is a kind of flattery not easy to resist. Besides, there was very little ladies' society in Venice in those times, and Ferris after trying the little he could get at, had gladly denied himself its pleasures, and consorted with the young men he met at the caffès, or in the Piazza. But when the Vervains came, they recalled to him the younger days in which he had delighted in the companionship of women. After so long disuse, it was charming to be with a beautiful girl who neither regarded him with distrust nor expected him to ask her in marriage because he sat alone with her, rode out with her in a gondola, walked with her, read with her. All young men like a house in which no ado is made about their coming and going, and Mrs. Vervain perfectly understood the art of letting him make himself at home. He perceived with amusement that this amiable lady, who never did an ungraceful thing nor wittingly said an ungracious one, was very much of a Bohemian at heart—the gentlest and most blameless of the tribe, but still lawless,—whether from her campaigning married life, or the rovings of her widowhood or by natural disposition; and that Miss Vervain was inclined to be conventionally strict, but with her irregular training was at a loss for rules by which to check her mother's little waywardnesses. Her anxious perplexity, at times, together with her heroic obedience and unswerving loyalty to her mother had something pathetic as well as amusing in it. He saw her tried almost to tears by her mother's helpless frankness—for Mrs. Vervain was apparently one of those ladies whom the intolerable surprise of having anything come into their heads causes instantly to say or do it—and he observed that she never tried to pass off her endurance with any feminine arts; but seemed to defy him to think what he would of it. Perhaps she was not able to do otherwise: he thought of her at times as a person wholly abandoned to the truth. Her pride was on the alert against him; she may have imagined that he was covertly smiling at her, and she no doubt tasted the ironical flavor of much of his talk and behavior, for in those days he liked to qualify his devotion to the Vervains with a certain nonchalant slight, which, while the mother openly enjoyed it, filled the daughter with anger and apprehension. Quite at random, she visited points of his informal manner with unmeasured reprisal; others, for which he might have blamed himself, she passed over with strange caprice. Sometimes this attitude of hers provoked him, and sometimes it disarmed him; but whether they were at feud, or keeping an armed truce, or, as now and then happened, were in an *entente cordiale* which he found very charming, the thing that he always contrived to treat with silent respect and forbearance in Miss Vervain was that sort of aggressive tenderness with which she hastened to shield the foibles of her mother. That was something very good in her pride, he finally decided. At the same time, he did not pretend to understand the curious filial self-sacrifice which it involved.

Another thing in her that puzzled him was her devoutness. Mrs. Vervain could with difficulty be got to church; but her daughter missed no service of the English ritual in the old palace where the British and American tourists assembled once a week with their guide-books in one pocket and their prayer-books in the other, and buried the tomahawk under the altar. Mr. Ferris was often sent with her, and then his thoughts, which were a young man's, wandered from the service to the beautiful girl at his side; the golden head that punctiliously bowed itself at the proper places in the liturgy; the full lips that murmured the responses; the silken lashes that swept her pale cheeks as she perused the morning lesson. He knew that the Vervains were not Episcopalians when at home, for Mrs. Vervain had told him so, and that Florida went to the English service because there was no other. He conjectured that perhaps her touch of ritualism came from mere love of any form she could make sure of.

The servants in Mrs. Vervain's lightly ordered household, with the sympathetic quickness of the Italians, learned to use him as the next friend of the family, and though they may have had their decorous surprise at his untrammeled footing, they probably excused the whole relation as a phase of that foreign eccentricity to which their nation is so amiable. If they were not able to cast the same mantle of charity over Don Ippolito's allegiance—and doubtless they had their reserves concerning such frankly familiar treatment of so dubious a character as a priest—still as a priest they stood somewhat in awe of him; they had the spontaneous loyalty of their race to the people they served, and they never intimated by a look that they found it strange when Don Ippolito freely came and went. Mrs. Vervain had quite adopted him into her family; while her daughter seemed more at ease with him than with Ferris, and treated him with a grave politeness which had something also of compassion and childlike reverence in it. Ferris observed that she was always particularly careful of his supposable sensibilities as a Roman Catholic, and that the priest was oddly indifferent to this deference, as if it would have mattered very little to him whether his church was spared or not. He had a way of lightly avoiding, Ferris fancied, not only religious points on which they could disagree, but all phases of religion as matters of indifference. At such times Miss Vervain relaxed her reverential attitude, and used him with something like rebuke, as if it did not please her to have the representative of even an alien religion slight his office; as if her respect were for his priesthood and her compassion for him personally. That was rather hard for Don Ippolito, Ferris thought, and waited to see him snubbed outright some day, when he should behave without sufficient gravity.

The blossoms came and went upon the pomegranate and almond trees in the garden, and some of the earliest roses were in their prime; everywhere was so full leaf that the wantonest of the strutting nymphs was forced into a sort of decent seclusion, but the careless naiad of the fountain burnt in sunlight that subtly increased its fervors, day by day, and it was no longer beginning to be warm, it was warm, when one morning Ferris and Miss Vervain sat on the steps of the terrace waiting for Don Ippolito to join them at breakfast.

By this time the painter was well on with the picture of Don Ippolito which the first sight of the priest had given him a longing to paint, and he had been just now talking of it with Miss Vervain.

"But why do you paint him simply as a priest?" she asked "I should think you would want to make him the centre of some famous or romantic scene," she added gravely looking into his eyes as he sat with his head thrown back against the balustrade.

"No, I doubt if you *think*," answered Ferris, "or you'd see that a Venetian priest doesn't need any tawdry accessaries. What do you want? Somebody administering the extreme unction to a victim of the Council of Ten? A priest stepping into a confessional at the Frari—tomb of Canova in the distance, perspective of one of the naves, and so forth—with his eye on a pretty devotee coming up to unburden her conscience? I've no patience with the follies people think and say about Venice!"

Florida stared in haughty question at the painter.

"You're no worse than the rest," he continued with indifference to her anger at his bluntness. "You all think that there can be no picture of Venice without a gondola or a Bridge of Sighs in it. Have you ever read the Merchant of Venice, or Othello? There isn't a boat nor a bridge, nor a canal mentioned in either of them; and yet they breathe and pulsate with the very life of Venice. I'm going to try to paint a Venetian priest so that you'll know him without a bit of conventional Venice near him."

"It was Shakespeare who wrote those plays," said Florida. Ferris bowed in mock suffering from her sarcasm. "You'd better have some sort of symbol in your picture of a Venetian priest, or people will wonder why you came so far to paint Father O'Brien."

"I don't say I shall succeed," Ferris answered. "In fact I've made one failure already, and I'm pretty well on with a second; but the principle is right, all the same. I don't expect everybody to see the difference between Don Ippolito and Father O'Brien. At any rate, what I'm going to paint *at* is the lingering pagan in the man, the renunciation first of the inherited nature, and then of a personality that would have enjoyed the world. I want to show that baffled aspiration, apathetic despair, and rebellious longing which you catch in his face when he's off his guard, and that suppressed look which is the characteristic expression of all Austrian Venice. Then," said Ferris, laughing, "I must work in that small suspicion of Jesuit, which there is in every priest. But it's quite possible I may make a Father O'Brien of him."

"You wont make a Don Ippolito of him," said Florida, after serious consideration of his face to see whether he was quite in earnest, "if you put all that into him. He has the simplest and openest look in the world," she added warmly, "and there's neither pagan, nor martyr nor rebel in it."

Ferris laughed again. "Excuse me; I don't think you know. I can convince you" . . .

Florida rose, and looking down the garden path, said, "He's coming," and as Don Ippolito drew near, his face lighting up with a joyous and innocent smile, she continued absently, "He's got on new stockings, and a different coat and hat."

The stockings were indeed new and the hat was not the accustomed *nicchio*, but a new silk cylinder with a very worldly, curling brim. Don Ippolito's coat, also, was of a more mundane cut than the *talare*; he wore a waistcoat and small-clothes, meeting the stockings at the knee with a sprightly buckle. His person showed no traces of the snuff with which it used to be so plentifully dusted; in fact he no longer took snuff in the presence of the ladies. The first week he had noted an inexplicable uneasiness in them when he drew forth that blue cotton handkerchief after the solace of a pinch; shortly afterwards, being alone with Florida, he saw her give a nervous start at its appearance. He blushed violently, and put it back into the pocket from which he had half drawn it, and whence it never emerged again in her presence. The contessina his former pupil had not shown any aversion to Don Ippolito's snuff or his blue handkerchief; but then the contessina had never rebuked his finger-nails by the tints of rose and ivory with which Miss Vervain's hands bewildered him. It was a little droll how anxiously he studied the ways of these Americans, and conformed to them as far as he knew. His English grew rapidly in their society, and it happened sometimes that the only Italian in the day's lesson was what he read with Florida, for she always yielded to her mother's wish to talk and Mrs. Vervain preferred the case of her native tongue. He was Americanizing in that good lady's hands as fast as she could transform him, and he listened to her with trustful reverence, as to a woman of striking though eccentric mind. Yet he seemed finally to refer every point to Florida as if with an intuition of steadier and stronger character in her; and now as he ascended the terrace steps in his modified costume, he looked intently at her. She swept him from head to foot with a glance, and then gravely welcomed him with unchanged countenance.

At the same moment Mrs. Vervain came out through one of the long windows, and adjusting her glasses, said with a start, "Why my dear Don Ippolito, I shouldn't have known you!"

"Indeed, Madama?" asked the priest with a painful smile. "Is it so great a change? We can wear this dress as well as the other, if we please."

"Why of course it's very becoming and all that; but it does look so out of character," Mrs. Vervain said leading the way to the breakfast room. "It's like seeing a military man in a civil coat."

"It must be a great relief to lay aside the uniform now and then, mother," said Florida, as they sat down. "I can remember that papa used to be glad to get out of his."

"Perfectly wild," assented Mrs. Vervain. "But he never seemed the same person. Soldiers and—clergymen—are so much more stylish in their own dress—not stylish, exactly, but taking; don't you know?"

"There, Don Ippolito," interposed Ferris, "you had better put on your *talare* and your *nicchio* again. Your *abbate's* dress isn't acceptable, you see."

The painter spoke in Italian, but Don Ippolito answered—with certain blunders which it would be tedious to reproduce—in his patient, conscientious English, half sadly, half playfully, and glancing at Florida before he turned to Mrs. Vervain, "You are as rigid as the rest of the world, Madama. I thought you would like this dress, but it seems that you think it a masquerade. As madamigella says, it is a relief to lay aside the uniform, now and then, for us who fight the spiritual enemies as well as for the other soldiers. There was one time, when I was younger and in the subdeaconate orders, that I put off the priest's dress altogether, and wore citizen's clothes—not an abbate's suit like this. We were in Padua, another young priest and I, my nearest and only friend, and for a whole night we walked about the streets in that dress, meeting the students, as they strolled singing through the moonlight; we went to the theatre and to the caffè,—we smoked cigars, all the time laughing and trembling to think of the tonsure under our hats. But in the morning we had to put on the stockings and the talare and the nicchio again."

Don Ippolito gave a melancholy laugh. He had thrust the corner of his napkin into his collar; seeing that Ferris had not his so, he twitched it out, and made a feint of its having been all the time in his lap. Every one was silent as if something shocking had been said; Florida looked with grave rebuke at Don Ippolito whose story affected Ferris like that of some girl's adventure in men's clothes. He was in terror lest Mrs. Vervain should be going to say it was like that; she was going to say something; he made haste to forestall her and turn the talk on other things.

The next day the priest came in his usual dress, and he did not again try to escape from it.

VI

ONE AFTERNOON as Don Ippolito was posing to Ferris for his picture of A Venetian Priest, the painter asked, to make talk, "Have you hit upon that new explosive yet, which is to utilize your breech-loading cannon? Or are you engaged upon something altogether new?"

"No," answered the other uneasily, "I have not touched the cannon since that day you saw it at my house; and as for other things I have not been able to put my mind to them. I have made a few trifles which I have ventured to offer the ladies."

Ferris had noticed the ingenious reading-desk which Don Ippolito had presented to Florida, and the foot stool contrived with springs and hinges, so that it would fold up into the compass of an ordinary portfolio, which Mrs. Vervain carried about with her.

An odd look which the painter caught at and missed, came into the priest's face, as he resumed: "I suppose it is the distraction of my new occupation, and of the new acquaintances so very strange to me in every way—that I have made in your amiable countrywomen, which hinders me from going about anything in earnest, now that their munificence has enabled me to pursue my aims with greater advantages than ever before. But this idle mood will pass, and in the meantime I am very happy. They are real angels, and madama is a true original."

"Mrs. Vervain is rather peculiar," said the painter, retiring a few paces from his picture, and quizzing it through his half-closed eyes. "She is a woman who has had affliction enough to turn a stronger head than hers could ever have been," he added kindly. "But she has the best heart in the world. In fact," he burst forth, "she is the most extraordinary combination of perfect fool and perfect lady, I ever saw."

"Excuse me; I don't understand," blankly faltered Don Ippolito.

"No; and I'm afraid I couldn't explain to you," answered Ferris.

53

There was a silence for a time, broken at last by Don Ippolito who asked, "Why do you not marry Madamigella?"

He seemed not to feel that there was anything out of the way in the question, and Ferris was too well used to the childlike directness of the most manoeuvering of races to be surprised. Yet he was displeased, as he would not have been if Don Ippolito were not a priest. He was not of the type of priests whom the American knew from the prejudice and distrust of the Italians; he was alienated from his clerical fellows by all the objects of his life, and by a reciprocal dislike. About other priests there were various scandals; but Don Ippolito was like that pretty match-girl of the Piazza of whom it was Venetianly answered when one asked if so sweet a face were not innocent, "O yes, she is mad!" He was of a purity so blameless that he was reputed crack-brained by the caffè-gossip that in Venice turns its searching light upon whoever you mention, and from his own association with the man Ferris perceived in him an apparent single-heartedness such as no man can have but the rarest of Italians. He was the albino of his species; a gray crow, a white fly; he was really this, or he knew how to seem it with an art far beyond any common deceit. It was the half-expectation of coming sometime upon the lurking duplicity in Don Ippolito that continually enfeebled the painter in his attempts to portray his Venetian priest and that gave its undecided, unsatisfactory character to the picture before him—its weak hardness, its provoking superficiality. He expressed the traits of melancholy and loss that he imagined in him, yet he always was tempted to leave the picture with a touch of something sinister in it, some airy and subtle shadow of selfish design.

He stared hard at Don Ippolito while this perplexity filled his mind, for the hundredth time; then he said stiffly, "I don't know. I don't want to marry anybody. Besides," he added, relaxing into a smile of helpless amusement, "it's possible that Miss Vervain might not want to marry me."

"As to that," replied Don Ippolito, "you never can tell. All young girls desire to be married, I suppose," he continued with a sigh. "She is very beautiful, is she not? It is seldom that we see such a blonde in Italy. Our blondes are dark; they have auburn hair and blue eyes, but their complexions are thick. Miss Vervain is blonde as the morning light; the sun's gold is in her hair, his noonday whiteness in her dazzling throat; the flush of his coming is on her lips; she might utter the dawn!"

"You're a poet, Don Ippolito," laughed the painter. "What property of the sun is in her angry-looking eyes?"

"His fire! Ah, that is her greatest charm! Those strange eyes of hers, they seem full of tragedies. She looks made to be the heroine of some stormy romance; and yet how simply patient and good she is!"

"Yes," said Ferris, who often responded in English to the priest's Italian; and he added half musingly in his own tongue, after a moment, "but I don't think it would be safe to count upon her. I'm afraid she has a bad temper. At any rate I always expect to see smoke somewhere when I look at those eyes of hers. She has wonderful self-control, however; and I don't exactly understand why. Perhaps people of strong impulses have strong wills to overrule them; it seems no more than fair."

"Is it the custom," asked Don Ippolito, after a moment, "for the American young ladies always to address their mammas as *mother*?"

"No; that seems to be a peculiarity of Miss Vervain's. It's a little formality that I should say served to hold Mrs. Vervain in check."

"Do you mean that it repulses her?"

"Not at all. I don't think I could explain," said Ferris with a certain air of regretting to have gone so far in comment on the Vervains. He added recklessly, "Don't you see that Mrs. Vervain sometimes does and says things that embarrass her daughter, and that Miss Vervain seems to try to restrain her?"

"I thought," returned Don Ippolito meditatively, "that the signorina was always very tenderly submissive to her mother."

"Yes, so she is," said the painter dryly, and looked in annoyance from the priest to the picture, and from the picture to the priest.

After a minute Don Ippolito said, "They must be very rich to live as they do."

"I don't know about that," replied Ferris. "Americans spend and save in ways different from the Italians. I dare say the Vervains find Venice very cheap after London and Paris and Berlin."

"Perhaps," said Don Ippolito, "if they were rich you would be in a position to marry her."

"I should not marry Miss Vervain for her money," answered the painter sharply.

"No, but if you loved her the money would enable you to marry her."

"Listen to me, Don Ippolito. I never said that I loved Miss Vervain, and I don't know how you feel warranted in speaking to me about the matter. Why do you do so?"

"I? Why? I could not but imagine that you must love her. Is there anything wrong in speaking of such things? Is it contrary to the American custom? I ask pardon with all my heart if I have done anything amiss."

"There is no offence," said the painter, with a laugh, "and I don't wonder you thought I ought to be in love with Miss Vervain. She *is* beautiful, and I believe she's good. But if men had to marry because women were beautiful and good, there isn't one of us could live single a day. Besides I'm the victim of another passion—I'm laboring under an unrequited affection for Art."

"Then you do *not* love her?" asked Don Ippolito eagerly.

"So far as I'm advised at present,—no, I don't."

"It is strange!" said the priest, absently, but with a glowing face.

He quitted the painter's and walked swiftly homeward with a triumphant buoyancy of step. A subtle content diffused itself over his face, and a joyful light burnt in his deep eyes. He sat down before the piano and organ as he had arranged them, and began to strike their keys in unison; this seemed to him for the first time childish. Then he played some lively bars on the piano alone; they sounded too light and trivial, and he turned to the other instrument. As the plaint of the reeds arose, it filled his sense like a solemn organ-music, and transfigured the place; the notes swelled to the ample vault of a church, and at the high altar he was celebrating the mass in his sacerdotal robes. He suddenly caught his fingers away from the keys; his breast heaved, he hid his face in his hands.

VII

FERRIS STOOD cleaning his palette, after Don Ippolito was gone, scraping the colors together with his knife, and neatly buttering them on the palette's edge, while he wondered what the priest meant by pumping him in that way. Nothing, he supposed, and yet it was odd. Of course she had a bad temper. . . .

He put on his hat and coat, and strolled vaguely forth and in an hour or two came by a roundabout course to the gondola station nearest his own house. There he stopped, and after an absent contemplation of the boats, from which the gondoliers were clamoring for his custom, he stepped into one, and ordered the man to row him to a gate on a small canal opposite. The gate opened, at his ringing, into the garden of the Vervains.

Florida was sitting alone on a bench near the fountain. It was no longer a ruined fountain; the broken-nosed naiad held a pipe above her head, and from this rose a willowy spray high enough to catch some colors of the sunset then striking into the garden, and fell again in a mist around her, making her almost modest.

"What does this mean?" asked Ferris carelessly taking the young girl's hand. "I thought this lady's occupation was gone."

"Don Ippolito repaired the fountain for the landlord, and he agreed to pay for filling the tank that feeds it," said Florida. "He seems to think it a hard bargain, for he only lets it play about half an hour a day. But he says it's very ingeniously mended. He didn't believe it could be done. It *is* pretty."

"It is, indeed," said the painter, with a singular desire, going through him like a pang, likewise to do something for Miss Vervain. "Did you go to Don Ippolito's house the other day to see his traps?"

"Yes, we were very much interested. I was sorry that I knew so very little about inventions. Do you think there are many practical ideas amongst his things? I hope there are—

he seemed so proud and pleased to show them. Shouldn't you think he had some real inventive talent?"

"Yes, I think he has; but I know as little about the matter as you do." He sat down beside her, and picking up a twig from the gravel, pulled the bark off in silence. Then, "Miss Vervain," he said, knitting his brows, as he always did when he had something on his conscience, and meant to ease it at any cost, "I'm the dog that fetches a bone and carries a bone: I talked Don Ippolito over with you, the other day, and now I've been talking you over with him. But I've the grace to say that I'm ashamed of myself."

"Why need you be ashamed?" asked Florida. "You said no harm of him. Did you of us?"

"Not exactly; but I don't think it was quite my business to discuss you at all. I think you can't let people alone, too much. For my part, if I try to characterize my friends, I fail to do them perfect justice, of course; and yet the imperfect result remains representative of them in my mind; it limits them and fixes them, and I can't get them back again into the undefined and the ideal where they really belong. One ought never to speak of the faults of one's friends: it mutilates them, they can never be the same afterwards."

"So you have been talking of my faults," said Florida, breathing quickly. "Perhaps you could tell me of them to my face."

"I should have to say that unfairness was one of them. But that is common to the whole sex. I never said I was talking of your faults. I declared against doing so, and you immediately infer that my motive is remorse. I don't know that you have any faults. They may be virtues in disguise. There is a charm even in unfairness. Well, I did say that I thought you had a quick temper"—

Florida colored violently.

—"But now I see that I was mistaken," said Ferris with a laugh.

"May I ask what else you said?" demanded the young girl haughtily.

"O that would be a betrayal of confidence," said Ferris, unaffected by her hauteur.

"Then why have you mentioned the matter to me at all?"

"I wanted to clear my conscience, I suppose, and sin again. I wanted to talk with you about Don Ippolito."

Florida looked with perplexity at Ferris's face, while her own slowly cooled and paled. "What did you want to say of him?" she asked calmly.

"I hardly know how to put it: that he puzzles me, to begin with. You know I feel somewhat responsible for him."

"Yes."

"Of course, I never should have thought of him, if it hadn't been for your mother's talk that morning coming back from San Lazzaro."

"I know," said Florida, with a faint blush.

"And yet, don't you see, it was as much a fancy of mine, a weakness for the man himself, as the desire to serve your mother that prompted me to bring him to you."

"Yes, I see," answered the young girl.

"I acted in the teeth of a bitter Venetian prejudice against priests. All my friends here—they're mostly young men with the modern Italian ideas, or old liberals—hate and despise the priests. They believe that priests are full of guile and deceit, that they are spies for the Austrians, and altogether evil."

"Don Ippolito is welcome to report our most secret thoughts to the police," said Florida, whose look of rising alarm relaxed into a smile.

"O," cried the painter, "how you leap to conclusions. I never intimated that Don Ippolito was a spy. On the contrary, it was his difference from other priests that made me think of him for a moment. He seems to be as much cut off from the church as from the world. And yet he is a priest, with a priest's education. What if I should have been altogether mistaken? He is either one of the openest souls in the world, as you have insisted, or he is one of the closest."

"I should not be afraid of him in any case," said Florida; "but I can't believe any wrong of him."

Ferris frowned in annoyance. "I don't want you to; I don't, myself. I've bungled the matter as I might have known I would. I was trying to put into words an undefined uneasiness of mine, a quite formless desire to have you possessed of the whole case as it had come up in my mind. I've made a mess of it," said Ferris rising, with a rueful air. "Besides, I ought to have spoken to Mrs. Vervain."

"O no," cried Florida, eagerly, springing to her feet beside him. "Don't! Little things wear upon my mother, so. I'm glad you didn't speak to her. I don't misunderstand you, I think; I expressed myself badly," she added with an anxious face. "I thank you very much. What do you want me to do?"

By Ferris's impulse they both began to move down the garden path toward the water-gate. The sunset had faded out of the fountain, but it still lit the whole heaven, in whose vast blue depths hung light whiffs of pinkish cloud, as ethereal as the draperies that floated after Miss Vervain as she walked with a splendid grace beside him, no awkwardness, now, or self-constraint in her. As she turned to Ferris, and asked in her deep tones, to which some latent feeling imparted a slight tremor, "What do you want me to do?" the sense of her willingness to be bidden by him gave him a delicious thrill. He looked at the superb creature, so proud, so helpless; so much a woman, so much a child; and he caught his breath before he answered. Her gauzes blew about his feet in the light breeze that lifted the foliage; she was a little near-sighted, and in her eagerness she drew closer to him, fixing her eyes full upon his with a bold innocence. "Good heavens, Miss Vervain," he cried, with a sudden blush, "it isn't a serious matter. I'm a fool to have spoken to you. Don't do anything. Let things go on as before. It isn't for me to instruct you."

"I should have been very glad of your advice," she said with a disappointed, almost wounded manner, keeping her eyes upon him. "It seems to me we are always going wrong"—

She stopped short, with a flush and then a pallor.

Ferris returned her look with one of comical dismay. This apparent readiness of Miss Vervain's to be taken command of, daunted him, on second thoughts. "I wish you'd dismiss all my stupid talk from your mind," he said. "I feel as if I'd been guiltily trying to set you against a man whom I like very much and have no reason not to trust, and who thinks me so much his friend that he couldn't dream of my making any sort of trouble for him. It would break his heart, I'm afraid, if you treated him in a different way from that in which you've treated him till now. It's really touching to listen to his gratitude to you and your mother. It's only conceivable on the ground that he has never had friends before in the world. He seems like another man, or the same man come to life. And it isn't his fault that he's a priest, I suppose," he added, with a sort of final throe, "that a Venetian family wouldn't use him with the frank hospitality you've shown, not because they distrusted him at all, perhaps, but because they would be afraid of other Venetian tongues."

This ultimate drop of venom, helplessly distilled, did not seem to rankle in Miss Vervain's mind. She walked now with her face turned from his, and she answered coldly, "We shall not be troubled. We don't care for Venetian tongues."

They were at the gate. "Good-bye," said Ferris abruptly, "I'm going."

"Wont you wait and see my mother?" asked Florida, with her awkward self-constraint again upon her.

"No, thanks," said Ferris gloomily. "I haven't time. I just dropped in for a moment, to blast an innocent man's reputation, and destroy a young lady's peace of mind."

"Then you needn't go, yet," answered Florida, coldly; "for you haven't succeeded."

"Well, I've done my worst," returned Ferris, drawing the bolt.

He went away hanging his head in amazement and disgust at himself, for his clumsiness and bad taste. It seemed to him a contemptible part, first to embarrass them with Don Ippolito's acquaintance, if it was an embarrassment, and then try to sneak out of his responsibility by these tardy cautions; and if it was not going to be an embarrassment, it was folly to have approached the matter at all.

What had he wanted to do, and with what motive? He hardly knew. As he battled the ground over and over again, nothing comforted him save the thought that bad as it was to have spoken to Miss Vervain, it must have been infinitely worse to speak to her mother.

VIII

IT WAS late before Ferris forgot his chagrin in sleep, and when he woke the next morning, the sun was making the solid green blinds at his window odorous of their native pine woods with its heat, and thrusting a golden spear at the heart of Don Ippolito's effigy where he had left it on the easel.

Marina brought a letter with his coffee. The letter was from Mrs. Vervain, and it entreated him to come to lunch at twelve, and then join them on an excursion, of which they had all often talked, up the Canal of the Brenta. "Don Ippolito has got his permission—think of his not being able to go to the mainland without the Patriarch's leave!—and can go with us to-day. So I try to make this hasty arrangement. You *must* come—it all depends upon you."

"Yes, so it seems," groaned the painter, and went.

In the garden he found Don Ippolito and Florida at the fountain where he had himself parted with her the evening before; and he observed with a guilty relief that Don Ippolito was talking to her in the happy unconsciousness habitual with him.

Florida cast at the painter a swift glance of latent appeal and intelligence, which he refused, and in the same instant, she met him with another look, as if she now saw him for the first time, and gave him her hand in greeting. It was a beautiful hand; he could not help worshipping its lovely forms, the lily whiteness and softness of the back, the rose of the palm and finger-tips.

She idly resumed the great Venetian fan which hung from her waist by a chain. "Don Ippolito has been talking about the *villeggiatura* on the Brenta in the old days," she explained.

"O yes," said the painter, "they used to have merry times in the villas then, and it was worth while being a priest, or at least an *abbate di casa*. I should think you would sigh for a return of those good old days, Don Ippolito. Just imagine: if you were *abbate di casa* with some patrician family about the close of the last century, you might be the instructor, companion and spiritual adviser of Illustrissima at the theatres,

62

card-parties, and masquerades, all winter; and at this season instead of going up the Brenta for a day's pleasure with us barbarous Yankees, you might be setting out with Illustrissima and all the 'Strissimi and 'Strissime, big and little, for a spring *villeggiatura*, there. You would be going in a gilded barge, with songs and fiddles and dancing, instead of a common gondola, and you would stay a month, walking, going to parties and caffès, drinking chocolate and lemonade, gaming, sonneteering, and butterflying about generally."

"It was doubtless a beautiful life," answered the priest, with simple indifference. "But I never have thought of it with regret, because I have been preoccupied with other ideas than those of social pleasures, though perhaps they were no wiser."

Florida had watched Don Ippolito's face while Ferris was speaking, and she now asked gravely, "But don't you think their life now-a-days is more becoming to the clergy?"

"Why, madamigella? What harm was there in those gayeties? I suppose the bad features of the old life are exaggerated to us."

"They couldn't have been worse than the amusements of the hard-drinking, hard-riding, hard-swearing fox-hunting English parsons about the same time," said Ferris. "Besides the *abbate di casa* had a charm of his own, the charm of all *rococo* things, which, whatever you may say of them are somehow elegant and refined, or at least refer to elegance and refinement. I don't say they're ennobling, but they're fascinating. I don't respect them, but I love them. When I think about the past of Venice, I don't care so much to see any of the heroically historical things, but I should like immensely to have looked in at the Ridotto, when the place was at its gayest, with wigs and masks, hoops and small-clothes, fans and rapiers, bows and courtseys, whispers and glances. I dare say I should have found Don Ippolito there in some becoming disguise."

Florida looked from the painter to the priest and back to the painter, as Ferris spoke, and then she turned a little anxiously toward the terrace, and a shadow slipped from her face, as her mother came rustling down the steps, catching at her drapery and shaking it into place. The young girl hurried to meet her, lifted her arms for what promised an embrace, and

with firm hands set the elder lady's bonnet straight with her
forehead.

"I'm always getting it on askew," Mrs. Vervain said for
greeting to Ferris; "How do you do, Don Ippolito? But I
suppose you think I've kept you long enough to get it on
straight for once. So I have. I *am* a fuss, and I don't deny it.
At my time of life, it's much harder to make yourself ship-
shape, than it is when you're younger. I tell Florida that anybody would take *her* for the *old* lady, she does seem to give
so little care to getting up an appearance."

"And yet she has the effect of a stylish young person in the
bloom of youth," observed Ferris, with a touch of caricature.

"We had better lunch with our things on," said Mrs. Vervain, "and then there needn't be any delay in starting. I
thought we would have it out here," she added, as Nina and
the house-servant appeared with trays of dishes and cups, "so
that we can start in a real picnicky spirit. I knew you'd think
it a womanish lunch, Mr. Ferris—Don Ippolito likes what *we*
do—and so I've provided you with a chicken salad—and I'm
going to ask you for a taste of it; I'm really hungry."

There was salad for all, in fact; and it was quite one o'clock
before the lunch was ended, and wraps of just the right thick-
ness and thinness were chosen, and the party were comfortably placed under the striped linen canopy of the gondola,
which they had from a public station, the house-gondola
being engaged that day. They rowed through the narrow
canal skirting the garden out into the expanse before the Giu-
decca, and then struck across the lagoon towards Fusina, past
the island church of San Giorgio in Alga, whose beautiful
tower has flushed and darkened in so many pictures of Venetian sunsets, and past the Austrian lagoon forts with their
coronets of guns threatening every point, and the Croatian
sentinels pacing to and fro on their walls. They stopped long
enough at one of the customs barges to declare to the swarthy
amicable officers the innocence of their freight, and at the
mouth of the Canal of the Brenta, they paused before the
station while a policeman came out and scanned them. He
bowed to Don Ippolito's cloth, and then they began to push
up the sluggish canal, shallow and overrun with weeds and
mosses, into the heart of the land.

The spring which in Venice comes in the softening air and the perpetual azure of the heavens, was renewed to their senses in all its miraculous loveliness. The garden of the Vervains had indeed confessed it in opulence of leaf and bloom, but there it seemed somehow only like a novel effect of the artifice which had been able to create a garden in that city of stone and sea. Here a vernal world suddenly opened before them, with wide-stretching fields of green under a dome of perfect blue; against its walls only the soft curves of far-off hills were traced, and near at hand the tender forms of full-foliaged trees. The long garland of vines that festoons all Italy seemed to begin in the neighboring orchards; the meadows waved their tall grasses in the sun, and broke in poppies as the sea-waves break in iridescent spray; the well-grown maize shook its gleaming blades in the light; the poplars marched in stately procession on either side of the straight white road to Padua till they vanished in the long perspective. The blossoms had fallen from the trees many weeks before, but the air was full of the vague sweetness of the perfect spring which here and there gathered and defined itself as the spicy odor of the grass cut on the shore of the canal, and drying in the mellow heat of the sun.

The voyagers spoke from time to time of some peculiarity of the villas that succeeded each other along the canal. Don Ippolito knew a few of them, the gondoliers knew others; but after all, their names were nothing. These haunts of old time splendor and idleness weary of themselves and unable to escape, are sadder than anything in Venice, and they belonged, as far as the Americans were concerned, to a world as strange as any to which they should go in another life,—the world of a faded fashion and an alien history. Some of the villas were kept in a sort of repair; some were even maintained in the state of old; but the most showed marks of greater or less decay, and here and there one was falling to ruin. They had gardens about them, tangled and wild-grown; a population of decrepit statues in the rococo taste strolled in their walks or simpered from their gates. Two or three houses seemed to be occupied, the rest stood empty, each

"Close latticed to the brooding heat,
And silent in its dusty vines."

The pleasure-party had no fixed plan for the day farther than to ascend the canal, and by and by take a carriage at some convenient village, and drive to the famous Villa Pisani at Strà. "These houses are very well," said Don Ippolito who had visited the villa once, and with whom it had remained a memory almost as signal as that night in Padua when he wore civil dress, "but it is at Strà that you see something really worthy of the royal splendor of the patricians of Venice. Royal? The villa is now one of the palaces of the ex-Emperor of Austria, who does not find it less imperial than his other palaces." Don Ippolito had celebrated the villa at Strà in this strain ever since they had spoken of going up the Brenta: now it was the magnificent conservatories and orangeries that he sang, now the vast garden with its statued walks between rows of clipt cedars and firs, now the stables with their stalls for numberless horses, now the palace itself with its frescoed halls and treasures of art and *vertu*. His enthusiasm for the villa at Strà had become an amiable jest with the Americans. Ferris laughed at his fresh outburst; he declared himself tired of the gondola, and he asked Florida to disembark with him, and walk under the trees of a pleasant street running on one side between the villas and the canal. "We are going to find something much grander than the Villa Pisani," he boasted, with a look at Don Ippolito.

As they sauntered along the path together, they came now and then to a stately palace like that of the Contarini, where the lions that give their name to one branch of the family, crouch in stone before the grand portal; but most of the houses were interesting only from their unstoried possibilities to the imagination. They were generally of stucco, and glared with fresh whitewash through the foliage of their gardens. When a peasant's cottage broke their line, it gave with its barns and straw-stacks, and its beds of potherbs, a homely relief from the decaying gentility of the villas.

"What a pity, Miss Vervain," said the painter, "that the blessings of this world should be so unequally divided! Why should all this sketchable adversity be lavished upon the neighborhood of a city that is so rich as Venice in picturesque dilapidation? It's pretty hard on us Americans, and forces people of sensibility into exile. What wouldn't cultivated persons give for a stretch of this street in the suburbs of Boston, or of your own Providence? I suppose the New Yorkers will be settling up something of the kind, one of these days, and giving it a French name—they'll call it *Aux bords du Brenta*. There was one of them carried back a gondola the other day to put on a pond in their new park. But the worst of it is you can't take home the sentiment of these things."

"I thought it was the business of painters to send home the sentiment of them in pictures," said Florida.

Ferris talked to her in this way because it was his way of talking; it always surprised him a little that she entered into the spirit of it; he was not quite sure that she did; he sometimes thought she waited till she could seize upon a point to turn against him, and so give herself the air of having comprehended the whole. He laughed: "O yes, a poor little, fragmentary, faded-out reproduction of their sentiment—which is 'as moonlight unto sunlight and as water unto wine,' when compared with the real thing. Suppose I made a picture of this very bit, ourselves in the foreground, looking at the garden over there where that amusing Vandal of an owner has just had his statues painted white: would our friends at home understand it? A whole history must be left unexpressed. I could only hint at an entire situation. Of course, people with a taste for olives would get the flavor; but even they would wonder that I chose such an unsuggestive bit. Why, it is just the most maddeningly suggestive thing to be found here! And if I may put it modestly for my share in it, I think we two young Americans looking on at this supreme excess of the rococo, are the very essence of the sentiment of the scene; but what would the honored connoisseurs—the good folks who get themselves up on Ruskin and try so honestly hard to have some little ideas about art—make of us? To be sure they might justifiably praise the grace of your pose, if I were so lucky as to catch it, and your way of putting your hand under the elbow of the arm that holds your parasol." . . . Florida seemed disdainfully to keep her attitude, and the painter smiled. "But they wouldn't know what it all meant, and couldn't imagine that we were inspired by this rascally little villa to sigh longingly over the wicked past"—

"Excuse me," interrupted Florida with a touch of trouble

in her proud manner, "I'm not sighing over it, for one, and
I don't want it back. I'm glad that I'm American and that
there is no past for me. I can't understand how you and Don
Ippolito can speak so tolerantly of what no one can respect,"
she added in almost an aggrieved tone.

If Miss Vervain wanted to turn the talk upon Don Ippolito, Ferris by no means did, he had had enough of that subject yesterday; he got as lightly away from it as he could.

"O, Don Ippolito's a pagan, I tell you; and I'm a painter,
and the rococo is my weakness. I wish I could paint it, but I
can't; I'm a hundred years too late. I couldn't even paint myself in the act of sentimentalizing it."

While he talked, he had been making a few lines in a small
pocket sketch book, with a furtive glance or two at Florida.
When they returned to the boat, he busied himself again with
the book, and presently he handed it to Mrs. Vervain.

"Why, it's Florida!" cried the lady. "How very nicely you
do sketch, Mr. Ferris."

"Thanks, Mrs. Vervain; you're always flattering me."

"No, but seriously. I *wish* that I had paid more attention to
my drawing when I was a girl. And now, Florida—she wont
touch a pencil. I wish you'd talk to her, Mr. Ferris."

"O, people who are pictures needn't trouble themselves to
be painters," said Ferris, with a little burlesque.

Mrs. Vervain began to look at the sketch through her
tubed hand; the painter made a grimace. "But you've made
her too proud, Mr. Ferris. She doesn't look like that."

"Yes she does—to those unworthy of her kindness. I have
taken Miss Vervain in the act of scorning the rococo, and its
humble admirer, me, with it."

"I'm sure *I* don't know what you mean, Mr. Ferris; but I
can't think that this proud look is habitual with Florida; and
I've heard people say—very good judges—that an artist
oughtn't to perpetuate a temporary expression. Something
like that."

"It can't be helped now, Mrs. Vervain: the sketch is irre-
trievably immortal. I'm sorry, but it's too late."

"O, stuff! As if you couldn't turn up the corners of the
mouth a little. Or something."

"And give her the appearance of laughing at me. Never!"

"Don Ippolito," said Mrs. Vervain, turning to the priest, who had been listening intently to all this trivial talk, "what do you think of this sketch?"

He took the book with an eager hand, and perused the sketch as if trying to read some secret there. After a minute he handed it back with a light sigh, apparently of relief, but said nothing.

"Well?" asked Mrs. Vervain.

"Oh! I ask pardon. No, it isn't my idea of madamigella. It seems to me that her likeness must be sketched in color. Those lines are true, but they need color to subdue them; they go too far, they are more than true."

"You're quite right, Don Ippolito," said Ferris.

"Then *you* don't think she always has this proud look?" pursued Mrs. Vervain.

The painter fancied that Florida quelled in herself a movement of impatience; he looked at her with an amused smile.

"Not always, no," answered Don Ippolito. "Sometimes her face expresses the greatest meekness in the world."

"But not at the present moment," thought Ferris, fascinated by the stare of angry pride which the girl bent upon the unconscious priest.

"Though I confess that I should hardly know how to characterize her habitual expression," added Don Ippolito.

"Thanks," said Florida, peremptorily. "I'm tired of the subject; it isn't an important one."

"O yes it is, my dear," said Mrs. Vervain. "At least it's important to me, if it isn't to you; for I'm your mother, and really, if I thought you looked like this, as a general thing, to a casual observer, I should consider it a reflection upon myself." Ferris gave a provoking laugh, as she continued sweetly, "I must insist, Don Ippolito: now did you *ever* see Florida look so!"

The girl leaned back, and began to wave her fan slowly to and fro before her face.

"I never saw her look so with *you*, dear madama," said the priest with an anxious glance at Florida, who let her fan fall folded into her lap, and sat perfectly still. He went on with priestly smoothness, and a touch of something like invoked authority, such as a man might show who could dispense indulgences and inflict penances. "No one could help seeing her devotedness to you, and I have admired from the first an obedience and tenderness that I have never known equalled. In all her relations to you, madamigella has seemed to me"—

Florida started forward. "You are not asked to comment on my behavior to my mother; you are not invited to speak of my conduct at all!" she burst out with sudden violence, her visage flaming, and her blue eyes burning upon Don Ippolito, who shrank from the astonishing rudeness as from a blow in the face. "What is it to you how I treat my mother?"

She sank back again upon the cushions, and opening the fan with a clash swept it swiftly before her.

"Florida!" said her mother gravely.

Ferris turned away in cold disgust like one who has witnessed a cruelty done to some helpless thing. Don Ippolito's speech was not fortunate at the best, but it might have come from a foreigner's misapprehension, and at the worst it was good-natured and well-meant. "The girl is a perfect brute, as I thought in the beginning," the painter said to himself. "How could I have ever thought differently? I shall have to tell Don Ippolito that I'm ashamed of her, and disclaim all responsibility. Pah! I wish I was out of this."

The pleasure of the day was dead. It could not rally from that stroke. They went on to Strà, as they had planned, but the glory of the Villa Pisani was eclipsed for Don Ippolito. He plainly did not know what to do. He did not address Florida again, whose savagery he would not probably have known how to resent if he had wished to resent it. Mrs. Vervain prattled away to him with unrelenting kindness; Ferris kept near him and with affectionate zeal tried to make him talk of the villa; but neither the frescoes, nor the orangeries, nor the greenhouses, nor the stables, nor the gardens could rouse him from the listless daze in which he moved, though Ferris found them all as wonderful as he had said. Amidst this heavy embarrassment no one seemed at ease but the author of it. She did not to be sure speak to Don Ippolito, but she followed her mother as usual with her assiduous cares, and she appeared tranquilly unconscious of the sarcastic civility with which Ferris rendered her any necessary service.

It was late in the afternoon when they got back to their

boat, and began to descend the canal towards Venice, and long before they reached Fusina, the day had passed. A sunset of melancholy red, streaked with level lines of murky cloud stretched across the flats behind them and faintly tinged with its reflected light the eastern horizon which the towers and domes of Venice had not yet begun to break. The twilight came, and then through the overcast heavens the moon shone dim; a light blossomed here and there in the villas, distant voices called musically; a cow lowed, a dog barked; the rich, sweet breath of the vernal land mingled its odors with the sultry air of the neighboring lagoon. The wayfarers spoke little; the time hung heavy on all no doubt; to Ferris it was a burden almost intolerable to hear the creak of the oars and the breathing of the gondoliers keeping time together. At last the boat stopped in front of the police-station in Fusina; a soldier, with a sword at his side and a lantern in his hand came out, and briefly parleyed with the gondoliers; they stepped ashore, and he marched them into the station before him.

"We have nothing left to wish for now," said Ferris, breaking into an ironical laugh.

"What does it all mean?" asked Mrs. Vervain.

"I think I had better go see."

"We will go with you," said Mrs. Vervain.

"Pazienza!" replied Ferris.

The ladies rose; but Don Ippolito remained seated. "Aren't you going too, Don Ippolito?" asked Mrs. Vervain.

"Thanks, madama; but I prefer to stay here."

Lamentable cries and shrieks, as if the prisoners had immediately been put to the torture came from the station, as Ferris opened the door. A lamp of petroleum lighted the scene, and shone upon the figures of two fishermen, who bewailed themselves unintelligibly in the vibrant accents of Chiozza, and from time to time advanced upon the gondoliers, and shook their heads and beat their breasts at them. A few police-guards reclined upon benches about the room, and surveyed the spectacle with mild impassibility.

Ferris politely asked one of them the cause of the detention.

"Why you see, signore," answered the guard amiably,

"these honest men accuse your gondoliers of having stolen a rope out of their boat at Dolo."

"It was my blood, you know," howled the elder of the fishermen, tossing his arms wildly abroad, "it was my own heart," he cried, letting the last vowel die away and rise again in mournful refrain, while he stared tragically into Ferris's face.

"What *is* the matter?" asked Mrs. Vervain, putting up her glasses, and trying with graceful futility to focus this melodrama.

"Nothing," said Ferris, "our gondoliers have had the heart's blood of this respectable Dervish; that is to say they have stolen a rope belonging to him."

"*Our* gondoliers? I don't believe it. They've no right to keep us here all night. Tell them you're the American consul."

"I'd rather not try my dignity on these underlings, Mrs. Vervain; there's no American squadron here that I could order to bombard Fusina if they didn't mind me. But I'll see what I can do further in quality of courteous foreigner. Can you perhaps tell me how long you will be obliged to detain us here?" he asked of the guard again.

"I am very sorry to detain you at all, signore. But what can I do? The commissary is unhappily absent. He may be here soon."

The guard renewed his apathetic contemplation of the gondoliers, who did not speak a word; the windy lamentation of the fishermen rose and fell fitfully. Presently they went out of doors and poured forth their wrongs to the moon.

The room was close, and with some trouble Ferris persuaded Mrs. Vervain to return to the gondola; Florida seconding his arguments with gentle good sense.

It seemed a long time till the commissary came, but his coming instantly simplified the situation. Perhaps because he had never been able to befriend a consul in trouble before, he befriended Ferris to the utmost. He had met him with rather a brow-beating air; but after a glance at his card, he gave a kind of roar of deprecation and apology. He had the ladies and Don Ippolito in out of the gondola, and led them to an upper chamber, where he made them all repose their honored persons upon his sofas. He ordered up his housekeeper to make them coffee, which he served with his own hands, excusing its hurried feebleness, and he stood by rubbing his palms together and smiling while they refreshed themselves.

"They need never tell me again that the Austrians are tyrants," said Mrs. Vervain in undertone to the consul.

It was not easy for Ferris to remind his host of the malefactors; but he brought himself to this ungraciousness. The commissary begged pardon, and asked him to accompany him below, where he confronted the accused and the accusers. The tragedy was acted over again with blood-curdling effectiveness by the Chiozzotti; the gondoliers maintaining the calm of conscious innocence.

Ferris felt outraged by the trumped-up charge against them.

"Listen, you others the prisoners," said the commissary. "Your padrone is anxious to return to Venice, and I wish to inflict no further displeasures upon him. Restore their rope to these honest men, and go about your business."

The injured gondoliers spoke in low tones together; then one of them shrugged his shoulders and went out. He came back in a moment and laid a rope before the commissary.

"Is that the rope?" he asked. "We found it floating down the canal, and picked it up that we might give it to the rightful owner. But now I wish to heaven we had let it sink to the bottom of the sea."

"O, a beautiful story!" wailed the Chiozzotti. They flung themselves upon the rope, and lugged it off to their boat; and the gondoliers went out, too.

The commissary turned to Ferris with an amiable smile. "I am sorry that those rogues should escape," said the American.

"O," said the Italian, "they are poor fellows; it is a little matter; I am glad to have served you."

He took leave of his involuntary guests with effusion, following them with a lantern to the gondola.

Mrs. Vervain, to whom Ferris gave an account of this trial as they set out again on their long-hindered return, had no mind save for the magical effect of his consular quality upon the commissary, and accused him of a vain and culpable modesty.

"Ah," said the diplomatist, "there's nothing like knowing

just *when* to produce your dignity. There are some officials
who know too little,—like those guards, and there are some
who know too much,—like the commissary's superiors. But
he is just in that golden mean of ignorance where he supposes
a consul is a person of importance."

Mrs. Vervain disputed this, and Ferris submitted in silence.
Presently as they skirted the shore to get their bearings for
the route across the lagoon, a fierce voice in Venetian shouted
from the darkness, "*Indrio, indrio!*" (Back, back!) and a gleam
of the moon through the pale watery clouds, revealed the figure of a gendarme on the nearest point of land. The gondoliers bent to their oars, and sent the boat swiftly out into the
lagoon.

"There, for example, is a person who would be quite insensible to my greatness, even if I had the consular seal in my
pocket. To him we are possible smugglers;* and I must say,"
he continued, taking out his watch, and staring hard at it,
"that if I were a disinterested person, and heard his suspicion
met with the explanation that we were a little party out here
for pleasure at half-past twelve p.m., I should say he was
right. At any rate we wont engage him in controversy. Quick,
quick!" he added to the gondoliers, glancing at the receding
shore, and then at the first of the lagoon-forts which they
were approaching. A dim shape moved along the top of the
wall, and seemed to linger and scrutinize them. As they drew
nearer, the challenge, "*Wer da?*" rang out.

The gondoliers eagerly answered with the one word of
German known to their craft, "*Freunde,*" and struggled to
urge the boat forward; the oar of the gondolier in front
slipped from the high row-lock, and fell out of his hand into
the water. The gondola lurched, and then suddenly ran
aground on the shallow. The sentry halted, dropped his gun
from his shoulder, and ordered them to go on, while the gondoliers clamored back in the high key of fear, and one of them
screamed out to his passengers to do something, saying that,
a few weeks before, a sentinel had fired upon a fisherman and
killed him.

"What's that he's talking about?" demanded Mrs. Vervain.

*Under the Austrians, Venice was a free port, but everything carried
thence to the mainland was liable to duty.

"If we don't get on, it will be that man's duty to fire on us; he has no choice," she said, nerved and interested by the presence of this danger.

The gondoliers leaped into the water and tried to push the boat off. It would not move, and without warning, Don Ippolito who had sat silent since they left Fusina, stepped over the side of the gondola, and thrusting an oar under its bottom lifted it free of the shallow.

"O, how very unnecessary!" cried Mrs. Vervain, as the priest and the gondoliers clambered back into the boat. "He will take his death of cold."

"It's ridiculous," said Ferris. "You ought to have told these worthless rascals what to do, Don Ippolito. You've got yourself wet for nothing. It's too bad!"

"It's nothing," said Don Ippolito taking his seat on the little prow-deck, and quietly dripping where the water would not incommode the others.

"O, here!" cried Mrs. Vervain, gathering some shawls together, "make him wrap those about him. He'll die, I know he will—with that reeking skirt of his. If you must go into the water, I wish you had worn your abbate's dress. How *could* you, Don Ippolito?"

The gondoliers set their oars, but before they had given a stroke, they were arrested by a sharp "Halt!" from the fort. Another figure had joined the sentry, and stood looking at them.

"Well," said Ferris, "*now* what, I wonder? That's an officer. If I had a little German about me, I might state the situation to him."

He felt a light touch on his arm. "I can speak German," said Florida, timidly.

"Then you had better speak it now," said Ferris.

She rose to her feet, and in a steady voice, briefly explained the whole affair. The figures listened motionless; then the last comer politely replied, begging her to be in no uneasiness, made her shadowy salute, and vanished. The sentry resumed his walk, and took no farther notice of them.

"Brava!" said Ferris, while Mrs. Vervain babbled her satisfaction, "I will buy a German Ollendorff tomorrow. The language is indispensable to a pleasure excursion in the lagoon."

Florida made no reply, but devoted herself to restoring her mother to that state of defence against the discomforts of the time and place, which the common agitation had impaired. She seemed to have no sense of the presence of any one else. Don Ippolito did not speak again save to protect himself from the anxieties and reproaches of Mrs. Vervain, renewed and reiterated at intervals. She drowsed after a while, and whenever she woke she thought they had just touched her own landing. By fits it was cloudy and moonlight; they began to meet peasants' boats going to the Rialto market; at last, they entered the Canal of the Zattere, then they slipped into a narrow way, and presently stopped at Mrs. Vervain's gate. This time she had not expected it.

Don Ippolito gave her his hand, and entered the garden with her, while Ferris lingered behind with Florida, helping her put together the wraps strewn about the gondola.

"Wait!" she commanded, as they moved up the garden walk. "I want to speak with you about Don Ippolito. What shall I do to him for my rudeness? You *must* tell me—you *shall*," she said in a fierce whisper, gripping the arm which Ferris had given to help her up the landing-stairs. "You are—older than I am!"

"Thanks. I was afraid you were going to say wiser. I should think your own sense of justice, your own sense of"—

"Decency. Say it, say it!" cried the girl passionately; "it was indecent, indecent—that was it!"

—"Would tell you what to do," concluded the painter, dryly.

She flung away the arm to which she had been clinging, and ran to where the priest stood with her mother at the foot of the terrace stairs. "Don Ippolito," she cried, "I want to tell you that I am sorry; I want to ask your pardon—how can you ever forgive me?—for what I said."

She instinctively stretched her hand towards him.

"Oh!" said the priest, with an indescribable long trembling sigh. He caught her hand in his, held it tight, and then pressed it for an instant against his breast.

Ferris made a little start forward.

"Now, that's right, Florida," said her mother, as the four stood in the pale, estranging moonlight. "I'm sure Don Ippolito can't cherish any resentment. If he does, he must come in and wash it out with a glass of wine—that's a good old fashion. I want you to have the wine at any rate, Don Ippolito: it'll keep you from taking cold. You really must."

"Thanks, madama; I cannot lose more time, now, I must go home at once. Good night."

Before Mrs. Vervain could frame a protest, or lay hold of him, he bowed and hurried out of the land-gate.

"How perfectly absurd for him to get into the water in that way," she said, looking mechanically in the direction in which he had vanished.

"Well, Mrs. Vervain, it isn't best to be too grateful to people," said Ferris, "but I think we must allow that if we were in any danger, sticking there in the mud, Don Ippolito got us out of it by putting his shoulder to the oar."

"Of course," assented Mrs. Vervain.

"In fact," continued Ferris, "I suppose we may say that, under Providence, we probably owe our lives to Don Ippolito's self-sacrifice and Miss Vervain's knowledge of German. At any rate, it's what I shall always maintain."

"Mother, don't you think you had better go in?" asked Florida, gently. Her gentleness ignored the presence, the existence of Ferris. "I'm afraid you will be sick after all this fatigue."

"There, Mrs. Vervain, it'll be no use offering *me* a glass of wine. I'm sent away, you see," said Ferris. "And Miss Vervain is quite right. Good night."

"O,—*good* night, Mr. Ferris," said Mrs. Vervain, giving her hand. "Thank you *so* much."

Florida did not look toward him. She gathered her mother's shawl about her shoulders for the twentieth time that day, and softly urged her indoors, while Ferris let himself out into the campo.

IX

FLORIDA BEGAN to prepare the bed for her mother's lying down.

"What are you doing that for, my dear?" asked Mrs. Vervain. "I can't go to bed at once."

"But mother"—

"No, Florida. And I mean it. You are too headstrong. I should think you would see yourself how you suffer in the end by giving way to your violent temper. What a day you have made for us!"

"I was very wrong," murmured the proud girl, meekly.

"And then the mortification of an apology; you might have spared yourself that."

"It didn't mortify me; I didn't care for it."

"No, I really believe you are too haughty to mind humbling yourself. And Don Ippolito had been so uniformly kind to us. I begin to believe that Mr. Ferris caught your true character in that sketch. But your pride will be broken some day, Florida."

"Wont you let me help you undress, mother? You can talk to me while you're undressing. You must try to get some rest."

"Yes, I am all unstrung. Why couldn't you have let him come in and talk awhile? It would have been the best way to get me quieted down. But no; you must always have your own way. Don't twitch me, my dear; I'd rather undress myself. You pretend to be very careful of me. I wonder if you really care for me."

"O mother, you are all I have in the world!"

Mrs. Vervain began to whimper. "You talk as if I were any better off. Have I anybody besides you? And I have lost so many."

"Don't think of those things now, mother."

Mrs. Vervain tenderly kissed the young girl. "You *are* good to your mother. Don Ippolito was right; no one ever saw you offer me disrespect or unkindness. There, there! Don't cry, my darling. I think I *had* better lie down, and I'll let you undress me."

She suffered herself to be helped into bed, and Florida

went softly about the room, putting it in order, and drawing the curtains closer to keep out the near dawn. Her mother talked a little while, and presently fell from incoherence to silence, and so to sleep.

Florida looked hesitatingly at her for a moment, and then set her candle on the floor, and sank wearily into an armchair beside the bed. Her hands fell into her lap; her head drooped sadly forward; the light flung the shadow of her face grotesquely exaggerated and foreshortened upon the ceiling.

By and by a bird piped in the garden; the shriek of a swallow made itself heard from a distance; the vernal day was beginning to stir from the light, brief drowse of the vernal night. A crown of angry red formed upon the candlewick, which toppled over in the socket and guttered out with a sharp hiss.

Florida started from her chair. A streak of sunshine pierced shutter and curtain. Her mother was supporting herself on one elbow in the bed, and looking at her as if she had just called to her.

"Mother, did you speak?" asked the girl.

Mrs. Vervain turned her face away; she sighed deeply, stretched her thin hands on the pillow, and seemed to be sinking, sinking down through the bed. She ceased to breathe and lay in a dead faint.

Florida felt rather than saw it all. She did not cry out nor call for help. She brought water and cologne, and bathed her mother's face, and then chafed her hands. Mrs. Vervain slowly revived; she opened her eyes, then closed them; she did not speak, but after a while she began to fetch her breath with the long and even respirations of sleep.

Florida noiselessly opened the door, and met the servant with a tray of coffee. She put her finger to her lip, and motioned her not to enter, asking in whisper: "What time is it Nina? I forgot to wind my watch."

"It's nine o'clock, signorina; and I thought you would be tired this morning, and would like your coffee in bed. O misericordia!" cried the girl, still in whisper, with a glance through the doorway, "you haven't been in bed at all!"

"My mother doesn't seem well. I sat down beside her, and fell asleep in my chair without knowing it."

"Ah, poor little thing! Then you must drink your coffee at once. It refreshes."

"Yes, yes," said Florida, closing the door, and pointing to a table in the next room, "put it down here. I will serve myself, Nina. Go call the gondola, please. I am going out, at once, and I want you to go with me. Tell Checa to come here and stay with my mother till I come back."

She poured out a cup of coffee with a trembling hand, and hastily drank it; then bathing her eyes, she went to the glass and bestowed a touch or two upon yesterday's toilet, studied the effect a moment and turned away. She ran back for another look, and the next moment she was walking down to the water-gate, where she found Nina waiting her in the gondola.

A rapid course brought them to Ferris's landing. "Ring," she said to the gondolier, "and say that one of the American ladies wishes to see the consul."

Ferris was standing on the balcony over her, where he had been watching her approach in mute wonder. "Why Miss Vervain," he called down, "what in the world is the matter?"

"I don't know. I want to see you," said Florida, looking up with a wistful face.

"I'll come down."

"Yes, please. Or no. I had better come up. Yes, Nina and I will come up."

Ferris met them at the lower door and led them to his apartment. Nina sat down in the outer room, and Florida followed the painter into his studio. Though her face was so wan, it seemed to him that he had never seen it lovelier, and he had a strange pride in her being there, though the disorder of the place ought to have humbled him. She looked over it with a certain childlike, timid curiosity and something of that lofty compassion with which young ladies regard the haunts of men, when they come into them by chance; in doing this she had a haughty, slow turn of the head that fascinated him.

"I hope," he said, "you don't mind the smell," which was a mingled one of oil-colors and tobacco-smoke. "The woman's putting my office to rights, and it's all in a cloud of dust. So I have to bring you in here."

Florida sat down on a chair fronting the easel, and found

herself looking into the sad eyes of Don Ippolito. Ferris brusquely turned the back of the canvas towards her. "I didn't mean you to see that. It isn't ready to show, yet," he said, and then he stood expectantly before her. He waited for her to speak, for he never knew how to take Miss Vervain; he was willing enough to make light of her grand moods, but now she was too evidently unhappy for mocking; at the same time he did not care to invoke a snub by a prematurely sympathetic demeanor. His mind ran on the events of the day before, and he thought this visit probably related somehow to Don Ippolito. But his visitor did not speak, and at last he said: "I hope there's nothing wrong at home, Miss Vervain. It's rather odd to have yesterday, last night and next morning all run together as they have been for me in the last twenty-four hours. I trust Mrs. Vervain is turning the whole thing into a good solid oblivion."

"It's about—it's about—I came to see you," said Florida hoarsely. "I mean," she hurried on to say, "that I want to ask you who is the best doctor here?"

Then it was not about Don Ippolito. "Is your mother sick?" asked Ferris, eagerly. "She must have been fearfully tired by that unlucky expedition of ours. I hope there's nothing serious?"

"No, no! But she is not well. She is very frail, you know. You must have noticed how frail she is," said Florida, tremulously.

Ferris had noticed that all his countrywomen, past their girlhood, seemed to be sick, he did not know how or why; he supposed it was all right, it was so common. In Mrs. Vervain's case, though she talked a great deal about her ill health, he had noticed it rather less than usual, she had so great spirit. He recalled now that he *had* thought her at times rather a shadowy presence, and that occasionally it had amused him that so slight a structure should hang together as it did—not only successfully, but triumphantly.

He said yes, he knew that Mrs. Vervain was not strong, and Florida continued, "It's only advice that I want for her, but I think we had better see some one—or know some one that we could go to in need. We are so far from any one we know, or from help of any kind." She seemed to be trying to account to herself, rather than to Ferris, for what she was doing. "We mustn't let anything pass unnoticed" . . . She looked at him entreatingly, but a shadow, as of some wounding memory, passed over her face, and she said no more.

"I'll go with you to a doctor's," said Ferris, kindly.

"No, please, I wont trouble you."

"It's no trouble."

"I don't *want* you to go with me, please. I'd rather go alone." Ferris looked at her perplexedly, as she rose. "Just give me the address, and I shall manage best by myself. I'm used to doing it."

"As you like. Wait a moment." Ferris wrote the address. "There," he said, giving it to her, "but isn't there anything I can do for you?"

"Yes," answered Florida with awkward hesitation, and a half-defiant, half-imploring look at him. "You must have all sorts of people applying to you, as a consul; and you look after their affairs—and try to forget them"—

"Well," said Ferris.

"I wish you wouldn't remember that I've asked this favor of you; that you'd consider it a"—

"Consular service? With all my heart," answered Ferris, thinking for the third or fourth time how very young Miss Vervain was.

"You are very good; you are kinder than I have any right," said Florida, smiling piteously. "I only mean, don't speak of it to my mother. Not," she added, "but what I want her to know everything I do; but it would worry her if she thought I was anxious about her. O! I wish I wouldn't."

She began a hasty search for her handkerchief; he saw her lips tremble and his soul trembled with them.

In another moment, "Good-morning," she said, briskly, with a sort of airy sob, "I don't want you to come down, please." She drifted out of the room and down the stairs, the servant-maid falling into her wake.

Ferris filled his pipe and went out on his balcony again, and stood watching the gondola in its course towards the address he had given, and smoking thoughtfully. It was really the same girl who had given poor Don Ippolito that cruel slap in the face, yesterday. But that seemed no more out of reason than her sudden, generous, exaggerated remorse; both were of a piece with her coming to him for help now, holding him at a distance, flinging herself upon his sympathy, and then trying to snub him, and breaking down in the effort. It was all of a piece, and the piece was bad; yes she had an ugly temper; and yet she had magnanimous traits too. These contradictions which in his reverie he felt rather than formulated, made him smile, as he stood on his balcony bathed by the morning air and sunlight, in fresh, strong ignorance, of the whole mystery of women's nerves. These caprices even charmed him. He reflected that he had gone on doing the Vervains one favor after another in spite of Florida's childish petulancies; and he resolved that he would not stop now; her whims should be nothing to him, as they had been nothing, hitherto. It is flattering to a man to be indispensable to a woman so long as he is not obliged to it; Miss Vervain's dependent relation to himself in this visit gave her a grace in Ferris's eyes which she had wanted before.

In the meantime he saw her gondola stop, turn round, and come back to the canal that bordered the Vervain garden.

"Another change of mind," thought Ferris, complacently, and rising superior to the whole fitful sex, he released himself from uneasiness on Mrs. Vervain's account. But in the evening he went to ask after her. He first sent his card to Florida, having written on it, "I hope Mrs. Vervain is better. Don't let me come in if it's any disturbance." He looked for a moment at what he had written, dimly conscious that it was patronizing; and when he entered he saw that Miss Vervain stood on the defensive and from some wilfulness meant to make him feel that he was presumptuous in coming. It did not comfort him to consider that she was very young. "Mother will be in directly," said Florida in a tone that relegated their morning's interview to the age of fable.

Mrs. Vervain came in smiling and cordial, apparently better and not worse for yesterday's misadventures. "O, I pick up quickly," she explained. "I'm an old campaigner, you know. Perhaps a little *too* old, now. Years *do* make a difference; and you'll find it out as you get on, Mr. Ferris."

"I suppose so," said Ferris, not caring to have Mrs. Vervain treat him so much like a boy. "Even at twenty-six I found it pleasant to take a nap this afternoon. How does one stand it at seventeen, Miss Vervain?" he asked.

"I haven't felt the need of sleep," replied Florida, indifferently, and he felt shelved, as an old fellow.

He had an empty, frivolous visit to his thinking. Mrs. Vervain asked if he had seen Don Ippolito, and wondered that the priest had not come about, all day. She told a long story, and at the end tapped herself on the mouth with her fan to punish a yawn.

Ferris rose to go. Mrs. Vervain wondered again in the same words why Don Ippolito had not been near them all day.

"Because he's a wise man," said Ferris with bitterness, "and knows when to time his visits." Mrs. Vervain did not notice his bitterness, but something made Florida follow him to the outer door.

"Why it's moonlight!" she exclaimed; and she glanced at him as though she had some purpose of atonement in her mind.

But he would not have it. "Yes, there's a moon," he said, moodily. "Good-night."

"Good-night," answered Florida, and she impulsively offered him her hand. He thought that it shook in his, but it was probably the agitation of his own nerves.

A soreness that had been lifted from his heart, came back; he walked home disappointed and defeated, he hardly knew why or in what. He did not laugh now to think how she had asked him that morning to forget her coming to him for help; he was outraged that he should have been repaid in this sort, and the rebuff with which his sympathy had just been met was vulgar; there was no other name for it but vulgarity. Yet he could not relate this quality to the face of the young girl as he constantly beheld it in his homeward walk. It did not defy him or repulse him; it looked up at him wistfully as from the gondola that morning. Nevertheless he hardened his heart. The Vervains should see him next when they had sent for him. After all, one is not so very old at twenty-six.

X

DON IPPOLITO has come, signorina," said Nina, the next morning, approaching Florida, where she sat, in an attitude of listless patience, in the garden.

"Don Ippolito!" echoed the young girl in a weary tone. She rose and went into the house, and they met with the constraint which was but too natural after the events of their last parting. It is hard to tell which has most to overcome in such a case, the forgiver or the forgiven. Pardon rankles even in a generous soul, and the memory of having pardoned embarrasses the sensitive spirit before the object of its clemency, humbling and making it ashamed. It would be well, I suppose, if there need be nothing of the kind between human creatures, who cannot sustain such a relation without mutual distrust. It is not so ill with them when apart, but when they meet they must be cold and shy at first.

"Now, I see what you two are thinking about," said Mrs. Vervain, and a faint blush tinged the cheek of the priest as she thus paired him off with her daughter. "You are thinking about what happened the other day; and you had better forget it. There is no use brooding over these matters. Dear me, if I had stopped to brood over every little unpleasant thing that happened, I wonder where I should be now? By the way, where were *you* all day yesterday, Don Ippolito?"

"I did not come to disturb you because I thought you must be very tired. Besides, I was quite busy."

"O yes, those inventions of yours. I think you are *so* ingenious! But you mustn't apply too closely. Now really, yesterday—after all you had been through it was too much for the brain." She tapped herself on the forehead with her fan.

"I was not busy with my inventions, madama," answered Don Ippolito, who sat in the womanish attitude priests get from their drapery, and fingered the cord round his three cornered hat. "I have scarcely touched them of late. But our parish takes part in the procession of Corpus Domini in the Piazza, and I had my share of the preparations."

"O, to be sure! When is it to be? We must all go. Our Nina

has been telling Florida of the grand sights,—little children dressed up like John the Baptist, leading lambs. I suppose it's a great event with you."

The priest shrugged his shoulders, and opened both his hands, so that his hat slid to the floor, bumping and tumbling some distance away. He recovered it and sat down again. "It's an observance," he said coldly.

"And shall you be in the procession?"

"I shall be there with the other priests of my parish."

"Delightful!" cried Mrs. Vervain. "We shall be looking out for you. I shall feel greatly honored to think I actually know some one in the procession. I'm going to give you a little nod. You wont think it very wrong?"

She saved him from any embarrassment he might have felt in replying by an abrupt lapse from all apparent interest in the subject. She turned to her daughter, and said with a querulous accent, "I wish you would throw the afghan over my feet, Florida, and make me a little comfortable before you begin your reading this morning." At the same time she feebly disposed herself among the sofa cushions on which she reclined, and waited for some final touches from her daughter. Then she said, "I'm just going to close my eyes, but I shall hear every word. You are getting a beautiful accent, my dear, I know you are. I should think Goldoni must have a very smooth, agreeable style; hasn't he now, in Italian?"

They began to read the comedy; after fifteen or twenty minutes Mrs. Vervain opened her eyes and said, "But before you commence, Florida, I wish you'd play a little to get me quieted down. I feel so very flighty. I suppose it's this sirocco. And I believe I'll lie down in the next room."

Florida followed her to repeat the arrangements for her comfort. Then she returned, and sitting down at the piano struck with a sort of soft firmness, a few low, soothing chords, out of which a lulling melody grew. With her fingers still resting on the keys she turned her stately head, and glanced through the open door at her mother.

"Don Ippolito," she asked softly, "is there anything in the air of Venice that makes people very drowsy?"

"I have never heard that, madamigella."

"I wonder," continued the young girl absently, "why my mother wants to sleep so much."

"Perhaps she has not recovered from the fatigues of the other night," suggested the priest.

"Perhaps," said Florida, sadly looking toward her mother's door.

She turned again to the instrument, and let her fingers wander over the keys, with a drooping head. Presently she lifted her face, and smoothed back from her temples some straggling tendrils of hair. Without looking at the priest she asked with the childlike bluntness that characterized her, "Why don't you like to walk in the procession of Corpus Domini?"

Don Ippolito's color came and went, and he answered evasively, "I have not said that I did not like to do so."

"No, that is true," said Florida, letting her fingers drop again on the keys.

Don Ippolito rose from the sofa where he had been sitting beside her, while they read, and walked the length of the room. Then he came towards her and said meekly, "Madamigella, I did not mean to repel any interest you feel in me. But it was a strange question to ask a priest, as I remembered I was when you asked it."

"Don't you always remember that?" demanded the girl, still without turning her head.

"No, sometimes I am suffered to forget it," he said with a tentative accent.

She did not respond, and he drew a long breath, and walked away in silence. She let her hands fall into her lap, and sat in an attitude of expectation. As Don Ippolito came near her again he paused a second time.

"It is in this house that I forget my priesthood," he began, "and it is the first of your kindnesses that you suffer me to do so, your good mother, there, and you. How shall I repay you? It cut me to the heart that you should ask forgiveness of me, when you did, though I was hurt by your rebuke. O had you not the right to rebuke me if I abused the delicate unreserve with which you had always treated me? But believe me, I meant no wrong, then."

His voice shook, and Florida broke in, "You did nothing wrong. It was I who was cruel for no cause."

"No, no. You shall not say that," he returned. "And why should I have cared for a few words, when all your acts had expressed a trust of me that is like heaven to my soul?"

She turned now and looked at him, and he went on. "Ah, I see you do not understand! How could you know what it is to be a priest in this most unhappy city? To be haunted by the strict espionage of all your own class, to be shunned as a spy by all who are not of it! But you two have not put up that barrier which everywhere shuts me out from my kind. You have been willing to see the man in me, and to let me forget the priest" . . .

"I do not know what to say, to you, Don Ippolito. I am only a foreigner, a girl, and I am very ignorant of these things," said Florida with a slight alarm. "I am afraid that you may be saying what you will be sorry for."

"O never! Do not fear for me if I am frank with you. It is my refuge from despair."

The passionate vibration of his voice increased as if it must break in tears. She glanced towards the other room with a little movement or stir.

"Ah, you needn't be afraid of listening to me!" cried the priest bitterly.

"I will not wake her," said Florida, calmly, after an instant.

"See how you speak the thing you mean, always, always, always! You could not deny that you meant to wake her, for you have the life-long habit of the truth. Do you know what it is to have the life-long habit of a lie? It is to be a priest. Do you know what it is to seem, to say, to do, the thing you are not, think not, will not? To leave what you believe unspoken, what you will undone, what you are unknown? It is to be a priest!"

Don Ippolito spoke in Italian and he uttered these words in a voice carefully guarded from every listener but the one before his face. "Do you know what it is when such a moment as this comes, and you would fling away the whole fabric of falsehood that has clothed your life—do you know what it is to keep still so much of it as will help you to unmask silently and secretly? It is to be a priest!"

His voice had lost its vehemence, and his manner was strangely subdued and cold. The sort of gentle apathy it expressed, together with a certain sad impersonal surprise at the difference between his own and the happier fortune with which he contrasted it, was more touching than any tragic demonstration.

As if she felt the fascination of the pathos which she could not fully analyze the young girl sat silent. After a time, in which she seemed to be trying to think it all out, she asked in a low deep murmur: "Why did you become a priest, then?"

"It is a long story," said Don Ippolito. "I will not trouble you with it now. Some other time."

"No; now," answered Florida, in English. "If you hate so to be a priest, I can't understand why you should have allowed yourself to become one. We should be very unhappy if we could not respect you, not trust you as we have done; and how could we, if we knew you were not true to yourself in being what you are?"

"Madamigella," said the priest, "I never dared believe that I was in the smallest thing necessary to your happiness. Is it true, then, that you care for my being rather this than that? That you are in the least grieved by any wrong of mine?"

"I scarcely know what you mean. How could we help being grieved by what you have said to me?"

"Thanks; but, why do you care whether a priest of my church loves his calling or not,—you a protestant? It is that you are sorry for me as an unhappy man, is it not?"

"Yes; it is that and more. I am no catholic, but we are both Christians"—

Don Ippolito gave the faintest movement of his shoulders.

—"And I cannot endure to think of your doing the things you must do as a priest, and yet hating to be a priest. It is terrible!"

"Are all the priests of your faith devotees?"

"They cannot be. But are none of yours so?"

"O, God forbid that I should say that. I have known real saints among them. That friend of mine in Padua, of whom I once told you, became such, and died an angel fit for Paradise. And I suppose that my poor uncle is a saint too in his way."

"Your uncle? A priest? You have never mentioned him to us."

"No," said Don Ippolito. After a certain pause he began abruptly, "We are of the people, my family, and in each generation we have sought to honor our blood by devoting one of the race to the church. When I was a child, I used to divert myself by making little figures out of wood and pasteboard, and I drew rude copies of the pictures I saw at church. We lived in the house where I live now, and where I was born, and my mother let me play in the small chamber where I now have my forge; it was anciently the oratory of the noble family that occupied the whole palace. I contrived an altar at one end of it; I stuck my pictures about the walls, and I ranged the puppets in the order of worshippers on the floor; then I played at saying mass, and preached to them all day long.

"My mother was a widow. She used to watch me with tears in her eyes. At last, one day, she brought my uncle to see: I remember it all far better than yesterday. 'Is it not the will of God?' she asked. My uncle called me to him, and asked me whether I should like to be a priest in good earnest, when I grew up? 'Shall I then be able to make as many little figures as I like, and to paint pictures, and carve an altar like that in your church?' I demanded. My uncle answered that I should have real men and women to preach to, as he had, and would not that be much finer? In my heart I did not think so, for I did not care for that part of it; I only liked to preach to my puppets because I had made them. But I said, 'O yes,' as children do. I kept on contriving the toys that I played with, and I grew used to hearing it told among my mates and about the neighborhood that I was to be a priest; I cannot remember any other talk with my mother, and I do not know how or when it was decided. Whenever I thought of the matter, I thought, 'That will be very well. The priests have very little to do, and they gain a great deal of money with their masses; and I shall be able to make whatever I like.' I only considered the office then as a means to gratify the passion that has always filled my soul for inventions and works of mechanical skill and ingenuity. My inclination was purely secular, but I was as inevitably becoming a priest as if I had been born to be one."

"But you were not forced? There was no pressure upon you?"

"No, there was merely an absence, so far as they were concerned, of any other idea. I think they meant justly, and assuredly they meant kindly by me. I grew in years, and the time came when I was to begin my studies. It was my uncle's influence that placed me in the Seminary of the Salute, and there I repaid his care by the utmost diligence. But it was not the theological studies that I loved, it was the mathematics and their practical application, and among the classics I loved best the poets and the historians. Yes, I can see that I was always a mundane spirit, and some of those in charge of me at once divined it, I think. They used to take us to walk,— you have seen the little creatures in their priest's gowns, which they put on when they enter the school,—with a couple of young priests at the head of the file; and once, for an uncommon pleasure, they took us to the Arsenal, and let us see the shipyards and the museum. You know the wonderful things that are there: the flags and the guns captured from the Turks; the strange weapons of all devices; the famous suits of armor. I came back half-crazed, I wept that I must leave the place. But I set to work the best I could, to carve out in wood an invention which the model of one of the antique galleys had suggested to me. They found it,—nothing can be concealed outside of your own breast in such a school,—and they carried me with my contrivance before the superior. He looked kindly but gravely at me: 'My son,' said he, 'do you wish to be a priest?' 'Surely, reverend father,' I answered in alarm, 'why not?' 'Because these things are not for priests. Their thoughts must be upon other things. Consider well of it, my son, while there is yet time,' he said, and he addressed me a long and serious discourse upon the life on which I was to enter. He was a just and conscientious and affectionate man; but every word fell like burning fire in my heart. At the end, he took my poor plaything, and thrust it down among the coals of his *scaldino*. It made the scaldino smoke, and he bade me carry it out with me, and so turned again to his book.

"My mother was by this time dead, but I could hardly have gone to her, if she had still been living. 'These things are not for priests!' kept repeating itself night and day in my brain. I was in despair, I was in a fury to see my uncle. I poured out my heart to him, and tried to make him understand the illusions and vain hopes in which I had lived. He received coldly my sorrow and the reproaches which I did not spare him; he bade me consider my inclinations as so many temptations to be overcome for the good of my soul, and the glory of God. He warned me against the scandal of now attempting to withdraw from the path marked out for me. I said that I never would be a priest, 'And what will you do?' he asked. Alas! what could I do? I went back to my prison, and in due course I became a priest. It was not without sufficient warning that I took one order after another, but my uncle's words 'What will you do?' made me deaf to these admonitions. All that is now past. I no longer resent nor hate; I seem to have lost the power; but those were days when my soul was filled with bitterness. Something of this must have showed itself to those who had me in their charge. I have heard that at one time my superiors had grave doubts whether I ought to be allowed to take orders. My examination, in which the difficulties of the sacerdotal life were brought before me with the greatest clearness was severe: I do not know how I passed it; it must have been in grace to my uncle. I spent the next ten days in a convent to meditate upon the step I was about to take. Poor helpless, friendless wretch! Madamigella, even yet I cannot see how I was to blame, that I came forth and received the first of the holy orders, and in their time the second and third.

"I was a priest, but no more a priest at heart than those Venetian conscripts whom you saw carried away last week, are Austrian soldiers. I was bound as they are bound, by an inexorable and inevitable law.

"You have asked me why I became a priest. Perhaps I have not told you why, but I have told you how—I have given you the slight outward events, not the processes of my mind—and that is all that I can do. If the guilt was mine, I have suffered for it. If it was not mine, still I have suffered for it. Some ban seems to have rested upon whatever I have attempted. My work,—O I know it well enough!—has all been cursed with futility; my labors are miserable failures or contemptible successes. I have had my unselfish dreams of blessing mankind by some great discovery or invention; but my life has been barren, barren, barren; and save for the kindness that I have known in this house, and that would not let me despair, it would now be without hope."

He ceased, and the young girl who had listened with her proud looks transfigured to an aspect of grieving pity, fetched a long sigh. "O, I am sorry for you!" she said, "more sorry than I know how to tell. But you must not lose courage, you must not give up!"

Don Ippolito resumed with a melancholy smile. "There are doubtless enough temptations to be false under the best of conditions in this world. But something—I do not know what or whom; perhaps no more my uncle or my mother than I, for they were only as the past had made them— caused me to begin by living a lie, do you not see?"

"Yes, yes," reluctantly assented the girl.

"Perhaps—who knows?—that is why no good has come of me, nor can come. My uncle's piety and repute have always been my efficient help. He is the principal priest of the church to which I am attached, and he has had infinite patience with me. My ambition and my attempted inventions are a scandal to him, for he is a priest of those like the Holy Father, who believe that all the wickedness of the modern world has come from the devices of science; my indifference to the things of religion is a terror and a sorrow to him which he combats with prayers and penances. He starves himself and goes cold and faint that God may have mercy and turn my heart to the things on which his own is fixed. He loves my soul, but not me, and we are scarcely friends."

Florida continued to look at him with steadfast, compassionate eyes. "It seems very strange—almost like some dream," she murmured, "that you should be saying all this to me, Don Ippolito, and I do not know why I should have asked you anything."

The pity of this virginal heart must have been very sweet to the man on whom she looked it. His eyes worshipped her, as he answered her devoutly, "It was due to the truth in you that I should seem to you what I am."

"Indeed, you make me ashamed!" she cried with a blush.

"It was selfish of me to ask you to speak. And now, after what you have told me, I am so helpless and I know so very little that I don't understand how to comfort or encourage you. But surely you can somehow help yourself. Are men, that seem so strong and able, just as powerless as women after all, when it comes to real trouble? Is a man"—

"I cannot answer. I am only a priest," said Don Ippolito coldly, letting his eyes drop to the gown that fell about him like a woman's skirt.

"Yes, but a priest should be a man, and so much more. A priest"—

Don Ippolito shrugged his shoulders.

"No, no!" cried the girl. "Your own schemes have all failed, you say; then why do you not think of becoming a priest in reality, and getting the good there must be in such a calling? It is singular that I should venture to say such a thing to you, and it must seem presumptuous and ridiculous for me, a protestant—but our ways are so different". . . . She paused, coloring deeply, then controlled herself, and added with grave composure, "If you were to pray"—

"To what, madamigella?" asked the priest, sadly.

"To what!" she echoed, opening her eyes full upon him. "To God!"

Don Ippolito made no answer. He let his head fall so low upon his breast that she could see the sacerdotal tonsure.

"You must excuse me," she said, blushing again. "I did not mean to wound your feelings as a Catholic. I have been very bold and intrusive. I ought to have remembered that people of your church have different ideas—that the saints" . . .

Don Ippolito looked up with pensive irony.

"O, the poor saints!"

"I don't understand you," said Florida, very gravely.

"I mean that I believe in the saints as little as you do."

"But you believe in your Church?"

"I have no Church."

There was a silence in which Don Ippolito again dropped his head upon his breast. Florida leaned forward in her eagerness, and murmured, "You believe in God?"

The priest lifted his eyes and looked at her beseechingly. "I do not know," he whispered.

She met his gaze with one of dumb bewilderment. At last she said: "Sometimes you baptize little children and receive them into the church in the name of God?"

"Yes."

"Poor creatures come to you and confess their sins, and you absolve them, or order them to do penances?"

"Yes."

"And sometimes when people are dying, you must stand by their deathbeds and give them the last consolations of religion?"

"It is true."

"Oh!" moaned the girl, and fixed on Don Ippolito a long look of wonder and reproach, which he met with eyes of silent anguish.

"It is terrible, madamigella," he said, rising. "I know it. I would fain have lived single-heartedly, for I think I was made so; but now you see how black and deadly a lie my life is. It is worse than you could have imagined, is it not? It is worse than the life of the cruelest bigot, for he at least believes in himself."

"Worse, far worse!"

"But at least, dear young lady," he went on piteously, "believe me that I have the grace to abhor myself. It is not much, it is very, very little, but it is something. Do not wholly condemn me!"

"Condemn? O I am sorry for you with my whole heart. Only, why must you tell me all this? No, no; you are not to blame. I made you speak; I made you put yourself to shame."

"Not that, dearest madamigella. I would unsay nothing now, if I could, unless to take away the pain I have given you. It has been more a relief than a shame to have all this known to you; and even if you should despise me" . . .

"I don't despise you; that isn't for me; but O, I wish that I could help you!"

Don Ippolito shook his head. "You cannot help me; but I thank you for your compassion; I shall never forget it." He lingered irresolutely with his hat in his hand. "Shall we go on with the reading, madamigella?"

"No, we will not read any more, to-day," she answered.

"Then I relieve you of the disturbance, madamigella," he

said, and after a moment's hesitation he bowed sadly and went.

She mechanically followed him to the door, with some little gestures and movements of a desire to keep him from going, yet let him go, and so turned back and sat down with her hands resting noiseless on the keys of the piano.

XI

THE NEXT MORNING Don Ippolito did not come, but in the afternoon the postman brought a letter for Mrs. Vervain, couched in the priest's English begging her indulgence until after the day of Corpus Christi, up to which time, he said, he should be too occupied for his visits of ordinary.

This letter reminded Mrs. Vervain that they had not seen Mr. Ferris for three days, and she sent to ask him to dinner. But he returned an excuse, and he was not to be had to breakfast the next morning for the asking. He was in open rebellion. Mrs. Vervain had herself rowed to the consular landing, and sent up her gondolier with another invitation to dinner.

The painter appeared on the balcony in the linen blouse which he wore at his work, and looked down with a frown on the smiling face of Mrs. Vervain for a moment without speaking. Then, "I'll come," he said gloomily.

"Come with *me*, then," returned Mrs. Vervain.

"I shall have to keep you waiting."

"I don't mind that. You'll be ready in five minutes."

Florida met the painter with such gentleness that he felt his resentment to have been a stupid caprice, for which there was no ground in the world. He tried to recall his fading sense of outrage, but he found nothing in his mind but penitence. The sort of distraught humility with which she behaved gave her a novel fascination.

The dinner was good, as Mrs. Vervain's dinners always were, and there was a compliment to the painter in the presence of a favorite dish. When he saw this, "Well, Mrs. Vervain, what is it?" he asked. "You needn't pretend that you're treating me so well, for nothing. You want something."

"We want nothing but that you should not neglect your friends. We have been utterly deserted for three or four days. Don Ippolito has not been here, either; but *he* has some excuse: he has to get ready for Corpus Christi. He's going to be in the procession."

"Is he to appear with his flying machine, or his portable dining-table, or his automatic camera?"

97

"For shame!" cried Mrs. Vervain, beaming reproach. Florida's face clouded, and Ferris made haste to say that he did not know these inventions were sacred, and that he had no wish to blaspheme them.

"You know well enough what I meant," answered Mrs. Vervain. "And now, we want you to get us a window to look out on the procession."

"O, *that's* what you want, is it? I thought you merely wanted me not to neglect my friends."

"Well, do you call that neglecting them?"

"Mrs. Vervain, Mrs. Vervain! What a mind you have! Is there anything else you want? Me to go with you for example?"

"We don't insist. You can take us to the window and leave us, if you like."

"This clemency is indeed unexpected," replied Ferris. "I'm really quite unworthy of it."

He was going on with the badinage customary between Mrs. Vervain and himself, when Florida protested,—

"Mother, I think we abuse Mr. Ferris's kindness."

"I know it, my dear, I know it," cheerfully assented Mrs. Vervain. "It's perfectly shocking. But what are we to do? We must abuse *somebody's* kindness."

"We had better stay at home. I'd much rather not go," said the girl, tremulously.

"Why, Miss Vervain," said Ferris gravely, "I'm very sorry if you've misunderstood my joking. I've never yet seen the procession to advantage, and I'd like very much to look on with you."

He could not tell whether she was grateful for his words, or annoyed. She resolutely said no more, but her mother took up the strain and discoursed long upon it, arranging all the particulars of their meeting and going together. Ferris was a little piqued, and began to wonder why Miss Vervain did not stay at home if she did not want to go. To be sure she went everywhere with her mother; but it was strange that she should, with her habitual violent submissiveness, have said anything in opposition to her mother's wish or purpose.

After dinner, Mrs. Vervain frankly withdrew for her nap, and Florida seemed to make a little haste to take some sewing in her hand, and sat down with the air of a woman willing to detain her visitor. Ferris was not such a stoic as not to be dimly flattered by this, but he was too much of a man to be fully aware how great an advance it might seem.

"I suppose we shall see most of the priests of Venice and what they are like, in the procession to morrow," she said. "Do you remember speaking to me about priests, the other day, Mr. Ferris?"

"Yes, I remember it very well. I think I overdid it; and I couldn't perceive afterwards that I had shown any motive but a desire to make trouble for Don Ippolito."

"I never thought that," answered Florida, seriously. "What you said was true, wasn't it?"

"Yes, it was and it wasn't, and I don't know that it differed from anything else in the world, in that respect. It is true that there is a great distrust of the priests amongst the Italians. The young men hate them—or think they do—or say they do. Most educated men in middle life are materialists, and of course unfriendly to the priests. There are even women who are skeptical about religion. But I suspect that the largest number of all those who talk loudest against the priests are really subject to them. You must consider how very intimately they are bound up with every family in the most solemn relations of life."

"Do you think the priests are generally bad men?" asked the young girl shyly.

"I don't, indeed. I don't see how things could hang together if it were so. There must be a great basis of sincerity and goodness in them, when all is said and done. It seems to me that at the worst they're merely professional people— poor fellows who have gone into the church for a living. You know it isn't often now that the sons of noble families take orders; the priests are mostly of humble origin; not that they're necessarily the worse for that: the patricians used to be just as bad in another way."

"I wonder," said Florida with her head on one side considering her seam, "why there is always something so dreadful to us in the idea of a priest."

"They *do* seem a kind of alien creature to us Protestants. I can't make out whether they seem so to Catholics, or not.

But we have a repugnance to all doomed people, haven't we? And a priest is a man under sentence of death to the natural ties between himself and the human race. He is dead to us. That makes him dreadful. The spectre of our dearest friend, father or mother, would be terrible. And yet," added Ferris, musingly, "a nun isn't terrible."

"No," answered the girl, "that's because a woman's life even in the world seems to be a constant giving up. No, a nun isn't unnatural, but a priest is."

She was silent for a time in which she sewed swiftly; then she suddenly dropped her work into her lap, and pressing it down with both hands, she asked, "Do you believe that priests themselves are ever skeptical about religion?"

"I suppose it must happen, now and then. In the best days of the church, it was a fashion to doubt, you know. I've often wanted to ask our friend Don Ippolito something about these matters, but I didn't see how it could be managed." Ferris did not note the change that passed over Florida's face, and he continued. "Our acquaintance hasn't become so intimate as I hoped it might. But you only get to a certain point with Italians. They like to meet you on the street; maybe they haven't any *indoors*."

"Yes, it must sometimes happen as you say," replied Florida, with a quick sigh, reverting to the beginning of Ferris's answer. "But is it any worse for a false priest than for a hypocritical minister?"

"It's bad enough for either, but it's worse for the priest. You see, Miss Vervain, a minister doesn't set up for so much. He doesn't pretend to forgive us our sins, and he doesn't ask us to confess them; he doesn't offer us the veritable body and blood at the sacrament, and he doesn't bear allegiance to the visible and tangible vice-gerent of Christ upon earth. A hypocritical parson may be absurd; but a skeptical priest is tragical."

"Yes, O yes, I see" murmured the girl with a grieving face. "Are they always to blame for it? They must be induced, sometimes to enter the church before they've seriously thought about it, and then don't know how to escape from the path that has been marked out for them from their childhood. Should you think such a priest as that was to blame for being a skeptic?" she asked very earnestly.

"No," said Ferris, with a smile at her seriousness, "I should think such a skeptic as that was to blame for being a priest."

"Shouldn't you be very sorry for him?" pursued Florida still more solemnly.

"I should, indeed, if I liked him. If I didn't, I'm afraid I shouldn't," said Ferris; but he saw that his levity jarred upon her. "Come, Miss Vervain, you're not going to look at those fat monks and sleek priests in the procession to-morrow as so many incorporate tragedies, are you? You'll spoil my pleasure if you do. I dare say they'll be all of them devout believers, accepting everything down to the animalculae in the holy water."

"If *you* were that kind of a priest," persisted the girl, without heeding his jests, "what should you do?"

"Upon my word, I don't know. I can't imagine it. Why," he continued, "think what a helpless creature a priest is in everything but his priesthood—more helpless than a woman, even. The only thing he could do would be to leave the church, and how could he do that? He's *in* the world, but he isn't *of* it, and I don't see what he could do with it, or it with him. If an Italian priest were to leave the church, even the liberals who distrust him now would despise him still more. Do you know that they have a pleasant fashion of calling the Protestant converts apostates? The first thing for such a priest would be exile. But I'm not supposably the kind of priest you mean, and I don't think just such a priest supposable. I dare say if a priest found himself drifting into doubt, he'd try to avoid the disagreeable subject, and if he couldn't, he'd philosophize it some way, and wouldn't let his skepticism worry him."

"Then you mean that they haven't consciences like us?"

"They have consciences, but not like us. The Italians are kinder people than we are, but they're not so just, and I should say that they don't think truth the chief good of life. They believe there are pleasanter and better things. Perhaps they're right."

"No, no; you don't believe that, you know you don't," said Florida, anxiously. "And you haven't answered my question."

"O yes, I have. I've told you it wasn't a supposable case."

"But suppose it was."

"Well, if I must," answered Ferris with a laugh. "With my unfortunate bringing up, I couldn't say less than that such a man ought to get out of his priesthood at any hazard. He should cease to be a priest if it cost him kindred, friends, good fame, country, everything. I don't see how there can be any living in such a lie, though I know there is. In all reason, it ought to eat the soul out of a man, and leave him helpless to do or be any sort of good. But there seems to be something, I don't know what it is, that is above all reason of ours, something that saves each of us for good in spite of the bad that's in us. It's very good practice, for a man who wants to be modest, to come and live in a Latin country. He learns to suspect his own topping virtues, and to be lenient to the novel combinations of right and wrong that he sees. But as for our insupposable priest, yes, I should say decidedly he ought to get out of it by all means."

Florida fell back in her chair with an aspect of such relief as comes to one from confirmation on an important point. She passed her hand over the sewing in her lap, but did not speak.

Ferris went on, with a doubting look at her, for he had been shy of introducing Don Ippolito's name since the day on the Brenta, and he did not know what effect a recurrence to him in this talk might have. "I've often wondered if our own clerical friend were not a little shaky in his faith. I don't think nature meant him for a priest. He always strikes me as an extremely secular-minded person. I doubt if he's ever put the question whether he is what he professes to be, squarely to himself—he's such a mere dreamer."

Florida changed her posture slightly, and looked down at her sewing. She asked, "But shouldn't you abhor him if he were a skeptical priest?"

Ferris shrugged his shoulders. "O, I don't find it such an easy matter to abhor people. It would be interesting," he continued musingly, "to have such a dreamer waked up, once, and suddenly confronted with what he recognized as perfect truthfulness, and couldn't help contrasting himself with. But it would be a little cruel."

"Would you rather have him left as he was?" asked Florida, lifting her eyes to his.

"As a moralist, no; as a humanitarian, yes, Miss Vervain. He'd be much happier as he was."

"What time ought we to be ready for you to-morrow?" demanded the girl in a tone of decision.

"We ought to be in the Piazza by nine o'clock," said Ferris carelessly accepting the change of subject; and he told her of his plan for seeing the procession from a window of the Old Procuratie. When he rose to go, he said lightly, "Perhaps, after all, we *may* see the type of tragical priest we've been talking about. Who can tell? I say his nose will be red."

"Perhaps," answered Florida with unheeding gravity.

XII

THE DAY was one of those which can come to the world only in early June at Venice. The heaven was without a cloud, but a blue haze made mystery of the horizon where the lagoon and sky met unseen. The breath of the sea bathed in freshness the city at whose feet her tides sparkled and slept.

The great Square of St. Mark was transformed from a mart, from a *salon* to a temple. The shops under the colonnades that enclose it upon three sides were shut; the caffès before which the circles of idle coffee-drinkers and sherbet-eaters ordinarily spread out into the piazza were repressed to the limits of their own doors; the stands of the water-vendors, the baskets of those that sold oranges of Palermo and black cherries of Padua had vanished from the base of the church of St. Mark, which with its dim splendor of mosaics and its carven luxury of pillar and arch and finial rose like the high-altar, ineffably rich and beautiful, of the vaster temple whose enclosure it completed. Before it stood the three great red flagstaffs, like painted tapers before an altar, and from them hung the Austrian flags of red and white, and yellow and black. In the middle of the square stood the Austrian military band motionless, encircling their leader with his gold-headed staff uplifted. During the night a light colonnade of wood, roofed with blue cloth, had been put up around the inside of the Piazza, and under this now paused the long pomp of the ecclesiastical procession: the priests of all the Venetian churches in their richest vestments, followed in their order by *facchini* in white sandals and gay robes with caps of scarlet, white, green, and blue, who bore huge painted candles and silken banners displaying the symbol or the portrait of the titular saints of the several churches and supported the canopies under which the host of each was elevated. Before the clergy went a company of Austrian soldiers, and behind the facchini came a long array of religious societies, charity-school boys in uniforms, old paupers in holiday dress, little naked urchins with shepherds' crooks and bits of fleece about their loins like John the Baptist in the wilderness, little girls with angels' wings and crowns, the monks of the various orders, and civilian penitents of all sorts in cloaks or dress coats, hooded or bareheaded, and carrying each a lighted taper. The corridors under the Imperial Palace and the New and Old Procuratie were packed with spectators; from every window up and down the fronts of the palaces, gay stuffs were flung; the startled doves of St. Mark perched upon the cornices, or fluttered uneasily to and fro above the crowd.

The baton of the band leader descended with a clash of martial music, the priests chanted, the charity-boys sang shrill, a vast noise of shuffling feet arose, mixed with the foliage-like rustling of the sheets of tinsel attached to the banners and candles in the procession: the whole strange, gorgeous picture came to life.

After all her plans and preparations, Mrs. Vervain had not felt well enough that morning to come to the spectacle which she had counted so much upon seeing, but she had therefore insisted the more that her daughter should go, and Ferris now stood with Florida alone at a window in the Old Procuratie.

"Well, what do you think, Miss Vervain?" he asked, when their senses had somewhat accustomed themselves to the noise of the procession, "do you say now that Venice is too gloomy a city to have ever had any possibility of gayety in her?"

"I *never* said that," answered Florida, opening her eyes upon him.

"Neither did I," returned Ferris, "but I've often thought it, and I'm not sure now but I'm right. There's something extremely melancholy to me in all this. I don't care so much for what one may call the deplorable superstition expressed in the spectacle, but the mere splendid sight and the music are enough to make one shed tears. I don't know anything more affecting except a procession of lantern-lit gondolas and barges on the Grand Canal. It's phantasmal. It's the spectral resurrection of the old dead forms into the present. It's not even the ghost, it's the corpse, of other ages that's haunting Venice. The city ought to have been destroyed by Napoleon when he destroyed the Republic, and thrown overboard St. Mark, Winged Lion, Bucentaur and all. There is no land like

America for true cheerfulness and light-heartedness. Think of our Fourth of Julys and our State Fairs. Selah!"

Ferris looked into the girl's serious face with twinkling eyes. He liked to embarrass her gravity with his antic speeches, and enjoyed her endeavors to find an earnest meaning in them, and her evident trouble when she could find none.

"I'm curious to know how our friend will look," he began again, as he arranged the cushion on the window sill for Florida's greater comfort in watching the spectacle, "but it wont be an easy matter to pick him out in this masquerade, I fancy. Candle-carrying, as well as the other acts of devotion, seems rather out of character with Don Ippolito, and I can't imagine his putting much soul into it. However, very few of the clergy appear to do that. Look at those holy men with their eyes to the wind! They are wondering who is the *bella bionda* at the window here."

Florida listened to his persiflage with an air of sad distraction. She was intent upon the procession as it approached from the other side of the Piazza, and she replied at random to his comments on the different bodies that formed it.

"It's very hard to decide which are my favorites," he continued, surveying the long column through an opera-glass. "My religious disadvantages have been such that I don't care much for priests or monks, or young John the Baptists or small female cherubim, but I do like little charity-boys with voices of pins and needles and hair cut *à la* dead-rabbit. I should like, if it were consistent with the consular dignity, to go down and rub their heads. I'm fond, also, of *old* charity-boys, I find. Those paupers make me in love with destitute and dependent age by their aspect of irresponsible enjoyment. See how briskly each of them topples along on the leg that he hasn't got in the grave! How attractive likewise are the civilian devotees in those imperishable dress-coats of theirs. Observe their high coat-collars of the era of the Holy Alliance: they and their fathers and their grandfathers before them have worn those dress-coats; in a hundred years from now their posterity will keep holiday in them. I should like to know the elixir, by which the dress coats of civil employees render themselves immortal. Those penitents in the cloaks and cowls, are not bad, either, Miss Vervain. Come, they add a very pretty touch of mystery to this spectacle. They're the sort of thing that painters are expected to paint in Venice— that people sigh over as so peculiarly Venetian. If you've a single sentiment about you, Miss Vervain, now is the time to produce it."

"But I haven't. I'm afraid I have no sentiment at all," answered the girl ruefully. "But this makes me dreadfully sad."

"Why that's just what I was saying a while ago. Excuse me, Miss Vervain, but your sadness lacks novelty; it's a sort of plagiarism."

"Don't, please," she pleaded yet more earnestly. "I was just thinking—I don't know why such an awful thought should come to me—that it might all be a mistake after all; perhaps there might not be any other world, and every bit of this power and display of the church—*our* church as well as the rest—might be only a cruel blunder, a dreadful mistake. Perhaps there isn't even any God! Do *you* think there is?"

"I don't *think* it," said Ferris gravely, "I *know* it. But I don't wonder that this sight makes you doubt. Great God! How far it is from Christ! Look there, at those troops who go before the followers of the Lamb: their trade is murder. In a minute, if a dozen men called out 'Long live the King of Italy!' it would be the duty of those soldiers to fire into the helpless crowd. Look at the silken and gilded pomp of the servants of the carpenter's son! Look at those miserable monks, voluntary prisoners, beggars, aliens to their kind! Look at those penitents who think that they can get forgiveness for their sins by carrying a candle round the Square! And it is nearly two thousand years since the world turned Christian! It *is* pretty slow. But I suppose God lets men learn him from their own experience of evil. I imagine the kingdom of Heaven is a sort of republic and that God draws men to Him only through their perfect freedom."

"Yes, yes, it must be so," answered the girl, staring down on the crowd with unseeing eyes, "but I can't fix my mind on it. I keep thinking the whole time of what we were talking about, yesterday. I never could have dreamt of a priest's disbelieving; but now I can't dream of anything else. It seems to me that none of these priests or monks can believe anything. Their faces look false and sly and bad—*all* of them!"

"No, no, Miss Vervain," said Ferris, smiling at her despair, "you push matters a little beyond—as a woman has a right to do, of course. I don't think their faces are bad, by any means. Some of them are dull and torpid and some are frivolous— just like the faces of other people. But I've been noticing the number of good, kind, friendly faces, and they're in the majority, just as they are amongst other people; for there are very few souls altogether out of drawing, in my opinion. I've even caught sight of some faces in which there was a real rapture of devotion, and now and then a very innocent one. Here, for instance, is a man I should like to bet on, if he'd only look up."

The priest whom Ferris indicated was slowly advancing toward the space immediately under their window. He was dressed in robes of high ceremony, and in his hand he carried a lighted taper. He moved with a gentle tread and the droop of his slender figure intimated a sort of despairing weariness. While most of his fellows stared carelessly or curiously about them, his face was downcast and averted.

Suddenly the procession paused, and a hush fell upon the vast assembly. Then the silence was broken by the rustle and stir of all those thousands going down upon their knees, as the cardinal-patriarch lifted his hands to bless them.

The priest upon whom Ferris and Florida had fixed their eyes faltered a moment, and before he knelt his next neighbor had to pluck him by the skirt. Then he too knelt hastily, mechanically lifting his head, and glancing along the front of the Old Procuratie. His face had that weariness in it which his figure and movement had suggested, and it was very pale, but it was yet more singular for the troubled innocence which its traits expressed.

"There," whispered Ferris, "that's what I call an uncommonly good face."

Florida raised her hand to silence him, and the heavy gaze of the priest rested on them coldly at first. Then a light of recognition shot into his eyes and a flush suffused his pallid visage, which seemed to grow the more haggard and desperate. His head fell again and he dropped the candle from his hand. One of those beggars who went by the side of the procession to gather the drippings of the tapers, restored it to him.

"Why," said Ferris aloud, "it's Don Ippolito! Did you know him at first?"

XIII

THE LADIES were sitting on the terrace when Don Ippolito came next morning to say that he could not read with Miss Vervain that day nor for several days after, alleging in excuse some priestly duties proper to the time. Mrs. Vervain began to lament that she had not been able to go to the procession of the day before. "I meant to have kept a sharp look-out, for you; Florida saw you, and so did Mr. Ferris. But it isn't at all the same thing, you know. Florida has no faculty for describing things; and now I shall probably go away from Venice without seeing you in your real character, once."

Don Ippolito suffered this and more in meek silence. He waited his opportunity with unfailing politeness, and then with gentle punctilio took his leave.

"Well, come again as soon as your duties will let you, Don Ippolito," cried Mrs. Vervain. "We shall miss you dreadfully, and I begrudge every one of your readings that Florida loses."

The priest passed with the sliding step which his impeding drapery imposed, down the garden walk, and was half-way to the gate, when Florida who had stood watching him, said to her mother, "I must speak to him again," and lightly descended the steps, and swiftly glided in pursuit.

"Don Ippolito!" she called.

He already had his hand upon the gate, but he turned, and rapidly went back to meet her.

She stood in the walk where she had stopped when her voice arrested him, breathing quickly. Their eyes met; a painful shadow overcast the face of the young girl, who seemed to be trying in vain to speak.

Mrs. Vervain put on her glasses and peered down at the two with good-natured curiosity.

"Well, madamigella," said the priest at last, "what do you command me?" He gave a faint, patient sigh.

The tears came into her eyes. "O," she began vehemently, "I wish there was some one who had the right to speak to you!"

"No one," answered Don Ippolito, "has so much the right as you."

"I saw you yesterday," she began again, "and I thought of what you had told me, Don Ippolito."

"Yes, I thought of it, too," answered the priest. "I have thought of it ever since."

"But haven't you thought of any hope for yourself? Must you still go on as before? How can you go back now to those things, and pretend to think them holy, and all the time have no heart or faith in them? It's terrible!"

"What would you, madamigella?" demanded Don Ippolito, with a moody shrug. "It is my profession, my trade, you know. You might say to the prisoner," he added bitterly, " 'It is terrible to see you chained here.' Yes, it is terrible. O, I don't reject your compassion! But what can I do?"

"Sit down with me here," said Florida in her blunt, child-like way, and sank upon the stone seat beside the walk. She clasped her hands together in her lap with some strong, bashful emotion, while Don Ippolito, obeying her command, waited for her to speak. Her voice was scarcely more than a hoarse whisper when she began.

"I don't know how to begin what I want to say. I am not fit to advise any one. I am so young, and so very ignorant of the world."

"I too know little of the world," said the priest as much to himself as to her.

"It may be all wrong, all wrong. Besides," she said abruptly, "how do I know that you are a good man, Don Ippolito? How do I know that you've been telling me the truth? It may be all a kind of trap" . . . .

He looked blankly at her.

"This is in Venice; and you may be leading me on to say things to you that will make trouble for my mother and me. You may be a spy" . . . .

"O no, no, no!" cried the priest springing to his feet with a kind of moan, and a shudder, "God forbid!" He swiftly touched her hand with the tips of his fingers, and then kissed them: an action of inexpressible humility. "Madamigella, I swear to you by everything you believe good that I would rather die than be false to you in a single breath or thought."

"O I know it, I know it," she murmured. "I don't see how I could say such a cruel thing". . .

"Not cruel, no, madamigella; not cruel," softly pleaded Don Ippolito.

"But—but, is there *no* escape for you?"

They looked stedfastly at each other for a moment, and then Don Ippolito spoke.

"Yes," he said very gravely, "there is one way of escape. I have often thought of it, and once I thought I had taken the first step towards it; but it is beset with many great obstacles, and to be a priest makes one timid and insecure."

He lapsed into his musing melancholy with the last words; but she would not suffer him to lose whatever heart he had begun to speak with. "That's nothing," she said, "you must think again of that way of escape, and never turn from it till you have tried it. Only take the first step and you can go on. Friends will rise up everywhere, and make it easy for you. Come," she implored him fervently, "you must promise."

He bent his dreamy eyes upon her.

"If I should take this only way of escape, and it seemed desperate to all others, would you still be my friend?"

"I should be your friend if the whole world turned against you."

"Would you be my friend," he asked eagerly in lower tones, and with signs of an inward struggle, "if this way of escape were for me to be no longer a priest?"

"O yes, yes! Why not?" cried the girl; and her face glowed with heroic sympathy and defiance. It is from this heaven-born ignorance in women of the insuperable difficulties of doing right that men take fire, and accomplish the sublime impossibilities. Our sense of details, our fatal habits of reasoning, paralyze us; we need the impulse of the pure ideal which we can get only from them. These two were alike children as regarded the world, but he had a man's dark prevision of the means, and she a heavenly scorn of everything but the end to be achieved.

He drew a long breath. "Then it does not seem terrible to you?"

"Terrible? No! I don't see how you can rest till it is done!"

"Is it true, then, that you urge me to this step, which indeed I have so long desired to take?"

"Yes it is true. Listen, Don Ippolito: it is the very thing that I hoped you would do, but I wanted you to speak of it first. You must have all the honor of it, and I am glad you thought of it before. You will never regret it!"

She smiled radiantly upon him, and he kindled at her enthusiasm. In another moment his face darkened again. "But it will cost much," he murmured.

"No matter," cried Florida. "Such a man as you ought to leave the priesthood at any risk or hazard. You should cease to be a priest, if it cost you kindred, friends, good fame, country, everything!" She blushed with irrelevant consciousness. "Why need you be downhearted? With your genius once free you can make country and fame and friends everywhere. Leave Venice. There are other places. Think how inventors succeed in America". . . .

"In America!" exclaimed the priest. "Ah, how long I have desired to be there!"

"You must go. You will soon be famous and honored there, and you shall not be a stranger, even at the first. Do you know that we are going home very soon? Yes, my mother and I have been talking of it to-day. We are both homesick, and you see that she is not well. You shall come to us there, and make our house your home till you have formed some plans of your own. Everything will be easy. God *is* good," she said in a breaking voice, "and you may be sure he will befriend you."

"Some one," answered Don Ippolito, with tears in his eyes, "has already been very good to me. I thought it was you, but I will call it God!"

"Hush! You mustn't say such things. But you must go, now. Take time to think, but not too much time. Only, be true to yourself."

They rose and she laid her hand on his arm with an instinctive gesture of appeal. He stood bewildered. Then, "Thanks, madamigella, thanks," he said, and caught her fragrant hand to his lips. He loosed it and lifted both his arms by a blind impulse in which he arrested himself with a burning blush, and turned away. He did not take leave of her with his wonted formalities, but hurried abruptly toward the gate.

A panic seemed to seize her as she saw him open it. She ran after him. "Don Ippolito, Don Ippolito," she said, coming up to him, and stammered and faltered. "I don't know: I am frightened. You must do nothing from me; I cannot let you; I'm not fit to advise you. It must be wholly from your own conscience. O no, don't look so! I *will* be your friend whatever happens. But if what you think of doing has seemed so terrible to you, perhaps it *is* more terrible than I can understand. If it is the only way, it is right. But is there no other? What I mean is, have you no one to talk all this over with? I mean can't you speak of it to—to Mr. Ferris? He is so true and honest and just."

"I was going to him," said Don Ippolito with a dim trouble in his face.

"O, I am so glad of that! Remember, I don't take anything back. No matter what happens, I will be your friend. But he will tell you just what to do."

Don Ippolito bowed and opened the gate.

Florida went back to her mother, who asked her, "What in the world have you and Don Ippolito been talking about so earnestly? what makes you so pale and out of breath?"

"I have been wanting to tell you, mother," said Florida. She drew her chair in front of the elder lady, and sat down.

XIV

ON IPPOLITO did not go directly to the painter's. He walked toward his house at first, and then turned aside, and wandered out through the noisy and populous district of Canaregio to the Campo di Marte. A squad of cavalry which had been going through some exercises there was moving off the parade ground; a few infantry soldiers were strolling about under the trees. Don Ippolito walked across the field to the border of the lagoon, where he began to pace to and fro, with his head sunk in deep thought. He moved rapidly, but sometimes he stopped, and stood still in the sun whose heat he did not seem to feel, though a perspiration bathed his pale face, and stood in drops on his forehead under the shadow of his nicchio. Some little dirty children of the poor with which this region swarms, looked at him from the sloping shore of the Campo di Giustizia, where the executions used to take place, and a small boy began to mock his movements and pauses, but was arrested by one of the girls who shook him and gesticulated warningly.

At this point, the long railroad bridge which connects Venice with the mainland, is in full sight, and now from the reverie in which he continued, whether he walked or stood still, Don Ippolito was roused by the whistle of an outward train. He followed it with his eye as it streamed along over the far-stretching arches, and struck out into the flat salt marshes beyond. When the distance hid it, he put on his hat, which he had unknowingly removed, and turned his rapid steps towards the railroad station. Arrived there, he lingered in the vestibule for half an hour, watching the people as they bought their tickets for departure, and had their baggage examined by the customs officers, and weighed and registered by the railroad porters, who passed it through the wicket shutting out the train, while the passengers gathered up their smaller parcels and took their way to the waiting-rooms. He followed a group of English people some paces in this direction, and then returned to the wicket, through which he looked long and wistfully at the train. The baggage was all passed through; the doors of the waiting-rooms were thrown open with harsh proclamation by the guards, and the passengers flocked into the carriages. Whistles and bells were sounded, and the train crept out of the station.

A man in the company's uniform approached the unconscious priest, and striking his hands softly together, said with a pleasant smile, "Your servant, Don Ippolito. Are you expecting some one?"

"Ah, good day!" answered the priest, with a little start. "No," he added, "I was not looking for any one."

"I see," said the other. "Amusing yourself as usual with the machinery. Excuse the freedom, Don Ippolito; but you ought to have been of our profession,—ha, ha! When you have the leisure, I should like to show you the drawing of an American locomotive which a friend of mine has sent me from Nuova York. It is very different from ours, very curious. But monstrous in size, you know, prodigious. May I come with it to your house, some evening?"

"You will do me a great pleasure," said Don Ippolito. He gazed dreamily in the direction of the vanished train. "Was that the train for Milan?" he asked presently.

"Exactly," said the man.

"Does it go all the way to Milan?"

"Oh no! It stops at Peschiera, where the passengers have their passports examined; and then another train backs down from Desenzano and takes them on to Milan. And after that," continued the man with animation, "if you are on the way to England, for example, another train carries you to Susa, and there you get the diligence over the mountain to St. Michel, where you take railroad again, and so on up through Paris to Boulogne-sur-Mer, and then by steamer to Folkestone, and then by railroad to London and to Liverpool. It is at Liverpool that you go on board the steamer for America, and piff! in ten days you are in Nuova York. My friend has written me all about it."

"Ah yes, your friend. Does he like it there in America?"

"Passably, passably. The Americans have no manners; but they are good devils. They are governed by the Irish. And the wine is dear. But he likes America, yes, he likes it. Nuova

York is a fine city. But immense, you know! Eight times as large as Venice!"

"Is your friend prosperous there?"

"Ah heigh! That is the prettiest part of the story. He has made himself rich. He is employed by a large house to make designs for mantelpieces, and marble tables, and tombs; and he has—listen!—six hundred francs a month!"

"O per Bacco!" cried Don Ippolito.

"Honestly. But you spend a great deal there. Still, it is magnificent, is it not? If it were not for that blessed war there, now, that would be the place for you, Don Ippolito. He tells me the Americans are actually mad for inventions. Your servant. Excuse the freedom, you know," said the man, bowing and moving away.

"Nothing, dear, nothing," answered the priest. He walked out of the station with a light step, and went to his own house where he sought the room in which his inventions were stored. He had not touched them for weeks. They were all dusty and many were cobwebbed. He blew the dust from some, and bringing them to the light, examined them critically, finding them mostly disabled in one way or other, except the models of the portable furniture, which he polished with his handkerchief, and set apart, surveying them from a distance with a look of hope. He took up the breech-loading cannon, and then suddenly put it down again with a little shiver, and went to the threshold of the perverted oratory, and glanced in at his forge. Veneranda had carelessly left the window open, and the draught had carried the ashes about the floor. On the cinder-heap lay the tools which he had used in mending the broken pipe of the fountain at Casa Vervain, and had not used since. The place seemed chilly even on that summer's day. He stood in the doorway with clenched hands. Then he called Veneranda, chid her for leaving the window open, and bade her close it, and so quitted the house and left her muttering.

Ferris seemed surprised to see him when he appeared at the consulate near the middle of the afternoon, and seated himself in the place where he was wont to pose for the painter.

"Were you going to give me a sitting?" asked the latter,

hesitating. "The light is horrible, just now, with this glare from the canal. Not that I manage much better when it's good. I don't get on with you, Don Ippolito. There are too many of you. I shouldn't have known you in the procession yesterday."

Don Ippolito did not respond. He rose and went towards his portrait on the easel, and examined it long, with a curious minuteness. Then he returned to his chair, and continued to look at it. "I suppose that it resembles me a great deal," he said, "and yet I do not *feel* like that. I hardly know what is the fault. It is as I should be if I were like other priests, perhaps?"

"I know it's not good," said the painter. "It *is* conventional, in spite of everything. But here's that first sketch I made of you."

He took up a canvas facing the wall, and set it on the easel. The character in this charcoal sketch was vastly sincerer and sweeter.

"Ah!" said Don Ippolito, with a sigh and smile of relief, "that is immeasurably better. I wish I could speak to you, dear friend, in a mood of yours as sympathetic as this picture records, of some matters that concern me very nearly. I have just come from the railroad station."

"Seeing some friends off?" asked the painter, indifferently, hovering near the sketch with a bit of charcoal in his hand, and hesitating whether to give it a certain touch. He glanced with half-shut eyes at the priest.

Don Ippolito sighed again. "I hardly know. I was seeing off my hopes, my desires, my prayers, that followed the train to America!"

The painter put down his charcoal, dusted his fingers, and looked at the priest without saying anything.

"Do you remember when I first came to you?" asked Don Ippolito.

"Certainly," said Ferris. "Is it of that matter you want to speak to me? I'm very sorry to hear it, for I don't think it practical."

"Practical, practical!" cried the priest hotly. "Nothing is practical till it has been tried. And why should I not go to America?"

"Because you can't get your passport, for one thing," answered the painter dryly.

"I have thought of that," rejoined Don Ippolito more patiently. "I can get a passport for France from the Austrian authorities here, and at Milan there must be ways by which I could change it for one from my own king"—it was by this title that patriotic Venetians of those days spoke of Victor Emmanuel—"that would carry me out of France into England."

Ferris pondered a moment. "That is quite true," he said. "Why hadn't you thought of that when you first came to me?"

"I cannot tell. I didn't know that I could even get a passport for France till the other day."

Both were silent, while the painter filled his pipe. "Well," he said presently, "I'm very sorry. I'm afraid you're dooming yourself to many bitter disappointments in going to America. What do you expect to do there?"

"Why, with my inventions"—

"I suppose," interrupted the other, putting a lighted match to his pipe, "that a painter must be a very poor sort of American: his first thought is of coming to Italy. So I know very little directly about the fortunes of my inventive fellow countrymen, or whether an inventor has any prospect of making a living. But once when I was at Washington I went into the Patent Office, where the models of the inventions are deposited; the building is about as large as the Ducal Palace, and it is full of them. The people there told me nothing was commoner than for the same invention to be repeated over and over again by different inventors. Some few succeed, and then they have law-suits with the infringers of their patents; some sell out their inventions for a trifle to companies that have capital, and that grow rich upon them; the great number can never bring their ideas to the public notice at all. You can judge for yourself what your chances would be. You have asked me why you should not go to America. Well, because I think you would starve there."

"I am used to that," said Don Ippolito; "and besides, until some of my inventions became known, I could give lessons in Italian."

"O, bravo!" said Ferris, "you prefer instant death, then?"

"But madamigella seemed to believe that my success as an inventor would be assured, there."

Ferris gave a very ironical laugh. "Miss Vervain must have been about twelve years old when she left America. Even a lady's knowledge of business at that age is limited. When did you talk with her about it? You had not spoken of it to me, of late, and I thought you were more contented than you used to be."

"It is true," said the priest. "Sometimes within the last two months I have almost forgotten it."

"And what has brought it so forcibly to your mind again?"

"That is what I so greatly desire to tell you," replied Don Ippolito, with an appealing look at the painter's face. He moistened his parched lips a little, waiting for further question from the painter, to whom he seemed a man fevered by some strong emotion and at that moment not quite wholesome. Ferris did not speak, and Don Ippolito began again: "Even though I have not said so in words to you, dear friend, has it not appeared to you that I have no heart in my vocation?"

"Yes. I have sometimes fancied that. I had no right to ask you why."

"Some day I will tell you, when I have the courage to go all over it again. It is partly my own fault, but it is more my miserable fortune. But wherever the wrong lies, it has at last become intolerable to me. I cannot endure it any longer and live. I must go away, I must fly from it."

Ferris shrank from him a little, as men instinctively do from one who has set himself upon some desperate attempt. "Do you mean, Don Ippolito, that you are going to renounce your priesthood?"

Don Ippolito opened his hands and let his priesthood, as it were, drop to the ground.

"You never spoke of this before when you talked of going to America. Though to be sure" . . .

"Yes, yes!" replied Don Ippolito with vehemence, "but now an angel has appeared and shown me the blackness of my life."

Ferris began to wonder if he or Don Ippolito were not perhaps mad.

"An angel, yes," the priest went on, rising from his chair, "an angel whose immaculate truth has mirrored my falsehood in all its vileness and distortion —to whom, if it destroys me I cannot devote less than a truthfulness like hers!"

"Hers, hers?" cried the painter, with a sudden pang. "Whose? Don't speak in these riddles. Whom do you mean?"

"Whom can I mean but only one—madamigella!" . . .

"Miss Vervain? Do you mean to say that Miss Vervain has advised you to renounce your priesthood?"

"In as many words she has bidden me forsake it at any risk,—at the cost of kindred, friends, good fame, country, everything."

The painter passed his hand confusedly over his face. These were his own words, the words he had used in speaking with Florida of the supposed skeptical priest. He grew very pale. "May I ask," he demanded in a hard, dry voice, "how she came to advise such a step?"

"I can hardly tell. Something had already moved her to learn from me the story of my life—to know that I was a man with neither faith nor hope. Her pure heart was torn by the thought of my wrong and of my error. I had never seen myself in such deformity as she saw me even when she used me with that divine compassion. I was almost glad to be what I was because of her angelic pity for me!"

The tears sprang to Don Ippolito's eyes, but Ferris asked in the same tone as before, "Was it then that she bade you be no longer a priest?"

"No, not then," patiently replied the other; "she was too greatly overwhelmed with my calamity to think of any cure for it. To-day it was that she uttered those words—words which I shall never forget, which will support and comfort me whatever happens!"

The painter was biting hard upon the stem of his pipe. He turned away and began ordering the color-tubes and pencils on a table against the wall,—putting them close together in very neat straight rows. Presently he said: "Perhaps Miss Vervain also advised you to go to America?"

"Yes," answered the priest reverently. "She had thought of everything. She has promised me a refuge under her mother's roof there until I can make my inventions known; and I shall follow them at once."

"Follow them?"

"They are going, she told me. Madama does not grow better. They are homesick. They—but you must know all this already?"—

"O not at all, not at all," said the painter with a very bitter smile. "You are telling me news. Pray go on."

"There is no more. She made me promise to come to you and listen to your advice before I took any step. I must not trust to her alone, she said; but if I took this step, then through whatever happened she would be my friend. Ah, dear friend, may I speak to you of the hope that these words gave me? You have seen—have you not?—you must have seen that". . . .

The priest faltered, and Ferris stared at him helpless. When the next words came he could not find any strangeness in the fact which yet gave him so great a shock. He found that to his nether consciousness it had been long familiar, ever since that day when he had first jestingly proposed Don Ippolito as Miss Vervain's teacher. Grotesque, tragic, impossible—it had still been the undercurrent of all his reveries; or so now it seemed to have been.

Don Ippolito anxiously drew nearer to him and laid an imploring touch upon his arm . . . "I love her". . . .

"What!" gasped the painter. "You . . . you! A priest?"

"Priest! Priest!" cried Don Ippolito violently. "From this day I am no longer a priest! From this hour I am a man, and I can offer her the honorable love of a man, the truth of a most sacred marriage, and fidelity to death!"

Ferris made no answer. He began to look very coldly and haughtily at Don Ippolito, whose heat died away under his stare, and who at last met it with a glance of tremulous perplexity. His hand had dropped from Ferris's arm, and he now moved some steps from him. "What is it, dear friend?" he besought him. "Is there something that offends you? I came to you for counsel, and you meet me with a repulse little short of enmity. I do not understand. Do I intend anything wrong without knowing it? O, I conjure you to speak plainly!"

"Wait. Wait a minute," said Ferris, waving his hand like a man tormented by a passing pain. "I am trying to think. What you say is . . . I cannot imagine it."

"Not imagine it? Not imagine it? And why? Is she not beautiful?"

"Yes."

"And good?"

"Without doubt."

"And young, and yet wise beyond her years? And true, and yet angelically kind?"

"It is all as you say, God knows. But . . . a priest" . . .

"Oh! Always that accursed word! And at heart, what is a priest, then, but a man?—a wretched, masked, imprisoned, banished man! Has he not blood and nerves like you? Has he not eyes to see what is fair, and ears to hear what is sweet? Can he live near so divine a flower and not know her grace, not inhale the fragrance of her soul, not adore her beauty? O great God! And if at last he would tear off his stifling mask, escape from his prison, return from his exile, would you gainsay him?"

"No!" said the painter with a kind of groan. He sat down in a tall carven gothic chair,—the furniture of one of his pictures,—and rested his head against its high back and looked at the priest across the room. "Excuse me," he continued with a strong effort. "I am ready to befriend you to the utmost of my power. What was it you wanted to ask me? I have told you truly what I thought of your scheme of going to America; but I may very well be mistaken. Was it about that Miss Vervain desired you to consult me?" His voice and manner hardened again in spite of him. "Or did she wish me to advise you about the renunciation of your priesthood? You must have thought that carefully over for yourself."

"Yes, I do not think you could make me see that as a greater difficulty than it has appeared to me." He paused with a confused and daunted air as if some important point had slipped his mind. "But I must take the step; the burden of the double part I play is unendurable, is it not?"

"You know better than I."

"But if you were such a man as I, with neither love for your vocation nor faith in it, should you not cease to be a priest?"

"If you ask me in that way: yes," answered the painter. "But I advise you nothing. I could not counsel another in such a case."

"But you think and feel as I do," said the priest, "and I am right, then."

"I do not say you are wrong."

Ferris was silent while Don Ippolito moved up and down the room, with his sliding step like some tall, gaunt, unhappy girl. Neither could put an end to this interview, so full of intangible, inconclusive misery. Ferris drew a long breath, and then said steadily, "Don Ippolito, I suppose you did not speak idly to me of your—your feeling for Miss Vervain, and that I may speak plainly to you in return."

"Surely," answered the priest, pausing in his walk, and fixing his eyes upon the painter. "It was to you as the friend of both that I spoke of my love, and my hope—which is oftener my despair."

"Then you have not much reason to believe that she returns your—feeling?"

"Ah, how could she consciously return it? I have been hitherto a priest to her, and the thought of me would have been impurity. But hereafter, if I can prove myself a man, if I can win my place in the world . . . . No, even now, why should she care so much for my escape from these bonds, if she did not care for me more than she knew?"

"Have you ever thought of that extravagant generosity of Miss Vervain's character?"

"It is divine!"

"Has it seemed to you that if such a woman knew herself to have once wrongly given you pain, her atonement might be as headlong and excessive as her offence? That she could have no reserves in her reparation?"

Don Ippolito looked at Ferris but did not interpose.

"Miss Vervain is very religious in her way, and she is truth itself. Are you sure that it is not concern for what seems to her your terrible position that has made her show so much anxiety on your account?"

"Do I not know that well? Have I not felt the balm of her most heavenly pity?"

"And may she not be only trying to appeal to something in you as high as the impulse of her own heart?"

"As high!" cried Don Ippolito, almost angrily, "Can there be any higher thing in heaven or on earth than love for such a woman?"

"Yes; both in heaven and on earth," answered Ferris.

"I do not understand you," said Don Ippolito with a puzzled stare.

Ferris did not reply. He fell into a dull revery in which he seemed to forget Don Ippolito and the whole affair. At last the priest spoke again. "Have you nothing to say to me, signore?"

"I? What is there to say?" returned the other blankly.

"Do you know any reason why I should not love her save that I am—have been—a priest?"

"No, I know none," said the painter, wearily.

"Ah," exclaimed Don Ippolito, "there is something on your mind that you will not speak. I beseech you not to let me go wrong. I love her so well that I would rather die than let my love offend her. I am a man with the passions and hopes of a man, but without a man's experience, or a man's knowledge of what is just and right in these relations. If you can be my friend in this so far as to advise or warn me; if you can be her friend" . . .

Ferris abruptly rose and went to his balcony and looked out upon the Grand Canal. The time-stained palace opposite had not changed in the last half hour. As on many another summer day he saw the black boats going by. A heavy, high-pointed barge from the Sile, with the captain's family at dinner in the shade of a matting on the roof moved sluggishly down the middle current. A party of Americans in a gondola, with their opera-glasses and guide-books in their hands, pointed out to each other the eagle on the consular arms. They were all like sights in a mirror, or things in a world turned upside down.

Ferris came back and looked dizzily at the priest, trying to believe that this unhuman, sacerdotal phantasm had been telling him that it loved a beautiful young girl of his own race, faith and language.

"Will you not answer me, signore?" meekly demanded Don Ippolito.

"In this matter," replied the painter, "I cannot advise or warn you. The whole affair is beyond my conception. I mean no unkindness; but I cannot consult with you about it. There are reasons why I should not. The mother of Miss Vervain is here with her, and I do not feel that her interests in such a matter are in my hands. If they come to me for help, that is different. What do you wish? You tell me that you are resolved to renounce the priesthood and go to America; and I have answered you to the best of my power. You tell me that you are in love with Miss Vervain. What can I have to say about that?"

Don Ippolito stood listening with a patient, and then a wounded air. "Nothing," he answered proudly. "I ask your pardon for troubling you with my affairs. Your former kindness emboldened me too much. I shall not trespass again. It was my ignorance, which I pray you to excuse. I take my leave, signore."

He bowed, and moved out of the room, and a dull remorse filled the painter, as he heard the outer door close after him. But he could do nothing. If he had given a wound to the heart that trusted him, it was in an anguish which he had not been able to master, and whose causes he could not yet define. It was all a shapeless torment; it held him like the memory of some hideous nightmare prolonging its horror beyond sleep. It seemed impossible that what had happened should have happened.

It was long, as he sat in the chair from which he had talked with Don Ippolito, before he could reason about what had been said; and then the worst phase presented itself first. He could not help seeing that the priest might have found cause for hope in the girl's behavior toward him. Her violent resentments and her equally violent repentances; her fervent interest in his unhappy fortunes and her anxiety that he should at once forsake the priesthood; her urging him to go to America, and her promising him a home under her mother's roof there, why might it not all be in fact a proof of her tenderness for him? She might have found it necessary to be thus coarsely explicit with him, for a man in

Don Ippolito's relation to her could not otherwise have imagined her interest in him. But her making use of Ferris to confirm her own purposes by his words, her repeating them so that they should come back to him from Don Ippolito's lips; her letting another man go with her to look upon the procession in which her priestly lover was to appear in his sacerdotal panoply, these things could not be accounted for except by that strain of insolent passionate defiance which he had noted in her from the beginning. Why should she first tell Don Ippolito of their going away? "Well, I wish him joy of his bargain," said Ferris aloud and rising, shrugged his shoulders, and tried to cast off all care of a matter that did not concern him. But one does not so easily cast off a matter that does not concern one. He found himself haunted by certain tones and looks and attitudes of the young girl, wholly alien to the character he had just constructed for her. They were childlike, trusting, unconscious, far beyond anything he had yet known in women, and they appealed to him now with a maddening pathos. She was standing there before Don Ippolito's picture as on that morning when she came to Ferris, looking anxiously at him, her innocent beauty, troubled with some hidden care, hallowing the place. Ferris thought of the young fellow who told him that he had spent three months in a dull German town because he had the room there that was once occupied by the girl who had refused him; the painter remembered that the young fellow said he had just read of her marriage in an American newspaper.

Why did Miss Vervain send Don Ippolito to him? Was it some scheme of her secret love for the priest; or mere coarse resentment of the cautions Ferris had once hinted, a piece of vulgar bravado? But if she had acted throughout in pure simplicity, in unwise goodness of heart? If Don Ippolito were altogether self-deceived, and nothing but her unknowing pity had given him grounds of hope? He himself had suggested this to the priest, and now with a different motive he looked at it in his own behalf. A great load began slowly to lift itself from Ferris's heart, which could ache now for this most unhappy priest. But if this conjecture were just, his duty would be different. He must not coldly acquiesce and let things take

their course. He had introduced Don Ippolito to the Vervains; he was in some sort responsible for him; he must save
them if possible from the painful consequences of the priest's
hallucination. But how to do this was by no means clear. He
blamed himself for not having been franker with Don Ippolito and tried to make him see that the Vervains might regard
his passion as a presumption upon their kindness to him, an
abuse of their hospitable friendship; and yet how could he
have done this without outrage to a sensitive and right-mean-
ing soul? For a moment it seemed to him that he must seek
Don Ippolito, and repair his fault, but they had hardly parted
as friends, and his action might be easily misconstrued. If he
shrank from the thought of speaking to him of the matter
again it appeared yet more impossible to bring it before the
Vervains. Like a man of the imaginative temperament as he
was, he exaggerated the probable effect, and pictured their
dismay in colors that made his interference seem a ludicrous
enormity; in fact it would have been an awkward business
enough for one not hampered by his intricate obligations. He
felt bound to the Vervains, the ignorant young girl, and the
addlepated mother; but if he ought to go to them and tell
them what he knew, to which of them ought he to speak, and
how? In an anguish of perplexity that made the sweat stand
in drops upon his forehead, he smiled to think it just possible
that Mrs. Vervain might take the matter seriously, and wish
to consider the propriety of Florida's accepting Don Ippolito.
But if he spoke to the daughter, how should he approach the
subject? "Don Ippolito tells me he loves you, and he goes to
America with the expectation that when he has made his fortune with a patent back-action apple-corer, you will marry
him." Should he say something to this purport? And in
heaven's name what right had he, Ferris, to say anything at
all? The horrible absurdity, the inexorable delicacy of his position made him laugh.

On the other hand, besides, he was bound to Don Ippolito,
who had come to him as the nearest friend of both, and confided in him. He remembered with a tardy, poignant intelligence how in their first talk of the Vervains Don Ippolito had
taken pains to inform himself that Ferris was not in love with
Florida. Could he be less manly and generous than this poor

priest, and violate the sanctity of his confidence? Ferris groaned aloud. No, contrive it as he would, call it by what fine name he chose, he could not commit this treachery. It was the more impossible to him because in this agony of doubt as to what he should do, he now at least read his own heart clearly, and had no longer a doubt what was in it. He pitied her for the pain she must suffer. He saw how her simple goodness, her blind sympathy with Don Ippolito, and only this must have led the priest to the mistaken pass at which he stood. But Ferris felt that the whole affair had been fatally carried beyond his reach; he could do nothing now but wait and endure. There are cases in which a man must not protect the woman he loves. This was one.

The afternoon wore away. In the evening he went to the Piazza, and drank a cup of coffee at Florian's. Then he walked to the Public Gardens, where he watched the crowd till it thinned in the twilight and left him alone. He hung upon the parapet, looking off over the lagoon that at last he perceived to be flooded with moonlight. He desperately called a gondola, and bade the man row him to the public landing nearest the Vervains', and so walked up the calle, and entered the palace from the campo, through the court that on one side opened into the garden.

Mrs. Vervain was alone in the room where he had always been accustomed to find her daughter with her, and a chill as of the impending change fell upon him. He felt how pleasant it had been to find them together; with a vain, piercing regret he felt how much like home the place had been to him. Mrs. Vervain, indeed, was not changed; she was even more than ever herself, though all that she said imported change. She seemed to observe nothing unwonted in him, and she began to talk in her way of things that she could not know were so near his heart.

"Now, Mr. Ferris, I have a little surprise for you. Guess what it is!"

"I'm not good at guessing. I'd rather not know what it is than have to guess it," said Ferris, trying to be light, under his heavy trouble.

"You wont try once, even? Well, you're going to be rid of us soon. We are going away."

"Yes, I knew that," said Ferris, quietly. "Don Ippolito told me so to-day."

"And is that all you have to say? Isn't it rather sad? Isn't it sudden? Come, Mr. Ferris, do be a little complimentary, for once!"

"It's sudden, and I can assure you it's sad enough for me," replied the painter in a tone which could not leave any doubt of his sincerity.

"Well, so it is for us," quavered Mrs. Vervain. "You have been very, very good to us," she went on more collectedly, "and we shall never forget it. Florida has been speaking of it too, and she's extremely grateful, and thinks we've quite imposed upon you."

"Thanks."

"I suppose we have, but as I always say, you're the representative of the country here. However, that's neither here nor there. We have no relatives on the face of the earth, you know; but I have a good many old friends in Providence, and we're going back there. We both think I shall be better at home; for I'm sorry to say, Mr. Ferris, that though I don't complain of Venice—it's really a beautiful place, and all that; not the least exaggerated—still I don't think it's done my health much good; or at least I don't seem to gain, don't you know; I don't seem to gain."

"I'm very sorry to hear it, Mrs. Vervain."

"Yes, I'm sure you are; but you see, don't you, that we must go? We are going next week. When we've once made up our minds, there's no object in prolonging the agony."

Mrs. Vervain adjusted her glasses with the thumb and finger of her right hand, and peered into Ferris's face with a gay smile. "But the greatest part of the surprise is," she resumed, lowering her voice a little, "that Don Ippolito is going with us."

"Ah!" cried Ferris sharply.

"I *knew* I should surprise you," laughed Mrs. Vervain. "We've been having a regular confab—*clave*, I mean—about it here, and he's all on fire to go to America; though it must be kept a great secret on his account, poor fellow. He's to join us in France, and then he can easily get into England, with us. You know he's to give up being a priest, and is going to devote himself to invention when he gets to America. Now, what *do* you think of it, Mr. Ferris? Quite strikes you dumb, doesn't it?" triumphed Mrs. Vervain. "I suppose it's what you would call a wild-goose chase—I used to pick up all those phrases—but we shall carry it through."

Ferris gasped, as though about to speak, but said nothing.

"Don Ippolito's been here the whole afternoon," continued Mrs. Vervain, "or rather ever since about five o'clock. He took dinner with us, and we've been talking it over and over. He's *so* enthusiastic about it, and yet he breaks down every little while, and seems quite to despair of the undertaking. But Florida wont let him do that; and really it's funny the way he defers to her judgment—you know *I* always regard Florida as such a mere child—and seems to take every word she says for gospel. But, shedding tears, now: it's dreadful in a man, isn't it? I wish Don Ippolito wouldn't do that. It makes one creep. I can't feel that it's manly; can you?"

Ferris found voice to say something about those things being different with the Latin races.

"Well, at any rate," said Mrs. Vervain, "I'm glad that *Americans* don't shed tears, as a general *rule*. Now, Florida: you'd think she was the man all through this business, she's so perfectly heroic about it, that is, outwardly: for I can see— women can, in each other, Mr. Ferris—just where she's on the point of breaking down, all the while. Has she ever spoken to you about Don Ippolito? She does think so highly of your opinion, Mr. Ferris."

"She does me too much honor," said Ferris, with ghastly irony.

"O, I don't think so," returned Mrs. Vervain. "She told me this morning that she'd made Don Ippolito promise to speak to you about it; but he didn't mention having done so, and . . . I hated, don't you know, to ask him . . . In fact, Florida had told me beforehand that I mustn't. She said he must be left entirely to himself in the matter, and". . . Mrs. Vervain looked suggestively at Ferris.

"He spoke to me about it," said Ferris.

"Then, why in the world did you let me run on? I suppose you advised him against it."

"I certainly did."

"Well, there's where I think woman's intuition is better than man's reason."

The painter silently bowed his head.

"Yes, I'm quite women's rights in that respect," said Mrs. Vervain.

"O, without doubt," answered Ferris, aimlessly.

"I'm perfectly delighted," she went on, "at the idea of Don Ippolito's giving up the priesthood, and I've told him he must get married to some good American girl. You ought to have seen how the poor fellow blushed! But really, you know there are lots of nice girls that would *jump* at him—so handsome and sad-looking and a genius."

Ferris could only stare helplessly at Mrs. Vervain, who continued:

"Yes, *I* think he's a genius, and I'm determined that he shall have a chance. I suppose we've got a job on our hands; but I'm not sorry. I'll introduce him into society, and if he needs money he shall have it. What does God give us money for, Mr. Ferris, but to help our fellow-creatures?"

So miserable, as he was, from head to foot, that it seemed impossible he could endure more, Ferris could not forbear laughing at this burst of piety.

"What are you laughing at?" asked Mrs. Vervain, who had cheerfully joined him. "Something I've been saying. Well, you wont have me to laugh at much longer. I do wonder whom you'll have next."

Ferris's merriment died away in something like a groan, and when Mrs. Vervain again spoke, it was in a tone of sudden querulousness. "I *wish* Florida would come! She went to bolt the land-gate after Don Ippolito—I wanted her to—but she ought to have been back long ago. It's odd you didn't meet them, coming in. She must be in the garden, somewhere—I suppose she's sorry to be leaving it. But I need her. Would you be so very kind, Mr. Ferris, as to go and ask her to come to me?"

Ferris rose heavily from the chair in which he seemed to have grown ten years older. He had hardly heard anything that he did not know already, but the clear vision of the affair with which he had come to the Vervains was hopelessly confused and darkened. He could make nothing of any phase of it. He did not know whether he cared now to see Florida or not. He mechanically obeyed Mrs. Vervain, and stepping out upon the terrace, slowly descended the stairway.

The moon was shining brightly into the garden.

XV

Florida and Don Ippolito had paused in the pathway which parted at the fountain and led in one direction to the water-gate, and in the other out through the palace-court into the campo.

"Now, you must not give way to despair again," she said to him. "You will succeed, I am sure, for you will deserve success."

"It is all your goodness, madamigella," sighed the priest, "and at the bottom of my heart I am afraid that all the hope and courage I have are also yours."

"You shall never want for hope and courage, then. We believe in you, and we honor your purpose, and we will be your stedfast friends. But now you must think only of the present—of how you are to get away from Venice. O, I can understand how you must hate to leave it! What a beautiful night! You mustn't expect such moonlights as this in America, Don Ippolito."

"It *is* beautiful, is it not?" said the priest, kindling from her. "But I think we Venetians are never so conscious of the beauty of Venice as you strangers are."

"I don't know. I only know that now since we have made up our minds to go, and fixed the day and hour, it is more like leaving my own country than anything else I've ever felt. This garden, I seem to have spent my whole life in it; and when we are settled in Providence, I'm going to have mother send back for some of these statues. I suppose Signor Cavaletti wouldn't mind our robbing his place of them if he were paid enough. At any rate we must have this one that belongs to the fountain. You shall be the first to set the fountain playing over there, Don Ippolito, and then we'll sit down on this stone bench before it, and imagine ourselves in the garden of Casa Vervain at Venice."

"No, no; let me be the last to set it playing here," said the priest, quickly stooping to the pipe at the foot of the figure, "and then we will sit down here, and imagine ourselves in the garden of Casa Vervain at Providence."

Florida put her hand on his shoulder: "You mustn't do it," she said simply. "The padrone doesn't like to waste the water."

"O we'll pray the saints to rain it back on him some day," cried Don Ippolito with wilful levity, and the stream leaped into the moonlight and seemed to hang there like a tangled skein of silver.

"But how shall I shut it off when you are gone?" asked the young girl, looking ruefully at the floating threads of splendor.

"O I will shut it off before I go," answered Don Ippolito. "Let it play a moment," he continued, gazing rapturously upon it, while the moon painted his lifted face with a pallor that his black robes heightened. He fetched a long, sighing breath as if he inhaled with that respiration all the rich odors of the flowers, blanched like his own visage in the white lustre; as if he absorbed into his heart at once the wide glory of the summer night, and the beauty of the young girl at his side. It seemed a supreme moment with him; he looked as a man might look who has climbed out of life-long defeat into a single instant of release and triumph.

Florida sank upon the bench before the fountain, indulging his caprice with that sacred motherly tolerance, some touch of which is in all womanly yielding to men's will, and which was perhaps present in greater degree in her feeling towards a man more than ordinarily orphaned and unfriended.

"Is Providence your native city?" asked Don Ippolito abruptly, after a little silence.

"O no, I was born at St. Augustine in Florida."

"Ah yes, I forgot; madama has told me about it: Providence is *her* city. But the two are near together?"

"No," said Florida, compassionately, "they are a thousand miles apart."

"A thousand miles? What a vast country!"

"Yes, it's a whole world."

"Ah, a world, indeed!" cried the priest softly. "I shall never comprehend it."

"You never will," answered the young girl gravely, "if you do not think about it more practically."

"Practically, practically!" lightly retorted the priest. "What a word with you Americans! That is the consul's word: *practical*."

"Then you have been to see him to-day?" asked Florida with eagerness. "I wanted to ask you". . . .

"Yes, I went to consult the oracle, as you bade me."

"Don Ippolito" . . .

"And he was averse to my going to America. He said it was not *practical*."

"Oh!" murmured the girl.

"I think," continued the priest with vehemence, "that Signor Ferris is no longer my friend."

"Did he treat you coldly,—harshly?" she asked, with a note of indignation in her voice. "Did he know that I—that you came" . . .

"Perhaps he was right. Perhaps I shall indeed go to ruin there. Ruin, ruin! Do I not *live* ruin here?"

"What did he say—what did he tell you?"

"No, no; not now madamigella! I do not want to think of that man, now. I want you to help me once more to realize myself in America, where I shall never have been a priest, where I shall at least battle even-handed with the world. Come, let us forget him—the thought of him palsies all my hope. He could not see me save in this robe, in this figure that I abhor."

"O it was strange, it was not like him, it was cruel. What did he say?"

"In everything but words, he bade me despair; he bade me look upon all that makes life dear and noble as impossible to me!"

"O, how? Perhaps he did not understand you. No, he did not understand you. What did you say to him, Don Ippolito? Tell me!" She leaned towards him, in anxious emotion as she spoke.

The priest rose, and stretched out his arms, as if he would gather something of courage from the infinite space. In his visage were the sublimity and the terror of a man who puts everything to the risk.

"How will it really be with me, yonder?" he demanded. "As it is with other men, whom their past life, if it has been guiltless, does not follow to that new world of freedom and justice?"

"Why should it not be so?" demanded Florida. "Did *he* say it would not?"

"Need it be known there that I have been a priest? Or if I tell it, will it make me appear a kind of monster, different from other men?"

"No, no!" she answered fervently. "Your story would gain friends and honor for you everywhere in America. Did *he*" . . .

"A moment, a moment!" cried Don Ippolito, catching his breath. "Will it ever be possible for me to win something more than honor and friendship there?"

She looked up at him askingly, confusedly.

"If I am a man, and the time should ever come that a face, a look, a voice, shall be to me what they are to other men, will *she* remember it against me that I have been a priest, when I tell her—say to her, madamigella—how dear she is to me, offer her my life's devotion, ask her to be my wife" . . .

Florida rose from the seat, and stood confronting him, in a helpless silence, which he seemed not to notice.

Suddenly he clasped his hands together, and desperately stretched them towards her.

"O my hope, my trust, my life, if it were *you* that I loved?" . . .

"What!" shuddered the girl, recoiling, with almost a shriek. "*You? A priest!*"

Don Ippolito gave a low cry—half laugh, half sob.

"His words, his words! It is true, I cannot escape, I am doomed, I must die as I have lived!"

He dropped his face into his hands, and stood with his head bowed before her; neither spoke for a long time, or moved.

Then Florida said absently, in the husky murmur to which her voice fell when she was strongly moved, "Yes, I see it all, how it has been," and was silent again, staring, as if a procession of the events and scenes of the past months were passing before her; and presently she moaned to herself, "O, O, O!" and wrung her hands.

The foolish fountain kept capering and babbling on. All at

once, now, as a flame flashes up and then expires, it leaped
and dropped extinct at the foot of the statue.

Its going out seemed somehow to leave them in darkness,
and under cover of that gloom, she drew nearer the priest,
and by such approaches as one makes toward a fancied apparition, when his fear will not let him fly, but it seems better
to suffer the worst from it at once than to live in terror of it
ever after, she lifted her hands to his, and gently taking them
away from his face, looked into his hopeless eyes.

"O Don Ippolito," she grieved. "What shall I say to you,
what can I do for you now?"

But there was nothing to do. The whole edifice of his
dreams, his wild imaginations had fallen into dust at a word;
no magic could rebuild it; the end that never seems the end
had come. He let her keep his cold hands, and presently he
returned the entreaty of her tears with his wan, patient smile.

"You cannot help me, there is no help for an error like
mine. Sometime, if ever the thought of me is a greater pain
than it is at this moment, you can forgive me. Yes, you can
do that for me."

"But who, *who* will ever forgive *me*," she cried, "for my
blindness! O you must believe that I never thought, I never
dreamt" . . .

"I know it well. It was your fatal truth that did it: truth
too high and fine for me to have discerned save through such
agony as . . . You too loved my soul, like the rest, and you
would have had me no priest for the reason that they would
have had me a priest—I see it. But you had no right to love
my soul and not me—you, a woman. A woman must not
love only the soul of a man."

"Yes, yes!" piteously explained the girl, "but you were a
priest to me!"

"That is true, madamigella, I was always a priest to you;
and now I see that I never could be otherwise. Ah, the wrong
began many years before we met. I was trying to blame you
a little"—

"Blame me, blame me; do!"

—"But there is no blame. Think that it was another way
of asking your forgiveness. . . . O my God, my God, my
God!"

He released his hands from her, and uttered this cry under his breath, with his face lifted towards the heavens. When he looked at her again, he said: "Madamigella, if my share of this misery gives me the right to ask of you"—

"O ask anything of me! I will give everything, do everything!"

He faltered, and then, "You do not love me," he said abruptly; "is there some one else that you love?"

She did not answer.

"Is it . . . he?"

She hid her face.

"I knew it," groaned the priest, "I knew that, too," and he turned away.

"Don Ippolito, Don Ippolito—O, poor, poor Don Ippolito!" cried the girl springing towards him. "Is *this* the way you leave me? Where are you going? What will you do now?"

"Did I not say? I am going to die a priest."

"Is there nothing that you will let me be to you, hope for you?"

"Nothing," said Don Ippolito, after a moment. "What could you?" He seized the hands imploringly extended towards him, and clasped them together and kissed them both: "Adieu!" he whispered; then he opened them, and passionately kissed either palm: "Adieu, adieu!"

A great wave of sorrow and compassion and despair for him swept through her. She flung her arms about his neck, and pulled his head down upon her heart, and held it tight there, weeping and moaning over him as over some hapless, harmless thing that she had unpurposely bruised or killed. Then she suddenly put her hand against his breast, and thrust him away, and turned and ran.

Ferris stepped back again into the shadow of the tree from which he had just emerged, and clung to its trunk lest he should fall. Another seemed to creep out of the court in his person, and totter across the white glare of the campo and down the blackness of the calle. In the intersected spaces where the moonlight fell, this alien, miserable man saw the figure of a priest gliding on before him.

XVI

FLORIDA SWIFTLY mounted the terrace steps, but she stopped with her hand on the door, panting, and turned and walked slowly away to the end of the terrace, drying her eyes with dashes of her handkerchief, and ordering her hair, some coils of which had been loosened by her flight. Then she went back to the door, waited, and softly opened it. Her mother was not in the parlor where she had left her, and she passed noiselessly into her own room, where some trunks stood open and half-packed against the wall. She began to gather up the pieces of dress that lay upon the bed and chairs, and to fold them with mechanical carefulness and put them in the boxes. Her mother's voice called from the other chamber, "Is that you, Florida?"

"Yes, mother," answered the girl, but remained kneeling before one of the boxes, with that pale green robe in her hand which she had worn on the morning when Ferris had first brought Don Ippolito to see them. She smoothed its folds and looked down at it without making any motion to pack it away, and so she lingered while her mother advanced with one question after another, "What are you doing, Florida? Where are you? Why didn't you come to me?" and finally stood in the doorway: "O, you're packing. Do you know, Florida, I'm getting very impatient about going. I wish we could be off at once."

A tremor passed over the young girl and she started from her languid posture, and laid the dress in the trunk. "So do I, mother. I would give the world if we could go to-morrow!"

"Yes, but we can't, you see. I'm afraid we've undertaken a great deal, my dear. It's quite a weight upon *my* mind, already; and I don't know what it *will* be. If we were free, now, I should say, go to-morrow, by all means. But we couldn't arrange it with Don Ippolito on our hands."

Florida waited a moment before she replied. Then she said coldly, "Don Ippolito is not going with us, mother."

"Not going with us? Why" . . .

"He is not going to America. He will not leave Venice; he is to remain a priest," said Florida doggedly.

Mrs. Vervain sat down in the chair that stood beside the door. "Not going to America; not leave Venice; remain a priest? Florida, you astonish me! But I am not the least surprised, not the least in the world. I thought Don Ippolito would give out, all along. He is not what I should call fickle, exactly, but he is weak, or timid, rather. He is a good man, but he lacks courage, resolution. I always doubted if he would succeed in America, he is too much of a dreamer. But this, really, goes a little beyond anything. I never expected this. What did he say, Florida? How did he excuse himself?"

"I hardly know; very little. What was there to say?"

"To be sure, to be sure. Did you try to reason with him, Florida?"

"No," answered the girl drearily.

"I am glad of that. I think you had said quite enough already. You owed it to yourself not to do so, and he might have misinterpreted it. These foreigners are very different from Americans. No doubt we should have had a time of it, if he had gone with us. It must be for the best. I'm sure it was ordered so. But all that doesn't relieve Don Ippolito from the charge of black ingratitude, and want of consideration for us. He's quite made fools of us."

"He was not to blame. It was a very great step for him. And if" . . .

"I know that. But he ought not to have talked of it. He ought to have known his own mind fully before speaking; that's the only safe way. Well, then; there is nothing to prevent our going to-morrow."

Florida drew a long breath, and rose to go on with the work of packing.

"Have you been crying, Florida? Well of course, you can't help feeling sorry for such a man. There's a great deal of good in Don Ippolito, a great deal. But when you come to my age you wont cry so easily, my dear. It's very trying," said Mrs. Vervain. She sat awhile in silence before she asked: "Will he come here to-morrow morning?"

Her daughter looked at her with a glance of terrified inquiry.

"Do have your wits about you, my dear! We can't go away without saying good-by to him, and we can't go away without paying him."

"Paying him?"

"Yes, paying him—paying him for your lessons. It's always been very awkward. He hasn't been like other teachers, you know: more like a guest, or friend of the family. He never seemed to want to take the money, and of late, I've been letting it run along, because I hated so to offer it, till now, it's quite a sum. I suppose he needs it, poor fellow. And how to get it to him is the question. He may not come to-morrow, as usual, and I couldn't trust it to the padrone. We might send it to him in a draft from Paris, but I'd rather pay him before we go. Besides, it would be rather rude, going away without seeing him again." Mrs. Vervain thought a moment; then, "I'll tell you," she resumed. "If he doesn't happen to come here to-morrow morning, we can stop on our way to the station and give him the money."

Florida did not answer.

"Don't you think that would be a good plan?"

"I don't know," replied the girl in a dull way.

"Why, Florida, if you think from anything Don Ippolito said that he would rather not see us again—that it would be painful to him—why we could ask Mr. Ferris to hand him the money."

"O no, no, no, mother!" cried Florida, hiding her face, "that would be too horribly indelicate!"

"Well, perhaps it wouldn't be quite good taste," said Mrs. Vervain perturbedly, "but you needn't express yourself so violently, my dear. It's not a matter of life and death. I'm sure I don't know what to do. We must stop at Don Ippolito's house, I suppose. Don't you think so?"

"Yes," faintly assented the daughter.

Mrs. Vervain yawned. "Well I can't think anything more about it to-night; I'm too stupid. But that's the way we shall do. Will you help me to bed, my dear? I shall be good for nothing to-morrow."

She went on talking of Don Ippolito's change of purpose till her head touched the pillow, from which she suddenly lifted it again, and called out to her daughter who had passed into the next room: "But Mr. Ferris—why didn't he come back with you?"

"Come back with me?"

"Why yes, child. I sent him out to call you, just before you came in. This Don Ippolito business put him quite out of my head. Didn't you see him—Oh! What's that?"

"Nothing: I dropped my candle."

"You're sure you didn't set anything on fire?"

"No. It went dead out."

"Light it again, and do look. Now is everything right?"

"Yes."

"It's queer he didn't come back to *say* he couldn't find you. What do you suppose became of him?"

"I don't know, mother."

"It's very perplexing. I wish Mr. Ferris were not so odd. It quite borders on affectation. I don't know what to make of it. We must send word to him the very first thing to-morrow morning, that we're going, and ask him to come to see us."

Florida made no reply. She sat staring at the black space of the doorway into her mother's room. Mrs. Vervain did not speak again. After a while her daughter softly entered her chamber, shading the candle with her hand; and seeing that she slept, softly withdrew, closed the door, and went about the work of packing again. When it was all done, she flung herself upon her bed and hid her face in the pillow.

The next morning was spent in bestowing those interminable last touches which the packing of ladies' baggage demands, and in taking leave with largess (in which Mrs. Vervain shone) of all the people in the house and out of it, who had so much as touched a hat to the Vervains during their sojourn. The whole was not a vast sum; nor did the sundry extortions of the padrone come to much, though the honest man racked his brain to invent injuries to his apartment and furniture. Being unmurmuringly paid, he gave way to his real good will for his tenants in many little useful offices. At the end he persisted in sending them to the station in his own gondola and could with difficulty be kept from going with them.

Mrs. Vervain had early sent a message to Ferris, but word

came back a first and a second time that he was not at home, and the forenoon wore away and he had not appeared. A certain indignation sustained her till the gondola pushed out into the Canal, and then it yielded to an intolerable regret that she should not see him.

"I *can't* go without saying good bye to Mr. Ferris, Florida," she said at last, "and it's no use asking me. He may have been wanting a little in politeness, but he's been *so* good all along; and we owe him too much not to make an effort to thank him before we go. We really must stop a moment at his house."

Florida, who had regarded her mother's efforts to summon Ferris to them with passive coldness, turned a look of agony upon her. But in a moment she bade the gondolier stop at the consulate, and dropping her veil over her face, fell back in the shadow of the tenda-curtains.

Mrs. Vervain sentimentalized their departure a little, but her daughter made no comment on the scene they were leaving.

The gondolier rang at Ferris's door and returned with the answer that he was not at home.

Mrs. Vervain gave way to despair. "O dear, O dear! This is too bad! What shall we do?"

"We'll lose the train, mother, if we loiter this way," said Florida.

"Well, wait. I *must* leave a message at least:" *"How could you be away,"* she wrote on her card, *"when we called to say good-by? We've changed our plans and we're going to-day. I shall write you a nice scolding letter from Verona—we're going over the Brenner—for your behavior last night. Who will keep you straight when I'm gone? You've been very, very kind. Florida joins me in a thousand thanks, regrets and good-bys."*

"There, I haven't said anything, after all," she fretted, with tears in her eyes.

The gondolier carried the card again to the door, where Ferris's servant let down a basket by a string and fished it up.

"If Don Ippolito shouldn't be in," said Mrs. Vervain, as the boat moved on again, "I don't know what I *shall* do with this money. It will be awkward beyond anything."

The gondola slipped from the Canalazzo into the net-work

of the smaller canals where the dense shadows were as old as
the palaces that cast them, and stopped at the landing of a
narrow quay. The gondolier dismounted and rang at Don Ippolito's door. There was no response; he rang again and
again. At last from a window of the uppermost story the head
of the priest himself peered out. The gondolier touched his
hat and said, "It is the ladies who ask for you, Don Ippolito."

It was a minute before the door opened, and the priest,
bare-headed and blinking in the strong light, came with a
stupefied air across the quay to the landing-steps.

"Well, Don Ippolito!" cried Mrs. Vervain, rising and giving him her hand, which she first waved at the trunks and
bags piled up in the vacant space in the front of the boat,
"what do you think of this? We are really going, immediately;
we can change our minds too; and I don't think it would have
been too much," she added with a friendly smile, "if we had
gone without saying good-by to you. What in the world does
it all mean, your giving up that grand project of yours so
suddenly?"

She sat down again, that she might talk more at her ease,
and seemed thoroughly happy to have Don Ippolito before
her again.

"It finally appeared best, madama," he said quietly, after a
quick, keen glance at Florida, who did not lift her veil.

"Well, perhaps you're partly right. But I can't help thinking
that you with your talent would have succeeded in America.
Inventors do get on there, in the most surprising way.
There's the Screw Company of Providence. It's such a simple
thing; and now the shares are worth eight hundred. Are you
well to-day, Don Ippolito?"

"Quite well, madama."

"I thought you looked rather pale. But I believe you're always a little pale. You mustn't work too hard. We shall miss
you a great deal, Don Ippolito."

"Thanks, madama."

"Yes, we shall be quite lost without you. And I wanted to
say this to you, Don Ippolito, that if ever you change your
mind again, and conclude to come to America, you must
write to me, and let me help you just as I had intended to
do."

The priest shivered, as if cold, and gave another look at Florida's veiled face. "You are too good," he said.

"Yes, I really think I am," replied Mrs. Vervain, playfully. "Considering that you were going to let me leave Venice without even trying to say good-by to me, I think I'm very good indeed."

Mrs. Vervain's mood became overcast, and her eyes filled with tears: "I hope you're sorry to have us going, Don Ippolito, for you know how very highly I prize your acquaintance. It was rather cruel of you, I think."

She seemed not to remember that he could not have known of their change of plans. Don Ippolito looked imploringly into her face, and made a touching gesture of deprecation, but did not speak.

"I'm really afraid you're *not* well; and I think it's too bad of us to be going," resumed Mrs. Vervain; "but it can't be helped now: we are all packed, don't you see. But I want to ask one favor of you, Don Ippolito; and that is," said Mrs. Vervain, covertly taking a little rouleau from her pocket, "that you'll leave these inventions of yours for a while, and give yourself a vacation. You need rest of mind. Go into the country, somewhere, do. That's what's preying upon you. But we must really be off, now. Shake hands with Florida—I'm going to be the last to part with you," she said, with a tearful smile.

Don Ippolito and Florida extended their hands. Neither spoke, and as she sank back upon the seat from which she had half risen, she drew more closely the folds of the veil which she had not lifted from her face.

Mrs. Vervain gave a little sob as Don Ippolito took her hand and kissed it; and she had some difficulty in leaving with him the rouleau, which she tried artfully to press into his palm. "Good-by, good-by," she said, "don't drop it," and attempted to close his fingers over it.

But he let it lie carelessly in his open hand, as the gondola moved off, and there it still lay as he stood watching the boat slip under a bridge at the next corner and disappear. While he stood there gazing at the empty arch, a man of a wild and savage aspect approached. It was said that this man's brain had been turned by the death of his brother who was betrayed to the Austrians after the revolution of '48, by his wife's confessor. He advanced with swift strides and at the moment he reached Don Ippolito's side he suddenly turned his face upon him and cursed him through his clenched teeth: "Dog of a priest!"

Don Ippolito, as if his whole race had renounced him in the maniac's words, uttered a desolate cry, and hiding his face in his hands, tottered into his house.

The rouleau had dropped from his palm; it rolled down the shelving marble of the quay, and slipped into the water.

The young beggar who had held Mrs. Vervain's gondola to the shore while she talked, looked up and down the deserted quay, and at the doors and windows. Then he began to take off his clothes for a bath.

XVII

FERRIS RETURNED at nightfall to his house, where he had not been since daybreak and flung himself exhausted upon the bed. His face was burnt red with the sun, and his eyes were bloodshot. He fell into a doze and dreamed that he was still at Malamocco, whither he had gone that morning in a sort of craze, with some fishermen who were to cast their nets there; then he was rowing back to Venice across the lagoon that seemed a molten fire under the keel. He woke with a heavy groan, and bade Marina fetch him a light.

She set it on the table, and handed him the card Mrs. Vervain had left. He read it and read it again, and then he laid it down, and putting on his hat, he took his cane and went out. "Do not wait for me, Marina," he said, "I may be late. Go to bed."

He returned at midnight, and lighting his candle took up the card and read it once more. He could not tell whether to be glad or sorry that he had failed to see the Vervains again. He took it for granted that Don Ippolito was to follow; he would not ask himself what motive had hastened their going. The reasons were all that he should never more look upon the woman so hatefully lost to him, but a strong instinct of his heart struggled against them.

He lay down in his clothes, and began to dream almost before he began to sleep. He woke early, and went out to walk. He did not rest all day. Once he came home, and found a letter from Mrs. Vervain, postmarked Verona, reiterating her lamentations and adieux, and explaining that the priest had relinquished his purpose, and should not go to America at all. The deeper mystery in which this news left him was not less sinister than before.

In the weeks that followed, Ferris had no other purpose than to reduce the days to hours, the hours to minutes. The burden that fell upon him when he woke, lay heavy on his heart till night, and oppressed him far into his sleep. He could not give his trouble certain shape; what was mostly with him was a formless loss, which he could not resolve into any definite shame or wrong. At times what he had seen seemed to him some baleful trick of the imagination, some lurid and foolish illusion.

But he could do nothing, he could not ask himself what the end was to be. He kept indoors all day, trying to work, trying to read, marvelling somewhat that he did not fall sick and die. At night he set out on long walks, which took him he cared not where, and often detained him till the gray lights of morning began to tremble through the nocturnal blue. But even by night he shunned the neighborhood in which the Vervains had lived. Their landlord sent him a package of trifles they had left behind, but he refused to receive them, sending back word that he did not know where the ladies were. He had half expected that Mrs. Vervain, though he had not answered her last letter, might write to him again from England, but she did not. The Vervains had passed out of his world; he knew that they had been in it only by the torment they had left him.

He wondered in a listless way that he should see nothing of Don Ippolito. Once at midnight he fancied that the priest was coming towards him across a campo he had just entered; he stopped and turned back into the calle: when the priest came up to him, it was not Don Ippolito.

In these days Ferris received a dispatch from the Department of State, informing him that his successor had been appointed, and directing him to deliver up the consular flags, seals, archives and other property of the United States. No reason for his removal was given; but as there had never been any reason for his appointment, he had no right to complain; the balance was exactly dressed by this simple device of our civil service. He determined not to wait for the coming of his successor before giving up the consular effects, and he placed them at once in the keeping of the worthy ship-chandler who had so often transferred them from departing to arriving consuls. Then being quite ready at any moment to leave Venice, he found himself in nowise eager to go; but he began in a desultory way to pack up his sketches and studies.

One morning as he sat idle in his dismantled studio, Marina came to tell him that an old woman waiting at the door below, wished to speak with him.

"Well, let her come up," said Ferris wearily, and presently Marina returned with a very ill-favored beldam, who stared hard at him while he frowningly puzzled himself as to where he had seen that malign visage before.

"Well?" he said, harshly.

"I come," answered the old woman, "on the part of Don Ippolito Rondinelli, who desires so much to see your Excellency."

Ferris made no response, while the old woman knotted the fringe of her shawl with quaking hands, and presently added with a tenderness in her voice which oddly discorded with the hardness of her face: "He has been very sick, poor thing, with a fever; but now he is in his senses again, and the doctors say he will get well. I hope so. But he is still very weak. He tried to write two lines to you, but he had not the strength; so he bade me bring you this word: That he had something to say which it greatly concerned you to hear, and that he prayed you to forgive his not coming to revere you, for it was impossible, and that you should have the goodness to do him this favor, to come to find him the quickest you could."

The old woman wiped her eyes with the corner of her shawl, and her chin wobbled pathetically while she shot a glance of baleful dislike at Ferris, who answered after a long dull stare at her, "Tell him I'll come."

He did not believe that Don Ippolito could tell him anything that greatly concerned him; but he was worn out with going round in the same circle of conjecture, and so far as he could be glad, he was glad of this chance to face his calamity. He would go, but not at once; he would think it over; he would go to-morrow, when he had got some grasp of the matter.

The old woman lingered.

"Tell him I'll come," repeated Ferris impatiently.

"A thousand excuses; but my poor master has been very sick. The doctors say he will get well. I hope so. But he is very weak indeed: a little shock, a little disappointment. . . . Is the signore very, *very* much occupied this morning? He greatly desired, he prayed that if such a thing were possible in the goodness of your excellency . . . But I am offending the signore!"

"What do you want?" demanded Ferris.

The old wretch set up a piteous whimper, and tried to possess herself of his hand; she kissed his coat-sleeve instead. "That you will return with me," she besought him.

"O, I'll go!" groaned the painter. "I might as well go first as last," he added in English. "There, stop that! Enough, enough, I tell you! Didn't I say I was going with you?" he cried to the old woman.

"God bless you!" she mumbled, and set off before him down the stairs and out of the door. She looked so miserably old and weary that he called a gondola to his landing and made her get into it with him.

It tormented Don Ippolito's idle neighborhood to see Veneranda arrive in such state, and a passionate excitement arose at the caffè, where the person of the consul was known, when Ferris entered the priest's house with her.

He had not often visited Don Ippolito, but the quaintness of the place had been so vividly impressed upon him, that he had a certain familiarity with the grape-arbor of the anteroom, the paintings of the parlor, and the puerile arrangement of the piano and melodeon. Veneranda led him through these rooms to the chamber where Don Ippolito had first shown him his inventions. They were all removed now, and on a bed set against the wall opposite the door, lay the priest with his hands on his breast, and a faint smile on his lips, so peaceful, so serene that the painter stopped with a sudden awe, as if he had unawares come into the presence of death.

"Advance, advance," whispered the old woman.

Near the head of the bed sat a white-haired priest wearing the red stockings of a canonico; his face was fanatically stern; but he rose, and bowed courteously to Ferris.

The stir of his robes roused Don Ippolito. He slowly and weakly turned his head, and his eyes fell upon the painter. He made a helpless gesture of salutation with his thin hand, and began to excuse himself for the trouble he had given with a gentle politeness that touched the painter's heart through all the complex resentments that divided them. It was indeed a strange ground on which the two men met. Ferris could not have described Don Ippolito as his enemy, for the priest had wittingly done him no wrong; he could not have logically hated him as a rival, for till it was too late he had not confessed to his own heart the love that was in it; he knew no evil of Don Ippolito, he could not accuse him of any betrayal of trust, or violation of confidence. He felt merely that this hapless creature, lying so deathlike before him had profaned, however involuntarily, what was sacredest in the world to him; beyond this all was chaos. He had heard of the priest's sickness with a fierce hardening of the heart; yet as he beheld him now, he began to remember things that moved him to a sort of remorse. He recalled again the simple loyalty with which Don Ippolito had first spoken to him of Miss Vervain and tried to learn his own feeling toward her; he thought how trustfully at their last meeting the priest had declared his love and hope, and how when he had coldly received his confession, Don Ippolito had solemnly adjured him to be frank with him; and Ferris could not. That pity for himself as the prey of fantastically cruel chances, which he had already vaguely felt, began now also to include the priest; ignoring all but that compassion, he went up to the bed and took the weak, chill, nerveless hand in his own.

The canonico rose and placed his chair for Ferris beside the pillow, on which lay a brass crucifix, and then softly left the room exchanging a glance of affectionate intelligence with the sick man.

"I might have waited a little while," said Don Ippolito weakly, speaking in a hollow voice that was the shadow of his old deep tones, "but you will know how to forgive the impatience of a man not yet quite master of himself. I thank you for coming. I have been very sick, as you see; I did not think to live; I did not care . . . I am very weak, now; let me say to you quickly what I want to say. Dear friend," continued Don Ippolito, fixing his eyes upon the painter's face, "I spoke to her that night after I had parted from you."

The priest's voice was now firm; the painter turned his face away.

"I spoke without hope," proceeded Don Ippolito, "and because I must. I spoke in vain; all was lost, all was past in a moment."

The coil of suspicions and misgivings and fears in which Ferris had lived was suddenly without a clew; he could not look upon the pallid visage of the priest lest he should now at last find there that subtle expression of deceit; the whirl of his thoughts kept him silent; Don Ippolito went on.

"Even if I had never been a priest, I would still have been impossible to her. She". . . .

He stopped as if for want of strength to go on. All at once he cried, "Listen!" and he rapidly recounted the story of his life, ending with the fatal tragedy of his love. When all was told, he said calmly, "But now everything is over with me on earth. I thank the Infinite Compassion for the sorrows through which I have passed. I, also, have proved the miraculous power of the Church, potent to save in all ages." He gathered the crucifix in his spectral grasp, and pressed it to his lips. "Many merciful things have befallen me on this bed of sickness. My uncle, whom the long years of my darkness divided from me, is once more at peace with me. Even that poor old woman whom I sent to call you, and who had served me as I believed with hate for me as a false priest in her heart, has devoted herself day and night to my helplessness; she has grown decrepit with her cares and vigils. Yes, I have had many and signal marks of the Divine pity to be grateful for." He paused, breathing quickly, and then added, "They tell that the danger of this sickness is past. But none the less I have died in it. When I rise from this bed, it shall be to take the vows of a Carmelite friar."

Ferris made no answer, and Don Ippolito resumed:

"I have told you how when I first owned to her the falsehood in which I lived, she besought me to try if I might not find consolation in the holy life to which I had been devoted. When you see her, dear friend, will you not tell her that I came to understand that this comfort, this refuge, awaited me in the call of the Carmelite? I have brought so much trouble into her life that I would fain have her know I have found peace where she bade me seek it, that I have mastered my affliction by reconciling myself to it. Tell her that but for her pity and fear for me, I believe that I must have died in my sins."

It was perhaps inevitable from Ferris's protestant association of monks and convents and penances chiefly with the machinery of fiction, that all this affected him as unreally as talk in a stage-play. His heart was cold as he answered: "I am glad that your mind is at rest concerning the doubts which so long troubled you. Not all men are so easily pacified; but, as you say, it is the privilege of your church to work miracles. As to Miss Vervain, I am sorry that I cannot promise to give her your message. I shall never see her again. Excuse me," he continued, "but your servant said there was something you wished to say that concerned me."

"You will never see her again!" cried the priest, struggling to lift himself upon his elbow, and falling back upon the pillow. "O, bereft! O, deaf and blind! It was *you* that she loved! She confessed it to me that night."

"Wait!" said Ferris, trying to steady his voice, and failing; "I was with Mrs. Vervain, that night; she sent me into the garden to call her daughter, and I saw how Miss Vervain parted from the man she did not love! I saw" . . . .

It was a horrible thing to have said it, he felt now that he had spoken; a sense of the indelicacy, the shamefulness seemed to alienate him from all high concern in the matter, and to leave him a mere self-convicted eaves-dropper. His face flamed; the wavering hopes, the wavering doubts alike died in his heart. He had fallen below the dignity of his own trouble.

"You saw, you saw," softly repeated the priest, without looking at him, and without any show of emotion; apparently, the convalescence that had brought him perfect clearness of reason had left his sensibilities still somewhat dulled. He closed his lips and lay silent. At last, he asked very gently, "And how shall I make you believe that what you saw was not a woman's love, but an angel's heavenly pity for me? Does it seem hard to believe this of her?"

"Yes," answered the painter doggedly, "it is hard."

"And yet it is the very truth. O, you do not know her, you never knew her! In the same moment that she denied me her love, she divined the anguish of my soul, and with that embrace she sought to console me for the friendlessness of a whole life, past and to come. But I know that I waste my words on you," he cried bitterly. "You never would see me as I was; you would find no singleness in me; and yet I had a heart as full of loyalty to you as love for her. In what have I been false to you?"

"You never were false to me," answered Ferris, "and God knows I have been true to you, and at what cost. We might well curse the day we met, Don Ippolito, for we have only done each other harm. But I never meant you harm. And now I ask you to forgive me, if I cannot believe you. I cannot—yet. I am of another race from you, slow to suspect, slow to trust. Give me a little time; let me see you again. I want to go away and think. I don't question your truth. I'm afraid you don't know. I'm afraid that the same deceit has tricked us both. I must come to you to-morrow. Can I?"

He rose and stood beside the couch.

"Surely, surely," answered the priest, looking into Ferris's troubled eyes with calm meekness. "You will do me the greatest pleasure. Yes, come again to-morrow. You know," he said with a sad smile, referring to his purpose of taking vows, "that my time in the world is short. Adieu, to meet again!"

He took Ferris's hand, hanging weak and hot by his side, and drew him gently down by it, and kissed him on either bearded cheek. "It is our custom, you know, among *friends*. Farewell."

The canonico in the ante-room bowed austerely to him as he passed through; the old woman refused with a harsh "Nothing!" the money he offered her at the door.

He bitterly upbraided himself for the doubts he could not banish, and he still flushed with shame that he should have declared his knowledge of a scene which ought, at its worst to have been inviolable by his speech. He scarcely cared now for the woman about whom these miseries grouped themselves; he realized that a fantastic remorse may be stronger than a jealous love.

He longed for the morrow to come that he might confess his shame and regret; but reaction to this violent repentance came before the night fell. As the sound of the priest's voice and the sight of his wasted face faded from the painter's sense, he began to see everything in the old light again. Then what Don Ippolito had said took a character of ludicrous, of insolent improbability.

After dark, Ferris set out upon one of his long rambling walks. He walked hard and fast, to try if he might not still by mere fatigue of body the anguish that filled his soul. But whichever way he went he came again and again to the house of Don Ippolito, and at last he stopped there, leaning against the parapet of the quay, and staring at the house, as though he would spell from the senseless stones the truth of the secret they sheltered. Far up in the chamber, where he knew that the priest lay, the windows were dimly lit.

As he stood thus, with his upturned face haggard in the moonlight, the soldier commanding the Austrian patrol which passed that way, halted his squad, and seemed about to ask him what he wanted there.

Ferris turned and walked swiftly homeward; but he did not even lie down. His misery took the shape of an intent that would not suffer him to rest. He meant to go to Don Ippolito and tell him that his story had failed of its effect, that he was not to be fooled so easily, and without demanding anything further to leave him in his lie.

At the earliest hour when he might hope to be admitted, he went, and rang the bell furiously. The door opened and he confronted the priest's servant. "I want to see Don Ippolito," said Ferris abruptly.

"It cannot be," she began.

"I tell you I must," cried Ferris, raising his voice. "I tell you" . . . .

"Madman!" fiercely whispered the old woman, shaking both her open hands in his face, "he's dead! He died last night!"

XVIII

THE TERRIBLE stroke sobered Ferris; he woke from his long debauch of hate and jealousy and despair; for the first time since that night in the garden, he faced his fate with a clear mind. Death had set his seal forever to a testimony which he had been able neither to refuse nor to accept; in abject sorrow and shame he thanked God that he had been kept from dealing that last cruel blow; but if Don Ippolito had come back from the dead to repeat his witness Ferris felt that the miracle could not change his own passive state. There was now but one thing in the world for him to do: to see Florida, to confront her with his knowledge of all that had been, and to abide by her word, whatever it was. At the worst, there was the war, whose drums had already called to him, for a refuge.

He thought at first that he might perhaps overtake the Vervains before they sailed for America, but he remembered that they had left Venice six weeks before. It seemed impossible that he could wait, but when he landed in New York, he was tormented in his impatience by a strange reluctance and hesitation. A fantastic light fell upon his plans; a sense of its wildness enfeebled his purpose. What was he going to do? Had he come four thousand miles to tell Florida that Don Ippolito was dead? Or was he going to say, "I have heard that you love me, but I don't believe it: is it true?"

He pushed on to Providence, stifling these antic misgivings as he might, and without allowing himself time to falter from his intent he set out to find Mrs. Vervain's house. He knew the street and the number, for she had often given him the address in her invitations against the time when he should return to America. As he drew near the house, a tender trepidation filled him and silenced all other senses in him; his heart beat thickly; the universe included only the fact that he was to look upon the face he loved, and this fact had neither past nor future.

But a terrible foreboding as of death seized him when he stood before the house, and glanced up at its close-shuttered front, and round upon the dusty grassplots and neglected flower-beds of the dooryard. With a cold hand, he rang and rang again, and no answer came. At last a man lounged up to the fence from the next house-door. "Guess you wont make anybody hear," he said, casually.

"Doesn't Mrs. Vervain live in this house?" asked Ferris, finding a husky voice in his throat that sounded to him like some other's voice lost there.

"She used to, but she isn't at home. Family's in Europe."

They had not come back yet.

"Thanks," said Ferris mechanically, and he went away. He laughed to himself at this keen irony of fortune: he was prepared for the confirmation of his doubts; he was ready for relief from them, Heaven knew; but this blank that the turn of the wheel had brought, this Nothing!

The Vervains were as lost to him as if Europe were in another planet. How should he find them there? Besides he was poor; he had no money to get back with, if he had wanted to return.

He took the first train to New York, and hunted up a young fellow of his acquaintance, who in the days of peace, had been one of the governor's aides. He was still holding this place, and was an ardent recruiter. He hailed with rapture the expression of Ferris's wish to go into the war. "Look here!" he said after a moment's thought, "didn't you have some rank as a consul?"

"Yes," replied Ferris with a dreary smile, "I have been equivalent to a commander in the navy and a colonel in the army—I don't mean both, but either."

"Good!" cried his friend. "We must strike high. The colonelcies are rather inaccessible, just at present and so are the lieutenant-colonelcies; but a majorship now" . . . .

"O no; don't!" pleaded Ferris. "Make me a corporal—or a cook. I shall not be so mischievous to our own side, then, and when the other fellows shoot me, I shall not be so much of a loss."

"O, they wont *shoot* you," expostulated his friend, highheartedly. He got Ferris a commission as second-lieutenant, and lent him money to buy a uniform.

———

Ferris's regiment was sent to a part of the southwest where he saw a good deal of fighting and fever and ague. At the end of two years, spent alternately in the field and the hospital, he was riding out near the camp one morning in unusual spirits, when two men in butternut fired at him: one had the mortification to miss him; the bullet of the other struck him in the arm. There was talk of amputation at first, but the case was finally managed without. In Ferris's state of health it was quite the same an end of his soldiering.

He came North sick and maimed and poor. He smiled now to think of confronting Florida in any imperative or challenging spirit, but the current of his hopeless melancholy turned more and more towards her. He had once, at a desperate venture, written to her at Providence, but he had got no answer. He asked of a Providence man among the artists in New York, if he knew the Vervains. The Providence man said that he did know them a little when he was much younger; they had been abroad a great deal; he believed in a dim way that they were still in Europe. The young one, he added, used to have a temper of her own.

"Indeed!" said Ferris stiffly.

The one fast friend whom he found in New York was the governor's dashing aide. The enthusiasm of this recruiter of regiments had not ceased with Ferris's departure for the front; the number of disabled officers forbade him to lionize any one of them, but he befriended Ferris; he made a feint of discovering the open secret of his poverty, and asked how he could help him.

"I don't know," said Ferris, "it looks like a hopeless case, to me."

"O no it isn't," retorted his friend, as cheerfully and confidently as he had promised him that he should not be shot. "Didn't you bring back any pictures from Venice with you?"

"I brought back a lot of sketches and studies. I'm sorry to say that I loafed a good deal there; I used to feel that I had eternity before me; and I was a theorist and a purist and an idiot generally. There are none of them fit to be seen."

"Never mind; let's look at them."

They hunted out Ferris's property from a catch-all closet in the studio of a sculptor with whom he had left them, and who expressed a polite pleasure in handing them over to Ferris rather than to his heirs and assigns.

"Well, I'm not sure that I share your satisfaction, old fellow," said the painter ruefully; but he unpacked the sketches.

Their inspection certainly revealed a disheartening condition of half-work. "And I can't do anything to help the matter for the present," groaned Ferris stopping midway in the business, and making as if to shut the case again.

"Hold on," said his friend. "What's this? Why, this isn't so bad." It was the study of Don Ippolito as a Venetian priest, which Ferris beheld with a stupid amaze, remembering that he had meant to destroy it, and wondering how it had got where it was, but not really caring much.

"It's worse than you can imagine," he said, still looking at it with this apathy.

"No matter; I want you to sell it to me. Come!"

"I can't!" replied Ferris piteously. "It would be flat burglary."

"Then put it into the Exhibition."

The sculptor who had gone back to scraping the chin of the famous public man on whose bust he was at work, stabbed him to the heart with his modeling-tool, and turned to Ferris and his friend. He slanted his broad red beard for a sidelong look at the picture, and said: "I know what you mean, Ferris. It's hard, and it's feeble in some ways; and it looks a little too much like experimenting. But it *isn't* so *infernally* bad."

"Don't be fulsome," responded Ferris, jadedly. He was thinking in a thoroughly vanquished mood what a tragicocomic end of the whole business it was that poor Don Ippolito should come to his rescue in this fashion, and as it were offer to succor him in his extremity. He perceived the shamefulness of suffering such help; it would be much better to starve; but he felt cowed, and he had not courage to take arms against this sarcastic destiny, which had pursued him with a mocking smile from one lower level to another. He rubbed his forehead and brooded upon the picture. At least it would be some comfort to be rid of it; and Don Ippolito was dead; and to whom could it mean more than the face of it?

His friend had his way about framing it, and it was got into the exhibition. The hanging-committee offered it the hospitalities of an obscure corner; but it was there, and it stood its chance. Nobody seemed to know that it was there, however, unless confronted with it by Ferris's friend, and then no one seemed to care for it, much less want to buy it. Ferris saw so many much worse pictures sold all round it, that he began gloomily to respect it. At first it had shocked him to see it on the Academy's wall; but it soon came to have no other relation to him than that of creatureship, like a poem in which a poet celebrates his love or laments his dead, and sells for a price. His pride as well as his poverty was set on having the picture sold; he had nothing to do, and he used to lurk about, and see if it would not interest somebody at last. But it remained unsold throughout May, and well into June, long after the crowds had ceased to frequent the exhibition and only chance visitors from the country straggled in by twos and threes.

One warm, dusty afternoon, when he turned into the Academy out of Fourth Avenue, the empty hall echoed to no footfall but his own. A group of weary women, who wore that look of wanting lunch which characterizes all picture-gallery-goers at home and abroad, stood faint before a certain large Venetian subject which Ferris abhorred, and the very name of which he spat out of his mouth with loathing for its unreality. He passed them with a sombre glance, as he took his way toward the retired spot where his own painting hung.

A lady whose crapes would have betrayed to her own sex the latest touch of Paris, stood a little way back from it, and gazed fixedly at it. The pose of her head, her whole attitude expressed a quiet dejection; without seeing her face one could know its air of pensive wistfulness. Ferris resolved to indulge himself in a near approach to this unwonted spectacle of interest in his picture, at the sound of his steps the lady slowly turned a face of somewhat heavily moulded beauty, and from low-growing, thick pale hair and level brows, stared at him with the sad eyes of Florida Vervain. She looked fully the last two years older.

As though she were listening to the sound of his steps in

the dark instead of having him there visibly before her, she kept her eyes upon him with dreamy unrecognition.

"Yes; it is I," said Ferris, as if she had spoken.

She recovered herself, and with a subdued, sorrowful quiet in her old directness, she answered, "I supposed you must be in New York," and she indicated that she had supposed so from seeing this picture.

Ferris felt the blood mounting to his head. "Do you think it is like?" he asked.

"No," she said, "it isn't just to him; it attributes things that didn't belong to him, and it leaves out a great deal."

"I could scarcely have hoped to please you in a portrait of Don Ippolito." Ferris saw the red light break out as it used on the girl's pale cheeks, and her eyes dilate angrily. He went on recklessly: "He sent for me after you went away, and gave me a message for you. I never promised to deliver it, but I will do so now. He asked me to tell you when we met, that he had acted on your desire, and had tried to reconcile himself to his calling and his religion; he was going to enter a Carmelite convent."

Florida made no answer, but she seemed to expect him to go on, and he was constrained to do so.

"He never carried out his purpose," Ferris said, with a keen glance at her; "he died the night after I saw him."

"Died?" The fan and the parasol and the two or three light packages she had been holding, slid down one by one, and lay at her feet. "Thank you for bringing me his last words," she said, but did not ask him anything more.

Ferris did not offer to gather up her things; he stood irresolute; presently he continued with a downcast look: "He had had a fever, but they thought he was getting well. His death must have been sudden." He stopped, and resumed fiercely, resolved to have the worst out: "I went to him, with no good will toward him the next day after I saw him; but I came too late. That was God's mercy to me. I hope you have your consolation, Miss Vervain."

It maddened him to see her so little moved, and he meant to make her share his remorse.

"Did he blame me for anything?" she asked.

"No!" said Ferris, with a bitter laugh, "he praised you."

"I am glad of that," returned Florida, "for I have thought it all over many times, and I know that I was not to blame, though at first I blamed myself. I never intended him anything but good. That is *my* consolation, Mr. Ferris. But you," she added, "you seem to make yourself my judge. Well, and what do *you* blame me for? I have a right to know what is in your mind."

The thing that was in his mind had rankled there for two years; in many a black reverie of those that alternated with his moods of abject self-reproach and perfect trust of her, he had confronted her and flung it out upon her in one stinging phrase. But he was now suddenly at a loss; the words would not come; his torment fell dumb before her; in her presence the cause was unspeakable. Her lips had quivered a little in making that demand, and there had been a corresponding break in her voice.

"Florida, Florida!" Ferris heard himself saying, "I loved you all the time!"

"O indeed, did you love me?" she cried, indignantly, while the tears shone in her eyes. "And was *that* why you left a helpless young girl to meet that trouble alone? Was *that* why you refused me your advice, and turned your back on me, and snubbed me? O, many thanks for your love!" She dashed the gathered tears angrily away, and went on. "Perhaps you knew, too, what that poor priest was thinking of?"

"Yes," said Ferris, stolidly, "I did at last: he told me."

"O then you acted generously and nobly to let him go on! It was kind to him, and very, very kind to me!"

"What could I do?" demanded Ferris, amazed and furious to find himself on the defensive. "His telling me put it out of my power to act."

"I'm glad that you can satisfy yourself with such a quibble! But I wonder that you can tell *me*—*any* woman of it!"

"By heavens, this is atrocious!" cried Ferris. "Do you think . . . Look here!" he went on rudely. "I'll put the case to you, and you shall judge it. Remember that I was such a fool as to be in love with you. Suppose Don Ippolito had told me that he was going to risk everything—going to give up home, religion, friends—on the ten thousandth part of a chance that you might some day care for him. I did not believe he had

even so much chance as that; but he had always thought me
his friend, and he trusted me. Was it a quibble that kept me
from betraying him? I don't know what honor is among
women; but no *man* could have done it. I confess to my
shame that I went to your house that night longing to betray
him. And then suppose your mother sent me into the garden
to call you, and I saw . . . what has made my life a hell of
doubt for the last two years; what . . . No; excuse me! I
can't put the case to you after all."

"What do you mean?" asked Florida. "I don't understand
you!"

"What do I mean? You don't understand? Are you so blind
as that, or are you making a fool of me? What could I think
but you had played that priest's heart till your own" . . .

"Oh!" cried Florida with a shudder, starting away from
him, "did you think I was such a wicked girl as that?"

It was no defence, no explanation, no denial; it simply left
the case with Ferris as before. He stood looking like a man
who does not know whether to bless or curse himself, to
laugh or blaspheme.

She stooped and tried to pick up the things she had let fall
upon the floor; but she seemed not able to find them. He
bent over and gathering them together, restored them to her
with his left hand, keeping the other in the breast of his coat.

"Thanks," she said, and then after a moment, "Have you
been hurt?" she asked timidly.

"Yes," said Ferris in a sulky way. "I have had my share."
He glanced down at his arm askance. "It's rather conventional," he added. "It isn't much of a hurt; but then, I wasn't
much of a soldier."

The girl's eyes looked reverently at the conventional arm;
those were the days, so long past, when women worshipped
men for such things. But she said nothing, and as Ferris's eyes
wandered to her, he received a novel and painful impression.
He said, hesitatingly, "I have not asked before: but your
mother, Miss Vervain—I hope she is well?"

"She is dead," answered Florida, with stony quiet.

They both were silent for a time. Then Ferris said, "I had
a great affection for your mother."

"Yes," said the girl, "she was fond of you, too. But you never wrote or sent her any word; it used to grieve her."

Her unjust reproach went to his heart so long preoccupied with its own troubles; he recalled with a tender remorse the old Venetian days and the kindliness of the gracious, silly woman who had seemed to like him so much; he remembered the charm of her perfect ladylikeness and of her winning weak-headed desire to make every one happy to whom she spoke, the beauty of the goodwill, the hospitable soul that in an imaginably better world than this will outvalue a merely intellectual or esthetic life. He humbled himself before her memory, and as keenly reproached himself as if he could have made her hear from him at any time during the past two years. He could only say, "I am sorry that I gave your mother pain; I loved her very truly. I hope that she did not suffer much before"—

"No," said Florida, "it was a peaceful end; but finally it was very sudden. She had not been well for many years, with that sort of decline; I used sometimes to feel troubled about her before we came to Venice; but I was very young. I never was really alarmed till that day I went to you."

"I remember," said Ferris contritely.

"She had fainted, and I thought we ought to see a doctor; but afterwards, because I thought that I ought not to do so without speaking to her, I did not go to the doctor; and that day we made up our minds to get home as soon as we could; and she seemed so much better, for a while; and then, everything seemed to happen at once. When we did start home, she could not go any further than Switzerland, and in the fall we went back to Italy. We went to Sorrento, where the climate seemed to do her good. But she was growing frailer, the whole time. She died in March. I found some old friends of hers in Naples, and came home with them."

The girl hesitated a little over the words, which she nevertheless uttered unbroken, while the tears fell quietly down her face. She seemed to have forgotten the angry words that had passed between her and Ferris, to remember him only as one who had known her mother, while she went on to relate some little facts in the history of her mother's last days, and she rose into a higher serener atmosphere, inaccessible to his resentment or his regret, as she spoke of her loss. The simple tale of sickness and death inexpressibly belittled his passionate woes, and made them look theatrical to him. He hung his head as they turned at her motion and walked away from the picture of Don Ippolito, and down the stairs toward the street-door; the people before the other Venetian picture had apparently yielded to their craving for lunch, and had vanished.

"I have very little to tell you of my own life," Ferris began awkwardly. "I came home soon after you started, and I went to Providence to find you, but you had not got back."

Florida stopped him and looked perplexedly into his face; and then moved on.

"Then I went into the army. I wrote once to you."

"I never got your letter," she said.

They were now in the lower hall, and near the door.

"Florida," said Ferris abruptly, "I'm poor and disabled; I've no more right than any sick beggar in the street to say it to you; but I loved you, I must always love you. I— Good-by."

She halted him again, and "You said," she grieved, "that you doubted me; you said that I had made your life a"—

"Yes, I said that; I know it," answered Ferris.

"You thought I could be such a false and cruel girl as that!"

"Yes, yes. I thought it all, God help me!"

"When I was only sorry for him, when it was you that I"—

"O I know it," answered Ferris in a heartsick, hopeless voice. "He knew it, too. He told me so the day before he died."

"And didn't you believe him?"

Ferris could not answer.

"Do you believe him now?"

"I believe anything you tell me. When I look at you, I can't believe I ever doubted you."

"Why?"

"Because—because—I love you."

"Oh! That's no reason."

"I know it; but I'm used to being without a reason."

Florida looked gravely at his penitent face, and a brave red color mantled her own, while she advanced an unanswerable argument: "Then what are you going away for?"

The world seemed to melt and float away from between them. It returned and solidified at the sound of the janitor's steps as he came towards them on his round through the empty building. Ferris caught her hand; she leaned heavily upon his arm as they walked out into the street. It was all they could do at the moment except to look into each other's faces, and walk swiftly on.

At last, after how long a time he did not know, Ferris cried: "Where are we going Florida?"

"Why, I don't know!" she replied. "I'm stopping with those friends of ours at the Fifth Avenue Hotel. We *were* going on to Providence to-morrow. We landed yesterday; and we staid to do some shopping"—

"And may I ask why you happened to give your first moments in America to the fine arts?"

"The fine arts? Oh! I thought I might find something of yours, there!"

At the hotel she presented him to her party as a friend whom her mother and she had known in Italy; and then went to lay aside her hat. The Providence people received him with the easy, half-southern warmth of manner, which seems to have floated northward as far as their city on the Gulf Stream bathing the Rhode Island shores. The matron of the party had, before Florida came back, an outline history of their acquaintance, which she evolved from him with so much tact that he was not conscious of parting with information; and she divined indefinitely more when she saw them together again. She was charming; but to Ferris's thinking she had a fault, she kept him too much from Florida, though she talked of nothing else, and at the last she was discreetly merciful.

"Do you think," whispered Florida, very close against his face, when they parted, "that I'll have a bad temper?"

"I hope you will—or I shall be killed with kindness," he replied.

She stood a moment, nervously buttoning his coat across his breast. "You mustn't let that picture be sold, Henry," she said, and by this touch alone did she express any sense, if she had it, of his want of feeling in proposing to sell it. He

winced, and she added with a soft pity in her voice, "He did
bring us together, after all. I wish you had believed him,
dear!"

"So do I," said Ferris, most humbly.

People are never equal to the romance of their youth in
after life, except by fits, and Ferris especially could not keep
himself at what he called the operatic pitch of their brief be-
trothal and the early days of their marriage. With his help, or
even his encouragement his wife might have been able to
maintain it. She had a gift for idealizing him, at least, and as
his hurt healed but slowly, and it was a good while before he
could paint with his wounded arm, it was an easy matter for
her to believe in the meanwhile that he would have been the
greatest painter of his time, but for his honorable disability:
to hear her, you would suppose no one else had ever been
shot in the service of his country.

It was fortunate for Ferris, since he could not work, that
she had money; in exalted moments he had thought this a
barrier to their marriage; yet he could not recall any one who
had refused the hand of a beautiful girl because of the accident of her wealth, and in the end, he silenced his scruples. It
might be said that in many other ways he was not her equal;
but one ought to reflect how very few men are worthy of
their wives in any sense. After his fashion he certainly loved
her always,—even when she tried him most, for it must be
owned that she really had that hot temper which he had
dreaded in her from the first. Not that her imperiousness directly affected him. For a long time after their marriage, she
seemed to have no other desire than to lose her outwearied
will in his. There was something a little pathetic in this; there
was a kind of bewilderment in her gentleness, as though the
relaxed tension of her long self-devotion to her mother left
her without a full motive; she apparently found it impossible
to give herself with a satisfactory degree of abandon to a man
who could do so many things for himself. When her children
came they filled this vacancy, and afforded her scope for the
greatest excesses of self-devotion. Ferris laughed to find her
protecting them and serving them with the same tigerish tenderness, the same haughty humility, as that with which she

used to care for poor Mrs. Vervain; and he perceived that this was merely the direction away from herself of that intense arrogance of nature which but for her power and need of loving, would have made her intolerable. What she chiefly exacted from them in return for her fierce devotedness was the truth in everything; she was content that they should be rather less fond of her than of their father, whom indeed they found much more amusing.

The Ferrises went to Europe some years after their marriage, revisiting Venice, but sojourning for the most part in Florence. Ferris had once imagined that the tragedy which had given him his wife would always invest her with the shadow of its sadness, but in this he was mistaken. There is nothing has really so strong a digestion as love, and this is very lucky, seeing what manifold experiences love has to swallow and assimilate; and when they got back to Venice, Ferris found that the customs of their joint life exorcised all the dark associations of the place. These simply formed a sombre background, against which their wedded happiness relieved itself. They talked much of the past, with free minds, unashamed and unafraid. If it is a little shocking, it is nevertheless true, and true to human nature, that they spoke of Don Ippolito as if he were a part of their love.

Ferris had never ceased to wonder at what he called the unfathomable innocence of his wife, and he liked to go over all the points of their former life in Venice, and bring home to himself the utter simplicity of her girlish ideas, motives and designs, which both confounded and delighted him.

"It's amazing, Florida," he would say, "it's perfectly amazing that you should have been willing to undertake the job of importing into America, that poor fellow with his whole stock of helplessness, dreamery and unpracticality. What *were* you about?"

"Why, I've often told you, Henry. I thought he oughtn't to continue a priest."

"Yes, yes; I know." Then he would remain lost in thought, softly whistling to himself. On one of these occasions he asked, "Do you think he was really very much troubled by his false position?"

"I can't tell, now. He seemed to be so."

"That story he told you of his childhood and of how he became a priest: didn't it strike you at the time like rather a made-up, melodramatic history?"

"No, no! How can you say such things, Henry? It was too simple not to be true."

"Well, well. Perhaps so. But he baffles me. He always did, for that matter."

Then came another pause, while Ferris lay back upon the gondola-cushions getting the level of the Lido just under his hat-brim.

"Do you think he was very much of a skeptic, after all, Florida?"

Mrs. Ferris turned her eyes reproachfully upon her husband. "Why Henry, how strange you are! You said yourself, once, that you used to wonder if he were not a skeptic."

"Yes; I know. But for a man who had lived in doubt so many years, he certainly slipped back into the bosom of mother church pretty suddenly. Don't you think he was a person of rather light feelings?"

"I can't talk with you, my dear, if you go on in that way."

"I don't mean any harm. I can see how in many things he was the soul of truth and honor. But it seems to me that even the life he lived was largely imagined. I mean that he was such a dreamer that once having fancied himself afflicted at being what he was he could go on and suffer as keenly as if he really were troubled by it. Why mightn't it be that all his doubts came from anger and resentment towards those who made him a priest, rather than from any examination of his own mind? I don't say it *was* so. But I don't believe he knew quite what he wanted. He must have felt that his failure as an inventor went deeper than the failure of his particular attempts. I once thought that perhaps he had a genius in that way, but I question now whether he had. If he had, it seems to me he had opportunity to prove it—certainly, as a priest he had leisure to prove it. But, when that sort of sub-consciousness of his own inadequacy came over him, it was perfectly natural for him to take refuge in the supposition that he had been baffled by circumstances."

Mrs. Ferris remained silently troubled. "I don't know how

to answer you, Henry; but I think that you're judging him narrowly and harshly."

"Not harshly. I feel very compassionate towards him. But now, even as to what one might consider the most real thing in his life,—his caring for you,—it seems to me there must have been a great share of imagined sentiment in it. It was not a passion; it was a gentle nature's dream of a passion."

"He didn't die of a dream," said the wife.

"No, he died of a fever."

"He had got well of the fever."

"That's very true, my dear. And whatever his head was, he had an affectionate and faithful heart. I wish I had been gentler with him. I must often have bruised that sensitive soul. God knows I'm sorry for it. But he's a puzzle, he's a puzzle!"

Thus lapsing more and more into a mere problem, as the years have passed, Don Ippolito has at last ceased to be even the memory of a man with a passionate love and a mortal sorrow. Perhaps this final effect in the mind of him who has realized the happiness of which the poor priest vainly dreamed is not the least tragic phase of the tragedy of Don Ippolito.

A MODERN INSTANCE

I

THE VILLAGE stood on a wide plain, and round it rose the mountains. They were green to their tops in summer, and in the winter white through their serried pines and drifting mists, but at every season serious and beautiful, furrowed with hollow shadows, and taking the light on masses and stretches of iron-gray crag. The river swam through the plain in long curves, and slipped away at last through an unseen pass to the southward, tracing a score of miles in its course over a space that measured but three or four. The plain was very fertile, and its features, if few and of purely utilitarian beauty, had a rich luxuriance, and there was a tropical riot of vegetation when the sun of July beat on those northern fields. They waved with corn and oats to the feet of the mountains, and the potatoes covered a vast acreage with the lines of their intense, coarse green; the meadows were deep with English grass to the banks of the river, that doubling and returning upon itself still marked its way with a dense fringe of alders and white birches.

But winter was full half the year. The snow began at Thanksgiving, and fell snow upon snow till Fast Day, thawing between the storms, and packing harder and harder against the break-up in the spring, when it covered the ground in solid levels three feet high, and lay heaped in drifts that defied the sun far into May. When it did not snow the weather was keenly clear and commonly very still. Then the landscape at noon had a stereoscopic glister under the high sun that burned in a heaven without a cloud, and at setting stained the sky and the white waste with freezing pink and violet. On such days the farmers and lumbermen came in to the village stores, and made a stiff and feeble stir about their doorways, and the school children gave the street a little life and color, as they went to and from the academy in their red and blue woollens. Four times a day the mill, the shrill wheeze of whose saws had become part of the habitual silence, blew its whistle for the hands to begin and leave off

175

work, in blasts that seemed to shatter themselves against the thin air. But otherwise an Arctic quiet prevailed.

Behind the black boles of the elms that swept the vista of the street with the fine gray tracery of their boughs, stood the houses deep-sunken in the accumulating drifts, through which each householder kept a path cut from his doorway to the road, white and clean as if hewn out of marble. Some cross-streets straggled away east and west with the poorer dwellings; but this that followed the northward and southward reach of the plain, was the main thoroughfare, and had its own impressiveness, with those square, white houses which they build so large in northern New England. They were all kept in scrupulous repair, though here and there the frost and thaw of many winters had heaved a fence out of plumb, and threatened the poise of the monumental urns of painted pine on the gate-posts. They had dark-green blinds of a color harmonious with that of the funereal evergreens in their door-yards; and they themselves had taken the tone of the snowy landscape as if by the operation of some such law as blanches the fur-bearing animals of the north. They seemed proper to its desolation, while some of more modern taste, painted to a warmer tone, looked, with their mansard roofs and jig-sawed piazzas and balconies, intrusive and alien.

At one end of the street stood the Academy with its classic façade and its belfry; midway was the hotel with the stores, the printing-office and the churches, and at the other extreme, one of the square white mansions stood advanced from the rank of the rest, at the top of a deep-plunging valley, defining itself against the mountain beyond, so sharply that it seemed as if cut out of its dark wooded side. It was from the gate before this house, distinct in the pink light which the sunset had left, that on a Saturday evening in February a cutter, gay with red-lined robes, dashed away and came musically clashing down the street under the naked elms. For the women who sat with their work, at the windows on either side of the way, hesitating whether to light their lamps, and drawing nearer and nearer to the dead-line of the outer cold, for the latest glimmer of the day, the passage of this ill-timed vehicle was a vexation little short of grievous. Every movement on the street was precious to them and with all the keenness of their starved curiosity these captives of the winter could not make out the people in the cutter. Afterwards it was a mortification to them that they should not have thought at once of Bartley Hubbard and Marcia Gaylord. They had seen him go up towards Squire Gaylord's house half an hour before, and they now blamed themselves for not reflecting that of course he was going to take Marcia over to the church-sociable at Lower Equity. Their identity being established, other little proofs of it reproached the inquirers; but these perturbed spirits were at peace, and the lamps were out in the houses, (where the smell of rats in the wainscot and of potatoes in the cellar strengthened with the growing night) when Bartley and Marcia drove back through the moon-lit silence to her father's door. Here, too, the windows were all dark, except for the light that sparely glimmered through the parlor blinds; and the young man slackened the pace of his horse, as if to still the bells, some distance away from the gate.

The girl took the hand he offered her when he dismounted at the gate, and as she jumped from the cutter, "Wont you come in?" she asked.

"I guess I can blanket my horse and stand him under the wood-shed," answered the young man, going round to the animal's head, and leading him away.

When he returned to the door the girl opened it, as if she had been listening for his step; and she now stood holding it ajar for him to enter, and throwing the light upon the threshold from the lamp which she lifted high in the other hand. The action brought her figure in relief, and revealed the outline of her bust and shoulders, while the lamp flooded with light the face she turned to him, and again averted for a moment, as if startled at some noise behind her. She thus showed a smooth low forehead, lips and cheeks deeply red, a softly rounded chin touched with a faint dimple, and in turn a nose short and aquiline; her eyes were dark, and her dusky hair flowed crinkling above her fine black brows, and vanished down the curve of a lovely neck. There was a peculiar charm in the form of her upper lip: it was exquisitely arched, and at the corners it projected a little over the lower lip, so that when she smiled it gave a piquant sweetness to her mouth, with a certain demure innocence that qualified the

Roman pride of her profile. For the rest, her beauty was of
the kind that coming years would only ripen and enrich: at
thirty she would be even handsomer than at twenty, and be
all the more southern in her type for the paling of that northern color in her cheeks. The young man who looked up at
her from the doorstep had a yellow moustache, shadowing
either side of his lip with a broad sweep like a bird's wing;
his chin, deep cut below his mouth, failed to come stren-
uously forward; his cheeks were filled to an oval contour; and
his face had otherwise the regularity common to Americans;
his eyes, a clouded gray, heavy-lidded and long-lashed, were
his most striking feature, and he gave her beauty a deliberate
look from them as he lightly stamped the snow from his feet,
and pulled the seal-skin gloves from his long hands.

"Come in!" she whispered, coloring with pleasure under
his gaze; and she made haste to shut the door after him with
a luxurious impatience of the cold. She led the way into the
room from which she had come, and set down the lamp on
the corner of the piano, while he slipped off his overcoat, and
swung it over the end of the sofa. They drew up chairs to the
stove, in which the smouldering fire, revived by the opened
draft, roared and snapped. It was midnight, as the sharp
strokes of a wooden clock declared from the kitchen; and they
were alone together and all the other inmates of the house
were asleep. The situation, scarcely conceivable to another
civilization, is so common in ours, where youth commands its
fate, and trusts solely to itself, that it may be said to be characteristic of the New England civilization wherever it keeps its simplicity. It was not stolen or clandestine; it would have interested
everyone but would have shocked no one in the village if the
whole village had known it; all that a girl's parents ordinarily
exacted was that they should not be waked up.

"Ugh!" said the girl, "it seems as if I never should get
warm." She leaned forward, and stretched her hands toward
the stove, and he presently rose from the rocking-chair in
which he sat somewhat lower than she, and lifted her sack to
throw it over her shoulders. But he put it down, and took up
his overcoat.

"Allow my coat the pleasure," he said, with the ease of a
man who is not too far lost to be really flattering.

"Much obliged to the coat," she replied, shrugging herself into it, and pulling the collar close about her throat. "I wonder you didn't put it on the sorrel. You could have tied the sleeves round her neck."

"Shall I tie them round yours?" He leaned forward from the low rocking-chair into which he had sunk again, and made a feint at what he had proposed.

But she drew back with a gay, "No!" and added, "Some day, father says, that sorrel will be the death of us. He says it's a bad color for a horse. They're always ugly, and when they get heated, they're crazy."

"You never seem to be very much frightened when you're riding after the sorrel," said Bartley.

"Oh, I've great faith in your driving."

"Thanks. But I don't believe in this notion about a horse being vicious because he's of a certain color. If your father didn't believe in it, I should call it a superstition. But the Squire has no superstitions."

"I don't know about that," said the girl. "I don't think he likes to see the new moon over his left shoulder."

"I beg his pardon, then," returned Bartley. "I ought to have said religions. The Squire has no religions."

The young fellow had a rich caressing voice, and a securely winning manner which comes from the habit of easily pleasing; in this charming tone and with this delightful insinuation, he often said things that hurt; but with such a humorous glance from his softly shaded eyes that people felt in some sort flattered at being taken into the joke, even while they winced under it.

The girl seemed to wince, as if, in spite of her familiarity with the fact, it wounded her to have her father's skepticism recognized just then. She said nothing, and he added, "I remember we used to think that a red-headed boy was worse-tempered on account of his hair. But I don't believe the sorrel-tops, as we called them were any fierier than the rest of us."

Marcia did not answer at once, and then she said with the vagueness of one not greatly interested by the subject, "You've got a sorrel-top in your office that's fiery enough if she's anything like what she used to be when she went to school."

"Hannah Morrison?"

"Yes."

"Oh, she isn't so bad. She's pretty lively; but she's very eager to learn the business, and I guess we shall get along. I think she wants to please me."

"*Does* she! But she must be going on seventeen, now."

"I dare say," answered the young man carelessly, but with perfect intelligence. "She's good-looking in her way, too."

"Oh! Then you admire red-hair."

He perceived the anxiety that the girl's pride could not keep out of her tone, but he answered indifferently: "I'm a little too near that color, myself. I hear that red hair's coming into fashion, but I guess it's natural I should prefer black."

She leaned back in her chair, and crushed the velvet collar of his coat under her neck in lifting her head to stare at the high-hung mezzotints and family photographs on the walls, while a flattered smile parted her lips, and there was a little thrill of joy in her voice. "I presume we must be a good deal behind the age in everything, at Equity."

"Well, you know my opinion of Equity," returned the young man. "If I didn't have you here to free my mind to, once in a while, I don't know what I should do."

She was so proud to be in the secret of his discontent with the narrow world of Equity, that she tempted him to disparage it farther by pretending to identify herself with it. "I don't see why you abuse Equity to me. I've never been anywhere else, except those two winters at school. You'd better look out: I might expose you," she threatened fondly.

"I'm not afraid. Those two winters make a great difference. You saw girls from other places—from Augusta and Bangor and Bath."

"Well, I couldn't see how they were so very different from Equity girls."

"I dare say they couldn't, either, if they judged from you."

She leaned forward again and begged for more flattery from him with her happy eyes. "Why, what *does* make me so different from all the rest? I should really like to know."

"Oh, you don't expect me to tell you to your face!"

"Yes, to my face! I don't believe it's anything complimentary."

"No, it's nothing that you deserve any credit for."

"Pshaw!" cried the girl. "I know you're only talking to make fun of me. How do I know but you make fun of me to other girls, just as you do of them to me. Everybody says you're sarcastic."

"Have I ever been sarcastic with you?"

"You know I wouldn't stand it."

He made no reply, but she admired the ease with which he now turned from her, and took one book after another from the table at his elbow, saying some words of ridicule about each. It gave her a still deeper sense of his intellectual command when he finally discriminated, and began to read out a poem with studied elocutionary effects. He read in a low tone, but at last some responsive noises came from the room overhead; he closed the book, and threw himself into an attitude of deprecation with his eyes cast up to the ceiling.

"Chicago," he said, laying the book on the table, and taking his knee between his hands, while he dazzled her by speaking from the abstraction of one who has carried on a train of thought quite different from that on which he seemed to be intent, "Chicago is the place for me. I don't think I can stand Equity much longer. You know that chum of mine I told you about: he's written to me to come out there and go into the law with him at once."

"Why don't you go?" the girl forced herself to ask.

"Oh, I'm not ready, yet. Should you write to me if I went to Chicago?"

"I don't think you'd find my letters very interesting. You wouldn't want any news from Equity."

"Your letters wouldn't be interesting if you gave me the Equity news; but they would if you left it out. Then you'd have to write about yourself."

"Oh, I don't think that would interest anybody."

"Well, I feel almost like going out to Chicago to see."

"But I haven't promised to write yet," said the girl, laughing for joy in his humor.

"I shall have to stay in Equity till you do, then. Better promise at once."

"Wouldn't that be too much like marrying a man to get rid of him?"

"I don't think that's always such a bad plan—for the man."
He waited for her to speak; but she had gone the length of
her tether, in this direction. "Byron says:

> " 'Man's love is of man's life a thing apart—
> 'Tis woman's whole existence.'

Do you believe that?" He dwelt upon her with his free look,
in the happy embarrassment with which she let her head
droop.

"I don't know," she murmured. "I don't know anything
about a man's life."

"It was the woman's I was asking about."

"I don't think I'm competent to answer."

"Well, I'll tell you, then. I think Byron was mistaken. My
experience is that when a man is in love, there's nothing else
of him. That's the reason I've kept out of it altogether, of late
years. My advice is, Don't fall in love: it takes too much
time." They both laughed at this. "But about corresponding,
now: you haven't said whether you would write to me, or
not. Will you?"

"Can't you wait and see?" she asked, stealing a look at him,
which she could not keep from being fond.

"No, no! Unless you wrote to me, I couldn't go to Chicago."

"Perhaps I ought to promise, then, at once."

"You mean that you wish me to go."

"You said that you were going. You oughtn't to let anything stand in the way of your doing the best you can for
yourself."

"But you would miss me a little, wouldn't you? You would
try to miss me, now and then?"

"Oh, you are here, pretty often. I don't think I should have
much difficulty in missing you."

"Thanks, thanks! I can go with a light heart, now. Good-
by!" He made a pretence of rising.

"What! Are you going at once?"

"Yes, this very night—or to-morrow. Or no, I can't go to-
morrow. There's something I was going to do to-morrow."

"Perhaps go to church."

"Oh, that, of course. But it was in the afternoon. Stop! I have it! I want you to go sleighriding with me in the afternoon."

"I don't know about that," Marcia began.

"But I do," said the young man. "Hold on: I'll put my request in writing." He opened her portefolio, which lay on the table. "What elegant stationery! May I use some of this elegant stationery? The letter is to a lady—to open a correspondence. May I?" She laughed her assent. "How ought I to begin? Dearest Miss Marcia, or just Dear Marcia: which is best?"

"You had better not put either"—

"But I must. You're one or the other, you know. You're dear,—to your family—and you're Marcia: you can't deny it. The only question is whether you're the dearest of all the Miss Marcias. I may be mistaken, you know. We'll err on the safe side: Dear Marcia." He wrote it down. "That looks well, and it reads well. It looks very natural, and it reads like poetry—blank verse; there's no rhyme for it that I can remember. Dear Marcia: Will you go sleigh-riding with me tomorrow afternoon at two o'clock sharp? Yours—Yours sincerely, or cordially, or affectionately, or what-ly? The Dear Marcia seems to call for something out of the common. I think it had better be affectionately." He suggested it with ironical gravity.

"And *I* think it had better be Truly," protested the girl.

"Truly, it shall be, then. Your word is law—statute in such case made and provided." He wrote "With unalterable devotion, Yours truly, Bartley J. Hubbard," and read it aloud.

She leaned forward, and lightly caught it away from him, and made a feint of tearing it. He seized her hands. "Mr. Hubbard," she cried in undertone, "let me go, please."

"On two conditions—Promise not to tear up my letter, and promise to answer it in writing."

She hesitated long, letting him hold her wrists. At last she said, "Well," and he released her wrists on whose whiteness his clasp left red circles. She wrote a single word on the paper, and pushed it across the table to him. He rose with it, and went round to her side. "This is very nice. But you haven't spelled it correctly. Anybody would say this was *No*, to look at it; and you meant to write *Yes*. Take the pencil in your hand, Miss Gaylord, and I will steady your trembling nerves, so that you can form the characters. Stop! At the slightest resistance on your part, I will call out and alarm the house; or I will"—He put the pencil into her fingers, and took her soft fist into his, and changed the word, while she submitted, helpless with her smothered laughter. "Now the address. Dear"—

"No, no!" she protested.

"Yes, yes! Dear Mr. Hubbard. There, that will do! Now the signature: Yours"—

"I *wont* write that. I wont, indeed!"

"Oh, yes you will. You only think you wont. Yours gratefully, Marcia Gaylord. That's right. The Gaylord is not very legible, on account of a slight tremor in the writer's arm, resulting from a constrained posture, perhaps. Thanks, Miss Gaylord, I will be here promptly at the hour indicated"—

The noises renewed themselves overhead; some one seemed to be moving about. Hubbard laid his hand on that of the girl still resting on the table, and grasped it in burlesque alarm; she could scarcely stifle her mirth. He released her hand, and reaching his chair with a theatrical stride, sat there cowering till the noises ceased. Then he began to speak soberly, in a low voice. He spoke of himself; but in application of a lecture which they had lately heard, so that he seemed to be speaking of the lecture. It was on the formation of character, and he told of the processes by which he had formed his own character. They appeared very wonderful to her, and she marvelled at the ease with which he dismissed the frivolity of his recent mood, and was now all seriousness. When he came to speak of the influence of others upon him, she almost trembled with the intensity of her interest. "But of all the women I have known, Marcia," he said, "I believe you have had the strongest influence upon me. I believe you could make me do anything; but you have always influenced me for good; your influence upon me has been ennobling and elevating."

She wished to refuse his praise; but her heart throbbed for bliss and pride in it; her voice dissolved on her lips. They sat in silence; and he took in his the hand that she let hang over the side of her chair.

The lamp began to burn low; and she found words to say, "I had better get another," but she did not move.

"No; don't," he said; "I must be going, too Look at the wick, there, Marcia: it scarcely reaches the oil. In a little while it will not reach it, and the flame will die out. That is the way the ambition to be good and great will die out of me when my life no longer draws its inspiration from your influence." This figure took her imagination; it seemed to her very beautiful; and his praise humbled her more and more. "Good-night," he said, in a low, sad voice. He gave her hand a last pressure, and rose to put on his coat. Her admiration of his words, her happiness in his flattery filled her brain like wine. She moved dizzily as she took up the lamp to light him to the door. "I have tired you," he said, tenderly, and he passed his hand around her to sustain the elbow of the arm with which she held the lamp; she wished to resist, but she could not try.

At the door he bent down his head and kissed her. "Good-night, dear—friend."

"Good night," she panted, and after the door had closed upon him, she stooped and kissed the knob on which his hand had rested.

As she turned, she started to see her father coming down the stairs with a candle in his hand. He had his black cravat tied round his throat, but no collar; otherwise he had on the rusty black clothes in which he ordinarily went about his affairs: the cassimere pantaloons, the satin vest, and the dress-coat which old fashioned country lawyers still wore, ten years ago, in preference to a frock or sack. He stopped on one of the lower steps, and looked sharply down into her uplifted face, and as they stood confronted, their consanguinity came out in vivid resemblances and contrasts; his high, hawklike profile was translated into the fine aquiline outline of hers; the harsh rings of black hair, now grizzled with age, which clustered tightly over his head, except where they had retreated from his deeply seamed and wrinkled forehead, were the crinkled flow above her smooth, white brow; and the line of the bristly tufts that overhung his eyes was the same as that of the low arches above hers. Her complexion was from her mother: his skin was dusky yellow; but they had the same mouth and hers showed how sweet his mouth must have been in his youth. His eyes, deep sunk in their cavernous sockets, had rekindled their dark fires in hers; his whole visage, softened to her sex and girlish years, looked up at him in his daughter's face.

"Why, father! Did we wake you?"

"No. I hadn't been asleep at all. I was coming down to read. But it's time you were in bed, Marcia."

"Yes, I'm going, now. There's a good fire in the parlor stove."

The old man descended the remaining steps but turned at the parlor door, and looked again at his daughter with a glance that arrested her with her foot on the lowest stair. "Marcia," he asked grimly, "are you engaged to Bartley Hubbard?"

The blood flashed up from her heart into her face like fire, and then as suddenly fell back again and left her white. She let her head droop and turn till her eyes were wholly averted from him, and she did not speak. He closed the door behind him and she went up stairs to her own room; in her shame she seemed to herself to crawl thither, with her father's glance burning upon her.

II

BARTLEY HUBBARD drove his sorrel colt back to the hotel stable through the moonlight, and woke up the ostler, asleep behind the counter on a bunk covered with buffalo robes. The half-grown boy did not wake easily: he conceived of the affair as a joke, and bade Bartley quit his fooling, till the young man took him by his collar, and stood him on his feet. Then he fumbled about the button of the lamp, turned low and smelling rankly, and lit his lantern, which contributed a rival stench to the choking air. He kicked together the embers that smouldered on the hearth of the Franklin stove, sitting down before it for his greater convenience, and having put a fresh pine root on the fire, fell into a doze, with his lantern in his hand. "Look here, young man!" said Bartley shaking him by the shoulder, "you had better go out and put that colt up, and leave this sleeping before the fire to me."

"Guess the colt can wait awhile," grumbled the boy; but he went out all the same, and Bartley, looking through the window saw his lantern wavering, a yellow blot in the white moonshine, towards the stable. He sat down in the ostler's chair, and in his turn kicked the pine-root with the heel of his shoe, and looked about the room. He had had, as he would have said, a grand good time; but it had left him hungry, and the table in the middle of the room, with the chairs huddled round it, was suggestive though he knew that it had been barrenly put there for the convenience of the landlord's friends, who came every night to play whist with him, and that nothing to eat or drink had ever been set out on it to interrupt the austere interest of the game. It was long since there had been anything on the shelves behind the counter cheerfuller than corn-balls and fancy-crackers for the children of the summer boarders; these dainties being out of the season the jars now stood there empty. The young man waited in a hungry reverie, in which it appeared to him that he was undergoing unmerited suffering, till the stable-boy came back, now wide awake and disposed to let the house share his vigils, as he stamped over the floor in his heavy boots.

"Andy," said Bartley in a pathetic tone of injury, "can't you scare me up something to eat?"

"There aint anything in the butt'ry but meat-pie," said the boy. He meant mince-pie, as Hubbard knew, and not a pasty of meat; and the hungry man hesitated.

"Well, fetch it," he said, finally. "I guess we can warm it up a little by the coals here." He had not been so long out of college but the idea of this irregular supper, when he had once formed it, began to have its fascination. He took up the broad fire shovel, and by the time the boy had clubbed to and from the pantry beyond the dining-room, Bartley had cleaned the shovel with a piece of newspaper, and was already heating it by the embers which he had raked out from under the pine-root. The boy silently transferred the half pie he had brought from its plate to the shovel; he pulled up a chair, and sat down to watch it; the pie began to steam and send out a savory odor; he himself in thawing emitted a stronger and stronger smell of stable. He was not without his disdain for the palate which must have its mince-pie warm at midnight; nor without his respect for it either: this fastidious taste must be part of the splendor which showed itself in Mr. Hubbard's city-cut clothes, and in his neck-scarfs, and the perfection of his finger nails and moustache. The boy had felt the original impression of these facts deepened rather than effaced by custom: they were for every day, and not, as he had at first conjectured, for some great occasion only.

"You don't suppose, Andy, there's such a thing as cold tea or coffee anywhere that we could warm up?" asked Bartley, gazing thoughtfully at the pie.

The boy shook his head. "Get you some milk," he said; and after he had let the dispiriting suggestion sink into the other's mind, he added, "Or some water."

"Oh, bring on the milk," groaned Bartley, but with the relief that a choice of evils affords.

The boy clubbed away for it, and when he came back the young man had got his pie on the plate again, and had drawn his chair up to the table. "Thanks," he said with his mouth full, as the boy set down the goblet of milk. Andy pulled his chair round so as to get an unrestricted view of a man who ate his pie with his fork as easily as another would with a knife. "That sister of yours is a smart girl," the young man added, making deliberate progress with the pie.

The boy made an inarticulate sound of satisfaction, and resolved in his heart to tell her what Mr. Hubbard had said. "She's as smart as time," continued Bartley. This was something concrete; the boy knew he should remember that comparison.

"Bring you anything else?" he asked, admiring the young man's skill in getting the last flakes of the crust on his fork: the pie had now vanished.

"Why, there isn't anything else, is there?" Bartley demanded with the plaintive dismay of a man who fears he has flung away his hunger upon one dish when he might have had something better.

"Cheese," replied the boy.

"Oh," said Bartley. He reflected a while. "I suppose I could toast a piece on this fork. But there isn't any more milk."

The boy took away the plate and goblet, and brought them again replenished.

Bartley contrived to get the cheese on his fork, and to rest it against one of the andirons so that it would not fall into the ashes. When it was done, he ate it as he had eaten the pie, without offering to share his feast with the boy. "There!" he said. "Yes, Andy, if she keeps on as she's been doing, she wont have any trouble. She's a bright girl." He stretched his legs before the fire again, and presently yawned.

"Want your lamp, Mr. Hubbard?" asked the boy.

"Well, yes, Andy," the young man consented, "I suppose I may as well go to bed."

But when the boy brought his lamp, he still remained with outstretched legs in front of the fire. Speaking of Hannah Morrison made him think of Marcia again and of the way in which she had spoken of the girl. He lolled his head on one side in such comfort as a young man finds in the conviction that a pretty girl is not only fond of him but is instantly jealous of any other girl whose name is mentioned. He smiled at the flame in his revery, and the boy examined, with clandestine minuteness, the set and pattern of his pantaloons, with glances of reference and comparison to his own.

There were many things about his relations with Marcia

Gaylord which were calculated to give Bartley satisfaction.
She was without question the prettiest girl in the place, and
she had more style than any other girl began to have. He
liked to go into a room with Marcia Gaylord; it was some
pleasure. Marcia was a lady; she had a good education; she
had been away two years to school; and when she came back
at the end of the second winter he knew that she had fallen
in love with him at sight; he believed that he could time it to
a second. He remembered how he had looked up at her as he
passed, and she had reddened and tried to turn away from
the window as if she had not seen him. Bartley was still free
as air; but if he could once make up his mind to settle down
in a hole like Equity he could have her by turning his hand.
Of course she had her drawbacks, like everybody. She was
proud, and she would be jealous; but with all her pride and
her distance she had let him see that she liked him; and not
a word on his part that any one could hold him to.

"Hullo!" he cried, with a suddenness that startled the boy,
who had finished his meditation upon Bartley's pantaloons,
and was now deeply dwelling on his boots. "Do you like 'em?
See what sort of shine you can give 'em for Sunday-go-to-
meeting to-morrow morning." He put out his hand and laid
hold of the boy's head, passing his fingers through the thick
red hair. "Sorrel-top!" he said, with a grin of agreeable reminiscence. "They emptied all the freckles they had left, into
your face, didn't they, Andy?"

This free, joking way of Bartley's was one of the things
that made him popular; he passed the time of day, and was
give and take right along, as his admirers expressed it, from
the first, in a community where his smartness had that honor
which gives us more smart men to the square mile than any
other country in the world. The fact of his smartness had
been affirmed and established in the strongest manner by the
authorities of the college at which he was graduated, in answer to the reference he made to them when negotiating with
the committee in charge for the place he now held as editor
of the Equity Free Press. The faculty spoke of the solidity and
variety of his acquirements; and the distinction with which he
had acquitted himself in every branch of study he had undertaken; they added that he deserved the greater credit because

his early disadvantages as an orphan, dependent on his own exertions for a livelihood, had been so great that he had entered college with difficulty and with heavy conditions. This turned the scale with a committee who had all been poor boys themselves and justly feared the encroachments of hereditary aristocracy. They perhaps had their misgivings when the young man in his well blacked boots, his gray pantaloons neatly fitting over them, and his diagonal coat buttoned high with one button stood before them with his thumbs in his waistcoat pockets and looked down over his moustache at the floor with sentiments concerning their wisdom which they could not explore; they must have resented the fashionable keeping of everything about him, for Bartley wore his one suit as if it were but one of many; but when they understood that he had come by everything through his own unaided smartness, they could no longer hesitate. One indeed still felt it a duty to call attention to the fact that the college authorities said nothing of the young man's moral characteristics, in a letter dwelling so largely upon his intellectual qualifications. The others referred this point by a silent look, to Squire Gaylord.

"I don't know," said the Squire, "as I ever heard that a great deal of morality was required by a newspaper editor." The rest laughed at the joke, and the Squire continued: "But I guess if he worked his own way through college, as they say, that he hain't had time to be up to a great deal of mischief. You know it's for idle hands that the devil provides, doctor."

"That's true, as far as it goes," said the doctor. "But it isn't the whole truth. The devil provides for some busy hands, too."

"There's a good deal of sense in that," the Squire admitted. "The worst scamps I ever knew were active fellows. Still, industry is in a man's favor. If the faculty knew anything against this young man they would have given us a hint of it. I guess we had better take him; we sha'n't do better. Is it a vote?"

The good opinion of Bartley's smartness which Squire Gaylord had formed was confirmed some months later by the development of the fact that the young man did not regard his management of the Equity Free Press as a final vocation.

The story went that he lounged into the lawyer's office one Saturday afternoon in October, and asked him to let him take his Blackstone into the woods with him. He came back with it a few hours later. "Well, sir," said the attorney, sardonically, "how much Blackstone have you read?"

"About forty pages," answered the young man, dropping into one of the empty chairs, and hanging his leg over the arm.

The lawyer smiled, and opening the book, asked half a dozen questions at random. Bartley answered without changing his indifferent countenance, or the careless posture he had fallen into. A sharper and longer examination followed: the very language seemed to have been unbrokenly transferred to his mind, and he often gave the author's words as well as his ideas.

"Ever looked at this before?" asked the lawyer, with a keen glance at him over his spectacles.

"No," said Bartley, gaping as if bored, and further relieving his weariness by stretching. He was without deference for any presence; and the old lawyer did not dislike him for this: he had no deference himself.

"You think of studying law?" he asked, after a pause.

"That's what I came to ask you about," said Bartley, swinging his leg.

The elder recurred to his book, and put some more questions. Then he said, "Do you want to study with me?"

"That's about the size of it."

He shut the book, and pushed it on the table towards the young man. "Go ahead. You'll get along—if you don't get along too easily."

It was in the spring after this that Marcia returned home from her last term at boarding-school, and first saw him.

III

BARTLEY WOKE on Sunday morning with the regrets that a supper of mince-pie and toasted cheese is apt to bring. He woke from a bad dream, and found that he had a dull headache. A cup of coffee relieved his pain, but it left him listless, and with a longing for sympathy, which he experienced in any mental or physical discomfort. The frankness with which he then appealed for compassion was one of the things that made people like him; he flung himself upon the pity of the first he met. It might be some one to whom he had said a cutting or mortifying thing at their last encounter, but Bartley did not mind that: what he desired was commiseration and he confidingly ignored the past in a trust that had rarely been abused. If his sarcasm proved that he was quick and smart, his recourse to those who had suffered from it proved that he did not mean anything by what he said; it showed that he was a man of warm feelings and that his heart was in the right place.

Bartley deplored his disagreeable sensations to the other boarders at breakfast, and affectionately excused himself to them for not going to church, when they turned into the office, and gathered there before the Franklin stove, sensible of the day in freshly shaven chins and newly blacked boots. The habit of church going was so strong and universal in Equity that even strangers stopping at the hotel found themselves the object of a sort of hospitable competition with the members of the different denominations, who took it for granted that they would wish to go somewhere, and only suffered them a choice between sects. There was no intolerance in their offer of pews, but merely a profound expectation, and one might continue to choose his place of worship Sabbath after Sabbath without offence. This was Bartley's custom, and it had worked to his favor rather than his disadvantage; for in the rather chaotic liberality into which religious sentiment had fallen in Equity, it was tacitly conceded that the editor of a paper devoted to the interests of the whole town, ought not to be of fixed theological opinions.

Religion there had largely ceased to be a fact of spiritual experience and the visible church flourished on condition of providing for the social needs of the community. It was practically held that the salvation of one's soul must not be made too depressing, or the young people would have nothing to do with it. Professors of the sternest creeds temporized with sinners, and did what might be done to win them to heaven by helping them to have a good time here. The church embraced and included the world. It no longer frowned even upon social dancing, a transgression once so heinous in its eyes; it opened its doors to popular lectures; and encouraged secular music in its basements, where during the winter oyster-suppers were given in aid of good objects. The Sunday School was made particularly attractive, both to the children and the young men and girls who taught them. Not only at Thanksgiving but at Christmas, and latterly even at Easter, there were special observances, which the enterprising spirits having the welfare of the church at heart, tried to make significant and agreeable to all, and promotive of good feeling. Christenings and marriages in the church were encouraged and elaborately celebrated; death alone, though treated with cut flowers in emblematic devices, refused to lend itself to the cheerful intentions of those who were struggling to render the idea of another and a better world less repulsive. In contrast with the relaxation and uncertainty of their doctrinal aim, the rude and bold infidelity of old Squire Gaylord had the greater affinity with the mood of the Puritanism they had outgrown. But Bartley Hubbard liked the religious situation well enough. He took a leading part in the entertainments, and did something to impart to them a literary cast, as in the series of readings from the poets which he gave, the first winter, for the benefit of each church in turn. At these lectures he commended himself to the sober elders, who were troubled by the levity of his behavior with young people on other occasions, by asking one of the ministers to open the exercises with prayer, and another, at the close, to invoke the divine blessing: there was no especial relevancy in this, but it pleased. He kept himself, from the beginning, pretty constantly in the popular eye. He was a speaker at all public meetings, where his declamation was admired, and at private parties, where the congealed particles of village society were united in a frozen mass, he was the first to break the ice, and set the angular fragments grating and grinding upon one another.

He now went to his room, and opened his desk with some vague purposes of bringing up the arrears of his correspondence. Formerly, before his interest in the newspaper had lapsed at all, he used to give his Sunday leisure to making selections and writing paragraphs for it; but he now let the pile of exchanges lie unopened on his desk, and began to rummage through the letters scattered about in it. They were mostly from young ladies, with whom he had corresponded, and some of them enclosed the photographs of the writers, doing their best to look as they hoped he might think they looked. They were not love-letters, but were of that sort which the laxness of our social life invites young people, who have met pleasantly, to exchange as long as they like without explicit intentions on either side: they commit the writers to nothing; they are commonly without result except in wasting time which is hardly worth saving. Every one who has lived the American life must have produced them in great numbers. While youth lasts, they afford an excitement whose charm is hard to realize afterwards.

Bartley's correspondents were young ladies of his college town, where he had first begun to see something of social life in days which he now recognized as those of his green youth. They were not so very far removed in point of time; but the experience of a larger world in the vacation he had spent with a Boston student had relegated them to a moral remoteness that could not readily be measured. His friend was the son of a family who had diverted him from the natural destiny of a Boston man at Harvard, and sent him elsewhere for sectarian reasons. They were rich people, devout in their way, and benevolent, after a fashion of their own; and their son always brought home with him for the holidays and other short vacations some fellow student accounted worthy of their hospitality through his religious intentions or his intellectual promise. These guests were indicated to the young man by one of the faculty, and he accepted their companionship for the time with what perfunctory civility he could muster. He and Bartley had amused themselves very well during that vacation. The Hallecks were not fashionable people, but they lived wealthily: they had a coachman and an inside man (whom Bartley at first treated with a consideration that it afterwards mortified him to think of); their house was richly furnished with cushioned seats, dense carpets and heavy curtains; and they were visited by other people of their denomination and of a like abundance. Some of these were infected with the prevailing culture of the city, and the young ladies especially dressed in a style and let fall ideas that filled the soul of the country student with wonder and worship. He heard a great deal of talk that he did not understand, but he eagerly treasured every impression, and pieced it out by question or furtive observation into an image often shrewdly true and often grotesquely untrue to the conditions into which he had been dropped. He civilized himself as rapidly as his light permitted. There was a great deal of church going; but he and young Halleck went also to lectures and concerts; they even went to the opera, and Bartley, with the privity of his friend, went to the theatre. Halleck said that he did not think there was much harm in a play; but that his people stayed away for the sake of the example: a reason that certainly need not hold with Bartley.

At the end of the vacation he returned to college, leaving his measure with Halleck's tailor, and his heart with all the splendors and elegancies of the town. He found the ceilings very low, and the fashions much belated in the village; but he reconciled himself as well as he could. The real stress came when he left college and the question of doing something for himself pressed upon him. He intended to study law, but he must meantime earn his living. It had been his fortune to be left when very young not only an orphan but an extremely pretty child, with an exceptional aptness for study; and he had been better cared for than if his father and mother had lived. He had been not only well housed and fed, and very well dressed, but pitied as an orphan, and petted for his beauty and talent, while he was always taught to think of himself as a poor boy, who was winning his own way through the world. But when his benefactor proposed to educate him for the ministry, with a view to his final use in missionary work, he revolted. He apprenticed himself to the printer of his village, and rapidly picked up a knowledge of the business, so that at nineteen he had laid by some money, and was able to think of going to college. There was a fund in aid of indigent students in the institution to which he turned, and the faculty favored him. He finished his course with great credit to himself and the college, and he was naturally inclined to look upon what had been done for him earlier, as an advantage taken of his youthful inexperience. He rebelled against the memory of that tutelage, in spite of which he had accomplished such great things. If he had not squandered his time or fallen into vicious courses in circumstances of so much discouragement, if he had come out of it all self-reliant and independent, he knew whom he had to thank for it. The worst of the matter was that there was some truth in all this.

The ardor of his satisfaction cooled in the two years following his graduation, when in intervals of teaching country schools he was actually reduced to work at his trade, on a village newspaper. But it was as a practical printer, through the free-masonry of the craft that Bartley heard of the wish of the Equity committee to place the Free Press in new hands, and he had to be grateful to his trade for a primary consideration from them which his collegiate honors would not have won him. There had not yet begun to be that talk of journalism as a profession which has since prevailed with our collegians, and if Bartley had thought, as other collegians think, of devoting himself to newspaper life, he would have turned his face towards the city where its prizes are won: the ten and fifteen dollar reporterships for which a four years' course of the classics is not too costly a preparation. But to tell the truth he had never regarded his newspaper as anything but a make-shift, by which he was to be carried over a difficult and anxious period of his life, and enabled to attempt something worthier his powers. He had no illusions concerning it: if he had ever thought of journalism as a grand and ennobling profession, these ideas had perished in his experience in a village printing-office. He came to his work in Equity with practical and immediate purposes which pleased the committee better. The paper had been established some time

before, in one of those flurries of ambition which from time
to time seized Equity, when its citizens reflected that it was
the central town in the county and yet not the shire-town.
The question of the removal of the county-seat had periodi-
cally arisen before; but it had never been so hotly agitated as
now. The paper had been a happy thought of a local politician whose conception of its management was that it might
be easily edited by a committee if a printer could be found to
publish it; but a few months' experience had made the Free
Press a terrible burden to its founders; it could not be sustained, and it could not be let die without final disaster to the
interests of the town; and the committee began to cast about
for a publisher who could also be editor. Bartley, to whom it
fell, could not be said to have thrown his heart and soul into
the work, but he threw all his energy, and he made it more
than its friends could have hoped. He espoused the cause of
Equity in the pending question with the zeal of a *condottiere*,
and did service no less faithful because of the cynical quality
latent in it. When the legislative decision against Equity put
an end to its ambitious hopes for the time being, he continued in control of the paper, with a fair prospect of getting
the property into his own hands at last, and with some growing question in his mind whether, after all, it might not be as
easy for him to go into politics from the newspaper as from
the law. He managed the office very economically, and by
having the work done by girl-apprentices, with the help of
one boy, he made it self-supporting. He modeled the newspaper upon the modern conception, through which the country press must cease to have any influence in public affairs,
and each paper become little more than an open letter of
neighborhood gossip. But while he filled his sheet with minute chronicles of the goings and comings of unimportant
persons, and with all attainable particulars of the ordinary life
of the different localities, he continued to make spicy hits at
the enemies of Equity in the late struggle, and kept the public
spirit of the town alive. He had lately undertaken to make
known its advantages as a summer resort, and had published
a series of encomiums upon the beauty of its scenery and the
healthfulness of its air and water which it was believed would
put it in a position of rivalry with some of the famous White

Mountain places. He invited the enterprise of outside capital, and advocated a narrow gauge road up the valley of the river through the Notch, so as to develop the picturesque advantages of that region. In all this, the color of mockery let the wise perceive that Bartley saw the joke and enjoyed it, and it deepened the popular impression of his smartness. This vein of cynicism was not characteristic, as it would have been in an older man: it might have been part of that spiritual and intellectual unruliness of youth, which people laugh at and forgive and which one generally regards in after-life as something almost alien to one's self. He wrote long bragging articles about Equity in a tone bordering on burlesque, and he had a department in his paper where he printed humorous squibs of his own and of other people; these were sometimes copied, and in the daily papers of the State he had been mentioned as "the funny man of the Equity Free Press." He also sent letters to one of the Boston journals, which he reproduced in his own sheet, and which gave him an importance that the best endeavor as a country editor would never have won him with the villagers. He would naturally, as the local printer, have ranked a little above the foreman of the saw mill in the social scale, and decidedly below the master of the Academy, but his personal qualities elevated him over the head even of the latter. But above all, the fact that he was studying law was a guaranty of his superiority that nothing else could have given: that science is the fountain of the highest distinction in a country town. Bartley's whole course implied that he was above editing the Free Press, but that he did it because it served his turn. That was admirable.

He sat a long time with these girls' letters before him, and lost himself in a pensive reverie over their photographs, and over the good times he used to have with them. He mused in that formless way in which a young man thinks about young girls; his soul is suffused with a sense of their sweetness and brightness, and unless he is distinctly in love there is no intention in his thoughts of them; even then there is often no intention. Bartley might very well have a good conscience about them; he had broken no hearts among them, and had only met them half way in flirtation. What he really regretted, as he held their letters in his hand was that he had never got up a correspondence with two or three of the girls whom he had met in Boston. Though he had been cowed by their magnificence in the beginning, he had never had any reverence for them: he believed that they would have liked very well to continue his acquaintance; but he had not known how to open a correspondence, and the point was one on which he was ashamed to consult Halleck. These college-belles, compared with them, were amusingly inferior; by a natural turn of thought, he realized that they were inferior to Marcia Gaylord, too, in looks and style, no less than in an impassioned preference for himself. A distaste for their somewhat veteran ways in flirtation grew upon him as he thought of her; he philosophized against them to her advantage; he could not blame her if she did not know how to hide her feelings for him. Yet he knew that Marcia would rather have died than let him suppose that she cared for him, if she had known that she was doing it. The fun of it was that she should not know; this charmed him, it touched him even; he did not think of it exultantly, as the night before, but sweetly, fondly, and with a final curiosity to see her again, and enjoy the fact in her presence. The acrid little jets of smoke which escaped from the joints of his stove from time to time, annoyed him; he shut his portfolio at last and went out to walk.

IV

T HE FORENOON sunshine, beating strong upon the thin
snow along the edges of the porch floor, tattered them
with a little thaw here and there; but it had no effect upon
the hard-packed levels of the street up the middle of which
Bartley walked in a silence intensified by the muffled voices of
exhortation that came to him out of the churches. It was in
the very heart of sermon time, and he had the whole street to
himself, on his way up to Squire Gaylord's house. As he drew
near, he saw smoke ascending from the chimney of the lawyer's office, a little white building that stood apart from the
dwelling on the left of the gate, and he knew that the old
man was within, reading there, with his hat on, and his long
legs flung out toward the stove, unshaven and unkempt, in a
grim protest against the prevalent Christian superstition. He
might be reading Hume, or Gibbon; or he might be reading
the Bible: a book in which he was deeply versed, and from
which he was furnished with texts for the demolition of its
friends, his adversaries. He professed himself a great admirer
of its literature, and in the heat of controversy he often found
himself a defender of its doctrine when he had occasion to
expose the fallacy of latitudinarian interpretations. For liberal
Christianity he had nothing but contempt, and refuted it with
a scorn which spared none of the worldly tendencies of the
church in Equity. The idea that souls were to be saved by
church sociables, filled him with inappeasable rancor; and he
maintained the superiority of the old Puritanic discipline
against them with a fervor which nothing but its re-establish-
ment could have abated. It was said that Squire Gaylord's
influence had largely helped to keep in place the last of the
rigidly orthodox ministers, under whom his liberalizing congregation chafed for years of discontent; but this was probably an exaggeration of the native humor. Mrs. Gaylord had
belonged to this church and had never formally withdrawn
from it; and the lawyer always contributed to pay the minister's salary; he also managed a little property for him so well

as to make him independent when he was at last asked to resign by his deacons.

In another mood, Bartley might have stepped aside to look in on the Squire, before asking at the house-door for Marcia. They relished each other's company, as people of contrary opinions and of no opinions are apt to do. Bartley loved to hear the Squire get going, as he said, and the old man felt a fascination in the youngster. Bartley was smart; he took a point quick as lightning; and the Squire did not mind his making friends with the Mammon of Righteousness, as he called the visible church in Equity: it amused him to see Bartley lending the church the zealous support of the press, with an impartial patronage of the different creeds. There had been times in his own career, when the silence of his opinions would have greatly advanced him, but he had not chosen to pay this price for success; he liked his freedom, or he liked the bitter tang of his own tongue too well, and he had remained a leading lawyer in Equity when he might have ended a judge, or even a Congressman. Of late years, however, since people whom he could have joined in their agnosticism so heartily, up to a certain point, had begun to make such fools of themselves about Darwinism and the brotherhood of all men in the monkey, he had grown much more tolerant. He still clung to his old-fashioned deistical opinions; but he thought no worse of a man for not holding them; he did not deny that a man might be a Christian and still be a very good man.

The audacious humor of his position sufficed with a people who like a joke rather better than any thing else; in his old age, his infidelity was something that would hardly have been changed, if possible, by a popular vote.

Even his wife, to whom it had once been a heavy cross, borne with secret prayer and tears, had long ceased to gainsay it in any wise. Her family had opposed her yoking with an unbeliever when she married him, but she had some such hopes of converting him, as women cherish who give themselves to men confirmed in drunkenness. She learned, as other women do that she could hardly change her husband in the least of his habits, and that in this great matter of his unbelief her love was powerless. It became easier at last for her to add self-sacrifice to self-sacrifice, than to vex him with her anxieties about his soul, and to act upon the feeling that if he must be lost, then she did not care to be saved. He had never interfered with her church-going; he had rather promoted it, for he liked to have women go; but the time came when she no longer cared to go without him; she lapsed from her membership, and it was now many years since she had worshipped with the people of her faith, if indeed she were still of any faith. Her life was silenced in every way, and as often happens with aging wives in country towns she seldom went out of her own door, and never appeared at the social or public solemnities of the village. Her husband and her daughter composed and bounded her world; she always talked of them, or of other things as related to them. She had grown an elderly woman, without losing the color of her yellow hair; and the bloom of girlhood had been stayed in her cheeks as if by the young habit of blushing which she had kept. She was still what her neighbors called very pretty-appearing, and she must have been a beautiful girl. The silence of her inward life subdued her manner, till now she seemed always to have come from some place on which a deep hush had newly fallen.

She answered the door when Bartley turned the crank that snapped the gong-bell in its centre; and the young man who was looking at the street while waiting for some one to come, confronted her with a start. "Oh!" he said. "I thought it was Marcia! Good-morning, Mrs. Gaylord. Isn't Marcia at home?"

"She went to church, this morning," replied her mother. "Wont you walk in?"

"Why, yes, I guess I will, thank you," faltered Bartley in the irresolution of his disappointment. "I hope I sha'n't disturb you."

"Come right into the sitting-room. She wont be gone a great while, now," said Mrs. Gaylord, leading the way to the large square room into which a door at the end of the narrow hall opened. A slumbrous heat from a sheet-iron wood-stove pervaded the place, and a clock ticked monotonously on a shelf in the corner. Mrs. Gaylord said, "Wont you take a chair," and herself sank into the rocker, with a deep feather cushion, in the seat, and a thinner feather cushion tied half way up the back. After the more active duties of her house-keeping were done, she sat every day in this chair with her knitting or sewing, and let the clock tick the long hours of her life away, with no more apparent impatience of them, or sense of their dulness than the cat on the braided rug at her feet, or the geraniums in their pots at the sunny window. "Are you pretty well to-day?" she asked.

"Well no, Mrs. Gaylord, I'm not," answered Bartley. "I'm all out of sorts. I haven't felt so dyspeptic for I don't know how long."

Mrs. Gaylord smoothed the silk dress across her lap: the thin old black silk, which she still instinctively put on for Sab-bath observance, though it was so long since she had worn it to church. "Mr. Gaylord used to have it when we were first married, though he ain't been troubled with it of late years. He seemed to think then, it was worse, Sundays."

"I don't believe Sunday has much to do with it in my case. I ate some mince pie and some toasted cheese, last night, and I guess they didn't agree with me very well," said Bartley, who did not spare himself the confession of his sins when seeking sympathy: it was this candor that went so far to con-vince people of his good heartedness.

"I don't know as I ever heard that meat-pie was bad," said Mrs. Gaylord thoughtfully. "Mr. Gaylord used to eat it right along all through his dyspepsia, and he never complained of it. And the cheese ought to have made it digest."

"Well, I don't know what it was," replied Bartley, plain-tively submitting to be exonerated, "but I feel perfectly used up. Oh, I suppose I shall get over it, or forget all about it by to-morrow," he added with strenuous cheerfulness. "It isn't anything worth minding."

Mrs. Gaylord seemed to differ with him on this point. "Head ache any?" she asked.

"It did, this morning when I first woke up," Bartley as-sented.

"I don't believe but what a cup of tea would be the best thing for you," she said critically.

Bartley had instinctively practiced a social art which ingra-tiated him with people at Equity as much as his demands for sympathy endeared him: he gave trouble in little unusual ways.

He now said, "Oh, I wish you would give me a cup, Mrs. Gaylord."

"Why, yes indeed! That's just what I was going to," she replied. She went to the kitchen which lay beyond another room, and re-appeared with the tea directly, proud of her promptness but having it on her conscience to explain it. "I 'most always keep the pot on the stove hearth, Sunday morning, so's to have it ready if Mr. Gaylord ever wants a cup. He's a master hand for tea, and always was. There: *I* guess you better take it without milk. I put some sugar in the saucer, if you want any." She dropped noiselessly upon her feather cushion again, and Bartley who had risen to receive the tea from her remained standing while he drank it.

"That does seem to go to the spot," he said, as he sipped it thoughtfully observant of its effect upon his disagreeable feelings. "I wish I had you to take care of me, Mrs. Gaylord, and keep me from making a fool of myself," he added, when he had drained the cup. "No, no!" he cried, at her offering to take it from him, "I'll set it down. I know it will fret you to have it in here, and I'll carry it out into the kitchen." He did so before she could prevent him, and came back, touching his moustache with his handkerchief. "I declare, Mrs. Gaylord, I should love to live in a kitchen like that."

"I guess you wouldn't, if you had to," said Mrs. Gaylord, flattered into a smile. "Marcia she likes to sit out there, she says, better than anywhere in the house. But I always tell her it's because she was there so much when she was little. I don't see as she seems over-anxious to do anything there *but* sit, I tell her. Not but what she knows how, well enough. Mr. Gaylord, too, he's great for being round in the kitchen. If he gets up in the night, when he has his waking spells, he rather take his lamp out there, if there's a fire left, and read, any time, than what he would in the parlor. Well, we used to sit there together a good deal when we were young, and he got the habit of it. There's everything in habit," she added, thoughtfully. "Marcia she's got quite in the way lately, of going to the Methodist church."

"Yes, I've seen her there. You know I board round at the

different churches, as the schoolmaster used to at the houses in the old times."

Mrs. Gaylord looked up at the clock, and gave a little nervous laugh. "I don't know what Marcia *will* say to my letting her company stay in the sitting-room. She's pretty late, to-day. But I guess you wont have much longer to wait, now." She spoke with that awe of her daughter and her judgments which is one of the pathetic idiosyncrasies of a certain class of American mothers. They feel themselves to be not so well-educated as their daughters whose fancied knowledge of the world they let outweigh their own experience of life; they are used to deferring to them, and they shrink willingly into household drudges before them, and leave them to order the social affairs of the family. Mrs. Gaylord was not much afraid of Bartley for himself, but as Marcia's company he made her more and more uneasy toward the end of the quarter of an hour in which she tried to entertain him with her simple talk, varying from Mr. Gaylord to Marcia and from Marcia to Mr. Gaylord again. When she recognized the girl's quick touch in the closing of the front door, and her elastic step approached through the hall, the mother made a little deprecatory noise in her throat, and fidgeted in her chair. As soon as Marcia opened the sitting-room door, Mrs. Gaylord modestly rose, and went out into the kitchen: the mother who remained in the room when her daughter had company was an oddity almost unknown in Equity.

Marcia's face flashed all into a light of joy at sight of Bartley, who scarcely waited for her mother to be gone before he drew her towards him by the hand she had given. She mechanically yielded, and then as if the recollection of some new resolution forced itself through her pleasure at sight of him, she freed her hand, and retreating a step or two, confronted him.

"Why, Marcia!" he cried, "what's the matter?"

"Nothing," she answered. It might have amused Bartley if he had felt quite well, to see the girl so defiant of him, when she was really so much in love with him, but it certainly did not amuse him now: it disappointed him in his expectation of finding her femininely soft and comforting and he did not know just what to do. He stood staring at her in discomfiture, while she gained in outward composure, though her cheeks were of the jacqueminot red of the ribbon at her throat.

"What have I done, Marcia?" he faltered.

"Oh, you haven't done anything."

"Some one has been talking to you against me!"

"No one has said a word to me about you."

"Then why are you so cold—so strange—so—so—different."

"Different?"

"Yes,—from what you were last night," he answered with an aggrieved air.

"Oh, we see some things differently by daylight," she lightly explained. "Wont you sit down?"

"No, thank you," Bartley replied, sadly but unresentfully. "I think I had better be going. I see there is something wrong"—

"I don't see why you say there is anything wrong," she retorted. "What have *I* done?"

"Oh, you have not *done* anything. I take it back. It is all right. But when I came here this morning, encouraged — hoping—that you had the same feeling as myself, and you seem to forget everything but a ceremonious acquaintance-ship—why it is all right, of course. I have no reason to complain; but I must say that I can't help being surprised." He saw her lips quiver and her bosom heave. "Marcia, do you blame me for feeling hurt at your coldness, when I came here to tell you—to tell you I—I love you." With his nerves all unstrung, and his hunger for sympathy, he really believed that he had come to tell her this. "Yes," he added bitterly, "I *will* tell you, though it seems to be the last word I shall speak to you. I'll go, now."

"Bartley! You shall *never* go!" she cried, throwing herself in his way. "Do you think I don't care for you, too? You may kiss me—you may *kill* me, now!" The passionate tears sprang to her eyes, without the sound of sobs, or the contortion of weeping, and she did not wait for his embrace: she flung her arms round his neck, and held him fast, crying, "I wouldn't let you for your own sake, darling; and if I had died for it—I thought I *should* die last night—I was never going to let you kiss me again till you said—till—till now! Don't you see?"

She caught him tighter, and hid her face in his neck, and cried and laughed for joy and shame, while he suffered her caresses with a certain bewilderment. "I want to tell you now, I want to explain," she said, lifting her face, and letting him from her as far as her arms, caught round his neck, would reach, and fervidly searching his eyes lest some ray of what he would think should escape her. "Don't speak a word first! Father saw us, at the door last night,—he happened to be coming down stairs, because he couldn't sleep—just when you— Oh, Bartley, don't!" she implored, at the little smile that made his moustache quiver. "And he asked me whether we were engaged; and when I couldn't tell him we were, I know what he thought. I know how he despised me, and I determined that if you didn't tell me that you cared for me— And that's the reason, Bartley; and not—not because I didn't care more for you than I do for the whole world. And— and—you don't mind it, now, do you? It was for your sake, dearest!"

Whether Bartley perfectly divined or not all the feeling at which her words hinted, it was delicious to be clung about by such a pretty girl as Marcia Gaylord, to have her now darting her face into his neck-scarf with intolerable consciousness and now boldly confronting him with all-defying fondness, while she lightly pushed him and pulled him here and there in the vehemence of her appeal. Perhaps such a man, in those fastnesses of his nature which psychology has not yet explored, never loses, even in the tenderest transports, the sense of prey as to the girl whose love he has won; but if this is certain, it is also certain that he has transports which are tender, and Bartley now felt his soul melted with affection that was very novel and sweet. "Why, Marcia!" he said, "what a strange girl you are!" He sank into his chair again, and putting his arms round her waist, drew her upon his knee, like a child.

She held herself apart from him at her arm's length, and said, "Wait! Let me say it before it seems as if we had always been engaged, and everything was as right then as it is now.

Did you despise me for letting you kiss me before we were engaged?"

"No," he laughed again. "I liked you for it."

"But if you thought I would let any one else, you wouldn't have liked it?"

This diverted him still more. "I shouldn't have liked that more than half as well."

"No," she said thoughtfully. She dropped her face awhile on his shoulder, and seemed to be struggling with herself. Then she lifted it, and, "Did you ever—did you"—she gasped.

"If you want me to say that all the other girls in the world are not worth a hair of your head, I'll say that, Marcia. Now let's talk business!"

This made her laugh, and—

"I shall want a little lock of yours," she said, as if they had hitherto been talking of nothing but each other's hair.

"And I shall want all of yours," he answered.

"No. Don't be silly." She critically explored his face. "How funny, to have a mole in your eyebrow!" She put her finger on it. "I never saw it before!"

"You never looked so closely. There's a scar at the corner of your upper lip, that I hadn't noticed."

"Can you see that?" she demanded, radiantly. "Well, you *have* got good eyes! The cat did it when I was a little girl."

The door opened, and Mrs. Gaylord surprised them in the celebration of these discoveries—or rather, she surprised herself, for she stood holding the door and helpless to move, though in her heart she had an apologetic impulse to retire, and she even believed that she made some murmurs of excuse for her intrusion. Bartley was equally abashed, but Marcia rose with the coolness of her sex in the intimate emergencies which confound a man.

"Oh, mother, it's you! I forgot about you. Come in! Or I'll set the table, if that's what you want." As Mrs. Gaylord continued to look from her to Bartley in her daze, Marcia added simply, "We're engaged, mother. You may as well know it first as last, and I guess you better know it first."

Her mother appeared not to think it safe to relax her hold

upon the door, and Bartley went filially to her rescue: if it was rescue to salute her blushing defencelessness as he did. A confused sense of the extraordinary nature and possible impropriety of the proceeding may have suggested her husband to her mind; or it may have been a feeling that some remark was expected of her, even in the mental destitution to which she was reduced. "Have you told Mr. Gaylord about it?" she asked, of either, or neither, or both, as they chose to take it.

Bartley left the word to Marcia, who answered, "Well, no, mother. We haven't yet. We've only just found it out ourselves. I guess father can wait till he comes in to dinner. I intend to keep Bartley here to prove it."

"He said," remarked Mrs. Gaylord, whom Bartley had led to her chair and placed on her cushion, " 't he had a headache when he first come in," and she appealed to him for corroboration, while she vainly endeavored to gather force to grapple again with the larger fact that he and Marcia were just engaged to be married.

Marcia stooped down and pulled her mother up out of her chair with a hug. "Oh, come, now, mother! You mustn't let it take your breath away," she said with patronizing fondness. "I'm not afraid of what father will say. You know what he thinks of Bartley—or Mr. Hubbard, as I presume you'll want me to call him! Now mother, you just run up stairs, and put on your best cap, and leave me to set the table and get up the dinner. I guess I can get Bartley to help me. Mother, mother, mother!" she cried, in happiness that was otherwise unutterable, and clasping her mother closer in her strong young arms she kissed her with a fervor that made her blush again before the young man.

"Marcia, Marcia! You hadn't ought to! It's ridiculous!" she protested. But she suffered herself to be thrust out of the room, grateful for exile in which she could collect her scattered wits, and set herself to realize the fact that had dispersed them. It was decorous also for her to leave Marcia alone with Mr. Hubbard, far more so now than when he was merely company; she felt that, and she fumbled over the dressing she was sent about, and once she looked out of her chamber window at the office where Mr. Gaylord sat, and wondered what Mr. Gaylord (she thought of him, and even dreamt of him as

Mr. Gaylord, and had never, in the most familiar moments, addressed him otherwise) *would* say! But she left the solution of the problem to him and Marcia: she was used to leaving them to the settlement of their own difficulties.

"Now, Bartley," said Marcia, in the business-like way that women assume in such matters as soon as the great fact is no longer in doubt, "you must help me to set the table. Put up that leaf and I'll put up this. I'm going to do more for mother, more than I used to," she said, repentant in her bliss. "It's a shame how much I've left to her." The domestic instinct was already astir in her heart.

Bartley pulled the table cloth straight for her, and vied with her in the rapidity and exactness with which he arranged the knives and forks at right angles beside the plates. When it came to some heavier dishes, they agreed to carry them turn about; but when it was her turn he put out his hand to support her elbow: "As I did last night, and saved you from dropping a lamp."

This made her laugh, and she dropped the first dish with a crash. "Poor mother!" she exclaimed. "I know she heard that, and she'll be in agony to know which one it is."

Mrs. Gaylord did indeed hear it far off in her chamber, and quaked with an anxiety which became intolerable at last. "Marcia! Marcia!" she quavered down the stairs, "what *have* you broken!"

Marcia opened the door long enough to call back, "Oh, only the old blue-edged platter, mother!" and then she flew at Bartley, crying, "For shame! For shame!" and pressing her hand over his mouth to stifle his laughter. "She'll hear you, Bartley, and think you're laughing at her." But she laughed herself at his struggles, and ended by taking him by the hand and pulling him out into the kitchen where neither of them could be heard. She abandoned herself in the extasy of her soul, and he thought she had never been so charming as in this wild gayety.

"Why, Marsh! I never saw you carry on so, before!"

"You never saw me engaged before! That's the way all girls act—if they get the chance. Don't you like me to be so?" she asked with quick anxiety.

"Rather!" he replied.

"Oh, Bartley," she exclaimed, "I feel like a child. I surprise myself as much as I do you; for I thought I had got very old, and I didn't suppose I should ever let myself go in this way. But there is something about this that lets me be as silly as I like. It's somehow as if I were a great deal more alone when I'm with you than when I'm by myself! How does it make you feel?"

"Good!" he answered, and that satisfied her better than if he had entered into those subtleties which she had tried to express: it was more like a man. He had his arm about her again, and she put down her hand on his to press it closer against her heart.

"Of course," she explained, recurring to his surprise at her frolic mood, "I don't expect you to be silly because I am."

"No," he assented, "but how can I help it?"

"Oh, I don't mean for the time being; I mean generally speaking. I mean that I care for you because I know you know a great deal more than I do, and because I respect you. I know that everybody expects you to be something great, and I do too."

Bartley did not deny the justness of her opinions concerning himself, or the reasonableness of the general expectation; though he probably could not see the relation of these cold abstractions to the pleasure of sitting there with a pretty girl in that way. But he said nothing.

"Do you know," she went on, turning her face prettily round toward him, but holding it a little way off, to secure attention as impersonal as might be under the circumstances, "what pleased me more than anything else you ever said to me?"

"No," answered Bartley. "Something you got out of me when you were trying to make me tell you the difference between you and the other Equity girls?"

She laughed in glad defiance of her own consciousness. "Well, I *was* trying to make you compliment me; I'm not going to deny it. But I must say I got my come-uppance: you didn't say a thing I cared for. But you did afterwards. Don't you remember?"

"No. When?"

She hesitated a moment. "When you told me that my influence had—had—made you better, you know"—

"Oh!" said Bartley. "That! Well," he added carelessly, "it's every word true. Didn't you believe it?"

"I was just as glad as if I did; and it made me resolve never to do or say a thing that could lower your opinion of me; and then you know, there at the door—it all seemed part of our trying to make each other better. But when father looked at me in that way, and asked me if we were engaged, I went down into the dust with shame. And it seemed to me that you had just been laughing at me, and amusing yourself with me, and I was so furious I didn't know what to do. Do you know what I wanted to do? I wanted to run down stairs to father and tell him what you had said, and ask him if he believed you had ever liked any other girl." She paused a little, but he did not answer, and she continued. "But now I'm glad I didn't. And I shall never ask you that, and I shall not care for anything that you—that's happened before to-day. It's all right. And you *do* think I shall always *try* to make you good and happy, don't you?"

"I don't think you can make me much happier than I am at present, and I don't believe anybody could make me feel better," answered Bartley.

She gave a little laugh at his refusal to be serious, and let her head for fondness fall upon his shoulder, while he turned round and round a ring he found on her finger.

"Ah, ha!" he said after while. "Who gave you this ring, Miss Gaylord?"

"Father—Christmas before last," she promptly answered without moving. "I'm glad you asked," she murmured in a lower voice, full of pride in the maiden love she could give him. "There's never been any one but you or the thought of any one." She suddenly started away. "Now, let's play we're getting dinner." It was quite time: in the next moment the coffee boiled up, and if she had not caught the lid off and stirred it down with her spoon it would have been spoiled. The steam ascended to the ceiling and filled the kitchen with the fragrant soul of the berry.

"I'm glad we're going to have coffee," she said. "You'll

have to put up with a cold dinner, except potatoes. But the coffee will make up, and I shall need a cup to keep me awake. I don't believe I slept last night till nearly morning. Do you like coffee?"

"I'd have given all I ever expect to be worth for a cup of it, last night," he said. "I was awfully hungry when I got back to the hotel, and I couldn't find anything but a piece of mince pie and some old cheese, and I had to be content with cold milk. I felt as if I had lost all my friends this morning, when I woke up."

A sense of remembered grievance trembled in his voice, and made her drop her head on his arm in pity and derision of him.

"Poor Bartley!" she cried. "And you came up here for a little petting from me, didn't you? I've noticed that in you! Well, you didn't get it, did you?"

"Well,—not at first," he said.

"Yes, you can't complain of any want of petting at last," she returned, delighted at his indirect recognition of the difference. The daring, the archness and caprice, that make coquetry in some women, and lurk a divine possibility in all, came out in her; the sweetness, kept back by the whole strength of her pride, overflowed that broken barrier now, and she seemed to lavish this revelation of herself upon him with a sort of tender joy in his bewilderment. She was not hurt when he crudely expressed the elusive sense which has been in other men's minds at such times: they cannot believe that this fascination is inspired, and not practiced. "Well," he said, "I'm glad you told me that I was the first. I should have thought you'd had a good deal of experience in flirtation."

"You wouldn't have thought so if you hadn't been a great flirt yourself," she answered, audaciously. "Perhaps I *have* been engaged before!"

Their talk was for the most part frivolous and their thoughts ephemeral, but again they were, with her at least, suddenly and deeply serious. Till then all things seemed to have been held in arrest, and impressions, ideas, feelings, fears, desires, released themselves simultaneously, and sought expression with a rush that defied coherence. "Oh, why do we try to talk?" she asked at last. "The more we say the more we leave unsaid. Let us keep still awhile!" But she could not. "Bartley! When did you first think you cared about me?"

"I don't know," said Bartley, "I guess it must have been the first time I saw you."

"Yes. That is when I first knew that I cared for you. But it seems to me that I must have always cared for you, and that I only found it out when I saw you going by the house that day." She mused a little time before she asked again, "Bartley!"

"Well."

"Did you ever use to be afraid   Or, no! Wait! I'll *tell* you first, and then I'll *ask* you. I'm not ashamed of it now, though once I thought I couldn't bear to have any one find it out. I used to be awfully afraid you didn't care for me! I would try to make out from things you did and said whether you did or not; but I never could be certain. I believe I used to find the most comfort in discouraging myself. I used to say to myself, 'Why of course he doesn't! How can he? He's been every where, and he's seen so many girls. He corresponds with lots of them. Altogether likely he's engaged to some of the young ladies he's met in Boston; and he just goes with me here for a blind.' And then when you would praise me, sometimes, I would just say, 'Oh, he's complimented plenty of girls. I know he's thinking this instant of the young lady he's engaged to in Boston.' And it would almost kill me; and when you did some little thing to show that you liked me, I would think, 'He doesn't like me! He hates, he despises me. He does, he does, he does!' And I would go on that way, with my teeth shut and my breath held, I don't know *how* long."

Bartley broke out into a broad laugh at this image of desperation, but she added tenderly, "I hope I never made you suffer in that way?"

"What way?" he asked.

"That's what I wanted you to tell me. Did you ever—did you use to be afraid sometimes that I—that you— Did you put off telling me that you cared for me, so long because you thought—you dreaded   Oh, I don't see what I can ever do to make it up to you if you did!— Were you afraid I didn't care for you?"

"No!" shouted Bartley. She had risen and stood before him

in the fervor of her entreaty, and he seized her arms, pinioning them to her side, and holding her helpless, while he laughed and laughed again. "I knew you were dead in love with me from the first moment."

"Bartley! Bartley Hubbard!" she exclaimed. "Let me go! Let me go, this instant! I never heard of such a shameless thing!" But she really made no effort to escape.

V

THE HOUSE seemed too little for Marcia's happiness, and after dinner she did not let Bartley forget his last night's engagement. She sent him off to get his horse at the hotel, and ran up to her room to put on her wraps for the drive. Her mother cleared away the dinner things; she pushed the table to the side of the room, and then sat down in her feather-cushioned chair and waited her husband's pleasure to speak. He ordinarily rose from the Sunday dinner and went back to his office; to-day he had taken a chair before the stove. But he had mechanically put his hat on, and he wore it, pushed off his forehead as he tilted his chair back on its hind legs, and braced himself against the hearth of the stove with his feet.

A man is master in his own house generally through the exercise of a certain degree of brutality, but Squire Gaylord maintained his predominance by an enlightened absenteeism. No man living always at home was ever so little under his own roof. While he was in more active business life he had kept an office in the heart of the village, where he spent all his days, and a great part of every night; but after he had become rich enough to risk whatever loss of business the change might involve, he bought this large old square house on the border of the village, and thenceforth made his home in the little detached office. If Mrs. Gaylord had dimly imagined that she should see something more of him, having him so near at hand, she really saw less: there was no weather, by day or night in which he could not go to his office, now. He went no more than his wife into the village society; she might have been glad now and then of a little glimpse of the world, but she never said so, and her social life had ceased like her religious life. Their house was richly furnished according to the local taste of the time; the parlor had a Brussels carpet, and heavy chairs of mahogany and haircloth; Marcia had a piano there, and since she had come home from school they had made company, as Mrs. Gaylord called it, two or three times for her; but they had held aloof from the festivity, the

Squire in his office, and Mrs. Gaylord in the family-room where they now sat in unwonted companionship.

"Well, Mr. Gaylord," said his wife, "I don't know as you can say but what *Marcia's* suited well enough." This was the first allusion they had made to the subject, but she let it take the argumentative form of her cogitations.

"Myes," sighed the Squire in long, nasal assent, "most too well, if anything." He rasped first one unshaven cheek and then the other, with his thin, quivering hand.

"He's smart enough," said Mrs. Gaylord, as before.

"Myes, most too smart," replied her husband, a little more quickly than before. "He's smart enough, even if she wasn't, to see from the start that she was crazy to have him, and that isn't the best way to begin life for a married couple, if I'm a judge."

"It would killed her, if she hadn't got him. I could see 'twas wearin' on her everyday, more and more. She used to fairly jump every knock she'd hear at the door; and I know sometimes, when she was afraid he wa'n't coming, she used to go out in hopes 't she sh'd meet him: I don't suppose she allowed to herself that she done it for that. Marcia's proud."

"Myes," said the Squire, "she's proud. And when a proud girl makes a fool of herself about a fellow, it's a matter of life and death with her. She can't help herself. She lets go everything."

"I declare," Mrs. Gaylord went on, "it worked me up considerable to have her come in some those times, and see by her face 't she'd seen him with some the other girls. She used to *look* so! And then I'd hear her up in her room, cryin' and cryin'. I shouldn't cared so much, if Marcia'd been like any other girl, kind of flirty like, about it. But she wa'n't. She was just bowed down before her idol."

A final assent came from the Squire as if wrung out of his heart, and he rose from his chair, and then sat down again. Marcia was his child, and he loved her with his whole soul. "Mwell!" he deeply sighed, "all that part's over, any way," but he tingled in an anguish of sympathy with what she had suffered. "You see, Miranda, how she looked at me when she first came in with him—so proud and independent, poor girl! and yet as if she was afraid I *mightn't* like it?"

"Yes, I see it."

He pulled his hat far down over his cavernous eyes, and worked his thin, rusty old jaws.

"I hope't she'll be able to school herself, so's't' not show out her feelings so much," said Mrs. Gaylord.

"I wish she could school herself so as to not have 'em so much; but I guess she'll have 'em, and I guess she'll show 'em out." They were both silent; after while he added, throwing at the stove a minute fragment of the cane he had pulled off the seat of his chair: "Miranda, I've expected something of this sort a good while, and I've thought over what Bartley had better do."

Mrs. Gaylord stooped forward and picked up the bit of wood which her husband had thrown down; her vigilance was rewarded by finding a thread on the oil-cloth near where it lay; she whipped this round her finger, and her husband continued: "He'd better give up his paper and go into the law. He's done well in the paper, and he's a smart writer; but editing a newspaper aint any work for a *man*. It's all well enough as long as he's single, but when he's got a wife to look after, he'd better get down to *work*. My business is in just such a shape now that I could hand it over to him in a lump; but come to wait a year or two longer, and this young man and that one'll eat into it, and it wont be the same thing at all. I shall want Bartley to push right along, and get admitted at once. He can do it, fast enough. He's bright enough," added the old man with a certain grimness. "Mwell!" he broke out, with a quick sigh, after a moment of musing. "It hasn't happened at any very bad time. I was just thinking this morning, that I should like to have my whole time, pretty soon, to look after my property. I sha'n't want Bartley to do *that*, for me. I'll give him a good start in money and in business; but I'll look after my property myself. I'll speak to him, the first chance I get."

A light step sounded on the stairs, and Marcia burst into the room ready for her drive. "I wanted to get a good warm before I started," she explained, stooping before the stove, and supporting herself with one hand on her father's knee. There had been no formal congratulations upon her engagement from either of her parents; but this was not requisite, and would have been a little affected: they were perhaps now ashamed to mention it outright before her alone. The Squire, however, went so far as to put his hand over the hand she had laid upon his knee, and to smooth it twice or thrice.

"You going to ride after that sorrel colt of Bartley's?" he asked.

"Of course!" she answered with playful pertness. "I guess Bartley can manage the sorrel colt! He's never had any trouble yet."

"He's always been able to give his whole mind to him before," said the Squire. He gave Marcia's hand a significant squeeze, and let it go.

She would not confess her consciousness of his meaning at once. She looked up at the clock, and then turned and pulled her father's watch out of his waistcoat pocket, and compared the time. "Why, you're both fast!"

"Perhaps Bartley's slow," said the Squire, and having gone as far as he intended in this direction, he permitted himself a low chuckle.

The sleigh-bells jingled without, and she sprang lightly to her feet. "*I* guess you don't think Bartley's slow," she exclaimed, and hung over her father long enough to rub her lips against his bristly cheek. "By, mother," she said over her shoulder, and went out of the room. She let her muff hang as far down in front of her as her arms would reach, in a stylish way, and moved with a little rhythmical tilt, as if to some inner music. Even in her furs she was elegantly slender in shape.

The old people remained silent and motionless till the clash of the bells died away. Then the Squire rose, and went to the wood shed beyond the kitchen, whence he re-appeared with an armful of wood. His wife started at the sight. "Mr. Gaylord, what *be* you doin'?"

"Oh, I'm going to make 'em up a little fire in the parlor stove. I guess they wont want us round a great deal, when they come back."

"Well, I never did!" said Mrs. Gaylord. When her husband returned from the parlor, she added, "I suppose some folks'd say it was rather of a strange way of spendin' the Sabbath."

"It's a very good way of spending the Sabbath. You don't

suppose that any of the people in church are half as happy, do you? Why old Jonathan Edwards himself used to allow 'all proper opportunity' for the young fellows that come to see his girls, 'and a room and fire, if needed.' His Life says so."

"I guess he didn't allow it on the Sabbath," retorted Mrs Gaylord.

"Well, the Life don't say," chuckled the Squire. "Why Miranda, I do it for Marcia! There's never but one first day to an engagement. You know that as well as I do." In saying this, Squire Gaylord gave way to his repressed emotion in an extravagance. He suddenly stooped over and kissed his wife; but he spared her confusion by going out to his office at once, where he staid the whole afternoon.

Bartley and Marcia took the Long Drive as it was called, at Equity. The road plunged into the darkly wooded gulch beyond the house, and then struck away eastward, crossing loop after loop of the river on the covered bridges, where the neighbors, who had broken it out with their ox-teams in the open, had thickly bedded it in snow. In the valleys and sheltered spots it remained free and so wide that encountering teams could easily pass each other, but where it climbed a hill, or crossed a treeless level it was narrowed to a single track, with turnouts at established points where the drivers of the sleighs waited to be sure that the stretch beyond was clear before going forward. In the country the winter which held the village in such close siege was an occupation under which nature seemed to cower helpless, and men made a desperate and ineffectual struggle. The houses, banked up with snow almost to the sills of the windows that looked out, blind with frost upon the lifeless world, were dwarfed in the drifts and seemed to founder in a white sea blotched with strange bluish shadows under the slanting sun. Where they fronted close upon the road, it was evident that the fight with the snow was kept up unrelentingly; spaces were shoveled out, and paths were kept open to the middle of the highway, and to the barn; but where they were somewhat removed, there was no visible trace of the conflict, and no sign of life except the faint, wreathed lines of smoke wavering upward from the chimneys.

In the hollows through which the road passed the lower

boughs of the pines and hemlocks were weighed down with the snowfall till they lay half submerged in the drifts, but wherever the wind could strike them, they swung free of this load and met in low, flat arches above the track. The river betrayed itself only when the swift current of a ripple broke through the white surface in long, irregular grayish blurs. It was all wild and lonesome, but to the girl alone in it with her lover, the solitude was sweet, and she did not wish to speak even to him. His hands were both busy with the reins, but it was agreed between them that she might lock hers through his arm. Cowering close to him under the robes, she laid her head on his shoulder and looked out over the flying landscape in measureless content, and smiled, with filling eyes, when he bent over, and warmed his cold red cheek on the top of her fur cap.

The moments of bliss that silence a woman rouse a man to make sure of his rapture. "How do you like it, Marsh?" he asked, trying at one of these times to peer round into her face. "Are you afraid?"

"No—only of getting back too soon."

He made the shivering echoes answer with his delight in this, and chirruped to the colt, who pulsed forward at a wilder speed, flinging his hoofs out before him with the straight thrust of the born trotter, and seeming to overtake them as they flew. "I should like this ride to last forever!"

"Forever!" she repeated. "That would do for a beginning."

"Marsh! What a girl you are! I never supposed you would be so free to let a fellow know how much you cared for him."

"Neither did I," she answered dreamily. "But now—now the only trouble is that I don't know *how* to let him know." She gave his arm to which she clung a little convulsive clutch, and pressed her head harder upon his shoulder.

"Well, that's pretty much my complaint, too," said Bartley, "though I couldn't have expressed it so well."

"Oh, *you* express!" she murmured with the pride in him which implied that there were no thoughts worth expressing, to which he could not give a monumental utterance. Her adoration flattered his self-love to the same passionate intensity, and to something like the generous complexion of her worship. "Marcia," he answered, "I am going to try to be all you expect of me. And I hope I shall never do anything unworthy of your ideal."

She could only press his arm again in speechless joy, but she said to herself that she should always remember these words.

The wind had been rising ever since they started, but they had not noticed it till now when the woods began to thin away on either side, and he stopped before striking out over one of the naked stretches of the plain—a white waste swept by blasts that sucked down through a gorge of the mountain, and flattened the snow-drifts as the tornado flattens the waves. Across this expanse ran the road, its stiff lines obliterated here and there, in the slight depressions, and showing dark along the rest of the track. It was a good half mile to the next body of woods, and mid way, there was one of those sidings where a sleigh approaching from the other quarter must turn out and yield the right of way. Bartley stopped his colt, and scanned the road.

"Anybody coming?" asked Marcia.

"No, I don't see anyone. But if there's any one in the woods yonder, they'd better wait till I get across. No horse in Equity can beat this colt to the turnout."

"Oh, well look carefully, Bartley. If we met any one beyond the turnout, I don't know what I should do," pleaded the girl.

"I don't know what *they* would do," said Bartley. "But it's their lookout, now, if they come. Wrap your face up well, or put your head under the robe; I've got to hold my breath the next half mile." He loosed the reins and sped the colt out of the shelter where he had halted. The wind struck them like an edge of steel, and catching the powdery snow that their horse's hoofs beat up, sent it spinning and swirling far along the glistering levels on their lee. They felt the thrill of the go as if they were in some light boat leaping over a swift current. Marcia disdained to cover her face, if he must confront the wind, but after a few gasps she was glad to bend forward, and bury it in the long hair of the bearskin robe. When she lifted it, they were already past the siding, and she saw a cutter dashing toward them from the cover of the woods. "Bartley!" she screamed, "The sleigh!"

"Yes," he shouted. "Some fool! There's going to be trouble, here," he added, checking his horse as he could. "They don't seem to know how to manage— It's a couple of women! Hold on, hold on!" he called. "Don't try to turn out: I'll turn out!"

The women pulled their horse's head this way and that, in apparent confusion, and then began to turn out into the trackless snow at the roadside, in spite of Bartley's frantic efforts to arrest them. They sank deeper and deeper into the drift; their horse plunged and struggled, and then their cutter went over, amidst their shrieks and cries for help.

Bartley drove up abreast of the wreck, and saying, "Still, Jerry! Don't be afraid, Marcia," he put the reins into her hands, and sprang out to the rescue.

One of the women had been flung out free of the sleigh, and had already gathered herself up, and stood crying and wringing her hands: "Oh, Mr. Hubbard, Mr. Hubbard! Help Hannah! She's under there!"

"All right! Keep quiet, Mrs. Morrison! Take hold of your horse's head!" Bartley had first of all seized him by the bit, and pulled him to his feet; he was old and experienced in obedience, and he now stood waiting orders, patiently enough. Bartley seized the cutter, and by an effort of all his strength righted it. The colt started and trembled, but Marcia called to him in Bartley's tone, "Still, Jerry!" and he obeyed her.

The girl who had been caught under the overturned cutter, escaped like a wild thing out of a trap, when it was lifted, and plunging some paces away, faced round upon her rescuer with the hood pulled straight and set comely to her face again, almost before he could ask: "Any bones broken, Hannah?"

"*No!*" she shouted. "Mother! Mother! Stop crying! Don't you see I'm not dead?" She leaped about, catching up this wrap and that, shaking the dry snow out of them, and flinging them back into the cutter, while she laughed in the wild tumult of her spirits. Bartley helped her pick up the fragments of the wreck, and joined her in her making fun of the adventure. The wind hustled them, but they were warm in defiance of it with their jollity and their bustle.

"Why didn't you let me turn out?" demanded Bartley, as he and the girl stood on opposite sides of the cutter, re-arranging the robes in it.

"Oh, I thought I could turn out, well enough. You had a right to the road."

"Well, the next time you see any one past the turn-out, you better not start from the woods."

"Why, there's no more room in the woods to get past than there is here," cried the girl.

"There's more shelter."

"Oh, I'm not cold!" She flashed a look at him from her brilliant face, warm with all the glow of her young health, and laughed, and before she dropped her eyes, she included Marcia in her glance. They had already looked at each other without any sign of recognition. "Come, mother! All right, now!"

Her mother left the horse's head, and heavily ploughing back to the cutter, tumbled herself in. The girl from her side, began to climb in, but her weight made the sleigh careen, and she dropped down with a gay shriek. Bartley came round and lifted her in; the girl called to her horse, and drove up into the road and away.

Bartley looked after her a moment, and continued to glance in that direction when he stood stamping the snow off his feet, and brushing it from his legs and arms before he re-mounted to Marcia's side. He was excited, and talked rapidly and loudly, as he took the reins from Marcia's passive hold, and let the colt out. "That girl is the pluckiest fool, yet! Wouldn't let me turn out because I had the right of way! And she wasn't going to let anybody else have a hand in getting that old ark of theirs afloat again. Good their horse wasn't anything like Jerry! How well Jerry behaved! Were you frightened, Marsh?" He bent over to see her face, but she had not her head on his shoulder, and she did not sit close to him, now. "Did you freeze?"

"Oh, no! I got along, very well," she answered dryly, and edged away as far as the width of the seat would permit. "It would have been better for you to lead their horse up onto the road, and then she could have got in without your help. Her mother got in alone."

He took the reins into his left hand, and passing his strong right around her, pulled her up to his side. She resisted, with diminishing force; at last she ceased to resist, and her head fell passively to its former place on his shoulder. He did not try to speak any word of comfort; he only held her close to him; when she looked up as they entered the village, she confronted him with a brilliant smile that ignored her tears.

But that night, when she followed him to the door, she looked him searchingly in the eyes. "I wonder if you really do despise me, Bartley?" she asked.

"Certainly," he answered, with a jesting smile. "What for?"

"For showing out my feelings so. For not even trying to pretend not to care everything for you."

"It wouldn't be any use, your trying: I should know that you did, any way."

"Oh, don't laugh, Bartley, don't laugh! I don't believe that I ought to. I've heard that it makes people tired of you. But I can't help it—I can't help it. And if—if you think I'm always going to be so; and that I'm going to keep on getting worse and worse, and making you so unhappy, why you'd better break your engagement now—while you have a chance."

"What have you been making me unhappy about, I should like to know? I thought I'd been having a very good time."

She hid her face against his breast. "It almost *killed* me to see you there with her! I was so cold,—my hands were half-frozen, holding the reins,—and I was so afraid of the colt I didn't know what to do; and I had been keeping up my courage on your account; and you seemed so long about it all; and she could have got in perfectly well—as well as her mother did—without your help"— Her voice broke in a miserable sob, and she clutched herself tighter to him.

He smoothed down her hair with his hand. "Why, Marsh! Did you think that made me unhappy? *I* didn't mind it a bit. I knew what the trouble was, at the time; but I wasn't going to say anything. I knew you would be all right as soon as you could think it over. You don't suppose I care anything for that girl?"

"No," answered a rueful sob. "But I *wish* you didn't have

anything to do with her. I know she'll make trouble for you, somehow."

"Well," said Bartley, "I can't very well turn her off as long as she does her work. But you needn't be worried about making me unhappy. If anything, I rather liked it. It showed how much you *did* care for me." He bent toward her with a look of bright raillery, for the parting kiss. "Now then: once, twice, three times—and good-night it is!"

VI

THE SPECTACLE of a love-affair in which the woman gives more of her heart than the man gives of his is so pitiable that we are apt to attribute a kind of merit to her, as if it were a voluntary self-sacrifice for her to love more than her share. Not only other men, but other women look on with this canonizing compassion; for women have a lively power of imagining themselves in the place of any sister who suffers in matters of sentiment, and are eager to espouse the common cause in commiserating her. Each of them pictures herself similarly wronged or slighted by the man she likes best, and feels how cruel it would be if he were to care less for her than she for him; and for the time being, in order to realize the situation, she loads him with all the sins of omission proper to the culprit in the alien case. But possibly there is a compensation in merely loving, even where the love given is out of all proportion to the love received.

If Bartley Hubbard's sensations and impressions of the day had been at all reasoned, that night as he lay thinking it over, he could unquestionably have seen many advantages for Marcia in the affair—perhaps more than for himself. But to do him justice he did not formulate these now, or in anywise explicitly recognize the favors he was bestowing. At twenty-six one does not naturally compute them in musing upon the girl to whom one is just betrothed; and Bartley's mind was a confusion of pleasure. He liked so well to think how fond of him Marcia was, that it did not occur to him then to question whether he were as fond of her. It is possible that as he drowsed, at last, there floated airily through the consciousness which was melting and dispersing itself before the approach of sleep, an intimation from somewhere to some one that perhaps the affair need not be considered too seriously. But in that mysterious limbo, one cannot be sure of what is thought and what is dreamed; and Bartley always acquitted himself, and probably with justice, of any want of seriousness.

What he did make sure of when he woke was that he was still out of sorts, and that he had again that dull headache;

and his instant longing for sympathy did more than anything else to convince him that he really loved Marcia, and had never, in his obscurest or remotest feeling, swerved in his fealty to her. In the atmosphere of her devotion yesterday, he had so wholly forgotten his sufferings that he had imagined himself well; but now he found that he was not well, and he began to believe that he was going to have what the country people call a fit of sickness. He felt that he ought to be taken care of, that he was unfit to work; and in his vexation at not being able to go to Marcia for comfort—it really amounted to nothing less—he entered upon the day's affairs with fretful impatience.

The Free Press was published on Tuesdays, and Monday was always a busy time of preparation. The hands were apt also to feel the demoralization that follows a holiday even when it has been a holy day. The girls who set the type of the Free Press had by no means foregone the rights and privileges of their sex in espousing their art, and they had their beaux on Sunday night like other young ladies. It resulted that on Monday morning they were nervous and impatient, alternating between fits of giggling delight in the interchange of fond reminiscences and the crossness which is pretty sure to disfigure human behavior from want of sleep. But ordinarily Bartley got on very well with them. In spite of the assumption of equality between all classes in Equity, they stood in secret awe of his personal splendor, and the tradition of his achievements at college and in the great world, and a flattering joke or a sharp sarcasm from him went a great way with them. Besides he had an efficient lieutenant in Henry Bird, the young printer who had picked up his trade in the office, and who acted as Bartley's foreman, so far as the establishment had an organization. Bird had industry and discipline which were contagious, and that love of his work which is said to be growing rare among artizans in the modern subdivision of trades. This boy—for he was only nineteen—worked at his craft early and late out of pleasure in it. He seemed one of those simple, subordinate natures which are happy in looking up to whatever assumes to be above them. He exulted to serve in a world where most people prefer to be served, and it is uncertain whether he liked his work better for its own sake, or Bartley's, for whom he did it. He was slight and rather delicate in health, and it came natural for Bartley to patronize him. He took him on the long walks of which he was fond and made him in some sort his humble confidant, talking to him of himself and his plans with large and braggart vagueness. He depended upon Bird in a great many things, and Bird never failed him; for he had a basis of constancy that was immovable. "No," said a philosopher from a neighboring logging-camp, who used to hang about the printing office a long time after he had got his paper, "there aint a great deal of natural push about Henry; but he stays put." In the confidences which Bartley used to make Bird, he promised that when he left the newspaper for the law, he would see that no one else succeeded him. The young fellow did not need this promise to make him Bartley's fast friend, but it colored his affection with ambitious enthusiasm: to edit and publish a newspaper—his dreams did not go beyond that; to devote it to Bartley's interest in the political life on which Bartley often hinted he might enter—that would be the sweetest privilege of realized success. Bird already wrote paragraphs for the Free Press, and Bartley let him make up a column of news from the city exchanges, which was partly written and partly selected.

Bartley came to the office rather late on Monday morning, bringing with him the papers from Saturday night's mail, which had lain unopened over Sunday, and went directly into his own room, without looking into the printing-office. He felt feverish and irritable, and he resolved to fill up with selections and let his editorial paragraphing go, or get Bird to do it. He was tired of the work, and sick of Equity: Marcia's face seemed to look sadly in upon his angry discontent, and he no longer wished to go to her for sympathy. His door opened, and without glancing from the newspaper which he held up before him he asked: "What is it, Bird? Do you want copy?"

"Well, no, Mr. Hubbard," answered Bird, "we have copy enough for the force we've got this morning."

"Why, what's up?" demanded Bartley, dropping his paper.

"Lizzie Sawyer has sent word that she is sick, and we haven't heard or seen anything of Hannah Morrison."

"Confound the girls!" said Bartley, "there's always something the matter with them." He rubbed his hand over his forehead, as if to rub out the dull pain there. "Well," he said, "I must go to work myself, then." He rose, and took hold of the lappels of his coat, to pull it off; but something in Bird's look arrested him. "What is it?" he asked.

"Old Morrison was here, just before you came in, and said he wanted to see you. I think he was drunk," said Bird, anxiously. "He said he was coming back again."

"All right; let him come," replied Bartley. "This is a free country—especially in Equity. I suppose he wants Hannah's wages raised, as usual. How much are we behind, on the paper, Henry?"

"We're not a great deal behind, Mr. Hubbard; if we were not so weak-handed."

"Perhaps we can get Hannah back, during the forenoon. At any rate we can ask her honored parent, when he comes."

Where Morrison got his liquor was a question that agitated Equity from time to time, and baffled the officer of the law empowered to see that no strong drink came into the town. Under conditions which made it impossible even in the logging-camps, and rendered the sale of spirits too precarious for the apothecary, who might be supposed to deal in them medicinally, Morrison never failed of his spree when the mysterious mechanism of his appetite enforced it. Probably it was some form of bedevilled cider that supplied the material of his debauch; but even cider was not easily to be had.

Morrison's spree was a movable feast, and recurred at irregular intervals of two, or three, or even six weeks, but it recurred often enough to keep him poor, and his family in a social outlawry against which the kindly instincts of their neighbors struggled in vain. Mrs. Morrison was that pariah who in a village like Equity cuts herself off from hope by taking in washing; and it was a decided rise in the world for Hannah, a wild girl at school, to get a place in the printing-office. Her father had applied for it humbly enough at the tremulous and penitent close of one of his long sprees, and was grateful to Bartley for taking the special interest in her which she reported at home.

But the independence of a drunken shoemaker is proverbial, and Morrison's meek spirit soared into lordly arrogance

with his earliest cups. The first warning which the community
had of his change of attitude was the conspicuous and even
defiant closure of his shop, and the scornful rejection of custom, however urgent or necessitous. All Equity might go in
broken shoes, for any patching or half-soling the people got
from him. He went about collecting his small dues, and paying up his debts, as long as the money lasted, in token of his
resolution not to take any favors from any man thereafter.
Then he retired to his house on one of the by-streets, and by
degrees drank himself past active offense. It was of course in
his defiant humor that he came to visit Bartley, who had
learned to expect him whenever Hannah failed to appear
promptly at her work. The affair was always easily arranged: Bartley instantly assented, with whatever irony he
liked, to Morrison's demands; he refused with overwhelming politeness even to permit him to give himself the
trouble to support them by argument; he complimented
Hannah inordinately as one of the most gifted and accomplished ladies of his acquaintance, and inquired affectionately after the health of each member of the Morrison family. When Morrison rose to go he always said, in shaking
hands: "Well, sir, if there was more like you in Equity a
poor man could get along. You're a gentleman, sir." After
getting some paces away from the street-door, he stumbled
back up the stairs to repeat, "You're a gentleman!" Hannah
came during the day, and the wages remained the same: neither of the contracting parties regarded the increase so elaborately agreed upon, and Morrison on becoming sober, gratefully ignored the whole transaction, though by a curious
juggle of his brain, he recurred to it in his next spree, and
advanced in his new demand from the last rise: his daughter
was now nominally in receipt of an income of forty dollars a
week, but actually accepted four.

Bartley, on his part, enjoyed the business as an agreeable
excitement and a welcome relief from the monotony of his
office life. He never hurried Morrison's visits, but amused
himself by treating him with the most flattering distinction,
and baffling his arrogance by immediate concession. But this
morning when Morrison came back, with a front of uncommon fierceness, he merely looked up from his newspapers, to

which he had recurred, and said coolly, "Oh, Mr. Morrison! Good-morning. I suppose it's that little advance that you wish to see me about. Take a chair. What is the increase you ask this time? Of course I agree to anything"—

He leaned forward, pencil in hand, to make a note of the figure Morrison should name, when the drunkard approached and struck the table in front of him with his fist, and blazed upon Bartley's face, suddenly uplifted, with his blue crazy eyes.

"No, sir! I wont take a seat, and I don't come on no such business! No, sir!" He struck the table again, and the violence of his blow upset the inkstand. Bartley saved himself by suddenly springing away.

"Hullo, here!" he shouted. "What do you mean by this infernal nonsense?"

"What do *you* mean," retorted the drunkard, "by makin' up to my girl?"

"You're a fool," cried Bartley, "and drunk!"

"I'll show you whether I'm a fool, and I'll show you whether I'm drunk," said Morrison. He opened the door, and beckoned to Bird with an air of mysterious authority. "Young man! Come here!"

Bird was used to the indulgence with which Bartley treated Morrison's tipsy freaks, and supposed that he had been called by his consent to witness another agreement to a rise in Hannah's wages. He came quickly, to help get Morrison out of the way, the sooner, and he was astonished to be met by Bartley with, "I don't want you, Bird."

"All right," answered the boy, and he turned to go out of the door. But Morrison had planted himself against it, and he waved Bird austerely back.

"*I* want you," he said, with drunken impressiveness, "for a witness—wick—witness—while I ask Mr. Hubbard what he means by"—

"Hold your tongue!" cried Bartley. "Get out of this!" He advanced a pace or two towards Morrison, who stood his ground without swerving.

"Now you—you keep quiet, Mr. Hubbard," said Morrison, with a swift drunken change of mood by which he passed from arrogant denunciation to a smooth, patronizing mastery of the situation. "*I* wish this thing all settled amic—ic—amelcabilly."

Bartley broke into a helpless laugh at Morrison's final failure on a word difficult to sober tongues, and the latter went on: "No 'casion for bad feeling on either side. All I want to know is, What you mean?"

"Well, go on!" cried Bartley, good-naturedly, and he sat down in his chair, which he tilted back, and clasping his hands behind his head, looked up into Morrison's face. "What do I mean by what?"

Probably Morrison had not expected to be categorical, or to bring anything like a bill of particulars against Bartley, and this demand gave him pause. "What you mean," he said at last, "by always praising her up, so?"

"What I said. She's a very good girl, and a very bright one. You don't deny that?"

"No—no matter what I deny. What—what you lend her all them books for?"

"To improve her mind. You don't object to that? I thought you once thanked me for taking an interest in her."

"Don't you mind what I object to, and what I thank you for," said Morrison, with dignity. "I know what I'm about."

"I begin to doubt. But, get on. I'm in a great hurry this morning," said Bartley.

Morrison seemed to be making a mental examination of his stock of charges, while the strain of keeping his upright position began to tell upon him, and he swayed to and fro against the door.

"What's that word you sent her by my boy, Sat'day night?"

"That she was a smart girl, and would be sure to get on if she was good—or words to that effect. I trust there was no offense in that, Mr. Morrison?"

Morrison surrendered himself to another season of cogitation, in which he probably found his vagueness growing upon him. He ended, by fumbling in all his pockets, and bringing up from the last a crumpled scrap of paper. "What you—what you say to that?"

Bartley took the extended scrap with an easy air. "Miss Morrison's handwriting, I think." He held it up before him, and read aloud, " 'I love my love with an H because he is Handsome.' This appears to be a confidence of Miss Morrison to her Muse. Whom do you think she refers to, Mr. Morrison?"

"What's—what's the first letter your name?" demanded Morrison, with an effort to collect his dispersing severity.

"B," promptly replied Bartley. "Perhaps this concerns you, Henry. Your name begins with an H." He passed the paper up over his head to Bird, who took it silently. "You see," he continued, addressing Bird, but looking at Morrison, as he spoke, "Mr. Morrison wishes to convict me of an attempt upon Miss Hannah's affections. Have you anything else to urge, Mr. Morrison?"

Morrison slid at last from his difficult position into a convenient chair, and struggled to keep himself from doubling forward. "I want to know what you mean," he said with dogged iteration.

"I'll show you what I mean," said Bartley with an ugly quiet, while his moustache began to twitch. He sprang to his feet and seized Morrison by the collar, pulling him up out of the chair till he held him clear of the floor, and opened the door with his other hand. "Don't show your face here again—you, or your girl either!" Still holding the man by the collar, he pushed him before him through the office, and gave him a final thrust out of the outer door.

Bartley returned to his room in a white heat: "Miserable tipsy rascal!" he panted. "I wonder who has set him on to this thing."

Bird stood pale and silent, still holding the crumpled scrap of paper in his hand.

"I shouldn't be surprised if that impudent little witch herself had put him up to it. She's capable of it," said Bartley, fumbling aimlessly about on his table, in his wrath, without looking at Bird.

"It's a lie!" said Bird.

Bartley started as if the other had struck him, and as he glared at Bird, the anger went out of his face, for pure amazement. "Are you out of your mind, Henry?" he asked calmly. "Perhaps you're drunk too, this morning? The devil seems to have got into pretty much everybody."

"It's a lie!" repeated the boy, while the tears sprang to his eyes. "She's as good a girl as Marcia Gaylord is, any day!"

"Better go away, Henry," said Bartley with a deadly sort of gentleness.

"I'm going away," answered the boy, his face twisted with weeping. "I've done my last day's work for *you*." He pulled down his shirt sleeves, and buttoned them at the wrists, while the tears ran out over his face: helpless tears, the sign of his womanish tenderness, his womanish weakness.

Bartley continued to glare at him. "Why, I do believe you're in love with her yourself, you little fool!"

"Oh, I've *been* a fool!" cried Bird. "A fool to think as much of you as I always have—a fool to believe that you were a gentleman, and wouldn't take a mean advantage. I was a fool to suppose you wanted to do her any good, when you came praising and flattering her, and turning her head!"

"Well, then," said Bartley with harsh insolence, "don't you be a fool any longer. If you're in love with her, you haven't any quarrel with me, my boy. She flies at higher game than humble newspaper editors. The head of Willett's lumbering gang is your man; and so you may go and tell that old sot, her father. Why, Henry! You don't mean to say you care anything for that girl?"

"And do you mean to say you haven't done everything you could, to turn her head, since she's been in this office? She used to like me well enough at school." All men are blind and jealous children alike, when it comes to question of a woman between them, and this poor boy's passion was turning him into a tiger. "Don't come to *me* with your lies, any more!" Here his rage culminated, and with a blind cry of "Ay!" he struck the paper, which he had kept in his hand into Bartley's face.

The demons, whatever they were, of anger, remorse, pride, shame, were at work in Bartley's heart too, and he returned the blow as instantly as if Bird's touch had set the mechanism of his arm in motion. In contempt of the other's weakness he struck with the flat of his hand; but the blow was enough. Bird fell headlong, and the concussion of his head upon the floor did the rest. He lay senseless.

VII

BARTLEY HUNG over the boy with such a terror in his soul
as he had never had before. He believed that he had
killed him, and in this conviction came with the simultaneity
of events in dream the sense of all his blame, of which the
blow given for a blow seemed the least part. He was not so
wrong in that, as he was wrong in what led to it. He did not
abhor in himself so much the wretch who had struck his
brother down as the light and empty fool who had trifled
with that silly hoyden. The follies that seemed so amusing
and resultless in their time had ripened to this bitter effect,
and he knew that he and not she was mainly culpable. Her
self-betrayal, however it came about, was proof that they were
more serious with her than with him, and he could not plead
to himself even the poor excuse that his fancy had been
caught. Amidst the anguish of his self-condemnation, the
need to conceal what he had done occurred to him. He had
been holding Bird's head in his arms, and imploring him,
"Henry! Henry! Wake up!" in a low husky voice; but now he
turned to the door and locked it, and the lie by which he
should escape sprang to his tongue. "He died in a fit." He
almost believed it, as it murmured itself from his lips. There
was no mark, no bruise, nothing to show that he had touched
the boy. Suddenly he felt the lie choke him. He pulled down
the window, to let in the fresh air, and this pure breath of
heaven blew into his darkened spirit and lifted there a little
the vapors which were thickening in it. The horror of having
to tell that lie, even if he should escape by it, all his life long,
till he was a gray old man, and to keep the truth forever from
his lips, presented itself to him as intolerable slavery. "O, my
God!" he spoke aloud, "how can I bear that?" and it was in
self-pity that he revolted from it. Few men love the truth for
its own sake, and Bartley was not one of these; but he practiced it because his experience had been that lies were difficult
to manage, and that they were a burden on the mind. He was
not candid; he did not shun concealments and evasions; but
positive lies he had kept from, and now he could not trust

one to save his life. He unlocked the door, and ran out to find help; he must do that at last; he must do it at any risk; no matter what he said afterwards. When our deeds and motives come to be balanced at the last day, let us hope that mercy and not justice may prevail.

It must have been mercy, that sent the doctor at that moment to the apothecary's on the other side of the street, and enabled Bartley to get him up into his office, without publicity or explanation other than that Henry Bird seemed to be in a fit. The doctor lifted the boy's head, and explored his bosom with his hand.

"Is he—is he dead?" gasped Bartley, and the words came so mechanically from his tongue that he began to believe he had not spoken them, when the doctor answered.

"No! How did this happen? Tell me exactly."

"We had a quarrel. He struck me. I knocked him down." Bartley delivered up the truth, as a prisoner of war—or a captive brigand, perhaps—parts with his weapons one by one.

"Very well," said the doctor. "Get some water."

Bartley poured some out of the pitcher on his table, and the doctor, wetting his handkerchief, drew it again and again over Bird's forehead.

"I never meant to hurt him," said Bartley. "I didn't even intend to strike him when he hit me"—

"Intentions have very little to do with physical effects," replied the doctor sharply. "Henry!"

The boy opened his eyes, and muttering feebly, "My head!" closed them again.

"There's a concussion, here," said the doctor. "We had better get him home. Drive my sleigh over, will you, from Smith's."

Bartley went out into the glare of the sun, which beat upon him like the eye of the world. But the street was really empty as it often was in the middle of the forenoon, at Equity. The apothecary, who saw him untying the doctor's horse, came to his door, and said jocosely, "Hello, Doc! Who's sick?"

"I am," said Bartley, solemnly, and the apothecary laughed at his readiness. Bartley drove round to the back of the printing-office, where the farmers delivered his wood. "I thought we could get him out better, that way," he explained, and the doctor, who had to befriend a great many concealments in his practice, silently spared Bartley's disingenuousness.

The rush of the cold air, as they drove rapidly down the street, with that limp shape between them, revived the boy, and he opened his eyes, and made an effort to hold himself erect; but he could not, and when they got him into the warm room at home, he fainted again. His mother had met them at the door of her poor little house, without any demonstration of grief or terror: she was far too well acquainted in her widowhood, bereft of all her children but for this son, with sickness and death, to show even surprise, if she felt it. When Bartley broke out into his lamentable confession, "Oh, Mrs. Bird! This is *my* work!" she only wrung her hands and answered, "*Your* work? Oh, Mr. Hubbard, he thought the world of *you*!" and did not ask him how or why he had done it. After they had got Henry on the bed, Bartley was no longer of use, there; but they let him remain, in the corner into which he had shrunk, and from which he watched all that went on, with a dry mouth and faltering breath. It began to appear to him that he was very young to be involved in a misfortune like this; he did not understand why it should have happened to him; but he promised himself that if Henry lived he would try to be a better man in every way.

After he had lost all hope, the time seemed so long, the boy on the bed opened his eyes, once more, and looked round, while Bartley still sat with his face in his hands. "Where — where is Mr. Hubbard?" he faintly asked, with a bewildered look at his mother and the doctor.

Bartley heard the weak voice, and staggered forward, and fell on his knees beside the bed. "Here, here! Here I am, Henry! Oh, Henry, I didn't intend"— He stopped at the word, and hid his face in the coverlet.

The boy lay as if trying to make out what had happened, and the doctor told him that he had fainted. After a time, he put out his hand and laid it on Bartley's head. "Yes; but I don't understand what makes him cry."

They looked at Bartley, who had lifted his head, and he went over the whole affair, except so far as it related to Hannah Morrison: he did not spare himself; he had often found that strenuous self-condemnation moved others to compassion; and besides, it was his nature to seek the relief of full confession. But Henry heard him through with a blank countenance. "Don't you remember?" Bartley implored at last.

"No, I don't remember. I only remember that there seemed to be something the matter with my head, this morning."

"That was the trouble with me, too," said Bartley. "I must have been crazy—I must have been insane—when I struck you. I can't account for it."

"I don't remember it," answered the boy.

"That's all right," said the doctor. "Don't try. I guess you better let him alone, now," he added to Bartley, with such a significant look that the young man retired from the bedside, and stood awkwardly apart. "He'll get along. You needn't be anxious about leaving him. He'll be better alone."

There was no mistaking this hint. "Well, well!" said Bartley humbly, "I'll go. But I'd rather stay and watch with him—I sha'n't eat or sleep till he's on foot again. And I can't leave till you tell me that you forgive me, Mrs. Bird. I never dreamt—I didn't intend"— He could not go on.

"I don't suppose you meant to hurt Henry," said the mother. "You always pretended to be so fond of him, and he thought the world of you. But I don't see how you could do it. I presume it was all right."

"No, it was all wrong,—or so nearly all wrong that I must ask your forgiveness on that ground. I loved him—I thought the world of him, too. I'd ten thousand times rather have hurt myself," pleaded Bartley. "Don't let me go till you say that you forgive me."

"I'll see how Henry gets along," said Mrs. Bird. "I don't know as I could rightly say I forgive you just yet." Doubtless she was dealing conscientiously with herself and with him. "I like to be sure of a thing when I say it," she added.

The doctor followed him into the hall, and Bartley could not help turning to him for consolation. "I think Mrs. Bird is very unjust, doctor. I've done everything I could—and said everything—to explain the matter; and I've blamed myself where I can't feel that I was to blame; and yet you see how she holds out against me."

"I dare say," answered the doctor dryly, "she'll feel differently, as she says, if the boy gets well."

Bartley dropped his hat to the floor. "Gets well! Why—why you think he'll get well, *now*, don't you doctor?"

"Oh, yes; I was merely using her words. He'll get well."

"And—and it wont affect his mind, will it? I thought it was very strange, his not remembering anything about it"—

"That's a very common phenomenon," said the doctor. "The patient usually forgets everything that occurred for some little time before the accident in cases of concussion of the brain." Bartley shuddered at the phrase, but he could not ask anything further. "What I wanted to say to you," continued the doctor, "was that this may be a long thing, and there may have to be an inquiry into it. You're lawyer enough to understand what that means. I should have to testify to what I know, and I only know what you've told me."

"Why, you don't doubt"—

"No, sir; I've no reason to suppose you haven't told me the truth, as far as it goes. If you have thought it advisable to keep anything back from me, you may wish to tell the whole story to an attorney."

"I haven't kept anything back, Doctor Wills," said Bartley. "I've told you everything—everything that concerned the quarrel. That drunken old scoundrel of a Morrison got us into it. He accused me of making love to his daughter; and Henry was jealous—I never knew he cared anything for her. I hated to tell you this before his mother. But this is the whole truth, so help me God."

"I supposed it was something of the kind," replied the doctor. "I'm sorry for you. You can't keep it from having an ugly look if it gets out; and it may have to be made public. I advise you to go and see Squire Gaylord; he's always stood your friend."

"I—I was just going there," said Bartley; and this was true. Through all, he had felt the need of some sort of retrieval; of re-establishing himself in his own esteem, by some signal stroke; and he could think of but one thing. It was not his fault if he believed that this must combine self-sacrifice with safety, and the greatest degree of humiliation with the largest sum of consolation. He was none the less resolved not to spare himself at all in offering to release Marcia from her engagement. The fact that he must now also see her father upon the legal aspect of his case, certainly complicated the affair, and detracted from its heroic quality. He could not tell which to see first, for he naturally wished his action to look as well as possible; and if he went first to Marcia, and she condemned him, he did not know in what figure he should approach her father. If on the other hand, he went first to Squire Gaylord the old lawyer might insist that the engagement was already at an end by Bartley's violent act, and might well refuse to let a man in his position even see his daughter. He lagged heavy-heartedly up the middle of the street, and left the question to solve itself at the last moment. But when he reached Squire Gaylord's gate, it seemed to him that it would be easier to face the father first; and this would be the right way, too.

He turned aside to the little office, and opened the door without knocking, and as he stood with the knob in his hand, trying to habituate his eyes, full of the snow-glare, to the dimmer light within, he heard a rapturous cry of "Why, Bartley!" and he felt Marcia's arms flung round his neck. His burdened heart yearned upon her with a tenderness he had not known before; he realized the preciousness of an embrace that might be the last; but he dared not put down his lips to hers. She pushed back her head in a little wonder, and saw the haggardness of his face, while he discovered her father looking at them. How strong and pure the fire in her must be when her father's presence could not abash her from this betrayal of her love! Bartley sickened, and he felt her arms slip from his neck. "Why—why—what is the matter?"

In spite of some vaguely magnanimous intention to begin at the beginning, and tell the whole affair just as it happened, Bartley found himself wishing to put the best face on it at first, and trust to chances to make it all appear well. He did not speak at once, and Marcia pressed him into a chair, and then like an eager child, who will not let its friend escape, till it has been told what it wishes to know, she set herself on his knee, and put her hand on his shoulder. He looked at her father, not at her, while he spoke hoarsely: "I have had trouble with Henry Bird, Squire Gaylord, and I've come to tell you about it."

The old Squire did not speak, but Marcia repeated in amazement, "With Henry Bird?"

"He struck me"—

"Henry Bird *struck* you!" cried the girl. "I should like to know why Henry Bird struck *you*, when you'd made so much of him, and he's always pretended to be so grateful!"

Bartley still looked at her father. "And I struck him back."

"You did perfectly right, Bartley," exclaimed Marcia, "and I should have despised you if you had let any one run over you. Struck you! I declare"—

He did not heed her, but continued to look at her father—"I didn't intend to hurt him—I hit him with my open hand—but he fell and struck his head on the floor. I'm afraid it hurt him pretty badly." He felt the pang that thrilled through the girl at his words, and her hand trembled on his shoulder; but she did not take it away.

The old man came forward from the pile of books which he and Marcia had been dusting, and sat down in a chair on the other side of the stove. He pushed back his hat from his forehead, and asked dryly, "What commenced it?"

Bartley hesitated. It was this part of the affair which he would rather have imparted to Marcia after seeing it with her father's eyes or possibly, if her father viewed it favorably, have had him tell her. The old man noticed his reluctance. "Hadn't you better go into the house, Marsh?" She merely gave him a look of utter astonishment for answer, and did not move. He laughed noiselessly, and said to Bartley: "Go on."

"It was that drunken old scoundrel of a Morrison, who began it!" cried Bartley, in angry desperation. Marcia dropped her hand from his shoulder, while her father worked his jaws upon the bit of stick he had picked up from the pile of wood, and put between his teeth. "You know that whenever he gets on a spree he comes to the office and wants Hannah's wages raised."

Marcia sprang to her feet. "Oh, I knew it! I knew it! I told you she would get you into trouble! I told you so!" She stood clinching her hands, and her father bent his keen scrutiny first upon her, and then upon the frowning face with which Bartley regarded her.

"Did he come to have her wages raised to-day?"

"No."

"What did he come for?" He involuntarily assumed the attitude of a lawyer cross-questioning a slippery witness.

"He came for— He came— He accused me of— He said I had—made love to his confounded girl."

Marcia gasped.

"What made him think you had?"

"It wasn't necessary for him to have any reason. He was drunk. I had been kind to the girl, and favored her all I could, because she seemed to be anxious to do her work well; and I praised her for trying."

"Um-umph," commented the squire. "And that made Henry Bird jealous?"

"It seems that he was fond of her. I never dreamed of such a thing, and when I put old Morrison out of the office, and came back he called me a liar, and struck me in the face." He did not lift his eyes to the level of Marcia's, who in her gray dress stood there like a gray shadow, and did not stir or speak.

"And you never had made up to the girl at all?"

"No."

"Kissed her, I suppose, now and then?" suggested the Squire.

Bartley did not reply.

"Flattered her up, and told her how much you thought of her, occasionally?"

"I don't see what that has to do with it," said Bartley with a sulky defiance.

"No, I suppose it's what you'd do with most any pretty girl," returned the Squire. He was silent awhile. "And so you knocked Henry down. What happened then?"

"I tried to bring him to, and then I went for the doctor. He revived, and we got him home to his mother's. The doctor says he will get well; but he advised me to come and see you."

"Any witnesses of the assault?"

"No; we were alone in my own room."

"Told any one else about it?"

"I told the doctor and Mrs. Bird. Henry couldn't remember it at all."

"Couldn't remember about Morrison, or what made him mad at you?"

"Nothing."

"And that's all about it?"

"Yes."

The two men had talked across the stove at each other, practically ignoring the girl, who stood apart from them, gray in the face as her dress, and suppressing a passion which had turned her as rigid as stone.

"Now, Marcia," said her father, kindly, "better go into the house. That's all there is of it."

"No, that isn't all," she answered. "Give me my ring, Bartley. Here's yours." She slipped it off her finger, and put it into his mechanically extended hand.

"Marcia!" he implored, confronting her.

"Give me my ring, please."

He obeyed, and put it into her hand. She slipped it back on the finger from which she had so fondly suffered him to take it yesterday, and replace it with his own.

"I'll go into the house, now, father. Good-by, Bartley." Her eyes were perfectly clear and dry, and her voice controlled; and as he stood passive before her, she took him round the neck, and pressed against his face, once, and twice, and thrice, her own gray face, in which all love and unrelenting and despair were painted. Once and again she held him, and looked him in the eyes, as if to be sure it was he. Then with a last pressure of her face to his, she released him, and passed out of the door. "She's been talking about you, here, all the morning," said the Squire with a sort of quiet absence, as if nothing in particular had happened, and he were commenting on a little fact that might possibly interest Bartley. He ruminated upon the fragment of wood in his mouth a while before he added: "I guess she wont want to talk about you any more. I drew you out a little, on that Hannah Morrison business, because I wanted her to understand just what kind of fellow you were. You see it isn't the trouble you've got into with Henry Bird that's killed her; it's the cause of the trouble. I guess if it had been anything else she'd have stood by you. But you see that's the one thing she couldn't bear, and I'm glad it's happened now instead of afterwards: I guess you're one of that *kind*, Mr. Hubbard."

"Squire Gaylord!" cried Bartley, "upon my sacred word of honor, there isn't any more of this thing than I've told you. And I think it's pretty hard to be thrown over for—for"—

"Fooling with a pretty girl, when you get a chance and the girl seems to like it? Yes, it *is* rather hard. And I suppose you haven't even seen her since you were engaged to Marcia?"

"Of course not! That is"—

"It's a kind of retroactive legislation on Marcia's part," said the Squire, rubbing his chin, "and that's against one of the first principles of law. But women don't seem to be able to grasp that idea. They're queer about some things. They appear to think they marry a man's whole life—his past as well as his future, and that makes 'em particular. And they distinguish between different kinds of men. You'll find 'em pinning their faith to a fellow who's been through pretty much everything, and swearing by him from the word go; and another chap, who's never *done* any thing very bad, they wont trust half a minute out of their sight. Well, I guess Marcia *is* of rather a jealous disposition," he concluded, as if Bartley had urged this point.

"She's very unjust to me," Bartley began.

"Oh, yes—she's *unjust*," said her father. "I don't deny that. But it wouldn't be any use talking to her. She'd probably turn round with some excuse about what she had suffered, and that would be the end of it. She would say that she couldn't go through it again. Well, it ought to be a comfort to you to think you don't care a great deal about it."

"But I *do* care!" exclaimed Bartley. "I care all the world for it. I"—

"Since when?" interrupted the Squire. "Do you mean to say that you didn't know till you asked her yesterday that Marcia was in love with you?" Bartley was silent. "I guess you knew it as much as a year ago, didn't you? Everybody else did. But you'd just as soon it had been Hannah Morrison or any other pretty girl. *You* didn't care! But Marcia did, you see. She wasn't one of the kind that let any good-looking fellow make love to them. It was because it was *you*; and you knew it. We're plain men, Mr. Hubbard; and I guess you'll get over this, in time. I shouldn't wonder if you began to mend, right away."

Bartley found himself helpless in the face of this passionless sarcasm. He could have met stormy indignation or any sort of invective in kind; but the contemptuous irony with which his pretensions were treated, the cold scrutiny with which his motives were searched was something he could not meet. He tried to pull himself together for some sort of protest, but he ended by hanging his head in silence. He always believed that Squire Gaylord had liked him, and here he was treating him like his bitterest enemy, and seeming to enjoy his misery. He could not understand it; he thought it extremely unjust, and past all the measure of his offense. This was true, perhaps; but it is doubtful if Bartley would have accepted any suffering no matter how nicely proportioned in punishment of his wrong-doing. He sat hanging his head, and taking his pain in rebellious silence, with a gathering hate in his heart for the old man.

"Mwell!" said the Squire at last, rising from his chair, "I guess I must be going."

Bartley sprang to his feet aghast. "You're not going to leave me in the lurch are you? You're not"—

"Oh, I shall take care of you, young man,—don't be afraid. I've stood your friend, too long, and your name's been mixed up too much with my girl's, for me to let you come to shame openly, if I can help it. I'm going to see Dr. Wills, about you, and I'm going to see Mrs. Bird, and try to patch it up, somehow."

"And—and—where shall I go?" gasped Bartley.

"You might go to the devil, for all I cared for you," said the old man, with the contempt which he no longer cared to make ironical. "But I guess you better go back to your office, and go to work as if nothing had happened—till something does happen. I shall close the paper out as soon as I can. I was thinking of doing that just before you came in. I was thinking of taking you into the law business with me. Marcia and I were talking about it, here. But I guess you wouldn't like the idea, now."

He seemed to get a bitter satisfaction out of these mocker-ies, from which, indeed, he must have suffered quite as much as Bartley. But he ended, sadly and almost compassionately, with, "Come, come! You must start sometime," and Bartley dragged his leaden weight out of the door. The Squire closed it after him; but he did not accompany him down the street. It was plain he did not wish to be any longer alone with Bartley, and the young man suspected with a sting of shame that he scorned to be seen with him.

VIII

THE MORE Bartley dwelt upon his hard case, during the week that followed, the more it appeared to him that he was punished out of all proportion to his offence. He was in no mood to consider such mercies as that he had been spared from seriously hurting Bird; and that Squire Gaylord and Doctor Wills had united with Henry's mother in saving him from open disgrace. The physician, indeed, had perhaps indulged a professional passion for hushing the matter up, rather than any pity for Bartley. He probably had the scientific way of looking at such questions; and saw much physical cause for moral effects. He refrained, with the physician's reticence, from inquiring into the affair; but he would not have thought Bartley without excuse under the circumstances. In regard to the relative culpability in matters of the kind his knowledge of women enabled him to take much the view of the woman's share that other women take.

But Bartley was ignorant of the doctor's leniency, and associated him with Squire Gaylord in the feeling that made his last week in Equity a period of social outlawry. There were moments in which he could not himself escape the same point of view. He could rebel against the severity of the condemnation he had fallen under in the eyes of Marcia and her father; he could, in the light of example and usage, laugh at the notion of harm in his behavior to Hannah Morrison; yet he found himself looking at it as a treachery to Marcia. Certainly she had no right to question his conduct before his engagement. Yet if he knew that Marcia loved him, and was waiting with life-and-death anxiety for some word of love from him, it was cruelly false to play with another at the passion which was such a tragedy to her. This was the point that, put aside however often, still presented itself, and its recurrence if he could have known it, was mercy and reprieve from the only source out of which these could come.

Hannah Morrison did not return to the printing-office, and Bird was still sick, though it was now only a question of time when he should be out again. Bartley visited him some hours every day, and sat and suffered under the quiet condemnation of his mother's eyes. She had kept Bartley's secret with the same hardness with which she had refused him her forgiveness, and the village had settled down into an ostensible acceptance of the theory of a faint as the beginning of Bird's sickness, with such other conjectures as the doctor freely permitted each to form. Bartley found his chief consolation in the work which kept him out of the way of a great deal of question. He worked far into the night, as he must, to make up for the force that was withdrawn from the office. At the same time he wrote more than ever in the paper, and he discovered in himself that dual life, of which every one who sins or sorrows is sooner or later aware: that strange separation of the intellectual activity from the suffering of the soul, by which the mind toils on in a sort of ironical indifference to the pangs that wring the heart; the realization that in some ways his brain can get on perfectly well without his conscience.

There was a great deal of sympathy felt for Bartley at this time, and his popularity in Equity was never greater than now when his life there was drawing to a close. The spectacle of his diligence was so impressive that when on the following Sunday the young minister who had succeeded to the pulpit of the orthodox church, preached a sermon on the beauty of industry from the text "Consider the Lilies," there were many who said that they thought of Bartley, the whole while, and one—a lady—asked Mr. Savin if he did not have Mr. Hubbard in mind in the picture he drew of the Heroic Worker. They wished that Bartley could have heard that sermon.

Marcia had gone away early in the week to visit in the town where she used to go to school, and Bartley took her going away as a sign that she wished to put herself wholly beyond his reach, or any danger of relenting at sight of him. He talked with no one about her; and going and coming irregularly to his meals, and keeping himself shut up in his room when he was not at work, he left people very little chance to talk with him. But they conjectured that he and Marcia had an understanding; and some of the ladies used such scant opportunity as he gave them to make sly allusions to her absence and his desolate condition. They were confirmed in their surmise, by the fact known from actual observation, that Bartley had not spoken a word to any other young lady since Marcia went away.

"Look here, my friend," said the philosopher from the logging-camp, when he came in for his paper on the Tuesday afternoon following, "seems to me from what I hear tell around here, you're tryin' to kill yourself on this newspaper. Now it wont do; I tell you it wont do."

Bartley was addressing for the mail the papers which one of the girls was folding. "What are you going to do about it?" he demanded of his sympathizer with whimsical sullenness, and not troubling himself to look up at him.

"Well, I hain't exactly settled, yet," replied the philosopher, who was of a tall, lank figure, and of a mighty brown beard. "But I've been around pretty much everywhere, and I find that about the poorest use you can put a man to is to kill him."

"It depends a good deal on the man," said Bartley. "But that's stale, Kinney. It's the old formula of the anti-capital-punishment fellows. Try something else. They're not talking of hanging me yet." He kept on writing, and the philosopher stood over him with a humorous twinkle of enjoyment at Bartley's readiness.

"Well, I'll allow it's old," he admitted. "So's Homer."

"Yes; but you don't pretend that you wrote Homer."

Kinney laughed mightily; then he leaned forward, and slapped Bartley on the shoulder with his newspaper. "Look here!" he exclaimed, "I *like* you!"

"Oh, try some other tack! Lots of fellows like me." Bartley kept on writing.

"I gave you your paper, didn't I, Kinney?"

"You mean that you want me to get out?" was the response.

"Far be it from me to say so."

This delighted Kinney as much as the last refinement of hospitality would have pleased another man.

"Look here!" he said, "I want you should come out and see our camp. I can't fool away any more time on you here; but I want you should come out and see us. Give you something to write about. Hey?"

"The invitation comes at a time when circumstances over

which I have no control oblige me to decline it. I admire your
prudence, Kinney."

"No, honest Injian, now," protested Kinney. "Take a day
off, and fill up with dead advertisements. That's the way they
used to do, out in Alkali City when they got short of help on
the Eagle, and we liked it just as well."

"Now you are talking sense," said Bartley looking up at
him. "How far is it to your settlement?"

"Two miles, if you're goin'; three and a half, if you ain't."

"When are you coming in again?"

"I'm in, now."

"I can't go with you to-day."

"Well, how'll to-morrow morning suit?"

"To-morrow morning will suit," said Bartley.

"All right. If anybody comes in to see the editor to-morrow
morning, Marrilla," said Kinney to the girl, "you tell 'em he's
sick, and gone a-loggin', and wont be back till Saturday. Say!"
he added, laying his hand on Bartley's shoulder, "you ain't
foolin'?"

"If I am," replied Bartley, "just mention it."

"Good!" said Kinney. "To-morrow it is, then."

Bartley finished addressing the newspapers, and then he put
them up in wrappers and packages, for the mail. "You can
go, now, Marrilla," he said to the girl. "I'll have some copy
for you and Kitty; you'll find it on my table in the morning."

"All right," answered the girl.

Bartley went to his supper, which he ate with more relish
than he had felt for his meals since his troubles began, and he
took part in the supper-table talk with something of his old
audacity. The change interested the lady-boarders and they
agreed that he must have had a letter. He returned to his
office, and worked till nine o'clock, writing and selecting matter out of his exchanges. He spent most of the time in preparing the funny column, which was a favorite feature in the
Free Press. Then he put the copy where the girls would find
it in the morning, and leaving the door unlocked, he took his
way up the street towards Squire Gaylord's.

He knew that he should find the lawyer in his office, and
he opened the office-door without knocking, and went in. He

had not met Squire Gaylord since the morning of his dismissal, and the old man had left him for the past eight days without any sign as to what he expected of Bartley, or of what he intended to do in his affair.

They looked at each other, but exchanged no sort of greeting, as Bartley, unbidden, took a chair on the opposite side of the stove; the Squire did not put down the book he had been reading. "I've come to see what you're going to do about the Free Press," said Bartley.

The old man rubbed his bristling jaw, that seemed even lanker than when Bartley saw it last. He waited almost a minute before he said: "I don't know as I've got any call to tell you."

"Then I'll tell you what *I'm* going to do about it," retorted Bartley. "I'm going to leave it. I've done my last day's work on that paper. Do you think," he cried, angrily, "that I'm going to keep on in the dark, and let you consult your pleasure as to my future? No, sir! You don't know your man, quite, Mr. Gaylord."

"You've got over your scare," said the lawyer.

"I've got over my scare," Bartley retorted.

"And you think, because you're not afraid, any longer, that you're out of danger. I know my man as well as you do, I guess."

"If you think I care for the danger, you don't. You may do what you please. Whatever you do, I shall know it isn't out of kindness for me. I didn't believe from the first that the law could touch me, and I wasn't uneasy on that account. But I didn't want to involve myself in a public scandal, for Miss Gaylord's sake. Miss Gaylord has released me from any obligations to her; and now you may go ahead and do what you like." Each of the men knew how much truth there was in this; but for the moment in his anger, Bartley believed himself sincere, and there is no question but his defiance was so. Squire Gaylord made him no answer, and after a minute of expectation Bartley added, "At any rate I've done with the Free Press. I advise you to stop the paper, and hand the office over to Henry Bird, when he gets about. I'm going out to Willett's logging-camp, to-morrow, and I'm coming back to

Equity on Saturday. You'll know where to find me till then, and after that you may look me up if you want me."

He rose to go, but stopped with his hand on the door-knob, at a sound, preliminary to speaking, which the old man made in his throat. Bartley stopped, hoping for a farther pretext of quarrel but the lawyer merely asked, "Where's the key?"

"It's in the office-door."

The old man now looked at him as if he no longer saw him, and Bartley went out, baulked of his purpose in part, and in that degree so much the more embittered.

Squire Gaylord remained an hour longer; then he blew out his lamp, and left the little office for the night. A light was burning in the kitchen, and he made his way round to the back door of the house, and let himself in. His wife was there, sitting before the stove, in those last delicious moments before going to bed, when all the house is mellowed to such a warmth that it seems hard to leave it to the cold and dark. In this poor lady, who had so long denied herself spiritual comfort, there was a certain obscure luxury: she liked little dainties of the table; she liked soft warmth, an easy cushion. It was doubtless in the disintegration of the finer qualities of her nature, that as they grew older together, she threw more and more the burden of acute feeling upon the husband to whose doctrine of life she had submitted, but had never been reconciled. Marriage is, with all its disparities a much more equal thing than appears, and the meek little wife, who has all the advantage of public sympathy, knows her power over her oppressor, and at some tender spot in his affections or his nerves can inflict an anguish that will avenge her for years of coarser aggression. Thrown in upon herself in so vital a matter as her religion, Mrs. Gaylord had involuntarily come to live largely for herself, though her talk was always of husband. She gave up for him, as she believed, her soul's salvation, but she held him to account for the uttermost farthing of the price. She padded herself round at every point where she could have suffered through her sensibilities, and lived soft and snug in the shelter of his iron will and indomitable courage. It was not apathy that she had felt when their children died one after another, but an obscure and formless expectation that Mr.

Gaylord would suffer enough for both. Marcia was the youngest, and her mother left her training almost wholly to her father; she sometimes said that she never supposed the child would live. She did not actually urge this in excuse, but she had the appearance of doing so; and she held aloof from them both in their mutual relations, with mildly critical reserves. They spoiled each other, as father and daughter are apt to do, when left to themselves. What was good in the child certainly received no harm from his indulgence; and what was naughty was after all not so very naughty. She was passionate, but she was generous; and if she showed a jealous temperament that must hereafter make her unhappy, for the time being it charmed and flattered her father to have her so fond of him that she could not endure any rivalry in his affection. Her education proceeded fitfully. He would not let her be forced to household tasks that she disliked; and as a little girl she went to school chiefly because she liked to go, and not because she would have been obliged to if she had not chosen. When she grew older, she wished to go away to school, and her father allowed her: he had no great respect for boarding-schools, but if Marcia wanted to try it, he was willing to humor the joke. What resulted was a great proficiency in the things that pleased her, and ignorance of the other things. Her father bought her a piano, on which she did not play much, and he bought her whatever dresses she fancied. He never came home from a journey, without bringing her something; and he liked to take her with him, when he went away to other places. She had been several times at Portland, and once at Montreal; he was very proud of her: he could not see that any one was better looking, or dressed any better than his girl.

He came into the kitchen, and sat down with his hat on, and taking his shin between his hands moved uneasily about on his chair.

"What's brought you in so early?" asked his wife.

"Well, I got through," he briefly explained. After a while he said, "Bartley Hubbard's been out there."

"You don't mean't he knew she"—

"No, he didn't know anything about that. He came to tell me he was going away."

"Well, I don't know what you're going to do, Mr. Gaylord," said his wife, shifting the responsibility wholly upon him. " 'D he seem to want to make it up?"

"Mno!" said the Squire, "he was on his high horse. He knows he ain't in any danger, now."

"Ain't you afraid she'll carry on dreadfully, when she finds out 't he's gone for good?" asked Mrs. Gaylord, with a sort of implied satisfaction that the carrying on was not to affect her.

"Myes," said the Squire, "I suppose she'll carry on. But I don't know what to do about it. Sometimes I almost wish I'd tried to make it up between 'em that day; but I thought she'd better see, once for all, what sort of man she was going in for, if she married him. It's too late, now, to do any thing. The fellow came in to-night for a quarrel, and nothing else; I could see that; and I didn't give him any chance."

"You feel sure," asked Mrs. Gaylord impartially, "that Marcia wa'n't too particular?"

"No, Miranda, I don't feel sure of anything, except that it's past your bedtime. You better go. I'll sit up a while, yet. I came in, because I couldn't settle my mind to anything, out there." He took off his hat in token of his intending to spend the rest of the evening at home, and put it on the table at his elbow.

His wife sewed at the mending in her lap, without offering to act upon his suggestion. "It's plain to be seen that she can't get along without him."

"She'll have to, now," replied the Squire.

"I'm afraid," said Mrs. Gaylord softly, "that she'll be down sick. She don't look as if she'd slept any great deal since she's been gone. I d'know as I like very much to see her looking, the way she does. I guess you've got to take her off, somewheres."

"Why, she's just been off, and couldn't stay!"

"That's because she thought he was here, yet. But if he's gone, it wont be the same thing."

"Well, we've got to fight it out, some way," said the Squire. "It wouldn't do to give in to it, now. It always *was* too much of a one-sided thing, at the best; and if we tried now to mend it up, it would be ridiculous. I don't believe he would come back at all, now, and if he did, he wouldn't come back on any equal terms. He'd want to have everything his own way. Mno!" said the Squire, as if confirming himself in a conclusion often reached already in his own mind, "I saw by the way he began to-night that there wa'n't anything to be done with him. It was fight from the word go."

"Well," said Mrs. Gaylord with gentle, skeptical interest in the outcome, "if you've made up your mind to that, I hope you'll be able to carry it through."

"That's what I've made up my mind to," said her husband.

Mrs. Gaylord rolled up the sewing in her work-basket, and packed it away against the side, bracing it with several pairs of newly darned socks and stockings neatly folded one into the other. She took her time for this, and when she rose at last to go out, with her basket in her hand, the door opened in her face, and Marcia entered. Mrs. Gaylord shrank back, and then slipped round behind her daughter and vanished. The girl took no notice of her mother, but went and sat down on her father's knee, throwing her arms round his neck, and dropping her haggard face on his shoulder. She had arrived at home a few hours earlier, having driven over from a station ten miles distant on a road that did not pass near Equity. After giving as much of a shock to her mother's mild nature as it was capable of receiving by her unexpected return, she had gone to her own room and remained ever since without seeing her father. He put up his thin old hand and passed it over her hair, but it was long before either of them spoke.

At last Marcia lifted her head, and looked her father in the face with a smile so pitiful that he could not bear to meet it. "Well, father?" she said.

"Well, Marsh," he answered huskily.

"What do you think of me now?"

"I'm glad to have you back again," he replied.

"You know why I came?"

"Yes, I guess I know."

She put down her head again, and moaned and cried, "Father! Father!" with dry sobs. When she looked up, confronting him with her tearless eyes, "What shall I do? What shall I do?" she demanded desolately.

He tried to clear his throat to speak, but it required more than one effort to bring the words.

"I guess you better go along with me up to Boston. I'm going up the first of the week."

"No," she said quietly.

"The change would do you good. It's a long while since you've been away from home," her father urged.

She looked at him in sad reproach of his uncandor. "You know there's nothing the matter with me, father. You know what the trouble is."

He was silent. He could not face the trouble.

"I've heard people talk of a heartache," she went on. "I never believed there was really such a thing. But I know there is, now. There's a pain here." She pressed her hand against her breast. "It's sore with aching. What shall I do? I shall have to live through it somehow."

"If you don't feel exactly well," said her father, "I guess you better see the doctor."

"What shall I tell him is the matter with me? That I want Bartley Hubbard?" He winced at the words, but she did not. "He knows that already. Everybody in town does. It's never been any secret. I couldn't hide it, from the first day I saw him. I'd just as lief as not they should say as I was dying for him. I shall not care what they say when I'm dead."

"You'd oughtn't—you'd oughtn't to talk that way, Marcia," said her father gently.

"What difference?" she demanded, scornfully.

There was truly no difference, so far as concerned any creed of his, and he was too honest to make further pretence.

"What shall I do?" she went on again. "I've thought of praying; but what would be the use?"

"I've never denied that there was a God, Marcia," said her father.

"Oh, I know. *That* kind of God! Well, well! I know that I talk like a crazy person! Do you suppose it was providential, my being with you in the office that morning when Bartley came in?"

"No," said her father, "I don't. I think it was an accident."

"Mother said it was Providential, my finding him out before it was too late."

"I think it was a good thing. The fellow has the making of a first-class scoundrel in him."

"Do you think he's a scoundrel now?" she asked quietly.

"He hasn't had any great opportunity yet," said the old man, conscientiously sparing him.

"Well, then, I'm sorry I found him out. Yes! If I hadn't, I might have married him, and perhaps if I had died soon I might *never* have found him out. He could have been good to me a year or two, and then if I died, I should have been safe. Yes, I wish he could have deceived me till after we were married. Then I *couldn't* have borne to give him up, may be."

"You *would* have given him up, even then. And that's the only thing that reconciles me to it now. I'm sorry for you, my girl; but you'd have made me sorrier then. Sooner or later he'd have broken your heart."

"He's broken it now," said the girl calmly.

"Oh, no, he hasn't," replied her father with a false cheerfulness that did not deceive her. "You're young, and you'll get over it. I mean to take you away from here, for a while. I mean to take you up to Boston; and on to New York. I shouldn't care if we went as far as Washington. I guess when you've seen a little more of the world you wont think Bartley Hubbard's the only one in it."

She looked at him so intently that he thought she must be pleased at his proposal. "Do you think I could get him back?" she asked.

Her father lost his patience; it was a relief to be angry. "No, I don't think it. I know you couldn't. And you ought to be ashamed of mentioning such a thing!"

"Oh, ashamed! No, I've got past that. I have no shame any more, where he's concerned. Oh, I'd give the world if I could call him back—if I could only undo what I did! I was wild. I wasn't reasonable; I wouldn't listen to him. I drove him away without giving him a chance to say a word! Of course he must hate me, now. What makes you think he wouldn't come back?"

"I know he wouldn't," answered her father, with a sort of groan. "He's going to leave Equity, for one thing, and"—

"Going to leave Equity?" she repeated absently. Then he

felt her tremble. "How do you know he's going?" She turned upon her father, and fixed him sternly with her eyes.

"Do you suppose he would stay, after what's happened, any longer than he could help?"

"How do you know he's going?" she repeated.

"He told me."

She stood up. "He told you? When?"

"To-night."

"Why, where—where did you see him?" she whispered.

"In the office."

"Since—since—I came? Bartley been here! And you didn't tell me—you didn't let me know?"

They looked at each other in silence. At last, "When is he going?" she asked.

"To-morrow morning."

She sat down in the chair which her mother had left, and clutched the back of another, on which her fingers opened and closed convulsively, while she caught her breath in irregular gasps. She broke into a low moaning, at last, the expression of abject defeat in the struggle she had waged with herself. Her father watched her with dumb compassion. "Better go to bed, Marcia," he said with the same dry calm as if he had been sending her away after some pleasant evening which she had suffered to run too far into the night.

"Don't you think—don't you think—he'll have to see you again before he goes?" she made out to ask.

"No; he's finished up with me," said the old man.

"Well, then," she cried desperately, "you'll have to go to him, father, and get him to come! I can't help it! I can't give him up! You've got to go to him, now, father—yes, yes, you have! You've got to go and tell him. Go and get him to come, for *mercy's* sake! Tell him that I'm sorry—that I beg his pardon—that I didn't think—I didn't understand—that I know he didn't do anything wrong"— She rose, and placing her hand on her father's shoulder, accented each entreaty with a little push.

He looked up into her face with a haggard smile of sympathy. "You're crazy, Marcia," he said, gently.

"Don't laugh!" she cried. "I'm not crazy, now. But I was, then—yes, stark, staring crazy. Look here, father! I want to tell you—I want to explain to you!" She dropped upon his knee again, and tremblingly passed her arm round his neck. "You see I had just told him the day before that I shouldn't care for anything that happened before we were engaged; and then at the very first thing I went and threw him off! And I had no right to do it. He knows that, and that's what makes him so hard towards me. But if you go and tell him that I see now I was all wrong, and that I beg his pardon; and then ask him to give me *one* more trial, just one *more*— You can do as much as that for me, can't you?"

"Oh, you poor, crazy girl!" groaned her father. "Don't you see that the trouble is in what the fellow *is*; and not in any particular thing that he's done? He's a scamp, through and through; and he's all the more a scamp when he doesn't know it. He hasn't got the first idea of anything but selfishness."

"No, no! Now, I'll tell you—now, I'll prove it to you. That very Sunday when we were out riding together; and we met her and her mother, and their sleigh upset, and he had to lift her back; and it made me wild to see him, and I wouldn't hardly touch him or speak to him afterwards, he didn't say one angry word to me. He just pulled me up to him, and wouldn't let me be mad; and he said that night he didn't mind it a bit because it showed how much I liked him. Now, doesn't that prove he's good—a good deal better than I am, and that he'll forgive me, if you'll go and ask him? I know he isn't in bed, yet; he always sits up late—he told me so; and you'll find him there in his room. Go straight to his room, father; don't let anybody see you down in the office; I couldn't bear it; and slip out with him as quietly as you can. But, oh do hurry, now! Don't lose another minute"—

A wild joy sprang into her face, as her father rose; a joy that it was terrible to him to see die out of it as he spoke: "I tell you it's no use, Marcia! He wouldn't come if I went to him"—

"Oh, yes—yes he would! I know he would! If"—

"He wouldn't! You're mistaken. I should have to get down in the dust for nothing. He's a bad fellow, I tell you; and you've got to give him up."

"You hate me!" cried the girl. The old man walked to and fro, clutching his hands. Their lives had always been in such intimate sympathy, his life had so long had her happiness for its sole pleasure, that the pang in her heart racked his with as sharp an agony. "Well, I shall die; and then I hope you will be satisfied."

"Marcia, Marcia!" pleaded her father. "You don't know what you're saying."

"You're letting him go away from me—you're letting me lose him—you're killing me!"

"He wouldn't come, my girl. It would be perfectly useless to go to him. You must—you *must* try to control yourself, Marcia. There's no other way—there's no other hope. You're disgraceful. You ought to be ashamed. You ought to have some pride about you. I don't know what's come over you since you've been with that fellow. You seem to be out of your senses. But try—try, my girl, to get over it. If you fight it, you'll conquer yet. You've got a spirit for anything. And I'll help you, Marcia. I'll take you anywhere. I'll do anything for you"—

"You wouldn't go to him, and ask him to come here, if it would save his life!"

"No," said the old man with a desperate quiet, "I wouldn't."

She stood looking at him, and then she sank suddenly, and straight down, as if she were sinking through the floor. When he lifted her, he saw that she was in a dead faint, and while the swoon lasted would be out of her misery. The sight of this had wrung him so that he had a kind of relief in looking at her lifeless face; and he was slow in laying her down again, like one that fears to wake a sleeping child. Then he went to the foot of the stairs and softly called to his wife: "Miranda! Miranda!"

IX

KINNEY CAME into town the next morning bright and early, as he phrased it; but he did not stop at the hotel for Bartley till nine o'clock. "Thought I'd give you time for breakfast," he explained, "and so I didn't hurry up any about gettin' in my supplies."

It was a beautiful morning, so blindingly sunny, that Bartley winked as they drove up through the glistening street, and was glad to dip into the gloom of the first woods, it was not cold: the snow felt the warmth, and packed moistly under their runners. The air was perfectly still; at a distance on the mountain sides it sparkled as if full of diamond-dust. Far overhead some crows called. "The sun's getting high," said Bartley, with the light sigh of one to whom the thought of spring brings no hope.

"Well, I shouldn't begin to plough for corn just yet," replied Kinney. "It's curious," he went on, "to see how anxious we are to have a thing over, it don't much matter what it is, whether it's summer or winter. I suppose we'd feel different if we wa'n't sure there was going to be another of 'em. I guess that's one reason why the Lord concluded not to keep us clearly posted on the question of another life. If it wa'n't for the uncertainty of the thing, there are a lot of fellows like you that wouldn't stand it here a minute. Why if we had a dead sure thing of over-the-river—good climate, plenty to eat and wear, and not much to do—I don't believe any of us would keep Darling Minnie waiting, well, a *great* while. But you see the thing's all on paper, and that makes us cautious, and willing to hang on here a while longer. Looks splendid on the map: streets regularly laid out; public squares; band-stands; churches; solid blocks of houses with all the modern improvements; but you can't tell whether there's any town there till you're on the ground; and then if you don't like it, there's no way of gettin' back to the States."

He turned round upon Bartley, and opened his mouth wide to imply that this was pleasantry.

"Do you throw your philosophy in, all under the same price, Kinney?" asked the young fellow.

"Well, yes; I never charge anything over," said Kinney. "You see I have a good deal of time to think when I'm around by myself all day, and the philosophy don't cost *me* anything, and the fellows like it. Roughing it the way they do, they can stand most anything. Hey?" He now not only opened his mouth upon Bartley, but thrust him in the side with his elbow; and then laughed noisily.

Kinney was the cook. He had been over pretty nearly the whole uninhabitable globe, starting as a gaunt and awkward boy from the Maine woods, and keeping until he came back to them in late middle-life the same gross and ridiculous optimism. He had been at sea, and had been shipwrecked on several islands in the Pacific; he had passed a rainy season at Panama, and a yellow-fever season at Vera Cruz, and had been carried far into the interior of Peru by a tidal wave during an earthquake season; he was in the Border Ruffian War of Kansas, and he clung to California till prosperity deserted her after the completion of the Pacific road. Wherever he went he carried or found adversity; but with a heart fed on the metaphysics of Horace Greeley, and buoyed up by a few wildly interpreted maxims of Emerson, he had always believed in other men, and their fitness for the terrestrial millennium which was never more than ten days or ten miles off. It is not necessary to say that he had continued as poor as he began, and that he was never able to contribute to those railroads, mills, elevators, towns, cities which were sure to be built, sir, sure to be built, wherever he went. When he came home at last to the woods some hundreds of miles north of Equity, he found that some one had realized his early dream of a summer hotel on the shore of the beautiful lake there; and he unenviously settled down to admire the landlord's thrift, and to act as guide and cook for parties of young ladies and gentlemen who started from the hotel to camp in the woods. This brought him into the society of cultivated people, for which he had a real passion. He had always had a few thoughts rattling round in his skull, and he liked to make sure of them in talk with those who had enjoyed greater advantages than himself. He never begrudged them their luck; he simply and sweetly admired them; he made studies of their several characters and was never tired of analyzing them to their advantage to the next summer's parties. Late in the fall, he went in, as it is called, with a camp of loggers, among whom he rarely failed to find some remarkable men. But he confessed that he did not enjoy the steady three or four months in the winter-woods, with no coming out at all till spring; and he had been glad of this chance in a logging-camp near Equity, in which he had been offered the cook's place by the owner, who had tested his fare in the northern woods the summer before. Its proximity to the village allowed him to loaf in upon civilization at least once a week, and he spent the greater part of his time at the Free Press office on publication-day. He had always sought the society of newspaper men, and wherever he could, he had given them his. He was not long in discovering that Bartley was smart as a steel trap, and by an early and natural transition from calling the young-lady compositors by their pet names, and patting them on their shoulders, he had arrived at a like affectionate intimacy with Bartley.

As they worked deep into the woods on their way to the camp, the road dwindled to a well-worn track between the stumps and bushes. The ground was rough, and they constantly plunged down the slopes of little hills, and climbed the sides of the little valleys, and from time to time they had to turn out for teams drawing logs to the mills in Equity, each with its equipage of four or five wild young fellows who saluted Kinney with an ironical cheer or jovial taunt, in passing.

"They're all just so," he explained, with pride, when the last party had passed. "They're gentlemen, every one of 'em—perfect gentlemen."

They came at last to a wider clearing than any they had yet passed through, and here on a level of the hillside stretched the camp: a long, low structure of logs, with the roof broken at one point by a stove pipe, and the walls irregularly pierced by small windows; around it crouched and burrowed in the drift the sheds that served as stables and storehouses. The sun shone and shone with dazzling brightness upon the opening, and the sound of distant shouts, and the rhythmical stroke of axes came to it out of the forest; but the camp was deserted, and in the stillness Kinney's voice seemed strange and alien. "Walk in, walk in!" he said hospitably. "I've got to look after my horse."

But Bartley remained at the door, blinking in the sunshine, and harking to the near silence that sang in his ears. A curious feeling possessed him: sickness of himself as of some one else; a longing, consciously helpless, to be something different; a sense of captivity to habits and thoughts and hopes that centred in himself, and served him alone.

"Terribly peaceful around here," said Kinney, coming back to him, and joining him in a survey of the landscape, with his hands on his hips, and a stem of timothy projecting from his lips.

"Yes, terribly," assented Bartley.

"But it *aint* a bad way for a man to live, as long as he's young; or ain't got anybody that wants his company more than his room. Be the place for you."

"On which ground?" Bartley asked dryly, without taking his eyes from a distant peak that showed through the notch in the forest.

Kinney laughed in as unselfish enjoyment as if he had made the turn himself. "Well that ain't exactly what I meant to say: what I meant was that any man engaged in intellectual pursuits wants to come out and commune with nature, every little while."

"You call the Equity Free Press intellectual pursuits?" demanded Bartley with scorn. "I suppose it is," he added. "Well, here I am—right on the commune. But nature's such a big thing, I think it takes two to commune with her."

"Well, a girl's a help," assented Kinney.

"I wasn't thinking of a girl, exactly," said Bartley, with a little sadness. "I mean that if you're not in first-rate spiritual condition, you're apt to get floored, if you undertake to commune with nature."

"I guess that's about so. If a man's got anything on his mind a big railroad depot's the place for *him*. But you're run down. You ought to come out here, and take a hand, and be a man amongst men." Kinney talked partly for quantity, and partly for pure, indefinite good feeling.

Bartley turned toward the door. "What have you got inside, here?"

Kinney flung the door open, and followed his guest within. The first two thirds of the cabin was used as a dormitory, and the sides were furnished with rough bunks, from the ground to the roof. The round, unhewn logs showed their form everywhere; the crevices were caulked with moss; and the walls were warm and tight. It was dark, between the bunks, but beyond it was lighter, and Bartley could see at the further end a vast cooking-stove, and three long tables with benches at their sides. A huge coffee-pot stood on the top of the stove, and various pots and kettles surrounded it.

"Come into the dining-room and sit down in the parlor," said Kinney, drawing off his coat, as he walked forward. "Take the sofa," he added, indicating a movable bench. He hung his coat on a peg, and rolled up his shirt-sleeves, and began to whistle cheerily, like a man who enjoys his work, as he threw open the stove-door, and poked in some sticks of fuel. A brooding warmth filled the place, and the wood made a pleasant crackling as it took fire.

"Here's my desk," said Kinney, pointing to a barrel that supported a broad smooth board top. "This is where I compose my favorite works." He turned round, and cut out of a mighty mass of dough in a tin trough, a portion which he threw down on his table, and attacked with a rolling-pin. "That means pie, Mr. Hubbard," he explained, "and pie means meat pie—or squash-pie, at a pinch. To-day's pie-baking day. But you needn't be troubled on that account. So's to-morrow and so was yesterday. Pie twenty-one times a week, is the word, and don't you forget it. They say old Agassiz," Kinney went on, in that easy familiar fondness with which our people like to speak of greatness that impresses their imagination, "they say old Agassiz recommended fish as the best food for the brain. Well, I don't suppose but what it is. But I don't know but what pie is more stimulating to the fancy. I *never* saw anything like meat-pie to make ye dream."

"Yes," said Bartley, nodding gloomily, "I've tried it."

Kinney laughed. "Well, I guess folks of sedentary pursuits, like you and me, don't need it; but these fellows that stamp round in the snow all day, they want something to keep their imagination goin'. And I guess pie does it. Anyway they can't seem to get enough of it. Ever try apples when you was at work? They say old Greeley kep' his desk full of 'em; kep' munchin' away, all the while, when he was writin' his editorials. And one of them German poets—I don't know but what it was old Gutty himself—kept *rotten* ones in *his* drawer; liked the smell of 'em. Well, there's a good deal of apple in meat-pie. May be it's the apple that does it. *I* don't know. But I guess if your pursuits are sedentary you better take the apple separate."

Bartley did not say anything; but he kept a lazily interested eye on Kinney as he rolled out his pie-crust, fitted it into his tins, filled these from a jar of mince-meat, covered them with a sheet of dough pierced in herring-bone pattern, and marshalled them at one side ready for the oven.

"If fish *is* any better for the brain," Kinney proceeded, "they can't complain of any want of it, at least in the salted form. They get fish-balls three times a week for breakfast, as reg'lar as Sunday, Tuesday and Thursday comes round. And Fridays I make up a sort of chowder for the Kanucks; they're Catholics, you know, and I don't believe in interferin' with *any* man's religion, it don't matter what it is."

"You ought to be a deacon in the First Church at Equity," said Bartley.

"Is that so? Why?" asked Kinney.

"Oh, they don't believe in interfering with any man's religion either."

"Well," said Kinney thoughtfully, pausing with the rolling-pin in his hand, "there's such a thing as being *too* liberal, I suppose."

"The world's tried the other thing a good while," said Bartley, with cynical amusement.

It seemed to chill the flow of the good fellow's optimism, so that he assented with but lukewarm satisfaction, "Well, that's so, too," and he made up the rest of his pies in silence.

"Well!" he exclaimed, at last, as if shaking himself out of an unpleasant revery, "I guess we shall get along, somehow. Do you like pork and beans?"

"Yes, I do," said Bartley.

"We're goin' to have 'em for dinner. You can hit beans,

any meal you drop in on us: beans twenty-one times a week, just like pie. Set 'em in to warm," he said, taking up a capacious earthen pot, near the stove, and putting it into the oven. "I been pretty much everywheres, and I don't know as I found anything for a stand-by that come up to beans. I'm goin' to give 'em potatoes and cabbage to-day—kind of a boiled-dinner day—but you'll see there aint one in ten'll touch 'em to what these will these old residenters. Potatoes and cabbage'll do for a kind of a delicacy—sort of a side-dish—on-*tree*, you know—but give 'em beans for a steady diet. Why off there in Chili, even, the people regularly live on beans—not exactly like ours; broad and flat; but they're beans. Wa'n't there some those ancients—old Horace, or Virgil, maybe—rung in something about beans in some their poems?"

"I don't remember anything of the kind," said Bartley, languidly.

"Well, I don't know as *I* can. I just have a dim recollection of language thrown out at the object—as old Matthew Arnold says. But it might have been something in Emerson."

Bartley laughed. "I didn't suppose you were such a reader, Kinney."

"Oh, I nibble round wherever I can get a chance. Mostly in the newspapers, you know. I don't get any time for books, as a general rule. But there's pretty much everything in the papers. I should call beans a brain-food."

"I guess you call anything a brain-food that you happen to like, don't you, Kinney?"

"No, sir," said Kinney, soberly, "but I like to see the philosophy of a thing when I get a chance. Now, there's tea, for example," he said, pointing to the great tin-pot on the stove.

"Coffee, you mean," said Bartley.

"No, sir, I mean tea. That's tea; and I give it to 'em three times a day, good and strong—molasses in it, and no milk. That's a brain-food, if ever there was one. Sets 'em up, right on end, every time. Clears their heads, and keeps the cold out."

"I should think you were running a seminary for young ladies, instead of a logging-camp," said Bartley.

"No, but look at it: I'm in earnest about tea. You look at

the tea-drinkers and the coffee-drinkers, all the world over! Look at 'em in our own country! All the Northern people and all the go-ahead people drink tea. The Pennsylvanians and the Southerners drink coffee. Why, our New England folks don't even know how to *make* coffee, so it's fit to drink! And it's just so, all over Europe. The Russians drink tea, and they'd e't up those coffee-drinkin' Turks long ago, if the tea-drinkin' English hadn't kept 'em from it. Go anywhere's you like, in the North, and you find 'em drinkin' tea. The Swedes and Norwegians in Aroostook county drink it; and they drink it at home."

"Well, what do you think of the French and Germans? They drink coffee, and they're pretty smart, active people too."

"French and Germans drink coffee?"

"Yes."

Kinney stopped short in his heated career of generalization, and scratched his shaggy head. "Well," he said finally, "I guess they're a kind of a missing link, as old Darwin says." He joined Bartley in his laugh cordially, and looked up at the round clock nailed to a log. "It's about time I set my tables, anyway. Well," he asked, apparently to keep the conversation from flagging, while he went about this work, "how is the good old Free Press getting along?"

"It's going to get along without me, from this out," said Bartley. "This is my last week in Equity."

"No!" retorted Kinney, in tremendous astonishment.

"Yes; I'm off at the end of the week. Squire Gaylord takes the paper back, for the committee; and I suppose Henry Bird will run it for a while; or perhaps they'll stop it altogether. It's been a losing business for the committee."

"Why, I thought you'd bought it of 'em."

"Well, that's what I expected to do; but the office hasn't made any money. All that I've saved is in my colt and cutter."

"That sorrel?"

Bartley nodded. "I'm going away about as poor as I came. I couldn't go much poorer."

"Well!" said Kinney in the exhaustion of adequate language. He went on laying the plates and knives and forks, in silence. These were of undisguised steel; the dishes and the drinking-mugs were of that dense and heavy make, which the keepers of cheap restaurants use to protect themselves against breakage, and which their servants chip to the quick at every edge. Kinney laid bread and crackers by each plate, and on each he placed a vast slab of cold corned-beef. Then he lifted the lid of the pot in which the cabbage and potatoes were boiling together, and pricked them with a fork. He dished up the beans in a succession of deep tins, and set them at intervals along the tables, and began to talk again.

"Well, now, I'm sorry. I'd just begun to feel real well acquainted with you. Tell you the truth, I didn't take much of a fancy, to *you*, first off."

"Is that so?" asked Bartley, not much disturbed by the confession.

"Yes, sir. Well, come to boil it down," said Kinney, with the frankness of the analytical mind that disdains to spare itself in the pursuit of truth, "I didn't like your good clothes. I don't suppose I ever had a suit of clothes to fit me. Feel kind of ashamed, you know, when I go into the store, and take the first thing the Jew wants to put off onto me. Now, I suppose you go to Macullar and Parker's in Boston, and you get what *you* want."

"No; I have my measure at a tailor's," said Bartley, with ill-concealed pride in the fact.

"You don't say so!" exclaimed Kinney. "Well!" he said, as if he might as well swallow this pill, too, while he was about it. "Well, what's the use? I never was the figure for clothes, anyway. Long, gangling boy to start with, and a lean, stoop-shouldered man. I found out sometime ago that a fellow wa'n't necessarily a bad fellow because he had money; or a good fellow because he hadn't. But I hadn't quite got over hating a man because he had style. Well, I suppose it was a kind of a *survival*, as old Tylor calls it. But I tell you, I sniffed round you a good while before I made up my mind to swallow you. And that turnout of yours, it kind of staggered me, after I got over the clothes. Why it wa'n't so much the colt— any man likes to ride after a sorrel colt; and it wa'n't so much the cutter: it was the red linin' with pinked edges that you had to your robe; and it was the red ribbon you had tied round the waist of your whip. When I see that ribbon on that whip, dumn you, I wanted to kill you." Bartley broke out into a laugh, but Kinney went on soberly. "But thinks I to myself: 'Here! Now you stop right here! You wait! You give the fellow a chance for his life. Let him have a chance to show whether that whip-ribbon goes all through him, first. If it does, kill him cheerfully; but give him a chance *first*.' Well, sir, I gave you the chance, and you showed that you deserved it. I guess you taught me a lesson. When I see you at work, pegging away, hard at something or other, every time I went into your office, up and coming with everybody, and just as ready to pass the time of day with me, as the biggest bug in town, thinks I: 'You'd have made a great mistake to kill that fellow, Kinney!' And I just made up my mind to like you."

"Thanks," said Bartley with ironical gratitude.

Kinney did not speak at once. He whistled thoughtfully through his teeth, and said: "I'll tell you what: if you're going away *very* poor, I know a wealthy chap you can raise a loan out of."

Bartley thought seriously, for a moment. "If your friend offers me twenty dollars, I'm not too well dressed to take it."

"All right," said Kinney. He now dished up the cabbage and potatoes; and throwing a fresh handful of tea into the pot, and filling it up with water, he took down a tin horn, with which he went to the door, and sounded a long, stertorous note.

X

Guess it was the clothes, again," said Kinney, as he began to wash his tins and dishes after the dinner was over, and the men had gone back to their work. "I could see 'em eyein' you over, when they first came in, and I could see that they didn't exactly like the looks of 'em. It would wear off in time, but it *takes* time for it to wear off; and it had to go pretty rusty, for a start-off. Well, I don't know as it makes much difference to you, does it?"

"Oh, I thought we got along very well," said Bartley with a careless yawn. "There wasn't much chance to get acquainted." Some of the loggers were as handsome and well-made as he, and were of as good origin and traditions, though he had some advantages of training. But his two-button cutaway, his well-fitting trowsers, his scarf with a pin in it, had been too much for these young fellows in their long stoga boots and flannel shirts. They looked at him askance, and dispatched their meal with more than their wonted swiftness, and were off again into the woods without any demonstrations of satisfaction in Bartley's presence.

He had perceived their grudge for he had felt it in his time. But it did not displease him; he had none of the pain with which Kinney, who had so long bragged of him to the loggers, saw that his guest was a failure. "I guess they'll come out all right in the end," he said. In this warm atmosphere, after the gross and heavy dinner he had eaten he yawned again and again. He folded his overcoat into a pillow for his bench, and lay down, and lazily watched Kinney about his work. Presently he saw Kinney seated on a block of wood beside the stove, with his elbow propped in one hand, and holding a magazine, out of which he was reading; he wore spectacles, which gave him a fresh and interesting touch of grotesqueness. Bartley found that an empty barrel had been placed on each side of him, evidently to keep him from rolling off his bench.

"Hello!" he said. "Much obliged to you, Kinney. I haven't

been taken such good care of since I can remember. Been asleep, haven't I?"

"About an hour," said Kinney, with a glance at the clock, and ignoring his agency in Bartley's comfort.

"Food for the brain!" said Bartley, sitting up. "I should think so. I've dreamt a perfect New American Cyclopedia and a pronouncing gazetteer, thrown in."

"Is *that* so?" said Kinney, as if pleased with the suggestive character of his cookery, now established by eminent experiment.

Bartley yawned a yawn of satisfied sleepiness, and rubbed his hand over his face.

"I suppose," he said, "if I'm going to write anything about Camp Kinney, I had better see all there is to see."

"Well, yes, I presume you had," said Kinney. "We'll go over to where they're cuttin', pretty soon, and you can see all there is in an hour. But I presume you'll *want* to see it so as to ring in some description, hey? Well, that's all right. But what you going to do with it, when you've done it, now you're out of the Free Press?"

"Oh, I shouldn't have printed it in the Free Press, anyway. Coals to Newcastle, you know. I'll tell you what I think I'll do, Kinney: I'll get my outlines, and then you post me with a lot of facts—queer characters, accidents, romantic incidents, snowings-up, threatened starvation, adventures with wild animals—and I can make something worth while; get out two or three columns, so they can print it in their Sunday edition. And then I'll take it up to Boston, with me, and seek my fortune with it."

"Well, sir, I'll do it," said Kinney, fired with the poetry of the idea. "I'll post you! Dumn 'f I don't wish *I* could write! Well, I *did* used to scribble once for an agricultural paper; but I don't call that writin'. I've set down, well, I guess as much as sixty times, to try to write out what I know about loggin'"—

"Hold on!" cried Bartley, whipping out his note-book. "That's first-rate. That'll do for the first line in the head: *What I Know about Logging*: large caps. Well!"

Kinney shut his magazine, and took his knee between his

hands, closing one of his eyes in order to sharpen his recollection. He poured forth a stream of reminiscence, mingled observation, and personal experience. Bartley followed him with
his pencil, jotting down points, striking in sub-head lines, and
now and then interrupting him with cries of "Good!" "Capital!" "It's a perfect mine—it's a mint!" "By Jove!" he exclaimed, "I'll make *six* columns of this! I'll offer it to one of
the magazines, and it'll come out illustrated! Go on, Kinney."

"Hark!" said Kinney, craning his neck forward to listen. "I
thought I heard sleigh-bells. But I guess it wasn't. Well, sir,
as I was sayin', they fetched that fellow into camp with both
feet frozen to the knees— Dumn 'f it *wa'n't* bells!" He unlim-
bered himself, and hurried to the door at the other end of the
cabin, which he opened, letting in a clear block of the afternoon sunshine, and a gush of sleigh-bell music, shot with
men's voices, and the cries and laughter of women.

"Well, sir," said Kinney, coming back, and making haste to
roll down his sleeves and put on his coat. "*Here's* a nuisance!
A whole party of folks—two sleigh-loads—right *on* us. I
don't know who they *be*, or where they're from. But I know
where I wish they *was*. Well, of course, it's natural they
should want to see a loggin' camp," added Kinney, taking
himself to task for his inhospitable mind, "and there ain't any
harm in it. But I wish they'd give a fellow a *little* notice!"

The voices and bells drew nearer, but Kinney seemed resolved to observe the decorum of not going to the door till
some one knocked.

"Kinney! Kinney! Hello, Kinney!" shouted a man's voice,
as the bells hushed before the door, and broke into a musical
clash, when one of the horses tossed his head.

"Well, sir," said Kinney, rising, "I guess it's old Willett
himself. He's the owner: lives up to Portland, and been
threatening to come down here all winter, with a party of
friends. You just stay still," he added; and he paid himself the
deference that every true American owes himself in his dealings with his employer: he went to the door very deliberately,
and made no haste on account of the repeated cries of "Kinney! Kinney!" in which others of the party outside now
joined.

When he opened the door again, the first voice saluted him with a roar of laughter: "Why, Kinney! I began to think you were dead!"

"No, sir," Bartley heard Kinney reply, "it takes more to kill me than you'd suppose." But now he stepped outside, and the talk became unintelligible. Finally, Bartley heard what was imaginably Mr. Willett's voice saying "Well, let's go in and have a look at it now," and with much outcry and laughter the ladies were invisibly helped to dismount, and presently the whole party came stamping and rustling in.

Bartley's blood tingled. He liked this, and he stood quite self-possessed, with his thumbs in his waistcoat pockets and his elbows dropped, while Mr. Willett advanced in a friendly way: "Ah, Mr. Hubbard! Kinney told us you were in here, and asked me to introduce myself while he looked after the horses. My name's Willett. These are my daughters: this is Mrs. Macallister of Montreal, Mrs. Witherby of Boston; Miss Witherby, and Mr. Witherby. *You* ought to know each other: Mr. Hubbard is the editor of the Equity Free Press; Mr. Witherby of the Boston Events, Mr. Hubbard. Oh! And *Mr.* Macallister."

Bartley bowed to the Willett and Witherby ladies, and shook hands with Mr. Witherby, a large, solemn man, with a purse-mouth and tight rings of white hair who treated him with the pomp inevitable to the owner of a city newspaper in meeting a country editor.

At the mention of his name Mr. Macallister, a slight little straight man in a long ulster and a seal-skin cap, tiddled farcically forward on his toes, and giving Bartley his hand said, "Ah, haow d'e-do, *haow* d'e-do!"

Mrs. Macallister fixed upon him the eye of the flirt who knows her man. She was of the dark-eyed English type; her eyes were very large and full, and her smooth black hair was drawn flatly backward, and fastened in a knot just under her dashing fur cap. She wore a fur sack, and she was equipped against the cold as exquisitely as her Southern sisters defend themselves from the summer. Bits of warm color, in ribbon and scarf flashed out here and there; when she flung open her sack, she showed herself much more lavishly buttoned and bugled and bangled than the Americans. She sat down on the movable bench which Bartley had vacated, and crossed her feet, very small and saucy even in their arctics, on a stick of firewood, and cast up her neat profile, and rapidly made eyes at every part of the interior. "Why, it's delicious, you know. I never saw anything so comfortable. I want to spend the rest of me life here, you know." She spoke very far down in her throat, and with a rising inflection in each sentence. "I'm going to have a quarrel with you, Mr. Willett, for not telling me what a delightful surprise you had for us here. Oh, but I'd no idea of it, I assure you!"

"Well, I'm glad you like it, Mrs. Macallister," said Mr. Willett with the clumsiness of American middle-age when summoned to say something gallant. "If I'd told you what a surprise I had for you, it wouldn't have been one."

"Oh, it's no good you're trying to get out of it *that* way," retorted the beauty. "There he comes now! I'm really in love with him, you know," she said, as Kinney opened the door, and came hulking forward.

Nobody said anything, at once, but Bartley laughed finally and ventured, "Well, I'll propose for you to Kinney."

"Oh, I dare say!" cried the beauty with a lively effect of wit. "Mr. Kinney, I've fallen in love with your camp, d'ye know," she added, as Kinney drew near, "and I'm beggin' Mr. Willett to let me come and live here among you."

"Well, ma'am," said Kinney, a little abashed at this proposition, "you couldn't do a better thing for your health, I *guess*."

The proprietor of the Boston Events turned about, and began to look over the arrangements of the interior; the other ladies went with him, conversing in low tones. "These must be the places where the men sleep," they said, gazing at the bunks.

"We must get Kinney to explain things to us," said Mr. Willett a little restlessly.

Mrs. Macallister jumped briskly to her feet. "Oh, yes, do, Mr. Willett, make him explain everything! I've been tryin' to coax it out of him, but he's *such* a tease!"

Kinney looked very sheepish, in this character, and Mrs. Macallister hooked Bartley to her side for the tour of the interior. "I can't let you away from me, Mr. Hubbard; your friend's so satirical, I'm afraid of him. Only fancy, Mr. Willett! He's been talkin' to *me* about brain-foods! I know he's makin' fun of me; and it isn't kind, is it, Mr. Hubbard?"

She did not give the least notice to the things that the others looked at, or to Kinney's modest lecture upon the manners and customs of the loggers. She kept a little apart with Bartley, and plied him with bravadoes, with pouts, with little cries of surprise. In the midst of these he heard Mr. Willett saying, "You ought to get some one to come and write about this for your paper, Witherby." But Mrs. Macallister was also saying something, with a significant turn of her floating eyes, and the thing that concerned Bartley, if he were to make his way among the newspapers, in Boston, slipped from his grasp like the idea which we try to seize in a dream. She made sure of him for the drive to the place which they visited to see the men felling the trees, by inviting him to a seat at her side in the sleigh; this crowded the others, but she insisted, and they all gave way, as people must to the caprices of a pretty woman. Her coquetries united British wilfulness to American nonchalance, and seemed to have been graduated to the appreciation of garrison and St. Lawrence River steamboat and watering-place society. The Willett ladies had already found it necessary to explain to the Witherby ladies that they had met her the summer before at the seaside; and that she had stopped at Portland on her way to England; they did not know her very well, but some friends of theirs did; and their father had asked her to come with them to the camp: they added that the Canadian ladies seemed to expect the gentlemen to be a great deal more attentive than ours were. They had known as little what to do with Mr. Macallister's small-talk and compliments, as his wife's audacities, but they did not view Bartley's responsiveness with pleasure. If Mrs. Macallister's arts were not subtle, as Bartley, even in the intoxication of her preference, could not keep from seeing, still in his mood it was consoling, to be singled out by her: it meant that even in a logging-camp he was recognizable by any person of fashion as a good-looking, well-dressed man of the world. It embittered him the more against Marcia, while in some sort it vindicated him to himself.

The early winter sunset was beginning to tinge the snow

with crimson, when the party started back to camp, where Kinney was to give them supper; he had it greatly on his conscience that they should have a good time, and he promoted it as far as hot mince-pie and newly-fried dough-nuts would go. He also opened a few canned goods, as he called some very exclusive sardines and peaches, and he made an entirely fresh pot of tea, and a pan of soda-biscuit. Mrs. Macallister made remarks across her plate which were for Bartley alone; and Kinney who was seriously waiting upon his guests, refused to respond to Bartley's joking reference to himself of some questions and comments of hers.

After supper, when the loggers had withdrawn to the other end of the long hut, she called out to Kinney, "Oh, *do* tell them to smoke: we shall not mind it at all, I assure you. Can't some of them do something? Sing or dance?"

Kinney unbent a little, at this. "There's a first-class clog-dancer, among them; but he's a little stuck-up, and I don't know as you could get him to dance," he said in a low tone.

"What a bloated aristocrat!" cried the lady. "Then the only thing is for us to dance first. Can they play?"

"One of 'em can whistle like a bird—he can whistle like a whole band," answered Kinney, warming. "And of course the Kanucks can fiddle."

"And what are Kanucks? Is *that* what you call us Canadians?"

"Well, ma'am, it aint quite the thing to do," said Kinney, penitently.

"It isn't at *all* the thing to do! Which are the Kanucks?"

She rose, and went forward with Kinney, in her spoiled way, and addressed a swarthy, gleaming-eyed young logger in French. He answered with a smile that showed all his white teeth, and turned to one of his comrades; then the two rose, and got violins out of the bunks, and came forward. Others of their race joined them, but the Yankees hung gloomily back; they clearly did not like these liberties, this patronage.

"I shall have your clog-dancer on his feet yet, Mr. Kinney," said Mrs. Macallister, as she came back to her place.

The Canadians began to play and sing those gay, gay airs of old France, which they have kept unsaddened through all the dark events that have changed the popular mood of the

mother-country. They have matched words to them in celebration of their life on the great rivers and in the vast forests
of the North, and in these blithe barcaroles and hunting
songs breathes the joyous spirit of a France that knows neither doubt nor care; France untouched by Revolution or Na-
poleonic wars: some of the airs still keep the very words that
came overseas with them two hundred years ago. The transition to the dance was quick and inevitable; a dozen slim
young fellows were gliding about behind the players, pounding the hard earthen floor, and singing in time. "Oh, come,
come!" cried the beauty, rising and stamping impatiently with
her little foot, "suppose we dance, too."

She pulled Bartley forward, by the hand; her husband followed with the taller Miss Willett; two of the Canadians, at
the instance of Mrs. Macallister came forward and politely
asked the honor of the other young ladies' hands in the
dance; their temper was infectious, and the cotillion was in
full life before their partners had time to wonder at their consent. Mrs. Macallister could sing some of the Canadian songs;
her voice, clear and fresh, rang through those of the men,
while in at the window thrown open for air, came the wild
cries of the forest: the wail of a catamount, and the solemn
hooting of a distant owl.

"Isn't it jolly good fun?" she demanded, when the figure
was finished; and now Kinney went up to the first-class clog-
dancer, and prevailed with him to show his skill. He seemed
to comply on condition that the whistler should furnish the
music: he came forward, with a bashful hauteur, bridling
stiffly like a girl, and struck into the laborious and monotonous jig which is perhaps our national dance; he was exquisitely shaped, and as he danced, he suppled more and more,
while the whistler warbled a wilder and swifter strain, and
kept time with his hands. There was something that stirred
the blood in the fury of the strain and dance: when it was
done, Mrs. Macallister caught off her cap and ran round the
spectators to make them pay; she excused no one, and she
gave the money to Kinney telling him to get his loggers
something to keep the cold out. "I should say whiskey, if I
were in the Canadian bush," she suggested.

"Well *I* guess we sha'n't say anything of that sort in *this* camp," said Kinney.

She turned upon Bartley, "I know Mr. Hubbard is dying to do something. Do something, Mr. Hubbard!" Bartley looked up in surprise at this interpretation of his tacit wish to distinguish himself before her. "Come, sing us some of your student songs." Bartley's vanity had confided the fact of his college training to her, and he was really thinking just then that he would like to give them a serio-comic song, for which he had been famous with his class. He borrowed the violin of a Kanuck, and sitting down strummed upon it banjo-wise. The song was one of those which is partly spoken and acted; he really did it very well; but the Willett and Witherby ladies did not seem to understand it, quite; and the gentlemen looked as if they thought this very undignified business for an educated American.

Mrs. Macallister feigned a yawn, and put up her hand to hide it. "*Oh*, what a styupid song!" she said. She sprang to her feet, and began to put on her wraps. The others were glad of this signal to go, and followed her example. "Good-bye!" she cried, giving her hand to Kinney. "*I* don't think your ideas are ridiculous. I think there's no end of good sense in them, I assure you. I hope you wont leave off that regard for the brain in your cooking. Good-bye!" She waved her hand to the Americans, and then to the Kanucks, as she passed out between their respectfully parted ranks. "Adieu, messieurs!" She merely nodded to Bartley; the others parted from him coldly, as he fancied, and it seemed to him that he had been made responsible for that woman's coquetries, when he was conscious, all the time of having forborne even to meet them half way. But this was not so much to his credit as he imagined. The flirt can only practice her audacities safely by grace of those upon whom she uses them, and if men really met them half way there could be no such thing as flirting.

XI

THE LOGGERS pulled off their boots and got into their bunks, where some of them lay and smoked, while others fell asleep directly.

Bartley made some indirect approaches to Kinney for sympathy in the snub which he had received, and which rankled in his mind with unabated keenness.

But Kinney did not respond. "Your bed's ready," he said. "You can turn in whenever you like."

"What's the matter?" asked Bartley.

"Nothing's the matter, if you say so," answered Kinney going about some preparations for the morning's breakfast.

Bartley looked at his resentful back. He saw that he was hurt, and he surmised that Kinney suspected him of making fun of his eccentricities to Mrs. Macallister. He *had* laughed at Kinney, and tried to amuse her with him; but he could not have made this appear as harmless as it was. He rose from the bench on which he had been sitting, and shut with a click the pen-knife with which he had been cutting a pattern on its edge. "I shall have to say good-night to you, I believe," he said going to the peg on which Kinney had hung his hat and overcoat. He had them on, and was buttoning the coat in an angry tremor before Kinney looked up and realized what his guest was about.

"Why, what—why, where—you goin'?" he faltered in dismay.

"To Equity," said Bartley, feeling in his coat-pockets for his gloves, and drawing them on, without looking at Kinney, whose great hands were in a pan of dough.

"Why—why—no, you ain't!" he protested, with a revulsion of feeling that swept away all his resentment, and left him nothing but remorse for his inhospitality.

"No?" said Bartley, putting up the collar of the first ulster worn by a native in that region.

"Why, look here!" cried Kinney, pulling his hands out of the dough, and making a fruitless effort to cleanse them upon each other. "I don't want you to go, this way."

"Don't you? I'm sorry to disoblige you; but I'm going," said Bartley.

Kinney tried to laugh. "Why, Hubbard—why, Bartley—why, Bart!" he exclaimed. "What's the matter with you? I ain't mad!"

"You have an unfortunate manner, then. Good-night." He strode out between the bunks full of snoring loggers. Kinney hurried after him, imploring and protesting in a low voice, trying to get before him, and longing to lay his floury paws upon him and detain him by main force, but even in his distress, respecting Bartley's overcoat too much to touch it.

He followed him out into the freezing air in his shirt-sleeves, and besought him not to be such a fool. "It makes me feel like the devil!" he exclaimed, pitifully. "You come back, now, half a minute, and I'll make it all right with you. I know I can; you're a gentleman; and you'll understand. *Do* come back! I shall never get over it, if you don't!"

"I'm sorry," said Bartley, "but I'm not going back. Good-night."

"Oh, good Lordy!" lamented Kinney. "What am I goin' to do? Why, man! It's a good three mile and more to Equity and the woods is full of catamounts. I tell ye 'tain't safe for ye." He kept following Bartley down the path to the road.

"I'll risk it," said Bartley.

Kinney had left the door of the camp open, and the yells and curses of the awakened sleepers recalled him to himself.

"Well, well! If you will *go*," he groaned in despair, "here's that money." He plunged his doughy hand into his pocket, and pulled out a roll of bills. "Here it is. I hain't time to count it; but it'll be all right, anyhow"—

Bartley did not even turn his head to look round at him.

"Keep your money!" he said, as he plunged forward through the snow. "I wouldn't touch a cent of it to save your life."

"All right," said Kinney, in hapless contrition, and he returned to shut himself in with the reproaches of the loggers and the upbraiding of his own heart.

Bartley dashed along the road in a fury that kept him unconscious of the intense cold; and he passed half the night when he was once more in his own room, packing up his effects against his departure next day. When all was done he went to bed half wishing that he might never rise from it again. It was not that he cared for Kinney; that fool's sulking was only the climax of a long series of injuries of which he was the victim at the hands of a hypercritical omnipotence.

Despite his conviction that it was useless to struggle longer against such injustice, he lived through the night, and came down late to breakfast, which he found stale, and without the compensating advantage of finding himself alone at the table. Some ladies had lingered there to clear up on the best authority the distracting rumors concerning him which they had heard the day before. Was it true that he had intended to spend the rest of the winter in logging; and *was* it true that he was going to give up the Free Press; and was it *true* that Henry Bird was going to be the editor? Bartley gave a sarcastic confirmation to all these reports; and went out to the printing office to gather up some things of his. He found Henry Bird there, looking pale and sick, but at work and seemingly in authority. This was what Bartley had always intended when he should go out, but he did not like it, and he resented some small changes that had already been made in the editor's room, in tacit recognition of his purpose not to occupy it again.

Bird greeted him stiffly, the printer-girls briefly nodded to him, suppressing some little hysterical titters, and tacitly let him feel that he was no longer master there. While he was in the composing-room, Hannah Morrison came in, apparently from some errand outside, and catching sight of him, stared, and pertly passed him in silence.

On his inkstand he found a letter from Squire Gaylord, briefly auditing his last account, and enclosing the balance due him. From this the old lawyer with the careful smallness of a village business man had deducted various little sums for things that Bartley had never expected to pay for. With a like thriftiness the landlord, when Bartley asked for his bill, had charged certain items that had not appeared in the bills before: Bartley felt that the charges were trumped up; but he was powerless to dispute them; besides he hoped to sell the landlord his colt and cutter, and he did not care to prejudice that matter. Some bills from storekeepers, which he thought he had paid, were handed to him by the landlord, and each of the churches had sent in a little account for pew rent for the past eighteen months: he had always believed himself dead headed at church. He outlawed the latter by tearing them to pieces in the landlord's presence, and dropping the fragments into a spittoon. It seemed to him that every soul in Equity was making a clutch at the rapidly diminishing sum of money which Squire Gaylord had enclosed to him, and which was all he had in the world. On the other hand, his popularity in the village seemed to have vanished over night. He had sometimes fancied a general and rebellious grief when it should become known that he was going away; but instead there was an acquiescence amounting to airiness. He wondered if anything about his affairs with Henry Bird and Hannah Morrison had leaked out. But he did not care. He only wished to shake the snow of Equity off his feet as soon as possible.

After dinner, when the boarders had gone out, and the loafers had not yet gathered in, he offered the landlord his colt and cutter. Bartley knew that the landlord wanted the colt; but now the latter said: "I don't know as I care to buy any hosses, right in the winter this way."

"All right," answered Bartley. "Just have the colt put into the cutter."

Andy Morrison brought it round. The boy looked at Bartley's set face with a sort of awe-stricken affection: his adoration for the young man survived all that he had heard said against him at home during the series of family quarrels that had ensued upon his father's interview with him; he longed to testify somehow his unabated loyalty, but he could not think of anything to do, much less to say.

Bartley pitched his valise into the cutter, and then as Andy left the horse's head to give him a hand with his trunk, offered him a dollar. "I don't want anything," said the boy, shyly refusing the money out of pure affection.

But Bartley mistook his motive, and thought it sulky resentment. "Oh, very well," he said. "Take hold."

The landlord came out. "Hold on a minute," he said. "Where you goin' to take the cars?"

"At the Junction," answered Bartley. "I know a man there that will buy the colt. What is it you want?"

The landlord stepped back a few paces, and surveyed the establishment: "I should like to ride after that hoss," he said, "if you ain't in any great of a hurry."

"Get in," said Bartley, and the landlord took the reins. From time to time, as he drove, he rose up and looked over the dashboard to study the gait of the horse. "I've noticed he strikes, some, when he first comes out in the spring."

"Yes," Bartley assented.

"Pulls consid'able."

"He pulls."

The landlord rose again, and scrutinized the horse's legs. "I don't know as I ever noticed 't he'd capped his hock before."

"Didn't you?"

"Done it kickin', nights, I guess."

"I guess so."

The landlord drew the whip lightly across the colt's rear: he shrank together, and made a little spring forward, but behaved perfectly well. "I don't know as I should always be sure he wouldn't kick in the daytime."

"No," said Bartley, "you never can be sure of anything."

They drove along in silence. At last the landlord said, "Well, he ain't so fast, as I *supposed*."

"He's not so fast a horse as some," answered Bartley.

The landlord leaned over sidewise for an inspection of the colt's action forward. "Hain't never thought he had a splint on that forrad off leg?"

"A splint? Perhaps he has a splint."

They returned to the hotel, and both alighted.

"Skittish devil," remarked the landlord, as the colt quivered under the hand he laid upon him.

"He's skittish," said Bartley.

The landlord retired as far back as the door, and regarded the colt critically. "Well, I s'pose you've always used him too well ever to winded him, but dumn 'f he don't *blow* like it."

"Look here, Simpson," said Bartley, very quietly. "You know this horse as well as I do, and you know there isn't an out about him. You want to buy him because you always have. Now make me an offer."

"Well," groaned the landlord, "what'll you take for the whole rig, just as it stands: colt, cutter, leathers and robe."

"Two hundred dollars," promptly replied Bartley.

"I'll give ye seventy-five," returned the landlord with equal promptness.

"Andy, take hold of the end of that trunk, will you." The landlord allowed them to put the trunk into the cutter. Bartley got in, too, and shifting the baggage to one side folded the robe around him from his middle down, and took his seat. "This colt can road you right along all day inside of five minutes, and he can trot inside of two-thirty, every time; and you know it as well as I do."

"Well," said the landlord, "make it an even hundred." Bartley leaned forward and gathered up the reins. "Let go his head, Andy," he quietly commanded.

"Make it one and a quarter," cried the landlord, not seeing that his chance was past. "What do you say."

What Bartley said as he touched the colt with the whip the landlord never knew. He stood watching the cutter's swift disappearance up the road, in a sort of stupid expectation of its return. When he realized that Bartley's departure was final, he said under his breath: "Sold, ye dumned old fool, and serve ye right," and went in-doors with a feeling of admiration for colt and man that bordered on reverence.

XII

THIS LAST DROP of the local meanness filled Bartley's bitter cup. As he passed the house at the end of the street, he seemed to drain it all. He knew that the old lawyer was there sitting by the office stove, drawing his hand across his chin, and Bartley hoped that he was still as miserable as he had looked when he last saw him; but he did not know that by the window in the house which he would not even look at, Marcia sat, self-prisoned in her room, with her eyes upon the road, famishing for the thousandth part of a chance to see him pass. She saw him now, for the instant of his coming and going; with eyes trained to take in every point, she saw the preparation which seemed like final departure, and with a gasp of "Bartley!" as if she were trying to call after him, she sank back into her chair, and shut her eyes.

He drove on, plunging into the deep hollow beyond the house, and keeping for several miles the road they had taken on that Sunday together; but he did not make the turn that brought them back to the village again. The pale sunset was slanting over the snow when he reached the Junction, for he had slackened his colt's pace, after he had put ten miles behind him; not choosing to reach a prospective purchaser with his horse all blown and bathed with sweat. He wished to be able to say, "Look at him! He's come fifteen miles since three o'clock, and he's as keen as when he started."

This was true, when, having left his baggage at the Junction, he drove another mile into the country to see the farmer of the gentleman who had his summer house here, and who had once bantered Bartley to sell him his colt. The farmer was away, and would not be at home till the up-train from Boston was in. Bartley looked at his watch, and saw that to wait would lose him the six o'clock down-train: there would be no other till eleven o'clock. But it was worth while: the gentleman had said, "When you want the money for that colt, bring him over any time; my farmer will have it ready for you." He waited for the up-train, but when the farmer arrived, he was full of all sorts of scruples and reluctances. He said he should not like to buy it till he had heard from Mr. Farnham; he ended by offering Bartley eighty dollars for the colt on his own account: he did not want the cutter. "You write to Mr. Farnham," said Bartley, "that you tried that plan with me, and it wouldn't work; he's lost the colt." He made this brave show of indifference, but he was disheartened, and having carried the farmer home from the Junction for the convenience of talking over the trade with him, he drove back again through the early nightfall in sullen desperation.

The weather had softened and was threatening rain or snow; the dark was closing in spiritlessly; the colt, shortening from a trot into a short, springy jolt, dropped into a walk, at last, as if he were tired, and gave Bartley time enough on his way back to the Junction for reflection upon the disaster into which his life had fallen. These passages of utter despair are commoner to the young than they are to those whom years have experienced in the impermanence of any fate, good, bad, or indifferent, unless, perhaps, the last may seem rather constant. Taken in reference to all that had been ten days ago, the present ruin was incredible, and had nothing reasonable in proof of its existence. Then he was prosperously placed and in the way to better himself indefinitely. Now, he was here in the dark, with fifteen dollars in his pocket, and an unsalable horse on his hands; outcast, deserted, homeless, hopeless: and by whose fault? He owned even then that he had committed some follies; but in his sense of Marcia's all-giving love he had risen for once in his life to a conception of self-devotion, and in taking herself from him as she did she had taken from him the highest incentive he had ever known, and had checked him in his first feeble impulse to do and be all in all for another. It was she who had ruined him.

As he jumped out of the cutter at the Junction, the station-master stopped with a cluster of parti-colored signal lanterns in his hand and cast their light over the sorrel. "Nice colt you got there."

"Yes," said Bartley blanketing the horse, "do you know anybody who wants to buy?"

"Whose is he?" asked the man.

"He's mine!" shouted Bartley. "Do you think I stole him?"

"*I* don't know where you got him," said the man, walking

off, and making a soft play of red and green lights on the snow beyond the narrow platform.

Bartley went into the great ugly barn of a station, trembling, and sat down in one of the gouged and whittled armchairs near the stove. A pomp of time-tables, and luminous advertisements of Western railroads and their land-grants decorated the wooden walls of the gentlemen's waiting room which had been sanded to keep the gentlemen from writing and sketching upon them. This was the more judicious because the ladies' room, in the absence of tourist travel, was locked in winter, and they were obliged to share the gentlemen's. In summer, the junction was a busy place, but after the snow fell and until the snow thawed, it was a desolation relieved only by the arrival of the sparsely-peopled through trains from the north and east; and by such local travellers as wished to take trains not stopping at their own stations. These broke in upon the solitude of the joint stationmaster and baggage-man and switch-tender with just sufficient frequency to keep him in a state of uncharitable irritation and unrest. To-night Bartley was the sole intruder, and he sat by the stove wrapped in a cloud of rebellious memories, when one side of a colloquy without made itself heard.

"What?"

Some question was repeated.

"No, it went down half an hour ago."

An inaudible question followed.

"Next down train at eleven."

There was now a faintly audible lament or appeal.

"Guess you'll have to come earlier next time. Most folks doos that wants to take it."

Bartley now heard the despairing moan of a woman; he had already divined the sex of the futile questioner whom the stationmaster was bullying; but he had divined it without compassion, and if he had not himself been a sufferer from the man's insolence he might even have felt a ferocious satisfaction in it. In a word he was at his lowest and worst when the door opened, and the woman came in, with a movement at once bewildered and daring, which gave him the impression of a despair as complete and final as his own. He doggedly kept his place; she did not seem to care for him, but in the uncertain light of the lamp above them she drew near the stove, and putting one hand to her pocket as if to find her handkerchief, she flung aside her veil with her other, and showed her tear-stained face.

He was on his feet, somehow. "Marcia!"

"Oh!—Bartley!"—

He had seized her by the arm, to make sure that she was there in verity of flesh and blood, and not by some trick of his own senses, as a cold chill running over him had made him afraid. At the touch their passion ignored all that they had made each other suffer; her head was on his breast, his embrace was round her; it was a moment of delirious bliss that intervened between the sorrows that had been, and the reasons that must come.

"What—what are you doing here, Marcia?" he asked at last. They sank on the benching that ran round the wall; he held her hands fast in one of his, and kept his other arm about her as they sat side by side.

"I don't know—I"— She seemed to rouse herself by an effort from her rapture. "I was going to see Netty Spaulding. And I saw you driving past our house; and I thought you were coming here; and I couldn't bear—I couldn't bear to let you go away without telling you that I was wrong; and asking—asking you to forgive me. I thought you would do it—I thought you would know that I had behaved that way because I—I—cared so much for you—I thought—I was afraid you had gone on the other train"— She trembled and sank back in his embrace from which she had lifted herself a little.

"How did you get here?" asked Bartley, as if willing to give himself all the proofs he could of the everyday reality of her presence.

"Andy Morrison brought me. Father sent him from the hotel. I didn't care what you would say to me. I wanted to tell you that I was wrong, and not let you go away feeling that— that—you were all to blame. I thought when I had done that you might drive me away—or laugh at me, or anything you pleased, if only you would let me take back"—

"Yes," he answered dreamily. All that wicked hardness was breaking up within him; he felt it melting drop by drop in his heart. This poor love-tossed soul, this frantic, unguided, reckless girl, was an angel of mercy to him, and in her folly and error a messenger of heavenly peace and hope. "I am a bad fellow, Marcia," he faltered. "You ought to know that. You did right to give me up. I made love to Hannah Morrison; I never promised to marry her, but I made her think that I was fond of her."

"I don't care for that," replied the girl. "I told you when we were first engaged that I would never think of anything that had gone before that; and then when I would not listen to a word from you that day, I broke my promise."

"When I struck Henry Bird, because he was jealous of me, I was as guilty as if I had killed him."

"If you had killed him, I was bound to you by my word. Your striking him was part of the same thing—part of what I had promised I never would care for." A gush of tears came into his eyes, and she saw them. "Oh, poor Bartley! Poor Bartley!" She took his head between her hands and pressed it hard against her heart, and then wrapped her arms tight about him, and softly bemoaned him.

They drew a little apart, when the man came in with his lantern, and set it down to mend the fire. But as a railroad employé he was far too familiar with the love that vaunts itself on all railroad trains to feel that he was an intruder. He scarcely looked at them, and went out, when he had mended the fire, and left it purring.

"Where is Andy Morrison?" asked Bartley. "Has he gone back?"

"No; he is at the hotel over there. I told him to wait till I found out when the train went north."

"So you inquired when it went to Boston," said Bartley with a touch of his old raillery. "Come," he added, taking her hand under his arm. He led her out of the room to where his cutter stood outside.

She was astonished to find the colt there. "I wonder I didn't see it. But if I had I should have thought that you had sold it and gone away; Andy told me you were coming here to sell the colt. When the man told me the express was gone, I knew you were on it."

They found the boy stolidly waiting for Marcia on the verandah of the hotel, stamping first upon one foot and then the other, and hugging himself in his greatcoat, as the coming snowfall blew its first flakes in his face.

"Is that you, Andy?" asked Bartley.

"Yes, sir," answered the boy without surprise at finding him with Marcia.

"Well, here! Just take hold of the colt's head a minute." As the boy obeyed, Bartley threw the reins on the dashboard, and leaped out of the cutter, and went within. He returned after a brief absence, followed by the landlord.

"Well, it ain't more'n a mile 'n' a half if it's that. You just keep straight along this street, and take your first turn to the left, and you're right at the house; it's the first house on the left hand side."

"Thanks," returned Bartley. "Andy: you tell the Squire that you left Marcia with me, and I said I would see about her getting back. You needn't hurry."

"All right," said the boy and he disappeared round the corner of the house, to get his horse from the barn.

"Well, I'll be all ready by the time you're here," said the landlord still holding the hall door ajar. "Luck to you!" he shouted, shutting it.

Marcia locked both her hands through Bartley's arm, and leaned her head on his shoulder. Neither spoke for some minutes. Then he asked, "Marcia, do you know where you are?"

"With you," she answered in a voice of utter peace.

"Do you know where we are going?" he asked, leaning over to kiss her cold, pure cheek.

"No," she answered in as perfect content as before.

"We are going to get married."

He felt her grow tense in her clasp upon his arm, and hold there rigidly for a moment, while the swift thoughts whirled through her mind. Then as if the struggle had ended, she silently relaxed, and leaned more heavily against him.

"There's still time to go back, Marcia," he said, "if you wish. That turn to the right, yonder, will take us to Equity, and you can be at home in two hours." She quivered. "I'm a poor man—I suppose you know that; I've only got fifteen dollars in the world, and the colt here. I know I can get on; I'm not afraid for myself; but if you would rather wait; if you're not perfectly certain of yourself— Remember, it's going to be a struggle; we're going to have some hard times"—

"You forgive me?" she huskily asked, for all answer, without moving her head from where it lay.

"Yes, Marcia."

"Then—hurry."

The minister was an old man, and he seemed quite dazed at the suddenness of their demand for his services. But he gathered himself together, and contrived to make them man and wife, and to give them his marriage-certificate.

"It seems as if there were something else," he said, absently, as he handed the paper to Bartley.

"Perhaps it's this," said Bartley, giving him a five-dollar note in return.

"Ah, perhaps," he replied, in unabated perplexity. He bade them serve God, and let them out into the snowy night, through which they drove back to the hotel.

The landlord had kindled a fire on the hearth of the Franklin stove in his parlor, and the blazing hickory snapped in electrical sympathy with the storm when they shut themselves into the bright room, and Bartley took Marcia fondly into his arms.

"Wife!"

"Husband!"

They sat down before the fire, hand in hand, and talked of the light things that swim to the top, and eddy round and round on the surface of our deepest moods. They made merry over the old minister's perturbation, which Bartley found endlessly amusing. Then he noticed that the dress Marcia had on was the one she had worn to the Sociable in Lower Equity, and she said, yes, she had put it on because he once said he liked it. He asked her when, and she said O, she knew; but if he could not remember, she was not going to tell him. Then she wanted to know if he recognized her by the dress before she lifted her veil in the station.

"No," he said, with a teasing laugh, "I wasn't thinking of you."

"Oh, Bartley!" she joyfully reproached him. "You must have been!"

"Yes, I was! I was so mad at you, that I was glad to have that brute of a station-master bullying *some* woman!"

"Bartley!"

He sat holding her hand. "Marcia," he said gravely, "we must write to your father at once, and tell him. I want to begin life in the right way, and I think it's only fair to him."

She was enraptured at his magnanimity. "Bartley! That's *like* you! Poor father! I declare—Bartley, I'm afraid I had forgotten him! It's dreadful; but—*you* put everything else out of my head. I do believe I've died and come to life somewhere else!"

"Well, *I* haven't," said Bartley, "and I guess you'd better write to your father. *You'd* better write; at present he and I are not on speaking terms. Here!" he took out his note-book, and gave her his stylographic pen after striking the fist that held it upon his other fist, in the fashion of the amateurs of that reluctant instrument, in order to bring down the ink.

"Oh, what's that?" she asked.

"It's a new kind of pen. I got it for a notice in the Free Press."

"Is Henry Bird going to edit the paper?"

"I don't know, and I don't care," answered Bartley. "I'll go out and get an envelope and ask the landlord what's the quickest way to get the letter to your father."

He took up his hat, but she laid her hand on his arm. "Oh, send for him!" she said.

"Are you afraid I sha'n't come back?" he demanded, with a laughing kiss. "I want to see him about something else, too."

"Well, don't be gone long." They parted with an embrace that would have fortified older married people for a year's separation. When Bartley came back, she handed him the leaf she had torn out of his book, and sat down beside him while he read it, with her arm over his shoulder.

"Dear father," the letter ran, "Bartley and I are married. We were married an hour ago, just across the New Hampshire line, by the Rev. Mr. Jessup. Bartley wants I should let you know the very first thing. I am going to Boston with Bartley to-night, and as soon as we get settled there, I will write again. I want you should forgive us both; but if you wont forgive Bartley, you mustn't me. You were mistaken about Bartley, and I was right. Bartley has told me everything and I am perfectly satisfied. Love to mother.

"Marcia.

"P.S. I *did* intend to visit Netty Spaulding. But I saw Bartley driving past on his way to the Junction, and I determined to see him if I could before he started for Boston, and tell him I was all wrong, no matter what he said or did afterwards. I ought to have told you I meant to see Bartley; but then you would not have let me come, and if I had not come I should have died."

"There's a good deal of Bartley in it," said the young man with a laugh.

"You don't like it!"

"Yes, I do; it's all right. Did you use to take the prize for composition at boarding-school?"

"Why, I think it's a very good letter for when I'm in such an excited state."

"It's beautiful," cried Bartley, laughing more and more. The tears started to her eyes.

"Marcia," said her husband fondly, "what a child you are! If ever I do anything to betray your trust in me"—

There came a shuffling of feet outside the door, a clinking of glass and crockery, and a jarring sort of blow, as if some one were trying to rap on the panel with the edge of a heavy laden waiter. Bartley threw the door open and found the landlord there, red and smiling with the waiter in his hand. "I thought I'd bring your supper in here, you know," he explained confidentially, "so's't you could have it a little more snug. And my wife she kind o' got wind o' what was goin' on—women will, you know," he said with a wink—"and she's sent ye in some hot biscuit and a little jell, and some of her cake." He set the waiter down on the table, and stood admiring its mystery of napkinned dishes. "She guessed you wouldn't object to some cold chicken, and she's put a little of that on. Sha'n't cost ye any more," he hastened to assure them. "Now, this is your room till the train comes, and there ain't agoin' anybody come in here. So you can make yourselves at home. And *I* hope you'll enjoy your supper, as much as we did our'n the night *we* was married. There! I guess I'll let the lady fix the table; she looks as if she knowed how."

He got himself out of the room again, and then Marcia, who had made him some embarrassed thanks, burst out in praise of his pleasantness.

"Well, he ought to be pleasant," said Bartley, "he's just beaten me on a horse-trade. I've sold him the colt."

"Sold him the colt!" cried Marcia, tragically dropping the napkin she had lifted from the plate of cold chicken.

"Well, we couldn't very well have taken him to Boston with us. And we couldn't have got there without selling him. You know you haven't married a millionaire, Marcia."

"How much did you get for the colt?"

"Oh, I didn't do so badly. I got a hundred and fifty for him."

"And you had fifteen besides."

"That was before we were married. I gave the minister five for you—I think you are worth it. I wanted to give fifteen."

"Well, then, you have a hundred and sixty now. Isn't that a great deal?"

"An everlasting lot," said Bartley with an impatient laugh. "Don't let the supper cool, Marcia!"

She silently set out the feast, but regarded it ruefully. "You oughtn't to have ordered so much, Bartley," she said. "You couldn't afford it."

"I can afford anything when I'm hungry. Besides I only ordered the oysters and coffee; all the rest is conscience money—or sentiment—from the landlord. Come, come! Cheer up, now! We sha'n't starve to-night, anyhow."

"Well, I know father will help us."

"We sha'n't count on him," said Bartley. "Now, *drop* it!" He put his arm round her shoulders and pressed her against him till she raised her face for his kiss.

"Well, I *will*!" she said, and the shadow lifted itself from their wedding feast, and they sat down and made merry as if they had all the money in the world to spend. They laughed and joked; they praised the things they liked, and made fun of the others.

"How strange! How perfectly impossible it all seems! Why last night I was taking supper at Kinney's logging-camp, and hating you at every mouthful with all my might. Everything seemed against me, and I was feeling ugly, and flirting like mad with a fool from Montreal: she had come out there from Portland for a frolic with the owner's party. You made me do it, Marcia!" he cried jestingly. "And remember that if you want me to be good, you must be kind. The other thing seems to make me worse and worse."

"I will—I will, Bartley," she said humbly, "I will try to be kind and patient with you. I will indeed."

He threw back his head and laughed and laughed. "Poor— poor old Kinney! He's the cook, you know, and he thought I'd been making fun of him to that woman, and he behaved so, after they were gone, that I started home in a rage; and he followed me out with his hands all covered with dough, and wanted to stop me, but he couldn't for fear of spoiling my clothes"— He lost himself in another paroxysm.

Marcia smiled a little. Then, "What sort of a looking person was she?" she tremulously asked.

Bartley stopped abruptly: "Not one ten thousandth part as good-looking, nor one millionth part as bright as Marcia Hubbard!" He caught her and smothered her against his breast.

"I don't care! I don't care!" she cried. "I was to blame more than you, if you flirted with her, and it serves me right. Yes, I will never say anything to you for anything that happened after I behaved so to you!"

"There wasn't anything else happened!" cried Bartley. "And the Montreal woman snubbed me soundly before she was done with me."

"Snubbed you!" exclaimed Marcia, with illogical indignation. This delighted Bartley so much that it was long before he left off laughing over her.

Then they sat down and were silent till she said, "And did you leave him in a temper?"

"Who? Kinney? In a perfect devil of a temper. I wouldn't even borrow some money he wanted to lend me."

"Write to him, Bartley!" said his wife, seriously. "I love you so I can't bear to have anybody bad friends with you!"

XIII

THE WHOLE THING was so crazy, as Bartley said, that it
made no difference if they kept up the expense a few days
longer. He took a hack from the depot, when they arrived in
Boston, and drove to the Revere House, instead of going up
in the horse-car. He entered his name on the register with a
flourish, "Bartley J. Hubbard and Wife, *Boston*," and asked
for a room and fire, with laconic gruffness; but the clerk knew
him at once for a country person, and when the call-boy followed him into the parlor where Marcia sat in the tremor
into which she now fell whenever Bartley was out of her
sight, the boy discerned her provinciality at a glance, and
made free to say that he guessed they had better let him take
their things up to their room, and come up themselves after
the porter had got their fire going.

"All right," said Bartley, with hauteur; and he added for no
reason, "Be quick about it."

"Yes, sir," said the boy.

"What time is supper—dinner, I mean?"

"It's ready now, sir."

"Good. Take up the things. Come just as you are, Marcia.
Let him take your cap—no, keep it on; a good many of them
come down in their bonnets."

Marcia put off her sack, and gloves, and hastily repaired the
ravages of travel as best she could. She would have liked to
go to her room just long enough to brush her hair a little,
and the fur cap made her head hot; but she was suddenly
afraid of doing something that would seem countrified, in
Bartley's eyes; and she promptly obeyed: they had come from
Portland in a parlor car, and she had been able to make a
traveler's toilet before they reached Boston.

She had been at Portland several times with her father; but
he stopped at a second-class hotel where he had always put
up when alone, and she was new to the vastness of hotel mir-
rors and chandeliers, the glossy paint, the frescoing, the fluted
pillars, the tessellated marble pavements upon which she
stepped when she left the brussels carpeting of the parlors.

299

She clung to Bartley's arm, silently praying that she might not do anything to mortify him, and admiring everything he did without question. He made a halt as they entered the glittering dining-room, and stood frowning till the head waiter ran respectfully up to them, and ushered them with sweeping bows to a table which they had to themselves. Bartley ordered their dinner with nonchalant ease, beginning with soup and going to black coffee with dazzling intelligence. While their waiter was gone with their order, he beckoned with one finger to another, and sent him out for a paper, which he unfolded and spread on the table, taking a toothpick into his mouth, and running the sheet over with his eye. "I just want to see what's going on to-night," he said without looking at Marcia.

She made a little murmur of acquiescence in her throat, but she could not speak for strangeness. She began to steal little timid glances about, and to notice the people at the other tables. In her heart she did not find the ladies so very well dressed, as she had expected the Boston ladies to be; and there was no gentleman there to compare with Bartley either in style or looks. She let her eyes finally dwell on him, wishing that he would put his paper away and say something; but afraid to ask, lest it should not be quite right: all the other gentlemen were reading papers. She was feeling lonesome and homesick, when he suddenly glanced at her and said, "How pretty you look, Marsh!"

"Do I?" she asked with a little, grateful throb, while her eyes joyfully suffused themselves.

"Pretty as a pink," he returned. "Gay—isn't it?" he continued, with a wink that took her again into his confidence, from which his study of the newspaper had seemed to exclude her. "I'll tell you what I'm going to do: I'm going to take you to the Museum, after dinner, and let you see Boucicault in the 'Colleen Bawn.'" He swept his paper off the table, and unfolded his napkin in his lap, and leaning back in his chair, began to tell her about the play. "We can walk: it's only just round the corner," he said at the end.

Marcia crept into the shelter of his talk—he sometimes spoke rather loud—and was submissively silent. When they got into their own room, which had gilt lambrequin frames, and a chandelier of three burners, and a marble mantel and marble-topped table, and washstand, and Bartley turned up the flaring gas, she quite broke down, and cried on his breast, to make sure that she had got him all back again.

"Why Marcia!" he said. "I know just how you feel. Don't you suppose I understand as well as you do that we're a country couple? But I'm not going to give myself away, and you mustn't, either. There wasn't a woman in that room that could compare with you—*dress* or looks!"

"You were splendid!" she whispered, "and just like the rest; and that made me feel somehow as if I had lost you."

"I know—I saw just how you felt; but I wasn't going to say anything for fear you'd give way right there. Come! There's plenty of time before the play begins. I call this *nice*! Old fashioned, rather, in the decorations," he said, "but pretty good for its time."

He had pulled up two armchairs in front of the glowing grate of anthracite; as he spoke, he cast his eyes about the room, and she followed his glance obediently. He had kept her hand in his, and now he held her slim finger-tips in the fist which he rested on his knee. "No; I'll tell you what, Marcia: if you want to get on in a city, there's no use being afraid of people. No use being afraid of *anything*, so long as we're good to each other. And you've got to believe in me, right along. Don't you let anything get you on the wrong track. I believe that as long as you have faith in me, I shall deserve it; and when you don't"—

"Oh, Bartley, you know I didn't doubt you! I just got to thinking, and I was a little worked up! I suppose I'm excited."

"I know it! I know it!" cried her husband. "Don't you suppose I understand *you*?"

They talked a long time together, and made each other loving promises of patience. They confessed their faults, and pledged each other that they would try hard to overcome them. They wished to be good; they both felt they had much to retrieve; but they had no concealments and they knew that was the best way to begin the future, of which they did their best to conceive seriously. Bartley told her his plans about

getting some newspaper work till he could complete his law-
studies. He meant to settle down to practice in Boston. "You
have to wait longer for it than you would in a country-place;
but when you get it it's worth while." He asked Marcia
whether she would look up his friend Halleck if she were in
his place; but he did not give her time to decide: "I guess I
wont do it. Not just yet, at any rate. He might suppose that
I wanted something of him. I'll call on him when I don't need
his help."

Perhaps, if they had not planned to go to the theatre they
would have stayed where they were; for they were tired, and
it was very cosy. But when they were once in the street, they
were glad they had come out. Bowdoin Square and Court
street, and Tremont Row were a glitter of gas-lights, and the
shops with their placarded bargains dazzled Marcia. "Is it one
of the principal streets?" she asked Bartley.

He gave the laugh of a veteran habitué of Boston. "Tremont Row? No! Wait till I show you Washington street to-
morrow! There's the Museum," he said, pointing to the long
row of globed lights on the façade of the building. "Here we
are in Scollay's Square. There's Hanover street; there's Corn-
hill; Court crooks down that way; here's Pemberton Square."
His familiarity with these names estranged him to her again;
she clung the closer to his arm, and caught her breath nervously as they turned in with the crowd that was climbing
the stairs to the box-office of the theatre. Bartley left her a
moment while he pushed his way up to the little window and
bought the tickets. "First-rate seats," he said, coming back to
her, and taking her hand under his arm again, "and a great
piece of luck. They were just returned for sale by the man in
front of me, or I should have had to take something way up
in the gallery. There's a regular jam. These are right in the
centre of the parquet." Marcia did not know what the parquet
was; she heard its name with the certainty that but for Bartley
she should not be equal to it. All her village pride was
quelled; she had only enough self-control to act upon Bartley's instructions not to give herself away by any conviction
of rusticity. They passed in through the long colonnaded vestibule, with its paintings and plaster casts and rows of birds
and animals in glass cases on either side and she gave scarcely

a glance at any of those objects endeared by association if not by intrinsic beauty to the Boston play-goer: Gulliver, with the Lilliputians swarming upon him; the painty-necked ostriches and pelicans; the mummied mermaid under a glass-bell; the governors' portraits; the stuffed elephant; Washington crossing the Delaware; Cleopatra applying the Asp; Sir William Pepperell, at full length on canvas and the pagan months and seasons in plaster,—if all these are indeed the subjects—were dim phantasmagoria, amid which she and Bartley moved scarcely more real. The usher in his dress coat, ran up the aisle to take their checks, and led them down to their seats; half a dozen elegant people stood to let them in to their places; the theatre was filled with faces: at Portland where she saw "The Lady of Lyons" with her father, three quarters of the house was empty. Bartley only had time to lean over and whisper, "The place is packed with Beacon street swells. It's a regular field night," when the bell tinkled and the curtain rose.

As the play went on the rich jacqueminot red flamed into her cheeks, and burnt there, a steady blaze, to the end. The people about her laughed and clapped, and at times they seemed to be crying. But Marcia sat through every part as stoical as a savage, and, except for the flaming color in her cheeks, making no sign of interest or intelligence. Bartley talked of the play all the way home, but she said nothing, and in their own room he asked: "Didn't you really like it? Were you disappointed? I haven't been able to get a word out of you about it. Didn't you like Boucicault?"

"I didn't know which he was," she answered with impassioned exultation. "I didn't care for him. I only thought of that poor girl, and her husband who despised her"—

She stopped. Bartley looked at her a moment, and then caught her to him and fell a laughing over her, till it seemed as if he never would end. "And you thought—you thought," he cried, trying to get his breath, "you thought you were Lily, and I was Hardress Cregan! Oh, I see, I see!" He went on making a mock and a burlesque of her tragical hallucination till she laughed with him at last.

When he put his hand up to turn out the gas, he began his joking afresh: "The real thing for Hardress to do," he said, fumbling for the key, "is to *blow* it out. That's what Hardress usually does when he comes up from the rural districts with Eily on their bridal tour. That finishes off Eily, without troubling Danny Mann. The only drawback is that it finishes off Hardress, too: they're *both* found suffocated in the morning."

XIV

THE NEXT DAY after breakfast, while they stood together before the parlor fire, Bartley proposed one plan after another for spending the day. Marcia rejected them all, with perfectly recovered self-composure. "Then what *shall* we do?" he asked, at last.

"Oh, I don't know," she answered rather absently. She added, after an interval, smoothing the warm front of her dress, and putting her foot on the fender, "What did those theatre-tickets cost?"

"Two dollars," he replied carelessly. "Why?"

Marcia gasped. "Two dollars! Oh, Bartley, we couldn't afford it!"

"It seems we did."

"And here—how much are we paying here?"

"That room with fire," said Bartley, stretching himself, "is seven dollars a day"—

"We must not stay another instant," said Marcia, all a woman's terror of spending money on anything but dress, all a wife's conservative instinct, rising within her. "How much have you got left?"

Bartley took out his pocket-book, and counted over the bills in it. "A hundred and twenty dollars."

"Why, what has become of it all? We had a hundred and sixty!"

"Well, our railroad tickets were nineteen, the sleeping car was three, the parlor car was three, the theatre was two, the hack was fifty cents; and we'll have to put down the other two and a half to refreshments."

Marcia listened in dismay. At the end she drew a long breath. "Well, we must go away from here, as soon as possible—*that* I know. We'll go out and find some boarding place. That's the first thing."

"Oh, now, Marcia, you're not going to be so severe as that, are you?" pleaded Bartley. "A few dollars, more or less, are not going to keep us out of the poorhouse. I just want to

305

stay here three days: that will leave us a clean hundred, and we can start fair"—

He was half joking, but she was wholly serious. "No, Bartley! Not another hour—not another minute! Come!" She took his arm, and bent it up into a crook, in which she put her hand and pulled him toward the door. "Well, after all," he said, "it will be some fun looking up a room." There was no one else in the parlor; in going to the door they took some waltzing steps together.

While she dressed to go out, he looked up places where rooms were let with or without board, in the newspaper. "There don't seem to be a great many," he said meditatively, bending over the open sheet. But he cut out half a dozen advertisements with his editorial scissors, and they started upon their search.

They climbed those pleasant old up-hill streets that converge to the State-house, and looked into the houses on the quiet Places that stretch from one thoroughfare to another. They had decided that they would be content with two small rooms, one for a chamber, and the other for a parlor, where they could have a fire. They found exactly what they wanted in the first house at which they applied, one flight up, with sunny windows, looking down the street; but it made Marcia's blood run cold, when the landlady said that the price was thirty dollars a week. At another place, the rooms were only twenty; the position was quite as good, and the carpet and furniture prettier.

This was still too dear, but it seemed comparatively reasonable till it appeared that this was the price without board. "I think we should prefer rooms with board, shouldn't we?" asked Bartley with a sly look at Marcia.

The prices were of all degrees of exorbitance, and they varied for no reason, from house to house; one landlady had been accustomed to take more and another less, but never little enough for Marcia, who overruled Bartley again and again when he wished to close with some small abatement of terms. She declared now that they must put up with one room, and they must not care what floor it was on. But the cheapest room with board was fourteen dollars a week, and Marcia had fixed her ideal at ten: even that was too high, for them.

"The best way will be to go back to the Revere House at seven dollars a day," said Bartley; he had lately been leaving the transaction of the business entirely to Marcia, who had rapidly acquired alertness and decision in it.

She could not respond to his joke. "What is there left?" she asked.

"There isn't anything left," he said; "we've got to the end."

They stood on the edge of the pavement, and looked up and down the street, and then by a common impulse they looked at the house opposite, where a placard in the window advertised "Apartments to let—to Gentlemen only."

"It would be of no use asking there," murmured Marcia with sad abstraction.

"Well, let's go over and try," said her husband. "They can't do more than turn us out of doors."

"I know it wont be of any use," Marcia sighed, as people do when they hope to gain something by forbidding themselves hope. But she helplessly followed, and stood at the foot of the doorsteps while he ran up and rang.

It was apparently the woman of the house who came to the door, and shrewdly scanned them.

"I see you have apartments to let," said Bartley.

"Well, yes," admitted the woman, as if she considered it useless to deny it, "I *have*."

"I should like to look at them," returned Bartley with promptness. "Come, Marcia!" and re-inforced by her he invaded the premises before the landlady had time to repel him. "I'll tell you what we want," he continued, turning into the little reception-room at the side of the door, "and if you haven't got it, there's no need to trouble you: we want a fair-sized room, anywhere between the cellar-floor and the roof, with a bed and a stove and a table in it, that sha'n't cost us more than ten dollars a week with board."

"Set down," said the landlady, herself setting the example, by sinking into the rocking-chair behind her, and beginning to rock, while she made a brief study of the intruders. "Want it for yourselves?"

"Yes," said Bartley.

"Well," returned the landlady, "I always *have* p'ferred single gentlemen."

"I inferred as much from a remark which you made in your front-window," said Bartley, indicating the placard.

The landlady smiled. They were certainly a very pretty-appearing young couple, and the gentleman was evidently up and coming. Mrs. Nash liked Bartley, as most people of her grade did, at once. "It's always b'en my exper'ence," she explained with the lazily rhythmical drawl, in which most half-bred New Englanders speak, "that I seemed to get along *ruther* better with gentlemen. They give less trouble as a general *rule*," she added, with a glance at Marcia, as if she did not deny that there were exceptions, and Marcia might be a striking one.

Bartley seized his advantage. "Well, my wife hasn't been married long enough to be unreasonable. I guess you'd get along."

They both laughed, and Marcia, blushing, joined them. "Well, I *thought* when you first come up the steps you hadn't been married, well, not a *great* while," said the landlady.

"No," said Bartley. "It seems a good while to my wife; but we were only married day before yesterday."

"The land!" cried Mrs. Nash.

"Bartley!" whispered Marcia, in soft upbraiding.

"What? Well, say last week, then. We were married last week, and we've come to Boston to seek our fortune."

His wit overjoyed Mrs. Nash. "You'll find Boston an awful hard place to get along," she said, shaking her head with a warning smile.

"I shouldn't think so, by the price Boston people ask for their rooms," returned Bartley. "If I had rooms to let I should get along pretty easily."

This again delighted the landlady. "I guess you aint goin' to get out of spirits, anyway," she said. "Well," she continued, "I *have* got a room 't I guess would suit you. Unexpectedly vacated." She seemed to recur to the language of an advertisement in these words, which she pronounced as if reading them. "It's pretty high up," she said with another warning shake of the head.

"Stairs to get to it?" asked Bartley.

"Plenty of *stairs*."

"Well, I like when a place is pretty high up to have plenty of stairs to get to it. I guess we'll see it, Marcia." He rose.

"Well, I'll just go up and see if it's *fit* to be seen, first," said the landlady.

"Oh, Bartley!" said Marcia, when she had left them alone, "how *could* you joke so, about our just being married!"

"Well, I saw she wanted awfully to ask. And anybody can tell it by looking at us, anyway. We can't keep that to ourselves, any more than we can our greenness. Besides, it's money in our pockets: she'll take something off our board for it, you'll see. Now, will you manage the bargaining from this on? I stepped forward because the rooms were for gentlemen only."

"I guess I'd better," said Marcia.

"All right; then I'll take a back seat, from this out."

"Oh, I do *hope* it wont be too much!" sighed the young wife. "I'm so *tired*, looking."

"You can come right along up," the landlady called down through the oval spire formed by the ascending handrail of the stairs. They found her in a broad low room whose ceiling sloped with the roof, and had the pleasant irregularity of the angles and recessions of two dormer windows. The room was clean and cosy; there was a table, and a stove that could be used open or shut; Marcia squeezed Bartley's arm to signify that it would do, perfectly, if only the price would suit.

The landlady stood in the middle of the floor and lectured: "Now, there! I get five dollars a week for this room; and I gen'ly let it to two gentlemen. It's just been vacated by two gentlemen, unexpectedly; but it's had to get gentlemen at this time the yea; and that's the reason I thought of takin' you. As I *say*, I don't much like ladies for inmates, and so I put in the window for gentlemen only. But it's no use bein' too particular; I can't have the room layin' empty on my hands. If it suits you, you can have it for four dollars. It's high up, and there's no use tryin' to deny it. But there ain't such anotha' view as them windes commands, anywheres. You can see the harbor, and pretty much the whole coast."

"Anything extra for the view?" said Bartley, glancing out.

"No, I throw that in."

"Does the price include gas and fire?" asked Marcia, sharpened as to all details by previous interviews.

"It includes the gas, but it don't include the fire," said the landlady, firmly. "And it's pretty low, at that, as you've found out, I guess."

"Yes, it *is* low," said Marcia. "Bartley, I think we'd better take it." She looked at him timidly, as if she were afraid he might not think it good enough; she did not think it good enough for him, but she felt that they must make their money go as far as possible.

"All *right!*" he said. "Then it's a bargain."

"And how much more will the board be?"

"Well, the'e," the landlady said, with candor; "I don't know as I can meet your views. I don't neve give boad. But there's plenty of houses, right on the street here, where you can get dayboard from four dollars a week, up."

"Oh, dear!" sighed Marcia; "and that would make it twelve dollars!"

"Why the dear suz, child!" exclaimed the landlady, "you didn't expect to get it for less?"

"We must," said Marcia.

"Then you'll have to go to a mechanics' boardin' house."

"I suppose we shall," she returned dejectedly. Bartley whistled.

"Look here," said the landlady, "ain't you from Down East, some'eres?"

Marcia started, as if the woman had recognized them. "Yes," she said.

"Well, now," said Mrs. Nash, "I'm from down Maine way, myself, and I'll tell you what I should do, if I was in your *place*. You don't want much of anything for breakfast or tea; you can boil you an egg on the stove here, and you can make your own tea or coffee; and if I was you, I'd go out for my dinners to an eatin' house. I heard some my lodgers tellin' how they done. Well, I heard the very gentlemen that occupied this room sayin' how they used to go to an eatin' house, and one'd order one thing and another another, and then they'd halve it between 'em, and make out a first rate meal, for about a quarter apiece. Plenty of places now where they give you a cut o' lamb or rib-beef for a shillin', and they bring you bread and butter and potato with it; an' it's always enough for two. That's what they *said*. I haint never tried it myself; but as long as you hain't got but yourselves to care for there aint any reason why *you* shouldn't."

They looked at each other.

"Well," added the landlady for a final touch, "*say* fire. That stove wont burn a great deal, anyway."

"All right," said Bartley, "we'll take the room—for a month, at least."

Mrs. Nash looked a little embarrassed. If she had made some concession to the liking she had conceived for this pretty young couple, she could not risk everything. "I always have to get the first week in advance,—where there aint no reference," she suggested.

"Of course," said Bartley, as he took out his pocket-book, which he had a boyish satisfaction in letting her see was well-filled. "Now, Marcia," he continued, looking at his watch, "I'll just run over to the hotel, and give up our room before they get us in for dinner."

Marcia accepted Mrs. Nash's invitation to come and sit with her till the chill was off the room; and she borrowed a pen and paper of her to write home. The note she sent was brief: she was not going to seem to ask anything of her father. But she was going to do what was right; she told him where she was, and she sent her love to her mother. She would not speak of her things; he might send them or not, as he chose; but she knew he would. This was the spirit of her letter; and her training had not taught her to soften and sweeten her phrase; but no doubt the old man who was like her, would understand that she felt no compunction for what she had done, and that she loved him though she still defied him.

Bartley did not ask her what her letter was when she demanded a stamp of him, on his return; but he knew. He inquired of Mrs. Nash where these cheap eating houses were to be found, and he posted the letter in the first box they came to, merely saying, "I hope you haven't been asking any favors, Marsh?"

"No, indeed!"

"Because I couldn't stand that."

Marcia had never dined in a restaurant, and she was somewhat bewildered by the one into which they turned. There was a great show of roast and steak and fish, and game and squash and cranberry pie in the window, and at the door a tack was driven through a mass of bills-of-fare, two of which Bartley plucked off as they entered, with a knowing air and then threw on the floor when he found the same thing on the table. The table had a marble top, and a silver-plated castor in the centre. The plates were laid, with a coarse red doyly in a cocked-hat on each, and a thinly plated knife and fork crossed beneath it; the plates were thick and heavy; the handle as well as the blade of the knife was metal and silvered. Besides the castor, there was a bottle of Leicestershire sauce on the table, and salt in what Marcia thought a pepper-box; the marble was of an unctuous translucence, in places, and showed the course of the cleansing napkin on its smeared surface. The place was hot, and full of confused smells of cooking; all the tables were crowded, so that they found places with difficulty, and pale, plain girls, of the Provincial and Irish-American type, in fashionable bangs and pull-backs, went about taking the orders which they wailed out towards a semi-circular hole opening upon a counter at the further end of the room; there they received the dishes ordered, and hurried with them to the customers, before whom they laid them with a noisy clacking of the heavy crockery. A great many of the people seemed to be taking hulled-corn and milk; baked beans formed another favorite dish, and squash-pie was in large request. Marcia was not critical; roast-turkey for Bartley and stewed chicken for herself with cranberry-pie for both seemed to her a very good and sufficient dinner, and better than they ought to have had. She asked Bartley if this were anything like Parker's; he had always talked to her about Parker's.

"Well, Marcia," he said, folding up his doyly, which does not betray use like the indiscreet white napkin, "I'll just take you round and show you the *outside* of Parker's; and some day we'll go there and get dinner."

He not only showed her Parker's but the City Hall; they walked down School street, and through Washington as far as Boylston; and Bartley pointed out the Old South, and brought Marcia home by the Common, where they stopped to see the boys coasting under the care of the police between two long lines of spectators. "The State House," said Bartley, with easy command of the facts, and pointing in the several directions; "Beacon street; Public Garden; Back Bay." She came home to Mrs. Nash joyfully admiring the city, but admiring still more her husband's masterly knowledge of it.

Mrs. Nash was one of those people who partake intimately of the importance of the place in which they live; to whom it is sufficient splendor and prosperity to be a Bostonian or New Yorker or Chicagoan, and who experience a delicious self-flattery in the celebration of the municipal grandeur. In his degree, Bartley was of this sort, and he exchanged compliments of Boston with Mrs. Nash till they grew into warm favor with each other.

After a while he said he must go up stairs and do some writing; and then he casually dropped the fact that he was an editor, and that he had come to Boston to get an engagement on a newspaper; he implied that he had come to take one.

"Well," said Mrs. Nash, smoothing the back of the cat which she had in her lap, "I guess there ain't anything like our Boston papers. And they say this new one—the Daily Events—is goin' to take the lead. You acquainted any with our Boston editors?"

Bartley hemmed. "Well, I know the proprietor of the Events."

"Oh, yes; Mr. Witherby. Well, they say he's got the money. I hear my lodgers talkin' about that paper consid'able. I hain't never seen it."

Bartley now went up stairs; he had an idea in his head. Marcia remained with Mrs. Nash a few moments. "He's been in Boston before," she said with proud satisfaction; "he visited here when he was in college."

"Gaw, is he college-bred?" cried Mrs. Nash. "Well, I thought he looked 'most too wide awake for that. He ain't a bit offish. He seems re'l practical. What you hurryin' off so, for?" she asked, as Marcia rose, and stood poised on the threshold, in act to follow her husband. "Why don't you set here with me, while he's at his writin'? You'll just keep talkin' to him and takin' his mind off, the whole while. You stay here!" she commanded hospitably. "You'll just be in the way, up there."

This was a novel conception to Marcia; but its good sense struck her. "Well, I will," she said. "I'll run up a minute to leave my things and then I'll come back."

She found Bartley dragging the table, on which he had already laid out his writing materials, into a good light, and she threw her arms round his neck, as if they had been a great while parted. "Come up to kiss me good luck?" he asked, finding her lips.

"Yes, and to tell you how splendid you are, going right to work this way," she answered fondly.

"Oh, I don't believe in losing time; and I've got to strike while the iron's hot, if I'm going to write out that logging-camp business. I'll take it over to that Events man, and hit him with it while it's fresh in his mind."

"Yes," said Marcia. "Are you going to write that out?"

"Why, I told you I was. Any objections?" He did not pay much attention to her and he asked his question jokingly, as he went on making his preparations.

"It's hard for me to realize that people can care for such things. I thought perhaps you'd begin with something else," she suggested, hanging up her sack and hat in the closet.

"No, that's the very thing to begin with," he answered carelessly. "What are you going to do? Want that book to read that I bought on the cars?"

"No, I'm going down to sit with Mrs. Nash, while you're writing."

"Well, that's a good idea."

"You can call me when you're done."

"Done!" cried Bartley. "I shan't be done till this time tomorrow. I'm going to make a lot about it."

"Oh!" said his wife. "Well, I suppose the more there is the more you will get for it. Shall you put in about those people coming to see the camp?"

"Yes, I think I can work that in so that old Witherby will like it. Something about a distinguished Boston newspaper proprietor and his refined and elegant ladies, as a sort of contrast to the rude life of the loggers."

"I thought you didn't admire them a great deal."

"Well, I didn't much. But I can work them up."

Marcia was quite ready to go; Bartley had seated himself at his table; but she still hovered about.

"And are you—shall you—put that Montreal woman in?"

"Yes, get it all in. She'll work up, first-rate."

Marcia was silent. Then she said:

"I shouldn't think you'd put her in if she was so silly and disagreeable."

Bartley turned round, and saw the look on her face that he could not mistake. He rose, and took her by the chin. "Look here, Marsh!" he said, "didn't you promise me you'd stop that?"

"Yes," she murmured, while the color flamed into her cheeks.

"And will you?"

"I *did* try"—

He looked sharply into her eyes. "Confound the Montreal woman! I wont put in a word about her. There!" He kissed Marcia, and held her in his arms, and soothed her as if she had been a jealous child.

"Oh, Bartley! Oh, Bartley!" she cried, "I love you so!"

"I think it's a remark you made before," he said, and with a final kiss and laugh, he pushed her out of the door; and she ran down stairs to Mrs. Nash again.

"Your husband ever write poetry, any?" enquired the landlady.

"No," returned Marcia; "he used to, in college. But he says it don't pay."

"One my lodgers—well she was a lady; you can't seem to get gentlemen oftentimes in the summer season, for *love* or money, and I was puttin' up with her,—breakin' joints,—as you may say, for the time *bein'—she* wrote poetry; 'n' I guess she found it pretty poor pickin'. Used to write for the weekly papers, she said, 'n' the child'n's magazines. Well, she couldn't get more'n a doll' or two, 'n' I dunno but what less, for a piece as long as that." Mrs. Nash held her hands about a foot apart. "Used to show 'em to me, and tell me about 'em. I declare, I used to pity her. I used tell her I ruther break stone for *my* livin'."

Marcia sat talking more than an hour to Mrs. Nash, informing herself upon the history of Mrs. Nash's past and present lodgers; and about the ways of the city, and the prices of provisions and dress-goods. The dearness of everything alarmed and even shocked her; but she came back to her faith in Bartley's ability to meet and overcome all difficulties. She grew drowsy in the close air which Mrs. Nash loved, after all her fatigues and excitements, and she said she guessed she would go up and see how Bartley was getting on. But when she stole into the room, and saw him busily writing, she said, "Now I wont speak a word, Bartley," and coiled herself down under a shawl on the bed, near enough to put her hand on his shoulder if she wished, and fell asleep.

XV

IT TOOK Bartley two days to write out his account of the logging camp. He worked it up to the best of his ability, giving all the facts that he had got out of Kinney, and relieving these with what he considered picturesque touches. He had the newspaper instinct, and he divined that his readers would not care for his picturesqueness without his facts. He therefore subordinated this, and he tried to give his description of the loggers a politico-economical interest, dwelling upon the variety of nationalities engaged in the industry, and the changes it had undergone in what he called its *personnel*; he enlarged upon its present character and its future development, in relation to what he styled in a line of small capitals, with an early use of the favorite newspaper possessive,

COLUMBIA'S MORIBUND SHIP-BUILDING.

And he interspersed his text plentifully with exclamatory headings intended to catch the eye with startling fragments of narration and statement such as,

THE PINE TREE STATE'S STORIED STAPLE,

MORE THAN A MILLION OF MONEY,

UNBROKEN WILDERNESS,

WILD CATS, LYNXES AND BEARS,

BITTEN OFF,

BOTH LEGS FROZEN TO THE KNEES,

CANADIAN SONGS,

JOY UNCONFINED,

THE LAMPLIGHT ON THEIR SWARTHY FACES.

He spent a final forenoon in polishing his article up and stuffing it full of telling points. But after dinner on this last day he took leave of Marcia with more trepidation than he was willing to show, or knew how to conceal. Her devout faith in his success seemed to unnerve him, and he begged her not to believe in it so much.

He seized what courage he had left in both hands, and

found himself, after the usual reluctance of the people in the business-office, face to face with Mr. Witherby in his private room. Mr. Witherby had lately dismissed his managing-editor for his neglect of the true interests of the paper as represented by the counting-room, and was managing the Events himself. He sat before a table strewn with newspapers and manuscripts, and as he looked up, Bartley saw that he did not recognize him.

"How do you do, Mr. Witherby? I had the pleasure of meeting you the other day in Maine—at Mr. Willett's logging-camp. Hubbard is my name; remember me as editor of the Equity Free Press."

"Oh, yes," said Mr. Witherby, rising and standing at his desk, as a sort of compromise between asking his visitor to sit down and telling him to go away. He shook hands in a loose way, and added, "I presume you would like to exchange. But the fact is our list is so large already, that we can't extend it, just now; we can't"—

Bartley smiled. "I don't want any exchange, Mr. Witherby. I'm out of the Free Press."

"Oh!" said the city journalist, with relief. He added, in a leading tone: "Then"—

"I've come to offer you an article—an account of lumbering in our State. It's a little sketch that I've prepared from what I saw in Mr. Willett's camp, and some facts and statistics I've picked up. I thought it might make an attractive feature of your Sunday edition."

"The Events," said Mr. Witherby, solemnly, "does not publish a Sunday edition."

"Of course not," answered Bartley, inwardly cursing his blunder, "I mean your Saturday evening supplement." He handed him his manuscript.

Mr. Witherby looked at it with the worry of a dull man who has assumed unintelligible duties. He had let the other papers "get ahead of him" on several important enterprises lately, and he would have been glad to retrieve himself; but he could not be sure that this was an enterprise. He began by saying that their last Saturday Supplement was just out, and the next was full; and ended by declaring with stupid pomp, that the Events preferred to send its own reporters to write up those matters. Then he hemmed, and looked at Bartley, and he would really have been glad to have him argue him out of this position; but Bartley could not divine what was in his mind. The cold fit which sooner or later comes to every form of authorship, seized him. He said awkwardly he was very sorry, and putting his manuscript back in his pocket, he went out, feeling curiously light-headed as if his rebuff had been a stunning blow. The affair was so quickly over that he might well have believed it had not happened. But he was sickeningly disappointed; he had counted upon the sale of his article to the Events; his hope had been founded upon actual knowledge of the proprietor's intention, and although he had rebuked Marcia's overweening confidence, he had expected that Witherby would jump at it. But Witherby had not even looked at it.

Bartley walked a long time in the cold winter sunshine. He would have liked to go back to his lodging, and hide his face in Marcia's hands, and let her pity him, but he could not bear the thought of her disappointment, and he kept walking. At last he regained courage enough to go to the editor of the paper for which he used to correspond in the summer, and which had always printed his letters. This editor was busy, too, but he apparently felt some obligations to civility with Bartley, and though he kept glancing over his exchanges as they talked, he now and then glanced at Bartley also. He said that he should be glad to print the sketch, but that they never paid for outside material, and he advised Bartley to go with it to the Events, or to the Daily Chronicle-Abstract; the Abstract and the Brief Chronicle had lately consolidated, and they were showing a good deal of enterprise. Bartley said nothing to betray that he had already been at the Events office, and upon this friendly editor's invitation to drop in again, sometime, he went away considerably re-inspirited. "If you should happen to go to the Chronicle-Abstract folks," the editor called after him, "you can tell 'em I suggested your coming."

The managing editor of the Chronicle-Abstract was reading a manuscript, and he did not desist from his work on Bartley's appearance which he gave no sign of welcoming. But he had a whimsical, shrewd, kind face, and Bartley felt that he should get on with him, though he did not rise and though he let Bartley stand.

"Yes," he said. "Lumbering, hey? Well, there's some interest in that, just now, on account of this talk about the decay of our ship-building interests. Anything on that point?"

"That's the very point I touch on first," said Bartley.

The editor stopped turning over his manuscript.

"Let's see," he said, holding out his hand for Bartley's article. He looked at the first head-line, "What I know about Logging," and smiled, "Old, but good." Then he glanced at the other headings, and ran his eye down the long strips on which Bartley had written; nibbled at the text here and there a little; returned to the first paragraph, and read that through; looked back at something else, and then read the close. "I guess you can leave it," he said, laying the manuscript on the table.

"No, I guess not," said Bartley, with equal coolness, gathering it up.

The editor looked fairly at him for the first time, and smiled. Evidently, he liked this. "What's the reason? Any particular hurry?"

"I happen to know that the Events is going to send a man down east to write up this very subject. And I don't propose to leave this article here till they steal my thunder, and then have it thrown back on my hands not worth the paper it's written on."

The editor tilted himself back in his chair, and braced his knees against his table. "Well, I guess you're right," he said. "What do you want for it?"

This was a terrible question. Bartley knew nothing about the prices that city papers paid; he feared to ask too much, but he also feared to cheapen his wares by asking too little. "Twenty-five dollars," he said, huskily.

"Let's look at it," said the editor, reaching out his hand for the manuscript again. "Sit down." He pushed a chair towards Bartley with his foot, having first swept a pile of newspapers from it to the floor. He now read the article more fully, and then looked up at Bartley, who sat still, trying to hide his anxiety. "You're not quite a new hand at the bellows, are you?"

"I've edited a country paper."

"Yes? Where?"

"Down in Maine."

The editor bent forward and took out a long narrow blank-book. "I guess we shall want your article. What name?"

"Bartley J. Hubbard." It sounded in his ears like some other's name.

"Going to be in Boston some time?"

"All the time," said Bartley, struggling to appear noncha-lant. The revulsion from the despair into which he had fallen after his interview with Witherby was still very great. The order on the counting-room which the editor had given him shook in his hand. He saw his way before him clearly now; he wished to propose some other things that he would like to write; but he was saved from this folly for the time by the editor's saying, in a tone of dismissal:

"Better come in, to-morrow, and see a proof. We shall put you into the Wednesday supplement."

"Thanks," said Bartley. "Good day."

The editor did not hear him, or did not think it necessary to respond from behind the newspaper which he had lifted up between them, and Bartley went out. He did not stop to cash his order; he made boyish haste to show it to Marcia, as something more authentic than the money itself, and more sacred. As he hurried homeward he figured Marcia's ecstasy in his thought. He saw himself flying up the stairs to their attic three steps at a bound, and bursting into the room, where she sat, eager and anxious, and flinging the order into her lap; and then when she had read it with rapture at the sum, and pride in the smartness with which he had managed the whole affair, he saw himself catching her up and dancing about the floor with her. He thought how fond of her he was, and he wondered that he could ever have been cold or lukewarm.

She was standing at the window of Mrs. Nash's little re-ception-room when he reached the house. It was not to be as he had planned, but he threw her a kiss, glad of the im-patience which would not let her wait till he could find her in their own room, and he had the precious order in his hand to dazzle her eyes as soon as he should enter. But as he sprang into the hall, his foot struck against a trunk, and some boxes.

"Hello!" he cried, "your things have come!"

Marcia lingered within the door of the room; she seemed afraid to come out. "Yes," she said faintly. "Father brought them. He has just been here."

He seemed there still, and the vision unnerved her as if Bartley and he had been confronted there in reality. Her husband had left her hardly a quarter of an hour when a hack drove up to the door and her father alighted. She let him in herself, before he could ring, and waited tremulously for what he should do or say. But he merely took her hand, and stooping over gave her the chary kiss with which he used to greet her at home when he returned from an absence.

She flung her arms round his neck: "Oh, father!"

"Well, well! There, there!" he said, and then he went into the reception-room with her; and there was nothing in his manner to betray that anything unusual had happened since they last met. He kept his hat on, as his fashion was, and he kept on his overcoat, below which the skirts of his dresscoat hung an inch or two; he looked old and weary and shabby.

"I can't leave Bartley, father!" she began hysterically.

"I haven't come to separate you from your husband, Marcia. What made you think so? It's your place to stay with him."

"He's out, now," she answered, in an incoherent hopefulness. "He's just gone. Will you wait and see him, father?"

"No, I guess I can't wait," said the old man. "It wouldn't do any good for us to meet now."

"Do you think he coaxed me away? He didn't. He took pity on me—he forgave me. And I didn't mean to deceive you when I left home, father. But I couldn't help trying to see Bartley again."

"I believe you, Marcia. I understand. The thing had to be. Let me see your marriage certificate." She ran up to her room and fetched it. Her father read it carefully. "Yes, that is all right," he said, and returned it to her. He added, after an absent pause: "I have brought your things, Marcia. Your mother packed all she could think of."

"How *is* mother?" asked Marcia, as if this had first reminded her of her mother.

"She is usually well," replied her father.

"Wont you—wont you come up and see our room, father?" Marcia asked after the interval following this feint of interest in her mother.

"No," said the old man rising restlessly from his chair, and buttoning at his coat, which was already buttoned. "I guess I sha'n't have time. I guess I must be going."

Marcia put herself between him and the door. "Wont you let me tell you about it, father?"

"About what?"

"How—I came to go off with Bartley. I want you should know!"

"I guess I know all I want to know about it, Marcia. I accept the facts. I told you how I felt. What you've done hasn't changed me towards you. I understand you better than you understand yourself; and I can't say that I'm surprised. Now I want you should make the best of it."

"You don't forgive Bartley!" she cried passionately. "Then I don't want you should forgive me!"

"Where did you pick up this nonsense about forgiving?" said her father knitting his shaggy brows. "A man does this thing or that, and the consequence follows. I couldn't forgive Bartley so that he could escape any consequence of what he's done; and you're not afraid I shall hurt him?"

"Stay and see him!" she pleaded. "He is so kind to me! He works night and day, and he has just gone out to sell something he has written for the papers."

"I never said he was lazy," returned her father. "Do you want any money, Marcia?"

"No, we have plenty. And Bartley is earning it all the time. I *wish* you would stay and see him!"

"No, I'm glad he didn't happen to be in," said the Squire. "I sha'n't wait for him to come back. It wouldn't do any good, just yet, Marcia; it would only do harm. Bartley and I haven't had time to change our minds about each other yet. But I'll say a good word for him to you. You're his wife; and it's your part to help him, not to hinder him. You can make him worse by being a fool; but you needn't be a fool. Don't worry him about other women; don't be jealous. He's your husband, now; and the worst thing you can do is to doubt him."

"I wont, father, I wont indeed! I will be good, and I will try to be sensible. Oh, I *wish* Bartley could know how you feel!"

"Don't tell him from *me*," said her father. "And don't keep making promises and breaking them. I'll help the man in with your things."

He went out, and came in again with one end of a trunk, as if he had been giving the man a hand with it into the house at home, and she suffered him as passively as she had suffered him to do her such services all her life. Then he took her hand laxly in his, and stooped down for another chary kiss. "Good-bye, Marcia."

"Why, father, are you going to *leave* me?" she faltered.

He smiled in melancholy irony at the bewilderment, the childish forgetfulness of the circumstances which her words expressed. "Oh, no! I'm going to take you with me."

His sarcasm restored her to a sense of what she had said, and she ruefully laughed at herself through her tears. "What am I talking about? Give my love to mother! When will you come again?" she asked, clinging about him, almost in the old playful way.

"When you want me," said the Squire, freeing himself.

"I'll write!" she cried after him, as he went down the steps; and if there had been at any moment a consciousness of her cruelty to him in her heart, she lost it, when he drove away, in her anxious waiting for Bartley's return. It seemed to her, that though her father had refused to see him his visit was of happy augury for future kindness between them, and she was proudly eager to tell Bartley what good advice her father had given her. But the sight of her husband suddenly turned these thoughts to fear. She trembled, and all that she could say was, "I know father will be all right, Bartley."

"How?" he retorted savagely. "By the way he abused me to you? Where is he?"

"He's gone—gone back."

"I don't care where he's gone, so he's gone. Did he come

to take you home with him? Why didn't you go?—Oh, Marcia!" The brutal words had hardly escaped him, when he ran to her as if he would arrest them before their sense should pierce her heart.

She thrust him back with a stiffly extended arm, "Keep away! Don't touch me!" She walked by him up the stairs without looking round at him, and he heard her close their door and lock it.

XVI

BARTLEY STOOD for a moment, and then went out and wandered aimlessly about till night-fall. He went out shocked and frightened at what he had done, and ready for any reparation. But this mood wore away, and he came back sullenly determined to let her make the advances toward reconciliation, if there was to be one. Her love had already made his peace, and she met him in the dimly lighted little hall with a kiss of silent penitence and forgiveness. She had on her hat and shawl, as if she had been waiting for him to come and take her out to tea; and on their way to the restaurant, she asked him of his adventure among the newspapers. He told her briefly, and when they sat down at their table he took out the precious order and showed it to her. But its magic was gone; it was only an order for twenty-five dollars, now; and two hours ago it had been success, rapture, a common hope and a common joy. They scarcely spoke of it, but talked soberly of indifferent things.

She could not recur to her father's visit at once, and he would not be the first to mention it. He did nothing to betray his knowledge of her intention, as she approached the subject through those feints that women use, and when they stood again in their little attic room she was obliged to be explicit.

"What hurt me, Bartley," she said, "was that you should think for an instant that I would let father ask me to leave you, or that he would ask such a thing. He only came to tell me to be good to you, and help you, and trust you; and not worry you with my silliness and—and—jealousy. And I don't ever mean to. And I know he will be good friends with you yet. He praised you for working so hard;"—she pushed it a little beyond the bare fact;—"he always did that; and I know he's only waiting for a good chance to make it up with you."

She lifted her eyes, glistening with tears, and it touched his peculiar sense of humor to find her offering him reparation, when he had felt himself so outrageously to blame; but he would not be outdone in magnanimity, if it came to that.

"It's all right, Marsh. I was a furious idiot, or I should have let you explain at once. But you see I had only one thought in my mind, and that was my luck, which I wanted to share with you; and when your father seemed to have come in between us again—"

"Oh, yes, yes!" she answered. "I understand." And she clung to him in the joy of this perfect intelligence, which she was sure could never be obscured again.

When Bartley's article came out, she read it with a fond admiration which all her praises seemed to leave unsaid. She bought a scrap-book, and pasted the article into it, and said that she was going to keep everything he wrote.

"What are you going to write the next thing?" she asked.

"Well, that's what I don't know," he answered. "I can't find another subject like that, so easily."

"Why, if people care to read about a logging camp, I should think they would read about almost anything. Nothing could be too common for them. You might even write about the trouble of getting cheap enough rooms in Boston."

"Marcia," cried Bartley, "you're a treasure! I'll write about that very thing! I know the Chronicle-Abstract will be glad to get it."

She thought he was joking till he came to her after a while for some figures which he did not remember. He had the true newspaper instinct, and went to work with a motive that was as different as possible from the literary motive. He wrote for the effect which he was to make, and not from any artistic pleasure in the treatment. He did not attempt to give it form, to imagine a young couple like himself and Marcia coming down from the country to place themselves in the city; he made no effort to throw about it the poetry of their ignorance and their poverty, or the pathetic humor of their dismay at the disproportion of the prices to their means. He set about getting all the facts he could, and he priced a great many lodgings in different parts of the city; then he went to a number of real-estate agents, and, giving himself out as a reporter of the Chronicle-Abstract, he interviewed them as to house rents, past and present. Upon these bottom facts, as he called them, he based a "spicy" sketch, which had also largely the character of an *exposé*. There is nothing the public enjoys so much as an *exposé*; it seems to be made in the reader's own interest; it somehow constitutes him a party to the attack upon the abuse, and its effectiveness redounds to the credit of all the newspaper's subscribers. After a week's stay in Boston, Bartley was able to assume the feelings of a native who sees his city falling into decay through the rapacity of its land-ladies. In the heading of ten or fifteen lines which he gave his sketch, the greater number were devoted to this feature of it; though the space actually allotted to it in the text was com-paratively small. He called his report "Boston's Boarding-Houses," and he spent a paragraph upon the relation of boarding-houses to civilization, before detailing his own ex-perience and observation. This part had many of those strokes of crude picturesqueness and humor which he knew how to give, and was really entertaining; but it was when he came to contrast the rates of house-rent and the cost of provisions with the landladies'

"PERPENDICULAR PRICES"

that Bartley showed all the virtue of a born reporter. The sen-tences were vivid and telling; the *ensemble* was very alarming; and the conclusion was inevitable that, unless this abuse could somehow be reached, we should lose a large and valuable portion of our population; especially those young married people of small means with whom the city's future prosperity so largely rested, and who must drift away to find homes in rival communities if the present exorbitant demands were maintained.

As Bartley had foretold, he had not the least trouble in selling this sketch to the Chronicle-Abstract. The editor prob-ably understood its essential cheapness perfectly well; but he also saw how thoroughly readable it was. He did not grumble at the increased price which Bartley put upon his work; it was still very far from dear; and he liked the young Downeaster's enterprise. He gave him as cordial a welcome as an over-worked man may venture to offer when Bartley came in with his copy, and he felt like doing him a pleasure. Some things out of the logging-camp sketch had been copied, and people had spoken to the editor about it, which was a still better sign that it was a hit.

"Don't you want to come round to our club to-night?"

asked the editor, as he handed Bartley the order for his money across the table. "We have a bad dinner, and we try to have a good time. We're all newspaper men together."

"Why, thank you," said Bartley, "I guess I should like to go."

"Well, come round at half-past five, and go with me."

Bartley walked homeward rather soberly. He had meant, if he sold this article, to make amends for the disappointment they had both suffered before, and to have a commemorative supper with Marcia at Parker's; he had ignored a little hint of hers about his never having taken her there yet, because he was waiting for this chance to do it in style. He resolved that, if she did not seem to like his going to the club, he would go back and withdraw his acceptance. But when he told her he had been invited,—he thought he would put the fact in this tentative way,—she said: "I hope you accepted!"

"Would you have liked me to?" he asked, with relief.

"Why, of course! It's a great honor. You'll get acquainted with all those editors, and perhaps some of them will want to give you a regular place."

A salaried employment was their common ideal of a provision for their future.

"Well, that's what I was thinking myself," said Bartley.

"Go and accept at once," she pursued.

"Oh, that isn't necessary. If I get round there by half-past five, I can go," he answered.

His lurking regret ceased when he came into the reception-room, where the members of the club were constantly arriving, and putting off their hats and overcoats, and then falling into groups for talk. His friend of the Chronicle-Abstract introduced him lavishly, as our American custom is. Bartley had a little strangeness, but no bashfulness, and, with his essentially slight opinion of people, he was promptly at his ease. These men liked his handsome face, his winning voice, the good-fellowship of his instant readiness to joke; he could see that they liked him, and that his friend Ricker was proud of the impression he made; before the evening was over he kept himself with difficulty from patronizing Ricker a little.

The club has grown into something much more splendid and expensive; but it was then content with a dinner certainly as bad as Ricker promised, but fabulously modest in price, at an old-fashioned hotel, whose site was long ago devoured by a dry-goods palace. The drink was commonly water or beer; occasionally, if a great actor or other distinguished guest honored the board, some spendthrift ordered champagne. But no one thought fit to go to this ruinous extreme for Bartley. Ricker offered him his choice of beer or claret, and Bartley temperately preferred water to either; he could see that this raised him in Ricker's esteem.

No company of men can fail to have a good time at a public dinner, and the good time began at once with these journalists, whose overworked week ended in this Saturday-evening jollity. They were mostly young men, who found sufficient compensation in the excitement and adventure of their underpaid labors, and in the vague hope of advancement; there were grizzled beards among them, for whom neither the novelty nor the expectation continued, but who loved the life for its own sake, and would hardly have exchanged it for prosperity. Here and there was an old fellow, for whom probably all illusion was gone; but he was proud of his vocation, proud even of the changes that left him somewhat superannuated in his tastes and methods. None, indeed, who have ever known it, can wholly forget the generous rage with which journalism inspires its followers. To each of those young men, beginning the strangely fascinating life as reporters and correspondents, his paper was as dear as his king once was to a French noble; to serve it night and day, to wear himself out for its sake, to merge himself in its glory, and to live in its triumphs without personal recognition from the public, was the loyal devotion which each expected his sovereign newspaper to accept as its simple right. They went and came, with the prompt and passive obedience of soldiers, wherever they were sent, and they struggled each to "get in ahead" of all the others with the individual zeal of heroes. They expanded to the utmost limits of occasion, and they submitted with an anguish that was silent to the editorial excision, compression, and mutilation of reports that were vitally dear to them. What becomes of these ardent young spirits, the inner history of journalism in any great city might pathetically show; but the outside world only knows them in the fine frenzy of interviewing, or of recording the midnight ravages of what they call the devouring element, or of working up horrible murders or tragical accidents, or of tracking criminals who have baffled all the detectives. Hearing their talk, Bartley began to realize that journalism might be a very different thing from what he had imagined it in a country printing-office, and that it might not be altogether wise to consider it merely as a stepping-stone to the law.

With the American eagerness to recognize talent, numbers of good fellows spoke to him about his logging sketch; even those who had not read it seemed to know about it as a hit. They were delighted to be able to say, "Ricker tells me that you offered it to old Witherby, and he wouldn't look at it!" He found that this fact, which he had doubtfully confided to Ricker, was not offensive to some of the Events people who were there; one of them got him aside, and darkly owned to him that Witherby was doing everything that any one man could to kill the Events, and that in fact the counting-room was running the paper.

All the club united in abusing the dinner, which in his rustic ignorance Bartley had not found so infamous; but they ate it with perfect appetite and with mounting good spirits. The president brewed punch in a great bowl before him, and, rising with a glass of it in his hand, opened a free parliament of speaking, story-telling, and singing. Whoever recollected a song or a story that he liked called upon the owner of it to sing it or tell it; and it appeared not to matter how old the fun or the music was: the company was resolved to be happy; it roared and clapped till the glasses rang. "You will like this song," Bartley's neighbors to right and left of him prophesied: or, "Just listen to this story of Mason's,—it's capital,"—as one or another rose in response to a general clamor. When they went back to the reception-room they carried the punch-bowl with them, and there, amid a thick cloud of smoke, two clever amateurs took their places at the piano, and sang and played to their hearts' content, while the rest, glass in hand, talked and laughed, or listened, as they chose. Bartley had not been called upon, but he was burning to try that song in which he had failed so dismally in the logging-camp. When the pianist rose at last, he slipped down into the chair, and, striking the chords of the accompaniment, he gave his piece with brilliant audacity. The room silenced itself, and then burst into a roar of applause, and cries of "Encore!" There could be no doubt of the success.

"Look here, Ricker," said a leading man, at the end of the repetition, "your friend must be one of us!"—and, rapping on the table, he proposed Bartley's name.

In that simple time the club voted *viva voce* on proposed members, and Bartley found himself elected by acclamation, and in the act of paying over his initiation fee to the treasurer, before he had well realized the honor done him. Everybody near him shook his hand, and offered to be of service to him. Much of this cordiality was merely collective good-feeling; something of it might justly be attributed to the punch; but the greater part was honest. In this civilization of ours, grotesque and unequal and imperfect as it is in many things, we are bound together in a brotherly sympathy unknown to any other. We new men have all had our hard rubs, but we do not so much remember them in soreness or resentment as in the wish to help forward any other who is presently feeling them. If he will but help himself too, a hundred hands are stretched out to him.

Bartley had kept his head clear of the punch, but he left the club drunk with joy and pride, and so impatient to be with Marcia and tell her of his triumphs, that he could hardly wait to read the proof of his boarding-house article, which Ricker had put in hand at once for the Sunday edition. He found Marcia sitting up for him, and she listened with a shining face while he hastily ran over the most flattering facts of the evening. She was not so much surprised at the honors done him as he had expected: but she was happier, and she made him repeat it all and give her the last details. He was afraid she would ask him what his initiation had cost; but she seemed to have no idea that it had cost anything, and though it had swept away a third of the money he had received for his sketch, he still resolved that she should have that supper at Parker's.

"I consider my future made," he said aloud, at the end of his swift cogitation on this point.

"Oh, yes!" she responded, rapturously. "We needn't have a moment's anxiety. But we must be very saving still till you get a place."

"Oh, certainly," said Bartley.

XVII

DURING several months that followed, Bartley's work consisted of interviewing, of special reporting in all its branches, of correspondence by mail and telegraph from points to which he was sent; his leisure he spent in studying subjects which could be treated like that of the boarding-houses. Marcia entered into his affairs with the keen half-intelligence which characterizes a woman's participation in business; whatever could be divined, she was quickly mistress of; she vividly sympathized with his difficulties and his triumphs; she failed to follow him in matters of political detail or of general effect; she could not be dispassionate or impartial; his relation to any enterprise was always more important than anything else about it. On some of his missions he took her with him, and then they made it a pleasure excursion; and if they came home late with the material still unwritten, she helped him with his notes, wrote from his dictation, and enabled him to give a fuller report than his rivals. She caught up with amusing aptness the technical terms of the profession, and was voluble about getting in ahead of the Events and the other papers, and she was indignant if any part of his report was cut out or garbled, or any feature was spoiled.

He made a "card" of grouping and treating with picturesque freshness the spring openings of the milliners and dry-goods people; and when he brought his article to Ricker, the editor ran it over, and said,

"Guess you took your wife with you, Hubbard."

"Yes, I did," Bartley owned. He was always proud of her looks, and it flattered him that Ricker should see the evidences of her feminine taste and knowledge in his account of the bonnets and dress-goods. "You don't suppose I could get at all these things by inspiration, do you?"

Marcia was already known to some of his friends whom he had introduced to her in casual encounters. They were mostly unmarried, or, if married, they lived at a distance, and they did not visit the Hubbards at their lodgings. Marcia was a little shy, and did not quite know whether they ought to call without being asked, or whether she ought to ask them; besides, Mrs. Nash's reception-room was not always at her disposal, and she would not have liked to take them all the way up to her own room. Her social life was, therefore, confined to the public places where she met these friends of her husband's. They sometimes happened together at a restaurant, or saw one another between the acts at the theatre, or on coming out of a concert. Marcia was not so much admired for her conversation by her acquaintance, as for her beauty and her style; a rustic reluctance still lingered in her; she was thin and dry in her talk with any one but Bartley, and she could not help letting even men perceive that she was uneasy when they interested him in matters foreign to her.

Bartley did not see why they could not have some of these fellows up in their room for tea; but Marcia told him it was impossible. In fact, although she willingly lived this irregular life with him, she was at heart not at all a Bohemian. She did not like being in lodgings or dining at restaurants; on their horse-car excursions into the suburbs, when the spring opened, she was always choosing this or that little house as the place where she would like to live, and wondering if it were within their means. She said she would gladly do the work herself; she hated to be idle so much as she now must. The city's novelty wore off for her sooner than for him: the concerts, the lectures, the theatres, had already lost their zest for her, and she went because he wished her to go, or in order to be able to help him with what he was always writing about such things.

As the spring advanced, Bartley conceived the plan of a local study, something in the manner of the boarding-house article, but on a much vaster scale: he proposed to Ricker a timely series on the easily accessible hot-weather resorts, to be called "Boston's Breathing-Places," and to relate mainly to the sea-side hotels and their surroundings. His idea was encouraged, and he took Marcia with him on most of his expeditions for its realization. These were largely made before the regular season had well begun; but the boats were already running, and the hotels were open, and they were treated with the hospitality which a knowledge of Bartley's mission must invoke. As he said, it was a matter of business, give and take on both sides, and the landlords took more than they gave in any such trade.

On her part, Marcia regarded dead-heading as a just and legitimate privilege of the press, if not one of its chief attributes; and these passes on boats and trains, this system of paying hotel bills by the presentation of a card, constituted distinguished and honorable recognition from the public. To her simple experience, when Bartley told how magnificently the reporters had been accommodated, at some civic or commercial or professional banquet, with a table of their own, where they were served with all the wines and courses, he seemed to have been one of the principal guests, and her fear was that his head should be turned by his honors. But, at the bottom of her heart, though she enjoyed the brilliancy of his present life, she did not think his occupation comparable to the law in dignity. Bartley called himself a journalist, now, but his newspaper connection still identified him in her mind with those country editors of whom she had always heard her father speak with such contempt: men dedicated to poverty and the despite of the local notables who used them. She could not shake off the old feeling of degradation, even when she heard Bartley and some of his fellow-journalists talking in their boastfulest vein of the sovereign character of journalism; and she secretly resolved never to relinquish her purpose of having him a lawyer. Till he was fairly this, in regular and prosperous practice, she knew that she should not have shown her father that she was right in marrying Bartley.

In the meantime their life went ignorantly on in the obscure channels where their isolation from society kept it longer than was natural. Three or four months after they came to Boston, they were still country people, with scarcely any knowledge of the distinctions and differences so important to the various worlds of any city. So far from knowing that they must not walk in the Common, they used to sit down on a bench there, in the pleasant weather, and watch the opening of the spring, among the lovers whose passion had a publicity that neither surprised nor shocked them. After they were a little more enlightened, they resorted to the Public Garden, where they admired the bridge, and the rockwork, and the statues. Bartley, who was already beginning to get up a taste for art, boldly stopped and praised the Venus, in the presence of the gardeners planting tulip-bulbs.

They went sometimes to the Museum of Fine Arts, where they found a pleasure in the worst things which the best never afterward gave them; and where she became as hungry and tired as if it were the Vatican. They had a pride in taking books out of the Public Library, where they walked about on tiptoe with bated breath; and they thought it a divine treat to hear the great organ play at noon. As they sat there in the Music Hall, and let the mighty instrument bellow over their strong young nerves, Bartley whispered Marcia the jokes he had heard about the organ; and then, upon the wave of aristocratic sensation from this experience, they went out and dined at Copeland's, or Weber's, or Fera's, or even at Parker's: they had long since forsaken the humble restaurant with its doilies and its ponderous crockery, and they had so mastered the art of ordering that they could manage a dinner as cheaply at these finer places as anywhere, especially if Marcia pretended not to care much for her half of the portion, and connived at its transfer to Bartley's plate.

In his hours of leisure, they were so perpetually together that it became a joke with the men who knew them to say, when asked if Bartley were married, "Very *much* married." It was not wholly their inseparableness that gave the impression of this extreme conjugality; as I said, Marcia's uneasiness when others interested Bartley in things alien to her, made itself felt even by these men. She struggled against it because she did not wish to put him to shame before them, and often with an aching sense of desolation she sent him off with them to talk apart, or left him with them if they met on the street, and walked home alone rather than let any one say that she kept her husband tied to her apron-strings. His club, after the first sense of its splendor and usefulness wore away, was an ordeal; she had failed to conceal that she thought the initiation and annual fees extravagant. She knew no other bliss like having Bartley sit down in their own room with her; it did not matter whether they talked; if he were busy, she would as lief sit and sew, or sit and silently look at him as he wrote. In these moments she liked to feign that she had lost him, that they had never been married, and then come back with a rush of joy to the reality. But on his club nights she heroically sent him off, and spent the evening with Mrs. Nash. Sometimes she went out by day with the landlady, who had a passion for auctions and cemeteries, and who led Marcia to an intimate acquaintance with such pleasures. At Mount Auburn, Marcia liked the marble lambs, and the emblematic hands pointing upward with the dexter finger, and the infants carved in stone, and the angels with folded wings and lifted eyes, better than the casts which Bartley said were from the antique, in the Museum. On this side her mind was as wholly dormant as that of Mrs. Nash herself. She always came home feeling as if she had not seen Bartley for a year, and fearful that something had happened to him. The hardest thing about their irregular life was that he must sometimes be gone two or three days at a time, when he could not take her with him. Then it seemed to her that she could not draw a full breath in his absence; and once he found her almost wild on his return: she had begun to fancy that he was never coming back again. He laughed at her when she betrayed her secret, but she was not ashamed; and when he asked her, "Well, what if I hadn't come back?" she answered passionately, "It wouldn't have made much difference to me: I should not have lived."

The uncertainty of his income was another cause of anguish to her. At times he earned forty or fifty dollars a week: oftener he earned ten; there was now and then a week when everything that he put his hand to failed, and he earned nothing at all. Then Marcia despaired; her frugality became a mania, and they had quarrels about what she called his extravagance. She imbittered his daily bread by blaming him for what he spent on it; she wore her oldest dresses, and would have had him go shabby in token of their adversity. Her economies were frantic child's-play,—methodless, inexperienced, fitful: and they were apt to be followed by remorse in which she abetted him in some wanton excess.

The future of any heroic action is difficult to manage; and the sublime sacrifice of her pride and all the conventional proprieties which Marcia had made in giving herself to Bartley was inevitably tried by the same sordid tests that every married life is put to.

That salaried place which he was always seeking on the staff

of some newspaper, proved not so easy to get as he had imagined in the flush of his first successes. Ricker willingly included him among the Chronicle-Abstract's own correspondents and special reporters; and he held the same off-and-on
relation to several other papers; but he remained without a
more definite position. He earned perhaps more money than
a salary would have given him, and in their way of living he
and Marcia laid up something out of what he earned. But it
did not seem to her that he exerted himself to get a salaried
place; she was sure that, if so many others who could not
write half so well had places, he might get one if he only kept
trying. Bartley laughed at these business-turns of Marcia's, as
he called them; but sometimes they enraged him, and he had
days of sullen resentment when he resisted all her advances
toward reconciliation. But he kept hard at work, and he always owned at last how disinterested her most ridiculous
alarm had been.

Once, when they had been talking as usual about that permanent place on some newspaper, she said,

"But I should only want that to be temporary, if you got
it. I want you should go on with the law, Bartley! I've been
thinking about that. I don't want you should always be a
journalist."

Bartley smiled.

"What could I do for a living, I should like to know, while
I was studying law?"

"You could do some newspaper work,—enough to support us,— while you were studying. You said when we first
came to Boston that you should settle down to the law."

"I hadn't got my eyes open, then. I've got a good deal
longer row to hoe than I supposed, before I can settle down
to the law."

"Father said you didn't need to study but a little more."

"Not if I were going into the practice at Equity. But it's a
very different thing, I can tell you, in Boston; I should have
to go in for a course in the Harvard Law School, just for a
little start-off."

Marcia was silenced, but she asked, after a moment:

"Then you're going to give up the law, altogether?"

"I don't know what I'm going to do; I'm going to do the

best I can for the present, and trust to luck. I don't like special reporting, for a finality; but I shouldn't like shystering, either."

"What's shystering?" asked Marcia.

"It's pettifogging in the city courts. Wait till I can get my basis,—till I have a fixed amount of money for a fixed amount of work,—and then I'll talk to you about taking up the law again. I'm willing to do it whenever it seems the right thing. I guess I should like it, though I don't see why it's any better than journalism, and I don't believe it has any more prizes."

"But you've been a long time trying to get your basis on a newspaper," she reasoned. "Why don't you try to get it in some other way? Why don't you try to get a clerk's place with some lawyer?"

"Well, suppose I was willing to starve along in that way, how should I go about to get such a place?" demanded Bartley, with impatience.

"Why don't you go to that Mr. Halleck you visited here? You used to tell me he was going to be a lawyer."

"Well, if you remember so distinctly what I said about going into the law when I first came to Boston," said her husband, angrily, "perhaps you'll remember that I said I shouldn't go to Halleck until I didn't need his help. I shall not go to him for *his* help."

Marcia gave way to spiteful tears.

"It seems as you were ashamed to let them know that you were in town. Are you afraid I shall want to get acquainted with them? Do you suppose I shall want to go to their parties, and disgrace you?"

Bartley took his cigar out of his mouth, and looked blackly at her.

"So, that's what you've been thinking, is it?"

She threw herself upon his neck.

"No! no, it isn't!" she cried, hysterically. "You know that I never thought it till this instant; you know I didn't think it at all; I just *said* it. My nerves are all gone; I don't know *what* I'm saying half the time, and you're as strict with me as if I were as well as ever! I may as well take off my things,—I'm not well enough to go with you, to-day, Bartley."

She had been dressing while they talked for an entertainment which Bartley was going to report for the Chronicle-Abstract, and now she made a feint of wishing to remove her hat. He would not let her. He said that if she did not go, he should not; he reproached her with not wishing to go with him any more; he coaxed her laughingly and fondly.

"It's only because I'm not so strong, now," she said, in a whisper that ended in a kiss on his cheek. "You must walk very slowly, and not hurry me."

The entertainment was to be given in aid of the Indigent Children's Surf-Bathing Society, and it was at the end of June, rather late in the season. But the Society itself was an after-thought, not conceived till a great many people had left town on whose assistance such a charity must largely depend. Strenuous appeals had been made, however: it was represented that ten thousand poor children could be transported to Nantasket Beach, and there, as one of the ladies on the committee said, bathed, clam-baked, and lemonaded three times during the summer at a cost so small that it was a saving to spend the money. Class Day falling about the same time, many exiles at Newport and on the North Shore came up and down; and the affair promised to be one of social distinction, if not pecuniary success. The entertainment was to be varied: a distinguished poet was to read an old poem of his, and a distinguished poetess was to read a new poem of hers; some professional people were to follow with comic singing; an elocutionist was to give impressions of noted public speakers; and a number of vocal and instrumental amateurs were to contribute their talent.

Bartley had instructions from Ricker to see that his report was very full socially. "We want something lively, and, at the same time, nice and tasteful, about the whole thing, and I guess you're the man to do it. Get Mrs. Hubbard to go with you, and keep you from making a fool of yourself about the costumes." He gave Bartley two tickets. "Mighty hard to get, I can tell you, for *love* or money, — especially love," he said; and Bartley made much of this difficulty in impressing Marcia's imagination with the uncommon character of the occasion. She had put on a new dress which she had just finished for herself, and which was a marvel not only of cheapness, but of elegance; she had plagiarized the idea from the costume of a lady with whom she stopped to look in at a milliner's window where she formed the notion of her bonnet. But Marcia had imagined the things anew in relation to herself, and made them her own; when Bartley first saw her in them, though he had witnessed their growth from the germ, he said that he was afraid of her, she was so splendid, and he did not quite know whether he felt acquainted. When they were seated at the concert, and had time to look about them, he whispered, "Well, Marsh, I don't see anything here that comes near you in style," and she flung a little corner of her drapery out over his hand so that she could squeeze it: she was quite happy again.

After the concert, Bartley left her for a moment, and went up to a group of the committee near the platform, to get some points for his report. He spoke to one of the gentlemen, note-book and pencil in hand, and the gentleman referred him to one of the ladies of the committee, who, after a moment of hesitation, demanded in a rich tone of injury and surprise, "Why! Isn't this Mr. Hubbard?" and, indignantly answering herself, "Of *course* it is!" gave her hand with a sort of dramatic cordiality, and flooded him with questions: "When did you come to Boston? Are you at the Hallecks'? Did you come— Or no, you're *not* Harvard. You're not *living* in Boston? And what in the world are *you* getting items for? Mr. Hubbard, Mr. Atherton."

She introduced him in a breathless climax to the gentleman to whom he had first spoken, and who had listened to her attack on Bartley with a smile which he was at no trouble to hide from her. "Which question are you going to answer first, Mr. Hubbard?" he asked quietly, while his eyes searched Bartley's for an instant with inquiry which was at once kind and keen. His face had the distinction which comes of being clean-shaven in our bearded times.

"Oh, the last," said Bartley. "I'm reporting the concert for the Chronicle-Abstract, and I want to interview some one in authority about it."

"Then interview *me*, Mr. Hubbard," cried the young lady. "*I'm* in authority about this affair,—it's my own invention, as the White Knight says,—and then I'll interview you after-ward. And you've gone into journalism, like all the Harvard men! So glad it's you, for you can be a perfect godsend to the cause if you will. The entertainment hasn't given us all the money we shall want, by any means, and we shall need all the help the press can give us. Ask me any questions you please, Mr. Hubbard: there isn't a soul here that I wouldn't sacrifice to the last personal particular if the press will only do its duty in return. You've no idea how we've been working during the last fortnight since this Old Man of the Sea-Bathing sprang upon us. I was sitting quietly at home, thinking of anything else in the world, I can assure you, when this atrocious idea occurred to me." She ran on to give a full sketch of the incep-tion and history of the scheme up to the present time. Sud-denly she arrested herself and Bartley's flying pencil: "Why, you're not putting all that nonsense down?"

"Certainly I am," said Bartley, while Mr. Atherton, with a laugh, turned and walked away to talk with some other ladies. "It's the very thing I want. I shall get in ahead of all the other papers on this; they haven't had anything like it, yet."

She looked at him for a moment in horror. Then:

"Well, go on; I would do anything for the cause!" she cried.

"Tell me who's been here, then," said Bartley.

She recoiled a little.

"I don't like giving names."

"But I can't say who the people were unless you do."

"That's true," said the young lady thoughtfully. She prided herself on her thoughtfulness, which sometimes came before and sometimes after the fact. "You're not obliged to say who told you?"

"Of course not."

She ran over a list of historical and distinguished names, and he slyly asked if this and that lady were not dressed so and so, and worked in the costumes from her unconsciously elaborate answers; she was afterward astonished that he should have known what people had on. Lastly he asked what the committee expected to do next, and was enabled to enrich his report with many authoritative expressions and intimations. The lady became all zeal in these confidences to the public; at last, she told everything she knew, and a great deal that she merely hoped.

"And now come into the committee-room and have a cup of coffee; I know you must be faint with all this talking," she concluded. "I want to ask you something about yourself." She was not older than Bartley, but she addressed him with the freedom we use in encouraging younger people.

"Thank you," he said coolly; "I can't very well. I must go back to my wife, and hurry up this report."

"Oh, is Mrs. Hubbard here?" asked the young lady, with well-controlled surprise. "Present me to her!" she cried, with that fearlessness of social consequences for which she was noted; she believed there were ways of getting rid of undesirable people without treating them rudely.

The audience had got out of the hall, and Marcia stood alone near one of the doors waiting for Bartley. He glanced proudly toward her, and said: "I shall be very glad."

Miss Kingsbury drifted by his side across the intervening space, and was ready to take Marcia impressively by the hand when she reached her; she had promptly decided her to be very beautiful and elegantly simple in dress, but she found her smaller than she had looked at a distance. Miss Kingsbury was herself rather large,—sometimes, she thought, rather too large: certainly too large if she had not had such perfect command of every inch of herself. In complexion she was richly blonde, with beautiful fair hair roughed over her forehead, as if by a breeze, and apt to escape in sunny tendrils over the peachy tints of her temples. Her features were massive rather than fine; and though she thoroughly admired her chin and respected her mouth, she had doubts about her nose which she frankly referred to friends for solution: had it not *too* much of a knob at the end? She seemed to tower over Marcia as she took her hand at Bartley's introduction, and expressed her pleasure at meeting her.

"I don't know why it need be such a surprise to find one's gentlemen friends married, but it always is, somehow. I don't think Mr. Hubbard would have known me if I hadn't insisted upon his recognizing me; I can't blame him: it's three years since we met. Do you help him with his reports? I know you do! You *must* make him lenient to our entertainment,—the cause is so good! How long have you been in Boston? Though I don't know why I should ask that,—you may have always been in Boston! One used to know everybody; but the place *is* so large, now. I should like to come and see you; but I'm going out of town to-morrow, for the summer. I'm not really here now, except *ex officio*; I ought to have been away weeks ago, but this Indigent Surf-Bathing has kept me. You've no idea what such an undertaking is. But you *must* let me have your address, and as soon as I get back to town in the fall, I shall insist upon looking you up. *Good*-bye! I must run away now, and leave you; there are a thousand things for me to look after yet to-day."

She took Marcia again by the hand, and superadded some bows and nods and smiles of parting, after she released her, but she did not ask her to come into the committee-room and have some coffee; and Bartley took his wife's hand under his arm and went out of the hall.

"Well," he said, with a man's simple pleasure in Miss Kingsbury's friendliness to his wife, "that's the girl I used to tell you about,—the rich one with the money in her own right, whom I met at the Hallecks'. She seemed to think you were about the thing, Marsh! I saw her eyes open as she came up, and I felt awfully proud of you: you never looked half so well. But why didn't you *say* something?"

"She didn't give me any chance," said Marcia, "and I had nothing to say, any way. I thought she was very disagreeable."

"Disagreeable!" repeated Bartley, in amaze.

Miss Kingsbury went back to the committee-room, where one of the amateurs had been lecturing upon her.

"Clara Kingsbury can say and do, from the best heart in the world, more offensive things in ten minutes than malice could invent in a week. Somebody ought to go out and drag her away from that reporter by main force. But I presume it's too late already; she's had time to destroy us all. You'll see that there wont be a shred left of us in *his* paper, at any rate. Really, I wonder that, in a city full of nervous and exasperated people like Boston, Clara Kingsbury has been suffered to live. She throws her whole soul into everything she undertakes, and she has gone so *en masse* into this Indigent Bathing, and splashed about in it so, that *I* can't understand how we got anybody to come to-day. Why, I haven't the least doubt that she's offered that poor man a ticket to go down to Nantasket and bathe with the other Indigents; she's treated *me* as if I ought to be personally surf-bathed for the last fortnight; and if there's any chance for us left by her tactlessness, you may be sure she's gone at it with her conscience, and simply swept it off the face of the earth."

XVIII

ONE HOT DAY in August, when Bartley had been doing nothing for a week, and Marcia was gloomily forecasting the future, when they would have to begin living upon the money they had put into the savings-bank, she reverted to the question of his taking up the law again. She was apt to recur to this in any moment of discouragement, and she urged him now to give up his newspaper work, with that wearisome persistence with which women can torment the men they love.

"My newspaper work seems to have given me up, my dear," said Bartley. "It's like asking a fellow not to marry a girl that wont have him." He laughed and then whistled; and Marcia burst into fretful, futile tears, which he did not attempt to assuage.

They had been all summer in town; the country would have been no change to them; and they knew nothing of the sea-side, except the crowded, noisy, expensive resorts near the city. Bartley wished her to go to one of these for a week or two, at any rate, but she would not; and in fact neither of them had the born citizen's conception of the value of a summer vacation. But they had found their attic intolerable; and, the single gentlemen having given up their rooms by this time, Mrs. Nash let Marcia have one lower down, where they sat looking out on the hot street.

"Well," cried Marcia at last, "you don't care for my feelings, or you would take up the law again."

Her husband rose with a sigh that was half a curse, and went out. After what she had said, he would not give her the satisfaction of knowing what he meant to do; but he had it in his head to go to that Mr. Atherton to whom Miss Kingsbury had introduced him, and ask his advice; he had found out that Mr. Atherton was a lawyer, and he believed that he would tell him what to do. He could at least give him some authoritative discouragement which he might use in these discussions with Marcia.

Mr. Atherton had his office in the Events building, and Bartley was on his way thither when he met Ricker.

"Seen Witherby?" asked his friend. "He was round looking for you."

"What does Witherby want with me?" asked Bartley, with a certain resentment.

"Wants to give you the managing-editorship of the Events," said Ricker, jocosely.

"Pshaw! Well, he knows where to find me, if he wants me very badly."

"Perhaps he doesn't," suggested Ricker. "In that case, you'd better look him up."

"Why, you don't advise"—

"Oh, *I* don't advise anything! But if *he* can let by-gones be by-gones, I guess *you* can afford to! I don't know just what he wants with you, but if he offers you anything like a basis, you'd better take it."

Bartley's basis had come to be a sort of by-word between them; Ricker usually met him with some such demand as, "Well, what about the basis?" or "How's your poor basis?" Bartley's ardor for a salaried position amused him, and he often tried to argue him out of it. "You're much better off as a free lance. You make as much money as most of the fellows in places, and you lead a pleasanter life. If you were on any one paper, you'd have to be on duty about fifteen hours out of the twenty-four; you'd be out every night till three or four o'clock; you'd have to do fires, and murders, and all sorts of police business; and now you work mostly on fancy jobs: something you suggest yourself, or something you're specially asked to do. That's a kind of a compliment, and it gives you scope."

Nevertheless, if Bartley had his heart set upon a basis, Ricker wanted him to have it. "Of course," he said, "I was only joking about the basis. But if Witherby should have something permanent to offer, don't quarrel with your bread and butter, and don't hold yourself *too* cheap. Witherby's going to get all he can, for as little as he can, every time."

Ricker was a newspaper man in every breath. His great interest in life was the Chronicle-Abstract, which paid him poorly and worked him hard. To get in ahead of the other papers was the object for which he toiled with unremitting zeal; but after that he liked to see a good fellow prosper, and he had for Bartley that feeling of comradery which comes out among journalists when their rivalries are off. He would hate to lose Bartley from the Chronicle-Abstract; if Witherby meant business, Bartley and he might be excoriating each other before a week passed, in sarcastic references to "our esteemed contemporary of the Events," and "our esteemed contemporary of the Chronicle-Abstract"; but he heartily wished him luck, and hoped it might be some sort of inside work.

When Ricker left him, Bartley hesitated. He was half minded to go home and wait for Witherby to look him up, as the most dignified and perhaps the most prudent course. But he was curious and impatient, and he was afraid of letting the chance, whatever it might be, slip through his fingers. He suddenly resolved upon a little ruse, which would still oblige Witherby to make the advance, and yet would risk nothing by delay. He mounted to Witherby's room in the Events building, and pushed open the door. Then he drew back embarrassed, as if he had made a mistake.

"Excuse me," he said, "isn't Mr. Atherton's office on this floor?"

Witherby looked up from the papers on his desk, and cleared his throat. When he overreached himself he was apt to hold any party to the transaction accountable for his error. Ever since he refused Bartley's paper on the logging-camp, he had accused him in his heart of fraud because he had sold the rejected sketch to another paper, and anticipated Witherby's tardy enterprise in the same direction. Each little success that Bartley made added to Witherby's dislike; and whilst Bartley had written for all the other papers, he had never got any work from the Events. Witherby had the guilty sense of having hated him as he looked up, and Bartley on his part was uneasily sensible of some mocking paragraphs of a more or less personal cast, which he had written in the Chronicle-Abstract, about the enterprise of the Events.

"Mr. Atherton is on the floor above," said Witherby. "But I'm very glad you happened to look in, Mr. Hubbard. I—I was just thinking about you. Ah—wont you take a chair?"

"Thanks," said Bartley, non-committally; but he sat down in the chair which the other rose to offer him.

Witherby fumbled about among the things on his desk before he resumed his own seat.

"I hope you have been well since I saw you?"

"Oh, yes, I'm always well. How have you been?"

Bartley wondered whither this exchange of civilities tended; but he believed he could keep it up as long as old Witherby could.

"Why, I have not been very well," said Witherby, getting into his chair and taking up a paper-weight to help him in talk. "The fact is, I find that I have been working too hard. I have undertaken to manage the editorial department of the Events in addition to looking after its business, and the care has been too great. It has told upon me. I flatter myself that I have not allowed either department to suffer"—

He referred this point so directly to him that Bartley made a murmur of assent, and Witherby resumed.

"But the care has told upon me. I am not so well as I could wish. I need rest, and I need help," he added.

Bartley had by this time made up his mind that, if Witherby had anything to say to him, he should say it unaided.

Witherby put down the paper-weight, and gave his attention for a moment to a paper-cutter.

"I don't know whether you have heard that Mr. Clayton is going to leave us?"

"No," Bartley said, "I hadn't heard that."

"Yes, he is going to leave us. Mr. Clayton and I have not agreed upon some points, and we have both judged it best that we should part." Witherby paused again, and changed the positions of his inkstand and mucilage-bottle. "Mr. Clayton has failed me, as I may say, at the last moment, and we have been compelled to part. I found Mr. Clayton—unpractical."

He looked again at Bartley, who said,

"Yes?"

"Yes. I found Mr. Clayton so much at variance in his views with—with my own views—that I could do nothing with him. He has used language to me which I am sure he will regret. But that is neither here nor there; he is going. I have had my eye on you, Mr. Hubbard, ever since you came to Boston, and have watched your career with interest. But I thought of Mr. Clayton, in the first instance, because he was already attached to the Events, and I wished to promote him. Office during good behavior, and promotion in the direct line: I'm *that* much of a civil-service reformer," said Witherby.

"Certainly," said Bartley.

"But, of course, my idea in starting the Events was to make money."

"Of course."

"I hold that the first duty of a public journal is to make money for the owner; all the rest follows naturally."

"You're quite right, Mr. Witherby," said Bartley. "Unless it makes money, there can be no enterprise about it, no independence,—nothing. That was the way I did with my little paper down in Maine. The first thing—I told the committee when I took hold of the paper—is to keep it from losing money; the next is to make money with it. First peaceable, then pure: that's what I told them."

"Precisely so!" Witherby was now so much at his ease with Bartley that he left off tormenting the things on his desk, and used his hands in gesticulating.

"Look at the churches themselves! No church can do any good till it's on a paying basis. As long as a church is in debt, it can't secure the best talent for the pulpit or the choir, and the members go about feeling discouraged and out of heart. It's just so with a newspaper. I say that a paper does no good till it pays; it has no influence, its motives are always suspected, and you've got to make it pay by hook or by crook before you can hope to—to—forward any good cause by it. That's what *I* say. Of course," he added, in a large, smooth way, "I'm not going to contend that a newspaper should be run *solely* in the interest of the counting-room. Not at all! But I do contend that when the counting-room protests against a certain course the editorial-room is taking, it ought to be respectfully listened to. There are always two sides to every question. Suppose all the newspapers pitch in—as they sometimes do—and denounce a certain public enterprise: a projected scheme of railroad legislation, or a peculiar system of banking, or a coöperative mining interest, and the counting-room sends up word that the company advertises heavily with us; shall *we* go and join indiscriminately in that hue and cry, or shall we give our friends the benefit of the doubt?"

"Give them the benefit of the doubt," answered Bartley. "That's what I say."

"And so would any other practical man!" said Witherby. "And that's just where Mr. Clayton and I differed. Well, I needn't allude to him any more," he added, leniently. "What I wish to say is this, Mr. Hubbard: I am overworked, and I feel the need of some sort of relief. I know that I have started the Events in the right line at last,—the only line in which it can be made a great, useful, and respectable journal, efficient in every good cause,—and what I want now is some sort of assistant in the management who shall be in full sympathy with my own ideas. I don't want a mere slave,—a tool; but I do want an independent, right-minded man, who shall be with me for the success of the paper the whole time and every time, and shall not be continually setting up his will against mine on all sorts of *doctrinaire* points. That was the trouble with Mr. Clayton. I have nothing against Mr. Clayton personally; he is an excellent young man in very many respects; but he was all wrong about journalism, all wrong, Mr. Hubbard. I talked with him a great deal, and tried to make him see where his interest lay. He had been on the paper as a reporter from the start, and I wished very much to promote him to this position; which he could have made the best position in the country. The Events is an evening paper; there is no night-work; and the whole thing is already thoroughly systematized. Mr. Clayton had plenty of talent, and all he had to do was to step in under my direction and put his hand on the helm. But, no! I should have been glad to keep him in a subordinate capacity; but I had to let him go. He said that he would not report the conflagration of a peanut-stand for a paper conducted on the principles I had developed to him. Now, that is no way to talk. It's absurd."

"Perfectly." Bartley laughed his rich, caressing laugh, in which there was the insinuation of all worldly-wise contempt for Clayton and all worldly-wise sympathy with Witherby. It made Witherby feel good, better, perhaps, than he had felt at any time since his talk with Clayton.

"Well, now, what do you say, Mr. Hubbard? Can't we make some arrangement with you?" he asked, with a burst of frankness.

"I guess you can," said Bartley. The fact that Witherby needed him was so plain that he did not care to practice any finesse about the matter.

"What are your present engagements?"

"I haven't any."

"Then you can take hold at once?"

"Yes."

"That's good."

Witherby now entered at large into the nature of the position which he offered Bartley. They talked a long time, and in becoming better acquainted with each other's views, as they called them, they became better friends. Bartley began to respect Witherby's business ideas, and Witherby, in recognizing all the admirable qualities of this clear-sighted and level-headed young man, began to feel that he had secretly liked him from the first, and had only waited a suitable occasion to unmask his affection. It was arranged that Bartley should come on as Witherby's assistant, and should do whatever he was asked to do in the management of the paper; he was to write on topics as they occurred to him, or as they were suggested to him. "I don't say whether this will lead to anything more, Mr. Hubbard, or not; but I do say that you will be in the direct line of promotion."

"Yes, I understand that," said Bartley.

"And now as to terms," continued Witherby, a little tremulously.

"And now as to terms," repeated Bartley to himself; but he said nothing aloud. He felt that Witherby had cut out a great deal of work for him, and work of a kind that he could not easily find another man both willing and able to do. He resolved that he would have all that his service was worth.

"What should you think of twenty dollars a week?" asked Witherby.

"I shouldn't think it was enough," said Bartley, amazed at

his own audacity, but enjoying it, and thinking how he had left Marcia with the intention of offering himself to Mr. Atherton as a clerk for ten dollars a week. "There is a great deal of labor in what you propose, and you command my whole time. You would not like to have me do any work outside of the Events."

"No," Witherby assented. "Would twenty-five be nearer the mark?" he inquired soberly.

"It would be nearer, certainly," said Bartley. "But I guess you had better make it thirty." He kept a quiet face, but his heart throbbed.

"Well, say thirty, then," replied Witherby, so promptly that Bartley perceived with a pang that he might as easily have got forty from him. But it was now too late, and a salary of fifteen hundred a year passed the wildest hopes he had cherished half an hour before.

"All right," he said quietly. "I suppose you want me to take hold at once?"

"Yes, on Monday. Oh, by the way," said Witherby, "there is one little piece of outside work which I should like you to finish up for us; and we'll agree upon something extra for it, if you wish. I mean our 'Solid Men' series. I don't know whether you've noticed the series in the Events?"

"Yes," said Bartley, "I have."

"Well, then, you know what they are. They consist of interviews—guarded and inoffensive as respects the sanctity of private life—with our leading manufacturers and merchant princes at their places of business and their residences, and include a description of these, and some account of the lives of the different subjects."

"Yes, I have seen them," said Bartley. "I've noticed the general plan."

"You know that Mr. Clayton has been doing them. He made them a popular feature. The parties themselves were very much pleased with them."

"Oh, people are always tickled to be interviewed," said Bartley. "I know they put on airs about it, and go round complaining to each other about the violation of confidence, and so on; but they all like it. You know I reported that Indigent Surf-Bathing entertainment, in June, for the Chronicle-

Abstract. I knew the lady who got it up, and I interviewed her after the entertainment."

"Miss Kingsbury?"

"Yes." Witherby made an inarticulate murmur of respect for Bartley in his throat, and involuntarily changed toward him, but not so subtly that Bartley's finer instinct did not take note of the change. "She was a fresh subject, and she told me everything. Of course I printed it all. She was awfully shocked—or pretended to be—and wrote me a very Oh-dear-how-could-you note about it. But I went round to the office the next day, and I found that nearly every lady mentioned in the interview had ordered half a dozen copies of that issue sent to her sea-side address, and the office had been full of Beacon-street swells the whole morning buying Chronicle-Abstracts—'the one with the report of the concert in it.'" These low views of high society, coupled with an apparent familiarity with it, modified Witherby more and more. He began to see that he had got a prize. "The way to do with such fellows as your 'Solid Men,'" continued Bartley, "is to submit a proof to 'em. They never know exactly what to do about it, and so you print the interview with their approval, and make 'em *particeps criminis*. I'll finish up the series for you, and I wont make any very heavy extra charge."

"I should wish to pay you whatever the work was worth," said Witherby, not to be outdone in nobleness.

"All right; we sha'n't quarrel about that, at any rate."

Bartley was getting toward the door, for he was eager to be gone now to Marcia, but Witherby followed him up as if willing to detain him.

"My wife," he said, "knows Miss Kingsbury. They have been on the same charities together."

"I met her a good while ago, when I was visiting a chum of mine at his father's house here. I didn't suppose she'd know me; but she did at once, and began to ask me if I was at the Hallecks',—as if I had never gone away."

"Mr. Ezra B. Halleck?" inquired Witherby reverently. "Leather trade?"

"Yes," said Bartley. "I believe his first name was Ezra. Ben Halleck was my friend. Do you know the family?" asked Bartley.

"Yes, we have met them—in society. I hope you're pleasantly situated where you are, Mr. Hubbard? Should be glad
to have you call at the house."

"Thank you," said Bartley; "my wife will be glad to have
Mrs. Witherby call."

"Oh!" cried Witherby. "I didn't know you were married!
That's good! There's nothing like marriage, Mr. Hubbard, to
keep a man going in the right direction. But you've begun
pretty young."

"Nothing like taking a thing in time," answered Bartley.
"But I haven't been married a great while; and I'm not so
young as I look. Well, good-afternoon, Mr. Witherby."

"*What* did you say was your address?" asked Witherby, taking out his note-book. "My wife will certainly call. She's
down at Nantasket now, but she'll be up the first part of September, and then she'll call. *Good*-afternoon."

They shook hands at last, and Bartley ran home to Marcia.
He burst into the room with a glowing face.

"Well, Marcia," he shouted, "I've got my basis!"

"Hush! No! Don't be so loud! You haven't!" she answered,
springing to her feet. "I don't believe it! How hot you are!"

"I've been running almost—all the way from the Events
office. I've got a place on the Events,—assistant managing-
editor,—thirty dollars a week," he panted.

"I knew you would succeed yet—I knew you would, if I
could only have a little patience. I've been scolding myself
ever since you went. I thought you were going to do something desperate, and I had driven you to it. But Bartley, Bartley! It can't be true, is it? Here, here! Do take this fan. Or
no, I'll fan you, if you'll let me sit on your knee! O poor
thing, how hot you are! But I thought you wouldn't write
for the Events; I thought you hated that old Witherby, who
acted so ugly to you when you first came."

"Oh, Witherby is a pretty good old fellow," said Bartley,
who had begun to get his breath again. He gave her a full
history of the affair, and they rejoiced together over it, and
were as happy as if Bartley had been celebrating a high and
honorable good fortune. She was too ignorant to feel the disgrace, if there were any, in the compact which Bartley had
closed, and he had no principles, no traditions by which to

perceive it. To them it meant unlimited prosperity, it meant provision for the future, which was to bring a new responsibility and a new care.

"We will take the parlor with the alcove, now," said Bartley. "Don't excite yourself," he added, with tender warning.

"No, no," she said, pillowing her head on his shoulder, and shedding peaceful tears.

"It doesn't seem as if we should ever quarrel again, does it?"

"No, no! We never shall," she murmured. "It has always come from my worrying you about the law, and I shall never do that any more. If you like journalism better, I shall not urge you any more to leave it, now you've got your basis."

"But I'm going on with the law, now, for that very reason. I shall read law all my leisure time. I feel independent, and I shall not be anxious about the time I give, because I shall know that I can afford it."

"Well, only you mustn't overdo." She put her lips against his cheek. "You're more to me than anything you can do for me."

"Oh, Marcia!"

XIX

Now that Bartley had got his basis, and had no favors to ask of any one, he was curious to see his friend Halleck again; but when, in the course of the "Solid Men Series," he went to interview the "Nestor of the Leather Interest," as he meant to call the elder Halleck, he resolved to let him make all the advances. On a legitimate business errand it should not matter to him whether Mr. Halleck welcomed him or not. The old man did not wait for Bartley to explain why he came; he was so simply glad to see him that Bartley felt a little ashamed to confess that he had been eight months in Boston without making himself known. He answered all the personal questions with which Mr. Halleck plied him; and in his turn he inquired after his college friend.

"Ben is in Europe," said his father. "He has been there all summer; but we expect him home about the middle of September. He's been a good while settling down," continued the old man, with an unconscious sigh. "He talked of the law at first, and then he went into business with me; but he didn't seem to find his calling in it; and now he's taken up the law again. He's been in the law school at Cambridge, and he's going back there for a year or two longer. I thought you used to talk of the law yourself when you were with us, Mr. Hubbard."

"Yes, I did," Bartley assented. "And I haven't given up the notion yet. I've read a good deal of law already; but when I came up to Boston, I had to go into newspaper work till I could see my way out of the woods."

"Well," said Mr. Halleck, "that's right. And you say you like the arrangement you've made with Mr. Witherby?"

"It's ideal—for me," answered Bartley.

"Well, that's good," said the old man. "And you've come to interview me. Well, that's all right. I'm not much used to being in print, but I shall be glad to tell you all I know about leather."

"You may depend upon my not asking anything that will be disagreeable to you, Mr. Halleck," said Bartley, touched

358

by the old man's trusting friendliness. When his inquisition ended, he slipped his note-book back into his pocket, and said with a smile:

"We usually say something about the victim's private residence, but I guess I'll spare you that, Mr. Halleck."

"Why, we live in the old place, and I don't suppose there is much to say. We are plain people, and we don't like to change. When I built there, thirty years ago, Rumford street was one of the most desirable streets in Boston. There was no Back Bay, then, you know, and we thought we were doing something very fashionable. But fashion has drifted away, and left us high and dry enough on Rumford street; though we don't mind it. We keep the old house and the old garden pretty much as you saw them. You can say whatever you think best. There's a good deal of talk about the intrusiveness of the newspapers; all I know is that they've never intruded upon me. We shall not be afraid that you will abuse our house, Mr. Hubbard, because we expect you to come there again. When shall it be? Mrs. Halleck and I have been at home all summer; we find it the most comfortable place; and we shall be very glad if you'll drop in any evening and take tea with us. We keep the old hours; we've never taken kindly to the late dinners. The girls are off at the mountains, and you'd see nobody but Mrs. Halleck. Come this evening!" cried the old man, with mounting cordiality.

His warmth, as he put his hand on Bartley's shoulder, made the young man blush again for the reserve with which he had been treating his own affairs. He stammered out, hoping that the other would see the relevancy of the statement:

"Why, the fact is, Mr. Halleck, I—I'm married."

"Married!" said Mr. Halleck. "Why didn't you tell me before? Of course we want Mrs. Hubbard, too. Where are you living? We wont stand upon ceremony among old friends. Mrs. Halleck will come with the carriage and fetch Mrs. Hubbard, and your wife must take that for a call. Why, you don't know how glad we shall be to have you both! I wish Ben was married. You'll come?"

"Of course we will," said Bartley. "But you mustn't let Mrs. Halleck send for us; we can walk perfectly well."

"*You* can walk if you want, but Mrs. Hubbard shall ride," said the old man.

When Bartley reported this to Marcia,

"Bartley!" she cried. "In her carriage? I'm afraid!"

"Nonsense! She'll be a great deal more afraid than you are. She's the bashfulest old lady you ever saw. All that I hope is that you wont overpower her."

"Bartley, hush! Shall I wear my silk, or"—

"Oh, wear the silk, by all means. Crush them at a blow!"

Rumford street is one of those old-fashioned thoroughfares at the west end of Boston, which are now almost wholly abandoned to boarding-houses of the poorer class. Yet they are charming streets, quiet, clean, and respectable, and worthy still to be the homes, as they once were, of solid citizens. The red brick houses, with their swell fronts, looking in perspective like a succession of round towers, are reached by broad granite steps, and their doors are deeply sunken within the wagon-roofs of white-painted Roman arches. Over the door there is sometimes the bow of a fine transom, and the parlor windows on the first floor of the swell front have the same azure gleam as those of the beautiful old houses which front the Common on Beacon street.

When her husband bought his lot there, Mrs. Halleck could hardly believe that a house on Rumford street was not too fine for her. They had come to the city simple and good young village people, and simple and good they had remained, through the advancing years which had so wonderfully—Mrs. Halleck hoped, with a trembling heart, not wickedly—prospered them. They were of faithful stock, and they had been true to their traditions in every way. One of these was constancy to the orthodox religious belief in which their young hearts had united, and which had blessed all their life; though their charity now abounded perhaps more than their faith. They still believed that for themselves there was no spiritual safety except in their church; but since their younger children had left it, they were forced tacitly to own that this might not be so in all cases. Their last endeavor for the church in Ben's case was to send him to the college where he and Bartley met; and this was such a failure on the main point, that it left them remorsefully indulgent. He had submitted, and had foregone his boyish dreams of Harvard, where all his mates were going; but the sacrifice seemed to have put him at odds with life. The years which had proved the old people mistaken would not come back upon their recognition of their error. He returned to the associations from which they had exiled him too much estranged to resume them, and they saw, with the unavailing regrets which visit fathers and mothers in such cases, that the young know their own world better than their elders can know it, and have a right to be in it and of it, superior to any theory of their advantage which their elders can form. Ben was not the fellow to complain; in fact, after he came home from college, he was allowed to shape his life according to his own rather fitful liking. His father was glad now to content him in anything he could, it was so very little that Ben asked. If he had suffered it, perhaps his family would have spoiled him.

The Halleck girls went early in July to the Profile House, where they had spent their summers for many years; but the old people preferred to stay at home, and only left their large, comfortable house for short absences. Their ways of life had been fixed in other times, and Mrs. Halleck liked better than mountain or sea the high-walled garden that stretched back of their house to the next street. They had bought through to this street when they built, but they had never sold the lot that fronted on it. They laid it out in box-bordered beds, and there were clumps of hollyhocks, sunflowers, lilies, and phlox in different corners; grapes covered the trellised walls; there were some pear-trees that bore blossoms and sometimes ripened their fruit beside the walk. Mrs. Halleck used to work in the garden; her husband seldom descended into it, but he liked to sit on the iron-railed balcony overlooking it from the back parlor.

As for the interior of the house, it had been furnished, once for all, in the worst style of that most tasteless period of household art which prevailed from 1840 to 1870; and it would be impossible to say which was most hideous, the carpets or the chandeliers, the curtains or the chairs and sofas; crude colors, lumpish and meaningless forms, abounded in a rich and horrible discord. The old people thought it all beautiful, and those daughters who had come into the new house as little girls revered it; but Ben and his youngest sister, who had been born in the house, used the right of children of their parents' declining years to laugh at it. Yet they laughed with a sort of filial tenderness.

"I suppose you know how frightful you have everything about you, Olive?" said Clara Kingsbury, one day after the Eastlake movement began, as she took a comprehensive survey of the Halleck drawing-room through her *pince-nez*.

"Certainly," answered the youngest Miss Halleck. "It's a perfect chamber of horrors. But I like it, because everything's so exquisitely in keeping."

"Really, I feel as if I had seen it all for the first time," said Miss Kingsbury. "I don't believe I ever realized it before."

She and Olive Halleck were great friends, though Clara was fashionable and Olive was not.

"It would all have been different," Ben used to say, in whimsical sarcasm of what he had once believed, "if I had gone to Harvard. Then the fellows in my class would have come to the house with me, and we should have got into the right set naturally. Now, we're outside of everything, and it makes me mad, because we've got money enough to be inside, and there's nothing to prevent it. Of course, I'm not going to say that leather is quite as blameless as cotton, socially, but taken in the wholesale form it isn't so very malodorous; and it's quite as good as other things that are accepted."

"It's not the leather, Ben," answered Olive, "and it's not your not going to Harvard altogether, though that has something to do with it. The trouble's in me. I was at school with all those girls Clara goes with, and I could have been in that set if I'd wanted; but I didn't really want to. I saw, at a very tender age, that it was going to be more trouble than it was worth, and I just quietly kept out of it. Of course, I couldn't have gone to Papanti's without a fuss, but mother would have let me go if I had made the fuss; and I could be hand and glove with those girls now, if I tried. They come here whenever I ask them; and when I meet them on charities, I'm awfully popular. No, if I'm not fashionable, it's my own fault. But what difference does it make to you, Ben? You dont want to marry any of those girls as long as your heart's set on that unknown charmer of yours." Ben had once seen his charmer in the street of a little Down-East town, where he met her walking with some other boarding-school girls; in a freak, with his fellow-students, he had bribed the village photographer to let him have the picture of this young lady, which he had sent home to Olive, marked, "My Lost Love."

"No, I don't want to marry anybody," said Ben. "But I hate to live in a town where I'm not first chop in everything."

"Pshaw!" cried his sister, "I guess it doesn't trouble you much."

"Well, I don't know that it does," he admitted.

Mrs. Halleck's black coachman drove her to Mrs. Nash's door on Canary Place, where she alighted and rang with as great perturbation as if it had been a palace, and these poor young people to whom she was going to be kind were princes. It was sufficient that they were strangers; but Marcia's anxiety, evident even to meekness like Mrs. Halleck's, restored her somewhat to her self-possession; and the thought that Bartley, in spite of his personal splendor, was a friend of Ben's, was a help, and she got home with her guests without great chasms in the conversation, though she never ceased to twist the window-tassel in her embarrassment.

Mr. Halleck came to her rescue at her own door, and let them in. He shook hands with Bartley again, and viewed Marcia with a fatherly friendliness that took away half her awe of the ugly magnificence of the interior. But still she admired that Bartley could be so much at his ease. He pointed to a stick at the foot of the hat-rack, and said, "How much that looks like Halleck!" which made the old man laugh, and clap him on the shoulder, and cry: "So it does! so it does! Recognized it, did you? Well, we shall soon have him with us again, now. Seems a long time to us since he went."

"Still limps a little?" asked Bartley.

"Yes, I guess he'll never quite get over that."

"I don't believe I should like him to," said Bartley. "He wouldn't seem natural without a cane in his hand, or hanging by the crook over his left elbow, while he stood and talked."

The old man clapped Bartley on the shoulder again, and laughed again at the image suggested.

"That's so! that's so! You're right, I *guess*!"

As soon as Marcia could lay off her things in the gorgeous chamber to which Mrs. Halleck had shown her, they went out to tea in the dining-room overlooking the garden.

"Seems natural, don't it?" asked the old man, as Bartley turned to one of the windows.

"Not changed a bit, except that I was here in winter, and I hadn't a chance to see how pretty your garden was."

"It *is* pretty, isn't it?" said the old man. "Mother—Mrs. Halleck, I mean—looks after it. She keeps it about right. Here's Cyrus!" he said, as the serving-man came into the room with something from the kitchen in his hands. "You remember Cyrus, I guess, Mr. Hubbard?"

"Oh, yes!" said Bartley, and when Cyrus had set down his dish, Bartley shook hands with the New Hampshire exemplar of freedom and equality; he was no longer so young as to wish to mark a social difference between himself and the inside man who had served Mr. Halleck with unimpaired self-respect for twenty-five years.

There was a vacant place at table, and Mr. Halleck said he hoped it would be taken by a friend of theirs. He explained that the possible guest was his lawyer, whose office Ben was going into after he left the law school; and presently Mr. Atherton came. Bartley was prepared to be introduced anew, but he was flattered and the Hallecks were pleased to find that he and Mr. Atherton were already acquainted; the latter was so friendly that Bartley was confirmed in his belief that you could not make an interview too strong, for he had celebrated Mr. Atherton among the other people present at the Indigent Surf-Bathing entertainment.

Mr. Atherton was put next to Marcia, and after a while he began to talk with her, feeling with a tacit skill for her highest note, and striking that with kindly perseverance. It was not a very high note, and it was not always a certain sound. She could not be sure that he was really interested in the simple matters he had set her to talking about, and from time to time she was afraid that Bartley did not like it; she would not have liked him to talk so long or so freely with a lady. But she found herself talking on, about boarding, and her own preference for keeping house; about Equity, and what sort of place it was, and how far from Crawford's; about Boston, and what she had seen and done there since she had come in the winter. Most of her remarks began or ended with Mr. Hubbard; many of her opinions, especially in matters of taste, were frank repetitions of what Mr. Hubbard thought; her conversation had the charm and pathos of that of the young wife who devotedly loves her husband, who lives in him and for him, tests everything by him, refers everything to him. She had a good mind, though it was as bare as it could well be of most of the things that the ladies of Mr. Atherton's world put into their minds.

Mrs. Halleck made from time to time a little murmur of satisfaction in Marcia's loyalty, and then sank back into the meek silence which she only emerged from to propose more tea to some one, or to direct Cyrus about offering this dish or that.

After they rose, she took Marcia about and showed her the house, ending with the room which Bartley had had when he visited there. They sat down in this room and had a long chat, and when they came back to the parlor they found Mr. Atherton already gone. Marcia inferred the early habits of the household from the departure of this older friend, but Bartley was in no hurry; he was enjoying himself, and he could not see that Mr. Halleck seemed at all sleepy.

Mrs. Halleck wished to send them home in her carriage, but they would not hear of this; they would far rather walk, and when they had been followed to the door, and bidden to mind the steps as they went down, the wide open night did not seem too large for their content in themselves and each other.

"Did you have a nice time?" asked Bartley, though he knew he need not.

"The best time I ever had in the world!" cried Marcia.

They discussed the whole affair; the two old people; Mr. Atherton, and how pleasant he was; the house and its splendors, which they did not know were hideous.

"Bartley," said Marcia at last, "I *told* Mrs. Halleck."

"Did you?" he returned, in trepidation; but after a while he laughed. "Well, all right, if you wanted to."

"Yes, I did; and you can't think how kind she was. She says we must have a house of our own somewhere, and she's going round with me in her carriage to help me to find one."

"Well," said Bartley, and he fetched a sigh, half of pride, half of dismay.

"Yes, I long to go to housekeeping. We can afford it now. She says we can get a cheap little house, or half a house, up at the South End, and it wont cost us any more than to board, hardly; and that's what I think, too."

"Go ahead, if you can find the house. I don't object to my own fireside. And I suppose we must."

"Yes, we must. Aint you glad of it?"

They were in the shadow of a tall house, and he dropped his face toward the face she lifted to his, and gave her a silent kiss that made her heart leap toward him.

XX

WITH the other news that Halleck's mother gave him on his return, she told him of the chance that had brought his old college comrade to them again, and how Bartley was now married, and was just settled in the little house she had helped his wife to find.

"He has married a very pretty girl," she said.

"Oh, I dare say!" answered her son. "He isn't the fellow to have married a plain girl."

"Your father and I have been to call upon them in their new house, and they seem very happy together. Mr. Hubbard wants you should come to see them. He talks a great deal about you."

"I'll look them up in good time," said the young man. "Hubbard's ardor to see me will keep."

That evening Mr. Atherton came to tea, and Halleck walked home with him to his lodgings, which were over the hill, and beyond the Public Garden.

"Yes, it's very pleasant, getting back," he said, as they sauntered down the Common side of Beacon street, "and the old town is picturesque after the best they can do across the water."

He halted his friend, and brought himself to a rest on his cane, for a look over the hollow of the Common and the level of the Garden, where the late September dark was keenly spangled with lamps. "'My heart leaps up,' and so forth, when I see that. Now that Athens and Florence and Edinburgh are past, I don't think there is any place quite so well worth being born in as Boston." He moved forward again, gently surging with his limp, in a way that had its charm for those that loved him. "It's more authentic and individual, more municipal, after the old pattern, than any other modern city. It gives its stamp, it characterizes. The Boston Irishman, the Boston Jew, is a quite different Irishman or Jew from those of other places. Even Boston provinciality is a precious testimony to the authoritative personality of the city. Cosmopolitanism is a modern vice, and we're antique, we're classic, in the other thing. Yes, I'd rather be a Bostonian, at odds with Boston, than one of the curled darlings of any other community."

A friend knows how to allow for mere quantity in your talk, and only replies to the quality; separates your earnest from your whimsicality, and accounts for some whimsicality in your earnest.

"I didn't know but you might have got that bee out of your bonnet on the other side," said Atherton.

"No, sir; we change our skies but not our bees. What should I amount to without my grievance? You wouldn't have known me. This talk to-night about Hubbard has set my bee to buzzing with uncommon liveliness; and the thought of the law school next week does nothing to allay him. The law school isn't Harvard; I realize that more and more, though I have tried to fancy that it was. No, sir, my wrongs are irreparable. I had the making of a real Harvard man in me, and of a Unitarian, nicely balanced between radicalism and amateur episcopacy. Now, I am an orthodox ruin, and the undutiful step-son of a Down-East *alma mater*. I belong nowhere; I'm at odds. Is Hubbard's wife really handsome, or is she only country-pretty?"

"She's beautiful,—I assure you, she's beautiful," said Atherton, with such earnestness that Halleck laughed.

"Well, that's right, as my father says. How's she beautiful?"

"That's difficult to tell. It's rather a superb sort of style; and—What did you really use to think of your friend?" Atherton broke off to ask.

"Who? Hubbard?"

"Yes."

"He was a poor, cheap sort of a creature. Deplorably smart, and regrettably handsome. A fellow that assimilated everything to a certain extent, and nothing thoroughly. A fellow with no more moral nature than a base-ball. The sort of chap you'd expect to find, the next time you met him, in Congress or the house of correction."

"Yes, that accounts for it," said Atherton, thoughtfully.

"Accounts for what?"

"The sort of look she had. A look as if she were naturally

above him, and had somehow fascinated herself with him, and were worshiping him in some sort of illusion."

"Doesn't that sound a little like refining upon the facts? Recollect, I've never seen her, and I don't say you're wrong."

"I'm not sure I'm not, though. I talked with her, and found her nothing more than honest and sensible and good; simple in her traditions, of course, and countrified yet, in her ideas, with a tendency to the intensely practical. I don't see why she mightn't very well be his wife. I suppose every woman hoodwinks herself about her husband in some degree."

"Yes; and we always like to fancy something pathetic in the fate of pretty girls that other fellows marry. I notice that we don't sorrow much over the plain ones. How's the divine Clara?"

"I believe she's well," said Atherton. "I haven't seen her, all summer. She's been at Beverly."

"Why, I should have supposed she would have come up and surf-bathed those indigent children with her own hand. She's equal to it. What made her falter in well-doing?"

"I don't know that we can properly call it faltering. There was a deficit in the appropriation necessary, and she made it up herself. After that, she consulted me seriously as to whether she ought not to stay in town and superintend the execution of the plan. But I told her she might fitly delegate that. She was all the more anxious to perform her whole duty, because she confessed that indigent children were personally unpleasant to her."

Halleck burst out laughing.

"That's like Clara! How charming women are! They're charming even in their goodness! I wonder the novelists don't take a hint from that fact, and stop giving us those scaly heroines they've been running lately. Why, a real woman can make righteousness delicious and virtue piquant. I like them for that!"

"Do you?" asked Atherton, laughing in his turn at the single-minded confession. He was some years older than his friend.

They had got down to Charles street, and Halleck took out his watch at the corner lamp.

"It isn't at all late yet; only half-past eight. The days are getting shorter."

"Well?"

"Suppose we go and call on Hubbard now? He's right up here on Clover street."

"I don't know," said Atherton. "It would do for you; you're an old friend. But for me,—wouldn't it be rather unceremonious?"

"Oh, come along! They'll not be punctilious. They'll like our dropping in, and I shall have Hubbard off my conscience. I must go to see him sooner or later, for decency's sake."

Atherton suffered himself to be led away.

"I suppose you wont stay long?"

"Oh, no; I shall cut it very short," said Halleck.

And they climbed the narrow little street where Marcia had at last found a house, after searching the South End quite to the Highlands, and ransacking Charlestown and Cambridgeport. These points all seemed to her terribly remote from where Bartley must be at work during the day, and she must be alone without the sight of him from morning till night. The accessibility of Canary Place had spoiled her for distances; she wanted Bartley at home for their one-o'clock dinner; she wanted to have him within easy call at all times; and she was glad when none of those far-off places yielded quite what they desired in a house. They took the house on Clover street, though it was a little dearer than they expected, for two years, and they furnished it, as far as they could, out of the three or four hundred dollars they had saved, including the remaining hundred from the colt and cutter, kept sacredly intact by Marcia. When you entered, the narrow staircase cramped you into the little parlor opening out of the hall; and back of the parlor was the dining-room. Overhead were two chambers, and overhead again were two chambers more; in the basement was the kitchen. The house seemed absurdly large to people who had been living for the last seven months in one room, and the view of the Back Bay from the little bow-window of the front chamber added all outdoors to their superfluous space.

Bartley came himself to answer Halleck's ring, and they met at once with such a "Why, Halleck!" and "How do you do, Hubbard?" as restored something of their old college comradery. Bartley welcomed Mr. Atherton under the gaslight he had turned up, and then they huddled into the little parlor, where Bartley introduced his old friend to his wife. Marcia wore a sort of dark robe, trimmed with bows of crimson ribbon, which she had made herself, and in which she looked a Roman patrician in an avatar of Boston domesticity; and Bartley was rather proud to see his friend so visibly dazzled by her beauty. It quite abashed Halleck, who limped helplessly about, after his cane had been taken from him, before he sat down, while Marcia, from the vantage of the sofa and the covert of her talk with Atherton, was content that Halleck should be plain and awkward, with close-cut drab hair and a dull complexion. She would not have liked even a man who knew Bartley before she did to be very handsome.

Halleck and Bartley had some talk about college days, from which their eyes wandered at times; and then Marcia excused herself to Atherton and went out, re-appearing after an interval at the sliding doors, which she rolled open between the parlor and dining-room. A table set for supper stood behind her, and, as she leaned a little forward, with her hands each on a leaf of the door, she said, with shy pride, "Bartley, I thought the gentlemen would like to join you," and he answered, "Of course they would," and led the way out, refusing to hear any demur. His heart swelled with satisfaction in Marcia; it was something like, having fellows drop in upon you, and be asked out to supper in this easy way. It made Bartley feel good, and he would have liked to give Marcia a hug on the spot. He could not help pressing her foot under the table, and exchanging a quiver of the eyelashes with her, as he lifted the lid of the white tureen, and looked at her across the glitter of their new crockery and cutlery. They made the jokes of the season about the oyster being promptly on hand for the first of the R months, and Bartley explained that he was sometimes kept at the Events office rather late, and that then Marcia waited supper for him, and always gave him an oyster stew, which she made herself. She could not stop him, and the guests praised the oysters, and then they praised the dining-room and the parlor. And when they rose from the table Bartley said, "Now we must show you the house," and persisted, against her deprecations, in making her lead the way. She was, in fact, willing enough to show it; her taste had made their money go to the utmost in furnishing it; and, though most people were then still in the period of green reps and tan terry, and of dull black-walnut movables, she had everywhere bestowed little touches that told. She had covered the marble parlor-mantel with cloth and fringed it, and she had set on it two vases in the Pompeiian colors then liked; her carpet was of wood colors and a moss pattern; she had done what could be done with folding carpet chairs to give the little room a specious air of luxury; the center-table was heaped with her sewing and Bartley's newspapers.

"We've just moved in, and we haven't furnished *all* the rooms yet," she said of two empty ones which Bartley perversely flung open.

"And I don't know that we shall. The house is much too big for us; but we thought we'd better take it," he added, as if it were a castle for vastness.

Halleck and Atherton were silent for some moments after they came away, and then:

"*I* don't believe he whips her," suggested the latter.

"No, I guess he's fond of her," said Halleck, gravely.

"Did you see how careful he was of her, coming up and down stairs? That was very pretty; and it was pretty to see them both so ready to show off their young housekeeping to us."

"Yes, it improves a man to get married," said Halleck, with a long, stifled sigh. "It's improved the most selfish hound I ever knew."

XXI

THE two elder Miss Hallecks were so much older than Olive, the youngest, that they seemed to be of a sort of intermediary generation between her and her parents, though Olive herself was well out of her teens, and was the senior of her brother Ben by two or three years. The elder sisters were always together, and they adhered in common to the religion of their father and mother. The defection of their brother was passive, but Olive, having conscientiously adopted an alien faith, was not a person to let others imagine her ashamed of it, and her Unitarianism was outspoken. In her turn she formed a kind of party with Ben inside the family, and would have led him on in her own excesses of independence if his somewhat melancholy indifferentism had consented. It was only in his absence that she had been with her sisters during their summer sojourn in the White Mountains; when they returned home, she vigorously went her way, and left them to go theirs. She was fond of them in her defiant fashion; but in such a matter as calling on Mrs. Hubbard, she chose not to be mixed up with her family, or in any way to countenance her family's prepossessions. Her sisters paid their visit together, and she waited for Clara Kingsbury to come up from the sea-side. Then she went with her to call upon Marcia, sitting observant and non-committal while Clara swooped through the little house, up stairs and down, clamoring over its prettiness, and admiring the art with which so few dollars could be made to go so far. "Think of finding such a bower on Clover street!" She made Marcia give her the cost of everything; and her heart swelled with pride in her sex when she heard that Marcia had put down all the carpets herself. "I wanted to make them up," Marcia explained, "but Mr. Hubbard wouldn't let me,—it cost so little at the store."

"Wouldn't let you!" cried Miss Kingsbury. "I should hope as much, indeed! Why, my child, you're a Roman matron!"

She came away in agony lest Marcia might think she meant her nose. She drove early the next morning to tell Olive Halleck that she had spent a sleepless night from this cause, and to ask her what she *should* do. "Do you think she will be hurt, Olive? Tell me what led up to it? How did I behave before that? The context is everything in such cases."

"Oh, you went about praising everything, and screaming and shouting, and my-dearing and my-childing her, and patronizing"—

"There, there! say no more! That's sufficient! I see,—I see it all! I've done the very most offensive thing I could, when I meant to be the most appreciative."

"These country people don't like to be appreciated down to the quick, in that way," said Olive. "I should think Mrs. Hubbard was rather a proud person."

"I know! I know!" moaned Miss Kingsbury. "It was ghastly."

"*I* don't suppose she's ashamed of her nose"—

"Olive!" cried her friend, "be still! Why, I can't *bear* it! why, you wretched thing!"

"I dare say all the ladies in Equity make up their own carpets, and put them down, and she thought you were laughing at her."

"*Will* you be still, Olive Halleck?" Miss Kingsbury was now a large blonde mass of suffering. "Oh, dear, dear! What shall I do? It was sacrilege—yes, it was nothing less than sacrilege—to go on as I did. And I meant so well; I did so admire, and respect, and revere her!" Olive burst out laughing. "You wicked girl!" whimpered Clara. "Should you—should you write to her?"

"And tell her you didn't mean her nose? Oh, by all means, Clara,—by all means! Quite an inspiration. Why not make her an evening party?"

"Olive," said Clara, with guilty meekness, "I have been thinking of that."

"*No*, Clara! Not seriously!" cried Olive, sobered at the idea.

"Yes, seriously. Would it be so very bad? Only just a *little* party," she pleaded. "Half a dozen people or so; just to show them that I really feel—friendly. I know that he's told her all about meeting me here, and I'm not going to have her think I want to drop him because he's married, and lives in a little house on Clover street."

"Noble Clara! So you wish to bring them out in Boston

society? What will you do with them after you've got them there?" Miss Kingsbury fidgeted in her chair a little. "Now look me in the eye, Clara! Whom were you going to ask to meet them? Your unfashionable friends, the Hallecks?"

"My friends, the Hallecks, of course."

"And Mr. Atherton, your legal adviser?"

"I had thought of asking Mr. Atherton. You needn't say what he is, if you please, Olive; you know that there's no one I prize so much."

"Very good. And Mr. Cameron?"

"He has got back,—yes. He's very nice."

"A Cambridge tutor; young and of recent attachment to the college, with no local affiliations, yet. What ladies?"

"Miss Strong is a nice girl; she is studying at the Conservatory."

"Yes. Poverty-stricken votary of Miss Kingsbury. Well?"

"Miss Clancy."

"Unfashionable elderly sister of fashionable artist. Yes?"

"The Brayhems."

"Young radical clergyman, and his wife, without a congregation, and hoping for a pulpit in Billerica. Parlor lectures on German literature in the meantime. Well?"

"And Mrs. Savage, I thought."

"Well-preserved young widow of uncertain antecedents tending to grassiness; outdoor *protégée* of the hostess. Yes, Clara, go on and give your party. It will be *perfectly safe!* But do you think it will *deceive* anybody?"

"Now, Olive Halleck!" cried Clara, "I am not going to have you talking to me in that way! You have no right to do it, and you have no business to do it," she added, trying to pluck up a spirit. "Is there anybody that I value more than I do you and your sisters, and Ben?"

"No. But you don't value us *just in that way*, and you know it. Don't you be a humbug, Clara. Now go on with your excuses."

"I'm not making excuses! Isn't Mr. Atherton in the most fashionable society?"

"Yes. Why don't you ask some other fashionable people?"

"Olive, this is all nonsense,—perfect nonsense! I can invite any one I like to meet any one I like, and if I choose to show Mr. Hubbard's wife a little attention, I can do it, can't I?"

"Oh, of course!"

"And what would be the use of inviting fashionable people—as you call them—to meet them? It would just embarrass them all round."

"Perfectly correct, Miss Kingsbury. All that I want you to do is to face the facts of the case. I want you to realize that, in showing Mr. Hubbard's wife this little attention, you're not doing it because you scorn to drop an old friend, and want to do him the highest honor; but because you think you can palm off your second-class acquaintance on them for first-class, and try to make up in that way for telling her she had a hooked nose!"

"You *know* that I didn't tell her she had a hooked nose."

"You told her that she was a Roman matron,—it's the same thing," said Olive.

Miss Kingsbury bit her lip and tried to look a dignified resentment. She ended by saying, with feeble spite, "I shall have the little evening for all you say. I suppose you wont refuse to come because I don't ask the whole Blue Book to meet them."

"Of course we shall come! I wouldn't miss it for anything. I always like to see how you manage your pieces of social duplicity, Clara. But you needn't expect that I will be a party to the swindle. No, Clara! I shall go to these poor young people and tell them plainly, 'This is not the *best* society; Miss Kingsbury keeps that for'"—

"Olive! I think I never saw even you in such a teasing humor." The tears came into Clara's large, tender blue eyes, and she continued, with an appeal that had no effect, "I'm sure I don't see why you should make it a question of anything of the sort. It's simply a wish to—to have a little company of no particular kind, for no partic— Because I want to."

"Oh, that's it, is it? Then I highly approve of it," said Olive. "When is it to be?"

"I sha'n't tell you, now! You may wait till I'm ready," pouted Clara, as she rose to go.

"Don't go away thinking I'm enough to provoke a saint because *you've* got mad at me, Clara!"

"Mad? You know I'm not mad! But I think you might be a *little* sympathetic *some*times, Olive!" said her friend, kissing her.

"Not in cases of social duplicity, Clara. My wrath is all that saves you. If you were not afraid of me, you would have been a lost worldling long ago."

"I know you always really love me," said Miss Kingsbury, tenderly.

"No, I don't," retorted her friend, promptly. "Not when you're humbugging. Don't expect it, for you wont get it." She followed Clara with a triumphant laugh as she went out of the door; and except for this parting taunt, Clara might have given up her scheme. She first ordered her *coupé* driven home, in fact, and then lowered the window to countermand the direction, and drove to Bartley's door on Clover street.

It was a very handsome equipage, and was in keeping with all the outward belongings of Miss Kingsbury, who mingled a sense of duty and a love of luxury in her life in very exact proportions. When her *coupé* was not standing before some of the wretchedest doors in the city, it was waiting at the finest; and Clara's days were divided between the extremes of squalor and of fashion.

She was the only child of parents who had early left her an orphan. Her father, who was much her mother's senior, was an old friend of Olive's father, and had made him his executor and the guardian of his daughter. Mr. Halleck had taken her into his own family, and, in the conscientious pursuance of what he believed would have been her father's preference, he gave her worldly advantages which he would not have desired for one of his own children. But the friendship that grew up between Clara and Olive was too strong for him in some things, and the girls went to the same fashionable school together.

When his ward came of age, he made over to her the fortune, increased by his careful management, which her father had left her, and advised her to put her affairs in the hands of Mr. Atherton. She had shown a quite ungirlish eagerness to manage them for herself. In the midst of her profusion she had odd accesses of stinginess, in which she fancied herself coming to poverty; and her guardian judged it best that she should have a lawyer who could tell her at any moment just where she stood. She hesitated, but she did as he advised; and having once intrusted her property to Atherton's care, she added her conscience and her reason in large degree, and obeyed him with embarrassing promptness in matters that did not interfere with her pleasures. Her pleasures were of various kinds. She chose to buy herself a fine house, and, having furnished it luxuriously, and unearthed a cousin of her father's in Vermont and brought her to Boston to matronize her, she kept house on a magnificent scale, pinching, however, at certain points with unexpected meanness. When she was alone, her table was of a Spartan austerity; she exacted a great deal from her servants, and paid them as small wages as she could. After that, she did not mind lavishing money upon them in kindness. A seamstress whom she had once employed fell sick, and Miss Kingsbury sent her to the Bahamas and kept her there till she was well, and then made her a guest in her house till the girl could get back her work. She watched her cook through the measles, caring for her like a mother; and, as Olive Halleck said, she was always portioning or burying the sisters of her second-girls. She was in all sorts of charities, but she was apt to cut her charities off with her pleasures at any moment, if she felt poor. She was fond of dress, and went a great deal into society: she suspected men generally of wishing to marry her for her money, but with those whom she did not think capable of aspiring to her hand, she was generously helpful with her riches. She liked to patronize; she had long supported an unpromising painter at Rome, and she gave orders to desperate artists at home.

The world had pretty well hardened one half of her heart, but the other half was still soft and loving, and into this side of her mixed nature she cowered when she believed she had committed some blunder or crime, and came whimpering to Olive Halleck for punishment. She made Olive her discipline partly in her lack of some fixed religion. She had not yet found a religion that exactly suited her, though she had many times believed herself about to be anchored in some faith forever.

She was almost sorry that she had put her resolution in effect when she rang at the door, and Marcia herself answered the bell, in place of the one servant, who was at that moment hanging out the wash. It seemed wicked to pretend to be showing this pretty creature a social attention, when she meant to palm off a hollow imitation of society upon her. Why should she not ask the very superfinest of her friends to meet such a brilliant beauty? It would serve Olive Halleck right if she should do this, and leave the Hallecks out, and Marcia would certainly be a sensation. She half-believed that she meant to do it when she quitted the house with Marcia's promise that she would bring her husband to tea on Wednesday evening, at eight; and she drove away so far penitent that she resolved at least to make her company distinguished, if not fashionable. She said to herself that she would make it fashionable yet, if she chose, and as a first move in this direction she easily secured Mr. Atherton: he had no engagements, so few people had got back to town. She called upon Mrs. Witherby, needlessly reminding her of the charity committees they had served on together; and then she went home and actually sent out notes to the plainest daughter and the maiden aunt of two of the most high-born families of her acquaintance. She added to her list an artist and his wife ("Now I shall *have* to let him paint me!" she reflected), a young author whose book had made talk, a teacher of Italian, with whom she was pretending to read Dante, and a musical composer.

Olive came late, as if to get a whole effect of the affair at once; and her smile revealed Clara's failure to her, if she had not realized it before. She read there that the aristocratic and æsthetic additions which she had made to the guests Olive originally divined had not availed; the party remained a humbug. It had seemed absurd to invite anybody to meet two such little, unknown people as the Hubbards; and then, to avoid marking them as the subjects of the festivity by the precedence to be observed in going out to supper, she resolved to have tea served in the drawing-room, and to make it literally tea, with bread and butter, and some thin, ascetic cake.

However sharp he was in business, Mr. Witherby was socially a dull man; and his wife and daughter seemed to partake of his qualities by affinition and heredity. They tried to make something of Marcia, but they failed through their want of art. Mrs. Witherby, finding the wife of her husband's assistant in Miss Kingsbury's house, conceived an awe of her, which Marcia would not have known how to abate if she had imagined it; and in a little while the Witherby family segregated themselves among the photograph albums and the bric-a-brac, from which Clara seemed to herself to be fruitlessly detaching them the whole evening. The plainest daughter and the maiden aunt of the patrician families talked to each other with unavailing intervals of the painter and the author. The radical clergyman and his wife were in danger of a conjugal devotion which society does not favor; the unfashionable sister of the fashionable artist conversed with the young Harvard tutor and the Japanese law-student, whom he had asked leave to bring with him, and whose small, mouse-like eyes continually twinkled away in pursuit of the blonde beauty of his hostess. The widow was winningly attentive, with a tendency to be confidential, to everybody. The Italian could not disabuse himself of the notion that he was expected to be light and cheerful, and when the pupil of the Conservatory sang, he abandoned himself to his error, and clapped and cried bravo with unseemly vivacity. But he was restored to reason when the composer sat down at the piano and played, amid the hush that falls on society at such times, something from Beethoven, and again something of his own, which was so like Beethoven that Beethoven himself would not have known the difference.

Mr. Atherton and Halleck moved about among the sufferers, and did their best to second Clara's efforts for their relief; but it was useless. In the desperation which owns defeat, she resolved to devote herself for the rest of the evening to trying to make at least the Hubbards have a good time; and then, upon the dangerous theory, of which young and pretty hostesses cannot be too wary, that a wife is necessarily flattered by attentions to her husband, she devoted herself exclusively to Bartley, to whom she talked long and with a reckless liveliness of the events of his former stay in Boston. Their laughter and scraps of their reminiscences reached Marcia where she sat in a feint of listening to Ben Halleck's perfunctory account of his college days with her husband, till she could bear it no longer. She rose abruptly, and, going to him, she said that it was time to say good-night.

"Oh, so soon!" cried Clara, mystified and a little scared at the look she saw on Marcia's face. "Good-night," she added, coldly

The assembly hailed this first token of its disintegration with relief; it became a little livelier; there was a fleeting moment in which it seemed as if it might yet enjoy itself; but its chance passed; it crumbled rapidly away, and Clara was left looking humbly into Olive Halleck's pitiless eyes.

"Thank you for a *delightful* evening, Miss Kingsbury! Congratulate you!" she mocked, with an unsparing laugh. "Such a success! But why didn't you give them something to eat, Clara? Those poor Hubbards have a one-o'clock dinner, and I famished for them. I wasn't hungry myself,—*we* have a two-o'clock dinner!"

XXII

B ARTLEY CAME home elate from Miss Kingsbury's entertainment. It was something like the social success which
he used to picture to himself. He had been flattered by the
attention specially paid him, and he did not detect the impo-
sition. He was half-starved, but he meant to have up some
cold meat and bottled beer, and talk it all over with Marcia.

She did not seem inclined to talk it over on their way
home, and when they entered their own door, she pushed in
and ran upstairs.

"Why, where are you going, Marcia?" he called after her.

"To bed!" she replied, closing the door after her with a
crash of unmistakable significance.

Bartley stood a moment in the fury that tempted him to
pursue her with a taunt, and then leave her to work herself
out of the transport of senseless jealousy she had wrought
herself into. But he set his teeth, and, full of inward cursing,
he followed her upstairs with a slow, dogged step. He took
her in his arms without a word, and held her fast, while his
anger changed to pity, and then to laughing. When it came
to that, she put up her arms, which she had kept rigidly at
her side, and laid them round his neck, and began softly to
cry on his breast.

"Oh, I'm not myself at all, any more!" she moaned penitently.

"Then this is very improper—for me," said Bartley.

The helpless laughter broke through her lamentation, but
she cried a little more to keep herself in countenance.

"But I guess, from a previous acquaintance with the party's
character, that it's really all you, Marcia. I don't blame you.
Miss Kingsbury's hospitality has left me as hollow as if I'd
had nothing to eat for a week; and I know you're perishing
from inanition. Hence these tears."

It delighted her to have him make fun of Miss Kingsbury's
tea, and she lifted her head to let him see that she was
laughing for pleasure now, before she turned away to dry her
eyes.

"Oh, poor fellow!" she cried, "I did pity you so when I saw those mean little slices of bread and butter coming round!"

"Yes," said Bartley, "I felt sorry myself. But don't speak of them any more, dearest."

"And I suppose," pursued Marcia, "that all the time she was talking to you there, you were simply ravening."

"I was casting lots in my own mind to see which of the company I should devour first."

His drollery appeared to Marcia the finest that ever was; she laughed and laughed again; when he made fun of the elderly aristocrat's conjecturable toughness, she implored him to stop if he did not want to kill her. Marcia was not in the state in which woman best convinces her enemies of her fitness for empire, but she was charming in her silly happiness, and Bartley felt very glad that he had not yielded to his first impulse to deal savagely with her.

"Come," he said, "let us go out somewhere, and get some oysters."

She began at once to take out her ear-rings and loosen her hair.

"No, I'll get something here in the house; I'm not very hungry. But *you* go, Bartley, and have a good supper, or you'll be sick to-morrow, and not fit to work. Go," she added to his hesitating image in the glass, "I insist upon it. I wont *have* you stay."

His reflected face approached from behind; she turned hers a little, and their mirrored lips met over her shoulder. "Oh, how *sweet* you are, Bartley!" she murmured.

"Yes, you will always find me obedient when commanded to go out and repair my wasted tissue."

"I don't mean *that*, dear," she said softly. "I mean—your not quarreling with me when I'm unreasonable. Why can't we always do so?"

"Well, you see," said Bartley, "it throws the whole burden on the fellow in his senses. It doesn't require any great degree of self-sacrifice to fly off at a tangent, but it's rather a maddening spectacle to the party that holds on."

"Now I will show you," said Marcia, "that I can be reasonable, too: I shall let you go alone to make our party call on Miss Kingsbury." She looked at him heroically.

"Marcia," said Bartley, "you're such a reasonable person when you're the most unreasonable, that I wonder I *ever* quarrel with you. I rather think I'll let *you* call on Miss Kingsbury alone. I shall suffer agonies of suspicion, but it will prove that I have perfect confidence in you." He threw her a kiss from the door, and ran down the stairs. When he returned, an hour later, he found her waiting up for him.

"Why, Marcia!" he exclaimed.

"Oh! I just wanted to say that we will both go to call on her *very soon*. If I sent you, she might think I was mad, and I wont give her that satisfaction."

"Noble girl!" cried Bartley, with irony that pleased her better than praise. Women like to be understood, even when they try not to be understood.

When Marcia went with Bartley to call, Miss Kingsbury received her with careful, perhaps anxious, politeness, but made no further effort to take her up. Some of the people whom Marcia met at Miss Kingsbury's called; and the Witherbys came, father, mother, and daughter together; but between the evident fact that the Hubbards were poor, and the other evident fact that they moved in the best society, the Witherbys did not quite know what to do about them. They asked them to dinner, and Bartley went alone; Marcia was not well enough to go.

He was very kind and tractable, now, and went whenever she bade him go without her, though tea at the Hallecks was getting to be an old story with him, and it was generally tea at the Hallecks to which she sent him. The Halleck ladies came faithfully to see her, and she got on very well with the two older sisters, who gave her all the kindness they could spare from their charities, and seemed pleased to have her so pretty and conjugal, though these things were far from them. But she was afraid of Olive at first, and disliked her as a friend of Miss Kingsbury. This rather attracted the odd girl. What she called Marcia's snubs enabled her to declare in her favor with a sense of disinterestedness, and to indulge her repugnance for Bartley with a good heart. She resented his odious good looks, and held it a shame that her mother should promote his visible tendency to stoutness by giving him such nice things for tea.

"Now, I like Mr. Hubbard," said her mother, placidly. "It's very kind of him to come to such plain folks as we are, whenever we ask him; now that his wife can't come, I know he does it because he likes us."

"Oh, he comes for the eating," said Olive, scornfully. Then another phase of her mother's remark struck her: "Why, mother!" she cried, "I do believe you think Bartley Hubbard's a distinguished man, somehow!"

"Your father says it's very unusual for such a young man to be in a place like his. Mr. Witherby really leaves everything to him, he says."

"Well, I think he'd better not, then! The Events has got to be perfectly horrid, of late. It's full of murders and all uncleanness."

"That seems to be the way with the papers, nowadays. Your father hears that the Events is making money."

"Why, mother! What a corrupt old thing you are! I believe you've been bought up by that disgusting interview with father. Nestor of the Leather Interest! Father ought to have turned him out of doors. Well, this family is getting a little *too* good, for me! And Ben's almost as bad as any of you, of late,—I haven't a bit of influence with him any more. He seems determined to be friendlier with that *person* than ever; he's always trying to do him good,—I can see it, and it makes me sick. One thing I know: I'm going to stop Mr. Hubbard's calling me Olive. Impudent!"

Mrs. Halleck shifted her ground with the pretense which women use, even amongst themselves, of having remained steadfast.

"He is a very good husband."

"Oh, because he likes to be!" retorted her daughter. "Nothing is easier than to be a good husband."

"Ah, my dear," said Mrs. Halleck, "wait till you have tried."

This made Olive laugh; but she answered with an argument that always had weight with her mother:

"Ben doesn't think he's a good husband."

"What makes you think so, Olive?" asked her mother.

"I know he dislikes him intensely."

"Why, you just said yourself, dear, that he was friendlier with him than ever."

"Oh, that's nothing. The more he disliked him, the kinder he would be to him."

"That's true," sighed her mother. "Did he ever say anything to you about him?"

"No," cried Olive shortly; "he never speaks of people he doesn't like."

The mother returned, with logical severity, "All that doesn't prove that Ben thinks he isn't a good husband."

"He dislikes him. Do you believe a bad man can be a good husband, then?"

"No," Mrs. Halleck admitted, as if confronted with indisputable proof of Bartley's wickedness.

In the meantime the peace between Bartley and Marcia continued unbroken, and these days of waiting, of suffering, of hoping and dreading, were the happiest of their lives. He did his best to be patient with her caprices and fretfulness, and he was at least manfully comforting and helpful, and instant in atonement for every failure. She said a thousand times that she should die without him; and when her time came, he thought that she was going to die before he could tell her of his sorrow for all that he had ever done to grieve her. He did not tell her, though she lived to give him the chance; but he took her and her baby both into his arms, with tears of as much fondness as ever a man shed. He even began his confession; but she said, "Hush! you never did a wrong thing yet that I didn't drive you to." Pale and faint, she smiled joyfully upon him, and put her hand on his head when he hid his face against hers on the pillow, and put her lips against his cheeks. His heart was full; he was grateful for the mercy that had spared him; he was so strong in his silent repentance that he felt like a good man.

"Bartley," she said, "I'm going to ask a great favor of you."

"There's nothing that I can do that I shall think a favor, darling!" he cried, lifting his face to look into hers.

"Write for mother to come. I want her!"

"Why, of course."

Marcia continued to look at him, and kept the quivering hold she had laid of his hand when he raised his head.

"Was that all?"

She was silent, and he added,

"I will ask your father to come with her."

She hid her face for the space of one sob.

"I wanted you to offer."

"Why, of course! of course!" he replied.

She did not acknowledge his magnanimity directly, but she lifted the coverlet and showed him the little head on her arm, and the little creased and crumpled face.

"Pretty?" she asked. "Bring me the letter before you send it."

"Yes, that is just right,—perfect!" she sighed, when he came back and read the letter to her, and she fell away to happy sleep.

Her father answered that he would come with her mother as soon as he got the better of a cold he had taken. It was now well into the winter, and the journey must have seemed more formidable in Equity than in Boston. But Bartley was not impatient of his father-in-law's delay, and he set himself cheerfully about consoling Marcia for it. She stole her white, thin hand into his, and now and then gave it a little pressure to accent the points she made in talking.

"Father was the first one I thought of—after you, Bartley. It seems to me as if baby came half to show me how unfeeling I had been to him. Of course I'm not sorry I ran away and asked you to take me back, for I couldn't have had you if I hadn't done it; but I never realized before how cruel it was to father. He always made such a pet of me; and I know that he thought he was acting for the best."

"I knew that *you* were," said Bartley, fervently.

"What sweet things you always say to me!" she murmured. "But don't you see, Bartley, that I didn't think enough of him? That's what baby seems to have come to teach me." She pulled a little away on the pillow, so as to fix him more earnestly with her eyes. "If baby should behave so to *you* when she grew up, I should hate her."

He laughed, and said,

"Well, perhaps your mother hates you."

"No, they don't—either of them," said Marcia with a sigh. "And I behaved very stiffly and coldly with him when he came up to see me,—more than I had any need to. I did it for your sake; but he didn't mean any harm to you,—he just wanted to make sure that I was safe and well."

"Oh, that's all right, Marsh."

"Yes, I know. But what if he had died!"

"Well, he didn't die," said Bartley, with a smile. "And you've corresponded with them regularly, ever since, and you know they've been getting along all right. And it's going to be altogether different from this out," he added, leaning back, a little weary with a matter in which he could not be expected to take a very cordial interest.

"Truly?" she asked, with one of the eagerest of those hand-pressures.

"It wont be my fault if it isn't," he replied, with a yawn.

"How good you are, Bartley!" she said, with an admiring look, as if it was the goodness of God she was praising.

Bartley released himself, and went to the new crib, in which the baby lay, and with his hands in his pockets stood looking down at it with a curious smile.

"Is it pretty?" she asked, envious of his bird's-eye view of the baby.

"Not definitively so," he answered. "I dare say she will smooth out in time; but she seems to be considerably puckered yet."

"Well," returned Marcia, with forced resignation, "I shouldn't let any one else say so."

Her husband set up a soft, low, thoughtful whistle.

"I'll tell you what, Marcia," he said, presently. "Suppose we name this baby after your father?"

She lifted herself on her elbow, and stared at him as if he must be making fun of her.

"Why, how could we?" she demanded. Squire Gaylord's parents had called his name Flavius Josephus, in a superstition once cherished by old-fashioned people, that the Jewish historian was somehow a sacred writer.

"We can't name her Josephus, but we can call her Flavia," said Bartley. "And if she makes up her mind to turn out a blonde, the name will just fit. Flavia,—it's a very pretty name." He looked at his wife, who suddenly turned her face down on the pillow.

"Bartley Hubbard," she cried, "you're the best man in the world!"

"Oh, no! Only the second-best," suggested Bartley.

In these days they took their fill of the delight of young fatherhood and motherhood. After its morning bath Bartley was called in, and allowed to revere the baby's mottled and dimpled back as it lay face downward on the nurse's lap, feebly wiggling its arms and legs, and responding with ineffectual little sighs and gurgles to her acceptable rubbings with warm flannel. When it was fully dressed, and its long clothes pulled snugly down, and its limp person stiffened into something tenable, he was suffered to take it into his arms, and to walk the room with it. After all, there is not much that a man can actually do with a small baby, either for its pleasure or his own, and Bartley's usefulness had its strict limitations. He was perhaps most beneficial when he put the child in its mother's arms, and sat down beside the bed, and quietly talked, while Marcia occasionally put up a slender hand and smoothed its golden-brown hair, bending her neck over to look at it where it lay, with the action of a mother bird. They examined with minute interest the details of the curious little creature: its tiny finger-nails, fine and sharp, and its small queer fist doubled so tight, and closing on one's finger like a canary's claw on a perch; the absurdity of its foot, the absurdity of its toes, the ridiculous inadequacy of its legs and arms to the work ordinarily expected of legs and arms, made them laugh. They could not tell yet whether its eyes would be black, like Marcia's, or blue, like Bartley's; those long lashes had the sweep of hers, but its mop of hair, which made it look so odd and old, was more like his in color.

"She will be a dark-eyed blonde," Bartley decided.

"Is that nice?" asked Marcia.

"With the telescope sight, they're warranted to kill at five hundred yards."

"Oh, for shame, Bartley! To talk of baby's ever killing!"

"Why, that's what they all come to. It's what you came to yourself."

"Yes, I know. But it's quite another thing with baby." She

began to mumble it with her lips, and to talk baby-talk to it. In their common interest in this puppet they already called each other papa and mamma.

Squire Gaylord came alone, and when Marcia greeted him with "Why, father! Where's mother?" he asked, "Did you expect her? Well, I guess your mother's feeling rather too old for such long winter journeys. You know she don't go out a great deal. *I* guess she expects your family down there in the summer."

The old man was considerably abashed by the baby when it was put into his arms, and being required to guess its name, he naturally failed.

"Flavia!" cried Marcia, joyfully. "Bartley named it after you."

This embarrassed the Squire still more.

"Is that so?" he asked, rather sheepishly. "Well, it's quite a compliment."

Marcia repeated this to her husband as evidence that her father was all right now. Bartley and the Squire were in fact very civil to each other; and Bartley paid the old man many marked attentions. He took him to the top of the State House, and walked him all about the city, to show him its points of interest, and introduced him to such of his friends as they met, though the Squire's dress-coat, whether fully revealed by the removal of his surtout, or betraying itself below the skirt of the latter, was a trial to a fellow of Bartley's style. He went with his father-in-law to see Mr. Warren in "Jefferson Scattering Batkins," and the Squire grimly appreciated the burlesque of the member from Cranberry Center; but he was otherwise not a very amusable person, and off his own ground he was not conversable; while he refused to betray his impressions of many things that Bartley expected to astonish him. The Events editorial rooms had no apparent effect upon him, though they were as different from most editorial dens as tapestry carpets, black-walnut desks, and swivel chairs could make them. Mr. Witherby covered him with urbanities and praises of Bartley that ought to have delighted him as a father-in-law; but apparently the great man of the Events was but a strange variety of the type with which he was familiar in the despised country editors. He got on better with Mr. Atherton, who was of a man's profession. The Squire wore his hat throughout their interview, and everywhere except at table and in bed; and as soon as he rose from either, he put it on.

Bartley tried to impress him with such novel traits of cosmopolitan life as a *table d'hôte* dinner at a French restaurant; but the Squire sat through the courses as if his barbarous old appetite had satisfied itself in that manner all his life. After that, Bartley practically gave him up; he pleaded his newspaper work, and left the Squire to pass the time as he could in the little house on Clover street, where he sat half a day at a stretch in the parlor with his hat on, reading the newspapers, his legs sprawled out toward the grate. In this way he probably reconstructed for himself some image of his wonted life in his office at home, and was for the time at peace; but otherwise he was very restless, except when he was with Marcia. He was as fond of her in his way as he had ever been, and though he apparently cared nothing for the baby, he enjoyed Marcia's pride in it; and he bore to have it thrust upon him with the surly mildness of an old dog receiving children's caresses. He listened with the same patience to all her celebrations of Bartley, which were often tedious enough, for she bragged of him constantly, of his smartness and goodness, and of the great success that had crowned the merit of both in him.

Mr. Halleck had called upon the Squire the morning after his arrival, and brought Marcia a note from his wife, offering to have her father stay with them if she found herself too much crowded at this eventful time.

"There! That is just the sort of people the Hallecks are!" she cried, showing the letter to her father. "And to think of our not going near them for months and months after we came to Boston, for fear they were stuck up! But Bartley is always just so proud. Now you must go right in, father, and not keep Mr. Halleck waiting. Give me your hat, or you'll be sure to wear it in the parlor." She made him stoop down to let her brush his coat-collar a little. "There! Now you look something like."

Squire Gaylord had never received a visit except on business in his life, and such a thing as one man calling socially upon another, as women did, was unknown to the civilization of Equity. But, as he reported to Marcia, he got along with

Mr. Halleck; and he got along with the whole family when he went with Bartley to tea, upon the invitation Mr. Halleck made him that morning. Probably it appeared to him an objectless hospitality; but he spent as pleasant an evening as he could hope to spend with his hat off and in a frock-coat, which he wore as a more ceremonious garment than the dress-coat of his every-day life. He seemed to take a special liking to Olive Halleck, whose habit of speaking her mind with vigor and directness struck him as commendable. It was Olive who made the time pass for him; and as the occasion was not one for personal sarcasm or question of the Christian religion, her task in keeping the old pagan out of rather abysmal silences must have had its difficulties.

"What did you talk about?" asked Marcia, requiring an account of his enjoyment from him the next morning, after Bartley had gone down to his work.

"Mostly about you, I guess," said the Squire, with a laugh. "There was a large, sandy-haired young woman there"—

"Miss Kingsbury," said Marcia, with vindictive promptness. Her eyes kindled, and she began to grow rigid under the coverlet. "Whom did *she* talk with?"

"Well, she talked a little with me; but she talked most of the time to the young man. She engaged to him?"

"No," said Marcia, relaxing. "She's a great friend of the whole family. I don't know what they meant by telling you it was to be just a family party, when they were going to have strangers in," she pouted.

"Perhaps they didn't count her."

"No."

But Marcia's pleasure in the affair was tainted, and she began to talk of other things.

Her father staid nearly a week, and they all found it rather a long week. After showing him her baby, and satisfying herself that he and Bartley were on good terms again, there was not much left for Marcia. Bartley had been banished to the spare room by the presence of the nurse; and he gave up his bed there to the Squire, and slept on a cot in the unfurnished attic room; the cook, and a small girl got in to help, had the other. The house that had once seemed so vast was full to bursting.

"I never knew how little it was till I saw your father coming down-stairs," said Bartley. "He's too tall for it. When he sits on the sofa, and stretches out his legs, his boots touch the mop-board on the other side of the room. Fact!"

"He wont stay over Sunday," began Marcia, with a rueful smile.

"Why, Marcia, you don't think I want him to go!"

"No; you're as good as can be about it. But I hope he wont stay over Sunday."

"Haven't you enjoyed his visit?" asked Bartley.

"Oh, yes, I've enjoyed it." The tears came into her eyes. "I've made it all up with father; and he doesn't feel hard to me. But, Bartley— Sit down, dear, here on the bed." She took his hand and gently pulled him down. "I see more and more that father and mother can never be what they used to be to me,— that you're all the world to me. Yes, my life is broken off from theirs forever. Could anything break it off from yours? You'll always be patient with me, wont you? And remember that I'd always rather be good when I'm behaving the worst?"

He rose, and went over to the crib, and kissed the head of their little girl.

"Ask Flavia," he said, from the door.

"Bartley!" she cried, in utter fondness, as he vanished from her happy eyes.

The next morning they heard the Squire moving about in his room, and he was late in coming down to breakfast, at which he was ordinarily so prompt.

"He's packing," said Marcia, sadly. "It's dreadful to be willing to have him go."

Bartley went out and met him at his door, bag in hand.

"Hollo!" he cried, and made a decent show of surprise and regret.

"Myes!" said the old man, as they went down-stairs. "I've made out a visit. But I'm an old fellow, and I aint easy away from home. I shall tell Mis' Gaylord how you're gettin' along, and she'll be pleased to hear it. Yes, she'll be pleased to hear it. I guess I shall get off on the ten-o'clock train."

The conversation between Bartley and his father-in-law was perfunctory. Men who have dealt so plainly with each other do not assume the conventional urbanities in their intercourse without effort. They had both been growing more impatient of the restraint; they could not have kept it up much longer.

"Well, I suppose it's natural you should want to be home again, but I can't understand how any one can want to go back to Equity when he has the privilege of staying in Boston."

"Boston will do for a young man," said the Squire, "but I'm too old for it. The city cramps me: it's too tight a fit; and yet I can't seem to find myself in it."

He suffered from the loss of identity which is a common affliction with country people coming to town. The feeling that they are of no special interest to any of the thousands they meet bewilders and harasses them; after the searching neighborhood of village life, the fact that nobody would meddle in their most intimate affairs if they could, is a vague distress. The Squire not only experienced this, but, after reigning so long as the censor of morals and religion in Equity, it was a deprivation for him to pass a whole week without saying a bitter thing to any one. He was tired of the civilities that smoothed him down on every side.

"Well, if you must go," said Bartley, "I'll order a hack."

"I guess I can walk to the depot," returned the old man.

"Oh, no, you can't."

Bartley drove to the station with him, and they bade each other adieu with a hand-shake. They were no longer enemies, but they liked each other less than ever.

"See you in Equity next summer, I suppose," suggested the Squire.

"So Marcia says," replied Bartley. "Well, take care of yourself.—You confounded tight-fisted old woodchuck!" he added, under his breath, for the Squire had allowed him to pay the hack-fare.

He walked home, composing variations on his parting malison, to find that the Squire had profited by his brief absence in ordering the hack to leave with Marcia a silver cup, knife, fork, and spoon, which Olive Halleck had helped him choose, for the baby. In the cup was a check for five hundred dollars. The Squire was embarrassed in presenting the gifts, and when

Marcia turned upon him with: "Now, look here, father, what do you mean?" he was at a loss how to explain.

"Well, it's what I always meant to do for you."

"Baby's things are all right," said Marcia. "But I'm not going to let Bartley take any money from you unless you think as well of him as I do, and say so, right out."

The Squire laughed.

"You couldn't quite expect me to do that, could you?"

"No, of course not. But what I mean is, do you think *now* that I did right to marry him?"

"Oh, *you're* all right, Marcia. I'm glad you're getting along so well."

"No, no! Is Bartley all right?"

The Squire laughed again, and rubbed his chin in enjoyment of her persistence.

"You can't expect me to own up to everything all at once."

"So you see, Bartley," said Marcia, in repeating these words to him, "it was quite a concession."

"Well, I don't know about the concession, but I guess there's no doubt about the check," replied Bartley, jocosely.

"Oh, don't say that, dear," protested his wife. "I think father was pleased with his visit every way. I know he's been anxious about me all the time; and yet it was a good deal for him to do, after what he had said, to come down here and as much as take it all back. Can't you look at it from his side?"

"Oh, I dare say it was a dose," Bartley admitted. The money had set several things in a better light. "If all the people that have abused me would take it back as handsomely as your father has,"—he held the check up,—"why, I wish there were twice as many of them."

She laughed for pleasure in his joke.

"I think father was impressed by everything about us,— beginning with baby," she said, proudly.

"Well, he kept his impressions to himself," said Bartley.

"Oh, that's nothing but his way. He never was demonstrative,—like me."

"No, he has his emotions under control—not to say under lock and key—not to add, in irons."

Bartley went on to give some instances of the Squire's for-

titude when apparently tempted to express pleasure or interest
in his Boston experiences.

They both undeniably felt freer now that he was gone.
Bartley staid longer than he ought from his work, in tacit
celebration of the Squire's departure, and they were very
merry together; but, when he left her, Marcia called for her
baby, and, gathering it close to her heart, sighed over it,
"Poor father! poor father!"

XXIII

WHEN the spring opened, Bartley pushed Flavia about the sunny pavements in a baby-carriage, while Marcia paced alongside, looking in under the calash top from time to time, arranging the bright afghan, and twitching the little one's lace hood into place. They never noticed that other perambulators were pushed by Irish nurse-girls, or French *bonnes*; they had paid somewhat more than they ought for theirs, and they were proud of it merely as a piece of property. It was rather Bartley's ideal, as it is that of most young American fathers, to go out with his wife and baby in that way; he liked to have his friends see him; and he went out every afternoon he could spare. When he could not go, Marcia went alone. Mrs. Halleck had given her a key to the garden, and on pleasant mornings she always found some of the family there, when she pushed the perambulator up the path, to let the baby sleep in the warmth and silence of the sheltered place. She chatted with Olive or the elder sisters, while Mrs. Halleck drove Cyrus on to the work of tying up the vines and trimming the shrubs, with the pitiless rigor of women when they get a man about some outdoor labor. Sometimes, Ben Halleck was briefly of the party; and one morning when Marcia opened the gate, she found him there alone with Cyrus, who was busy at some belated tasks of horticulture. The young man turned at the unlocking of the gate, and saw Marcia lifting the front wheels of the perambulator to get it over the steps of the pavement outside. He limped hastily down the walk to help her, but she had the carriage in the path before he could reach her, and he had nothing to do but to walk back at its side, as she propelled it toward the house. "You see what a useless creature a cripple is," he said.

Marcia did not seem to have heard him. "Is your mother at home?" she asked.

"I think she is," said Halleck. "Cyrus, go in and tell mother that Mrs. Hubbard is here, wont you?"

Cyrus went, after a moment of self-respectful delay, and Marcia sat down on a bench under a pear-tree beside the

walk. Its narrow young leaves and blossoms sprinkled her
with shade shot with vivid sunshine, and in her light dress,
she looked like a bright, fresh figure from some painter's
study of spring. She breathed quickly from her exertion, and
her cheeks had a rich, dewy bloom. She had pulled the perambulator round so that she might see her baby while she
waited, and she looked at the baby now, and not at Halleck,
as she said:

"It is quite hot in the sun to-day."

She had a way of closing her lips, after speaking, in that
sweet smile of hers, and then of glancing sidelong at the person to whom she spoke.

"I suppose it is," said Halleck, who remained on foot. "But
I haven't been out yet. I gave myself a day off from the law-
school, and I hadn't quite decided what to do with it."

Marcia leaned forward, and brushed a tendril of the baby's
hair out of its eye.

"She's the greatest little sleeper that ever was when she gets
into her carriage," she half mused, leaning back with her
hands folded in her lap, and setting her head on one side for
the effect of the baby without the stray ringlet. "She's getting
so fat," she said, proudly.

Halleck smiled.

"Do you find it makes a difference in pushing her carriage,
from day to day?"

Marcia took his question in earnest, as she must take anything but the most obvious pleasantry concerning her baby.

"The carriage runs very easily; we picked out the lightest
one we could, and I never have any trouble with it, except
getting up curb-stones and crossing Cambridge street. I don't
like to cross Cambridge street; there are always so many
horse-cars. But it's all down-hill coming here; that's one
good thing."

"That makes it a very bad thing going home, though," said
Halleck.

"Oh, I go round by Charles street and come up the hill
from the other side; it isn't so steep there."

There was no more to be said upon this point, and in the
lapse of their talk, Halleck broke off some boughs of the
blooming pear, and dropped them on the baby's afghan.

"Your mother wont like your spoiling her pear-tree," said Marcia, seriously.

"She will when she knows that I did it for Miss Hubbard."

"Miss Hubbard!" repeated the young mother, and she laughed in fond derision. "How funny to hear *you* saying that! I thought you hated babies."

Halleck looked at her with strong self-disgust, and he dropped the bough which he had in his hand upon the ground. There is something in a young man's ideal of women, at once passionate and ascetic, so fine that any words are too gross for it. The event which intensified the interest of his mother and sisters in Marcia, had abashed Halleck; when she came so proudly to show her baby to them all, it seemed to him like a mockery of his pity for her captivity to the love that profaned her. He went out of the room in angry impatience, which he could hardly hide when one of his sisters tried to make him take the baby. Little by little his compassion adjusted itself to the new conditions; it accepted the child as an element of her misery in the future, when she must realize the hideous deformity of her marriage. His prophetic sense of this, and of her inaccessibility to human help here and hereafter, made him sometimes afraid of her; but all the more severely he exacted of his ideal of her that she should not fall beneath the tragic dignity of her fate through any levity of her own. Now, at her innocent laugh, a subtle irreverence, which he was not able to exorcise, infused itself into his sense of her.

He stood looking at her, after he dropped the pear-bough, and seeing her mere beauty as he had never seen it before. The bees hummed in the blossoms, which gave out a dull, sweet smell; the sunshine had the luxurious, enervating warmth of spring. He started suddenly from his revery: Marcia had said something.

"I beg your pardon?" he queried.

"Oh, nothing. I asked if you knew where I went to church yesterday?"

Halleck flushed, ashamed of the wrong his thoughts, or rather his emotions, had done.

"No, I don't," he answered.

"I was at your church."

"I ought to have been there myself," he returned, gravely, "and then I should have known."

She took his self-reproach literally.

"You couldn't have seen me. I was sitting pretty far back, and I went out before any of your family saw me. Don't you go there?"

"Not always, I'm sorry to say. Or, rather, I'm sorry not to be sorry. What church do you generally go to?"

"Oh, I don't know. Sometimes to one, and sometimes to another. Bartley used to report the sermons and we went round to all the churches then. That is the way I did at home, and it came natural to me. But I don't like it very well. I want Flavia should belong to some particular church."

"There are enough to choose from," said Halleck, with pensive sarcasm.

"Yes, that's the difficulty. But I shall make up my mind to one of them, and then I shall always keep to it. What I mean is that I should like to find out where most of the good people belong, and then have her be with them," pursued Marcia. "I think it's best to belong to some church, don't you?"

There was something so bare, so spiritually poverty-stricken in these confessions and questions, that Halleck found nothing to say to them.

He was troubled, moreover, as to what the truth was in his own mind. He answered, with a sort of mechanical adhesion to the teachings of his youth: "I should be a recreant not to think so. But I'm not sure that I know what you mean by belonging to some church," he added. "I suppose you would want to believe in the creed of the church, whichever it was."

"I don't know that I should be particular," said Marcia, with perfect honesty.

Halleck laughed sadly.

"I'm afraid *they* would, then, unless you joined the Broad Church."

"What is that?"

He explained as well as he could. At the end she repeated, as if she had not followed him very closely:

"I should like her to belong to the church where most of

the good people go. I think that would be the right one, if you could only find which it is."

Halleck laughed again.

"I suppose what I say must sound very queer to you; but I've been thinking a good deal about this lately."

"I beg your pardon," said Halleck. "I had no reason to laugh, either on your account or my own. It's a serious subject."

She did not reply, and he asked, as if she had left the subject:

"Do you intend to pass the summer in Boston?"

"No; I'm going down home pretty early, and I wanted to ask your mother what is the best way to put away my winter things."

"You'll find my mother very good authority on such matters," said Halleck. Through an obscure association with moths that corrupt, he added: "She's a good authority on church matters, too."

"I guess I shall talk with her about Flavia," said Marcia.

Cyrus came out of the house.

"Mis' Halleck will be here in a minute. She's got to get red of a lady that's calling, first," he explained.

"I will leave you, then," said Halleck, abruptly.

"Good-by," answered Marcia, tranquilly. The baby stirred; she pushed the carriage to and fro, without glancing after him as he walked away.

His mother came down the steps from the house, and kissed Marcia for welcome, and looked under the carriage top at the sleeping baby.

"How she *does* sleep!" she whispered.

"Yes," said Marcia, with the proud humility of a mother who cannot deny the merit of her child, "and she sleeps the whole night through. I'm *never* up with her. Bartley says she's a perfect Seven Sleeper. It's a regular joke with him— her sleeping."

"Ben was a good baby for sleeping, too," said Mrs. Halleck, retrospectively emulous. "It's one of the best signs. It shows that the child is strong and healthy."

They went on to talk of their children, and in their community of motherhood, they spoke of the young man as if he were still an infant.

"He has never been a moment's care to me," said Mrs. Halleck. "A well baby will be well even in teething."

"And I had somehow thought of him as sickly!" said Marcia, in self-derision.

Tears of instant intelligence sprang into his mother's eyes.

"And did you suppose he was *always* lame?" she demanded with gentle indignation. "He was the brightest and strongest boy that ever was, till he was twelve years old. That's what makes it so hard to bear; that's what makes me wonder at the way the child bears it! Did you never hear how it happened? One of the big boys, as he called him, tripped him up at school, and he fell on his hip. It kept him in bed for a year, and he's never been the same since; he will always be a cripple," grieved the mother. She wiped her eyes; she never could think of her boy's infirmity without weeping. "And what seemed the worst of all," she continued, "was that the boy who did it, never expressed any regret for it, or acknowledged it by word or deed, though he must have known that Ben knew who hurt him. He's a man, here, now; and sometimes Ben meets him. But Ben always says that he can stand it if the other one can. He was always just so from the first! He wouldn't let us blame the boy; he said that he didn't mean any harm, and that all was fair in play. And now he says he knows the man is sorry, and would own to what he did, if he didn't have to own to what came of it. Ben says that very few of us have the courage to face the consequences of the injuries we do, and that's what makes people seem hard and indifferent when they are really not so. There!" cried Mrs. Halleck. "I don't know as I ought to have told you about it; I know Ben wouldn't like it. But I can't bear to have any one think he was always lame, though I don't know why I shouldn't: I'm prouder of him since it happened than ever I was before. I thought he was here with you," she added abruptly.

"He went out just before you came," said Marcia, nodding toward the gate. She sat listening to Mrs. Halleck's talk about Ben; Mrs. Halleck took herself to task from time to time, but only to go on talking about him again. Sometimes Marcia commented on his characteristics, and compared them with

Bartley's, or with Flavia's, according to the period of Ben's life under consideration. At the end Mrs. Halleck said: "I haven't let you get in a word! Now you must talk about *your* baby. Dear little thing! I feel that she's been neglected. But I'm always just so selfish when I get to running on about Ben. They all laugh at me."

"Oh, I like to hear about other children," said Marcia, turning the perambulator round. "I don't think any one can know too much that has the care of children of their own." She added, as if it followed from something they had been saying of vaccination: "Mrs. Halleck, I want to talk with you about getting Flavia christened. You know I never was christened."

"Weren't you?" said Mrs. Halleck, with a dismay which she struggled to conceal.

"No," said Marcia, "father doesn't believe in any of those things, and mother had got to letting them go, because he didn't take any interest in them. They did have the first children christened, but I was the last."

"I didn't speak with your father on the subject," faltered Mrs. Halleck. "I didn't know what his persuasion was."

"Why, father doesn't belong to *any* church! He believes in a God, but he doesn't believe in the Bible." Mrs. Halleck sank down on the garden-seat too much shocked to speak, and Marcia continued: "I don't know whether the Bible is true or not; but I've often wished that I belonged to church."

"You couldn't, unless you believed in the Bible," said Mrs. Halleck.

"Yes, I know that. Perhaps I should, if anybody proved it to me. I presume it could be explained. I never talked much with any one about it. There must be a good many people who don't belong to church, although they believe in the Bible. I should be perfectly willing to try, if I only knew how to begin."

In view of this ruinous open-mindedness, Mrs. Halleck could only say,

"The way to begin is to read it."

"Well, I will try. How do you know, after you've become so that you believe the Bible, whether you're fit to join the church?"

"It's hard to tell you, my dear. You have to feel first that you have a Saviour,—that you've given your whole heart to him,—that he can save you, and that no one else can; that all you can do yourself wont help you. It's an experience."

Marcia looked at her attentively, as if this were all a very hard saying.

"Yes, I've heard of that. Some of the girls had it at school. But I never did. Well," she said at last, "I don't feel so anxious about myself, just at present, as I do about Flavia. I want to do everything I can for Flavia, Mrs. Halleck. I want her to be christened,—I want her to be baptized into some church. I think a good deal about it. I think sometimes, what if she should die, and I hadn't done that for her, when may be it was one of the most important things"—Her voice shook, and she pressed her lips together.

"Of course," said Mrs. Halleck, tenderly. "I think it is the *most* important thing."

"But there are so many churches," Marcia resumed. "And I don't know about any of them. I told Mr. Halleck, just now, that I should like her to belong to the church where the best people go, if I could find it out. Of course, it was a ridiculous way to talk; I knew he thought so. But what I meant was that I wanted she should be with good people all her life; and I didn't care what she believed."

"It's very important to believe the truth, my dear," said Mrs. Halleck.

"But the truth is so hard to be certain of, and you know goodness as soon as you see it. Mrs. Halleck, I'll tell you what I want: I want Flavia should be baptized into your church. Will you let her?"

"*Let* her? Oh, my dear child, we shall be humbly thankful that it has been put into your heart to choose for her what *we* think is the true church," said Mrs. Halleck, fervently.

"I don't know about that," returned Marcia. "I can't tell whether it's the true church or not, and I don't know that I ever could; but I shall be satisfied, if it's made you what you are," she added simply.

Mrs. Halleck did not try to turn away her praise with vain affectations of humility. "We try to do right, Marcia," she said. "Whenever we do it, we must be helped to it by some power outside of ourselves. I can't tell you whether it's our church; I'm not so sure of that as I used to be. I once thought that there could be no real good out of it; but I *can't* think that, any more: Olive and Ben are as good children as ever lived; I *know* they wont be lost; but neither of them belongs to our church."

"Why, what church does he belong to?"

"He doesn't belong to any, my dear," said Mrs. Halleck, sorrowfully.

Marcia looked at her absently.

"I knew Olive was a Unitarian; but I thought—I thought he"—

"No, he doesn't," returned Mrs. Halleck. "It has been a great cross to his father and me. He is a good boy; but we think the *truth* is in our church!"

Marcia was silent a moment. Then she said, decisively:

"Well, I should like Flavia to belong to your church."

"She couldn't belong to it now," Mrs. Halleck explained. "That would have to come later, when she could understand. But she could be christened in it—dear little thing!"

"Well, christened, then. It must be the training he got in it. I've thought a great deal about it, and I think my worst trouble is that I've been left too free in everything. One mustn't be left too free. I've never had any one to control me, and now I can't control myself at the very times when I need to do it the most, with—with—when I'm in danger of vexing—when Bartley and I"—

"Yes," said Mrs. Halleck, sympathetically.

"And Bartley is just so, too. He's always been left to himself. And Flavia will need all the control we can give her—I know she will. And I shall have her christened in your church, and I shall teach her all about it. She shall go to the Sunday-school, and I will go to church, so that she can have an example. I told father I should do it when he was up here, and he said there couldn't be any harm in it. And I've told Bartley, and *he* doesn't care."

They were both far too single-minded and too serious to find anything droll in the terms of the adhesion of Marcia's family to her plan, and Mrs. Halleck entered into its execution with affectionate zeal.

"Ben, dear," she said, tenderly, that evening, when they

were all talking it over in family council, "I hope you didn't drop anything, when that poor creature spoke to you about it this morning, that could unsettle her mind in any way?"

"No, mother," said Halleck, gently.

"I was sure you didn't," returned his mother, repentantly. They had been talking a long time of the matter, and Halleck now left the room.

"Mother! How could you say such a thing to Ben?" cried Olive, in a quiver of indignant sympathy. "Ben say anything to unsettle anybody's religious purposes! He's got more religion now than all the rest of the family put together!"

"Speak for yourself, Olive," said one of the intermediary sisters.

"Why, Olive, I spoke because I thought she seemed to place more importance on Ben's belonging to the church than anything else, and she seemed so surprised when I told her he didn't belong to any."

"I dare say she thinks Ben is good when she compares him with that mass of selfishness of a husband of hers," said Olive. "But I will thank her," she added, hotly, "not to compare Ben with Bartley Hubbard, even to Bartley Hubbard's disadvantage. I don't feel flattered by it."

"Of course, she thinks all the world of her husband," said Mrs. Halleck. "And I know Ben is good; and as you say, he is religious; I feel that, though I don't understand how, exactly. I wouldn't hurt his feelings for the world, Olive, you know well enough. But it was a stumbling-block when I had to tell that poor, pretty young thing that Ben didn't belong to church; and I could see that it puzzled her. I couldn't have believed," continued Mrs. Halleck, "that there was any person in a Christian land, except among the very lowest, that seemed to understand so little about the Christian religion, or any scheme of salvation. Really, she talked to me like a pagan. She sat there much better dressed and better educated than I was; but I felt like a missionary talking to a South Sea Islander."

"I wonder the old Bartlett pear didn't burst into a palm-tree over your heads," said Olive. Mrs. Halleck looked grieved at her levity, and she hastened to add:

"Don't put up your lip, mother. I understood just what

you meant, and I can imagine just how shocking Mrs. Hubbard's heathen remarks must have been. We should all be shocked if we knew how many people there are just like her, and we should all try to deny it, and so would they. I guess Christianity is about as uncommon as civilization—and that's *very* uncommon. If her poor, feeble mind was such a chaos, what do you suppose her husband's is?"

This would certainly not have been easy for Mrs. Halleck to say, then, or to say afterward, when Bartley walked up to the font in her church, with Marcia at his side, and Flavia in his arms, and a faintly ironical smile on his face, as if he had never expected to be got in for this, but was going to see it through now. He had, in fact, said, "Well, let's go the whole figure," when Marcia had expressed a preference for having the rite performed in church, instead of in their own house.

He was unquestionably growing stout, and even Mrs. Halleck noticed that his blonde face was unpleasantly red that day. He was, of course, not intemperate. He always had beer with his lunch, which he had begun to take down town, since the warm weather had come on and made the walk up the hill to Clover street irksome: and he drank beer at his dinner—he liked a late dinner, and they dined at six, now—because it washed away the fatigues of the day and freshened you up. He was rather particular about his beer, which he had sent in by the gross—it came cheaper that way; after trying both the Cincinnati and the Milwaukee lagers, and making a cursory test of the Boston brand, he had settled down upon the American Tivoli; it was cheap, and you could drink a couple of bottles without feeling it. Freshened up by his two bottles, he was apt to spend the evening in an amiable drowse and get early to bed, when he did not go out on newspaper duty. He joked about the three fingers of fat on his ribs, and frankly guessed it was the beer that did it; at such times he said that perhaps he should have to cut down on his Tivoli.

Marcia and he had not so much time together as they used to have; she was a great deal taken up with the baby, and he found it dull at home, not doing anything or saying anything; and, when he did not feel sleepy, he sometimes invented work that took him out at night. But he always came upstairs after putting his hat on, and asked Marcia if he could help her about anything.

He usually met other newspaper men on these excursions, and talked newspaper with them, airing his favorite theories. He liked to wander about with reporters who were working up cases; to look in at the police stations, and go to the fires; and he was often able to give the Events men points that had escaped the other reporters. If asked to drink, he always said, "Thanks, no; I don't do anything in that way. But if you'll make it beer, I don't mind." He took nothing but beer when he hurried out of the theatre into one of the neighboring resorts, just as the great platters of stewed kidneys and *lyonnaise* potatoes came steaming up out of the kitchen, prompt to the drop of the curtain on the last act. Here, sometimes, he met a friend, and shared with him his dish of kidneys and his schooner of beer; and he once suffered himself to be lured by the click of the balls into the back room. He believed that he played a very good game of billiards; but he was badly beaten that night. He came home at daylight fifty dollars out. But he had lost like a gentleman in a game with gentlemen; and he never played again.

By day he worked hard, and since his expenses had been increased by Flavia's coming, he had undertaken more work for more pay. He still performed all the routine labor of a managing editor, and he now wrote the literary notices of The Events, and sometimes, especially if there was anything new, the dramatic criticisms; he brought to the latter task all the freshness of a man who, till the year before, had not been half a dozen times inside a theatre.

He attributed the fat on his ribs to the Tivoli; perhaps it was also owing in some degree to a good conscience, which is a much easier thing to keep than people imagine. At any rate, he now led a tranquil, industrious, and regular life, and a life which suited him so well that he was reluctant to interrupt it by the visit to Equity which he and Marcia had talked of in the early spring. He put it off from time to time, and one day, when she was pressing him to fix some date for it, he said:

"Why can't you go, Marcia?"

"Alone?" she faltered.

"Well, no; take the baby, of course. And I'll run down for a day or two when I get a chance."

Marcia seemed in these days to be schooling herself against the impulses that once brought on her quarrels with Bartley.

"A day or two"—she began, and then stopped and added gravely, "I thought you said you were going to have several weeks' vacation."

"Oh, don't tell me what I *said!*" cried Bartley. "That was before I undertook this extra work, or before I knew what a grind it was going to be. Equity is a good deal of a dose for me, anyway. It's all well enough for you, and I guess the change from Boston will do you good, and do the baby good, but *I* shouldn't look forward to three weeks in Equity with unmitigated hilarity."

"I know it will be stupid for you. But you need the rest. And the Hallecks are going to be at North Conway; and they said they would come over," urged Marcia. "I know we should have a good time."

Bartley grinned.

"Is that your idea of a good time, Marsh? Three weeks of Equity, relieved by a visit from such heavy weights as Ben Halleck and his sisters? Not any in mine, thank you."

"How can you—how *dare* you speak so of them!" cried Marcia, lightening upon him. "Such good friends of yours—such good people"—

Her voice shook with indignation and wounded feeling.

Bartley rose and took a turn about the room, pulling down his waistcoat and contemplating its outward slope with a smile.

"Oh, I've got more friends than I can shake a stick at. And with pleasure at the helm, goodness is a drug in the market—if you'll excuse the mixed metaphor. Look here, Marcia," he added, severely. "If you like the Hallecks, all well and good; I sha'n't interfere with you; but they bore me. I outgrew Ben Halleck years ago. He's duller than death. As for the old people, there's no harm in them,—though *they're* bores, too,—nor in the old girls; but Olive Halleck doesn't treat me decently. I suppose that just suits you: I've noticed that you never like the women that *do* treat me decently."

"They don't treat me decently!" retorted Marcia.

"Oh, Miss Kingsbury treated you very well that night. She couldn't imagine your being jealous of her politeness to me."

Marcia's temper fired at his treacherous recurrence to a grievance which he had once so sacredly and sweetly ignored.

"If you wish to take up by-gones, why don't you go back to Hannah Morrison at once? She treated you even better than Miss Kingsbury."

"I should have been very willing to do that," said Bartley, "but I thought it might remind you of a disagreeable little episode in your own life, when you flung me away, and had to go down on your knees to pick me up again."

These thrusts which they dealt each other in their quarrels, however blind and misdirected, always reached their hearts: it was the wicked will that hurt, rather than the words. Marcia rose, bleeding inwardly, and her husband felt the remorse of a man who gets the best of it in such an encounter.

"Oh, I'm sorry I said that, Marcia! I didn't mean it; indeed I"—She disdained to heed him as she swept out of the room and up the stairs; and his anger flamed out again.

"I give you fair warning," he called after her, "not to try that trick of locking the door, or I will smash it in."

Her answer was to turn the key in the door with a click which he could not fail to hear.

The peace in which they had been living of late was very comfortable to Bartley; he liked it; he hated to have it broken; he was willing to do what he could to restore it at once. If he had no better motive than this, he still had this motive; and he choked down his wrath, and followed Marcia softly upstairs. He intended to reason with her, and he began, "I say, Marsh," as he turned the door-knob. But you cannot reason through a keyhole, and before he knew he found himself saying, "Will you open this?" in a tone whose quiet was deadly. She did not answer; he heard her stop in her movements about the room, and wait, as if she expected him to ask again. He hesitated a moment whether to keep his threat of breaking the door in; but he turned away and went downstairs, and so into the street. Once outside, he experienced the sense of release that comes to a man from the violation of his better impulses; but he did not know what to do or where to go. He walked rapidly away; but Marcia's eyes and voice seemed to follow him, and plead with him for his forbearance. He answered his conscience, as if it had been some such presence, that he had forborne too much already, and that now he should not humble himself: that he was right and should stand upon his right. There was not much comfort in it, and he had to brace himself again and again with vindictive resolution.

XXIV

B ARTLEY WALKED about the streets for a long time, without purpose or direction, brooding fiercely on his
wrongs, and reminding himself how Marcia had determined
to have him, and had indeed flung herself upon his mercy,
with all sorts of good promises; and had then at once taken
the whiphand, and goaded and tormented him ever since. All
the kindness of their common life counted for nothing in this
furious reverie, or rather it was never once thought of; he
cursed himself for a fool that he had ever asked her to marry
him, and for doubly a fool that he had married her when she
had as good as asked him. He was glad, now, that he had
taunted her with that; he only regretted that he had told her
he was sorry. He was presently aware of being so tired that
he could scarcely pull one leg after another; and yet he felt
hopelessly wide awake. It was in simple despair of anything
else to do that he climbed the stairs to Ricker's lofty perch in
the Chronicle-Abstract office. Ricker turned about as he entered, and stared up at him from beneath the green pasteboard visor with which he was shielding his eyes from the
gas; his hair, which was of the harshness and color of hay,
was stiffly poked up and strewn about on his skull, as if it
were some foreign product.

"Hello!" he said. "Going to issue a morning edition of the
Events?"

"What makes you think so?"

"Oh, I supposed you evening paper gents went to bed with
the hens. What has kept you up, esteemed contemporary?"

He went on working over some dispatches which lay upon
his table.

"Don't you want to come out and have some oysters?"
asked Bartley.

"Why this princely hospitality? I'll come with you in half a
minute," Ricker said, going to the slide that carried up the
copy to the composing-room, and thrusting his manuscript
into the box.

"Where are you going?" he asked, when they found themselves out in the soft starlit autumnal air; and Bartley answered with the name of an oyster-house, obscure, but of singular excellence.

"Yes, that's the best place," Ricker commented. "What I continually wonder at in you is the rapidity with which you've taken on the city. You were quite in the green wood when you came here, and now you know your Boston like a little man. I suppose it's your newspaper work that's familiarized you with the place. Well, how do you like friend Witherby, as far as you've gone?"

"Oh, we shall get along, I guess," said Bartley. "He still keeps me in the background, and plays at being editor himself, but he pays me pretty well."

"Not too well, I hope."

"I should like to see him try it."

"I shouldn't," said Ricker. "He'd expect certain things of you, if he did. You'll have to look out for Witherby."

"You mean that he's a scamp?"

"No; there isn't a better conscience than Witherby carries in the whole city. He's perfectly honest. He not only believes that he has a right to run the Events in his way, but he sincerely believes that he is right in doing it. There's where he has the advantage of you, if you doubt him. I don't suppose he ever did a wrong thing in his life; he'd persuade himself that the thing was right before he did it."

"That's a common phenomenon, isn't it?" sneered Bartley. "Nobody sins."

"You're right, partly. But some of us sinners have our misgivings, and Witherby never has. You know he offered me your place?"

"No, I didn't," said Bartley, astonished and not pleased.

"I thought he might have told you. He made me inducements; but I was afraid of him: Witherby is the counting-room incarnate. I talked you into him for some place or other; but he didn't seem to wake up to the value of my advice at once. Then I couldn't tell what he was going to offer you."

"Thank you for letting me in for a thing you were afraid of!"

"I didn't believe he would get you under his thumb, as he

would me. You've got more backbone than I have. I have to keep out of temptation; you have noticed that I never drink, and I would rather not look upon Witherby when he is red and giveth his color in the cup. I'm sorry if I've let you in for anything that you regret. But Witherby's sincerity makes him dangerous—I own that."

"I think he has some very good ideas about newspapers," said Bartley, rather sulkily.

"Oh, very," assented Ricker. "Some of the very best going. He believes that the press is a great moral engine, and that it ought to be run in the interest of the engineer."

"And I suppose you believe that it ought to be run in the interest of the public?"

"Exactly—after the public has paid."

"Well, I don't; and I never did. A newspaper is a private enterprise."

"It's private property, but it isn't a private enterprise, and in its very nature it can't be. You know I never talk 'journalism' and stuff; it amuses me to hear the young fellows at it, though I think they might be doing something worse than magnifying their office; they might be decrying it. But I've got a few ideas and principles of my own in my back pantaloons-pocket."

"Haul them out," said Bartley.

"I don't know that they're very well formulated," returned Ricker, "and I don't contend that they're very new. But I consider a newspaper a public enterprise, with certain distinct duties to the public. It's sacredly bound not to do anything to deprave or debauch its readers; and it's sacredly bound not to mislead or betray them, not merely as to questions of morals and politics, but as to questions of what we may lump as 'advertising.' Has friend Witherby developed his great ideas of advertisers' rights to you?" Bartley did not answer, and Ricker went on: "Well, then, you can understand my position, when I say it's exactly the contrary."

"You ought to be on a religious newspaper, Ricker," said Bartley, with a scornful laugh.

"Thank you, a secular paper is bad enough for me."

"Well, I don't pretend that I make the Events just what I want," said Bartley. "At present the most I can do is to indulge in a few cheap dreams of what I should do, if I had a paper of my own."

"What are your dreams? Haul out, as you say."

"I should make it pay, to begin with; and I should make it pay by making it such a thorough newspaper, that every class of people *must* have it. I should cater to the lowest class first, and as long as I was poor, I would have the fullest and best reports of every local accident and crime; that would take *all* the rabble. Then, as I could afford it, I'd rise a little, and give first-class non-partisan reports of local political affairs; that would fetch the next largest class, the ward politicians of all parties. I'd lay for the local religious world, after that—religion comes right after politics in the popular mind, and it interests the women like murder: I'd give the minutest religious intelligence, and not only that, but the religious gossip, and the religious scandal. Then I'd go in for fashion and society—that comes next. I'd have the most reliable and thorough-going financial reports that money could buy. When I'd got my local ground perfectly covered, I'd begin to ramify. Every fellow that could spell, in any part of the country, should understand that if he sent me an account of a suicide, or an elopement, or a murder, or an accident, he should be well paid for it; and I'd rise on the same scale through all the departments. I'd add art criticisms, dramatic and sporting news, and book-reviews, more for the looks of the thing than for anything else; they don't any of 'em appeal to a large class. I'd get my paper into such a shape that people of every kind and degree would have to say, no matter what particular objection was made to it, "Yes, that's so; but it's the best *news*paper in the world, *and we can't get along without it.*"

"And then," said Ricker, "you'd begin to clean up, little by little—let up on your murders and scandals, and purge and live cleanly like a gentleman? The trick's been tried before."

They had arrived at the oyster-house, and were sitting at their table, waiting for the oysters to be brought to them. Bartley tilted his chair back. "I don't know about the cleaning up. I should want to keep all my audience. If I cleaned up, the dirty fellows would go off to some one else; and the fellows that pretended to be clean would be disappointed."

"Why don't you get Witherby to put your ideas in force?" asked Ricker, dryly.

Bartley dropped his chair to all fours, and said with a smile, "He belongs to church."

"Ah, he has his limitations. What a pity! He has the money to establish this great moral engine of yours, and you haven't. It's a loss to civilization."

"One thing, I know," said Bartley, with a certain effect of virtue, "nobody should buy or sell me; and the advertising element shouldn't spread beyond the advertising page."

"Isn't that rather high ground?" inquired Ricker.

Bartley did not think it worth while to answer. "I don't believe that a newspaper is obliged to be superior in tone to the community," he said.

"I quite agree with you."

"And if the community is full of vice and crime, a newspaper can't do better than reflect its condition."

"Ah, there I should distinguish, esteemed contemporary. There are several tones in every community, and it will keep any newspaper scratching to rise above the highest. But if it keeps out of the mud at all it can't help rising above the lowest. And no community is full of vice and crime any more than it is full of virtue and good works. Why not let your model newspaper mirror these?"

"They're not snappy."

"No, that's true."

"You must give the people what they want."

"Are you sure of that?"

"Yes, I am."

"Well, it's a beautiful dream," said Ricker, "nourished on a youth sublime. Why do not these lofty imaginings visit us later in life? You make me quite ashamed of my own ideal newspaper. Before you began to talk I had been fancying that the vice of our journalism was its intense localism. I have doubted a good while whether a drunken Irishman who breaks his wife's head, or a child who falls into a tub of hot water, has really established a claim on the public interest. Why should I be told by telegraph how three negroes died on the gallows in North Carolina? Why should an accurate correspondent inform me of the elopement of a married man with his maid-servant in East Machias? Why should I sup on all the horrors of a railroad accident, and have the bleeding fragments hashed up for me at breakfast? Why should my newspaper give a succession of shocks to my nervous system, as I pass from column to column, and poultice me between shocks with the nastiness of a distant or local scandal? You reply, because I like spice. But I don't. I am sick of spice; and I believe that most of our readers are."

"Cater to them with milk-toast, then," said Bartley.

Ricker laughed with him, and they fell to upon their oysters.

When they parted, Bartley still found himself wakeful. He knew that he should not sleep if he went home, and he said to himself that he could not walk about all night. He turned into a gayly lighted basement, and asked for something in the way of a night-cap

The bar-keeper said there was nothing like a hot-scotch to make you sleep; and a small man, with his hat on, who had been talking with the bar-keeper, and coming up to the counter occasionally to eat a bit of cracker or a bit of cheese out of the two bowls full of such fragments that stood at the end of the counter, said that this was so.

It was very cheerful in the bar-room, with the light glittering on the rows of decanters behind the bar-keeper, a large, stout, clean, pale man in his shirt-sleeves, after the manner of his kind; and Bartley made up his mind to stay there till he was drowsy, and to drink as many hot-scotches as were necessary to the result. He had his drink put on a little table and sat down to it easily, stirring it to cool it a little, and feeling its flattery in his brain from the first sip.

The man who was munching cheese and crackers wore a hat rather large for him, pulled down over his eyes. He now said that he did not care if he took a gin-sling, and the bar-keeper promptly set it before him on the counter, and saluted with "Good evening, Colonel," a large man who came in, carrying a small dog in his arms. Bartley recognized him as the manager of a variety combination playing at one of the theatres, and the manager recognized the little man with the gin-sling as Tommy. He did not return the bar-keeper's salutation, but he asked, as he sat down at a table:

"What do I want for supper, Charley?"

The bar-keeper said, oracularly, as he leaned forward to wipe his counter with a napkin:

"Fricasee chicken."

"Fricassee devil," returned the manager. "Get me a Welsh rabbit."

The bar-keeper, unperturbed by this rejection, called into the tube behind him:

"One Welsh rabbit!"

"I want some cold chicken for my dog," said the manager.

"One cold chicken," repeated the bar-keeper, in his tube.

"White meat," said the manager.

"White meat," repeated the bar-keeper.

"I went into the Parker House one night about midnight, and I saw four doctors there eating lobster salad, and deviled crab, and washing it down with champagne; and I made up my mind that the doctors needn't talk to me any more about what was wholesome. I was going in for what was *good*. And there aint anything better for supper than Welsh rabbit in *this* world."

As the manager addressed this philosophy to the company at large, no one commented upon it, which seemed quite the same to the manager, who hitched one elbow over the back of his chair, and caressed with the other hand the dog lying in his lap.

The little man in the large hat continued to walk up and down, leaving his gin-sling on the counter, and drinking it between his visits to the cracker and cheese.

"What's that new piece of yours, Colonel?" he asked, after awhile. "I aint seen it yet."

"Legs, principally," sighed the manager. "That's what the public wants. I give the public what it wants. I don't pretend to be any better than the public. Nor any worse," he added, stroking his dog.

These ideas struck Bartley in their accordance with his own ideas of journalism as he had propounded them to Ricker. He had drunk half of his hot-scotch.

"That's what I say," assented the little man. "All that a theatre has got to do is to keep even with the public."

"That's so, Tommy," said the manager of a school of morals, with wisdom that impressed more and more the manager of a great moral engine.

"The same principle runs through everything," observed Bartley, speaking for the first time.

The drink had stiffened his tongue somewhat, but it did not incommode his utterance; it rather gave dignity to it, and his head was singularly clear. He lifted his empty glass from the table, and, catching the bar-keeper's eye, said, "Do it again." The man brought it back full.

"It runs through the churches as well as the theatres. As long as the public wanted hell-fire, the ministers gave them hell-fire. But you couldn't get hell-fire—not the pure, old-fashioned brimstone article—out of a popular preacher now, for love or money."

The little man said, "I guess you've got about the size of it there;" and the manager laughed.

"It's just so with the newspapers, too," said Bartley. "Some newspapers used to stand out against publishing murders, and personal gossip, and divorce trials. There aint a newspaper that pretends to keep anyways up with the times, now, that don't do it! The public want spice, and they will have it!"

"Well, sir," said the manager, "that's my way of looking at it. I say if the public don't want Shakspere, give 'em burlesque till they're sick of it. I believe in what Grant said: 'The quickest way to get rid of a bad law is to enforce it.'"

"That's so," said the little man, "every time."

He added to the bar-keeper that he guessed he would have some brandy and soda, and Bartley found himself at the bottom of his second tumbler. He ordered it replenished.

The little man seemed to be getting further away. He said, from the distance to which he had withdrawn:

"You want to go to bed with three night-caps on, like an old-clothes-man."

Bartley felt like resenting the freedom, but he was anxious to pour his ideas of journalism into the manager's sympathetic ear, and he began to talk, with an impression that it behooved him to talk fast. His brain was still very clear, but his tongue was getting stiffer. The manager now had his Welsh rabbit before him; but Bartley could not make out how it had got there, nor when. He was talking fast, and he knew by the way everybody was listening, that he was talking well. Sometimes he left his table, glass in hand, and went and laid down the law to the manager, who smilingly assented to all he said. Once he heard a low growling at his feet, and looking down, he saw the dog with his plate of cold chicken, that had also been conjured into the room somehow.

"Look out," said the manager, "he'll nip you in the leg."

"Curse the dog! he seems to be on all sides of you," said Bartley. "I can't stand anywhere."

"Better sit down then," suggested the manager.

"Good idea," said the little man, who was still walking up and down. It appeared as if he had not spoken for several hours; his hat was further over his eyes. Bartley had thought he was gone.

"What business is it of yours?" he demanded fiercely, moving toward the little man.

"Come, none of that," said the bar-keeper, steadily.

Bartley looked at him in amazement.

"Where's your hat?" he asked.

The others laughed; the bar-keeper smiled.

"Are you a married man?"

"Never mind!" said the bar-keeper, severely.

Bartley turned to the little man:

"You married?"

"Not *much*," replied the other. He was now topping off with a whisky-straight.

Bartley referred himself to the manager:

"You?"

"*Pas si bête*," said the manager, who did his own adapting from the French.

"Well, you're scholar, and you're gentleman," said Bartley. The indefinite articles would drop out, in spite of all his efforts to keep them in. " 'N' I want ask you what you do—to—ask—you—what—would—you—do," he repeated with painful exactness, but he failed to make the rest of the sentence perfect, and he pronounced it all in a word, " 'fyour-wifelockyouout."

"I'd take a walk," said the manager.

"I'd bu'st the door in," said the little man.

Bartley turned and gazed at him as if the little man were a much more estimable person than he had supposed. He passed his arm through the little man's, which the other had just crooked to lift his whisky to his mouth.

"Look here," said Bartley, "tha's jus' what *I* told her. I want you to go home 'th me; I want t' introduce you to my wife."

"All right," answered the little man. "Don't care if I do." He dropped his tumbler to the floor. "Hang it up, Charley, glass and all. Hang up this gentleman's night-caps—my account. Gentleman asks me home to his house, I'll hang him—I'll get him hung—well, fix it to suit yourself—every time!"

They got themselves out of the door, and the manager said to the bar-keeper, who came round to gather up the fragments of the broken tumbler,

"Think his wife will be glad to see 'em, Charley?"

"Oh, they'll be taken care of before they reach his house."

XXV

WHEN they were once out under the stars, Bartley, who still felt his brain clear, said that he would not take his friend home at once, but would show him where he visited when he first came to Boston. The other agreed to the indulgence of this sentiment, and they set out to find Rumford street together.

"You've heard of old man Halleck—Lestor Neather Interest? Tha's place—there's where I staid. His son's my frien'—damn stuck-up supercilious beast he is, too. *I* do' care f'r him! I'll show you place, so's't you'll know it when you come to it,—'f I can ever find it."

They walked up and down the street, looking, while Bartley poured his sorrows into the ear of his friend, who grew less and less responsive, and at last ceased from his side altogether. Bartley then dimly perceived that he was himself sitting on a doorstep, and that his head was hanging far down between his knees, as if he had been sleeping in that posture.

"Locked out—locked out of my own door, and by my own wife!" He shed tears, and fell asleep again. From time to time he woke, and bewailed himself to Ricker as a poor boy who had fought his own way; he owned that he had made mistakes, as who had not? Again he was trying to convince Squire Gaylord that they ought to issue a daily edition of the Equity Free Press, and at the same time persuading Mr. Halleck to buy the Events for him, and let him put it on a paying basis. He shivered, sighed, hiccupped, and was dozing off again, when Henry Bird knocked him down, and he fell with a cry, which at last brought to the door the uneasy sleeper who had been listening to him within, and trying to realize his presence, catching his voice in waking intervals, doubting it, drowsing when it ceased, and then catching it and losing it again.

"Hallo, here! What do you want? Hubbard! Is it you? What in the world are you doing here?"

"Halleck," said Bartley, who was unsteadily straightening himself upon his feet, "glad to find you at home. Been looking for your house all night. Want to introduce you to partic-

ic-ular friend of mine. Mr. Halleck, Mr. —. Curse me if I
know your name"—

"Hold on a minute," said Halleck.

He ran into the house for his hat and coat, and came out
again, closing the door softly after him. He found Bartley in
the grip of a policeman, whom he was asking his name that
he might introduce him to his friend Halleck.

"Do you know this man, Mr. Halleck?" asked the policeman.

"Yes—yes, I know him," said Ben, in a low voice. "Let's
get him away quietly, please. He's all right. It's the first time
I ever saw him so. Will you help me with him up to Johnson's
stable? I'll get a carriage there and take him home."

They had begun walking Bartley along between them; he
dozed and paid no attention to their talk.

The policeman laughed.

"I was just going to run him in, when you came out. You
didn't come a minute too soon."

They got Bartley to the stable, and he slept heavily in one
of the chairs in the office, while the hostlers were putting the
horses to the carriage. The policeman remained at the office-
door, looking in at Bartley, and philosophizing the situation
to Halleck.

"Your speakin' about its bein' the first time you ever saw
him so made me think 't I rather help take home a regular
habitual drunk to his family, any day, than a case like this.
They always seem to take it so much harder the first time.
Boards with his mother, I presume?"

"He's married," said Halleck, sadly. "He has a house of his
own."

"Well!" said the policeman.

Bartley slept all the way to Clover street, and when the
carriage stopped at his door, they had difficulty in waking
him sufficiently to get him out.

"Don't come in, please," said Halleck, to the policeman,
when this was done. "The man will carry you back to your
beat. Thank you, ever so much!"

"All right, Mr. Halleck. Don't mention it," said the policeman, and he leaned back in the hack with an air of luxury, as
it rumbled softly away.

Halleck remained on the pavement with Bartley falling limply against him in the dim light of the dawn.

"What you want? What you doing with me?" he demanded with sullen stupidity.

"I've got you home, Hubbard. Here we are at your house."

He pulled him across the pavement, to the threshold, and put his hand on the bell, but the door was thrown open before he could ring, and Marcia stood there, with her face white, and her eyes red with watching and crying.

"Oh, Bartley, oh, Bartley!" she sobbed. "Oh, Mr. Halleck, what is it? Is he hurt? I did it—yes, I did it! It's my fault! Oh, will he die? Is he sick?"

"He isn't very well. He'd better go to bed," said Halleck.

"Yes, yes! I will help you upstairs with him."

"Do' need any help," said Bartley, sulkily. "Go upstairs myself."

He actually did so, with the help of the hand-rail, Marcia running before, to open the door, and smooth the pillows which her head had not touched, and Halleck following him to catch him if he should fall. She unlaced his shoes and got them off, while Halleck removed his coat.

"Oh, Bartley, where do you feel badly, dear? Oh, what shall I do?" she moaned, as he tumbled himself on the bed, and lapsed into a drunken stupor.

"Better—better come out, Mrs. Hubbard," said Halleck. "Better let him alone, now. You only make him worse, talking to him."

Quelled by the mystery of his manner, she followed him out and down the stairs.

"Oh, *do* tell me what it is," she implored, in a low voice, "or I shall go wild! But tell me and I can bear it! I can bear anything if I know what it is!" She came close to him in her entreaty, and fixed her eyes beseechingly on his, while she caught his hand in both of hers. "Is he—is he insane?"

"He isn't quite in his right mind, Mrs. Hubbard," Halleck began, softly releasing himself, and retreating a little from her, but she pursued him, and put her hand on his arm.

"Oh, then go for the doctor—go instantly! Don't lose a minute! I shall not be afraid to stay alone. Or if you think I'd better not, I will go for the doctor myself."

"No, no," said Halleck, smiling, sadly: the case certainly had its ludicrous side. "He doesn't need a doctor. You mustn't think of calling a doctor. Indeed you mustn't. He'll come out all right of himself. If you sent for a doctor, it would make him very angry."

She burst into tears. "Well, I will do what you say," she cried. "It would never have happened, if it hadn't been for me. I want to tell you what I did," she went on wildly. "I want to tell"—

"Please don't tell me anything, Mrs. Hubbard! It will all come right—and very soon. It isn't anything to be alarmed about. He'll be well in a few hours. I—ah— Good-by!" He had found his cane, and he made a limp toward the door, but she swiftly interposed herself.

"Why," she panted in mixed reproach and terror, "you're not going away? You're not going to leave me before Bartley is well? He may get worse—he may die! You mustn't go, Mr. Halleck!"

"Yes, I must,—I can't stay,—I oughtn't to stay—it wont do! He wont get worse, he wont die"—The perspiration broke out on Halleck's face, which he lifted to hers with a distress as great as her own.

She only answered, "I can't let you go. It would kill me. I wonder at your wanting to go."

There was something ghastly comical in it all, and Halleck stood in fear of its absurdity hardly less than of its tragedy. He rapidly revolved in his mind the possibilities of the case. He thought at first that it might be well to call a doctor, and having explained the situation to him, pay him to remain in charge; but he reflected that it would be insulting to ask a doctor to see a man in Hubbard's condition. He took out his watch, and saw that it was six o'clock; and he said desperately: "You can send for me, if you get anxious"—

"I can't let you go!"

"I must really get my breakfast"—

"The girl will get something for you here. Oh, *don't* go away!" Her lip began to quiver again, and her bosom to rise.

He could not bear it. "Mrs. Hubbard, will you believe what I say?"

"Yes," she faltered, reluctantly.

"Well, I tell you that Mr. Hubbard is in no sort of danger; and I know that it would be extremely offensive to him if I staid."

"Then you must go," she answered promptly, and opened the door, which she had closed for fear he might escape. "I will send for a doctor."

"No, *don't* send for a doctor, don't send for anybody; don't speak of the matter to any one: it would be very mortifying to him. It's merely a—a—kind of—seizure, that a great many people—men—are subject to; but he wouldn't like to have it known." He saw that his words were making an impression upon her; perhaps her innocence was beginning to divine the truth. "Will you do what I say?"

"Yes," she murmured.

Her head began to droop, and her face to turn away in a dawning shame too cruel for him to see.

"I—I will come back as soon as I get my breakfast, to make sure that everything is right."

She let him find his own way out, and Halleck issued upon the street, as miserable as if the disgrace were his own. It was easy enough for him to get back into his own room without alarming the family. He ate his breakfast absently, and then went out while the others were still at table.

"I don't think Ben seems very well," said his mother, anxiously, and she looked to her husband for the denial he always gave.

"Oh, I guess he's all right. What's the matter with him?"

"It's nothing but his ridiculous, romantic way of taking the world to heart," Olive interposed. "You may be sure he's troubled about something that doesn't concern him in the least. It's what comes of the life-long conscientiousness of his parents. If Ben doesn't turn out a philanthropist of the deepest dye yet, you'll have me to thank for it. I see more and more every day that I was providentially born wicked, so as to keep this besottedly righteous family's head above water."

She feigned an angry impatience with the condition of things; but, when her father went out, she joined her mother in earnest conjectures as to what Ben had on his mind.

Halleck wandered about till nearly ten o'clock, and then he

went to the little house on Clover street. The servant-girl answered his ring, and when he asked for Mrs. Hubbard, she said that Mr. Hubbard wished to see him, and please would he step upstairs.

He found Bartley seated at the window, with a wet towel round his head and his face pale with headache.

"Well, old man," he said, with an assumption of comradery that was nauseous to Halleck, "you've done the handsome thing by me. I know all about it. I knew something about it all the time." He held out his hand, without rising, and Halleck forced himself to touch it. "I appreciate your delicacy in not telling my wife. Of course you *couldn't* tell," he said, with depraved enjoyment of what he conceived of Halleck's embarrassment. "But I guess she must have smelt a rat. As the fellows say," he added, seeing the disgust that Halleck could not keep out of his face, "I shall make a clean breast of it, as soon as she can bear it. She's pretty high-strung. Lying down, now," he explained. "You see I went out to get something to make me sleep, and the first thing I knew I had got too much. Good thing I turned up on your door-step; might have been waltzing into the police-court about now. How did you happen to hear me?"

Halleck briefly explained, with an air of abhorrence for the facts.

"Yes, I remember most of it," said Bartley. "Well, I want to thank you, Halleck. You've saved me from disgrace—from ruin, for all I know. Whew, how my head aches!" he said, making an appeal to Halleck's pity, with closed eyes. "Halleck," he murmured, feebly, "I wish you would do me a favor."

"Yes? What is it?" asked Halleck, dryly.

"Go round to the Events office and tell old Witherby that I sha'n't be able to put in an appearance to-day. I'm not up to writing a note, even, and he'd feel flattered at your coming personally. It would make it all right for me."

"Of course, I will go," said Halleck.

"Thanks," returned Bartley plaintively, with his eyes closed.

XXVI

Bartley would willingly have passed this affair over with Marcia, like some of their quarrels, and allowed a reconciliation to effect itself through mere lapse of time and daily custom. But there were difficulties in the way to such an end; his shameful escapade had given the quarrel a character of its own, which could not be ignored. He must keep his word about making a clean breast of it to Marcia, whether he liked or not; but she facilitated his confession by the meek and dependent fashion in which she hovered about, anxious to do something or anything for him. If, as he suggested to Halleck, she had divined the truth, she evidently did not hold him wholly to blame for what had happened, and he was not without a self-righteous sense of having given her a useful and necessary lesson. He was inclined to a severity to which his rasped and shaken nerves contributed, when he spoke to her that night, as they sat together after tea; she had some sewing in her lap, little mysteries of soft muslin for the baby, which she was edging with lace, and her head drooped over her work, as if she could not confront him with her swollen eyes.

"Look here, Marcia," he said, "do you know what was the matter with me this morning?"

She did not answer in words; her hands quivered a moment; then she caught up the things out of her lap, and sobbed into them. The sight unmanned Bartley; he hated to see any one cry, even his wife, to whose tears he was accustomed. He dropped down beside her on the sofa, and pulled her head over on his shoulder.

"It was my fault, it was my fault, Bartley!" she sobbed. "Oh, how can I ever get over it?"

"Well, don't cry, don't cry! It wasn't altogether your fault," returned Bartley. "We were both to blame."

"No! I began it. If I hadn't broken my promise about speaking of Hannah Morrison, it never would have happened." This was so true that Bartley could not gainsay it. "But I couldn't seem to help it; and you were—you were—

so quick with me; you didn't give me time to think; you—
But I was the one to blame, I was to blame!"

"Oh, well, never mind about it; don't take on so," coaxed
Bartley. "It's all over now, and it can't be helped. And I can
promise you," he added, "that it shall never happen again, no
matter what you do," and in making this promise, he felt the
glow of virtuous performance. "I think we've both had a lesson. I suppose," he continued sadly, as one might from impersonal reflection upon the temptations and depravity of
large cities, "that it's *common* enough. I dare say it isn't the
first time Ben Halleck has taken a fellow home in a hack."
Bartley got so much comfort from the conjecture he had
thrown out for Marcia's advantage, that he felt a sort of self-
approval in the fact with which he followed it up. "And
there's this consolation about it, if there isn't any other: that
it wouldn't have happened now, if it had ever happened before."

Marcia lifted her head and looked into his face:

"What—what do you mean, Bartley?"

"I mean that I never was overcome before in my life by—
wine." He delicately avoided saying whisky.

"Well?" she demanded.

"Why, don't you see? If I'd had the habit of drinking, I
shouldn't have been affected by it."

"I don't understand," she said, anxiously.

"Why, I knew I shouldn't be able to sleep, I was so mad at
you"—

"Oh!"

"And I dropped into the hotel bar-room for a night-cap—
for something to make me sleep."

"Yes, yes!" she urged, eagerly.

"I took what wouldn't have touched a man that was in the
habit of it."

"Poor Bartley!"

"And the first thing I knew I had got too much. I was
drunk—wild drunk," he said, with magnanimous frankness.

She had been listening intensely, exculpating him at every
point, and now his innocence all flashed upon her.

"I see—I see!" she cried. "And it was because you had
never tasted it before"—

"Well, I had tasted it once or twice," interrupted Bartley, with heroic veracity.

"No matter! It was because you had never more than hardly tasted it that a very little overcame you in an instant. I see!" she repeated, contemplating him, in her ecstasy, as the one habitually sober man in a Boston full of inebriates. "And now I shall never regret it; I shall never care for it; I never shall think about it again! Or, yes! I shall always remember it, because it shows—because it *proves*—that you are always strictly temperance. It was worth happening for that. I am *glad* it happened!"

She rose from his side, and took her sewing nearer the lamp, and resumed her work upon it with shining eyes.

Bartley remained in his place on the sofa, feeling, and perhaps looking, rather sheepish. He had made a clean breast of it, and the confession had redounded only too much to his credit. To do him justice, he had not intended to bring the affair to quite such a triumphant conclusion; and perhaps something better than his sense of humor was also touched when he found himself not only exonerated but transformed into an exemplar of abstinence.

"Well," he said, "it isn't exactly a thing to be glad of, but it certainly isn't a thing to worry yourself about. You know the worst of it, and you know the best of it. It never happened before, and it never shall happen again; that's all. Don't lament over it, don't accuse yourself; just let it go, and we'll both see what we can do after this in the way of behaving better."

He rose from the sofa, and began to walk about the room.

"Does your head still ache?" she asked, fondly. "I *wish* I could do something for it!"

"Oh, I shall sleep it off," returned Bartley.

She followed him with her eyes.

"Bartley!"

"Well?"

"Do you suppose—do you believe—that Mr. Halleck—that he was ever"—

"No, Marcia, I don't," said Bartley, stopping. "I *know* he never was. Ben Halleck is slow; but he's good. I couldn't imagine his being drunk any more than I could imagine your being so. I'd willingly sacrifice his reputation to console you," added Bartley, with a comical sense of his own regret that Halleck was not, for the occasion, an habitual drunkard, "but I cannot tell a lie."

He looked at her with a smile, and broke into a sudden laugh.

"No, my dear, the only person I think of just now, as having suffered similarly with myself, is the great and good Andrew Johnson. Did you ever hear of him?"

"Was he the one they impeached?" she faltered, not knowing what Bartley would be at, but smiling faintly in sympathy with his mirth.

"He was the one they impeached. He was the one who was overcome by wine on his inauguration day, because he had never been overcome before. It's a parallel case!"

Bartley got a great deal more enjoyment out of the parallel case than Marcia. The smile faded from her face, and, "Come, come," he coaxed, "be satisfied with Andrew Johnson, and let Halleck go. Ah, Marcia!" he added, seriously, "Ben Halleck is the kind of man you ought to have married! Don't you suppose that I know I'm not good enough for you? I'm pretty good by fits and starts; but he would have been good right straight along. I should never have had to bring *him* home in a hack to you!"

His generous admission had the just effect. "Hush, Bartley! Don't talk so! You know that you're better for me than the best man in the world, dear, and even if you were not, I should love you the best. Don't talk, please, that way, of any one else, or it will make me hate you!"

He liked that; and after all he was not without an obscure pride in his last night's adventure as a somewhat hazardous but decided assertion of manly supremacy. It was not a thing to be repeated; but for once in a way it was not wholly to be regretted, especially as he was so well out of it.

He pulled up a chair in front of her, and began to joke about the things she had in her lap; and the shameful and sorrowful day ended in the bliss of a more perfect peace between them than they had known since the troubles of their married life began.

"I tell you," said Bartley, "I shall stick to Tivoli after this, religiously."

It was several weeks later that Halleck limped into Atherton's lodgings, and dropped into one of his friend's easy chairs. The room had a bachelor comfort of aspect, and the shaded lamp on the table shed a mellow light on the green leather-covered furniture, wrinkled and creased, and worn full of such hospitable hollows as that which welcomed Halleck. Some packages of law papers were scattered about on the table; but the hour of the night had come when a lawyer permits himself a novel. Atherton looked up from his as Halleck entered, and stretched out a hand, which the latter took on his way to the easy chair across the table.

"How do you do?" said Atherton, after allowing him to sit for a certain time in the frank silence which expressed better than words the familiarity that existed between them in spite of the lawyer's six or seven years of seniority.

Halleck leaned forward and tapped the floor with his stick; then he fell back again, and laid his cane across the arms of his chair, and drew a long breath.

"Atherton," he said, "if you had found a blackguard of your acquaintance drunk on your doorstep early one morning, and had taken him home to his wife, how would you have expected her to treat you the next time you saw her?"

The lawyer was too much used to the statement, direct and hypothetical, of all sorts of cases, to be startled at this. He smiled slightly, and said:

"That would depend a good deal upon the lady."

"Oh, but generalize! From what you know of women as Woman, what should you expect? Shouldn't you expect her to make you pay somehow for your privity to her disgrace, to revenge her misery upon you? Isn't there a theory that women forgive injuries, but never ignominies?"

"That's what the novelists teach, and we bachelors get most of our doctrine about women from them."

He closed his novel on the paper-cutter, and laying the book upon the table, clasped his hands together at the back of his head.

"We don't go to nature for our impressions; but neither do the novelists, for that matter. Now and then, however, in the way of business, I get a glimpse of realities that make me doubt my prophets. Who had this experience?"

"I did."

"I'm sorry for that," said Atherton.

"Yes," returned Halleck, with whimsical melancholy; "I'm not particularly adapted for it. But I don't know that it would be a very pleasant experience for anybody."

He paused drearily, and Atherton said:

"And how did she actually treat you?"

"I hardly know. I hadn't been at the pains to look them up since the thing happened, and I had been carrying their squalid secret round for a fortnight, and suffering from it as if it were all my own."

Atherton smiled at the touch of self-characterization.

"When I met her and her husband and her baby to-day— a family party—well, she made me ashamed of the melodramatic compassion I had been feeling for her: It seemed that I had been going about unnecessarily, not to say impertinently, haggard with the recollection of her face as I saw it when she opened the door for her blackguard and me that morning. She looked as if nothing unusual had happened at our last meeting: I couldn't brace up all at once: I behaved like a sneak, in view of her serenity."

"Perhaps nothing unusual had happened," suggested Atherton.

"No, that theory isn't tenable," said Halleck. "It was the one fact in the blackguard's favor that she had evidently never seen him in that state before, and didn't know what was the matter. She was wild at first; she wanted to send for a doctor. I think towards the last she began to suspect. But I don't know how she looked *then*: I couldn't look at her."

He stopped, as if still in the presence of the pathetic figure, with its sidelong, drooping head.

Atherton respected his silence a moment before he again suggested, as lightly as before:

"Perhaps she is magnanimous."

"No," said Halleck, with the effort of having also given that theory consideration. "She's not magnanimous, poor soul. I fancy she is rather a narrow-minded person, with strict limitations in regard to people who think ill—or too well— of her husband."

"Then perhaps," said Atherton, with the air of having exhausted conjecture, "she's obtuse."

"I have tried to think that too," replied Halleck, "but I can't manage it. No, there are only two ways out of it: the fellow has abused her innocence and made her believe it's a common and venial affair to be brought home in that state, or else she's playing a part. He's capable of telling her that neither you nor I, for example, ever go to bed sober. But she isn't obtuse: I fancy she's only too keen in all the sensibilities that women suffer through; and I'd rather think that he had deluded her in that way than that she was masquerading about it, for she strikes me as an uncommonly truthful person. I suppose you know whom I'm talking about, Atherton?" he said, with a sudden look at his friend's face, across the table.

"Yes, I know," said the lawyer. "I'm sorry it's come to this already. Though I suppose you're not altogether surprised."

"No, something of the kind was to be expected," Halleck sighed, and rolled his cane up and down on the arms of his chair. "I hope we know the worst."

"Perhaps we do. But I recollect a wise remark you made the first time we talked of these people," said Atherton, replying to the mood rather than the speech of his friend. "You suggested that we rather liked to grieve over the pretty girls that other fellows marry, and that we never thought of the plain ones as suffering."

"Oh, I hadn't any data for my pity in this case, then," replied Halleck. "I'm willing to allow that a plain woman would suffer under the same circumstances; and I think I should be capable of pitying her. But I'll confess that the notion of a pretty woman's sorrow is more intolerable; there's no use denying a fact so universally recognized by the male consciousness. I take my share of shame for it. I wonder why it is? Pretty women always seem to appeal to us as more dependent and child-like. I dare say they're not."

"Some of them are quite able to take care of themselves," said Atherton. "I've known striking instances of the kind. How do you know but the object of your superfluous pity was cheerful because fate had delivered her husband, bound forever, into her hand, through this little escapade of his?"

"Isn't that rather a coarse suggestion?" asked Halleck.

"Very likely. I suggest it; I don't assert it. But I fancy that wives sometimes like a permanent grievance that is always at hand, no matter what the mere passing occasion of the particular disagreement is. It seems to me that I have detected obscure appeals to such a weapon in domestic interviews at which I've assisted in the way of business."

"Don't, Atherton!" cried Halleck.

"Don't, how? In this particular case, or in regard to wives generally? We can't do women a greater injustice than not to account for a vast deal of human nature in them. You may be sure that things haven't come to the present pass with those people, without blame on both sides."

"Oh, do you defend a man for such beastliness by that stale old plea of blame on both sides?" demanded Halleck, indignantly.

"No; but I should like to know what she had said or done to provoke it before I excused her altogether."

"You would! Imagine the case reversed!"

"It isn't imaginable."

"You think there is a special code of morals for women; sins and shames for them that are no sins and shames for us!"

"No, I don't think that. I merely suggest that you don't idealize the victim in this instance. I dare say she hasn't suffered half as much as you have. Remember that she's a person of commonplace traditions, and probably took a simple view of the matter, and let it go as something that could not be helped."

"No, that would not do either," said Halleck.

"You're hard to please. Suppose we imagine her proud enough to face you down on the fact for his sake; too proud to revenge her disgrace on you"—

"Oh, you come back to your old plea of magnanimity! Atherton, it makes me sick at heart to think of that poor creature. That look of hers haunts me! I can't get rid of it!"

Atherton sat considering his friend with a curious smile.

"Well, I'm sorry this has happened to *you*, Halleck."

"Oh, why do you say that to me?" demanded Halleck, impatiently. "Am I a nervous woman, that I must be kept from unpleasant sights and disagreeable experiences? If there's anything of the man about me, you insult it! Why not be a little sorry for her?"

"I'm sorry enough for her; but I suspect that so far you have been the principal sufferer. She's simply accepted the fact and survived it."

"So much the worse, so much the worse!" groaned Halleck. "She'd better have died!"

"Well, perhaps. I dare say she thinks it will never happen again, and has dismissed the subject; while you've had it happening ever since, whenever you've thought of her."

Halleck struck the arms of his chair with his clenched hands.

"Confound the fellow! What business has he to come back into my way, and make me think about his wife? Oh, very likely, it's quite as you say! I dare say she's stupidly content with him; that she's forgiven it and forgotten all about it. Probably she's told him how I behaved, and they've laughed over me together. But does that make it any easier to bear?"

"It ought," said Atherton. "What did the husband do when you met them?"

"Everything but tip me the wink—everything but say in so many words: 'You see I've made it all right with her. Don't you wish you knew how?' "

Halleck dropped his head, with a wrathful groan.

"I fancy," said Atherton, thoughtfully, "that if we really knew how, it would surprise us. Married life is as much a mystery to us outsiders as the life to come, almost. The ordinary motives don't seem to count; it's the realm of unreason. If a man only makes his wife suffer enough, she finds out that she loves him so much she *must* forgive him. And then, there's a great deal in their being bound. They can't live together in enmity, and they must live together. I dare say the offense had merely worn itself out between them."

"Oh, I dare say," Halleck assented, wearily. "That isn't my idea of marriage though."

"It's not mine, either," returned Atherton. "The question is whether it isn't often the fact in regard to such people's marriages."

"Then, they are so many hells," cried Halleck, "where self-respect perishes with resentment, and the husband and wife are enslaved to each other. They ought to be broken up!"

"I don't think so," said Atherton, soberly. "The sort of men and women that marriage enslaves would be vastly more wretched and mischievous, if they were set free. I believe that the hell people make for themselves isn't at all a bad place for them. It's the best place for them."

"Oh, I know your doctrine," said Halleck, rising. "It's horrible. How a man with any kindness in his heart can harbor such a cold-blooded philosophy, *I* don't understand. I wish you joy of it. Good-night," he added, gloomily, taking his hat from the table. "It serves me right for coming to you with a matter that I ought to have been man enough to keep to myself."

Atherton followed him toward the door.

"It wont do you any harm to consider your perplexity in the light of my philosophy. An unhappy marriage isn't the only hell, nor the worst."

Halleck turned.

"What could be a worse hell than marriage without love?" he demanded, fiercely.

"Love without marriage," said Atherton.

Halleck looked sharply at his friend. Then he shrugged his shoulders as he turned again and swung out of the door.

"You're too esoteric for me. It's quite time I was gone."

The way through Clover street was not the shortest way home; but he climbed the hill and passed the little house. He wished to rehabilitate in its pathetic beauty the image which his friend's conjectures had jarred, distorted, insulted; and he lingered for a moment before the door where this vision had claimed his pity for anguish that no after serenity could repudiate. The silence in which the house was wrapt was like another fold of the mystery which involved him. The night wind rose in a sudden gust, and made the neighboring lamp flare, and his shadow wavered across the pavement like the figure of a drunken man. This and not that other was the image which he saw.

XXVII

O F COURSE," said Marcia, when she and Bartley recurred
to the subject of her visit to Equity, "I have always felt
as if I should like to have you with me, so as to keep people
from talking, and show that it's all right between you and
father. But if you don't wish to go, I can't ask it."

"I understand what you mean, and I should like to gratify
you," said Bartley. "Not that I care a rap what all the people
in Equity think. I'll tell you what I'll do: I'll go down there
with you and hang round a day or two; and then I'll come
after you, when your time's up, and stay a day or two there.
I *couldn't* stand three weeks in Equity."

In the end, he behaved very handsomely. He dressed Flavia
out to kill, as he said, in lace hoods and embroidered long-
clothes, for which he tossed over half the ready-made stock of
the great dry-goods stores; and he made Marcia get herself a
new suit throughout, with a bonnet to match, which she
thought she could not afford; but he said he should manage
it somehow. In Equity he spared no pains to deepen the
impression of his success in Boston, and he was affable with
everybody. He hailed his friends across the street, waving his
hand to them, and shouting out a jolly greeting. He visited
the hotel office and the stores to meet the loungers there; he
stepped into the printing-office and congratulated Henry Bird
on having stopped the Free Press and devoted himself to job-
work. He said "Hallo, Marilla! Hallo, Hannah!" and he stood
a good while beside the latter at her case, joking and laughing. He had no resentments. He stopped old Morrison on the
street and shook hands with him. "Well, Mr. Morrison, do
you find it as easy to get Hannah's wages advanced nowadays
as you used to?"

As for his relations with Squire Gaylord, he flattened public
conjecture out like a pancake, as he told Marcia, by making
the old gentleman walk arm-and-arm with him the whole
length of the village street the morning after his arrival. "And
I never saw your honored father look as if he enjoyed a thing
less," added Bartley. "Well, what's the use? He couldn't help

himself." They had arrived on Friday evening, and after spending Saturday in this social way, Bartley magnanimously went with Marcia to church. He was in good spirits, and he shook hands, right and left, as he came out of church. In the afternoon he had up the best team from the hotel stable, and took Marcia the Long Drive, which they had taken the day of their engagement. He could not be contented without pushing the perambulator out after tea, and making Marcia walk beside it, to let people see them with the baby.

He went away the next morning on an early train, after a parting which he made very cheery, and a promise to come down again as soon as he could manage it. Marcia watched him drive off toward the station in the hotel barge, and then she went upstairs to their room, where she had been so long a young girl, and where now their child lay sleeping. The little one seemed the least part of all the change that had taken place. In this room she used to sit and think of him; she used to fly up thither when he came unexpectedly, and order her hair or change a ribbon or her dress, that she might please him better; at these windows she used to sit and watch and long for his coming; from these she saw him go by that day when she thought she should see him no more, and took heart of her despair to risk the wild chance that made him hers. There was a deadly, unsympathetic stillness in the room, which seemed to leave to her all the responsibility for what she had done.

The days began to go by in a sunny, still, midsummer monotony. She pushed the baby out in its carriage, and saw the summer boarders walking or driving through the streets; she returned the visits that the neighbors paid her, in-doors she helped her mother about the house-work. An image of her maiden life reinstated itself. At times it seemed almost as if she had dreamed her marriage. When she looked at her baby in these moods, she thought she was dreaming yet. A young wife, suddenly parted for the first time from her husband, in whose intense possession she has lost her individual existence, and devolving upon her old separate personality, must have strong fancies, strange sensations. Marcia's marriage had been full of such shocks and storms as might well have left her dazed in their entire cessation.

"She seems to be pretty well satisfied here," said her father, one evening when she had gone upstairs with her sleeping baby in her arms.

"She seems to be pretty quiet," her mother non-committally assented.

"Myes," snarled the Squire, and he fell into a long revery, while Mrs. Gaylord went on crocheting the baby a bib, and the smell of the petunia-bed under the window came in through the mosquito-netting. "Myes," he resumed, "I guess you're right. I guess it's only quiet. I guess she aint any more likely to be satisfied than the rest of us."

"I don't see why she shouldn't be," said Mrs. Gaylord, resenting the compassion in the Squire's tone with that curious jealousy a wife feels for her husband's indulgence of their daughter. "She's had her way."

"She's had her way, poor girl,—yes. But I don't know as it satisfies people to have their way always."

Doubtless Mrs. Gaylord saw that her husband wished to talk about Marcia, and must be helped to do so by a little perverseness.

"I don't know but what most of folks would say't she'd made out pretty well. I guess she's got a good provider."

"She didn't need any provider," said the Squire haughtily.

"No; but so long as she would have something, it's well enough that she should have a provider." Mrs. Gaylord felt that this was reasoning, and she smoothed out so much of the bib as she had crocheted across her knees with an air of self-content. "You can't have everything in a husband," she added, "and Marcia ought to know that by this time."

"I've no doubt she knows it," said the Squire.

"Why, what makes you think she's disappointed any?" Mrs. Gaylord came plump to the question at last.

"Nothing she ever said," returned her husband promptly. "She'd die first. When I was up there I thought she talked about him too much to be feeling just right about him. It was Bartley this and Bartley that, the whole while. She was always wanting me to say that I thought she had done right to marry him. I *did* sort of say it, at last—to please her—but I kept thinking that if she felt sure of it, she wouldn't want to talk it into me so. Now, she never mentions him at all, if she can help it. She writes to him every day, and she hears from him often enough—postals, mostly—but she don't talk about Bartley. Bartley!" The Squire stretched his lips back from his teeth, and inhaled a long breath, as he rubbed his chin.

"You don't suppose anything's happened since you was up there," said Mrs. Gaylord.

"Nothing but what's happened from the start. *He's* happened. He keeps happening right along, I guess."

Mrs. Gaylord found herself upon the point of experiencing a painful emotion of sympathy, but she saved herself by saying:

"Well, Mr. Gaylord, I don't know as you've got anybody but yourself to thank for it all. You got him here, in the first *place*."

She took one of the kerosene lamps from the table and went upstairs, leaving him to follow at his will.

Marcia sometimes went out to the Squire's office in the morning, carrying her baby with her, and propping her with law-books on a newspaper in the middle of the floor, while she dusted the shelves, or sat down for one of the desultory talks or the satisfactory silences which she had with her father.

He usually found her there when he came up from the post-office, with the morning mail in the top of his hat: the last evening's Events,—which Bartley had said must pass for a letter from him when he did not write,—and a letter or a postal card from him. She read these, and gave her father any news or message that Bartley sent; and then she sat down at his table to answer them. But one morning, after she had been at home nearly a month, she received a letter for which she postponed Bartley's postal. "It's from Olive Halleck!" she said, with a glance at the handwriting on the envelope; and she tore it open, and ran it through. "Yes, and they'll come here, any time I let them know. They've been at Niagara, and they've come down the St. Lawrence to Quebec, and they will be at North Conway the last of next week. Now, father, I want to do something for them!" she cried, feeling an American daughter's right to dispose of her father and all his possessions for the behoof of her friends at any time. "I want they should come to the house."

"Well, I guess there wont be any trouble about that, if you

think they can put up with our way of living." He smiled at her over his spectacles.

"Our way of living! Put up with it! I should hope as *much*! They're just the kind of people that will put up with anything, because they've had everything, and because they're all as sweet and good as they can be. You don't know them, father, you don't half know them! Now, just get right away"—she pushed him out of the chair he had taken at the table—"and let me write to Bartley this instant. He's *got* to come when they're here and I'll invite them to come over at once before they get settled at North Conway."

He gave his dry chuckle to see her so fired with pleasure, and he enjoyed the ardor with which she drove him up out of his chair and dashed off her letters. This was her old way; he would have liked the prospect of the Hallecks' coming, because it made his girl so happy, if for nothing else.

"Father, I will tell you about Ben Halleck," she said, pounding her letter to Olive with the thick of her hand to make the envelope stick. "You know that lameness of his?"

"Yes."

"Well, it came from his being thrown down by another boy when he was at school. He knew the boy that did it; and the boy must have known that Mr. Halleck knew it; but he never said a word to show that he was sorry, or did anything to make up for it. He's a man, now, and lives there in Boston, and Ben Halleck often meets him. He says that if the man can stand it *he* can. Don't you think that's grand? When I heard that I made up my mind that I wanted Flavia to belong to Ben Halleck's church—or the church he did belong to; he doesn't belong to any now!"

"He couldn't have got any damages for such a thing anyway," the Squire said.

Marcia paid no heed to this legal opinion of the case. She took off her father's hat to put the letters into it, and replacing it on his head,—"Now, don't you forget them, father," she cried.

She gathered up her baby and hurried into the house, where she began her preparations for her guests.

The elder Miss Hallecks had announced with much love, through Olive, that they should not be able to come to Eq-

uity, and Ben was to bring Olive alone. Marcia decided that
Ben should have the guest chamber and Olive should have
her room; she and Bartley could take the little room in the L,
while their guests remained.

But when the Hallecks came, it appeared that Ben had engaged quarters for himself at the hotel, and no expostulation
would prevail with him to come to Squire Gaylord's house.

"We have to humor him in such things, Mrs. Hubbard,"
Olive explained to Marcia's distress. "And most people get on
very well without him."

This explanation was, of course, given in Halleck's presence. His sister added, behind his back:

"Ben has a perfectly morbid dread of giving trouble in a
house. He wont let us do anything to make him comfortable
at home, and the idea that you should attempt it drove him
distracted. You *mustn't* mind it. I don't believe he'd have
come if his bachelor freedom couldn't have been respected;
and we both wanted to come very much."

The Hallecks arrived in the forenoon and Bartley was due
in the evening. But during the afternoon Marcia had a tele-
gram, saying that he could not come till two days later, and
asking her to postpone the picnic she had planned. The Hallecks were only going to stay three days, and the suspicion
that Bartley had delayed in order to leave himself as little time
as possible with them, rankled in her heart so that she could
not keep it to herself when they met.

"Was that what made you give me such a cool reception?"
he asked, with cynical good-nature. "Well, you're mistaken;
I don't suppose I mind the Hallecks any more than they do
me. I'll tell you why I staid. Some people dropped down on
Witherby, who were a little out of his line —fashionable people that he had asked to let him know if they ever came to
Boston; and when they did come and let him know he didn't
know what to do about it, and he called on me to help him
out. I've been almost boarding with Witherby for the last
three days; and I've been barouching round all over the moral
vine-yard with his friends: out to Mount Auburn and the
Washington Elm and Bunker Hill and Brookline and the Art
Museum and Lexington; we've been down the harbor, and
we haven't left a monumental stone unturned. They were

going north, and they came down here with me; and I got them to stop over a day for the picnic."

"You got them to stop over for the picnic? Why, *I* don't want anybody but ourselves, Bartley! This spoils everything."

"The Hallecks are not ourselves," said Bartley. "And these are jolly people; they'll help to make it go off."

"Who are they?" asked Marcia, with provisional self-control.

"Oh, some people that Witherby met in Portland at Willett's, who used to have the logging camp out here."

"That Montreal woman!" cried Marcia, with fatal divination.

Bartley laughed.

"Yes, Mrs. Macallister and her husband. She's a regular case. She'll amuse you."

Marcia's passionate eyes blazed.

"She shall never come to my picnic in the world!"

"No?" Bartley looked at her in a certain way. "She shall come to mine, then. There will be two picnics. The more the merrier."

Marcia gasped, as if she felt the clutch, in which her husband had her, tightening on her heart. She saw that she could only carry her point against him at the cost of disgraceful division before the Hallecks, for which he would not care in the least. She moved her head a little from side to side, like one that breathes a stifling air. "Oh, let her come," she said quietly, at last.

"Now you're talking business," said Bartley. "I haven't forgotten the little snub Mrs. Macallister gave me, and you'll see me pay her off."

Marcia made no answer, but went down stairs to put what face she could upon the matter to Olive, whom she had left alone in the parlor, while she ran up with Bartley immediately upon his arrival to demand an explanation of him. In her wrathful haste she had forgotten to kiss him, and she now remembered that he had not looked at the baby, which she had all the time had in her arms.

The picnic was to be in a pretty glen three or four miles north of the village, where there was shade on a bit of level green, and a spring bubbling out of a fern-hung bluff: from which you looked down the glen over a stretch of the river. Marcia had planned that they were to drive thither in a four-seated carryall, but the addition of Bartley's guests disarranged this.

"There's only one way," said Mrs. Macallister, who had driven up with her husband from the hotel to the Squire's house in a buggy. "Mr. Halleck tells me he doesn't know how to drive, and me husband doesn't know the way. Mr. Hubbard must get in here with me, and you must take Mr. Macallister in your party." She looked authoritatively at the others.

"First-rate!" cried Bartley, climbing to the seat which Mr. Macallister left vacant. "We'll lead the way."

Those who followed had difficulty in keeping their buggy in sight. Sometimes Bartley stopped long enough for them to come up, and then, after a word or two of gay banter, was off again.

They had taken possession of the picnic grounds, and Mrs. Macallister was disposing shawls for rugs and drapery, while Bartley, who had got the horse out, and tethered where he could graze, was pushing the buggy out of the way by the shafts when the carryall came up.

"Don't we look quite domestic?" she asked of the arriving company, in her neat English tone, and her rising English inflection. "You know I like this," she added, singling Halleck out for her remark, and making it as if it were brilliant. "I like being out of doors, don't you know. But there's one thing I don't like: we weren't able to get a drop of champagne at that ridiculous hotel. They told us they were not allowed to keep 'intoxicating liquors.' Now I call that jolly stupid, you know. I don't know whatever we shall do if you haven't brought something."

"I believe this is a famous spring," said Halleck.

"How droll you are! Spring, indeed!" cried Mrs. Macallister. "Is *that* the way you let your brother make game of people, Miss Halleck?" She directed a good deal of her rattle at Olive; she scarcely spoke to Marcia, but she was nevertheless furtively observant of her. Mr. Macallister had his rattle, too, which after trying it unsatisfactorily upon Marcia he plied almost exclusively for Olive. He made puns; he asked

conundrums; he had all the accomplishments which keep people going in a lively, unintellectual, colonial society; and he
had the idea that he must pay attentions and promote repar-
tee. His wife and he played into each other's hands in their
jeux d'esprit; and kept Olive's inquiring Boston mind at work
in the vain endeavor to account for and to place them socially.
Bartley hung about Mrs. Macallister, and was nearly as obedient as her husband. He felt that the Hallecks disapproved
his behavior, and that made him enjoy it; he was almost
rudely negligent of Olive.

The composition of the party left Marcia and Halleck necessarily to each other, and she accepted this arrangement in a
sort of passive seriousness; but Halleck saw that her thoughts
wandered from her talk with him, and that her eyes were always turning with painful anxiety to Bartley. After their
lunch, which left them with the whole afternoon before them,
Marcia said, in a timid effort to resume her best leadership of
the affair:

"Bartley, don't you think they would like to see the view
from the Devil's Backbone?"

"Would you like to see the view from the Devil's Backbone?" he asked in turn of Mrs. Macallister.

"And *what* is the Devil's Backbone?" she inquired.

"It's a ridge of rocks on the bluff above here," said Bartley,
nodding his head vaguely toward the bank.

"And *how* do you get to it?" asked Mrs. Macallister, pointing her pretty chin at him in lifting her head to look.

"Walk."

"Thanks; then I shall try to be satisfied with me own backbone," said Mrs. Macallister, who had that freedom in allud-
ing to her anatomy which marks the superior civilization of
Great Britain and its colonial dependencies.

"Carry you," suggested Bartley.

"I dare say you'd be very sure-footed; but I'd quite enough
of donkeys in the hills at home."

Bartley roared with the resolution of a man who will enjoy
a joke at his own expense.

Marcia turned away, and referred her invitation with a
glance to Olive.

"I don't believe Miss Halleck wants to go," said Mr. Macallister.

"I couldn't," said Olive, regretfully. "I've neither the feet nor the head for climbing over high rocky places."

Marcia was about to sink down on the grass again, from which she had risen in the hopes that her proposition would succeed, when Bartley called out:

"Why don't you show Ben the Devil's Backbone? The view is worth seeing, Halleck."

"Would you like to go?" asked Marcia, listlessly.

"Yes, I should, very much," said Halleck, scrambling to his feet, "if it wont tire you too much?"

"Oh, no," said Marcia, gently, and led the way. She kept ahead of him in the climb, as she easily could, and she answered briefly to all he said. When they arrived at the top, "There is the view," she said coldly. She waved her hand toward the valley; she made a sound in her throat as if she would speak again, but her voice died in one broken sob.

Halleck stood with downcast eyes and trembled. He durst not look at her, not for what he should see in her face, but for what she should see in his: the anguish of intelligence, the helpless pity. He beat the rock at his feet with the ferule of his stick, and could not lift his head again. When he did, she stood turned from him and drying her eyes on her handkerchief. Their looks met, and she trusted her self-betrayal to him without any attempt at excuse or explanation.

"I will send Hubbard up to help you down," said Halleck.

"Well," she answered, sadly.

He clambered down the side of the bluff, and Bartley started to his feet in guilty alarm when he saw him approach. "What's the matter?"

"Nothing. But I think you had better help Mrs. Hubbard down the bluff."

"Oh!" cried Mrs. Macallister, "A panic! How interesting!"

Halleck did not respond. He threw himself on the grass, and left her to change or pursue the subject as she liked. Bartley showed more *savoir-faire* when he came back with Marcia, after an absence long enough to let her remove the traces of her tears.

"Pretty rough on your game foot, Halleck. But Marcia had got it into her head that it wasn't safe to trust you to help her down, even after you had helped her up."

"Ben," said Olive, when they were seated in the train the next day, "why *did* you send Marcia's husband up there to her?" She had the effect of not having rested till she could ask him.

"She was crying," he answered.

"What do you suppose could have been the matter?"

"What you do: she was miserable about his coquetting with that woman."

"Yes. I could see that she hated terribly to have her come; and that she felt put down by her all the time. What kind of person *is* Mrs. Macallister?"

"Oh, a fool," replied Halleck. "All flirts are fools."

"I think she's more wicked than foolish."

"Oh, no, flirts are better than they seem—perhaps because men are better than flirts think. But they make misery just the same."

"Yes," sighed Olive. "Poor Marcia, poor Marcia! But I suppose that if it were not Mrs. Macallister it would be some one else."

"Given Bartley Hubbard,—yes."

"And given Marcia. Well,—I don't like being mixed up with other people's unhappiness, Ben. It's dangerous."

"I don't like it either. But you can't very well keep out of people's unhappiness in this world."

"No," assented Olive, ruefully.

The talk fell, and Halleck attempted to read a newspaper, while Olive looked out of the window. She presently turned to him.

"Did you ever fancy any resemblance between Mrs. Hubbard and the photograph of that girl we used to joke about—your lost love?"

"Yes," said Halleck.

"What's become of it—the photograph? I can't find it any more; I wanted to show it to her, one day."

"I destroyed it. I burnt it the first evening after I had met Mrs. Hubbard. It seemed to me that it wasn't right to keep it."

"Why, you don't think it was *her* photograph!"

"I think it was," said Halleck.

He took up his paper again, and read on till they left the cars.

That evening, when Halleck came to his sister's room to bid her good-night, she threw her arms round his neck, and kissed his plain, common face, in which she saw a heavenly beauty.

"Ben, dear," she said, "if you don't turn out the happiest man in the world, I shall say there's no use in being good!"

"Perhaps you'd better say that after all I wasn't good," he suggested, with a melancholy smile.

"I shall know better," she retorted.

"Why, what's the matter, now?"

"Nothing. I was only thinking. Good-night!"

"Good-night," said Halleck. "You seem to think my room is better than my company, good as I am."

"Yes," she said, laughing, in that breathless way, which means weeping next, with women. Her eyes glistened.

"Well," said Halleck, limping out of the room, "you're quite good-looking with your hair down, Olive."

"All girls are," she answered. She leaned out of her doorway to watch him as he limped down the corridor to his own room. There was something pathetic, something disappointed and weary in the movement of his figure, and when she shut her door, and ran back to her mirror, she could not see the good-looking girl there for her tears.

XXVIII

Hello!" said Bartley, one day after the autumn had brought back all the summer wanderers to the city, "I haven't seen you for a month of Sundays." He had Ricker by the hand, and he pulled him into a door-way to be a little out of the rush on the crowded pavement, while they chatted.

"That's because I can't afford to go to the White Mountains, and swell round at the aristocratic summer resorts like some people," returned Ricker. "I'm a horny-handed son of toil, myself."

"Pshaw!" said Bartley. "Who isn't? I've been here hard at it, except for three days at one time and five at another."

"Well, all I can say is that I saw in the Record personals, that Mr. Hubbard, of the Events, was spending the summer months with his father-in-law, Judge Gaylord, among the spurs of the White Mountains. I supposed you wrote it yourself. You're full of ideas about journalism."

"Oh, come! I wouldn't work that joke any more. Look here, Ricker, I'll tell you what I want. I want you to dine with me."

"Dines people!" said Ricker, in an awe-stricken aside.

"No,—I mean business! You've never seen my kid yet, and you've never seen my house. I want you to come. We've all got back, and we're in nice running order. What day are you disengaged?"

"Let me see," said Ricker, thoughtfully. "So many engagements! Wait! I could squeeze your dinner in some time next month, Hubbard."

"All right. But suppose we say next Sunday. Six is the hour."

"Six? Oh, I can't dine in the middle of the forenoon that way! Make it later!"

"Well, we'll say one P.M., then. I know your dinner hour. We shall expect you."

"Better not, till I come." Bartley knew that this was Ricker's way of accepting, and he said nothing, but he answered his next question with easy joviality. "How are you making it with old Witherby?"

"Oh, hand over hand! Witherby and I were formed for each other. By-by!"

"No, hold on! Why don't you come to the club any more?"

"We-e-ll! The club isn't what it used to be," said Bartley, confidentially.

"Why, of course! It isn't just the thing for a gentleman moving in the select circles of Clover street, as you do; but why not come, sometimes, in the character of distinguished guest, and encourage your humble friends? I was talking with a lot of the fellows about you the other night."

"Were they abusing me?"

"They were speaking the truth about you, and I stopped them. I told them that sort of thing wouldn't do. Why, you're getting fat!"

"You're behind the times, Ricker," said Bartley. "I began to get fat six months ago. I don't wonder the Chronicle-Abstract is running down on your hands. Come round and try my Tivoli on Sunday. That's what gives a man girth, my boy." He tapped Ricker lightly on his hollow waistcoat, and left him with a wave of his hand.

Ricker leaned out of the door-way and followed him down the street with a troubled eye. He had taken stock in Bartley, as the saying is, and his heart misgave him that he should lose on the investment; he could not have sold out to any of their friends for twenty cents on the dollar. Nothing that any one could lay his finger on had happened, and yet there had been a general loss of confidence in that particular stock. Ricker himself had lost confidence in it, and when he lightly mentioned that talk at the club, with a lot of the fellows, he had a serious wish to get at Bartley some time, and see what it was that was beginning to make people mistrust him. The fellows who liked him at first and wished him well, and believed in his talent, had mostly dropped him. Bartley's associates were now the most raffish set on the press, or the green hands; and something had brought this to pass in less than two years. Ricker had believed that it was Witherby; at the Club he had contended that it was Bartley's association with Witherby that made people doubtful of him. As for those ideas that Bartley had advanced in their discussion of journalism, he had considered it all mere young man's nonsense that

Bartley would outgrow. But now, as he looked at Bartley's back, he had his misgivings; it struck him as the back of a degenerate man, and that increasing bulk seemed not to represent an increase of wholesome substance, but a corky, buoyant tissue, materially responsive to some sort of moral dry-rot.

Bartley pushed on to the Events office in a blithe humor. Witherby had recently advanced his salary; he was giving him fifty dollars a week now; and Bartley had made himself necessary in more ways than one. He was not only readily serviceable, but since he had volunteered to write those advertising articles for an advance of pay, he was in possession of business facts that could be made very uncomfortable to Witherby in the event of a disagreement. Witherby not only paid him well, but treated him well; he even suffered Bartley to bully him a little, and let him foresee the day when he must be recognized as the real editor of the Events.

At home everything went on smoothly. The baby was well and growing fast; she was beginning to explode airy bubbles on her pretty lips that a fond superstition might interpret as papa and mamma. She had passed that stage in which a man regards his child with despair; she had passed out of slippery and evasive doughiness into a firm tangibility that made it some pleasure to hold her.

Bartley liked to take her on his lap, to feel the spring of her little legs, as she tried to rise on her feet; he liked to have her stretch out her arms to him from her mother's embrace. The innocent tenderness which he experienced at these moments, was satisfactory proof to him that he was a very good fellow, if not a good man. When he spent an evening at home, with Flavia in his lap for half an hour after dinner, he felt so domestic that he seemed to himself to be spending all his evenings at home now. Once or twice it had happened, when the house-maid was out, that he went to the door with the baby on his arm, and answered the ring of Olive and Ben Halleck, or of Olive and one or both of the intermediary sisters.

The Hallecks were the only people at all apt to call in the evening, and Bartley ran so little chance of meeting any one else, when he opened the door with Flavia on his arm, that

probably he would not have thought it worth while to put
her down, even if he had not rather enjoyed meeting them in
that domestic phase. He had not only long felt how intensely
Olive disliked him, but he had observed that somehow it embarrassed Ben Halleck to see him in his character of devoted
young father. At those times he used to rally his old friend
upon getting married, and laughed at the confusion to which
the joke put him. He said more than once afterward that he
did not see what fun Ben Halleck got out of coming there; it
must bore even such a dull fellow as he was to sit a whole
evening like that and not say twenty words. "Perhaps he's
livelier when I'm not here, though," he suggested. "I always
did seem to throw a wet blanket on Ben Halleck." He did
not at all begrudge Halleck's having a better time in his absence if he could.

One night when the bell rung Bartley rose, and saying, "I
wonder which of the tribe it is this time," went to the door.
But when he opened it, instead of hearing the well-known
voices, Marcia listened through a hesitating silence, which
ended in a loud laugh from without, and a cry from her husband of "Well, I swear! Why, you infamous old scoundrel,
come in out of the wet!" There ensued, amidst Bartley's voluble greetings, a noise of shy shuffling about in the hall, as of
a man not perfectly master of his footing under social pressure, a sound of husky, embarrassed whispering, a dispute
about doffing an overcoat, and question as to the disposition
of a hat, and then Bartley re-appeared, driving before him the
lank, long figure of a man who blinked in the flash of gaslight, as Bartley turned it all up in the chandelier overhead,
and rubbed his immense hands in cruel embarrassment at the
beauty of Marcia, set like a jewel in the pretty comfort of the
little parlor.

"Mr. Kinney, Mrs. Hubbard," said Bartley, and, having accomplished the introduction, he hit Kinney a thwack between
the shoulders with the flat of his hand that drove him stum-
bling across Marcia's foot-stool into the seat on the sofa to
which she had pointed him. "You old fool, where did you
come from?"

The refined warmth of Bartley's welcome seemed to make

Kinney feel at home, in spite of his trepidations at Marcia's presence. He bobbed his head forward, and stretched his mouth wide, in one of his vast, silent laughs. "Better ask where I'm goin' to."

"Well, I'll ask that, if it'll be any accommodation. Where you going?"

"Illinois."

"For a divorce?"

"Try again."

"To get married?"

"Maybe, after I've made my pile." Kinney's eyes wandered about the room, and took in its evidences of prosperity, with simple, unenvious admiration; he ended with a furtive glimpse of Marcia, who seemed to be a climax of good-luck too dazzling for contemplation; he withdrew his glance from her as if hurt by her splendor, and became serious.

"Well, you're the *last* man I ever expected to see again," said Bartley, sitting down with the baby in his lap, and contemplating Kinney with deliberation. Kinney was dressed in a long frock coat of cheap diagonals, black cassimere pantaloons, a blue neck-tie, and a celluloid collar. He had evidently had one of his encounters with a cheap clothier, in which the Jew had triumphed; but he had not yet visited a barber, and his hair and beard were as shaggy as they were in the logging camp; his hands and face were as brown as leather. "But I'm as glad," Bartley added, "as if you had telegraphed you were coming. Of course, you're going to put up with us." He had observed Kinney's awe of Marcia, and he added this touch to let Kinney see that he was master in his house, and lord even of that radiant presence.

Kinney started in real distress.

"Oh, no! I couldn't do it! I've got all my things round at the Quincy House."

"Trunk or bag?" asked Bartley.

"Well, it's a bag; but"—

"All right. We'll step round and get it together. I generally take a little stroll out, after dinner," said Bartley, tranquilly.

Kinney was beginning again when Marcia, who had been stealing some covert looks at him under her eyelashes, while she put together the sewing she was at work on, preparatory to going up-stairs with the baby, joined Bartley in his invitation.

"You wont make us the least trouble, Mr. Kinney," she said. "The guest-chamber is all ready, and we shall be glad to have you stay."

Kinney must have felt the note of sincerity in her words. He hesitated, and Bartley clinched his tacit assent with a quotation:

" 'The chief ornament of a house is the guests who frequent it.' Who says that?"

Kinney's little blue eyes twinkled.

"Old Emerson."

"Well, I agree with him. We don't care anything about your company, Kinney; but we want you for decorative purposes."

Kinney opened his mouth for another noiseless laugh, and said:

"Well, fix it to suit yourselves."

"I'll carry her up for you," said Bartley to Marcia, who was stooping forward to take the baby from him, "if Mr. Kinney will excuse us a moment."

"All right," said Kinney.

Bartley ventured upon this bold move, because he had found that it was always best to have things out with Marcia at once, and if she was going to take his hospitality to Kinney in bad part, he wanted to get through the trouble.

"That was very nice of you, Marcia," he said, when they were in their own room. "My invitation rather slipped out, and I didn't know how you would like it."

"Oh, I'm very glad to have him stay. I never forget about his wanting to lend you money that time," said Marcia, opening the baby's crib.

"You're a mighty good fellow, Marcia!" cried Bartley, kissing her over the top of the baby's head as she took it from him. "And I'm not half good enough for you. You never forget a benefit. Nor an injury, either," he added, with a laugh. "And I'm afraid that I forget one about as easily as the other."

Marcia's eyes suffused themselves at this touch of self-analysis which, coming from Bartley, had its sadness; but she said nothing, and he was eager to escape and get back to their guest. He told her he should go out with Kinney, and that she was not to sit up, for they might be out late.

In his pride, he took Kinney down to the Events office, and unlocked it, and lit the gas, so as to show him the editorial rooms; and then he passed him into one of the theatres, where they saw part of an Offenbach opera; after that they went to the Parker House and had a New York stew. Kinney said he must be off by the Sunday-night train, and Bartley thought it well to concentrate as many dazzling effects upon him as he could in the single evening at his disposal. He only regretted that it was not the club night, for he would have liked to take Kinney round and show him some of the fellows.

"But never mind," he said. "I'm going to have one of them dine with us to-morrow, and you'll see about the best of the lot."

"Well, sir," observed Kinney, when they had got back into Bartley's parlor, and he was again drinking in its prettiness in the subdued light of the shaded Argand burner. "I hain't seen anything yet that suits me much better than this."

"It isn't bad," said Bartley. He had got up a plate of crackers and two bottles of Tivoli, and was opening the first. He offered the beaded goblet to Kinney.

"Thank you," said Kinney. "Not any. I never do."

Bartley quaffed half of it in tolerant content.

"I *always* do. Find it takes my nerves down at the end of a hard week's work. Well, now, tell me something about yourself. What are you going to do in Illinois?"

"Well, sir, I've got a friend out there that's got a coal mine, and he thinks he can work me in somehow. I guess he can; I've tried pretty much everything. Why don't you come out there and start a newspaper? We've got a town that's bound to grow."

It amused Bartley to hear Kinney bragging already of a town that he had never seen. He winked a good-natured disdain over the rim of the goblet which he tilted on his lips. "And give up my chances here?" he said, as he set the goblet down.

"Well, that's so!" said Kinney, responding to the sense of

the wink. "I'll tell you what, Bartley, I didn't know as you'd speak to me when I rung your bell to-night. But thinks I to myself, 'Dumn it! look here! He can't more'n slam the door in your face, anyway. And you've hankered after him so long—go and take your chances, you old buzzard!' And so I got your address at the Events office pretty early this morning; and I went round all day screwing my courage up, as old Macbeth says—or Ritch-loo; I don't know which it was—and at last I *did* get myself so that I toed the mark like a little man."

Bartley laughed so that he could hardly get the cork out of the second bottle.

"You see," said Kinney, leaning forward, and taking Bartley's plump, soft knee between his thumb and forefinger, "I felt awfully about the way we parted that night. I felt *bad*. I hadn't acted well, just to my own mind; and it cut me to have you refuse my money; it cut me all the worse because I saw that you was partly right; I *hadn't* been quite fair with you. But I always did admire you, and you know it. Some them little things you used to get off in the old Free Press—well, I could see't you was *smart*. And I liked you; and it kind o' hurt me when I thought you'd been makin' fun o' me to that woman. Well, I could see't I was a dumned old fool, afterward. And I always wanted to tell you so. And I always *did* hope that I should be able to offer you that money again, twice over, and get you to take it just to show that you didn't bear malice." Bartley looked up, with quickened interest. "But I can't do it now, sir," added Kinney.

"Why, what's happened?" asked Bartley, in a disappointed tone, pouring out his second glass from his second bottle.

"Well, sir," said Kinney, with a certain reluctance, "I undertook to provision the camp on spec, last winter, and,—well, you know, I always run a little on food for the brain"—Bartley broke into a reminiscent cackle, and Kinney smiled forlornly,—"and thinks I 'Dumn it, I'll give 'em the real thing, every time.' And I got hold of a health-food circular; and I sent on for a half a dozen barrels of their crackers and half a dozen of their flour, and a lot of cracked cocoa, and I put the camp on a health-food basis. I calculated to bring those fellows out in the spring physically vigorous and mentally enlightened. But my goodness! After the first bakin' o' that flour and the first round o' them crackers it was all up! Fellows got so mad that I suppose if I hadn't gone back to doughnuts and sody biscuits and Japan tea, they'd 'a' burnt the camp down. Of course I yielded. But it ruined me, Bartley; it bu'st me."

Bartley dropped his arms upon the table, and, hiding his face upon them, laughed and laughed again.

"Well, sir," said Kinney, with sad satisfaction, "I'm glad to see that you don't need any money from me." He had been taking another survey of the parlor and the dining-room beyond. "I don't know as I ever saw anybody much better fixed. I should say that you was a success; and you deserve it. You're a smart fellow, Bart, and you're a good fellow. You're a generous fellow." Kinney's voice shook with emotion.

Bartley having lifted his wet and flushed face, managed to say: "Oh, there's nothing mean about *me*, Kinney," as he felt blindly for the beer bottles, which he shook in succession with an evident surprise at finding them empty.

"You've acted like a brother to me, Bartley Hubbard," continued Kinney, "and I shan't forget it in a hurry. I guess it would about broke my heart if you hadn't taken it just the way you did to-night. I should like to see the man that didn't use you well; or the woman, either!" said Kinney, with vague defiance. "Though *they* don't seem to have done so bad by you," he added, in recognition of Marcia's merit. "I should say *that* was the biggest part of your luck. She's a lady, sir, every inch of her. Mighty different stripe from that Montreal woman that cut up so that night."

"Oh, Mrs. Macallister wasn't such a scamp, after all," said Bartley, with magnanimity.

"Well, sir, *you* can say so. I ain't going to be too strict with a *girl*; but I like to see a married woman *act* like a married woman. Now, I don't think you'd catch Mrs. Hubbard flirting with a young fellow the way that woman carried on with you, that night?"

Bartley grinned.

"Well, sir, you're getting along, and you're happy."

"Perfect clam," said Bartley.

"Such a position as you've got—such a house, such a wife, *and* such a baby. Well," said Kinney, rising, "it's a little too much for *me*."

"Want to go to bed?" asked Bartley.

"Yes, I guess I better turn in," returned Kinney, despairingly.

"Show you the way."

Bartley tripped upstairs with Kinney's bag, which they had left standing in the hall, while Kinney creaked carefully after him; and so led the way to the guest chamber, and turned up the gaslight, which had been left burning low.

Kinney stood erect, dwarfing the room, and looked round on the pink chintzing and soft carpet and white coverleted bed and lace-hooded dressing-mirror, with meek veneration.

"Well, I swear!"

He said no more, but sat hopelessly down, and began to pull off his boots.

He was in the same humble mood the next morning, when, having got up inordinately early, he was found trying to fix his mind on a newspaper by Bartley, who came down late to the Sunday breakfast, and led his guest into the dining-room. Marcia, in a bewitching morning-gown, was already there, having put the daintier touches to the meal herself, and the baby in a fresh white dress was there, tied into its arm-chair with a napkin, and beating on the table with a spoon. Bartley's nonchalance amidst all this impressed Kinney with yet more poignant sense of his superiority, and almost deprived him of the powers of speech. When, after breakfast, Bartley took him out to Cambridge on the horse-cars, and showed him the College Buildings and Memorial Hall and the Washington Elm and Mount Auburn, Kinney fell into such a cowed and broken condition that something had to be specially done to put him in repair against Ricker's coming to dinner. Marcia luckily thought of asking him if he would like to see her kitchen. In this region Kinney found himself at home, and praised its neat perfection with professional intelligence. Bartley followed them round with Flavia on his arm, and put in a jocose word here and there, when he saw Kinney about to fall a prey to his respect for Marcia, and so kept him

going till Ricker rang. He contrived to give Ricker a hint of
the sort of man he had on his hands, and by their joint effort
they had Kinney talking about himself at dinner before he
knew what he was about. He could not help talking well
upon this theme, and he had them so vividly interested, as he
poured out adventure after adventure in his strange career,
that Bartley began to be proud of him.

"Well, sir," said Ricker, when he came to a pause, "you've
lived a romance."

"Yes," replied Kinney, looking at Bartley for his approval,
"and I've always thought that if I ever got run clean ashore,
high and dry, I'd make a stagger to write it out and do something with it. Do you suppose I could?"

"I promise to take it for the Sunday edition of the Chronicle-Abstract, whenever you get it ready," said Ricker.

Bartley laid his hand on his friend's arm.

"It's bought up, old fellow. That narrative—'Confessions
of an Average American'—belongs to the Events."

They had their laugh at this, and then Ricker said to Kinney:

"But look here, my friend! What's to prevent our interviewing you on this little personal history of yours, and using
your material any way we like? It seems to me that you've put
your head in the lion's mouth."

"Oh, I'm amongst gentlemen," said Kinney, with an innocent swagger. "I understand that."

"Well, I don't know about it," said Ricker. "Hubbard,
here, is used to all sorts of hard names; but I've never had
that epithet applied to me before."

Kinney doubled himself up over the side of his chair in
recognition of Ricker's joke; and when Bartley rose and asked
him if he would come into the parlor and have a cigar, he
said, with a wink, no, he guessed he would stay with the
ladies. He waited with great mystery till the folding-doors
were closed and Bartley had stopped peeping through the
crevice between them, and then he began to disengage from
his watch-chain the golden nugget, shaped to a rude sphere,
which hung there. This done, he asked if he might put it on
the little necklace—a christening gift from Mrs. Halleck—
which the baby had on, to see how it looked. It looked very

well, like an old Roman *bolla*, though neither Kinney nor Marcia knew it.

"Guess we'll let it stay there," he suggested, timidly.

"Mr. Kinney!" cried Marcia, in amaze, "I can't let you!"

"Oh, *do* now, ma'am!" pleaded the big fellow, simply. "If you knew how much good it does me, you would. Why, it's been like heaven to me to get into such a home as this, for a day; it has indeed."

"Like heaven?" said Marcia, turning pale. "Oh, my!"

"Well, I don't mean any harm. What I mean is, I've knocked about the world so much, and never had any home of my own, that to see folks as happy as you be makes me happier than I've been since I don't know when. Now, you let it stay. It was the first piece of gold I picked up in Californy when I went out there in '50, and it's about the last; I didn't have very good luck. Well, of course! I know I aint fit to give it; but I want to do it. I think Bartley's about the greatest fellow, and he's the best fellow this world can show. That's the way I feel about him. And I want to do it. Sho! the thing wa'n't no use to me!"

Marcia always gave her maid of all work Sunday afternoon, and she would not trespass upon her rule because she had guests that day. Except for the confusion to which Kinney's unexpected gift had put her, she would have waited for him to join the others before she began to clear away the dinner; but now she mechanically began, and Kinney, to whom these domestic occupations were a second nature, joined her in the work, equally absent-minded in the fervor of his petition.

Bartley suddenly flung open the doors. "My dear, Mr. Ricker says he must be go"— He discovered Marcia with the dish of potatoes in her hand, and Kinney in the act of carrying off the platter of turkey. "Look here, Ricker!"

Kinney came to himself, and opening his mouth above the platter, wide enough to swallow the remains of the turkey, slapped his leg with the hand that he released for the purpose, and shouted, "The ruling passion, Bartley, the ruling passion!"

The men roared; but Marcia, even while she took in the situation, did not see anything so ridiculous in it as they. She smiled a little in sympathy with their mirth, and then said, with a look and tone which he had not seen or heard in her since the day of their picnic at Equity, "Come, see what Mr. Kinney has given baby, Bartley."

They sat up talking Kinney over after he was gone; but even at ten o'clock Bartley said he should not go to bed; he felt like writing.

XXIX

Bartley lived well, now. He felt that he could afford it, on fifty dollars a week; and yet somehow he had always a sheaf of unpaid bills on hand. Rent was so much, the butcher so much, the grocer so much; these were the great outlays, and he knew just what they were; but the sum total was always much larger than he expected. At a pinch, he borrowed; but he did not let Marcia know of this, for she would have starved herself to pay the debt; what was worse, she would have wished him to starve with her. He kept the purse and he kept the accounts; he was master in his house, and he meant to be so.

The pinch always seemed to come in the matter of clothes, and then Marcia gave up whatever she wanted, and said she must make the old things do. Bartley hated this; in his position he must dress well, and as there was nothing mean about him, he wished Marcia to dress well too. Just at this time he had set his heart on her having a certain sacque which they had noticed in a certain window one day when they were on Washington Street together. He surprised her a week later by bringing the sacque home to her, and he surprised himself with a scalskin cap which he had long coveted: it was coming winter, now, and for half a dozen days of the season he would really need the cap. There would be many days when it would be comfortable, and many others when it would be tolerable; and he looked so handsome in it that Marcia herself could not quite feel that it was an extravagance. She asked him how they could afford both of the things at once, but he answered with easy mystery that he had provided the funds; and she went gaily round with him to call on the Hallecks that evening and show off her sacque. It was so stylish and pretty that it won her a compliment from Ben Halleck, which she noticed because it was the first compliment, or anything like it, that he had ever paid her. She repeated it to Bartley. "He said that I looked like a Hungarian Princess that he saw in Vienna."

"Well, I suppose it has a hussar kind of look, with that fur trimming and that broad braid. Did anybody say anything about my cap?" asked Bartley with burlesque eagerness.

"Oh, poor Bartley!" she cried in laughing triumph. "I don't believe any of them noticed it; and you kept twirling it round in your hands all the time to make them look."

"Yes, I did my level best," said Bartley.

They had a jolly time about that. Marcia was proud of her sacque; when she took it off and held it up by the loop in the neck, so as to realize its prettiness, she said she should make it last three winters at least; and she leaned over and gave Bartley a sweet kiss of gratitude and affection, and told him not to try to make up for it by extra work, but to help her scrimp for it.

"I'd rather do the extra work," he protested. In fact he already had the extra work done. It was something that he felt he had the right to sell outside of the Events, and he carried his manuscript to Ricker and offered it to him for his Sunday edition.

Ricker read the title and ran his eye down the first slip, and then glanced quickly at Hubbard. "You don't mean it?"

"Yes, I do," said Bartley. "Why not?"

"I thought he was going to use the material himself some time."

Bartley laughed. "He use the material! Why he can't write, any more than a hen; he can make tracks on paper, but nobody would print 'em, much less buy 'em. I know him; he's all right. It wouldn't hurt the material for his purpose, any way; and he'll be tickled to death when he sees it, if he ever does. Look here, Ricker!" added Bartley, with a touch of anger at the hesitation in his friend's face, "if you're going to spring any conscientious scruples on me, I prefer to offer my manuscript elsewhere. I give you the first chance at it; but it needn't go begging. Do you suppose I'd do this if I didn't understand the man and know just how he'd take it?"

"Why, of course, Hubbard! I beg your pardon. If you say it's all right I'm bound to be satisfied. What do you want for it?"

"Fifty dollars."

"That's a good deal, isn't it?"

"Yes, it is. But I can't afford to do a dishonorable thing for less money," said Bartley with a wink.

The next Sunday, when Marcia came home from church, she went into the parlor a moment to speak to Bartley, before she ran upstairs to the baby. He was writing, and she put her left hand on his back while with her right she held her sacque slung over her shoulder by the loop, and leaned forward with a wandering eye on the papers that strewed the table. In that attitude he felt her pause and grow absorbed, and then rigid; her light caress tightened into a grip. "Why how base! How shameful! That man shall never enter my doors again! Why, it's stealing!"

"What's the matter? What are you talking about?" Bartley looked up with a frown of preparation.

"This!" cried Marcia, snatching up the Chronicle-Abstract at which she had been looking. "Haven't you seen it? Here's Mr. Kinney's life all written out! And when he said that he was going to keep it, and write it out himself. That thief has stolen it!"

"Look out how you talk," said Bartley. "Kinney's an old fool, and he never could have written it out in the world"—

"That makes no difference. He said that he told the things because he knew he was among gentlemen. A great gentleman Mr. Ricker is! And I thought he was so nice!" The tears sprang to her eyes, which flashed again. "I want you to break off with him, Bartley; I don't want you to have anything to do with such a *thief*! And I shall be proud to tell everybody that you've broken off with him *because* he was a thief. Oh, Bartley"—

"Hold your tongue!" shouted her husband.

"I *wont* hold my tongue! And if you defend"—

"Don't you say a word against Ricker. It's all right, I tell you. You don't understand such things. You don't know what you're talking about. I—I—I wrote the thing myself."

He could face her, but she could not face him. There was a subsidence in her proud attitude, as if her physical strength had snapped with her breaking spirit.

"There's no theft about it," Bartley went on. "Kinney

would never write it out, and if he did, I've put the material in better shape for him here than he could ever have given it. Six weeks from now nobody will remember a word of it; and he could tell the same things right over again, and they would be just as good as new." He went on to argue the point.

She seemed not to have listened to him. When he stopped, she said in a quiet, passionless voice:

"I suppose you wrote it to get money for this sacque."

"Yes; I did," replied Bartley.

She dropped it on the floor at his feet.

"I shall never wear it again," she said in the same tone, and a little sigh escaped her.

"Use your pleasure about that," said Bartley, sitting down to his writing again, as she turned and left the room.

She went upstairs and came down immediately, with the gold nugget, which she had wrenched from the baby's necklace, and laid it on the paper before him.

"Perhaps you would like to spend it for Tivoli beer," she suggested. "Flavia shall not wear it."

"I'll get it fitted on to my watch-chain." Bartley slipped it into his waistcoat pocket.

The sacque still lay on the floor at his feet; he pulled his chair a little forward and put his feet on it. He feigned to write awhile longer, and then he folded up his papers and went out, leaving Marcia to make her Sunday dinner alone. When he came home late at night, he found the sacque where she had dropped it, and with a curse he picked it up and hung it on the hat-rack in the hall.

He slept in the guest-chamber, and at times during the night the child cried in Marcia's room and waked him; and then he thought he heard a sound of sobbing which was not the child's. In the morning, when he came down to breakfast, Marcia met him with swollen eyes.

"Bartley," she said tremulously, "I wish you would tell me how you felt justified in writing out Mr. Kinney's life in that way."

"My dear," said Bartley, with perfect amiability, for he had slept off his anger, and he really felt sorry to see her so unhappy, "I would tell you almost anything you want on any other subject; but I think we had better remand that one to the safety of silence, and go upon the general supposition that I know what I'm about."

"I can't, Bartley!"

"Can't you? Well, that's a pity." He pulled his chair to the breakfast table. "It seems to me that girl's imagination always fails her on Mondays. Can she never give us anything but hash and corn-bread when she's going to wash? However, the coffee's good. I suppose *you* made it?"

"Bartley!" persisted Marcia, "I want to believe in everything you do—I want to be proud of it"—

"That will be difficult," suggested Bartley, with an air of thoughtful impartiality, "for the wife of a newspaper man."

"No, no! It needn't be! It mustn't be! If you will only tell me"—

She stopped, as if she feared to repeat her offense.

Bartley leaned back in his chair and looked at her intense face with a smile.

"Tell you that in some way I had Kinney's authority to use his facts? Well, I should have done that yesterday if you had let me. In the first place, Kinney's the most helpless ass in the world. He could never have used his own facts. In the second place, there was hardly anything in his rigmarole the other day that he hadn't told me down there in the lumber camp, with full authority to use it in any way I liked; and I don't see how he could revoke that authority. That's the way I reasoned about it."

"I see—I see!" said Marcia, with humble eagerness.

"Well, that's all there is about it. What I've done can't hurt Kinney. If he ever does want to write his old facts out, he'll be glad to take my report of them, and—spoil it," said Bartley, ending with a laugh.

"And if—if there had been anything wrong about it," said Marcia, anxious to justify him to herself, "Mr. Ricker would have told you so when you offered him the article."

"I don't think Mr. Ricker would have ventured on any impertinence with me," said Bartley, with grandeur. But he lapsed into his wonted, easy way of taking everything. "What are you driving at, Marsh? I don't care particularly for what happened yesterday. We've had rows enough before, and I dare say we shall have them again. You gave me a bad quarter of an hour, and you gave yourself"—he looked at her tear-stained eyes—"a bad night, apparently. That's all there is about it."

"Oh, no, that isn't all! It isn't like the other quarrels we've had. When I think how I've felt toward you ever since, it *scares* me. There can't be anything sacred in our marriage unless we trust each other in everything."

"Well, *I* haven't done any of the mistrusting," said Bartley, with humorous lightness. "But isn't sacred rather a strong word to use in regard to our marriage, anyway?"

"Why—why—what do you mean, Bartley? We were married by a minister."

"Well, yes, by what was left of one," said Bartley. "He couldn't seem to shake himself together sufficiently to ask for the proof that we had declared our intention to get married."

Marcia looked mystified.

"Don't you remember his saying there was something else, and my suggesting to him that it was the fee?"

Marcia turned white.

"Father said the certificate was all right"—

"Oh, he asked to see it, did he? He is a prudent old gentleman. Well, it is all right."

"And what difference did it make about our not proving that we had declared our intention?" asked Marcia, as if only partly reassured.

"No difference to us; and only a difference of sixty dollars fine to him, if it was ever found out."

"And you let the poor old man run that risk?"

"Well, you see, it couldn't be helped. We hadn't declared our intention, and the lady seemed very anxious to be married. You needn't be troubled. We are married, right and tight enough; but I don't know that there's anything *sacred* about it."

"No," Marcia wailed out, "it's tainted with fraud from the beginning."

"If you like to say so," Bartley assented, putting his napkin into its ring.

Marcia hid her face in her arms on the table; the baby left off drumming with its spoon, and began to cry.

Witherby was reading the Sunday edition of the Chronicle-

Abstract when Bartley got down to the Events office; and he
cleared his throat with a premonitory cough as his assistant
swung easily into the room. "Good-morning, Mr. Hubbard,"
he said. "There is quite an interesting article in yesterday's
Chronicle-Abstract. Have you seen it?"

"Yes," said Bartley. "What article?"

"This 'Confessions of an Average American.'" Witherby
held out the paper, where Bartley's article, vividly head-lined
and sub-headed, filled half a page. "What is the reason *we*
cannot have something of this kind?"

"Well, I don't know," Bartley began.

"Have you any idea who wrote this?"

"Oh, yes, I wrote it."

Witherby had the task before him of transmuting an
expression of rather low cunning into one of wounded confidence, mingled with high-minded surprise. "I thought it had
your ear-marks, Mr. Hubbard; but I preferred not to believe
it till I heard the fact from your own lips. I suppose that our
contract covered such contributions as this."

"I wrote it out of time, and on Sunday night. You pay me
by the week, and all that I do throughout the week belongs
to you. The next day after that Sunday I did a full day's work
on the Events. I don't see what you have to complain of. You
told me when I began that you would not expect more than
a certain amount of work from me. Have I ever done less?"

"No, but"—

"Haven't I always done more?"

"Yes; I have never complained of the amount of work. But
upon this theory of yours, what you did in your summer vacation would not belong to the Events, or what you did on
legal holidays."

"I never have any summer vacation or holidays, legal or
illegal. Even when I was down at Equity last summer I sent
you something for the paper every day."

This was true, and Witherby could not gainsay it. "Very
well, sir. If this is to be your interpretation of our understanding for the future, I shall wish to revise our contract," he said,
pompously.

"You can tear it up if you like," returned Bartley. "I dare
say Ricker would jump at a little study of the true inwardness

of counting-room journalism. Unless you insist upon having it for the Events." Bartley gave a chuckle of enjoyment as he sat down at his desk; Witherby rose and stalked away.

He returned in half an hour and said, with an air of frank concession, touched with personal grief: "Mr. Hubbard, I can see how, from your point of view, you were perfectly justifiable in selling your article to the Chronicle-Abstract. My point of view is different, but I shall not insist upon it; and I wish to withdraw—and—and apologize for—any hasty expressions I may have used."

"All right," said Bartley, with a wicked grin. He had triumphed; but his triumph was one to leave some men with an uneasy feeling, and there was not altogether a pleasant taste in Bartley's mouth. After that his position in the Events office was whatever he chose to make it, but he did not abuse his ascendency, and he even made a point of increased deference toward Witherby. Many courtesies passed between them; each took some trouble to show the other that he had no ill feeling.

Three or four weeks later Bartley received a letter with an Illinois postmark which gave him a disagreeable sensation, at first, for he knew it must be from Kinney. But the letter was so amusingly characteristic, so helplessly ill-spelled and ill-constructed, that he could not help laughing. Kinney gave an account of his travels to the mining town, and of his present situation and future prospects; he was full of affectionate messages and inquiries for Bartley's family, and he said he should never forget that Sunday he had passed with them. In a postscript he added: "They copied that String of lies into our paper, here, out of the Chron.-Ab. It was pretty well done, but if your friend Mr. Ricker done it, I'm not goen to Insult him soon again by calling him a gentleman."

This laconic reference to the matter in a postscript was delicious to Bartley; he seemed to hear Kinney saying the words, and imagined his air of ineffective sarcasm. He carried the letter about with him, and the first time he saw Ricker he showed it to him. Ricker read it without appearing greatly diverted; when he came to the postscript he flushed, and demanded, "What have you done about it?"

"Oh, I haven't done anything. It wasn't necessary. You see,

now, what Kinney could have done with his facts if we had left them to him. It would have been a wicked waste of material. I thought the sight of some of his literature would help you wash up your uncleanly scruples on that point."

"How long have you had this letter?" pursued Ricker.

"*I* don't know. A week or ten days."

Ricker folded it up and returned it to him. "Mr. Hubbard," he said, "the next time we meet will you do me the favor to cut my acquaintance?"

Bartley stared at him; he thought he must be joking. "Why, Ricker, what's the matter? I didn't suppose you'd care anything about old Kinney. I thought it would amuse you. Why confound it! I'd just as soon write out and tell him that I did the thing." He began to be angry. "But I can cut your acquaintance fast enough, or any man's, if you're really on your ear!"

"I'm on my ear," said Ricker. He left Bartley standing where they had met.

It was peculiarly unfortunate, for Bartley had occasion within that week to ask Ricker's advice, and he was debarred from doing so by this absurd displeasure. Since their recent perfect understanding, Witherby had slighted no opportunity to cement their friendship, and to attach Bartley more and more firmly to the Events. He now offered him some of the Events stock on extremely advantageous terms, with the avowed purpose of attaching him to the paper. There seemed nothing covert in this, and Bartley had never heard any doubts of the prosperity of the Events, but he would have especially liked to have Ricker's mind upon this offer of stock. Witherby had urged him not to pay for the whole outright, but to accept a somewhat lower salary, and trust to his dividends to make up the difference. The shares had paid fifteen per cent. the year before, and Bartley could judge for himself of the present chances from that showing. Witherby advised him to borrow only fifteen hundred dollars on the three thousand of stock which he offered him, and to pay up the balance in three years by dropping five hundred a year from his salary. It was certainly a flattering proposal; and, under his breath, where Bartley still did most of his blaspheming, he cursed Ricker for an old fool, and resolved to close with Witherby on his own responsibility. After he had done so he told Marcia of the step he had taken.

Since their last quarrel there had been an alienation in her behavior toward him, different from any former resentment. She was submissive and quiescent; she looked carefully after his comfort, and was perfect in her housekeeping; but she held aloof from him somehow, and left him to a solitude in her presence, in which he fancied, if he did not divine, her contempt. But in this matter of common interest, something of their community of feeling revived; they met on a lower level, but they met, for the moment, and Marcia joined eagerly in the discussion of ways and means.

The notion of dropping five hundred from his salary delighted her, because they must now cut down their expenses as much; and she had long grieved over their expenses without being able to make Bartley agree to their reduction. She went upstairs at once and gave the little nurse-maid a week's warning; she told the maid-of-all-work that she must take three dollars a week hereafter, instead of four, or else find another place; she mentally forewent new spring dresses for herself and the baby, and arranged to do herself all of the wash she had been putting out; she put a note in the mouth of the can at the back-door, telling the milkman to leave only two quarts in future; and she came radiantly back to tell Bartley that she had saved half of the lost five hundred a year already. But her countenance fell. "Why, where are you to get the other fifteen hundred dollars, Bartley?"

"Oh, I've thought of that," said Bartley, laughing at her swift alternations of triumph and despair. "You trust to me for that."

"You're not—not going to ask father for it?" she faltered.

"Not very much," said Bartley, as he took his hat to go out.

He meant to make a raise out of Ben Halleck, as he phrased it to himself. He knew that Halleck had plenty of money; he could make the stock itself over to him as security; he did not see why Halleck should hesitate. But when he entered Halleck's room, having asked Cyrus to show him directly there, Halleck gave a start which seemed ominous to Bartley. He had scarcely the heart to open his business, and Halleck lis-

tened with changing color, and something only too like the
embarrassment of a man who intends a refusal. He would not
look Bartley in the face, and when Bartley had made an end
he sat for a time without speaking. At last he said, with a
quick sigh, as if at the close of an internal conflict: "I will
lend you the money!"

Bartley's heart gave a bound, and he broke out into an
immense laugh of relief, and clapped Halleck on the shoulder.
"You looked deucedly as if you *wouldn't*, old man! By
George, you had on such a dismal, hang-dog expression that
I didn't know but *you'd* come to borrow money of *me*, and
I'd made up my mind not to let you have it! But I'm ever-
lastingly obliged to you, Halleck, and I promise you that you
won't regret it."

"I shall have to speak to my father about this," said Halleck, responding coldly to Bartley's robust pressure of his
hand.

"Of course—of course."

"How soon shall you want the money?"

"Well, the sooner the better, now. Bring the check round,
—can't you?—to-morrow night, and take dinner with us,
you and Olive; and we'll celebrate a little. I know it will
please Marcia when she finds out who my hard-hearted
creditor is!"

"Well," assented Halleck, with a smile so ghastly that Bartley noticed it even in his joy.

"Curse me," he said to himself, "if ever I saw a man so
ashamed of doing a good action!"

XXX

THE PRESIDENTIAL canvas of the summer which followed upon these events in Bartley's career was not very active. Sometimes, in fact, it languished so much that people almost forgot it, and a good field was afforded the Events for the practice of independent journalism. To hold a course of strict impartiality, and yet come out on the winning side, was a theory of independent journalism which Bartley illustrated with cynical enjoyment. He developed into something rather artistic the gift which he had always shown in his newspaper work for ironical persiflage. Witherby was not a man to feel this burlesque himself; but when it was pointed out to him by others, he came to Bartley in some alarm for its effect upon the fortunes of the paper. "We can't afford, Mr. Hubbard," he said, with virtuous trepidation, "we can't *afford* to make fun of our friends!"

Bartley laughed at Witherby's anxiety. "They're no more our friends than the other fellows are. We are independent journalists; and this way of treating the thing leaves us perfectly free hereafter to claim, just as we choose, that we were in fun or in earnest on any particular question if we're ever attacked. See?"

"I see," said Witherby, with not wholly subdued misgiving. But after due time for conviction no man enjoyed Bartley's irony more than Witherby when once he had mastered an instance of it. Sometimes it happened that Bartley found him chuckling over a perfectly serious paragraph, but he did not mind that; he enjoyed Witherby's mistake even more than his appreciation.

In these days Bartley was in almost uninterrupted good humor, as he had always expected to be when he became fairly prosperous. He was at no time an unamiable fellow, as he saw it; he had his sulks, he had his moments of anger; but generally he felt good, and he had always believed, and he had promised Marcia, that when he got squarely on his legs he should feel good perpetually. This sensation he now agreeably realized; and he was also now in that position in which he had proposed to himself some little moral reforms. He was not much in the habit of taking stock; but no man wholly escapes the contingencies in which he is confronted with himself and sees certain habits, traits, tendencies, which he would like to change for the sake of his peace of mind hereafter. To some souls these contingencies are full of anguish, of remorse for the past, of despair; but Bartley had never yet seen the time when he did not feel himself perfectly able to turn over a new leaf and blot the old one. There were not many things in his life which he really cared to have very different; but there were two or three shady little corners which he always intended to clean up. He had meant some time or other to have a religious belief of some sort, he did not much care what; since Marcia had taken to the Hallecks' church, he did not see why he should not go with her, though he had never yet done so. He was not quite sure whether he was always as candid with her as he might be, or as kind; though he maintained against this question that in all their quarrels it was six of one and half a dozen of the other. He had never been tipsy but once in his life, and he considered that he had repented and atoned for that enough, especially as nothing had ever come of it; but sometimes he thought he might be overdoing the beer; yes, he thought he must cut down on the Tivoli; he was getting ridiculously fat. If ever he met Kinney again he should tell him that it was he and not Ricker who had appropriated his facts; and he intended to make it up with Ricker somehow.

He had not found just the opportunity yet, but in the meantime he did not mind telling the real cause of their alienation to good fellows who could enjoy a joke. He had his following, though so many of his brother journalists had cooled toward him, and those of his following considered him as smart as chain-lightning and bound to rise. These young men and not very wise elders roared over Bartley's frank declaration of the situation between himself and Ricker, and they contended that if Ricker had taken the article for the Chronicle-Abstract he ought to take the consequences. Bartley told them that of course he should explain the facts to Kinney; but that he meant to let Ricker enjoy his virtuous indignation a while. Once, after a confidence of this kind at the club, where Ricker had refused to speak to him, he came away with a curious sense of moral decay. It did not pain him a great deal, but it certainly surprised him that now with all these prosperous conditions, so favorable for cleaning up, he had so little disposition to clean up. He found himself quite willing to let the affair with Ricker go, and he suspected that he had been needlessly virtuous in his intentions concerning church-going and beer. As to Marcia, it appeared to him that he could not treat a woman of her disposition otherwise than as he did. At any rate, if he had not done everything he could to make her happy she seemed to be getting along well enough, and was probably quite as happy as she deserved to be. They were getting on very quietly now; there had been no violent outbreak on her part since the trouble about Kinney, and then she had practically confessed herself in the wrong, as Bartley looked at it. At last, there was now what might be called a perfect business amity between them. If her life with him was no longer an expression of that intense devotion which she used to show him, it was more like what married life generally comes to, and he accepted her tractability and what seemed her common-sense view of their relations as greatly preferable. With his growth in flesh, Bartley liked peace more and more.

Marcia had consented to go down to Equity alone, that summer, for he had convinced her that during a heated political contest it would not do for him to be away from the paper. He promised to go down for her when she wished to come home; and it was easily arranged for her to travel as far as the Junction under Halleck's escort, when he went to join his sisters in the White Mountains. Bartley missed her and the baby at first. But he soon began to adjust himself with resignation to his solitude. They had determined to keep their maid over the summer, for they had so much trouble in replacing her the last time after their return; and Bartley said he should live very economically. It was quiet, and the woman kept the house cool and clean; she was a good cook, and when Bartley brought a man home to dinner she took an interest in serving it well. Bartley let her order the things from the grocer and butcher, for she knew what they were used to getting, and he had heard so much talk from Marcia about bills since he bought that Events stock, that he was sick of the prices of things. There was no extravagance, and yet he seemed to live very much better after Marcia went. There is no doubt but he lived very much more at his ease. One little restriction after another fell away from him; he went and came with absolute freedom, not only without having to account for his movements, but without having a pang for not doing so. He had the sensation of stretching himself after a cramping posture; and he wrote Marcia the cheerfullest letters, charging her not to cut short her visit from anxiety on his account. He said that he was working hard, but hard work evidently agreed with him, for he was never better in his life. In this high content he maintained a feeling of loyalty by going to the Hallecks, where Mrs. Halleck often had him to tea in pity of his loneliness. They were dull company, certainly; but Marcia liked them, and the cooking was always good. Other evenings he went to the theatres, where there were amusing variety bills; and sometimes he passed the night at Nantasket, or took a run for a day to Newport; he always reported these excursions to Marcia, with expressions of regret that Equity was too far away to run down to for a day.

Marcia's letters were longer and more regular than his; but he could have forgiven some want of constancy, for the sake of a less searching anxiety on her part. She was anxious not only for his welfare, which was natural and proper, but she was anxious about the housekeeping and the expenses, things Bartley could not afford to let trouble him, though he did what he could in a general way to quiet her mind. She wrote fully of the visit which Olive Halleck had paid her, but said that they had not gone about much, for Ben Halleck had only been able to come for a day. She was very well, and so was Flavia.

Bartley realized Flavia's existence with an effort, and for the rest this letter bored him. What could he care about Olive Halleck's coming, or Ben Halleck's staying away? All that he asked of Ben Halleck was a little extension of time when his interest fell due. The whole thing was disagreeable; and he resented what he considered Marcia's endeavor to clap the domestic harness on him again. His thoughts wandered to conditions, to contingencies of which a man does not permit

himself even to think without a degree of moral disintegration. In these ill-advised reveries he mused upon his life as it
might have been if he had never met her, or if they had never
met after her dismissal of him. As he recalled the facts, he was
at that time in an angry and embittered mood, but he was in
a mood of entire acquiescence; and the reconciliation had
been of her own seeking. He could not blame her for it; she
was very much in love with him, and he had been fond of
her. In fact, he was still very fond of her; when he thought of
little ways of hers, it filled him with tenderness. He did justice
to her fine qualities, too: her generosity, her truthfulness, her
entire loyalty to his best interests; he smiled to realize that he
himself preferred his second-best interests, and in her absence
he remembered that her virtues were tedious and even painful
at times. He had his doubts whether there was sufficient compensation in them. He sometimes questioned whether he had
not made a great mistake to get married; he expected now to
stick it through; but this doubt occurred to him. A moment
came in which he asked himself, What if he had never come
back to Marcia that night when she locked him out of her
room? Might it not have been better for both of them? She
would soon have reconciled herself to the irreparable; he even
thought of her happy in a second marriage; and the thought
did not enrage him; he generously wished Marcia well. He
wished—he hardly knew what he wished. He wished nothing
at all but to have his wife and child back again as soon as
possible; and he put aside with a laugh the fancies which
really found no such distinct formulation as I have given
them; which were mere vague impulses, arrested mental tendencies, scraps of undirected reverie. Their recurrence had
nothing to do with what he felt to be his sane and waking
state. But they recurred, and he even amused himself in turning them over.

XXXI

ONE MORNING in September, not long before Marcia returned, Bartley found Witherby at the office waiting for him. Witherby wore a pensive face, which had the effect of being studied. "Good-morning, Mr. Hubbard," he said, and when Bartley answered, "Good-morning," cheerfully ignoring his mood, he added, "What is this I hear, Mr. Hubbard, about a personal misunderstanding between you and Mr. Ricker?"

"I'm sure I don't know," said Bartley; "but I suppose that, if you have heard anything, *you* know."

"I have heard," proceeded Witherby, a little dashed by Bartley's coolness, "that Mr. Ricker accuses you of having used material in that article you sold him which had been intrusted to you under the seal of confidence, and that you had left it to be inferred by the party concerned that Mr. Ricker had written the article himself."

"All right," said Bartley.

"But, Mr. Hubbard," said Witherby, struggling to rise into virtuous supremacy, "what am I to think of such a report?"

"I can't say; unless you should think that it wasn't your affair. That would be the easiest thing."

"But I *can't* think that, Mr. Hubbard! Such a report reflects through you upon the Events; it reflects upon *me!*" Bartley laughed. "I can't approve of such a thing. If you admit the report, it appears to me that you have—a—done a—a—wrong action, Mr. Hubbard."

Bartley turned upon him with a curious look; at the same time he felt a pang, and there was a touch of real anguish in the sarcasm of his demand, "Have I fallen so low as to be rebuked by *you?*"

"I—I don't know what you mean by such an expression as that, Mr. Hubbard," said Witherby. "I don't know what I've done to forfeit your esteem,—to justify you in using such language to me."

"I don't suppose you really do," said Bartley. "Go on."

"I have nothing more to say, Mr. Hubbard, except—except

to add that this has given me a great blow,—a *great* blow. I had begun to have my doubts before as to whether we were quite adapted to each other, and this has—increased them. I pass no judgment upon what you have done, but I will say that it has made me anxious and—a—unrestful. It has made me ask myself whether upon the whole we should not be happier apart. I don't say that we should; but I only feel that nine out of ten business men would consider you, in the position you occupy on the Events,—a—a—dangerous person."

Bartley got up from his desk, and walked toward Witherby, with his hands in his pockets; he halted a few paces from him, and looked down on him with a sinister smile. "I don't think they'd consider *you* a dangerous person in *any* position."

"May be not, may be not," said Witherby, striving to be easy and dignified. In the effort he took up an open paper from the desk before him, and, lifting it between Bartley and himself, feigned to be reading it.

Bartley struck it out of his trembling hands. "You impudent old scoundrel! Do you pretend to be reading when I speak to you? For half a cent"—

Witherby, slipping and sliding in his swivel-chair, contrived to get to his feet. "No violence, Mr. Hubbard, no violence *here!*"

"Violence!" laughed Bartley. "I should have to *touch* you! Come! Don't be afraid! But don't you put on airs of any sort! I understand your game. You want, for some reason, to get rid of me, and you have seized the opportunity with a sharpness that does credit to your cunning. I don't condescend to deny this report,"—speaking in this lofty strain, Bartley had a momentary sensation of its being a despicable slander,— "but I see that, as far as you are concerned, it answers all the purposes of truth. You think that, with the chance of having this thing exploited against me, I wont expose your nefarious practices, and you can get rid of me more safely now than ever you could again. Well, you're right. I dare say you heard of this report a good while ago, and you've waited till you could fill my place without inconvenience to yourself. So I can go at once. Draw your check for all you owe me, and pay me back the money I put into your stock, and I'll clear out at once."

He went about putting together a few personal effects on his desk.

"I must protest against any allusion to nefarious practices, Mr Hubbard," said Witherby, "and I wish you to understand that I part from you without the slightest ill-feeling. I shall always have a high regard for your ability, and—and—your social qualities."

While he made these expressions he hastened to write two checks.

Bartley, who had paid no attention to what Witherby was saying, came up and took the checks.

"This is all right," he said of one; but, looking at the other, he added, "Fifteen hundred dollars!—where is the dividend?"

"That is not due till the end of the month," said Witherby. "If you withdraw your money now, you lose it."

Bartley looked at the face to which Witherby did his best to give a high judicial expression.

"*You* old thief!" he said good-humoredly, almost affectionately. "I *have* a mind to tweak your nose!"

But he went out of the room without saying or doing anything more. He wondered a little at his own amiability; but, with the decay of whatever was right-principled in him, he was aware of growing more and more incapable of indignation. Now, his flash of rage over, he was not at all discontented. With these checks in his pocket, with his youth, his health, and his practised hand, he could have faced the world, with a light heart, if he had not also had to face his wife. But when he thought of the inconvenience of explaining to her, of pacifying her anxiety, of clearing up her doubts on a thousand points, and of getting her simply to eat or sleep till he found something else to do, it dismayed him.

"Good Lord!" he said to himself, "I wish I was dead—or some one."

That conclusion made him smile again.

He decided not to write to Marcia of the change in his affairs, but to take the chance of finding something better before she returned. There was very little time for him to turn round, and he was still without a place or any prospect when she came home. It had sufficed with his acquaintance when he said that he had left the Events because he could not get on with Witherby; but he was very much astonished when it seemed to suffice with her.

"Oh, well," she said, "I am glad of it. You will do better by yourself; and I know you can earn just as much by writing on the different papers."

Bartley knew better than this, but he said:

"Yes, I shall not be in a hurry to take another engagement just yet. But, Marsh," he added, "I was afraid you would blame me—think I had been reckless, or at fault"—

"No," she answered, after a little pause, "I shall not do that any more. I have been thinking all these things over, while I was away from you, and I'm going to do differently after this. I shall believe that you've acted for the best,—that you've not meant to do wrong in anything,—and I shall never question you or doubt you any more."

"Isn't that giving me rather too *much* rope?" asked Bartley, with lightness that masked a vague alarm lest the old times of exaction should be coming back with the old times of devotion.

"No; I see where my mistake has always been. I've always asked too much, and expected too much, even when I didn't ask it. Now, I shall be satisfied with what you don't do, as well as what you do."

"I shall try to live up to my privileges," said Bartley, with a sigh of relief. He gave her a kiss, and then he unclasped Kinney's nugget from his watch-chain, and fastened it on the baby's necklace, which lay in a box Marcia had just taken from her trunk. She did not speak; but Bartley felt better to have the thing off him; Marcia's gentleness, the tinge of sadness in her tone, made him long to confess himself wrong in the whole matter, and justly punished by Ricker's contempt and Witherby's dismissal. But he did not believe that he could trust her to forgive him, and he felt himself unable to go through all that without the certainty of her forgiveness.

As she took the things out of her trunk, and laid them away in this drawer and that, she spoke of events in the village, and told who was dead, who was married, and who had gone away.

"I staid longer than I expected—a little, because father seemed to want me to. I don't think mother's so well as she used to be. I—I'm afraid she seems to be failing, somehow."

Her voice dropped to a lower key, and Bartley said:

"I'm sorry to hear that, I guess she isn't failing. But of course she's getting on, and every year makes a difference."

"Yes, that must be it," she answered, looking at a bundle of collars she had in her hand, as if absorbed in the question as to where she should put them.

Before they slept that night she asked:

"Bartley, did you hear about Hannah Morrison?"

"No. What about her?"

"She's gone—gone away. The last time she was seen was in Portland. They don't know what's become of her. They say that Henry Bird is about heart-broken; but everybody knows she never cared for him. I hated to write to you about it."

Bartley experienced so disagreeable a sensation that he was silent for a time. Then he gave a short, bitter laugh.

"Well, that's what it was bound to come to, sooner or later, I suppose. It's a piece of good luck for Bird."

Bartley went about picking up work from one paper and another, but not securing a basis on any. In that curious and unwholesome leniency which corrupt natures manifest, he and Witherby met at their next encounter on quite amicable terms. Bartley reported some meetings for the Events, and experienced no resentment when Witherby at the office introduced him to the gentleman with whom he had replaced him. Of course Bartley expected that Witherby would insinuate things to his disadvantage, but he did not mind that. He heard of something of the sort being done in Ricker's presence, and of Ricker's saying that in any question of honor and veracity between Witherby and Hubbard he should decide for Hubbard. Bartley was not very grateful for this generous defense; he thought that if Ricker had not been such an ass in the first place there would have been no trouble between them, and Witherby would not have had that handle against him.

He was enjoying himself very well, and he felt entitled to the comparative rest which had not been of his seeking. He wished that Halleck would come back, for he would like to ask his leave to put that money into some other enterprise. His credit was good, and he had not touched the money to pay any of his accumulated bills; he would have considered it dishonorable to do so. But it annoyed him to have the money lying idle. In his leisure he studied the stock market, and he believed that he had several points which were infallible. He put a few hundreds—two or three—of Halleck's money into a mining stock which was so low that it *must* rise. In the meantime he tried a new kind of beer—Norwegian beer,— which he found a little lighter even than Tivoli. It was more expensive, but it was *very* light, and it was essential to Bartley to drink the lightest beer he could find.

He staid a good deal at home now, for he had leisure, and it was a much more comfortable place since Marcia had ceased to question or reproach him. She did not interfere with some bachelor habits he had formed, in her absence, of sleeping far into the forenoon; he now occasionally did night-work on some of the morning papers, and the rest was nec-essary; he had his breakfast whenever he got up, as if he had been at a hotel. He wondered upon what new theory she was really treating him; but he had always been apt to accept what was comfortable in life without much question, and he did not wonder long. He was immensely good-natured now. In his frequent leisure he went out to walk with Marcia and Fla-via, and sometimes he took the little girl alone. He even went to church with them one Sunday, and called at the Hallecks as often as Marcia liked. The young ladies had returned, but Ben Halleck was still away. It made Bartley smile to hear his wife talking of Halleck with his mother and sisters, and falling quite into the family way of regarding him as if he were somehow a saint and martyr.

Bartley was still dabbling in stocks with Halleck's money; some of it had lately gone to pay an assessment which had unexpectedly occurred in place of a dividend. He told Marcia that he was holding the money ready to return to Halleck when he came back, or to put it into some other enterprise where it would help to secure Bartley a new basis. They were now together more than they had been since the first days of their married life in Boston; but the perfect intimacy of those days was gone; he had his reserves, and she her preoccupations,—with the house, with the little girl, with her anxiety about her mother. Sometimes they sat a whole evening together, with almost nothing to say to each other, he reading and she sewing. After an evening of this sort, Bartley felt himself worse bored than if Marcia had spent it in taking him to task as she used to do. Once he looked at her over the top of his paper, and distinctly experienced that he was tired of the whole thing.

But the political canvass was growing more interesting now. It was almost the end of October, and the speech-making had become very lively. The Democrats were hopeful and the Republicans resolute, and both parties were active in getting out their whole strength, as the saying is at such times. This was done not only by speech-making, but by long nocturnal processions of torch-lights; by day as well as by night, drums throbbed and horns brayed, and the feverish excitement spread its contagion through the whole population. But it did not affect Bartley. He had cared nothing about the canvass from the beginning, having an equal contempt for the "bloody shirt" of the Republicans and the reform pretensions of the Democrats. The only thing that he took an interest in was the betting; he laid his wages with so much apparent science and sagacity that he had a certain following of young men who bet as Hubbard did. Hubbard, they believed, had a long head; he disdained bets of hats, and of barrels of apples, and ordeals by wheelbarrows; he would bet only with people who could put up their money, and his followers honored him for it; when asked where he got his money, being out of place, and no longer instant to do work that fell in his way, they answered from a ready faith that he had made a good thing in mining stocks.

In her heart, Marcia probably did not share this faith. But she faithfully forbore to harass Bartley with her doubts, and on those evenings when he found her such dull company she was silent because if she spoke she must express the trouble in her mind. Women are more apt to theorize their husbands than men in their stupid self-absorption ever realize. When a man is married, his wife almost ceases to be exterior to his consciousness; she afflicts or consoles him like a condition of health or sickness; she is literally part of him in a spiritual sense, even when he is rather indifferent to her; but the most devoted wife has always a corner of her soul in which she thinks of her husband as *him*; in which she philosophizes him wholly aloof from herself. In such an obscure fastness of her being, Marcia had meditated a great deal upon Bartley during her absence at Equity,—meditated painfully and, in her sort, prayerfully upon him. She perceived that he was not her young dream of him; and since it appeared to her that she could not forego that dream and live, she could but accuse herself of having somehow had a perverse influence upon him. She knew that she had never reproached him except for his good, but she saw too that she had always made him worse, and not better. She recurred to what he said the first night they arrived in Boston: "I believe that, if you have faith in me, I shall get along; and when you don't, I shall go to the bad." She could reason to no other effect, than that hereafter, no matter what happened, she must show perfect faith in him by perfect patience. It was hard, far harder than she had thought. But she did forbear; she did use patience.

The election day came and went. Bartley remained out until the news of Tilden's success could no longer be doubted, and then came home jubilant. Marcia seemed not to understand. "I didn't know you cared so much for Tilden," she said, quietly. "Mr. Halleck is for Hayes; and Ben Halleck was coming home to vote."

"That's all right: a vote in Massachusetts makes no difference. I'm for Tilden, because I have the most money up on him. The success of that noble old reformer is worth seven hundred dollars to me in bets." Bartley laughed, rubbed her cheeks with his chilly hands, and went down into the cellar for some beer. He could not have slept without that, in his excitement; but he was out very early the next morning, and in the raw damp of the rainy November day he received a more penetrating chill when he saw the bulletins at the newspaper offices intimating that a fair count might give the Republicans enough Southern States to elect Hayes. This appeared to Bartley the most impudent piece of political effrontery in the whole history of the country, and among those who went about denouncing Republican chicanery at the Democratic club-rooms, no one took a loftier tone of moral indignation than he. The thought that he might lose so much of Halleck's money through the machinations of a parcel of carpet-bagging tricksters filled him with a virtue at which he afterward smiled when he found that people were declaring their bets off. "I laid a wager on the popular result, not on the decision of the Returning Boards," he said in reclaiming his money from the referees. He had some difficulty in getting it all back, but he had got it when he walked homeward at night, after having been out all day; and there now ensued in his soul a struggle as to what he should do with this money. He had it all except the three hundred he had ventured on the mining stock, which would eventually be worth everything he had paid for it. After his frightful escape from losing half of it on those bets, he had an intense longing to be rid of it, to give it back to Halleck, who never would ask him for it, and then to go home and tell Marcia everything, and throw himself on her mercy. Better poverty, better disgrace before Halleck and her, better her condemnation, than this life of temptation that he had been leading. He saw how hideous it was in the retrospect, and he shuddered; his good instincts awoke, and put forth their strength, such as it was; tears came into his eyes; he resolved to write to Kinney and exonerate Ricker, he resolved humbly to beg Ricker's pardon. He must leave Boston; but if Marcia would forgive him, he would go back with her to Equity, and take up the study of the law in her father's office again, and fulfil all her wishes. He would have a hard time to overcome the old man's prejudices, but he deserved a hard time, and he knew he should finally succeed. It would be bitter, returning to that stupid little town, and he imagined the intrusive conjecture and sarcastic comment that would attend his return; but he believed that he could live this down, and he trusted himself to laugh it down. He already saw himself there, settled in the Squire's office, reinstated in public opinion, a leading lawyer of the place, with Congress open before him whenever he chose to turn his face that way.

He had thought of going first to Halleck, and returning the money, but he was willing to give himself the encouragement of Marcia's pleasure, of her forgiveness and her praise in an affair that had its difficulties and would require all his manfulness. The maid met him at the door with little Flavia, and told him that Marcia had gone out to the Hallecks', but had left word that she would soon return, and that then they would have supper together. Her absence dashed his warm impulse, but he recovered himself, and took the little one from the maid. He lighted the gas in the parlor, and had a frolic with Flavia in kindling a fire in the grate, and making the room bright and cheerful. He played with the child and made her laugh; he already felt the pleasure of a good conscience, though with a faint nether ache in his heart which was perhaps only his wish to have the disagreeable preliminaries to his better life over as soon as possible. He drew two easy-chairs up at opposite corners of the hearth, and sat down in one, leaving the other for Marcia; he had Flavia standing on his knees, and clinging fast to his fingers, laughing and crowing while he danced her up and down, when he heard the front door open, and Marcia burst into the room.

She ran to him and plucked the child from him, and then went back as far as she could from him in the room, crying, "Give *me* the child!" and facing him with the look he knew. Her eyes were dilated, and her visage white with the transport that had whirled her far beyond the reach of reason. The frail structure of his good resolutions dropped to ruin at the sight, but he mechanically rose and advanced upon her till she forbade him with a muffled shriek of "Don't *touch* me! So!" she went on, gasping and catching her breath, "it was *you*! I might have known it! I might have guessed it from the first! *You!* Was *that* the reason why you didn't care to have me hurry home this summer? Was that—was that"— She choked, and convulsively pressed her face into the neck of the child, which began to cry.

Bartley closed the doors, and then, with his hands in his pockets, confronted her with a smile of wicked coolness.

"Will you be good enough to tell me what you're talking about?"

"Do you pretend that you don't know? I met a woman at the bottom of the street, just now. Do you know who?"

"No; but it's very dramatic. Go on!"

"It was Hannah Morrison! She reeled against me; and

when I— such a fool as I was!—pitied her, because I was on my way home to you, and was thinking about you, and loving you, and was so happy in it, and asked her how she came to that, she *struck* me, and told me to—to—ask my—husband!"

The transport broke in tears; the denunciation had turned to entreaty in everything but words; but Bartley had hardened his heart now past all entreaty. The idiotic penitent that he had been a few moments ago—the soft, well-meaning dolt—was so far from him now as to be scarce within the reach of his contempt. He was going to have this thing over once for all; he would have no mercy upon himself or upon her; the Devil was in him and uppermost in him, and the Devil is fierce and proud, and knows how to make many base emotions feel like a just self-respect.

"And did you believe a woman like that?" he sneered.

"Do I believe a man like this?" she demanded, with a dying flash of her fury. "You—you don't dare to deny it."

"Oh, no, I don't deny it. For one reason it would be of no use. For all practical purposes, I admit it. What then?"

"What then?" she asked bewildered. "Bartley! You don't mean it!"

"Yes, I do. I mean it. I *don't* deny it. What then? What are you going to do about it?" She gazed at him in incredulous horror. "Come! I mean what I say. What will you do?"

"Oh, merciful God! what shall I do?" she prayed aloud.

"That's just what I'm curious to know. When you leaped in here, just now, you must have meant to do something, if I couldn't convince you that the woman was lying. Well, you see that I don't try. I give you leave to believe whatever she said. What then?"

"Bartley!" she besought him in her despair. "Do you drive me from you?"

"Oh, no, certainly not. That isn't my way. You have driven me from you, and I might claim the right to retaliate, but I don't. I've no expectation that you'll go away, and I want to see what else you'll do. You would have me, before we were married; you were tolerably shameless in getting me; when your jealous temper made you throw me away, you couldn't live till you got me back again; you ran after me. Well, I suppose you've learnt wisdom, now. At least you wont try *that* game again. But what *will* you do?"

He looked at her smiling, while he dealt her these stabs one by one.

She set down the child, and went out to the entry where its hat and cloak hung. She had not taken off her own things, and now she began to put on the little one's garments with shaking hands, kneeling before it.

"I will never live with you again, Bartley," she said.

"Very well. I doubt it, as far as you're concerned; but if you go away now, you certainly *wont* live with me again, for I shall not let you come back. Understand that."

Each had most need of the other's mercy, but neither would have mercy.

"It isn't for what you won't deny. I don't believe that. It's for what you've said now."

She could not make the buttons and the button-holes of the child's sack meet with her quivering fingers; he actually stooped down and buttoned the little garment for her as if they had been going to take the child out for a walk between them. She caught it up in her arms, and sobbing "Good-by, Bartley!" ran out of the room.

"Recollect that if you go, you don't come back," he said.

The outer door crashing to behind her was his answer.

He sat down to think, before the fire he had built for her. It was blazing brightly now, and the whole room had a hideous cosiness. He could not think—he must act. He went up to their room, where the gas was burning low, as if she had lighted it and then frugally turned it down as her wont was. He did not know what his purpose was, but it developed itself. He began to pack his things in a traveling-bag which he took out of the closet, and which he had bought for her when she set out for Equity in the summer; it had the perfume of her dresses yet.

When this was finished, he went down-stairs again, and being now strangely hungry, he made a meal of such things as he found set out on the tea-table. Then he went over the papers in his secretary; he burnt some of them, and put others into his bag.

After all this was done he sat down by the fire again, and

gave Marcia a quarter of an hour longer in which to return. He did not know whether he was afraid that she would or would not come. But when the time ended, he took up his bag and went out of the house. It began to rain, and he went back for an umbrella; he gave her that one chance more, and he ran up into their room. But she had not come back. He went out again, and hurried away, through the rain, to the Albany Depot, where he bought a ticket for Chicago. There was as yet nothing definite in his purpose, beyond the fact that he was to be rid of her: whether for a long or short time, or forever, he did not yet know; whether he meant ever to communicate with her, or seek or suffer a reconciliation, the locomotive that leaped westward into the dark with him knew as well as he.

Yet all the mute, obscure forces of habit, which are doubtless the strongest forces in human nature, were dragging him back to her. Because their lives had been united so long, it seemed impossible to sever them, though their union had been so full of misery and discord; the custom of marriage was so subtile and so pervasive, that his heart demanded her sympathy for what he was suffering in abandoning her. The solitude into which he had plunged stretched before him so vast, so sterile and hopeless, that he had not the courage to realize it; he insensibly began to give it limits: he would return after so many months, weeks, days.

He passed twenty-four hours on the train, and left it at Cleveland for the half-hour it stopped for supper. But he could not eat; he had to own to himself that he was beaten, and that he must return, or throw himself into the lake. He ran hastily to the baggage-car, and effected the removal of his bag; then he went to the ticket-office and waited at the end of a long queue for his turn at the window. His turn came at last, and he confronted the nervous and impatient ticket-agent, without speaking.

"Well, sir, what do you want?" demanded the agent. Then, with rising temper, "What is it? Are you deaf? Are you dumb? You can't expect to stand there all night!"

The policeman outside the rail laid his hand on Bartley's shoulder:

"Move on, my friend."

He obeyed, and reeled away in a fashion that confirmed the policeman's suspicions. He searched his pockets again and again; but his porte-monnaie was in none of them. It had been stolen, and Halleck's money with the rest. Now he could not return; nothing remained for him but the ruin he had chosen.

XXXII

HALLECK prolonged his summer vacation beyond the end of October. He had been in town from time to time, and then had set off again on some new absence; he was so restless and so far from well during the last of these flying visits, that the old people were glad when he wrote them that he should stay as long as the fine weather continued. He spoke of an interesting man whom he had met at the mountain resort where he was staying—a Spanish-American, attached to one of the legations at Washington, who had a scheme for Americanizing popular education in his own country. "He has made a regular set at me," Halleck wrote, "and if I had not fooled away so much time already on law and on leather, I should like to fool away a little more on such a cause as this."

He did not mention the matter again in his letters; but the first night after his return, when they all sat together in the comfort of having him at home again, he asked his father:

"What would you think of my going to South America?"

The old man started up from the pleasant after-supper drowse into which he was suffering himself to fall, content with Halleck's presence, and willing to leave the talk to the women folk.

"I don't know what you mean, Ben?"

"I suppose it's my having the matter so much in mind that makes me feel as if we had talked it over. I mentioned it in one of my letters."

"Yes," returned his father; "but I presumed you were joking."

Halleck frowned impatiently; he would not meet the gaze of his mother and sisters, but he addressed himself again to his father.

"I don't know that I was in earnest." His mother dropped her eyes to her mending, with a faint sigh of relief. "But I can't say," he added, "that I was joking, exactly. The man himself was very serious about it."

He stopped, apparently to govern an irritable impulse, and

493

then he went on to set the project of his Spanish-American acquaintance before them, explaining it in detail.

At the end:

"That's good," said his father, "but why need *you* have gone, Ben?"

The question seemed to vex Halleck; he did not answer at once. His mother could not bear to see him crossed, and she came to his help against herself and his father, since it was only supposing the case.

"I presume," she said, "that we could have looked at it as a missionary work."

"It isn't a missionary work, mother," answered Halleck, severely, "in any sense that you mean. I should go down there to teach, and I should be paid for it. And I want to say at once that they have no yellow fever nor earthquakes, and that they have not had a revolution for six years. The country's perfectly safe every way, and so wholesome that it will be a good thing for me. But I shouldn't expect to convert anybody."

"Of course not, Ben," said his mother, soothingly.

"I hope you wouldn't object to it if it *were* a missionary work," said one of the elder sisters.

"No, Anna," returned Ben.

"I merely wanted to know," said Anna.

"Then I hope you're satisfied, Anna," Olive cut in. "Ben won't *refuse* to convert the Uruguayans, if they apply in a proper spirit."

"I think Anna had a right to ask," said Miss Louisa, the eldest.

"Oh, undoubtedly, Miss Halleck," said Olive. "I like to see Ben reproved for misbehavior to his mother, myself."

Her father laughed at Olive's prompt defense.

"Well, it's a cause that we've all got to respect; but I don't see why *you* should go, Ben, as I said before. It would do very well for some young fellow who had no settled prospects, but you've got your duties here. I presume you looked at it in that light. As you said in your letter, you've fooled away so much time on leather and law"—

"I shall never amount to anything in the law!" Ben broke out. His mother looked at him in anxiety; his father kept a steady smile on his face; Olive sat alert for any chance that offered to put down her elder sisters, who drew in their breath, and grew silently a little primmer. "I'm not well"—

"Oh, I know you're not, dear," interrupted his mother, glad of another chance to abet him.

"I'm not strong enough to go on with the line of work I've marked out, and I feel that I'm throwing away the feeble powers I have."

His father answered with less surprise than Halleck had evidently expected, for he had thrown out his words with a sort of defiance; probably the old man had watched him closely enough to surmise that it might come to this with him at last. At any rate, he was able to say, without seeming to assent too readily, "Well, well, give up the law, then, and come back into leather, as you call it. Or take up something else. We don't wish to make anything a burden to you; but take up some useful work at home. There are plenty of things to be done."

"Not for me," said Halleck gloomily.

"Oh, yes, there are," said the old man.

"I see you are not willing to have me go," said Halleck, rising in uncontrollable irritation. "But I wish you wouldn't all take this tone with me!"

"We haven't taken any tone with you, Ben," said his mother, with pleading tenderness.

"I think Anna has decidedly taken a tone," said Olive.

Anna did not retort, but "What tone?" demanded Louisa, in her behalf.

"Hush, children," said their mother.

"Well, well," suggested his father to Ben, "think it over, think it over. There's no hurry."

"I've thought it over; there *is* hurry," retorted Halleck. "If I go, I must go at once."

His mother arrested her thread, half drawn through the seam, letting her hand drop, while she glanced at him.

"It isn't so much a question of your giving up the law, Ben, as of your giving up your family and going so far from us all," said his father. "That's what I shouldn't like."

"I don't like that, either. But I can't help it." He added, "Of course, mother, I shall not go without your full and free consent. You and father must settle it between you." He fetched a quick, worried sigh as he put his hand on the door.

"Ben isn't himself at all," said Mrs. Halleck, with tears in her eyes, after he had left the room.

"No," said her husband. "He's restless. He'll get over this idea in a few days." He urged this hope against his wife's despair, and argued himself into low spirits.

"I don't believe but what it *would* be the best thing for his health, may be," said Mrs. Halleck, at the end.

"I've always had my doubts whether he would ever come to anything in the law," said the father.

The elder sisters discussed Halleck's project apart between themselves, as their wont was with any family interest, and they bent over a map of South America, so as to hide what they were doing from their mother.

Olive had left the room by another door, and she intercepted Halleck before he reached his own.

"What is the matter, Ben?" she whispered.

"Nothing," he answered, coldly. But he added, "Come in, Olive."

She followed him, and hovered near after he turned up the gas.

"I can't stand it here,—I must go," he said, turning a dull, weary look upon her.

"Who was at the Elm House that you knew this last time?" she asked, quickly.

"Laura Dixmore isn't driving me away, if you mean that," replied Halleck.

"I *couldn't* believe it was she! I should have despised you if it was. But I shall hate her, whoever it was."

Halleck sat down before his table, and his sister sank upon the corner of a chair near it, and looked wistfully at him.

"I know there is some one!"

"If you think I've been fool enough to offer myself to any one, Olive, you're very much mistaken."

"Oh, it needn't have come to that," said Olive, with indignant pity.

"My life is a failure here," cried Halleck, moving his head uneasily from side to side. "I feel somehow as if I could go out there and pick up the time I've lost. Great Heaven!" he cried, "if I were only running away from some innocent young girl's rejection, what a happy man I should be!"

"It's some horrid married thing, then, that's been flirting with you!"

He gave a forlorn laugh.

"I'd almost confess it to please you, Olive. But I prefer to get out of the matter without lying, if I could. Why need you suppose any reason but the sufficient one I've given?—Don't afflict me! don't imagine things about me, don't make a mystery of me! I've been blunt and awkward, and I've bungled the business with father and mother; but I want to get away because I'm a miserable fraud here, and I think I might rub on a good while there before I found myself out again."

"Ben," demanded Olive, regardless of his words, "what have you been doing?"

"The old story,—nothing."

"Is that true, Ben?"

"You used to be satisfied with asking once, Olive."

"You *haven't* been so wicked, so careless, as to get some poor creature in love with you, and then want to run away from the misery you've made?"

"I suppose if I look it there's no use denying it," said Halleck, letting his sad eyes meet hers, and smiling drearily. "You insist upon having a lady in the case?"

"Yes. But I see you wont tell me anything; and I *wont* afflict you. Only I'm afraid it's just some silly thing that you've got to brooding over, and that you'll let drive you away."

"Well, you have the comfort of reflecting that I can't get away, whatever the pressure is."

"You know better than that, Ben; and so do I. You know that, if you haven't got father and mother's consent already, it's only because you haven't had the heart to ask for it. As far as that's concerned, you're gone already. But I hope you won't go without thinking it over, as father says,—and talking it over. I hate to have you seem unsteady and fickleminded, when I know you're not; and I'm going to set myself against this project till I know what's driving you from us,—or till I'm sure that it's something worth while. You needn't expect that I shall help to make it easy for you; I shall help to make it hard."

Her loving looks belied her threats; if the others could not resist Ben when any sort of desire showed itself through his habitual listlessness, how could she, who understood him best and sympathized with him most? "There was something I was going to talk to you about, to-night, if you hadn't scared us all with this ridiculous scheme, and ask you whether you couldn't do something." She seemed to suggest the change of interest with the hope of winning his thoughts away from the direction they had taken; but he listened apathetically, and left her to go farther or not, as she chose. "I think," she added abruptly, "that some trouble is hanging over those wretched Hubbards."

"Some new one?" asked Halleck, with sad sarcasm, turning his eyes toward her, as if with the resolution of facing her.

"You know he's left his place on that newspaper."

"Yes, I heard that when I was at home before."

"There are some very disagreeable stories about it. They say he was turned away by Mr. Witherby for behaving badly—for printing something he oughtn't to have done."

"That was to have been expected," said Halleck.

"He hasn't found any other place, and Marcia says he gets very little work to do. He must be running into debt, terribly. I feel very anxious about them. I don't know what they're living on."

"Probably on some money I lent him," said Halleck, quietly. "I lent him fifteen hundred in the spring. It ought to make him quite comfortable for the present."

"Oh, Ben! Why did you lend him money? You might have known he wouldn't do any good with it."

Halleck explained how and why the loan had been made, and added, "If he's supporting his family with it, he's doing some good. I lent it to him for her sake."

Halleck looked hardily into his sister's face, but he dropped his eyes when she answered, simply:

"Yes, of course. But I don't believe she knows anything about it; and I'm glad of it; it would only add to her trouble. She worships you, Ben!"

"Does she?"

"She seems to think you are perfect, and she never comes here but she asks when you're to be home. I suppose she thinks you have a good influence on that miserable husband of hers. He's going from bad to worse, I guess. Father heard that he is betting on the election. That's what he's doing with your money."

"It would be somebody else's money if it wasn't mine," said Halleck. "Bartley Hubbard must live, and he must have the little excitements that make life agreeable."

"Poor thing!" sighed Olive, "I don't know what she would do if she heard that you were going away. To hear her talk, you would think she had been counting the days and hours till you got back. It's ridiculous, the way she goes on with mother; asking everything about you as if she expected to make Bartley Hubbard over again on your pattern. I should hate to have anybody think me such a saint as she does you. But there isn't much danger, thank goodness! I could laugh, sometimes, at the way she questions us all about you, and is so delighted when she finds that you and that wretch have anything in common. But it's all too miserably sad. She certainly *is* the most single-hearted creature alive," continued Olive, reflectively. "Sometimes she *scares* me with her innocence. I don't believe that even her jealousy ever suggested a wicked idea to her: she's furious because she feels the injustice of giving so much more than he does. She hasn't really a thought for anybody else: I do believe that, if she were free to choose from now to doomsday, she would always choose Bartley Hubbard, bad as she knows him to be. And if she were a widow, and anybody else proposed to her, she would be utterly shocked and astonished."

"Very likely," said Halleck, absently.

"I feel very unhappy about her," Olive resumed. "I know that she's anxious and troubled all the time. *Can't* you do something, Ben? Have a talk with that disgusting thing, and see if you can't put him straight again, somehow?"

"No!" exclaimed Halleck, bursting violently from his abstraction. "I shall have nothing to do with them! Let him go his own way and the sooner he goes to the—. I wont interfere,—I can't, I mustn't! I wonder at you, Olive!" He pushed away from the table, and went limping about the room, searching here and there for his hat and stick, which were on the desk where he had put them, in plain view. As he laid hand on them at last, he met his sister's astonished eyes. "If I interfered, I should not interfere because I cared for *him* at all!" he cried.

"Of course not," said Olive. "But I don't see anything to make you *wonder* at me about that."

"It would be because I cared for her"—

"Certainly! You didn't suppose I expected you to interfere from any other motive?"

He stood looking at her in stupefaction, with his hand on his hat and stick, like a man who doubts whether he has heard aright. Presently a shiver passed over him, another light came into his eyes, and he said quietly, "I'm going out to see Atherton."

"To-night?" said his sister, accepting provisionally, as women do, the apparent change of subject. "Don't go to-night, Ben! You're too tired."

"I'm not tired. I intended to see him to-night, at any rate. I want to talk over this South-American scheme with him."

He put on his hat and moved quickly toward the door.

"Ask him about the Hubbards," said Olive. "Perhaps he can tell you something."

"I don't want to know anything. I shall ask him nothing."

She slipped between him and the door.

"Ben, you haven't heard anything against poor Marcia, have you?"

"No!"

"You don't think she's to blame in any way for his going wrong, do you?"

"How could I?"

"Then I don't understand why you wont do anything to help her."

He looked at her again, and opened his lips to speak once, but closed them before he said:

"I've got my own affairs to worry me. Isn't that reason enough for not interfering in theirs?"

"Not for you, Ben."

"Then I don't choose to mix myself up in other people's misery. I don't like it, as you once said."

"But you can't help it sometimes, as *you* said."

"I can this time, Olive. Don't you see"—he began.

"I see there's something you wont tell me. But I shall find it out," she threatened him half playfully.

"I wish you could," he answered. "Then perhaps you'd let me know." She opened the door for him now, and as he passed out he said gently, "I *am* tired, but I sha'n't begin to rest till I have had this talk with Atherton. I'd better go."

"Yes," Olive assented, "you'd better." She added in banter. "You're altogether too mysterious to be of much comfort at home."

The family heard him close the outside door behind him after Olive came back to them, and she explained;

"He's gone out to talk it over with Mr. Atherton."

His father gave a laugh of relief.

"Well, if he leaves it to Atherton, I guess we needn't worry about it."

"The child isn't at all well," said his mother.

XXXIII

H ALLECK met Atherton at the door of his room with his hat and coat on.

"Why, Halleck! I was just going to see if you had come home!"

"You needn't now," said Halleck, pushing by him into the room. "I want to see you, Atherton, on business."

Atherton took off his hat and closed the door with one hand, while he slipped the other arm out of his overcoat sleeve.

"Well, to tell the truth, I was going to mingle a little business myself with the pleasure of seeing you."

He turned up the gas in his drop-light, and took the chair from which he had looked across the table at Halleck, when they talked there before.

"It's the old subject," he said, with a sense of repetition in the situation. "I learn from Witherby that Hubbard has taken that money of yours out of the Events, and from what I hear elsewhere he is making ducks and drakes of it on election bets. What shall you do about it?"

"Nothing," said Halleck.

"Oh! Very well," returned Atherton, with the effect of being a little snubbed, but resolved to take his snub professionally. He broke out, however, in friendly exasperation: "Why in the world did you lend the fellow that money?"

Halleck lifted his brooding eyes, and fixed them half pleadingly, half defiantly upon his friend's face.

"I did it for his wife's sake."

"Yes, I know," returned Atherton. "I remember how you felt. I couldn't share your feeling, but I respected it. However, I doubt if your loan was a benefit to either of them. It probably tempted him to count upon money that he hadn't earned, and that's always corrupting."

"Yes," Halleck replied. "But I can't say that, so far as he's concerned, I'm very sorry. I don't suppose it would do her any good if I forced him to disgorge any balance he may have left from his wagers?"

"No, hardly."

"Then I shall let him alone."

The subject was dismissed, and Atherton waited for Halleck to speak of the business on which he had come. But Halleck only played with the paper-cutter which his left hand had found on the table near him, and, with his chin sunk on his breast, seemed lost in an unhappy reverie.

"I hope you won't accuse yourself of doing him an injury," said Atherton, at last, with a smile.

"Injury?" demanded Halleck, quickly. "What injury? How?"

"By lending him that money."

"Oh! I had forgotten that; I wasn't thinking of it," returned Halleck, impatiently. "I was thinking of something different. I'm aware of disliking the man so much that I should be willing to have greater harm than that happen to him—the greatest, for that matter. Though I don't know, after all, that it would be harm. In another life, if there is one, he might start in a new direction; but that isn't imaginable of him here; he can only go from bad to worse; he can only make more and more sorrow and shame. Why shouldn't one wish him dead, when his death could do nothing but good?"

"I suppose you don't expect me to answer such a question seriously."

"But suppose I did?"

"Then I should say that no man ever wished any such good as that, except from the worst motive; and the less one has to do with such questions, even as abstractions, the better."

"You're right," said Halleck. "But why do you call it an abstraction?"

"Because, in your case, nothing else is conceivable."

"I told you I was willing the worst should happen to him."

"And I didn't believe you."

Halleck lay back in his chair, and laughed wearily.

"I wish I could convince somebody of my wickedness. But it seems to be useless to try. I say things that ought to raise the roof, both to you here and to Olive at home, and you tell me you don't believe me, and she tells me that Mrs. Hubbard thinks me a saint. I suppose now, that if I took you by the button-hole and informed you confidentially that I had stopped long enough at 129 Clover street to put a knife into Hubbard in a quiet way, you wouldn't send for a policeman."

"I should send for a doctor," said Atherton.

"Such is the effect of character! And yet, out of the fulness of the heart the mouth speaketh. Out of the heart proceed all those unpleasant things enumerated in Scripture; but if you bottle them up there, and keep your label fresh, it's all that's required of you—by your fellow-beings, at least. What an amusing thing morality would be if it were not—otherwise. Atherton, do you believe that such a man as Christ ever lived?"

"I know you do, Halleck," said Atherton.

"Well, that depends upon what you call *me*. If what I was,—if my well Sunday-schooled youth—is I, I do. But if I, poising dubiously on the momentary present between the past and future, am I—I'm afraid I don't. And yet it seems to me that I have a fairish sort of faith. I know that, if Christ never lived on earth, some One lived who imagined him, and that One must have been a God. The historical fact oughtn't to matter. Christ being imagined, can't you see what a comfort, what a rapture, it must have been to all these poor souls to come into such a presence and be looked through and through? The relief, the rest, the complete exposure of Judgment Day"—

"Every day is Judgment Day," said Atherton.

"Yes, I know your doctrine. But I mean the Last Day. We ought to have something in anticipation of it, here, in our social system. Character is a superstition, a wretched fetish. Once a year wouldn't be too often to seize upon sinners whose blameless life has placed them above suspicion, and turn them inside out before the community, so as to show people how the smoke of the Pit had been quietly blackening their interior. That would destroy character as a cult."

He laughed again.

"Well, this isn't business—though it isn't pleasure, either, exactly. What I came for was to ask you something. I've finished at the law school, and I'm just ready to begin here in the office with you. Don't you think it would be a good time for me to give up the law? Wait a moment!" he said, arresting in Atherton an impulse to speak. "We will take the decent surprise, the friendly demur, the conscientious scruple, for granted. Now, honestly, do you believe I've got the making of a lawyer in me?"

"I don't think you're very well, Halleck," Atherton began.

"Ah, *you're* a lawyer! You won't give me a direct answer!"

"I will if you wish," retorted Atherton.

"Well."

"Do you want to give it up?"

"Yes."

"Then do it. No man ever prospered in it yet who wanted to leave it. And now, since it's come to this, I'll tell you what I really *have* thought all along. I've thought that, if your heart was really set on the law, you would overcome your natural disadvantages for it; but if the time ever came when you were tired of it, your chance was lost: you never would make a lawyer. The question is, whether that time has come."

"It has," said Halleck.

"Then stop, here and now. You've wasted two years' time, but you can't get it back by throwing more after it. I shouldn't be your friend, I shouldn't be an honest man, if I let you go on with me, after this. A bad lawyer is such a very bad thing. This isn't altogether a surprise to me, but it will be a blow to your father," he added, with a questioning look at Halleck, after a moment.

"It might have been, if I hadn't taken the precaution to deaden the place by a heavier blow first."

"Ah! you have spoken to him already?"

"Yes, I've had it out in a sneaking, hypothetical way. But I could see that, so far as the law was concerned, it was enough; it served. Not that he's consented to the other thing; there's where I shall need your help, Atherton. I'll tell you what my plan is." He stated it bluntly at first; and then went over the ground and explained it fully, as he had done at home. Atherton listened without permitting any sign of surprise to escape him; but he listened with increasing gravity, as if he heard something not expressed in Halleck's slow, somewhat nasal monotone, and at the end he said, "I approve of any plan that will take you away for a while. Yes, I'll speak to your father about it."

"If you think you need any conviction, I could use arguments to bring it about in you," said Halleck, in recognition of his friend's ready concurrence.

"No, I don't need any arguments to convince me, I believe," returned Atherton.

"Then I wish you'd say something to bring *me* round! Unless argument is used by somebody, the plan always produces a cold chill in me." Halleck smiled, but Atherton kept a sober face. "I wish my Spanish-American was here! What makes you think it's a good plan? Why should I disappoint my father's hopes again, and wring my mother's heart by proposing to leave them for any such uncertain good as this scheme promises?" He still challenged his friend with a jesting air, but a deeper and stronger feeling of some sort trembled in his voice.

Atherton would not reply to his emotion; he answered, with obvious evasion: "It's a good cause; in some sort—the best sort—it's a missionary work."

"That's what my mother said to me."

"And the change will be good for your health."

"That's what I said to my mother!"

Atherton remained silent, waiting apparently for Halleck to continue, or to end the matter there, as he chose.

It was some moments before Halleck went on: "You would say, wouldn't you, that my first duty was to my own undertakings, and to those who had a right to expect their fulfillment from me? You would say that it was an enormity to tear myself away from the affection that clings to me in that home of mine, yonder, and that nothing but some supreme motive could justify me? And yet you pretend to be satisfied with the reasons I've given you. You're not dealing honestly with me, Atherton!"

"No," said Atherton, keeping the same scrutiny of Halleck's face which he had bent upon him throughout, but seeming now to hear his thoughts rather than his words. "I knew that you would have some supreme motive; and if I have pretended to approve your scheme on the reasons you have given me, I haven't dealt honestly with you. But perhaps a little dishonesty is the best thing under the circumstances. You haven't told me your real motive, and I can't ask it."

"But you imagine it?"

"Yes."

"And what do you imagine? That I have been disappointed in love? That I have been rejected? That the girl who had accepted me has broken her engagement? Something of that sort?" demanded Halleck, scornfully.

Atherton did not answer.

"Oh, how far you are from the truth! How blest and proud and happy I should be if it were the truth!" He looked into his friend's eyes, and added bitterly: "You're not curious, Atherton: you don't ask me what my trouble really is! Do you wish me to tell you what it is without asking?"

Atherton kept turning a pencil end for end between his fingers, while a compassionate smile slightly curved his lips.

"No," he said, finally, "I think you had better not tell me your trouble. I can believe very well, without knowing it, that it's serious"—

"Oh, tragic!" said Halleck, self-contemptuously.

"But I doubt if it would help you to tell it. I've too much respect for your good sense to suppose that it's an unreality; and I suspect that confession would only weaken you. If you told me, you would feel that you had made me a partner in your responsibility, and you would be tempted to leave the struggle to me. If you're battling with some temptation, some self-betrayal, you must make the fight alone: you would only turn to an ally to be flattered into disbelief of your danger or your culpability."

Halleck assented with a slight nod to each point that the lawyer made.

"You are right," he said, "but a man of your subtlety can't pretend that he doesn't know what the trouble is in such a simple case as mine."

"I don't know anything certainly," returned Atherton, "and, as far as I can, I refuse to imagine anything. If your trouble concerns some one besides yourself,—and no great trouble can concern one man alone,—you've no right to tell it."

"Another Daniel come to judgment!"

"You must trust to your principles, your self-respect, to keep you right"—

Halleck burst into a harsh laugh, and rose from his chair:

"Ah, there you abdicate the judicial function! Principles, self-respect! Against *that*? Don't you suppose I was approached *through* my principles and self-respect? Why, the Devil always takes a man on the very highest plane. *He* knows all about our principles and self-respect, and what they're made of. How the noblest and purest attributes of our nature, with which we trap each other so easily, must amuse him! Pity, rectitude, moral indignation, a blameless life,—he knows that they're all instruments for him! No, sir! No more principles and self-respect for me,—I've had enough of them; there's nothing for me but to *run*, and that's what I'm going to do. But you're quite right about the other thing, Atherton, and I give you a beggar's thanks for telling me that my trouble isn't mine alone, and I've no right to confide it to you. It *is* mine in the sense that no other soul is defiled with the knowledge of it, and I'm glad you saved me from the ghastly profanation, the sacrilege, of telling it. I *was* sneaking round for your sympathy; I *did* want somehow to shift the responsibility onto you; to get you—God help me!—to flatter me out of my wholesome fear and contempt for myself. Well! That's past, now, and— Good-night!"

He abruptly turned away from Atherton, and swung himself on his cane toward the door.

Atherton took up his hat and coat. "I'll walk home with you," he said.

"All right," returned Halleck, listlessly.

"How soon shall you go?" asked the lawyer, when they were in the street.

"Oh, there's a ship sailing from New York next week," said Halleck, in the same tone of weary indifference. "I shall go in that."

They talked desultorily of other things.

When they came to the foot of Clover Street, Halleck plucked his hand out of Atherton's arm. "I'm going up through here!" he said, with sullen obstinacy.

"Better not," returned his friend, quietly.

"Will it hurt her if I stop to look at the outside of the house where she lives?"

"It will hurt you," said Atherton.

"I don't wish to spare myself!" retorted Halleck. He shook

off the touch that Atherton had laid upon his shoulder, and started up the hill; the other overtook him, and, like a man who has attempted to rule a drunkard by thwarting his freak, and then hopes to accomplish his end by humoring it, he passed his arm through Halleck's again, and went with him. But when they came to the house, Halleck did not stop, he did not even look at it; but Atherton felt the deep shudder that passed through him.

In the week that followed, they met daily, and Halleck's broken pride no longer stayed him from the shame of open self-pity and wavering purpose. Atherton found it easier to persuade the clinging reluctance of the father and mother, than to keep Halleck's resolution for him: Halleck could no longer keep it for himself. "Not much like the behavior of people we read of in similar circumstances," he said once. "*They* never falter when they see the path of duty: they push forward without looking to either hand; or else," he added, with a hollow laugh at his own satire, "they turn their backs on it,—like men! Well!"

He grew gaunt and visibly feeble. In this struggle the two men changed places. The plan for Halleck's flight was no longer his own, but Atherton's; and when he did not rebel against it, he only passively acquiesced. The decent pretense of ignorance on Atherton's part necessarily disappeared: in all but words the trouble stood openly confessed between them, and it came to Atherton's saying, in one of Halleck's lapses of purpose, from which it had required all the other's strength to lift him: "Don't come to me any more, Halleck, with the hope that I shall somehow justify your evil against your good. I pitied you at first; but I blame you now."

"You're atrocious," said Halleck, with a puzzled, baffled look. "What do you mean?"

"I mean that you secretly think you have somehow come by your evil virtuously; and you want me to persuade you that it is different from other evils of exactly the same kind,— that it is beautiful and sweet and pitiable, and not ugly as hell and bitter as death, to be torn out of you mercilessly and flung from you with abhorrence. Well, I tell you that you are suffering guiltily, for no man suffers innocently from such a cause. You must *go*, and you can't go too soon. Don't suppose that I find anything noble in your position. I should do you a great wrong if I didn't do all I could to help you realize that you're in disgrace, and that you're only making a choice of shames in running away. Suppose the truth was known,—suppose that those who hold you dear could be persuaded of it,—could you hold up your head?"

"Do I hold up my head as it is?" asked Halleck. "Did you ever see a more abject dog than I am at this moment? Your wounds are faithful, Atherton; but perhaps you might have spared me this last stab. If you want to know, I can assure you that I don't feel any melodramatic vainglory. I know that I'm running away because I'm beaten, but no other man can know the battle I've fought. Don't you suppose I know how hideous this thing is? No one else can know it in all its ugliness!" He covered his face with his hands. "You are right," he said, when he could find his voice. "I suffer guiltily. I must have known it when I seemed to be suffering for pity's sake; I knew it before, and when you said that love without marriage was a worse hell than any marriage without love, you left me without refuge: I had been trying not to face the truth, but I had to face it then. I came away in hell, and I have lived in hell ever since. I tried to think it was a crazy fancy, and put it on my failing health; I used to make believe that some morning I should wake and find the illusion gone. I abhorred it from the beginning as I do now; it has been torment to me; and yet somewhere in my lost soul—the blackest depth, I dare say!—this shame has been so sweet,—it is so sweet,—the one sweetness of life— Ah!" He dashed the weak tears from his eyes, and rose and buttoned his coat about him. "Well, I shall go. And I hope I shall never come back. Though you needn't mention this to my father as an argument for my going when you talk me over with him," he added, with a glimmer of his wonted irony. He waited a moment, and then turned upon his friend, in sad upbraiding: "When I came to you a year and a half ago, after I had taken that ruffian home drunk to her—Why didn't you warn me then, Atherton? Did you see any danger?"

Atherton hesitated: "I knew that, with your habit of suffering for other people, it would make you miserable; but I couldn't have dreamed this would come of it. But you've never been out of your own keeping for a moment. You are responsible, and you are to blame if you are suffering now, and can find no safety for yourself but in running away."

"That's true," said Halleck, very humbly, "and I won't trouble you any more. I can't go on sinning against her belief in me here, and live. I shall go on sinning against it there, as long as I live; but it seems to me the harm will be a little less. Yes, I will go."

But the night before he went, he came to Atherton's lodging to tell him that he should not go; Atherton was not at home, and Halleck was spared this last dishonor. He returned to his father's house through the rain that was beginning to fall lightly, and as he let himself in with his key, Olive's voice said, "It's Ben!" and at the same time she laid her hand upon his arm with a nervous, warning clutch. "Hush! Come in here!" She drew him from the dimly lighted hall into the little reception-room near the door. The gas was burning brighter there, and in the light he saw Marcia, white and still, where she sat holding her baby in her arms. They exchanged no greeting: it was apparent that her being there transcended all usage, and that they need observe none.

"Ben will go home with you," said Olive, soothingly. "Is it raining?" she asked, looking at her brother's coat. "I will get my waterproof."

She left them a moment. "I have been been walking—walking about," Marcia panted. "It has got so dark—I'm—afraid to go home. I hate to—take you from them—the last— night."

Halleck answered nothing; he sat staring at her till Olive came back with the water-proof and an umbrella. Then, while his sister was putting the water-proof over Marcia's shoulders, he said, "Let me take the little one," and gathered it, with or without her consent, from her arms into his. The baby was sleeping; it nestled warmly against him with a luxurious quiver under the shawl that Olive threw around it. "You can carry the umbrella," he said to Marcia.

They walked fast, when they got out into the rainy dark, and it was hard to shelter Halleck as he limped rapidly on. Marcia ran forward once, to see if her baby were safely kept from the wet, and found that Halleck had its little face pressed close between his neck and cheek. "Don't be afraid," he said. "I'm looking out for it."

His voice sounded broken and strange, and neither of them spoke again till they came in sight of Marcia's door. Then she tried to stop him. She put her hand on his shoulder.

"Oh, I'm afraid—afraid to go in," she pleaded.

He halted, and they stood confronted in the light of a street lamp; her face was twisted with weeping.

"Why are you afraid?" he demanded harshly.

"We had a quarrel, and I—I ran away—I said that I would never come back. I left him"—

"You must go back to him," said Halleck. "He's your husband!"

He pushed on again, saying over and over, as if the words were some spell in which he found safety, "You must go back, you must go back, you must go back!"

He dragged her with him now, for she hung helpless on his arm, which she had seized, and moaned to herself. At the threshold, "I can't go in!" she broke out. "I'm afraid to go in! What will he say? What will he do? Oh, come in with me! You are good,—and then I shall not be afraid!"

"You must go in alone! No man can be your refuge from your husband! Here!"

He released himself, and, kissing the warm little face of the sleeping child, he pressed it into her arms. His fingers touched hers under the shawl; he tore his hand away with a shiver.

She stood a moment looking at the closed door; then she flung it open, and, pausing as if to gather her strength, vanished into the brightness within.

He turned, and ran crookedly down the street, wavering from side to side in his lameness, and flinging up his arms to save himself from falling as he ran, with a gesture that was like a wild and hopeless appeal.

XXXIV

M ARCIA pushed into the room where she had left Bartley.
She had no escape from her fate; she must meet it,
whatever it was. The room was empty, and she began
doggedly to search the house for him, upstairs and down,
carrying the child with her. She would not have been afraid
now to call him, but she had no voice, and she could not ask
the servant anything when she looked into the kitchen. She
saw the traces of the meal he had made in the dining-room,
and when she went a second time to their chamber to lay the
little girl down in her crib, she saw the drawers pulled open,
and the things as he had tossed them about in packing his
bag. She looked at the clock on the mantel—an extravagance
of Bartley's, for which she had scolded him—and it was only
half-past eight; she had thought it must be midnight.

She sat all night in a chair beside the bed; in the morning
she drowsed and dreamed that she was weeping on Bartley's
shoulder, and he was joking her and trying to comfort her, as
he used to do when they were first married; but it was the
little girl, sitting up in her crib, and crying loudly for her
breakfast. She put on the child a pretty frock that Bartley
liked, and when she had dressed her own tumbled hair she
went down-stairs, feigning to herself that they should find
him in the parlor. The servant was setting the table for breakfast, and the little one ran forward:

"Baby's chair; mamma's chair; papa's chair!"

"Yes," answered Marcia, so that the servant might hear too.
"Papa will soon be home."

She persuaded herself that he had gone as before for the
night, and in this pretense she talked with the child at the
table, and she put aside some of the breakfast to be kept
warm for Bartley. "I don't know just when he may be in," she
explained to the girl. The utterance of her pretense that she
expected him encouraged her, and she went about her work
almost cheerfully.

At dinner she said, "Mr. Hubbard must have been called

away, somewhere. We must get his dinner for him when he comes; the things dry up so in the oven."

She put Flavia to bed early, and then trimmed the fire, and made the parlor cozy against Bartley's coming. She did not blame him for staying away the night before; it was a just punishment for her wickedness, and she should tell him so, and tell him that she knew he never was to blame for anything about Hannah Morrison. She enacted over and over in her mind the scenes of their reconciliation. In every step on the pavement he approached the door; at last all the steps died away, and the second night passed.

Her head was light, and her brain confused with loss of sleep. When the child called her from above, and awoke her out of her morning drowse, she went to the kitchen and begged the servant to give the little one its breakfast, saying that she was sick and wanted nothing herself. She did not say anything about Bartley's breakfast and she would not think anything; the girl took the child into the kitchen with her, and kept it there all day.

Olive Halleck came during the forenoon, and Marcia told her that Bartley had been unexpectedly called away.

"To New York," she added, without knowing why.

"Ben sailed from there to-day," said Olive sadly.

"Yes," assented Marcia.

"We want you to come and take tea with us this evening," Olive began.

"Oh, I can't," Marcia broke in. "I mustn't be away when Bartley gets back." The thought was something definite in the sea of uncertainty on which she was cast away; she never afterward lost her hold of it; she confirmed herself in it by other inventions; she pretended that he had told her where he was going, and then that he had written to her. She almost believed these childish fictions as she uttered them. At the same time, in all her longing for his return, she had a sickening fear that when he came back he would keep his parting threat and drive her away; she did not know how he could do it, but this was what she feared.

She seldom left the house, which at first she kept neat and pretty, and then let fall into slatternly neglect. She ceased to care for her dress or the child's; the time came when it seemed as if she could scarcely move in the mystery that beset her life, and she yielded to a deadly lethargy which paralyzed all her faculties but the instinct of concealment.

She repelled the kindly approaches of the Hallecks, sometimes sending word to the door when they came, that she was sick and could not see them; or when she saw any of them, repeating those hopeless lies concerning Bartley's whereabouts, and her expectations of his return.

For the time she was safe against all kindly misgivings; but there were some of Bartley's creditors who grew impatient of his long absence, and refused to be satisfied with her fables. She had a few dollars left from some money that her father had given her at home, and she paid these all out upon the demand of the first-comer. Afterward, as other bills were pressed, she could only answer with incoherent promises and evasions that scarcely served for the moment. The pursuit of these people dismayed her. It was nothing that certain of them refused further credit; she would have known, both for herself and her child, how to go hungry and cold; but there was one of them who threatened her with the law if she did not pay. She did not know what he could do; she had read somewhere that people who did not pay their debts were imprisoned, and if that disgrace were all she would not care. But if the law were enforced against her the truth would come out; she would be put to shame before the world as a deserted wife; and this when Bartley had *not* deserted her. The pride that had bidden her heart break in secret rather than suffer this shame, even before itself, was baffled; her one blind device had been concealment, and this poor refuge was possible no longer. If all were not to know, some one must know.

The law with which she had been threatened might be instant in its operation; she could not tell. Her mind wavered from fear to fear. Even while the man stood before her, she perceived the necessity that was upon her, and when he left her she would not allow herself a moment's delay.

She reached the Events building, in which Mr. Atherton had his office, just as a lady drove away in her coupé. It was Miss Kingsbury, who made a point of transacting all business matters with her lawyer at his office, and of keeping her social relations with him entirely distinct, as she fancied, by this means. She was only partly successful, but at least she never talked business with him at her house, and doubtless she would not have talked anything else with him at his office, but for that increasing dependence upon him in everything which she certainly would not have permitted herself if she had realized it. As it was, she had now come to him in a state of nervous exaltation, which was not business-like. She had been greatly shocked by Ben Halleck's sudden freak; she had sympathized with his family till she herself felt the need of some sort of condolence, and she had promised herself this consolation from Atherton's habitual serenity. She did not know what to do when he received her with what she considered an impatient manner, and did not seem at all glad to see her. There was no reason why he should be glad to see a lady calling on business and no doubt he often found her troublesome, but he had never shown it before. She felt like crying at first; then she passed through an epoch of resentment, and then through a period of compassion for him. She ended by telling him with dignified severity that she wanted some money: they usually made some jokes about her destitution when she came upon that errand. He looked surprised and vexed, and:

"I have spent what you gave me last month," she explained.

"Then you wish to anticipate the interest on your bonds?"

"Certainly not," said Clara, rather sharply. "I wish to have the interest up to the present time."

"But I told you," said Atherton, and he could not, in spite of himself, help treating her somewhat as a child, "I told you then that I was paying you the interest up to the first of November. There is none due now. Didn't you understand that?"

"No, I didn't understand," answered Clara. She allowed herself to add, "It is very strange!" Atherton struggled with his irritation, and made no reply. "I can't be left without money," she continued. "What am I to do without it?" she demanded with an air of unanswerable argument. "Why, I *must* have it!"

"I felt that I ought to understand you fully," said Atherton, with cold politeness. "It's only necessary to know what sum you require."

Clara flung up her veil and confronted him with an excited face.

"Mr. Atherton, I don't wish a *loan*; I can't *permit* it; and you know that my principles are entirely against anticipating interest."

Atherton, from stooping over his table, pencil in hand, leaned back in his chair, and looked at her with a smile that provoked her:

"Then may I ask what you wish me to do?"

"No! I can't instruct you. My affairs are in your hands. But I must *say*"— She bit her lip, however, and did not say it. On the contrary she asked, rather feebly, "Is there nothing due on anything?"

"I went over it with you, last month," said Atherton patiently, "and explained all the investments. I could sell some stocks, but this election trouble has disordered everything, and I should have to sell at a heavy loss. There are your mortgages and there are your bonds. You can have any amount of money you want, but you will have to borrow it."

"And that you know I wont do. There should always be a sum of money in the bank," said Clara decidedly.

"I do my very best to keep a sum there, knowing your theory; but your practice is against me. You draw too many checks," said Atherton, laughing.

"Very well!" cried the lady, pulling down her veil. "Then I'm to have nothing?"

"You wont allow yourself to have anything," Atherton began. But she interrupted him haughtily.

"It is certainly very odd that my affairs should be in such a state that I can't have all the money of my own that I want, whenever I want it."

Atherton's thin face paled a little more than usual.

"I shall be glad to resign the charge of your affairs, Miss Kingsbury."

"And I shall accept your resignation," cried Clara, magnificently, "whenever you offer it." She swept out of the office, and descended to her coupé like an incensed goddess. She drew the curtains and began to cry. At her door, she bade the servant deny her to everybody, and went to bed, where she was visited a little later by Olive Halleck, whom no ban excluded. Clara lavishly confessed her sin and sorrow. "Why, I *went* there, more than half, to sympathize with him about Ben; I don't need any money, just yet; and the first thing I knew, I was accusing him of neglecting my interests, and I don't know what all! Of course he had to say he wouldn't have anything more to do with them, and I should have despised him if he hadn't. And now I don't care what becomes of the property: it's never been anything but misery to me ever since I had it, and I always knew it would get me into trouble sooner or later." She whirled her face over into her pillow, and sobbed. "But I *didn't* suppose it would ever make me insult and outrage the best friend I ever had,—and the truest man,—and the noblest gentleman! Oh, *what* will he think of me?"

Olive remained sadly quiet, as if but superficially interested in these transports, and Clara lifted her face again to say in her handkerchief:

"It's a shame, Olive, to burden you with all this at a time when you've care enough of your own."

"Oh, I'm rather glad of somebody else's care; it helps to take my mind off," said Olive.

"Then what would you do?" asked Clara, tempted by the apparent sympathy with her in the effect of her naughtiness.

"You might make a party for him, Clara," suggested Olive, with lack-luster irony.

Clara gave way to a loud burst of grief.

"Oh, Olive Halleck! I didn't suppose you could be *so* cruel!"

Olive rose impatiently.

"Then write to him, or go to him and tell him that you're ashamed of yourself, and ask him to take your property back again."

"Never!" cried Clara, who had listened with fascination. "What would he think of me?"

"Why need you care? It's purely a matter of business!"

"Yes."

"And you needn't mind what he thinks."

"Of course," admitted Clara, thoughtfully.

"He will naturally despise you," added Olive, "but I suppose he does that, now."

Clara gave her friend as piercing a glance as her soft blue eyes could emit, and, detecting no sign of jesting in Olive's sober face, she answered haughtily:

"I don't see what right Mr. Atherton has to despise me!"

"Oh, no! He must admire a girl who has behaved to him as you've done."

Clara's hauteur collapsed, and she began to truckle to Olive.

"If he were *merely* a business man, I shouldn't mind it; but knowing him socially, as I do, and as a—friend, and—an acquaintance, that way, I don't see how I can do it."

"I wonder you didn't think of that before you accused him of fraud and peculation, and all those things."

"I *didn't* accuse him of fraud and peculation!" cried Clara, indignantly.

"You said you didn't know what all you'd called him," said Olive with her hand on the door.

Clara followed her down-stairs.

"Well, I shall never do it in the world," she said, with reviving hope in her voice.

"Oh, I don't expect you to go to him this morning," said Olive, dryly. "That would be a little *too* barefaced."

Her friend kissed her.

"Olive Halleck, you're the strangest girl that ever was. I do believe you'd joke at the point of death! But I'm *so* glad you have been perfectly frank with me, and of course it's worth worlds to know that you think I've behaved horridly, and ought to make *some* reparation."

"I'm glad you value my opinion, Clara. And if you come to me for frankness, you can always have all you want; it's a drug in the market with me."

She meagerly returned Clara's embrace, and left her in a reverie of tactless scheming for the restoration of peace with Mr. Atherton.

Marcia came in upon the lawyer before he had thought, after parting with Miss Kingsbury, to tell the clerk in the outer office to deny him; but she was too full of her own trouble to see the reluctance which it taxed all his strength to quell, and she sank into the nearest chair unbidden. At sight of her Atherton became the prey of one of those fantastic repulsions in which men visit upon women the blame of others' thoughts about them: he censured her for Halleck's wrong; but in another instant he recognized his cruelty, and atoned by relenting a little in his intolerance of her presence. She sat gazing at him with a face of blank misery, to which he could not refuse the charity of a prompting question:

"Is there something I can do for you, Mrs. Hubbard?"

"Oh, I don't know,—I don't know!"

She had a folded paper in her hands, which lay helpless in her lap. After a moment she resumed, in a hoarse, low voice:

"They have all begun to come for their money, and this one—this one says he will have the law of me—I don't know what he means—if I don't pay him."

Marcia could not know how hard Atherton found it to govern the professional suspicion which sprung up at the question of money. But he overruled his suspicion by an effort that was another relief to the struggle in which he was wrenching his mind from Miss Kingsbury's outrageous behavior.

"What have you got there?" he asked, gravely, and not unkindly, and being used to prompt the reluctance of lady clients, he put out his hand for the paper she held.

It was the bill of the threatening creditor, for indefinitely repeated dozens of Tivoli beer.

"Why do they come to *you* with this?"

"Mr. Hubbard is away."

"Oh, yes. I heard. When do you expect him home?"

"I don't know."

"Where is he?"

She looked at him piteously without speaking.

Atherton stepped to his door, and gave the order forgotten before. Then he closed the door, and came back to Marcia.

"Don't you know where your husband is, Mrs. Hubbard?"

"Oh, he will come back! He *couldn't* leave me! He's dead,—I know he's dead; but he will come back! He only went away for the night, and something must have happened to him."

The whole tragedy of her life for the past fortnight was

expressed in these wild and inconsistent words; she had not been able to reason beyond the pathetic absurdities which they involved; they had the effect of assertions confirmed in the belief by incessant repetition, and doubtless she had said them to herself a thousand times. Atherton read in them, not only the confession of her despair, but a prayer for mercy, which it would have been inhuman to deny, and for the present he left her to such refuge from herself as she had found in them. He said, quietly:

"You had better give me that paper, Mrs. Hubbard," and took the bill from her. "If the others come with their accounts again, you must send them to me. When did you say Mr. Hubbard left home?"

"The night after the election," said Marcia.

"And he didn't say how long he should be gone?" pursued the lawyer, in the feint that she had known he was going.

"No," she answered.

"He took some things with him?"

"Yes."

"Perhaps you could judge how long he meant to be absent from the preparation he made?"

"I've never looked to see. I couldn't!"

Atherton changed the line of his inquiry. "Does any one else know of this?"

"No," said Marcia, quickly, "I told Mrs. Halleck and all of them that he was in New York, and I said that I had heard from him. I came to you because you were a lawyer, and you would not tell what I told you."

"Yes," said Atherton.

"I want it kept a secret. Oh, do you think he's dead?" she implored.

"No," returned Atherton, gravely. "I don't think he's dead."

"Sometimes it seems to me I could bear it better if I knew he was dead. If he isn't dead, he's out of his mind! He's out of his mind, don't you think, and he's wandered off somewhere."

She besought him so pitifully to agree with her, bending forward and trying to read the thoughts in his face, that he could not help saying, "Perhaps."

A gush of grateful tears blinded her, but she choked down her sobs.

"I said things to him that night that were enough to drive him crazy. I was always the one in fault, but he was always the one to make up first, and he never would have gone away from me if he had known what he was doing! But he will come back, I know he will," she said, rising. "And oh, you won't say anything to anybody, will you? And he'll get back before they find out. I will send those men to you, and Bartley will see about it as soon as he comes home"—

"Don't go, Mrs. Hubbard," said the lawyer. "I want to speak with you a little longer." She dropped again in her chair, and looked at him inquiringly. "Have you written to your father about this?"

"Oh, no," she answered quickly, with an effect of shrinking back into herself.

"I think you had better do so. You can't tell when your husband will return, and you can't go on in this way."

"I will never tell *father*," she replied, closing her lips inexorably.

The lawyer forbore to penetrate the family trouble he divined. "Are you all alone in the house?" he asked.

"The girl is there. And the baby."

"That won't do, Mrs. Hubbard," said Atherton, with a compassionate shake of the head. "You can't go on living there alone."

"Oh, yes, I can. I'm not afraid to be alone," she returned with the air of having thought of this.

"But he may be absent some time yet," urged the lawyer; "he may be absent indefinitely. You must go home to your father and wait for him there."

"I can't do that. He must find me here when he comes," she answered firmly.

"But how will you stay?" pleaded Atherton; he had to deal with an unreasonable creature who could not be driven, and he must plead. "You have no money, and how can you live?"

"Oh," replied Marcia, with an air of having thought of this too, "I will take boarders."

Atherton smiled at the hopeless practicality and shook his head; but he did not oppose her directly. "Mrs. Hubbard," he said, earnestly, "you have done well in coming to me, but let me convince you that this is a matter which can't be kept. It must be known. Before you can begin to help yourself, you must let others help you. Either you must go home to your father and let your husband find you there"—

"He must find me here, in our own house"—

"Then you must tell your friends here that you don't know where he is, nor when he will return, and let them advise together as to what can be done. You must tell the Hallecks"—

"I will *never* tell them!" cried Marcia. "Let me go! I can starve there and freeze, and if he finds me dead in the house, none of them shall have the right to blame him,—to say that he left me,—that he deserted his little child! Oh! oh! oh! oh! What shall I do?"

The hapless creature shook with the thick-coming sobs that overpowered her now, and Atherton refrained once more. She did not seem ashamed before him of the sorrows which he felt it a sacrilege to know, and in a blind, instinctive way he perceived that in proportion as he was a stranger it was possible for her to bear her disgrace in his presence. He spoke at last from the hint he found in this fact: "Will you let me mention the matter to Miss Kingsbury?"

She had looked at him with sad intensity in the eyes, as if trying to fathom any nether thought that he might have. It must have seemed to her at first that he was mocking her, but his words brought her the only relief from her self-upbraiding she had known. To suffer kindness from Miss Kingsbury would be in some sort an atonement to Bartley for the wrong her jealousy had done him; it would be self-sacrifice for his sake; it would be expiation. "Yes, tell her," she answered with a promptness whose obscure motive was not illumined by the flash of passionate pride with which she added, "I shall not care for *her*."

She rose again, and Atherton did not detain her; but when she had left him he lost no time in writing to her father the facts of the case as her visit had revealed them. He spoke of her reluctance to have her situation known to her family, but assured the Squire that he need have no anxiety about her for the present. He promised to keep him fully informed in regard to her, and to telegraph the first news of Mr. Hubbard. He left the Squire to form his own conjectures, and to take whatever action he thought best. For his own part, he had no question that Hubbard had abandoned his wife, and had stolen Halleck's money; and the detectives to whom he went were clear that it was a case of European travel.

XXXV

ATHERTON went from the detectives to Miss Kingsbury, and boldly resisted the interdict at her door, sending up his name with the message that he wished to see her immediately on business. She kept him waiting while she made a frightened toilet, and leaving the letter to him which she had begun half finished on her desk, she came down to meet him in a flutter of despondent conjecture. He took her mechanically yielded hand, and seated himself on the sofa beside her. "I sent word that I had come on business," he said, "but it is no affair of yours,"—she hardly knew whether to feel relieved or disappointed,—"except as you make all unhappy people's affairs your own."

"Oh!" she murmured in meek protest, and at the same time she remotely wondered if these affairs were his.

"I came to you for help," he began again, and again she interrupted him in deprecation.

"You are very good, after—after—what I—what happened,—I'm sure." She put up her fan to her lips, and turned her head a little aside. "Of course I shall be glad to help you in anything, Mr. Atherton; you know I always am."

"Yes, and that gave me courage to come to you, even after the way in which we parted this morning. I knew you would not misunderstand me"—

"No," said Clara softly, doing her best to understand him.

"Or think me wanting in delicacy"—

"Oh, no, no!"

"If I believed that we need not have any embarrassment in meeting in behalf of the poor creature who came to see me just after you left me. The fact is," he went on, "I felt a little freer to promise your interest since I had no longer any business relation to you, and could rely on your kindness like—like—any other."

"Yes," assented Clara, faintly; and she forbore to point out to him, as she might fitly have done, that he had never had the right to advise or direct her at which he hinted, except as she expressly conferred it from time to time. "I shall be only too glad"—

"And I will have a statement of your affairs drawn up to-morrow, and sent to you." Her heart sank; she ceased to move the fan which she had been slowly waving back and forth before her face. "I was going to set about it this morning, but Mrs. Hubbard's visit"—

"Mrs. Hubbard!" cried Clara, and a little air of pique qualified her despair.

"Yes; she is in trouble,—the greatest: her husband has deserted her."

"*Oh*, Mr. Atherton!" Clara's mind was now far away from any concern for herself. The woman whose husband has deserted her supremely appeals to all other women. "I can't believe it! What makes you think so?"

"What she concealed, rather than what she told me, I believe," answered Atherton. He ran over the main points of their interview, and summed up his own conjectures. "I know from things Halleck has let drop that they haven't always lived happily together; Hubbard has been speculating with borrowed money, and he's in debt to everybody. She's been alone in her house for a fortnight, and she only came to me because people had begun to press her for money. She's been pretending to the Hallecks that she hears from her husband, and knows where he is."

"Oh, poor, poor thing!" said Clara, too shocked to say more. "Then they don't know?"

"No one knows but ourselves. She came to me because I was a comparative stranger, and it would cost her less to confess her trouble to me than to them, and she allowed me to speak to you for very much the same reason."

"But I know she dislikes me!"

"So much the better! She can't doubt your goodness"—

"Oh!"

"And if she dislikes you, she can keep her pride better with you."

Clara let her eyes fall, and fingered the edges of her fan. There was reason in this, and she did not care that the opportunity of usefulness was personally unflattering, since he thought her capable of rising above the fact. "What do you want me to do?" she asked, lifting her eyes docilely to his.

"You must find some one to stay with her, in her house, till she can be persuaded to leave it, and you must lend her some money till her father can come to her or write to her. I've just written to him, and I've told her to send all her bills to me; but I'm afraid she may be in immediate need."

"Terrible!" sighed Clara, to whom the destitution of an acquaintance was appalling after all her charitable knowledge of want and suffering. "Of course, we mustn't lose a moment," she added; but she lingered in her corner of the sofa to discuss ways and means with him, and to fathom that sad enjoyment which comfortable people find in the contemplation of alien sorrows. It was not her fault if she felt too kindly toward the disaster that had brought Atherton back to her on the old terms; or if she arranged her plans for befriending Marcia in her desolation with too buoyant a cheerfulness. But she took herself to task for the radiant smile she found on her face, when she ran upstairs and looked into her glass to see how she looked in parting with Atherton: she said to herself that he would think her perfectly heartless.

She decided that it would be indecent to drive to Marcia's under the circumstances, and she walked; though with all the time this gave her for reflection she had not wholly banished this smile when she looked into Marcia's woe-begone eyes. But she found herself incapable of the awkwardnesses she had deliberated, and fell back upon the native motherliness of her heart, into which she took Marcia with sympathy that ignored everything but her need of help and pity. Marcia's bruised pride was broken before the goodness of the girl she had hated, and she performed her sacrifice to Bartley's injured memory, not with the haughty self-devotion which she intended should humiliate Miss Kingsbury, but with the prostration of a woman spent with watching and fasting and despair. She held Clara away for a moment of scrutiny, and then submitted to the embrace in which they recognized and confessed all.

It was scarcely necessary for Clara to say that Mr. Atherton had told her; Marcia already knew that; and Clara became a partisan of her theory of Bartley's absence almost without an effort, in spite of the facts that Atherton had suggested to the contrary. "Of *course*! He has wandered off somewhere, and as soon as he comes to his senses he will hurry home. Why I was reading of such a case only the other day,—the case of a minister who wandered off in just the same way, and found himself out in Western New York somewhere, after he had been gone three months."

"Bartley wont be gone three months," protested Marcia.

"Certainly not!" cried Clara, in severe self-rebuke. Then she talked of his return for a while as if it might be expected at any moment. "In the mean time," she added, "you must stay here; you're quite right about that, too, but you mustn't stay here alone: he'd be quite as much shocked at that as if he found you gone when he came back. I'm going to ask you to let my friend Miss Strong stay with you; and she must pay her board; and you must let me lend you all the money you need. And, dear,"—Clara dropped her voice to a lower and gentler note,—"you mustn't try to keep this from your friends. You must let Mr. Atherton write to your father; you must let me tell the Hallecks: they'll be hurt if you don't. You needn't be troubled; of *course* he wandered off in a temporary hallucination, and nobody will think differently."

She adopted the fiction of Bartley's aberration with so much fervor that she even silenced Atherton's injurious theories with it when he came in the evening to learn the result of her intervention. She had forgotten, or she ignored, the facts as he had stated them in the morning; she was now Bartley's valiant champion, as well as the tender protector of Marcia: she was the equal friend of the whole exemplary Hubbard family.

Atherton laughed, and she asked what he was laughing at.

"Oh," he answered, "at something Ben Halleck once said: a real woman can make righteousness delicious and virtue piquant."

Clara reflected. "I don't know whether I like that," she said finally.

"No?" said Atherton. "Why not?"

She was serving him with an after-dinner cup of tea, which she had brought into the drawing-room, and in putting the second lump of sugar into his saucer she paused again, thoughtfully, holding the little cube in the tongs. She was rather elaborately dressed for so simple an occasion, and her silken train coiled itself far out over the mossy depth of the moquette carpet; the pale blue satin of the furniture, and the delicate white and gold of the decorations, became her wonderfully.

"I can't say, exactly. It seems depreciatory, somehow, as a generalization. But a man might say it of the woman he was in love with," she concluded.

"And you wouldn't approve of a man's saying it of the woman his friend was in love with?" pursued Atherton, taking his cup from her.

"If they were very close friends." She did not know why, but she blushed, and then grew a little pale.

"I understand what you mean," he said, "and I shouldn't have liked the speech from another kind of man. But Halleck's innocence characterized it." He stirred his tea, and then let it stand untasted in his abstraction.

"Yes, he is good," sighed Clara. "If he were not so good, it would be hard to forgive him for disappointing all their hopes in the way he's done."

"It's the best thing he could have done," said Atherton gravely, even severely.

"I know you advised it," asserted Clara. "But it's a great blow to them. How strange that Mr. Hubbard should have disappeared the last night Ben was at home! I'm glad that he got away without knowing anything about it."

Atherton drank off his tea, and refused a second cup with a gesture of his hand. "Yes, so am I," he said. "I'm glad of every league of sea he puts behind him." He rose, as if eager to leave the subject.

Clara rose, too, with the patient acquiescence of a woman, and took his hand proffered in parting. They had certainly talked out, but there seemed no reason why he should go. He held her hand, while he asked, "How shall I make my peace with you?"

"My peace? What for?" She flushed joyfully. "I was the one in fault."

He looked at her mystified. "Why, surely, *you* didn't repeat Halleck's remark?"

"Oh!" she cried indignantly, withdrawing her hand. "I meant *this morning*. It doesn't matter," she added. "If you still wish to resign the charge of my affairs, of course I must submit. But I thought—I thought"— She did not go on, she was too deeply hurt. Up to this moment she had imagined that she had befriended Marcia, and taken all that trouble upon herself for goodness' sake; but now she was ready to upbraid him for ingratitude in not seeing that she had done it for his sake. "You can send me the statement, and then— and then—I don't know what I *shall* do! *Why* do you mind what I said? I've often said quite as much before, and you know that I didn't mean it. I want you to take my property back again, and never to mind anything I say: I'm not worth minding." Her intended upbraiding had come to this pitiful effect of self-contempt, and her hand somehow was in his again. "Do take it back!"

"If I do that," said Atherton, gravely, "I must make my conditions," and now they sat down together on the sofa from which he had risen. "I can't be subjected again to your—disappointments,"—he arrested with a motion of his hand the profuse expression of her penitence and good intentions,—"and I've felt for a long time that this was no attitude for your attorney. You ought to have the right to question and censure; but I confess I can't grant you this. I've allowed myself to make your interests too much my own in everything to be able to bear it. I've thought several times that I ought to give up the trust; but it seemed like giving up so much more, that I never had the courage to do it in cold blood. This morning you gave me my chance to do it in hot blood, and if I resume it, I must make my terms."

It seemed a long speech to Clara, who sometimes thought she knew whither it tended, and sometimes not. She said in a low voice, "Yes."

"I must be relieved," continued Atherton, "of the sense I've had that it was indelicate in me to keep it, while I felt as I've grown to feel—toward you." He stopped: "If I take it back, you must come with it!" he suddenly concluded.

The inconsistency of accepting these conditions ought to have struck a woman who had so long imagined herself the chase of fortune-hunters. But Clara apparently found nothing

alarming in the demand of a man who openly acted upon his knowledge of what could only have been matter of conjecture to many suitors she had snubbed. She found nothing incongruous in the transaction, and she said, with as tremulous breath and as swift a pulse as if the question had been solely of herself, "I accept— the conditions."

In the long, happy talk that lasted till midnight, they did not fail to recognize that, but for their common pity of Marcia, they might have remained estranged, and they were decently ashamed of their bliss when they thought of misery like hers. When Atherton rose to bid Clara good-night, Marcia was still watching for Bartley, indulging for the last time the folly of waiting for him as if she definitely expected him that night.

Every night since he disappeared, she had kept the lights burning in the parlor and hall, and drowsed before the fire till the dawn drove her to a few hours of sleep in bed. But with the coming of the stranger who was to be her companion, she must deny herself even this consolation, and openly accept the fact that she no longer expected Bartley at any given time. She bitterly rebelled at the loss of her solitude, in which she could be miserable in whatever way her sorrow prompted, and the pangs with which she had submitted to Miss Kingsbury's kindness grew sharper hour by hour till she maddened in a frenzy of resentment against the cruelty of her expiation. She longed for the day to come that she might go to her, and take back her promises and her submission, and fling her insulting good-will in her face. She said to herself that no one should enter her door again till Bartley opened it; she would die there in the house, she and her baby, and as she stood wringing her hands and moaning over the sleeping little one, a hideous impulse made her brain reel; she wished to look if Bartley had left his pistol in its place; a cry for help against herself broke from her; she dropped upon her knees.

The day came, and the hope and strength which the mere light so strangely brings to the sick in spirit as well as the sick in body visited Marcia. She abhorred the temptation of the night like the remembrance of a wicked dream, and she went about with a humble and grateful prayer—to something, to some one—in her heart. Her housewifely pride stirred again: that girl should not think she was a slattern; and Miss Strong, when she preceded her small trunk in the course of the forenoon, found the parlor and the guest-chamber, which she was to have, swept and dusted, and set in perfect order by Marcia's hands. She had worked with fury, and kept her heartache still, but it began again at sight of the girl. Fortunately, the conservatory pupil had embraced with even more than Miss Kingsbury's ardor the theory of Bartley's aberration, and she met Marcia with a sympathy in her voice and eyes that could only have come from sincere conviction. She was a simple country thing, who would never be a prima-donna; but the overflowing sentimentality which enabled her to accept herself at the estimate of her enthusiastic fellow-villagers made her of far greater comfort to Marcia than the sublimest musical genius would have done. She worshiped the heroine of so tragic a fact, and her heart began to go out to her in honest helpfulness from the first. She broke in upon the monotony of Marcia's days with the offices and interests of wholesome commonplace, and exorcised the ghostly silence with her first stroke on the piano,—which Bartley had bought on the installment plan and had not yet paid for.

In fine, life adjusted itself with Marcia to the new conditions, as it does with women less wofully widowed by death, who promise themselves reunion with their lost in another world, and suffer through the first weeks and days in the hope that their parting will be for but days or weeks, and then gradually submit to indefinite delay. She prophesied Bartley's return, and fixed it in her own mind for this hour and that. "Now, in the morning, I shall wake and find him standing by the bed. No, at night he will come in and surprise us at dinner." She cheated herself with increasing faith at each renewal of her hopes. When she ceased to formulate them at last, it was because they had served their end, and left her established, if not comforted, in the superstition by which she lived. His return at any hour or any moment was the fetish which she let no misgiving blaspheme; everything in her of woman and of wife consecrated it. She kept the child in continual remembrance of him by talking of him, and by making her recognize the photographs in which Bartley had abundantly perpetuated himself; at night, when she folded the little one's hands for prayer, she made her pray God to take care of poor papa and send him home soon to mamma. She was beginning to canonize him.

Her father came to see her as soon as he thought it best after Atherton's letter; and the old man had to endure talk of Bartley to which all her former praises were as refreshing shadows of defamation. She required him to agree with everything she said, and he could not refuse; she reproached him for being with herself the cause of all Bartley's errors, and he had to bear it without protest. At the end he could say nothing but "Better come home with me, Marcia," and he suffered in meekness the indignation with which she rebuked him: "I will stay in Bartley's house till he comes back to me. If he is dead, I will die here."

The old man had satisfied himself that Bartley had absconded in his own rascally right mind, and he accepted with tacit grimness the theory of the detectives that he had not gone alone to Europe. He paid back the money which Bartley had borrowed from Halleck, and he set himself as patiently as he could to bear with Marcia's obstinacy. It was a mania which must be indulged for the time, and he could only trust to Atherton to keep him advised concerning her. When he offered her money at parting, she hesitated. But she finally took it, saying, "Bartley will pay it back, every cent, as soon as he gets home. And if," she added, "he doesn't get back soon, I will take some other boarders and pay it myself."

He could see that she was offended with him for asking her to go home. But she was his girl; he only pitied her. He shook hands with her as usual, and kissed her with the old stoicism; but his lips, set to fierceness by the life-long habit of sarcasm, trembled as he turned away. She was eager to have him go; for she had given him Miss Strong's room, and had taken the girl into her own, and Bartley would not like it if he came back and found her there.

Bartley's disappearance was scarcely a day's wonder with people outside his own circle in that time of anxiety for a fair count in Louisiana and Florida, and long before the Returning Boards had partly relieved the tension of the public mind by their decision he had quite dropped out of it. The reporters who called at his house to get the bottom facts in the case, adopted Marcia's theory, given them by Miss Strong, and whatever were their own suspicions or convictions, paragraphed him with merciful brevity as having probably wandered away during a temporary hallucination. They spoke of the depression of spirits which many of his friends had observed in him, and of pecuniary losses as the cause. They mentioned his possible suicide only to give the report the authoritative denial of his family; and they added, that the case was in the hands of the detectives, who believed themselves in possession of important clews. The detectives in fact remained constant to their original theory, that Bartley had gone to Europe, and they were able to name with reasonable confidence the person with whom he had eloped. But these were matters hushed up among the force and the press. In the meantime, Bartley had been simultaneously seen at Montreal and Cincinnati, at about the same time that an old friend had caught a glimpse of him on a train bound westward from Chicago.

So far as the world was concerned, the surmise with which Marcia saved herself from final despair was the only impression that even vaguely remained of the affair. Her friends, who had compassionately acquiesced in it at first, waited for the moment when they could urge her to relinquish it and go home to her father; but while they waited, she gathered strength to establish herself immovably in it, and to shape her life more and more closely about it. She had no idea, no instinct, but to stay where he had left her till he came back. She opposed this singly and solely against all remonstrance, and treated every suggestion to the contrary as an instigation to crime. Her father came from time to time during the winter to see her, but she would never go home with him even for a day. She put her plan in force; she took other boarders: other girl students like Miss Strong, whom her friends brought her when they found that it was useless to oppose her and so began to abet her; she worked hard, and she actually supported herself at last in a frugal independence. Her father consulted with Atherton and the Hallecks; he saw that she was with good and faithful friends, and he submitted to what he could not help. When the summer came, he made a last attempt to induce her to go home with him. He told her that her mother wished to see her. She would not understand. "I'll come," she said, "if mother gets seriously sick. But I can't go home for the summer. If I hadn't been at home last summer, *he* would never have got into that way, and *it* would never have happened."

She went home at last, in obedience to a peremptory summons; but her mother was too far gone to know her when she came. Her quiet, narrow life had grown colder and more inward to the end, and it passed without any apparent revival of tenderness for those once dear to her; the funeral publicity that followed seemed a final touch of the fate by which all her preferences had been thwarted in the world.

Marcia stayed only till she could put the house in order after they had laid her mother to rest among the early reddening sumacs under the hot glare of the August sun; and when she came away, she brought her father with her to Boston, where he spent his days as he might, taking long and aimless walks, devouring heaps of newspapers, rusting in idleness, and aging fast, as men do in the irksomeness of disuse.

Halleck's father was beginning to show his age, too; and Halleck's mother lived only in her thoughts of him, and her hopes of his return; but he did not even speak of this in his letters to them. He said very little of himself, and they could merely infer that the experiment to which he had devoted himself was becoming less and less satisfactory. Their sense of this added its pang to their unhappiness in his absence.

One day Marcia said to Olive Halleck:

"Has any one noticed that you are beginning to look like your sisters?"

"*I've* noticed it," answered the girl. "I always *was* an old maid, and now I'm beginning to show it."

Marcia wondered if she had not hurt Olive's feelings; but she would never have known how to excuse herself; and latterly she had been growing more and more like her father in certain traits. Perhaps her passion for Bartley had been the one spring of tenderness in her nature, and, if ever it were spent, she would stiffen into the old man's stern aridity.

XXXVI

IT WAS nearly two years after Atherton's marriage that Halleck one day opened the door of the lawyer's private office, and, turning the key in the lock, limped forward to where the latter was sitting at his desk. Halleck was greatly changed: the full beard that he had grown scarcely hid the savage gauntness of his face; but the change was not so much in lines and contours as in that expression of qualities which we call looks.

"Well, Atherton!"

"Halleck! *You!*"

The friends looked at each other; and Atherton finally broke from his amaze and offered his hand, with an effect, even then, of making conditions. But it was Halleck who was the first to speak again.

"How *is* she? Is she well? Is she still here? Have they heard anything from him yet?"

"No," said Atherton, answering the last question with the same provisional effect as before.

"Then he is *dead*. That's what I knew; that's what I *said*! And here I am. The fight is over, and that's the end of it. I'm beaten."

"You look it," said Atherton, sadly.

"Oh, yes; I look it. That's the reason I can afford to be frank, in coming back to my friends. I knew that with this look in my face I should make my own welcome; and it's cordial even beyond my expectations."

"I'm not glad to see you, Halleck," said Atherton. "For your own sake I wish you were at the other end of the world."

"Oh, I know that. How are my people? Have you seen my father lately? Or my mother? Or—Olive?"

A pathetic tremor shook his voice.

"Why, haven't *you* seen them yet?" demanded Atherton.

Halleck laughed cynically.

"My dear friend, my steamer arrived this morning, and I'm just off the New York train. I've hurried to your office in all

536

the impatience of friendship. I'm very lucky to find you here so late in the day! You can take me home to dinner, and let your domestic happiness preach to me. Come, I rather like the notion of that!"

"Halleck," said Atherton, without heeding his banter, "I wish you would go away again! No one knows you are here, you say, and no one need ever know it."

Halleck set his lips and shook his head, with a mocking smile.

"I'm surprised at you, Atherton, with your knowledge of human nature. I've come to stay; you must know that. You must know that I had gone through everything before I gave up, and that I haven't the strength to begin the struggle over again. I tell you I'm beaten, and I'm glad of it; for there is rest in it. You would waste your breath if you talked to me in the old way; there's nothing in me to appeal to, any more. If I was wrong— But I don't admit, any more, that I was wrong: by heaven, I was *right*!"

"You *are* beaten, Halleck," said Atherton, sorrowfully.

He pushed himself back in his chair, and clasped his hands together behind his head, as his habit was in reasoning with obstinate clients.

"What do you propose to do?"

"I propose to stay."

"What for?"

"What for? Till I can prove that he is dead."

"And then?"

"Then I shall be free to ask her." He added, angrily: "You know what I've come back for; why do you torment me with these questions? I did what I could; I ran away. And the last night I saw her, I thrust her back into that hell she called her home, and I told her that no man could be her refuge from that devil, her husband, when she had begged me in her mortal terror to go in with her and save her from him. *That* was the recollection I had to comfort me when I tried to put her out of my mind,—out of my soul! When I heard that he was gone, I respected her days of mourning. God knows how I endured it, now it's over; but I did endure it. I waited, and here I am. And you ask me to go away again. Ah!" He fetched his breath through his set teeth, and struck his fist on his knee. "He is *dead*! And now, if she will, she can marry me. Don't look at me as if I had killed him! There hasn't been a time in these two infernal years when I wouldn't have given my life to save his—for *her* sake. I know that; and that gives me courage, it gives me hope."

"But if he isn't dead?"

"Then he has abandoned her, and she has the right to be free. She can get a divorce!"

"Oh!" said Atherton, compassionately, "has that poison got into *you*, Halleck? You might ask her, if she were a widow, to marry you; but how will you ask her, if she's still a wife, to get a divorce and then marry you? How will you suggest that to a woman whose constancy to her mistake has made her sacred to you?" Halleck seemed about to answer; but he only panted, dry-lipped and open-mouthed, and Atherton continued: "You would have to corrupt her soul first. I don't know what change you've made in yourself during these two years; you look like a desperate and defeated man, but you don't look like *that*. You don't *look* like one of those scoundrels who lure women from their duty, ruin homes, and destroy society—not in the old libertine fashion in which the seducer had at least the grace to risk his life, but safely, smoothly, under the shelter of our infamous laws. Have you really come back here to give your father's honest name, and the example of a man of your own blameless life, in support of conditions that tempt people to marry with a mental reservation, and that weaken every marriage bond with the guilty hope of escape whenever a fickle mind, or secret lust, or wicked will may dictate? Have you come to join yourself to those miserable specters who go shrinking through the world, afraid of their own past, and anxious to hide it from those they hold dear; or do you propose to defy the world, to help form within it the community of outcasts with whom shame is not shame, nor dishonor dishonor? How will you like the society of those uncertain men, those certain women?"

"You are very eloquent," said Halleck, "but I ask you to observe that these little abstractions don't interest me. I've a concrete purpose, and I can't contemplate the effect of other people's actions upon American civilization. When you ask me to believe that I oughtn't to try to rescue a woman from the misery to which a villain has left her, simply because some justice of the peace consecrated his power over her, I decline to be such a fool. I use my reason, and I see who it was that defiled and destroyed that marriage, and I know that she is as free in the sight of God as if he had never lived. If the world doesn't like my open shame, let it look to its own secret shame—the marriages made and maintained from interest and ambition and vanity and folly. I will take my chance with the men and women who have been honest enough to own their mistake, and to try to repair it, and I will preach by my life that marriage has no sanctity but what love gives it, and that, when love ceases, marriage ceases, before heaven. If the laws have come to recognize that, by whatever fiction, so much the better for the laws!" Halleck rose.

"Well, then," cried Atherton, rising too, "you shall meet me on your own ground! This poor creature is constant in every breath she draws, to the ruffian who has abandoned her. I must believe, since you say it, that you are ready to abet her in getting a divorce, even one of those divorces that are 'obtained without publicity, and for any cause,'"—Halleck winced,—"that you are willing to put your sisters to shame before the world, to break your mother's heart and your father's pride—to insult the ideal of goodness that she herself has formed of you; but how will you begin? The love on her part, at least, hasn't ceased; has the marriage?"

"She shall tell me," answered Halleck. He left Atherton without another word, and in resentment that effaced all friendship between them, though after this parting they still kept up its outward forms, and the Athertons took part in the rejoicings with which the Hallecks celebrated Ben's return. His meeting with the lawyer was the renewal of the old conflict on terms of novel and hopeless degradation. He had mistaken for peace that exhaustion of spirit which comes to a man in battling with his conscience; he had fancied his struggle over, and he was to learn now that its anguish had just begun. In that delusion his love was to have been a law to itself, able to loose and to bind, and potent to beat down all regrets, all doubts, all fears, that questioned it; but the words with which Marcia met him struck his passion dumb.

"Oh, I am so glad you have come back!" she said. "Now I

know that we can find him. You were such friends with him, and you understood him so well, that you will know just what to do. Yes, we shall find him now, and we should have found him long ago, if you had been here. Oh, if you had never gone away! But I can never be grateful enough for what you said to me that night when you would not come in with me. The words have rung in my ears ever since; they showed that you had faith in him, more faith than I had, and I've made them my rule and my guide. No one has been my refuge from him, and no one ever shall be. And I thank you— yes, I thank you on my bended knees—for making me go into the house alone; it's my one comfort that I had the strength to come back to him, and let him do anything he would to me, after I had treated him so; but I've never pretended it was my own strength. I have always told everybody that the strength came from you!"

Halleck had brought Olive with him; she and Marcia's father listened to these words with the patience of people who had heard them many times before; but at the end Olive glanced at Halleck's downcast face with fond pride in the satisfaction she imagined they must give him. The old man ruminated upon a bit of broom-straw, and absently let the little girl catch by his hands, as she ran to and fro between him and her mother while her mother talked. Halleck made a formless sound in his throat, for answer, and Marcia went on.

"I've got a new plan now, but it seems as if father took a pleasure in discouraging *all* my plans. I *know* that Bartley's shut up, somewhere, in some asylum, and I want them to send detectives to all the asylums in the United States and in Canada,—you can't tell how far off he would wander in that state,—and inquire if any stray insane person has been brought to them. Doesn't it seem to you as if that would be the right way to find him? I want to talk it all over with you, Mr. Halleck, for I know *you* can sympathize with me; and if need be I will go to the asylums myself; I will walk to them, I will crawl to them on my knees! When I think of him shut up there among those raving maniacs, and used as they use people in some of the asylums—oh, oh, oh, oh!"

She broke out into sobs, and caught her little girl to her breast. The child must have been accustomed to her mother's tears; she twisted her head round, and looked at Halleck with a laughing face.

Marcia dried her eyes, and asked, with quivering lips, "Isn't she like him?"

"Yes," replied Halleck huskily.

"She has his long eyelashes exactly, and his hair and complexion, hasn't she?"

The old man sat chewing his broom-straw in silence; but when Marcia left the room to get Bartley's photograph, so that Halleck might see the child's resemblance to him, her father looked at Halleck from under his beetling brows: "I don't think we need trouble the *asylums* much for Bartley Hubbard. But if it was to search the State's-prisons and the jails, the rum-holes and the gambling-hells, or if it was to dig up the scoundrels who have been hung under assumed names during the last two years, I should have some hopes of identifying him."

Marcia came back, and the old man sat in cast-iron quiet, as if he had never spoken; it was clear that, whatever hate he felt for Bartley, he spared her; and that if he discouraged her plans, as she said, it was because they were infected by the craze in which she canonized Bartley.

"You see how she is," said Olive, when they came away.

"Yes, yes, yes," Halleck desolately assented.

"Sometimes she seems to me just like a querulous, vulgar, middle-aged woman in her talk; she repeats herself in the same scolding sort of way; and she's so eager to blame somebody besides Bartley for Bartley's wickedness, that, when she can't punish herself, she punishes her father. She's merciless to that wretched old man, and he's wearing his homesick life out here in the city for her sake. You heard her just now about his discouraging her plans?"

"Yes," said Halleck, as before.

"She's grown commoner and narrower, but it's hardly her fault, poor thing! and it seems terribly unjust that she should be made so by what she has suffered. But that's just the way it has happened. She's so undisciplined, that she couldn't get any good out of her misfortunes—she's only got harm; they've made her selfish, and there seems to be nothing left of what she was two years ago but her devotion to that miserable wretch. You mustn't let it turn you against her, Ben; you mustn't forget what she might have been. She had a rich nature; but how it's been wasted and turned back upon itself! Poor, untrained, impulsive, innocent creature—my heart aches for her! It's been hard to bear with her at times, terribly hard, and you'll find it so, Ben. But you *must* bear with her. The awfulest thing about people in trouble is that they are such *bores*; they tire you to death. But you'll only have to stand her praises of what Bartley was; and we had to stand them, and her hopes of what you would be if you were only at home, besides. I don't know what all she expects of you, but you must try not to disappoint her; she worships the ground you tread on, and I really think she believes you can do anything you will, just because you're good."

Halleck listened in silence. He was indeed helpless to be otherwise than constant. With shame and grief in his heart, he could only vow her there the greater fealty because of the change he found in her.

He was doomed at every meeting to hear her glorify a man whom he believed a heartless traitor, to plot with her for the rescue from imaginary captivity of the wretch who had cruelly forsaken her. He actually took some of the steps she urged: he addressed inquiries to the insane asylums, far and near; and in these futile endeavors, made only with the desire of failure, his own reason seemed sometimes to waver. She insisted that Atherton should know all the steps they were taking; and his sense of his old friend's exact and perfect knowledge of his motives was a keener torture than even her father's silent scorn of his efforts, or the worship in which his own family held him for them.

XXXVII

HALLECK had come home in broken health, and had promised his family, with the self-contempt that depraves, not to go away again, since the change had done him no good. There was no talk for the present of his trying to do anything but get well; and for a while, under the strong excitement, he seemed to be better. But suddenly he failed; he kept his room, and then he kept his bed; and the weeks stretched into months before he left it.

When the spring weather came, he was able to go out again, and he spent most of his time in the open air, feeling every day a fresh accession of strength. At the end of one long April afternoon, he walked home with a light heart, whose right to rejoice he would not let his conscience question. He had met Marcia in the public garden, where they sat down on a bench and talked, while her father and the little girl wandered away in the restlessness of age and the restlessness of childhood.

"We are going home to Equity this summer," she said, "and perhaps we shall not come back. No, we shall not come back. *I have given up*. I have waited, hoping—hoping. But now I know that it is no use waiting any longer: *he is dead*."

She spoke in tearless resignation, and the peace of accepted widowhood seemed to diffuse itself around her.

Her words repeated themselves to Halleck as he walked homeward. He found the postman at the door with a newspaper, which he took from him with a smile at its veteran appearance and its probable adventures in reaching him. The wrapper seemed to have been several times slipped off, and then slit up; it was tied with a string now, and was scribbled with rejections in the hands of various Hallocks and Halletts, one of whom had finally indorsed upon it, "Try 97 Rumford street." It was originally addressed, as he made out, to "Mr. B. Halleck, Boston, Mass.," and he carried it to his room before he opened it, with a careless surmise as to its interest for him. It proved to be a flimsy, shabbily printed country newspaper, with an advertisement marked in one corner.

nant compassion for Marcia to know anything else. She tried
to speak.

"Don't you understand, Olive? This is the notice that the
law requires she shall have to come and defend her cause, and
it has been sent by the clerk of the court there, to the address
that villain must have given in the knowledge that it could
reach her only by one chance in ten thousand."

"And it has come to you! Oh, Ben! Who sent it to *you*?"
The brother and sister looked at each other, but neither spoke
the awe-stricken thought that was in both their hearts. "Ben,"
she cried, in a solemn ecstasy of love and pride, "I would
rather be you this minute than any other man in the world!"

"Don't!" pleaded Halleck. His head dropped, and then he
lifted it by a sudden impulse. "Olive!"—but the impulse
failed, and he only said, "I want you to go to Atherton with
me. We mustn't lose time. Have Cyrus get a carriage. Go
down and tell them we're going out. I'll be ready as soon as
you are."

But when she called to him from below that the carriage
had come and she was waiting, he would have refused to go
with her if he durst. He no longer wished to keep back the
fact, but he felt an invalid's weariness of it, a sick man's inadequacy to the further demands it should make upon him.
He crept slowly down the stairs, keeping a tremulous hold
upon the rail; and he sank with a sigh against the carriage
cushions, answering Olive's eager questions and fervid comments with languid monosyllables.

They found the Athertons at coffee, and Clara would have
them come to the dining-room and join them. Halleck refused the coffee, and, while Olive told what had happened,
he looked listlessly about the room, aware of a perverse sympathy with Bartley, from Bartley's point of view; Bartley
might never have gone wrong if he had had all that luxury;
and why should he not have had it, as well as Atherton? What
right had the untempted prosperity of such a man to judge
the guilt of such men as himself and Bartley Hubbard?

Olive produced the newspaper from her lap, where she
kept both hands upon it, and opened it in dramatic corroboration of what she had been telling Atherton. He read it and
passed it to Clara.

"When did this come to you?"

Olive answered for him. "This evening—just now. Didn't I say that?"

"No," said Atherton, and he added to Halleck, gently; "I beg your pardon. Did you notice the dates?"

"Yes," answered Halleck, with cold refusal of Atherton's tone of reparation.

"The cause is set for hearing on the 11th," said Atherton. "This is the 8th. The time is very short."

"It's long enough," said Halleck, wearily.

"Oh, telegraph!" cried Clara. "Telegraph them instantly that she never dreamt of leaving him! Abandonment! Oh, if they only knew how she had been slaving her fingers off for the last two years to keep a home for him to come back to, they'd give *her* the divorce!"

Atherton smiled and turned to Halleck: "Do you know what their law is now? It was changed two years ago."

"Yes," said Halleck, replying to the question Atherton had asked and the subtler question he had looked, "I have read up the whole subject since I came home. The divorce is granted only upon proof, even when the defendant fails to appear, and if this were to go against us,"—he instinctively identified himself with Marcia's cause,—"we can have the default set aside, and a new trial granted, for cause shown."

The women listened in awe of the legal phrases; but when Atherton rose, and asked, "Is your carriage here?" his wife sprang to her feet.

"Why, where are you going?" she demanded, anxiously.

"Not to Indiana, immediately," answered her husband. "We're first going to Clover street, to see Squire Gaylord and Mrs. Hubbard. Better let me take the paper, dear," he said, softly withdrawing it from her hands.

"Oh, it's a cruel, cruel law!" she moaned, deprived of this moral support. "To suppose that such a notice as this is sufficient! Women couldn't have made such a law."

"No, women only profit by such laws after they're made: they work both ways. But it's not such a bad law, as divorce laws go. We do worse, now, in some New England States."

They found the Squire alone in the parlor, and, with a few words of explanation, Atherton put the paper in his hands, and he read the notice in emotionless quiet. Then he took off his spectacles, and shut them in their case, which he put back into his waistcoat pocket. "This is all right," he said. He cleared his throat, and lifting the fierce glimmer of his eyes to Atherton's, he asked, drily, "What is the law, at present?"

Atherton briefly recapitulated the points as he had them from Halleck.

"That's good," said the old man. "We will fight this gentleman." He rose, and from his gaunt height looked down on both of them, with his sinuous lips set in a bitter smile. "Bartley must have been disappointed when he found a divorce so hard to get in Indiana. He must have thought that the old law was still in force there. He's not the fellow to swear to a lie if he can help it; but I guess he expects to get this divorce by perjury."

Marcia was putting little Flavia to bed. She heard the talking below; she thought she heard Bartley's name. She ran to the stairs, and came hesitantly down, the old wild hope and wild terror fluttering her pulse and taking her breath. At sight of the three men, apparently in counsel, she crept toward them, holding out her hands before her like one groping his way. "What—what is it?" She looked from Atherton's face to her father's; the old man stopped, and tried to smile reassuringly; he tried to speak; Atherton turned away.

It was Halleck who came forward, and took her wandering hands. He held them quivering in his own, and said gravely and steadily, using her name for the first time in the deep pity which cast out all fear and shame, "Marcia, we have found your husband."

"Dead?" she made with her lips.

"He is alive," said Halleck. "There is something in this paper for you to see,—something you *must* see"—

"I can bear anything, if he is not dead. Where—what is it? Show it to me." The paper shook in the hands which Halleck released; her eyes strayed blindly over its columns; he had to put his finger on the place before she could find it. Then her tremor ceased, and she seemed without breath or pulse while she read it through. She fetched a long, deep sigh, and passed her hand over her eyes, as if to clear them; staying herself unconsciously against Halleck's breast, and, laying her trem-

bling arm along his arm till her fingers knit themselves among
his fingers, she read it a second time and a third. Then she
dropped the paper, and turned to look up at him. "Why!"
she cried, as if she had made it out at last, while an awful,
joyful light of hope flashed into her face, "*It is a mistake!*
Don't you see? He thinks that I never came back! He thinks
that I meant to abandon him. That I—that I—But you *know*
that I came back,—you came back *with* me! Why, I wasn't
gone an hour,—a *half*-hour, hardly. O Bartley! poor Bartley!
He thought I could leave him, and take his child from him;
that I could be so wicked, so heartless— Oh, no, no, no.
Why, I only stayed away that little time because I was *afraid*
to go back! Don't you remember how I told you I was afraid,
and wanted you to come in with me?" Her exultation broke
in a laugh. "But we can explain it now, and it will be all right.
He will see—he will understand—I will tell him just how it
was— Oh, Flavia, Flavia, we've found papa, we've found
papa! Quick!"

She whirled away toward the stairs, but her father caught
her by the arm. "Marcia!" he shouted, in his old raucous
voice, "you've got to understand! This"—he hesitated, as if
running over all terms of opprobrium in his mind, and he
resumed as if he had found them each too feeble—"*Bartley*
hasn't acted under any mistake."

He set the facts before her with merciless clearness, and she
listened with an audible catching of the breath at times, while
she softly smoothed her forehead with her left hand. "I don't
believe it," she said, when he had ended. "Write to him, tell
him what I say, and you will see."

The old man uttered something between a groan and a
curse. "Oh, you poor, crazy child! Can nothing make you
understand that Bartley wants to get rid of you, and that he's
just as ready for one lie as another? He thinks he can make
out a case of abandonment with the least trouble, and so he
accuses you of that; but he'd just as soon accuse you of anything else. *Write* to him? You've got to *go* to him! You've got
to go out there and fight him in open court, with facts and
witnesses. Do you suppose Bartley Hubbard wants any explanation from you? Do you think he's been waiting these two
years to hear that you didn't really abandon him, but came

back to this house an hour after you left it, and that you've waited for him here ever since? When he knows that, will he withdraw this suit of his and come home? He'll want the proof, and the way to do it is to go out there and let him have it. If I had him on the stand for five minutes," said the old man, between his set teeth—"*just five minutes*—I'd undertake to convince him from his own lips that he was wrong about you! But I am afraid he wouldn't mind a letter. You think I say so because I hate him, and you don't believe me. Well, ask either of these gentlemen here whether I'm telling you the truth."

She did not speak, but, with a glance at their averted faces, she sank into a chair, and passed one hand over the other, while she drew her breath in long, shuddering respirations, and stared at the floor with knit brows and starting eyes, like one stifling a deadly pang. She made several attempts to speak before she could utter any sound; then she lifted her eyes to her father's: "Let us—let us—go—home! Oh, let us go home! I will give him up. I *had* given him up already; I told you," she said, turning to Halleck, and speaking in a slow, gentle tone, "only an hour ago, that he was dead. And this—this that's happened, it makes no difference. Why did you bring the paper to me when you knew that I thought he was dead?"

"God knows I wished to keep it from you."

"Well, no matter now. Let him go free if he wants to. I can't help it."

"You *can* help it," interrupted her father. "You've got the facts on your side, and you've got the witnesses."

"Would you go out with me, and tell him that I never meant to leave him?" she asked simply, turning to Halleck. "You—and Olive?"

"We would do anything for you, Marcia!"

She sat musing, and drawing her hands one over the other again, while her quivering breath came and went on the silence. She let her hands fall nervelessly on her lap. "I can't go; I'm too weak; I couldn't bear the journey. No!" She shook her head. "I can't go!"

"Marcia," began her father, "it's your *duty* to go!"

"Does it say in the law that I have to go if I don't choose?" she asked of Halleck.

"No, you certainly need not go if you don't choose!"

"Then I will stay. Do you think it's my duty to go?" she asked, referring her question first to Halleck, and then to Atherton. She turned from the silence by which they tried to leave her free. "I don't care for my duty any more. I don't want to keep him, if it's so that he—left me—and—and meant it—and he doesn't—care for me any—more."

"Care for you? He *never* cared for you, Marcia! And you may be sure he doesn't care for you now!"

"Then let him go, and let us go home."

"Very well," said the old man; "we will go home, then, and before the week's out Bartley Hubbard will be a perjured bigamist."

"Bigamist?" Marcia leaped to her feet.

"Yes, bigamist! Don't you suppose he had his eye on some other woman out there before he began this suit?"

The languor was gone from Marcia's limbs. As she confronted her father, the wonderful likeness in the outline of their faces appeared. His was dark and wrinkled with age, and hers was gray with the anger that drove the blood back to her heart; but one impulse animated those fierce profiles, and the hoarded hate in the old man's soul seemed to speak in Marcia's thick whisper, "I will go."

XXXVIII

THE ATHERTONS sat late over their breakfast in the luxurious dining-room, where the April sun came in at the windows overlooking the Back Bay, and commanding at that stage of the tide a long stretch of shallow with a flight of white gulls settled upon it.

They had let Clara's house on the hill, and she had bought another on the new land; she insisted upon the change, not only because everybody was leaving the hill, but also because, as she said, it would seem too much like taking Mr. Atherton to board, if they went to housekeeping where she had always lived; she wished to give him the effect before the world of having brought her to a house of his own. She had even furnished it anew for the most part, and had banished as far as possible the things that reminded her of the time when she was not his wife. He humored her in this fantastic self-indulgence, and philosophized her wish to give him the appearance of having the money, as something orderly in its origin, and not to be deprecated on other grounds, since probably it deceived nobody. They lived a very tranquil life, and Clara had no grief of her own, unless it was that there seemed to be no great things she could do for him. One day, when she whimsically complained of this, he said: "I'm very glad of that. Let's try to be equal to the little sacrifices we must make for each other; they will be quite enough. Many a woman, who would be ready to die for her husband, makes him wretched because she wont live for him. Don't despise the day of small things."

"Yes, but when every day seems the day of small things!" she pouted.

"Every day *is* the day of small things," said Atherton, "with people who are happy. We're never so prosperous as when we can't remember what happened last Monday."

"Oh, but I can't bear to be always living in the present."

"It's not so spacious, I know, as either the past or the future; but it's all we have."

"There!" cried Clara, "that's *fatalism*! It's *worse* than fatalism!"

"And is fatalism so very bad?" asked her husband.

"It's Mahometanism!"

"Well, it isn't necessarily a plurality of wives," returned Atherton, in subtle anticipation of her next point. "And it's really only another name for resignation, which is certainly a good thing."

"Resignation? Oh, I don't know about that!"

Atherton laughed, and put his arm round her waist— an argument that no woman can answer in a man she loves: it seems to deprive her of her reasoning faculties. In the atmosphere of affection which she breathed, she sometimes feared that her mental powers were really weakening. As a girl she had lived a life full of purposes, which, if somewhat vague, were unquestionably large. She had then had great interests,—art, music, literature,—the symphony concerts, Mr. Hunt's classes, the novels of George Eliot, and Mr. Fiske's lectures on the cosmic philosophy; and she had always felt that they expanded and elevated existence. In her moments of question as to the shape which her life had taken since, she tried to think whether the happiness which seemed so little dependent on these things was not beneath the demands of a spirit which was probably immortal and was certainly cultivated. They all continued to be part of her life, but only a very small part; and she would have liked to ask her husband whether his influence upon her had been wholly beneficial. She was not sure that it had; but neither was she sure that it had not. She had never fully consented to the distinctness with which he classified all her emotions and ideas as those of a woman; in her heart she doubted whether a great many of them might not be those of a man, though she had never found any of them exactly like his. She could not complain that he did not treat her as an equal; he deferred to her, and depended upon her good sense to an extent that sometimes alarmed her, for she secretly knew that she had a very large streak of silliness in her nature. He seemed to tell her everything, and to be greatly ruled by her own advice, especially in matters of business; but she could not help observing that he often kept matters involving certain moral questions from her till the moment for deciding them was past. When she accused him of this, he confessed that it was so, but defended

himself by saying that he was afraid her conscience might
sway him against his judgment.

Clara now recurred to these words of his as she sat looking
at him through her tears across the breakfast table. "Was that
the reason you never told me about poor Ben before?"

"Yes, and I expect you to justify me. What good would it
have done to tell you?"

"I could have told you, at least, that if Ben had any such
feeling as that, it wasn't *his* fault altogether!"

"But you wouldn't have believed that, Clara," said Atherton. "You know that, whatever that poor creature's faults are,
coquetry isn't one of them."

Clara only admitted this fact passively.

"How did he excuse himself for coming back?" she asked.

"He didn't excuse himself; he defied himself. We had a
stormy talk, and he ended by denying that he had any social
duty in the matter."

"And I think he was quite right!" Clara flashed out. "It was
his own affair."

"He said he had a concrete purpose, and wouldn't listen to
abstractions. Yes, he talked like a woman. But you know he
wasn't right, Clara, though *you* talk like a woman too. There
are a great many things that are not wrong except as they
wrong others. I've no doubt that, as compared with the highest love her husband ever felt for her, Ben's passion was as
light to darkness. But, if he could only hope for its return
through the perversion of her soul,—through teaching her to
think of escape from her marriage by a divorce,—then it was
a crime against her and against society."

"Ben couldn't do such a thing!"

"No, he could only dream of doing it. When it came to the
attempt, everything that was good in him revolted against it
and conspired to make him help her in the efforts that would
defeat his hopes if they succeeded. It was a ghastly ordeal, but
it was sublime; and when the climax came,—that paper,
which he had only to conceal for a few days or weeks,—he
was equal to the demand upon him. But suppose a man of
his pure training and traditions had yielded to temptation,—
suppose he had so far depraved himself that he could have set
about persuading her that she owed no allegiance to her hus-

band, and might rightfully get a divorce and marry him,—
what a ruinous blow it would have been to all who knew of
it! It would have disheartened those who abhorred it, and
encouraged those who wanted to profit by such an example.
It doesn't matter much, socially, what undisciplined people
like Bartley and Marcia Hubbard do; but if a man like Ben
Halleck goes astray, it's calamitous; it 'confounds the human
conscience,' as Victor Hugo says. All that careful nurture in
the right since he could speak, all that lifelong decency of
thought and act, that noble ideal of unselfishness and responsibility to others, trampled under foot and spit upon,—it's
horrible!"

"Yes," answered Clara, deeply moved, even as a woman
may be in a pretty breakfast-room, "and such a good soul as
Ben always was naturally. Will you have some more tea?"

"Yes, I will take another cup. But as for natural goodness"—

"Wait! I will ring for some hot water."

When the maid had appeared, disappeared, reappeared, and
finally vanished, Atherton resumed. "The natural goodness
doesn't count. The natural man is a wild beast, and his natural
goodness is the amiability of a beast basking in the sun when
his stomach is full. The Hubbards were full of natural goodness, I dare say, when they didn't happen to cross each
other's wishes. No, it's the implanted goodness that saves,—
the seed of righteousness treasured from generation to generation, and carefully watched and tended by disciplined fathers and mothers in the hearts where they had dropped it.
The flower of this implanted goodness is what we call civilization, the condition of general uprightness that Halleck declared he owed no allegiance to. But he was better than his
word."

Atherton lifted, with his slim, delicate hand, the cup of
translucent china, and drained off the fragrant Souchong,
sweetened, and tempered with Jersey cream to perfection.
Something in the sight went like a pang to his wife's heart.
"Ah!" she said, "it is easy enough for us to condemn. *We*
have everything we want!"

"I don't forget that, Clara," said Atherton, gravely. "Sometimes when I think of it, I am ready to renounce all judgment

of others. The consciousness of our comfort, our luxury, almost paralyzes me at those times, and I am ashamed and afraid even of our happiness."

"Yes, what right," pursued Clara, rebelliously, "have we to be happy and united, and these wretched creatures so"—

"No right—none in the world! But somehow the effects follow their causes. In some sort they chose misery for themselves,—we make our own hell in this life and the next,—or it was chosen for them by undisciplined wills that they inherited. In the long run their fate must be a just one."

"Ah, but I have to look at things in the *short* run, and I can't see any justice in Marcia's husband using her so!" cried Clara. "Why shouldn't you use me badly? I don't believe any woman ever meant better by her husband than she did."

"Oh, the meaning doesn't count! It's our deeds that judge us. He is a thoroughly bad fellow, but you may be sure she has been to blame. Though I don't blame the Hubbards, either of them, so much as I blame Halleck. He not only had everything he wished, but the training to know what he ought to wish."

"I don't know about his having everything. I think Ben must have been disappointed some time," said Clara evasively.

"Oh, that's nothing," replied Atherton, with the contented husband's indifference to sentimental grievances.

Clara did not speak for some moments, and then she summed up a turmoil of thoughts in a profound sigh. "Well, I don't like it! I thought it was bad enough having a man, even on the outskirts of my acquaintance, abandon his wife; but now, Ben Halleck, who has been like a brother to me—to have him mixed up in such an affair in the way he is—it's intolerable!"

"I agree with you," said Atherton, playing with his spoon. "You know how I hate anything that sins against order, and this whole thing is disorderly. It's intolerable, as you say. But we must bear our share of it. We're all bound together. No one sins or suffers to himself in a civilized state, or religious state—it's the same thing. Every link in the chain feels the effect of the violence more or less intimately. We rise or fall together in Christian society. It's strange that it should be so hard to realize a thing that every experience of life teaches.

We keep on thinking of offenses against the common good as if they were abstractions!"

"Well, *one* thing," said Clara, "I shall always think unnecessarily shocking and disgraceful about it, and that is Ben's going out with her on this journey. I don't see how you could allow that, Eustace."

"Yes," said Atherton, after a thoughtful silence, "it *is* shocking. The only consolation is that it is *not* unnecessarily shocking. I'm afraid that it's necessarily so. When any disease of soul or body has gone far enough, it makes its own conditions, and other things must adjust themselves to it. Besides, no one knows the ugliness of the situation but Halleck himself. I don't see how I could have interfered; and upon the whole I don't know that I ought to have interfered, if I could. She would be helpless without him, and he can get no harm from it. In fact, it's part of his expiation, which must have begun as soon as he met her again after he came home."

Clara was convinced, but not reconciled. She only said, "I don't like it."

Her husband did not reply; he continued musingly: "When the old man made that final appeal to her jealousy,—all that there is really left, probably, of her love for her husband,— and she responded with a face as wicked as his, I couldn't help looking at Halleck."

"Oh, poor Ben! *How* did he take it? It must have scared, it must have disgusted him!"

"That's what I had expected. But there was nothing in his face but pity. He understood, and he pitied her. That was all."

Clara rose, and turned to the window, where she remained looking through her tears at the gulls on the shallow. It seemed much more than twenty-four hours since she had taken leave of Marcia and the rest at the station, and saw them set out on their long journey with its uncertain and unimaginable end. She had deeply sympathized with them all, but at the same time she had felt very keenly the potential scandalousness of the situation; she shuddered inwardly when she thought what if people knew; she had always revolted from contact with such social facts as their errand involved. She got Olive aside for a moment and asked her, "Don't you *hate* it, Olive? Did you ever dream of being mixed up in such a thing? I should die—simply *die*!"

"I shall not think of dying, unless we fail," answered Olive. "And, as for hating it, I haven't consulted my feelings a great deal; but I rather think I like it."

"Like going out to be a witness in an Indiana divorce case!"

"I don't look at it in that way, Clara. It's a crusade to me; it's a holy war; it's the cause of an innocent woman against a wicked oppression. I know how *you* would feel about it, Clara; but I never *was* as respectable as you are, and I'm quite satisfied to do what Ben, and father, and Mr. Atherton approve. They think it's my duty, and I am glad to go, and to be of all the use I can. But you shall have my heart-felt sympathy through all, Clara, for your involuntary acquaintance with our proceedings."

"Olive! You *know* that I'm proud of your courage and Ben's goodness, and that I fully appreciate the sacrifice you're making. And I'm not ashamed of your business: I think it's grand and sublime, and I would just as soon scream it out at the top of my voice, right here in the Albany Depot."

"Don't," said Olive. "It would frighten the child."

She had Flavia by the hand, and she made the little girl her special charge throughout the journey. The old Squire seemed anxious to be alone, and he restlessly escaped from Marcia's care. He sat all the first day apart, chewing upon some fragment of wood that he had picked up, and now and then putting up a lank hand to rasp his bristling jaw, glancing furtively at people who passed him, and lapsing into his ruminant abstraction. He had been vexed that they did not start the night before; and every halt the train made visibly afflicted him. He would not leave his place to get anything to eat when they stopped for refreshment, though he hungrily devoured the lunch that Marcia brought into the car for him. At New York he was in a tumult of fear lest they should lose the connecting train on the Pennsylvania road, and the sigh of relief with which he sank into his seat in the sleeping-car expressed the suffering he had undergone. He said he was not tired, but he went to bed early, as if to sleep away as much of the time as he could.

When Halleck came into their car, the next morning, he found Marcia and her father sitting together, and looking out of the window at the wooded slopes of the Alleghanies through which the train was running. The old man's impatience had relaxed; he let Marcia lay her hand on his, and he answered her with quiet submission, when she spoke now and then of the difference between these valleys, where the wild rhododendrons were growing, and the frozen hollows of the hills at home, which must be still choked with snow.

"But, oh! how much I would rather see them!" she said at last with a homesick throb.

"Well," he assented, "we can go right back—afterward."

"Yes," she whispered.

"Well, sir, good morning," said the old man to Halleck, "we are getting along, sir. At this rate, unless our calculations were mistaken, we shall be there by midnight. We are on time, the porter tells me."

"Yes, we shall soon be at Pittsburg," said Halleck, and he looked at Marcia, who turned away her face. She had not spoken of the object of the journey to him since they left Boston, and it had not been so nearly touched by either of them before. He could see that she recoiled from it; but the old man, once having approached it, could not leave it.

"If everything goes well, we shall have our grip on that fellow's throat in less than forty-eight hours." He looked down mechanically at his withered hands, lean and yellow like the talons of a bird, and lifted his accipitral profile with a predatory alertness. "I didn't sleep very well the last part of the night, but I thought it all out. I shan't care whether I get there before or after judgment is rendered; all I want is to get there before he has a chance to clear out. I think I shall be able to convince Bartley Hubbard that there is a God in Israel yet! Don't you be anxious, Marcia; I've got this thing at my fingers' ends as clear as a bell. I intend to give Bartley a little surprise!"

Marcia kept her face averted, and Halleck relinquished his purpose of sitting down with them, and went forward to the state-room that Marcia and Olive had occupied with the little girl. He tapped on the door, and found his sister dressed, but the child still asleep.

"What is the matter, Ben?" she asked. "You don't look well. You oughtn't to have undertaken this journey."

"Oh, I'm all right. But I've been up a good while, with nothing to eat. That old man is terrible, Olive!"

"Her father? Yes, he's a terrible old man!"

"It sickened me to hear him talk, just now—throwing out his threats of vengeance against Hubbard. It made me feel a sort of sympathy for that poor dog. Do you suppose she has the same motive? I couldn't forgive her!" he said, with a kind of passionate weakness. "I couldn't forgive myself!"

"We've got nothing to do with their motive, Ben. We are to be her witnesses for justice against a wicked wrong. I don't believe in special providences, of course; but it does seem as if we had been called to this work, as mother would say. Your happening to go home with her, that night and then that paper happening to come to you—doesn't it look like it?"

"It looks like it, yes."

"We couldn't have refused to come. That's what consoles me for being here this minute. I put on a bold face with Clara Atherton, yesterday morning at the depot; but I was in a cold chill all the time. Our coming off, in this way, on such an errand, is something so different from the rest of our whole life! And I *do* like quiet, and orderly ways, and all that we call respectability! I've been thinking that the trial will be reported by some such interviewing wretch as Bartley himself, and that we shall figure in the newspapers. But I've concluded that we mustn't care. It's right, and we must do it. I don't shut my eyes to the kind of people we're mixed up with. I pity Marcia, and I love her—poor, helpless, unguided thing!—but that old man *is* terrible! He's as cruel as the grave where he thinks he's been wronged, and crueller where he thinks *she's* been wronged. You've forgiven so much, Ben, that you can't understand a man who forgives nothing; but *I* can, for I'm a pretty good hater myself. And Marcia's just like her father, at times. I've seen her look at Clara Atherton as if she could kill her!"

The little girl stirred in her berth, and then lifted herself on her hands, and stared around at them through her tangled golden hair. "Is it morning, yet?" she asked sleepily. "Is it to-morrow?"

"Yes; it's to-morrow, Flavia," said Olive. "Do you want to get up?"

"And is next day the day after to-morrow?"

"Yes."

"Then it's only one day till I shall see papa. That's what mamma said. Where is mamma?" asked the child, rising to her knees, and sweeping back her hair from her face with either hand.

"I will go and send her to you," said Halleck.

At Pittsburg the Squire was eager for his breakfast, and made amends for his fast of the day before. He ate grossly of the heterogeneous abundance of the railroad restaurant, and drank two cups of coffee that in his thin, native air would have disordered his pulse for a week. But he resumed his journey with a tranquil strength that seemed the physical expression of a mind clear and content. He was willing and even anxious to tell Halleck what his theories and plans were; but the young man shrank from knowing them. He wished only to know whether Marcia were privy to them, and this, too, he shrank from knowing.

XXXIX

THEY left Pittsburg under the dun pall of smoke that hangs perpetually over the city, and ran out of a world where the earth seemed turned to slag and cinders, and the coal-grime blackened even the sheathing from which the young leaves were unfolding their vivid green. Their train twisted along the banks of the Ohio, and gave them now and then a reach of the stream, forgetful of all the noisy traffic that once fretted its waters, and losing itself in almost primitive wildness among its softly rounded hills. It is a beautiful land, and it had, even to their loath eyes, a charm that touched their hearts. They were on the borders of the illimitable West, whose lands stretch like a sea beyond its hilly Ohio shore; but as yet this vastness, which appalls and wearies all but the born Westerner, had not burst upon them; they were still among heights and hollows, and in a milder and softer New England.

"I have a strange feeling about this journey," said Marcia, turning from the window at last, and facing Halleck on the opposite seat. "I want it to be over, and yet I am glad at every little stop. I feel like some one that has been called to a death-bed, and is hurrying on and holding back with all her might, at the same time. I shall have no peace till I am there, and then shall I have peace?" She fixed her eyes imploringly on his. "Say something to me, if you can! What do you think?"

"Whether you will—succeed?" He was confounding what he knew of her father's feeling with what he had feared of hers.

"Do you mean about the lawsuit? I don't care for that! Do you think he will hate me when he sees me? Do you think he will believe me when I tell him that I never meant to leave him, and that I'm sorry for what I did to drive him away?"

She seemed to expect him to answer, and he answered as well as he could: "He ought to believe that—yes, he must believe it."

"Then all the rest may go," she said. "I don't care who gains the case. But if he shouldn't believe me—if he should drive me away from him, as I drove him from me"— She held her breath in the terror of such a possibility, and an awe of her ignorance crept over Halleck. Apparently she had not understood the step that Bartley had taken, except as a stage in their quarrel from which they could both retreat, if they would, as easily as from any other dispute; she had not realized it as a final, an almost irrevocable act on his part, which could only be met by reprisal on hers. All those points of law which had been so sharply enforced upon her must have fallen blunted from her longing to be at one with him; she had, perhaps, not imagined her defense in open court, except as a sort of public reconciliation.

But at another time she recurred to her wrongs in all the bitterness of her father's vindictive purpose. A young couple entered the car at one of the country stations, and the bride made haste to take off her white bonnet, and lay her cheek on her husband's shoulder, while he passed his arm round her silken waist, and drew her close to him on the seat, in the loving rapture which is nowise inconvenienced by publicity on our railroad trains. Indeed, after the first general recognition of their condition, no one noticed them except Marcia, who seemed fascinated by the spectacle of their unsophisticated happiness; it must have recalled the blissful abandon of her own wedding journey to her.

"Oh, poor fool!" she said to Olive. "Let her wait, and it will not be long before she will know that she had better lean on the empty air than on him. Some day he will let her fall to the ground, and when she gathers herself up all bruised and bleeding— But he hasn't got the all-believing simpleton to deal with that he used to have; and he shall pay me back for all—drop by drop, and ache for ache!"

She was in that strange mental condition into which women fall who brood long upon opposing purposes and desires. She wished to be reconciled, and she wished to be revenged, and she recurred to either wish for the time as vehemently as if the other did not exist. She took Flavia on her knee, and began to prattle to her of seeing papa to-morrow, and presently she turned to Olive, and said:

"I know he will find us both a great deal changed. Flavia looks so much older—and so do I. But I shall soon show

him that I can look young again. I presume he's changed
too."

Marcia held the little girl up at the window. They had now
left the river-hills and the rolling country beyond, and had
entered the great plain which stretches from the Ohio to the
Mississippi; and mile by mile, as they ran southward and
westward, the spring unfolded in the mellow air under the
dull, warm sun. The willows were in perfect leaf, and wore
their delicate green like veils caught upon their boughs; the
May-apples had already pitched their tents in the woods, beginning to thicken and darken with the young foliage of the
oaks and hickories; suddenly, as the train dashed from a
stretch of forest, the peach orchards flushed pink beside the
brick farmsteads. The child gave a cry of delight, and pointed;
and her mother seemed to forget all that had gone before,
and abandoned herself to Flavia's joy in the blossoms, as if
there were no trouble for her in the world.

Halleck rose and went into the other car; he felt giddy, as
if her fluctuations of mood and motive had somehow turned
his own brain. He did not come back till the train stopped at
Columbus for dinner. The old Squire showed the same appetite as at breakfast: he had the effect of falling upon his
food like a bird of prey; and as soon as the meal was dispatched he went back to his seat in the car, where he lapsed
into his former silence and immobility, his lank jaws working
with fresh activity upon the wooden toothpick he had
brought away from the table. While they waited for a train
from the north which was to connect with theirs, Halleck
walked up and down the vast, noisy station with Olive and
Marcia, and humored the little girl in her explorations of the
place. She made friends with a red-bird that sang in its cage
in the dining-hall, and with an old woman, yellow and wrinkled, and sunken-eyed, sitting on a bundle tied up in a quilt
beside the door, and smoking her clay pipe as placidly as if
on her own cabin threshold. " 'Pears like you ain't much
afeard of strangers, honey," said the old woman, taking her
pipe out of her mouth, to fill it. "Where do you live at when
you're home?"

"Boston," said the child, promptly. "Where do *you* live?"

"I *used* to live in Old Virginia. But my son he's takin' me

out to Illinoy, now. He's settled out there." She treated the
child with the serious equality which simple old people use
with children; and spat neatly aside in resuming her pipe.
"Which o' them ladies yonder is your maw, honey?"

"My mamma?"

The old woman nodded.

Flavia ran away and laid her hand on Marcia's dress, and
then ran back to the old woman.

"That your paw, with her?" Flavia looked blank, and the
old woman interpreted, "Your father."

"No! We're going out to see papa—out West. We're going
to see him to-morrow, and then he's coming back with us.
My grandpa is in that car."

The old woman now laid her folded arms on her knees,
and smoked obliviously. The little girl lingered a moment,
and then ran off laughing to her mother, and pulled her skirt.
"Wasn't it funny, mamma? She thought Mr. Halleck was my
papa!" She hung forward by the hold she had taken, as children do, and tilted her head back to look into her mother's
face. "What *is* Mr. Halleck, mamma?"

"What is he?" The group halted involuntarily.

"Yes, what is he? Is he my uncle, or my cousin, or what? Is
he going out to see papa, too? What is *he* going for? Oh,
look, look!" The child plucked away her hand, and ran off to
join the circle of idle men and half-grown boys who were
forming about two shining negroes with banjos. The negroes
flung their hands upon the strings with an ecstatic joy in the
music, and lifted their black voices in a wild plantation strain.
The child began to leap and dance, and her mother ran after
her.

"Naughty little girl!" she cried. "Come into the car with
me, this minute."

Halleck did not see Marcia again till the train had run far
out of the city, and was again sweeping through the thick
woods, and flashing out upon the levels of the fields where
the farmers were riding their sulky-plows up and down the
long furrows in the pleasant afternoon sun. There is something in this transformation of man's old-time laborious dependence into a lordly domination over the earth, which
strikes the westward journeyer as finally expressive of human

destiny in the whole mighty region, and which penetrated even to Halleck's sore and jaded thoughts. A different type of men began to show itself in the car, as the Western people gradually took the places of his fellow-travelers from the East. The men were often slovenly and sometimes uncouth in their dress; but they made themselves at home in the exaggerated splendor and opulence of the car, as if born to the best in every way; their faces suggested the security of people who trusted the future from the past, and had no fears of the life that had always used them well; they had not that eager and intense look which the Eastern faces wore; there was energy enough to spare in them, but it was not an anxious energy. The sharp accent of the seaboard yielded to the rounded, soft, and slurring tones, and the prompt address was replaced by a careless and confident neighborliness of manner.

Flavia fretted at her return to captivity in the car, and demanded to be released with a teasing persistence from which nothing she was shown out of the window could divert her. A large man leaned forward at last from a seat near by, and held out an orange.

"Come here to me, little Trouble," he said, and Flavia made an eager start toward this unlooked-for friend.

Marcia wished to check her; but Halleck pleaded to have her go.

"It will be a relief to you," he said.

"Well, let her go," Marcia consented. "But she was no trouble, and she is no relief." She sat looking dully at the little girl after the Westerner had gathered her up into his lap. "Should I have liked to tell her," she said, as if thinking aloud, "how we were really going to meet her father, and that you were coming with me to be my witness against him in a court—to put him down and disgrace him—to fight him, as father says?"

"You mustn't think of it in that way," said Halleck gently, but, as he felt, feebly and inadequately.

"Oh, I shall not think of it in that way long," she answered. "My head is in a whirl, and I can't hold what we're doing before my mind in any one shape for a minute at a time. I don't know what will become of me—I don't know what will become of me!"

But in another breath she rose from this desolation, and was talking with impersonal cheerfulness of the sights that the car-window showed. As long as the light held, they passed through the same opulent and monotonous landscape; through little towns full of signs of material prosperity, and then farms and farms again; the brick houses set in the midst of evergreens, and compassed by vast acreages of corn-land, where herds of black pigs wandered, and the farmers were riding their plows, or heaping into vast winrows for burning the winter-worn stalks of the last year's crop. Where they came to a stream the landscape was roughened into low hills, from which it sank again luxuriously to a plain. If there was any difference between Ohio and Indiana, it was that in Indiana the spring night, whose breath softly buffeted their cheeks through the open window, had gathered over those eternal corn-fields, where the long, crooked winrows, burning on either hand, seemed a trail of fiery serpents writhing away from the train as it roared and clamored over the track.

They were to leave their car at Indianapolis, and take another road which would bring them to Tecumseh by daylight next morning. Olive went away with the little girl, and put her to bed on the sofa in the state-room, and Marcia suffered them to go alone; it was only by fits that she had cared for the child, or even noticed it.

"Now tell me again," she said to Halleck, "why we are going."

"Surely you know."

"Yes, yes, I know; but I can't think—I don't seem to remember. Didn't I give it up once? Didn't I say that I would rather go home, and let Bartley get the divorce, if he wanted?"

"Yes, you said that, Marcia."

"I used to make him very unhappy; I was very strict with him, when I knew he couldn't bear any kind of strictness. And he was always so patient with me; though he never really cared for me. Oh, yes, I knew that from the first! He used to try; but he must have been glad to get away. Poor Bartley! It was cruel, cruel, to put that in about my abandoning him when he knew I would come back; but perhaps the lawyers told him he must; he had to put in something! Why shouldn't

I let him go? Father said he only wanted to get rid of me, so that he could marry some one else— Yes, yes; it was that that made me start! Father knew it would! Oh," she grieved, with a wild self-pity that tore Halleck's heart, "he knew it would!" She fell wearily back against the seat, and did not speak for some minutes. Then she said, in a slow, broken utterance: "But now I don't seem to mind even that any more. Why shouldn't he marry some one else that he really likes, if he doesn't care for me?"

Halleck laughed in bitterness of soul, as his thought recurred to Atherton's reasons.

"Because," he said, "you have a *public* duty in the matter. You must keep him bound to you, for fear some other woman, whose husband doesn't care for her, would let *him* go, too, and society be broken up and civilization destroyed. In a matter like this, which seems to concern yourself alone, you are only to regard others."

His reckless irony did not reach her through her manifold sorrow.

"Well," she said, simply, "It must be that. But, oh! how can I bear it? how can I bear it?"

The time passed; Olive did not return for an hour; then she merely said that the little girl had just fallen asleep, and that she should go back and lie down with her—that she was sleepy too.

Marcia did not answer, but Halleck said he would call her in good time before they reached Indianapolis.

The porter made up the berths of such as were going through to St. Louis, and Marcia was left sitting alone with Halleck.

"I will go and get your father to come here," he said.

"I don't want him to come! I want to talk to you—to say something— What was it? I can't think!"

She stopped, like one trying to recover a faded thought; he waited, but she did not speak again. She had laid a nervous clutch upon his arm, to detain him from going for her father, and she kept her hand there mechanically; but after a while he felt it relax; she drooped against him, and fell away into a sleep in which she started now and then like a frightened child. He could not release himself without waking her; but

it did not matter; her sorrow had unsexed her; only the tenderness of his love for this hapless soul remained in his heart,
which ached and evermore heavily sank within him.

He woke her at last when he must go to tell Olive that they
were running into Indianapolis. Marcia struggled to her feet:
"Oh, oh! Are we there? Are we there?"

"We are at Indianapolis," said Halleck.

"I thought it was Tecumseh!" She shuddered. "We can go
back; oh, yes, we can still go back!"

They alighted from the train in the chilly midnight air, and
found their way through the crowd to the eating-room of the
station. The little girl cried with broken sleep and the strangeness, and Olive tried to quiet her. Marcia clung to Halleck's
arm, and shivered convulsively. Squire Gaylord stalked beside
them with a demoniac vigor. "A few more hours—a few
more hours, sir!" he said. He made a hearty supper, while the
rest scalded their mouths with hot tea, which they forced with
loathing to their lips.

Some women who were washing the floor of the ladies'
waiting-room told them they must go into the men's room,
and wait there for their train, which was due at one o'clock.
They obeyed, and found the room full of emigrants, and the
air thick with their tobacco-smoke. There was no choice;
Olive went in first and took the child on her lap, where it
straightway fell asleep; the Squire found a seat beside them,
and sat erect, looking round on the emigrants with the air of
being amused at their outlandish speech, into which they
burst clamorously from their silence at intervals. Marcia
stopped Halleck at the threshold. "Stay out here with me,"
she whispered. "I want to tell you something," she added, as
he turned mechanically and walked away with her up the vast
lamp-shot darkness of the depot. "*I am not going on!* I am
going back. We will take the train that goes to the East; father will never know till it is too late. We needn't speak to
him about it."

Halleck set himself against this delirious folly: he consented
to her return; she could do what she would; but he would
not consent to cheat her father. "We must go and tell him,"
he said, for all answer to all her entreaties. He dragged her
back to the waiting-room; but at the door she started at the

figure of a man who was bending over a group of emigrant children asleep in the nearest corner—poor, uncouth, stubbed little creatures, in old-mannish clothes, looking like children roughly blocked out of wood, and stiffly stretched on the floor, or resting woodenly against their mother.

"There!" said the man, pressing a mug of coffee on the woman. "You drink that! It'll do you good,—every drop of it! I've seen the time," he said, turning round with the mug, when she had drained it, in his hand, and addressing Marcia and Halleck, as the most accessible portion of the English-speaking public, "when I used to be down on coffee—I thought it was bad for the nerves; but I tell you, when you're travelin', it's a brain-food if ever there was a brain"—

He dropped the mug, and stumbled back into the heap of sleeping children, fixing a ghastly stare on Marcia.

She ran toward him.

"Mr. Kinney!"

"No, you don't! No, you don't."

"Why, don't you know me—Mrs. Hubbard?"

"He—he—told me you—was dead!" roared Kinney.

"He told you I was dead?"

"More'n a year ago! The last time I seen him! Before I went out to Leadville!"

"He told you I was dead," repeated Marcia huskily. "He must have wished it!" she whispered. "Oh, mercy, mercy, mercy!" She stopped, and then she broke into a wild laugh: "Well, you see he was wrong. I'm on my way to him now to show him that I'm alive!"

XL

HALLECK woke at daybreak from the drowse into which he had fallen. The train was creeping slowly over the track, feeling its way, and he heard fragments of talk among the passengers about a broken rail that the conductor had been warned of. He turned to ask some question, when the pull of rising speed came from the locomotive, and at the same moment the car stopped with a jolting pitch. It settled upon the track again; but the two cars in front were overturned, and the passengers were still climbing from their windows, when Halleck got his bewildered party to the ground. Children were crying, and a woman was led by with her face cut and bleeding from the broken glass; but it was reported that no one else was hurt, and the trainmen gave their helplessness to the inspection of the rotten cross-tie that had caused the accident. One of the passengers kicked the decayed wood with his boot. "Well," he said, "I always like a little accident like this, early; it makes us safe the rest of the day." The sentiment apparently commended itself to popular acceptance. Halleck went forward with part of the crowd to see what was the matter with the locomotive; it had kept the track, but seemed to be injured somehow; the engineer was working at it, hammer in hand; he exchanged some dry pleasantries with a passenger who asked him if there was any chance of hiring a real fast ox-team in that neighborhood, in case a man was in a hurry to get on to Tecumseh.

They were in the midst of a level prairie that stretched all round to the horizon, where it was broken by patches of timber; the rising sun slanted across the green expanse, and turned its distance to gold; the grass at their feet was full of wild flowers, upon which Flavia flung herself as soon as they got out of the car. By the time Halleck returned to them, she was running with cries of joy and wonder toward a windmill that rose beautiful above the roofs of a group of commonplace houses, at a little distance from the track; it stirred its mighty vanes in the thin, sweet inland breeze, and took the sun gayly on the light gallery that encircled it.

A vision of Belgian plains swept before Halleck's eyes. "There ought to be storks on its roof," he said absently.

"How strange that it should be here, away out in the West!" said Olive.

"If it were less strange than we are here, I couldn't stand it," he answered.

A brakeman came up with a flag in his hand, and nodded toward Flavia. "She's on the right track for breakfast," he said. "There's an old Dutchman at that mill, and his wife knows how to make coffee like a fellow's mother. You'll have plenty of time. This train has come here to stay—till somebody can walk back five miles and telegraph for help."

"How far are we from Tecumseh?" asked Halleck.

"Fifty miles," the brakeman called back over his shoulder.

"Don't you worry any, Marcia," said her father, moving off in pursuit of Flavia. "This accident makes it all right for us, if we don't get there for a week."

Marcia answered nothing. Halleck began to talk to her of that Belgian landscape in which he had first seen a windmill, and he laughed at the blank unintelligence with which she received his reminiscence of travel. For the moment, the torturing stress was lifted from his soul; he wished that the breakfast in the miller's house might never come to an end; he explored the mill with Flavia; he bantered the Squire on his saturnine preference for steam power in the milling business; he made the others share his mood; he pushed far from him the series of tragic or squalid facts which had continually brought the end to him in reveries in which he found himself holding his breath, as if he might hold it till the end really came.

But this respite could not last. A puff of white steam showed on the horizon, and after an interval the sound of the locomotive's whistle reached them, as it came backing down a train of empty cars toward them. They were quickly on their journey again, and a scanty hour before noon they arrived at Tecumseh.

The pretty town, which in prospect had worn to Olive Halleck's imagination the blended hideousness of Sodom and Gomorrah, was certainly very much more like a New England village in fact. After the brick farmsteads and coal-smoked towns of Central Ohio, its wooden houses, set back from the street with an ample depth of door-yard, were appealingly familiar, and she exchanged some homesick whispers with Marcia about them, as they drove along under the full-leaved maples which shadowed the way. The grass was denser and darker than in New England, and, pretty as the town was, it wore a more careless and unscrupulous air than the true New England village; the South had touched it, and here and there it showed a wavering line of fence and a faltering conscientiousness in its paint. Presently all aspects of village quiet and seclusion ceased, and a section of conventional American city, with flat-roofed brick blocks, showy hotel, stores, paved street, and stone sidewalks, expressed the readiness of Tecumseh to fulfill the destiny of every Western town, and become a metropolis at a day's notice, if need be. The second-hand omnibus, which reflected the actuality of Tecumseh, set them down at the broad steps of the court-house, fronting on an avenue which for a city street was not very crowded or busy. Such passers as there were had leisure and inclination, as they loitered by, to turn and stare at the strangers; and the voice of the sheriff, as he called from an upper window of the court-house the names of absentee litigants or witnesses required to come into court, easily made itself heard above all the other noises.

It seemed to Halleck as if the sheriff were calling them; he lifted his head and looked at Olive, but she would not meet his eye; she led by the hand the little girl, who kept asking, "Is this the house where papa lives?" with the merciless iteration of a child. Halleck dragged lamely after the Squire, who had mounted the steps with unnatural vigor; he promptly found his way to the clerk's office, where he examined the docket, and then returned to the party triumphant. "We are in time," he said, and he led them on up into the court-room.

A few spectators, scattered about on the rows of benching, turned to look at them as they walked up the aisle, where the cocoa matting, soaked and dried, and soaked again with perpetual libations of tobacco-juice, mercifully silenced their footsteps; most of the faces turned upon them showed a slow and thoughtful movement of the jaws, and, as they were dropped or averted, a general discharge of tobacco-juice seemed to express the general adoption of the new-comers, whoever they were, as a necessary element of the scene, which it was useless to oppose and about which it was idle to speculate. Before the Squire had found his party seats on one of the benches next the bar, the spectators had again given their languid attention to the administration of justice, which is everywhere informal with us, and is only a little more informal in the West than in the East. An effect of serene disoccupation pervaded the place, such as comes at the termination of an interesting affair; and no one seemed to care for what the clerk was reading aloud in a set, mechanical tone. The judge was busy with his docket; the lawyers, at their several little tables within the bar, lounged in their chairs, or stalked about laughing and whispering to each other; the prosecuting attorney leaned upon the shoulder of a jolly-looking man, who lifted his face to joke up at him, as he tilted his chair back; a very stout, youngish person, who sat next him, kept his face dropped, while the clerk proceeded:

"And now, on motion of plaintiff, it is ordered by the Court that said defendant be now here three times called, which is done in open court, and she comes not; but wholly makes default therein. And this cause is now submitted to the Court for trial, and the Court having heard the evidence, and being fully advised, find for the plaintiff—that the allegations of his complaint are true, and that he is entitled to a divorce. It is therefore considered by the Court that said plaintiff be and he is hereby divorced, and the bonds of matrimony heretofore existing between said parties are dissolved and held for naught."

As the clerk closed the large volume before him, the jolly lawyer, as if the record had been read at his request, nodded to the Court, and said, "The record of the decree seems correct, your honor." He leaned forward, and struck the fat man's expanse of back with the flat of his hand. "Congratulate you, my dear boy!" he said in a stage whisper that was heard through the room. "Many happy returns of the day!"

A laugh went round, and the judge said severely:

"Mr. Sheriff, see that order is kept in the court-room."

The fat man rose to shake hands with another friend, and at the same moment Squire Gaylord stretched himself to his full height before stooping over to touch the shoulder of one of the lawyers within the bar, and his eyes encountered those of Bartley Hubbard in mutual recognition.

It was not the fat on Bartley's ribs only that had increased: his broad cheeks stood out and hung down with it, and his chin descended by the three successive steps to his breast. His complexion was of a tender pink, on which his blonde moustache showed white; it almost vanished in the tallowy pallor to which the pink turned as he saw his father-in-law, and then the whole group which the intervening spectators had hitherto hidden from him. He dropped back into his chair, and intimated to his lawyer, with a wave of his hand and a twist of his head, that some hopeless turn in his fortunes had taken place. That jolly soul turned to him for explanation, and at the same time the lawyer whom Squire Gaylord had touched on the shoulder responded to a few whispered words from him by beckoning to the prosecuting attorney, who stepped briskly across to where they stood. A brief dumb-show ensued, and the prosecutor ended by taking the Squire's hand, and inviting him within the bar; the other attorney politely made room for him at his table, and the prosecutor returned to his place near the jury-box, where he remained standing for a moment.

"If it please the Court," he began, in a voice breaking heavily upon the silence that had somehow fallen upon the whole room, "I wish to state that the defendant in the case of Hubbard *vs.* Hubbard is now and here present, having been prevented, by an accident on the road between this place and Indianapolis, from arriving in time to make defense. She desires to move the Court to set aside the default."

The prosecutor retired a few paces, and nodded triumphantly at Bartley's lawyer, who could not wholly suppress his enjoyment of the joke, though it told so heavily against him and his client. But he was instantly on his feet with a technical objection.

The judge heard him through, and then opened his docket at the case of Hubbard *vs.* Hubbard. "What name shall I enter for the defense?" he inquired formally.

Squire Gaylord turned with an old-fashioned state and deliberation which had their effect, and cast a glance of professional satisfaction in the situation at the attorneys and the spectators. "I ask to be allowed to appear for the defense in this case, if the Court please. My friend, Mr. Hathaway, will move my admission to this bar."

The attorney to whom the Squire had first introduced himself promptly complied: "Your honor, I move the admission of Mr. F. J. Gaylord, of Equity, Equity County, Maine, to practice at this bar."

The judge bowed to the Squire, and directed the clerk to administer the usual oath. "I have entered your name for the defense, Mr. Gaylord. Do you desire to make any motion in the case?" he pursued, the natural courtesy of his manner further qualified by a feeling which something pathetic in the old Squire's bearing inspired.

"Yes, your honor, I move to set aside the default, and I shall offer in support of this motion my affidavit, setting forth the reasons for the non-appearance of the defendant at the calling of the cause."

"Shall I note your motion as filed?" asked the judge.

"Yes, your honor," replied the old man. He made a futile attempt to prepare the paper; the pen flew out of his trembling hand. "*I* can't write," he said in despair that made other hands quick to aid him. A young lawyer at the next desk rapidly drew up the paper, and the Squire duly offered it to the clerk of the Court. The clerk stamped it with the file-mark of the Court, and returned it to the Squire, who read aloud the motion and affidavit, setting forth the facts of the defendant's failure to receive the notice in time to prepare for her defense, and of the accident which had contributed to delay her appearance, declaring that she had a just defense to the plaintiff's bill, and asking to be heard upon the facts.

Bartley's attorney was prompt to interpose again. He protested that the printed advertisement was sufficient notice to the defendant, whenever it came to her knowledge, or even if it never came to her knowledge, and that her plea of failure to receive it in time was not a competent excuse. This might be alleged in any case, and any delay of travel might be brought forward to account for non-appearance as plausibly as this trumped-up accident in which nobody was hurt. He did his best, which was also his worst, and the judge once more addressed the Squire, who stood waiting for Bartley's counsel to close. "I was about to adjourn the Court," said the judge, in that accent which is the gift of the South to some parts of the West; it is curiously soft and gentle, and expressive, when the speaker will, of a caressing deference. "But we have still some minutes before noon in which we can hear you in support of your motion, if you are ready."

"I am mready, your honor!" The old man's nasals cut across the judge's rounded tones, almost before they had ceased. His lips compressed themselves to a waving line, and his high hawk-beak came down over them; the fierce light burned in his cavernous eyes, and his grizzled hair erected itself like a crest. He swayed slightly back and forth at the table, behind which he stood, and paused as if waiting for his hate to gather head.

In this interval it struck several of the spectators, who had appreciative friends outside, that it was a pity they should miss the coming music, and they risked the loss of some strains themselves that they might step out and inform these *dilettanti*. One of them was stopped by a man at the door. "What's up, now?" The other impatiently explained; but the inquirer, instead of hurrying in to enjoy the fun, turned quickly about, and ran down the stairs. He crossed the street, and, by a system of alleys and by-ways, modestly made his way to the outlying fields of Tecumseh, which he traversed at heightened speed, plunging at last into the belt of timber beyond. This excursion, which had so much the appearance of a chase, was an exigency of the witness who had corroborated on oath the testimony of Bartley in regard to his wife's desertion. Such an establishment of facts, purely imaginary with the witness, was simple enough in the absence of rebutting testimony; but, confronted with this, it became another affair—it had its embarrassments, its risks.

"Mready," repeated Squire Gaylord, "mready with facts and *witnesses!*" The word, in which he exulted till it rang and echoed through the room, drew the eyes of all to the little group on the bench next the bar, where Marcia, heavily veiled in the black which she had worn ever since Bartley's disappearance, sat with Halleck and Olive. The little girl, spent with her long journey, rested her head on her mother's lap, and the mother's hand tremulously smoothed her hair, and tried to hush the grieving whisper in which she incessantly repeated, "Where is papa? I want to see papa!"

Olive looked straight before her, and Halleck's eyes were fixed upon the floor. After the first glance at them, Bartley did not lift his head, but held it bent forward where he sat, and showed only a fold of fat red neck above his coat-collar. Marcia might have seen his face in that moment before it blanched and he sank into his chair; she did not look toward him again.

"Mr. Sheriff, keep silence in the Court!" ordered the judge, in reprimand of the stir that ensued upon the general effort to catch sight of the witnesses.

"Silence in the Court! Keep your seats, gentlemen!" cried the sheriff.

"And I thank the Court," resumed the Squire, "for this immediate opportunity to redress an atrocious wrong, and to vindicate an innocent and injured woman. Sir, I think it will prejudice our cause with no one, when I say that we are here not only in the relation of attorney and client, but in that of father and daughter, and that I stand in this place singularly and sacredly privileged to demand justice for my own child!"

"Order, order!" shouted the sheriff. But he could not quell the sensation that followed; the point had been effectively made, and it was some moments before the noise of the people beginning to arrive from the outside permitted the Squire to continue. He waited, with one lean hand hanging at his side, and the other resting in a loosely folded fist on the table before him. He took this fist up as if it were some implement he had laid hold of, and swung it in the air.

"By a chance which *I* shall not be the last to describe as providential,"—he paused, and looked round the room as if defying any one there to challenge the sincerity of his assertion,—"the notice, which your law requires to be given by newspaper advertisement to the non-resident defendant in such a case as this, came, by one chance in millions, to her hand. By one chance more or less, it would not have reached her, and a monstrous crime against justice would have been irrevocably accomplished. For she had mourned this man as dead,—dead to the universal frame of things, when he was only dead to honor, dead to duty, and dead to her; and it was that newspaper, sent almost at random through the mail, and wandering from hand to hand, and everywhere rejected, for weeks, before it reached her at last, which convinced her that he was still in such life as a man may live who has survived his own soul. We are therefore *here*, standing upon our right, and prepared to prove it God's right and the everlasting truth. Two days ago, a thousand miles and a thousand uncertainties intervened between us and this right, but *now* we are here to show that the defendant, basely defamed by the plea of abandonment, returned to her home within an hour after she had parted there with the plaintiff, and has remained there day and night ever since." He stopped. "Did I say she had never absented herself during all this time? I was wrong. I spoke hastily. I forgot." He dropped his voice. "She did absent herself at one time,—for three days,—while she could come home to close her mother's dying eyes, and help me to lay her in the grave!" He tried to close his lips firmly again, but the sinuous line was broken by a convulsive twitching. "Perhaps," he resumed with the utmost gentleness, "the plaintiff returned in this interval, and, finding her gone, was confirmed in his belief that she had abandoned him."

He felt blindly about on the table with his trembling hands, and his whole figure had a pathos that gave the old dress coat statuesque dignity. The spectators quietly changed their places, and occupied the benches near him, till Bartley was left sitting alone with his counsel. We are beginning to talk here at the East of the decline of oratory; but it is still a passion in the West, and his listeners now clustered about the Squire in keen appreciation of his power; it seemed to summon even the loiterers in the street, whose ascending tramp on the stairs continually made itself heard; the lawyers, the officers of the court, the judge, forgot their dinner, and posed themselves anew in their chairs to listen.

No doubt the electrical sphere of sympathy and admiration penetrated to the old man's consciousness. When he pulled off his black satin stock—the relic of ancient fashion which the piety of his daughter kept in repair—and laid it on the table, there was a deep, inarticulate murmur of satisfaction which he could not have mistaken. His voice rose again:

"If the plaintiff indeed came at that time, the walls of those empty rooms, into which he peered like a thief in the night, might have told him—if walls had tongues to speak as they have ears to hear—a tale that would have melted even *his* heart with remorse and shame. They might have told him of a woman waiting in hunger and cold for his return, and willing to starve and freeze, rather than own herself forsaken; waiting till she was hunted from her door by the creditors whom he had defrauded, and forced to confess her disgrace and her despair, in order to save herself from the unknown terrors of the law invoked upon her innocent head by his villainy. This is the history of the first two weeks of those two years, during which, as his perjured lips have sworn, he was using every effort to secure her return to him. I will not enlarge now upon this history, nor upon that of the days and weeks and months that followed, wringing the heart and all but crazing the brain of the wife who would not, in the darkest hours of her desolation, believe herself willfully abandoned. But we have the record, unbroken and irrefragable, which shall not only right his victim, but shall bring yonder perjurer to justice."

The words had an iron weight; they fell like blows. Bartley did not stir; but Marcia moved uneasily in her chair, and a low, pitiful murmur broke from behind her veil. Her father stopped again, panting, and his dry lips closed and parted several times before he could find his voice again. But at that sound of grief he partly recovered himself, and went on brokenly.

"I now ask this Court, for due cause, to set aside the default upon which judgment has been rendered against the defendant, and I shall then ask leave to file her cross-petition for divorce."

Marcia started half-way from her chair, and then fell back again; she looked round at Halleck as if for help, and hid her face in her hands. Her father cast a glance at her as if for her approval of this development of his plan.

"Then, may it please the Court, upon the rendition of judgment in our favor upon that petition—a result of which I have no more doubt than of my own existence—I shall demand under your law the indictment of yonder perjurer for his crime, and I shall await in security the sentence which shall consign him to a felon's cell in a felon's garb"—

Marcia flung herself upon her father's arm, outstretched toward Bartley.

"No! No! No!" she cried with deep, shuddering breaths, in a voice thick with horror. "Never! Let him go! I will not have it! I didn't understand! I never meant to harm him! Let him go! It is *my* cause, and I say"—

The old man's arm dropped; he fixed a ghastly, bewildered look upon his daughter, and fell across the table at which he stood. The judge started from his chair; the people leaped over the benches, and crushed about the Squire, who fetched his breath in convulsive gasps. "Keep back!" "Give him air!" "Open the window!" "Get a doctor!" cried those next him.

Even Bartley's counsel had joined the crowd about the Squire, from the midst of which broke the long, frightened wail of a child. This was Bartley's opportunity. When his counsel turned to look for him, and advise his withdrawal from a place where he could do no good, and where possibly he might come to harm, he found that his advice had been anticipated: Bartley's chair was vacant.

XLI

THAT NIGHT, when Halleck had left the old man to the care of Marcia and Olive, for the time, a note was brought to him from Bartley's lawyer, begging the favor of a few moments' interview on very important business. It might be some offer of reparation or advance in Marcia's interest, and Halleck went with the bearer of the note. The lawyer met him hospitably at the door of his office. "How do you do, sir?" he said, shaking hands. Then he indicated a bulk withdrawn into a corner of the dimly lighted room; the blinds were drawn, and he locked the door after Halleck's entrance. "Mr. Hubbard, whom I think you know," he added. "I'll just step into the next room, gentlemen, and will be subject to your call at any moment."

The bulk lifted itself and moved some paces toward Halleck; Bartley even raised his hand, with the vague expectation of taking Halleck's, but seeing no responsive gesture on his part, he waved a salutation and dropped it again to his side.

"How d'ye do, Halleck? Rather a secret, black, and midnight interview," he said jocosely. "But I couldn't very well manage it otherwise. I'm *not* just in the position to offer you the freedom of the city."

"What do you want, Hubbard?" asked Halleck, bluntly.

"How is the old Squire?"

"The doctor thinks he may rally from the shock."

"Paralysis?"

"Yes."

"I have spent the day in the 'tall timber,' as our friends out here say, communing with nature; and I've only just come into town since dark, so I hadn't any particulars." He paused, as if expecting that Halleck might give them; but, upon his remaining silent, he resumed. "Of course, as the case now stands, I know very well that the law can't touch me. But I didn't know what the popular feeling might be. The Squire laid it on pretty hot, and he might have made it livelier for me than he intended: he isn't aware of the inflammable nature of the material out here." He gave a nervous chuckle. "I wanted to see you, Halleck, to tell you that I haven't forgotten that money I owe you, and that I mean to pay it all up some time yet. If it hadn't been for some expenses I've had lately,—doctor's bills, and so forth,—I haven't been very well, myself,"—he made a sort of involuntary appeal for Halleck's sympathy,—"and I've had to pay out a good deal of money,—I should be able to pay most of it now. As it is, I can only give you five hundred of it." He tugged his portemonnaie with difficulty up the slope of his pantaloons. "That will leave me just three hundred to begin the world with; for of course I've got to clear out of *here*. And I'd got very comfortably settled after two years of pretty hard work at the printing business, and hard reading at the law. Well, it's all right. And I want to pay you this money, now, and I'll pay you the rest whenever I can. And I want you to tell Marcia that I did it. I always meant to do it."

"Hubbard," interrupted Halleck, "you don't owe me any money. Your father-in-law paid that debt two years ago. But you owe some one else a debt that no one can pay for you. We needn't waste words. What are you going to do to repair the wrong you have done the woman and the child"— He stopped; the effort had perhaps been too much.

Bartley saw his emotion, and in his benighted way he honored it. "Halleck, you are a good fellow. You are *such* a good fellow that you can't understand this thing. But it's played out. I felt badly about it myself, at one time; and if I hadn't been robbed of that money you lent me on my way here, I'd have gone back inside of forty-eight hours. I was sorry for Marcia; it almost broke my heart to think of the little one; but I knew they were in the hands of friends; and the more time I had to think it over, the more I was reconciled to what I had done. That was the only way out for either of us. We had tried it for three years, and we couldn't make it go; we never could have made it go; we were incompatible. Don't you suppose I knew Marcia's good qualities? No one knows them better, or appreciates them more. You might think that I applied for this divorce because I had some one else in view. Not any more in mine at present! But I thought we ought to be free, both of us; and if our marriage had become a chain, that we ought to break it." Bartley paused, apparently to give these facts and reasons time to sink into Halleck's mind. "But there's one thing I should like to have you tell her, Halleck: she was wrong about that girl; I never had anything to do with her. Marcia will understand." Halleck made no reply, and Bartley resumed, in a burst of generosity, which marked his fall into the abyss as nothing else could have done. "Look here, Halleck, I can't marry again for two years. But, as I understand the law, Marcia isn't bound in any way. I know that she always had a very high opinion of you, and that she thinks you are the best man in the world: why don't *you* fix it up with Marcia?"

Bartley was in effect driven into exile by the accidents of his suit for divorce which have been described. He was not in bodily danger after the first excitement passed off, if he was ever in bodily danger at all; but he could not reasonably hope to establish himself in a community which had witnessed such disagreeable facts concerning him; before which, indeed, he stood attainted of perjury, and only saved from the penalty of his crime by the refusal of his wife to press her case.

As soon as her father was strong enough to be removed, Marcia returned to the East with him, in the care of the friends who continued with them. They did not go back to Boston, but went directly to Equity, where in the first flush of the young and jubilant summer, they opened the dim old house at the end of the village street, and resumed their broken lives. Her father, with one side palsy-stricken, wavered out every morning to his office, and sat there all day, the tremulous shadow of his former will. Sometimes his old friends came in to see him, but no one expected now to hear the Squire "get going." He no longer got going on any topic; he had become as a little child—as the little child that played about him there, in the still, warm summer days and built houses with his law-books on the floor. He laughed feebly at her pranks, and submitted to her rule with pathetic meekness in everything where Marcia had not charged them both to the contrary. He was very obedient to Marcia, who looked vigilantly after his welfare, and knew all his goings and comings, as she knew those of her little comrade. Two or three times a day she ran out to see that they were safe; but for the rest she kept herself closely housed, and saw no one whom she was not forced to see; only the meat-man and the fish-man could speak authoritatively concerning her appearance and behavior before folks. They reported the latter as dry, cold, and uncommunicative. Doubtless the bitter experiences of her life had wrought their due effect in that passionate heart; but probably it was as much a morbid sensitiveness as a hardened indifference that turned her from her kind. The village inquisitiveness that invades, also suffers much eccentricity; and after it had been well ascertained that Marcia was as queer as her mother, she was allowed to lead her mother's unmolested life in the old house, which had always turned so cold a shoulder to the world. Toward the end of the summer the lame young man and his sister, who had been several times in Equity before, paid her a visit; but stayed only a day or two, as was accurately known by persons who had noted the opening and closing of the spare-chamber blinds. In the winter he came again, but this time he came alone, and stayed at the hotel. He remained over a Sunday, and sat in the pulpit of the Orthodox church, where the minister extended to him the right hand of fellowship, and invited him to make the opening prayer. It was considered a good prayer, generally speaking, but it was criticised as not containing anything attractive to young people. He was understood to be on his way to take charge of a backwoods church down in Aroostook County, where probably his prayers would be more acceptable to the popular taste.

That winter Squire Gaylord had another stroke of paralysis, and late in the following spring he succumbed to a third. The old minister who had once been Mrs. Gaylord's pastor was now dead; and the Squire was buried by the lame man, who came up to Equity for that purpose, at the wish, often expressed, of the deceased. This at least was the common report, and it is certain that Halleck officiated.

In entering the ministry, he had returned to the faith which had been taught him almost before he could speak. He did not defend or justify this course on the part of a man who had once thrown off all allegiance to creeds; he said simply that for him there was no other course. He freely granted that he had not reasoned back to his old faith; he had fled to it as to a city of refuge. His unbelief had been helped, and he no longer suffered himself to doubt; he did not ask if the truth was here or there, any more; he only knew that he could not find it for himself, and he rested in his inherited belief. He accepted everything; if he took one jot or tittle away from the Book, the curse of doubt was on him. He had known the terrors of the law, and he preached them to his people; he had known the Divine mercy, and he also preached that.

The Squire's death occurred a few months before the news came of another event to which the press of the State referred with due recognition, but without great fullness of detail. This was the fatal case of shooting which occurred at Whited Sepulchre, Arizona, where Bartley Hubbard pitched his tent, and set up a printing-press after leaving Tecumseh. He began with the issue of a Sunday paper, and made it so spicy and so indispensable to all the residents of Whited Sepulchre, who enjoyed the study of their fellow-citizens' affairs, that he was looking hopefully forward to the establishment of a daily edition, when he unfortunately chanced to comment upon the domestic relations of "one of Whited Sepulchre's leading citizens." The leading citizen promptly took the war-path, as an esteemed contemporary expressed it, in reporting the difficulty with the cynical lightness and the profusion of felicitous head-lines with which our journalism often alleviates the history of tragic occurrences: the parenthetical truth in the closing statement, that "Mr. Hubbard leaves a (divorced) wife and child somewhere at the East," was quite in Bartley's own manner.

Marcia had been widowed so long before that this event,—consequence or penalty, as we choose to think it,—could make no outward change in her. What inner change, if any, it wrought, is one of those facts which fiction must seek in vain to disclose. But, if love such as hers had been did not deny his end the pang of a fresh grief, we may be sure that her sorrow was not unmixed with self-accusal as unavailing as it was passionate, and perhaps as unjust.

One evening, a year later, the Athertons sat talking over a letter from Halleck, which Atherton had brought from Boston with him. It was summer, and they were at their place on the Beverly shore. It was a long letter, and Atherton had read parts of it several times already, on his way down in the cars, and had since read it all to his wife. "It's a very morbid letter," he said, with a perplexed air, when he had finished.

"Yes," she assented. "But it's a very *good* letter. Poor Ben!"

Her husband took it up again, and read here and there a passage from it.

"But I am turning to you now for help in a matter on which my own conscience throws such a fitful and uncertain light that I cannot trust it. I know that you are a good man, Atherton, and I humbly beseech you to let me have your judgment without mercy: though it slay me, I will abide by it. . . . Since her father's death, she lives there quite alone with her child. I have seen her only once, but we write to each other, and there are times when it seems to me at last that I have the right to ask her to be my wife. The words give me a shock as I write them; and the things which I used to think reasons for my right rise up in witness against me. Above all, I remember with horror that *he* approved it, that he advised it!

". . . . It is true that I have never, by word or deed, suffered her to know what was in my heart; but has there ever been a moment when I could do so? It is true that I have waited for his death; but, if I have been willing he should die, am I not a potential murderer!"

"Oh, what ridiculous nonsense!" Clara indignantly protested.

Atherton read on: "These are the questions which I ask myself in my despair. She is free, now; but am I free? Am I not rather bound by the past to perpetual silence? There are times when I rebel against these tortures; when I feel a sanction for my love of her, an assurance from somewhere that it is right and good to love her; but then I sink again, for, if I ask whence this assurance comes—I beseech you to tell me what you think. Has my offence been so great that nothing can atone for it? Must I sacrifice to this fear all my hopes of what I could be to her, and for her?"

Atherton folded up the letter, and put it back into its envelope, with a frown of exasperation. "I can't see what should have infatuated Halleck with that woman. I don't believe now that he loves her; I believe he only pities her. She is altogether inferior to him: passionate, narrow-minded, jealous—she would make him miserable. He'd much better stay as he is. If it were not pathetic to have him deifying her in this way, it would be laughable."

"She had a jealous temperament," said Clara, looking down. "But all the Hallecks are fond of her. They think there is a great deal of good in her. I don't suppose Ben himself thinks she is perfect. But"—

"I dare say," interrupted her husband, "that he thinks he's entirely sincere in asking my advice. But you can see how he *wishes* to be advised."

"Of course. He wishes to marry her. It isn't so much a question of what a man ought to have, as what he wants to have, in marrying, is it? Even the best of men. If she *is* exacting and quick-tempered, he is good enough to get on with her. If she had a husband that she could thoroughly trust, she would be easy enough to get on with. There is no woman good enough to get on with a bad man. It's terrible to think of that poor creature living there by herself, with no one to look after her and her little girl; and if Ben"—

"What do you mean, Clara? Don't you see that his being in love with her when she was another man's wife is what he feels it to be—an indelible stain?"

"She never knew it; and no one ever knew it but you. You said it was our deeds that judged us. Didn't Ben go away when he realized his feeling for her?"

"He came back."

"But he did everything he could to find that poor wretch, and he tried to prevent the divorce. Ben is morbid about it; but there is no use in our being so."

"There was a time when he would have been glad to profit by a divorce."

"But he never did. You said the will didn't count. And now she is a widow, and any man may ask her to marry him."

"Any man but the one who loved her during her husband's life. That is, if he is such a man as Halleck. Of course, it isn't a question of mere right and wrong, of gross black and white—there are degrees, there are shades; there might be redemption for another sort of man in such a marriage; but for Halleck there could only be loss—deterioration—lapse from the ideal. I should think he might suffer something of this even in her eyes"—

"Oh, how hard you are! I wish Ben hadn't asked your advice. Why, you are worse than he is! You're *not* going to write that to him?"

Atherton flung the letter upon the table, and drew a troubled sigh. "Ah, I don't know! I don't know!"

INDIAN SUMMER

I

MIDWAY of the Ponte Vecchio at Florence, where three
arches break the line of the little jewellers' booths glittering on either hand, and open an approach to the parapet,
Colville lounged against the corner of a shop and stared out
upon the river. It was the late afternoon of a day in January,
which had begun bright and warm, but had suffered a change
of mood as its hours passed, and now from a sky dimmed
with flying gray clouds was threatening rain. There must already have been rain in the mountains, for the yellow torrent
that seethed and swirled around the piers of the bridge was
swelling momently on the wall of the Lung' Arno, and rolling
a threatening flood toward the Cascine, where it lost itself
under the ranks of the poplars that seemed to file across its
course, and let their delicate tops melt into the pallor of the
low horizon.

The city, with the sweep of the Lung' Arno on either hand,
and its domes and towers hung in the dull air, and the country with its white villas and black cypresses breaking the gray
stretches of the olive orchards on its hill-sides, had alike been
growing more and more insufferable; and Colville was finding a sort of vindictive satisfaction in the power to ignore the
surrounding frippery of landscape and architecture. He isolated himself so perfectly from it, as he brooded upon the
river, that, for any sensible difference, he might have been
standing on the Main Street Bridge at Des Vaches, Indiana,
looking down at the tawny sweep of the Wabash. He had no
love for that stream, nor for the ambitious town on its banks,
but ever since he woke that morning he had felt a growing
conviction that he had been a great ass to leave them. He
had, in fact, taken the prodigious risk of breaking his life
sharp off from the course in which it had been set for many
years, and of attempting to renew it in a direction from which
it had long been diverted. Such an act could be precipitated only by a strong impulse of conscience, or a profound
disgust, and with Colville it sprang from disgust. He had
experienced a bitter disappointment in the city to whose pros-

perity he had given the energies of his best years, and in whose favor he imagined that he had triumphantly established himself.

He had certainly made the Des Vaches *Democrat-Republican* a very good paper; its ability was recognized throughout the State, and in Des Vaches people of all parties were proud of it. They liked every morning to see what Colville said; they believed that in his way he was the smartest man in the State, and they were fond of claiming that there was no such writer on any of the Indianapolis papers. They forgave some political heresies to the talent they admired; they permitted him the whim of free trade, they laughed tolerantly when he came out in favor of civil service reform, and no one had much fault to find when the *Democrat-Republican* bolted the nomination of a certain politician of its party for Congress. But when Colville permitted his own name to be used by the opposing party, the people arose in their might and defeated him by a tremendous majority. That was what the regular nominee said. It was a withering rebuke to treason, in the opinion of this gentleman; it was a good joke, anyway, with the Democratic managers who had taken Colville up, being all in the Republican family; whichever it was, it was a mortification for Colville which his pride could not brook. He stood disgraced before the community not only as a theorist and unpractical doctrinaire, but as a dangerous man; and what was worse, he could not wholly acquit himself of a measure of bad faith; his conscience troubled him even more than his pride. Money was found, and a printer bought up with it to start a paper in opposition to the *Democrat-Republican*. Then Colville contemptuously offered to sell out to the Republican committee in charge of the new enterprise, and they accepted his terms.

In private life he found much of the old kindness returning to him; and his successful opponent took the first opportunity of heaping coals of fire on his head in the public street, when he appeared to the outer eye to be shaking hands with Colville. During the months that he remained to close up his affairs after the sale of his paper, the *Post-Democrat-Republican* (the newspaper had agglutinated the titles of two of its predecessors, after the fashion of American journals) was fulsome in its complimentary allusions to him. It politely invented the fiction that he was going to Europe for his health, impaired by his journalistic labors, and adventurously promised its readers that they might hope to hear from him from time to time in its columns. In some of its allusions to him Colville detected the point of a fine irony, of which he had himself introduced the practice in the *Democrat-Republican*; and he experienced, with a sense of personal impoverishment, the curious fact that a journalist of strong characteristics leaves the tradition of himself in such degree with the journal he has created that he seems to bring very little away. He was obliged to confess in his own heart that the paper was as good as ever. The assistants, who had trained themselves to write like him, seemed to be writing quite as well, and his honesty would not permit him to receive the consolation offered him by the friends who told him that there was a great falling off in the *Post-Democrat-Republican*. Except that it was rather more Stalwart in its Republicanism, and had turned quite round on the question of the tariff, it was very much what it had always been. It kept the old decency of tone which he had given it, and it maintained the literary character which he was proud of. The new management must have divined that its popularity, with the women at least, was largely due to its careful selections of verse and fiction, its literary news, and its full and piquant criticisms, with their long extracts from new books. It was some time since he had personally looked after this department, and the young fellow in charge of it under him had remained with the paper. Its continued excellence, which he could not have denied if he had wished, seemed to leave him drained and feeble, and it was partly from the sense of this that he declined the overtures, well backed up with money, to establish an independent paper in Des Vaches. He felt that there was not fight enough in him for the work, even if he had not taken that strong disgust for public life which included the place and its people. He wanted to get away, to get far away, and with the abrupt and total change in his humor he reverted to a period in his life when journalism and politics and the ambition of Congress were things undreamed of.

At that period he was a very young architect, with an inclination toward the literary side of his profession, which made it seem profitable to linger, with his Ruskin in his hand, among the masterpieces of Italian Gothic, when perhaps he might have been better employed in designing red-roofed, many-verandaed, consciously-mullioned sea-side cottages on the New England coast. He wrote a magazine paper on the zoology of the Lombardic pillars in Verona, very Ruskinian, very scornful of modern motive. He visited every part of the peninsula, but he gave the greater part of his time to North Italy, and in Venice he met the young girl whom he followed to Florence. His love did not prosper; when she went away she left him in possession of that treasure to a man of his temperament, a broken heart. From that time his vague dreams began to lift, and to let him live in the clear light of common day; but he was still lingering at Florence, ignorant of the good which had befallen him, and cowering within himself under the sting of wounded vanity, when he received a letter from his elder brother suggesting that he should come and see how he liked the architecture of Des Vaches. His brother had been seven years at Des Vaches, where he had lands, and a lead mine, and a scheme for a railroad, and had lately added a daily newspaper to his other enterprises. He had, in fact, added two newspapers; for having unexpectedly and almost involuntarily become the owner of the Des Vaches *Republican*, the fancy of building up a great local journal seized him, and he bought the *Wabash Valley Democrat*, uniting them under the name of the *Democrat-Republican*. But he had trouble almost from the first with his editors, and he naturally thought of the brother with a turn for writing who had been running to waste for the last year or two in Europe. His real purpose was to work Colville into the management of his paper when he invited him to come out and look at the architecture of Des Vaches.

Colville went, because he was at that moment in the humor to go anywhere, and because his money was running low, and he must begin work somehow. He was still romantic enough to like the notion of the place a little because it bore the name given to it by the old French *voyageurs* from a herd of buffalo cows which they had seen grazing on the site of their camp there; but when he came to the place itself he did not like it.

He hated it; but he staid, and as an architect was the last thing any one wanted in Des Vaches, since the jail and courthouse had been built, he became, half without his willing it, a newspaper man. He learned in time to relish the humorous intimacy of the life about him, and when it was decided that he was no fool—there were doubts, growing out of his Eastern accent and the work of his New York tailor, at first—he found himself the object of a pleasing popularity. In due time he bought his brother out; he became very fond of newspaper life, its constant excitements and its endless variety; and six weeks before he sold his paper he would have scoffed at a prophecy of his return to Europe for the resumption of any artistic purpose whatever. But here he was, lounging on the Ponte Vecchio at Florence, whither he had come with the intention of rubbing up his former studies, and of perhaps getting back to put them in practice at New York ultimately. He had said to himself before coming abroad that he was in no hurry; that he should take it very easily—he had money enough for that; yet he would keep architecture before him as an object, for he had lived long in a community where every one was intensely occupied, and he unconsciously paid to Des Vaches the tribute of feeling that an objectless life was disgraceful to a man.

In the mean time he suffered keenly and at every moment the loss of the occupation of which he had bereaved himself: in thinking of quite other things, in talk of totally different matters, from the dreams of night, he woke with a start to the realization of the fact that he had no longer a newspaper. He perceived now, as never before, that for fifteen years almost every breath of his life had been drawn with reference to his paper, and that without it he was in some sort lost and as it were extinct. A tide of ridiculous homesickness, which was an expression of this passionate regret for the life he had put behind him, rather than any longing for Des Vaches, swept over him, and the first passages of a letter to the *Post-Democrat-Republican* began to shape themselves in his mind. He had always, when he left home for New York or Washington, or for his few weeks of summer vacation on the Canadian rivers or the New England coast, written back to his readers, in whom he knew he could count upon quick sympathy in all he saw and felt, and he now found himself addressing them with that frank familiarity which comes to the journalist, in minor communities, from the habit of print. He began by confessing to them the defeat of certain expectations with which he had returned to Florence, and told them that they must not look for anything like the ordinary letters of travel from him. But he was not so singular in his attitude toward the place as he supposed; for any tourist who comes to Florence with the old-fashioned expectation of impressions will probably suffer a disappointment, unless he arrives very young and for the first time. It is a city superficially so well known that it affects one somewhat like a collection of views of itself: they are from the most striking points, of course, but one has examined them before, and is disposed to be critical of them. Certain emotions, certain sensations, failed to repeat themselves to Colville at sight of the familiar monuments, which seemed to wear a hardy and indifferent air, as if being stared at so many years by so many thousands of travellers had extinguished in them that sensibility which one likes to fancy in objects of interest everywhere.

The life which was as vivid all about him as if caught by the latest instantaneous process made the same comparatively ineffective appeal. The operatic spectacle was still there. The people, with their cloaks statuesquely draped over their left shoulders, moved down the street, or posed in vehement dialogue on the sidewalks; the drama of bargaining, with the customer's scorn, the shop-man's pathos, came through the open shop door; the handsome, heavy-eyed ladies, the bareheaded girls, thronged the ways; the caffès were full of the well-remembered figures over their newspapers and little cups; the officers were as splendid as of old, with their long cigars in their mouths, their swords kicking against their beautiful legs, and their spurs jingling; the dandies, with their little dogs and their flower-like smiles, were still in front of the confectioners' for the inspection of the ladies who passed; the old beggar still crouched over her *scaldino* at the church door, and the young man with one leg, whom he thought to escape by walking fast, had timed him to a second from the other side of the street. There was the wonted warmth in the sunny squares, and the old familiar damp and stench in the deep, narrow streets. But some charm had gone out of all this. The artisans coming to the doors of their shallow booths for the light on some bit of carpentering, or cobbling, or tinkering; the crowds swarming through the middle of the streets on perfect terms with the wine carts and cab horses; the ineffective grandiosity of the palaces huddled upon the crooked thoroughfares; the slight but insinuating cold of the southern winter, gathering in the shade and dispersing in the sun, and denied everywhere by the profusion of fruit and flowers, and by the greenery of gardens showing through the grated portals and over the tops of high walls; the groups of idle poor permanently or temporarily propped against the bases of edifices with a southern exposure; the priests and monks and nuns in their gliding passage; the impassioned snapping of the cabmen's whips; the clangor of bells that at some hours inundated the city, and then suddenly subsided and left it to the banging of coppersmiths; the open-air frying of cakes, with its primitive smell of burning fat; the tramp of soldiery, and the fanfare of bugles blown to gay measures—these and a hundred other characteristic traits and facts still found a response in the consciousness where they were once a rapture of novelty; but the response was faint and thin; he could not warm over the old mood in which he once treasured them all away as of equal preciousness.

Of course there was a pleasure in recognizing some details of former experience in Florence as they recurred. Colville had been met at once by a *festa*, when nothing could be done, and he was more than consoled by the caressing sympathy with which he was assured that his broken trunk could not be mended till the day after to-morrow; he had quite forgotten about the festas and the sympathy. That night the piazza on which he lodged seemed full of snow to the casual glance he gave it; then he saw that it was the white Italian moonlight, which he had also forgotten. . . .

II

COLVILLE had reached this point in that sarcastic study of his own condition of mind for the advantage of his late readers in the *Post-Democrat-Republican*, when he was aware of a polite rustling of draperies, with an ensuing well-bred murmur, which at once ignored him, deprecated intrusion upon him, and asserted a common right to the prospect on which he had been dwelling alone. He looked round with an instinctive expectation of style and poise, in which he was not disappointed. The lady, with a graceful lift of the head and a very erect carriage, almost Bernhardtesque in the backward fling of her shoulders and the strict compression of her elbows to her side, was pointing out the different bridges to the little girl who was with her.

"That first one is the Santa Trinità, and the next is the Carraja, and that one quite down by the Cascine is the iron bridge. The Cascine, you remember—the park where we were driving—that clump of woods there—"

A vagueness expressive of divided interest had crept into the lady's tone rather than her words. Colville could feel that she was waiting for the right moment to turn her delicate head, sculpturesquely defined by its toque, and steal an imperceptible glance at him; and he involuntarily afforded her the coveted excuse by the slight noise he made in changing his position in order to be able to go away as soon as he had seen whether she was pretty or not. At forty-one the question is still important to every man with regard to every woman.

"Mr. Colville!"

The gentle surprise conveyed in the exclamation, without time for recognition, convinced Colville, upon a cool review of the facts, that the lady had known him before their eyes met.

"Why, Mrs. Bowen!" he said.

She put out her round, slender arm, and gave him a frank clasp of her gloved hand. The glove wrinkled richly up the sleeve of her dress half-way to her elbow. She bent on his face a demand for just what quality and degree of change he found in hers, and apparently she satisfied herself that his inspection was not to her disadvantage, for she smiled brightly, and devoted the rest of her glance to an electric summary of the facts of Colville's physiognomy: the sufficiently good outline of his visage, with its full, rather close-cut drabbish-brown beard and mustache, both shaped a little by the ironical self-conscious smile that lurked under them; the non-committal, rather weary-looking eyes; the brown hair, slightly frosted, that showed while he stood with his hat still off. He was a little above the middle height, and if it must be confessed, neither his face nor his figure had quite preserved their youthful lines. They were both much heavier than when Mrs. Bowen saw them last, and the latter here and there swayed beyond the strict bounds of symmetry. She was herself in that moment of life when, to the middle-aged observer, at least, a woman's looks have a charm which is wanting to her earlier bloom. By that time her character has wrought itself more clearly out in her face, and her heart and mind confront you more directly there. It is the youth of her spirit which has come to the surface.

"I should have known you anywhere," she exclaimed, with friendly pleasure in seeing him.

"You are very kind," said Colville. "I didn't know that I had preserved my youthful beauty to that degree. But I can imagine it—if you say so, Mrs. Bowen."

"Oh, I assure you that you have!" she protested; and now she began gently to pursue him with one fine question after another about himself, till she had mastered the main facts of his history since they had last met. He would not have known so well how to possess himself of hers, even if he had felt the same necessity; but in fact it had happened that he had heard of her from time to time at not very long intervals. She had married a leading lawyer of her Western city, who in due time had gone to Congress, and after his term was out, had "taken up his residence" in Washington, as the newspapers said, "in his elegant mansion at the corner of & Street and Idaho Avenue." After that he remembered reading that Mrs. Bowen was going abroad for the education of her daughter, from which he made his own inferences concerning her marriage. And "You knew Mr. Bowen was no longer living?" she said, with fit obsequy of tone.

"Yes, I knew," he answered, with decent sympathy.

"This is my little Effie," said Mrs. Bowen, after a moment; and now the child, hitherto keeping herself discreetly in the background, came forward and promptly gave her hand to Colville, who perceived that she was not so small as he had thought her at first; an effect of infancy had possibly been studied in the brevity of her skirts and the immaturity of her corsage, but both were in good taste, and really to the advantage of her young figure. There was reason and justice in her being dressed as she was, for she was really not so old as she looked by two or three years; and there was reason in Mrs. Bowen's carrying in the hollow of her left arm the India shawl sacque she had taken off and hung there; the deep cherry silk lining gave life to the sombre tints prevailing in her dress, which its removal left free to express all the grace of her extremely lady-like person. Lady-like was the word for Mrs. Bowen throughout—for the turn of her head, the management of her arm from the elbow, the curve of her hand from wrist to finger-tips, the smile, subdued, but sufficiently sweet, playing about her little mouth, which was yet not too little, and the refined and indefinite perfume which exhaled from the ensemble of her silks, 'her laces, and her gloves, like an odorous version of that otherwise impalpable quality which women call style. She had, with all her flexibility, a certain charming stiffness, like the stiffness of a very tall feather.

"And have you been here a great while?" she asked, turning her head slowly toward Colville, and looking at him with a little difficulty she had in raising her eyelids: when she was younger the glance that shyly stole from under the covert of their lashes was like a gleam of sunshine, and it was still like a gleam of paler sunshine.

Colville, whose mood was very susceptible to the weather, brightened in the ray. "I only arrived last night," he said, with a smile.

"How glad you must be to get back! Did you ever see Florence more beautiful than it was this morning?"

"Not for years," said Colville, with another smile for her pretty enthusiasm. "Not for seventeen years at the least calculation."

"Is it so many?" cried Mrs. Bowen, with lovely dismay. "Yes, it is," she sighed, and she did not speak for an appreciable interval.

He knew that she was thinking of that old love affair of his, to which she was privy in some degree, though he never could tell how much; and when she spoke he perceived that she purposely avoided speaking of a certain person, whom a woman of more tact or of less would have insisted upon naming at once. "I never can believe in the lapse of time when I get back to Italy; it always makes me feel as young as when I left it last."

"I could imagine you'd never left it," said Colville.

Mrs. Bowen reflected a moment. "Is that a compliment?"

"I had an obscure intention of saying something fine; but I don't think I've quite made it out," he owned.

Mrs. Bowen gave her small, sweet smile. "It was very nice of you to try. But I haven't really been away for some time; I've taken a house in Florence, and I've been here two years. Palazzo Pinti, Lung' Arno della Zecca. You must come and see me. Thursdays from four till six."

"Thank you," said Colville.

"I'm afraid," said Mrs. Bowen, remotely preparing to offer her hand in adieu, "that Effie and I broke in upon some very important cogitations of yours." She shifted the silken burden of her arm a little, and the child stirred from the correct pose she had been keeping, and smiled politely.

"I don't think they deserve a real dictionary word like that," said Colville. "I was simply mooning. If there was anything definite in my mind, I was wishing that I was looking down on the Wabash in Des Vaches, instead of the Arno in Florence."

"Oh! And I supposed you must be indulging all sorts of historical associations with the place. Effie and I have been walking through the Via de' Bardi, where Romola lived, and I was bringing her back over the Ponte Vecchio, so as to impress the origin of Florence on her mind."

"Is that what makes Miss Effie hate it?" asked Colville, looking at the child, whose youthful resemblance to her mother was in all things so perfect that a fantastic question whether she could ever have had any other parent swept through him. Certainly, if Mrs. Bowen were to marry again, there was nothing in this child's looks to suggest the idea of a predecessor to the second husband.

"Effie doesn't hate any sort of useful knowledge," said her mother, half jestingly. "She's just come to me from school at Vevay."

"Oh, then, I think she might," persisted Colville. "Don't you hate the origin of Florence a little?" he asked of the child.

"I don't know enough about it," she answered, with a quick look of question at her mother, and checking herself in a possibly indiscreet smile.

"Ah, that accounts for it," said Colville, and he laughed. It amused him to see the child referring even this point of propriety to her mother, and his thoughts idled off to what Mrs. Bowen's own untrammelled girlhood must have been in her Western city. For her daughter there were to be no buggy rides or concerts or dances at the invitation of young men; no picnics, free and unchaperoned as the casing air; no sitting on the steps at dusk with callers who never dreamed of asking for her mother; no lingering at the gate with her youthful escort home from the ball—nothing of that wild, sweet liberty which once made American girlhood a long rapture. But would she be any the better for her privations, for referring not only every point of conduct, but every thought and feeling, to her mother? He suppressed a sigh for the inevitable change, but rejoiced that his own youth had fallen in the earlier time, and said, "You will hate it as soon as you've read a little of it."

"The difficulty *is* to read a little of Florentine history. I can't find anything in less than ten or twelve volumes," said Mrs. Bowen. "Effie and I were going to Vieusseux's Library again, in desperation, to see if there wasn't something shorter in French."

She now offered Colville her hand, and he found himself very reluctant to let it go. Something in her looks did not forbid him, and when she took her hand away, he said, "Let me go to Vieusseux's with you, Mrs. Bowen, and give you the advantage of my unprejudiced ignorance in the choice of a book on Florence."

"Oh, I was longing to ask you!" said Mrs. Bowen, frankly. "It is really such a serious matter, especially when the book is for a young person. Unless it's very dry, it's so apt to be—objectionable."

"Yes," said Colville, with a smile at her perplexity. He moved off down the slope of the bridge with her, between the jewellers' shops, and felt a singular satisfaction in her company. Women of fashion always interested him; he liked them; it diverted him that they should take themselves seriously. Their resolution, their suffering for their ideal, such as it was, their energy in dressing and adorning themselves, the pains they were at to achieve the trivialties they passed their lives in, were perpetually delightful to him. He often found them people of great simplicity, and sometimes of singularly good sense; their frequent vein of piety was delicious.

Ten minutes earlier, he would have said that nothing could have been less welcome to him than this encounter, but now he felt unwilling to leave Mrs. Bowen.

"Go before, Effie," she said; and she added, to Colville, "How very Florentine all this is! If you dropped from the clouds on this spot without previous warning, you would know that you were on the Ponte Vecchio, and nowhere else."

"Yes, it's very Florentine," Colville assented. "The bridge is very well as a bridge, but as a street I prefer the Main Street Bridge at Des Vaches. I was looking at the jewelry before you came up, and I don't think it's pretty, even the old pieces of peasant jewelry. Why do people come here to look at it? If you were going to buy something for a friend, would you dream of coming here for it?"

"Oh *no*!" replied Mrs. Bowen, with the deepest feeling.

They quitted the bridge, and turning to the left, moved down the street, which with difficulty finds space between the parapet of the river and the shops of the mosaicists and dealers in statuary cramping it on the other hand.

"Here's something distinctively Florentine too," said Colville. "These table-tops, and paper-weights, and caskets, and photograph frames, and lockets, and breast-pins; and here, this ghostly glare of under-sized Psyches and Hebes and Graces in alabaster."

"Oh, you mustn't think of any of them!" Mrs. Bowen broke in, with horror. "If your friend wishes you to get her something characteristically Florentine, and at the same time very tasteful, you must go—"

Colville gave a melancholy laugh. "My friend is an abstraction, Mrs. Bowen, without sex or any sort of entity."

"Oh!" said Mrs. Bowen. Some fine drops had begun to sprinkle the pavement. "What a ridiculous blunder! It's raining! Effie, I'm afraid we must give up your book for to-day. We're not dressed for damp weather, and we'd better hurry home as soon as possible." She got promptly into the shelter of a doorway, and gathered her daughter to her, while she flung her sacque over her shoulder, and caught her draperies from the ground for the next movement. "Mr. Colville, will you please stop the first closed carriage that comes in sight?"

A figure of *primo tenore* had witnessed the manœuvre from the box of his cab; he held up his whip, and at a nod from Colville he drove abreast of the doorway his broken-kneed, tremulous little horse, gay in brass-mounted harness, and with a stiff turkey feather stuck upright at one ear in his head-stall.

Mrs. Bowen had no more scruple than another woman in stopping travel and traffic in a public street for her convenience. She now entered into a brisk parting conversation with Colville, such as ladies love, blocking the narrow side-walk with herself, her daughter, and her open carriage door, and making people walk round her cab, in the road, which they did meekly enough, with the Florentine submissiveness to the pretensions of any sort of vehicle. She said a dozen important things that seemed to have just come into her head, and, "Why, how stupid I am!" she called out, making Colville check the driver in his first start, after she had got into the cab. "We are to have a few people to-night. If you have no engagement, I should be so glad to have you come. Can't you?"

"Yes, I can," said Colville, admiring the whole transaction and the parties to it with a passive smile.

After finding her pocket, she found that her card-case was not in it, but in the purse she had given Effie to carry; but she got her address at last, and gave it to Colville, though he said he should remember it without. "Any time between nine and eleven," she said. "It's so nice of you to promise!"

She questioned him from under her half-lifted eyelids, and he added, with a laugh, "I'll come!" and was rewarded with two pretty smiles, just alike, from mother and daughter, as they drove away.

III

Twenty years earlier, when Mrs. Bowen was Miss Lina Ridgely, she used to be the friend and confidante of the girl who jilted Colville. They were then both so young that they could scarcely have been a year out of school before they left home for the year they were spending in Europe; but to the young man's inexperience they seemed the wisest and maturest of society women. His heart quaked in his breast when he saw them talking and laughing together, for fear they should be talking and laughing about him; he was even a little more afraid of Miss Ridgely than of her friend, who was dashing and effective, where Miss Ridgely was serene and elegant, according to his feeling at that time. He never saw her after his rejection, and it was not till he read of her marriage with the Hon. Mr. Bowen that certain vague impressions began to define themselves. He then remembered that Lina Ridgely in many fine little ways had shown a kindness, almost a compassion, for him, as for one whose unconsciousness a hopeless doom impended over. He perceived that she had always seemed to like him—a thing that had not occurred to him in the stupid absorption of his passion for the other—and fragments of proof that she had probably defended and advocated him occurred to him, and inspired a vain and retrospective gratitude; he abandoned himself to regrets, which were proper enough in regard to Miss Ridgely, but were certainly a little unlawful concerning Mrs. Bowen.

As he walked away toward his hotel he amused himself with the conjecture whether he, with his forty-one years and his hundred and eighty-five pounds, were not still a pathetic and even a romantic figure to this pretty and kindly woman, who probably imagined him as heart-broken as ever. He was very willing to see more of her, if she wished; but with the rain beginning to fall more thick and chill in the darkening street, he could have postponed their next meeting till a pleasanter evening without great self-denial. He felt a little twinge of rheumatism in his shoulder when he got into his room, for your room in a Florentine hotel is always some degrees colder than out-doors, unless you have fire in it; and with the sun shining on his windows when he went out after lunch, it had seemed to Colville ridiculous to have his morning fire kept up. The sun was what he had taken the room for. It was in it, the landlord assured him, from ten in the morning till four in the afternoon; and so, in fact, it was, when it shone; but even then it was not fully in it, but had a trick of looking in at the sides of the window, and painting the chamber wall with a delusive glow. Colville raked away the ashes of his fire-place, and throwing on two or three fagots of broom and pine sprays, he had a blaze that would be very pretty to dress by after dinner, but that gave out no warmth for the present. He left it, and went down to the Reading-Room, as it was labelled over the door, in homage to a predominance of English-speaking people among the guests; but there was no fire there; that was kindled only by request, and he shivered at the bare aspect of the apartment, with its cold piano, its locked book-cases, and its table, where the London *Times*, the *Neue Freie Presse* of Vienna, and the *Italie* of Rome exposed their titles, one just beyond the margin of the other. He turned from the door and went into the dining-room, where the stove was ostentatiously roaring over its small logs and its lozenges of peat. But even here the fire had been so recently lighted that the warmth was potential rather than actual. By stooping down before the stove, and pressing his shoulder against its brass doors, Colville managed to lull his enemy, while he studied the figures of the woman-headed, woman-breasted hounds developing into vines and foliage that covered the frescoed trellising of the quadrangularly vaulted ceiling. The waiters, in their veteran dress-coats, were putting the final touches to the table, and the sound of voices outside the door obliged Colville to get up. The effort involved made him still more reluctant about going out to Mrs. Bowen's.

The door opened, and some English ladies entered, faintly acknowledging, provisionally ignoring, his presence, and talking of what they had been doing since lunch. They agreed that it was really too cold in the churches for any pleasure in the pictures, and that the Pitti Gallery, where they had those braziers, was the only place you could go with comfort. A French lady and her husband came in; a Russian lady fol-

lowed; an Italian gentleman, an American family, and three
or four detached men of the English-speaking race, whose
language at once became the law of the table.

As the dinner progressed from soup to fish, and from the
entrée to the roast and salad, the combined effect of the pleasant cheer and the increasing earnestness of the stove made the
room warmer and warmer. They drank Chianti wine from the
wicker-covered flasks, tied with tufts of red and green silk, in
which they serve table wine at Florence, and said how pretty
the bottles were, but how the wine did not seem very good.

"It certainly isn't so good as it used to be," said Colville.

"Ah, then you have been in Florhence beforhe," said the
French lady, whose English proved to be much better than
the French that he began to talk to her in.

"Yes, a great while ago; in a state of pre-existence, in fact,"
he said.

The lady looked a little puzzled, but interested. "In a state
of prhe-existence?" she repeated.

"Yes; when I was young," he added, catching the gleam in
her eye. "When I was twenty-four. A great while ago."

"You must be an Amerhican," said the lady, with a laugh.

"Why do you think so? From my accent?"

"Frhom your metaphysics too. The Amerhicans like to talk
in that way."

"I didn't know it," said Colville.

"They like to strhike the key of perhsonality; they can't endure not being interhested. They must rhelate everything to
themselves or to those with whom they are talking."

"And the French, no?" asked Colville.

The lady laughed again. "There is a large Amerhican colony
in Parhis. Perhaps we have learned to be like you."

The lady's husband did not speak English, and it was probably what they had been saying that she interpreted to him,
for he smiled, looking forward to catch Colville's eye in a
friendly way, and as if he would not have him take his wife's
talk too seriously.

The Italian gentleman on Colville's right was politely offering him the salad, which had been left for the guests to pass
to one another. Colville thanked him in Italian, and they began to talk of Italian affairs. One thing led to another, and he

found that his new friend, who was not yet his acquaintance, was a member of Parliament, and a republican.

"That interests me as an American," said Colville. "But why do you want a republic in Italy?"

"When we have a constitutional king, why should we have a king?" asked the Italian.

An Englishman across the table relieved Colville from the difficulty of answering this question by asking him another that formed talk about it between them. He made his tacit observation that the English, since he met them last, seemed to have grown in the grace of facile speech with strangers; it was the American family which kept its talk within itself, and hushed to a tone so low that no one else could hear it. Colville did not like their mumbling; for the honor of the country, which we all have at heart, however little we think it, he would have preferred that they should speak up, and not seem afraid or ashamed; he thought the English manner was better. In fact, he found himself in an unexpectedly social mood; he joined in helping to break the ice; he laughed and hazarded comment with those who were new-comers like himself, and was very respectful of the opinions of people who had been longer in the hotel, when they spoke of the cook's habit of under-doing the vegetables. The dinner at the Hôtel d'Atene made an imposing show on the *carte du jour*; it looked like ten or twelve courses, but in fact it was five, and even when eked out with roast chestnuts and butter into six, it seemed somehow to stop very abruptly, though one seemed to have had enough. You could have coffee afterward if you ordered it. Colville ordered it, and was sorry when the last of his commensals, slightly bowing him good-night, left him alone to it.

He had decided that he need not fear the damp in a cab rapidly driven to Mrs. Bowen's. When he went to his room he had his doubts about his dress-coat; but he put it on, and he took the crush hat with which he had provided himself in coming through London. That was a part of the social panoply unknown in Des Vaches; he had hardly been a dozen times in evening dress there in fifteen years, and his suit was as new as his hat. As he turned to the glass he thought himself personable enough, and in fact he was one of those men who look better in evening dress than in any other: the broad expanse of shirt bosom, with its three small studs of gold dropping, points of light, one below the other, softened his strong, almost harsh face, and balanced his rather large head. In his morning coat, people had to look twice at him to make sure that he did not look common; but now he was not wrong in thinking that he had an air of distinction, as he took his hat under his arm and stood before the pier-glass in his room. He was almost tempted to shave, and wear his mustache alone, as he used to do: he had let his beard grow because he found that under the lax social regimen at Des Vaches he neglected shaving, and went about days at a time with his face in an offensive stubble. Taking his chin between his fingers, and peering closer into the mirror, he wondered how Mrs. Bowen should have known him; she must have remembered him very vividly. He would like to take off his beard and put on the youthfulness that comes of shaving, and see what she would say. Perhaps, he thought, with a last glance at his toilet, he was overdoing it, if she were only to have a few people, as she promised. He put a thick neckerchief over his chest so as not to provoke that abominable rheumatism by any sort of exposure, and he put on his ulster instead of the light spring overcoat that he had gone about with all day.

He found that Palazzo Pinti, when you came to it, was rather a grand affair, with a gold-banded porter eating salad in the lodge at the great doorway, and a handsome gate of iron cutting you off from the regions above till you had rung the bell of Mrs. Bowen's apartment, when it swung open of itself, and you mounted. At her door a man in modified livery received Colville, and helped him off with his overcoat so skillfully that he did not hurt his rheumatic shoulder at all; there were half a dozen other hats and coats on the carved chests that stood at intervals along the wall, and some gayer wraps that exhaled a faint, fascinating fragrance on the chilly air. Colville experienced the slight exhilaration, the mingled reluctance and eagerness, of a man who formally re-enters an assemblage of society after long absence from it, and rubbing his hands a little nervously together, he put aside the yellow Abruzzi blanket portière and let himself into the brilliant interior.

Mrs. Bowen stood in front of the fire in a brown silk of subdued splendor, and with her hands and fan and handkerchief tastefully composed before her. At sight of Colville she gave a slight start, which would have betrayed to him, if he had been another woman, that she had not really believed he would come, and came forward with a rustle and murmur of pleasure to meet him: he had politely made a rush upon her, so as to spare her this exertion, and he was tempted to a long-forgotten foppishness of attitude as he stood talking with her during the brief interval before she introduced him to any of the company. She had been honest with him; there were not more than twenty-five or thirty people there; but if he had overdone it in dressing for so small an affair, he was not alone, and he was not sorry. He was sensible of a better personal effect than the men in frock-coats and cut-aways were making, and he perceived with self-satisfaction that his evening dress was of better style than that of the others who wore it; at least no one else carried a crush hat.

At forty-one a man is still very much of a boy, and Colville was obscurely willing that Mrs. Bowen, whose life since they last met at an evening party had been passed chiefly at New York and Washington, should see that he was a man of the world in spite of Des Vaches. Before she had decided which of the company she should first present him to, her daughter came up to his elbow with a cup of tea and some bread and butter on a tray, and gave him good-evening with charming correctness of manner. "Really," he said, turning about to take the cup, "I thought it was you, Mrs. Bowen, who had got round to my side with a sash on. How do you and Miss Effie justify yourselves in looking so bewitchingly alike?"

"You notice it, then?" Mrs. Bowen seemed delighted.

"I did every moment you were together to-day. You don't mind my having been so personal in my observations?"

"Oh, not at all," said Mrs. Bowen, and Colville laughed.

"It must be true," he said, "what a French lady said to me at the *table d'hôte* dinner to-night: 'the Amerhicans always strhike the note of perhsonality.'" He neatly imitated the French lady's guttural accent.

"I suppose we do," mused Mrs. Bowen, "and that we don't mind it in each other. I wish *you* would say which I shall introduce you to," she said, letting her glance stray invisibly over her company, where all the people seemed comfortably talking.

"Oh, there's no hurry; put it off till to-morrow," said Colville.

"Oh no; that won't do," said Mrs. Bowen, like a woman who has public duties to perform, and is resolute to sacrifice her private pleasure to them. But she postponed them a moment longer. "I hope you got home before the rain," she said.

"Yes," returned Colville. "That is, I don't mind a little sprinkling. Who is the Junonian young person at the end of the room?"

"Ah," said Mrs. Bowen, "you can't be introduced to *her* first. But *isn't* she lovely?"

"Yes. It's a wonderful effect of white and gold."

"You mustn't say that to her. She was doubtful about her dress because she says that the ivory white with her hair makes her look just like white and gold furniture."

"Present me at once, then; before I forget not to say it to her."

"No; I must keep you for some other person: anybody can talk to a pretty girl."

Colville said he did not know whether to smile or shed tears at this imbittered compliment, and pretended an eagerness for the acquaintance denied him.

Mrs. Bowen seemed disposed to intensify his misery. "Did you ever see a more statuesque creature—with those superb broad shoulders and that little head, and that thick braid brought round over the top? Doesn't her face, with that calm look in those starry eyes, and that peculiar fall of the corners of the mouth, remind you of some of those exquisite great Du Maurier women? That style of face is very fashionable now: you might think he had made it so."

"Is there a fashion in faces?" asked Colville.

"Why, certainly. You must know that."

"Then why aren't all the ladies in the fashion?"

"It isn't one that can be put on. Besides, every one hasn't got Imogene Graham's figure to carry it off."

"That's her name, then—Imogene Graham. It's a very pretty name."

"Yes. She's staying with me for the winter. Now that's all I can allow you to know for the present. Come! You must!"

"But this is worse than nothing." He made a feint of protesting as she led him away, and named him to the lady she wished him to know. But he was not really sorry; he had his modest misgivings whether he were equal to quite so much young lady as Miss Graham seemed. When he no longer looked at her he had a whimsical impression of her being a heroic statue of herself.

The lady whom Mrs. Bowen left him with had not much to say, and she made haste to introduce her husband, who had a great deal to say. He was an Italian, but master of that very efficient English which the Italians get together with unimaginable sufferings from our orthography, and Colville repeated the republican deputy's saying about a constitutional king, which he had begun to think was neat.

"I might prefer a republic myself," said the Italian, "but I think that gentleman is wrong to be a republican where he is, and for the present. The monarchy is the condition of our unity; nothing else could hold us together, and we must remain united if we are to exist as a nation. It's a necessity, like our army of half a million men. We may not like it in itself, but we know that is our salvation." He began to speak of the economic state of Italy, of the immense cost of freedom and independence to a people whose political genius enables them to bear quietly burdens of taxation that no other government would venture to impose. He spoke with that fond, that appealing patriotism which expresses so much to the sympathetic foreigner in Italy: the sense of great and painful uncertainty of Italy's future through the complications of diplomacy, the memory of her sufferings in the past, the spirit of quiet and inexhaustible patience for trials to come. This resolution, which is almost resignation, poetizes the attitude of the whole people; it made Colville feel as if we had done nothing and borne nothing yet.

"I am ashamed," he said, not without a remote resentment of the unworthiness of the Republican voters of Des Vaches, "when I hear of such things, to think of what we are at home, with all our resources and opportunities."

The Italian would have politely excused us to him, but Col-

ville would have no palliation of our political and moral na-
kedness; and he framed a continuation of the letter he began
on the Ponte Vecchio to the *Post-Democrat-Republican*, in
which he made a bitterly ironical comparison of the achievements of Italy and America in the last ten years.

He forgot about Miss Graham, and had only a vague sense
of her splendor as he caught sight of her in the long mirror
which she stood before. She was talking to a very handsome
young clergyman, and smiling upon him. The company
seemed to be mostly Americans, but there were a good many
evident English also, and Colville was dimly aware of a question in his mind whether this clergyman was English or
American. There were three or four Italians and there were
some Germans, who spoke English.

Colville moved about from group to group as his enlarging
acquaintance led, and found himself more interested in society than he could ever have dreamed of being again. It was
certainly a defect of the life at Des Vaches that people, after
the dancing and love-making period, went out rarely or
never. He began to see that the time he had spent so busily
in that enterprising city had certainly been in some sense
wasted.

At a certain moment in the evening, which perhaps marked
its advancement, the tea-urn was replaced by a jug of the rum
punch, mild or strong according to the custom of the house,
which is served at most Florentine receptions. Some of the
people went immediately after, but the young clergyman remained talking with Miss Graham.

Colville, with his smoking glass in his hand, found himself
at the side of a friendly old gentleman who had refused the
punch. They joined in talk by a common impulse, and the old
gentleman said, directly, "You are an American, I presume?"

His accent had already established the fact of his own nationality, but he seemed to think it the part of candor to say,
when Colville had acknowledged his origin, "I'm an American myself."

"I've met several of our countrymen since I arrived," suggested Colville.

The old gentleman seemed to like this way of putting it.
"Well, yes, we're not unfairly represented here in numbers, I

must confess. But I'm bound to say that I don't find our countrymen so aggressive, so loud, as our international novelists would make out. I haven't met any of their peculiar heroines as yet, sir."

Colville could not help laughing. "I wish *I* had. But perhaps they avoid people of our years and discretion, or else take such a filial attitude toward us that we can't recognize them."

"Perhaps, perhaps," cried the old gentleman, with cheerful assent.

"I was talking with one of our German friends here just now, and he complained that the American girls—especially the rich ones—seem very calculating and worldly and conventional. I told him I didn't know how to account for that. I tried to give him some notion of the ennobling influences of society in Newport, as I've had glimpses of it."

The old gentleman caressed his elbows, which he was holding in the palms of his hands, in high enjoyment of Colville's sarcasm. "Ah! very good! very good!" he said. "I quite agree with you; and I think the other sort are altogether preferable."

"I think," continued Colville, dropping his ironical tone, "that we've much less to regret in their unsuspecting, unsophisticated freedom than in the type of hard materialism which we produce in young girls, perfectly wide awake, disenchanted, unromantic, who prefer the worldly vanities and advantages deliberately and on principle, recognizing something better merely to despise it. I've sometimes seen them—"

Mrs. Bowen came up in her gentle, inquiring way, "I'm glad that you and Mr. Colville have made acquaintance," she said to the old gentleman.

"Oh, but we haven't," said Colville. "We're entire strangers."

"Then I'll introduce you to Rev. Mr. Waters. And take you away," she added, putting her hand through Colville's arm with a delicate touch that flattered his whole being, "for your time's come at last, and I'm going to present you to Miss Graham."

"I don't know," he said. "Of course, as there *is* a Miss Graham, I can't help being presented to her, but I had almost worked myself up to the point of wishing there were none. I believe I'm afraid."

"Oh, I don't believe that at all. A simple school-girl like that!" Mrs. Bowen's sense of humor had not the national acuteness. She liked joking in men, but she did not know how to say funny things back. "You'll see, as you come up to her."

IV

MISS GRAHAM did, indeed, somehow diminish in the nearer perspective. She ceased to be overwhelming. When Colville lifted his eyes from bowing before her he perceived that she was neither so very tall nor so very large, but possessed merely a generous amplitude of womanhood. But she was even more beautiful, with a sweet and youthful radiance of look that was very winning. If she had ceased to be the goddess she looked across the length of the salon, she had gained much by becoming an extremely lovely young girl; and her teeth, when she spoke, showed a fascinating little irregularity that gave her the last charm.

Mrs. Bowen glided away with the young clergyman, but Effie remained at Miss Graham's side, and seemed to have hold of the left hand, which the girl let hang carelessly behind her in the volume of her robe. The child's face expressed an adoration of Miss Graham far beyond her allegiance to her mother.

"I began to doubt whether Mrs. Bowen was going to bring you at all," she said, frankly, with an innocent, nervous laugh, which made favor for her with Colville. "She promised it early in the evening."

"She has used me much worse, Miss Graham," said Colville. "She has kept me waiting from the beginning of time. So that I have grown gray on my way up to you," he added, by an inspiration. "I was a comparatively young man when Mrs. Bowen first told me she was going to introduce me."

"Oh, how *good*!" said Miss Graham, joyously. And her companion, after a moment's hesitation, permitted herself a polite little titter. She had made a discovery: she had discovered that Mr. Colville was droll.

"I'm very glad you like it," he said, with a gravity that did not deceive them.

"Oh yes," sighed Miss Graham, with generous ardor. "Who but an American could say just such things? There's the loveliest old lady here in Florence, who's lived here thirty years, and she's always going back and never getting back, and she's so homesick she doesn't know what to do, and she always says that Americans may not be *better* than other people, but they are *different*."

"That's very pretty. They're different in everything but thinking themselves better. Their native modesty prevents that."

"I don't exactly know what you mean," said Miss Graham, after a little hesitation.

"Well," returned Colville, "I haven't thought it out very clearly myself yet. I may mean that the Americans differ from other people in not thinking well of themselves, or they may differ from them in not thinking well enough. But what I said had a very epigrammatic sound, and I prefer not to investigate it too closely."

This made Miss Graham and Miss Effie both cry out "Oh!" in delighted doubt of his intention. They both insensibly drifted a little nearer to him.

"There was a French lady said to me at the *table d'hôte* this evening that she knew I was an American because the Americans always strike the key of personality." He practiced these economies of material in conversation quite recklessly, and often made the same incident or suggestion do duty round a whole company.

"Ah, I don't believe that," said Miss Graham.

"Believe what?"

"That the Americans always talk about themselves."

"I'm not sure she meant that. You never can tell what a person means by what he says—or *she*."

"How shocking!"

"Perhaps the French lady meant that we always talk about other people. That's in the key of personality too."

"But I don't believe we do," said Miss Graham. "At any rate, *she* was talking about *us*, then."

"Oh, she accounted for that by saying there was a large American colony in Paris, who had corrupted the French, and taught them our pernicious habit of introspection."

"Do you think we're very introspective?"

"Do you?"

"I know I'm not. I hardly ever think about myself at all. At any rate, not till it's too late. That's the great trouble. I wish I could. But I'm always studying other people. They're so much more interesting."

"Perhaps if you knew yourself better you wouldn't think so," suggested Colville.

"Yes, I know they are. I don't think any young person can be interesting."

"Then what becomes of all the novels? They're full of young persons."

"They're ridiculous. If I were going to write a novel, I should take an old person for a hero—thirty-five or forty." She looked at Colville, and blushing a little, hastened to add: "I don't believe that they begin to be interesting much before that time. Such flat things as young men are always saying! Don't you remember that passage somewhere in Heine's Pictures of Travel, where he sees the hand of a lady coming out from under her mantle, when she's confessing in a church, and he knows that it's the hand of a young person who has enjoyed nothing and suffered nothing, it's so smooth and flower like? After I read that I hated the look of my hands— I was only sixteen, and it seemed as if I had had no more experience than a child. Oh, I like people to be *through* something. Don't you?"

"Well, yes, I suppose I do. Other people."

"No; but don't you like it for yourself?"

"I can't tell; I haven't been through anything worth speaking of yet."

Miss Graham looked at him dubiously, but pursued with ardor: "Why, just getting back to Florence, after not having been here for so long—I should think it would be so romantic. Oh dear! I wish I were here for the second time."

"I'm afraid you wouldn't like it so well," said Colville. "I wish I were here for the first time. There's nothing like the first time in everything."

"Do you really think so?"

"Well, there's nothing like the first time in Florence."

"Oh, I can't imagine it. I should think that recalling the old emotions would be perfectly fascinating."

"Yes, if they'd come when you do call them. But they're as

contrary-minded as spirits from the vasty deep. I've been shouting around here for my old emotions all day, and I haven't had a responsive squeak."

"Oh!" cried Miss Graham, staring full-eyed at him. "How delightful!" Effie Bowen turned away her pretty little head and laughed, as if it might not be quite kind to laugh at a person's joke to his face.

Stimulated by their appreciation, Colville went on with more nonsense. "No; the only way to get at your old emotions in regard to Florence is to borrow them from somebody who's having them fresh. What do *you* think about Florence, Miss Graham?"

"I? I've been here two months."

"Then it's too late?"

"No, I don't know that it is. I keep feeling the strangeness all the time. But I can't tell you. It's very different from Buffalo, I can assure you."

"Buffalo? I can imagine the difference. And it's not altogether to the disadvantage of Buffalo."

"Oh, have you been there?" asked Miss Graham, with a touching little eagerness. "Do you know anybody in Buffalo?"

"Some of the newspaper men; and I pass through there once a year on my way to New York—or used to. It's a lively place."

"Yes, it is," sighed Miss Graham, fondly.

"Do the girls of Buffalo still come out at night and dance by the light of the moon?"

"What!"

"Ah, I see," said Colville, peering at her under his thoughtfully knitted brows, "you do belong to another era. You don't remember the old negro minstrel song."

"No," said Miss Graham. "I can only remember the end of the war."

"How divinely young!" said Colville. "Well," he added, "I wish that French lady could have overheard us, Miss Graham. I think she would have changed her mind about Americans striking the note of personality in their talk."

"Oh!" exclaimed the girl, reproachfully, after a moment of swift reflection and recognition, "I don't see how you could let me do it! You don't suppose that I should have talked so with every one? It was because you were another American, and such an old friend of Mrs. Bowen's."

"That is what I shall certainly tell the French lady if she attacks me about it," said Colville. He glanced carelessly toward the end of the room, and saw the young clergyman taking leave of Mrs. Bowen; all the rest of the company were gone. "Bless me!" he said, "I must be going."

Mrs. Bowen had so swiftly advanced upon him that she caught the last words. "Why?" she asked.

"Because it's to-morrow, I suspect, and the invitation was for one day only."

"It was a season ticket," said Mrs. Bowen, with gay hospitality, "and it isn't to-morrow for half an hour yet. I can't think of letting you go. Come up to the fire, all, and let's sit down by it. It's at its very best."

Effie looked a pretty surprise and a pleasure in this girlish burst from her mother, whose habitual serenity made it more striking in contrast, and she forsook Miss Graham's hand and ran forward and disposed the easy-chairs comfortably about the hearth.

Colville and Mrs. Bowen suddenly found themselves upon those terms which often succeed a long separation with people who have felt kindly toward each other at a former meeting and have parted friends: they were much more intimate than they had supposed themselves to be, or had really any reason for being.

"Which one of your guests do you wish me to offer up, Mrs. Bowen?" he asked, from the hollow of the arm-chair, not too low, which he had sunk into. With Mrs. Bowen in a higher chair at his right hand, and Miss Graham intent upon him from the sofa on his left, a sense of delicious satisfaction filled him from head to foot. "There isn't one I would spare if you said the word."

"And there isn't one I want destroyed, I'm sorry to say," answered Mrs. Bowen. "Don't you think they were all very agreeable?"

"Yes, yes; agreeable enough—agreeable enough, I suppose. But they staid too long. When I think we might have been sitting here for the last half-hour, if they'd only gone sooner, I find it pretty hard to forgive them."

Mrs. Bowen and Miss Graham exchanged glances above his head—a glance which demanded, "Didn't I tell you?" for a glance that answered, "Oh, he *is!*" Effie Bowen's eyes widened; she kept them fastened upon Colville in silent worship.

He asked who were certain of the company that he had noticed, and Mrs. Bowen let him make a little fun of them: the fun was very good-natured. He repeated what the German had said about the worldly ambition of American girls; but she would not allow him so great latitude in this. She said they were no worldlier than other girls. Of course they were fond of society, and some of them got a little spoiled. But they were in no danger of becoming too conventional.

Colville did not insist. "I missed the military to-night, Mrs. Bowen," he said. "I thought one couldn't get through an evening in Florence without officers?"

"We have them when there is dancing," returned Mrs. Bowen.

"Yes, but they don't know anything but dancing," Miss Graham broke in. "I like some one who can talk something besides compliments."

"You are very peculiar, you know, Imogene," urged Mrs. Bowen, gently. "I don't think our young men at home do much better in conversation, if you come to that, though."

"Oh, *young* men, yes! They're the same everywhere. But here, even when they're away along in the thirties, they think that girls can only enjoy flattery. *I* should like a gentleman to talk to me without a single word or look to show that he thought I was good-looking."

"Ah, how could he?" Colville insinuated, and the young girl colored.

"I mean if I were pretty. This everlasting adulation is insulting."

"Mr. Morton doesn't flatter," said Mrs. Bowen, thoughtfully, turning the feather screen she held at her face, now edgewise, now flatwise, toward Colville.

"Oh no," owned Miss Graham. "He's a clergyman."

Mrs. Bowen addressed herself to Colville. "You must go to hear him some day. He's very interesting, if you don't mind his being rather Low-Church."

Colville was going to pretend to an advanced degree of

ritualism, but it occurred to him that it might be a serious matter to Mrs. Bowen, and he asked instead who was the Rev. Mr. Waters.

"Oh, isn't he lovely?" cried Miss Graham. "There, Mrs. Bowen! Mr. Waters's manner is what I call *truly* complimentary. He always talks to you as if he expected you to be interested in serious matters, and as if you were his intellectual equal. And he's so *happy* here in Florence! He gives you the impression of feeling every breath he breathes here a privilege. You ought to hear him talk about Savonarola, Mr. Colville."

"Well," said Colville, "I've heard a great many people talk about Savonarola, and I'm rather glad he talked to me about American girls."

"American girls!" uttered Miss Graham, in a little scream. "Did Mr. Waters talk to you about *girls*?"

"Yes. Why not? He was probably in love with one once."

"Mr. Waters?" cried the girl. "What nonsense!"

"Well, then, with some old lady. Would you like that better?"

Miss Graham looked at Mrs. Bowen for permission, as it seemed, and then laughed, but did not attempt any reply to Colville.

"You find even that incredible of such pyramidal antiquity," he resumed. "Well, it *is* hard to believe. I told him what that German said, and we agreed beautifully about another type of American girl which we said we preferred."

"Oh! What could it be?" demanded Miss Graham.

"Ah, it wouldn't be so easy to say right off-hand," answered Colville, indolently.

Mrs. Bowen put her hand under the elbow of the arm holding her screen. "I don't believe I should agree with you so well," she said, apparently with a sort of didactic intention.

They entered into a discussion which is always fruitful with Americans—the discussion of American girlhood, and Colville contended for the old national ideal of girlish liberty as wide as the continent, as fast as the Mississippi. Mrs. Bowen withstood him with delicate firmness. "Oh," he said, "you're Europeanized."

"I certainly prefer the European plan of bringing up girls," she replied, steadfastly. "I shouldn't think of letting a daughter of mine have the freedom I had."

"Well, perhaps it will come right in the next generation, then; she will let her daughter have the freedom she hadn't."

"Not if I'm alive to prevent it," cried Mrs. Bowen.

Colville laughed. "Which plan do you prefer, Miss Graham?"

"I don't think it's quite the same now as it used to be," answered the girl, evasively.

"Well, then, all I can say is that if I had died before this change, I had lived a blessed time. I perceive more and more that I'm obsolete. I'm in my dotage; I prattle of the good old times, and the new spirit of the age flouts me. Miss Effie, do you prefer the Amer—"

"No, thank you," said her mother, quickly. "Effie is out of the question. It's time you were in bed, Effie."

The child came with instant submissiveness and kissed her mother good-night; she kissed Miss Graham, and gave her hand to Colville. He held it a moment, letting her pull shyly away from him, while he lolled back in his chair, and laughed at her with his sad eyes. "It's past the time *I* should be in bed, my dear, and I'm sitting up merely because there's nobody to send me. It's not that I'm really such a very bad boy. Good-night. Don't put me into a disagreeable dream; put me into a nice one." The child bridled at the mild pleasantry, and when Colville released her hand she suddenly stooped forward and kissed him.

"You're so *funny*!" she cried, and ran and escaped beyond the *portière*.

Mrs. Bowen stared in the same direction, but not with severity. "Really, Effie has been carried a little beyond herself."

"Well," said Colville, "that's *one* conquest since I came to Florence. And merely by being funny! When I was in Florence before, Mrs. Bowen," he continued, after a moment, "there were two ladies here, and I used to go about quite freely with either of them. They were both very pretty, and we were all very young. Don't you think it was charming?" Mrs. Bowen colored a lovely red, and smiled, but made no other response. "Florence has changed very much for the worse since that time. There used to be a pretty flower girl,

with a wide flapping straw hat, who flung a heavy bough full
of roses into my lap when she met me driving across the Carraja bridge. I spent an hour looking for that girl to-day, and
couldn't find her. The only flower girl I could find was a fat
one of fifty, who kept me fifteen minutes in Via Tornabuoni
while she was fumbling away at my button-hole, trying to
poke three second-hand violets and a sickly daisy into it. Ah,
youth! youth! I suppose a young fellow could have found
that other flower girl at a glance; but *my* old eyes! No, we
belong, each of us, to our own generation. Mrs. Bowen," he
said, with a touch of tragedy—whether real or affected he
did not well know himself—in his hardiness, "what has become of Mrs. Pilsbury?"

"Mrs. Milbury, you mean?" gasped Mrs. Bowen, in affright
at his boldness.

"Milbury, Bilbury, Pilsbury—it's all one, so long as it
isn't—"

"They're living in Chicago!" she hastened to reply, as if she
were afraid he was going to say, "so long as it isn't Colville,"
and she could not have borne that.

Colville clasped his hands at the back of his head and
looked at Mrs. Bowen with eyes that let her know that he
was perfectly aware she had been telling Miss Graham of his
youthful romance, and that he had now touched it purposely.
"And you wouldn't," he said, as if that were quite relevant to
what they had been talking about—"you wouldn't let Miss
Graham go out walking alone with a dotard like me?"

"Certainly not," said Mrs. Bowen.

Colville got to his feet by a surprising activity. "Good-by,
Miss Graham." He offered his hand to her with burlesque
despair, and then turned to Mrs. Bowen. "Thank you for *such*
a pleasant evening! What was your day, did you say?"

"Oh, any day!" said Mrs. Bowen, cordially, giving her
hand.

"Do you know whom you look like?" he asked, holding it.

"No."

"Lina Ridgely."

The ladies stirred softly in their draperies after he was gone.
They turned and faced the hearth, where a log burned in a
bed of hot ashes, softly purring and ticking to itself, and

whilst they stood pressing their hands against the warm fronts of their dresses, as the fashion of women is before a fire, the clock on the mantel began to strike twelve.

"Was that her name?" asked Miss Graham, when the clock had had its say. "Lina Ridgely?"

"No; that was *my* name," answered Mrs. Bowen.

"Oh yes!" murmured the young girl, apologetically.

"She led him on; she certainly encouraged him. It was shocking. He was quite wild about it."

"She must have been a cruel girl. How *could* he speak of it so lightly?"

"It was best to speak of it, and have done with it," said Mrs. Bowen. "He knew that I must have been telling you something about it."

"Yes. How bold it was! A *young* man couldn't have done it! Yes, he's fascinating. But how old and sad he looked as he lay back there in the chair!"

"Old? I didn't think he looked old. He looked sad. Yes, it's left its mark on him."

The log burned quite through to its core, and fell asunder, a bristling mass of embers. They had been looking at it with downcast heads. Now they lifted their faces, and saw the pity in each other's eyes, and the beautiful girl impulsively kissed the pretty woman good-night.

V

COLVILLE fell asleep with the flattered sense which abounds in the heart of a young man after his first successful evening in society, but which can visit maturer life only upon some such conditions of long exile and return as had been realized in his. The looks of these two charming women followed him into his dreams; he knew he must have pleased them, the dramatic homage of the child was evidence of that; and though it had been many years since he had found it sufficient cause of happiness to have pleased a woman, the desire to do so was by no means extinct in him. The eyes of the girl hovered above him like stars; he felt in their soft gaze that he was a romance to her young heart, and this made him laugh; it also made him sigh.

He woke at dawn with a sharp twinge in his shoulder, and he rose to give himself the pleasure of making his own fire with those fagots of broom and pine twigs which he had enjoyed the night before, promising himself to get back into bed when the fire was well going, and sleep late. While he stood before the open stove, the jangling of a small bell outside called him to the window, and he saw a procession which had just issued from the church, going to administer the extreme unction to some dying person across the piazza. The parish priest went first, bearing the consecrated wafer in its vessel, and at his side an acolyte holding a yellow silk umbrella over the Eucharist; after them came a number of *facchini* in white robes and white hoods that hid their faces; their tapers burned sallow and lifeless in the new morning light; the bell jangled dismally.

"They even die dramatically in this country," thought Colville, in whom the artist was taken with the effectiveness of the spectacle before his human pity was stirred for the poor soul who was passing. He reproached himself for that, and instead of getting back to bed, he dressed and waited for the mature hour which he had ordered his breakfast for. When it came at last, picturesquely borne on the open hand of Giovanni, steaming coffee, hot milk, sweet butter in delicate

629

disks, and two white eggs coyly tucked in the fold of a
napkin, and all grouped upon the wide salver, it brought
him a measure of the consolation which good cheer imparts
to the ridiculous human heart even in the house where
death is. But the sad incident tempered his mind with a
sort of pensiveness that lasted throughout the morning, and
quite till lunch. He spent the time in going about the
churches; but the sunshine which the day began with was
overcast, as it was the day before, and the churches were
rather too dark and cold in the afternoon. He went to
Vieusseux's reading-room and looked over the English papers, which he did not care for much; and he also made a
diligent search of the catalogue for some book about Florence for little Effie Bowen: he thought he would like to
surprise her mother with his interest in the matter. As the
day waned toward dark, he felt more and more tempted to
take her at her word, when she had said that any day was
her day to him, and go to see her. If he had been a younger man he would have anxiously considered this indulgence and denied himself, but after forty a man denies himself no reasonable and harmless indulgence; he has learned
by that time that it is a pity and a folly to do so.

Colville found Mrs. Bowen's room half full of arriving and
departing visitors, and then he remembered that it was this
day she had named to him on the Ponte Vecchio, and when
Miss Graham thanked him for coming his first Thursday, he
made a merit of not having forgotten it, and said he was
going to come every Thursday during the winter. Miss Graham drew him a cup of tea from the Russian samovar which
replaces in some Florentine houses the tea-pot of Occidental
civilization, and Colville smiled upon it and upon her, bending over the brazen urn with a flower-like tilt of her beautiful
head. She wore an æsthetic dress of creamy camel's-hair,
whose color pleased the eye as its softness would have flattered the touch.

"What a very Tourguéneffish effect the samovar gives!" he
said, taking a biscuit from the basket Effie Bowen brought
him, shrinking with redoubled shyness from the eyebrows
which he arched at her. "I wonder you can keep from calling
me Fedor Colvillitch. Where is your mother, Effie Bowen-

ovna?" he asked of the child, with a temptation to say Imogene Grahamovna.

They both looked mystified, but Miss Graham said, "I'm sorry to say you won't see Mrs. Bowen to-day. She has a very bad headache, and has left Effie and me to receive. We feel very incompetent, but she says it will do us good."

There were some people there of the night before, and Colville had to talk to them. One of the ladies asked him if he had met the Inglehart boys as he came in.

"The Inglehart boys? No. What are the Inglehart boys?"

"They were here all last winter, and they've just got back. It's rather exciting for Florence." She gave him a rapid sketch of that interesting exodus of a score of young painters from the art school at Munich, under the lead of the singular and fascinating genius by whose name they became known. "They had their own school for a while in Munich, and then they all came down into Italy in a body. They had their studio things with them, and they travelled third class, and they made the greatest excitement everywhere, and had the greatest fun. They were a great sensation in Florence. They went everywhere, and were such favorites. I hope they are going to stay."

"I hope so too," said Colville. "I should like to see them."

"Dear me!" said the lady, with a glance at the clock. "It's five! I must be going."

The other ladies went, and Colville approached to take leave, but Miss Graham detained him.

"What is Tourguéneffish?" she demanded.

"The quality of the great Russian novelist Tourguéneff," said Colville, perceiving that she had not heard of him.

"Oh!"

"You ought to read him. The samovar sends up its agreeable odor all through his books. Read *Lisa* if you want your heart really broken."

"I'm glad you approve of heart-breaks in books. So many people won't read anything but cheerful books. It's the only quarrel I have with Mrs. Bowen. She says there are so many sad things in life that they ought to be kept out of books."

"Ah, there I perceive a divided duty," said Colville. "I should like to agree with both of you. But if Mrs. Bowen were here I should remind her that if there are so many sad things in life, that is a very good reason for putting them in books too."

"Of course I shall tell her what you said."

"Why, I don't object to a certain degree of cheerfulness in books; only don't carry it too far—that's all."

This made the young girl laugh, and Colville was encouraged to go on. He told her of the sight he had seen from his window at daybreak, and he depicted it all very graphically, and made her feel its pathos perhaps more keenly than he had felt it. "Now that little incident kept with me all day, tempering my boisterous joy in the Giottos, and reducing me to a decent composure in the presence of the Cimabues; and it's pretty hard to keep from laughing at some of them—don't you think?"

The young people perceived that he was making fun again; but he continued with an air of greater seriousness. "Don't you see what a very good thing that was to begin one's day with? Why, even in Santa Croce, with the thermometer ten degrees below zero in the shade of Alfieri's monument, I was no gayer than I should have been in a church at home. I suppose Mrs. Bowen would object to having that procession go by under one's window in a book; but I can't really see how it would hurt the reader, or damp his spirits permanently. A wholesome reaction would ensue, such as you see now in me, whom the thing happened to in real life."

He stirred his tea, and shook with an inward laugh as he carried it to his lips.

"Yes," said Miss Graham, thoughtfully, and she looked at him searchingly in the interval of silence that ensued. But she only added: "I wish it would get warmer in the churches. I've seen hardly anything of them yet."

"From the way I felt in them to-day," sighed Colville, "I should think the churches would begin to thaw out about the middle of May. But if one goes well wrapped up in furs, and has a friend along to rouse him and keep him walking when he is about to fall into that lethargy which precedes death by freezing, I think they may be visited even now with safety. Have you been in Santa Maria Novella yet?"

"No," said Miss Graham, with a shake of the head that expressed her resolution to speak the whole truth if she died for it, "not even in Santa Maria Novella."

"What a wonderful old place it is! That curious façade, with the dials and its layers of black and white marble soaked golden red in a hundred thousand sunsets! That exquisite grand portal!" He gesticulated with the hand that the tea-cup left free, to suggest form and measurement, as artists do. "Then the inside! The great Cimabue, with all that famous history on its back—the first divine Madonna by the first divine master, carried through the streets in a triumph of art and religion! Those frescoes of Ghirlandajo's, with real Florentine faces and figures in them, and all lavished upon the eternal twilight of that choir—but I suppose that if the full day were let in on them once, they would vanish like ghosts at cock-crow! You must be sure to see the Spanish chapel; and the old cloister itself is such a pathetic place. There's a boys' school, as well as a military college, in the suppressed convent now, and the colonnades were full of boys running and screaming and laughing and making a joyful racket; it was so much more sorrowful than silence would have been there. One of the little scamps came up to me and the young monk that was showing me round, and bobbed us a mocking bow and bobbed his hat off; then they all burst out laughing again and raced away, and the monk looked after them and said, so sweetly and wearily, 'They're at their diversions; we must have patience.' There are only twelve monks left there; all the rest are scattered and gone." He gave his cup to Miss Graham for more tea.

"Don't you think," she asked, drawing it from the samovar, "that it is very sad having the convents suppressed?"

"It was very sad having slavery abolished—for some people," suggested Colville: he felt the unfairness of the point he had made.

"Yes," sighed Miss Graham.

Colville stood stirring his second cup of tea, when the *portière* parted, and showed Mrs. Bowen wistfully pausing on the threshold. Her face was pale, but she looked extremely pretty there.

"Ah, come in, Mrs. Bowen!" he called gayly to her. "I won't give you away to the other people. A cup of tea will do you good."

"Oh, I'm a great deal better," said Mrs. Bowen, coming forward to give him her hand. "I heard your voice, and I couldn't resist looking in."

"That was very kind of you," said Colville, gratefully; and her eyes met his in a glance that flushed her face a deep red. "You find me here —*I* don't know why!—in my character of old family friend, doing my best to make life a burden to the young ladies."

"I wish you would stay to a family dinner with us," said Mrs. Bowen, and Miss Graham brightened in cordial support of the hospitality. "Why can't you?"

"I don't know, unless it's because I'm a humane person, and have some consideration for your headache."

"Oh, that's all gone," said Mrs. Bowen. "It was one of those convenient headaches—if you ever had them, you'd know—that go off at sunset."

"But you'd have another to-morrow."

"No, I'm safe for a whole fortnight from another."

"Then you leave me without an excuse, and I was just wishing I had none," said Colville.

After dinner Mrs. Bowen sent Effie to bed early to make up for the late hours of the night before, but she sat before the fire with Miss Graham rather late, talking Colville over, when he was gone.

"He's very puzzling to me," said Miss Graham. "Sometimes you think he's nothing but an old cynic, from his talk, and then something so sweet and fresh comes out that you don't know what to do. Don't you think he has really a very poetical mind, and that he's putting all the rest on?"

"I think he likes to make little effects," said Mrs. Bowen, judiciously. "He always did, rather."

"Why, was he like this when he was young?"

"I don't consider him very old now."

"No, of course not. I meant when you knew him before." Miss Graham had some needle-work in her hand; Mrs. Bowen, who never even pretended to work at that kind of thing, had nothing in hers but the feather screen.

"He is old, compared with you, Imogene, but you'll find, as you live along, that your contemporaries are always young. Mr. Colville is very much improved. He used to be painfully shy, but he put on a bold front, and now the bold front seems to have become a second nature with him."

"I like it," said Miss Graham, to her needle.

"Yes; but I suspect he's still shy, at heart. He used to be very sentimental, and was always talking Ruskin. I think if he hadn't talked Ruskin so much, Jenny Milbury might have treated him better. It was very priggish in him."

"Oh, I can't imagine Mr. Colville's being priggish!"

"He's very much improved. He used to be quite a sloven in his dress: you know how very slovenly most American gentlemen are in their dress, at any rate. I think that influenced her against him too."

"He isn't slovenly now," suggested Miss Graham.

"Oh no; he's quite swell," said Mrs. Bowen, depriving the adjective of slanginess by the refinement of her tone.

"Well," said Miss Graham, "I don't see how you could have endured her after that. It was atrocious."

"It was better for her to break with him, if she found out she didn't love him, than to marry him. That," said Mrs. Bowen, with a depth of feeling uncommon for her, "would have been a thousand times worse."

"Yes, but she ought to have found out before she led him on so far."

"Sometimes girls can't. They don't know themselves; they think they're in love when they're not. She was very impulsive, and of course she was flattered by it; he was so intellectual. But at last she found that she couldn't bear it, and she had to tell him so."

"Did she ever say why she didn't love him?"

"No; I don't suppose she could. The only thing I remember her saying was that he was 'too much of a mixture.'"

"What *did* she mean by that?"

"I don't know exactly."

"Do you think he's insincere?"

"Oh no. Perhaps she meant that he wasn't single-minded."

"Fickle?"

"No. He certainly wasn't that in her case."

"Undecided?"

"He was decided enough with her—at last."

Imogene dropped the hopeless quest. "How can a man ever stand such a thing?" she sighed.

"He stood it very nobly. That was the best thing about it; he took it in the most delicate way. She showed me his letter. There wasn't a word or a hint of reproach in it; he seemed to be anxious about nothing but her feeling badly for him. Of course he couldn't help showing that he was mortified for having pursued her with attentions that were disagreeable to her; but that was delicate too. Yes, it was a very large-minded letter."

"It was shocking in her to show it."

"It wasn't very nice. But it was a letter that any girl might have been proud to show."

"Oh, she *couldn't* have done it to gratify her vanity!"

"Girls are very queer, my dear," said Mrs. Bowen, as if the fact were an abstraction. She mused upon the flat of her screen, while Miss Graham plied her needle in silence.

The latter spoke first. "Do you think he was very much broken by it?"

"You never can tell. He went out West then, and there he has staid ever since. I suppose his life would have been very different if nothing of the kind had happened. He had a great deal of talent. I always thought I should hear of him in some way."

"Well, it was a heartless, shameless thing! I don't see how you can speak of it so leniently as you do, Mrs. Bowen. It makes all sorts of coquetry and flirtation more detestable to me than ever. Why, it has ruined his life!"

"Oh, he was young enough then to outlive it. After all, they were a boy and girl."

"A boy and girl! How old were they?"

"He must have been twenty-three or four, and she was twenty."

"*My* age! Do you call that being a girl?"

"She was old enough to know what she was about," said Mrs. Bowen, justly.

Imogene fell back in her chair, drawing out her needle the

full length of its thread, and then letting her hand fall. "I don't know. It seems as if I never should be grown up, or anything but a child. Yes, when I think of the way young men talk, they do seem boys. Why can't they talk like Mr. Colville? I wish I could talk like him. It makes you forget how old and plain he is."

She remained with her eyelids dropped in an absent survey of her sewing, while Mrs. Bowen regarded her with a look of vexation, impatience, resentment, or the last refinement of these emotions, which she banished from her face before Miss Graham looked up and said, with a smile: "How funny it is to see Effie's infatuation with him! She can't take her eyes off him for a moment, and she follows him round the room so as not to lose a word he is saying. It was heroic of her to go to bed without a murmur before he left to-night."

"Yes, she sees that he is good," said Mrs. Bowen.

"Oh, she sees that he's something very much more! Mr. Waters is good."

Miss Graham had the best of the argument, and so Mrs. Bowen did not reply.

"I feel," continued the young girl, "as if it were almost a shame to have asked him to go to that silly dancing party with us. It seems as if we didn't appreciate him. I think we ought to have kept him for high æsthetic occasions and historical researches."

"Oh, I don't think Mr. Colville was very deeply offended at being asked to go with us."

"No," said Imogene, with another sigh, "he didn't seem so. I suppose there's always an under-current of sadness—of tragedy—in everything for him."

"I don't suppose anything of the kind," cried Mrs. Bowen, gayly. "He's had time enough to get over it."

"Do people *ever* get over such things?"

"Yes—men."

"It must be because he was young, as you say. But if it had happened *now?*"

"Oh, it *couldn't* happen now. He's altogether too cool and calculating."

"Do you think he's cool and calculating?"

"No. He's too old for a broken heart—a new one."

"Mrs. Bowen," demanded the girl, solemnly, "could *you* forgive yourself for such a thing, if you had done it?"

"Yes, perfectly well, if I wasn't in love with him."

"But if you'd made him *think* you were?" pursued the girl, breathlessly.

"If I were a flirt—yes."

"*I* couldn't," said Imogene, with tragic depth.

"Oh, be done with your intensities, and go to bed, Imogene," said Mrs. Bowen, giving her a playful push.

VI

IT WAS so long since Colville had been at a dancing party
that Mrs. Bowen's offer to take him to Madame Uccelli's
had first struck his sense of the ludicrous. Then it had begun
to flatter him; it implied that he was still young enough to
dance if he would, though he had stipulated that they were
not to expect anything of the kind from him. He liked also
the notion of being seen and accepted in Florentine society as
the old friend of Mrs. Bowen, for he had not been long in
discovering that her position in Florence was, among the foreign residents, rather authoritative. She was one of the very
few Americans who were asked to Italian houses, and Italian
houses lying even beyond the neutral ground of English-
speaking intermarriages. She was not, of course, asked to the
great Princess Strozzi ball, where the Florentine nobility appeared in the mediæval pomp—the veritable costumes—of
their ancestors; only a rich American banking family went,
and their distinction was spoken of under the breath; but any
glory short of this was within Mrs. Bowen's reach. So an old
lady who possessed herself of Colville the night before had
told him, celebrating Mrs. Bowen at length, and boasting of
her acceptance among the best English residents, who, next
after the natives, seem to constitute the social ambition of
Americans living in Italian cities.

It interested him to find that some geographical distinctions which are fading at home had quite disappeared in Florence. When he was there before, people from quite small
towns in the East had made pretty Lina Ridgely and her
friend feel the disadvantage of having come from the western
side of an imaginary line; he had himself been at the pains
always to let people know, at the American watering-places
where he spent his vacations, that though presently from Des
Vaches, Indiana, he was really born in Rhode Island; but in
Florence it was not at all necessary. He found in Mrs.
Bowen's house people from Denver, Chicago, St. Louis, Boston, New York, and Baltimore, all meeting as of apparently
the same civilization, and whether Mrs. Bowen's own origin

was, like that of the Etruscan cities, lost in the mists of antiquity, or whether she had sufficiently atoned for the error of her birth by subsequent residence in the national capital and prolonged sojourn in New York, it seemed certainly not to be remembered against her among her Eastern acquaintance. The time had been when the fact that Miss Graham came from Buffalo would have gone far to class her with the animal from which her native city had taken its name; but now it made no difference, unless it was a difference in her favor. The English spoke with the same vague respect of Buffalo and of Philadelphia; and to a family of real Bostonians Colville had the courage to say simply that he lived in Des Vaches, and not to seek to palliate the truth in any sort. If he wished to prevaricate at all, it was rather to attribute himself to Mrs. Bowen's city in Ohio.

She and Miss Graham called for him with her carriage the next night, when it was time to go to Madame Uccelli's.

"This gives me a very patronized and effeminate feeling," said Colville, getting into the odorous dark of the carriage, and settling himself upon the front seat with a skill inspired by his anxiety not to tear any of the silken spreading white wraps that inundated the whole interior. "Being come for by ladies!" They both gave some nervous joyful laughs as they found his hand in the obscurity, and left the sense of a gloved pressure upon it. "Is this the way you used to do in Vespucius, Mrs. Bowen?"

"Oh no, indeed!" she answered. "The young gentlemen used to find out whether I was going, and came for me with a hack; and generally, if the weather was good, we walked home."

"That's the way we still do in Des Vaches. Sometimes, as a tremendous joke, the ladies come for us in leap-year. How do you go to balls in Buffalo, Miss Graham? Or, no; I withdraw the embarrassing question." Some gleams from the street lamps, as they drove along, struck in through the carriage windows, and flitted over the ladies' faces and were gone again. "Ah! this is very trying. Couldn't you stop him at the next corner, and let me see how radiant you ladies really are? I may be in very great danger; I'd like to know just how much."

"It wouldn't be of any use," cried the young girl, gayly. "We're all wrapped up, and you couldn't form any idea of us. You must wait, and let us burst upon you when we come out of the dressing-room at Madame Uccelli's."

"But then it may be too late," he urged. "Is it very far?"

"Yes," said Mrs. Bowen. "It's ridiculously far. It's outside the Roman Gate. I don't see why people live at that distance."

"In order to give the friends you bring the more pleasure of your company, Mrs. Bowen."

"Ah! that's very well. But you're not logical."

"No," said Colville; "you can't be logical and complimentary at the same time. It's too much to ask. How delicious your flowers are!" The ladies each had a bouquet in her hand, which she was holding in addition to her fan, the edges of her cloak, and the skirt of her train.

"Yes," said Mrs. Bowen; "we are so much obliged to you for them."

"Why, I sent you no flowers," said Colville, startled into untimely earnest.

"Didn't you?" triumphed Mrs. Bowen. "I thought gentlemen always sent flowers to ladies when they were going to a ball with them. They used to, in Columbus."

"And in Buffalo they always do," Miss Graham added.

"Ah! they don't in Des Vaches," said Colville.

They tried to mystify him further about the bouquets; they succeeded in being very gay, and in making themselves laugh a great deal. Mrs. Bowen was even livelier than the young girl.

Her carriage was one of the few private equipages that drove up to Madame Uccelli's door; most people had not even come in a *remise*, but, after the simple Florentine fashion, had taken the little cabs, which stretched in a long line up and down the way; the horses had let their weary heads drop, and were easing their broken knees by extending their forelegs while they drowsed; the drivers, huddled in their great-coats, had assembled around the doorway to see the guests alight, with that amiable, unenvious interest of the Italians in the pleasure of others. The deep sky glittered with stars; in the corner of the next villa garden the black plumes of some cypresses blotted out their space among them.

"*Isn't* it Florentine?" demanded Mrs. Bowen, giving the hand which Colville offered in helping her out of the carriage a little vivid pressure, full of reminiscence and confident sympathy. A flush of youth warmed his heart; he did not quail even when the porter of the villa intervened between her and her coachman, whom she was telling when to come back, and said that the carriages were ordered for three o'clock.

"Did you ever sit up so late as that in Des Vaches?" asked Miss Graham, mischievously.

"Oh yes; I was editor of a morning paper," he explained. But he did not like the imputation of her question.

Madame Uccelli accepted him most hospitably among her guests when he was presented. She was an American who had returned with her Italian husband to Italy, and had long survived him in the villa which he had built with her money. Such people grow very queer with the lapse of time. Madame Uccelli's character remained inalienably American, but her manners and customs had become largely Italian; without having learned the language thoroughly, she spoke it very fluently, and its idioms marked her Philadelphia English. Her house was a menagerie of all the nationalities; she was liked in Italian society, and there were many Italians; English-speaking Russians abounded; there were many genuine English, Germans, Scandinavians, Protestant Irish, American Catholics, and then Americans of all kinds. There was a superstition of her exclusiveness among her compatriots, but one really met every one there sooner or later; she was supposed to be a convert to the religion of her late husband, but no one really knew what religion she was of, probably not even Madame Uccelli herself. One thing you were sure of at her house, and that was a substantial supper: it is the example of such resident foreigners which has corrupted the Florentines, though many native families still hold out against it.

The dancing was just beginning, and the daughter of Madame Uccelli, who spoke both English and Italian much better than her mother, came forward and possessed herself of Miss Graham, after a polite feint of pressing Mrs. Bowen to let her find a partner for her.

Mrs. Bowen cooed a gracious refusal, telling Fanny Uccelli that she knew very well that she never danced now. The girl had not much time for Colville; she welcomed him, but she was full of her business of starting the dance, and she hurried away without asking him whether she should introduce him to some lady for the quadrille that was forming. Her mother, however, asked him if he would not go out and get himself some tea, and she found a lady to go with him to the supper-room. This lady had daughters whom apparently she wished to supervise while they were dancing, and she brought Colville back very soon. He had to stand by the sofa where she sat till Madame Uccelli found him and introduced him to another mother of daughters. Later he joined a group formed by the father of one of the dancers and the non-dancing husband of a dancing wife. Their conversation was perfunctory; they showed one another that they had no pleasure in it.

Presently the father went to see how his daughter looked while dancing; the husband had evidently no such curiosity concerning his wife; and Colville went with the father, and looked at Miss Graham. She was very beautiful, and she obeyed the music as if it were her breath; her face was rapt, intense, full of an unsmiling delight, which shone in her dark eyes, glowing like low stars. Her abandon interested Colville, and then awed him; the spectacle of that young, unjaded capacity for pleasure touched him with a profound sense of loss. Suddenly Imogene caught sight of him, and with the coming of a second look in her eyes the light of an exquisite smile flashed over her face. His heart was in his throat.

"*Your* daughter?" asked the fond parent at his elbow. "That is mine yonder, in red."

Colville did not answer, nor look at the young lady in red. The dance was ceasing; the fragments of those kaleidoscopic radiations were dispersing themselves; the tormented piano was silent.

The officer whom Imogene had danced with brought her to Mrs. Bowen, and resigned her with the regulation bow, hanging his head down before him as if submitting his neck to the axe. She put her hand in Colville's arm, where he stood beside Mrs. Bowen. "Oh, *do* take me to get something to eat!"

In the supper-room she devoured salad and ices with a childish joy in them. The place was jammed, and she laughed from her corner at Colville's struggles in getting the things for her and bringing them to her. While she was still in the midst of an ice, the faint note of the piano sounded. "Oh, they're beginning again! It's the Lancers!" she said, giving him the plate back. She took his arm again; she almost pulled him along on their return. "Why don't *you* dance?" she demanded, mockingly.

"I would, if you'd let me dance with you."

"Oh, that's impossible! I'm engaged ever so many deep." She dropped his arm instantly at sight of a young Englishman who seemed to be looking for her. This young Englishman had a zeal for dancing that was unsparing; partners were nothing to him except as a means of dancing; his manner expressed a supreme contempt for people who made the slightest mistake, who danced with less science or less conscience than himself. "I've been looking for you," he said, in a tone of cold rebuke, without looking at her. "We've been waiting."

Colville wished to beat him, but Imogene took his rebuke meekly, and murmured some apologies about not hearing the piano before. He hurried off with her without recognizing Colville's existence in any way.

The undancing husband of the dancing wife was boring himself in a corner; Colville decided that the chances with him were better than with the fond father, and joined him, just as a polite officer came up and entreated him to complete a set. "Oh, I never danced in my life," he replied; and then he referred the officer to Colville. "Don't *you* dance?"

"I used to dance," Colville began, while the officer stood looking patiently at him. This was true. He used to dance the Lancers too, and very badly, seventeen years before. He had danced it with Lina Ridgely and the other one, Mrs. Milbury. His glance wandered to the vacant place on the floor; it was the same set which Miss Graham was in; she smiled and beckoned derisively. A vain and foolish ambition fired him. "Oh yes, I can dance a little," he said.

A little was quite enough for the eager officer. He had Colville a partner in an instant, and the next he was on the floor.

"Oh, what fun!" cried Miss Graham; but the fun had not really begun yet.

Colville had forgotten everything about the Lancers. He walked round like a bear in a pen; he capered to and fro with a futile absurdity; people poked him hither and thither; his progress was attended by rending noises from the trains over which he found his path. He smiled and cringed, and apologized to the hardening faces of the dancers; even Miss Graham's face had become very grave.

"This won't do," said the Englishman at last, with cold insolence. He did not address himself to any one; he merely stopped; they all stopped, and Colville was effectively expelled the set; another partner was found for his lady, and he wandered giddily away. He did not know where to turn; the whole room must have seen what an incredible ass he had made of himself, but Mrs. Bowen looked as if she had not seen.

He went up to her, resolved to make fun of himself at the first sign she gave of being privy to his disgrace. But she only said, "Have you found your way to the supper-room yet?"

"Oh yes; twice," he answered, and kept on talking with her and Madame Uccelli. After five minutes or so something occurred to Colville. "Have *you* found the way to the supper-room yet, Mrs. Bowen?"

"No!" she owned, with a small, pathetic laugh, which expressed a certain physical faintness, and reproached him with insupportable gentleness for his selfish obtuseness.

"Let me show you the way," he cried.

"Why, I *am* rather hungry," said Mrs. Bowen, taking his arm, with a patient arrangement first of her fan, her bouquet, and her train, and then moving along by his side with a delicate-footed pace, which insinuated and deprecated her dependence upon him.

There were only a few people in the supper-room, and they had it practically to themselves. She took a cup of tea and a slice of buttered bread, with a little salad, which she excused herself from eating because it was the day after her headache. "I shouldn't have thought you *were* hungry, Mrs. Bowen," he said, "if you hadn't told me so," and he recalled that, as a young girl, her friend used to laugh at her for having such a butterfly appetite; she was in fact one of those women who go through life the marvels of such of our brutal sex as ob-

serve the ethereal nature of their diet. But in an illogical revulsion of feeling, Colville, who was again cramming himself
with all the solids and fluids in reach, and storing up a vain
regret against the morrow, preferred her delicacy to the magnificent rapacity of Miss Graham: Imogene had passed from
salad to ice, and at his suggestion had frankly reverted to
salad again, and then taken a second ice, with the robust appetite of perfect health and perfect youth. He felt a desire to
speak against her to Mrs. Bowen, he did not know why and
he did not know how; he veiled his feeling in an open attack.
"Miss Graham has just been the cause of my playing the fool,
with her dancing. She dances so superbly that she makes you
want to dance too—she made me feel as if I *could* dance."

"Yes," said Mrs. Bowen; "it was very kind of you to complete the set. I saw you dancing," she added, without a glimmer of guilty consciousness in her eyes.

It was very sweet, but Colville had to protest. "Oh no; you
didn't see me *dancing*; you saw me *not* dancing. I am a ruined
man, and I leave Florence to-morrow; but I have the sad satisfaction of reflecting that I don't leave an unbroken train
among the ladies of that set. And I have made one young
Englishman so mad that there is a reasonable hope of his not
recovering."

"Oh no; you *don't* think of going away for that!" said Mrs.
Bowen, not heeding the rest of his joking.

"Well, the time has been when I have left Florence for
less," said Colville, with the air of preparing himself to listen
to reason.

"You mustn't," said Mrs. Bowen, briefly.

"Oh, very well, then, I won't," said Colville, whimsically,
as if that settled it.

Mrs. Bowen would not talk of the matter any more; he
could see that with her kindness, which was always more than
her tact, she was striving to get away from the subject. As he
really cared for it no longer, this made him persist in clinging
to it; he liked this pretty woman's being kind to him. "Well,"
he said, finally, "I consent to stay in Florence on condition
that you suggest some means of atonement for me which I
can also make a punishment to Miss Graham."

Mrs. Bowen did not respond to the question of placating and punishing her *protégée* with sustained interest. They went back to Madame Uccelli and to the other elderly ladies, in the room that opened by archways upon the dancing-room.

Imogene was on the floor, dancing not merely with unabated joy, but with a zest that seemed only to freshen from dance to dance. If she left the dance, it was to go out on her partner's arm to the supper-room. Colville could not decently keep on talking to Mrs. Bowen the whole evening; it would be too conspicuous; he devolved from frump to frump; he bored himself; he yawned in his passage from one of these mothers or fathers to another. The hours passed; it was two o'clock; Imogene was going out to the supper-room again. He was taking out his watch. She saw him, and "Oh, don't!" she cried, laughing, as she passed.

The dancing went on; she was waltzing now in the interminable german. Some one had let down a window in the dancing-room, and he was feeling it in his shoulder. Mrs. Bowen, across the room, looked heroically patient, but weary. He glanced down at the frump on the sofa near, and realized that she had been making a long speech to him, which, he could see from her look, had ended in some sort of question.

Three o'clock came, and they had to wait till the german was over. He felt that Miss Graham was behaving badly, ungratefully, selfishly; on the way home in the carriage he was silent from utter boredom and fatigue, but Mrs. Bowen was sweetly sympathetic with the girl's rapture. Imogene did not seem to feel his moodiness; she laughed, she joked, she told a number of things that happened, she hummed the air of the last waltz. "Isn't it divine?" she asked. "Oh! I feel as if I could dance for a week." She was still dancing; she gave Colville's foot an accidental tap in keeping time on the floor of the carriage to the tune she was humming. No one said anything about a next meeting when they parted at the gate of Palazzo Pinti, and Mrs. Bowen bade her coachman drive Colville to his hotel. But both the ladies' voices called good-night to him as he drove away. He fancied a shade of mocking in Miss Graham's voice.

The great outer door of the hotel was locked, of course,

and the poor little porter kept Colville thumping at it some time before he unlocked it, full of sleepy smiles and apologies. "I'm sorry to wake you up," said Colville, kindly.

"It is my duty," said the porter, with amiable heroism. He discharged another duty by lighting a whole new candle, which would be set down to Colville's account, and went before him to his room up the wide stairs, cold in their white linen path, and on through the crooked corridors haunted by the ghosts of extinct *tables d'hôte*, and full of goblin shadows. He had recovered a noonday suavity by the time he reached Colville's door, and bowed himself out, after lighting the candles within, with a sweet plenitude of politeness, which Colville, even in his gloomy mood, could not help admiring in a man in his shirt sleeves, with only one suspender up.

If there had been a fire, Colville would have liked to sit down before it, and take an account of his feelings, but the atmosphere of a bed-chamber in a Florentine hotel at half past three o'clock on a winter morning is not one that invites to meditation; and he made haste to get into bed, with nothing clearer in his mind than a shapeless sense of having been trifled with. He ought not to have gone to a dancing party, to begin with, and then he certainly ought not to have attempted to dance; so far he might have been master of the situation, and was responsible for it; but he was, over and above this, aware of not having wished to do either, of having been wrought upon against his convictions to do both. He regarded now with supreme loathing a fantastic purpose which he had formed while tramping round on those women's dresses, of privately taking lessons in dancing, and astonishing Miss Graham at the next ball where they met. Miss Graham! What did he care for that child? Or Mrs. Bowen either, for the matter of that? Had he come four thousand miles to be used, to be played with, by them? At this point Colville was aware of the brutal injustice of his mood. They were ladies, both of them, charming and good, and he had been a fool; that was all. It was not the first time he had been a fool for women. An inexpressible bitterness for that old wrong, which, however he had been used to laugh at it and despise it, had made his life solitary and barren, poured upon his soul; it was as if it had happened to him yesterday.

A band of young men burst from one of the narrow streets leading into the piazza and straggled across it, letting their voices flare out upon the silence, and then drop extinct one by one. A whole world of faded associations flushed again in Colville's heart This was Italy; this was Florence; and he execrated the hour in which he had dreamed of returning.

VII

THE NEXT morning's sunshine dispersed the black mood of the night before; but enough of Colville's self-disgust remained to determine him not to let his return to Florence be altogether vain, or his sojourn so idle as it had begun being. The vague purpose which he had cherished of studying the past life and character of the Florentines in their architecture shaped itself anew in the half-hour which he gave himself over his coffee; and he turned it over in his mind with that mounting joy in its capabilities which attends the contemplation of any sort of artistic endeavor. No people had ever more distinctly left the impress of their whole temper in their architecture, or more sharply distinguished their varying moods from period to period in their palaces and temples. He believed that he could not only supply that brief historical sketch of Florence which Mrs. Bowen had lamented the want of, but he could make her history speak an intelligible, an unmistakable tongue in every monument of the past, from the Etruscan wall at Fiesole to the cheap, plain, and tasteless shaft raised to commemorate Italian Unity in the next piazza. With sketches from his own pencil, illustrative of points which he could not otherwise enforce, he could make such a book on Florence as did not exist, such a book as no one had yet thought of making. With this object in his mind, making and keeping him young, he could laugh with any one who liked at the vanity of the middle-aged Hoosier who had spoiled a set in the Lancers at Madame Uccelli's party; he laughed at him now alone, with a wholly impersonal sense of his absurdity.

After breakfast, he went without delay to Vieusseux's reading-room, to examine his catalogue, and see what there was in it to his purpose. While he was waiting his turn to pay his subscription, with the people who surrounded the proprietor, half a dozen of the acquaintances he had made at Mrs. Bowen's passed in and out. Vieusseux's is a place where sooner or later you meet every one you know among the foreign residents at Florence; the natives in smaller proportion resort there too; and Colville heard a lady asking for a book in that perfect Italian which strikes envy to the heart of the stranger sufficiently versed in the language to know that he never shall master it. He rather rejoiced in his despair, however, as an earnest of his renewed intellectual life. Henceforth his life would be wholly intellectual. He did not regret his little excursion into society; it had shown him with dramatic sharpness how unfit for it he was.

"Good-*morning*!" said some one in a bland under-tone full of a pleasant recognition of the claims to quiet of a place where some others were speaking in their ordinary tones.

Colville looked round on the Rev. Mr. Waters, and took his friendly hand. "Good-morning—glad to see you," he answered.

"Are you looking for that short Florentine history for Mrs. Bowen's little girl?" asked Mr. Waters, inclining his head slightly for the reply. "She mentioned it to me."

By day Colville remarked more distinctly that the old gentleman was short and slight, with a youthful eagerness in his face surviving on good terms with the gray locks that fell down his temples from under the brim of his soft felt hat. With the boyish sweetness of his looks blended a sort of appreciative shrewdness, which pointed his smiling lips slightly aslant in what seemed the expectation rather than the intention of humor.

"Not exactly," said Colville, experiencing a difficulty in withholding the fact that in some sort he was just going to write a short Florentine history, and finding a certain pleasure in Mrs. Bowen's having remembered that he had taken an interest in Effie's reading. He had a sudden wish to tell Mr. Waters of his plan, but this was hardly the time or place.

They now found themselves face to face with the librarian, and Mr. Waters made a gesture of waiving himself in Colville's favor.

"No, no!" said the latter; "you had better ask. I am going to put this gentleman through rather an extended course of sprouts."

The librarian smiled with the helplessness of a foreigner who knows his interlocutor's English but not the meaning of it.

"Oh, I merely wanted to ask," said Mr. Waters, addressing the librarian, and explaining to Colville, "whether you had received that book on Savonarola yet. The German one."

"I shall see," said the librarian, and he went upon a quest that kept him some minutes.

"You're not thinking of taking Savonarola's life, I suppose?" suggested Colville.

"Oh no. Villari's book has covered the whole ground forever, it seems to me. It's a wonderful book. You've read it?"

"Yes. It's a thing that makes you feel that, after all, the Italians have only to make a real effort in any direction, and they go ahead of everybody else. What biography of the last twenty years can compare with it?"

"You're right, sir—you're right," cried the old man, enthusiastically. "They're a gifted race, a people of genius."

"I wish for their own sakes they'd give their minds a little to generalship," said Colville, pressed by the facts to hedge somewhat. "They did get so badly smashed in their last war, poor fellows."

"Oh, I don't think I should like them any better if they were better soldiers. Perhaps the lesson of noble endurance that they've given our times is all that we have the right to demand of them in the way of heroism; no one can say they lack courage. And sometimes it seems to me that in simply outgrowing the different sorts of despotism that had fastened upon them, till their broken bonds fell away without positive effort on their part, they showed a greater sublimity than if they had violently conquered their freedom. Most nations sink lower and lower under tyranny; the Italians grew steadily more and more civilized, more noble, more gentle, more grand. It was a wonderful spectacle—like a human soul perfected through suffering and privation. Every period of their history is full of instruction. I find my ancestral puritanism particularly appealed to by the puritanism of Savonarola."

"Then Villari hasn't satisfied you that Savonarola wasn't a Protestant?"

"Oh yes, he has. I said his puritanism. Just now I'm interested in justifying his failure to myself, for it's one of the things in history that I've found it hardest to accept. But no doubt his puritanic state fell because it was dreary and ugly, as the puritanic state always has been. It makes its own virtues intolerable; puritanism won't let you see how good and beautiful the Puritans often are. It was inevitable that Savonarola's enemies should misunderstand and hate him."

"You are one of the last men I should have expected to find among the *Arrabiati*," said Colville.

"Oh, there's a great deal to be said for the Florentine Arrabiati, as well as for the English Malignants, though the Puritans in neither case would have known how to say it. Savonarola perished because he was excessive. I am studying him in this aspect; it is fresh ground. It is very interesting to inquire just at what point a man's virtues become mischievous and intolerable."

These ideas interested Colville; he turned to them with relief from the sense of his recent trivialities; in this old man's earnestness he found support and encouragement in the new course he had marked out for himself. Sometimes it had occurred to him not only that he was too old for the interests of his youth at forty, but that there was no longer time for him to take up new ones. He considered Mr. Waters's gray hairs, and determined to be wiser. "I should like to talk these things over with you—and some other things," he said.

The librarian came toward them with the book for Mr. Waters, who was fumbling near-sightedly in his pocket-book for his card. "I shall be very happy to see you at my room," he said. "Ah, thank you," he added, taking his book, with a simple relish as if it were something whose pleasantness was sensible to the touch. He gave Colville the scholar's far-off look as he turned to go; he was already as remote as the fifteenth century through the magic of the book, which he opened and began to read at once. Colville stared after him; he did not wish to come to just that yet either. Life, active life, life of his own day, called to him; he had been one of its busiest children: could he turn his back upon it for any charm or use that was in the past? Again that unnerving doubt, that paralyzing distrust, beset him, and tempted him to curse the day in which he had returned to this outworn Old World. Idler on its modern surface, or delver in its deep-hearted past, could he reconcile himself to it? What did he care for the Italians of to-day, or the history of the Florentines as expressed in their architectural monuments? It was the problems of the vast, tumultuous American life, which he had turned his back on, that really concerned him. Later he might take up the study that fascinated yonder old man, but for the present it was intolerable.

He was no longer young, that was true; but with an ache of old regret he felt that he had not yet lived his life, that his was a baffled destiny, an arrested fate. A lady came up and took his turn with the librarian, and Colville did not stay for another. He went out and walked down the Lung' Arno toward the Cascine. The sun danced on the river, and bathed the long line of pale buff and gray houses that followed its curve, and ceased in the mist of leafless tree-tops where the Cascine began. It was not the hour of the promenade, and there was little driving; but the sidewalks were peopled thickly enough with persons, in groups or singly, who had the air of straying aimlessly up or down, with no purpose but to be in the sun, after the rainy weather of the past week. There were faces of invalids, wistful and thin, and here and there a man, muffled to the chin, lounged feebly on the parapet and stared at the river. Colville hastened by them; they seemed to claim him as one of their ailing and aging company, and just then he was in the humor of being very young and strong.

A carriage passed before him through the Cascine gates, and drove down the road next the river. He followed, and when it had got a little way it stopped at the road-side, and a lady and little girl alighted, who looked about and caught sight of him, and then obviously waited for him to come up with them. It was Imogene and Effie Bowen, and the young girl called to him: "We *thought* it was you. Aren't you astonished to find us here at this hour?" she demanded, as soon as he came up, and gave him her hand. "Mrs. Bowen sent us for our health—or Effie's health—and I was just making the man stop and let us out for a little walk."

"My health is very much broken too, Miss Effie," said Colville. "Will you let me walk with you?" The child smiled, as she did at Colville's speeches, which she apparently considered all jokes, but diplomatically referred the decision to Imogene with an upward glance.

"We shall be very glad indeed," said the girl.

"That's very polite of you. But Miss Effie makes no effort to conceal her dismay," said Colville.

The little girl smiled again, and her smile was so like the smile of Lina Ridgely, twenty years ago, that his next words were inevitably tinged with reminiscence.

"Does one still come for one's health to the Cascine? When I was in Florence before, there was no other place if one went to look for it with young ladies—the Cascine or the Boboli Gardens. Do they keep the fountain of youth turned on here during the winter still?"

"I've never seen it," said Imogene, gayly.

"Of course not. You never looked for it. Neither did I when I was here before. But it wouldn't escape me now."

Since he had met them he had aged again, in spite of his resolutions to the contrary; somehow, beside their buoyancy and bloom, the youth in his heart faded.

Imogene had started forward as soon as he joined them, and Colville, with Effie's gloved hand stolen shyly in his, was finding it quite enough to keep up with her in her elastic advance.

She wore a long habit of silk, whose fur-trimmed edge wandered diagonally across her breast and down to the edge of her walking dress. To Colville, whom her girlish slimness in her ball costume had puzzled after his original impressions of Junonian abundance, she did not so much dwindle as seem to vanish from the proportions his vision had assigned her that first night when he saw her standing before the mirror. In this out-door avatar, this companionship with the sun and breeze, she was new to him again, and he found himself searching his consciousness for his lost acquaintance with her, and feeling as if he knew her less and less. Perhaps, indeed, she had no very distinctive individuality; perhaps at her age no woman has, but waits for it to come to her through life, through experience. She was an expression of youth, of health, of beauty, and of the moral loveliness that comes from a fortunate combination of these; but beyond this she was elusive in a way that seemed to characterize her even materially. He could not make anything more of the mystery as he walked at her side, and he went thinking—formlessly, as people always think—that with the child or with her mother he would have had a community of interest and feeling which he lacked with this splendid girlhood; he was both too young and too old for it; and then, while he answered this or that to Imogene's talk aptly enough, his mind went back to the time when this mystery was no mystery, or when he was contemporary with it, and if he did not understand it, at least accepted it as if it were the most natural thing in the world. It seemed a longer time now since it had been in his world than it was since he was a child.

"Should you have thought," she asked, turning her face back toward him, "that it would be so hot in the sun to-day? *Oh*, that beautiful river! How it twists and writhes along! Do you remember that sonnet of Longfellow's—the one he wrote in Italian about the Ponte Vecchio, and the Arno twisting like a dragon underneath it? They say that Hawthorne used to live in a villa just behind the hill over there; we're going to look it up as soon as the weather is settled. Don't you think his books are perfectly fascinating?"

"Yes," said Colville; "only I should want a good while to say it."

"*I* shouldn't!" retorted the girl. "When you've said fascinating, you've said everything. There's no other word for them. Don't you like to talk about the books you've read?"

"I would, if I could remember the names of the characters. But I get them mixed up."

"Oh, *I* never do! I remember the least one of them, and all they do and say."

"I used to."

"It seems to me you *used* to do everything."

"It seems to me as if I did.

"   'I remember, when I think,
        That my youth was half divine.' "

"Oh, Tennyson—yes! *He's* fascinating. Don't you think he's fascinating?"

"Very," said Colville. He was wondering whether this were the kind of talk that he thought was literary when he was a young fellow.

"How perfectly weird the 'Vision of Sin' is!" Imogene continued. "Don't you like *weird* things?"

"Weird things?" Colville reflected. "Yes; but I don't see very much in them any more. The fact is, they don't seem to come to anything in particular."

"Oh, *I* think they do! I've had dreams that I've lived on for days. Do you ever have prophetic dreams?"

"Yes; but they never come true. When they do, I know that I didn't have them."

"What *do* you mean?"

"I mean that we are all so fond of the marvellous that we can't trust ourselves about any experience that seems supernatural. If a ghost appeared to me I should want him to prove it by at least two other reliable, disinterested witnesses before I believed my own account of the matter."

"Oh!" cried the girl, half puzzled, half amused. "Then of course you don't believe in ghosts?"

"Yes; I expect to be one myself some day. But I'm in no hurry to mingle with them."

Imogene smiled vaguely, as if the talk pleased her, even when it mocked the fancies and whims which, after so many generations that have indulged them, she was finding so fresh and new in her turn.

"Don't you like to walk by the side of a river?" she asked, increasing her eager pace a little "I feel as if it were bearing me along."

"I feel as if I were carrying it," said Colville. "It's as fatiguing as walking on railroad ties."

"Oh, that's too bad!" cried the girl. "How can you be so prosaic? Should you ever have believed that the sun could be so hot in January? And look at those ridiculous green hillsides over the river there! Don't you like it to be winter when it *is* winter?"

She did not seem to have expected anything from Colville but an impulsive acquiescence, but she listened while he defended the mild weather. "I think it's very well for Italy," he said. "It has always seemed to me—that is, it seems to me now for the first time, but one has to begin the other way—as if the seasons here had worn themselves out like the turbulent passions of the people. I dare say the winter was much fiercer in the times of the Bianchi and Neri."

"Oh, how delightful! Do you really believe that?"

"No, I don't know that I do. But I shouldn't have much difficulty in proving it, I think, to the sympathetic understanding."

"I wish you would prove it to mine. It sounds so pretty, I'm sure it must be true."

"Oh, then, it isn't necessary. I'll reserve my arguments for Mrs. Bowen."

"You had better. She isn't at all romantic. She says it's very well for me she isn't—that her being matter-of-fact lets me be as romantic as I like."

"Then Mrs. Bowen isn't as romantic as she would like to be if she hadn't charge of a romantic young lady?"

"Oh, I don't say that. Dear me! I'd no idea it *could* be so hot in January." As they strolled along beside the long hedge of laurel, the carriage slowly following them at a little distance, the sun beat strong upon the white road, blotched here and there with the black irregular shadows of the ilexes. The girl undid the pelisse across her breast, with a fine impetuosity, and let it swing open as she walked. She stopped suddenly. "Hark! What bird was that?"

" 'It was the nightingale, and not the lark,' " suggested Colville, lazily.

"Oh, *don't* you think *Romeo and Juliet* is divine?" demanded Imogene, promptly dropping the question of the bird.

"I don't know about Romeo," returned Colville, "but it's sometimes occurred to me that Juliet was rather forth-putting."

"You *know* she wasn't. It's my favorite play. I could go every night. It's perfectly amazing to me that they can play anything else."

"You would like it five hundred nights in the year, like *Hazel Kirke*? That would be a good deal of Romeo, not to say Juliet."

"They ought to do it out of respect to Shakespeare. Don't you like Shakespeare?"

"Well, I've seen the time when I preferred Alexander Smith," said Colville, evasively.

"Alexander Smith? Who in the world is Alexander Smith?"

"How recent you are! Alexander Smith was an immortal who flourished about the year 1850."

"That was before I was born. How could I remember him? But I don't feel so very recent for all that."

"Neither do I, this morning," said Colville. "I was up at one of Pharaoh's balls last night, and I danced too much."

He gave Imogene a droll glance, and then bent it upon Effie's discreet face. The child dropped her eyes with a blush like her mother's, having first sought provisional counsel of Imogene, who turned away. He rightly inferred that they all had been talking him over at breakfast, and he broke into a laugh which they joined in, but Imogene said nothing in recognition of the fact.

With what he felt to be haste for his relief she said, "Don't you hate to be told to read a book?"

"I used to—quarter of a century ago," said Colville, recognizing that this was the way young people talked, even then.

"Used to?" she repeated. "Don't you now?"

"No; I'm a great deal more tractable now. I always say that I shall get the book out of the library. I draw the line at buying. I still hate to *buy* a book that people recommend."

"What kind of books *do* you like to buy?"

"Oh, no kind. I think we ought to get all our books out of the library."

"Do you never like to talk in earnest?"

"Well, not often," said Colville. "Because, if you do, you can't say with a good conscience afterward that you were only in fun."

"Oh! And do you always like to talk so that you can get out of things afterward?"

"No. I didn't say that, did I?"

"Very nearly, I should think."

"Then I'm glad I didn't quite."

"I like people to be outspoken—to say everything they think," said the girl, regarding him with a puzzled look.

"Then I foresee that I shall become a favorite," answered Colville. "I say a great deal more than I think."

She looked at him again, with envy, with admiration, qualifying her perplexity. They had come to a point where some moss-grown, weather-beaten statues stood at the corners of the road that traversed the bosky stretch between the avenues of the Cascine. "Ah, how beautiful they are!" he said, halting, and giving himself to the rapture that a blackened garden statue imparts to one who beholds it from the vantage-ground of sufficient years and experience.

"Do you remember that story of Heine's," he resumed, after a moment, "of the boy who steals out of the old castle by moonlight, and kisses the lips of the garden statue, fallen among the rank grass of the ruinous parterres? And long afterward, when he looks down on the sleep of the dying girl where she lies on the green sofa, it seems to him that she and that statue are the same?"

"Oh!" deeply sighed the young girl. "No; I never read it. Tell me what it is. I *must* read it."

"The rest is all talk—very good talk, but I doubt whether it would interest you. He goes on to talk of a great many things—of the way Bellini spoke French, for example. He says it was blood-curdling, horrible, cataclysmal. He brought out the poor French words and broke them upon the wheel, till you thought the whole world must give way with a thunder-crash. A dead hush reigned in the room; the women did not know whether to faint or fly; the men looked down at their pantaloons, and tried to realize what they had on."

"Oh, how perfectly delightful! how shameful!" cried the girl. "I *must* read it. What is it in? What is the name of the story?"

"It isn't a story," said Colville. "Did you ever see anything lovelier than these statues?"

"No," said Imogene. "*Are* they good?"

"They are much better than good—they are the very worst rococo."

"What makes you say they are beautiful, then?"

"Why, don't you see? They commemorate youth, gayety, brilliant, joyous life. That's what that kind of statues was made for—to look on at rich, young, beautiful people and their gallantries; to be danced before by fine ladies and gentlemen playing at shepherds and shepherdesses; to be driven past by marcheses and contessinas flirting in carriages; to be hung with scarfs and wreaths; to be parts of eternal *fêtes champêtres*. Don't you see how bored they look? When I first came to Italy I should have detested and ridiculed their bad art; but now they're exquisite—the worse, the better."

"I don't know what in the world you *do* mean," said Imogene, laughing uneasily.

"Mrs. Bowen would. It's a pity Mrs. Bowen isn't here with us. Miss Effie, if I lift you up to one of those statues, will you kindly ask it if it doesn't remember a young American signore who was here just before the French Revolution? I don't believe it's forgotten me."

"No, no," said Imogene. "It's time we were walking back. Don't you like Scott?" she added. "I should think you would if you like those romantic things. I used to like Scott so *much*! When I was fifteen I wouldn't read anything but Scott. Don't you like Thackeray? Oh, he's so *cynical*! It's perfectly delightful."

"Cynical?" repeated Colville, thoughtfully. "I was looking into *The Newcomes* the other day, and I thought he was rather sentimental."

"Sentimental! Why, what an idea! That is the strangest thing I ever heard of. Oh!" she broke in upon her own amazement, "don't you think Browning's 'Statue and the Bust' is splendid? Mr. Morton read it to us—to Mrs. Bowen, I mean."

Colville resented this freedom of Mr. Morton's, he did not know just why; then his pique was lost in sarcastic recollection of the time when he too used to read poems to ladies. He had read that poem to Lina Ridgely and the other one.

"Mrs. Bowen asked him to read it," Imogene continued.

"Did she?" asked Colville, pensively.

"And then we discussed it afterward. We had a long discussion. And then he read us the 'Legend of Pornic,' and we had a discussion about that. Mrs. Bowen says it was real gold they found in the coffin; but I think it was the girl's 'gold hair.' I don't know which Mr. Morton thought. Which do you? Don't you think the 'Legend of Pornic' is splendid?"

"Yes, it's a great poem, and deep," said Colville. They had come to a place where the bank sloped invitingly to the river.

"Miss Effie," he asked, "wouldn't you like to go down and throw stones into the Arno? That's what a river is for," he added, as the child glanced toward Imogene for authorization—"to have stones thrown into it."

"Oh, let us!" cried Imogene, rushing down to the brink. "I don't want to throw stones into it, but to get near it—to get near to any bit of nature. They do pen you up so from it in Europe!" She stood and watched Colville skim stones over the current. "When you stand by the shore of a swift river like this, or near a railroad train when it comes whirling by, don't you ever have a morbid impulse to fling yourself forward?"

"Not at my time of life," said Colville, stooping to select a flat stone. "Morbid impulses are one of the luxuries of youth." He threw the stone, which skipped triumphantly far out into the stream. "That was beautiful, wasn't it, Miss Effie?"

"Lovely!" murmured the child.

He offered her a flat pebble. "Would you like to try one?"

"It would spoil my gloves," she said, in deprecating refusal.

"Let *me* try it!" cried Imogene. "I'm not afraid of my gloves."

Colville yielded the pebble, looking at her with the thought of how intoxicating he should once have found this bit of willful abandon, but feeling rather sorry for it now. "Oh, perhaps not," he said, laying his hand upon hers and looking into her eyes.

She returned his look, and then she dropped the pebble and put her hand back in her muff, and turned and ran up the bank. "There's the carriage. It's time we should be going." At the top of the bank she became a mirror of dignity, a transparent mirror to his eye. "Are you going back to town, Mr. Colville?" she asked, with formal state. "We could set you down anywhere."

"Thank you, Miss Graham. I shall be glad to avail myself of your very kind offer. Allow me." He handed her ceremoniously to the carriage; he handed Effie Bowen even more ceremoniously to the carriage, holding his hat in one hand while he offered the other. Then he mounted to the seat in front of them. "The weather has changed," he said.

Imogene hid her face in her muff, and Effie Bowen bowed hers against Imogene's shoulder.

A sense of the girl's beauty lingered in Colville's thought all day, and recurred to him again and again; and the ambitious intensity and enthusiasm of her talk came back in touches of amusement and compassion. How divinely young it all was, and how lovely! He patronized it from a height far aloof.

He was not in the frame of mind for the hotel table, and he went to lunch at a restaurant. He chose a simple trattoria, the first he came to, and he took his seat at one of the bare, rude tables, where the joint saucers for pepper and salt, and a small glass for tooth-picks, with a much-scraped porcelain box for matches, expressed an uncorrupted Florentinity of custom. But when he gave his order in off-hand Italian, the waiter answered in the French which waiters get together for the traveller's confusion in Italy, and he resigned himself to whatever chance of acquaintance might befall him. The place had a companionable smell of stale tobacco, and the dim light showed him on the walls of a space dropped a step or two lower, at the end of the room, a variety of sketches and caricatures. A waiter was laying a large table in this space, and when Colville came up to examine the drawings he jostled him, with due apologies, in the haste of a man working against time for masters who will brook no delay. He was hurrying still when a party of young men came in and took their places at the table, and began to rough him for his delay. Colville could recognize several of them in the vigorous burlesques on the walls, and as others dropped in the grotesque portraitures made him feel as if he had seen them before. They all talked at once, each man of his own interests, except when they joined in a shout of mockery and welcome for some new-comer. Colville, at his *risotto*, almost the room's length away, could hear what they thought, one and another, of Botticelli and Michelangelo; of old Piloty's things at Munich; of the dishes they had served to them, and of the quality of the Chianti; of the respective merits of German and Italian tobacco; of whether Inglehart had probably got to Venice yet; of the personal habits of Billings, and of the question whether the want of modelling in Simmons's nose had anything to do with his Italian accent; of the overrated coloring of some of those Venetian fellows; of the delicacy of Mino da Fiesole, and of the genius of Babson's tailor. Babson was there to defend the cut of his trousers, and Billings and Simmons were present to answer for themselves at the expense of the pictures of those who had called their habits and features into question. When it came to this, all the voices joined in a jolly uproar. Derision and denial broke out of the tumult, and presently they were all talking quietly of a reception which some of them were at the day before. Then Colville heard one of them saying that he would like a chance to paint some lady whose name he did not catch, and "She looks awfully sarcastic," one of the young fellows said.

"They say she *is*," said another. "They say she's awfully intellectual."

"Boston?" queried a third.

"No; Kalamazoo. The centre of culture is out there now."

"She knows how to dress, anyhow," said the first commentator. "I wonder what Parker would talk to her about when he was painting her? He's never read anything but Poe's 'Ullalume.' "

"Well, that's a good subject—'Ullalume.' "

"I suppose she's read it?"

"She's read 'most everything, they say."

"What's an Ullalume, anyway, Parker?"

One of the group sprang up from the table and drew on the wall what he labelled "An Ullalume." Another rapidly depicted Parker in the moment of sketching a young lady; her portrait had got as far as the eyes and nose when some one protested: "Oh, hello! No personalities."

The draughtsman said, "Well, all right!" and sat down again.

"Hall talked with her the most. What did she say, Hall?"

"Hall can't remember words in three syllables, but he says it was mighty brilliant and mighty deep."

"They say she's a niece of Mrs. Bowen's. She's staying with Mrs. Bowen."

Then it was the wisdom and brilliancy and severity of Imogene Graham that these young men stood in awe of! Colville remembered how the minds of girls of twenty had once daz-zled him. "And, yes," he mused, "she must have believed that we were talking literature in the Cascine. Of course I should have thought it an intellectual time when I was at that age," he owned to himself with forlorn irony.

The young fellows went on to speak of Mrs. Bowen, whom it seemed they had known the winter before. She had been very polite to them; they praised her as if she were quite an old woman.

"But she must have been a very pretty girl," one of them put in.

"Well, she has a good deal of style yet."

"Oh yes, but she never could have been a beauty like the other one."

On her part, Imogene was very sober when she met Mrs. Bowen, though she had come in flushed and excited from the air and the morning's adventure. Mrs. Bowen was sitting by the fire, placidly reading; a vase of roses on the little table near her diffused the delicate odor of winter roses through the room; all seemed very still and dim, and of another time, somehow.

Imogene kept away from the fire, sitting down, in the pro-visional fashion of women, with her things on; but she un-buttoned her pelisse and flung it open. Effie had gone to her room.

"Did you have a pleasant drive?" asked Mrs. Bowen.

"Very," said the girl.

"Mr. Morton brought you these roses," continued Mrs. Bowen.

"Oh," said Imogene, with a cold glance at them.

"The Flemmings have asked us to a party Thursday. There is to be dancing."

"The Flemmings?"

"Yes." As if she now saw reason to do so, Mrs. Bowen laid the book face downward in her lap. She yawned a little, with her hand on her mouth. "Did you meet any one you knew?"

"Yes; Mr. Colville." Mrs. Bowen cut her yawn in half. "We got out to walk in the Cascine, and we saw him coming in at the gate. He came up and asked if he might walk with us."

"Did you have a pleasant walk?" asked Mrs. Bowen, a breath more chillily than she had asked if they had a pleasant drive.

"Yes, pleasant enough. And then we came back and went down the river-bank, and he skipped stones, and we took him to his hotel."

"Was there anybody you knew in the Cascine?"

"Oh no; the place was a howling wilderness. I never saw it so deserted," said the girl, impatiently. "It was terribly hot walking. I thought I should burn up."

Mrs. Bowen did not answer anything; she let the book lie in her lap.

"What an odd person Mr. Colville is!" said Imogene, after a moment. "Don't you think he's very different from other gentlemen?"

"Why?"

"Oh, he has such a peculiar way of talking."

"What peculiar way?"

"Oh, I don't know. Plenty of the young men I see talk cynically, and I do sometimes myself—desperately, don't you know. But then I know very well we don't mean anything by it."

"And do you think Mr. Colville does? Do you think he talks cynically?"

Imogene leaned back in her chair and reflected. "No," she returned, slowly, "I can't say that he does. But he talks lightly, with a kind of touch and go that makes you feel that he has exhausted all feeling. He doesn't parade it at all. But you hear between the words, don't you know, just as you read between the lines in some kinds of poetry. Of course it's everything in knowing what he's been through. He's perfectly unaffected; and don't you think he's good?"

"Oh yes," sighed Mrs. Bowen. "In his way."

"But he sees through you. Oh, quite! Nothing escapes him, and pretty soon he lets out that he has seen through you, and then you feel so *flat*! Oh, it's perfectly intoxicating to be with him. I would give the world to talk as he does."

"What was your talk all about?"

"Oh, I don't know. I suppose it would have been called rather intellectual."

Mrs. Bowen smiled infinitesimally. But after a moment she said, gravely: "Mr. Colville is very much older than you. He's old enough to be your father."

"Yes, I know that. You feel that he feels old, and it's perfectly tragical. Sometimes when he turns that slow, dull, melancholy look on you, he seems a thousand years old."

"I don't mean that he's positively old," said Mrs. Bowen. "He's only old comparatively."

"Oh yes; I understand that. And I don't mean that he really seems a thousand years old. What I meant was, he seems a thousand years off, as if he were still young, and had got left behind somehow. He seems to be on the other side of some impassable barrier, and you want to get over there and help him to our side, but you can't do it. I suppose his talking in that light way is merely a subterfuge to hide his feeling, to make him forget."

Mrs. Bowen fingered the edges of her book. "You mustn't let your fancy run away with you, Imogene," she said, with a little painful smile.

"Oh, I *like* to let it run away with me. And when I get such a subject as Mr. Colville, there's no stopping. I can't stop, and I don't *wish* to stop. Shouldn't you have thought that he would have been perfectly crushed at the exhibition he made of himself in the Lancers last night? He wasn't the least embarrassed when he met me, and the only allusion he made to it was to say that he had been up late, and had danced too much. Wasn't it wonderful he could do it? Oh, if *I* could do that!"

"I wish he could have avoided the occasion for his bravado," said Mrs. Bowen.

"I think I was a little to blame, perhaps," said the girl. "I beckoned him to come and take the vacant place."

"I don't see that that was an excuse," returned Mrs. Bowen, primly.

Imogene seemed insensible to the tone, as it concerned herself; it only apparently reminded her of something. "Guess what Mr. Colville said, when I had been silly, and then tried to make up for it by being very dignified all of a sudden?"

"I don't know. How had you been silly?"

The servant brought in some cards. Imogene caught up the

pelisse which she had been gradually shedding as she sat talking to Mrs. Bowen, and ran out of the room by another door.

They did not recur to the subject. But that night, when Mrs. Bowen went to say good-night to Effie, after the child had gone to bed, she lingered.

"Effie," she said at last, in a husky whisper, "what did Imogene say to Mr. Colville to-day that made him laugh?"

"I don't know," said the child. "They kept laughing at so many things."

"Laughing?"

"Yes; he laughed. Do you mean toward the last, when he had been throwing stones into the river?"

"It must have been then."

The child stretched herself drowsily. "Oh, I couldn't understand it all. She wanted to throw a stone in the river, but he told her she had better not. But that didn't make *him* laugh. She was so very stiff just afterward that he said the weather had changed, and that made *us* laugh."

"Was that all?"

"We kept laughing ever so long. I never saw any one like Mr. Colville. How queerly the fire shines on your face! It gives you such a beautiful complexion."

"Does it?"

"Yes, lovely." The child's mother stooped over and kissed her. "You're the prettiest mamma in the world," she said, throwing her arms round her neck. "Sometimes I can't tell whether Imogene is prettier or not, but to-night I'm certain you are. Do you like to have me think that?"

"Yes, yes. But don't pull me down so; you hurt my neck. Good-night."

The child let her go. "I haven't said my prayer yet, mamma. I was thinking."

"Well, say it now, then," said the mother, gently.

When the child had finished she turned upon her cheek. "Good-night, mamma."

Mrs. Bowen went about the room a little while, picking up its pretty disorder. Then she sat down in a chair by the hearth, where a log was still burning. The light of the flame flickered upon her face, and threw upon the ceiling a writhing, fantastic shadow, the odious caricature of her gentle beauty.

VIII

IN THAT still air of the Florentine winter time seems to share
the arrest of the natural forces, the repose of the elements.
The pale blue sky is frequently overcast, and it rains two days
out of five; sometimes, under extraordinary provocation from
the north, a snow-storm whirls along under the low gray
dome, and whitens the brown roofs, where a growth of spin-
dling weeds and grass clothes the tiles the whole year round,
and shows its delicate green above the gathered flakes. But
for the most part the winds are laid, and the sole change is
from quiet sun to quiet shower. This at least is the impression
which remains in the senses of the sojourning stranger, whose
days slip away with so little difference one from another that
they seem really not to have passed, but, like the grass that
keeps the hill-sides fresh round Florence all the winter long,
to be waiting some decisive change of season before they
begin.

The first of the Carnival sights, that marked the lapse of a
month since his arrival, took Colville by surprise. He could
not have believed that it was February yet if it had not been
for the straggling maskers in armor whom he met one day in
Via Borgognissanti, with their visors up for their better convenience in smoking. They were part of the chorus at one of
the theatres, and they were going about to eke out their sal-
aries with the gifts of people whose windows the festival season privileged them to play under. The silly spectacle stirred
Colville's blood a little, as any sort of holiday preparation was
apt to do. He thought that it afforded him a fair occasion to
call at Palazzo Pinti, where he had not been so much of late
as in the first days of his renewed acquaintance with Mrs.
Bowen. He had at one time had the fancy that Mrs. Bowen
was cool toward him. He might very well have been mistaken
in this; in fact, she had several times addressed him the politest reproaches for not coming; but he made some evasion,
and went only on the days when she was receiving other people, and when necessarily he saw very little of the family.

Miss Graham was always very friendly, but always very

busy, drawing tea from the samovar, and looking after others. Effie Bowen dropped her eyes in re-established strangeness when she brought the basket of cake to him. There was one moment when he suspected that he had been talked over in family council, and put under a certain regimen. But he had no proof of this, and it had really nothing to do with his keeping away, which was largely accidental. He had taken up, with as much earnestness as he could reasonably expect of himself, that notion of studying the architectural expression of Florentine character at the different periods. He had spent a good deal of money in books, he had revived his youthful familiarity with the city, and he had made what acquaintance he could with people interested in such matters. He met some of these in the limited but very active society in which he mingled daily and nightly. After the first strangeness to any sort of social life had worn off, he found himself very fond of the prompt hospitalities which his introduction at Mrs. Bowen's had opened to him. His host—or more frequently it was his hostess—had sometimes merely an apartment at a hotel; perhaps the family was established in one of the fur-nished lodgings which stretch the whole length of the Lung' Arno on either hand, and abound in all the new streets ap-proaching the Cascine, and had set up the simple and facile housekeeping of the sojourner in Florence for a few months; others had been living in the villa or the palace they had taken for years.

The more recent and transitory people expressed something of the prevailing English and American æstheticism in the decoration of their apartments, but the greater part accepted the Florentine drawing-room as their landlord had imagined it for them, with furniture and curtains in yellow satin, a cheap ingrain carpet thinly covering the stone floor, and a fire of little logs ineffectually blazing on the hearth, and flickering on the carved frames of the pictures on the wall and the na-kedness of the frescoed allegories in the ceiling. Whether of longer or shorter stay, the sojourners were bound together by a common language and a common social tradition; they all had a Day, and on that day there was tea and bread and but-ter for every comer. They had one another to dine; there were evening parties, with dancing and without dancing. Colville even went to a fancy ball, where he was kept in countenance by several other Florentines of the period of Romola. At all these places he met nearly the same people, whose alien life in the midst of the native community struck him as one of the phases of modern civilization worthy of note, if not particular study; for he fancied it destined to a wider future throughout Europe, as the conditions in England and America grow more tiresome and more onerous. They seemed to see very little of Italian society, and to be shut out from practical knowledge of the local life by the terms upon which they had themselves insisted. Our race finds its simplified and cheapened London or New York in all its Continental resorts now, but nowhere has its taste been so much studied as in Italy, and especially in Florence. It was not, perhaps, the real Englishman or American who had been considered, but a *forestiere* conventionalized from the Florentine's observation of many Anglo-Saxons. But he had been so well conjectured that he was hemmed round with a very fair illusion of his national circumstances.

It was not that he had his English or American doctor to prescribe for him when sick, and his English or American apothecary to compound his potion; it was not that there was an English tailor and an American dentist, an English bookseller and an English baker, and chapels of every shade of Protestantism, with Catholic preaching in English every Sunday. These things were more or less matters of necessity, but Colville objected that the barbers should offer him an American shampoo; that the groceries should abound in English biscuit and our own canned fruit and vegetables, and that the grocers' clerks should be ambitious to read the labels of the Boston baked beans. He heard—though he did not prove this by experiment—that the master of a certain trattoria had studied the doughnut of New England till he had actually surpassed the original in the qualities that have undermined our digestion as a people. But above all it interested him to see that intense expression of American civilization, the horse-car, triumphing along the magnificent avenues that mark the line of the old city walls; and he recognized an instinctive obedience to an abstruse natural law in the fact that whereas the omnibus, which the Italians have derived from the En glish, was not filled beyond its seating capacity, the horse-car was overcrowded without and within at Florence just as it is with us who invented it.

"I wouldn't mind even that," he said one day to the lady who was drawing him his fifth or sixth cup of tea for that afternoon, and with whom he was naturally making this absurd condition of things a matter of personal question; "but you people here pass your days in a round of unbroken English, except when you talk with your servants. I'm not sure you don't speak English with the shop people. I can hardly get them to speak Italian to me."

"Perhaps they think you can speak English better," said the lady.

This went over Florence; in a week it was told to Colville as something said to some one else. He fearlessly reclaimed it as said to himself, and this again was told. In the houses where he visited he had the friendly acceptance of any intelligent and reasonably agreeable person who comes promptly and willingly when he is asked, and seems always to have enjoyed himself when he goes away. But besides this sort of general favor, he enjoyed a very pleasing little personal popularity which came from his interest in other people, from his good-nature, and from his inertness. He slighted no acquaintance, and talked to every one with the same apparent wish to be entertaining. This was because he was incapable of the cruelty of open indifference when his lot was cast with a dull person, and also because he was mentally too lazy to contrive pretenses for getting away; besides, he did not really find anybody altogether a bore, and he had no wish to shine. He listened without shrinking to stories that he had heard before, and to things that had already been said to him; as has been noted, he had himself the habit of repeating his ideas with the recklessness of maturity, for he had lived long enough to know that this can be done with almost entire safety.

He haunted the studios a good deal, and through a retrospective affinity with art, and a human sympathy with the sacrifice which it always involves, he was on friendly terms with sculptors and painters who were not in every case so friendly with one another. More than once he saw the scars of old rivalries, and he might easily have been an adherent of two or three parties. But he tried to keep the freedom of the different camps without taking sides; and he felt the pathos of the case when they all told the same story of the disaster which the taste for bric-à-brac had wrought to the cause of art; how people who came abroad no longer gave orders for statues and pictures, but spent their money on curtains and carpets, old chests and chairs, and pots and pans. There were some among these artists whom he had known twenty years before in Florence, ardent and hopeful beginners; and now the backs of their gray or bald heads, as they talked to him with their faces toward their work, and a pencil or a pinch of clay held thoughtfully between their fingers, appealed to him as if he had remained young and prosperous, and they had gone forward to age and hard work. They were very quaint at times. They talked the American slang of the war days and of the days before the war; without a mastery of Italian, they often used the idioms of that tongue in their English speech. They were dim and vague about the country, with whose affairs they had kept up through the newspapers. Here and there one thought he was going home very soon; others had finally relinquished all thoughts of return. These had, perhaps, without knowing it, lost the desire to come back; they cowered before the expensiveness of life in America, and doubted of a future with which, indeed, only the young can hopefully grapple. But in spite of their accumulated years, and the evil times on which they had fallen, Colville thought them mostly very happy men, leading simple and innocent lives in a world of the ideal, and rich in the inexhaustible beauty of the city, the sky, the air. They all, whether they were ever going back or not, were fervent Americans, and their ineffaceable nationality marked them, perhaps, all the more strongly for the patches of something alien that overlaid it in places. They knew that he was or had been a newspaper man; but if they secretly cherished the hope that he would bring them to the *dolce lume* of print, they never betrayed it; and the authorship of his letter about the American artists in Florence, which he printed in the *American Register* at Paris, was not traced to him for a whole week.

Colville was a frequent visitor of Mr. Waters, who had a lodging in Piazza San Marco, of the poverty which can always be decent in Italy. It was bare, but for the books that furnished it; with a table for his writing, on a corner of which he breakfasted, a wide sofa with cushions in coarse white linen that frankly confessed itself a bed by night, and two chairs of plain Italian walnut; but the windows, which had no sun, looked out upon the church and the convent sacred to the old Socinian for the sake of the meek, heroic mystic whom they keep alive in all the glory of his martyrdom. No two minds could well have been farther apart than the New England minister and the Florentine monk, and no two souls nearer together, as Colville recognized with a not irreverent smile.

When the old man was not looking up some point of his saint's history in his books, he was taking with the hopefulness of youth and the patience of age a lesson in colloquial Italian from his landlady's daughter, which he pronounced with a scholarly scrupulosity and a sincere atonic Massachusetts accent. He practiced the language wherever he could, especially at the trattoria where he dined, and where he made occasions to detain the waiter in conversation. They humored him, out of their national good-heartedness and sympathy, and they did what they could to realize a strange American dish for him on Sundays—a combination of stock-fish and potatoes boiled, and then fried together in small cakes. They revered him as a foreign gentleman of saintly amiability and incomprehensible preferences; and he was held in equal regard at the next green-grocer's, where he spent every morning five centesimi for a bunch of radishes and ten for a little pat of butter to eat with his bread and coffee: he could not yet accustom himself to mere bread and coffee for breakfast, though he conformed as completely as he could to the Italian way of living. He respected the abstemiousness of the race; he held that it came from a spirituality of nature to which the North was still strange, with all its conscience and sense of individual accountability. He contended that he never suffered in his small dealings with these people from the dishonesty which most of his countrymen complained of; and he praised their unfailing gentleness of manner: this could arise only from goodness of heart, which was perhaps the best kind of goodness, after all.

None of these humble acquaintance of his could well have accounted for the impression they all had that he was some sort of ecclesiastic. They could never have understood—nor, for that matter, could any one have understood through European tradition—the sort of sacerdotal office that Mr. Waters had filled so long in the little deeply book-clubbed New England village where he had outlived most of his flock, till one day he rose in the midst of the surviving dyspeptics and consumptives and, following the example of Mr. Emerson, renounced his calling forever. By that time even the pale Unitarianism thinning out into paler doubt was no longer tenable with him. He confessed that while he felt the Divine goodness more and more, he believed that it was a mistake to preach any specific creed or doctrine, and he begged them to release him from their service. A young man came to fill his place in their pulpit, but he kept his place in their hearts. They raised a subscription of seventeen hundred dollars and thirty-five cents, and this being submitted to the new button manufacturer, who had founded his industry in the village, he promptly rounded it out to three thousand, and Mr. Waters came to Florence. His people parted with him in terms of regret as delicate as they were awkward, and their love followed him. He corresponded regularly with two or three ladies, and his letters were sometimes read from his pulpit.

Colville took the Piazza San Marco in on his way to Palazzo Pinti on the morning when he had made up his mind to go there, and he stood at the window looking out with the old man when some more maskers passed through the place—two young fellows in old Florentine dress, with a third habited as a nun.

"Ah," said the old man, gently, "I wish they hadn't introduced the nun! But I suppose they can't help signalizing their escape from the domination of the Church on all occasions. It's a natural reaction. It will all come right in time."

"You preach the true American gospel," said Colville.

"Of course. That *is* the gospel."

"Do you suppose that Savonarola would think it had all come out right," asked Colville, a little maliciously, "if he could look from the window with us here and see the wicked old Carnival, that he tried so hard to kill four hundred years ago, still alive? And kicking?" he added, in cognizance of the caper of one of the maskers.

"Oh yes; why not? By this time he knows that his puritanism was all a mistake, unless as a thing for the moment only. I should rather like to have Savonarola here with us; he would find these costumes familiar; they are of his time. I shall make a point of seeing all I can of the Carnival, as part of my study of Savonarola, if nothing else."

"I'm afraid you'll have to give yourself limitations," said Colville, as one of the maskers threw his arm round the mock-nun's neck. But the old man did not see this, and Colville did not feel it necessary to explain himself.

The maskers had passed out of the piazza now, and "Have you seen our friends at Palazzo Pinti lately?" said Mr. Waters.

"Not very," said Colville. "I was just on my way there."

"I wish you would make them my compliments. Such a beautiful young creature."

"Yes," said Colville, "she is certainly a beautiful girl."

"I meant Mrs. Bowen," returned the old man, quietly.

"Oh; I thought you meant Miss Graham. Mrs. Bowen is my contemporary, and so I didn't think of her when you said young. I should have called her pretty rather than beautiful."

"No; she's beautiful. The young girl is good-looking—I don't deny that; but she is very crude yet."

Colville laughed. "Crude in looks? I should have said Miss Graham was rather crude in mind, though I'm not sure I wouldn't have stopped at saying *young*."

"No," mildly persisted the old man; "she couldn't be crude in mind without being crude in looks."

"You mean," pursued Colville, smiling, but not wholly satisfied, "that she hasn't a lovely nature?"

"You never can know what sort of nature a young girl has. Her nature depends so much upon that of the man whose fate she shares."

"The woman is what the man makes her? That is convenient for the woman, and relieves her of all responsibility."

"The man is what the woman makes him, too, but not so much so. The man was cast into a deep sleep, you know—"

"And the woman was what he dreamed her. I wish she were!"

"In most cases she is," said Mr. Waters.

They did not pursue the matter. The truth that floated in the old minister's words pleased Colville by its vagueness, and flattered the man in him by its implication of the man's superiority. He wanted to say that if Mrs. Bowen were what the late Mr. Bowen had dreamed her, then the late Mr. Bowen, when cast into his deep sleep, must have had Lina Ridgely in his eye. But this seemed to be personalizing the fantasy unwarrantably, and pushing it too far. For like reason he forbore to say that if Mr. Waters's theory were correct, it would be better to begin with some one whom nobody else had dreamed before; then you could be sure at least of not having a wife to somebody else's mind rather than your own. Once on his way to Palazzo Pinti, he stopped, arrested by a thought that had not occurred to him before in relation to what Mr. Waters had been saying, and then pushed on with the sense of security which is the compensation the possession of the initiative brings to our sex along with many responsibilities. In the enjoyment of this, no man stops to consider the other side, which must wait his initiative, however they mean to meet it.

In the Por San Maria, Colville found masks and dominoes filling the shop windows and dangling from the doors. A devil in red and a clown in white crossed the way in front of him from an intersecting street; several children in pretty masquerading dresses flashed in and out among the crowd. He hurried to the Lung' Arno, and reached the palace where Mrs. Bowen lived with these holiday sights fresh in his mind. Imogene turned to meet him at the door of the apartment, running from the window where she had left Effie Bowen still gazing.

"We saw you coming," she said, gayly, without waiting to exchange formal greetings. "We didn't know at first but it might be somebody else disguised as you. We've been watching the maskers go by. Isn't it exciting?"

"Awfully," said Colville, going to the window with her, and putting his arm on Effie's shoulder, where she knelt in a chair looking out. "What have you seen?"

"Oh, only two Spanish students with mandolins," said Imogene; "but you can see they're *beginning* to come."

"They'll stop now," murmured Effie, with gentle disappointment; "it's commencing to rain."

"Oh, too bad!" wailed the young girl. But just then two mediæval men-at-arms came in sight, carrying umbrellas. "Isn't that too delicious? Umbrellas and chain armor!"

"You can't expect them to let their chain armor get rusty," said Colville. "You ought to have been with me—minstrels in scale armor, Florentines of Savonarola's times, nuns, clowns, demons, fairies—no end to them."

"It's very well saying we ought to have been with you; but we can't go anywhere alone."

"I didn't say alone," said Colville. "Don't you think Mrs. Bowen would trust you with me to see these Carnival beginnings?" He had not meant at all to do anything of this kind, but that had not prevented his doing it.

"How do we know, when she hasn't been asked?" said Imogene, with a touch of burlesque dolor, such as makes a dignified girl enchanting, when she permits it to herself. She took Effie's hand in hers, the child having faced round from the window, and stood smoothing it, with her lovely head pathetically tilted on one side.

"What haven't I been asked yet?" demanded Mrs. Bowen, coming lightly toward them from a door at the side of the salon. She gave her hand to Colville with the prettiest grace, and a cordiality that brought a flush to her cheek. There had really been nothing between them but a little unreasoned coolness, if it were even so much as that; say rather a dryness, aggravated by time and absence, and now, as friends do, after a thing of that kind, they were suddenly glad to be good to each other.

"Why, you haven't been asked how you have been this long time," said Colville.

"I have been wanting to tell you for a whole week," returned Mrs. Bowen, seating the rest in taking a chair for herself. "Where have you been?"

"Oh, shut up in my cell at Hôtel d'Atene, writing a short history of the Florentine people for Miss Effie."

"Effie, take Mr. Colville's hat," said her mother. "We're going to make you stay to lunch," she explained to him.

"Is that so?" he asked, with an effect of polite curiosity.

"Yes." Imogene softly clapped her hands, unseen by Mrs. Bowen, for Colville's instruction that all was going well. If it delights women to pet an undangerous friend of our sex, to use him like one of themselves, there are no words to paint the soft and flattered content with which his spirit purrs under their caresses. "You must have nearly finished the history," added Mrs. Bowen.

"Well, I could have finished it," said Colville, "if I had only begun it. You see, writing a short history of the Florentine people is such quick work that you have to be careful how you actually put pen to paper, or you're through with it before you've had any fun out of it."

"I think Effie will like to read that kind of history," said her mother.

The child hung her head, and would not look at Colville; she was still shy with him; his absence must have seemed longer to a child, of course.

At lunch they talked of the Carnival sights that had begun to appear. He told of his call upon Mr. Waters and of the old minister's purpose to see all he could of the Carnival in order to judge intelligently of Savonarola's opposition to it.

"Mr. Waters is a very good man," said Mrs. Bowen, with the air of not meaning to approve him quite, nor yet to let any notion of his be made fun of in her presence. "But for my part I wish there were not going to be any Carnival; the city will be in such an uproar for the next two weeks."

"Oh, Mrs. Bowen!" cried Imogene, reproachfully. Effie looked at her mother in apparent anxiety lest she should be meaning to put forth an unquestionable power and stop the Carnival.

"The last Carnival, I thought there was never going to be any end to it; I was so glad when Lent came."

"Glad when *Lent* came!" breathed Imogene, in astonishment; but she ventured upon nothing more insubordinate, and Colville admired to see this spirited girl as subject to Mrs. Bowen as her own child. There is no reason why one woman should establish another woman over her, but nearly all women do it in one sort or another, from love of a voluntary submission, or from a fear of their own ignorance, if they are younger and more inexperienced than their lieges. Neither the one passion nor the other seems to reduce them to a like passivity as regards their husbands. They must apparently have a fetich of their own sex. Colville could see that Imogene obeyed Mrs. Bowen not only as a protégée but as a devotee.

"Oh, I suppose *you* will have to go through it all," said Mrs. Bowen, in reward of the girl's acquiescence.

"You're rather out of the way of it up here," said Colville. "You had better let me go about with the young ladies—if you can trust them to the care of an old fellow like me."

"Oh, I don't think you're so very old, at all times," replied Mrs. Bowen, with a peculiar look, whether indulgent or reproachful he could not quite make out.

But he replied, boldly, in his turn: "I have certainly my moments of being young still; I don't deny it. There's always a danger of their occurrence."

"I was thinking," said Mrs. Bowen, with a graceful effect of not listening, "that you would let me go too. It would be quite like old times."

"Only too much honor and pleasure," returned Colville, "if you will leave out the old times. I'm not particular about having them along." Mrs. Bowen joined in laughing at the joke, which they had to themselves. "I was only consulting an explicit abhorrence of yours in not asking you to go at first," he explained.

"Oh yes; I understand that."

The excellence of the whole arrangement seemed to grow upon Mrs. Bowen. "Of course," she said, "Imogene ought to see all she can of the Carnival. She may not have another chance, and perhaps if she had, *he* wouldn't consent."

"I'll engage to get *his* consent," said the girl. "What I was afraid of was that I couldn't get yours, Mrs. Bowen."

"Am I so severe as that?" asked Mrs. Bowen, softly.

"Quite," replied Imogene.

"Perhaps," thought Colville, "it isn't always silent submission."

For no very good reason that any one could give, the Carnival that year was not a brilliant one. Colville's party seemed to be always meeting the same maskers on the street, and the maskers did not greatly increase in numbers. There were a few more of them after night-fall, but they were then a little more bacchanal, and he felt it was better the ladies had gone home by that time. In the pursuit of the tempered pleasure of looking up the maskers he was able to make the reflection that their fantastic and vivid dresses sympathized in a striking way with the architecture of the city, and gave him an effect of Florence which he could not otherwise have had. There came by-and-by a little attempt at a *corso* in Via Cerratani and Via Tornabuoni. There were some masks in carriages, and from one they actually threw plaster *confetti*; half a dozen bare-legged boys ran before and beat one another with bladders. Some people, but not many, watched the show from the windows, and the footways were crowded.

Having proposed that they should see the Carnival together, Colville had made himself responsible for it to the Bowen household. Imogene said, "Well, is *this* the famous Carnival of Florence?"

"It certainly doesn't compare with the Carnival last year," said Mrs. Bowen.

"Your reproach is just, Mrs. Bowen," he acknowledged. "I've managed it badly. But you know I've been out of practice a great while there in Des Vaches."

"Oh, poor Mr. Colville!" cried Imogene. "He isn't altogether to blame."

"I don't know," said Mrs. Bowen, humoring the joke in her turn. "It seems to me that if he had consulted us a little earlier, he might have done better."

He drove home with the ladies, and Mrs. Bowen made him stay to tea. As if she felt that he needed to be consoled for the failure of his Carnival, she was especially indulgent with him. She played to him on the piano some of the songs that were in fashion when they were in Florence together before. Imogene had never heard them; she had heard her mother speak of them. One or two of them were negro songs, such as very pretty young ladies used to sing without harm to themselves or offense to others; but Imogene decided that they were rather rowdy. "Dear me, Mrs. Bowen! Did *you* sing such songs? You wouldn't let Effie!"

"No, I wouldn't let Effie. The times are changed. I wouldn't let Effie go to the theatre alone with a young gentleman."

"The times are changed for the worse," Colville began. "What harm ever came to a young man from a young lady's going alone to the theatre with him?"

He staid till the candles were brought in, and then went away only because, as he said, they had not asked him to stay to dinner.

He came nearly every day, upon one pretext or another, and he met them oftener than that at the teas and on the days of other ladies in Florence; for he was finding the busy idleness of the life very pleasant, and he went everywhere. He formed the habit of carrying flowers to the Palazzo Pinti, excusing himself on the ground that they were so cheap and so abundant as to be impersonal. He brought violets to Effie and roses to Imogene; to Mrs. Bowen he always brought a bunch of the huge purple anemones which grow so abundantly all winter long about Florence. "I wonder why *purple* anemones?" he asked her one day in presenting them to her.

"Oh, it is quite time I should be wearing purple," she said, gently.

"Ah, Mrs. Bowen!" he reproached her. "Why do I bring purple violets to Miss Effie?"

"You must ask Effie!" said Mrs. Bowen, with a laugh.

After that he staid away forty-eight hours, and then appeared with a bunch of the red anemones, as large as tulips, which light up the meadow grass when it begins to stir from its torpor in the spring. "They grew on purpose to set me right with you," he said, "and I saw them when I was in the country."

It was a little triumph for him, which she celebrated by putting them in a vase on her table, and telling people who exclaimed over them that they were some Mr. Colville gathered in the country. He enjoyed his privileges at her house with the futureless satisfaction of a man. He liked to go about with the Bowens; he was seen with the ladies, driving and walking, in most of their promenades. He directed their visits to the churches and the galleries; he was fond of strolling about with Effie's daintily gloved little hand in his. He took her to Giacosa's and treated her to ices; he let her choose from the confectioner's prettiest caprices in candy; he was allowed to bring the child presents in his pockets. Perhaps he was not as conscientious as he might have been in his behavior with the little girl. He did what he could to spoil her, or at least to relax the severity of the training she had received; he liked to see the struggle that went on in the mother's mind against this, and then the other struggle with which she overcame her opposition to it. The worst he did was to teach Effie some picturesque Western phrases, which she used with innocent effectiveness; she committed the crimes against convention which he taught her with all the conventional elegance of her training. The most that he ever gained for her were some concessions in going out in weather that her mother thought unfit, or sitting up for half-hours after her bed-time. He ordered books for her from Goodban's, and it was Colville now, and not the Rev. Mr. Morton, who read poetry aloud to the ladies on afternoons when Mrs. Bowen gave orders that she and Miss Graham should be denied to all other comers.

It was an intimacy; and society in Florence is not blind, and especially it is not dumb. The old lady who had celebrated Mrs. Bowen to him the first night at Palazzo Pinti led a life of active question as to what was the supreme attraction to Colville there, and she referred her doubt to every friend with whom she drank tea. She philosophized the situation very scientifically, and if not very conclusively, how few are the absolute conclusions of science upon any point!

"He is a bachelor, and there is a natural affinity between bachelors and widows—much more than if he were a widower too. If he were a widower, I should say it was undoubtedly mademoiselle. If he were a little *bit* younger, I should have no doubt it was madame; but men of that age have such an ambition to marry young girls! I suppose that they think it proves they are not so very old, after all. And certainly he isn't too old to marry. If he were wise—which he probably isn't, if he's like other men in such matters—there wouldn't be any question about Mrs. Bowen. Pretty creature! And so much sense! Too much for him. Ah, my dear, how we are wasted upon that sex!"

Mrs. Bowen herself treated the affair with masterly frankness. More than once in varying phrase she said: "You are very good to give us so much of your time, Mr. Colville, and

I won't pretend I don't know it. You're helping me out with a very hazardous experiment. When I undertook to see Imogene through a winter in Florence, I didn't reflect what a very gay time girls have at home, in Western towns especially. But I haven't heard her breathe Buffalo once. And I'm sure it's doing her a great deal of good here. She's naturally got a very good mind; she's very ambitious to be cultivated. She's read a good deal, and she's anxious to know history and art; and your advice and criticism are the greatest possible advantage to her."

"Thank you," said Colville, with a fine, remote dissatisfaction. "I supposed I was merely enjoying myself."

He had lately begun to haunt his banker's for information in regard to the Carnival balls, with the hope that something might be made out of them. But either there were to be no great Carnival balls, or it was a mistake to suppose that his banker ought to know about them. Colville went experimentally to one of the people's balls at a minor theatre, which he found advertised on the house walls. At half past ten the dancing had not begun, but the masks were arriving; young women in gay silks and dirty white gloves; men in women's dresses, with enormous hands; girls as pages; clowns, pantaloons, old women, and the like. They were all very good-humored; the men, who far outnumbered the women, danced contentedly together. Colville liked two cavalry soldiers who waltzed with each other for an hour, and then went off to a battery on exhibition in the pit, and had as much electricity as they could hold. He liked also two young citizens who danced together as long as he staid, and did not leave off even for electrical refreshment. He came away at midnight, pushing out of the theatre through a crowd of people at the door, some of whom were tipsy. This certainly would not have done for the ladies, though the people were civilly tipsy.

IX

THE NEXT MORNING Paolo, when he brought up Colville's breakfast, brought the news that there was to be a *veglione* at the Pergola Theatre. This news revived Colville's courage. "Paolo," he said, "you ought to open a banking house." Paolo was used to being joked by foreigners who could not speak Italian very well; he smiled as if he understood.

The banker had his astute doubts of Paolo's intelligence; the banker in Europe doubts all news not originating in his house; but after a day or two the advertisements in the newspapers carried conviction even to the banker.

When Colville went to the ladies with news of the veglione he found that they had already heard of it. "Should you like to go?" he asked Mrs. Bowen.

"I don't know. What do you think?" she asked in turn.

"Oh, it's for you to do the thinking. I only know what I want."

Imogene said nothing, while she watched the internal debate as it expressed itself in Mrs. Bowen's face.

"People go in boxes," she said, thoughtfully; "but you would feel that a box wasn't the same thing exactly?"

"*We* went on the floor," suggested Colville.

"It was very different then. And, besides, Mrs. Finley had absolutely *no* sense of propriety." When a woman has explicitly condemned a given action, she apparently gathers courage for its commission under a little different conditions. "Of course, if we went upon the floor, I shouldn't wish it to be known at all, though foreigners can do almost anything they like."

"Really," said Colville, "when it comes to that, I don't see any harm in it."

"And you say go?"

"I say whatever you say."

Mrs. Bowen looked from him to Imogene. "I don't either," she said finally, and they understood that she meant the harm which he had not seen.

"Which of us has been so good as to deserve this?" asked Colville.

"Oh, you have all been good," she said. "We shall go in masks and dominoes," she continued. "Nothing will happen; and who should know us if anything did?" They had received tickets to the great Borghese ball, which is still a fashionable and desired event of the Carnival to foreigners in Florence; but their preconceptions of the veglione threw into the shade the entertainment which the gentlemen of Florence offer to favored sojourners.

"Come," said Mrs. Bowen, "you must go with us and help us choose our dominoes."

A prudent woman does not do an imprudent thing by halves. Effie was to be allowed to go to the veglione too, and she went with them to the shop where they were to hire their dominoes. It would be so much more fun, Mrs. Bowen said, to choose the dresses in the shop than to have them sent home for you to look at. Effie was to be in black; Imogene was to have a light blue domino, and Mrs. Bowen chose a purple one: even where their faces were not to be seen they considered their complexions in choosing the colors. If you happened to find a friend, and wanted to unmask, you would not want to look horrid. The shop people took the vividest interest in it all, as if it were a new thing to them, and these were the first foreigners they had ever served with masks and dominoes. They made Mrs. Bowen and Imogene go into an inner room and come out for the mystification of Colville, hulking about in the front shop with his mask and domino on.

"Which is which?" the ladies both challenged him, in the mask's conventional falsetto, when they came out.

With a man's severe logic he distinguished them according to their silks; but there had been time for them to think of changing, and they took off their masks to laugh in his face.

They fluttered so airily about among the pendent masks and dominoes, from which they shook a ghostly perfume of old carnivals, that his heart leaped.

"Ah, you'll never be so fascinating again!" he cried. He wanted to take them in his arms, they were both so delicious; a man has still only that primitive way of expressing his supreme satisfaction in women. "Now, which am I?" he demanded of them, and that made them laugh again. He had really put his arm about Effie.

"Do you think you will know your papa at the veglione?" asked one of the shop-women, with a mounting interest in the amiable family party.

They all laughed; the natural mistake seemed particularly droll to Imogene.

"Come," cried Mrs. Bowen; "it's time we should be going."

That was true; they had passed so long a time in the shop that they did not feel justified in seriously attempting to beat down the price of their dresses. They took them at the first price. The woman said with reason that it was Carnival, and she could get her price for the things.

They went to the veglione at eleven, the ladies calling for Colville, as before, in Mrs. Bowen's carriage. He felt rather sheepish, coming out of his room in his mask and domino, but the corridors of the hotel were empty, and for the most part dark; there was no one up but the porter, who wished him a pleasant time in as matter-of-fact fashion as if he were going out to an evening party in his dress-coat. His spirits mounted in the atmosphere of adventure which the ladies diffused about them in the carriage; Effie Bowen laughed aloud when he entered, in childish gayety of heart.

The narrow streets roared with the wheels of cabs and carriages coming and going; the street before the theatre was so packed that it was some time before they could reach the door. Masks were passing in and out; the nervous joy of the ladies expressed itself in a deep-drawn quivering sigh. Their carriage door was opened by a servant of the theatre, who wished them a pleasant veglione, and the next moment they were in the crowded vestibule, where they paused a moment, to let Imogene and Effie really feel that they were part of a masquerade.

"Now, keep all together," said Mrs. Bowen, as they passed through the inner door of the vestibule, and the brilliantly lighted theatre flashed its colors and splendors upon them. The floor of the pit had been levelled to that of the stage, which, stripped of the scenic apparatus, opened vaster spaces for the motley crew already eddying over it in the waltz. The boxes, tier over tier, blazed with the light of candelabra which added their sparkle to that of the gas jets.

"You and Effie go before," said Mrs. Bowen to Imogene. She made them take hands like children, and mechanically passed her own hand through Colville's arm.

A mask in red from head to foot attached himself to the party, and began to make love to her in excellent pantomime.

Colville was annoyed. He asked her if he should tell the fellow to take himself off.

"Not on any account!" she answered. "It's perfectly delightful. It wouldn't be the veglione without it. Did you ever see such good acting?"

"I don't think it's remarkable for anything but its fervor," said Colville.

"I should like to see *you* making love to some lady," she rejoined, mischievously.

"I will make love to you, if you like," he said, but he felt in an instant that his joke was in bad taste.

They went the round of the theatre. "That is Prince Strozzi, Imogene," said Mrs. Bowen, leaning forward to whisper to the girl. She pointed out other people of historic and aristocratic names in the boxes, where there was a democracy of beauty among the ladies, all painted and powdered to the same *marquise* effect.

On the floor were gentlemen in evening dress without masks, and here and there ladies waltzing who had masks but no dominoes. But for the most part people were in costume; the theatre flushed and flowered in gay variety of tint that teased the eye with its flow through the dance.

Mrs. Bowen had circumscribed the adventure so as to exclude dancing from it. Imogene was not to dance. One might go to the veglione and look on from a box; if one ventured further and went on the floor, decidedly one was not to dance.

This was thoroughly understood beforehand, and there were to be no petitions or murmurs at the theatre. They found a quiet corner, and sat down to look on.

The mask in red followed, and took his place at a little

distance, where, whenever Mrs. Bowen looked that way, he continued to protest his passion.

"You're sure he doesn't bore you?" suggested Colville.

"No, indeed. He's very amusing."

"Oh, all right!"

The waltz ceased; the whirling and winding confusion broke into an irregular streaming hither and thither, up and down. They began to pick out costumes and characters that interested them. Clowns in white, with big noses, and harlequins in their motley, with flat black masks, abounded. There were some admirable grasshoppers in green, with long antennæ quivering from their foreheads. Two or three Mephistos reddened through the crowd. Several knights in armor got about with difficulty, apparently burdened by their greaves and breastplates.

A group of leaping and dancing masks gathered around a young man in evening dress, with long hair, who stood leaning against a pillar near them, and who underwent their mockeries with a smile of patience, half amused, half tormented.

When they grew tired of baiting him, and were looking about for other prey, the red mask redoubled his show of devotion to Mrs. Bowen, and the other masks began to flock round and approve.

"Oh, *now*," she said, with a little embarrassed laugh, in which there was no displeasure, "I think you may ask him to go away. But don't be harsh with him," she added, at a brusque movement which Colville made toward the mask.

"Oh, why should I be harsh with him? We're not rivals." This was not in good taste either, Colville felt. "Besides, I'm an Italian too," he said, to retrieve himself. He made a few paces toward the mask, and said in a low tone, with gentle suggestion, "Madame finds herself a little incommoded."

The mask threw himself into an attitude of burlesque despair, bowed low with his hand on his heart, in token of submission, and vanished into the crowd. The rest dispersed with cries of applause.

"How very prettily you did it, both of you!" said Mrs. Bowen. "I begin to believe you *are* an Italian, Mr. Colville. I shall be afraid of you."

"You weren't afraid of *him*."

"Oh, he was a *real* Italian."

"It seems to me that mamma is getting all the good of the veglione," said Effie, in a plaintive murmur. The well-disciplined child must have suffered deeply before she lifted this seditious voice.

"Why, so I am, Effie," answered her mother, "and I don't think it's fair myself. What shall we do about it?"

"I should like something to eat," said the child.

"So should I," said Colville. "That's reparation your mother owes us all. Let's make her take us and get us something. Wouldn't you like an ice, Miss Graham?"

"Yes, an *ice*," said Imogene, with an effect of adding, "nothing more for worlds," that made Colville laugh. She rose slowly, like one in a dream, and cast a look as impassioned as a look could be made through a mask on the scene she was leaving behind her. The band was playing a waltz again, and the wide floor swam with circling couples.

The corridor where the tables were set was thronged with people, who were drinking beer and eating cold beef and boned turkey and slices of huge round sausages. "Oh, how *can* they?" cried the girl, shuddering.

"I didn't know you were so ethereal-minded about these things," said Colville. "I thought you didn't object to the salad at Madame Uccelli's."

"Oh, but at the veglione!" breathed the girl for all answer. He laughed again; but Mrs. Bowen did not laugh with him: he wondered why.

When they returned to their corner in the theatre they found a mask in a black domino there, who made place for them, and remained standing near. They began talking freely and audibly, as English-speaking people incorrigibly do in Italy, where their tongue is all but the language of the country.

"Really," said Colville, "I think I shall stifle in this mask. If you ladies will do what you can to surround me and keep me secret, I'll take it off a moment."

"I believe I will join you, Mr. Colville," said the mask near them. He pushed up his little visor of silk, and discovered the mild, benignant features of Mr. Waters.

"Bless my soul!" cried Colville.

Mrs. Bowen was apparently too much shocked to say anything.

"You didn't expect to meet me here?" asked the old man, as if otherwise it should be the most natural thing in the world. After that they could only unite in suppressing their astonishment. "It's extremely interesting," he went on, "extremely! I've been here ever since the exercises began, and I have not only been very greatly amused, but greatly instructed. It seems to me the key to a great many anomalies in the history of this wonderful people."

If Mr. Waters took this philosophical tone about the Carnival, it was not possible for Colville to take any other.

"And have you been able to divine from what you have seen here," he asked, gravely, "the grounds of Savonarola's objection to the Carnival?"

"Not at all," said the old man, promptly. "I have seen nothing but the most harmless gayety throughout the evening."

Colville hung his head. He remembered reading once in a passage from Swedenborg that the most celestial angels had scarcely any power of perceiving evil.

"Why aren't you young people dancing?" asked Mr. Waters, in a cheerful general way, of Mrs. Bowen's party.

Colville was glad to break the silence. "Mrs. Bowen doesn't approve of dancing at vegliones."

"No?—why not?" inquired the old man, with invincible simplicity.

Mrs. Bowen smiled her pretty, small smile below her mask. "The company is apt to be rather mixed," she said, quietly.

"Yes," pursued Mr. Waters; "but you could dance with one another. The company seems very well-behaved."

"Oh, quite so," Mrs. Bowen assented.

"Shortly after I came," said Mr. Waters, "one of the masks asked me to dance. I was really sorry that my age and traditions forbade my doing so. I tried to explain, but I'm afraid I didn't make myself quite clear."

"Probably it passed for a joke with her," said Colville, in order to say something.

"Ah, very likely; but I shall always feel that my impressions of the Carnival would have been more definite if I could have danced. Now, if I were a young man like you—"

Imogene turned and looked at Colville through the eye-holes of her mask; even in that sort of isolation he thought her eyes expressed surprise.

"It never occurred to you before that I was a young man," he suggested, gravely.

She did not reply.

After a little interval, "Imogene," asked Mrs. Bowen, "would you like to dance?"

Colville was astonished. "The veglione has gone to your head, Mrs. Bowen," he tacitly made his comment. She had spoken to Imogene, but she glanced at him as if she expected him to be grateful to her for this stroke of liberality.

"What would be the use?" returned the girl.

Colville rose. "After my performance in the Lancers, I can't expect you to believe me, but I really *do* know how to waltz." He had but to extend his arms, and she was hanging upon his shoulder, and they were whirling away through a long orbit of delight to the girl.

"Oh, why have you let me do you such injustice?" she murmured, intensely. "I never shall forgive myself."

"It grieved me that you shouldn't have divined that I was really a magnificent dancer in disguise, but I bore it as best I could," said Colville, really amused at her seriousness. "Perhaps you'll find out after a while that I'm not an old fellow either, but only a 'Lost Youth.'"

"Hush," she said; "I don't like to hear you talk so."

"How?"

"About—age!" she answered. "It makes me feel— Don't to-night!"

Colville laughed. "It isn't a fact that my blinking is going to change materially. You had better make the most of me as a lost youth. I'm old enough to be two of them."

She did not answer, and as they wound up and down through the other orbing couples he remembered the veglione of seventeen years before, when he had dreamed through the waltz with the girl who jilted him; she was very docile and submissive that night; he believed afterward that if he had spoken frankly then, she would not have refused him. But he had veiled his passion in words and phrases that, taken in themselves, had no meaning—that neither committed him nor claimed her. He could not help it; he had not the courage at any moment to risk the loss of her forever, till it was too late, till he must lose her.

"Do you believe in pre-existence?" he demanded of Imogene.

"Oh yes!" she flashed back. "This very instant it was just as if I had been here before, long ago."

"Dancing with me?"

"With you? Yes—yes—I think so."

He had lived long enough to know that she was making herself believe what she said, and that she had not lived long enough to know this.

"Then you remember what I said to you—tried to say to you—that night?" Through one of those psychological juggles which we all practice with ourselves at times, it amused him, it charmed him, to find her striving to realize this past.

"No; it was so long ago. What was it?" she whispered, dreamily.

A turn of the waltz brought them near Mrs. Bowen; her mask seemed to wear a dumb reproach. He began to be weary; one of the differences between youth and later life is that the latter wearies so soon of any given emotion.

"Ah, I can't remember, either! Aren't you getting rather tired of the waltz and me?"

"Oh no; go on!" she deeply murmured. "Try to remember."

The long, pulsating stream of the music broke and fell. The dancers crookedly dispersed in wandering lines. She took his arm; he felt her heart leap against it; those innocent, trustful throbs upbraided him. At the same time his own heart beat with a sort of fond, protecting tenderness; he felt the witchery of his power to make this young, radiant, and beautiful creature hang flattered and bewildered on his talk; he liked the compassionate worship with which his tacit confidence had inspired her, even while he was not without some satirical sense of the crude sort of heart-broken hero he must be in the fancy of a girl of her age.

"Let us go and walk in the corridor a moment," he said.

But they walked there till the alluring melancholy music of the waltz began again. In a mutual caprice, they rejoined the dance.

It came into his head to ask, "Who is *he*?" and as he had got past denying himself anything, he asked it.

"He? What he?"

"He that Mrs. Bowen thought might object to your seeing the Carnival?"

"Oh!—oh yes! That was the not impossible he."

"Is that all?"

"Yes."

"Then he's not even the not improbable he?"

"No, indeed."

They waltzed in silence. Then, "Why did you ask me that?" she murmured.

"I don't know. Was it such a strange question?"

"I don't know. You ought to."

"Yes, if it was wrong, I'm old enough to know better."

"You promised not to say 'old' any more."

"Then I suppose I mustn't. But you mustn't get me to ignore it, and then laugh at me for it."

"Oh!" she reproached him, "you think I could do that?"

"You could if it was you who were here with me once before."

"Then I know I wasn't."

Again they were silent, and it was he who spoke first. "I wish you would tell me why you object to the interdicted topic?"

"Because—because I like every time to be perfect in itself."

"Oh! And this wouldn't be perfect in itself if I were—not so young as some people?"

"I didn't mean that. No; but if you didn't mention it, no one else would think of it or care for it."

"Did any one ever accuse you of flattering, Miss Graham?"

"Not till now. And you are unjust."

"Well, I withdraw the accusation."

"And will you ever pretend such a thing again?"

"Oh, never!"

"Then I have your promise."

The talk was light word-play, such as depends upon the

talker's own mood for its point or its pointlessness. Between two young people of equal years it might have had meanings to penetrate, to sigh over, to question. Colville found it delicious to be pursued by the ingenuous fervor of this young girl, eager to vindicate her sincerity in prohibiting him from his own ironical depreciation. Apparently, she had a sentimental mission of which he was the object: he was to be convinced that he was unnecessarily morbid; he was to be cheered up, to be kept in heart.

"I must believe in you after this," he said, with a smile which his mask hid.

"Thanks," she breathed. It seemed to him that her hand closed convulsively upon his in their light clasp.

The pressure sent a real pang to his heart. It forced her name from his lips. "Imogene! Ah, I've no right to call you that."

"Yes."

"From this out I promise to be twenty years younger. But no one is to know it but you. Do you think you will know it? I shouldn't like to keep the secret to myself altogether."

"No; I will help you. It shall be *our* secret."

She gave a low laugh of delight. He convinced himself that she had entered into the light spirit of banter in which he believed that he was talking.

The music ceased again. He whirled her to the seat where he had left Mrs. Bowen. She was not there, nor the others.

Colville felt the meanness of a man who has betrayed his trust, and his self-contempt was the sharper because the trust had been as tacit and indefinite as it was generous. The effect of Mrs. Bowen's absence was as if she had indignantly flown, and left him to the consequences of his treachery.

He sat down rather blankly with Imogene to wait for her return; it was the only thing they could do.

It had grown very hot. The air was thick with dust. The lights burned through it as through a fog.

"I believe I will take off my mask," she said. "I can scarcely breathe."

"No, no," protested Colville; "that won't do."

"I feel faint," she gasped.

His heart sank. "Don't," he said, incoherently. "Come with me into the vestibule, and get a breath of air."

He had almost to drag her through the crowd, but in the vestibule she revived, and they returned to their place again. He did not share the easy content with which she recognized the continued absence of Mrs. Bowen.

"Why, they must be lost. But isn't it perfect, sitting here and watching the maskers?"

"Perfect," said Colville, distractedly.

"Don't you like to make romances about the different ones?"

It was on Colville's tongue to say that he had made all the romances he wished for that evening, but he only answered, "Oh, very."

"Poor Mrs. Bowen," laughed the girl. "It will be such a joke on her, with her punctilious notions, getting lost from her protégée at a Carnival ball! I shall tell every one."

"Oh no, don't," said Colville, in horror that his mask scarcely concealed.

"Why not?"

"It wouldn't be at all the thing."

"Why, are *you* becoming Europeanized too?" she demanded. "I thought you went in for all sorts of unconventionalities. Recollect your promise. You must be as impulsive as I am."

Colville, staring anxiously about in every direction, made for the first time the reflection that most young girls probably conform to the proprieties without in the least knowing why.

"Do you think," he asked, in desperation, "that you would be afraid to be left here a moment while I went about in the crowd and tried to find them?"

"Not at all," she said. But she added: "Don't be gone long."

"Oh no," he answered, pulling off his mask. "Be sure not to move from here on any account."

He plunged into the midst of the crowd that buffeted him from side to side as he struck against its masses. The squeaking and gibbering masks mocked in their falsetto at his wild-eyed, naked face thrusting hither and thither among them.

"I saw your lady wife with another gentleman," cried one of them, in a subtle misinterpretation of the cause of his distraction.

The throng had immensely increased; the clowns and harlequins ran shrieking up and down, and leaped over one another's heads.

It was useless. He went back to Imogene with a heart-sickening fear that she too might have vanished.

But she was still there.

"You ought to have come sooner," she said, gayly. "That red mask has been here again. He looked as if he wanted to make love to *me* this time. But he didn't. If you'd been here you might have asked him where Mrs. Bowen was."

Colville sat down. He had done what he could to mend the matter, and the time had come for philosophical submission. It was now his duty to keep up Miss Graham's spirits. They were both Americans, and from the national stand-point he was simply the young girl's middle-aged bachelor friend. There was nothing in the situation for him to beat his breast about.

"Well, all that we can do is to wait for them," he said.

"Oh yes," she answered, easily. "They'll be sure to come back in the course of time."

They waited a half-hour, talking somewhat at random, and still the others did not come. But the red mask came again. He approached Colville, and said, politely,

"La signora è partita."

"The lady gone?" repeated Colville, taking this to be part of the red mask's joke.

"La bambina pareva poco bene."

"The little one not well?" echoed Colville again, rising. "Are you joking?"

The mask made a deep murmur of polite deprecation. "I am not capable of such a thing in a serious affair. Perhaps you know me?" he said, taking off his mask; and in further sign of good faith he gave the name of a painter sufficiently famous in Florence.

"I beg your pardon, and thank you," said Colville. He had no need to speak to Imogene; her hand was already trembling on his arm.

They drove home in silence through the white moonlight of the streets, filled everywhere with the gay voices and figures of the Carnival.

Mrs. Bowen met them at the door of her apartment, and received them with a manner that justly distributed the responsibility and penalty for their escapade. Colville felt that a meaner spirit would have wreaked its displeasure upon the girl alone. She made short, quiet answers to all his eager inquiries. Most probably it was some childish indisposition; Effie had been faint. No, he need not go for the doctor. Mr. Waters had called the doctor, who had just gone away. There was nothing else that he could do for her. She dropped her eyes, and in everything but words dismissed him. She would not even remain with him till he could decently get himself out of the house. She left Imogene to receive his adieux, feigning that she heard Effie calling.

"I'm—I'm very sorry," faltered the girl, "that we didn't go back to her at once."

"Yes; I was to blame," answered the humiliated hero of her Carnival dream. The clinging regret with which she kept his hand at parting scarcely consoled him for what had happened.

"I will come round in the morning," he said. "I must know how Effie is."

"Yes; come."

X

COLVILLE went to Palazzo Pinti next day with the feeling that he was defying Mrs. Bowen. Upon a review of the facts he could not find himself so very much to blame for the occurrences of the night before, and he had not been able to prove to his reason that Mrs. Bowen had resented his behavior. She had not made a scene of any sort when he came in with Imogene; it was natural that she should excuse herself, and should wish to be with her sick child: she had done really nothing. But when a woman has done nothing she fills the soul of the man whose conscience troubles him with an instinctive apprehension. There is then no safety, his nerves tell him, except in bringing the affair, whatever it is, to an early issue—in having it out with her. Colville subdued the cowardly impulse of his own heart, which would have deceived him with the suggestion that Mrs. Bowen might be occupied with Effie, and it would be better to ask for Miss Graham. He asked for Mrs. Bowen, and she came in directly.

She smiled in the usual way, and gave her hand, as she always did; but her hand was cold, and she looked tired, though she said Effie was quite herself again, and had been asking for him. "Imogene has been telling her about your adventure last night, and making her laugh."

If it had been Mrs. Bowen's purpose to mystify him, she could not have done it more thoroughly than by this bold treatment of the affair. He bent a puzzled gaze upon her. "I'm glad any of you have found it amusing," he said; "I confess that I couldn't let myself off so lightly in regard to it." She did not reply, and he continued: "The fact is, I don't think I behaved very well. I abused your kindness to Miss Graham."

"Abused my kindness to Miss Graham?"

"Yes. When you allowed her to dance at the veglione, I ought to have considered that you were stretching a point. I ought to have taken her back to you very soon, instead of tempting her to go and walk with me in the corridor."

"Yes," said Mrs. Bowen. "So it was you who proposed it? Imogene was afraid that she had. What exemplary young peo-

ple you are! The way each of you confesses and assumes all
the blame would leave the severest chaperon without a
word."

Her gayety made Colville uncomfortable. He said, gravely,
"What I blame myself most for is that I was not there to be
of use to you when Effie—"

"Oh, you mustn't think of that at all. Mr. Waters was most
efficient. My admirer in the red mask was close at hand, and
between them they got Effie out without the slightest disturbance. I fancy most people thought it was a Carnival joke.
Please don't think of that again."

Nothing could be politer than all this.

"And you won't allow me to punish myself for not being
there to give you even a moral support?"

"Certainly not. As I told Imogene, young people *will* be
young people; and I knew how fond you were of dancing."

Though it pierced him, Colville could not help admiring
the neatness of this thrust. "I didn't know you were so ironical, Mrs. Bowen."

"Ironical? Not at all."

"Ah! I see I'm not forgiven."

"I'm sure I don't know what you mean."

Imogene and Effie came in. The child was a little pale, and
willingly let him take her on his knee and lay her languid head
on his shoulder. The girl had not aged overnight like himself
and Mrs. Bowen; she looked as fresh and strong as yesterday.

"Miss Graham," said Colville, "if a person to whom you
had done a deadly wrong insisted that you hadn't done any
wrong at all, should you consider yourself forgiven?"

"It would depend upon the person," said the girl, with innocent liveliness, recognizing the extravagance in his tone.

"Yes," he said, with an affected pensiveness, "so very much
depends upon the person in such a case."

Mrs. Bowen rose. "Excuse me a moment; I will be back
directly. Don't get up, please," she said, and prevented him
with a quick withdrawal to another room, which left upon
his sense the impression of elegant grace, and a smile and
sunny glance. But neither had any warmth in it.

Colville heaved an involuntary sigh. "Do you feel very
much used up?" he asked Imogene.

"Not at all," she laughed. "Do you?"

"Not in the least. My veglione hasn't ended yet. I'm still practically at the Pergola. It's easy to keep a thing of that sort up if you don't sleep after you get home."

"Didn't you sleep? I expected to lie awake a long time thinking it over. But I dropped asleep at once. I suppose I was very tired. I didn't even dream."

"You must have slept hard. You're pretty apt to dream when you're waking."

"How do you know?"

"Ah, I've noticed when you've been talking to me. Better not! It's a bad habit; it gives you false views of things. I used—"

"But you mustn't say you *used*! That's forbidden now. Remember your promise."

"My promise? What promise?"

"Oh, if you've forgotten already!"

"I remember. But that was last night."

"No, no! It was for all time. Why should dreams be so very misleading? I think there's ever so much in dreams. The most wonderful thing is the way you make people talk in dreams. It isn't strange that you should talk yourself, but that other people should say this and that when you aren't at all expecting what they say."

"That's when you're sleeping. But when you're waking, you make people say just what you want. And that's why day dreams are so bad. If you make people say what you want, they probably don't mean it."

"Don't you think so?"

"Half the time. Do you ever have day dreams?" he asked Effie, pressing her cheek against his own.

"I don't know what they are," she murmured, with a soft little note of polite regret for her ignorance, if possibly it incommoded him.

"You will, by-and-by," he said, "and then you must look out for them. They're particularly bad in this air. I had one of them in Florence once that lasted three months."

"What was it about?" asked the child.

Imogene involuntarily bent forward.

"Ah, I can't tell you now. She's trying to hear us."

"No, no," protested the girl, with a laugh. "I was thinking of something else."

"Oh, we know her, don't we?" he said to the child, with a playful appeal to that passion for the joint possession of a mystery which all children have.

"We might whisper it," she suggested.

"No; better wait for some other time." They were sitting near a table where a pencil and some loose leaves of paper lay. He pulled his chair a little closer, and with the child still upon his knee, began to scribble and sketch at random. "Ah, there's San Miniato," he said, with a glance from the window. "Must get its outline in. You've heard how there came to be a church up there? No? Well, it shows the sort of man San Miniato really was. He was one of the early Christians, and he gave the poor pagans a great deal of trouble. They first threw him to the wild beasts in the amphitheatre, but the moment those animals set eyes on him they saw it would be of no use; they just lay down and died. Very well; then the pagans determined to see what effect the axe would have upon San Miniato; but as soon as they struck off his head he picked it up, set it back on his shoulders again, waded across the Arno, walked up the hill, and when he came to a convenient little oratory up there he knelt down and expired. Isn't that a pretty good story? It's like fairies, isn't it?"

"Yes," whispered the child.

"What nonsense!" said Imogene. "You made it up."

"Oh, did I? Perhaps I built the church that stands there to commemorate the fact. It's all in the history of Florence. Not in all histories; some of them are too proud to put such stories in, but I'm going to put every one I can find into the history I'm writing for Effie. San Miniato was beheaded where the church of Santa Candida stands now, and he walked all that distance."

"Did he have to die when he got to the oratory?" asked the child, with gentle regret.

"It appears so," said Colville, sketching. "He would have been dead by this time, anyway, you know."

"Yes," she reluctantly admitted.

"I never quite like those things either, Effie," he said, pressing her to him. "There were people cruelly put to death two or three thousand years ago that I can't help feeling would be alive yet if they had been justly treated. There are a good many fairy stories about Florence; perhaps they used to be true stories: the truth seems to die out of stories after a while, simply because people stop believing them. Saint Ambrose of Milan restored the son of his host to life when he came down here to dedicate the Church of San Giovanni. Then there was another saint, San Zenobi, who worked a very pretty miracle after he was dead. They were carrying his body from the Church of San Giovanni to the Church of Santa Reparata, and in Piazza San Giovanni his bier touched a dead elm-tree that stood there, and the tree instantly sprang into leaf and flower, though it was in the middle of the winter. A great many people took the leaves home with them, and a marble pillar was put up there, with a cross and an elm-tree carved on it. Oh, the case is very well authenticated."

"I shall really begin to think you believe such things," said Imogene. "Perhaps you *are* a Catholic."

Mrs. Bowen returned to the room, and sat down.

"There's another fairy story, prettier yet," said Colville, while the little girl drew a long deep breath of satisfaction and expectation. "You've heard of the Buondelmonti?" he asked Imogene.

"Oh, it seems to me as if I'd had *nothing* but the Buondelmonti dinned into me since I came to Florence!" she answered, in lively despair.

"Ah, this happened some centuries before the Buondelmonte you've been bored with was born. This was Giovanni Gualberto of the Buondelmonti, and he was riding along one day in 1001, near the Church of San Miniato, when he met a certain man named Ugo, who had killed one of his brothers. Gualberto stopped and drew his sword; Ugo saw no other chance of escape, and he threw himself face downward on the ground, with his arms stretched out in the form of the cross. 'Gualberto, remember Jesus Christ, who died upon the cross praying for his enemies.' The story says that these words went to Gualberto's heart; he got down from his horse, and in sign of pardon lifted his enemy and kissed and embraced him. Then they went together into the church, and fell on their knees before the figure of Christ upon the cross, and the fig-

ure bowed its head in sign of approval and pleasure in Gualberto's noble act of Christian piety."

"Beautiful!" murmured the girl; the child only sighed.

"Ah, yes; it's an easy matter to pick up one's head from the
ground and set it back on one's shoulders, or to bring the
dead to life, or to make a tree put forth leaves and flowers in
mid-winter; but to melt the heart of a man with forgiveness
in the presence of his enemy—that's a different thing; *that's*
no fairy story; that's a real miracle; and I believe this one
happened—it's so impossible."

"Oh yes, it must have happened," said the girl.

"Do you think it's so very hard to forgive, then?" asked
Mrs. Bowen, gravely.

"Oh, not for ladies," replied Colville.

She flushed, and her eyes shone when she glanced at him.

"I'm sorry to put you down," he said to the child; "but I
can't take you with me, and I must be going."

Mrs. Bowen did not ask him to stay to lunch; he thought
afterward that she might have relented as far as that but for
the last little thrust, which he would better have spared.

"Effie dear," said her mother, when the door closed upon
Colville, "don't you think you'd better lie down awhile? You
look so tired."

"Shall I lie down on the sofa here?"

"No; on your bed."

"Well."

"I'll go with you, Effie," said Imogene, "and see that you're
nicely tucked in."

When she returned alone, Mrs. Bowen was sitting where
she had left her, and seemed not to have moved. "I think
Effie will drop off to sleep," she said; "she seems drowsy."
She sat down, and after a pensive moment continued, "I wonder what makes Mr. Colville seem so gloomy?"

"Does he seem gloomy?" asked Mrs. Bowen, unsympa-
thetically.

"No, not gloomy exactly. But different from last night. I
wish people could always be the same! He was so gay and full
of spirits; and now he's so self-absorbed. He thinks you're
offended with him, Mrs. Bowen."

"I don't think he was very much troubled about it. I only

thought he was flighty from want of sleep. At your age you don't mind the loss of a night."

"Do you think Mr. Colville seems so very old?" asked Imogene, anxiously.

Mrs. Bowen appeared not to have heard her. She went to the window and looked out. When she came back, "Isn't it almost time for you to have a letter from home?" she asked.

"Why, no. I had one from mother day before yesterday. What made you think so?"

"Imogene," interrupted Mrs. Bowen, with a sudden excitement which she tried to control, but which made her lips tremble, and break a little from her restraint, "you know that I am here in the place of your mother, to advise you and look after you in every way?"

"Why, yes, Mrs. Bowen," cried the girl, in surprise.

"It's a position of great responsibility in regard to a young lady. I can't have anything to reproach myself with afterward."

"No."

"Have I always been kind to you, and considerate of your rights and your freedom? Have I ever interfered with you in any way that you think I oughtn't?"

"What an idea! You've been loveliness itself, Mrs. Bowen!"

"Then I want you to listen to me, and answer me frankly, and not suspect my motives."

"Why, how *could* I do that?"

"Never mind!" cried Mrs. Bowen, impatiently, almost angrily. "People can't help their suspicions! Do you think Mr. Morton cares for you?"

The girl hung her head.

"Imogene, answer me!"

"I don't know," answered Imogene, coldly; "but if you're troubled about that, Mrs. Bowen, you needn't be; I don't care anything for Mr. Morton."

"If I thought you were becoming interested in any one, it would be my duty to write to your mother and tell her."

"Of course; I should expect you to do it."

"And if I saw you becoming interested in any one in a way that I thought would make you unhappy, it would be my duty to warn you."

"Yes."

"Of course, I don't mean that any one would knowingly try to make you unhappy."

"No."

"Men don't go about nowadays trying to break girls' hearts. But very good men can be thoughtless and selfish."

"Yes, I understand that," said Imogene, in a falling accent.

"I don't wish to prejudice you against any one. I should consider it very wrong and wicked. Besides, I don't care to interfere with you to that degree. You are old enough to see and judge for yourself."

Imogene sat silent, passing her hand across the front of her dress. The clock ticked audibly from the mantel.

"I will not have it left to me!" cried Mrs. Bowen. "It is hard enough, at any rate. Do you think I like to speak to you?"

"No."

"Of course it makes me seem inhospitable, and distrustful, and—detestable."

"I never thought of accusing you," said the girl, slowly lifting her eyes.

"I will never, never speak to you of it again," said Mrs. Bowen, "and from this time forth I insist upon your feeling just as free as if I hadn't spoken." She trembled upon the verge of a sob, from which she repelled herself.

Imogene sat still, with a sort of serious, bewildered look.

"You shall have every proper opportunity of meeting any one you like."

"Oh yes."

"And I shall be only too gl-glad to take back everything!"

Imogene sat motionless and silent. Mrs. Bowen broke out again with a sort of violence: the years teach us something of self-control, perhaps, but they weaken and unstring the nerves. In this opposition of silence to silence, the woman of the world was no match for the inexperienced girl.

"Have you nothing to say, Imogene?"

"I never thought of him in that way at all. I don't know what to say yet. It—confuses me. I—I can't imagine it. But if you think that he is trying to amuse himself—"

"I never said that!"

"No, I know it."

"He likes to make you talk, and to talk with you. But he is perfectly idle here, and—there is too much difference, every way. The very good in him makes it the worse. I suppose that after talking with him every one else seems insipid."

"Yes."

Mrs. Bowen rose and ran suddenly from the room.

Imogene remained sitting cold and still.

No one had been named since they spoke of Mr. Morton.

XI

COLVILLE had not done what he meant in going to Mrs. Bowen's; in fact, he had done just what he had not meant to do, as he distinctly perceived in coming away. It was then that in a luminous retrospect he discovered his motive to have been a wish to atone to her for behavior that must have distressed her, or at least to explain it to her. She had not let him do this at once; an instant willingness to hear and to condone was not in a woman's nature; she had to make him feel, by the infliction of a degree of punishment, that she had suffered. But before she ended she had made it clear that she was ready to grant him a tacit pardon, and he had answered with a silly sarcasm the question that was to have led to peace. He could not help seeing that throughout the whole Carnival adventure she had yielded her cherished reluctances to please him, to show him that she was not stiff or prudish, to convince him that she would not be a killjoy through her devotion to conventionalities which she thought he despised. He could not help seeing that he had abused her delicate generosity, insulted her subtile concessions. He strolled along down the Arno, feeling flat and mean, as a man always does after a contest with a woman in which he has got the victory; our sex can preserve its self-respect only through defeat in such a case. It gave him no pleasure to remember that the glamour of the night before seemed still to rest on Imogene unbroken; that, indeed, was rather an added pain. He surprised himself in the midst of his poignant reflections by a yawn. Clearly the time was past when these ideal troubles could keep him awake, and there was, after all, a sort of brutal consolation in the fact. He was forty-one years old, and he was sleepy, whatever capacity for suffering remained to him. He went to his hotel to catch a little nap before lunch. When he woke it was dinner-time. The mists of slumber still hung about him, and the events of the last forty-eight hours showed vast and shapelessly threatening through them.

When the drama of the *table d'hôte* reached its climax of roast chestnuts and butter, he determined to walk over to San

Marco and pay a visit to Mr. Waters. He found the old minister from Haddam East Village, Massachusetts, Italianate outwardly in almost ludicrous degree. He wore a fur-lined overcoat in-doors; his feet, cased in thick woollen shoes, rested on a strip of carpet laid before his table; a man who had lived for forty years in the pungent atmosphere of an airtight stove, succeeding a quarter of a century of roaring hearth fires, contented himself with the spare heat of a scaldino, which he held his clasped hands over in the very Italian manner; the lamp that cast its light on the book open before him was the classic *lucerna*, with three beaks, fed with olive oil. He looked up at his visitor over his spectacles, without recognizing him, till Colville spoke. Then, after their greeting, "Is it snowing heavily?" he asked.

"It isn't snowing at all. What made you think that?"

"Perhaps I was drowsing over my book and dreamed it. We become very strange and interesting studies to ourselves as we live along."

He took up the metaphysical consideration with the promptness of a man who has no small-talk, and who speaks of the mind and soul as if they were the gossip of the neighborhood.

"At times the forty winters that I passed in Haddam East Village seem like an alien experience, and I find myself pitying the life I lived there quite as if it were the life of some one else. It seems incredible that men should still inhabit such climates."

"Then you're not homesick for Haddam East Village?"

"Ah! for the good and striving souls there, yes; especially the souls of some women there. They used to think that it was I who gave them consolation and spiritual purpose, but it was they who really imparted it. Women souls—how beautiful they sometimes are! They seem truly like angelic essences. I trust that I shall meet them somewhere some time, but it will never be in Haddam East Village. Yes, I must have been dreaming when you came in. I thought that I was by my fire there, and all round over the hills and in the streets the snow was deep and falling still. How distinctly," he said, closing his eyes, as artists do in looking at a picture, "I can see the black wavering lines of the walls in the fields sinking into the drifts! the snow billowed over the graves by the church where I preached! the banks of snow around the houses! the white desolation everywhere! I ask myself at times if the people are still there. Yes, I feel as blessedly remote from that terrible winter as if I had died away from it and were in the weather of heaven."

"Then you have no reproach for feeble-spirited fellow-citizens who abandon their native climate and come to live in Italy?"

The old man drew his fur coat closer about him and shrugged his shoulders in true Florentine fashion. "There may be something to say against those who do so in the heyday of life, but I shall not be the one to say it. The race must yet revert in its decrepitude, as I have in mine, to the climates of the South. Since I have been in Italy I have realized what used to occur to me dimly at home—the cruel disproportion between the end gained and the means expended in reclaiming the savage North. Half the human endeavor, half the human suffering, would have made the whole South Protestant and the whole East Christian, and our civilization would now be there. No, I shall never go back to New England. New England? New Ireland—New Canada! Half the farms in Haddam are in the hands of our Irish friends, and the labor on the rest is half done by French Canadians. That is all right and well. New England must come to me here, by way of the great middle West and the Pacific coast."

Colville smiled at the Emersonian touch, but he said, gravely, "I can never quite reconcile myself to the thought of dying out of my own country."

"Why not? It is very unimportant where one dies. A moment after your breath is gone you are in exile forever—or at home forever."

Colville sat musing upon this phase of Americanism, as he had upon many others. At last he broke the silence they had both let fall, far away from the topic they had touched.

"Well," he asked, "how did you enjoy the veglione?"

"Oh, I'm too old to go to such places for pleasure," said the minister, simply. "But it was very interesting, and certainly very striking; especially when I went back, toward daylight, after seeing Mrs. Bowen home."

"Did you go back?" demanded Colville, in some amaze.

"Oh yes. I felt that my experience was incomplete without some knowledge of how the Carnival ended at such a place."

"Oh! And do you still feel that Savonarola was mistaken?"

"There seemed to be rather more boisterousness toward the close, and, if I might judge, the excitement grew a little unwholesome. But I really don't feel myself very well qualified to decide. My own life has been passed in circumstances so widely different that I am at a certain disadvantage."

"Yes," said Colville, with a smile, "I dare say the Carnival at Haddam East Village was quite another thing."

The old man smiled responsively. "I suppose that some of my former parishioners might have been scandalized at my presence at a Carnival ball, had they known the fact merely in the abstract; but in my letters home I shall try to set it before them in an instructive light. I should say that the worst thing about such a scene of revelry would be that it took us too much out of our inner quiet. But I suppose the same remark might apply to almost any form of social entertainment."

"Yes."

"But human nature is so constituted that some means of expansion must be provided, or a violent explosion takes place. The only question is, what means are most innocent. I have been looking about," added the old man, quietly, "at the theatres lately."

"Have you?" asked Colville, opening his eyes in suppressed surprise.

"Yes; with a view to determining the degree of harmless amusement that may be derived from them. It's rather a difficult question. I should be inclined to say, however, that I don't think the ballet can ever be instrumental for good."

Colville could not deny himself the pleasure of saying, "Well, not the highest, I suppose."

"No," said Mr. Waters, in apparent unconsciousness of the irony. "But I think the Church has made a mistake in condemning the theatre in toto. It appears to me that it might always have countenanced a certain order of comedy, in which the motive and plot are unobjectionable. Though I don't deny that there are moods when all laughter seems low and unworthy and incompatible with the most advanced state of being. And I confess," he went on, with a dreamy thoughtfulness, "that I have very great misgivings in regard to tragedy. The glare that it throws upon the play of the passions—jealousy in its anguish, revenge glutting itself, envy eating its heart, hopeless love—their nakedness is terrible. The terror may be salutary; it may be very mischievous. I am afraid that I have left some of my inquiries till it is too late. I seem to have no longer the materials of judgment left in me. If I were still a young man like you—"

"Am I still a young man?" interrupted Colville, sadly.

"You are young enough to respond to the appeals that sometimes find me silent. If I were of your age I should certainly investigate some of these interesting problems."

"Ah, but if you become personally interested in the problems, it's as bad as if you hadn't the materials of judgment left; you're prejudiced. Besides, I doubt my youthfulness very much."

"You are fifty, I presume?" suggested Mr. Waters, in a leading way.

"Not very near—only too near," laughed Colville. "I'm forty-one."

"You are younger than I supposed. But I remember now that at your age I had the same feeling which you intimate. It seemed to me then that I had really passed the bound which separates us from the farther possibility of youth. But I've lived long enough since to know that I was mistaken. At forty, one has still a great part of youth before him—perhaps the richest and sweetest part. By that time the turmoil of ideas and sensations is over; we see clearly and feel consciously. We are in a sort of quiet in which we peacefully enjoy. We have enlarged our perspective sufficiently to perceive things in their true proportion and relation; we are no longer tormented with the lurking fear of death, which darkens and imbitters our earlier years; we have got into the habit of life; we have often been ailing and we have not died. Then we have time enough behind us to supply us with the materials of reverie and reminiscence; the terrible solitude of inexperience is broken; we have learned to smile at many things besides the fear of death. We ought also to have learned pity and patience.

Yes," the old man concluded, in cheerful self-corroboration, "it is a beautiful age."

"But it doesn't look so beautiful as it is," Colville protested. "People in that rosy prime don't produce the effect of garlanded striplings upon the world at large. The women laugh at us; they think we are fat old fellows; they don't recognize the slender and elegant youth that resides in our unwieldy bulk."

"You take my meaning a little awry. Besides, I doubt if even the ground you assume is tenable. If a woman has lived long enough to be truly young herself, she won't find a man at forty either decrepit or grotesque. He can even make himself youthful to a girl of thought and imagination."

"Yes," Colville assented, with a certain discomfort.

"But to be truly young at forty," resumed Mr. Waters, "a man should be already married."

"Yes?"

"I sometimes feel," continued the old man, "that I made a mistake in yielding to a disappointment that I met with early in life, and in not permitting myself the chance of retrieval. I have missed a beautiful and consoling experience in my devotion to a barren regret."

Colville said nothing, but he experienced a mixed feeling of amusement, of repulsion, and of curiosity at this.

"We are put into the world to be of it. I am more and more convinced of that. We have scarcely a right to separate ourselves from the common lot in any way. I justify myself for having lived alone only as a widower might. I—lost her. It was a great while ago."

"Yes," said Colville, after the pause which ensued, "I agree with you that one has no right to isolate himself, to refuse his portion of the common lot; but the effects of even a rebuff may last so long that one has no heart to put out his hand a second time—for a second rap over the knuckles. Oh, I know how trivial it is in the retrospect, and how what is called a disappointment is something to be humbly grateful for in most cases; but for a while it certainly makes you doubtful whether you were ever really intended to share the common lot." He was aware of an insincerity in his words; he hoped that it might not be perceptible, but he did not greatly care.

Mr. Waters took no notice of what he had been saying. He resumed from another point. "But I should say that it would be unwise for a man of mature life to seek his happiness with one much younger than himself. I don't deny that there are cases in which the disparity of years counts for little or nothing, but, generally speaking, people ought to be as equally mated in age as possible. They ought to start with the same advantages of ignorance. A young girl can only live her life through a community of feeling, an equality of inexperience in the man she gives her heart to. If he is tired of things that still delight her, the chances of unhappiness are increased."

"Yes, that's true," answered Colville, gravely. "It's apt to be a mistake and a wrong."

"Oh, not always—not always," said the old minister. "We mustn't look at it in that way quite. Wrongs are of the will." He seemed to lapse into a greater intimacy of feeling with Colville. "Have you seen Mrs. Bowen to-day? Or—ah! true! I think you told me."

"No," said Colville. "Have we spoken of her? But I have seen her."

"And was the little one well?"

"Very much better."

"Pretty creatures, both of them," said the minister, with as fresh a pleasure in his recognition of the fact as if he had not said nearly the same thing once before. "You've noticed the very remarkable resemblance between mother and daughter?"

"Oh yes."

"There is a gentleness in Mrs. Bowen which seems to me the last refinement of a gracious spirit," suggested Mr. Waters. "I have never met any lady who reconciled more exquisitely what is charming in society with what is lovely in nature."

"Yes," said Colville. "Mrs. Bowen always had that gentle manner. I used to know her here as a girl a great while ago."

"Did you? I wonder you allowed her to become Mrs. Bowen."

This sprightliness of Mr. Waters amused Colville greatly. "At that time I was preoccupied with my great mistake, and I had no eyes for Mrs. Bowen."

"It isn't too late yet," said Mr. Waters, with open insinuation.

A bachelor of forty is always flattered by any suggestion of marriage; the suggestion that a beautiful and charming woman would marry him is too much for whatever reserves of modesty and wisdom he may have stored up. Colville took leave of the old minister in better humor with himself than he had been for forty-eight hours, or than he had any very good reason for being now.

Mr. Waters came with him to the head of the stairs and held up the lamp for him to see. The light fell upon the white locks thinly straggling from beneath his velvet skull-cap, and he looked like some mediæval scholar of those who lived and died for learning in Florence when letters were a passion there almost as strong as love.

The next day Colville would have liked to go at once and ask about Effie, but upon the whole he thought he would not go till after he had been at the reception where he was going in the afternoon. It was an artist who was giving the reception; he had a number of pictures to show, and there was to be tea. There are artists and artists. This painter was one who had a distinct social importance. It was felt to be rather a nice thing to be asked to his reception; one was sure at least to meet the nicest people.

This reason prevailed with Colville so far as it related to Mrs. Bowen, whom he felt that he would like to tell he had been there. He would speak to her of this person and that very respected and recognized social figures—so that she might see he was not the outlaw, the Bohemian, he must sometimes have appeared to her. It would not be going too far to say that something like an obscure intention to show himself the next Sunday at the English chapel, where Mrs. Bowen went, was forming itself in his mind. As he went along it began to seem not impossible that she would be at the reception. If Effie's indisposition was no more serious than it appeared yesterday, very probably Mrs. Bowen would be there. He even believed that he recognized her carriage among those which were drawn up in front of the old palace, under the painter's studio windows.

There were a great number of people of the four nationalities that mostly consort in Italy. There were English and Americans and Russians and the sort of Italians resulting from the native intermarriages with them; here and there were Italians of pure blood, borderers upon the foreign life through a literary interest, or an artistic relation, or a matrimonial intention; here and there, also, the large stomach of a German advanced the bounds of the new empire and the new ideal of duty. There were no Frenchmen; one may meet them in more strictly Italian assemblages, but it is as if the sorrows and uncertainties of France in these times discouraged them from the international society in which they were always an infrequent element. It is not, of course, imaginable that as Frenchmen they have doubts of their merits, but that they have their misgivings as to the intelligence of others. The language that prevailed was English—in fact, one heard no other—and the tea which our civilization carries everywhere with it steamed from the cups in all hands. This beverage, in fact, becomes a formidable factor in the life of a Florentine winter. One finds it at all houses, and more or less mechanically drinks it.

"I am turning out a terrible tea toper," said Colville, stirring his cup in front of the old lady whom his relations to the ladies at Palazzo Pinti had interested so much. "I don't think I drink less than ten cups a day; seventy cups a week is a low average for me. I'm really beginning to look down at my boots a little anxiously."

Mrs. Amsden laughed. She had not been in America for forty years, but she liked the American way of talking better than any other. "Oh, didn't you hear about Inglehart when he was here? He was so good-natured that he used to drink all the tea people offered him, and then the young ladies made tea for him in his studio when they went to look at his pictures. It almost killed him. By the time spring came he trembled so that the brush flew out of his hands when he took it up. He had to hurry off to Venice to save his life. It's just as bad at the Italian houses; they've learned to like tea."

"When I was here before, they never offered you anything but coffee," said Colville. "They took tea for medicine, and there was an old joke that I thought I should die of, I heard it so often, about the Italian that said to the English woman when she offered him tea, 'Grazie; sto bene.' "

"Oh, that's all changed now."

"Yes; I've seen the tea, and I haven't heard the joke."

The flavor of Colville's talk apparently encouraged his companion to believe that he would like to make fun of their host's paintings with her; but whether he liked them, or whether he was principled against that sort of return for hospitality, he chose to reply seriously to some ironical lures she threw out.

"Oh, if you're going to be good," she exclaimed, "I shall have nothing more to say to you. Here comes Mr. Thurston; I can make *him* abuse the pictures. There! You had better go away to a young lady I see alone over yonder, though I don't know what you will do with *one* alone." She laughed and shook her head in a way that had once been arch and lively, but that was now puckery and infirm—it is affecting to see these things in women—and welcomed the old gentleman who came up and superseded Colville.

The latter turned, with his cup still in his hand, and wandered about through the company, hoping he might see Mrs. Bowen among the groups peering at the pictures or solidly blocking the view in front of them. He did not find her, but he found Imogene Graham standing somewhat apart near a window. He saw her face light up at sight of him, and then darken again as he approached.

"Isn't this rather an unnatural state of things?" he asked when he had come up. "I ought to be obliged to fight my way to you through successive phalanxes of young men crowding round with cups of tea outstretched in their imploring hands. Have you *had* some tea?"

"Thank you, no; I don't wish any," said the young girl, so coldly that he could not help noticing, though commonly he was man enough to notice very few things.

"How is Effie to-day?" he asked, quickly.

"Oh, quite well," said Imogene.

"I don't see Mrs. Bowen," he ventured further.

"No," answered the girl, still very lifelessly; "I came with Mrs. Fleming." She looked about the room as if not to look at him.

He now perceived a distinct intention to snub him. He smiled. "Have you seen the pictures? There are two or three really lovely ones."

"Mrs. Fleming will be here in a moment, I suppose," said Imogene, evasively, but not with all her first coldness.

"Let us steal a march on her," said Colville, briskly. "When she comes, you can tell her that I showed you the pictures."

"I don't know," faltered the girl.

"Perhaps it isn't necessary you should," he suggested.

She glanced at him with questioning trepidation.

"The respective duties of chaperon and protégée are rather undefined. When the chaperon isn't there to command, the protégée isn't there to obey. I suppose you'd know if you were at home?"

"Oh yes!"

"Let me imagine myself at a loan exhibition in Buffalo. Ah! that appeal is irresistible. You'll come, I see."

She hesitated; she looked at the nearest picture, then followed him to another. He now did what he had refused to do for the old lady who tempted him to it; he made fun of the pictures a little, but so amiably and with so much justice to their good points that the painter himself would not have minded his jesting. From time to time he made Imogene smile, but in her eyes lurked a look of uneasiness, and her manner expressed a struggle against his will which might have had its pathos for him in different circumstances, but now it only incited him to make her forget herself more and more; he treated her as one does a child that is out of sorts—coaxingly, ironically.

When they had made the round of the rooms, Mrs. Fleming was not at the window where she had left Imogene; the girl detected the top of her bonnet still in the next room.

"The chaperon is never there when you come back with the protégée," said Colville. "It seems to be the nature of the chaperon."

Imogene turned very grave. "I think I ought to go to her," she murmured.

"Oh no; she ought to come to you; I stand out for protégées' rights."

"I suppose she will come directly."

"She sees me with you; she knows you are safe."

"Oh, of course," said the girl. After a constraint which she marked by rather a long silence, she added, "How strange a roomful of talking sounds, doesn't it? Just like a great caldron boiling up and bubbling over. Wouldn't you like to know what they're all saying?"

"Oh, it's quite bad enough to see them," replied Colville, frivolously.

"I think a company of gentlemen with their hats off look very queer, don't you?" she asked, after another interval.

"Well, really," said Colville, laughing, "I don't know that the spectacle ever suggested any metaphysical speculations to me. I rather think they look queerer with their hats on."

"Oh yes."

"Though there is not very much to choose. We're a queer-looking set, anyway."

He got himself another cup of tea, and coming back to her, allowed her to make the efforts to keep up the conversation, and was not without a malicious pleasure in her struggles. They interested him as social exercises which, however abrupt and undexterous now, were destined, with time and practice, to become the finesse of a woman of society, and to be accepted, even while they were still abrupt and undexterous, as touches of character. He had broken up that coldness with which she had met him at first, and now he let her adjust the fragments as she could to the new situation. He wore that air of a gentleman who has been talking a long time to a lady, and who will not dispute her possession with a new-comer.

But no one came, though, as he cast his eyes carelessly over the company, he found that it had been increased by the accession of eight or ten young fellows, with a refreshing light of originality in their faces, and little touches of difference from the other men in their dress.

"Oh, there are the Inglehart boys!" cried the girl, with a flash of excitement.

There was a sensation of interest and friendliness in the company as these young fellows, after their moment of social intimidation, began to gather round the pictures, and to fling their praise and blame about, and talk the delightful shop of the studio.

The sight of their fresh young faces, the sound of their voices, struck a pang of regret that was almost envy to Colville's heart.

Imogene followed them with eager eyes. "Oh," she sighed, "shouldn't you like to be an artist?"

"I should, very much."

"Oh, I beg your pardon; I forgot. I knew you were an architect."

"I should say I used to be, if you hadn't objected to my perfects and preterits."

What came next seemed almost an accident.

"I didn't suppose you cared for my objections, so long as I amused you." She suddenly glanced at him, as if terrified at her own words.

"Have you been trying to amuse me?" he asked.

"Oh no. I thought—"

"Oh, then," said Colville, sharply, "you meant that I was amusing myself with you?" She glanced at him in terror of his divination, but could not protest. "Has any one told you that?" he pursued, with sudden angry suspicion.

"No, *no* one," began Imogene. She glanced about her, frightened. They stood quite alone where they were; the people had mostly wandered off into the other rooms. "Oh, don't—I didn't mean—I didn't intend to say anything—"

"But you *have* said something—something that surprises me from *you*, and hurts me. I wish to know whether you say it from yourself."

"I don't know—yes. That is, not— Oh, I wish Mrs. Fleming—"

She looked as if another word of pursuit would put it beyond her power to control herself.

"Let me take you to Mrs. Fleming," said Colville, with freezing hauteur, and led the way where the top of Mrs. Fleming's bonnet still showed itself. He took leave at once, and hastily parting with his host, found himself in the street, whirled in many emotions. The girl had not said that from herself, but it was from some woman; he knew that by the directness of the phrase and its excess, for he had noticed that women, who like to beat about the bush in small matters, have a prodigious straightforwardness in more vital affairs, and will even call gray black in order clearly to establish the presence of the black in that color. He could hardly keep himself from going to Palazzo Pinti.

But he contrived to go to his hotel instead, where he ate a moody dinner, and then, after an hour's solitary bitterness in his room, went out and passed the evening at the theatre. The play was one of those fleering comedies which render contemptible for the time all honest and earnest intention, and which surely are a whiff from the bottomless pit itself. It made him laugh at the serious strain of self-question that had mingled with his resentment; it made him laugh even at his resentment, and with its humor in his thoughts, sent him off to sleep in a sottish acceptance of whatever was trivial in himself as the only thing that was real and lasting.

He slept late, and when Paolo brought up his breakfast, he brought with it a letter which he said had been left with the porter an hour before. A faint appealing perfume of violets exhaled from the note, and mingled with the steaming odors of the coffee and boiled milk, when Colville, after a glance at the unfamiliar handwriting of the superscription, broke the seal.

"DEAR MR. COLVILLE,—I don't know what you will think of my writing to you, but perhaps you can't think worse of me than you do already, and anything will be better than the misery that I am in. I have not been asleep all night. I hate myself for telling you, but I do want you to understand how I have felt. I would give worlds if I could take back the words that you say wounded you. I didn't mean to wound you. Nobody is to blame for them but me; nobody ever breathed a word about you that was meant in unkindness.

"I am not ashamed of writing this, *whatever* you think, and I will sign my name in full.

IMOGENE GRAHAM."

Colville had commonly a good appetite for his breakfast, but now he let his coffee stand long untasted. There were several things about this note that touched him—the childlike simplicity and directness, the generous courage, even the imperfection and crudity of the literature. However he saw it afterward, he saw it then in its true intention. He respected that intention; through all the sophistications in which life had wrapped him, it awed him a little. He realized that if he had been younger he would have gone to Imogene herself with her letter. He felt for the moment a rush of the emotion which he would once not have stopped to examine, which he would not have been capable of examining. But now his duty was clear; he must go to Mrs. Bowen. In the noblest human purpose there is always some admixture, however slight, of less noble motive, and Colville was not without the willingness to see whatever embarrassment she might feel when he showed her the letter, and to invoke her finest tact to aid him in re-assuring the child.

She was alone in her drawing-room, and she told him in response to his inquiry for their health that Imogene and Effie had gone out to drive. She looked so pretty in the quiet house dress in which she rose from the sofa and stood, letting him come the whole way to greet her, that he did not think of any other look in her, but afterward he remembered an evidence of inner tumult in her brightened eyes.

He said, smiling, "I'm so glad to see you alone," and this brought still another look into her face, which also he afterward remembered. She did not reply, but made a sound in her throat like a bird when it stirs itself for flight or song. It was a strange, indefinite little note, in which Colville thought he detected trepidation at the time, and recalled for the sort of expectation suggested in it. She stood waiting for him to go on.

"I have come to get you to help me out of trouble."

"Yes?" said Mrs. Bowen, with a vague smile. "I always supposed you would be able to help yourself out of trouble. Or perhaps wouldn't mind it if you were in it."

"Oh yes, I mind it very much," returned Colville, refusing her banter, if it were banter. "Especially this sort of trouble, which involves some one else in the discomfort." He went on abruptly: "I have been held up to a young lady as a person who was amusing himself with her, and I was so absurd as to be angry when she told me, and demanded the name of my friend, whoever it was. My behavior seems to have given the young lady a bad night, and this morning she writes to tell me so, and to take all the blame on herself, and to assure me that no harm was meant me by any one. Of course I don't want her to be distressed about it. Perhaps you can guess who has been writing to me."

Colville said all this looking down, in a fashion he had. When he looked up he saw a severity in Mrs. Bowen's pretty face such as he had not seen there before.

"I didn't know she had been writing to you, but I know that you are talking of Imogene. She told me what she had said to you yesterday, and I blamed her for it, but I'm not sure that it wasn't best."

"Oh, indeed!" said Colville. "Perhaps you can tell me who put the idea into her head?"

"Yes; I did."

A dead silence ensued, in which the fragments of the situation broken by these words revolved before Colville's thought with kaleidoscopic variety, and he passed through all the phases of anger, resentment, wounded self-love, and accusing shame.

At last, "I suppose you had your reasons," he said, simply.

"I am in her mother's place here," she replied, tightening the grip of one little hand upon another, where she held them laid against the side of her waist.

"Yes, I know that," said Colville; "but what reason had you to warn her against me as a person who was amusing himself with her? I don't like the phrase; but she seems to have got it from you; I use it at third hand."

"I don't like the phrase, either; I didn't invent it."

"You used it."

"No, it wasn't I who used it. I should have been glad to use another, if I could," said Mrs. Bowen, with perfect steadiness.

"Then you mean to say that you believe I've been trifling with the feelings of this child?"

"I mean to say nothing. You are very much older; and she is a romantic girl, very extravagant. You have tried to make her like you."

"I certainly have. I have tried to make Effie Bowen like me, too."

Mrs. Bowen passed this over in serenity that he felt was not far from contempt.

He gave a laugh that did not express enjoyment.

"You have no right to laugh!" she cried, losing herself a little, and so making her first gain upon him.

"It appears not. Perhaps you will tell me what I am to do about this letter?"

"That is for you to decide." She recovered herself, and lost ground with him in proportion.

"I thought perhaps that since you were able to judge my motives so clearly, you might be able to advise me."

"I don't judge your motives," Mrs. Bowen began. She added suddenly, as if by an after-thought, "I don't think you had any."

"I'm obliged to you."

"But you are as much to blame as if you had."

"And perhaps I'm as much to blame as if I had really wronged somebody?"

"Yes."

"It's rather paradoxical. You don't wish me to see her any more?"

"I haven't any wish about it; you must not *say* that I have," said Mrs. Bowen, with dignity.

Colville smiled. "May I *ask* if you have?"

"Not for myself."

"You put me on very short allowance of conjecture."

"I will not let you trifle with the matter!" she cried. "You have made me speak, when a word, a look, ought to have been enough. Oh, I didn't think you had the miserable vanity to wish it!"

Colville stood thinking a long time, and she waiting. "I see that everything is at an end. I am going away from Florence. Good-by, Mrs. Bowen." He approached her, holding out his hand. But if he expected to be rewarded for this, nothing of the kind happened. She shrank swiftly back.

"No, no. You shall not touch me."

He paused a moment, gazing keenly at her face, in which, whatever other feeling showed, there was certainly no fear of him. Then with a slight bow he left the room.

Mrs. Bowen ran from it by another door, and shut herself

into her own room. When she returned to the salotto, Imogene and Effie were just coming in. The child went to lay aside her hat and sacque; the girl, after a glance at Mrs. Bowen's face, lingered inquiringly.

"Mr. Colville came here with your letter, Imogene."

"Yes," said Imogene, faintly. "Do you think I oughtn't to have written it?"

"Oh, it makes no difference now. He is going away from Florence."

"Yes?" breathed the girl.

"I spoke openly with him."

"Yes?"

"I didn't spare him. I made him think I hated and despised him."

Imogene was silent. Then she said, "I know that whatever you have done, you have acted for the best."

"Yes, I have a right that you should say that—I have a right that you should always say it. I think he has behaved very foolishly, but I don't blame him—"

"No; I was to blame."

"I don't *know* that he was to blame, and I won't let you think he was."

"Oh, he is the best man in the world!"

"He gave up at once; he didn't try to defend himself. It's nothing for you to lose a friend at your age; but at mine—"

"I *know* it, Mrs. Bowen."

"And I wouldn't even shake hands with him when he was going, I—"

"Oh, I don't see how you could be so hard!" cried Imogene. She put up her hands to her face and broke into tears. Mrs. Bowen watched her, dry-eyed, with her lips parted, and an intensity of question in her face.

"Imogene," she said at last, "I wish you to promise me one thing."

"Yes."

"Not to write to Mr. Colville again."

"No, no; indeed I won't, Mrs. Bowen!" The girl came up to kiss her; Mrs. Bowen turned her cheek.

Imogene was going from the room, when Mrs. Bowen spoke again: "But I wish you to promise me this only because you don't feel sure of yourself about him. If you care for him—if you think you care for him—then I leave you perfectly free."

The girl looked up, scared. "No, no; I'd rather you wouldn't leave me free—you mustn't; I shouldn't know what to do."

"Very well, then," said Mrs. Bowen.

They both waited a moment, as if each were staying for the other to speak. Then Imogene asked, "Is he—going soon?"

"I don't know," said Mrs. Bowen. "Why should he want to delay? He had better go at once. And I hope he will go home—as far from Florence as he can. I should think he would *hate* the place."

"Yes," said the girl, with a quivering sigh; "it must be hateful to him." She paused, and then she rushed on with bitter self-reproach: "And I—*I* have helped to make it so! Oh, Mrs. Bowen, perhaps it's *I* who have been trifling with *him*? Trying to make him believe—no, not trying to do that, but letting him see that I sympathized— Oh, do you think I have?"

"You know what you have been doing, Imogene," said Mrs. Bowen, with the hardness it surprises men to know women use with each other, they seem such tender creatures in the abstract. "You have no need to ask me."

"No, no."

"As you say, I warned you from the first."

"Oh yes; you did."

"I couldn't do more than hint; it was too much to expect—"

"Oh, yes, yes."

"And if you couldn't take my hints, I was helpless."

"Yes; I see it."

"I was only afraid of saying too much, and all through that miserable veglione business I was trying to please you and him, because I was afraid I *had* said too much—gone too far. I wanted to show you that I disdained to be suspicious, that I was ashamed to suppose that a girl of your age could care for the admiration of a man of his."

"Oh, I didn't care for his admiration. I admired *him*—and pitied him."

Mrs. Bowen apparently would not be kept now from saying all that had been rankling in her breast. "I didn't approve of going to the veglione. A great many people would be shocked if they knew I went; I wouldn't at all like to have it known. But I was not going to have him thinking that I was severe with you, and wanted to deny you any really harmless pleasure."

"Oh, who could think that? You're only too good to me. You see," said the girl, "what a return I have made for your trust! I knew you didn't want to go to the veglione. If I hadn't been the most selfish girl in the world I wouldn't have let you. But I did. I *forced* you to go, and then, after we got there, I seized every advantage, and abused your kindness till I wonder I didn't sink through the floor. Yes! I ought to have refused to dance—if I'd had a spark of generosity or gratitude I would have done it; and I ought to have come straight back to you the instant the waltz was done. And now see what has come of it! I've made you think he was trifling with me, and I've made him think that I'm a false and hollow-hearted thing."

"You know best what you have done, Imogene," said Mrs. Bowen, with a smiling tearfulness that was somehow very bitter. She rose from the sofa, as if to indicate that there was no more to be said, and Imogene, with a fresh burst of grief, rushed away to her own room.

She dropped on her knees beside her bed, and stretched out her arms upon it, an image of that desolation of soul which, when we are young, seems limitless, but which in later life we know has comparatively narrow bounds beyond the clouds that rest so blackly around us.

XII

In his room Colville was devouring as best he might the chagrin with which he had come away from Palazzo Pinti, while he packed his trunk for departure. Now that the thing was over, the worst was past. Again he observed that his emotions had no longer the continuity that the emotions of his youth possessed. As he remembered, a painful or pleasant impression used to last indefinitely; but here he was with this humiliating affair hot in his mind, shrugging his shoulders with a sense of relief, almost a sense of escape. Does the soul really wear out with the body? The question flitted across his mind as he took down a pair of trousers, and noticed that they were considerably frayed about the feet; he determined to give them to Paolo, and this reminded him to ring for Paolo, and send word to the office that he was going to take the evening train for Rome.

He went on packing, and putting away with the different garments the unpleasant thoughts that he knew he should be sure to unpack with them in Rome; but they would then have less poignancy. For the present he was doing the best he could, and he was not making any sort of pretenses. When his trunk was locked he kindled himself a fire, and sat down before it to think of Imogene. He began with her, but presently it seemed to be Mrs. Bowen that he was thinking of; then he knew he was dropping off to sleep by the manner in which their two ideas mixed. The fatigues and excitements of the week had been great, but he would not give way; it was too disgraceful.

Some one rapped at his door. He called out "Avanti!" and he would have been less surprised to see either of those ladies than Paolo with the account he had ordered to be made out. It was a long, pendulous, minutely itemed affair, such as the traveller's recklessness in candles and fire-wood comes to in the books of the Continental landlord, and it almost swept the floor when its volume was unrolled. But it was not the sum total that dismayed Colville when he glanced at the final figure; that, indeed, was not so very great, with all the items; it was the conviction, suddenly flashing upon him, that he had not money enough by him to pay it. His watch, held close to the fire, told him that it was five o'clock; the banks had been closed an hour, and this was Saturday afternoon.

The squalid accident had all the effect of intention, as he viewed it from without himself, and considered that the money ought to have been the first thing in his thoughts after he determined to go away. He must get the money somehow, and be off to Rome by the seven-o'clock train. A whimsical suggestion, which was so good a bit of irony that it made him smile, flashed across him: he might borrow it of Mrs. Bowen. She was, in fact, the only person in Florence with whom he was at all on borrowing terms, and a sad sense of the sweetness of her lost friendship followed upon the antic notion. No; for once he could not go to Mrs. Bowen. He recollected now the many pleasant talks they had had together, confidential in virtue of their old acquaintance, and harmlessly intimate in many things. He recalled how, when he was feeling dull from the Florentine air, she had told him to take a little quinine, and he had found immediate advantage in it. These memories did not strike him as grotesque or ludicrous; he only felt their pathos. He was ashamed even to seem in any wise recreant farther. If she should ever hear that he had lingered for thirty-six hours in Florence after he had told her he was going away, what could she think but that he had repented his decision? He determined to go down to the office of the hotel, and see if he could not make some arrangement with the landlord. It would be extremely distasteful, but his ample letter of credit would be at least a voucher of his final ability to pay. As a desperate resort, he could go and try to get the money of Mr. Waters.

He put on his coat and hat, and opened the door to some one who was just in act to knock at it, and whom he struck against in the obscurity.

"I beg your pardon," said the visitor.

"Mr. Waters! Is it possible?" cried Colville, feeling something fateful in the chance. "I was just going to see you."

"I'm fortunate in meeting you, then. Shall we go to my room?" he asked, at a hesitation in Colville's manner.

"No, no," said the latter; "come in here." He led the way back into his room, and struck a match to light the candles on his chimney. Their dim rays fell upon the disorder his packing had left. "You must excuse the look of things," he said. "The fact is, I'm just going away. I'm going to Rome at seven o'clock."

"Isn't this rather sudden?" asked the minister, with less excitement than the fact might perhaps have been expected to create in a friend. "I thought you intended to pass the winter in Florence."

"Yes, I did—sit down, please—but I find myself obliged to cut my stay short. Won't you take off your coat?" he asked, taking off his own.

"Thank you; I've formed the habit of keeping it on indoors," said Mr. Waters. "And I oughtn't to stay long, if you're to be off so soon."

Colville gave a very uncomfortable laugh. "Why, the fact is, I'm not off so very soon unless you help me."

"Ah?" returned the old gentleman, with polite interest.

"Yes, I find myself in the absurd position of a man who has reckoned without his host. I have made all my plans for going, and have had my hotel bill sent to me in pursuance of that idea, and now I discover that I not only haven't money enough to pay it and get to Rome, but I haven't much more than half enough to pay it. I have credit galore," he said, trying to give the situation a touch of liveliness, "but the bank is shut."

Mr. Waters listened to the statement with a silence concerning which Colville was obliged to form his conjectures. "That is unfortunate," he said, sympathetically, but not encouragingly.

Colville pushed on desperately. "It is, unless you can help me, Mr. Waters. I want you to lend me fifty dollars for as many hours."

Mr. Waters shook his head with a compassionate smile. "I haven't fifty francs in cash. You are welcome to what there is. I'm very forgetful about money matters, and haven't been to the bankers."

"Oh, don't excuse yourself to me, unless you wish to imbitter my shame. I'm obliged to you for offering to share your destitution with me. I must try to run my face with the land-lord," said Colville.

"Oh no," said Mr. Waters, gently. "Is there such haste as all that?"

"Yes; I must go at once."

"I don't like to have you apply to a stranger," said the old man, with fatherly kindness. "Can't you remain over till Monday? I had a little excursion to propose."

"No; I can't possibly stay; I must go to-night," cried Colville.

The minister rose. "Then I really mustn't detain you, I suppose. Good-by." He offered his hand. Colville took it, but could not let it go at once. "I would like extremely to tell you why I'm leaving Florence in such haste. But I don't see what good it would do, for I don't want you to persuade me to stay."

The old gentleman looked at him with friendly interest.

"The fact is," Colville proceeded, as if he had been encouraged to do so, "I have had the misfortune—yes, I'm afraid I've had the fault—to make myself very displeasing to Mrs. Bowen, and in such a way that the very least I can do is to take myself off as far and as soon as I conveniently can."

"Yes?" said Mr. Waters, with the cheerful note of incredulity in his voice with which one is apt to respond to others' confession of extremity. "Is it so bad as that? I've just seen Mrs. Bowen, and she told me you were going."

"Oh," said Colville, with a disagreeable sensation, "perhaps she told you why I was going?"

"No," answered Mr. Waters; "she didn't do that." Colville imagined a consciousness in him which perhaps did not exist. "She didn't allude to the subject farther than to state the fact, when I mentioned that I was coming to see you."

Colville had dropped his hand. "She was very forbearing," he said, with bitterness that might well have been incomprehensible to Mr. Waters upon any theory but one.

"Perhaps," he suggested, "you are precipitate; perhaps you have mistaken; perhaps you have been hasty. These things are often the result of impulse in women. I have often wondered how they could make up their minds; I believe they certainly ought to be allowed to change them at least once."

Colville turned very red. "What in the world do you mean? Do you imagine that I have been offering myself to Mrs. Bowen?"

"Wasn't it that which you wished to—which you said you would like to tell me?"

Colville was suddenly silent, on the verge of a self-derisive laugh. When he spoke he said, gently: "No, it wasn't that. I never thought of offering myself to her. We have always been very good friends. But now I'm afraid we can't be friends any more—at least we can't be acquaintances."

"Oh!" exclaimed Mr. Waters. He waited awhile as if for Colville to say more, but the latter remained silent, and the old man gave his hand again in farewell. "I must really be going. I hope you won't think me intrusive in my mistaken conjecture?"

"Oh no."

"It was what I supposed you had been telling me—"

"I understand. You mustn't be troubled," said Colville, though he had to own to himself that it seemed superfluous to make this request of Mr. Waters, who was taking the affair with all the serenity of age concerning matters of sentiment. "I wish you were going to Rome with me," he added, to disembarrass the moment of parting.

"Thank you. But I shall not go to Rome for some years. Shall you come back on your way in the spring?"

"No; I shall not come to Florence again," said Colville, sadly.

"Ah, I'm sorry. Good-by, my dear young friend. It's been a great pleasure to know you." Colville walked down to the door of the hotel with his visitor, and parted with him there. As he turned back he met the landlord, who asked him if he would have the omnibus for the station. The landlord bowed smilingly, after his kind, and rubbed his hands. He said he hoped Colville was pleased with his hotel, and ran to his desk in the little office to get some cards for him, so that he might recommend it accurately to American families.

Colville looked absently at the cards. "The fact is," he said to the little bowing, smiling man, "I don't know but I shall be obliged to postpone my going till Monday." He smiled too, trying to give the fact a jocose effect, and added, "I find myself out of money, and I've no means of paying your bill till I can see my bankers."

After all his heroic intention, this was as near as he could come to asking the landlord to let him send the money from Rome.

The little man set his head on one side. "Oh, well, occupy the room until Monday, then," he cried, hospitably. "It is quite at your disposition. You will not want the omnibus?"

"No, I shall not want the omnibus," said Colville, with a laugh, doubtless not perfectly intelligible to the landlord, who respectfully joined him in it.

He did not mean to stop that night without writing to Mrs. Bowen, and assuring her that though an accident had kept him in Florence till Monday, she need not be afraid of seeing him again. But he could not go back to his room yet; he wandered about the town, trying to pick himself up from the ruin into which he had fallen again, and wondering with a sort of alien compassion what was to become of his aimless, empty existence. As he passed through the Piazza San Marco he had half a mind to pick a pebble from the gardened margin of the fountain there and toss it against the Rev. Mr. Waters's window, and when he put his skull-cap out, to ask that optimistic agnostic what a man had best do with a life that had ceased to interest him. But, for the time being, he got rid of himself as he best could by going to the opera. They professed to give *Rigoletto*, but it was all Mrs. Bowen and Imogene Graham to Colville.

It was so late when he got back to his hotel that the outer gate was shut, and he had to wake up the poor little porter, as on that night when he returned from Madame Uccelli's. The porter was again equal to his duty, and contrived to light a new candle to show him the way to his room. The repetition, almost mechanical, of this small chicane made Colville smile, and this apparently encouraged the porter to ask, as if he supposed him to have been in society somewhere,

"You have amused yourself this evening?"

"Oh, very much."

"I am glad. There is a letter for you."

"A letter! Where?"

"I sent it to your room. It came just before midnight."

XIII

Mrs. Bowen sat before the hearth in her salon, with her hands fallen in her lap. At thirty-eight the emotions engrave themselves more deeply in the face than they do in our first youth, or than they will when we have really aged, and the pretty woman looked haggard.

Imogene came in, wearing a long blue robe, flung on as if with desperate haste; her thick hair fell crazily out of a careless knot, down her back. "I couldn't sleep," she said, with quivering lips, at the sight of which Mrs. Bowen's involuntary smile hardened. "Isn't it eleven yet?" she added, with a glance at the clock. "It seems years since I went to bed."

"It's been a long day," Mrs. Bowen admitted. She did not ask Imogene why she could not sleep, perhaps because she knew already, and was too honest to affect ignorance.

The girl dropped into a chair opposite her, and began to pull her fingers through the long tangle of her hair, while she drew her breath in sighs that broke at times on her lips; some tears fell down her cheeks unheeded. "Mrs. Bowen," she said at length, "I should like to know what right we have to drive any one from Florence? I should think people would call it rather a high-handed proceeding if it were known."

Mrs. Bowen met this feebleness promptly. "It isn't likely to be known. But we are not driving Mr. Colville away."

"He is going."

"Yes; he said he would go."

"Don't you believe he will go?"

"I believe he will do what he says."

"He has been very kind to us all; he has been as *good*!"

"No one feels that more than I," said Mrs. Bowen, with a slight tremor in her voice. She faltered a moment. "I can't let you say those things to me, Imogene."

"No; I know it's wrong. I didn't know what I was saying. Oh, I wish I could tell what I ought to do! I wish I could make up my mind. Oh, I can't let him go—*so*. I—I don't know what to think any more. Once it was clear, but now I'm not sure; no, I'm not sure."

"Not sure about what?"

"I think I am the one to go away, if any one."

"You know you can't go away," said Mrs. Bowen, with weary patience.

"No, of course not. Well, I shall never see any one like him."

Mrs. Bowen made a start in her chair, as if she had no longer the power to remain quiet, but only placed herself a little more rigidly in it.

"No," the girl went on, as if uttering a hopeless reverie. "He made every moment interesting. He was always thinking of us—he never thought of himself. He did as much for Effie as for any one; he tried just as hard to make himself interesting to her. He was unselfish. I have seen him at places being kind to the stupidest people. You never caught him choosing out the stylish or attractive ones, or trying to shine at anybody's expense. Oh, he's a true gentleman—I shall always say it. How delicate he was, never catching you up, or if you said a foolish thing, trying to turn it against you. No, never, never, never! Oh dear! And now, what can he think of me? Oh, how frivolous and fickle and selfish he must think me!"

"Imogene!" Mrs. Bowen cried out, but quelled herself again.

"Yes," pursued the girl, in the same dreary monotone. "He thinks I couldn't appreciate him because he was old. He thinks that I cared for his not being handsome! Perhaps—perhaps—" She began to catch her breath in the effort to keep back the sobs that were coming. "Oh, I can't bear it! I would rather die than let him think it—such a thing as that!" She bent her head aside, and cried upon the two hands with which she clutched the top of her chair.

Mrs. Bowen sat looking at her distractedly. From time to time she seemed to silence a word upon her lips, and in fact she did not speak.

Imogene lifted her head at last, and softly dried her eyes. Then, as she pushed her handkerchief back into the pocket of her robe, "What sort of looking girl was that other one?"

"That other one?"

"Yes; you know what I mean: the one who behaved so badly to him before."

"Imogene!" said Mrs. Bowen, severely, "this is nonsense, and I can't let you go on so. I might pretend not to know what you mean; but I won't do that; and I tell you that there is no sort of likeness—of comparison—"

"No, no," wailed the girl, "there *is* none. I feel that. She had nothing to warn her—he hadn't suffered then; he was young; he was able to bear it—you said it yourself, Mrs. Bowen. But now—*now*, what will he do? He could make fun of that, and not hate her so much, because she didn't know how much harm she was doing. But I did; and what can he think of me?"

Mrs. Bowen looked across the barrier between them, that kept her from taking Imogene into her arms, and laughing and kissing away her craze, with cold dislike, and only said, "You know whether you've really anything to accuse yourself of, Imogene. I can't and won't consider Mr. Colville in the matter; I *didn't* consider him in what I said to-day. And I tell you again that I will not interfere with you in the slightest degree beyond appearances and the responsibility I feel to your mother. And it's for you to know your own mind. You are old enough. I will do what you say. It's for you to be sure that you wish what you say."

"Yes," said Imogene, huskily, and she let an interval that was long to them both elapse before she said anything more. "Have I always done what you thought best, Mrs. Bowen?"

"Yes; I have never complained of you."

"Then why can't you tell me now what you think best?"

"Because there is nothing to be done. It is all over."

"But if it were not, would you tell me?"

"No."

"Why?"

"Because I—couldn't."

"Then I take back my promise not to write to Mr. Colville. I am going to ask him to stay."

"Have you made up your mind to that, Imogene?" asked Mrs. Bowen, showing no sign of excitement, except to take a faster hold of her own wrists with the slim hands in which she had caught them.

"Yes."

"You know the position it places you in?"

"What position?"

"Has he offered himself to you?"

"No!" The girl's face blazed.

"Then, after what's passed, this is the same as offering yourself to him."

Imogene turned white. "I must write to him, unless you forbid me."

"Certainly I shall not forbid you." Mrs. Bowen rose and went to her writing-desk. "But if you have fully made up your mind to this step, and are ready for the consequences, whatever they are—" She stopped, before sitting down, and looked back over her shoulder at Imogene.

"Yes," said the girl, who had also risen.

"Then I will write to Mr. Colville for you, and render the proceeding as little objectionable as possible."

Imogene made no reply. She stood motionless while Mrs. Bowen wrote.

"Is this what you wished?" asked the latter, offering the sheet.

> "DEAR MR. COLVILLE,—I have reasons for wishing to recall my consent to your going away. Will you not come and lunch with us to-morrow, and try to forget everything that has passed during a few days?
>
> "Yours very sincerely,
>
> "EVALINA BOWEN."

"Yes, that will do," gasped Imogene.

Mrs. Bowen rang the bell for the porter, and stood with her back to the girl, waiting for him at the salon door. He came after a delay that sufficiently intimated the lateness of the hour. "This letter must go at once to the Hôtel d'Atene," said Mrs. Bowen, peremptorily.

"You shall be served," said the porter, with fortitude.

As Mrs. Bowen turned, Imogene ran toward her with clasped hands. "Oh, how merciful—how good—"

Mrs. Bowen shrank back. "Don't touch me, Imogene, please!"

It was her letter which Colville found on his table and read by the struggling light of his newly acquired candle. Then he sat down and replied to it.

"DEAR MRS. BOWEN,—I know that you mean some sort of kindness by me, and I hope you will not think me prompted by any poor resentment in declining to-morrow's lunch. I am satisfied that it is best for me to go; and I am ashamed not to be gone already. But a ridiculous accident has kept me, and when I came in and found your note I was just going to write and ask your patience with my presence in Florence till Monday morning.

"Yours sincerely,

"THEODORE COLVILLE."

He took his note down to the porter, who had lain down again in his little booth, but sprang up with a cheerful request to be commanded. Colville consulted him upon the propriety of sending the note to Palazzo Pinti at once, and the porter, with his head laid in deprecation upon one of his lifted shoulders, owned that it was perhaps the very least little bit in the world late.

"Send it the first thing in the morning, then," said Colville.

Mrs. Bowen received it by the servant who brought her coffee to the room, and she sent it without any word to Imogene. The girl came instantly back with it. She was fully dressed, as if she had been up a long time, and she wore a very plain, dull dress, in which one of her own sex might have read the expression of a potential self-devotion.

"It's just as I wish it, Mrs. Bowen," she said, in a low key of impassioned resolution. "*Now*, my conscience is at rest. And you have done this for me, Mrs. Bowen!" She stood timidly with the door in her hand, watching Mrs. Bowen's slight smile; then, as if at some sign in it, she flew to the bed and kissed her, and so fled out of the room again.

Colville slept late, and awoke with a vague sense of self-reproach, which faded afterward to such poor satisfaction as comes to us from the consciousness of having made the best of a bad business; some pangs of softer regret mixed with this. At first he felt a stupid obligation to keep in-doors, and he really did not go out till after lunch. The sunshine had looked cold from his window, and with the bright fire which he found necessary in his room, he fancied a bitterness in the gusts that caught up the dust in the piazza, and blew it against the line of cabs on the other side; but when he got out into the weather he found the breeze mild and the sun warm. The streets were thronged with people, and at all the corners there were groups of cloaked and overcoated talkers, soaking themselves full of the sunshine. The air throbbed, as always, with the sound of bells, but it was a mellower and opener sound than before, and looking at the purple bulk of one of those hills which seem to rest like clouds at the end of each avenue in Florence, Colville saw that it was clear of snow. He was going up through Via Cavour to find Mr. Waters and propose a walk, but he met him before he had got half-way to San Marco.

The old man was at a momentary stand-still looking up at the Riccardi Palace, and he received Colville with apparent forgetfulness of anything odd in his being still in Florence. "Upon the whole," he said, without preliminary talk of any sort, as Colville turned and joined him in walking on, "I don't know any homicide that more distinctly proves the futility of assassination as a political measure than that over yonder." He nodded his head sidewise toward the palace as he shuffled actively along at Colville's elbow. "You might say that the moment when Lorenzino killed Alessandro was the most auspicious for a deed of that kind. The Medici had only recently been restored; Alessandro was the first ruler in Florence who had worn a title; no more reckless, brutal, and insolent tyrant ever lived, and his right, even such as the Medici might have, to play the despot was involved in the doubt of his origin; the heroism of the great siege ought still to have survived in the people who withstood the forces of the whole German Empire for fifteen months. It seems as if the taking off of that single wretch should have ended the whole Medicean domination; but there was not a voice raised to second the homicide's appeal to the old love of liberty in Florence. The Medici party were able to impose a boy of eighteen upon the most fiery democracy that ever existed, and to hunt down and destroy Alessandro's murderer at their leisure. No," added the old man, thoughtfully, "I think that the friends of progress must abandon assassination as invariably useless. The trouble was not that Alessandro was alive, but that Florence was dead. Assassination always comes too early or too late in any popular movement. It may be," said Mr. Waters, with a carefulness to do justice to assassination which made Colville smile, "that the modern scientific spirits may be able to evolve something useful from the principle, but considering the enormous abuses and perversions to which it is liable, I am very doubtful of it—very doubtful."

Colville laughed. "I like your way of bringing a fresh mind to all these questions in history and morals, whether they are conventionally settled or not. Don't you think the modern scientific spirit could evolve something useful out of the old classic idea of suicide?"

"Perhaps," said Mr. Waters; "I haven't yet thought it over. The worst thing about suicide—and this must always rank it below political assassination—is that its interest is purely personal. No man ever kills himself for the good of others."

"That's certainly against it. We oughtn't to countenance such an abominably selfish practice. But you can't bring that charge against euthanasy. What have you to say of that?"

"I have heard one of the most benevolent and tenderhearted men I ever knew defend it in cases of hopeless suffering. But I don't know that I should be prepared to take his ground. There appears to be something so sacred about human life that we must respect it even in spite of the prayers of the sufferer who asks us to end his irremediable misery."

"Well," said Colville, "I suspect we must at least class murder with the ballet as a means of good. One might say there was still some virtue in the primal, eldest curse against bloodshed."

"Oh, I don't by any means deny those things," said the old man, with the air of wishing to be scrupulously just. "Which way are you walking?"

"Your way, if you will let me," replied Colville. "I was going to your house to ask you to take a walk with me."

"Ah, that's good. I was reading of the great siege last night, and I thought of taking a look at Michelangelo's bastions. Let us go together, if you don't think you'll find it too fatiguing."

"I shall be ashamed to complain if I do."

"And you didn't go to Rome, after all?" said Mr. Waters.

"No; I couldn't face the landlord with a petition so preposterous as mine. I told him that I found I had no money to pay his bill till I had seen my banker, and as he didn't propose that I should send him the amount back from Rome, I staid. Landlords have their limitations; they are not imaginative, as a class."

"Well, a day more will make no great difference to you, I suppose," said the old man, "and a day less would have been a loss to me. I shall miss you."

"Shall you, indeed?" asked Colville, with a grateful stir of the heart. "It's very nice of you to say that."

"Oh no. I meet few people who are willing to look at life objectively with me, and I have fancied some such willingness in you. What I chiefly miss, over here, is a philosophic lift in the human mind, but probably that is because my opportunities of meeting the best minds are few, and my means of conversing with them are small. If I had not the whole past with me, I should feel lonely at times."

"And is the past such good company always?"

"Yes; in a sense it is. The past is humanity set free from circumstance, and history studied where it was once life is the past rehumanized."

As if he found this rarefied air too thin for his lungs, Colville made some ineffectual gasps at response, and the old man continued: "What I mean is that I meet here the characters I read of, and commune with them before their errors were committed, before they had condemned themselves to failure, while they were still wise and sane, and still active and vital forces."

"Did they all fail? I thought some of the bad fellows had a pretty fair worldly success?"

"The blossom of decay."

"Oh! what black pessimism!"

"Not at all! Men fail, but man succeeds. I don't know what it all means, or any part of it; but I have had moods in which it seemed as if the whole secret of the mystery were about to flash upon me. Walking along in the full sun, in the midst of men, or sometimes in the solitude of midnight, poring over a book, and thinking of quite other things, I have felt that I had almost surprised it."

"But never quite?"

"Oh, it isn't too late yet."

"I hope you won't have your revelation before I get away from Florence, or I shall see them burning you here like the great *frate*."

They had been walking down the Via Calzioli from the Duomo, and now they came out into the Piazza della Signoria, suddenly, as one always seems to do, upon the rise of the old palace and the leap of its tower into the blue air. The history of all Florence is there, with memories of every great time in bronze or marble, but the supreme presence is the martyr who hangs forever from the gibbet over the quenchless fire in the midst.

"Ah, they *had* to kill him!" sighed the old man. "It has always been so with the benefactors. They have always meant mankind more good than any one generation can bear, and it must turn upon them and destroy them."

"How will it be with you, then, when you have read us 'the riddle of the painful earth'?"

"That will be so simple that every one will accept it willingly and gladly, and wonder that no one happened to think of it before. And perhaps the world is now grown old enough and docile enough to receive the truth without resentment."

"I take back my charge of pessimism," said Colville. "You are an optimist of the deepest dye."

They walked out of the piazza and down to the Lung' Arno, through the corridor of the Uffizi, where the illustrious Florentines stand in marble under the arches, all reconciled and peaceful and equal at last. Colville shivered a little as he passed between the silent ranks of the statues.

"I can't stand those fellows, to-day. They seem to feel such a smirk satisfaction at having got out of it all."

They issued upon the river, and he went to the parapet and looked down on the water. "I wonder," he mused aloud, "if it has the same Sunday look to these Sabbathless Italians as it has to us?"

"No; nature isn't puritan," replied the old minister.

"Not at Haddam East Village?"

"No: there less than here; for she's had to make a harder fight for her life there."

"Ah, then you believe in nature—you're a friend of nature?" asked Colville, following the lines of an oily swirl in the current with indolent eye.

"Only up to a certain point." Mr. Waters seemed to be patient of any direction which the other might be giving the talk. "Nature is a savage. She has good impulses, but you can't trust her altogether."

"Do you know," said Colville, "I don't think there's very much of her left in us after we reach a certain point in life. She drives us on at a great pace for a while, and then some fine morning we wake up and find that nature has got tired of us and has left us to taste and conscience. And taste and conscience are by no means so certain of what they want you to do as nature was."

"Yes," said the minister, "I see what you mean." He joined Colville in leaning on the parapet, and he looked out on the river as if he saw his meaning there. "But by the time we reach that point in life most of us have got the direction which nature meant us to take, and there's no longer any need of her driving us on."

"And what about the unlucky fellows who haven't got the direction, or haven't kept it?"

"They had better go back to it."

"But if nature herself seemed to change her mind about you?"

"Ah, you mean persons of weak will. They are a great curse to themselves and to everybody else."

"I'm not so sure of that," said Colville. "I've seen cases in which a strong will looked very much more like the devil."

"Yes, a perverted will. But there can be no good without a strong will. A weak will means inconstancy. It means, even in good, good attempted and relinquished, which is always a terrible thing, because it is sure to betray some one who relied upon its accomplishment."

"And in evil? Perhaps the evil attempted and relinquished turns into good."

"Oh, never!" replied the minister, fervently. "There is something very mysterious in what we call evil. Apparently it has infinitely greater force and persistence than good. I don't know why it should be so. But so it appears."

"You'll have the reason of that along with the rest of the secret when your revelation comes," said Colville, with a smile. He lifted his eyes from the river, and looked up over the clustering roofs beyond it to the hills beyond them, flecked to the crest of their purple slopes with the white of villas and villages. As if something in the beauty of the wonderful prospect had suggested the vision of its opposite, he said, dreamily: "I don't think I shall go to Rome to-morrow, after all. I will go to Des Vaches! Where did you say you were walking, Mr. Waters? Oh yes! You told me. I will cross the bridge with you. But I couldn't stand anything quite so vigorous as the associations of the siege this afternoon. I'm going to the Boboli Gardens, to debauch myself with a final sense of nerveless despotism, as it expressed itself in marble allegory and formal alleys. The fact is that if I stay with you any longer I shall tell you something that I'm too old to tell and you're too old to hear." The old man smiled, but offered no urgence or comment, and at the thither end of the bridge Colville said, hastily: "Good-by. If you ever come to Des Vaches, look me up."

"Good-by," said the minister. "Perhaps we shall meet in Florence again."

"No, no. Whatever happens, that won't."

They shook hands and parted. Colville stood a moment, watching the slight bent figure of the old man as he moved briskly up the Via de' Bardi, turning his head from side to side, to look at the palaces as he passed, and so losing himself in the dim, cavernous curve of the street. As soon as he was out of sight, Colville had an impulse to hurry after him and rejoin him; then he felt like turning about and going back to his hotel.

But he shook himself together into the shape of resolution, however slight and transient. "I must do *something* I intended to do," he said, between his set teeth, and pushed on up through the Via Guicciardini. "I will go to the Boboli because I *said* I would."

As he walked along he seemed to himself to be merely crumbling away in this impulse and that, in one abortive intent and another. What did it all mean? Had he been his whole life one of those weak wills which are a curse to themselves and others, and most a curse when they mean the best? Was that the secret of his failure in life? But for many years he had seemed to succeed, to be as other men were, hard, practical men; he had once made a good newspaper, which was certainly not a dream of romance. Had he given that up at last because he was a weak will? And now was he running away from Florence because his will was weak? He could look back to that squalid tragedy of his youth and see that a more violent, a more determined man could have possessed himself of the girl whom he had lost. And now would it not be more manly, if more brutal, to stay here, where a hope, however fleeting, however fitful, of what might have been, had revisited him in the love of this young girl? He felt sure, if anything were sure, that something in him, in spite of their wide disparity of years, had captured her fancy, and now in his abasement he felt again the charm of his own power over her. They were no farther apart in years than many a husband and wife; they would grow more and more together; there was youth enough in his heart yet; and who was pushing him away from her, forbidding him this treasure that he had but to put out his hand and make his own? Some one whom through all his thoughts of another he was trying to please, but whom he had made finally and inexorably his enemy. Better stay, then, something said to him, and when he answered, "I will," something else reminded him that this also was not willing but unwilling.

XIV

WHEN he entered the beautiful old garden, its benison of peace fell upon his tumult, and he began to breathe a freer air, reverting to his purpose to be gone in the morning and resting in it, as he strolled up the broad curve of its alley from the gate. He had not been there since he walked there with one now more like a ghost to him than any of the dead who had since died. It was there that she had refused him: he recalled with a grim smile the awkwardness of getting back with her to the gate from the point, far within the garden, where he had spoken. Except that this had happened in the fall, and now it was early spring, there seemed no change since then; the long years that had elapsed were like a winter between.

He met people in groups and singly loitering through the paths, and chiefly speaking English; but no one spoke to him, and no one invaded the solitude in which he walked. But the garden itself seemed to know him, and to give him a tacit recognition; the great, foolish grotto before the gate, with its statues by Bandinelli, and the fantastic effects of drapery and flesh in party-colored statues lifted high on either side of the avenue; the vast shoulder of wall, covered thick with ivy and myrtle, which he passed on his way to the amphitheatre behind the palace; the alternate figures and urns on their pedestals in the hemicycle, as if the urns were placed there to receive the ashes of the figures when they became extinct; the white statues or the colossal busts set at the ends of the long alleys against black curtains of foliage; the big fountain with its group in the centre of the little lake, and the meadow, quiet and sad, that stretched away on one side from this; the keen light under the levels of the dense pines and ilexes; the paths striking straight on either hand from the avenue through which he sauntered, and the walk that coiled itself through the depths of the plantations; all knew him; and from them, and from the winter neglect which was upon the place, distilled a subtle influence, a charm, an appeal, belonging to that combination of artifice and nature which is perfect

only in an Italian garden under an Italian sky. He was right
in the name which he mockingly gave the effect before he felt
it; it was a debauch, delicate, refined, of unserious pensiveness, a smiling melancholy, in which he walked emancipated
from his harassing hopes, and keeping only his shadowy regrets.

Colville did not care to scale the easy height from which
you have the magnificent view, conscious of many photographs, of Florence. He wandered about the skirts of that
silent meadow, and seeing himself unseen, he invaded its borders far enough to pluck one of those large scarlet anemones,
such as he had given his gentle enemy. It was tilting there in
the breeze above the unkempt grass; and the grass was beginning to feel the spring, and to stir and stretch itself after its
winter sleep; it was sprinkled with violets, but these he did
not molest. He came back to a stained and mossy stone bench
on the avenue, fronting a pair of rustic youths carved in
stone, who had not yet finished some game in which he remembered seeing them engaged when he was there before.
He had not walked fast, but he had walked far, and was warm
enough to like the whiffs of soft wind on his uncovered head.
The spring was coming; that was its breath, which you know
unmistakably in Italy after all the kisses that winter gives.
Some birds were singing in the trees. Down an alley into
which he could look, between the high walls of green, he
could see two people in flirtation: he waited patiently till the
young man should put his arm round the girl's waist for the
fleeting embrace, from which she pushed it and fled farther
down the path.

"Yes, it's spring," thought Colville; and then, with the selfishness of the troubled soul, he wished that it might be winter
still and indefinitely. It occurred to him now that he should
not go back to Des Vaches, for he did not know what he
should do there. He would go to New York; though he did
not know what he should do in New York, either.

He became tired of looking at the people who passed, and
of speculating about them through the second consciousness
which enveloped the sad substance of his misgivings like an
atmosphere; and he let his eyelids fall, as he leaned his head
back against the tree behind his bench. Then their voices pur-

sued him through the twilight that he had made himself, and forced him to the same weary conjecture as if he had seen their faces. He heard gay laughter, and laughter that affected gayety; the tones of young men in earnest disquisition reached him through the veil, and the talk, falling to whisper, of girls, with the names of men in it; sums of money, a hundred francs, forty thousand francs, came in high tones; a husband and wife went by quarrelling in the false security of English, and snapping at each other as confidingly as if in the sanctuary of home. The man bade the woman not be a fool, and she asked him how she was to endure his company if she was not a fool.

Colville opened his eyes to look after them, when a voice that he knew called out, "Why, it *is* Mr. Colville!"

It was Mrs. Amsden, and pausing with her, as if they had passed him in doubt, and arrested themselves when they had got a little way by, were Effie Bowen and Imogene Graham. The old lady had the child by the hand, and the girl stood a few paces apart from them. She was one of those beauties who have the property of looking very plain at times, and Colville, who had seen her in more than one transformation, now beheld her somehow clumsy of feature, and with the youth gone from her aspect. She seemed a woman of thirty, and she wore an unbecoming walking dress of a fashion that contributed to this effect of age. Colville was aware afterward of having wished that she was really as old and plain as she looked.

He had to come forward, and put on the conventional delight of a gentleman meeting lady friends.

"It's remarkable how your having your eyes shut estranged you," said Mrs. Amsden. "Now if you had let me see you oftener in church, where people close their eyes a good deal for one purpose or another, I should have known you at once."

"I hope you haven't lost a great deal of time, as it is, Mrs. Amsden," said Colville. "Of course I should have had my eyes open if I had known you were going by."

"Oh, don't apologize!" cried the old thing, with ready enjoyment of his tone.

"I don't apologize for not being recognizable; I apologize for being visible," said Colville, with some shapeless impression that he ought to excuse his continued presence in Florence to Imogene, but keeping his eyes upon Mrs. Amsden, to whom what he said could not be intelligible. "I ought to be in Turin to-day."

"In Turin! Are you going away from Florence?"

"I'm going home."

"Why, did *you* know that?" asked the old lady of Imogene, who slightly nodded, and then of Effie, who also assented. "Really, the silence of the Bowen family in regard to the affairs of others is extraordinary. There never was a family more eminently qualified to live in Florence. I dare say that if I saw a little more of them, I might hope to reach the years of discretion myself some day. *Why* are you going away? (You see I haven't reached them yet!) Are you tired of Florence already?"

"No," said Colville, passively; "Florence is tired of me."

"You're quite sure?"

"Yes; there's no mistaking one of her sex on such a point."

Mrs. Amsden laughed. "Ah, a great many people mistake us, both ways. And you're really going back to America? What in the world for?"

"I haven't the least idea."

"Is America fonder of you than Florence?"

"She's never told her love. I suspect it's merely that she's more used to me."

They were walking, without any volition of his, down the slope of the broad avenue to the fountain, where he had already been.

"Is your mother well?" he asked of the little girl. It seemed to him that he had better not speak to Imogene, who still kept that little distance from the rest, and get away as soon as he decently could.

"She has a headache," said Effie.

"Oh, I'm sorry," returned Colville.

"Yes, she deputed me to take her young people out for an airing," said Mrs. Amsden; "and Miss Graham decided us for the Boboli, where she hadn't been yet. I've done what I could to make the place attractive. But what is an old woman to do for a girl in a garden? We ought to have brought some other young people—some of the Inglehart boys. But we're respectable, we Americans abroad; we're decorous, above all things; and I don't know about meeting *you* here, Mr. Colville. It has a very bad appearance. Are you sure that you didn't know I was to go by here at exactly half past four?"

"I was living from breath to breath in the expectation of seeing you. You must have noticed how eagerly I was looking out for you."

"Yes, and with a single red anemone in your hand, so that I should know you without being obliged to put on my spectacles."

"You divine everything, Mrs. Amsden," he said, giving her the flower.

"I shall make my brags to Mrs. Bowen when I see her," said the old lady. "How far into the country did you walk for this?"

"As far as the meadow yonder."

They had got down to the sheet of water from which the sea-horses of the fountain sprang, and the old lady sank upon a bench near it. Colville held out his hand toward Effie. "I saw a lot of violets over there in the grass."

"Did you?" She put her hand eagerly into his, and they strolled off together. After a first motion to accompany them, Imogene sat down beside Mrs. Amsden, answering quietly the talk of the old lady, and seeming in no wise concerned about the expedition for violets. Except for a dull first glance, she did not look that way. Colville stood in the border of the grass, and the child ran quickly hither and thither in it, stooping from time to time upon the flowers. Then she came out to where he stood, and showed her bunch of violets, looking up into the face which he bent upon her, while he trifled with his cane. He had a very fatherly air with her.

"I think I'll go and see what they've found," said Imogene, irrelevantly, to a remark of Mrs. Amsden's about the expensiveness of Madame Bossi's bonnets.

"Well," said the old lady. Imogene started, and the little girl ran to meet her. She detained Effie with her admiration of the violets till Colville lounged reluctantly up. "Go and show them to Mrs. Amsden," she said, giving back the violets, which she had been smelling. The child ran on. "Mr. Colville, I want to speak with you."

"Yes," said Colville, helplessly.

"Why are you going away?"

"Why? Oh, I've accomplished the objects or no-objects I came for," he said, with dreary triviality, "and I must hurry away to other fields of activity." He kept his eyes on her face, which he saw full of a passionate intensity, working to some sort of overflow.

"That is not true, and you needn't say it to spare me. You are going away because Mrs. Bowen said something to you about me."

"Not quite that," returned Colville, gently.

"No; it was something that she said to me about you. But it's the same thing. It makes no difference. I ask you not to go for that."

"Do you know what you are saying, Imogene?"

"Yes."

Colville waited a long moment. "Then, I thank you, you dear girl, and I am going to-morrow, all the same. But I sha'n't forget this; whatever my life is to be, this will make it less unworthy and less unhappy. If it could buy anything to give you joy, to add some little grace to the good that must come to you, I would give it. Some day you'll meet the young fellow whom you're to make immortal, and you must tell him of an old fellow who knew you afar off, and understood how to worship you for an angel of pity and unselfishness. Ah, I hope he'll understand, too! Good-by." If he was to fly, that was the sole instant. He took her hand, and said again, "Good-by." And then he suddenly cried, "Imogene, do you wish me to stay?"

"Yes!" said the girl, pouring all the intensity of her face into that whisper.

"Even if there had been nothing said to make me go away—should you still wish me to stay?"

"Yes."

He looked her in the starry, lucid eyes, where a divine fervor deepened. He sighed in nerveless perplexity; it was she who had the courage.

"It's a mistake! You mustn't! I am too old for you! It would be a wrong and a cruelty! Yes, you must let me go, and forget me. I have been to blame. If Mrs. Bowen has blamed me, she was right—I deserved it; I deserved all she could say against me."

"She never said anything against you. Do you think I would have let her? No; it was I that said it, and I blamed you. It was because I thought that you were—you were"—

"Trifling with you? How could you think that?"

"Yes, I know now how it was, and it makes you seem all the grander to me. Did you think I cared for your being older than I was? I never cared for it—I never hardly thought of it after the very first. I tried to make you understand that, and how it hurt me to have you speak of it. Don't you think that I could see how good you were? Do you suppose that all I want is to be happy? I don't care for that—I despise it, and I always hate myself for seeking my own pleasure, if I find myself doing it. I have seen enough of life to know what *that* comes to! And what hurt me worst of all was that you seemed to believe that I cared for nothing but amusing myself, when I wished to be something better, higher. It's nothing whether you are of my age or not, if—if—you care for me."

"Imogene!"

"All that I ask is to be with you, and try to make you forget what's been sad in your life, and try to be of use to you in whatever you are doing, and I shall be prouder and gladder of that than anything that people *call* happiness."

Colville stood holding her hand, while she uttered these ideas and incoherent repetitions of them, with a deep sense of powerlessness. "If I believed that I could keep you from regretting this—"

"What should I regret? I won't let you depreciate yourself—make yourself out not good enough for the best. Oh, I know how it happened! But now you shall never think of it again. No; I will not let you. That is the only way you could make me regret anything."

"I am going to stay," said Colville. "But on my own terms. I will be bound to you, but you shall not be bound to me."

"You doubt me! I would rather have you go! No; stay. And let me prove to you how wrong you are. I mustn't ask

more than that. Only give me the chance to show you how
different I am from what you think—how different you are
too."

"Yes. But you must be free."

"Well."

"What are they doing so long there?" asked Mrs. Amsden
of Effie, putting her glasses to her eyes. "I can't see."

"They are just holding hands," said the child, with an easy
satisfaction in the explanation, which perhaps the old lady did
not share. "He always holds my hand when he is with me."

"Does he, indeed?" exclaimed Mrs. Amsden, with a cackle.
She added, "That's very polite of him, isn't it? You must be
a great favorite with Mr. Colville. You will miss him when
he's gone."

"Yes. He's very nice."

Colville and Imogene returned, coming slowly across the
loose, neglected grass toward the old woman's seat. She rose
as they came up.

"You don't seem to have succeeded so well in getting flowers for Miss Graham as for the other ladies. But perhaps you
didn't find her favorite over there. What is your favorite
flower, Miss Graham? Don't say you have none! I didn't
know that I preferred scarlet anemones. Were there no forget-
me-nots over there in the grass?"

"There was no occasion for them," answered Colville.

"You always did make such pretty speeches!" said the old
lady. "And they have such an Orphic character, too; you can
interpret them in so many different ways. Should you mind
saying just what you meant by that one?"

"Yes, very much," replied Colville.

The old lady laughed with cheerful resignation. She would
as lief report that reply of his as another. Even more than a
man whom she could entangle in his speech she liked a man
who could slip through the toils with unfailing ease. Her talk
with such a man was the last consolation which remained to
her from a life of harmless coquetries.

"I will refer it to Mrs. Bowen," she said. "She is a very wise
woman, and she used to know you a great while ago."

"If you like, I will do it for you, Mrs. Amsden. I'm going
to see her."

"To renew your adieux? Well, why not? Parting is such sweet sorrow! And if I were a young man I would go to say good-by to Mrs. Bowen as often as she would let me. Now tell me honestly, Mr. Colville, did you ever see such an exquisite, perfect *creature*?"

"Oh, that's asking a good deal."

"What?"

"To tell you a thing honestly. How did you come here, Mrs. Amsden?"

"In Mrs. Bowen's carriage. I sent it round from the Pitti entrance to the Porta Romana. It's waiting there now, I suppose."

"I thought you had been corrupted somehow. Your zeal is carriage-bought. It *is* a delightful vehicle. Do you think you could give me a lift home in it?"

"Yes, indeed. I have always a seat for you in my carriage. To Hotel d'Atene?"

"No; to Palazzo Pinti."

"This is deliciously mysterious," said Mrs. Amsden, drawing her shawl up about her shoulders, which, if no longer rounded, had still a charming droop. One realizes in looking at such old ladies that there are women who could manage their own skeletons winningly. She put up her glasses, which were an old-fashioned sort, held to the nose by a handle, and perused the different persons of the group. "Mr. Colville concealing an inward trepidation under a bold front; Miss Graham agitated but firm; the child as much puzzled as the old woman. I feel that we are a very interesting group—almost dramatic."

"Oh, call us a passage from a modern novel," suggested Colville, "if you're in the romantic mood. One of Mr. James's."

"Don't you think we ought to be rather more of the great world for that? I hardly feel up to Mr. James. I should have said Howells. Only nothing happens in that case!"

"Oh, very well; that's the most comfortable way. If it's only Howells, there's no reason why I shouldn't go with Miss Graham to show her the view of Florence from the cypress grove up yonder."

"No; he's very particular when he's on Italian ground," said

Mrs. Amsden, rising. "You must come another time with Miss Graham, and bring Mrs. Bowen. It's quite time we were going home."

The light under the limbs of the trees had begun to grow more liquid. The currents of warm breeze streaming through the cooler body of the air had ceased to ruffle the lakelet round the fountain, and the naiads rode their sea-horses through a perfect calm. A damp, pierced with the fresh odor of the water and of the springing grass, descended upon them. The saunterers through the different paths and alleys were issuing upon the main avenues, and tending in gathering force toward the gate.

They found Mrs. Bowen's carriage there, and drove first to her house, beyond which Mrs. Amsden lived in a direct line. On the way Colville kept up with her the bantering talk that they always carried on together, and found in it a respite from the formless future pressing close upon him. He sat with Effie on the front seat, and he would not look at Imogene's face, which, nevertheless, was present to some inner vision. When the porter opened the iron gate below, and rang Mrs. Bowen's bell, and Effie sprang up the stairs before them to give her mother the news of Mr. Colville's coming, the girl stole her hand into his.

"Shall you— tell her?"

"Of course. She must know without an instant's delay."

"Yes, yes; that is right. Oh!— Shall I go with you?"

"Yes; come!"

XV

Mrs. Bowen came in to them, looking pale and pain-worn, as she did that evening when she would not let Colville go away with the other tea-taking callers to whom she had made her headache an excuse. The eyelids which she had always a little difficulty in lifting were heavy with suffering, and her pretty smile had an effect of very great remoteness. But there was no consciousness of anything unusual or unexpected in his presence expressed in her looks or manner. Colville had meant to take Imogene by the hand and confront Mrs. Bowen with an immediate declaration of what had happened; but he found this impossible, at least in the form of his intention; he took, instead, the hand of conventional welcome which she gave him, and he obeyed her in taking provisionally the seat to which she invited him. At the same time the order of his words was dispersed in that wonder whether she suspected anything with which he listened to her placid talk about the weather; she said she had thought it was a chilly day out-doors; but her headaches always made her very sensitive.

"Yes," said Colville, "I supposed it was cold myself till I went out, for I woke with a twinge of rheumatism." He felt a strong desire to excuse, to justify, what had happened, and he went on, with a painful sense of Imogene's eyes bent in bewildered deference upon him. "I started out for a walk with Mr. Waters, but I left him after we got across the Ponte Vecchio; he went up to look at the Michelangelo bastions, and I strolled over to the Boboli Gardens—where I found your young people."

He had certainly brought himself to the point, but he seemed actually farther from it than at first, and he made a desperate plunge, trying at the same time to keep something of his habitual nonchalance. "But that doesn't account for my being here. Imogene accounts for that. She has allowed me to stay in Florence."

Mrs. Bowen could not turn paler than her headache had left her, and she now underwent no change of complexion.

But her throat was not clear enough to say to the end, "Allowed you to stay in——" The trouble in her throat arrested her again.

Colville became very red. He put out his hand and took Imogene's, and now his eyes and Mrs. Bowen's met in the kind of glance in which people intercept and turn each other aside before they have reached a resting-place in each other's souls. But at the girl's touch his courage revived—in some physical sort. "Yes; and if she will let me stay with her, we are not going to part again."

Mrs. Bowen did not answer at once, and in the hush Colville heard the breathing of all three.

"Of course," he said, "we wished you to know at once, and I came in with Imogene to tell you."

"What do you wish me," asked Mrs. Bowen, "to do?"

Colville forced a nervous laugh. "Really, I'm so little used to this sort of affair that I don't know whether I have any wish. Imogene is here with you, and I suppose I supposed you would wish to do something."

"I will do whatever you think best."

"Thank you: that's very kind of you." He fell into a silence, in which he was able only to wish that he knew what was best, and from which he came to the surface with, "Imogene's family ought to know, of course."

"Yes; they put her in my charge. They will have to know. Shall I write to them?"

"Why, if you will."

"Oh, certainly."

"Thank you."

He had taken to stroking with his right hand the hand of Imogene which he held in his left, and now he looked round at her with a glance which it was a relief not to have her meet. "And till we can hear from them, I suppose you will let me come to see her?"

"You know you have always been welcome here."

"Thank you very much." It seemed as if there ought to be something else to say, but Colville could not think of anything, except: "We wish to act in every way with your approval, Mrs. Bowen. And I know that you are very particular in some things"—the words, now that they were said, struck him as unfortunate and even vulgar—"and I shouldn't wish to annoy you—"

"Oh, I understand. I think it will be—I have no doubt you will know how to manage all that. It isn't as if you were both—"

"Young?" asked Colville. "No; one of us is quite old enough to be thoroughly up in the *convenances*. We are qualified, I'm afraid, as far as that goes," he added, bitterly, "to set all Florence an example of correct behavior."

He knew there must be pain in the face which he would not look at; he kept looking at Mrs. Bowen's face, in which certainly there was not much pleasure, either.

There was another silence, which became very oppressive before it ended in a question from Mrs. Bowen, who stirred slightly in her chair, and bent forward as if about to rise in asking it. "Shall you wish to consider it an engagement?"

Colville felt Imogene's hand tremble in his, but he received no definite prompting from the tremor. "I don't believe I know what you mean."

"I mean, till you have heard from Imogene's mother."

"I hadn't thought of that. Perhaps under the circumstances—" The tremor died out of the hand he held; it lay lax between his. "What do you say, Imogene?"

"I can't say anything. Whatever you think will be right—for me."

"I wish to do what will seem right and fair to your mother."

"Yes."

Colville heaved a hopeless sigh. Then, with a deep inward humiliation, he said, "Perhaps, if you know Imogene's mother, Mrs. Bowen, you can suggest—advise— You—"

"You must excuse me; I can't suggest or advise anything. I must leave you perfectly free." She rose from her chair, and they both rose too, from the sofa on which he had seated himself at Imogene's side. "I shall have to leave you, I'm afraid; my head aches still a little. Imogene!" She advanced toward the girl, who stood passively letting her come the whole distance. As if sensible of the rebuff expressed in this attitude, she halted a very little. Then she added, "I hope you will be very happy," and suddenly cast her arms round the girl, and stood long pressing her face into her neck. When she released her, Colville trembled lest she should be going to give him her hand in congratulation. But she only bowed slightly to him, with a sidelong, aversive glance, and walked out of the room with a slow, rigid pace, like one that controls a tendency to giddiness.

Imogene threw herself on Colville's breast. It gave him a shock, as if he were letting her do herself some wrong. But she gripped him fast, and began to sob and to cry. "Oh! oh! oh!"

"What is it?—what is it, my poor girl?" he murmured. "Are you unhappy? Are you sorry? Let it all end, then!"

"No, no; it isn't that! But I am very unhappy—yes, very, very unhappy! Oh, I didn't suppose I should ever feel so toward any one. I hate her!"

"You hate her?" gasped Colville.

"Yes, I hate her. And she—she is so good to me! It must be that I've done her some deadly wrong, without knowing it, or I couldn't hate her as I know I do."

"Oh no," said Colville, soothingly; "that's just your fancy. You haven't harmed her, and you don't hate her."

"Yes, yes, I do! You can't understand how I feel toward her."

"But you can't feel so toward her long," he urged, dealing as he might with what was wholly a mystery to him. "She is so good—"

"It only makes my badness worse, and makes me hate her more."

"I don't understand. But you're excited now. When you're calmer you'll feel differently, of course. I've kept you restless and nervous a long time, poor child; but now our peace begins, and everything will be bright and—" He stopped: the words had such a very hollow sound.

She pushed herself from him, and dried her eyes. "Oh yes."

"And, Imogene—perhaps—perhaps— Or, no; never mind now. I must go away—" She looked at him, frightened but submissive. "But I will be back to-night, or perhaps to-morrow morning. I want to think—to give you time to think. I don't want to be selfish about you. I want to consider you, all the more because you won't consider yourself.

Good-by." He stooped over and kissed her hair. Even in this he felt like a thief; he could not look at the face she lifted to his.

Mrs. Bowen sent word from her room that she was not coming to dinner, and Imogene did not come till the dessert was put on. Then she found Effie Bowen sitting alone at the table, and served in serious formality by the man, whom she had apparently felt it right to repress, for they were both silent. The little girl had not known how to deny herself an excess of the less wholesome dishes, and she was perhaps anticipating the regret which this indulgence was to bring, for she was very pensive.

"Isn't mamma coming at *all*?" she asked, plaintively, when Imogene sat down, and refused everything but a cup of coffee. "Well," she went on, "I can't make out what is coming to this family. You were all crying last night because Mr. Colville was going away, and now, when he's going to stay, it's just as bad. I don't think you make it very pleasant for *him*. I should think he would be perfectly puzzled by it, after he's done so much to please you all. I don't believe he thinks it's very polite. I suppose it *is* polite, but it doesn't seem so. And he's always so cheerful and nice. I should think he would want to visit in some family where there was more amusement. There used to be plenty in this family, but now it's as dismal! The first of the winter you and mamma used to be so pleasant when he came, and would try everything to amuse him, and would let me come in to get some of the good of it; but now you seem to fly every way as soon as he comes in sight of the house, and I'm poked off in holes and corners before he can open his lips. And I've borne it about as long as I can. I would rather be back in Vevay. Or anywhere." At this point her own pathos overwhelmed her, and the tears rolling down her cheeks moistened the crumbs of pastry at the corners of her pretty mouth. "What was so strange, I should like to know, about his staying, that mamma should pop up like a ghost, when I told her he had come home with us, and grab me by the wrist, and twitch me about, and ask me all sorts of questions I couldn't answer, and frighten me almost to death? I haven't got over it yet. And I don't think it's very nice. It used to be a very polite family, and pleasant with each other, and always having something agreeable going on in it; but if it keeps on *very* much longer in this way, I shall think the Bowens are beginning to lose their good-breeding. I suppose that if Mr. Colville were to go down on his knees to mamma and ask her to let him take me somewhere now, she wouldn't do it." She pulled her handkerchief out of her pocket, and dried her eyes on a ball of it. "I don't see what *you've* been crying about, Imogene. *You've* got nothing to worry you."

"I'm not very well, Effie," returned the girl, gently. "I haven't been well all day."

"It seems to me that nobody is well any more. I don't believe Florence is a very healthy place. Or at least this house isn't. *I* think it must be the drainage. If we keep on, I suppose we shall all have diphtheria. Don't you, Imogene?"

"Yes," asserted the girl, distractedly.

"The girls had it at Vevay frightfully. And none of them were as strong afterward. Some of the parents came and took them away; but Madame Schebres never let mamma know. Do you think that was right?"

"No; it was very wrong."

"I suppose Mr. Colville will have it if we do. That is, if he keeps coming here. Is he coming any more?"

"Yes; he's coming to-morrow morning."

"*Is* he?" A smile flickered over the rueful face. "What time is he coming?"

"I don't know exactly," said Imogene, listlessly stirring her coffee. "Some time in the forenoon."

"Do you suppose he's going to take us anywhere?"

"Yes—I think so. I can't tell exactly."

"If he asks me to go somewhere, will you tease mamma? She always lets you, Imogene, and it seems sometimes as if she just took a pleasure in denying me."

"You mustn't talk so of your mother, Effie."

"No; I wouldn't to *every*body. I know that she means for the best; but I don't believe she understands how much I suffer when she won't let me go with Mr. Colville. Don't you think he's about the nicest gentleman we know, Imogene?"

"Yes; he's very kind."

"And I think he's handsome. A good many people would

consider him old-looking, and of course he isn't so young as Mr. Morton was, or the Inglehart boys; but that makes him all the easier to get along with. And his being just a little fat, that way, seems to suit so well with his character." The smiles were now playing across the child's face, and her eyes sparkling. "*I* think Mr. Colville would make a good Saint Nicholas—the kind they have going down chimneys in America. I'm going to tell him, for the next veglione. It would be such a nice surprise."

"No, better not tell him that," suggested Imogene.

"Do you think he wouldn't like it?"

"Yes."

"Well, it would become him. How old do you suppose he is, Imogene? Seventy-five?"

"What an idea!" cried the girl, fiercely. "He's forty-one."

"I didn't know they had those little jiggering lines at the corners of their eyes so quick. But forty-one is pretty old, isn't it? Is Mr. Waters—"

"Effie," said her mother's voice at the door behind her, "will you ring for Giovanni, and tell him to bring me a cup of coffee in here?" She spoke from the *portière* of the salotto.

"Yes, mamma. I'll bring it to you myself."

"Thank you, dear," Mrs. Bowen called from within.

The little girl softly pressed her hands together. "I *hope* she'll let me stay up! I feel so excited, and I hate to lie and think so long before I get to sleep. Couldn't you just hint a little to her that I might stay up? It's Sunday night."

"I can't, Effie," said Imogene. "I oughtn't to interfere with any of your mother's rules."

The child sighed submissively and took the coffee that Giovanni brought to her. She and Imogene went into the salotto together. Mrs. Bowen was at her writing-desk. "You can bring the coffee here, Effie," she said.

"Must I go to bed at once, mamma?" asked the child, setting the cup carefully down.

The mother looked distractedly up from her writing. "No; you may sit up awhile," she said, looking back to her writing.

"How long, mamma?" pleaded the little girl.

"Oh, till you're sleepy. It doesn't matter *now*."

She went on writing; from time to time she tore up what she had written.

Effie softly took a book from the table, and perching herself on a stiff, high chair, bent over it and began to read.

Imogene sat by the hearth, where a small fire was pleasant in the in-door chill of an Italian house, even after so warm a day as that had been. She took some large beads of the strand she wore about her neck into her mouth, and pulled at the strand listlessly with her hand while she watched the fire. Her eyes wandered once to the child.

"What made you take such an uncomfortable chair, Effie?"

Effie shut her book over her hand. "It keeps me wakeful longer," she whispered, with a glance at her mother from the corner of her eye.

"I don't see why any one should wish to be wakeful," sighed the girl.

When Mrs. Bowen tore up one of her half-written pages, Imogene started nervously forward, and then relapsed again into her chair. At last Mrs. Bowen seemed to find the right phrases throughout, and she finished rather a long letter, and read it over to herself. Then she said, without leaving her desk, "Imogene, I've been trying to write to your mother. Will you look at this?"

She held the sheet over her shoulder, and Imogene came languidly and took it; Mrs. Bowen dropped her face forward on the desk, into her hands, while Imogene was reading.

"FLORENCE, *March* 10, 18—.

"DEAR MRS. GRAHAM,—I have some very important news to give you in regard to Imogene, and as there is no way of preparing you for it, I will tell you at once that it relates to her marriage.

"She has met at my house a gentleman whom I knew in Florence when I was here before, and of whom I never knew anything but good. We have seen him very often, and I have seen nothing in him that I could not approve. He is Mr. Theodore Colville, of Prairie des Vaches, Indiana, where he was for many years a newspaper editor; but he was born somewhere in New England. He is a very cultivated, interesting man, and though not exactly a society man, he is very agreeable and refined in his manners. I am sure his character is irreproachable, though he is not a member of any church. In regard to his means I know nothing whatever, and can only infer from his way of life that he is in easy circumstances.

"The whole matter has been a surprise to me, for Mr. Colville is some twenty-one or two years older than Imogene, who is very young in her feelings for a girl of her age. If I could have realized anything like a serious attachment between them sooner, I would have written before. Even now I do not know whether I am to consider them engaged or not. No doubt Imogene will write you more fully.

"Of course I would rather not have had anything of the kind happen while Imogene was under my charge, though I am sure that you will not think I have been careless or imprudent about her. I interfered as far as I could, at the first moment I could, but it appears that it was then too late to prevent what has followed. Yours sincerely,

"EVALINA BOWEN."

Imogene read the letter twice over, and then she said, "Why isn't he a society man?"

Probably Mrs. Bowen expected this sort of approach. "I don't think a society man would have undertaken to dance the Lancers as he did at Madame Uccelli's," she answered, patiently, without lifting her head.

Imogene winced, but "I should despise him if he were merely a society man," she said. "I have seen enough of them. I think it's better to be intellectual and good." Mrs. Bowen made no reply, and the girl went on. "And as to his being older, I don't see what difference it makes. If people are in sympathy, then they are of the same age, no difference how much older than one the other is. I have always heard that." She urged this as if it were a question.

"Yes," said Mrs. Bowen.

"And how should his having been a newspaper editor be anything against him?"

Mrs. Bowen lifted her face and stared at the girl in astonishment. "Who said it was against him?"

"You hint as much. The whole letter is against him."

"Imogene!"

"Yes! Every word! You make him out perfectly detestable. I don't know why you should hate *him*. He's done everything he could to satisfy you."

Mrs. Bowen rose from her desk, putting her hand to her forehead, as if to soften a shock of headache that her change of posture had sent there. "I will leave the letter with you, and you can send it or not, as you think best. It's merely a formality my writing to your mother. Perhaps you'll see it differently in the morning. Effie!" she called to the child, who with her book shut upon her hand had been staring at them and listening intently. "It's time to go to bed now."

When Effie stood before the glass in her mother's room, and Mrs. Bowen was braiding her hair and tying it up for the night, she asked, ruefully, "What's the matter with Imogene, mamma?"

"She isn't very happy to-night."

"*You* don't seem very happy either," said the child, watching her own face as it quivered in the mirror. "I should think that now Mr. Colville's concluded to stay, we would all be happy again. But we don't seem to. We're—we're perfectly demoralized!" It was one of the words she had picked up from Colville.

The quivering face in the glass broke in a passion of tears, and Effie sobbed herself to sleep.

Imogene sat down at Mrs. Bowen's desk, and pushing her letter away, began to write.

"FLORENCE, *March* 10, 18—.

"DEAR MOTHER,—I inclose a letter from Mrs. Bowen which will tell you better than I can what I wish to tell. I do not see how I can add anything that would give you more of an idea of him, or less, either. No person can be put down in cold black and white, and not seem like a mere inventory. I do not suppose you expected me to become engaged when you sent me out to Florence, and, as Mrs. Bowen says, I don't know whether I am engaged or not. I will leave it entirely to Mr. Colville; if he says we are engaged, we are. I am sure he will do what is best. I only know that he was going away from Florence because he thought I supposed he was not in earnest, and I asked him to stay.

"I am a good deal excited to-night, and can not write very clearly. But I will write soon again, and more at length.

"Perhaps something will be decided by that time. With much love to father,

"Your affectionate daughter,

"IMOGENE."

She put this letter into an envelope with Mrs. Bowen's, and leaving it unsealed to show her in the morning, she began to write again. This time she wrote to a girl with whom she had been on terms so intimate that when they left school they had agreed to know each other by names expressive of their extremely confidential friendship, and to address each other respectively as Diary and Journal. They were going to write every day, if only a line or two; and at the end of a year they were to meet and read over together the records of their lives as set down in these letters. They had never met since, though it was now three years since they parted, and they had not written since Imogene came abroad; that is, Imogene had not answered the only letter she had received from her friend in Florence. This friend was a very serious girl, and had wished to be a minister, but her family would not consent, or even accept the compromise of studying medicine, which she proposed, and she was still living at home in a small city of central New York. Imogene now addressed her:

"DEAR DIARY,—You can not think how far away the events of this day have pushed the feelings and ideas of the time when I agreed to write to you under this name. Till now it seems to me as if I had not changed in the least thing since we parted, and now I can hardly know myself for the same person. Oh, dear Di! something very wonderful has come into my life, and I feel that it rests with me to make it the greatest blessing to myself and others, or the greatest misery. If I prove unworthy of it or unequal to it, then I am sure that nothing but wretchedness will come of it.

"I am engaged—yes!—and to a man more than twice my own age. It is so easy to tell *you* this, for I know that your large-mindedness will receive it very differently from most people, and that you will see it as I do. He is the noblest of men, though he tries to conceal it under the light, ironical manner with which he has been faithful to a cruel disappointment. It was here in Florence, twenty years ago, that a girl—I am ashamed to call her a girl—trifled with the priceless treasure that has fallen to me, and flung it away. *You*, Di, will understand how I was first fascinated with the idea of trying to atone to him here for all the wrong he had suffered. At first it was only the vaguest suggestion—something like what I had read in a poem or novel—that had nothing to do with me personally, but it grew upon me more and more the more I saw of him, and felt the witchery of his light, indifferent manner, which I learned to see was tense with the anguish he had suffered. She had killed his youth; she had spoiled his life: if I could revive them, restore them! It came upon me like a great flash of light at last, and as soon as this thought took possession of me, I felt my whole being elevated and purified by it, and I was enabled to put aside with contempt the selfish considerations that had occurred to me at first. At first the difference between our ages was very shocking to me; for I had always imagined it would be some one young; but when this light broke upon me, I saw that *he* was young, younger even than I, as a man is at the same age with a girl. Sometimes, with my experiences, the fancies and flirtations that every one has and *must* have, however one despises them, I felt so *old* beside him; for he had been true to one love all his life, and he had not wavered for a moment. If I could make him forget it, if I could lift every feather's weight of sorrow from his breast, if I could help him to complete the destiny, grand and beautiful as it would have been, which another had arrested, broken off— don't you see, Di dear, how rich my reward would be?

"And he, how forbearing, how considerate, how anxious for me, how full of generous warning he has been! always putting me in mind, at every step, of the difference in years between us; never thinking of himself, and shrinking so much from even seeming to control me or sway me, that I don't know really whether I have not made all the advances!

"I can not write his name yet, and you must not ask it till I can; and I can not tell you anything about his looks or his life without seeming to degrade him, somehow, and make him a common man like others.

"How can I make myself his companion in everything? How can I convince him that there is no sacrifice for me, and that he alone is giving up? These are the thoughts that keep whirling through my mind. I hope I shall be helped, and I hope that I shall be tried, for that is the only way for me to be helped. I feel strong enough for anything that people can say. I should *welcome* criticism and opposition from any quarter. But I can see that *he* is very sensitive—it comes from his keen sense of the ridiculous—and if I suffer it will be on account of this grand, unselfish nature, and I shall be glad of that.

"I know you will understand me, Di, and I am not afraid of your laughing at these ravings. But if you did I should not care. It is such a comfort to say these things about him, to exalt him, and get him in the true light at last.

"Your faithful   JOURNAL.

"I shall tell him about you, one of the first things, and perhaps he can suggest some way out of your trouble, he has had so much experience of every kind. You will worship him, as I do, when you see him; for you will feel at once that he understands you, and that is such a *rest*.

"J."

Before Imogene fell asleep, Mrs. Bowen came to her in the dark, and softly closed the door that opened from the girl's room into Effie's. She sat down on the bed, and began to speak at once, as if she knew Imogene must be awake. "I thought you would come to *me*, Imogene; but as you didn't, I have come to you, for if you can go to sleep with hard thoughts of me to-night, I can't let you. You need me for your friend, and I wish to be your friend; it would be wicked in me to be anything else. I would give the world if your mother were here; but I tried to make my letter to her every-thing that it should be. If you don't think it is, I will write it over in the morning."

"No," said the girl, coldly; "it will do very well. I don't wish to trouble you so much."

"Oh, how can you speak so to me? Do you think that I blame Mr. Colville? Is that it? I don't ask you—I shall never ask you—how he came to remain, but I know that he has acted truthfully and delicately. I knew him long before you did, and no one need take his part with me." This was not perhaps what Mrs. Bowen meant to say when she began. "I have told you all along what I thought, but if you imagine that I am not satisfied with Mr. Colville, you are very much mistaken. I can't burst out into praises of him to your mother; that would be very patronizing, and very bad taste. Can't you see that it would?"

"Oh yes."

Mrs. Bowen lingered, as if she expected Imogene to say something more, but she did not, and Mrs. Bowen rose. "Then I hope we understand each other," she said, and went out of the room.

XVI

W HEN Colville came in the morning, Mrs. Bowen received him. They shook hands, and their eyes met in the intercepting glance of the night before.

"Imogene will be here in a moment," she said, with a naturalness that made him awkward and conscious.

"Oh, there is no haste," he answered, uncouthly. "That is, I am very glad of the chance to speak a moment with you, and to ask your—to profit by what you think best. I know you are not very well pleased with me, and I don't know that i can ever put myself in a better light with you—the true light. It seems that there are some things we must not do even for the truth's sake. But that's neither here nor there. What I am most anxious for is not to take a shadow of advantage of this child's—of Imogene's inexperience, and her remoteness from her family. I feel that I must in some sort protect her from herself. Yes—that is my idea. But I have to do this in so many ways that I hardly know how to begin. I should be very willing, if you thought best, to go away and stay away till she has heard from her people, and let her have that time to think it all over again. She is very young—so much younger than I! Or, if you thought it better, I would stay, and let her remain free while I held myself bound to any decision of hers. I am anxious to do what is right. At the same time"—he smiled ruefully—"there is such a thing as being so *dis*interested that one may seem *un*interested. I may leave her so very free that she may begin to suspect that I want a little freedom myself. What shall I do? I wish to act with your approval."

Mrs. Bowen had listened with acquiescence and intelligence that might well have looked like sympathy, as she sat fingering the top of her hand-screen, with her eyelids fallen. She lifted them to say: "I have told you that I will not advise you in any way. I can not. I have no longer any wish in this matter. I must still remain in the place of Imogene's mother; but I will do only what you wish. Please understand that, and don't ask me for advice any more. It is painful." She drew her lower lip in a little, and let the screen fall into her lap.

"I'm sorry, Mrs. Bowen, to do anything—say anything—that is painful to you," Colville began. "You know that I would give the world to please you—" The words escaped him and left him staring at her.

"What are you saying to me, Theodore Colville?" she exclaimed, flashing a full-eyed glance upon him, and then breaking into a laugh, as unnatural for her. "Really, I don't believe you know!"

"Heaven knows I meant nothing but what I said," he answered, struggling stupidly with a confusion of desires which every man but no woman will understand. After eighteen hundred years, the man is still imperfectly monogamous. "Is there anything wrong in it?"

"Oh no! Not for you," she said, scornfully.

"I am very much in earnest," he went on, hopelessly, "in asking your opinion, your help, in regard to how I shall treat this affair."

"And I am still more in earnest in telling you that I will give you no opinion, no help. I forbid you to recur to the subject." He was silent, unable to drop his eyes from hers. "But for her," continued Mrs. Bowen, "I will do anything in my power. If she asks my advice I will give it, and I will give her all the help I can."

"Thank you," said Colville, vaguely.

"I will not have your thanks," promptly retorted Mrs. Bowen, "for I mean you no kindness. I am trying to do my duty to Imogene, and when that is ended, all is ended. There is no way now for you to please me—as you call it—except to keep her from regretting what she has done."

"Do you think I shall fail in that?" he demanded, indignantly.

"I can offer you no opinion. I can't tell what you will do."

"There are two ways of keeping her from regretting what she has done; and perhaps the simplest and best way would be to free her from the consequences, as far as they're involved in me," said Colville.

Mrs. Bowen dropped herself back in her arm-chair. "If you choose to force these things upon me, I am a woman, and can't help myself. Especially, I can't help myself against a guest."

"Oh, I will relieve you of my presence," said Colville. "I've no wish to force anything upon you—least of all myself." He rose, and moved toward the door.

She hastily intercepted him. "Do you think I will let you go without seeing Imogene? Do you understand me so little as that? It's *too late* for you to go! You know what I think of all this, and I know, better than you, what you think. I shall play my part, and you shall play yours. I have refused to give you advice or help, and I never shall do it. But I know what my duty to her is, and I will fulfill it. No matter how distasteful it is to either of us, you must come here as before. The house is as free to you as ever—freer. And we are to be as good friends as ever—better. You can see Imogene alone or in my presence; and, as far as I am concerned, you shall consider yourself engaged or not, as you choose. Do you understand?"

"Not in the least," said Colville, in the ghost of his old bantering manner. "But don't explain, or I shall make still less of it."

"I mean simply that I do it for Imogene, and not for you."

"Oh, I understand that you don't do it for me."

At this moment Imogene appeared between the folds of the *portière*, and her timid, embarrassed glance from Mrs. Bowen to Colville was the first gleam of consolation that had visited him since he parted with her the night before. A thrill of inexplicable pride and fondness passed through his heart, and even the compunction that followed could not spoil its sweetness. But if Mrs. Bowen discreetly turned her head aside that she need not witness a tender greeting between them, the precaution was unnecessary. He merely went forward and took the girl's hand, with a sigh of relief. "Good-morning, Imogene," he said, with a kind of compassionate admiration.

"Good-morning," she returned, half-inquiringly.

She did not take a seat near him, and turned, as if for instruction, to Mrs. Bowen. It was probably the force of habit. In any case, Mrs. Bowen's eyes gave no response. She bowed slightly to Colville, and began, "I must leave Imogene to entertain you for the present, Mr.—"

"No!" cried the girl, impetuously; "don't go." Mrs. Bowen stopped. "I wish to speak with you—with you and Mr. Colville together. I wish to say—I don't know how to say it exactly; but I wish to know— You asked him last night, Mrs. Bowen, whether he wished to consider it an engagement?"

"I thought perhaps you would rather hear from your mother—"

"Yes, I would be glad to know that my mother approved; but if she didn't, I couldn't help it. Mr. Colville said he was bound, but I was not. That can't be. I *wish* to be bound, if he is."

"I don't quite know what you expect me to say."

"Nothing," said Imogene. "I merely wished you to know. And I don't wish you to sacrifice anything to us. If you think best, Mr. Colville will not see me till I hear from home; though it won't make any difference with me *what* I hear."

"There's no reason why you shouldn't meet," said Mrs. Bowen, absently.

"If you wish it to have the same appearance as an Italian engagement—"

"No," said Mrs. Bowen, putting her hand to her head with a gesture she had; "that would be quite unnecessary. It would be ridiculous—under the circumstances. I have thought of it, and I have decided that the American way is the best."

"Very well, then," said Imogene, with the air of summing up; "then the only question is whether we shall make it known or not to other people."

This point seemed to give Mrs. Bowen greater pause than any. She was a long time silent, and Colville saw that Imogene was beginning to chafe at her indecision. Yet he did not see the moment to intervene in a debate in which he found himself somewhat ludicrously ignored, as if the affair were solely the concern of these two women, and none of his.

"Of course, Mrs. Bowen," said the girl, haughtily, "if it will be disagreeable to you to have it known—"

Mrs. Bowen blushed delicately—a blush of protest and of generous surprise, or so it seemed to Colville. "I was not thinking of myself, Imogene. I only wish to consider you. And I was thinking whether, at this distance from home, you wouldn't prefer to have your family's approval before you made it known."

"I am sure of their approval. Father will do what mother says, and she has always said that she would never interfere with me in—in—such a thing."

"Perhaps you would like all the more, then, to show her the deference of waiting for her consent."

Imogene started as if stopped short in swift career; it was not hard for Colville to perceive that she saw for the first time the reverse side of a magnanimous impulse. She suddenly turned to him.

"I think Mrs. Bowen is right," he said, gravely, in answer to the eyes of Imogene. He continued, with a flicker of his wonted mood: "You must consider me a little in the matter. I have some small shreds of self-respect about me somewhere, and I would rather not be put in the attitude of defying your family, or ignoring them."

"No," said Imogene, in the same effect of arrest.

"When it isn't absolutely necessary," continued Colville. "Especially as you say there will be no opposition."

"Of course," Imogene assented; and in fact what he said was very just, and he knew it; but he could perceive that he had suffered loss with her. A furtive glance at Mrs. Bowen did not assure him that he had made a compensating gain in that direction, where, indeed, he had no right to wish for any.

"Well, then," the girl went on, "it shall be so. We will wait. It will only be waiting. I ought to have thought of you before: I make a bad beginning," she said, tremulously. "I supposed I *was* thinking of you; but I see that I was only thinking of myself." The tears stood in her eyes. Mrs. Bowen, quite overlooked in this apology, slipped from the room.

"Imogene!" said Colville, coming toward her.

She dropped herself upon his shoulder. "Oh, why, why, *why* am I so miserable?"

"Miserable, Imogene!" he murmured, stroking her beautiful hair.

"Yes, yes! Utterly miserable! It must be because I'm unworthy of you—unequal every way. If you think so, cast me off at once. Don't be weakly merciful!"

The words pierced his heart. "I would give the world to

make you happy, my child!" he said, with perfidious truth, and a sigh that came from the bottom of his soul. "Sit down here by me," he said, moving to the sofa; and with whatever obscure sense of duty to her innocent self-abandon, he made a space between them, and reduced her embrace to a clasp of the hand she left with him. "Now tell me," he said, "what is it makes you unhappy?"

"Oh, I don't know," she answered, drying her averted eyes. "I suppose I am overwrought from not sleeping, and from thinking how we should arrange it all."

"And now that it's all arranged, can't you be cheerful again?"

"Yes."

"You're satisfied with the way we've arranged it? Because if—"

"Oh, perfectly—perfectly!" She hastily interrupted. "I wouldn't have it otherwise. Of course," she added, "it wasn't very pleasant having some one else suggest what I ought to have thought of myself, and seem more delicate about you than I was."

"Some one else?"

"You know! Mrs. Bowen."

"Oh! But I couldn't see that she was anxious to spare me. It occurred to me that she was concerned about your family."

"It led up to the other; it's all the same thing."

"Well, even in that case, I don't see why you should mind it. It was certainly very friendly of her, and I know that she has your interest at heart entirely."

"Yes, she knows how to make it seem so."

Colville hesitated in bewilderment. "I don't—" he cried at last, "I don't understand this. Don't you think Mrs. Bowen likes you?"

"She detests me."

"Oh, no, no, no! That's too cruel an error. You mustn't think that. I can't let you. It's morbid. I'm sure that she's devotedly kind and good to you."

"Being kind and good isn't liking. I know what she thinks. But of course I can't expect to convince you of it; no one else could see it."

"No!" said Colville, with generous fervor. "Because it

doesn't exist, and you mustn't imagine it. You are as sincerely and unselfishly regarded in this house as you could be in your own home. I'm sure of that. I know Mrs. Bowen. She has her little worldlinesses and unrealities of manner, but she is truth and loyalty itself. She would rather die than be false, or even unfair. I knew her long ago—"

"Yes," cried the girl, "long before you knew me!"

"And I know her to be the soul of honor," said Colville, ignoring the childish outburst. "Honor—like a man's," he added. "And, Imogene, I want you to promise me that you'll not think of her any more in that way. I want you to think of her as faithful and loving to you, for she is so. Will you do it?"

Imogene did not answer him at once. Then she turned upon him a face of radiant self-abnegation. "I will do anything you tell me. Only tell me things to do."

The next time he came he again saw Mrs. Bowen alone before Imogene appeared. The conversation was confined to two sentences.

"Mr. Colville," she said, with perfectly tranquil point, while she tilted a shut book to and fro on her knee, "I will thank you not to defend me."

Had she overheard? Had Imogene told her? He answered, in a fury of resentment for her ingratitude that stupefied him, "I will never speak of you again."

Now they were enemies; he did not know how or why, but he said to himself, in the bitterness of his heart, that it was better so; and when Imogene appeared, and Mrs. Bowen vanished, as she did without another word to him, he folded the girl in a vindictive embrace.

"What is the matter?" she asked, pushing away from him.

"With me?"

"Yes; you seem so excited."

"Oh, nothing," he said, shrinking from the sharpness of that scrutiny in a woman's eyes which, when it begins the perusal of a man's soul, astonishes and intimidates him; he never perhaps becomes able to endure it with perfect self-control. "I suppose a slight degree of excitement in meeting you may be forgiven me." He smiled under the unrelaxed severity of her gaze.

"Was Mrs. Bowen saying anything about me?"

"Not a word," said Colville, glad of getting back to the firm truth again, even if it were mere literality.

"We have made it up," she said, her scrutiny changing to a lovely appeal for his approval. "What there was to make up."

"Yes?"

"I told her what you had said. And now it's all right between us, and you mustn't be troubled at that any more. I did it to please you."

She seemed to ask him with the last words whether she really had pleased him, as if something in his aspect suggested a doubt; and he hastened to re-assure her. "That was very good of you. I appreciate it highly. It's extremely gratifying."

She broke into a laugh of fond derision. "I don't believe you really cared about it, or else you're not thinking about it now. Sit down, here; I want to tell you of something I've thought out." She pulled him to the sofa, and put his arm about her waist, with a simple fearlessness and matter-of-course promptness that made him shudder. He felt that he ought to tell her not to do it, but he did not quite know how without wounding her. She took hold of his hand and drew his lax arm taut. Then she looked up into his eyes, as if some sense of his misgiving had conveyed itself to her, but she did not release her hold of his hand.

"Perhaps we oughtn't, if we're not engaged?" she suggested, with such utter trust in him as made his heart quake.

"Oh," he sighed, from a complexity of feeling that no explanation could wholly declare, "we're engaged enough for that, I suppose."

"I'm glad you think so," she answered, innocently. "I knew you wouldn't let me if it were not right." Having settled the question, "Of course," she continued, "we shall all do our best to keep our secret; but in spite of everything it may get out. Do you see?"

"Well?"

"Well, of course it will make a great deal of remark."

"Oh yes; you must be prepared for that, Imogene," said Colville, with as much gravity as he could make comport with his actual position.

"I am prepared for it, and prepared to despise it," answered the girl. "I shall have no trouble except the fear that you will mind it." She pressed his hand as if she expected him to say something to this.

"I shall never care for it," he said, and this was true enough. "My only care will be to keep you from regretting. I have tried from the first to make you see that I was very much older than you. It would be miserable enough if you came to see it too late."

"I have never seen it, and I never shall see it, because there's no such difference between us. It isn't the years that make us young or old—who is it says that? No matter, it's true. And I want you to believe it. I want you to feel that *I* am your youth—the youth you were robbed of—given back to you. Will you do it? Oh, if you could, I should be the happiest girl in the world." Tears of fervor dimmed the beautiful eyes which looked into his. "Don't speak!" she hurried on. "I won't let you till I have said it all. It's been this idea, this hope, with me always—ever since I knew what happened to you here long ago—that you might go back in my life and take up yours where it was broken off; that I might make your life what it would have been—complete your destiny—"

Colville wrenched himself loose from the hold that had been growing more tenderly close and clinging. "And do you think I could be such a vampire as to let you? Yes, yes: I have had my dreams of such a thing; but I see now how hideous they were. You shall make no such sacrifice to me. You must put away the fancies that could never be fulfilled, or if by some infernal magic they could, would only bring sorrow to you and shame to me. God forbid! And God forgive me if I have done or said anything to put this in your head! And thank God it isn't too late yet for you to take yourself back."

"Oh," she murmured. "Do you think it is self-sacrifice for me to give myself to *you*? It's self-glorification! You don't understand—I haven't told you what I mean, or else I've told it in such a way that I've made it hateful to you. Do you think I don't care for you except to be something to you? I'm not so generous as that. You are all the world to me. If I take myself back from you, as you say, what shall I do with myself?"

"Has it come to that?" asked Colville. He sat down again with her, and this time he put his arm around her and drew her to him, but it seemed to him he did it as if she were his child. "I was going to tell you just now that each of us lived to himself in this world, and that no one could hope to enter into the life of another and complete it. But now I see that I was partly wrong. We two are bound together, Imogene, and whether we become all in all or nothing to each other, we can have no separate fate."

The girl's eyes kindled with rapture. "Then let us never speak of it again. I was going to say something, but now I won't say it."

"Yes, say it."

"No; it will make you think that I am anxious on my own account about appearances before people."

"You poor child, I shall never think you are anxious on your own account about anything. What were you going to say?"

"Oh, nothing! It was only   are you invited to the Phillipses' fancy ball?"

"Yes," said Colville, silently making what he could of the diversion, "I believe so."

"And are you going— did you mean to go?" she asked, timidly.

"Good heavens, no! What in the world should I do at another fancy ball? I walked about with the airy grace of a bull in a china shop at the last one."

Imogene did not smile. She faintly sighed. "Well, then, I won't go either."

"Did you intend to go?"

"Oh no!"

"Why, of course you did, and it's very right you should. Did you want me to go?"

"It would bore you."

"Not if you're there." She gave his hand a grateful pressure. "Come, I'll go, of course, Imogene. A fancy ball to please you is a very different thing from a fancy ball in the abstract."

"Oh, what nice things you say! Do you know, I always admired your compliments. I think they're the most charming compliments in the world."

"I don't think they're half so pretty as yours; but they're more sincere."

"No, honestly. They flatter, and at the same time they make fun of the flattery a little; they make a person feel that you like them, even while you laugh at them."

"They appear to be rather an intricate kind of compliment—sort of *salsa agradolce* affair—*tutti frutti* style—species of moral mayonnaise."

"No—be quiet! You know what I mean. What were we talking about? Oh! I was going to say that the most fascinating thing about you always was that ironical way of yours."

"Have I an ironical way? You were going to tell me something more about the fancy ball."

"I don't care for it. I would rather talk about you."

"And I prefer the ball. It's a fresher topic—to me."

"Very well, then. But this I *will* say. No matter how happy you should be, I should always want you to keep that tone of persiflage. You've no idea how perfectly intoxicating it is."

"Oh yes, I have. It seems to have turned the loveliest and wisest head in the world."

"Oh, do you really think so? I would give anything if you did."

"What?"

"Think I was pretty," she pleaded, with full eyes. "Do you?"

"No; but I think you are wise. Fifty per cent. of truth—it's a large average in compliments. What are you going to wear?"

"Wear? Oh! At the ball! Something Egyptian, I suppose. It's to be an Egyptian ball. Didn't you understand that?"

"Oh yes. But I supposed you could go in any sort of dress."

"You can't. You must go in some Egyptian character."

"How would Moses do? In the bulrushes, you know. You could be Pharaoh's daughter, and recognize me by my three hats. And toward the end of the evening, when I became very much bored, I could go round killing Egyptians."

"No, no. Be serious. Though I like you to joke, too. I shall always want you to joke. Shall you, always?"

"There may be emergencies when I shall fail—like family prayers, and grace before meat, and dangerous sickness."

"Why, of course. But I mean when we're together, and there's no reason why you shouldn't?"

"Oh, at such times I shall certainly joke."

"And before people, too. I won't have them saying that it's sobered you—that you used to be very gay, and now you're cross and never say anything."

"I will try to keep it up sufficiently to meet the public demand."

"And I shall want you to joke *me*, too. You must satirize me. It does more to show me my faults than anything else, and it will show other people how perfectly submissive I am, and how I think everything you do is just right."

"If I were to beat you a little in company, don't you think it would serve the same purpose?"

"No, no; be serious."

"About joking?"

"No, about me. I know that I'm very intense, and you must try to correct that tendency in me."

"I will, with pleasure. Which of *my* tendencies are you going to correct?"

"You have none."

"Well, then, neither have you. I'm not going to be outdone in civilities."

"Oh, if people could only hear you talk in this light way, and then know what *I* know!"

Colville broke out into a laugh at the deep sigh which accompanied these words. As a whole, the thing was grotesque and terrible to him, but, after a habit of his, he was finding a strange pleasure in its details.

"No, no," she pleaded. "Don't laugh. There are girls that would give their eyes for it."

"As pretty eyes as yours?"

"Do you think they're nice?"

"Yes, if they were not so mysterious."

"Mysterious?"

"Yes; I feel that your eyes can't really be as honest as they look. That was what puzzled me about them the first night I saw you."

"No—did it, really?"

"I went home saying to myself that no girl could be so sincere as that Miss Graham seemed."

"Did you say that?"

"Words to that effect."

"And what do you think now?"

"Ah, I don't know. You had better go as the Sphinx."

Imogene laughed in simple gayety of heart. "How far we've got from the ball!" she said, as if the remote excursion were a triumph. "What shall we really go as?"

"Isis and Osiris."

"Weren't they gods of some kind?"

"Little one-horse deities—not very much."

"It won't do to go as gods of any kind. They're always failures. People expect too much of them."

"Yes," said Colville. "That's human nature under all circumstances. But why go to an Egyptian ball at all?"

"Oh, we *must* go. If we both staid away it would make talk at once, and my object is to keep people in the dark till the very last moment. Of course it's unfortunate your having told Mrs. Amsden that you were going away, and then telling her just after you came back with me that you were going to stay. But it can't be helped now. And I don't really care for it. But don't you see why I want you to go to all these things?"

"*All* these things?"

"Yes; everything you're invited to after this. It's not merely for a blind as regards ourselves now, but if they see that you're very fond of all sorts of gayeties, they will see that you are—they will understand—"

There was no need for her to complete the sentence. Colville rose. "Come, come, my dear child," he said, "why don't you end all this at once? I don't blame you. Heaven knows I blame no one but myself! I ought to have the strength to break away from this mistake, but I haven't. I couldn't bear to see you suffer from pain that I should give you even for your good. But do it yourself, Imogene, and for pity's sake don't forbear from any notion of sparing me. I have no wish except for your happiness. And now I tell you clearly that no appearance we can put on before the world will deceive the world. At the end of all our trouble I shall still be forty—"

She sprang to him and put her hand over his mouth. "I know what you're going to say, and I won't let you say it, for you've promised over and over again not to speak of that any more. Oh, do you think I care for the world, or what it will think or say?"

"Yes; very much."

"That shows how little you understand me. It's because I wish to *defy* the world—"

"Imogene! Be as honest with yourself as you are with me."

"I *am* honest."

"Look me in the eyes, then."

She did so for an instant, and then hid her face on his shoulder.

"You silly girl!" he said. "What is it you really do wish?"

"I wish there was no one in the world but you and me."

"Ah, you'd find it very crowded at times," said Colville, sadly. "Well, well," he added, "I'll go to your fandangoes, because you want me to go."

"That's all I wished you to say," she replied, lifting her head, and looking him radiantly in the face. "I don't want you to go at all! I only want you to promise that you'll come here every night that you're invited out, and read to Mrs. Bowen and me."

"Oh, I can't do that," said Colville; "I'm too fond of society. For example, I've been invited to an Egyptian fancy ball, and I couldn't think of giving that up."

"Oh, how delightful you are! They couldn't any of them talk like you."

He had learned to follow the processes of her thought now. "Perhaps they can when they come to my age."

"There!" she exclaimed, putting her hand on his mouth again, to remind him of another broken promise. "Why can't you give up the Egyptian ball?"

"Because I expect to meet a young lady there—a very beautiful young lady."

"But how shall you know her if she's disguised?"

"Why, I shall be disguised too, you know."

"Oh, what delicious nonsense you *do* talk! Sit down here and tell me what you are going to wear."

She tried to pull him back to the sofa. "What character shall you go in?"

"No, no," he said, resisting the gentle traction. "I can't; I have urgent business down-town."

"Oh! Business in *Florence!*"

"Well, if I staid, I should tell you what disguise I'm going to the ball in."

"I knew it was that. What do you think would be a good character for me?"

"I don't know. The serpent of old Nile would be pretty good for you."

"Oh, I know you don't think it!" she cried, fondly. She had now let him take her hand, and he stood holding it at arm's-length. Effie Bowen came into the room. "Good-by," said Imogene, with an instant assumption of society manner.

"Good-by," said Colville, and went out.

"Oh, Mr. Colville!" she called, before he got to the outer door.

"Yes," he said, starting back.

She met him midway of the dim corridor. "Only to—" She put her arms about his neck and sweetly kissed him.

Colville went out into the sunlight feeling like some strange, newly invented kind of scoundrel—a rascal of such recent origin and introduction that he had not yet had time to classify himself and ascertain the exact degree of his turpitude. The task employed his thoughts all that day, and kept him vibrating between an instinctive conviction of monstrous wickedness and a logical and well-reasoned perception that he had all the facts and materials for a perfectly good conscience. He was the betrothed lover of this poor child, whose affection he could not check without a degree of brutality for which only a better man would have the courage. When he thought of perhaps refusing her caresses, he imagined the shock it would give her, and the look of grief and mystification that would come into her eyes, and he found himself incapable of that cruel rectitude. He knew that these were the impulses of a white and loving soul; but at the end of all his argument they remained a terror to him, so that he lacked nothing but the will to fly from Florence and shun her altogether till she had heard from her family. This, he recalled, with bitter self-reproach, was what had been his first inspiration; he had spoken of it to Mrs. Bowen, and it had still everything in its favor except that it was impossible.

Imogene returned to the salotto, where the little girl was standing with her face to the window, drearily looking out; her back expressed an inner desolation, which revealed itself in her eyes when Imogene caught her head between her hands and tilted up her face to kiss it.

"What is the matter, Effie?" she demanded, gayly.

"Nothing."

"Oh yes, there is."

"Nothing that you will care for. As long as he's pleasant to you, you don't care what he does to me."

"What has he done to you?"

"He didn't take the slightest notice of me when I came into the room. He didn't speak to me, or even look at me."

Imogene caught the little grieving, quivering face to her breast. "He is a wicked, wicked wretch! And I will give him the awfulest scolding he ever had when he comes here again. I will teach him to neglect my pet! I will let him understand that if he doesn't notice you, he needn't notice me. I will tell you, Effie—I've just thought of a way. The next time he comes we will both receive him. We will sit up very stiffly on the sofa together, and just answer Yes, No, Yes, No, to everything he says, till he begins to take the hint, and learns how to behave himself. Will you?"

A smile glittered through the little girl's tears; but she asked, "Do you think it would be very polite?"

"No matter, polite or not, it's what he deserves. Of course, as soon as he begins to take the hint, we will be just as we always are."

Imogene dispatched a note, which Colville got the next morning, to tell him of his crime, and apprise him of his punishment, and of the sweet compunction that had pleaded for him in the breast of the child. If he did not think he could help play the comedy through, he must come prepared to offer Effie some sort of atonement.

It was easy to do this: to come with his pockets full of presents, and take the little girl on his lap, and pour out all his troubled heart in the caresses and tendernesses which would bring him no remorse. He humbled himself to her thoroughly, and with a strange sincerity in the harmless duplicity, and promised, if she would take him back into favor, that he would never offend again. Mrs. Bowen had sent word that she was not well enough to see him; she had another of her headaches; and he sent back a sympathetic and respectful message by Effie, who stood thoughtfully at her mother's pillow after she had delivered it, fingering the bouquet Colville had brought her, and putting her head first on this side and then on that to admire it.

"I think Mr. Colville and Imogene are much more affectionate than they used to be," she said.

Mrs. Bowen started up on her elbow. "What do you mean, Effie?"

"Oh, they're both so good to me."

"Yes," said her mother, dropping back to her pillow. "Both?"

"Yes. He's the *most* affectionate."

The mother turned her face the other way. "Then he must be," she murmured.

"What?" asked the child.

"Nothing. I didn't know I spoke."

The little girl stood awhile still playing with her flowers. "*I* think Mr. Colville is about the pleasantest gentleman that comes here. Don't you, mamma?"

"Yes."

"He's so interesting, and says such nice things. I don't know whether children ought to think of such things, but I wish I was going to marry some one like Mr. Colville. Of course I should want to be tolerably old if I did. How old do you think a person ought to be to marry him?"

"You mustn't talk of such things, Effie," said her mother.

"No; I suppose it isn't very nice." She picked out a bud in her bouquet, and kissed it; then she held the nosegay at arm's-length before her, and danced away with it.

XVII

IN THE ensuing fortnight a great many gayeties besides the
Egyptian Ball took place, and Colville went wherever he
and Imogene were both invited. He declined the quiet dinners which he liked, and which his hearty appetite and his
habit of talk fitted him to enjoy, and accepted invitations to
all sorts of evenings and At Homes, where dancing occupied
a modest corner of the card, and usurped the chief place in
the pleasures. At these places it was mainly his business to see
Imogene danced with by others, but sometimes he waltzed
with her himself, and then he was complimented by people
of his own age, who had left off dancing, upon his vigor.
They said they could not stand that sort of thing, though they
supposed, if you kept yourself in practice, it did not come so
hard. One of his hostesses, who had made a party for her
daughters, told him that he was an example to everybody,
and that if middle-aged people at home mingled more in the
amusements of the young, American society would not be the
silly, insipid, boy-and-girl affair that it was now. He went to
these places in the character of a young man, but he was not
readily accepted or recognized in that character. They gave
him frumps to take out to supper, mothers and maiden aunts,
and if the mothers were youngish, they threw off on him, and
did not care for his talk.

At one of the parties Imogene seemed to become aware for
the first time that the lapels of his dress-coat were not faced
with silk.

"Why don't you have them so?" she asked. "All the *other*
young men have. And you ought to wear a *boutonnière*."

"Oh, I think a man looks rather silly in silk lapels at my—"
He arrested himself, and then continued: "I'll see what the
tailor can do for me. In the mean time, give me a bud out of
your bouquet."

"How sweet you are!" she sighed. "You do the least thing
so that it is ten times as good as if any one else did it."

The same evening, as he stood leaning against a doorway,

behind Imogene and a young fellow with whom she was beginning a quadrille, he heard her taking him to task.

"Why do you say 'Sir' to Mr. Colville?"

"Well, I know the English laugh at us for doing it, and say it's like servants; but I never feel quite right answering just 'Yes' and 'No' to a man of his age."

This was one of the Inglehart boys, whom he met at nearly all of these parties, and not all of whom were so respectful. Some of them treated him upon an old-boy theory, joking him as freely as if he were one of themselves, laughing his antiquated notions of art to scorn, but condoning them because he was good-natured, and because a man could not help being of his own epoch anyway. They put a caricature of him among the rest on the walls of their *trattoria*, where he once dined with them.

Mrs. Bowen did not often see him when he went to call upon Imogene, and she was not at more than two or three of the parties. Mrs. Amsden came to chaperon the girl, and apparently suffered an increase of unrequited curiosity in regard to his relations to the Bowen household, and the extraordinary development of his social activity. Colville not only went to all those evening parties, but he was in continual movement during the afternoon at receptions and at "days," of which he began to think each lady had two or three. Here he drank tea, cup after cup, in reckless excitement, and at night, when he came home from the dancing parties, dropping with fatigue, he could not sleep till toward morning. He woke at the usual breakfast hour, and then went about drowsing throughout the day till the tea began again in the afternoon. He fell asleep whenever he sat down, not only in the reading-room at Vieusseux's, where he disturbed the people over their newspapers by his demonstrations of somnolence, but even at church, whither he went one Sunday to please Imogene, and started awake during the service with the impression that the clergyman had been making a joke. Everybody but Imogene was smiling. At the café he slept without scruple, selecting a corner seat for the purpose, and proportioning his *buona-mano* to the indulgence of the *giovane*. He could not tell how long he slept at these places, but sometimes it seemed to him hours.

One day he went to see Imogene, and while Effie Bowen stood prattling to him as he sat waiting for Imogene to come in, he faded light-headedly away from himself on the sofa, as if he had been in his corner at the café. Then he was aware of some one saying " 'Sh!" and he saw Effie Bowen, with her finger on her lip, turned toward Imogene, a figure of beautiful despair in the doorway. He was all tucked up with sofa pillows, and made very comfortable, by the child no doubt. She slipped out, seeing him awake, so as to leave him and Imogene alone, as she had apparently been generally instructed to do, and Imogene came forward.

"What is the matter, Theodore?" she asked, patiently. She had taken to calling him Theodore when they were alone. She owned that she did not like the name, but she said it was right she should call him by it, since it was his. She came and sat down beside him, where he had raised himself to a sitting posture, but she did not offer him any caress.

"Nothing," he answered. "But this climate is making me insupportably drowsy; or else the spring weather."

"Oh no; it isn't that," she said, with a slight sigh. He had left her in the middle of a german at three o'clock in the morning, but she now looked as fresh and lambent as a star. "It's the late hours. They're killing you."

Colville tried to deny it; his incoherencies dissolved themselves in a yawn, which he did not succeed in passing for a careless laugh.

"It won't do," she said, as if speaking to herself; "no, it won't do."

"Oh yes, it will," Colville protested. "I don't mind being up. I've been used to it all my life on the paper. It's just some temporary thing. It'll come all right."

"Well, no matter," said Imogene. "It makes you ridiculous, going to all those silly places, and I'd rather give it up."

The tears began to steal down her cheeks, and Colville sighed. It seemed to him that somebody or other was always crying. A man never quite gets used to the tearfulness of women.

"Oh, don't mind it," he said. "If you wish me to go, I will go! Or die in the attempt," he added, with a smile.

Imogene did not smile with him. "I don't wish you to go

any more. It was a mistake in the first place, and from this out I will adapt myself to you."

"And give up all your pleasures? Do you think I would let you do that? No, indeed! Neither in this nor in anything else. I will not cut off your young life in any way, Imogene—not shorten it or diminish it. If I thought I should do that, or you would try to do it for me, I should wish I had never seen you."

"It isn't that. I know how good you are, and that you would do anything for me."

"Well, then, why don't you go to these fandangoes alone? I can see that you have me on your mind all the time, when I'm with you."

"Oughtn't I?"

"Yes, up to a certain point, but not up to the point of spoiling your fun. I will drop in now and then, but I won't try to come to all of them, after this; you'll get along perfectly well with Mrs. Amsden, and I shall be safe from her for a while. That old lady has marked me for her prey: I can see it in her glittering eye-glass. I shall fall asleep some evening between dances, and then she will get it all out of me."

Imogene still refused to smile. "No; I shall give it up. I don't think it's well, going so much without Mrs. Bowen. People will begin to talk."

"Talk?"

"Yes; they will begin to say that I had better stay with her a little more, if she isn't well."

"Why, isn't Mrs. Bowen well?" asked Colville, with trepidation.

"No; she's miserable. Haven't you noticed?"

"She sees me so seldom now. I thought it was only her headaches—"

"It's much more than that. She seems to be failing every way. The doctor has told her she ought to get away from Florence." Colville could not speak; Imogene went on: "She's always delicate, you know. And I feel that all that's keeping her here now is the news from home that I—we're waiting for."

Colville got up. "This is ghastly! She mustn't do it!"

"How can you help her doing it? If she thinks anything is right, she can't help doing it. Who could?"

Colville thought to himself that he could have said; but he was silent. At the moment he was not equal to so much joke or so much truth; and Imogene went on:

"She'd be all the more strenuous about it if it were disagreeable; and rather than accept any relief from *me*, she would die."

"Is she—unkind to you?" faltered Colville.

"She is only *too* kind. You can feel that she's determined to be so—that she's said she will have nothing to reproach herself with; and she won't. You don't suppose Mrs. Bowen would be unkind to any one she disliked?"

"Ah, I didn't know," sighed Colville.

"The more she disliked them, the better she would use them. It's because our engagement is so distasteful to her that she's determined to feel that she did nothing to oppose it."

"But how can you tell that it's distasteful, then?"

"She lets you feel it by—not saying anything about it."

"I can't see how—"

"She never speaks of you. I don't believe she ever mentions your name. She asks me about the places where I've been, and about the people—every one but you. It's very uncomfortable."

"Yes," said Colville, "it's uncomfortable."

"And if I allude to letters from home, she merely presses her lips together. It's perfectly wretched."

"I see. It's I whom she dislikes, and I would do anything to please her. She must know that," mused Colville, aloud, "Imogene!" he exclaimed, with a sudden inspiration. "Why shouldn't I go away?"

"Go away?" she palpitated. "What should *I* do?"

The colors faded from his brilliant proposal. "Oh, I only meant till something was settled—determined—concluded; till this terrible suspense was over." He added, hopelessly, "But nothing can be done!"

"I proposed," said Imogene, "that we should *all* go away. I suggested Via Reggio—the doctor said she ought to have sea air—or Venice; but she wouldn't hear of it. No; we must wait."

"Yes, we must wait," repeated Colville, hollowly. "Then nothing can be done?"

"Why, haven't you said it?"

"Oh yes—yes. I can't go away, and you can't. But couldn't we do something—get up something?"

"I don't know what you mean."

"I mean, couldn't we—amuse her somehow—help her to take her mind off herself?"

Imogene stared at him rather a long time. Then, as if she had satisfied herself in her own mind, she shook her head. "She wouldn't submit to it."

"No; she seems to take everything amiss that I do," said Colville.

"She has no right to do that," cried Imogene. "I'm sure that you're always considering her, and proposing to do things for her. I won't let you humble yourself, as if you had wronged her."

"Oh, I don't call it humbling. I—I should only be too happy if I could do *anything* that was agreeable to her."

"Very well, I will tell her," said the girl, haughtily. "Shall you object to my joining you in your amusements, whatever they are? I assure you I will be very unobtrusive."

"I don't understand all this," replied Colville. "Who has proposed to exclude you? Why did you tell me anything about Mrs. Bowen, if you didn't want me to say or do something? I supposed you did; but I'll withdraw the offensive proposition, whatever it was."

"There was nothing offensive. But if you pity her so much, why can't you pity me a little?"

"I didn't know anything was the matter with you. I thought that you were enjoying yourself—"

"Enjoying? Keeping you up at dances till you drop asleep whenever you sit down? And then coming home and talking to a person who won't mention your name! Do you call that enjoying? I can't speak of you to any one; and no one speaks to me—"

"If you like, I will talk to you on the subject," Colville essayed, in dreary jest.

"Oh, don't joke about it! This perpetual joking, I believe it's that that's wearing me out. When I come to you for a little comfort in circumstances that drive me almost distracted, you want to amuse Mrs. Bowen; and when I ask to be allowed to share in the amusement, you laugh at me! If you don't understand it all, I'm sure *I* don't."

"Imogene!"

"No! It's very strange. There's only one explanation. You don't care for me."

"Not care for you!" cried Colville, thinking of his sufferings in the past fortnight.

"And I would have made any—*any* sacrifice for you. At least I wouldn't have made you show yourself a mean and grudging person if you had come to me for a little sympathy."

"Oh, poor child!" he cried, and his heart ached with the sense that she really was nothing but an unhappy child. "I do sympathize with you, and I see how hard it is for you to manage with Mrs. Bowen's dislike for me. But you mustn't think of it. I dare say it will be different; I've no doubt we can get her to look at me in some brighter light. I—" He did not know what he should urge next, but he goaded his invention, and was able to declare that if they loved each other they need not regard any one else. This flight, when accomplished, did not strike him as of very original effect, and it was with a dull surprise that he saw it sufficed for her.

"No, no one!" she exclaimed, accepting the platitude as if it were now uttered for the first time. She dried her eyes and smiled. "I will tell Mrs. Bowen how you feel and what you've said, and I know she will appreciate your generosity."

"Yes," said Colville, pensively; "there's nothing I won't *propose* doing for people."

She suddenly clung to him, and would not let him go. "Oh, what is the matter?" she moaned afresh. "I show out the worst that is in me, and only the worst. Do you think I shall always be so narrow-minded with you? I thought I loved you enough to be magnanimous. *You* are. It seemed to me that our lives together would be grand and large; and here I am, grovelling in the lowest selfishness! I am worrying and scolding you because you wish to please some one that has been as good as my own mother to me. Do you call that noble?"

Colville did not venture any reply to a demand evidently addressed to her own conscience.

But when she asked if he really thought he had better go away, he said, "Oh no; that was a mistake."

"Because, if you do, you shall—to punish me."

"My dearest girl, why should I wish to punish you?"

"Because I've been low and mean. Now I want you to do something for Mrs. Bowen—something to amuse her; to show that we appreciate her. And I don't want you to sympathize with me at all. When I ask for your sympathy, it's a sign that I don't deserve it."

"Is that so?"

"Oh, be serious with me. I mean it. And I want to beg your pardon for something."

"Yes; what's that?"

"Can't you guess?"

"No."

"You needn't have your lapels silk-lined. You needn't wear *boutonnières*."

"Oh, but I've had the coat changed."

"No matter! Change it back! It isn't for me to make you over. I must make myself over. It's my right, it's my sacred privilege, to conform to you in every way, and I humble myself in the dust for having forgotten it at the very start. Oh, *do* you think I can ever be worthy of you? I *will* try; indeed I will! I shall not wear my light dresses another time! From this out, I shall dress more in keeping with you. I boasted that I should live to comfort and console you, to recompense you for the past, and what have I been doing? Wearying and degrading you!"

"Oh no," pleaded Colville. "I am very comfortable. I don't need any compensation for the past. I need—sleep. I'm going to bed to-night at eight o'clock, and I am going to sleep twenty-four hours. Then I shall be fresh for Mrs. Fleming's ball."

"I'm not going," said Imogene, briefly.

"Oh yes, you are. I'll come round to-morrow evening and see."

"No. There are to be no more parties."

"Why?"

"I can't endure them."

She was looking at him and talking at him, but she seemed far aloof in the abstraction of a sublime regret; she seemed puzzled, bewildered at herself.

Colville got away. He felt the pathos of the confusion and question to which he left her, but he felt himself powerless against it. There was but one solution to it all, and that was impossible. He could only grieve over her trouble, and wait; grieve for the irrevocable loss which made her trouble remote and impersonal to him, and submit.

XVIII

The young clergyman whom Colville saw talking to Imogene on his first evening at Mrs. Bowen's had come back from Rome, where he had been spending a month or two, and they began to meet at Palazzo Pinti again. If they got on well enough together, they did not get on very far. The suave house-priest manners of the young clergyman offended Colville; he could hardly keep from sneering at his taste in art and books, which in fact was rather conventional; and no doubt Mr. Morton had his own reserves, under which he was perfectly civil, and only too deferential, to Colville, as to an older man. Since his return, Mrs. Bowen had come back to her salon. She looked haggard; but she did what she could to look otherwise. She was always polite to Colville, and she was politely cordial with the clergyman. Sometimes Colville saw her driving out with him and Effie; they appeared to make excursions; and he had an impression, very obscure, that Mrs. Bowen lent the young clergyman money; that he was a superstition of hers, and she a patron of his; he must have been ten years younger than she—not more than twenty-five.

The first Sunday after his return, Colville walked home with Mr. Waters from hearing a sermon of Mr. Morton's, which they agreed was rather well judged, and simply and fitly expressed.

"And he spoke with the authority of the priest," said the old minister. "His Church alone of all the Protestant Churches has preserved that to its ministers. Sometimes I have thought it was a great thing."

"Not always?" asked Colville, with a smile.

"These things are matters of mood rather than conviction with me," returned Mr. Waters. "Once they affected me very deeply; but now I shall so soon know all about it that they don't move me. But at times I think that if I were to live my life over again, I would prefer to be of some formal, some inflexibly ritualized, religion. At solemnities—weddings and funerals—I have been impressed with the advantage of the Anglican rite: it is the Church speaking to and for humanity—or seems so," he added, with cheerful indifference. "Something in its favor," he continued, after a while, "is the influence that every ritualized faith has with women. If they apprehend those mysteries more subtly than we, such a preference of theirs must mean a good deal. Yes; the other Protestant systems are men's systems. Women must have form. They don't care for freedom."

"They appear to like the formalist, too, as well as the form," said Colville, with scorn not obviously necessary.

"Oh yes; they must have everything in the concrete," said the old gentleman, cheerfully.

"I wonder where Mr. Morton met Mrs. Bowen first," said Colville.

"Here, I think. I believe he had letters to her. Before you came I used often to meet him at her house. I think she has helped him with money at times."

"Isn't that rather an unpleasant idea?"

"Yes, it's disagreeable. And it places the ministry in a dependent attitude. But under our system it's unavoidable. Young men devoting themselves to the ministry frequently receive gifts of money."

"I don't like it," cried Colville.

"They don't feel it as others would. I didn't myself. Even at present I may be said to be living on charity. But sometimes I have fancied that in Mr. Morton's case there might be peculiarly mitigating circumstances."

"What do you mean?"

"When I met him first at Mrs. Bowen's I used to think that it was Miss Graham in whom he was interested—"

"I can assure you," interrupted Colville, "that she was never interested in him."

"Oh no; I didn't suppose that," returned the old man, tranquilly. "And I've since had reason to revise my opinion. I think he is interested in Mrs. Bowen."

"Mrs. Bowen! And you think that would be a mitigating circumstance in his acceptance of money from her? If he had the spirit of a man at all, it would make it all the more revolting."

"Oh no, oh no," softly pleaded Mr. Waters. "We must not look at these things too romantically. He probably reasons that she would give him all her money if they were married."

"But he has no right to reason in that way," retorted Colville, with heat. "They are not married; it's ignoble and unmanly for him to count upon it. It's preposterous. She must be ten years older than he."

"Oh, I don't say that they're to be married," Mr. Waters replied. "But these disparities of age frequently occur in marriage. I don't like them, though sometimes I think the evil is less when it is the wife who is the elder. We look at youth and age in a gross, material way too often. Women remain young longer than men. They keep their youthful sympathies; an old woman understands a young girl. Do you—or do I—understand a young man?"

Colville laughed harshly. "It isn't *quite* the same thing, Mr. Waters. But yes, I'll admit, for the sake of argument, that I don't understand young men. I'll go farther, and say that I don't like them; I'm afraid of them. And you wouldn't think," he added, abruptly, "that it would be well for me to marry a girl twenty years younger than myself."

The old man glanced up at him with innocent slyness. "I prefer always to discuss these things in an impersonal way."

"But you can't discuss them impersonally with me: I'm engaged to Miss Graham. Ever since you first found me here after I told you I was going away I have wished to tell you this, and this seems as good a time as any—or as bad." The defiance faded from his voice, which dropped to a note of weary sadness. "Yes, we're engaged—or shall be, as soon as she can hear from her family. I wanted to tell you because it seemed somehow your due, and because I fancied you had a friendly interest in us both."

"Yes, that is true," returned Mr. Waters. "I wish you joy." He went through the form of offering his hand to Colville, who pressed it with anxious fervor.

"I confess," he said, "that I feel the risks of the affair. It's not that I have any dread for my own part: I have lived my life, such as it is. But the child is full of fancies about me that can't be fulfilled. She dreams of restoring my youth somehow, of retrieving the past for me, of avenging me at her own cost for an unlucky love affair that I had here twenty years ago.

It's pretty of her, but it's terribly pathetic—it's tragic. I know very well that I'm a middle-aged man, and that there's no more youth for me. I'm getting gray, and I'm getting fat. I wouldn't be young if I could; it's a bore. I suppose I could keep up an illusion of youthfulness for five or six years more; and then if I could be quietly chloroformed out of the way, perhaps it wouldn't have been so very bad."

"I have always thought," said Mr. Waters, dreamily, "that a good deal might be said for abbreviating hopeless suffering. I have known some very good people advocate its practice by science."

"Yes," answered Colville. "Perhaps I've presented that point too prominently. What I wished you to understand was that I don't care for myself; that I consider only the happiness of this young girl that's somehow—I hardly know how— been put in my keeping. I haven't forgotten the talks that we've had heretofore on this subject, and it would be affectation and bad taste in me to ignore them. Don't be troubled at anything you've said; it was probably true, and I'm sure it was sincere. Sometimes I think that the kindest—the least cruel—thing I could do would be to break with her, to leave her. But I know that I shall do nothing of the kind; I shall drift. The child is very dear to me. She has great and noble qualities; she's supremely unselfish; she loves me through her mistaken pity, and because she thinks she can sacrifice herself to me. But she can't. Everything is against that; she doesn't know how; and there is no reason why. I don't express it very well. I think nobody clearly understands it but Mrs. Bowen, and I've somehow alienated her."

He became aware that his self-abnegation was taking the character of self-pity, and he stopped.

Mr. Waters seemed to be giving the subject serious attention in the silence that ensued. "There is this to be remembered," he began, "which we don't consider in our mere speculations upon any phase of human affairs, and that is the wonderful degree of amelioration that any given difficulty finds in the realization. It is the anticipation, not the experience, that is the trial. In a case of this kind, facts of temperament, of mere association, of union, work unexpected mitigations; they not only alleviate, they allay. You say that she cherishes an illusion concerning you: well, with women, nothing is so indestructible as an illusion. Give them any chance at all, and all the forces of their nature combine to preserve it. And if, as you say, she is so dear to you, that in itself is almost sufficient. I can well understand your misgivings, springing as they do from a sensitive conscience; but we may reasonably hope that they are exaggerated. Very probably there will not be the rapture for her that there would be if—if you were younger; but the chances of final happiness are great—yes, very considerable. She will learn to appreciate what is really best in you, and you already understand her. Your love for her is the key to the future. Without that, of course—"

"Oh, of course," interrupted Colville, hastily. Every touch of this comforter's hand had been a sting; and he parted with him in that feeling of utter friendlessness involving a man who has taken counsel upon the confession of half his trouble.

Something in Mrs. Bowen's manner when he met her next made him think that perhaps Imogene had been telling her of the sympathy he had expressed for her ill health. It was in the evening, and Imogene and Mr. Morton were looking over a copy of *The Marble Faun*, which he had illustrated with photographs at Rome. Imogene asked Colville to look at it too, but he said he would examine it later; he had his opinion of people who illustrated *The Marble Faun* with photographs; it surprised him that she seemed to find something novel and brilliant in the idea.

Effie Bowen looked round where she was kneeling on a chair beside the couple with the book, and seeing Colville wandering neglectedly about before he placed himself, she jumped down and ran and caught his hand.

"Well, what now?" he asked, with a dim smile, as she began to pull him toward the sofa. When he should be expelled from Palazzo Pinti he would really miss the worship of that little thing. He knew that her impulse had been to console him for his exclusion from the pleasures that Imogene and Mr. Morton were enjoying.

"Nothing. Just talk," she said, making him fast in a corner of the sofa by crouching tight against him.

"What about? About which is the pleasantest season?"

"Oh no; we've talked about that so often. Besides, of course you'd say spring, now that it's coming on so nicely."

"Do you think I'm so changeable as that? Haven't I always said winter when this question of the seasons was up? And I say it now. Sha'n't you be awfully sorry when you can't have a pleasant little fire on the hearth like this any more?"

"Yes; I know. But it's very nice having the flowers, too. The grass was all full of daisies to-day—perfectly powdered with them."

"To-day? Where?"

"At the Cascine. And in under the trees there were millions of violets and crows-feet. Mr. Morton helped me to get them for mamma and Imogene. And we staid so long that when we drove home the daisies had all shut up, and the little pink leaves outside made it look like a field of red clover. Are you never going there any more?"

Mrs. Bowen came in. From the fact that there was no greeting between her and Mr. Morton, Colville inferred that she was returning to the room after having already been there. She stood a moment, with a little uncertainty, when she had shaken hands with him, and then dropped upon the sofa beyond Effie. The little girl ran one hand through Colville's arm, and the other through her mother's, and gripped them fast. "Now I have got you both," she triumphed, and smiled first into her face, and then into his.

"Be quiet, Effie," said her mother, but she submitted.

"I hope you're better for your drive to-day, Mrs. Bowen. Effie has been telling me about it."

"We staid out a long time. Yes, I think the air did me good; but I'm not an invalid, you know."

"Oh no."

"I'm feeling a little fagged. And the weather was tempting. I suppose you've been taking one of your long walks."

"No; I've scarcely stirred out. I usually feel like going to meet the spring a little more than half-way; but this year I don't, somehow."

"A good many people are feeling rather languid, I believe," said Mrs. Bowen.

"I hope you'll get away from Florence," said Colville.

"Oh," she returned, with a faint flush, "I'm afraid Imogene exaggerated that a little." She added, "You are very good."

She was treating him more kindly than she had ever done since that Sunday afternoon when he came in with Imogene to say that he was going to stay. It might be merely because she had worn out her mood of severity, as people do, returning in good humor to those with whom they were offended, merely through the reconciling force of time. She did not look at him, but this was better than meeting his eye with that interceptive glance. A strange peace touched his heart. Imogene and the young clergyman at the table across the room were intent on the book still; he was explaining and expatiating, and she listening. Colville saw that he had a fine head, and an intelligent, handsome, gentle face. When he turned again to Mrs. Bowen it was with the illusion that she had been saying something; but she was, in fact, sitting mute, and her face, with its bright color, showed pathetically thin.

"I should imagine that Venice would be good for you," he said.

"It's still very harsh there, I hear. No; when we leave Florence, I think we will go to Switzerland."

"Oh, not to Madame Schebres's!" pleaded the child, turning upon her.

"No, not to Madame Schebres's," consented the mother. She continued, addressing Colville: "I was thinking of Lausanne. Do you know Lausanne at all?"

"Only from Gibbon's report. It's hardly up to date."

"I thought of taking a house there for the summer," said Mrs. Bowen, playing with Effie's fingers. "It's pleasant by the lake, I suppose."

"It's lovely by the lake!" cried the child. "Oh, do go, mamma! I could get a boat and learn to row. Here you can't row, the Arno's so swift."

"The air would bring you up," said Colville to Mrs. Bowen. "Switzerland's the only country where you're perfectly sure of waking new every morning."

This idea interested the child. "Waking new!" she repeated.

"Yes; perfectly made over. You wake up another person. Shouldn't you think that would be nice?"

"No."

"Well, I shouldn't, in your place. But in mine, I much prefer to wake up another person. Only it's pretty hard on the other person."

"How queer you are!" The child set her teeth for fondness of him, and seizing his cheeks between her hands, squeezed them hard, admiring the effect upon his features, which in some respects was not advantageous.

"Effie!" cried her mother, sternly; and she dropped to her place again, and laid hold of Colville's arm for protection. "You are really very rude. I shall send you to bed."

"Oh no, don't, Mrs. Bowen," he begged. "I'm responsible for these violences. Effie used to be a very well behaved child before she began playing with me. It's all my fault."

They remained talking on the sofa together, while Imogene and Mr. Morton continued to interest themselves in the book. From time to time she looked over at them, and then turned again to the young clergyman, who, when he had closed the book, rested his hands on its top and began to give an animated account of something, conjecturably his sojourn in Rome.

In a low voice, and with pauses adjusted to the occasional silences of the young people across the room, Mrs. Bowen told Colville how Mr. Morton was introduced to her by an old friend who was greatly interested in him. She said, frankly, that she had been able to be of use to him, and that he was now going back to America very soon: it was as if she were privy to the conjecture that had come to the surface in his talk with Mr. Waters, and wished him to understand exactly how matters stood with the young clergyman and herself. Colville, indeed, began to be more tolerant of him; he succeeded in praising the sermon he had heard him preach.

"Oh, he has talent," said Mrs. Bowen.

They fell into the old, almost domestic strain, from which she broke at times with an effort, but returning as if helplessly to it. He had the gift of knowing how not to take an advantage with women; that sense of unconstraint in them fought in his favor; when Effie dropped her head wearily against his arm, her mother even laughed in sending her off to bed; she had hitherto been serious. Imogene said she would go to see her tucked in, and that sent the clergyman to say good-night to Mrs. Bowen, and to put an end to Colville's audience.

In these days, when Colville came every night to Palazzo Pinti, he got back the tone he had lost in the past fortnight. He thought that it was the complete immunity from his late pleasures, and the regular and sufficient sleep, which had set him firmly on his feet again, but he did not inquire very closely. Imogene went two or three times, after she had declared she would go no more, from the necessity women feel of blunting the edge of comment; but Colville profited instantly and fully by the release from the parties which she offered him. He did not go even to afternoon tea-drinkings: the "days" of the different ladies, which he had been so diligent to observe, knew him no more. At the hours when society assembled in this house or that and inquired for him, or wondered about him, he was commonly taking a nap, and he was punctually in bed every night at eleven, after his return from Mrs. Bowen's.

He believed, of course, that he went there because he now no longer met Imogene elsewhere, and he found the house pleasanter than it had ever been since the veglione. Mrs. Bowen's relenting was not continuous, however. There were times that seemed to be times of question and of struggle with her, when she vacillated between the old cordiality and the later alienation; when she went beyond the former, or lapsed into moods colder and more repellent than the latter. It would have been difficult to mark the moment when these struggles ceased altogether, and an evening passed in unbroken kindness between them. But afterward Colville could remember an emotion of grateful surprise at a subtle word or action of hers in which she appeared to throw all restraint—scruple or rancor, whichever it might be—to the winds, and become perfectly his friend again. It must have been by compliance with some wish or assent to some opinion of his; what he knew was that he was not only permitted, he was invited, to feel himself the most favored guest. The charming smile, so small and sweet, so very near to bitterness, came back to her lips, the deeply fringed eyelids were lifted to let the sunny eyes stream upon him. She did, now, whatever he asked her. She consulted his taste and judgment on many points; she consented to resume, when she should be a little stronger, their visits to the churches and galleries: it would be a shame to go away from Florence without knowing them thoroughly. It came to her asking him to drive with her and Imogene in the Cascine; and when Imogene made some excuse not to go, Mrs. Bowen did not postpone the drive, but took Colville and Effie.

They drove quite down to the end of the Cascine, and got out there to admire the gay monument, with the painted bust, of the poor young Indian prince who died in Florence. They strolled all about, talking of the old times in the Cascine, twenty years before; and walking up the road beside the canal, while the carriage slowly followed, they stopped to enjoy the peasants lying asleep in the grass on the other bank. Colville and Effie gathered wild flowers, and piled them in her mother's lap when she remounted to the carriage and drove along, while they made excursions into the little dingles beside the road. Some people who overtook them in these sylvan pleasures reported the fact at a reception to which they were going, and Mrs. Amsden, whose mind had been gradually clearing under the simultaneous withdrawal of Imogene and Colville from society, professed herself again as thickly clouded as a weather-glass before a storm. She appealed to the sympathy of others against this hardship.

Mrs. Bowen took Colville home to dinner; Mr. Morton was coming, she said, and he must come too. At table the young clergyman made her his compliment on her look of health; and she said, Yes, she had been driving, and she believed that she needed nothing but to be in the air a little more, as she very well could, now the spring weather was really coming. She said that they had been talking all winter of going to Fiesole, where Imogene had never been yet; and, upon comparison, it appeared that none of them had yet been to Fiesole except herself. Then they must all go together, she said; the carriage would hold four very comfortably.

"Ah! that leaves me out," said Colville, who had caught sight of Effie's fallen countenance.

"Oh no. How is that? It leaves Effie out."

"It's the same thing. But I might ride, and Effie might give me her hand to hold over the side of the carriage; that would sustain me."

"We could take her between us, Mrs. Bowen," suggested Imogene. "The back seat is wide."

"Then the party is made up," said Colville, "and Effie hasn't 'demeaned' herself by asking to go where she wasn't invited."

The child turned inquiringly toward her mother, who met her with an indulgent smile, which became a little flush of grateful appreciation when it reached Colville; but Mrs. Bowen ignored Imogene in the matter altogether.

The evening passed delightfully. Mr. Morton had another book which he had brought to show Imogene, and Mrs. Bowen sat a long time at the piano, striking this air and that of the songs which she used to sing when she was a girl: Colville was trying to recall them. When he and Imogene were left alone for their adieux they approached each other in an estrangement through which each tried to break.

"Why don't you scold me?" she asked. "I have neglected you the whole evening."

"How have you neglected me?"

"How? Ah! if you don't know——"

"No. I dare say I must be very stupid. I saw you talking with Mr. Morton, and you seemed interested. I thought I'd better not intrude."

She seemed uncertain of his intention, and then satisfied of its simplicity.

"Isn't it pleasant to have Mrs. Bowen in the old mood again?" he asked.

"Is she in the old mood?"

"Why, yes. Haven't you noticed how cordial she is?"

"I thought she was rather colder than usual."

"Colder!" The chill of the idea penetrated even through the density of Colville's selfish content. A very complex emotion, which took itself for indignation, throbbed from his heart. "Is she cold with you, Imogene?"

"Oh, if you saw nothing——"

"No; and I think you must be mistaken. She never speaks of you without praising you."

"Does she speak of me?" asked the girl, with her honest eyes wide open upon him.

"Why, no," Colville acknowledged. "Come to reflect, it's I who speak of you. But how—how is she cold with you?"

"Oh, I dare say it's a delusion of mine. Perhaps I'm cold with her."

"Then don't be so, my dear! Be sure that she's your friend—true and good. Good-night."

He caught the girl in his arms and kissed her tenderly. She drew away, and stood a moment with her repellent fingers on his breast.

"Is it all for me?" she asked.

"For the whole obliging and amiable world," he answered, gayly.

XIX

T HE NEXT TIME Colville came he found himself alone with Imogene, who asked him what he had been doing all day.

"Oh, living along till evening. What have you?"

She did not answer at once, nor praise his speech for the devotion implied in it. After a while she said: "Do you believe in courses of reading? Mr. Morton has taken up a course of reading in Italian poetry. He intends to master it."

"Does he?"

"Yes. Do you think something of the kind would be good for me?"

"Oh, if you thirst for conquest. But I should prefer to rest on my laurels if I were you."

Imogene did not smile. "Mr. Morton thinks I should enjoy a course of Kingsley. He says he's very earnest."

"Oh, immensely. But aren't you earnest enough already, my dear?"

"Do you think I'm too earnest?"

"No; I should say you were just right."

"You know better than that. I wish you would criticise me sometimes."

"Oh, I'd rather not."

"Why? Don't you see anything to criticise in me? Are you satisfied with me in every way? You ought to think. You ought to think now. Do you think that I am doing right in all respects? Am I all that I could be to you, and to you alone? If I am wrong in the least thing, criticise me, and I will try to be better."

"Oh, you might criticise back, and I shouldn't like that."

"Then you don't approve of a course of Kingsley?" asked the girl.

"Does that follow? But if you're going in for earnestness, why don't you take up a course of Carlyle?"

"Do you think that would be better than Kingsley?"

"Not a bit. But Carlyle's so earnest that he can't talk straight."

"I can't make out what you mean. Wouldn't you like me to improve?"

"Not much," laughed Colville. "If you did, I don't know what I should do. I should have to begin to improve too, and I'm very comfortable as I am."

"I should wish to do it to—to be more worthy of you," grieved the girl, as if deeply disappointed at his frivolous behavior.

He could not help laughing, but he was sorry, and would have taken her hand; she kept it from him, and removed to the farthest corner of the sofa. Apparently, however, her ideal did not admit of open pique, and she went on trying to talk seriously with him.

"You think, don't you, that we oughtn't to let a day pass without storing away some thought—suggestion—"

"Oh, there's no hurry," he said, lazily. "Life is rather a long affair—if you live. There appears to be plenty of time, though people say not, and I think it would be rather odious to make every day of use. Let a few of them go by without doing anything for you! And as for reading, why not read when you're hungry, just as you eat? Shouldn't you hate to take up a course of roast beef, or a course of turkey?"

"Very well, then," said Imogene. "I shall not begin Kingsley."

"Yes, do it. I dare say Mr. Morton's quite right. He will look at these things more from your own point of view. All the Kingsley novels are in the Tauchnitz. By all means do what he says."

"I will do what *you* say."

"Oh, but I say nothing."

"Then I will do nothing."

Colville laughed at this too, and soon after the clergyman appeared. Imogene met him so coldly that Colville felt obliged to make him some amends by a greater show of cordiality than he felt. But he was glad of the effort, for he began to like him as he talked to him; it was easy for him to like people; the young man showed sense and judgment, and if he was a little academic in his mind and manners, Colville tolerantly reflected that some people seemed to be born so, and that he was probably not artificial, as he had once imagined from the ecclesiastical scrupulosity of his dress.

Imogene ebbed away to the piano in the corner of the room, and struck some chords on it. At each stroke the young clergyman, whose eyes had wandered a little toward her from the first, seemed to vibrate in response. The conversation became incoherent before Mrs. Bowen joined them. Then, by a series of illogical processes, the clergyman was standing beside Imogene at the piano, and Mrs. Bowen was sitting beside Colville on the sofa.

"Isn't there to be any Effie to-night?" he asked.

"No. She has been up too much of late. And I wished to speak with you—about Imogene."

"Yes," said Colville, not very eagerly. At that moment he could have chosen another topic.

"It is time that her mother should have got my letter. In less than a fortnight we ought to have an answer."

"Well?" said Colville, with a strange constriction of the heart.

"Her mother is a person of very strong character; her husband is absorbed in business, and defers to her in everything."

"It isn't an uncommon American situation," said Colville, relieving his tension by this excursion.

Mrs. Bowen ignored it. "I don't know how she may look at the affair. She may give her assent at once, or she may decide that nothing has taken place till—she sees you."

"I could hardly blame her for that," he answered, submissively.

"It isn't a question of that," said Mrs. Bowen. "It's a question of—others. Mr. Morton was here before you came, and I know he was interested in Imogene—I am certain of it. He has come back, and he sees no reason why he should not renew his attentions."

"No—o—o," faltered Colville.

"I wish you to realize the fact."

"But what would you—"

"I told you," said Mrs. Bowen, with a full return of that severity whose recent absence Colville had found so comfortable, "that I can't advise or suggest anything at all."

He was long and miserably silent. At last, "Did you ever think," he asked, "did you ever suppose—that is to say, did you ever suspect that—she—that Imogene was—at all interested in him?"

"I think she was—at one time," said Mrs. Bowen, promptly.

Colville sighed, with a wandering disposition to whistle.

"But that is nothing," she went on. "People have many passing fancies. The question is, what are you going to do now? I want to know, as Mr. Morton's friend."

"Ah, I wish you wanted to know as *my* friend, Mrs. Bowen!" A sudden thought flashed upon him. "Why shouldn't I go away from Florence till Imogene hears from her mother? That seemed to me right in the first place. There is no tie that binds her to me. I hold her to nothing. If she finds in my absence that she likes this young man better—" An expression of Mrs. Bowen's face stopped him. He perceived that he had said something very shocking to her; he perceived that the thing was shocking in itself; but it was not that which he cared for. "I don't mean that I won't hold myself true to her as long as she will. I recognize my responsibility fully. I know that I am answerable for all this, and that no one else is; and I am ready to bear any penalty. But what I can't bear is that you should misunderstand me, that you should—I have been so wretched ever since you first began to blame me for my part in this, and so happy this past fortnight, that I can't—I *won't*—go back to that state of things. No; you have no right to relent toward me, and then fling me off as you have tried to do to-night! I have some feeling too—some rights. You shall receive me as a friend, or not at all! How can I live if you—"

She had been making little efforts as if to rise; now she forced herself to her feet, and ran from the room.

The young people looked up from their music; some wave of the sensation had spread to them, but seeing Colville remain seated, they went on with their playing till he rose. Then Imogene called out, "Isn't Mrs. Bowen coming back?"

"I don't know; I think not," answered Colville, stupidly, standing where he had risen.

She hastened questioningly toward him. "What is the matter? Isn't she well?"

Mr. Morton's face expressed a polite share in her anxiety.

"Oh yes; quite, I believe," Colville replied.

"She heard Effie call, I suppose," suggested the girl.

"Yes, yes; I think so; that is—yes. I must be going. Good-night."

He took her hand and went away, leaving the clergyman still there; but he lingered only for a report from Mrs. Bowen, which Imogene hurried to get. She sent word that she would join them presently. But Mr. Morton said that it was late already, and he would beg Miss Graham to say good-night for him. When Mrs. Bowen returned, Imogene was alone.

She did not seem surprised or concerned at that. "Imogene, I have been talking to Mr. Colville about you and Mr. Morton."

The girl started and turned pale.

"It is almost time to hear from your mother, and she may consent to your engagement. Then you must be prepared to act."

"Act?"

"To make it known. Matters can't go on as they have been going. I told Mr. Colville that Mr. Morton ought to know at once."

"Why ought he to know?" asked Imogene, doubtless with that impulse to temporize which is natural to the human soul in questions of right and interest. She sank into the chair beside which she had been standing.

"If your mother consents, you will feel bound to Mr. Colville?"

"Yes," said the girl.

"And if she refuses?"

"He has my word. I will keep my word to him," replied Imogene, huskily. "Nothing shall make me break it."

"Very well, then!" exclaimed Mrs. Bowen. "We need not wait for your mother's answer. Mr. Morton ought to know, and he ought to know at once. Don't try to blind yourself, Imogene, to what you see as plainly as I do. He is in love with you."

"Oh," moaned the girl.

"Yes; you can't deny it. And it's cruel, it's treacherous, to let him go on thinking that you are free."

"I will never see him again."

"Ah! that isn't enough. He has a claim to know why. I will not let him be treated so."

They were both silent. Then, "What did Mr. Colville say?" asked Imogene.

"He? I don't know that he said anything. He—" Mrs. Bowen stopped.

Imogene rose from her chair.

"I will not let him tell Mr. Morton. It would be too indelicate."

"And shall you let it go on so?"

"No. I will tell him myself."

"How will you tell him?"

"I will tell him if he speaks to me."

"You will let it come to that?"

"There is no other way. I shall suffer more than he."

"But you will deserve to suffer, and your suffering will not help him."

Imogene trembled into her chair again.

"I see," said Mrs. Bowen, bitterly, "how it will be at last. It will be as it has been from the first." She began to walk up and down the room, mechanically putting the chairs in place, and removing the disorder in which the occupancy of several people leaves a room at the end of an evening. She closed the piano, which Imogene had forgot to shut, with a clash that jarred the strings from their silence. "But I will do it, and I wonder "

"You will speak to him?" faltered the girl.

"Yes!" returned Mrs. Bowen, vehemently, and arresting herself in her rapid movements. "It won't do for you to tell him, and you won't let Mr. Colville."

"No, I can't," said Imogene, slowly shaking her head. "But I will discourage him; I will not see him any more." Mrs. Bowen silently confronted her. "I will not see any one now till I have heard from home."

"And how will that help? He must have some explanation, and I will have to make it. What shall it be?"

Imogene did not answer. She said: "I will not have any one know what is between me and Mr. Colville till I have heard from home. If they try to refuse, then it will be for him to take me against their will. But if he doesn't choose to do that, then he shall be free, and I won't have him humiliated a second time before the world. *This* time *he* shall be the one to reject. And I don't care who suffers. The more I prize the person, the gladder I shall be; and if I could suffer before everybody, I would. If people ever find it out, I will tell them that it was he who broke it off." She rose again from her chair, and stood flushed and thrilling with the notion of her self-sacrifice. Out of the tortuous complexity of the situation she had evolved this brief triumph, in which she rejoiced as if it were enduring success. But she suddenly fell from it in the dust. "Oh, what can I do for him? How can I make him feel more and more that I would give up anything, everything, for him! It's because he asks nothing and wants nothing that it's so hard! If I could see that he was unhappy, as I did once! If I could see that he was at all different since—since— Oh, what I dread is this smooth tranquillity! If our lives could only be stormy and full of cares and anxieties and troubles that I could take on myself, then, then I shouldn't be afraid of the future! But I'm afraid they won't be so—no, I'm afraid that they will be easy and quiet, and then what shall I do? Oh, Mrs. Bowen, do you think he cares for me?"

Mrs. Bowen turned white; she did not speak.

The girl wrung her hands. "Sometimes it seems as if he didn't—as if I had forced myself on him through a mistake, and he had taken me to save me from the shame of knowing that I had made a mistake. Do you think that is true? If you can only tell me that it isn't— Or, no! If it is true, tell me that! *That* would be real mercy."

The other trembled as if physically beaten upon by this appeal. But she gathered herself together rigidly. "How can I answer you such a thing as that? I mustn't listen to you; you mustn't ask me." She turned and left the girl standing still in her attitude of imploring. But in her own room, where she locked herself in, sobs mingled with the laughter which broke crazily from her lips as she removed this ribbon and that jewel, and pulled the bracelets from her wrists. A man would have plunged from the house and walked the night away; a woman must wear it out in her bed.

XX

IN THE MORNING Mrs. Bowen received a note from her banker covering a dispatch by cable from America. It was from Imogene's mother; it acknowledged the letters they had written, and announced that she sailed that day for Liverpool. It was dated at New York, and it was to be inferred that after perhaps writing in answer to their letters, she had suddenly made up her mind to come out.

"Yes, that is it," said Imogene, to whom Mrs. Bowen hastened with the dispatch. "Why should she have telegraphed to *you*?" she asked, coldly, but with a latent fire of resentment in her tone.

"You must ask her when she comes," returned Mrs. Bowen, with all her gentleness. "It won't be long now."

They looked as if they had neither of them slept; but the girl's vigil seemed to have made her wild and fierce, like some bird that has beat itself all night against its cage, and still from time to time feebly strikes the bars with its wings. Mrs. Bowen was simply worn to apathy.

"What shall you do about this?" she asked.

"Do about it? Oh, I will think. I will try not to trouble you."

"Imogene!"

"I shall have to tell Mr. Colville. But I don't know that I shall tell him at once. Give me the dispatch, please." She possessed herself of it greedily, offensively. "I shall ask you not to speak of it."

"I will do whatever you wish."

"Thank you."

Mrs. Bowen left the room, but she turned immediately to re-open the door she had closed behind her.

"We were to have gone to Fiesole to-morrow," she said, inquiringly.

"We can still go if the day is fine," returned the girl. "Nothing is changed. I wish very much to go. Couldn't we go to-day?" she added, with eager defiance.

"It's too late to-day," said Mrs. Bowen, quietly. "I will write to remind the gentlemen."

"Thank you. I wish we could have gone to-day."

"You can have the carriage if you wish to drive anywhere," said Mrs. Bowen.

"I will take Effie to see Mrs. Amsden." But Imogene changed her mind, and went to call upon two Misses Guicciardi, the result of an international marriage, whom Mrs. Bowen did not like very well. Imogene drove with them to the Cascine, where they bowed to a numerous military acquaintance, and they asked her if Mrs. Bowen would let her join them in a theatre party that evening: they were New-Yorkers by birth, and it was to be a theatre party in the New York style; they were to be chaperoned by a young married lady; two young men cousins of theirs, just out from America, had taken the box.

When Imogene returned home she told Mrs. Bowen that she had accepted this invitation. Mrs. Bowen said nothing, but when one of the young men came up to hand Imogene down to the carriage, which was waiting with the others at the gate, she could not have shown a greater toleration of his second-rate New-Yorkiness if she had been a Boston dowager offering him the scrupulous hospitalities of her city.

Imogene came in at midnight; she hummed an air of the opera as she took off her wraps and ornaments in her room, and this in the quiet of the hour had a terrible, almost profane effect: it was as if some other kind of girl had whistled. She showed the same nonchalance at breakfast, where she was prompt, and answered Mrs. Bowen's inquiries about her pleasure the night before with a liveliness that ignored the polite resolution that prompted them.

Mr. Morton was the first to arrive, and if his discouragement began at once, the first steps masked themselves in a reckless welcome, which seemed to fill him with joy, and Mrs. Bowen with silent perplexity. The girl ran on about her evening at the opera, and about the weather, and the excursion they were going to make; and after an apparently needless ado over the bouquet which he brought her, together with one for Mrs. Bowen, she put it in her belt, and made Colville notice it when he came: he had not thought to bring flowers.

He turned from her hilarity with anxious question to Mrs. Bowen, who did not meet his eye, and who snubbed Effie when the child found occasion to whisper: "*I* think Imogene is acting very strangely, for *her*; don't you, mamma? It seems as if going with those Guicciardi girls just once had spoiled her."

"Don't make remarks about people, Effie," said her mother, sharply. "It isn't nice in little girls, and I don't want you to do it. You talk too much lately."

Effie turned grieving away from this rejection, and her face did not light up even at the whimsical sympathy in Colville's face, who saw that she had met a check of some sort; he had to take her on his knee and coax and kiss her before her wounded feelings were visibly healed. He put her down with a sighing wish that some one could take him up and soothe his troubled sensibilities too, and kept her hand in his while he sat waiting for the last of those last moments in which the hurrying delays of ladies preparing for an excursion seem never to end.

When they were ready to get into the carriage, the usual contest of self-sacrifice arose, which Imogene terminated by mounting to the front seat; Mr. Morton hastened to take the seat beside her, and Colville was left to sit with Effie and her mother. "You old people will be safer back there," said Imogene. It was a little joke which she addressed to the child, but a gleam from her eye as she turned to speak to the young man at her side visited Colville in desperate defiance. He wondered what she was about in that allusion to an idea which she had shrunk from so sensitively hitherto. But he found himself in a situation which he could not penetrate at any point. When he spoke with Mrs. Bowen it was with a dark under-current of conjecture as to how and when she expected him to tell Mr. Morton of his relation to Imogene, or whether she still expected him to do it; when his eyes fell upon the face of the young man, he despaired as to the terms in which he should put the fact: any form in which he tacitly dramatized it remained very embarrassing, for he felt bound to say that while he held himself promised in the matter, he did not allow her to feel herself so.

A sky of American blueness and vastness, a mellow sun,

and a delicate breeze did all that these things could for them, as they began the long, devious climb of the hills crowned by the ancient Etruscan city. At first they were all in the constraint of their own and one another's moods, known or imagined, and no talk began till the young clergyman turned to Imogene and asked, after a long look at the smiling landscape, "What sort of weather do you suppose they are having at Buffalo to-day?"

"At Buffalo?" she repeated, as if the place had only a dim existence in her remotest consciousness. "Oh! the ice isn't near out of the lake yet. You can't count on it before the first of May."

"And the first of May comes sooner or later, according to the season," said Colville. "I remember coming on once in the middle of the month, and the river was so full of ice between Niagara Falls and Buffalo that I had to shut the car window that I'd kept open all the way through southern Canada. But we have very little of that local weather at home; our weather is as democratic and continental as our political constitution. Here it's March or May any time from September till June, according as there's snow on the mountains or not."

The young man smiled. "But don't you like," he asked, with deference, "this slow, orderly advance of the Italian spring, where the flowers seem to come out one by one, and every blossom has its appointed time?"

"Oh yes; it's very well in its way; but I prefer the rush of the American spring: no thought of mild weather this morning; a warm, gusty rain to-morrow night; day after to-morrow a burst of blossoms and flowers and young leaves and birds. I don't know whether we were made for our climate or our climate was made for us, but its impatience and lavishness seem to answer some inner demand of our go-ahead souls. This happens to be the week of the peach blossoms here, and you see their pink everywhere to-day, and you don't see anything else in the blossom line. But imagine the American spring abandoning a whole week of her precious time to the exclusive use of peach blossoms! She wouldn't do it; she's got too many other things on hand."

Effie had stretched out over Colville's lap, and with her elbow sunk deep in his knee, was resting her chin in her hand and taking the facts of the landscape thoroughly in. "Do they have just a week?" she asked.

"Not an hour more or less," said Colville. "If they found an almond blossom hanging round anywhere after their time came, they would make an awful row; and if any lazy little peach-blow hadn't got out by the time their week was up, it would have to stay in till next year; the pear blossoms wouldn't let it come out."

"Wouldn't they?" murmured the child, in dreamy sympathy with this belated peach-blow.

"Well, that's what people say. In America it would be allowed to come out any time. It's a free country."

Mrs. Bowen offered to draw Effie back to a posture of more decorum, but Colville put his arm round the little girl. "Oh, let her stay! It doesn't incommode me, and she must be getting such a novel effect of the landscape."

The mother fell back into her former attitude of jaded passivity. He wondered whether she had changed her mind about having him speak to Mr. Morton; her quiescence might well have been indifference; one could have said, knowing the whole situation, that she had made up her mind to let things take their course, and struggle with them no longer.

He could not believe that she felt content with him; she must feel far otherwise; and he took refuge, as he had the power of doing, from the discomfort of his own thoughts in jesting with the child, and mocking her with this extravagance and that; the discomfort then became merely a dull ache that insisted upon itself at intervals, like a grumbling tooth.

The prospect was full of that mingled wildness and subordination that gives its supreme charm to the Italian landscape; and without elements of great variety, it combined them in infinite picturesqueness. There were olive orchards and vineyards, and again vineyards and olive orchards. Closer to the farm-houses and cottages there were peaches and other fruit trees and kitchen-gardens; broad ribbons of grain waved between the ranks of trees; around the white villas the spires of the cypresses pierced the blue air. Now and then they came to a villa with weather-beaten statues strutting about its parterres. A mild, pleasant heat brooded upon the fields and roofs, and the city, dropping lower and lower as they mounted, softened and blended its towers and monuments in a sombre mass shot with gleams of white.

Colville spoke to Imogene, who withdrew her eyes from it with a sigh, after long brooding upon the scene. "You can do nothing with it, I see."

"With what?"

"The landscape. It's too full of every possible interest. What a history is written all over it, public and private! If you don't take it simply, like any other landscape, it becomes an oppression. It's well that tourists come to Italy so ignorant, and keep so. Otherwise they couldn't live to get home again: the past would crush them."

Imogene scrutinized him as if to extract some personal meaning from his words, and then turned her head away. The clergyman addressed him with what was like a respectful toleration of the drolleries of a gifted but eccentric man, the flavor of whose talk he was beginning to taste.

"You don't really mean that one shouldn't come to Italy as well informed as possible?"

"Well, I did," said Colville; "but I don't."

The young man pondered this, and Imogene started up with an air of rescuing them from each other—as if she would not let Mr. Morton think Colville trivial, or Colville consider the clergyman stupid, but would do what she could to take their minds off the whole question. Perhaps she was not very clear as to how this was to be done; at any rate she did not speak, and Mrs. Bowen came to her support, from whatever motive of her own. It might have been from a sense of the injustice of letting Mr. Morton suffer from the complications that involved herself and the others. The affair had been going very hitchily ever since they started, with the burden of the conversation left to the two men and that helpless girl; if it were not to be altogether a failure, she must interfere.

"Did you ever hear of Gratiano when you were in Venice?" she asked Mr. Morton.

"Is he one of their new water-colorists?" returned the young man. "I heard they had quite a school there now."

"No," said Mrs. Bowen, ignoring her failure as well as she

could; "he was a famous talker; he loved to speak an infinite deal of nothing more than any man in Venice."

"An ancestor of mine, Mr. Morton," said Colville; "a poor, honest man, who did his best to make people forget that the ladies were silent. Thank you, Mrs. Bowen, for mentioning him. I wish he were with us to-day."

The young man laughed. "Oh, in the *Merchant of Venice!*"

"No other," said Colville.

"I confess," said Mrs. Bowen, "that I *am* rather stupid this morning. I suppose it's the softness of the air; it's been harsh and irritating so long. It makes me drowsy."

"Don't mind *us*," returned Colville. "We will call you at important points." They were driving into a village at which people stop sometimes to admire the works of art in its church. "Here, for example, is— What place is this?" he asked of the coachman.

"San Domenico."

"I should know it again by its beggars." Of all ages and sexes they swarmed round the carriage, which the driver had instinctively slowed to oblige them, and thrust forward their hands and hats. Colville gave Effie his small change to distribute among them, at sight of which they streamed down the street from every direction. Those who had received brought forward the halt and blind, and did not scruple to propose being rewarded for this service. At the same time they did not mind his laughing in their faces; they laughed too, and went off content, or as nearly so as beggars ever are. He buttoned up his pocket as they drove on more rapidly. "I am the only person of no principle—except Effie—in the carriage, and yet I am at this moment carrying more blessings out of this village than I shall ever know what to do with. Mrs. Bowen, I know, is regarding me with severe disapproval. She thinks that I ought to have sent the beggars of San Domenico to Florence, where they would all be shut up in the Pia Casa di Ricovero, and taught some useful occupation. It's terrible in Florence. You can walk through Florence now and have no appeal made to your better nature that is not made at the appellant's risk of imprisonment. When I was there before, you had opportunities of giving at every turn."

"You can send a check to the Pia Casa," said Mrs. Bowen.

"Ah, but what good would that do me? When I give I want the pleasure of it; I want to see my beneficiary cringe under my bounty. But I've tried in vain to convince you that the world has gone wrong in other ways. Do you remember the one-armed man whom we used to give to on the Lung' Arno? That persevering sufferer has been repeatedly arrested for mendicancy, and obliged to pay a fine out of his hard earnings to escape being sent to your Pia Casa."

Mrs. Bowen smiled, and said, Was he living yet? in a pensive tone of reminiscence. She was even more than patient of Colville's nonsense. It seemed to him that the light under her eyelids was sometimes a grateful light. Confronting Imogene and the young man whose hopes of her he was to destroy at the first opportunity, the lurid moral atmosphere which he breathed seemed threatening to become a thing apparent to sense, and to be about to blot the landscape. He fought it back as best he could, and kept the hovering cloud from touching the earth by incessant effort. At times he looked over the side of the carriage, and drew secretly a long breath of fatigue. It began to be borne in upon him that these ladies were using him ill in leaving him the burden of their entertainment. He became angry, but his heart softened, and he forgave them again, for he conjectured that he was the cause of the cares that kept them silent. He felt certain that the affair had taken some new turn. He wondered if Mrs. Bowen had told Imogene what she had demanded of him. But he could only conjecture and wonder in the dreary under-current of thought that flowed evenly and darkly on with the talk he kept going. He made the most he could of the varying views of Florence which the turns and mounting levels of the road gave him. He became affectionately grateful to the young clergyman when he replied promptly and fully, and took an interest in the objects or subjects he brought up.

Neither Mrs. Bowen nor Imogene was altogether silent. The one helped on at times wearily, and the other broke at times from her abstraction. Doubtless the girl had undertaken too much in insisting upon a party of pleasure with her mind full of so many things, and doubtless Mrs. Bowen was sore with a rankling resentment at her insistence, and vexed at herself for having yielded to it. If at her time of life and with all her experience of it she could not rise under this inner load, Imogene must have been crushed by it.

Her starts from the dreamy oppression, if that were what kept her silent, took the form of aggression, when she disagreed with Colville about things he was saying, or attacked him for this or that thing which he had said in times past. It was an unhappy and unamiable self-assertion, which he was not able to compassionate so much when she resisted or defied Mrs. Bowen, as she seemed seeking to do at every point. Perhaps another would not have felt it so; it must have been largely in his consciousness; the young clergyman seemed not to see anything in these bursts but the indulgence of a gay caprice, though his laughing at them did not alleviate the effect to Colville, who, when he turned to Mrs. Bowen for her alliance, was astonished with a prompt snub, unmistakable to himself, however imperceptible to others.

He found what diversion and comfort he could in the party of children who beset them at a point near the town, and followed the carriage, trying to sell them various light and useless trifles made of straw—fans, baskets, parasols, and the like. He bought recklessly of them and gave them to Effie, whom he assured, without the applause of the ladies, and with the grave question of the young clergyman, that the venders were little Etruscan girls, all at least twenty-five hundred years old. "It's very hard to find any Etruscans under that age; most of the grown-up people are three thousand."

The child humored his extravagance with the faith in fable which children are able to command, and said, "Oh, tell me about them!" while she pushed up closer to him, and began to admire her presents, holding them up before her, and dwelling fondly upon them one by one.

"Oh, there's very little to tell," answered Colville. "They're mighty close people, and always keep themselves very much *to* themselves. But wouldn't you like to see a party of Etruscans of all ages, even down to little babies only eleven or twelve hundred years old, come driving into an American town? It would make a great excitement, wouldn't it?"

"It would be splendid."

"Yes; we would give them a collation in the basement of the City Hall, and drive them out to the cemetery. The Americans and Etruscans are very much alike in that—they always show you their tombs."

"Will they in Fiesole?"

"How you always like to burrow into the past!" interrupted Imogene.

"Well, it's rather difficult burrowing into the future," returned Colville, defensively. Accepting the challenge, he added: "Yes, I should really like to meet a few Etruscans in Fiesole this morning. I should feel as if I'd got amongst my contemporaries at last; they would understand me."

The girl's face flushed. "Then no one else can understand you?"

"Apparently not. I am the great American *incompris*."

"I'm sorry for you," she returned, feebly; and, in fact, sarcasm was not her strong point.

When they entered the town they found the Etruscans preoccupied with other visitors, whom at various points in the quaint little piazza they surrounded in dense groups, to their own disadvantage as guides and beggars and dealers in straw goods. One of the groups reluctantly dispersed to devote itself to the new arrivals, and these then perceived that it was a party of artists, scattered about and sketching, which had absorbed the attention of the population. Colville went to the restaurant to order lunch, leaving the ladies to the care of Mr. Morton. When he came back he found the carriage surrounded by the artists, who had turned out to be the Inglehart boys. They had walked up to Fiesole the afternoon before, and they had been sketching there all the morning. With the artist's indifference to the conventional objects of interest, they were still ignorant of what ought to be seen in Fiesole by tourists, and they accepted Colville's proposition to be of his party in going the rounds of the Cathedral, the Museum, and the view from that point of the wall called the Belvedere. They found that they had been at the Belvedere before without knowing that it merited particular recognition, and some of them had made sketches from it—of bits of architecture and landscape, and of figure amongst the women with straw fans and baskets to sell, who thronged round the whole party again, and interrupted the prospect. In the church they differed amongst themselves as to the best bits for study, and Colville listened in whimsical despair to the enthusiasm of their likings and dislikings. All that was so far from him now; but in the Museum, which had only a thin interest based upon a small collection of art and archæology, he suffered a real affliction in the presence of a young Italian couple, who were probably plighted lovers. They went before a gray-haired pair, who might have been the girl's father and mother, and they looked at none of the objects, though they regularly stopped before them and waited till their guide had said his say about them. The girl, clinging tight to the young man's arm, knew nothing but him; her mouth and eyes were set in a passionate concentration of her being upon him, and he seemed to walk in a dream of her. From time to time they peered upon each others' faces, and then they paused, rapt, and indifferent to all besides.

The young painters had their jokes about it; even Mr. Morton smiled, and Mrs. Bowen recognized it. But Imogene did not smile; she regarded the lovers with an interest in them scarcely less intense than their interest in each other; and a cold perspiration of question broke out on Colville's forehead. Was that her ideal of what her own engagement should be? Had she expected him to behave in that way to her, and to accept from her a devotion like that girl's? How bitterly he must have disappointed her! It was so impossible to him that the thought of it made him feel that he must break all ties which bound him to anything like it. And yet he reflected that the time was when he could have been equal to that, and even more.

After lunch the painters joined them again, and they all went together to visit the ruins of the Roman theatre and the stretch of Etruscan wall beyond it. The former seems older than the latter, whose huge blocks of stone lie as firmly and evenly in their courses as if placed there a year ago; the turf creeps to the edge at top, and some small trees nod along the crest of the wall, whose ancient face, clean and bare, looks sternly out over a vast prospect, now young and smiling in the first delight of spring. The piety or interest of the community, which guards the entrance to the theatre by a fee of certain centesimi, may be concerned in keeping the wall free from the grass and vines which are stealing the half-excavated arena back to forgetfulness and decay; but whatever agency it was, it weakened the appeal that the wall made to the sympathy of the spectators. They could do nothing with it; the artists did not take their sketch-blocks from their pockets. But in the theatre, where a few broken columns marked the place of the stage, and the stone benches of the auditorium were here and there reached by a flight of uncovered steps, the human interest returned.

"I suspect that there is such a thing as a ruin's being too old," said Colville. "Our Etruscan friends made the mistake of building their wall several thousand years too soon for our purpose."

"Yes," consented the young clergyman. "It seems as if our own race became alienated from us through the mere effect of time—don't you think, sir? I mean, of course, terrestrially."

The artists looked uneasy, as if they had not counted upon anything of this kind, and they began to scatter about for points of view. Effie got her mother's leave to run up and down one of the stairways, if she would not fall. Mrs. Bowen sat down on one of the lower steps, and Mr. Morton took his place respectfully near her.

"I wonder how it looks from the top?" Imogene asked this of Colville, with more meaning than seemed to belong to the question properly.

"There is nothing like going to see," he suggested. He helped her up, giving her his hand from one course of seats to another. When they reached the point which commanded the best view of the whole, she sat down, and he sank at her feet, but they did not speak of the view.

"Theodore, I want to tell you something," she said, abruptly. "I have heard from home."

"Yes?" he replied, in a tone in which he did his best to express a readiness for any fate.

"Mother has telegraphed. She is coming out. She is on her way now. She will be here very soon."

Colville did not know exactly what to say to these passionately consecutive statements. "Well?" he said at last.

"Well"—she repeated his word—"what do you intend to do?"

"Intend to do in what event?" he asked, lifting his eyes for the first time to the eyes which he felt burning down upon him.

"If she should refuse?"

Again he could not command an instant answer, but when it came it was a fair one. "It isn't for me to say what I shall do," he replied, gravely. "Or, if it is, I can only say that I will do whatever you wish."

"Do *you* wish nothing?"

"Nothing but your happiness."

"Nothing but my happiness!" she retorted. "What is my happiness to me? Have I ever sought it?"

"I can't say," he answered; "but if I did not think you would find it—"

"I shall find it, if ever I find it, in yours," she interrupted. "And what shall you do if my mother will not consent to our engagement?"

The experienced and sophisticated man—for that in no ill way was what Colville was—felt himself on trial for his honor and his manhood by this simple girl, this child. He could not endure to fall short of her ideal of him at that moment, no matter what error or calamity the fulfillment involved. "If you feel sure that you love me, Imogene, it will make no difference to me what your mother says. I would be glad of her consent; I should hate to go counter to her will; but I know that I am good enough man to be true and keep you all my life the first in all my thoughts, and that's enough for me. But if you have any fear, any doubt of yourself, now is the time—"

Imogene rose to her feet as in some turmoil of thought or emotion that would not suffer her to remain quiet.

"Oh, keep still!" "Don't get up yet!" "Hold on a minute, please!" came from the artists in different parts of the theatre, and half a dozen imploring pencils were waved in the air.

"They are sketching you," said Colville, and she sank compliantly into her seat again.

"I have no doubt for myself—no," she said, as if there had been no interruption.

"Then we need have no anxiety in meeting your mother," said Colville, with a light sigh, after a moment's pause. "What makes you think she will be unfavorable?"

"I don't think that; but I thought—I didn't know but—"

"What?"

"Nothing, now." Her lips were quivering; he could see her struggle for self-control, but he could not see it unmoved.

"Poor child!" he said, putting out his hand toward her.

"Don't take my hand; they're all looking," she begged.

He forbore, and they remained silent and motionless a little while, before she had recovered herself sufficiently to speak again.

"Then we are promised to each other, whatever happens," she said.

"Yes."

"And we will never speak of this again. But there is one thing. Did Mrs. Bowen ask you to tell Mr. Morton of our engagement?"

"She said that I ought to do so."

"And did you say you would?"

"I don't know. But I suppose I ought to tell him."

"I don't wish you to!" cried the girl.

"You don't wish me to tell him?"

"No; I will not have it!"

"Oh, very well; it's much easier not. But it seems to me that it's only fair to him."

"Did you think of that yourself?" she demanded, fiercely.

"No," returned Colville, with sad self-recognition. "I'm afraid I'm not apt to think of the comforts and rights of other people. It was Mrs. Bowen who thought of it."

"I knew it!"

"But I must confess that I agreed with her, though I would have preferred to postpone it till we heard from your family." He was thoughtfully silent a moment; then he said, "But if their decision is to have no weight with us, I think he ought to be told at once."

"Do you think that I am flirting with him?"

"Imogene!" exclaimed Colville, reproachfully.

"That's what you imply; that's what she implies."

"You're very unjust to Mrs. Bowen, Imogene."

"Oh, you always defend her! It isn't the first time you've told me I was unjust to her."

"I don't mean that you are willingly unjust, or could be so,

to any living creature, least of all to her. But I—we—owe
her so much; she has been so patient."

"What do we owe her? How has she been patient?"

"She has overcome her dislike to me."

"Oh, indeed!"

"And—and I feel under obligation to her for—in a thousand little ways; and I should be glad to feel that we were
acting with her approval; I should like to please her."

"You wish to tell Mr. Morton?"

"I think I ought."

"To please Mrs. Bowen! Tell him, then! You always cared
more to please her than me. Perhaps you staid in Florence to
please her!"

She rose and ran down the broken seats and ruined steps
so recklessly and yet so sure-footedly that it seemed more like
a flight than a pace, to the place where Mrs. Bowen and Mr.
Morton were talking together.

Colville followed as he could, slowly and with a heavy
heart. A good thing develops itself in infinite and unexpected
shapes of good; a bad thing into manifold and astounding
evils. This mistake was whirling away beyond his recall in
hopeless mazes of error. He saw this generous young spirit
betrayed by it to ignoble and unworthy excess, and he knew
that he and not she was to blame.

He was helpless to approach her, to speak with her, to set
her right, great as the need of that was, and he could see that
she avoided him. But their relations remained outwardly un-
disturbed. The artists brought their sketches for inspection
and comment, and, without speaking to each other, he and
Imogene discussed them with the rest.

When they started homeward the painters said they were
coming a little way with them for a send-off, and then going
back to spend the night in Fiesole. They walked beside the
carriage, talking with Mrs. Bowen and Imogene, who had
taken their places, with Effie between them, on the back seat;
and when they took their leave, Colville and the young clergyman, who had politely walked with them, continued on
foot a little farther, till they came to the place where the highway to Florence divided into the new road and the old. At
this point it steeply overtops the fields on one side, which is

shored up by a wall some ten or twelve feet deep; and here round a sharp turn of the hill on the other side came a peasant driving a herd of the black pigs of the country.

Mrs. Bowen's horses were, perhaps, pampered beyond the habitual resignation of Florentine horses to all manner of natural phenomena; they reared at sight of the sable crew, and backing violently up-hill, set the carriage across the road, with its hind wheels a few feet from the brink of the wall. The coachman sprang from his seat; the ladies and the child remained in theirs as if paralyzed.

Colville ran forward to the side of the carriage. "Jump, Mrs. Bowen! jump, Effie! Imogene—"

The mother and the little one obeyed. He caught them in his arms and set them down. The girl sat still, staring at him with reproachful, with disdainful eyes.

He leaped forward to drag her out; she shrank away, and then he flew to help the coachman, who had the maddened horses by the bit.

"Let go!" he heard the young clergyman calling to him; "she's safe!" He caught a glimpse of Imogene, whom Mr. Morton had pulled from the other side of the carriage. He struggled to free his wrist from the curb-bit chain of the horse, through which he had plunged it in his attempt to seize the bridle. The wheels of the carriage went over the wall; he felt himself whirled into the air, and then swung ruining down into the writhing and crashing heap at the bottom of the wall.

XXI

WHEN Colville came to himself, his first sensation was delight in the softness and smoothness of the turf on which he lay; then the strange color of the grass commended itself to his notice; and presently he perceived that the thing under his head was a pillow, and that he was in bed. He was supported in this conclusion by the opinion of the young man who sat watching him a little way off, and who now smiled cheerfully at the expression in the eyes which Colville turned inquiringly upon him.

"Where am I?" he asked, with what appeared to him very unnecessary feebleness of voice.

The young man begged his pardon in Italian, and when Colville repeated his question in that tongue, he told him that he was in Palazzo Pinti, whither he had been brought from the scene of his accident. He added that Colville must not talk till the doctor had seen him and given him leave, and he explained that he was himself a nurse from the hospital, who had been taking care of him.

Colville moved his head and felt the bandage upon it; he desisted in his attempt to lift his right arm to it before the attendant could interfere in behalf of the broken limb. He recalled dimly and fragmentarily long histories that he had dreamed, but he forbore to ask how long he had been in his present case, and he accepted patiently the apparition of the doctor and other persons who came and went, and were at his bedside or not there, as it seemed to him, between the opening and closing of an eye. As the days passed they acquired greater permanence and maintained a more uninterrupted identity. He was able to make quite sure of Mr. Morton and of Mr. Waters; Mrs. Bowen came in, leading Effie, and this gave him a great pleasure. Mrs. Bowen seemed to have grown younger and better. Imogene was not among the phantoms who visited him; and he accepted her absence as quiescently as he accepted the presence of the others. There was a cheerfulness in those who came that permitted him no anxiety, and he was too weak to invite it by any conjecture.

He consented to be spared and to spare himself; and there were some things about the affair which gave him a singular and perhaps not wholly sane content. One of these was the man-nurse, who had evidently taken care of him throughout. He celebrated, whenever he looked at this capable person, his escape from being, in the odious helplessness of sickness, a burden upon the strength and sympathy of the two women for whom he had otherwise made so much trouble. His satisfaction in this had much to do with his recovery, which, when it once began, progressed rapidly to a point where he was told that Imogene and her mother were at a hotel in Florence, waiting till he should be strong enough to see them. It was Mrs. Bowen who told him this, with an air which she visibly strove to render non-committal and impersonal, but which betrayed, nevertheless, a faint apprehension for the effect upon him. The attitude of Imogene and her mother was certainly not one to have been expected of people holding their nominal relation to him, but Colville had been revising his impressions of events on the day of his accident; Imogene's last look came back to him, and he could not think the situation altogether unaccountable.

"Have I been here a long time?" he asked, as if he had not heeded what she told him.

"About a fortnight," answered Mrs. Bowen.

"And Imogene—how long has she been away?"

"Since they knew you would get well."

"I will see them any time," he said, quietly.

"Do you think you are strong enough?"

"I shall never be stronger till I have seen them," he returned, with a glance at her. "Yes; I want them to come today. I shall not be excited; don't be troubled—if you were going to be," he added. "Please send to them at once."

Mrs. Bowen hesitated, but after a moment left the room. She returned in half an hour with a lady who revealed even to Colville's languid regard evidences of the character which Mrs. Bowen had attributed to Imogene's mother. She was a large, robust person, laced to sufficient shapeliness, and she was well and simply dressed. She entered the room with a waft of some clean, wholesome perfume, and a quiet temperament and perfect health looked out of her clear, honest eyes—the eyes of Imogene Graham, though the girl's were dark and the woman's were blue. When Mrs. Bowen had named them to each other, in withdrawing, Mrs. Graham took Colville's weak left hand in her fresh, strong right, and then lifted herself a chair to his bedside, and sat down.

"How do you do to-day, sir?" she said, with a touch of old-fashioned respectfulness in the last word. "Do you think you are quite strong enough to talk with me?"

"I think so," said Colville, with a faint smile. "At least I can listen with fortitude."

Mrs. Graham was not apparently a person adapted to joking. "I don't know whether it will require much fortitude to hear what I have to say or not," she said, with her keen gaze fixed upon him. "It's simply this: I am going to take Imogene home."

She seemed to expect that Colville would make some reply to this, and he said, blankly, "Yes?"

"I came out prepared to consent to what she wished, after I had seen you, and satisfied myself that she was not mistaken; for I had always promised myself that her choice should be perfectly untrammelled, and I have tried to bring her up with principles and ideas that would enable her to make a good choice."

"Yes," said Colville again. "I'm afraid you didn't take her temperament and her youth into account, and that she disappointed you."

"No, I can't say that she did. It isn't that at all. I see no reason to blame her for her choice. Her mistake was of another kind."

It appeared to Colville that this very sensible and judicial lady found an intellectual pleasure in the analysis of the case, which modified the intensity of her maternal feeling in regard to it, and that, like many people who talk well, she liked to hear herself talk in the presence of another appreciative listener. He did not offer to interrupt her, and she went on. "No, sir, I am not disappointed in her choice. I think her chances of happiness would have been greater, in the abstract, with one nearer her own age; but that is a difference which other things affect so much that it did not alarm me greatly. Some people are younger at your age than at hers. No, sir, that is not the point." Mrs. Graham fetched a sigh, as if she found it easier to say what was not the point than to say what was, and her clear gaze grew troubled. But she apparently girded herself for the struggle. "As far as you are concerned, Mr. Colville, I have not a word to say. Your conduct throughout has been most high-minded and considerate and delicate."

It is hard for any man to deny merits attributed to him, especially if he has been ascribing to himself the opposite demerits. But Colville summoned his dispersed forces to protest against this.

"Oh, no, no," he cried. "Anything but that. My conduct has been selfish and shameful. If you could understand all—"

"I think I do understand all—at least far more, I regret to say, than my daughter has been willing to tell me. And I am more than satisfied with you. I thank you and honor you."

"Oh no; don't say that," pleaded Colville. "I really can't stand it."

"And when I came here it was with the full intention of approving and confirming Imogene's decision. But I was met at once by a painful and surprising state of things. You are aware that you have been very sick?"

"Dimly," said Colville.

"I found you very sick, and I found my daughter frantic at the terror which she had discovered in herself—discovered too late, as she felt." Mrs. Graham hesitated, and then added, abruptly, "She had found out that she did not love you."

"Didn't love me?" repeated Colville, feebly.

"She had been conscious of the truth before, but she had stifled her misgivings insanely, and, as I feel, almost wickedly, pushing on, and saying to herself that when you were married, then there would be no escape, and she *must* love you."

"Poor girl! poor child! I see, I see."

"But the accident that was almost your death saved her from that miserable folly and iniquity. Yes," she continued, in answer to the protest in his face, "folly and iniquity. I found her half crazed at your bedside. She was fully aware of your danger, but while she was feeling all the remorse that she ought to feel—that any one could feel—she was more and more convinced that she never had loved you and never should. I can give you no idea of her state of mind."

"Oh, you needn't! you needn't! Poor, poor child!"

"Yes, a child indeed. If it had not been for the pity I felt for her— But no matter about that. She saw at last that if your heroic devotion to her"—Colville did his best to hang his pillowed head for shame—"if your present danger did not awaken her to some such feeling for you as she had once imagined she had; if they both only increased her despair and self-abhorrence—then the case was indeed hopeless. She was simply distracted. I had to tear her away almost by force. She has had a narrow escape from brain-fever. And now I have come to implore, to *demand*"—Mrs. Graham, with all her poise and calm, was rising to the hysterical key—"her release from a fate that would be worse than death for such a girl. I mean marrying without the love of her whole soul. She esteems you, she respects you, she admires you, she likes you; but—" Mrs. Graham pressed her lips together, and her eyes shone.

"She is free," said Colville, and with the words a mighty load rolled from his heart. "There is no need to demand anything."

"I know."

"There hasn't been an hour, an instant, during—since I— we—spoke together that I wouldn't have released her if I could have known what you tell me now."

"Of course!—of course!"

"I have had my fears—my doubts; but whenever I approached the point I found no avenue by which we could reach a clearer understanding. I could not say much without seeming to seek for myself the release I was offering her."

"Naturally. And what added to her wretchedness was the suspicion at the bottom of all that she had somehow forced herself upon you—misunderstood you, and made you say and do things to spare her that you would not have done voluntarily." This was advanced tentatively. In the midst of his sophistications Colville had, as most of his sex have, a native, fatal, helpless truthfulness, which betrayed him at the most unexpected moments, and this must now have appeared in his countenance. The lady rose haughtily. She had apparently been considering him, but, after all, she must have been really considering her daughter. "If anything of the kind was the case," she said, "I will ask you to spare her the killing knowledge. It's quite enough for *me* to know it. And allow me to say, Mr. Colville, that it would have been far kinder in you—"

"Ah, *think*, my dear madam!" he exclaimed. "How *could* I?"

She did think, evidently, and when she spoke it was with a generous emotion, in which there was no trace of pique.

"You couldn't. You have done right; I feel that, and I will trust you to say anything you will to my daughter."

"To your daughter? Shall I see her?"

"She came with me. She wished to beg your forgiveness."

Colville lay silent. "There is no forgiveness to be asked or granted," he said at length. "Why should she suffer the pain of seeing me?—for it would be nothing else. What do you think? Will it do her any good hereafter? I don't care for myself."

"I don't know what to think," said Mrs. Graham. "She is a strange child. She may have some idea of reparation."

"Oh, beseech her from me not to imagine that any reparation is due! Where there has been an error there must be blame; but wherever it lies in ours, I am sure it isn't at her door. Tell her I say this; tell her that I acquit her with all my heart of every shadow of wrong; that I am not unhappy, but glad for her sake and my own that this has ended as it has." He stretched his left hand across the coverlet to her, and said, with the feebleness of exhaustion: "Good-by. Bid her good-by for me."

Mrs. Graham pressed his hand and went out. A moment after the door was flung open, and Imogene burst into the room. She threw herself on her knees beside his bed. "I will *pray* to you!" she said, her face intense with the passions working in her soul. She seemed choking with words which would not come; then, with an inarticulate cry that must stand for all, she caught up the hand that lay limp on the coverlet; she crushed it against her lips, and ran out of the room.

He sank into a deathly torpor, the physical refusal of his

brain to take account of what had passed. When he woke from it, little Effie Bowen was airily tiptoeing about the room, fondly retouching its perfect order. He closed his eyes, and felt her come to him and smooth the sheet softly under his chin. Then he knew she must be standing with clasped hands admiring the effect. Some one called her in whisper from the door. It closed, and all was still again.

XXII

COLVILLE got himself out of the comfort and quiet of Mrs. Bowen's house as soon as he could. He made the more haste because he felt that if he could have remained with the smallest trace of self-respect, he would have been glad to stay there forever.

Even as it was, the spring had advanced to early summer, and the sun was lying hot and bright in the piazzas, and the shade dense and cool in the narrow streets, before he left Palazzo Pinti; the Lung' Arno was a glare of light that struck back from the curving line of the buff houses; the river had shrivelled to a rill in its bed; the black cypresses were dim in the tremor of the distant air on the hill-slopes beyond; the olives seemed to swelter in the sun, and the villa walls to burn whiter and whiter. At evening the mosquito began to wind his tiny horn. It was the end of May, and nearly everybody but the Florentines had gone out of Florence, dispersing to Villa Reggio by the sea, to the hills of Pistoja, and to the high, cool air of Siena. More than once Colville had said that he was keeping Mrs. Bowen after she ought to have got away, and she had answered that she liked hot weather, and that this was not comparable to the heat of Washington in June. She was looking very well, and younger and prettier than she had since the first days of their renewed acquaintance in the winter. Her southern complexion enriched itself in the sun; sometimes when she came into his room from out-doors the straying brown hair curled into loose rings on her temples, and her cheeks glowed a deep red.

She said those polite things to appease him as long as he was not well enough to go away, but she did not try to detain him after his strength sufficiently returned. It was the blow on the head that kept him longest. After his broken arm and his other bruises were quite healed he was aware of physical limits to thinking of the future or regretting the past, and this sense of his powerlessness went far to reconcile him to a life of present inaction and oblivion. Theoretically he ought to have been devoured by remorse and chagrin, but as a matter

of fact he suffered very little from either. Even in people who
are in full possession of their capacity for mental anguish one
observes that after they have undergone a certain amount of
pain they cease to feel.

Colville amused himself a good deal with Effie's endeavors
to entertain him and take care of him. The child was with
him every moment that she could steal from her tasks, and
her mother no longer attempted to stem the tide of her devotion. It was understood that Effie should joke and laugh
with Mr. Colville as much as she chose; that she should fan
him as long as he could stand it; that she should read to him
when he woke, and watch him when he slept. She brought
him his breakfast, she petted him and caressed him, and
wished to make him a monster of dependence and self-indulgence. It seemed to grieve her that he got well so fast.

The last night before he left the house she sat on his knee
by the window looking out beyond the fire-fly twinkle of
Oltrarno to the silence and solid dark of the solemn company
of hills beyond. They had not lighted the lamps because of
the mosquitoes, and they had talked till her head dropped
against his shoulder.

Mrs. Bowen came in to get her. "Why, is she asleep?"

"Yes. Don't take her yet," said Colville.

Mrs. Bowen rustled softly into the chair which Effie had
left to get into Colville's lap. Neither of them spoke, and he
was so richly content with the peace, the tacit sweetness of
the little moment, that he would have been glad to have it
silently endure forever. If any troublesome question of his
right to such a moment of bliss obtruded itself upon him, he
did not concern himself with it.

"We shall have another hot day, to-morrow," said Mrs.
Bowen at length. "I hope you will find your room comfortable."

"Yes; it's at the back of the hotel, mighty high and wide,
and no sun ever comes into it except when they show it to
foreigners in winter. Then they get a few rays to enter as a
matter of business, on condition that they won't detain them.
I dare say I shall stay there some time. I suppose you will be
getting away from Florence very soon?"

"Yes. But I haven't decided where to go yet."

"Should you like some general expression of my gratitude for all you've done for me, Mrs. Bowen?"

"No; I would rather not. It has been a great pleasure—to Effie."

"Oh, a luxury beyond the dreams of avarice." They spoke in low tones, and there was something in the hush that suggested to Colville the feasibility of taking into his unoccupied hand one of the pretty hands which the pale night light showed him lying in Mrs. Bowen's lap. But he forbore, and only sighed. "Well, then, I will say nothing. But I shall keep on thinking, all my life."

She made no answer.

"When you are gone, I shall have to make the most of Mr. Waters," he said.

"He is going to stop all summer, I believe."

"Oh yes. When I suggested to him the other day that he might find it too hot, he said that he had seventy New England winters to thaw out of his blood, and that all the summers he had left would not be more than he needed. One of his friends told him that he could cook eggs in his piazza in August, and he said that he should like nothing better than to cook eggs there. He's the most delightfully expatriated compatriot I've ever seen."

"Do you like it?"

"It's well enough for him. Life has no claims on him any more. I think it's very pleasant over here, now that everybody's gone," added Colville, from a confused resentfulness of collectively remembered Days and Afternoons and Evenings. "How still the night is!"

A few feet clapping by on the pavement below alone broke the hush.

"Sometimes I feel very tired of it all, and want to get home," sighed Mrs. Bowen.

"Well, so do I."

"I can't believe it's right staying away from the country so long." People often say such things in Europe.

"No, I don't, either, if you've got anything to do there."

"You can always make something to do there."

"Oh yes." Some young men, breaking from a street near

by, began to sing. "We shouldn't have that sort of thing at home."

"No," said Mrs. Bowen, pensively.

"I heard just such singing before I fell asleep the night after that party at Madame Uccelli's, and it filled me with fury."

"Why should it do that?"

"I don't know. It seemed like voices from our youth— Lina."

She had no resentment of his use of her name in the tone with which she asked: "Did you hate that so much?"

"No; the loss of it."

They both fetched a deep breath.

"The Uccellis have a villa near the Baths of Lucca," said Mrs. Bowen. "They have asked me to go."

"Do you think of going?" inquired Colville. "I've always fancied it must be pleasant there."

"No; I declined. Sometimes I think I will just stay on in Florence."

"I dare say you'd find it perfectly comfortable. There's nothing like having the range of one's own house in summer." He looked out of the window on the blue-black sky.

" 'And deepening through their silent spheres,
    Heaven over heaven rose the night,' "

he quoted. "It's wonderful! Do you remember how I used to read 'Mariana in the South' to you and poor Jenny? How it must have bored her! What an ass I was!"

"Yes," said Mrs. Bowen, breathlessly, in sympathy with his reminiscence rather than in agreement with his self-denunciation.

Colville broke into a laugh, and then she began to laugh too, but not quite willingly, as it seemed.

Effie started from her sleep. "What—what is it?" she asked, stretching and shivering as half-wakened children do.

"Bed-time," said her mother, promptly, taking her hand to lead her away. "Say good-night to Mr. Colville."

The child turned and kissed him. "Good-night," she murmured.

"Good-night, you sleepy little soul!" It seemed to Colville that he must be a pretty good man, after all, if this little thing loved him so.

"Do you always kiss Mr. Colville good-night?" asked her mother when she began to undo her hair for her in her room.

"Sometimes. Don't you think it's nice?"

"Oh yes, nice enough."

Colville sat by the window a long time, thinking Mrs. Bowen might come back; but she did not return.

Mr. Waters came to see him the next afternoon at his hotel. "Are you pretty comfortable here?" he asked.

"Well, it's a change," said Colville. "I miss the little one awfully."

"She's a winning child," admitted the old man. "That combination of conventionality and *naïveté* is very captivating. I notice it in the mother."

"Yes, the mother has it too. Have you seen them to-day?"

"Yes; Mrs. Bowen was sorry to be out when you came."

"I had the misfortune to miss them. I had a great mind to go again to-night." The old man said nothing to this. "The fact is," Colville went on, "I'm so habituated to being there that I'm rather spoiled."

"Ah, it's a nice place," Mr. Waters admitted.

"Of course I made all the haste I could to get away, and I have the reward of a good conscience. But I don't find that the reward is very great."

The old gentleman smiled. "The difficulty is to know conscience from self-interest."

"Oh, there's no doubt of it in my case," said Colville. "If I'd consulted my own comfort and advantage, I should still be at Palazzo Pinti."

"I dare say they would have been glad to keep you."

"Do you really think so?" asked Colville, with sudden seriousness. "I wish you would tell me why. Have you any reason—grounds? Pshaw! I'm absurd!" He sank back into the easy-chair from whose depths he had pulled himself in the eagerness of his demand, and wiped his forehead with his handkerchief. "Mr. Waters, you remember my telling you of my engagement to Miss Graham?"

"Yes."

"That is broken off—if it were ever really on. It was a great mistake for both of us—a tragical one for her, poor child, a ridiculous one for me. My only consolation is that it *was* a mistake and no more; but I don't conceal from myself that I might have prevented it altogether if I had behaved with greater wisdom and dignity at the outset. But I'm afraid I was flattered by an illusion of hers that ought to have pained and alarmed me, and the rest followed inevitably, though I was always just on the point of escaping the consequences of my weakness—my wickedness."

"Ah, there is something extremely interesting in all that," said the old minister, thoughtfully. "The situation used to be figured under the old idea of a compact with the devil. His debtor was always on the point of escaping, as you say, but I recollect no instance in which he did not pay at last. The myth must have arisen from man's recognition of the inexorable sequence of effect from cause in the moral world, which even repentance can not avert. Goethe tries to imagine an atonement for Faust's trespass against one human soul in his benefactions to the race at large; but it is a very cloudy business."

"It isn't quite a parallel case," said Colville, rather sulkily. He had, in fact, suffered more under Mr. Waters's generalization than he could from a more personal philosophy of the affair.

"Oh no; I didn't think that," consented the old man.

"And I don't think I shall undertake any extended scheme of drainage or subsoiling in atonement for my little dream," Colville continued, resenting the parity of outline that grew upon him in spite of his protest. They were both silent for a while, and then Colville cried out: "Yes, yes; they are alike. *I* dreamed, too, of recovering and restoring my own lost and broken past in the love of a young soul, and it was in essence the same cruelly egotistic dream; and it's nothing in my defense that it was all formless and undirected at first, and that as soon as I recognized it I abhorred it."

"Oh yes, it is," replied the old man, with perfect equanimity. "Your assertion is the hysterical excess of Puritanism, in all times and places. In the moral world we are responsible only for the wrong that we intend. It can't be otherwise."

"And the evil that's suffered from the wrong we didn't intend?"

"Ah, perhaps that isn't evil."

"It's pain!"

"It's pain, yes."

"And to have wrung a young and innocent heart with the anguish of self-doubt, with the fear of wrong to another, with the shame of an error such as I allowed, perhaps encouraged, her to make—"

"Yes," said the old man. "The young suffer terribly. But they recover. Afterward we don't suffer so much, but we don't recover. I wouldn't defend you against yourself if I thought you seriously in the wrong. If you know yourself to be, you shouldn't let me."

Thus put upon his honor, Colville was a long time thoughtful. "How can I tell?" he asked. "You know the facts; you can judge."

"If I were to judge at all, I should say you were likely to do a greater wrong than any you have committed."

"I don't understand you."

"Miss Graham is a young girl, and I have no doubt that the young clergyman—what was his name?"

"Morton. Do you think—do you suppose there was anything in that?" demanded Colville, with eagerness that a more humorous observer than Mr. Waters might have found ludicrous. "He was an admirable young fellow, with an excellent head and a noble heart. I underrated him at one time, though I recognized his good qualities afterward; but I was afraid she did not appreciate him."

"I'm not so sure of that," said the old man, with an astuteness of manner which Colville thought authorized by some sort of definite knowledge.

"I would give the world if it were so!" he cried, fervently.

"But you are really very much more concerned in something else."

"In what else?"

"Can't you imagine?"

"No," said Colville; but he felt himself growing very red in the face.

"Then I have no more to say."

"Yes, speak!" And after an interval Colville added, "Is it anything about—you hinted at something long ago—Mrs. Bowen?"

"Yes;" the old man nodded his head. "Do you owe her nothing?"

"Owe her nothing? Everything! My life! What self-respect is left me! Immeasurable gratitude! The homage of a man saved from himself as far as his stupidity and selfishness would permit! Why, I—I love her!" The words gave him courage. "In every breath and pulse! She is the most beautiful and gracious and wisest and best woman in the world! I have loved her ever since I met her here in Florence last winter. Good heavens! I must have always loved her! But," he added, falling from the rapture of this confession, "she simply loathes *me!*"

"It was certainly not to your credit that you were willing at the same time to marry some one else."

"Willing! I wasn't willing! I was bound hand and foot! Yes—I don't care what you think of my weakness—I was not a free agent. It's very well to condemn one's self, but it may be carried too far; injustice to others is not the only injustice, or the worst. What I was willing to do was to keep my word—to prevent that poor child, if possible, from ever finding out her mistake."

If Colville expected this heroic confession to impress his listener, he was disappointed. Mr. Waters made him no reply, and he was obliged to ask, with a degree of sarcastic impatience, "I suppose you scarcely blame me for that?"

"Oh, I don't know that I blame people for things. There are times when it seems as if we were all puppets, pulled this way or that, without control of our own movements. Hamlet was able to browbeat Rosencrantz and Guildenstern with his business of the pipe; but if they had been in a position to answer they might have told him that it required far less skill to play upon a man than any other instrument. Most of us, in fact, go sounding on without any special application of breath or fingers, repeating the tunes that were played originally upon other men. It appears to me that you suffered yourself to do something of the kind in this affair. We are a long time learning to act with common-sense, or even common sanity, in what are called matters of the affections. A broken engagement *may* be a bad thing in some cases, but I am inclined to think that it is the very best thing that could happen in most cases where it happens. The evil is done long before; the broken engagement is merely sanative, and so far beneficent."

The old gentleman rose, and Colville, dazed by the recognition of his own cowardice and absurdity, did not try to detain him. But he followed him down to the outer gate of the hotel. The afternoon sun was pouring into the piazza a sea of glimmering heat, into which Mr. Waters plunged with the security of a salamander. He wore a broad-brimmed Panama hat, a sack-coat of black alpaca, and loose trousers of the same material, and Colville fancied him doubly defended against the torrid waves not only by the stored cold of half a century of winters at Haddam East Village, but by an inner coolness of spirit, which appeared to diffuse itself in an appreciable atmosphere about him. It was not till he was gone that Colville found himself steeped in perspiration and glowing with a strange excitement.

XXIII

COLVILLE went back to his own room, and spent a good deal of time in the contemplation of a suit of clothes, adapted to the season, which had been sent home from the tailor's just before Mr. Waters came in. The coat was of the lightest serge, the trousers of a pearly gray tending to lavender, the waistcoat of cool white duck. On his way home from Palazzo Pinti he had stopped in Via Tornabuoni and bought some silk gauze neck-ties, of a tasteful gayety of tint which he had at the time thought very well of. But now, as he spread out the whole array on his bed, it seemed too emblematic of a light and blameless spirit for his wear. He ought to put on something as nearly analogous to sackcloth as a modern stock of dry-goods afforded; he ought, at least, to wear the grave materials of his winter costume. But they were really insupportable in this sudden access of summer. Besides, he had grown thin during his sickness, and the things bagged about him. If he were going to see Mrs. Bowen that evening, he ought to go in some decent shape. It was perhaps providential that he had failed to find her at home in the morning, when he had ventured thither in the clumsy attire in which he had been loafing about her drawing-room for the past week. He now owed it to her to appear before her as well as he could. How charmingly punctilious she always was herself!

As he put on his new clothes he felt the moral support which the becomingness of dress alone can give. With the blue silk gauze lightly tied under his collar, and the lapels of his thin coat thrown back to admit his thumbs to his waistcoat pockets, he felt almost cheerful before his glass. Should he shave? As once before, this important question occurred to him. His thinness gave him some advantages of figure, but he thought that it made his face older. What effect would cutting off his beard have upon it? He had not seen the lower part of his face for fifteen years. No one could say what recent ruin of a double chin might not be lurking there. He decided not to shave, at least till after dinner, and after dinner he was too impatient for his visit to brook the necessary delay.

He was shown into the salotto alone, but Effie Bowen came running in to meet him. She stopped suddenly, bridling.

"You never expected to see me looking quite so pretty," said Colville, tracing the cause of her embarrassment to his summer splendor. "Where is your mamma?"

"She is in the dining-room," replied the child, getting hold of his hand. "She wants you to come and have coffee with us."

"By all means—not that I haven't had coffee already, though."

She led the way, looking up at him shyly over her shoulder as they went.

Mrs. Bowen rose, napkin in lap, and gave him a hand of welcome. "How are you feeling to-day?" she asked, politely ignoring his finery.

"Like a new man," he said. And then he added, to relieve the strain of the situation, "Of the best tailor's make in Florence."

"You look very well," she smiled.

"Oh, I always do when I take pains," said Colville. "The trouble is that I don't always take pains. But I thought I would to-night, in calling upon a lady."

"Effie will feel very much flattered," said Mrs. Bowen.

"Don't refuse a portion of the satisfaction," he cried.

"Oh, is it for me too?"

This gave Colville consolation which no religion or philosophy could have brought him; and his pleasure was not marred, but rather heightened, by the little pangs of expectation, bred by long custom, that from moment to moment Imogene would appear. She did not appear, and a thrill of security succeeded upon each alarm. He wished her well with all his heart; such is the human heart that he wished her arrived home the betrothed of that excellent, that wholly unobjectionable young man, Mr. Morton.

"Will you have a little of the ice before your coffee?" asked Mrs. Bowen, proposing one of the moulded creams with her spoon.

"Yes, thank you. Perhaps I will take it in place of the coffee. They forgot to offer us any ice at the *table d'hôte* this evening."

"This is rather luxurious for us," said Mrs. Bowen. "It's a compromise with Effie. She wanted me to take her to Giacosa's this afternoon."

"I *thought* you would come," whispered the child to Colville.

Her mother made a little face of mock surprise at her. "Don't give yourself away, Effie."

"Why, let us go to Giacosa's too," said Colville, taking the ice. "We shall be the only foreigners there, and we shall not even feel ourselves foreign. It's astonishing how the hot weather has dispersed the tourists. I didn't see a Baedeker on the whole way up here, and I walked down Via Tornabuoni, across through Porta Rosso, and the Piazza della Signoria, and the Uffizzi. You've no idea how comfortable and home-like it was—all the statues loafing about in their shirt sleeves, and the objects of interest stretching and yawning round, and having a good rest after their winter's work."

Effie understood Colville's way of talking well enough to enjoy this; her mother did not laugh.

"Walked?" she asked.

"Certainly. Why not?"

"You are getting well again. You'll soon be gone too."

"I've *got* well. But as to being gone, there's no hurry. I rather think I shall wait now to see how long you stay."

"We may keep you all summer," said Mrs. Bowen, drooping her eyelids indifferently.

"Oh, very well. All summer it is, then. Mr. Waters is going to stay, and he is such a very cool old gentleman that I don't think one need fear the wildest antics of the mercury where he is."

When Colville had finished his ice, Mrs. Bowen led the way to the salotto; and they all sat down by the window there and watched the sunset die on San Miniato. The bronze copy of Michelangelo's David, in the Piazzale below the church, blackened in perfect relief against the pink sky and then faded against the gray while they talked. They were so domestic that Colville realized with difficulty that this was an image of what might be rather than what really was; the very ease with which he could apparently close his hand upon the happiness within his grasp unnerved him. The talk strayed hither and thither, and went and came aimlessly. A sound of singing floated in from the kitchen, and Effie eagerly asked her mother if she might go and see Maddalena. Maddalena's mother had come to see her, and she was from the mountains.

"Yes, go," said Mrs. Bowen; "but don't stay too long."

"Oh, I will be back in time," said the child; and Colville remembered that he had proposed going to Giacosa's.

"Yes; don't forget." He had forgotten it himself.

"Maddalena is the cook," explained Mrs. Bowen. "She sings ballads to Effie that she learned from her mother, and I suppose Effie wants to hear them at first hand."

"Oh yes," said Colville, dreamily.

They were alone now, and each little silence seemed freighted with a meaning deeper than speech.

"Have you seen Mr. Waters to-day?" asked Mrs. Bowen, after one of these lapses.

"Yes; he came this afternoon."

"He is a very strange old man. I should think he would be lonely here."

"He seems not to be. He says he finds company in the history of the place. And his satisfaction at having got out of Haddam East Village is perennial."

"But he will want to go back there before he dies."

"I don't know. He thinks not. He's a strange old man, as you say. He has the art of putting all sorts of ideas into people's heads. Do you know what we talked about this afternoon?"

"No, I don't," murmured Mrs. Bowen.

"About you. And he encouraged me to believe—imagine—that I might speak to you—ask—tell you that—I loved you, Lina." He leaned forward and took one of the hands that lay in her lap. It trembled with a violence inconceivable in relation to the perfect quiet of her attitude. But she did not try to take it away. "Could you—do you love me?"

"Yes," she whispered; but here she sprang up and slipped from his hold altogether as, with an inarticulate cry of rapture, he released her hand to take her in his arms.

He followed her a pace or two. "And you will—will be my wife?" he pursued, eagerly.

"Never!" she answered; and now Colville stopped short, while a cold bewilderment bathed him from head to foot. It must be some sort of jest, though he could not tell where the humor was, and he could not treat it otherwise than seriously.

"Lina, I have loved you from the first moment that I saw you this winter, and Heaven knows how long before!"

"Yes; I know that."

"And every moment."

"Oh, I know that too."

"Even if I had no sort of hope that you cared for me, I loved you so much that I must tell you before we parted—"

"I expected that—I intended it."

"You intended it! and you do love me! And yet you won't—Ah, I don't understand!"

"How could you understand? I love you—I blush and burn for shame to think that I love you. But I will never marry you: I can at least help doing that, and I can still keep some little trace of self-respect. How you must really despise me, to think of anything else, after all that has happened! Did you suppose that I was merely waiting till that poor girl's back was turned, as you were? Oh, how can you be yourself, and still be yourself? Yes, Jenny Wheelwright was right. You are too much of a mixture, Theodore Colville"—her calling him so showed how often she had thought of him so—"too much for her, too much for Imogene, too much for me; too much for any woman except some wretched creature who enjoys being trampled on and dragged through the dust, as you have dragged me."

"I dragged you through the dust? There hasn't been a moment in the past six months when I wouldn't have rolled myself in it to please you."

"Oh, I knew that well enough! And do you think that was flattering to me?"

"That has nothing to do with it. I only know that I love you, and that I couldn't help wishing to show it even when I wouldn't acknowledge it to myself. That is all. And now when I am free to speak, and you own that you love me, you won't— I give it up!" he cried, desperately. But in the next breath he implored, "*Why* do you drive me from you, Lina?"

"Because you have humiliated me too much." She was perfectly steady, but he knew her so well that in the twilight he knew what bitterness there must be in the smile which she must be keeping on her lips. "I was here in the place of her mother, her best friend, and you made me treat her like an enemy. You made me betray her and cast her off."

"I?"

"Yes, you! I knew from the very first that you did not really care for her, that you were playing with yourself, as you were playing with her, and I ought to have warned her."

"It appears to me you did warn her," said Colville, with some resentful return of courage.

"I tried," she said, simply, "and it made it worse. It made it worse because I knew that I was acting for my own sake more than hers, because I wasn't—disinterested." There was something in this explanation, serious, tragic, as it was to Mrs. Bowen, which made Colville laugh. She might have had some perception of its effect to him, or it may have been merely from a hysterical helplessness, but she laughed too a little.

"But why," he gathered courage to ask, "do you still dwell upon that? Mr. Waters told me that Mr. Morton—that there was—"

"He is mistaken. He offered himself, and she refused him. He told me."

"Oh!"

"Do you think she would do otherwise, with you lying here between life and death? No: you can have no hope from that."

Colville, in fact, had none. This blow crushed and dispersed him. He had not strength enough to feel resentment against Mr. Waters for misleading him with this *ignis fatuus*.

"No one warned him, and it came to that," said Mrs. Bowen. "It was of a piece with the whole affair. I was weak in that too."

Colville did not attempt to reply on this point. He feebly

reverted to the inquiry regarding himself, and was far enough from mirth in resuming it.

"I couldn't imagine," he said, "that you cared anything for me when you warned another against me. If I could—"

"You put me in a false position from the beginning. I ought to have sympathized with her and helped her, instead of making the poor child feel that somehow I hated her. I couldn't even put her on guard against herself, though I knew all along that she didn't really care for you, but was just in love with her own fancy for you. Even after you were engaged I ought to have broken it off; I ought to have been frank with her; it was my duty; but I couldn't without feeling that I was acting for myself too, and I would not submit to that degradation. No! I would rather have died. I dare say you don't understand. How could you? You are a man, and the kind of man who couldn't. At every point you made me violate every principle that was dear to me. I loathed myself for caring for a man who was in love with me when he was engaged to another. Don't think it was gratifying to me. It was detestable; and yet I did let you see that I cared for you. Yes, I even *tried* to make you care for me—falsely, cruelly, treacherously."

"You didn't have to try very hard," said Colville, with a sort of cold resignation to his fate.

"Oh no; you were quite ready for any hint. I could have told her for her own sake that she didn't love you, but that would have been for my sake too; and I would have told you if I hadn't cared for you and known how you cared for me. I've saved at least the consciousness of this from the wreck."

"I don't think it's a great treasure," said Colville. "I wish that you had saved the consciousness of having been frank even to your own advantage."

"Do you dare to reproach me, Theodore Colville? But perhaps I've deserved this too."

"No, Lina, you certainly don't deserve it, if it's unkindness, from me. I won't afflict you with my presence: but will you listen to me before I go?"

She sank into a chair in sign of assent. He also sat down. He had a dim impression that he could talk better if he took her hand, but he did not venture to ask for it. He contented himself with fixing his eyes upon as much of her face as he could make out in the dusk, a pale blur in a vague outline of dark.

"I want to assure you, Lina—Lina, my love, my dearest, as I shall call you for the first and last time!—that I *do* understand everything, as delicately and fully as you could wish, all that you have expressed and all that you have left unsaid. I understand how high and pure your ideals of duty are, and how heroically, angelically, you have struggled to fulfill them, broken and borne down by my clumsy and stupid selfishness from the start. I want you to believe, my dearest love—you must forgive me!—that if I didn't see everything at the time, I do see it now, and that I prize the love you kept from me far more than any love you could have given me to the loss of your self-respect. It isn't logic—it sounds more like nonsense, I am afraid—but you know what I mean by it. You are more perfect, more lovely, to me than any being in the world, and I accept whatever fate you choose for me. I would not win you against your will if I could. You are sacred to me. If you say we must part, I know that you speak from a finer discernment than mine, and I submit. I will try to console myself with the thought of your love, if I may not have you. Yes, I submit."

His instinct of forbearance had served him better than the subtlest art. His submission was the best defense. He rose with a real dignity, and she rose also. "Remember," he said, "that I confess all you accuse me of, and that I acknowledge the justice of what you do—because you do it." He put out his hand and took the hand which hung nerveless at her side. "You are quite right. Good-by." He hesitated a moment. "May I kiss you, Lina?" He drew her to him, and she let him kiss her on the lips.

"Good-by," she whispered. "Go—"

"I am going."

Effie Bowen ran into the room from the kitchen. "Aren't you going to take—" She stopped and turned to her mother. She must not remind Mr. Colville of his invitation; that was what her gesture expressed.

Colville would not say anything. He would not seize his

advantage, and play upon the mother's heart through the feelings of her child, though there is no doubt that he was tempted to prolong the situation by any means. Perhaps Mrs. Bowen divined both the temptation and the resistance. "Tell her," she said, and turned away.

"I can't go with you to-night, Effie," he said, stooping toward her for the inquiring kiss that she gave him. "I am—going away, and I must say good-by."

The solemnity of his voice alarmed her. "Going away!" she repeated.

"Yes—away from Florence. I'm afraid I shall not see you again."

The child turned from him to her mother again, who stood motionless. Then, as if the whole calamitous fact had suddenly flashed upon her, she plunged her face against her mother's breast. "I can't *bear* it!" she sobbed out, and the reticence of her lamentation told more than a storm of cries and prayers.

Colville wavered.

"Oh, you must stay!" said Lina, in the self-contemptuous voice of a woman who falls below her ideal of herself.

XXIV

IN THE LEVITIES which the most undeserving husbands permit themselves with the severest of wives, there were times after their marriage when Colville accused Lina of never really intending to drive him away, but of meaning, after a disciplinary ordeal, to marry him in reward of his tested self-sacrifice and obedience. He said that if the appearance of Effie was not a *coup de théâtre* contrived beforehand, it was an accident of no consequence whatever; that if she had not come in at that moment, her mother would have found some other pretext for detaining him. This is a point which I would not presume to decide. I only know that they were married early in June before the syndic of Florence, who tied a tricolor sash round his ample waist for the purpose, and never looked more paternal or venerable than when giving the sanction of the Italian state to their union. It is not, of course, to be supposed that Mrs. Colville was contented with the civil rite, though Colville may have thought it quite sufficient. The religious ceremony took place in the English chapel, the assistant clergyman officiating in the absence of the incumbent, who had already gone out of town.

The Rev. Mr. Waters gave away the bride, and then went home to Palazzo Pinti with the party, the single and singularly honored guest at their wedding feast, for which Effie Bowen went with Colville to Giacosa's to order the ices in person. She has never regretted her choice of a step-father, though when Colville asked her how she would like him in that relation she had a moment of hesitation, in which she reconciled herself to it; as to him she had no misgivings. He has sometimes found himself the object of little jealousies on her part, but by promptly deciding all questions between her and her mother in Effie's favor, he has convinced her of the groundlessness of her suspicions.

In the absence of any social pressure to the contrary, the Colvilles spent the summer in Palazzo Pinti. Before their fellow-sojourners returned from the *villeggiature* in the fall, however, they had turned their faces southward, and they are now in Rome, where, arriving as a married couple, there was no inquiry and no interest in their past.

It is best to be honest, and own that the affair with Imogene has been the grain of sand to them. No one was to blame, or very much to blame; even Mrs. Colville says that. It was a thing that happened, but one would rather it had not happened.

Last winter, however, Mrs. Colville received a letter from Mrs. Graham which suggested, if it did not impart, consolation. "Mr. Morton was here the other day, and spent the morning. He has a parish at Erie, and there is talk of his coming to Buffalo."

"Oh, Heaven grant it!" said Colville, with sudden piety.

"Why?" demanded his wife.

"Well, I wish she was married."

"You have nothing whatever to do with her."

It took him some time to realize that this was the fact.

"No," he confessed; "but what do you think about it?"

"There is no telling. We are such simpletons! If a man will keep on long enough— But if it isn't Mr. Morton, it will be some one else—some *young* person."

Colville rose and went round the breakfast table to her. "I hope so," he said. "*I* have married a young person, and it would only be fair."

This magnanimity was irresistible.

THE RISE OF SILAS LAPHAM

I

WHEN BARTLEY HUBBARD went to interview Silas Lapham for the "Solid Men of Boston" series, which he undertook to finish up in "The Events," after he replaced their original projector on that newspaper, Lapham received him in his private office by previous appointment.

"Walk right in!" he called out to the journalist, whom he caught sight of through the door of the counting-room.

He did not rise from the desk at which he was writing, but he gave Bartley his left hand for welcome, and he rolled his large head in the direction of a vacant chair. "Sit down! I'll be with you in just half a minute."

"Take your time," said Bartley, with the ease he instantly felt. "I'm in no hurry." He took a note-book from his pocket, laid it on his knee, and began to sharpen a pencil.

"There!" Lapham pounded with his great hairy fist on the envelope he had been addressing. "William!" he called out, and he handed the letter to a boy who came to get it. "I want that to go right away. Well, sir," he continued, wheeling round in his leather-cushioned swivel-chair, and facing Bartley, seated so near that their knees almost touched, "so you want my life, death, and Christian sufferings, do you, young man?"

"That's what I'm after," said Bartley. "Your money or your life."

"I guess you wouldn't want my life without the money," said Lapham, as if he were willing to prolong these moments of preparation.

"Take 'em both," Bartley suggested. "Don't want your money without your life, if you come to that. But you're just one million times more interesting to the public than if you hadn't a dollar; and you know that as well as I do, Mr. Lapham. There's no use beating about the bush."

"No," said Lapham, somewhat absently. He put out his huge foot and pushed the ground-glass door shut between his little den and the book-keepers, in their larger den outside.

"In personal appearance," wrote Bartley in the sketch for

which he now studied his subject, while he waited patiently for him to continue, "Silas Lapham is a fine type of the successful American. He has a square, bold chin, only partially concealed by the short, reddish-gray beard, growing to the edges of his firmly closing lips. His nose is short and straight; his forehead good, but broad rather than high; his eyes blue, and with a light in them that is kindly or sharp according to his mood. He is of medium height, and fills an average arm-chair with a solid bulk, which, on the day of our interview, was unpretentiously clad in a business suit of blue serge. His head droops somewhat from a short neck, which does not trouble itself to rise far from a pair of massive shoulders."

"I don't know as I know just where you want me to begin," said Lapham.

"Might begin with your birth; that's where most of us begin," replied Bartley.

A gleam of humorous appreciation shot into Lapham's blue eyes.

"I didn't know whether you wanted me to go quite so far back as that," he said. "But there's no disgrace in having been born, and I was born in the State of Vermont, pretty well up under the Canada line—so well up, in fact, that I came very near being an adoptive citizen; for I was bound to be an American of *some* sort, from the word Go! That was about—well, let me see!—pretty near sixty years ago: this is '75, and that was '20. Well, say I'm fifty-five years old; and I've *lived* 'em, too; not an hour of waste time about *me*, anywheres! I was born on a farm, and——"

"Worked in the fields summers and went to school winters: regulation thing?" Bartley cut in.

"Regulation thing," said Lapham, accepting this irreverent version of his history somewhat dryly.

"Parents poor, of course," suggested the journalist. "Any barefoot business? Early deprivations of any kind, that would encourage the youthful reader to go and do likewise? Orphan myself, you know," said Bartley, with a smile of cynical good comradery.

Lapham looked at him silently, and then said with quiet self-respect, "I guess if you see these things as a joke, my life wont inter*est* you."

"Oh, yes, it will," returned Bartley, unabashed. "You'll see; it'll come out all right." And in fact it did so, in the interview which Bartley printed.

"Mr. Lapham," he wrote, "passed rapidly over the story of his early life, its poverty and its hardships, sweetened, however, by the recollections of a devoted mother, and a father who, if somewhat her inferior in education, was no less ambitious for the advancement of his children. They were quiet, unpretentious people, religious, after the fashion of that time, and of sterling morality, and they taught their children the simple virtues of the Old Testament and Poor Richard's Almanac."

Bartley could not deny himself this gibe; but he trusted to Lapham's unliterary habit of mind for his security in making it, and most other people would consider it sincere reporter's rhetoric.

"You know," he explained to Lapham, "that we have to look at all these facts as material, and we get the habit of classifying them. Sometimes a leading question will draw out a whole line of facts that a man himself would never think of." He went on to put several queries, and it was from Lapham's answers that he generalized the history of his childhood. "Mr. Lapham, although he did not dwell on his boyish trials and struggles, spoke of them with deep feeling and an abiding sense of their reality." This was what he added in the interview, and by the time he had got Lapham past the period where risen Americans are all pathetically alike in their narrow circumstances, their sufferings, and their aspirations, he had beguiled him into forgetfulness of the check he had received, and had him talking again in perfect enjoyment of his autobiography.

"Yes, sir," said Lapham, in a strain which Bartley was careful not to interrupt again, "a man never sees all that his mother has been to him till it's too late to let her know that he sees it. Why, *my* mother—" he stopped. "It gives me a lump in the throat," he said apologetically, with an attempt at a laugh. Then he went on: "She was a little, frail thing, not bigger than a good-sized intermediate school-girl; but she did the whole work of a family of boys, and boarded the hired men besides. She cooked, swept, washed, ironed, made and mended from daylight till dark—and from dark till daylight, I was going to say; for I don't know how she got any time for sleep. But I suppose she did. She got time to go to church, and to teach us to read the Bible, and to misunderstand it in the old way. She was *good*. But it aint her on her knees in church that comes back to me so much like the sight of an angel, as her on her knees before me at night, washing my poor, dirty little feet, that I'd run bare in all day, and making me decent for bed. There were six of us boys; it seems to me we were all of a size; and she was just so careful with all of us. I can feel her hands on my feet yet!" Bartley looked at Lapham's No. 10 boots and softly whistled through his teeth. "We were patched all over; but we wa'n't ragged. *I* don't know how she got through it. She didn't seem to think it was anything; and I guess it was no more than my father expected of her. *He* worked like a horse in doors and out— up at daylight, feeding the stock, and groaning round all day with his rheumatism, but not stopping."

Bartley hid a yawn over his note-book, and probably, if he could have spoken his mind, he would have suggested to Lapham that he was not there for the purpose of interviewing his ancestry. But Bartley had learned to practice a patience with his victims which he did not always feel, and to feign an interest in their digressions till he could bring them up with a round turn.

"I tell you," said Lapham, jabbing the point of his penknife into the writing-pad on the desk before him, "when I hear women complaining nowadays that their lives are stunted and empty, I want to tell 'em about my *mother's* life. *I* could paint it out for 'em."

Bartley saw his opportunity at the word paint, and cut in. "And you say, Mr. Lapham, that you discovered this mineral paint on the old farm yourself?"

Lapham acquiesced in the return to business. "*I* didn't discover it," he said, scrupulously. "My father found it one day, in a hole made by a tree blowing down. There it was, laying loose in the pit, and sticking to the roots that had pulled up a big cake of dirt with 'em. *I* don't know what give him the idea that there was money in it, but he did think so from the start. I guess, if they'd had the word in those days, they'd considered him pretty much of a crank about it. He was trying as long as he lived to get that paint introduced; but he couldn't make it go. The country was so poor they couldn't paint their houses with anything; and father hadn't any facilities. It got to be a kind of joke with us; and I guess that paint-mine did as much as any one thing to make us boys clear out as soon as we got old enough. All my brothers went West and took up land; but I hung on to New England, and I hung on to the old farm, not because the paint-mine was on it, but because the old house was—and the graves. Well," said Lapham, as if unwilling to give himself too much credit, "there wouldn't been any market for it, anyway. You can go through that part of the State and buy more farms than you can shake a stick at for less money than it cost to build the barns on 'em. Of course, it's turned out a good thing. I keep the old house up in good shape, and we spend a month or so there every summer. M' wife kind of likes it, and the girls. Pretty place; sightly all round it. I've got a force of men at work there the whole time, and I've got a man and his wife in the house. Had a family meeting there last year; the whole connection from out West. There!" Lapham rose from his seat and took down a large warped, unframed photograph from the top of his desk, passing his hand over it, and then blowing vigorously upon it, to clear it of the dust. "There we are, *all* of us."

"I don't need to look twice at *you*," said Bartley, putting his finger on one of the heads.

"Well, that's Bill," said Lapham, with a gratified laugh. "He's about as brainy as any of us, I guess. He's one of their leading lawyers, out Dubuque way; been judge of the Common Pleas once or twice. That's his son—just graduated at Yale—alongside of my youngest girl. Good-looking chap, aint he?"

"*She's* a good-looking chap," said Bartley, with prompt irreverence. He hastened to add, at the frown which gathered between Lapham's eyes, "What a beautiful creature she is! What a lovely, refined, sensitive face! And she looks *good*, too."

"She *is* good," said the father, relenting.

"And, after all, that's about the best thing in a woman,"

said the potential reprobate. "If my wife wasn't good enough to keep both of us straight, I don't know what would become of me."

"My other daughter," said Lapham, indicating a girl with eyes that showed large, and a face of singular gravity. "Mis' Lapham," he continued, touching his wife's effigy with his little finger. "My brother Willard and his family—farm at Kankakee. Hazard Lapham and his wife—Baptist preacher in Kansas. Jim and his three girls—milling business at Minneapolis. Ben and his family—practicing medicine in Fort Wayne."

The figures were clustered in an irregular group in front of an old farm-house, whose original ugliness had been smartened up with a coat of Lapham's own paint and heightened with an incongruous piazza. The photographer had not been able to conceal the fact that they were all decent, honest-looking, sensible people, with a very fair share of beauty among the young girls; some of these were extremely pretty, in fact. He had put them into awkward and constrained attitudes, of course; and they all looked as if they had the instrument of torture which photographers call a head-rest under their occiputs. Here and there an elderly lady's face was a mere blur; and some of the younger children had twitched themselves into wavering shadows, and might have passed for spirit-photographs of their own little ghosts. It was the standard family-group photograph, in which most Americans have figured at some time or other; and Lapham exhibited a just satisfaction in it. "I presume," he mused aloud, as he put it back on top of his desk, "that we sha'n't soon get together again, all of us."

"And you say," suggested Bartley, "that you staid right along on the old place, when the rest cleared out West?"

"No-o-o-o," said Lapham, with a long, loud drawl; "I cleared out West too, first off. Went to Texas. Texas was all the cry in those days. But I got enough of the Lone Star in about three months, and I come back with the idea that Vermont was good enough for me."

"Fatted calf business?" queried Bartley, with his pencil poised above his note-book.

"I presume they were glad to see me," said Lapham, with

dignity. "Mother," he added gently, "died that winter, and I staid on with father. I buried him in the spring; and then I came down to a little place called Lumberville, and picked up what jobs I could get. I worked round at the saw-mills, and I was ostler awhile at the hotel—I always *did* like a good horse. Well, I *wa'n't* exactly a college graduate, and I went to school odd times. I got to driving the stage after while, and by and by I *bought* the stage and run the business myself. Then I hired the tavern-stand, and—well, to make a long story short, then I got married. Yes," said Lapham, with pride, "I married the school-teacher. We did pretty well with the hotel, and my wife she was always at me to paint up. Well, I put it off, and *put* it off, as a man will, till one day I give in, and says I, 'Well, *let's* paint up. Why, Pert,'— m'wife's name's Persis,—'I've got a whole paint-mine out on the farm. Let's go out and look at it.' So we drove out. I'd let the place for seventy-five dollars a year to a shif'less kind of a Kanuck that had come down that way; and I'd hated to see the house with him in it; but we drove out one Saturday afternoon, and we brought back about a bushel of the stuff in the buggy-seat, and I tried it crude, and I tried it burnt; and I liked it. M'wife she liked it, too. There wa'n't any painter by trade in the village, and I mixed it myself. Well, sir, that tavern's got that coat of paint on it yet, and it haint ever had any other, and I don't know's it ever will. Well, you know, I felt as if it was a kind of a harumscarum experiment, all the while; and I presume I shouldn't have tried it, but I kind of liked to do it because father'd always set so much store by his paint-mine. And when I'd got the first coat on,"—Lapham called it *cut*,—"I presume I must have set as much as half an hour, looking at it and thinking how he would have enjoyed it. I've had my share of luck in this world, and I aint a-going to complain on my *own* account, but I've noticed that most things get along too late for most people. It made me feel bad, and it took all the pride out my success with the paint, thinking of father. Seemed to me I might 'a' taken more interest in it when he was by to see; but we've got to live and learn. Well, I called my wife out,—I'd tried it on the back of the house, you know,—and she left her dishes,—I can remember she came out with her sleeves rolled up and set down alongside of me on the trestle,—and says I, 'What do you think, Persis?' And says she, 'Well, you haint got a paint-mine, Silas Lapham; you've got a *gold*-mine.' She always was just so enthusiastic about things. Well, it was just after two or three boats had burnt up out West, and a lot of lives lost, and there was a great cry about non-inflammable paint, and I guess that was what was in her mind. 'Well, I guess it aint any gold-mine, Persis,' says I; 'but I guess it *is* a paint-mine. I'm going to have it analyzed, and if it turns out what I think it is, I'm going to work it. And if father hadn't had such a long name, I should call it the Nehemiah Lapham Mineral Paint. But, any rate, every barrel of it, and every keg, and every bottle, and every package, big or little, has got to have the initials and figures N. L. f. 1835, S. L. t. 1855, on it. Father found it in 1835, and I tried it in 1855.'"

" 'S. T.—1860—X.' business," said Bartley.

"Yes," said Lapham, "but I hadn't heard of Plantation Bitters then, and I hadn't seen any of the fellow's labels. I set to work and I got a man down from Boston; and I carried him out to the farm, and he analyzed it—made a regular job of it. Well, sir, we built a kiln, and we kept a lot of that paint-ore red-hot for forty-eight hours; kept the Kanuck and his family up, firing. The presence of iron in the ore showed with the magnet from the start; and when he came to test it, he found out that it contained about seventy-five per cent. of the peroxide of iron."

Lapham pronounced the scientific phrases with a sort of reverent satisfaction, as if awed through his pride by a little lingering uncertainty as to what peroxide was. He accented it as if it were purr-ox-*eyed*; and Bartley had to get him to spell it.

"Well, and what then?" he asked, when he had made a note of the percentage.

"What then?" echoed Lapham. "Well, then, the fellow set down and told me, 'You've got a paint here,' says he, 'that's going to drive every other mineral paint out of the market. Why,' says he, 'it'll drive 'em right into the Back Bay!' Of course, *I* didn't know what the Back Bay was then; but I begun to open my eyes; thought I'd had 'em open before, but I guess I hadn't. Says he, 'That paint has got hydraulic cement in it, and it can stand fire and water and acids'; he named over a lot of things. Says he, 'It'll mix easily with linseed oil, whether you want to use it boiled or raw; and it aint a-going to crack nor fade any; and it aint a-going to scale. When you've got your arrangements for burning it properly, you're going to have a paint that will stand like the everlasting hills, in every climate under the sun.' Then he went into a lot of particulars, and I begun to think he was drawing a long bow, and meant to make his bill accordingly. So I kept pretty cool; but the fellow's bill didn't amount to anything hardly—said I might pay him after I got going; young chap, and pretty easy; but every word he said was gospel. Well, I aint a-going to brag up my paint; I don't suppose you came here to hear me blow——"

"Oh, yes, I did," said Bartley. "That's what I want. Tell all there is to tell, and I can boil it down afterward. A man can't make a greater mistake with a reporter than to hold back anything out of modesty. It may be the very thing we want to know. What we want is the whole truth, and more; we've got so much modesty of our own that we can temper almost any statement."

Lapham looked as if he did not quite like this tone, and he resumed a little more quietly. "Oh, there isn't really very much more to say about the paint itself. But you can use it for almost anything where a paint is wanted, inside or out. It'll prevent decay, and it'll stop it, after it's begun, in tin or iron. You can paint the inside of a cistern or a bath-tub with it, and water wont hurt it; and you can paint a steam-boiler with it, and heat wont. You can cover a brick wall with it, or a railroad car, or the deck of a steam-boat, and you can't do a better thing for either."

"Never tried it on the human conscience, I suppose," suggested Bartley.

"No, sir," replied Lapham, gravely. "I guess you want to keep that as free from paint as you can, if you want much use of it. I never cared to try any of it on mine." Lapham suddenly lifted his bulk up out of his swivel-chair, and led the way out into the wareroom beyond the office partitions, where rows and ranks of casks, barrels, and kegs stretched dimly back to the rear of the building, and diffused an honest, clean, wholesome smell of oil and paint. They were labeled and branded as containing each so many pounds of Lapham's Mineral Paint, and each bore the mystic devices, *N. L. f. 1835—S. L. t. 1855.* "There!" said Lapham, kicking one of the largest casks with the toe of his boot, "that's about our biggest package; and here," he added, laying his hand affectionately on the head of a very small keg, as if it were the head of a child, which it resembled in size, "this is the smallest. We used to put the paint on the market dry, but now we grind every ounce of it in oil—very best quality of linseed oil—and warrant it. We find it gives more satisfaction. Now, come back to the office, and I'll show you our fancy brands."

It was very cool and pleasant in that dim wareroom, with the rafters showing overhead in a cloudy perspective, and darkening away into the perpetual twilight at the rear of the building; and Bartley had found an agreeable seat on the head of a half-barrel of the paint, which he was reluctant to leave. But he rose and followed the vigorous lead of Lapham back to the office, where the sun of a long summer afternoon was just beginning to glare in at the window. On shelves opposite Lapham's desk were tin cans of various sizes, arranged in tapering cylinders, and showing, in a pattern diminishing toward the top, the same label borne by the casks and barrels in the wareroom. Lapham merely waved his hand toward these; but when Bartley, after a comprehensive glance at them, gave his whole attention to a row of clean, smooth jars, where different tints of the paint showed through flawless glass, Lapham smiled and waited in pleased expectation.

"Hello!" said Bartley. "That's pretty!"

"Yes," assented Lapham, "it is rather nice. It's our latest thing, and we find it takes with customers first-rate. Look here!" he said, taking down one of the jars, and pointing to the first line of the label.

Bartley read, "THE PERSIS BRAND," and then he looked at Lapham and smiled.

"After *her*, of course," said Lapham. "Got it up and put the first of it on the market her last birthday. She was pleased."

"I should think she might have been," said Bartley, while he made a note of the appearance of the jars.

"I don't know about your mentioning it in your interview," said Lapham, dubiously.

"That's going into the interview, Mr. Lapham, if nothing else does. Got a wife myself, and I know just how you feel." It was in the dawn of Bartley's prosperity on the "Boston Events," before his troubles with Marcia had seriously begun.

"Is that so?" said Lapham, recognizing with a smile another of the vast majority of married Americans; a few underrate their wives, but the rest think them supernal in intelligence and capability. "Well," he added, "we must see about that. Where'd you say you lived?"

"We don't live; we board. Mrs. Nash, 13 Canary Place."

"Well, we've all got to commence that way," suggested Lapham, consolingly.

"Yes; but we've about got to the end of our string. I expect to be under a roof of my own on Clover street before long. I suppose," said Bartley, returning to business, "that you didn't let the grass grow under your feet much after you found out what was in your paint-mine?"

"No, sir," answered Lapham, withdrawing his eyes from a long stare at Bartley, in which he had been seeing himself a young man again, in the first days of his married life. "I went right back to Lumberville and sold out everything, and put all I could rake and scrape together into paint. And Mis' Lapham was with me every time. No hang back about *her*. I tell you she was a *woman*!"

Bartley laughed. "That's the sort most of us marry."

"No, we don't," said Lapham. "Most of us marry silly little girls grown up to *look* like women."

"Well, I guess that's about so," assented Bartley, as if upon second thought.

"If it hadn't been for her," resumed Lapham, "the paint wouldn't have come to anything. I used to tell her it wa'n't the seventy-five per cent. of purr-ox-eyed of iron in the *ore* that made that paint go; it was the seventy-five per cent. of purr-ox-eyed of iron in *her*."

"Good!" cried Bartley. "I'll tell Marcia that."

"In less'n six months there wa'n't a board-fence, nor a bridge-girder, nor a dead wall, nor a barn, nor a face of rock in that whole region that didn't have 'Lapham's Mineral Paint—Specimen' on it in the three colors we begun by making." Bartley had taken his seat on the window-sill, and Lapham, standing before him, now put up his huge foot close to Bartley's thigh; neither of them minded that.

"I've heard a good deal of talk about that S. T.—1860—X. man, and the stove-blacking man, and the kidney-cure man, because they advertised in that way; and I've read articles about it in the papers; but I don't see where the joke comes in, exactly. So long as the people that own the barns and fences don't object, I don't see what the public has got to do with it. And I never saw anything so very sacred about a big rock, along a river or in a pasture that it wouldn't do to put mineral paint on it in three colors. I wish some of the people that talk about the landscape, and *write* about it, had to bu'st one of them rocks *out* of the landscape with powder, or dig a hole to bury it in, as we used to have to do up on the farm; I guess they'd sing a little different tune about the profanation of scenery. There aint any man enjoys a sightly bit of nature—a smooth piece of interval, with half a dozen good-sized wine-glass elms in it—more than *I* do. But I aint a-going to stand up for every big ugly rock I come across, as if we were all a set of dumn Druids. I say the landscape was made for man, and not man for the landscape."

"Yes," said Bartley, carelessly; "it was made for the stove-polish man and the kidney-cure man."

"It was made for any man that knows how to use it," Lapham returned, insensible to Bartley's irony. "Let 'em go and live with nature in the *winter*, up there along the Canada line, and I guess they'll get enough of her for one while. Well—where was I?"

"Decorating the landscape," said Bartley.

"Yes, sir; I started right there at Lumberville, and it give the place a start, too. You wont find it on the map now; and you wont find it in the gazetteer. I give a pretty good lump of money to build a town-hall, about five years back, and the first meeting they held in it they voted to change the name,—Lumberville *wa'n't* a name,—and it's Lapham now."

"Isn't it somewhere up in that region that they get the old Brandon red?" asked Bartley.

"We're about ninety miles from Brandon. The Brandon's a good paint," said Lapham, conscientiously. "Like to show you round up at our place some odd time, if you get off."

"Thanks. I should like it first-rate. Works there?"

"Yes; Works there. Well, sir, just about the time I got started, the war broke out; and it knocked my paint higher than a kite. The thing dropped perfectly dead. I presume that if I'd had any sort of influence, I might have got it into government hands, for gun-carriages and army-wagons, and may be on board government vessels. But I hadn't, and we had to face the music. I was about broken-hearted, but m'wife she looked at it another way. 'I guess it's a providence,' says she. 'Silas, I guess you've got a country that's worth fighting for. Any rate, you better go out and give it a chance.' Well, sir, I went. I knew she meant business. It might kill her to have me go, but it would kill her sure if I staid. She was one of that kind. I went. Her last words was, 'I'll look after the paint, Si.' We hadn't but just one little girl then,—boy'd died,—and Mis' Lapham's mother was livin' with us; and I knew if times *did* anyways come up again, m'wife'd know just what to do. So I went. I got through; and you can call me Colonel, if you want to. Feel there!" Lapham took Bartley's thumb and forefinger and put them on a bunch in his leg, just above the knee. "Anything hard?"

"Ball?"

Lapham nodded. "Gettysburg. That's my thermometer. If it wa'n't for that, I shouldn't know enough to come in when it rains."

Bartley laughed at a joke which betrayed some evidences of wear. "And when you came back, you took hold of the paint and rushed it."

"I took hold of the paint and rushed it—all I could," said Lapham, with less satisfaction than he had hitherto shown in his autobiography. "But I found that I had got back to another world. The day of small things was past, and I don't suppose it will ever come again in this country. My wife was at me all the time to take a partner—somebody with capital; but I couldn't seem to bear the idea. That paint was like my own blood to me. To have anybody else concerned in it was like—well, I don't know what. I saw it was the thing to do;

but I tried to fight it off, and I tried to joke it off. I used to say, 'Why didn't you take a partner yourself, Persis, while I was away?' And she'd say, 'Well, if you hadn't come back, I should, Si.' Always *did* like a joke about as well as any woman *I* ever saw. Well, I had to come to it. I took a partner." Lapham dropped the bold blue eyes with which he had been till now staring into Bartley's face, and the reporter knew that here was a place for asterisks in his interview, if interviews were faithful. "He had money enough," continued Lapham, with a suppressed sigh; "but he didn't know anything about paint. We hung on together for a year or two. And then we quit."

"And he had the experience," suggested Bartley, with companionable ease.

"I had some of the experience too," said Lapham, with a scowl; and Bartley divined, through the freemasonry of all who have sore places in their memories, that this was a point which he must not touch again.

"And since that, I suppose, you've played it alone."

"I've played it alone."

"You must ship some of this paint of yours to foreign countries, Colonel?" suggested Bartley, putting on a professional air.

"We ship it to all parts of the world. It goes to South America, lots of it. It goes to Australia, and it goes to India, and it goes to China, and it goes to the Cape of Good Hope. It'll stand any climate. Of course, we don't export these fancy brands much. They're for home use. But we're introducing them elsewhere. Here." Lapham pulled open a drawer, and showed Bartley a lot of labels in different languages—Spanish, French, German, and Italian. "We expect to do a good business in all those countries. We've got our agencies in Cadiz now, and in Paris, and in Hamburg, and in Leghorn. It's a thing that's bound to make its way. Yes, sir. Wherever a man has got a ship, or a bridge, or a dock, or a house, or a car, or a fence, or a pig-pen, anywhere in God's universe, to paint, that's the paint for him, and he's bound to find it out sooner or later. You pass a ton of that paint dry through a blast-furnace, and you'll get a quarter of a ton of pig-iron. I believe in my paint. I believe it's a blessing to the world.

When folks come in, and kind of smell round, and ask me what I mix it with, I always say, 'Well, in the first place, I mix it with *Faith*, and after that I grind it up with the best quality of boiled linseed oil that money will buy.'"

Lapham took out his watch and looked at it, and Bartley perceived that his audience was drawing to a close. "'F you ever want to run down and take a look at our Works, pass you over the road,"—he called it *rud*,—"and it sha'n't cost you a cent."

"Well, may be I shall, sometime," said Bartley. "Good afternoon, Colonel."

"Good afternoon. Or—hold on! My horse down there yet, William?" he called to the young man in the counting-room, who had taken his letter at the beginning of the interview. "Oh! All right!" he added, in response to something the young man said. "Can't I set you down somewhere, Mr. Hubbard? I've got my horse at the door, and I can drop you on my way home. I'm going to take Mis' Lapham to look at a house I'm driving piles for, down on the New Land."

"Don't care if I do," said Bartley.

Lapham put on a straw hat, gathered up some papers lying on his desk, pulled down its rolling cover, turned the key in it, and gave the papers to an extremely handsome young woman at one of the desks in the outer office. She was stylishly dressed, as Bartley saw, and her smooth, yellow hair was sculpturesquely waved over a low, white forehead. "Here," said Lapham, with the same prompt, gruff kindness that he had used in addressing the young man, "I want you should put these in shape, and give me a type-writer copy to-morrow."

"What an uncommonly pretty girl!" said Bartley, as they descended the rough stairway and found their way out to the street, past the dangling rope of a block and tackle wandering up into the cavernous darkness overhead.

"She does her work," said Lapham, shortly.

Bartley mounted to the left side of the open buggy standing at the curb-stone, and Lapham, gathering up the hitching-weight, slid it under the buggy-seat and mounted beside him.

"No chance to speed a horse here, of course," said Lapham,

while the horse with a spirited gentleness picked her way, with a high, long action, over the pavement of the street. The streets were all narrow, and most of them crooked, in that quarter of the town; but at the end of one the spars of a vessel penciled themselves delicately against the cool blue of the afternoon sky. The air was full of a smell pleasantly compounded of oakum, of leather, and of oil. It was not the busy season, and they met only two or three trucks heavily straggling toward the wharf with their long string teams; but the cobble-stones of the pavement were worn with the dint of ponderous wheels, and discolored with iron-rust from them; here and there, in wandering streaks over its surface, was the gray stain of the salt water with which the street had been sprinkled.

After an interval of some minutes, which both men spent in looking round the dashboard from opposite sides to watch the stride of the horse, Bartley said, with a light sigh, "I had a colt once down in Maine that stepped just like that mare."

"Well!" said Lapham, sympathetically recognizing the bond that this fact created between them. "Well, now, I tell you what you do. You let me come for you 'most any afternoon, now, and take you out over the Milldam, and speed this mare a little. I'd like to show you what this mare can do. Yes, I would."

"All right," answered Bartley; "I'll let you know my first day off."

"Good," cried Lapham.

"Kentucky?" queried Bartley.

"No, sir. I don't ride behind anything but Vermont; never did. Touch of Morgan, of course; but you can't have much Morgan in a horse if you want speed. Hambletonian mostly. Where'd you say you wanted to get out?"

"I guess you may put me down at the 'Events' office, just round the corner here. I've got to write up this interview while it's fresh."

"All right," said Lapham, impersonally assenting to Bartley's use of him as material.

He had not much to complain of in Bartley's treatment, unless it was the strain of extravagant compliment which it involved. But the flattery was mainly for the paint, whose vir-

tues Lapham did not believe could be overstated, and himself
and his history had been treated with as much respect as Bartley was capable of showing any one. He made a very picturesque thing of the discovery of the paint-mine. "Deep in the
heart of the virgin forests of Vermont, far up toward the line
of the Canadian snows, on a desolate mountain-side, where
an autumnal storm had done its wild work, and the great
trees, strewn hither and thither, bore witness to its violence,
Nehemiah Lapham discovered, just forty years ago, the mineral which the alchemy of his son's enterprise and energy has
transmuted into solid ingots of the most precious of metals.
The colossal fortune of Colonel Silas Lapham lay at the bottom of a hole which an uprooted tree had dug for him, and
which for many years remained a paint-mine of no more appreciable value than a soap-mine."

Here Bartley had not been able to forego another grin; but
he compensated for it by the high reverence with which he
spoke of Colonel Lapham's record during the war of the rebellion, and of the motives which impelled him to turn aside
from an enterprise in which his whole heart was engaged and
take part in the struggle. "The Colonel bears imbedded in the
muscle of his right leg a little memento of the period in the
shape of a minie-ball, which he jocularly referred to as his
thermometer, and which relieves him from the necessity of
reading 'The Probabilities' in his morning paper. This saves
him just so much time; and for a man who, as he said, has
not a moment of waste time on him anywhere, five minutes
a day are something in the course of a year. Simple, clear,
bold, and straightforward in mind and action, Colonel Silas
Lapham, with a prompt comprehensiveness and a never-fail-
ing business sagacity, is, in the best sense of that much-abused
term, one of nature's noblemen, to the last inch of his five
eleven and a half. His life affords an example of single-minded
application and unwavering perseverance which our young
business men would do well to emulate. There is nothing
showy or meretricious about the man. He believes in mineral
paint, and he puts his heart and soul into it. He makes it a
religion; though we would not imply that it *is* his religion.
Colonel Lapham is a regular attendant at the Rev. Dr. Langworthy's church. He subscribes liberally to the Associated

Charities, and no good object or worthy public enterprise fails to receive his support. He is not now actively in politics, and his paint is not partisan; but it is an open secret that he is, and always has been, a stanch Republican. Without violating the sanctities of private life, we cannot speak fully of various details which came out in the free and unembarrassed interview which Colonel Lapham accorded our representative. But we may say that the success of which he is justly proud he is also proud to attribute in great measure to the sympathy and energy of his wife—one of those women who, in whatever walk of life, seem born to honor the name of American Woman, and to redeem it from the national reproach of Daisy Millerism. Of Colonel Lapham's family, we will simply add that it consists of two young lady daughters.

"The subject of this very inadequate sketch is building a house on the water side of Beacon street, after designs by one of our leading architectural firms, which, when complete, will be one of the finest ornaments of that exclusive avenue. It will, we believe, be ready for the occupancy of the family sometime in the spring."

When Bartley had finished his article, which he did with a good deal of inward derision, he went home to Marcia, still smiling over the thought of Lapham, whose burly simplicity had peculiarly amused him.

"He regularly turned himself inside out to me," he said, as he sat describing his interview to Marcia.

"Then I know you could make something nice out of it," said his wife; "and that will please Mr. Witherby."

"Oh, yes, I've done pretty well; but I couldn't let myself loose on him the way I wanted to. Confound the limitations of decency, anyway! I should like to have told just what Colonel Lapham thought of landscape advertising in Colonel Lapham's own words. I'll tell you one thing, Marsh: he had a girl there at one of the desks that you wouldn't let *me* have within gunshot of *my* office. Pretty? It aint any name for it!" Marcia's eyes began to blaze, and Bartley broke out into a laugh, in which he arrested himself at sight of a formidable parcel in the corner of the room.

"Hello! What's that?"

"Why, I don't know what it is," replied Marcia, tremulously. "A man brought it just before you came in, and I didn't like to open it."

"Think it was some kind of infernal machine?" asked Bartley, getting down on his knees to examine the package. "*Mrs. B. Hubbard*, heigh?" He cut the heavy hemp string with his penknife. "We must look into this thing. I should like to know who's sending packages to Mrs. Hubbard in my absence." He unfolded the wrappings of paper, growing softer and finer inward, and presently pulled out a handsome square glass jar, through which a crimson mass showed richly. "The Persis Brand!" he yelled. "I knew it!"

"Oh, what is it, Bartley?" quavered Marcia. Then, courageously drawing a little nearer: "Is it some kind of jam?" she implored.

"Jam? No!" roared Bartley. "It's *paint*! It's mineral paint—Lapham's paint!"

"Paint?" echoed Marcia, as she stood over him while he stripped their wrappings from the jars which showed the dark blue, dark green, light brown, dark brown, and black, with the dark crimson, forming the gamut of color of the Lapham paint. "Don't *tell* me it's paint that *I* can use, Bartley!"

"Well, I shouldn't advise you to use much of it—all at once," replied her husband. "But it's paint that you can use in moderation."

Marcia cast her arms round his neck and kissed him. "O Bartley, I think I'm the happiest girl in the world! I was just wondering what I should do. There are places in that Clover street house that need touching up so dreadfully. I shall be very careful. You needn't be afraid I shall overdo. But this just saves my life. Did you *buy* it, Bartley? You know we couldn't afford it, and you oughtn't to have done it! And what does the Persis Brand mean?"

"Buy it?" cried Bartley. "No! The old fool's sent it to you as a present. You'd better wait for the facts before you pitch into me for extravagance, Marcia. Persis is the name of his wife; and he named it after her because it's his finest brand. You'll see it in my interview. Put it on the market her last birthday for a surprise to her."

"What old fool?" faltered Marcia.

"Why, Lapham—the mineral paint man."

"Oh, what a good man!" sighed Marcia from the bottom of her soul. "Bartley! you *wont* make fun of him, as you do of some of those people? *Will* you?"

"Nothing that *he*'ll ever find out," said Bartley, getting up and brushing off the carpet-lint from his knees.

II

AFTER dropping Bartley Hubbard at the "Events" building, Lapham drove on down Washington street to Nankeen Square at the South End, where he had lived ever since the mistaken movement of society in that direction ceased. He had not built, but had bought very cheap of a terrified gentleman of good extraction who discovered too late that the South End was not the thing, and who in the eagerness of his flight to the Back Bay threw in his carpets and shades for almost nothing. Mrs. Lapham was even better satisfied with their bargain than the Colonel himself, and they had lived in Nankeen Square for twelve years. They had seen the saplings planted in the pretty oval round which the houses were built flourish up into sturdy young trees, and their two little girls in the same period had grown into young ladies; the Colonel's tough frame had expanded into the bulk which Bartley's interview indicated; and Mrs. Lapham, while keeping a more youthful outline, showed the sharp print of the crow's-foot at the corners of her motherly eyes, and certain slight creases in her wholesome cheeks. The fact that they lived in an unfashionable neighborhood was something that they had never been made to feel to their personal disadvantage, and they had hardly known it till the summer before this story opens, when Mrs. Lapham and her daughter Irene had met some other Bostonians far from Boston, who made it memorable. They were people whom chance had brought for the time under a singular obligation to the Lapham ladies, and they were gratefully recognizant of it. They had ventured—a mother and two daughters—as far as a rather wild little Canadian watering-place on the St. Lawrence, below Quebec, and had arrived some days before their son and brother was expected to join them. Two of their trunks had gone astray, and on the night of their arrival the mother was taken violently ill. Mrs. Lapham came to their help, with her skill as nurse, and with the abundance of her own and her daughter's wardrobe, and a profuse, single-hearted kindness. When a doctor could be got at, he said that but for Mrs. Lapham's timely care, the lady would hardly have lived. He was a very effusive little Frenchman, and fancied he was saying something very pleasant to everybody.

A certain intimacy inevitably followed, and when the son came he was even more grateful than the others. Mrs. Lapham could not quite understand why he should be as attentive to her as to Irene; but she compared him with other young men about the place, and thought him nicer than any of them. She had not the means of a wider comparison; for in Boston, with all her husband's prosperity, they had not had a social life. Their first years there were given to careful getting on Lapham's part, and careful saving on his wife's. Suddenly the money began to come so abundantly that she need not save; and then they did not know what to do with it. A certain amount could be spent on horses, and Lapham spent it; his wife spent on rich and rather ugly clothes and a luxury of household appointments. Lapham had not yet reached the picture-buying stage of the rich man's development, but they decorated their house with the costliest and most abominable frescoes; they went upon journeys, and lavished upon cars and hotels; they gave with both hands to their church and to all the charities it brought them acquainted with; but they did not know how to spend on society. Up to a certain period Mrs. Lapham had the ladies of her neighborhood in to tea, as her mother had done in the country in her younger days. Lapham's idea of hospitality was still to bring a heavy-buying customer home to pot-luck; neither of them imagined dinners.

Their two girls had gone to the public schools, where they had not got on as fast as some of the other girls; so that they were a year behind in graduating from the grammar-school, where Lapham thought that they had got education enough. His wife was of a different mind; she would have liked them to go to some private school for their finishing. But Irene did not care for study; she preferred housekeeping, and both the sisters were afraid of being snubbed by the other girls, who were of a different sort from the girls of the grammar-school; these were mostly from the parks and squares, like themselves. It ended in their going part of a year. But the elder had an odd taste of her own for reading, and she took some private lessons, and read books out of the circulating library; the whole family were amazed at the number she read, and rather proud of it.

They were not girls who embroidered or abandoned themselves to needle-work. Irene spent her abundant leisure in shopping for herself and her mother, of whom both daughters made a kind of idol, buying her caps and laces out of their pin-money, and getting her dresses far beyond her capacity to wear. Irene dressed herself very stylishly, and spent hours on her toilet every day. Her sister had a simpler taste, and, if she had done altogether as she liked, might even have slighted dress. They all three took long naps every day, and sat hours together minutely discussing what they saw out of the window. In her self-guided search for self-improvement, the elder sister went to many church lectures on a vast variety of secular subjects, and usually came home with a comic account of them, and that made more matter of talk for the whole family. She could make fun of nearly everything; Irene complained that she scared away the young men whom they got acquainted with at the dancing-school sociables. They were, perhaps, not the wisest young men.

The girls had learned to dance at Papanti's; but they had not belonged to the private classes. They did not even know of them, and a great gulf divided them from those who did. Their father did not like company, except such as came informally in their way; and their mother had remained too rustic to know how to attract it in the sophisticated city fashion. None of them had grasped the idea of European travel; but they had gone about to mountain and sea-side resorts, the mother and the two girls, where they witnessed the spectacle which such resorts present throughout New England, of multitudes of girls, lovely, accomplished, exquisitely dressed, humbly glad of the presence of any sort of young man; but the Laphams had no skill or courage to make themselves noticed, far less courted by the solitary invalid, or clergyman, or artist. They lurked helplessly about in the hotel parlors, looking on and not knowing how to put themselves forward. Perhaps they did not care a great deal to do so. They had not a conceit of themselves, but a sort of content in their own ways that one may notice in certain families. The very strength of their mutual affection was a barrier to worldly knowledge; they dressed for one another; they equipped their house for their own satisfaction; they lived richly to themselves, not because they were selfish, but because they did not know how to do otherwise. The elder daughter did not care for society, apparently. The younger, who was but three years younger, was not yet quite old enough to be ambitious of it. With all her wonderful beauty, she had an innocence almost vegetable. When her beauty, which in its immaturity was crude and harsh, suddenly ripened, she bloomed and glowed with the unconsciousness of a flower; she not merely did not feel herself admired, but hardly knew herself discovered. If she dressed well, perhaps too well, it was because she had the instinct of dress; but till she met this young man who was so nice to her at Baie St. Joan, she had scarcely lived a detached, individual life, so wholly had she depended on her mother and her sister for her opinions, almost her sensations. She took account of everything he did and said, pondering it, and trying to make out exactly what he meant, to the inflection of a syllable, the slightest movement or gesture. In this way she began for the first time to form ideas which she had not derived from her family, and they were none the less her own because they were often mistaken.

Some of the things that he partly said, partly looked, she reported to her mother, and they talked them over, as they did everything relating to these new acquaintances, and wrought them into the novel point of view which they were acquiring. When Mrs. Lapham returned home, she submitted all the accumulated facts of the case, and all her own conjectures, to her husband, and canvassed them anew.

At first he was disposed to regard the whole affair as of small importance, and she had to insist a little beyond her own convictions in order to counteract his indifference.

"Well, I can tell you," she said, "that if you think they were not the nicest people *you* ever saw, you're mightily mistaken. They had about the best manners; and they had been everywhere, and knew everything. I declare it made me feel as if we had always lived in the backwoods. I don't know but the mother and the daughters would have *let* you feel so a little, if they'd showed out all they thought; but they never did; and the son—well, I can't express it, Silas! But that young man had about perfect ways."

"Seem struck up on Irene?" asked the Colonel.

"How can *I* tell? He seemed just about as much struck up on me. Anyway, he paid me as much attention as he did her. Perhaps it's more the way, now, to notice the mother than it used to be."

Lapham ventured no conjecture, but asked, as he had asked already, who the people were.

Mrs. Lapham repeated their name. Lapham nodded his head. "Do you know them? What business is he in?"

"I guess he aint in anything," said Lapham.

"They were very nice," said Mrs. Lapham, impartially.

"Well, they'd ought to be," returned the Colonel. "Never done anything else."

"They didn't seem stuck up," urged his wife.

"They'd no need to—with you. I could buy him and sell him, twice over."

This answer satisfied Mrs. Lapham rather with the fact than with her husband. "Well, I guess I wouldn't brag, Silas," she said.

In the winter the ladies of this family, who returned to town very late, came to call on Mrs. Lapham. They were again very polite. But the mother let drop, in apology for their calling almost at nightfall, that the coachman had not known the way exactly.

"Nearly all our friends are on the New Land or on the Hill."

There was a barb in this that rankled after the ladies had gone; and on comparing notes with her daughter, Mrs. Lapham found that a barb had been left to rankle in her mind also.

"They said they had never been in this part of the town before."

Upon a strict search of her memory, Irene could not report that the fact had been stated with anything like insinuation, but it was that which gave it a more penetrating effect.

"Oh, well, of course," said Lapham, to whom these facts

were referred. "Those sort of people haven't got much business up our way, and they don't come. It's a fair thing all round. We don't trouble the Hill or the New Land much."

"We know where they are," suggested his wife, thoughtfully.

"Yes," assented the Colonel. "*I* know where they are. I've got a lot of land over on the Back Bay."

"You have?" eagerly demanded his wife.

"Want me to build on it?" he asked in reply, with a quizzical smile.

"I guess we can get along here for a while."

This was at night. In the morning Mrs. Lapham said:

"I suppose we ought to do the best we can for the children, in every way."

"I supposed we always had," replied her husband.

"Yes, we have, according to our light."

"Have you got some new light?"

"I don't know as it's light. But if the girls are going to keep on living in Boston and marry here, I presume we ought to try to get them into society, some way; or ought to do something."

"Well, who's ever done more for their children than we have?" demanded Lapham, with a pang at the thought that he could possibly have been outdone. "Don't they have everything they want? Don't they dress just as you say? Don't you go everywhere with 'em? Is there ever anything going on that's worth while that they don't see it or hear it? *I* don't know what you mean. Why don't you get them into society? There's money enough!"

"There's got to be something besides money, I guess," said Mrs. Lapham, with a hopeless sigh. "I presume we didn't go to work just the right way about their schooling. We ought to have got them into some school where they'd have got acquainted with city girls—girls who could help them along. Nearly everybody at Miss Smillie's was from somewhere else."

"Well, it's pretty late to think about that now," grumbled Lapham.

"And we've always gone our own way, and not looked out for the future. We ought to have gone out more, and had people come to the house. Nobody comes."

"Well, is that my fault? I guess nobody ever makes people welcomer."

"We ought to have invited company more."

"Why don't you do it now? If it's for the girls, I don't care if you have the house full all the while."

Mrs. Lapham was forced to a confession full of humiliation. "I don't know who to ask."

"Well, you can't expect me to tell you."

"No; we're both country people, and we've kept our country ways, and we don't, either of us, know what to do. You've had to work so hard, and your luck was so long coming, and then it came with such a rush, that we haven't had any chance to learn what to do with it. It's just the same with Irene's looks; I didn't expect she was ever going to have any, she *was* such a plain child, and, all at once, she's blazed out this way. As long as it was Pen that didn't seem to care for society, I didn't give much mind to it. But I can see it's going to be different with Irene. I don't believe but what we're in the wrong neighborhood."

"Well," said the Colonel, "there aint a prettier lot on the Back Bay than mine. It's on the water side of Beacon, and it's twenty-eight feet wide and a hundred and fifty deep. Let's build on it."

Mrs. Lapham was silent awhile. "No," she said finally; "we've always got along well enough here, and I guess we better stay."

At breakfast she said, casually: "Girls, how would you like to have your father build on the New Land?"

The girls said they did not know. It was more convenient to the horse-cars where they were.

Mrs. Lapham stole a look of relief at her husband, and nothing more was said of the matter.

The mother of the family who had called upon Mrs. Lapham brought her husband's cards, and when Mrs. Lapham returned the visit she was in some trouble about the proper form of acknowledging the civility. The Colonel had no card but a business card, which advertised the principal depot and the several agencies of the mineral paint; and Mrs. Lapham doubted, till she wished to goodness that she had never seen nor heard of those people, whether to ignore her husband in the transaction altogether, or to write his name on her own card. She decided finally upon this measure, and she had the relief of not finding the family at home. As far as she could judge, Irene seemed to suffer a little disappointment from the fact.

For several months there was no communication between the families. Then there came to Nankeen Square a litho-graphed circular from the people on the Hill, signed in ink by the mother, and affording Mrs. Lapham an opportunity to subscribe for a charity of undeniable merit and acceptability. She submitted it to her husband, who promptly drew a check for five hundred dollars.

She tore it in two. "I will take a check for a hundred, Silas," she said.

"Why?" he asked, looking up guiltily at her.

"Because a hundred is enough; and I don't want to show off before them."

"Oh, I thought may be you did. Well, Pert," he added, having satisfied human nature by the preliminary thrust, "I guess you're about right. When do you want I should begin to build on Beacon street?" He handed her the new check, where she stood over him, and then leaned back in his chair and looked up at her.

"I don't want you should begin at all. What do you mean, Silas?" She rested against the side of his desk.

"Well, I don't know as I mean anything. But shouldn't you like to build? Everybody builds, at least once in a life-time."

"Where is your lot? They say it's unhealthy over there."

Up to a certain point in their prosperity Mrs. Lapham had kept strict account of all her husband's affairs; but as they expanded, and ceased to be of the retail nature with which women successfully grapple, the intimate knowledge of them made her nervous. There was a period in which she felt that they were being ruined, but the crash had not come; and, since his great success, she had abandoned herself to a blind confidence in her husband's judgment, which she had hitherto felt needed her revision. He came and went, day by day, un-questioned. He bought and sold and got gain. She knew that he would tell her if ever things went wrong, and he knew that she would ask him whenever she was anxious.

"It ain't unhealthy where I've bought," said Lapham, rather

enjoying her insinuation. "I looked after that when I was
trading; and I guess it's about as healthy on the Back Bay as
it is here, anyway. I got that lot for *you*, Pert; I thought you'd
want to build on the Back Bay some day."

"Pshaw!" said Mrs. Lapham, deeply pleased inwardly, but
not going to show it, as she would have said. "I guess you
want to build there yourself." She insensibly got a little nearer
to her husband. They liked to talk to each other in that blunt
way; it is the New England way of expressing perfect confidence and tenderness.

"Well, I guess I do," said Lapham, not insisting upon the
unselfish view of the matter. "I always did like the water side
of Beacon. There aint a sightlier place in the world for a
house. And some day there's bound to be a drive-way all
along behind them houses, between them and the water, and
then a lot there is going to be worth the gold that will cover
it—*coin*. I've had offers for that lot, Pert, twice over what I
give for it. Yes, I *have*. Don't you want to ride over there
some afternoon with me and see it?"

"I'm satisfied where we be, Si," said Mrs. Lapham, recurring to the parlance of her youth in her pathos at her husband's kindness. She sighed anxiously, for she felt the trouble
a woman knows in view of any great change. They had often
talked of altering over the house in which they lived, but they
had never come to it; and they had often talked of building,
but it had always been a house in the country that they had
thought of. "I wish you had sold that lot."

"I haint," said the Colonel, briefly

"I don't know as I feel much like changing our way of
living."

"Guess we could live there pretty much as we live here.
There's all kinds of people on Beacon street; you mustn't
think they're all big-bugs. I know one party that lives in a
house he built to sell, and his wife don't keep any girl. You
can have just as much style there as you want, or just as little.
I guess we live as well as most of 'em now, and set as good a
table. And if you come to style, I don't know as anybody has
got more of a right to put it on than what we have."

"Well, I don't want to build on Beacon street, Si," said
Mrs. Lapham, gently.

"Just as you please, Persis. I aint in any hurry to leave."

Mrs. Lapham stood flapping the check which she held in her right hand against the edge of her left.

The Colonel still sat looking up at her face, and watching the effect of the poison of ambition which he had artfully instilled into her mind.

She sighed again—a yielding sigh. "What are you going to do this afternoon?"

"I'm going to take a turn on the Brighton road," said the Colonel.

"I don't believe but what I should like to go along," said his wife.

"All right. You haint ever rode behind that mare yet, Pert, and I want you should see me let her out once. They say the snow's all packed down already, and the going is A 1."

At four o'clock in the afternoon, with a cold, red winter sunset before them, the Colonel and his wife were driving slowly down Beacon street in the light, high-seated cutter, where, as he said, they were a pretty tight fit. He was holding the mare in till the time came to speed her, and the mare was springily jolting over the snow, looking intelligently from side to side, and cocking this ear and that, while from her nostrils, her head tossing easily, she blew quick, irregular whiffs of steam.

"Gay, aint she?" proudly suggested the Colonel.

"She *is* gay," assented his wife.

They met swiftly dashing sleighs, and let them pass on either hand, down the beautiful avenue narrowing with an admirably even skyline in the perspective. They were not in a hurry. The mare jounced easily along, and they talked of the different houses on either side of the way. They had a crude taste in architecture, and they admired the worst. There were women's faces at many of the handsome windows, and once in a while a young man on the pavement caught his hat suddenly from his head, and bowed in response to some salutation from within.

"I don't think our girls would look very bad behind one of those big panes," said the Colonel.

"No," said his wife, dreamily.

"Where's the *young* man? Did he come with them?"

"No; he was to spend the winter with a friend of his that has a ranch in Texas. I guess he's got to do something."

"Yes; gentlemaning as a profession has got to play out in a generation or two."

Neither of them spoke of the lot, though Lapham knew perfectly well what his wife had come with him for, and she was aware that he knew it. The time came when he brought the mare down to a walk, and then slowed up almost to a stop, while they both turned their heads to the right and looked at the vacant lot, through which showed the frozen stretch of the Back Bay, a section of the Long Bridge, and the roofs and smoke-stacks of Charlestown.

"Yes, it's sightly," said Mrs. Lapham, lifting her hand from the reins, on which she had unconsciously laid it.

Lapham said nothing, but he let the mare out a little.

The sleighs and cutters were thickening round them. On the Milldam it became difficult to restrict the mare to the long, slow trot into which he let her break. The beautiful landscape widened to right and left of them, with the sunset redder and redder, over the low, irregular hills before them. They crossed the Milldam into Longwood; and here, from the crest of the first upland, stretched two endless lines, in which thousands of cutters went and came. Some of the drivers were already speeding their horses, and these shot to and fro on inner lines, between the slowly moving vehicles on either side of the road. Here and there a burly mounted policeman, bulging over the pommel of his McClellan saddle, jolted by, silently gesturing and directing the course, and keeping it all under the eye of the law. It was what Bartley Hubbard called "a carnival of fashion and gayety on the Brighton road," in his account of it. But most of the people in those elegant sleighs and cutters had so little the air of the great world that one knowing it at all must have wondered where they and their money came from; and the gayety of the men, at least, was expressed, like that of Colonel Lapham, in a grim, almost fierce, alertness; the women wore an air of courageous apprehension. At a certain point the Colonel said, "I'm going to let her out, Pert," and he lifted and then dropped the reins lightly on the mare's back.

She understood the signal, and, as an admirer said, "she

laid down to her work." Nothing in the immutable iron of Lapham's face betrayed his sense of triumph, as the mare left everything behind her on the road. Mrs. Lapham, if she felt fear, was too busy holding her flying wraps about her, and shielding her face from the scud of ice flung from the mare's heels, to betray it; except for the rush of her feet, the mare was as silent as the people behind her; the muscles of her back and thighs worked more and more swiftly, like some mechanism responding to an alien force, and she shot to the end of the course, grazing a hundred encountered and rival sledges in her passage, but unmolested by the policemen, who probably saw that the mare and the Colonel knew what they were about, and, at any rate, were not the sort of men to interfere with trotting like that. At the end of the heat Lapham drew her in, and turned off on a side street into Brookline.

"Tell you what, Pert," he said, as if they had been quietly jogging along, with time for uninterrupted thought since he last spoke, "I've about made up my mind to build on that lot."

"All right, Silas," said Mrs. Lapham; "I suppose you know what you're about. Don't build on it for me, that's all."

When she stood in the hall at home, taking off her things, she said to the girls, who were helping her, "Some day your father will get killed with that mare."

"Did he speed her?" asked Penelope, the elder. She was named after her grandmother, who had in her turn inherited from another ancestress the name of the Homeric matron whose peculiar merits won her a place even among the Puritan Faiths, Hopes, Temperances, and Prudences. Penelope was the girl whose odd, serious face had struck Bartley Hubbard in the photograph of the family group Lapham showed him on the day of the interview. Her large eyes, like her hair, were brown; they had the peculiar look of near-sighted eyes which is called mooning; her complexion was of a dark pallor.

Her mother did not reply to a question which might be considered already answered. "He says he's going to build on that lot of his," she next remarked, unwinding the long veil which she had tied round her neck to hold her bonnet on. She put her hat and cloak on the hall table, to be carried upstairs later, and they all went in to tea: creamed oysters, birds, hot biscuit, two kinds of cake, and dishes of stewed and canned fruit and honey. The women dined alone at one, and the Colonel at the same hour down-town. But he liked a good hot meal when he got home in the evening. The house flared with gas, and the Colonel, before he sat down, went about shutting the registers, through which a welding heat came voluming up from the furnace.

"I'll be the death of that darkey *yet*," he said, "if he don't stop making on such a fire. The only way to get any comfort out of your furnace is to take care of it yourself."

"Well," answered his wife from behind the tea-pot, as he sat down at table with this threat, "there's nothing to prevent you, Si. And you can shovel the snow, too, if you want to—till you get over to Beacon street, anyway."

"I guess I can keep my own sidewalk on Beacon street clean, if I take the notion."

"I should like to see you at it," retorted his wife.

"Well, you keep a sharp lookout, and may be you will."

Their taunts were really expressions of affectionate pride in each other. They liked to have it, give and take, that way, as they would have said, right along.

"A man can be a man on Beacon street as well as anywhere, I guess."

"Well, I'll do the wash, as I used to in Lumberville," said Mrs. Lapham. "I presume you'll let me have set tubs, Si. You know I aint so young, any more." She passed Irene a cup of Oolong tea,—none of them had a sufficiently cultivated palate for Souchong,—and the girl handed it to her father.

"Papa," she asked, "you don't really mean that you are going to build over there?"

"Don't I? You wait and see," said the Colonel, stirring his tea.

"I don't believe you do," pursued the girl.

"Is that so? I presume you'd hate to have me. Your mother does." He said *doos*, of course.

Penelope took the word. "I go in for it. I don't see any use in not enjoying money, if you've got it *to* enjoy. That's what it's for, I suppose; though you mightn't always think so." She had a slow, quaint way of talking, that seemed a pleasant personal modification of some ancestral Yankee drawl, and her voice was low and cozy, and so far from being nasal that it was a little hoarse.

"I guess the ayes has it, Pen," said her father. "How would it do to let Irene and your mother stick in the old place here, and us go into the new house?" At times the Colonel's grammar failed him.

The matter dropped, and the Laphams lived on as before, with joking recurrences to the house on the water side of Beacon. The Colonel seemed less in earnest than any of them about it; but that was his way, his girls said; you never could tell when he really meant a thing.

III

OWARD the end of the winter there came a newspaper addressed to Miss Irene Lapham; it proved to be a Texas newspaper, with a complimentary account of the ranch of the Hon. Loring G. Stanton, which the representative of the journal had visited.

"It must be his friend," said Mrs. Lapham, to whom her daughter brought the paper; "the one he's staying with."

The girl did not say anything, but she carried the paper to her room, where she scanned every line of it for another name. She did not find it, but she cut the notice out and stuck it into the side of her mirror, where she could read it every morning when she brushed her hair, and the last thing at night when she looked at herself in the glass just before turning off the gas. Her sister often read it aloud, standing behind her and rendering it with elocutionary effects.

"The first time I ever heard of a love-letter in the form of a puff to a cattle-ranch. But perhaps that's the style on the Hill."

Mrs. Lapham told her husband of the arrival of the paper, treating the fact with an importance that he refused to see in it.

"How do you know the fellow sent it, anyway?" he demanded.

"Oh, I know he did."

"I don't see why he couldn't write to 'Rene, if he really meant anything."

"Well, I guess that wouldn't be their way," said Mrs. Lapham; she did not at all know what their way would be.

When the spring opened Colonel Lapham showed that he had been in earnest about building on the New Land. His idea of a house was a brown-stone front, four stories high, and a French roof with an air-chamber above. Inside, there was to be a reception-room on the street and a dining-room back. The parlors were to be on the second floor, and finished in black walnut or parti-colored paint. The chambers were to be on the three floors above, front and rear, with side rooms over the front door. Black walnut was to be used everywhere except in the attic, which was to be painted and grained to look like black walnut. The whole was to be very high-studded, and there were to be handsome cornices and elaborate center-pieces throughout, except, again, in the attic.

These ideas he had formed from the inspection of many new buildings which he had seen going up, and which he had a passion for looking into. He was confirmed in his ideas by a master-builder who had put up a great many houses on the Back Bay as a speculation, and who told him that if he wanted to have a house in the style, that was the way to have it.

The beginnings of the process by which Lapham escaped from the master-builder and ended in the hands of an architect are so obscure that it would be almost impossible to trace them. But it all happened, and Lapham promptly developed his ideas of black-walnut finish, high-studding, and cornices. The architect was able to conceal the shudder which they must have sent through him. He was skillful, as nearly all architects are, in playing upon that simple instrument Man. He began to touch Colonel Lapham's stops.

"Oh, certainly, have the parlors high-studded. But you've seen some of those pretty, old-fashioned country-houses, haven't you, where the entrance-story is very low-studded?"

"Yes," Lapham assented.

"Well, don't you think something of that kind would have a very nice effect? Have the entrance-story low-studded, and your parlors on the next floor as high as you please. Put your little reception-room here beside the door, and get the whole width of your house frontage for a square hall, and an easy low-tread staircase running up three sides of it. I'm sure Mrs. Lapham would find it much pleasanter." The architect caught toward him a scrap of paper lying on the table at which they were sitting and sketched his idea. "Then have your dining-room behind the hall, looking on the water."

He glanced at Mrs. Lapham, who said, "Of course," and the architect went on:

"That gets you rid of one of those long, straight, ugly staircases,"—until that moment Lapham had thought a long, straight staircase the chief ornament of a house,—"and gives you an effect of amplitude and space."

"That's so!" said Mrs. Lapham. Her husband merely made a noise in his throat.

"Then, were you thinking of having your parlors together, connected by folding doors?" asked the architect deferentially.

"Yes, of course," said Lapham. "They're always so, aint they?"

"Well, nearly," said the architect. "I was wondering how would it do to make one large square room at the front, taking the whole breadth of the house, and, with this hall-space between, have a music-room back for the young ladies?"

Lapham looked helplessly at his wife, whose quicker apprehension had followed the architect's pencil with instant sympathy. "First-rate!" she cried.

The Colonel gave way. "I guess that would do. It'll be kind of odd, wont it?"

"Well, I don't know," said the architect. "Not so odd, I hope, as the other thing will be a few years from now." He went on to plan the rest of the house, and he showed himself such a master in regard to all the practical details that Mrs. Lapham began to feel a motherly affection for the young man, and her husband could not deny in his heart that the fellow seemed to understand his business. He stopped walking about the room, as he had begun to do when the architect and Mrs. Lapham entered into the particulars of closets, drainage, kitchen arrangements, and all that, and came back to the table. "I presume," he said, "you'll have the drawing-room finished in black walnut?"

"Well, yes," replied the architect, "if you like. But some less expensive wood can be made just as effective with paint. Of course you can paint black walnut, too."

"Paint it?" gasped the Colonel.

"Yes," said the architect quietly. "White, or a little off white."

Lapham dropped the plan he had picked up from the table. His wife made a little move toward him of consolation or support.

"Of course," resumed the architect, "I know there has been a great craze for black walnut. But it's an ugly wood; and for a drawing-room there is really nothing like white paint. We should want to introduce a little gold here and there. Perhaps we might run a painted frieze round under the cornice—garlands of roses on a gold ground; it would tell wonderfully in a white room."

The Colonel returned less courageously to the charge. "I presume you'll want Eastlake mantel-shelves and tiles?" He meant this for a sarcastic thrust at a prevailing foible of the profession.

"Well, no," gently answered the architect. "I was thinking perhaps a white marble chimney-piece, treated in the refined Empire style, would be the thing for that room."

"White marble!" exclaimed the Colonel. "I thought that had gone out long ago."

"Really beautiful things can't go out. They may disappear for a little while, but they must come back. It's only the ugly things that stay out after they've had their day."

Lapham could only venture very modestly, "Hard-wood floors?"

"In the music-room, of course," consented the architect.

"And in the drawing-room?"

"Carpet. Some sort of moquette, I should say. But I should prefer to consult Mrs. Lapham's taste in that matter."

"And in the other rooms?"

"Oh, carpets, of course."

"And what about the stairs?"

"Carpet. And I should have the rail and banisters white—banisters turned or twisted."

The Colonel said under his breath, "Well, I'm dumned!" but he gave no utterance to his astonishment in the architect's presence. When he went at last,—the session did not end till eleven o'clock,—Lapham said, "Well, Pert, I guess that fellow's fifty years behind, or ten years ahead. I wonder what the Ongpeer style is?"

"I don't know. I hated to ask. But he seemed to understand what he was talking about. I declare, he knows what a woman wants in a house better than she does herself."

"And a man's simply nowhere in comparison," said Lapham. But he respected a fellow who could beat him at every point, and have a reason ready, as this architect had; and when he recovered from the daze into which the complete upheaval of all his preconceived notions had left him, he was in a fit state to swear by the architect. It seemed to him that he had discovered the fellow (as he always called him) and owned him now, and the fellow did nothing to disturb this impression. He entered into that brief but intense intimacy with the Laphams which the sympathetic architect holds with his clients. He was privy to all their differences of opinion and all their disputes about the house. He knew just where to insist upon his own ideas, and where to yield. He was really building several other houses, but he gave the Laphams the impression that he was doing none but theirs.

The work was not begun till the frost was thoroughly out of the ground, which that year was not before the end of April. Even then it did not proceed very rapidly. Lapham said they might as well take their time to it; if they got the walls up and the thing closed in before the snow flew, they could be working at it all winter. It was found necessary to dig for the kitchen; at that point the original salt marsh lay near the surface, and before they began to put in the piles for the foundation they had to pump. The neighborhood smelt like the hold of a ship after a three years' voyage. People who had cast their fortunes with the New Land went by professing not to notice it; people who still "hung on to the Hill" put their handkerchiefs to their noses, and told each other the old terrible stories of the material used in filling up the Back Bay.

Nothing gave Lapham so much satisfaction in the whole construction of his house as the pile-driving. When this began, early in the summer, he took Mrs. Lapham every day in his buggy and drove round to look at it; stopping the mare in front of the lot, and watching the operation with even keener interest than the little loafing Irish boys who superintended it in force. It pleased him to hear the portable engine chuckle out a hundred thin whiffs of steam, in carrying the big iron weight to the top of the framework above the pile, then seem to hesitate, and cough once or twice in pressing the weight against the detaching apparatus. There was a moment in which the weight had the effect of poising before it fell; then it dropped with a mighty whack on the iron-bound head of the pile and drove it a foot into the earth.

"By gracious!" he would say, "there aint anything like that in *this* world for *business*, Persis!"

Mrs. Lapham suffered him to enjoy the sight twenty or thirty times before she said, "Well, now drive on, Si."

By the time the foundation was in and the brick walls had begun to go up, there were so few people left in the neighborhood that she might indulge with impunity her husband's passion for having her clamber over the floor-timbers and the skeleton staircases with him. Many of the householders had boarded up their front doors before the buds had begun to swell and the assessor to appear in early May; others had followed soon; and Mrs. Lapham was as safe from remark as if she had been in the depth of the country. Ordinarily she and her girls left town early in July, going to one of the hotels at Nantasket, where it was convenient for the Colonel to get to and from his business by the boat. But this summer they were all lingering a few weeks later, under the novel fascination of the new house, as they called it, as if there were no other in the world.

Lapham drove there with his wife after he had set Bartley Hubbard down at the "Events" office, but on this day something happened that interfered with the solid pleasure they usually took in going over the house. As the Colonel turned from casting anchor at the mare's head with the hitching-weight, after helping his wife to alight, he encountered a man to whom he could not help speaking, though the man seemed to share his hesitation if not his reluctance at the necessity. He was a tallish, thin man, with a dust-colored face, and a dead, clerical air, which somehow suggested at once feebleness and tenacity.

Mrs. Lapham held out her hand to him.

"Why, Mr. Rogers!" she exclaimed, and then, turning toward her husband, seemed to refer the two men to each other. They shook hands, but Lapham did not speak. "I didn't know you were in Boston," pursued Mrs. Lapham. "Is Mrs. Rogers with you?"

"No," said Mr. Rogers, with a voice which had the flat, succinct sound of two pieces of wood clapped together. "Mrs. Rogers is still in Chicago."

A little silence followed, and then Mrs. Lapham said:

"I presume you are quite settled out there."

"No; we have left Chicago. Mrs. Rogers has merely remained to finish up a little packing."

"Oh, indeed! Are you coming back to Boston?"

"I cannot say as yet. We some think of so doing."

Lapham turned away and looked up at the building. His wife pulled a little at her glove, as if embarrassed or even pained. She tried to make a diversion.

"We are building a house," she said, with a meaningless laugh.

"Oh, indeed," said Mr. Rogers, looking up at it.

Then no one spoke again, and she said, helplessly:

"If you come to Boston, I hope I shall see Mrs. Rogers."

"She will be happy to have you call," said Mr. Rogers.

He touched his hat-brim, and made a bow forward rather than in Mrs. Lapham's direction.

She mounted the planking that led into the shelter of the bare brick walls, and her husband slowly followed. When she turned her face toward him her cheeks were burning, and tears that looked hot stood in her eyes.

"You left it all to me!" she cried. "Why couldn't you speak a word?"

"I hadn't anything to say to him," replied Lapham sullenly.

They stood awhile, without looking at the work which they had come to enjoy, and without speaking to each other.

"I suppose we might as well go on," said Mrs. Lapham at last, as they returned to the buggy. The Colonel drove recklessly toward the Milldam. His wife kept her veil down and her face turned from him. After a time she put her handkerchief up under her veil and wiped her eyes, and he set his teeth and squared his jaw.

"I don't see how he always manages to appear just at the moment when he seems to have gone fairly out of our lives, and blight everything," she whimpered.

"I supposed he was dead," said Lapham.

"Oh, don't *say* such a thing! It sounds as if you wished it."

"Why do you mind it? What do you let him blight everything for?"

"I can't help it, and I don't believe I ever shall. I don't

know as his being dead would help it any. I can't ever see him without feeling just as I did at first."

"I tell you," said Lapham, "it was a perfectly square thing. And I wish, once for all, you would quit bothering about it. My conscience is easy as far as he's concerned, and it always was."

"And I can't look at him without feeling as if you'd ruined him, Silas."

"Don't look at him, then," said her husband with a scowl. "I want you should recollect in the first place, Persis, that I never wanted a partner."

"If he hadn't put his money in when he did, you'd 'a' broken down."

"Well, he got his money out again, and more too," said the Colonel with a sulky weariness.

"He didn't want to take it out."

"I gave him his choice: buy out or go out."

"You know he couldn't buy out then. It was no choice at all."

"It was a business chance."

"No; you had better face the truth, Silas. It was no chance at all. You crowded him out. A man that had saved you! No, you had got greedy, Silas. You had made your paint your god, and you couldn't bear to let anybody else share in its blessings."

"I tell you he was a drag and a brake on me from the word go. You say he saved me. Well, if I hadn't got him out he'd 'a' ruined me sooner or later. So it's an even thing, as far forth as that goes."

"No, it aint an even thing, and you know it, Silas. Oh, if I could only get you once to acknowledge that you did wrong about it, then I should have some hope. I don't say you meant wrong exactly, but you took an advantage. Yes, you took an advantage! You had him where he couldn't help himself, and then you wouldn't show him any mercy."

"I'm sick of this," said Lapham. "If you'll 'tend to the house, I'll manage my business without your help."

"You were very glad of my help once."

"Well, I'm tired of it now. Don't meddle."

"I *will* meddle. When I see you hardening yourself in a

wrong thing, it's time for me to meddle, as you call it, and I will. I can't ever get you to own up the least bit about Rogers, and I feel as if it was hurting you all the while."

"What do you want I should own up about a thing for when I don't feel wrong? I tell you Rogers haint got anything to complain of, and that's what I told you from the start. It's a thing that's done every day. I was loaded up with a partner that didn't know anything, and couldn't do anything, and I unloaded; that's all."

"You unloaded just at the time when you knew that your paint was going to be worth about twice what it ever had been; and you wanted all the advantage for yourself."

"I had a right to it. I made the success."

"Yes, you made it with Rogers's money; and when you'd made it you took his share of it. I guess you thought of that when you saw him, and that's why you couldn't look him in the face."

At these words Lapham lost his temper.

"I guess you don't want to ride with me any more to-day," he said, turning the mare abruptly round.

"I'm as ready to go back as what you are," replied his wife. "And don't you ask me to go to that house with you any more. You can sell it, for all me. I sha'n't live in it. There's blood on it."

IV

THE silken texture of the marriage tie bears a daily strain of wrong and insult to which no other human relation can be subjected without lesion; and sometimes the strength that knits society together might appear to the eye of faltering faith the curse of those immediately bound by it. Two people by no means reckless of each other's rights and feelings, but even tender of them for the most part, may tear at each other's heart-strings in this sacred bond with perfect impunity; though if they were any other two they would not speak or look at each other again after the outrages they exchange. It is certainly a curious spectacle, and doubtless it ought to convince an observer of the divinity of the institution. If the husband and wife are blunt, outspoken people like the Laphams, they do not weigh their words; if they are more refined, they weigh them very carefully, and know accurately just how far they will carry, and in what most sensitive spot they may be planted with most effect.

Lapham was proud of his wife, and when he married her it had been a rise in life for him. For a while he stood in awe of his good fortune, but this could not last, and he simply remained supremely satisfied with it. The girl who had taught school with a clear head and a strong hand was not afraid of work; she encouraged and helped him from the first, and bore her full share of the common burden. She had health, and she did not worry his life out with peevish complaints and vagaries; she had sense and principle, and in their simple lot she did what was wise and right. Their marriage was hallowed by an early sorrow: they lost their boy, and it was years before they could look each other in the face and speak of him. No one gave up more than they when they gave up each other, and Lapham went to the war. When he came back and began to work, her zeal and courage formed the spring of his enterprise. In that affair of the partnership she had tried to be his conscience, but perhaps she would have defended him if he had accused himself; it was one of those things in this life which seem destined to await justice, or at least judgment, in the next. As he said, Lapham had dealt fairly by his partner in money; he had let Rogers take more money out of the business than he put into it; he had, as he said, simply forced out of it a timid and inefficient participant in advantages which he had created. But Lapham had not created them all. He had been dependent at one time on his partner's capital. It was a moment of terrible trial. Happy is the man forever after who can choose the ideal, the unselfish part in such an exigency! Lapham could not rise to it. He did what he could maintain to be perfectly fair. The wrong, if any, seemed to be condoned to him, except when from time to time his wife brought it up. Then all the question stung and burned anew, and had to be reasoned out and put away once more. It seemed to have an inextinguishable vitality. It slept, but it did not die.

His course did not shake Mrs. Lapham's faith in him. It astonished her at first, and it always grieved her that he could not see that he was acting solely in his own interest. But she found excuses for him, which at times she made reproaches. She vaguely perceived that his paint was something more than business to him; it was a sentiment, almost a passion. He could not share its management and its profit with another without a measure of self-sacrifice far beyond that which he must make with something less personal to him. It was the poetry of that nature, otherwise so intensely prosaic; and she understood this, and for the most part forbore. She knew him good and true and blameless in all his life, except for this wrong, if it were a wrong; and it was only when her nerves tingled intolerably with some chance renewal of the pain she had suffered that she shared her anguish with him in true wifely fashion.

With those two there was never anything like an explicit reconciliation. They simply ignored a quarrel; and Mrs. Lapham had only to say a few days after at breakfast, "I guess the girls would like to go round with you this afternoon, and look at the new house," in order to make her husband grumble out as he looked down into his coffee-cup, "I guess we better all go, hadn't we?"

"Well, I'll see," she said.

There was not really a great deal to look at when Lapham

arrived on the ground in his four-seated beach-wagon. But the walls were up, and the studding had already given skeleton shape to the interior. The floors were roughly boarded over, and the stairways were in place, with provisional treads rudely laid. They had not begun to lath and plaster yet, but the clean, fresh smell of the mortar in the walls mingling with the pungent fragrance of the pine shavings neutralized the Venetian odor that drew in over the water. It was pleasantly shady there, though for the matter of that the heat of the morning had all been washed out of the atmosphere by a tide of east wind setting in at noon, and the thrilling, delicious cool of a Boston summer afternoon bathed every nerve.

The foreman went about with Mrs. Lapham, showing her where the doors were to be; but Lapham soon tired of this, and having found a pine stick of perfect grain, he abandoned himself to the pleasure of whittling it in what was to be the reception-room, where he sat looking out on the street from what was to be the bay-window. Here he was presently joined by his girls, who, after locating their own room on the water side above the music-room, had no more wish to enter into details than their father.

"Come and take a seat in the bay-window, ladies," he called out to them, as they looked in at him through the ribs of the wall. He jocosely made room for them on the trestle on which he sat.

They came gingerly and vaguely forward, as young ladies do when they wish not to seem to be going to do a thing they have made up their minds to do. When they had taken their places on their trestle, they could not help laughing with scorn, open and acceptable to their father; and Irene curled her chin up, in a little way she had, and said, "How ridiculous!" to her sister.

"Well, I can tell you what," said the Colonel, in fond enjoyment of their young-ladyishness, "your mother wasn't ashamed to sit with me on a trestle when I called her out to look at the first coat of my paint that I ever tried on a house."

"Yes; we've heard that story," said Penelope, with easy security of her father's liking what she said. "We were brought up on that story."

"Well, it's a good story," said her father.

At that moment a young man came suddenly in range, who began to look up at the signs of building as he approached. He dropped his eyes in coming abreast of the bay-window, where Lapham sat with his girls, and then his face lightened, and he took off his hat and bowed to Irene. She rose mechanically from the trestle, and her face lightened too. She was a very pretty figure of a girl, after our fashion of girls, round and slim and flexible, and her face was admirably regular. But her great beauty—and it was very great—was in her coloring. This was of an effect for which there is no word but delicious, as we use it of fruit or flowers. She had red hair, like her father in his earlier days, and the tints of her cheeks and temples were such as suggested May-flowers and apple-blossoms and peaches. Instead of the gray that often dulls this complexion, her eyes were of a blue at once intense and tender, and they seemed to burn on what they looked at with a soft, lambent flame. It was well understood by her sister and mother that her eyes always expressed a great deal more than Irene ever thought or felt; but this is not saying that she was not a very sensible girl and very honest.

The young man faltered perceptibly, and Irene came a little forward, and then there gushed from them both a smiling exchange of greeting, of which the sum was that he supposed she was out of town, and that she had not known that he had got back. A pause ensued, and flushing again in her uncertainty as to whether she ought or ought not to do it, she said, "My father, Mr. Corey; and my sister."

The young man took off his hat again, showing his shapely head, with a line of wholesome sunburn ceasing where the recently and closely clipped hair began. He was dressed in a fine summer check, with a blue white-dotted neckerchief, and he had a white hat, in which he looked very well when he put it back on his head. His whole dress seemed very fresh and new, and, in fact, he had cast aside his Texan habiliments only the day before.

"How do you do, sir?" said the Colonel, stepping to the window, and reaching out of it the hand which the young man advanced to take. "Wont you come in? We're at home here. House I'm building."

"Oh, indeed?" returned the young man; and he came promptly up the steps, and through its ribs into the reception-room.

"Have a trestle?" asked the Colonel, while the girls exchanged little shocks of terror and amusement at the eyes.

"Thank you," said the young man, simply, and sat down.

"Mrs. Lapham is upstairs interviewing the carpenter, but she'll be down in a minute."

"I hope she's quite well," said Corey. "I supposed—I was afraid she might be out of town."

"Well, we are off to Nantasket next week. The house kept us in town pretty late."

"It must be very exciting, building a house," said Corey to the elder sister.

"Yes, it is," she assented, loyally refusing in Irene's interest the opportunity of saying anything more.

Corey turned to the latter. "I suppose you've all helped to plan it?"

"Oh, no; the architect and mamma did that."

"But they allowed the rest of us to agree, when we were good," said Penelope.

Corey looked at her, and saw that she was shorter than her sister, and had a dark complexion.

"It's very exciting," said Irene.

"Come up," said the Colonel, rising, "and look round if you'd like to."

"I should like to, very much," said the young man.

He helped the young ladies over crevasses of carpentry and along narrow paths of planking, on which they had made their way unassisted before. The elder sister left the younger to profit solely by these offices as much as possible. She walked between them and her father, who went before, lecturing on each apartment and taking the credit of the whole affair more and more as he talked on.

"There!" he said, "we're going to throw out a bay-window here, so as get the water all the way up and down. This is my girls' room," he added, looking proudly at them both.

It seemed terribly intimate. Irene blushed deeply and turned her head away.

But the young man took it all, apparently, as simply as their father. "What a lovely lookout," he said. The Back Bay spread its glassy sheet before them, empty but for a few smaller boats and a large schooner, with her sails close-furled and dripping like snow from her spars, which a tug was rapidly towing toward Cambridge. The carpentry of that city, embanked and embowered in foliage, shared the picturesqueness of Charlestown in the distance.

"Yes," said Lapham, "I go in for using the best rooms in your house yourself. If people come to stay with you, they can put up with the second best. Though we don't intend to have any second best. There aint going to be an unpleasant room in the whole house, from top to bottom."

"Oh, I wish papa wouldn't brag so!" breathed Irene to her sister, where they stood a little apart looking away together.

The Colonel went on. "No, sir," he swelled out, "I have gone in for making a regular job of it. I've got the best architect in Boston, and I'm building a house to suit myself. And if money can do it, I guess I'm going to be suited."

"It seems very delightful," said Corey, "and very original."

"Yes, sir. That fellow hadn't talked five minutes before I saw that he knew what he was about every time."

"I wish mamma would come!" breathed Irene again. "I shall certainly go through the floor if papa says anything more."

"They are making a great many very pretty houses nowadays," said the young man. "It's very different from the old-fashioned building."

"Well," said the Colonel, with a large toleration of tone and a deep breath that expanded his ample chest, "we spend more on our houses nowadays. I started out to build a forty-thousand-dollar house. Well, sir! that fellow has got me in for more than sixty thousand already, and I doubt if I get out of it much under a hundred. You can't have a nice house for nothing. It's just like ordering a picture of a painter. You pay him enough, and he can afford to paint you a first-class picture; and if you don't, he can't. That's all there is of it. Why, they tell me that A. T. Stewart gave one of those French fellows sixty thousand dollars for a little seven-by-nine picture the other day. Yes, sir, give an architect money enough and he'll give you a nice house, every time."

"I've heard that they're sharp at getting money to realize their ideas," assented the young man, with a laugh.

"Well, I should say so!" exclaimed the Colonel. "They come to you with an improvement that you can't resist. It has good looks and common sense and everything in its favor, and it's like throwing money away to refuse. And they always manage to get you when your wife is around, and then you're helpless."

The Colonel himself set the example of laughing at this joke, and the young man joined him less obstreperously. The girls turned, and he said: "I don't think I ever saw this view to better advantage. It's surprising how well the Memorial Hall and the Cambridge spires work up, over there. And the sunsets must be magnificent."

Lapham did not wait for them to reply.

"Yes, sir, it's about the sightliest view I know of. I always did like the water side of Beacon. Long before I owned property here, or ever expected to, m'wife and I used to ride down this way, and stop the buggy to get this view over the water. When people talk to me about the Hill, I can understand 'em. It's snug, and it's old-fashioned, and it's where they've always lived. But when they talk about Commonwealth Avenue, I don't know what they mean. It don't hold a candle to the water side of Beacon. You've got just as much wind over there, and you've got just as much dust, and all the view you've got is the view across the street. No, sir! When you come to the Back Bay at all, give me the water side of Beacon."

"Oh, I think you're quite right," said the young man. "The view here is everything."

Irene looked "I wonder what papa is going to say next!" at her sister, when their mother's voice was heard overhead, approaching the opening in the floor where the stairs were to be; and she presently appeared, with one substantial foot a long way ahead. She was followed by the carpenter, with his rule sticking out of his overalls pocket, and she was still talking to him about some measurements they had been taking, when they reached the bottom, so that Irene had to say, "Mamma, Mr. Corey," before Mrs. Lapham was aware of him.

He came forward with as much grace and speed as the uncertain footing would allow, and Mrs. Lapham gave him a stout squeeze of her comfortable hand.

"Why, Mr. Corey! When did you get back?"

"Yesterday. It hardly seems as if I *had* got back. I didn't expect to find you in a new house."

"Well, you are our first caller. I presume you won't expect I should make excuses for the state you find it in. Has the Colonel been doing the honors?"

"Oh, yes. And I've seen more of your house than I ever shall again, I suppose."

"Well, I hope not," said Lapham. "There'll be several chances to see us in the old one yet, before we leave."

He probably thought this a neat, off-hand way of making the invitation, for he looked at his womankind as if he might expect their admiration.

"Oh, yes, indeed!" said his wife. "We shall be very glad to see Mr. Corey, any time."

"Thank you; I shall be glad to come."

He and the Colonel went before, and helped the ladies down the difficult descent. Irene seemed less sure-footed than the others; she clung to the young man's hand an imperceptible moment longer than need be, or else he detained her. He found opportunity of saying, "It's so pleasant seeing you again," adding, "All of you."

"Thank you," said the girl. "They must all be glad to have you at home again."

Corey laughed.

"Well, I suppose they would be; if they were at home to have me. But the fact is, there's nobody in the house but my father and myself, and I'm only on my way to Bar Harbor."

"Oh! Are they there?"

"Yes; it seems to be the only place where my mother can get just the combination of sea and mountain air that she wants."

"We go to Nantasket—it's convenient for papa; and I don't believe we shall go anywhere else this summer, mamma's so taken up with building. We do nothing but talk house; and Pen says we eat and sleep house. She says it would be a sort of relief to go and live in tents for a while."

"She seems to have a good deal of humor," the young man ventured, upon the slender evidence.

The others had gone to the back of the house a moment, to look at some suggested change. Irene and Corey were left standing in the doorway. A lovely light of happiness played over her face and etherealized its delicious beauty. She had some ado to keep herself from smiling outright, and the effort deepened the dimples in her cheeks; she trembled a little, and the pendants shook in the tips of her pretty ears.

The others came back directly, and they all descended the front steps together. The Colonel was about to renew his invitation, but he caught his wife's eye, and, without being able to interpret its warning exactly, was able to arrest himself, and went about gathering up the hitching-weight, while the young man handed the ladies into the beach-wagon. Then he lifted his hat, and the ladies all bowed, and the Laphams drove off, Irene's blue ribbons fluttering backward from her hat, as if they were her clinging thoughts.

"So that's young Corey, is it?" said the Colonel, letting the stately stepping, tall coupé horse make his way homeward at will with the beach-wagon. "Well, he aint a bad-looking fellow, and he's got a good, fair and square, honest eye. But I don't see how a fellow like that, that's had every advantage in this world, can hang round home and let his father support him. Seems to me, if I had his health and his education, I should want to strike out and do something for myself."

The girls on the back seat had hold of each other's hands, and they exchanged electrical pressures at the different points their father made.

"I presume," said Mrs. Lapham, "that he was down in Texas looking after something."

"He's come back without finding it, I guess."

"Well, if his father has the money to support him, and don't complain of the burden, I don't see why *we* should."

"Oh, I know it's none of my business; but I don't like the principle. I like to see a man *act* like a man. I don't like to see him taken care of like a young lady. Now, I suppose that fellow belongs to two or three clubs, and hangs around 'em all day, lookin' out the window,—I've seen 'em,—instead of tryin' to hunt up something to do for an honest livin'."

"If I was a young man," Penelope struck in, "I would belong to twenty clubs, if I could find them, and I would hang around them all, and look out the window till I dropped."

"Oh, you would, would you?" demanded her father, delighted with her defiance, and twisting his fat head around over his shoulder to look at her. "Well, you wouldn't do it on *my* money, if you were a son of *mine*, young lady."

"Oh, you wait and see," retorted the girl.

This made them all laugh. But the Colonel recurred seriously to the subject that night, as he was winding up his watch preparatory to putting it under his pillow.

"I could make a man of that fellow, if I had him in the business with me. There's stuff in him. But I spoke up the way I did because I didn't choose Irene should think I would stand any kind of a loafer 'round—I don't care who he is, or how well educated or brought up. And I guess, from the way Pen spoke up, that 'Rene saw what I was driving at."

The girl, apparently, was less anxious about her father's ideas and principles than about the impression which he had made upon the young man. She talked it over and over with her sister before they went to bed, and she asked in despair, as she stood looking at Penelope brushing out her hair before the glass,

"Do you suppose he'll think papa always talks in that bragging way?"

"He'll be right if he does," answered her sister. "It's the way father always does talk. You never noticed it so much, that's all. And I guess if he can't make allowance for father's bragging, he'll be a little too good. *I* enjoyed hearing the Colonel go on."

"I know you did," returned Irene in distress. Then she sighed. "Didn't you think he looked very nice?"

"Who? The Colonel?" Penelope had caught up the habit of calling her father so from her mother, and she used his title in all her jocose and perverse moods.

"You know very well I don't mean papa," pouted Irene.

"Oh! Mr. Corey! Why didn't you say Mr. Corey if you meant Mr. Corey? If I meant Mr. Corey, I should say Mr. Corey. It isn't swearing! Corey, Corey, Co——"

Her sister clapped her hand over her mouth. "Will you

hush, you wretched thing?" she whimpered. "The whole house can hear you."

"Oh, yes, they can hear me all over the square. Well, I think he looked well enough for a plain youth, who hadn't taken his hair out of curl-papers for some time."

"It *was* clipped pretty close," Irene admitted; and they both laughed at the drab effect of Mr. Corey's skull, as they remembered it. "Did you like his nose?" asked Irene, timorously.

"Ah, now you're *coming* to something," said Penelope. "I don't know whether, if I had so much of a nose, I should want it all Roman."

"I don't see how you can expect to have a nose part one kind and part another," argued Irene.

"Oh, *I* do. Look at mine!" She turned aside her face, so as to get a three-quarters view of her nose in the glass, and crossing her hands, with the brush in one of them, before her, regarded it judicially. "Now, my nose started Grecian, but changed its mind before it got over the bridge, and concluded to be snub the rest of the way."

"You've got a very pretty nose, Pen," said Irene, joining in the contemplation of its reflex in the glass.

"Don't say that in hopes of getting me to compliment *his*, Mrs."—she stopped, and then added deliberately—"C.!"

Irene also had her hair-brush in her hand, and now she sprang at her sister and beat her very softly on the shoulder with the flat of it. "You mean thing!" she cried, between her shut teeth, blushing hotly.

"Well, *D.*, then," said Penelope. "You've nothing to say against D.? Though I think C. is just as nice an initial."

"Oh!" cried the younger, for all expression of unspeakable things.

"I think he has very good eyes," admitted Penelope.

"Oh, he *has*! And didn't you like the way his sack-coat set? So close to him, and yet free—kind of peeling away at the lapels?"

"Yes, I should say he was a young man of great judgment. He knows how to choose his tailor."

Irene sat down on the edge of a chair. "It was so nice of you, Pen, to come in, that way, about clubs."

"Oh, I didn't mean anything by it except opposition," said Penelope. "I couldn't have father swelling on so, without saying something."

"How he *did* swell!" sighed Irene. "Wasn't it a relief to have mamma come down, even if she did seem to be all stocking at first?"

The girls broke into a wild giggle and hid their faces in each other's necks. "I thought I *should* die," said Irene.

" 'It's just like ordering a painting,' " said Penelope, recalling her father's talk, with an effect of dreamy absent-mindedness. " 'You give the painter money enough, and he can afford to paint you a first-class picture. Give an architect money enough, and he'll give you a first-class house, every time.' "

"Oh, wasn't it awful!" moaned her sister. "No one would ever have supposed that he had fought the very idea of an architect for weeks, before he gave in."

Penelope went on. " 'I always did like the water side of Beacon—long before I owned property there. When you come to the Back Bay at all, give me the water side of Beacon.' "

"Ow-w-w-w!" shrieked Irene. "*Do* stop!"

The door of their mother's chamber opened below, and the voice of the real Colonel called, "What are you doing up there, girls? Why don't you go to bed?"

This extorted nervous shrieks from both of them. The Colonel heard a sound of scurrying feet, whisking drapery, and slamming doors. Then he heard one of the doors opened again, and Penelope said, "I was only repeating something you said when you talked to Mr. Corey."

"Very well, now," answered the Colonel. "You postpone the rest of it till to-morrow at breakfast, and see that you're up in time to let *me* hear it."

V

A<small>T THE</small> same moment young Corey let himself in at his own door with his latch-key, and went to the library, where he found his father turning the last leaves of a story in the "Revue des Deux Mondes." He was a white-mustached old gentleman, who had never been able to abandon his *pince-nez* for the superior comfort of spectacles, even in the privacy of his own library. He knocked the glasses off as his son came in, and looked up at him with lazy fondness, rubbing the two red marks that they always leave on the side of the nose.

"Tom," he said, "where did you get such good clothes?"

"I stopped over a day in New York," replied the son, finding himself a chair. "I'm glad you like them."

"Yes, I always do like your clothes, Tom," returned the father thoughtfully, swinging his glasses. "But I don't see how you can afford 'em. *I* can't."

"Well, sir," said the son, who dropped the sir into his speech with his father, now and then, in an old-fashioned way that was rather charming, "you see I have an indulgent parent."

"Smoke?" suggested the father, pushing toward his son a box of cigarettes, from which he had taken one.

"No, thank you," said the son. "I've dropped that."

"Ah, is that so?" The father began to feel about on the table for matches, in the purblind fashion of elderly men. His son rose, lighted one, and handed it to him. "Well,—oh, thank you, Tom!—I believe some statisticians prove that if you will give up smoking you can dress very well on the money your tobacco costs, even if you haven't got an indulgent parent. But I'm too old to try. Though, I confess, I should rather like the clothes. Whom did you find at the club?"

"There were a lot of fellows there," said young Corey, watching the accomplished fumigation of his father in an absent way.

"It's astonishing what a hardy breed the young club-men are," observed his father. "All summer through, in weather that sends the sturdiest female flying to the sea-shore, you

916

find the clubs filled with young men, who don't seem to mind the heat in the least."

"Boston isn't a bad place, at the worst, in summer," said the son, declining to take up the matter in its ironical shape.

"I dare say it isn't, compared with Texas," returned the father, smoking tranquilly on. "But I don't suppose you find many of your friends in town outside of the club."

"No; you're requested to ring at the rear door, all the way down Beacon street and up Commonwealth Avenue. It's rather a blank reception for the returning prodigal."

"Ah, the prodigal must take his chance if he comes back out of season. But I'm glad to have you back, Tom, even as it is, and I hope you're not going to hurry away. You must give your energies a rest."

"I'm sure you never had to reproach me with abnormal activity," suggested the son, taking his father's jokes in good part.

"No, I don't know that I have," admitted the elder. "You've always shown a fair degree of moderation, after all. What do you think of taking up next? I mean after you have embraced your mother and sisters at Mount Desert. Real estate? It seems to me that it is about time for you to open out as a real-estate broker. Or did you ever think of matrimony?"

"Well, not just in that way, sir," said the young man. "I shouldn't quite like to regard it as a career, you know."

"No, no. I understand that. And I quite agree with you. But you know I've always contended that the affections could be made to combine pleasure and profit. I wouldn't have a man marry for money,—that would be rather bad,—but I don't see why, when it comes to falling in love, a man shouldn't fall in love with a rich girl as easily as a poor one. Some of the rich girls are very nice, and I should say that the chances of a quiet life with them were rather greater. They've always had everything, and they wouldn't be so ambitious and uneasy. Don't you think so?"

"It would depend," said the son, "upon whether a girl's people had been rich long enough to have given her position before she married. If they hadn't, I don't see how she would be any better than a poor girl in that respect."

"Yes, there's sense in that. But the suddenly rich are on a

level with any of us nowadays. Money buys position at once. I don't say that it isn't all right. The world generally knows what it's about, and knows how to drive a bargain. I dare say it makes the new rich pay too much. But there's no doubt but money is to the fore now. It is the romance, the poetry of our age. It's the thing that chiefly strikes the imagination. The Englishmen who come here are more curious about the great new millionaires than about any one else, and they respect them more. It's all very well. I don't complain of it."

"And you would like a rich daughter-in-law, quite regardless, then?"

"Oh, not quite so bad as that, Tom," said his father. "A little youth, a little beauty, a little good sense and pretty behavior—one mustn't object to those things; and they go just as often with money as without it. And I suppose I should like her people to be rather grammatical."

"It seems to me that you're exacting, sir," said the son. "How can you expect people who have been strictly devoted to business to be grammatical? Isn't that rather too much?"

"Perhaps it is. Perhaps you're right. But I understood your mother to say that those benefactors of hers, whom you met last summer, were very passably grammatical."

"The father isn't."

The elder, who had been smoking with his profile toward his son, now turned his face full upon him. "I didn't know you had seen him?"

"I hadn't until to-day," said young Corey, with a little heightening of his color. "But I was walking down street this afternoon, and happened to look round at a new house some one was putting up, and I saw the whole family in the window. It appears that Mr. Lapham is building the house."

The elder Corey knocked the ash of his cigarette into the holder at his elbow. "I am more and more convinced, the longer I know you, Tom, that we are descended from Giles Corey. The gift of holding one's tongue seems to have skipped me, but you have it in full force. I can't say just how you would behave under *peine forte et dure*, but under ordinary pressure you are certainly able to keep your own counsel. Why didn't you mention this encounter at dinner? You weren't asked to plead to an accusation of witchcraft."

"No, not exactly," said the young man. "But I didn't quite see my way to speaking of it. We had a good many other things before us."

"Yes, that's true. I suppose you wouldn't have mentioned it now if I hadn't led up to it, would you?"

"I don't know, sir. It was rather on my mind to do so. Perhaps it was I who led up to it."

His father laughed. "Perhaps you did, Tom; perhaps you did. Your mother would have known you were leading up to something, but I'll confess that I didn't. What is it?"

"Nothing very definite. But do you know that in spite of his syntax I rather liked him?"

The father looked keenly at the son; but unless the boy's full confidence was offered, Corey was not the man to ask it. "Well?" was all that he said.

"I suppose that in a new country one gets to looking at people a little out of our tradition; and I dare say that if I hadn't passed a winter in Texas I might have found Colonel Lapham rather too much."

"You mean that there are worse things in Texas?"

"Not that exactly. I mean that I saw it wouldn't be quite fair to test him by our standards."

"This comes of the error which I have often deprecated," said the elder Corey. "In fact I am always saying that the Bostonian ought never to leave Boston. Then he knows—and then only—that there can *be* no standard but ours. But we are constantly going away, and coming back with our convictions shaken to their foundations. One man goes to England, and returns with the conception of a grander social life; another comes home from Germany with the notion of a more searching intellectual activity; a fellow just back from Paris has the absurdest ideas of art and literature; and you revert to us from the cowboys of Texas, and tell us to our faces that we ought to try Papa Lapham by a jury of his peers. It ought to be stopped—it ought, really. The Bostonian who leaves Boston ought to be condemned to perpetual exile."

The son suffered the father to reach his climax with smiling patience. When he asked finally, "What are the characteristics of Papa Lapham that place him beyond our jurisdiction?" the younger Corey crossed his long legs, and leaned forward to take one of his knees between his hands.

"Well, sir, he bragged, rather."

"Oh, I don't know that bragging should exempt him from the ordinary processes. I've heard other people brag in Boston."

"Ah, not just in that personal way—not about money."

"No, that was certainly different."

"I don't mean," said the young fellow, with the scrupulosity which people could not help observing and liking in him, "that it was more than an indirect expression of satisfaction in the ability to spend."

"No. I should be glad to express something of the kind myself, if the facts would justify me."

The son smiled tolerantly again. "But if he was enjoying his money in that way, I didn't see why he shouldn't show his pleasure in it. It might have been vulgar, but it wasn't sordid. And I don't know that it was vulgar. Perhaps his successful strokes of business were the romance of his life——"

The father interrupted with a laugh. "The girl must be uncommonly pretty. What did she seem to think of her father's brag?"

"There were two of them," answered the son evasively.

"Oh, two! And is the sister pretty, too?"

"Not pretty, but rather interesting. She is like her mother."

"Then the pretty one isn't the father's pet?"

"I can't say, sir. I don't believe," added the young fellow, "that I can make you see Colonel Lapham just as I did. He struck me as very simple-hearted and rather wholesome. Of course he could be tiresome; we all can; and I suppose his range of ideas is limited. But he is a force, and not a bad one. If he hasn't got over being surprised at the effect of rubbing his lamp——"

"Oh, one could make out a case. I suppose you know what you are about, Tom. But remember that we are Essex County people, and that in savor we are just a little beyond the salt of the earth. I will tell you plainly that I don't like the notion of a man who has rivaled the hues of nature in her wildest haunts with the tints of his mineral paint; but I don't say there are not worse men. He isn't to my taste, though he might be ever so much to my conscience."

"I suppose," said the son, "that there is nothing really to be ashamed of in mineral paint. People go into all sorts of things."

His father took his cigarette from his mouth and once more looked his son full in the face. "Oh, is *that* it?"

"It has crossed my mind," admitted the son. "I must do something. I've wasted time and money enough. I've seen much younger men all through the West and Southwest taking care of themselves. I don't think I was particularly fit for anything out there, but I am ashamed to come back and live upon you, sir."

His father shook his head with an ironical sigh. "Ah, we shall never have a real aristocracy while this plebeian reluctance to live upon a parent or a wife continues the animating spirit of our youth. It strikes at the root of the whole feudal system. I really think you owe me an apology, Tom. I supposed you wished to marry the girl's money, and here you are, basely seeking to go into business with her father."

Young Corey laughed again like a son who perceives that his father is a little antiquated, but keeps a filial faith in his wit. "I don't know that it's quite so bad as that; but the thing had certainly crossed my mind. I don't know how it's to be approached, and I don't know that it's at all possible. But I confess that I 'took to' Colonel Lapham from the moment I saw him. He looked as if he 'meant business,' and I mean business too."

The father smoked thoughtfully. "Of course people do go into all sorts of things, as you say, and I don't know that one thing is more ignoble than another, if it's decent, and large enough. In my time you would have gone into the China trade or the India trade—though *I* didn't; and a little later cotton would have been your manifest destiny—though it wasn't mine; but now a man may do almost anything. The real-estate business *is* pretty full. Yes, if you have a deep inward vocation for it, I don't see why mineral paint shouldn't do. I fancy it's easy enough approaching the matter. We will invite Papa Lapham to dinner, and talk it over with him."

"Oh, I don't think that would be exactly the way, sir," said the son, smiling at his father's patrician unworldliness.

"No? Why not?"

"I'm afraid it would be a bad start. I don't think it would strike him as business-like."

"I don't see why he should be punctilious, if we're not."

"Ah, we might say that if he were making the advances."

"Well, perhaps you are right, Tom. What is your idea?"

"I haven't a very clear one. It seems to me I ought to get some business friend of ours, whose judgment he would respect, to speak a good word for me."

"Give you a character?"

"Yes. And of course I must go to Colonel Lapham. My notion would be to inquire pretty thoroughly about him, and then, if I liked the look of things, to go right down to Republic street and let him see what he could do with me, if anything."

"That sounds tremendously practical to me, Tom, though it may be just the wrong way. When are you going down to Mount Desert?"

"To-morrow, I think, sir," said the young man. "I shall turn it over in my mind while I'm off."

The father rose, showing something more than his son's height, with a very slight stoop, which the son's figure had not. "Well," he said, whimsically, "I admire your spirit, and I don't deny that it is justified by necessity. It's a consolation to think that while I've been spending and enjoying, I have been preparing the noblest future for you—a future of industry and self-reliance. You never could draw, but this scheme of going into the mineral-paint business shows that you have inherited something of my feeling for color."

The son laughed once more, and waiting till his father was well on his way upstairs, turned out the gas and then hurried after him and preceded him into his chamber. He glanced over it, to see that everything was there, to his father's hand. Then he said, "Good-night, sir," and the elder responded, "Good-night, my son," and the son went to his own room.

Over the mantel in the elder Corey's room hung a portrait which he had painted of his own father, and now he stood a moment and looked at this as if struck by something novel in

it. The resemblance between his son and the old India merchant, who had followed the trade from Salem to Boston
when the larger city drew it away from the smaller, must have
been what struck him. Grandfather and grandson had both
the Roman nose which appears to have flourished chiefly at
the formative period of the republic, and which occurs more
rarely in the descendants of the conscript fathers, though it
still characterizes the profiles of a good many Boston ladies.
Bromfield Corey had not inherited it, and he had made his
straight nose his defense when the old merchant accused him
of a want of energy. He said, "What could a man do whose
unnatural father had left his own nose away from him?" This
amused but did not satisfy the merchant. "You must do
something," he said; "and it's for you to choose. If you don't
like the India trade, go into something else. Or, take up law
or medicine. No Corey yet ever proposed to do nothing."
"Ah, then, it's quite time one of us made a beginning," urged
the man who was then young, and who was now old, looking
into the somewhat fierce eyes of his father's portrait. He had inherited as little of the fierceness as of the nose, and there was
nothing predatory in his son either, though the aquiline beak
had come down to him in such force. Bromfield Corey liked his
son Tom for the gentleness which tempered his energy.

"Well, let us compromise," he seemed to be saying to his
father's portrait. "I will travel." "Travel? How long?" the
keen eyes demanded. "Oh, indefinitely. I wont be hard with
you, father." He could see the eyes soften, and the smile of
yielding come over his father's face; the merchant could not
resist a son who was so much like his dead mother. There
was some vague understanding between them that Bromfield
Corey was to come back and go into business after a time,
but he never did so. He traveled about over Europe, and traveled handsomely, frequenting good society everywhere, and
getting himself presented at several courts, at a period when
it was a distinction to do so. He had always sketched, and
with his father's leave he fixed himself at Rome, where he
remained studying art and rounding the being inherited from
his Yankee progenitors, till there was very little left of the
ancestral angularities. After ten years he came home and
painted that portrait of his father. It was very good, if a little

amateurish, and he might have made himself a name as a painter of portraits if he had not had so much money. But he had plenty of money, though by this time he was married and beginning to have a family. It was absurd for him to paint portraits for pay, and ridiculous to paint them for nothing; so he did not paint them at all. He continued a dilettante, never quite abandoning his art, but working at it fitfully, and talking more about it than working at it. He had his theory of Titian's method; and now and then a Bostonian insisted upon buying a picture of him. After a while he hung it more and more inconspicuously, and said apologetically, "Oh, yes! that's one of Bromfield Corey's things. It has nice qualities, but it's amateurish."

In process of time the money seemed less abundant. There were shrinkages of one kind and another, and living had grown much more expensive and luxurious. For many years he talked about going back to Rome, but he never went, and his children grew up in the usual way. Before he knew it his son had him out to his class-day spread at Harvard, and then he had his son on his hands. The son made various unsuccessful provisions for himself, and still continued upon his father's hands, to their common dissatisfaction, though it was chiefly the younger who repined. He had the Roman nose and the energy without the opportunity, and at one of the reversions his father said to him, "You ought not to have that nose, Tom; then you would do very well. You would go and travel, as I did."

Lapham and his wife continued talking after he had quelled the disturbance in his daughters' room overhead; and their talk was not altogether of the new house.

"I tell you," he said, "if I had that fellow in the business with me I would make a man of him."

"Well, Silas Lapham," returned his wife, "I do believe you've got mineral paint on the brain. Do you suppose a fellow like young Corey, brought up the way he's been, would touch mineral paint with a ten-foot pole?"

"Why not?" haughtily asked the Colonel.

"Well, if you don't know already, there's no use trying to tell you."

VI

THE COREYS had always had a house at Nahant, but after letting it for a season or two they found they could get on without it, and sold it at the son's instance, who foresaw that if things went on as they were going, the family would be straitened to the point of changing their mode of life altogether. They began to be of the people of whom it was said that they staid in town very late; and when the ladies did go away, it was for a brief summering in this place and that. The father remained at home altogether; and the son joined them in the intervals of his enterprises, which occurred only too often.

At Bar Harbor, where he now went to find them, after his winter in Texas, he confessed to his mother that there seemed no very good opening there for him. He might do as well as Loring Stanton, but he doubted if Stanton was doing very well. Then he mentioned the new project which he had been thinking over. She did not deny that there was something in it, but she could not think of any young man who had gone into such a business as that, and it appeared to her that he might as well go into a patent medicine or a stove-polish.

"There was one of his hideous advertisements," she said, "painted on a reef that we saw as we came down."

Corey smiled. "Well, I suppose, if it was in a good state of preservation, that is proof positive of the efficacy of the paint on the hulls of vessels."

"It's very distasteful to me, Tom," said his mother; and if there was something else in her mind, she did not speak more plainly of it than to add: "It's not only the kind of business, but the kind of people you would be mixed up with."

"I thought you didn't find them so very bad," suggested Corey.

"I hadn't seen them in Nankeen Square then."

"You can see them on the water side of Beacon street when you go back."

Then he told of his encounter with the Lapham family in their new house. At the end his mother merely said, "It is getting very common down there," and she did not try to oppose anything further to his scheme.

The young man went to see Colonel Lapham shortly after his return to Boston. He paid his visit at Lapham's office, and if he had studied simplicity in his summer dress he could not have presented himself in a figure more to the mind of a practical man. His hands and neck still kept the brown of the Texan suns and winds, and he looked as business-like as Lapham himself.

He spoke up promptly and briskly in the outer office, and caused the pretty girl to look away from her copying at him. "Is Mr. Lapham in?" he asked; and after that moment for reflection which an array of book-keepers so addressed likes to give the inquirer, a head was lifted from a ledger and nodded toward the inner office.

Lapham had recognized the voice, and he was standing, in considerable perplexity of mind, to receive Corey, when the young man opened his painted glass door. It was a hot afternoon, and Lapham was in his shirt-sleeves. Scarcely a trace of the boastful hospitality with which he had welcomed Corey to his house a few days before lingered in his present address. He looked at the young man's face, as if he expected him to dispatch whatever unimaginable affair he had come upon.

"Wont you sit down? How are you? You'll excuse me," he added, in brief allusion to the shirt-sleeves. "I'm about roasted."

Corey laughed. "I wish you'd let me take off *my* coat."

"Why, *take* it off!" cried the Colonel, with instant pleasure. There is something in human nature which causes the man in his shirt-sleeves to wish all other men to appear in the same dishabille.

"I will, if you ask me after I've talked with you two minutes," said the young fellow, companionably pulling up the chair offered him toward the desk where Lapham had again seated himself. "But perhaps you haven't got two minutes to give me?"

"Oh, yes, I have," said the Colonel. "I was just going to knock off. I can give you twenty, and then I shall have fifteen minutes to catch the boat."

"All right," said Corey. "I want you to take me into the mineral paint business."

The Colonel sat dumb. He twisted his thick neck, and looked round at the door to see if it was shut. He would not have liked to have any of those fellows outside hear him, but there is no saying what sum of money he would not have given if his wife had been there to hear what Corey had just said.

"I suppose," continued the young man, "I could have got several people whose names you know to back my industry and sobriety, and say a word for my business capacity. But I thought I wouldn't trouble anybody for certificates till I found whether there was a chance, or the ghost of one, of your wanting me. So I came straight to you."

Lapham gathered himself together as well as he could. He had not yet forgiven Corey for Mrs. Lapham's insinuation that he would feel himself too good for the mineral paint business; and though he was dispersed by that astounding shot at first, he was not going to let any one even hypothetically despise his paint with impunity. "How do you think I am going to take you on?" They took on hands at the works; and Lapham put it as if Corey were a hand coming to him for employment. Whether he satisfied himself by this or not, he reddened a little after he had said it.

Corey answered, ignorant of the offense: "I haven't a very clear idea, I'm afraid; but I've been looking a little into the matter from the outside——"

"I hope you haint been paying any attention to that fellow's stuff in the 'Events'?" Lapham interrupted. Since Bartley's interview had appeared, Lapham had regarded it with very mixed feelings. At first it gave him a glow of secret pleasure, blended with doubt as to how his wife would like the use Bartley had made of her in it. But she had not seemed to notice it much, and Lapham had experienced the gratitude of the man who escapes. Then his girls had begun to make fun of it; and though he did not mind Penelope's jokes much, he did not like to see that Irene's gentility was wounded. Business friends met him with the kind of knowing smile about it that implied their sense of the fraudulent character of its praise—the smile of men who had been there and who knew how it was themselves. Lapham had his misgivings as to how his clerks and underlings looked at it; he treated them with stately severity for a while after it came out, and he ended by feeling rather sore about it. He took it for granted that everybody had read it.

"I don't know what you mean," replied Corey. "I don't see the 'Events' regularly."

"Oh, it was nothing. They sent a fellow down here to interview me, and he got everything about as twisted as he could."

"I believe they always do," said Corey. "I hadn't seen it. Perhaps it came out before I got home."

"Perhaps it did."

"My notion of making myself useful to you was based on a hint I got from one of your own circulars."

Lapham was proud of those circulars; he thought they read very well. "What was that?"

"I could put a little capital into the business," said Corey, with the tentative accent of a man who chances a thing. "I've got a little money, but I didn't imagine you cared for anything of that kind."

"No, sir, I don't," returned the Colonel bluntly. "I've had one partner, and one's enough."

"Yes," assented the young man, who doubtless had his own ideas as to eventualities—or perhaps rather had the vague hopes of youth. "I didn't come to propose a partnership. But I see that you are introducing your paint into the foreign markets, and there I really thought I might be of use to you, and to myself, too."

"How?" asked the Colonel scantly.

"Well, I know two or three languages pretty well. I know French, and I know German, and I've got a pretty fair sprinkling of Spanish."

"You mean that you can talk them?" asked the Colonel, with the mingled awe and slight that such a man feels for such accomplishments.

"Yes; and I can write an intelligible letter in either of them."

Lapham rubbed his nose. "It's easy enough to get all the letters we want translated."

"Well," pursued Corey, not showing his discouragement if he felt any, "I know the countries where you want to introduce this paint of yours. I've been there. I've been in Germany and France, and I've been in South America and Mexico; I've been in Italy, of course. I believe I could go to any of those countries and place it to advantage."

Lapham had listened with a trace of persuasion in his face, but now he shook his head.

"It's placing itself as fast as there's any call for it. It wouldn't pay us to send anybody out to look after it. Your salary and expenses would eat up about all we should make on it."

"Yes," returned the young man intrepidly, "if you had to pay me any salary and expenses."

"You don't propose to work for nothing?"

"I propose to work for a commission." The Colonel was beginning to shake his head again, but Corey hurried on. "I haven't come to you without making some inquiries about the paint, and I know how it stands with those who know best. I believe in it."

Lapham lifted his head and looked at the young man, deeply moved.

"It's the best paint in God's universe," he said, with the solemnity of prayer.

"It's the best in the market," said Corey; and he repeated, "I believe in it."

"You believe in it," began the Colonel, and then he stopped. If there had really been any purchasing power in money, a year's income would have bought Mrs. Lapham's instant presence. He warmed and softened to the young man in every way, not only because he must do so to any one who believed in his paint, but because he had done this innocent person the wrong of listening to a defamation of his instinct and good sense, and had been willing to see him suffer for a purely supposititious offense.

Corey rose.

"You mustn't let me outstay my twenty minutes," he said, taking out his watch. "I don't expect you to give a decided answer on the spot. All that I ask is that you'll consider my proposition."

"Don't hurry," said Lapham. "Sit still! I want to tell you about this paint," he added, in a voice husky with the feeling that his hearer could not divine. "I want to tell you *all* about it."

"I could walk with you to the boat," suggested the young man.

"Never mind the boat! I can take the next one. Look here!" The Colonel pulled open a drawer, as Corey sat down again, and took out a photograph of the locality of the mine. "Here's where we get it. This photograph don't half do the place justice," he said, as if the imperfect art had slighted the features of a beloved face. "It's one of the sightliest places in the country, and here's the very spot"—he covered it with his huge forefinger—"where my father found that paint, more than forty—years—ago. Yes, sir!"

He went on, and told the story in unsparing detail, while his chance for the boat passed unheeded, and the clerks in the outer office hung up their linen office coats and put on their seersucker or flannel street coats. The young lady went, too, and nobody was left but the porter, who made from time to time a noisy demonstration of fastening a distant blind, or putting something in place. At last the Colonel roused himself from the autobiographical delight of the history of his paint. "Well, sir, that's the story."

"It's an interesting story," said Corey, with a long breath, as they rose together, and Lapham put on his coat.

"That's what it is," said the Colonel. "Well!" he added, "I don't see but what we've got to have another talk about this thing. It's a surprise to me, and I don't see exactly how you're going to make it pay."

"I'm willing to take the chances," answered Corey. "As I said, I believe in it. I should try South America first. I should try Chili."

"Look here!" said Lapham, with his watch in his hand. "I like to get things over. We've just got time for the six o'clock boat. Why don't you come down with me to Nantasket? I can give you a bed as well as not. And then we can finish up."

The impatience of youth in Corey responded to the impatience of temperament in his elder.

"Why, I don't see why I shouldn't," he allowed himself to

say. "I confess I should like to have it finished up myself, if it could be finished up in the right way."

"Well, we'll see. Dennis!" Lapham called to the remote porter, and the man came. "Want to send any word home?" he asked Corey.

"No; my father and I go and come as we like, without keeping account of each other. If I don't come home, he knows that I'm not there. That's all."

"Well, that's convenient. You'll find you can't do that when you're married. Never mind, Dennis," said the Colonel.

He had time to buy two newspapers on the wharf before he jumped on board the steam-boat with Corey. "Just made it," he said; "and that's what I like to do. I can't stand it to be aboard much more than a minute before she shoves out." He gave one of the newspapers to Corey as he spoke, and set him the example of catching up a camp-stool on their way to that point on the boat which his experience had taught him was the best. He opened his paper at once and began to run over its news, while the young man watched the spectacular recession of the city, and was vaguely conscious of the people about him, and of the gay life of the water round the boat. The air freshened; the craft thinned in number; they met larger sail, lagging slowly inward in the afternoon light, the islands of the bay waxed and waned as the steamer approached and left them behind.

"I hate to see them stirring up those Southern fellows again," said the Colonel, speaking into the paper on his lap. "Seems to me it's time to let those old issues go."

"Yes," said the young man. "What are they doing now?"

"Oh, stirring up the Confederate brigadiers in Congress. I don't like it. Seems to me, if our party haint got any other stock-in-trade, we better shut up shop altogether." Lapham went on, as he scanned his newspaper, to give his ideas of public questions, in a fragmentary way, while Corey listened patiently, and waited for him to come back to business. He folded up his paper at last, and stuffed it into his coat pocket. "There's one thing I always make it a rule to do," he said, "and that is to give my mind a complete rest from business while I'm going down on the boat. I like to get the fresh air all through me, soul and body. I believe a man can give his mind a rest, just the same as he can give his legs a rest, or his back. All he's got to do is to use his will-power. Why, I suppose, if I hadn't adopted some such rule, with the strain I've had on me for the last ten years, I should 'a' been a dead man long ago. That's the reason I like a horse. You've got to give your mind to the horse; you can't help it, unless you want to break your neck; but a boat's different, and there you got to use your will-power. You got to take your mind right up and put it where you want it. I make it a rule to read the paper on the boat— Hold on!" he interrupted himself to prevent Corey from paying his fare to the man who had come round for it. "I've got tickets. And when I get through the paper, I try to get somebody to talk to, or I watch the people. It's an astonishing thing to me where they all come from. I've been riding up and down on these boats for six or seven years, and I don't know but very few of the faces I see on board. Seems to be a perfectly fresh lot every time. Well, of course! Town's full of strangers in the summer season, anyway, and folks keep coming down from the country. They think it's a great thing to get down to the beach, and they've all heard of the electric light on the water, and they want to see it. But you take faces now! The astonishing thing to me is not what a face tells, but what it don't tell. When you think of what a man is, or a woman is, and what most of 'em have been through before they get to be thirty, it seems as if their experience would burn right through. But it don't. I like to watch the couples, and try to make out which are engaged, or going to be, and which are married, or better be. But half the time I can't make any sort of guess. Of course, where they're young and kittenish, you can tell; but where they're anyways on, you can't. Heigh?"

"Yes, I think you're right," said Corey, not perfectly reconciled to philosophy in the place of business, but accepting it as he must.

"Well," said the Colonel, "I don't suppose it was meant we should know what was in each other's minds. It would take a man out of his own hands. As long as he's in his own hands, there's some hopes of his doing something with himself; but if a fellow has been found out—even if he hasn't been found out to be so very bad—it's pretty much all up with him. No, sir. I don't want to know people through and through."

The greater part of the crowd on board—and, of course, the boat was crowded—looked as if they might not only be easily but safely known. There was little style and no distinction among them; they were people who were going down to the beach for the fun or the relief of it, and were able to afford it. In face they were commonplace, with nothing but the American poetry of vivid purpose to light them up, where they did not wholly lack fire. But they were nearly all shrewd and friendly-looking, with an apparent readiness for the humorous intimacy native to us all. The women were dandified in dress, according to their means and taste, and the men differed from each other in degrees of indifference to it. To a straw-hatted population, such as ours is in summer, no sort of personal dignity is possible. We have not even the power over observers which comes from the fantasticality of an Englishman when he discards the conventional dress. In our straw hats and our serge or flannel sacks we are no more imposing than a crowd of boys.

"Some day," said Lapham, rising as the boat drew near the wharf of the final landing, "there's going to be an awful accident on these boats. Just look at that jam."

He meant the people thickly packed on the pier, and under strong restraint of locks and gates, to prevent them from rushing on board the boat and possessing her for the return trip before she had landed her Nantasket passengers.

"Overload 'em every time," he continued, with a sort of dry, impersonal concern at the impending calamity, as if it could not possibly include him. "They take about twice as many as they ought to carry, and about ten times as many as they could save if anything happened. Yes, sir, it's bound to come. Hello! There's my girl!" He took out his folded newspaper and waved it toward a group of phaetons and barouches drawn up on the pier a little apart from the pack of people, and a lady in one of them answered with a flourish of her parasol.

When he had made his way with his guest through the crowd, she began to speak to her father before she noticed

Corey. "Well, Colonel, you've improved your last chance. We've been coming to every boat since four o'clock,—or Jerry has,—and I told mother that I would come myself once, and see if *I* couldn't fetch you; and if I failed, you could walk next time. You're getting perfectly spoiled."

The Colonel enjoyed letting her scold him to the end before he said, with a twinkle of pride in his guest and satisfaction in her probably being able to hold her own against any discomfiture, "I've brought Mr. Corey down for the night with me, and I was showing him things all the way, and it took time."

The young fellow was at the side of the open beach-wagon, making a quick, gentlemanly bow, and Penelope Lapham was cozily drawling, "Oh, how do you do, Mr. Corey?" before the Colonel had finished his explanation.

"Get right in there, alongside of Miss Lapham, Mr. Corey," he said, pulling himself up into the place beside the driver. "No, no," he had added quickly, at some signs of polite protest in the young man, "I don't give up the best place to anybody. Jerry, suppose you let me have hold of the leathers a minute."

This was his way of taking the reins from the driver; and in half the time he specified, he had skillfully turned the vehicle on the pier, among the crooked lines and groups of foot-passengers, and was spinning up the road toward the stretch of verandaed hotels and restaurants in the sand along the shore. "Pretty gay down here," he said, indicating all this with a turn of his whip, as he left it behind him. "But I've got about sick of hotels; and this summer I made up my mind that I'd take a cottage. Well, Pen, how are the folks?" He looked half-way round for her answer, and with the eye thus brought to bear upon her he was able to give her a wink of supreme content. The Colonel, with no sort of ulterior design, and nothing but his triumph over Mrs. Lapham definitely in his mind, was feeling, as he would have said, about right.

The girl smiled a daughter's amusement at her father's boyishness. "I don't think there's much change since morning. Did Irene have a headache when you left?"

"No," said the Colonel.

"Well, then, there's that to report."

"Pshaw!" said the Colonel, with vexation in his tone.

"I'm sorry Miss Irene isn't well," said Corey politely.

"I think she must have got it from walking too long on the beach. The air is so cool here that you forget how hot the sun is."

"Yes, that's true," assented Corey.

"A good night's rest will make it all right," suggested the Colonel, without looking round. "But you girls have got to look out."

"If you're fond of walking," said Corey, "I suppose you find the beach a temptation."

"Oh, it isn't so much that," returned the girl. "You keep walking on and on because it's so smooth and straight before you. We've been here so often that we know it all by heart— just how it looks at high tide, and how it looks at low tide, and how it looks after a storm. We're as well acquainted with the crabs and stranded jelly-fish as we are with the children digging in the sand and the people sitting under umbrellas. I think they're always the same, all of them."

The Colonel left the talk to the young people. When he spoke next it was to say, "Well, here we are!" and he turned from the highway and drove up in front of a brown cottage with a vermilion roof, and a group of geraniums clutching the rock that cropped up in the loop formed by the road. It was treeless and bare all round, and the ocean, unnecessarily vast, weltered away a little more than a stone's cast from the cottage. A hospitable smell of supper filled the air, and Mrs. Lapham was on the veranda, with that demand in her eyes for her belated husband's excuses, which she was obliged to check on her tongue at sight of Corey.

VII

THE EXULTANT Colonel swung himself lightly down from his seat. "I've brought Mr. Corey with me," he nonchalantly explained.

Mrs. Lapham made their guest welcome, and the Colonel showed him to his room, briefly assuring himself that there was nothing wanting there. Then he went to wash his own hands, carelessly ignoring the eagerness with which his wife pursued him to their chamber.

"What gave Irene a headache?" he asked, making himself a fine lather for his hairy paws.

"Never you mind Irene," promptly retorted his wife. "How came he to come? Did you press him? If you *did*, I'll never forgive you, Silas!"

The Colonel laughed, and his wife shook him by the shoulder to make him laugh lower. " 'Sh!" she whispered. "Do you want him to hear *every* thing? *Did* you urge him?"

The Colonel laughed the more. He was going to get all the good out of this. "No, I didn't urge him. Seemed to want to come."

"I don't believe it. Where did you meet him?"

"At the office."

"What office?"

"Mine."

"Nonsense! What was he doing there?"

"Oh, nothing much."

"What did he come for?"

"Come for? Oh! He *said* he wanted to go into the mineral paint business."

Mrs. Lapham dropped into a chair, and watched his bulk shaken with smothered laughter. "Silas Lapham," she gasped, "if you try to get off any more of those things on me——"

The Colonel applied himself to the towel. "Had a notion he could work it in South America. *I* don't know what he's up to."

"Never mind!" cried his wife. "I'll get even with you *yet*."

"So I told him he had better come down and talk it over," continued the Colonel, in well-affected simplicity. "I knew he wouldn't touch it with a ten-foot pole."

"Go on!" threatened Mrs. Lapham.

"Right thing to do, wa'n't it?"

A tap was heard at the door, and Mrs. Lapham answered it. A maid announced supper. "Very well," she said, "come to tea now. But I'll make you pay for this, Silas."

Penelope had gone to her sister's room as soon as she entered the house.

"Is your head any better, 'Rene?" she asked.

"Yes, a little," came a voice from the pillows. "But I shall not come to tea. I don't want anything. If I keep still, I shall be all right by morning."

"Well, I'm sorry," said the elder sister. "He's come down with father."

"He hasn't! Who?" cried Irene, starting up in simultaneous denial and demand.

"Oh, well, if you say he hasn't, what's the use of my telling you who?"

"Oh, how can you treat me so!" moaned the sufferer. "What do you mean, Pen?"

"I guess I'd better not tell you," said Penelope, watching her like a cat playing with a mouse. "If you're not coming to tea, it would just excite you for nothing."

The mouse moaned and writhed upon the bed.

"Oh, I wouldn't treat *you* so!"

The cat seated herself across the room and asked quietly:

"Well, what could you do if it *was* Mr. Corey? You couldn't come to tea, you say. But *he*'ll excuse you. *I*'ve told him you had a headache. Why, of course you can't come! It would be too barefaced. But you needn't be troubled, Irene; I'll do my best to make the time pass pleasantly for him." Here the cat gave a low titter, and the mouse girded itself up with a momentary courage and self-respect.

"I should think you would be ashamed to come here and tease me so."

"I don't see why you shouldn't believe me," argued Penelope. "Why shouldn't he come down with father, if father asked him? and he'd be sure to if he thought of it. I don't see any p'ints about that frog that's any better than any other frog."

The sense of her sister's helplessness was too much for the tease; she broke down in a fit of smothered laughter, which convinced her victim that it was nothing but an ill-timed joke.

"Well, Pen, I wouldn't use you so," she whimpered.

Penelope threw herself on the bed beside her.

"Oh, poor Irene! He *is* here. It's a solemn fact." And she caressed and soothed her sister, while she choked with laughter. "You must get up and come out. I don't know what brought him here, but here he *is*."

"It's too late now," said Irene, desolately. Then she added, with a wilder despair: "What a fool I was to take that walk!"

"Well," coaxed her sister, "come out and get some tea. The tea will do you good."

"No, no; I can't come. But send me a cup here."

"Yes, and then perhaps you can see him later in the evening."

"I shall not see him at all."

An hour after Penelope came back to her sister's room and found her before her glass. "You might as well have kept still, and been well by morning, 'Rene," she said. "As soon as we were done father said, 'Well, Mr. Corey and I have got to talk over a little matter of business, and we'll excuse you, ladies.' He looked at mother in a way that I guess was pretty hard to bear. 'Rene, you ought to have heard the Colonel swelling at supper. It would have made you feel that all he said the other day was nothing."

Mrs. Lapham suddenly opened the door.

"Now, see here, Pen," she said, as she closed it behind her, "I've had just as much as I can stand from your father, and if you don't tell me this instant what it all means——"

She left the consequences to imagination, and Penelope replied, with her mock soberness:

"Well, the Colonel does seem to be on his high horse, ma'am. But you mustn't ask me what his business with Mr. Corey is, for I don't know. All that I know is that I met them at the landing, and that they conversed all the way down—on literary topics."

"Nonsense! What do you think it is?"

"Well, if you want my candid opinion, I think this talk about business is nothing but a blind. It seems a pity Irene shouldn't have been up to receive him," she added.

Irene cast a mute look of imploring at her mother, who was too much preoccupied to afford her the protection it asked.

"Your father said he wanted to go into the business with him."

Irene's look changed to a stare of astonishment and mystification, but Penelope preserved her imperturbability.

"Well, it's a lucrative business, I believe."

"Well, I don't believe a word of it!" cried Mrs. Lapham. "And so I told your father."

"Did it seem to convince him?" inquired Penelope.

Her mother did not reply. "I know one thing," she said. "He's got to tell me every word, or there'll be no sleep for him *this* night."

"Well, ma'am," said Penelope, breaking down in one of her queer laughs, "I shouldn't be a bit surprised if you were right."

"Go on and dress, Irene," ordered her mother, "and then you and Pen come out into the parlor. They can have just two hours for business, and then we must all be there to receive him. You haven't got headache enough to hurt you."

"Oh, it's all gone now," said the girl.

At the end of the limit she had given the Colonel, Mrs. Lapham looked into the dining-room, which she found blue with his smoke.

"I think you gentlemen will find the parlor pleasanter now, and we can give it up to you."

"Oh, no, you needn't," said her husband. "We've got about through." Corey was already standing, and Lapham rose too. "I guess we can join the ladies now. We can leave that little point till to-morrow."

Both of the young ladies were in the parlor when Corey entered with their father, and both were frankly indifferent to the few books and the many newspapers scattered about on the table where the large lamp was placed. But after Corey had greeted Irene he glanced at the novel under his eye, and said, in the dearth that sometimes befalls people at such times: "I see you're reading 'Middlemarch.' Do you like George Eliot?"

"Who?" asked the girl.

Penelope interposed. "I don't believe Irene's read it yet. I've just got it out of the library; I heard so much talk about it. I wish she would let you find out a little about the people for yourself," she added. But here her father struck in:

"I can't get the time for books. It's as much as I can do to keep up with the newspapers; and when night comes, I'm tired, and I'd rather go out to the theater, or a lecture, if they've got a good stereopticon to give you views of the places. But I guess we all like a play better than 'most anything else. I want something that'll make me laugh. I don't believe in tragedy. I think there's enough of that in real life without putting it on the stage. Seen 'Joshua Whitcomb'?"

The whole family joined in the discussion, and it appeared that they all had their opinions of the plays and actors. Mrs. Lapham brought the talk back to literature. "I guess Penelope does most of our reading."

"Now, mother, you're not going to put it all on me!" said the girl, in comic protest.

Her mother laughed, and then added, with a sigh: "I used to like to get hold of a good book when I was a girl; but we weren't allowed to read many novels in those days. My mother called them all *lies*. And I guess she wasn't so very far wrong about some of them."

"They're certainly fictions," said Corey, smiling.

"Well, we do buy a good many books, first and last," said the Colonel, who probably had in mind the costly volumes which they presented to one another on birthdays and holidays. "But I get about all the reading I want in the newspapers. And when the girls want a novel, I tell 'em to get it out of the library. That's what the library's for. Phew!" he panted, blowing away the whole unprofitable subject. "How close you women-folks like to keep a room! You go down to the sea-side or up to the mountains for a change of air, and then you cork yourselves into a room so tight you don't have any air at all. Here! You girls get on your bonnets and go and show Mr. Corey the view of the hotels from the rocks."

Corey said that he should be delighted. The girls exchanged looks with each other, and then with their mother. Irene curved her pretty chin in comment upon her father's incorrigibility, and Penelope made a droll mouth, but the Colonel remained serenely content with his finesse. "I got 'em out of the way," he said, as soon as they were gone, and before his wife had time to fall upon him, "because I've got through my talk with him, and now I want to talk with *you*. It's just as I said, Persis; he wants to go into the business with me."

"It's lucky for you," said his wife, meaning that now he would not be made to suffer for attempting to hoax her. But she was too intensely interested to pursue that matter further. "What in the world do you suppose he means by it?"

"Well, I should judge by his talk that he had been trying a good many different things since he left college, and he haint found just the thing he likes —or the thing that likes him. It aint so easy. And now he's got an idea that he can take hold of the paint and push it in other countries—push it in Mexico and push it in South America. He's a splendid Spanish scholar,"—this was Lapham's version of Corey's modest claim to a smattering of the language, —"and he's been among the natives enough to know their ways. And he believes in the paint," added the Colonel.

"I guess he believes in something else besides the paint," said Mrs. Lapham.

"What do you mean?"

"Well, Silas Lapham, if you can't see *now* that he's after Irene, I don't know what ever *can* open your eyes. That's all."

The Colonel pretended to give the idea silent consideration, as if it had not occurred to him before. "Well, then, all I've got to say is, that he's going a good way round. I don't say you're wrong, but if it's Irene, I don't see why he should want to go off to South America to get her. And that's what he proposes to do. I guess there's some paint about it too, Persis. He says he believes in it,"—the Colonel devoutly lowered his voice,—"and he's willing to take the agency on his own account down there, and run it for a commission on what he can sell."

"Of course! He isn't going to take hold of it any way so as to feel beholden to you. He's got too much pride for that."

"He aint going to take hold of it at all, if he don't mean paint in the first place and Irene afterward. I don't object to him, as I know, either way, but the two things wont mix; and I don't propose he shall pull the wool over my eyes—or anybody else. But, as far as heard from, up to date, he means paint first, last, and all the time. At any rate, I'm going to take him on that basis. He's got some pretty good ideas about it, and he's been stirred up by this talk, just now, about getting our manufactures into the foreign markets. There's an overstock in everything, and we've got to get rid of it, or we've got to shut down till the home demand begins again. We've had two or three such flurries before now, and they didn't amount to much. They say we can't extend our commerce under the high tariff system we've got now, because there aint any sort of reciprocity on our side,—we want to have the other fellows show all the reciprocity,—and the English have got the advantage of us every time. I don't know whether it's so or not; but I don't see why it should apply to my paint. Anyway, he wants to try it, and I've about made up my mind to let him. Of course I aint going to let him take all the risk. I believe in the paint *too*, and I shall pay his expenses anyway."

"So you want another partner after all?" Mrs. Lapham could not forbear saying.

"Yes, if that's your idea of a partner. It isn't mine," returned her husband dryly.

"Well, if you've made up your mind, Si, I suppose you're ready for advice," said Mrs. Lapham.

The Colonel enjoyed this. "Yes, I *am*. What have you got to say against it?"

"I don't know as I've got anything. I'm satisfied if you are."

"Well?"

"When is he going to start for South America?"

"I shall take him into the office awhile. He'll get off some time in the winter. But he's got to know the business first."

"Oh, indeed! Are you going to take him to board in the family?"

"What are you after, Persis?"

"Oh, nothing! I presume he will feel free to visit in the family, even if he don't board with us."

"I presume he will."

"And if he don't use his privileges, do you think he'll be a fit person to manage your paint in South America?"

The Colonel reddened consciously. "I'm not taking him on that basis."

"Oh, yes, you are! You may pretend you aint to yourself, but you mustn't pretend so to me. Because I know you."

The Colonel laughed. "Pshaw!" he said.

Mrs. Lapham continued: "I don't see any harm in hoping that he'll take a fancy to her. But if you really think it wont do to mix the two things, I advise you not to take Mr. Corey into the business. It will do all very well if he *does* take a fancy to her; but if he don't, you know how you'll feel about it. And I know you well enough, Silas, to know that you can't do him justice if that happens. And I don't think it's right you should take this step unless you're pretty sure. I can see that you've set your heart on this thing——"

"I haven't set my heart on it at all," protested Lapham.

"And if you can't bring it about, you're going to feel unhappy over it," pursued his wife, regardless of his protest.

"Oh, very well," he said. "If you know more about what's in my mind than I do, there's no use arguing, as I can see."

He got up, to carry off his consciousness, and sauntered out of the door on to his piazza. He could see the young people down on the rocks, and his heart swelled in his breast. He had always said that he did not care what a man's family was, but the presence of young Corey as an applicant to him for employment, as his guest, as the possible suitor of his daughter, was one of the sweetest flavors that he had yet tasted in his success. He knew who the Coreys were very well, and, in his simple, brutal way, he had long hated their name as a symbol of splendor which, unless he should live to see at least three generations of his descendants gilded with mineral paint, he could not hope to realize in his own. He was acquainted in a business way with the tradition of old Phillips Corey, and he had heard a great many things about the Corey who had spent his youth abroad and his father's money everywhere, and done nothing but say smart things. Lapham could not see the smartness of some of them which had been repeated to him. Once he had encountered the fellow, and it seemed to Lapham that the tall, slim, white-mustached man, with the slight stoop, was everything that was offensively aristocratic. He had bristled up aggressively at the name when his wife told how she had made the acquaintance of the fellow's family the summer before, and he had treated the notion of young Corey's caring for Irene with the contempt which such a ridiculous superstition deserved. He had made up his mind about young Corey beforehand; yet when he met him he felt an instant liking for him, which he frankly acknowledged, and he had begun to assume the burden of his wife's superstition, of which she seemed now ready to accuse him of being the inventor.

Nothing had moved his thick imagination like this day's events since the girl who taught him spelling and grammar in the school at Lumberville had said she would have him for her husband.

The dark figures, stationary on the rocks, began to move, and he could see that they were coming toward the house. He went indoors so as not to appear to have been watching them.

VIII

A WEEK after she had parted with her son at Bar Harbor,
Mrs. Corey suddenly walked in upon her husband in
their house in Boston. He was at breakfast, and he gave her
the patronizing welcome with which the husband who has
been staying in town all summer receives his wife when she
drops down upon him from the mountains or the sea-side.
For a little moment she feels herself strange in the house, and
suffers herself to be treated like a guest, before envy of his
comfort vexes her back into possession and authority. Mrs.
Corey was a lady, and she did not let her envy take the form
of open reproach.

"Well, Anna, you find me here in the luxury you left me
to. How did you leave the girls?"

"The girls were well," said Mrs. Corey, looking absently at
her husband's brown velvet coat, in which he was so handsome. No man had ever grown gray more beautifully. His
hair, while not remaining dark enough to form a theatrical
contrast with his mustache, was yet some shades darker, and,
in becoming a little thinner, it had become a little more gracefully wavy. His skin had the pearly tint which that of elderly
men sometimes assumes, and the lines which time had traced
upon it were too delicate for the name of wrinkles. He had
never had any personal vanity, and there was no consciousness in his good looks now.

"I am glad of that. The boy I have with me," he returned;
"that is, when he *is* with me."

"Why, where is he?" demanded the mother.

"Probably carousing with the boon Lapham somewhere.
He left me yesterday afternoon to go and offer his allegiance
to the Mineral Paint King, and I haven't seen him since."

"Bromfield!" cried Mrs. Corey. "Why didn't you stop
him?"

"Well, my dear, I'm not sure that it isn't a very good
thing."

"A good thing? It's horrid!"

"No, I don't think so. It's decent. Tom had found out—

without consulting the landscape, which I believe proclaims it everywhere——"

"Hideous!"

"That it's really a good thing; and he thinks that he has some ideas in regard to its dissemination in the parts beyond seas."

"Why shouldn't he go into something else?" lamented the mother.

"I believe he has gone into nearly everything else, and come out of it. So there is a chance of his coming out of this. But as I had nothing to suggest in place of it, I thought it best not to interfere. In fact, what good would my telling him that mineral paint was nasty have done? I dare say *you* told him it was nasty."

"Yes! I did."

"And you see with what effect, though he values your opinion three times as much as he values mine. Perhaps you came up to tell him again that it was nasty?"

"I feel very unhappy about it. He is throwing himself away. Yes, I should like to prevent it if I could!"

The father shook his head.

"If Lapham hasn't prevented it, I fancy it's too late. But there may be some hopes of Lapham. As for Tom's throwing himself away, I don't know. There's no question but he is one of the best fellows under the sun. He's tremendously energetic, and he has plenty of the kind of sense which we call horse; but he isn't brilliant. No, Tom is not brilliant. I don't think he would get on in a profession, and he's instinctively kept out of everything of the kind. But he has got to do something. What shall he do? He says mineral paint, and really I don't see why he shouldn't. If money is fairly and honestly earned, why should we pretend to care what it comes out of, when we don't really care? That superstition is exploded everywhere."

"Oh, it isn't the paint alone," said Mrs. Corey; and then she perceptibly arrested herself, and made a diversion in continuing: "I wish he had married some one."

"With money?" suggested her husband. "From time to time I have attempted Tom's corruption from that side, but I suspect Tom has a conscience against it, and I rather like him for it. I married for love myself," said Corey, looking across the table at his wife.

She returned his look tolerantly, though she felt it right to say, "What nonsense!"

"Besides," continued her husband, "if you come to money, there is the paint princess. She will have plenty."

"Ah, that's the worst of it," sighed the mother. "I suppose I could get on with the paint——"

"But not with the princess? I thought you said she was a very pretty, well-behaved girl?"

"She is very pretty, and she is well-behaved; but there is nothing of her. She is insipid; she is very insipid."

"But Tom seemed to like her flavor, such as it was?"

"How can I tell? We were under a terrible obligation to them, and I naturally wished him to be polite to them. In fact, I asked him to be so."

"And he was too polite?"

"I can't say that he was. But there is no doubt that the child is extremely pretty."

"Tom says there are two of them. Perhaps they will neutralize each other."

"Yes, there is another daughter," assented Mrs. Corey. "I don't see how you can joke about such things, Bromfield," she added.

"Well, I don't either, my dear, to tell you the truth. My hardihood surprises me. Here is a son of mine whom I see reduced to making his living by a shrinkage in values. It's very odd," interjected Corey, "that some values should have this peculiarity of shrinking. You never hear of values in a picture shrinking; but rents, stocks, real estate—all those values shrink abominably. Perhaps it might be argued that one should put all his values into pictures; I've got a good many of mine there."

"Tom needn't earn his living," said Mrs. Corey, refusing her husband's jest. "There's still enough for all of us."

"That is what I have sometimes urged upon Tom. I have proved to him that with economy, and strict attention to business, he need do nothing as long as he lives. Of course he would be somewhat restricted, and it would cramp the rest of us; but it is a world of sacrifices and compromises. He couldn't agree with me, and he was not in the least moved by the example of persons of quality in Europe, which I alleged in support of the life of idleness. It appears that he wishes to do something—to do something for himself. I am afraid that Tom is selfish."

Mrs. Corey smiled wanly. Thirty years before, she had married the rich young painter in Rome, who said so much better things than he painted—charming things, just the things to please the fancy of a girl who was disposed to take life a little too seriously and practically. She saw him in a different light when she got him home to Boston; but he had kept on saying the charming things, and he had not done much else. In fact, he had fulfilled the promise of his youth. It was a good trait in him that he was not actively but only passively extravagant. He was not adventurous with his money; his tastes were as simple as an Italian's; he had no expensive habits. In the process of time he had grown to lead a more and more secluded life. It was hard to get him out anywhere, even to dinner. His patience with their narrowing circumstances had a pathos which she felt the more the more she came into charge of their joint life. At times it seemed too bad that the children and their education and pleasures should cost so much. She knew, besides, that if it had not been for them she would have gone back to Rome with him, and lived princely there for less than it took to live respectably in Boston.

"Tom hasn't consulted me," continued his father, "but he has consulted other people. And he has arrived at the conclusion that mineral paint is a good thing to go into. He has found out all about it, and about its founder or inventor. It's quite impressive to hear him talk. And if he must do something for himself, I don't see why his egotism shouldn't as well take that form as another. Combined with the paint princess, it isn't so agreeable; but that's only a remote possibility, for which your principal ground is your motherly solicitude. But even if it were probable and imminent, what could you do? The chief consolation that we American parents have in these matters is that we can do nothing. If we were Europeans, even English, we should take some cognizance of our children's love affairs, and in some measure teach their young affections how to shoot. But it is our custom to ignore them

until they have shot, and then they ignore us. We are altogether too delicate to arrange the marriages of our children;
and when they have arranged them we don't like to say anything, for fear we should only make bad worse. The right way
is for us to school ourselves to indifference. That is what the
young people have to do elsewhere, and that is the only logical result of our position here. It is absurd for us to have any
feeling about what we don't interfere with."

"Oh, people do interfere with their children's marriages
very often," said Mrs. Corey.

"Yes, but only in a half-hearted way, so as not to make it
disagreeable for themselves if the marriages go on in spite of
them, as they're pretty apt to do. Now, my idea is that I
ought to cut Tom off with a shilling. That would be very
simple, and it would be economical. But you would never
consent, and Tom wouldn't mind it."

"I think our whole conduct in regard to such things is
wrong," said Mrs. Corey.

"Oh, very likely. But our whole civilization is based upon
it. And who is going to make a beginning? To which father
in our acquaintance shall I go and propose an alliance for
Tom with his daughter? I should feel like an ass. And will
you go to some mother, and ask her sons in marriage for our
daughters? You would feel like a goose. No; the only motto
for us is, Hands off altogether."

"I shall certainly speak to Tom when the time comes," said
Mrs. Corey.

"And I shall ask leave to be absent from your discomfiture,
my dear," answered her husband.

The son returned that afternoon, and confessed his surprise
at finding his mother in Boston. He was so frank that she had
not quite the courage to confess in turn why she had come,
but trumped up an excuse.

"Well, mother," he said promptly, "I have made an engagement with Mr. Lapham."

"Have you, Tom?" she asked faintly.

"Yes. For the present I am going to have charge of his
foreign correspondence, and if I see my way to the advantage
I expect to find in it, I am going out to manage that side of
his business in South America and Mexico. He's behaved very

handsomely about it. He says that if it appears for our common interest, he shall pay me a salary as well as a commission. I've talked with Uncle Jim, and he thinks it's a good opening."

"Your Uncle Jim does?" queried Mrs. Corey in amaze.

"Yes; I consulted him the whole way through, and I've acted on his advice."

This seemed an incomprehensible treachery on her brother's part.

"Yes; I thought you would like to have me. And besides, I couldn't possibly have gone to any one so well fitted to advise me."

His mother said nothing. In fact, the mineral paint business, however painful its interest, was, for the moment, superseded by a more poignant anxiety. She began to feel her way cautiously toward this.

"Have you been talking about your business with Mr. Lapham all night?"

"Well, pretty much," said her son, with a guiltless laugh. "I went to see him yesterday afternoon, after I had gone over the whole ground with Uncle Jim, and Mr. Lapham asked me to go down with him and finish up."

"Down?" repeated Mrs. Corey.

"Yes, to Nantasket. He has a cottage down there."

"At Nantasket?" Mrs. Corey knitted her brows a little. "What in the world can a cottage at Nantasket be like?"

"Oh, very much like a 'cottage' anywhere. It has the usual allowance of red roof and veranda. There are the regulation rocks by the sea; and the big hotels on the beach about a mile off, flaring away with electric lights and roman-candles at night. We didn't have them at Nahant."

"No," said his mother. "Is Mrs. Lapham well? And her daughter?"

"Yes, I think so," said the young man. "The young ladies walked me down to the rocks in the usual way after dinner, and then I came back and talked paint with Mr. Lapham till midnight. We didn't settle anything till this morning coming up on the boat."

"What sort of people do they seem to be at home?"

"What sort? Well, I don't know that I noticed." Mrs. Corey

permitted herself the first part of a sigh of relief; and her son laughed, but apparently not at her. "They're just reading 'Middlemarch.' They say there's so much talk about it. Oh, I suppose they're very good people. They seemed to be on very good terms with each other."

"I suppose it's the plain sister who's reading 'Middlemarch.' "

"Plain? Is she plain?" asked the young man, as if searching his consciousness. "Yes, it's the older one who does the reading, apparently. But I don't believe that even she overdoes it. They like to talk better. They reminded me of Southern people in that." The young man smiled, as if amused by some of his impressions of the Lapham family. "The living, as the country people call it, is tremendously good. The Colonel— he's a colonel—talked of the coffee as his wife's coffee, as if she had personally made it in the kitchen, though I believe it was merely inspired by her. And there was everything in the house that money could buy. But money has its limitations."

This was a fact which Mrs. Corey was beginning to realize more and more unpleasantly in her own life; but it seemed to bring her a certain comfort in its application to the Laphams. "Yes, there is a point where taste has to begin," she said.

"They seemed to want to apologize to me for not having more books," said Corey. "I don't know why they should. The Colonel said they bought a good many books, first and last; but apparently they don't take them to the sea-side."

"I dare say they *never* buy a *new* book. I've met some of these moneyed people lately, and they lavish on every conceivable luxury, and then borrow books, and get them in the cheap paper editions."

"I fancy that's the way with the Lapham family," said the young man, smilingly. "But they are very good people. The other daughter is humorous."

"Humorous?" Mrs. Corey knitted her brows in some perplexity. "Do you mean like Mrs. Sayre?" she asked, naming the lady whose name must come into every Boston mind when humor is mentioned.

"Oh, no; nothing like that. She never says anything that you can remember; nothing in flashes or ripples; nothing the least literary. But it's a sort of droll way of looking at things;

or a droll medium through which things present themselves.
I don't know. She tells what she's seen, and mimics a little."

"Oh," said Mrs. Corey, coldly. After a moment she asked:
"And is Miss Irene as pretty as ever?"

"She's a wonderful complexion," said the son, unsatisfactorily. "I shall want to be by when father and Colonel Lapham meet," he added, with a smile.

"Ah, yes, your father!" said the mother, in that way in
which a wife at once compassionates and censures her husband to their children.

"Do you think it's really going to be a trial to him?" asked
the young man, quickly.

"No, no, I can't say it is. But I confess I wish it was some
other business, Tom."

"Well, mother, I don't see why. The principal thing looked
at now is the amount of money; and while I would rather
starve than touch a dollar that was dirty with any sort of dishonesty——"

"Of course you would, my son!" interposed his mother,
proudly.

"I shouldn't at all mind its having a little mineral paint on
it. I'll use my influence with Colonel Lapham—if I ever have
any—to have his paint scraped off the landscape."

"I suppose you wont begin till the autumn."

"Oh, yes, I shall," said the son, laughing at his mother's
simple ignorance of business. "I shall begin to-morrow
morning."

"To-morrow morning!"

"Yes. I've had my desk appointed already, and I shall be
down there at nine in the morning to take possession."

"Tom!" cried his mother, "why do you think Mr. Lapham
has taken you into business so readily? I've always heard that
it was so hard for young men to get in."

"And do you think I found it easy with him? We had about
twelve hours' solid talk."

"And you don't suppose it was any sort of—personal consideration?"

"Why, I don't know exactly what you mean, mother. I suppose he likes me."

Mrs. Corey could not say just what she meant. She answered, ineffectually enough:

"Yes. You wouldn't like it to be a favor, would you?"

"I think he's a man who may be trusted to look after his own interest. But I don't mind his beginning by liking me. It'll be my own fault if I don't make myself essential to him."

"Yes," said Mrs. Corey.

"Well," demanded her husband, at their first meeting after her interview with their son, "what did you say to Tom?"

"Very little, if anything. I found him with his mind made up, and it would only have distressed him if I had tried to change it."

"That is precisely what I said, my dear."

"Besides, he had talked the matter over fully with James, and seems to have been advised by him. I can't understand James."

"Oh! it's in regard to the paint, and not the princess, that he's made up his mind. Well, I think you were wise to let him alone, Anna. We represent a faded tradition. We don't really care what business a man is in, so it is large enough, and he doesn't advertise offensively; but we think it fine to affect reluctance."

"Do you really feel so, Bromfield?" asked his wife, seriously.

"Certainly I do. There was a long time in my misguided youth when I supposed myself some sort of porcelain; but it's a relief to be of the common clay, after all, and to know it. If I get broken, I can be easily replaced."

"If Tom must go into such a business," said Mrs. Corey, "I'm glad James approves of it."

"I'm afraid it wouldn't matter to Tom if he didn't; and I don't know that I should care," said Corey, betraying the fact that he had perhaps had a good deal of his brother-in-law's judgment in the course of his life. "You had better consult him in regard to Tom's marrying the princess."

"There is no necessity at present for that," said Mrs. Corey, with dignity. After a moment, she asked, "Should you feel quite so easy if it were a question of that, Bromfield?"

"It would be a little more personal."

"You feel about it as I do. Of course, we have both lived too long, and seen too much of the world, to suppose we can control such things. The child is good, I haven't the least doubt, and all those things can be managed so that they wouldn't disgrace us. But she has had a certain sort of bringing up. I should prefer Tom to marry a girl with another sort, and this business venture of his increases the chances that he wont. That's all."

" 'Tis not so deep as a well, nor so wide as a church door, but 'twill serve.' "

"I shouldn't like it."

"Well, it hasn't happened yet."

"Ah, you never can realize anything beforehand."

"Perhaps that has saved me some suffering. But you have at least the consolation of two anxieties at once. I always find that a great advantage. You can play one off against the other."

Mrs. Corey drew a long breath as if she did not experience the suggested consolation; and she arranged to quit, the following afternoon, the scene of her defeat, which she had not had the courage to make a battle-field. Her son went down to see her off on the boat, after spending his first day at his desk in Lapham's office. He was in a gay humor, and she departed in a reflected gleam of his good spirits. He told her all about it, as he sat talking with her at the stern of the boat, lingering till the last moment, and then stepping ashore, with as little waste of time as Lapham himself, on the gang-plank which the deck-hands had laid hold of. He touched his hat to her from the wharf to reassure her of his escape from being carried away with her, and the next moment his smiling face hid itself in the crowd.

He walked on smiling up the long wharf, encumbered with trucks and hacks and piles of freight, and, taking his way through the deserted business streets beyond this bustle, made a point of passing the door of Lapham's warehouse, on the jambs of which his name and paint were lettered in black on a square ground of white. The door was still open, and Corey loitered a moment before it, tempted to go upstairs and fetch away some foreign letters which he had left on his desk, and which he thought he might finish up at home. He was in love with his work, and he felt the enthusiasm for it which nothing but the work we can do well inspires in us. He believed that he had found his place in the world, after a good deal of looking, and he had the relief, the repose, of fitting into it. Every little incident of the momentous, uneventful day was a pleasure in his mind, from his sitting down at his desk, to which Lapham's boy brought him the foreign letters, till his rising from it an hour ago. Lapham had been in view within his own office, but he had given Corey no formal reception, and had, in fact, not spoken to him till toward the end of the forenoon, when he suddenly came out of his den with some more letters in his hand, and after a brief "How d'ye do?" had spoken a few words about them, and left them with him. He was in his shirt-sleeves again, and his sanguine person seemed to radiate the heat with which he suffered. He did not go out to lunch, but had it brought to him in his office, where Corey saw him eating it before he left his own desk to go out and perch on a swinging seat before the long counter of a down-town restaurant. He observed that all the others lunched at twelve, and he resolved to anticipate his usual hour. When he returned, the pretty girl who had been clicking away at a type writer all the morning was neatly putting out of sight the evidences of pie from the table where her machine stood, and was preparing to go on with her copying. In his office Lapham lay asleep in his arm-chair, with a newspaper over his face.

Now, while Corey lingered at the entrance to the stairway, these two came down the stairs together, and he heard Lapham saying, "Well, then, you better get a divorce."

He looked red and excited, and the girl's face, which she veiled at sight of Corey, showed traces of tears. She slipped round him into the street.

But Lapham stopped, and said, with the show of no feeling but surprise: "Hello, Corey! Did you want to go up?"

"Yes; there were some letters I hadn't quite got through with."

"You'll find Dennis up there. But I guess you better let them go till to-morrow. I always make it a rule to stop work when I'm done."

"Perhaps you're right," said Corey, yielding.

"Come along down as far as the boat with me. There's a little matter I want to talk over with you."

It was a business matter, and related to Corey's proposed connection with the house.

The next day the head book-keeper, who lunched at the long counter of the same restaurant with Corey, began to talk with him about Lapham. Walker had not apparently got his place by seniority; though, with his bald head, and round, smooth face, one might have taken him for a plump elder, if he had not looked equally like a robust infant. The thick, drabbish-yellow mustache was what arrested decision in either direction, and the prompt vigor of all his movements was that of a young man of thirty, which was really Walker's age. He knew, of course, who Corey was, and he had waited for a man who might look down on him socially to make the overtures toward something more than business acquaintance; but, these made, he was readily responsive, and drew freely on his philosophy of Lapham and his affairs.

"I think about the only difference between people in this world is that some know what they want, and some don't. Well, now," said Walker, beating the bottom of his salt-box to make the salt come out, "the old man knows what he wants every time. And generally he gets it. Yes, sir, he generally gets it. He knows what he's about, but I'll be blessed if the rest of us do half the time. Anyway, we don't till he's ready to let us. You take my position in most business houses. It's confidential. The head book-keeper knows right along pretty much everything the house has got in hand. I'll give you my word *I* don't. He may open up to you a little more in your department, but, as far as the rest of us go, he don't open up any more than an oyster on a hot brick. They say he had a partner once; I guess he's dead. *I* wouldn't like to be the old man's partner. Well, you see, this paint of his is like his heart's blood. Better not try to joke him about it. I've seen people come in occasionally and try it. They didn't get much fun out of it."

While he talked, Walker was plucking up morsels from his plate, tearing off pieces of French bread from the long loaf, and feeding them into his mouth in an impersonal way, as if he were firing up an engine.

"I suppose he thinks," suggested Corey, "that if he doesn't tell, nobody else will."

Walker took a draught of beer from his glass, and wiped the foam from his mustache.

"Oh, but he carries it too far! It's a weakness with him. He's just so about everything. Look at the way he keeps it up about that type-writer girl of his. You'd think she was some princess traveling incognito. There isn't one of us knows who she is, or where she came from, or who she belongs to. He brought her and her machine into the office one morning, and set 'em down at a table, and that's all there is about it, as far as we're concerned. It's pretty hard on the girl, for I guess she'd like to talk; and to any one that didn't know the old man—" Walker broke off and drained his glass of what was left in it.

Corey thought of the words he had overheard from Lapham to the girl. But he said, "She seems to be kept pretty busy."

"Oh, yes," said Walker; "there aint much loafing round the place, in any of the departments, from the old man's down. That's just what I say. He's got to work just twice as hard, if he wants to keep everything in his own mind. But he aint afraid of work. That's one good thing about him. And Miss Dewey has to keep step with the rest of us. But she don't look like one that would take to it naturally. Such a pretty girl as that generally thinks she does enough when she looks her prettiest."

"She's a pretty girl," said Corey, non-committally. "But I suppose a great many pretty girls have to earn their living."

"Don't any of 'em like to do it," returned the book-keeper. "They think it's a hardship, and I don't blame 'em. They have got a right to get married, and they ought to have the chance. And Miss Dewey's smart, too. She's as bright as a biscuit. I guess she's had trouble. I shouldn't be much more than half surprised if Miss Dewey wasn't Miss Dewey, or hadn't always been. Yes, sir," continued the book-keeper, who prolonged the talk as they walked back to Lapham's warehouse together,

"I don't know exactly what it is,—it isn't any one thing in particular,—but I should say that girl had been married. I wouldn't speak so freely to any of the rest, Mr. Corey,—I want you to understand that,—and it isn't any of my business, anyway; but that's my opinion."

Corey made no reply, as he walked beside the book-keeper, who continued:

"It's curious what a difference marriage makes in people. Now, I know that I don't look any more like a bachelor of my age than I do like the man in the moon, and yet I couldn't say where the difference came in, to save me. And it's just so with a woman. The minute you catch sight of her face, there's something in it that tells you whether she's married or not. What do you suppose it is?"

"I'm sure I don't know," said Corey, willing to laugh away the topic. "And from what I read occasionally of some people who go about repeating their happiness, I shouldn't say that the intangible evidences were always unmistakable."

"Oh, of course," admitted Walker, easily surrendering his position. "All signs fail in dry weather. Hello! What's that?" He caught Corey by the arm, and they both stopped.

At a corner, half a block ahead of them, the summer noon solitude of the place was broken by a bit of drama. A man and woman issued from the intersecting street, and at the moment of coming into sight the man, who looked like a sailor, caught the woman by the arm, as if to detain her. A brief struggle ensued, the woman trying to free herself, and the man half coaxing, half scolding. The spectators could now see that he was drunk; but before they could decide whether it was a case for their interference or not, the woman suddenly set both hands against the man's breast and gave him a quick push. He lost his footing and tumbled into a heap in the gutter. The woman faltered an instant, as if to see whether he was seriously hurt, and then turned and ran.

When Corey and the book-keeper reëntered the office, Miss Dewey had finished her lunch, and was putting a sheet of paper into her type-writer. She looked up at them with her eyes of turquoise blue, under her low white forehead, with the hair neatly rippled over it, and then began to beat the keys of her machine.

IX

LAPHAM had the pride which comes of self-making, and he would not openly lower his crest to the young fellow he had taken into his business. He was going to be obviously master in his own place to every one; and during the hours of business he did nothing to distinguish Corey from the half-dozen other clerks and book-keepers in the outer office, but he was not silent about the fact that Bromfield Corey's son had taken a fancy to come to him. "Did you notice that fellow at the desk facing my type-writer girl? Well, sir, that's the son of Bromfield Corey—old Phillips Corey's grandson. And I'll say this for him, that there isn't a man in the office that looks after his work better. There isn't anything he's too good for. He's right here at nine every morning, before the clock gets in the word. I guess it's his grandfather coming out in him. He's got charge of the foreign correspondence. We're pushing the paint everywhere." He flattered himself that he did not lug the matter in. He had been warned against that by his wife, but he had the right to do Corey justice, and his brag took the form of illustration. "Talk about training for business—I tell you it's all in the man himself! I used to believe in what old Horace Greeley said about college graduates being the poorest kind of horned cattle; but I've changed my mind a little. You take that fellow Corey. He's been through Harvard, and he's had about every advantage that a fellow could have. Been everywhere, and talks half a dozen languages like English. I suppose he's got money enough to live without lifting a hand, any more than his father does; son of Bromfield Corey, you know. But the thing was in him. He's a natural-born business man; and I've had many a fellow with me that had come up out of the street, and worked hard all his life, without ever losing his original opposition to the thing. But Corey likes it. I believe the fellow would like to stick at that desk of his night and day. I don't know where he got it. I guess it must be his grandfather, old Phillips Corey; it often skips a generation, you know. But what I say is, a thing has got to be born in a man; and if it ain't born in him, all the privations in the world won't put it there, and if it is, all the college training won't take it out."

Sometimes Lapham advanced these ideas at his own table, to a guest whom he had brought to Nantasket for the night. Then he suffered exposure and ridicule at the hands of his wife, when opportunity offered. She would not let him bring Corey down to Nantasket at all.

"No, indeed!" she said. "I am not going to have them think we're running after him. If he wants to see Irene, he can find out ways of doing it for himself."

"Who wants him to see Irene?" retorted the Colonel angrily.

"I do," said Mrs. Lapham. "And I want him to see her without any of your connivance, Silas. I'm not going to have it said that I put my girls *at* anybody. Why don't you invite some of your other clerks?"

"He ain't just like the other clerks. He's going to take charge of a part of the business. It's quite another thing."

"Oh, indeed!" said Mrs. Lapham vexatiously. "Then you *are* going to take a partner."

"I shall ask him down if I choose!" returned the Colonel, disdaining her insinuation.

His wife laughed with the fearlessness of a woman who knows her husband.

"But you won't choose when you've thought it over, Si." Then she applied an emollient to his chafed surface. "Don't you suppose I feel as you do about it? I know just how proud you are, and I'm not going to have you do anything that will make you feel meeching afterward. You just let things take their course. If he wants Irene, he's going to find out some way of seeing her; and if he don't, all the plotting and planning in the world isn't going to make him."

"Who's plotting?" again retorted the Colonel, shuddering at the utterance of hopes and ambitions which a man hides with shame, but a woman talks over as freely and coolly as if they were items of a milliner's bill.

"Oh, not *you*!" exulted his wife. "I understand what *you* want. You want to get this fellow, who is neither partner nor clerk, down here to talk business with him. Well, now, you just talk business with him at the office."

The only social attention which Lapham succeeded in offering Corey was to take him in his buggy, now and then, for a spin out over the Milldam. He kept the mare in town, and on a pleasant afternoon he liked to knock off early, as he phrased it, and let the mare out a little. Corey understood something about horses, though in a passionless way, and he would have preferred to talk business when obliged to talk horse. But he deferred to his business superior with the sense of discipline which is innate in the apparently insubordinate American nature. If Corey could hardly have helped feeling the social difference between Lapham and himself, in his presence he silenced his traditions, and showed him all the respect that he could have exacted from any of his clerks. He talked horse with him, and when the Colonel wished he talked house. Besides himself and his paint Lapham had not many other topics; and if he had a choice between the mare and the edifice on the water side of Beacon street, it was just now the latter. Sometimes, in driving in or out, he stopped at the house, and made Corey his guest there, if he might not at Nantasket; and one day it happened that the young man met Irene there again. She had come up with her mother alone, and they were in the house, interviewing the carpenter as before, when the Colonel jumped out of his buggy and cast anchor at the pavement. More exactly, Mrs. Lapham was interviewing the carpenter, and Irene was sitting in the bow-window on a trestle, and looking out at the driving. She saw him come up with her father, and bowed and blushed. Her father went on upstairs to find her mother, and Corey pulled up another trestle which he found in the back part of the room. The first floorings had been laid throughout the house, and the partitions had been lathed so that one could realize the shape of the interior.

"I suppose you will sit at this window a good deal," said the young man.

"Yes, I think it will be very nice. There's so much more going on than there is in the Square."

"It must be very interesting to you to see the house grow."

"It is. Only it doesn't seem to grow so fast as I expected."

"Why, I'm amazed at the progress your carpenter has made every time I come."

The girl looked down, and then lifting her eyes she said, with a sort of timorous appeal:

"I've been reading that book since you were down at Nantasket."

"Book?" repeated Corey, while she reddened with disappointment. "Oh, yes. 'Middlemarch.' Did you like it?"

"I haven't got through with it yet. Pen has finished it."

"What does she think of it?"

"Oh, I think she likes it very well. I haven't heard her talk about it much. Do you like it?"

"Yes; I liked it immensely. But it's several years since I read it."

"I didn't know it was so old. It's just got into the Seaside Library," she urged, with a little sense of injury in her tone.

"Oh, it hasn't been out such a very great while," said Corey, politely. "It came a little before 'Daniel Deronda.' "

The girl was again silent. She followed the curl of a shaving on the floor with the point of her parasol.

"Do you like that Rosamond Vincy?" she asked, without looking up.

Corey smiled in his kind way.

"I didn't suppose she was expected to have any friends. I can't say I liked her. But I don't think I disliked her so much as the author does. She's pretty hard on her good-looking"— he was going to say girls, but as if that might have been rather personal, he said—"people."

"Yes, that's what Pen says. She says she doesn't give her any chance to be good. She says she should have been just as bad as Rosamond if she had been in her place."

The young man laughed. "Your sister is very satirical, isn't she?"

"I don't know," said Irene, still intent upon the convolutions of the shaving. "She keeps us laughing. Papa thinks there's nobody that can talk like her." She gave the shaving a little toss from her, and took the parasol up across her lap. The unworldliness of the Lapham girls did not extend to their dress; Irene's costume was very stylish, and she governed her head and shoulders stylishly. "We are going to have the back room upstairs for a music-room and library," she said abruptly.

"Yes?" returned Corey. "I should think that would be charming."

"We expected to have book-cases, but the architect wants to build the shelves in."

The fact seemed to be referred to Corey for his comment.

"It seems to me that would be the best way. They'll look like part of the room then. You can make them low, and hang your pictures above them."

"Yes, that's what he said." The girl looked out of the window in adding, "I presume with nice bindings it will look very well."

"Oh, nothing furnishes a room like books."

"No. There will have to be a good many of them."

"That depends upon the size of your room and the number of your shelves."

"Oh, of course! I presume," said Irene, thoughtfully, "we shall have to have Gibbon."

"If you want to read him," said Corey, with a laugh of sympathy for an imaginable joke.

"We had a great deal about him at school. I believe we had one of his books. Mine's lost, but Pen will remember."

The young man looked at her, and then said, seriously, "You'll want Greene, of course, and Motley, and Parkman."

"Yes. What kind of writers are they?"

"They're historians, too."

"Oh, yes; I remember now. That's what Gibbon was. Is it Gibbon or Gibbons?"

The young man decided the point with apparently superfluous delicacy. "Gibbon, I think."

"There used to be so many of them," said Irene, gayly. "I used to get them mixed up with each other, and I couldn't tell them from the poets. Should you want to have poetry?"

"Yes; I suppose some edition of the English poets."

"We don't any of us like poetry. Do you like it?"

"I'm afraid I don't very much," Corey owned. "But, of course, there was a time when Tennyson was a great deal more to me than he is now."

"We had something about him at school, too. I think I remember the name. I think we ought to have *all* the American poets."

"Well, not all. Five or six of the best: you want Longfellow and Bryant and Whittier and Holmes and Emerson and Lowell."

The girl listened attentively, as if making mental note of the names.

"And Shakspere," she added. "Don't you like Shakspere's plays?"

"Oh, yes, very much."

"I used to be perfectly crazy about his plays. Don't you think 'Hamlet' is splendid? We had ever so much about Shakspere. Weren't you perfectly astonished when you found out how many other plays of his there were? I always thought there was nothing but 'Hamlet' and 'Romeo and Juliet' and 'Macbeth' and 'Richard III.' and 'King Lear,' and that one that Robeson and Crane have—oh, yes! 'Comedy of Errors.' "

"Those are the ones they usually play," said Corey.

"I presume we shall have to have Scott's works," said Irene, returning to the question of books.

"Oh, yes."

"One of the girls used to think he was *great*. She was always talking about Scott." Irene made a pretty little, amiably contemptuous mouth. "He isn't American, though?" she suggested.

"No," said Corey; "he's Scotch, I believe."

Irene passed her glove over her forehead. "I always get him mixed up with Cooper. Well, papa has got to get them. If we have a library, we have got to have books in it. Pen says it's perfectly ridiculous having one. But papa thinks whatever the architect says is right. He fought him hard enough at first. I don't see how any one can keep the poets and the historians and novelists separate in their mind. Of course papa will buy them if we say so. But I don't see how I'm ever going to tell him which ones." The joyous light faded out of her face and left it pensive.

"Why, if you like," said the young man, taking out his pencil, "I'll put down the names we've been talking about."

He clapped himself on his breast pockets to detect some lurking scrap of paper.

"Will you?" she cried delightedly. "Here! take one of my cards," and she pulled out her card-case. "The carpenter writes on a three-cornered block and puts it into his pocket, and it's so uncomfortable he can't help remembering it. Pen says she's going to adopt the three-cornered-block plan with papa."

"Thank you," said Corey. "I believe I'll use your card." He crossed over to her, and after a moment sat down on the trestle beside her. She looked over the card as he wrote. "Those are the ones we mentioned, but perhaps I'd better add a few others."

"Oh, thank you," she said, when he had written the card full on both sides. "He has got to get them in the nicest binding, too. I shall tell him about their helping to furnish the room, and then he can't object." She remained with the card, looking at it rather wistfully.

Perhaps Corey divined her trouble of mind.

"If he will take that to any book-seller, and tell him what bindings he wants, he will fill the order for him."

"Oh, thank you very much," she said, and put the card back into her card-case with great apparent relief. Then she turned her lovely face toward the young man, beaming with the triumph a woman feels in any bit of successful manœuvring, and began to talk with recovered gayety of other things, as if, having got rid of a matter annoying out of all proportion to its importance, she was now going to indemnify herself.

Corey did not return to his own trestle. She found another shaving within reach of her parasol, and began poking that with it, and trying to follow it through its folds. Corey watched her awhile.

"You seem to have a great passion for playing with shavings," he said. "Is it a new one?"

"New what?"

"Passion."

"I don't know," she said, dropping her eyelids, and keeping on with her effort. She looked shyly aslant at him. "Perhaps you don't approve of playing with shavings?"

"Oh, yes, I do. I admire it very much. But it seems rather difficult. I've a great ambition to put my foot on the shaving's tail and hold it for you."

"Well," said the girl.

"Thank you," said the young man. He did so, and now she

ran her parasol point easily through it. They looked at each other and laughed. "That was wonderful. Would you like to try another?" he asked.

"No, I thank you," she replied. "I think one will do."

They both laughed again, for whatever reason or no reason, and then the young girl became sober. To a girl everything a young man does is of significance; and if he holds a shaving down with his foot while she pokes through it with her parasol, she must ask herself what he means by it.

"They seem to be having rather a long interview with the carpenter to-day," said Irene, looking vaguely toward the ceiling. She turned with polite ceremony to Corey. "I'm afraid you're letting them keep you. You mustn't."

"Oh, no. You're letting me stay," he returned.

She bridled, and bit her lip for pleasure. "I presume they will be down before a great while. Don't you like the smell of the wood and the mortar? It's so fresh."

"Yes, it's delicious." He bent forward and picked up from the floor the shaving with which they had been playing, and put it to his nose. "It's like a flower. May I offer it to you?" he asked, as if it had been one.

"Oh, thank you, thank you!" She took it from him and put it into her belt, and then they both laughed once more.

Steps were heard descending. When the elder people reached the floor where they were sitting, Corey rose and presently took his leave.

"What makes you so solemn, 'Rene?" asked Mrs. Lapham.

"Solemn?" echoed the girl. "I'm not a *bit* solemn. What *can* you mean?"

Corey dined at home that evening, and as he sat looking across the table at his father, he said, "I wonder what the average literature of non-cultivated people is."

"Ah," said the elder, "I suspect the average is pretty low even with cultivated people. You don't read a great many books yourself, Tom."

"No, I don't," the young man confessed. "I read more books when I was with Stanton, last winter, than I had since I was a boy. But I read them because I must—there was nothing else to do. It wasn't because I was fond of reading.

Still, I think I read with some sense of literature and the difference between authors. I don't suppose that people generally do that; I have met people who had read books without troubling themselves to find out even the author's name, much less trying to decide upon his quality. I suppose that's the way the vast majority of people read."

"Yes. If authors were not almost necessarily recluses, and ignorant of the ignorance about them, I don't see how they could endure it. Of course they are fated to be overwhelmed by oblivion at last, poor fellows; but to see it weltering all round them while they are in the very act of achieving immortality must be tremendously discouraging. I don't suppose that we who have the habit of reading, and at least a nodding acquaintance with literature, can imagine the bestial darkness of the great mass of people—even people whose houses are rich, and whose linen is purple and fine. But occasionally we get glimpses of it. I suppose you found the latest publications lying all about in Lapham cottage when you were down there?"

Young Corey laughed. "It wasn't exactly cumbered with them."

"No?"

"To tell the truth, I don't suppose they ever buy books. The young ladies get novels that they hear talked of out of the circulating library."

"Had they knowledge enough to be ashamed of their ignorance?"

"Yes, in certain ways—to a certain degree."

"It's a curious thing, this thing we call civilization," said the elder, musingly. "We think it is an affair of epochs and of nations. It's really an affair of individuals. One brother will be civilized and the other a barbarian. I've occasionally met young girls who were so brutally, insolently, willfully indifferent to the arts which make civilization that they ought to have been clothed in the skins of wild beasts and gone about barefoot with clubs over their shoulders. Yet they were of polite origin, and their parents were at least respectful of the things that these young animals despised."

"I don't think that is exactly the case with the Lapham family," said the son, smiling. "The father and mother rather apologized about not getting time to read, and the young ladies by no means scorned it."

"They are quite advanced!"

"They are going to have a library in their Beacon street house."

"Oh, poor things! How are they ever going to get the books together?"

"Well, sir," said the son, coloring a little, "*I* have been indirectly applied to for help."

"You, Tom!" His father dropped back in his chair and laughed.

"I recommended the standard authors," said the son.

"Oh, I never supposed your *prudence* would be at fault, Tom!"

"But seriously," said the young man, generously smiling in sympathy with his father's enjoyment, "they're not unintelligent people. They are very quick, and they are shrewd and sensible."

"I have no doubt that some of the Sioux are so. But that is not saying that they are civilized. All civilization comes through literature now, especially in our country. A Greek got his civilization by talking and looking, and in some measure a Parisian may still do it. But we, who live remote from history and monuments, we must read or we must barbarize. Once we were softened, if not polished, by religion; but I suspect that the pulpit counts for much less now in civilizing."

"They're enormous devourers of newspapers, and theatergoers; and they go a great deal to lectures. The Colonel prefers them with the stereopticon."

"They might get a something in that way," said the elder, thoughtfully. "Yes, I suppose one must take those things into account—especially the newspapers and the lectures. I doubt if the theater is a factor in civilization among us. I dare say it doesn't deprave a great deal, but from what I've seen of it I should say that it was intellectually degrading. Perhaps they might get some sort of lift from it; I don't know. Tom!" he added, after a moment's reflection. "I really think I ought to see this patron of yours. Don't you think it would be rather decent in me to make his acquaintance?"

"Well, if you have the fancy, sir," said the young man. "But there's no sort of obligation. Colonel Lapham would be the last man in the world to want to give our relation any sort of social character. The meeting will come about in the natural course of things."

"Ah, I didn't intend to propose anything immediate," said the father. "One can't do anything in the summer, and I should prefer your mother's superintendence. Still, I can't rid myself of the idea of a dinner. It appears to me that there ought to be a dinner."

"Oh, pray don't feel that there's any necessity."

"Well," said the elder, with easy resignation, "there's at least no hurry."

"There is one thing I don't like," said Lapham, in the course of one of those talks which came up between his wife and himself concerning Corey, "or at least I don't understand it; and that's the way his father behaves. I don't want to force myself on any man; but it seems to me pretty queer the way he holds off. I should think he would take enough interest in his son to want to know something about his business. What is he afraid of?" demanded Lapham angrily. "Does he think I'm going to jump at a chance to get in with him, if he gives me one? He's mightily mistaken if he does. _I_ don't want to know him."

"Silas," said his wife, making a wife's free version of her husband's words, and replying to their spirit rather than their letter, "I hope you never said a word to Mr. Corey to let him know the way you feel."

"I never mentioned his father to him!" roared the Colonel. "That's the way I feel about it!"

"Because it would spoil everything. I wouldn't have them think we cared the least thing in the world for their acquaintance. We shouldn't be a bit better off. We don't know the same people they do, and we don't care for the same kind of things."

Lapham was breathless with resentment of his wife's implication. "Don't I tell you," he gasped, "that I don't want to know them? Who began it? They're friends of yours if they're anybody's."

"They're distant acquaintances of mine," returned Mrs. Lapham quietly; "and this young Corey is a clerk of yours. And I want we should hold ourselves so that when they get ready to make the advances we can meet them half-way or not just as we choose."

"That's what grinds me," cried her husband. "Why should we wait for them to make the advances? Why shouldn't we make 'em? Are they any better than we are? My note of hand would be worth ten times what Bromfield Corey's is on the street to-day. And I made *my* money. I haven't loafed my life away."

"Oh, it isn't what you've got, and it isn't what you've done exactly. It's what you are."

"Well, then, what's the difference?"

"None that really amounts to anything, or that need give you any trouble, if you don't think of it. But he's been all his life in society, and he knows just what to say and what to do, and he can talk about the things that society people like to talk about, and you—can't."

Lapham gave a furious snort. "And does that make him any better?"

"No. But it puts him where he can make the advances without demeaning himself, and it puts you where you can't. Now, look here, Silas Lapham! You understand this thing as well as I do. You know that I appreciate you, and that I'd sooner die than have you humble yourself to a living soul. But I'm not going to have you coming to me, and pretending that you can meet Bromfield Corey as an equal on his own ground. You can't. He's got a better education than you, and if he hasn't got more brains than you, he's got different. And he and his wife, and their fathers and grandfathers before 'em, have always had a high position, and you can't help it. If you want to know them, you've got to let them make the advances. If you don't, all well and good."

"I guess," said the chafed and vanquished Colonel, after a moment for swallowing the pill, "that they'd have been in a pretty fix if you'd waited to let them make the advances last summer."

"That was a different thing altogether. I didn't know who they were, or may be I should have waited. But all I say now is that if you've got young Corey into business with you, in hopes of our getting into society with his father, you better ship him at once. For I ain't going to have it on that basis."

"Who wants to have it on that basis?" retorted her husband.

"Nobody, if you don't," said Mrs. Lapham tranquilly.

Irene had come home with the shaving in her belt, unnoticed by her father, and unquestioned by her mother. But her sister saw it at once, and asked her what she was doing with it.

"Oh, nothing," said Irene, with a joyful smile of self-betrayal, taking the shaving carefully out, and laying it among the laces and ribbons in her drawer.

"Hadn't you better put it in water, 'Rene? It'll be all wilted by morning," said Pen.

"You mean thing!" cried the happy girl "It isn't a flower!"

"Oh, I thought it was a whole bouquet. Who gave it to you?"

"I sha'n't tell you," said Irene saucily.

"Oh, well, never mind. Did you know Mr. Corey had been down here this afternoon, walking on the beach with me?"

"He wasn't—he wasn't at all! He was at the house with *me*. There! I've caught you fairly."

"Is that so?" drawled Penelope. "Then I never could guess who gave you that precious shaving."

"No, you couldn't!" said Irene, flushing beautifully. "And you may guess, and you may guess, and you may guess!" With her lovely eyes she coaxed her sister to keep on teasing her, and Penelope continued the comedy with the patience that women have for such things.

"Well, I'm not going to try, if it's no use. But I didn't know it had got to be the fashion to give shavings instead of flowers. But there's some sense in it. They can be used for kindlings when they get old, and you can't do anything with old flowers. Perhaps he'll get to sending 'em by the barrel."

Irene laughed for pleasure in this tormenting. "Oh, Pen, I want to tell you how it all happened."

"Oh, he *did* give it to you, then? Well, I guess I don't care to hear."

"You shall, and you've got to!" Irene ran and caught her

sister, who feigned to be going out of the room, and pushed her into a chair. "There, now!" She pulled up another chair, and hemmed her in with it. "He came over, and sat down on the trestle alongside of me——"

"What? As close as you are to me now?"

"You wretch! I will *give* it to you! No, at a proper distance. And here was this shaving on the floor, that I'd been poking with my parasol——"

"To hide your embarrassment."

"Pshaw! I wasn't a bit embarrassed. I was just as much at my ease! And then he asked me to let him hold the shaving down with his foot, while I went on with my poking. And I said yes he might——"

"What a bold girl! You said he might hold a shaving down for you?"

"And then—and then—" continued Irene, lifting her eyes absently, and losing herself in the beatific recollection, "and then— Oh, yes! Then I asked him if he didn't like the smell of pine shavings. And then he picked it up, and said it smelt like a flower. And then he asked if he might offer it to me— just for a joke, you know. And I took it, and stuck it in my belt. And we had such a laugh! We got into a regular gale. And oh, Pen, what do you suppose he meant by it?" She suddenly caught herself to her sister's breast, and hid her burning face on her shoulder.

"Well, there used to be a book about the language of flowers. But I never knew much about the language of shavings, and I can't say exactly——"

"Oh, don't— *don't*, Pen!" and here Irene gave over laughing, and began to sob in her sister's arms.

"Why, 'Rene!" cried the elder girl.

"You *know* he didn't mean anything. He doesn't care a bit about me. He hates me! He despises me! Oh, what shall I do?"

A trouble passed over the face of the sister as she silently comforted the child in her arms; then the drolling light came back into her eyes. "Well, 'Rene, *you* haven't got to do *any*-thing. That's one advantage girls have got—if it *is* an advantage. I'm not always sure."

Irene's tears turned to laughing again. When she lifted her

head it was to look into the mirror confronting them, where her beauty showed all the more brilliant for the shower that had passed over it. She seemed to gather courage from the sight.

"It must be awful to have to *do*," she said, smiling into her own face. "I don't see how they ever can."

"Some of 'em can't—especially when there's such a tearing beauty around."

"Oh, pshaw, Pen! You know that isn't so. You've got a real pretty mouth, Pen," she added thoughtfully, surveying the feature in the glass, and then pouting her own lips for the sake of that effect on them.

"It's a useful mouth," Penelope admitted; "I don't believe I could get along without it now, I've had it so long."

"It's got such a funny expression—just the mate of the look in your eyes; as if you were just going to say something ridiculous. He said, the very first time he saw you, that he knew you were humorous."

"Is it possible? It must be so, if the Grand Mogul said it. Why didn't you tell me so before, and not let me keep on going round just like a common person?"

Irene laughed as if she liked to have her sister take his praises in that way rather than another. "I've got such a stiff, prim kind of mouth," she said, drawing it down, and then looking anxiously at it.

"I hope you didn't put on that expression when he offered you the shaving. If you did, I don't believe he'll ever give you another splinter."

The severe mouth broke into a lovely laugh, and then pressed itself in a kiss against Penelope's cheek.

"There! Be done, you silly thing! I'm not going to have you accepting *me* before I've offered myself, *anyway*." She freed herself from her sister's embrace, and ran from her round the room.

Irene pursued her, in the need of hiding her face against her shoulder again. "Oh, Pen! Oh, Pen!" she cried.

The next day, at the first moment of finding herself alone with her eldest daughter, Mrs. Lapham asked, as if knowing that Penelope must have already made it subject of inquiry:

"What was Irene doing with that shaving in her belt yesterday?"

"Oh, just some nonsense of hers with Mr. Corey. He gave it to her at the new house." Penelope did not choose to look up and meet her mother's grave glance.

"What do you think he meant by it?"

Penelope repeated Irene's account of the affair, and her mother listened without seeming to derive much encouragement from it.

"He doesn't seem like one to flirt with her," she said at last. Then, after a thoughtful pause: "Irene is as good a girl as ever breathed, and she's a perfect beauty. But I should hate the day when a daughter of mine was married for her beauty."

"You're safe as far as I'm concerned, mother."

Mrs. Lapham smiled ruefully. "She isn't really equal to him, Pen. I misdoubted that from the first, and it's been borne in upon me more and more ever since. She hasn't mind enough."

"I didn't know that a man fell in love with a girl's intellect," said Penelope quietly.

"Oh, no. He hasn't fallen in love with Irene at all. If he had, it wouldn't matter about the intellect."

Penelope let the self-contradiction pass.

"Perhaps he has, after all."

"No," said Mrs. Lapham. "She pleases him when he sees her. But he doesn't try to see her."

"He has no chance. You won't let father bring him here."

"He would find excuses to come without being brought, if he wished to come," said the mother. "But she isn't in his mind enough to make him. He goes away and doesn't think anything more about her. She's a child. She's a good child, and I shall always say it; but she's nothing but a child. No, she's got to forget him."

"Perhaps that won't be so easy."

"No, I presume not. And now your father has got the notion in his head, and he will move heaven and earth to bring it to pass. I can see that he's always thinking about it."

"The Colonel has a will of his own," observed the girl, rocking to and fro where she sat looking at her mother.

"I wish we had never met them!" cried Mrs. Lapham. "I

wish we had never thought of building! I wish he had kept away from your father's business!"

"Well, it's too late now, mother," said the girl. "Perhaps it isn't so bad as you think."

"Well, we must stand it, anyway," said Mrs. Lapham, with the grim antique Yankee submission.

"Oh, yes, we've got to stand it," said Penelope, with the quaint modern American fatalism.

X

IT WAS late June, almost July, when Corey took up his life in Boston again, where the summer slips away so easily. If you go out of town early, it seems a very long summer when you come back in October; but if you stay, it passes swiftly, and, seen foreshortened in its flight, seems scarcely a month's length. It has its days of heat, when it is very hot, but for the most part it is cool, with baths of the east wind that seem to saturate the soul with delicious freshness. Then there are stretches of gray, westerly weather, when the air is full of the sentiment of early autumn, and the frying of the grasshopper in the blossomed weed of the vacant lots on the Back Bay is intershot with the carol of crickets; and the yellowing leaf on the long slope of Mt. Vernon street smites the sauntering observer with tender melancholy. The caterpillar, gorged with the spoil of the lindens on Chestnut, and weaving his own shroud about him in his lodgment on the brickwork, records the passing of summer by mid-July; and if after that comes August, its breath is thick and short, and September is upon the sojourner before he has fairly had time to philosophize the character of the town out of season.

But it must have appeared that its most characteristic feature was the absence of everybody he knew. This was one of the things that commended Boston to Bromfield Corey during the summer; and if his son had any qualms about the life he had entered upon with such vigor, it must have been a relief to him that there was scarcely a soul left to wonder or pity. By the time people got back to town the fact of his connection with the mineral paint man would be an old story, heard afar off with different degrees of surprise, and considered with different degrees of indifference. A man has not reached the age of twenty-six in any community where he was born and reared without having had his capacity pretty well ascertained; and in Boston the analysis is conducted with an unsparing thoroughness which may fitly impress the un-Bostonian mind, darkened by the popular superstition that the Bostonians blindly admire one another. A man's qualities are

sifted as closely in Boston as they doubtless were in Florence
or Athens; and, if final mercy was shown in those cities because a man was, with all his limitations, an Athenian or Florentine, some abatement might as justly be made in Boston for
like reason. Corey's powers had been gauged in college, and
he had not given his world reason to think very differently of
him since he came out of college. He was rated as an energetic fellow, a little indefinite in aim, with the smallest
amount of inspiration that can save a man from being commonplace. If he was not commonplace, it was through nothing remarkable in his mind, which was simply clear and practical, but through some combination of qualities of the heart
that made men trust him, and women call him sweet—a
word of theirs which conveys otherwise indefinable excel-
lences. Some of the more nervous and excitable said that Tom
Corey was as sweet as he could live; but this perhaps meant
no more than the word alone. No man ever had a son less
like him than Bromfield Corey. If Tom Corey had ever said a
witty thing, no one could remember it; and yet the father had
never said a witty thing to a more sympathetic listener than
his own son. The clear mind which produced nothing but
practical results reflected everything with charming lucidity;
and it must have been this which endeared Tom Corey to
every one who spoke ten words with him. In a city where
people have good reason for liking to shine, a man who did
not care to shine must be little short of universally acceptable
without any other effort for popularity; and those who admired and enjoyed Bromfield Corey loved his son. Yet, when
it came to accounting for Tom Corey, as it often did in a
community where every one's generation is known to the remotest degrees of cousinship, they could not trace his sweetness to his mother, for neither Anna Bellingham nor any of
her family, though they were so many blocks of Wenham ice
for purity and rectangularity, had ever had any such savor;
and, in fact, it was to his father, whose habit of talk wronged
it in himself, that they had to turn for this quality of the son's.
They traced to the mother the traits of practicality and common sense in which he bordered upon the commonplace, and
which, when they had dwelt upon them, made him seem
hardly worth the close inquiry they had given him.

While the summer wore away he came and went methodically about his business, as if it had been the business of his life, sharing his father's bachelor liberty and solitude, and expecting with equal patience the return of his mother and sisters in the autumn. Once or twice he found time to run down to Mt. Desert and see them; and then he heard how the Philadelphia and New York people were getting in everywhere, and was given reason to regret the house at Nahant which he had urged to be sold. He came back and applied himself to his desk with a devotion that was exemplary rather than necessary; for Lapham made no difficulty about the brief absences which he asked, and set no term to the apprenticeship that Corey was serving in the office before setting off upon that mission to South America in the early winter, for which no date had yet been fixed.

The summer was a dull season for the paint as well as for everything else. Till things should brisk up, as Lapham said, in the fall, he was letting the new house take a great deal of his time. Æsthetic ideas had never been intelligibly presented to him before, and he found a delight in apprehending them that was very grateful to his imaginative architect. At the beginning, the architect had foreboded a series of mortifying defeats and disastrous victories in his encounters with his client; but he had never had a client who could be more reasonably led on from one outlay to another. It appeared that Lapham required but to understand or feel the beautiful effect intended, and he was ready to pay for it. His bull-headed pride was concerned in a thing which the architect made him see, and then he believed that he had seen it himself, perhaps conceived it. In some measure the architect seemed to share his delusion, and freely said that Lapham was very suggestive. Together they blocked out windows here, and bricked them up there; they changed doors and passages; pulled down cornices and replaced them with others of different design; experimented with costly devices of decoration, and went to extravagant lengths in novelties of finish. Mrs. Lapham, beginning with a woman's adventurousness in the unknown region, took fright at the reckless outlay at last, and refused to let her husband pass a certain limit. He tried to make her believe that a far-seeing economy dictated the expense; and that if he put the money into the house, he could get it out any time by selling it. She would not be persuaded.

"I don't want you should sell it. And you've put more money into it now than you'll ever get out again, unless you can find as big a goose to buy it, and that isn't likely. No, sir! You just stop at a hundred thousand, and don't you let him get you a cent beyond. Why, you're perfectly bewitched with that fellow! You've lost your head, Silas Lapham, and if you don't look out you'll lose your money too."

The Colonel laughed; he liked her to talk that way, and promised he would hold up awhile.

"But there's no call to feel anxious, Pert. It's only a question what to do with the money. I can reinvest it; but I never had so much of it to spend before."

"Spend it, then," said his wife; "don't throw it away! And how came you to have so much more money than you know what to do with, Silas Lapham?" she added.

"Oh, I've made a very good thing in stocks lately."

"In stocks? When did you take up gambling for a living?"

"Gambling? Stuff! What gambling? Who said it was gambling?"

"You have; many a time."

"Oh, yes, buying and selling on a margin. But this was a *bona fide* transaction. I bought at forty-three for an investment, and I sold at a hundred and seven; and the money passed both times."

"Well, you better let stocks alone," said his wife, with the conservatism of her sex. "Next time you'll buy at a hundred and seven and sell at forty-three. Then where'll you be?"

"Left," admitted the Colonel.

"You better stick to paint awhile yet."

The Colonel enjoyed this, too, and laughed again with the ease of a man who knows what he is about. A few days after that he came down to Nantasket with the radiant air which he wore when he had done a good thing in business and wanted his wife's sympathy. He did not say anything of what had happened till he was alone with her in their own room; but he was very gay the whole evening, and made several jokes which Penelope said nothing but very great prosperity could excuse: they all understood these moods of his.

"Well, what is it, Silas?" asked his wife when the time came. "Any more big-bugs wanting to go into the mineral paint business with you?"

"Something better than that."

"I could think of a good many better things," said his wife, with a sigh of latent bitterness. "What's this one?"

"I've had a visitor."

"Who?"

"Can't you guess?"

"I don't want to try. Who was it?"

"Rogers."

Mrs. Lapham sat down with her hands in her lap, and stared at the smile on her husband's face, where he sat facing her.

"I guess you wouldn't want to joke on that subject, Si," she said, a little hoarsely, "and you wouldn't grin about it unless you had some good news. I don't know what the miracle is, but if you could tell quick——"

She stopped like one who can say no more.

"I will, Persis," said her husband, and with that awed tone in which he rarely spoke of anything but the virtues of his paint. "He came to borrow money of me, and I lent him it. That's the short of it. The long——"

"Go on," said his wife, with gentle patience.

"Well, Pert, I was never so much astonished in my life as I was to see that man come into my office. You might have knocked me down with—I don't know what."

"I don't wonder. Go on!"

"And he was as much embarrassed as I was. There we stood, gaping at each other, and I hadn't hardly sense enough to ask him to take a chair. I don't know just how we got at it. And I don't remember just how it was that he said he came to come to me. But he had got hold of a patent right that he wanted to go into on a large scale, and there he was wanting me to supply him the funds."

"Go on!" said Mrs. Lapham, with her voice further in her throat.

"I never felt the way you did about Rogers, but I know how you always did feel, and I guess I surprised him with my answer. He had brought along a lot of stock as security——"

"You didn't take it, Silas!" his wife flashed out.

"Yes, I did, though," said Lapham. "You wait. We settled our business, and then we went into the old thing, from the very start. And we talked it all over. And when we got through we shook hands. Well, I don't know when it's done me so much good to shake hands with anybody."

"And you told him—you owned up to him that you were in the wrong, Silas?"

"No, I didn't," returned the Colonel, promptly; "for I wasn't. And before we got through, I guess he saw it the same as I did."

"Oh, no matter! so you had the chance to show how you felt."

"But I never felt that way," persisted the Colonel. "I've lent him the money, and I've kept his stocks. And he got what he wanted out of me."

"Give him back his stocks!"

"No, I sha'n't. Rogers came to borrow. He didn't come to beg. You needn't be troubled about his stocks. They're going to come up in time; but just now they're so low down that no bank would take them as security, and I've got to hold them till they do rise. I hope you're satisfied now, Persis," said her husband; and he looked at her with the willingness to receive the reward of a good action which we all feel when we have performed one. "I lent him the money you kept me from spending on the house."

"Truly, Si? Well, I'm satisfied," said Mrs. Lapham, with a deep, tremulous breath. "The Lord has been good to you, Silas," she continued, solemnly. "You may laugh if you choose, and I don't know as I believe in his interfering a great deal; but I believe he's interfered this time; and I tell you, Silas, it ain't always he gives people a chance to make it up to others in this life. I've been afraid you'd die, Silas, before you got the chance; but he's let you live to make it up to Rogers."

"I'm glad to be let live," said Lapham, stubbornly; "but I hadn't anything to make up to Milton K. Rogers. And if God has let me live for that——"

"Oh, say what you please, Si! Say what you please, now you've done it! I sha'n't stop you. You've taken the one spot—the one *speck*—off you that was ever there, and I'm satisfied."

"There wa'n't ever any speck there," Lapham held out, lapsing more and more into his vernacular; "and what I done, I done for you, Persis."

"And I thank you for your own soul's sake, Silas."

"I guess my soul's all right," said Lapham.

"And I want you should promise me one thing more."

"Thought you said you were satisfied?"

"I am. But I want you should promise me this: that you won't let anything tempt you—anything!—to ever trouble Rogers for that money you lent him. No matter what happens—no matter if you lose it all. Do you promise?"

"Why, I don't ever *expect* to press him for it. That's what I said to myself when I lent it. And of course I'm glad to have that old trouble healed up. I don't *think* I ever did Rogers any wrong, and I never did think so; but if I *did* do it—*if* I did—I'm willing to call it square, if I never see a cent of my money back again."

"Well, that's all," said his wife.

They did not celebrate his reconciliation with his old enemy—for such they had always felt him to be since he ceased to be an ally—by any show of joy or affection. It was not in their tradition, as stoical for the woman as for the man, that they should kiss or embrace each other at such a moment. She was content to have told him that he had done his duty, and he was content with her saying that. But before she slept she found words to add that she always feared the selfish part he had acted toward Rogers had weakened him, and left him less able to overcome any temptation that might beset him; and that was one reason why she could never be easy about it. Now she should never fear for him again.

This time he did not explicitly deny her forgiving impeachment.

"Well, it's all past and gone now, anyway; and I don't want you should think anything more about it."

He was man enough to take advantage of the high favor in which he stood when he went up to town, and to abuse it by bringing Corey down to supper. His wife could not help condoning the sin of disobedience in him at such a time. Penelope said that between the admiration she felt for the Colonel's boldness and her mother's forbearance, she was hardly in a state to entertain company that evening; but she did what she could.

Irene liked being talked to better than talking, and when her sister was by she was always, tacitly or explicitly, referring to her for confirmation of what she said. She was content to sit and look pretty as she looked at the young man and listened to her sister's drolling. She laughed, and kept glancing at Corey to make sure that he was understanding her. When they went out on the veranda to see the moon on the water, Penelope led the way and Irene followed.

They did not look at the moonlight long. The young man perched on the rail of the veranda, and Irene took one of the red-painted rocking-chairs where she could conveniently look at him and at her sister, who sat leaning forward lazily and running on, as the phrase is. That low, crooning note of hers was delicious; her face, glimpsed now and then in the moonlight as she turned it or lifted it a little, had a fascination which kept his eye. Her talk was very unliterary, and its effect seemed hardly conscious. She was far from epigram in her funning. She told of this trifle and that; she sketched the characters and looks of people who had interested her, and nothing seemed to have escaped her notice; she mimicked a little, but not much; she suggested, and then the affair represented itself as if without her agency. She did not laugh; when Corey stopped, she made a soft cluck in her throat, as if she liked his being amused, and went on again.

The Colonel, left alone with his wife for the first time since he had come from town, made haste to take the word. "Well, Pert, I've arranged the whole thing with Rogers, and I hope you'll be satisfied to know that he owes me twenty thousand dollars, and that I've got security from him to the amount of a fourth of that, if I was to force his stocks to a sale."

"How came he to come down with you?" asked Mrs. Lapham.

"Who? Rogers?"

"Mr. Corey."

"Corey? Oh!" said Lapham, affecting not to have thought she could mean Corey. "He proposed it."

"Likely!" jeered his wife, but with perfect amiability.

"It's so," protested the Colonel. "We got talking about a matter just before I left, and he walked down to the boat with me; and then he said if I didn't mind he guessed he'd come along down and go back on the return boat. Of course I couldn't let him do that."

"It's well for you you couldn't."

"And I couldn't do less than bring him here to tea."

"Oh, certainly not."

"But he ain't going to stay the night—unless," faltered Lapham, "you want him to."

"Oh, of course, I want him to! I guess he'll stay, probably."

"Well, you know how crowded that last boat always is, and he can't get any other now."

Mrs. Lapham laughed at the simple wile. "I hope you'll be just as well satisfied, Si, if it turns out he doesn't want Irene after all."

"Pshaw, Persis! What are you always bringing that up for?" pleaded the Colonel. Then he fell silent, and presently his rude, strong face was clouded with an unconscious frown.

"There!" cried his wife, startling him from his abstraction. "I see how you'd feel; and I hope that you'll remember who you've got to blame."

"I'll risk it," said Lapham, with the confidence of a man used to success.

From the veranda the sound of Penelope's lazy tone came through the closed windows, with joyous laughter from Irene and peals from Corey.

"Listen to that!" said her father within, swelling up with inexpressible satisfaction. "That girl can talk for twenty, right straight along. She's better than a circus any day. I wonder what she's up to now."

"Oh, she's probably getting off some of those yarns of hers, or telling about some people. She can't step out of the house without coming back with more things to talk about than most folks would bring back from Japan. There ain't a ridiculous person she's ever seen but what she's got something from them to make you laugh at; and I don't believe we've ever had anybody in the house since the girl could talk that she hain't got some saying from, or some trick that'll pint

'em out so't you can see 'em and hear 'em. Sometimes I want
to stop her; but when she gets into one of her gales there
ain't any standing up against her. I guess it's lucky for Irene
that she's got Pen there to help entertain her company. I can't
ever feel down where Pen is."

"That's so," said the Colonel. "And I guess she's got about
as much culture as any of them. Don't you?"

"She reads a great deal," admitted her mother. "She seems
to be at it the whole while. I don't want she should injure her
health, and sometimes I feel like snatchin' the books away
from her. I don't know as it's good for a girl to read so much,
anyway, especially novels. I don't want she should get notions."

"Oh, I guess Pen'll know how to take care of herself," said
Lapham.

"She's got sense enough. But she ain't so practical as Irene.
She's more up in the clouds—more of what you may call a
dreamer. Irene's wide-awake every minute; and I declare, any
one to see these two together when there's anything to be
done, or any lead to be taken, would say Irene was the oldest,
nine times out of ten. It's only when they get to talking that
you can see Pen's got twice as much brains."

"Well," said Lapham, tacitly granting this point, and leaning back in his chair in supreme content. "Did you ever see
much nicer girls anywhere?"

His wife laughed at his pride. "I presume they're as much
swans as anybody's geese."

"No; but honestly, now!"

"Oh, they'll do; but don't you be silly, if you can help it,
Si."

The young people came in, and Corey said it was time for
his boat. Mrs. Lapham pressed him to stay, but he persisted,
and he would not let the Colonel send him to the boat; he
said he would rather walk. Outside, he pushed along toward
the boat, which presently he could see lying at her landing in
the bay, across the sandy tract to the left of the hotels. From
time to time he almost stopped in his rapid walk, as a man
does whose mind is in a pleasant tumult; and then he went
forward at a swifter pace.

"She's charming!" he said, and he thought he had spoken

aloud. He found himself floundering about in the deep sand, wide of the path; he got back to it, and reached the boat just before she started. The clerk came to take his fare, and Corey looked radiantly up at him in his lantern-light, with a smile that he must have been wearing a long time; his cheek was stiff with it. Once some people who stood near him edged suddenly and fearfully away, and then he suspected himself of having laughed outright.

XI

COREY put off his set smile with the help of a frown, of which he first became aware after reaching home, when his father asked:

"Anything gone wrong with your department of the fine arts to-day, Tom?"

"Oh, no—no, sir," said the son, instantly relieving his brows from the strain upon them, and beaming again. "But I was thinking whether you were not perhaps right in your impression that it might be well for you to make Colonel Lapham's acquaintance before a great while."

"Has he been suggesting it in any way?" asked Bromfield Corey, laying aside his book and taking his lean knee between his clasped hands.

"Oh, not at all!" the young man hastened to reply. "I was merely thinking whether it might not begin to seem intentional, your not doing it."

"Well, Tom, you know I have been leaving it altogether to you——"

"Oh, I understand, of course, and I didn't mean to urge anything of the kind——"

"You are so very much more of a Bostonian than I am, you know, that I've been waiting your motion in entire confidence that you would know just what to do, and when to do it. If I had been left quite to my own lawless impulses, I think I should have called upon your *padrone* at once. It seems to me that *my* father would have found some way of showing that he expected as much as that from people placed in the relation to him that we hold to Colonel Lapham."

"Do you think so?" asked the young man.

"Yes. But you know I don't pretend to be an authority in such matters. As far as they go, I am always in the hands of your mother and you children."

"I'm very sorry, sir. I had no idea I was overruling your judgment. I only wanted to spare you a formality that didn't seem quite a necessity yet. I'm very sorry," he said again, and this time with more comprehensive regret. "I shouldn't like to have seemed remiss with a man who has been so considerate of me. They are all very good-natured."

"I dare say," said Bromfield Corey, with the satisfaction which no elder can help feeling in disabling the judgment of a younger man, "that it won't be too late if I go down to your office with you to-morrow."

"No, no. I didn't imagine your doing it at once, sir."

"Ah, but nothing can prevent me from doing a thing when once I take the bit in my teeth," said the father, with the pleasure which men of weak will sometimes take in recognizing their weakness. "How does their new house get on?"

"I believe they expect to be in it before New Year's."

"Will they be a great addition to society?" asked Bromfield Corey, with unimpeachable seriousness.

"I don't quite know what you mean," returned the son, a little uneasily.

"Ah, I see that you do, Tom."

"No one can help feeling that they are all people of good sense and—right ideas."

"Oh, that won't do. If society took in all the people of right ideas and good sense, it would expand beyond the calling capacity of its most active members. Even your mother's social conscientiousness could not compass it. Society is a very different sort of thing from good sense and right ideas. It is based upon them, of course, but the airy, graceful, winning superstructure which we all know demands different qualities. Have your friends got these qualities,—which may be felt, but not defined?"

The son laughed. "To tell you the truth, sir, I don't think they have the most elemental ideas of society, as we understand it. I don't believe Mrs. Lapham ever gave a dinner."

"And with all that money!" sighed the father.

"I don't believe they have the habit of wine at table. I suspect that when they don't drink tea and coffee with their dinner, they drink ice-water."

"Horrible!" said Bromfield Corey.

"It appears to me that this defines them."

"Oh, yes. There are people who give dinners, and who are not cognoscible. But people who have never yet given a dinner, how is society to assimilate them?"

"It digests a great many people," suggested the young man.

"Yes; but they have always brought some sort of sauce pi-quante with them. Now, as I understand you, these friends of yours have no such sauce."

"Oh, I don't know about that!" cried the son.

"Oh, rude, native flavors, I dare say. But that isn't what I mean. Well, then, they must spend. There is no other way for them to win their way to general regard. We must have the Colonel elected to the Ten O'clock Club, and he must put himself down in the list of those willing to entertain. Any one can manage a large supper. Yes, I see a gleam of hope for him in that direction."

In the morning Bromfield Corey asked his son whether he should find Lapham at his place as early as eleven.

"I think you might find him even earlier. I've never been there before him. I doubt if the porter is there much sooner."

"Well, suppose I go with you, then?"

"Why, if you like, sir," said the son, with some depreca-tion.

"Oh, the question is, will *he* like?"

"I think he will, sir"; and the father could see that his son was very much pleased.

Lapham was rending an impatient course through the morning's news when they appeared at the door of his inner room. He looked up from the newspaper spread on the desk before him, and then he stood up, making an indifferent feint of not knowing that he knew Bromfield Corey by sight.

"Good-morning, Colonel Lapham," said the son, and Lap-ham waited for him to say further, "I wish to introduce my father."

Then he answered "Good-morning," and added rather sternly for the elder Corey, "How do you do, sir? Will you take a chair?" and he pushed him one.

They shook hands and sat down, and Lapham said to his subordinate, "Have a seat"; but young Corey remained stand-ing, watching them in their observance of each other with an amusement which was a little uneasy. Lapham made his visi-tor speak first by waiting for him to do so.

"I'm glad to make your acquaintance, Colonel Lapham, and I ought to have come sooner to do so. My father in your place would have expected it of a man in my place at once, I believe. But I can't feel myself altogether a stranger as it is. I hope Mrs. Lapham is well? And your daughter?"

"Thank you," said Lapham, "they're quite well."

"They were very kind to my wife——"

"Oh, that was nothing!" cried Lapham. "There's nothing Mrs. Lapham likes better than a chance of that sort. Mrs. Corey and the young ladies well?"

"Very well, when I heard from them. They're out of town."

"Yes, so I understood," said Lapham, with a nod toward the son. "I believe Mr. Corey, here, told Mrs. Lapham." He leaned back in his chair, stiffly resolute to show that he was not incommoded by the exchange of these civilities.

"Yes," said Bromfield Corey. "Tom has had the pleasure which I hope for of seeing you all. I hope you're able to make him useful to you here?" Corey looked round Lapham's room vaguely, and then out at the clerks in their railed inclosure, where his eye finally rested on an extremely pretty girl, who was operating a type-writer.

"Well, sir," replied Lapham, softening for the first time with this approach to business, "I guess it will be our own fault if we don't. By the way, Corey," he added, to the younger man, as he gathered up some letters from his desk, "here's something in your line. Spanish or French, I guess."

"I'll run them over," said Corey, taking them to his desk.

His father made an offer to rise.

"Don't go," said Lapham, gesturing him down again. "I just wanted to get him away a minute. I don't care to say it to his face,—I don't like the principle,—but since you ask me about it, I'd just as lief say that I've never had any young man take hold here equal to your son. I don't know as you care——"

"You make me very happy," said Bromfield Corey. "Very happy indeed. I've always had the idea that there was something in my son, if he could only find the way to work it out. And he seems to have gone into your business for the love of it."

"He went to work in the right way, sir! He told me about it. He looked into it. And that paint is a thing that will bear looking into."

"Oh, yes. You might think he had invented it, if you heard him celebrating it."

"Is that so?" demanded Lapham, pleased through and through. "Well, there ain't any other way. You've got to believe in a thing before you can put any heart in it. Why, I had a partner in this thing once, along back just after the war, and he used to be always wanting to tinker with something else. 'Why,' says I, 'you've got the best thing in God's universe now. Why ain't you satisfied?' I had to get rid of him at last. I stuck to my paint, and that fellow's drifted round pretty much all over the whole country, whittling his capital down all the while, till here the other day I had to lend him some money to start him new. No, sir, you've got to believe in a thing. And I believe in your son. And I don't mind telling you that, so far as he's gone, he's a success."

"That's very kind of you."

"No kindness about it. As I was saying the other day to a friend of mine, I've had many a fellow right out of the street that had to work hard all his life, and didn't begin to take hold like this son of yours."

Lapham expanded with profound self-satisfaction. As he probably conceived it, he had succeeded in praising, in a perfectly casual way, the supreme excellence of his paint, and his own sagacity and benevolence; and here he was sitting face to face with Bromfield Corey, praising his son to him, and receiving his grateful acknowledgments as if he were the father of some office-boy whom Lapham had given a place half out of charity.

"Yes, sir, when your son proposed to take hold here, I didn't have much faith in his ideas, that's the truth. But I had faith in him, and I saw that he meant business from the start. I could see it was born in him. Any one could."

"I'm afraid he didn't inherit it directly from me," said Bromfield Corey; "but it's in the blood, on both sides."

"Well, sir, we can't help those things," said Lapham, compassionately. "Some of us have got it, and some of us haven't. The idea is to make the most of what we *have* got."

"Oh, yes; that is the idea. By all means."

"And you can't ever tell what's in you till you try. Why, when I started this thing, I didn't more than half understand my own strength. I wouldn't have said, looking back, that I could have stood the wear and tear of what I've been through. But I developed as I went along. It's just like exercising your muscles in a gymnasium. You can lift twice or three times as much after you've been in training a month as you could before. And I can see that it's going to be just so with your son. His going through college won't hurt him,— he'll soon slough all that off,—and his bringing up won't; don't be anxious about it. I noticed in the army that some of the fellows that had the most go-ahead were fellows that hadn't ever had much more to do than girls before the war broke out. Your son will get along."

"Thank you," said Bromfield Corey, and smiled—whether because his spirit was safe in the humility he sometimes boasted, or because it was triply armed in pride against anything the Colonel's kindness could do.

"He'll get along. He's a good business man and he's a fine fellow. *Must* you go?" asked Lapham, as Bromfield Corey now rose more resolutely. "Well, glad to see you. It was natural you should want to come and see what he was about, and I'm glad you did. I should have felt just so about it. Here is some of our stuff," he said, pointing out the various packages in his office, including the Persis Brand.

"Ah, that's very nice, very nice indeed," said his visitor. "That color through the jar—very rich—delicious. Is Persis Brand a name?"

Lapham blushed.

"Well, Persis is. I don't know as you saw an interview that fellow published in the 'Events' awhile back?"

"What is the 'Events'?"

"Well, it's that new paper Witherby's started."

"No," said Bromfield Corey, "I haven't seen it. I read 'The Daily,'" he explained; by which he meant "The Daily Advertiser," the only daily there is in the old-fashioned Bostonian sense.

"He put a lot of stuff in my mouth that I never said," resumed Lapham; "but that's neither here nor there, so long as you haven't seen it. Here's the department your son's in," and he showed him the foreign labels. Then he took him out into the warehouse to see the large packages. At the head of the stairs, where his guest stopped to nod to his son and say "Good-bye, Tom," Lapham insisted upon going down to the lower door with him. "Well, call again," he said in hospitable dismissal. "I shall always be glad to see you. There ain't a great deal doing at this season." Bromfield Corey thanked him, and let his hand remain perforce in Lapham's lingering grasp. "If you ever like to ride after a good horse—— " the Colonel began.

"Oh, no, no, no; thank you! The better the horse, the more I should be scared. Tom has told me of your driving!"

"Ha, ha, ha!" laughed the Colonel. "Well! every one to his taste. Well, good-morning, sir!" and he suffered him to go.

"Who is the old man blowing to this morning?" asked Walker, the book-keeper, making an errand to Corey's desk.

"My father."

"Oh! That your father? I thought he must be one of your Italian correspondents that you'd been showing round, or Spanish."

In fact, as Bromfield Corey found his way at his leisurely pace up through the streets on which the prosperity of his native city was founded, hardly any figure could have looked more alien to its life. He glanced up and down the façades and through the crooked vistas like a stranger, and the swarthy fruiterer of whom he bought an apple, apparently for the pleasure of holding it in his hand, was not surprised that the purchase should be transacted in his own tongue.

Lapham walked back through the outer office to his own room without looking at Corey, and during the day he spoke to him only of business matters. That must have been his way of letting Corey see that he was not overcome by the honor of his father's visit. But he presented himself at Nantasket with the event so perceptibly on his mind that his wife asked: "Well, Silas, has Rogers been borrowing any more money of you? I don't want you should let that thing go too far. You've done enough."

"You needn't be afraid. I've seen the last of Rogers for one while." He hesitated, to give the fact an effect of no importance. "Corey's father called this morning."

"Did he?" said Mrs. Lapham, willing to humor his feint of indifference. "Did *he* want to borrow some money too?"

"Not as I understood." Lapham was smoking at great ease, and his wife had some crocheting on the other side of the lamp from him.

The girls were on the piazza looking at the moon on the water again. "There's no man in it to-night," Penelope said, and Irene laughed forlornly.

"What *did* he want, then?" asked Mrs. Lapham.

"Oh, I don't know. Seemed to be just a friendly call. Said he ought to have come before."

Mrs. Lapham was silent awhile. Then she said: "Well, I hope you're satisfied now."

Lapham rejected the sympathy too openly offered. "I don't know about being satisfied. I wa'n't in any hurry to see him."

His wife permitted him this pretense also. "What sort of a person is he, anyway?"

"Well, not much like his son. There's no sort of business about him. I don't know just how you'd describe him. He's tall; and he's got white hair and a mustache; and his fingers are very long and limber. I couldn't help noticing them as he sat there with his hands on the top of his cane. Didn't seem to be dressed very much, and acted just like anybody. Didn't talk much. Guess I did most of the talking. Said he was glad I seemed to be getting along so well with his son. He asked after you and Irene; and he said he couldn't feel just like a stranger. Said you had been very kind to his wife. Of course I turned it off. Yes," said Lapham thoughtfully, with his hands resting on his knees, and his cigar between the fingers of his left hand, "I guess he meant to do the right thing, every way. Don't know as I ever saw a much pleasanter man. Dunno but what he's about the pleasantest man I ever did see." He was not letting his wife see in his averted face the struggle that revealed itself there—the struggle of stalwart achievement not to feel flattered at the notice of sterile elegance, not to be sneakingly glad of its amiability, but to stand up and look at it with eyes on the same level. God, who made us so much like himself, but out of the dust, alone knows when that struggle will end. The time had been when Lapham could not have imagined any worldly splendor which his dollars could not buy if he chose to spend them for it; but his wife's half discoveries, taking form again in his ignorance of the world, filled him with helpless misgiving. A cloudy vision of something unpurchasable, where he had supposed there was nothing, had cowed him in spite of the burly resistance of his pride.

"I don't see why he shouldn't be pleasant," said Mrs. Lapham. "He's never done anything else."

Lapham looked up consciously, with an uneasy laugh. "Pshaw, Persis! you never forget anything!"

"Oh, I've got more than that to remember. I suppose you asked him to ride after the mare?"

"Well," said Lapham, reddening guiltily, "he said he was afraid of a good horse."

"Then, of course, you hadn't asked him." Mrs. Lapham crocheted in silence, and her husband leaned back in his chair and smoked.

At last he said, "I'm going to push that house forward. They're loafing on it. There's no reason why we shouldn't be in it by Thanksgiving. I don't believe in moving in the dead of winter."

"We can wait till spring. We're very comfortable in the old place," answered his wife. Then she broke out on him: "What are you in such a hurry to get into that house for? Do you want to invite the Coreys to a house-warming?"

Lapham looked at her without speaking.

"Don't you suppose I can see through you? I declare, Silas Lapham, if I didn't know different, I should say you *were* about the biggest fool! Don't you know *any*thing? Don't you know that it wouldn't do to ask those people to our house before they've asked us to theirs? They'd laugh in our faces!"

"I don't believe they'd laugh in our faces. What's the difference between our asking them and their asking us?" demanded the Colonel, sulkily.

"Oh, well! If you don't see!"

"Well, I *don't* see. But *I* don't want to ask them to the house. I suppose, if I want to, I can invite him down to a fish dinner at Taft's."

Mrs. Lapham fell back in her chair, and let her work drop in her lap with that "Tckk!" in which her sex knows how to express utter contempt and despair.

"What's the matter?"

"Well, if you *do* such a thing, Silas, I'll never speak to you again! It's no *use*! It's *no* use! I did think, after you'd behaved so well about Rogers, I might trust you a little. But I see I can't. I presume as long as you live you'll have to be nosed about like a perfect—*I* don't know what!"

"What are you making such a fuss about?" demanded Lapham, terribly crest-fallen, but trying to pluck up a spirit. "I haven't done anything yet. I can't ask your advice about anything any more without having you fly out. Confound it! I shall do as I please after this."

But as if he could not endure that contemptuous atmosphere, he got up, and his wife heard him in the dining-room pouring himself out a glass of ice-water, and then heard him mount the stairs to their room, and slam its door after him.

"Do you know what your father's wanting to do now?" Mrs. Lapham asked her eldest daughter, who lounged into the parlor a moment with her wrap stringing from her arm, while the younger went straight to bed. "He wants to invite Mr. Corey's father to a fish dinner at Taft's!"

Penelope was yawning with her hand on her mouth; she stopped, and, with a laugh of amused expectance, sank into a chair, her shoulders shrugged forward.

"Why! what in the world has put the Colonel up to that?"

"Put him up to it! There's that fellow, who ought have come to see him long ago, drops into his office this morning, and talks five minutes with him, and your father is flattered out of his five senses. He's crazy to get in with those people, and I shall have a perfect battle to keep him within bounds."

"Well, Persis, ma'am, you can't say but what you began it," said Penelope.

"Oh, yes, I began it," confessed Mrs. Lapham. "Pen," she broke out, "what do you suppose he means by it?"

"Who? Mr. Corey's father? What does the Colonel think?"

"Oh, the Colonel!" cried Mrs. Lapham. She added tremulously: "Perhaps he *is* right. He *did* seem to take a fancy to her last summer, and now if he's called in that way—" She left her daughter to distribute the pronouns aright, and resumed: "Of course, I should have said once that there wasn't any question about it. I should have said so last year; and I don't know what it is keeps me from saying so now. I suppose I know a little more about things than I did; and your father's being so bent on it sets me all in a twitter. He thinks his money can do everything. Well, I don't say but what it can, a good many. And 'Rene is as good a child as ever there was; and I don't see but what she's pretty-appearing enough to suit any one. She's pretty-behaved, too; and she *is* the most capable girl. I presume young men don't care very much for such things nowadays; but there ain't a great many girls can go right into the kitchen, and make such a custard as she did yesterday. And look at the way she does, through the whole house! She can't seem to go into a room without the things fly right into their places. And if she had to do it to-morrow, she could make all her own dresses a great deal better than them we pay to do it. I don't say but what he's about as nice a fellow as ever stepped. But there! I'm ashamed of going on so."

"Well, mother," said the girl after a pause, in which she looked as if a little weary of the subject, "why do you worry about it? If it's to be it'll be, and if it isn't——"

"Yes, that's what I tell your father. But when it comes to myself, I see how hard it is for him to rest quiet. I'm afraid we shall all do something we'll repent of afterwards."

"Well, ma'am," said Penelope, "*I* don't intend to do anything wrong; but if I do, I promise not to be sorry for it. I'll go that far. And I think I wouldn't be sorry for it beforehand, if I were in your place, mother. Let the Colonel go on! He likes to manœuvre, and he isn't going to hurt any one. The Corey family can take care of themselves, I guess."

She laughed in her throat, drawing down the corners of her mouth, and enjoying the resolution with which her mother tried to fling off the burden of her anxieties. "Pen! I believe you're right. You always do see things in such a light! There! I don't care if he brings him down every day."

"Well, ma'am," said Pen, "I don't believe 'Rene would, either. She's just so indifferent!"

The Colonel slept badly that night, and in the morning Mrs. Lapham came to breakfast without him.

"Your father ain't well," she reported. "He's had one of his turns."

"I should have thought he had two or three of them," said

Penelope, "by the stamping round I heard. Isn't he coming to breakfast?"

"Not just yet," said her mother. "He's asleep, and he'll be all right if he gets his nap out. I don't want you girls should make any great noise."

"Oh, we'll be quiet enough," returned Penelope. "Well, I'm glad the Colonel isn't sojering. At first I thought he might be sojering." She broke into a laugh, and, struggling indolently with it, looked at her sister. "You don't think it'll be necessary for anybody to come down from the office and take orders from him while he's laid up, do you, mother?" she inquired.

"Pen!" cried Irene.

"He'll be well enough to go up on the ten o'clock boat," said the mother, sharply.

"I think papa works too hard all through the summer. Why don't you make him take a rest, mamma?" asked Irene.

"Oh, take a rest! The man slaves harder every year. It used to be so that he'd take a little time off now and then; but I declare, he hardly ever seems to breathe now away from his office. And this year he says he doesn't intend to go down to Lapham, except to see after the works for a few days. *I* don't know what to do with the man any more! Seems as if the more money he got, the more he wanted to get. It scares me to think what would happen to him if he lost it. I know one thing," concluded Mrs. Lapham. "He shall not go back to the office to-day."

"Then he won't go up on the ten o'clock boat," Pen reminded her.

"No, he won't. You can just drive over to the hotel as soon as you're through, girls, and telegraph that he's not well, and won't be at the office till to-morrow. I'm not going to have them send anybody down here to bother him."

"That's a blow," said Pen. "I didn't know but they might send——" she looked demurely at her sister— "Dennis!"

"Mamma!" cried Irene.

"Well, I declare, there's no living with this family any more," said Penelope.

"There, Pen, be done!" commanded her mother. But perhaps she did not intend to forbid her teasing. It gave a pleasant sort of reality to the affair that was in her mind, and made what she wished appear not only possible but probable.

Lapham got up and lounged about, fretting and rebelling as each boat departed without him, through the day; before night he became very cross, in spite of the efforts of the family to soothe him, and grumbled that he had been kept from going up to town. "I might as well have gone as not," he repeated, till his wife lost her patience.

"Well, you shall go to-morrow, Silas, if you have to be carried to the boat."

"I declare," said Penelope, "the Colonel don't pet worth a cent."

The six o'clock boat brought Corey. The girls were sitting on the piazza, and Irene saw him first.

"Oh, Pen!" she whispered, with her heart in her face; and Penelope had no time for mockery before he was at the steps.

"I hope Colonel Lapham isn't ill," he said, and they could hear their mother engaged in a moral contest with their father indoors.

"Go and put on your coat! I say you shall! It don't matter *how* he sees you at the office, shirt-sleeves or not. You're in a gentleman's house now—or you ought to be and you sha'n't see company in your dressing-gown."

Penelope hurried in to subdue her mother's anger.

"Oh, he's very much better, thank you!" said Irene, speaking up loudly to drown the noise of the controversy.

"I'm glad of that," said Corey, and when she led him indoors the vanquished Colonel met his visitor in a double-breasted frock-coat, which he was still buttoning up. He could not persuade himself at once that Corey had not come upon some urgent business matter, and when he was clear that he had come out of civility, surprise mingled with his gratification that he should be the object of solicitude to the young man. In Lapham's circle of acquaintance they complained when they were sick, but they made no womanish inquiries after one another's health, and certainly paid no visits of sympathy till matters were serious. He would have enlarged upon the particulars of his indisposition if he had been allowed to do so; and after tea, which Corey took with them, he would have remained to entertain him if his wife had not sent him to bed. She followed him to see that he took some medicine she had prescribed for him, but she went first to Penelope's room, where she found the girl with a book in her hand, which she was not reading.

"You better go down," said the mother. "I've got to go to your father, and Irene is all alone with Mr. Corey; and I know she'll be on pins and needles without you're there to help make it go off."

"She'd better try to get along without me, mother," said Penelope soberly. "I can't always be with them."

"Well," replied Mrs. Lapham, "then *I* must. There'll be a perfect Quaker meeting down there."

"Oh, I guess 'Rene will find something to say if you leave her to herself. Or if she don't, *he* must. It'll be all right for you to go down when you get ready; but I sha'n't go till toward the last. If he's coming here to see Irene—and I don't believe he's come on father's account—he wants to see her and not me. If she can't interest him alone, perhaps he'd as well find it out now as any time. At any rate, I guess you'd better make the experiment. You'll know whether it's a success if he comes again."

"Well," said the mother, "may be you're right. I'll go down directly. It does seem as if he did mean something, after all."

Mrs. Lapham did not hasten to return to her guest. In her own girlhood it was supposed that if a young man seemed to be coming to see a girl, it was only common sense to suppose that he wished to see her alone; and her life in town had left Mrs. Lapham's simple traditions in this respect unchanged. She did with her daughter as her mother would have done with her.

Where Penelope sat with her book, she heard the continuous murmur of voices below, and after a long interval she heard her mother descend. She did not read the open book that lay in her lap, though she kept her eyes fast on the print. Once she rose and almost shut the door, so that she could scarcely hear; then she opened it wide again with a self-disdainful air, and resolutely went back to her book, which again she did not read. But she remained in her room till it was nearly time for Corey to return to his boat.

When they were alone again, Irene made a feint of scolding her for leaving her to entertain Mr. Corey.

"Why! didn't you have a pleasant call?" asked Penelope.

Irene threw her arms round her. "Oh, it was a *splendid* call! I didn't suppose I could make it go off so well. We talked nearly the whole time about you!"

"I don't think *that* was a very interesting subject."

"He kept asking about you. He asked everything. You don't know how much he thinks of you, Pen. Oh, Pen! what do you think made him come? Do you think he really did come to see how papa was?" Irene buried her face in her sister's neck.

Penelope stood with her arms at her side, submitting. "Well," she said, "I don't think he did, altogether."

Irene, all glowing, released her. "Don't you—don't you *really*? Oh! Pen, don't you think he *is* nice? Don't you think he's handsome? Don't you think I behaved horridly when we first met him this evening, not thanking him for coming? I know he thinks I've no manners. But it seemed as if it would be thanking him for coming to see me. Ought I to have asked him to come again, when he said good-night? I didn't; I couldn't. Do you believe he'll think I don't want him to? You don't believe he would keep coming if he didn't—want to——"

"He hasn't kept coming a great deal, yet," suggested Penelope.

"No; I know he hasn't. But if he—if he should?"

"Then I should think he wanted to."

"Oh, would you —*would* you? Oh, how good you always are, Pen! And you always say what you think. I wish there was some one coming to see you too. That's all that I don't like about it. Perhaps—— He was telling about his friend there in Texas——"

"Well," said Penelope, "his friend couldn't call often from Texas. You needn't ask Mr. Corey to trouble about me, 'Rene. I think I can manage to worry along, if you're satisfied."

"Oh, I *am*, Pen. When do you suppose he'll come again?" Irene pushed some of Penelope's things aside on the dressing-case, to rest her elbow and talk at ease. Penelope came up and put them back.

"Well, not to-night," she said; "and if that's what you're sitting up for——"

Irene caught her round the neck again, and ran out of the room.

The Colonel was packed off on the eight o'clock boat the next morning; but his recovery did not prevent Corey from repeating his visit in a week. This time Irene came radiantly up to Penelope's room, where she had again withdrawn herself. "You must come down, Pen," she said. "He's asked if you're not well, and mamma says you've got to come."

After that Penelope helped Irene through with her calls, and talked them over with her far into the night after Corey was gone. But when the impatient curiosity of her mother pressed her for some opinion of the affair, she said, "You know as much as I do, mother."

"Don't he ever say anything to you about her—praise her up, any?"

"He's never mentioned Irene to me."

"He hasn't to me, either," said Mrs. Lapham, with a sigh of trouble. "Then what makes him keep coming?"

"I can't tell you. One thing, he says there isn't a house open in Boston where he's acquainted. Wait till some of his friends get back, and then if he keeps coming, it'll be time to inquire."

"Well!" said the mother; but as the weeks passed she was less and less able to attribute Corey's visits to his loneliness in town, and turned to her husband for comfort.

"Silas, I don't know as we ought to let young Corey keep coming so. I don't quite like it, with all his family away."

"He's of age," said the Colonel. "He can go where he pleases. It don't matter whether his family's here or not."

"Yes, but if they don't want he should come? Should you feel just right about letting him?"

"How're you going to stop him? I swear, Persis, I don't know what's got over you! What is it? You didn't use to be so. But to hear you talk, you'd think those Coreys were too good for this world, and we wa'n't fit for 'em to walk on."

"I'm not going to have 'em say we took an advantage of their being away and tolled him on."

"I should like to *hear* 'em say it!" cried Lapham. "Or anybody!"

"Well," said his wife, relinquishing this point of anxiety, "I can't make out whether he cares anything for her or not. And Pen can't tell either; or else she won't."

"Oh, I guess he cares for her, fast enough," said the Colonel.

"I can't make out that he's said or done the first thing to show it."

"Well, I was better than a year getting *my* courage up."

"Oh, that was different," said Mrs. Lapham, in contemptuous dismissal of the comparison, and yet with a certain fondness. "I guess, if he cared for her, a fellow in his position wouldn't be long getting up his courage to speak to Irene."

Lapham brought his fist down on the table between them.

"Look here, Persis! Once for all, now, don't you ever let me hear you say anything like that again! I'm worth nigh on to a million, and I've made it every cent myself; and my girls are the equals of anybody, I don't care who it is. He ain't the fellow to take on any airs; but if he ever tries it with me, I'll send him to the right about mighty quick. I'll have a talk with him, if——"

"No, no; don't do that!" implored his wife. "I didn't mean anything. I don't know as I meant *anything*. He's just as unassuming as he can be, and I think Irene's a match for anybody. You just let things go on. It'll be all right. You never can tell how it is with young people. Perhaps *she's* offish. Now you ain't—you ain't going to say anything?"

Lapham suffered himself to be persuaded, the more easily, no doubt, because after his explosion he must have perceived that his pride itself stood in the way of what his pride had threatened. He contented himself with his wife's promise that she would never again present that offensive view of the case, and she did not remain without a certain support in his sturdy self-assertion.

XII

MRS. COREY returned with her daughters in the early days of October, having passed three or four weeks at Intervale after leaving Bar Harbor. They were somewhat browner than they were when they left town in June, but they were not otherwise changed. Lily, the elder of the girls, had brought back a number of studies of kelp and toadstools, with accessory rocks and rotten logs, which she would never finish up and never show any one, knowing the slightness of their merit. Nanny, the younger, had read a great many novels with a keen sense of their inaccuracy as representations of life, and had seen a great deal of life with a sad regret for its difference from fiction. They were both nice girls, accomplished, well dressed of course, and well-enough looking; but they had met no one at the seaside or the mountains whom their taste would allow to influence their fate, and they had come home to the occupations they had left, with no hopes and no fears to distract them.

In the absence of these they were fitted to take the more vivid interest in their brother's affairs, which they could see weighed upon their mother's mind after the first hours of greeting.

"Oh, it seems to have been going on, and your father has never written a word about it," she said, shaking her head.

"What good would it have done?" asked Nanny, who was little and fair, with rings of light hair that filled a bonnet-front very prettily; she looked best in a bonnet. "It would only have worried you. He could not have stopped Tom; you couldn't, when you came home to do it."

"I dare say papa didn't know much about it," suggested Lily. She was a tall, lean, dark girl, who looked as if she were not quite warm enough, and whom you always associated with wraps of different æsthetic effect after you had once seen her.

It is a serious matter always to the women of his family when a young man gives them cause to suspect that he is interested in some other woman. A son-in-law or brother-in-law does not enter the family; he need not be caressed or made anything of; but the son's or brother's wife has a claim upon his mother and sisters which they cannot deny. Some convention of their sex obliges them to show her affection, to like or to seem to like her, to take her to their intimacy, however odious she may be to them. With the Coreys it was something more than an affair of sentiment. They were by no means poor, and they were not dependent money-wise upon Tom Corey; but the mother had come, without knowing it, to rely upon his sense, his advice in everything, and the sisters, seeing him hitherto so indifferent to girls, had insensibly grown to regard him as altogether their own till he should be released, not by his marriage, but by theirs, an event which had not approached with the lapse of time. Some kinds of girls—they believed that they could readily have chosen a kind—might have taken him without taking him from them; but this generosity could not be hoped for in such a girl as Miss Lapham.

"Perhaps," urged their mother, "it would not be so bad. She seemed an affectionate little thing with her mother, without a great deal of character, though she was so capable about some things."

"Oh, she'll be an affectionate little thing with Tom too, you may be sure," said Nanny. "And that characterless capability becomes the most intense narrow-mindedness. She'll think we were against her from the beginning."

"She has no cause for that," Lily interposed, "and we shall not give her any."

"Yes, we shall," retorted Nanny. "We can't help it; and if we can't, her own ignorance would be cause enough."

"I can't feel that she's altogether ignorant," said Mrs. Corey, justly.

"Of course she can read and write," admitted Nanny.

"I can't imagine what he finds to talk about with her," said Lily.

"Oh, *that's* very simple," returned her sister. "They talk about themselves, with occasional references to each other. I have heard people 'going on' on the hotel piazzas. She's embroidering, or knitting, or tatting, or something of that kind; and he says she seems quite devoted to needle-work; and she says, yes, she has a perfect passion for it, and everybody laughs at her for it; but she can't help it, she always was so from a child, and supposes she always shall be,—with remote and minute particulars. And she ends by saying that perhaps he does not like people to tat, or knit, or embroider, or whatever. And he says, oh, yes, he does; what could make her think such a thing? but for his part he likes boating rather better, or if you're in the woods camping. Then she lets him take up one corner of her work, and perhaps touch her fingers; and that encourages him to say that he supposes nothing could induce her to drop her work long enough to go down on the rocks, or out among the huckleberry bushes; and she puts her head on one side, and says she doesn't know really. And then they go, and he lies at her feet on the rocks, or picks huckleberries and drops them in her lap, and they go on talking about themselves, and comparing notes to see how they differ from each other. And——"

"That will do, Nanny," said her mother.

Lily smiled autumnally. "Oh, disgusting!"

"Disgusting? Not at all!" protested her sister. "It's very amusing when you see it, and when you do it——"

"It's always a mystery what people see in each other," observed Mrs. Corey, severely.

"Yes," Nanny admitted, "but I don't know that there is much comfort for us in the application."

"No, there isn't," said her mother.

"The most that we can do is to hope for the best till we know the worst. Of course we shall make the best of the worst when it comes."

"Yes, and perhaps it would not be so very bad. I was saying to your father when I was here in July that those things can always be managed. You must face them as if they were nothing out of the way, and try not to give any cause for bitterness among ourselves."

"That's true. But I don't believe in too much resignation beforehand. It amounts to concession," said Nanny.

"Of course we should oppose it in all proper ways," returned her mother.

Lily had ceased to discuss the matter. In virtue of her artistic temperament, she was expected not to be very practical. It was her mother and her sister who managed, submitting to the advice and consent of Corey what they intended to do.

"Your father wrote me that he had called on Colonel Lapham at his place of business," said Mrs. Corey, seizing her first chance of approaching the subject with her son.

"Yes," said Corey. "A dinner was father's idea, but he came down to a call, at my suggestion."

"Oh," said Mrs. Corey, in a tone of relief, as if the statement threw a new light on the fact that Corey had suggested the visit. "He said so little about it in his letter that I didn't know just how it came about."

"I thought it was right they should meet," explained the son, "and so did father. I was glad that I suggested it, afterward; it was extremely gratifying to Colonel Lapham."

"Oh, it was quite right in every way. I suppose you have seen something of the family during the summer."

"Yes, a good deal. I've been down at Nantasket rather often."

Mrs. Corey let her eyes droop. Then she asked: "Are they well?"

"Yes, except Lapham himself, now and then. I went down once or twice to see him. He hasn't given himself any vacation this summer; he has such a passion for his business that I fancy he finds it hard being away from it at any time, and he's made his new house an excuse for staying——"

"Oh, yes, his house! Is it to be something fine?"

"Yes; it's a beautiful house. Seymour is doing it."

"Then, of course, it will be very handsome. I suppose the young ladies are very much taken up with it; and Mrs. Lapham."

"Mrs. Lapham, yes. I don't think the young ladies care so much about it."

"It must be for them. Aren't they ambitious?" asked Mrs. Corey, delicately feeling her way.

Her son thought awhile. Then he answered with a smile:

"No, I don't really think they are. They are unambitious, I should say." Mrs. Corey permitted herself a long breath. But her son added, "It's the parents who are ambitious for them," and her respiration became shorter again.

"Yes," she said.

"They're very simple, nice girls," pursued Corey. "I think you'll like the elder, when you come to know her."

When you come to know her. The words implied an expectation that the two families were to be better acquainted.

"Then she is more intellectual than her sister?" Mrs. Corey ventured.

"Intellectual?" repeated her son. "No; that isn't the word, quite. Though she certainly has more mind."

"The younger seemed very sensible."

"Oh, sensible, yes. And as practical as she's pretty. She can do all sorts of things, and likes to be doing them. Don't you think she's an extraordinary beauty?"

"Yes—yes, she is," said Mrs. Corey, at some cost.

"She's good, too," said Corey, "and perfectly innocent and transparent. I think you will like her the better the more you know her."

"I thought her very nice from the beginning," said the mother, heroically; and then nature asserted itself in her. "But I should be afraid that she might perhaps be a little bit tiresome at last; her range of ideas seemed so extremely limited."

"Yes, that's what I was afraid of. But, as a matter of fact, she isn't. She interests you by her very limitations. You can see the working of her mind, like that of a child. She isn't at all conscious even of her beauty."

"I don't believe young men can tell whether girls are conscious or not," said Mrs. Corey. "But I am not saying the Miss Laphams are not—" Her son sat musing, with an inattentive smile on his face. "What is it?"

"Oh, nothing. I was thinking of Miss Lapham and something she was saying. She's very droll, you know."

"The elder sister? Yes, you told me that. Can you see the workings of her mind too?"

"No; she's everything that's unexpected." Corey fell into another revery, and smiled again; but he did not offer to explain what amused him, and his mother would not ask.

"I don't know what to make of his admiring the girl so frankly," she said afterward to her husband. "That couldn't come naturally till after he had spoken to her, and I feel sure that he hasn't yet."

"You women haven't risen yet—it's an evidence of the

backwardness of your sex—to a conception of the Bismarck idea in diplomacy. If a man praises one woman, you still think he's in love with another. Do you mean that because Tom didn't praise the elder sister so much, he *has* spoken to *her*?"

Mrs. Corey refused the consequence, saying that it did not follow. "Besides, he did praise her."

"You ought to be glad that matters are in such good shape, then. At any rate, you can do absolutely nothing."

"Oh! I know it," sighed Mrs. Corey. "I wish Tom would be a little opener with me."

"He's as open as it's in the nature of an American-born son to be with his parents. I dare say if you'd ask him plumply what he meant in regard to the young lady, he would have told you—if he knew."

"Why, don't you think he does know, Bromfield?"

"I'm not at all sure he does. You women think that because a young man dangles after a girl, or girls, he's attached to them. It doesn't at all follow. He dangles because he must, and doesn't know what to do with his time, and because they seem to like it. I dare say that Tom has dangled a good deal in this instance because there was nobody else in town."

"Do you really think so?"

"I throw out the suggestion. And it strikes me that a young lady couldn't do better than stay in or near Boston during the summer. Most of the young men are here, kept by business through the week, with evenings available only on the spot, or a few miles off. What was the proportion of the sexes at the seashore and the mountains?"

"Oh, twenty girls at least for even an excuse of a man. It's shameful."

"You see, I am right in one part of my theory. Why shouldn't I be right in the rest?"

"I wish you were. And yet I can't say that I do. Those things are very serious with girls. I shouldn't like Tom to have been going to see those people if he meant nothing by it."

"And you wouldn't like it if he did. You are difficult, my dear." Her husband pulled an open newspaper toward him from the table.

"I feel that it wouldn't be at all like him to do so," said Mrs. Corey, going on to entangle herself in her words, as women often do when their ideas are perfectly clear. "Don't go to reading, please, Bromfield! I am really worried about this matter. I must know how much it means. I can't let it go on so. I don't see how you can rest easy without knowing."

"I don't in the least know what's going to become of me when I die; and yet I sleep well," replied Bromfield Corey, putting his newspaper aside.

"Ah, but this is a very different thing."

"So much more serious? Well, what can you do? We had this out when you were here in the summer, and you agreed with me then that we could do nothing. The situation hasn't changed at all."

"Yes, it has; it has continued the same," said Mrs. Corey, again expressing the fact by a contradiction in terms. "I think I must ask Tom outright."

"You know you can't do that, my dear."

"Then why doesn't he tell us?"

"Ah, that's what *he* can't do, if he's making love to Miss Irene—that's her name, I believe—on the American plan. He will tell us after he has told *her*. That was the way I did. Don't ignore our own youth, Anna. It was a long while ago, I'll admit."

"It was very different," said Mrs. Corey, a little shaken.

"I don't see how. I dare say Mamma Lapham knows whether Tom is in love with her daughter or not; and no doubt Papa Lapham knows it at second hand. But we shall not know it until the girl herself does. Depend upon that. Your mother knew, and she told your father; but my poor father knew nothing about it till we were engaged; and I had been hanging about—dangling, as you call it——"

"No, no; *you* called it that."

"Was it I?—for a year or more."

The wife could not refuse to be a little consoled by the image of her young love which the words conjured up, however little she liked its relation to her son's interest in Irene Lapham. She smiled pensively. "Then you think it hasn't come to an understanding with them yet?"

"An understanding? Oh, probably."

"An explanation, then?"

"The only logical inference from what we've been saying is

that it hasn't. But I don't ask you to accept it on that account. May I read now, my dear?"

"Yes, you may read now," said Mrs. Corey, with one of those sighs which perhaps express a feminine sense of the unsatisfactoriness of husbands in general, rather than a personal discontent with her own.

"Thank you, my dear; then I think I'll smoke too," said Bromfield Corey, lighting a cigar.

She left him in peace, and she made no further attempt upon her son's confidence. But she was not inactive for that reason. She did not, of course, admit to herself, and far less to others, the motive with which she went to pay an early visit to the Laphams, who had now come up from Nantasket to Nankeen Square. She said to her daughters that she had always been a little ashamed of using her acquaintance with them to get money for her charity, and then seeming to drop it. Besides, it seemed to her that she ought somehow to recognize the business relation that Tom had formed with the father; they must not think that his family disapproved of what he had done.

"Yes, business is business," said Nanny, with a laugh. "Do you wish us to go with you again?"

"No; I will go alone this time," replied the mother with dignity.

Her coupé now found its way to Nankeen Square without difficulty, and she sent up a card, which Mrs. Lapham received in the presence of her daughter Penelope.

"I presume I've got to see her," she gasped.

"Well, don't look so guilty, mother," joked the girl; "you haven't been doing anything so *very* wrong."

"It seems as if I *had*. I don't know what's come over me. I wasn't afraid of the woman before, but now I don't seem to feel as if I could look her in the face. He's been coming here of his own accord, and I fought against his coming long enough, goodness knows. I didn't want him to come. And as far forth as that goes, we're as respectable as they are; and your father's got twice their money, any day. We've no need to go begging for their favor. I guess they were glad enough to get him in with your father."

"Yes, those are all good points, mother," said the girl; "and if you keep saying them over, and count a hundred every time before you speak, I guess you'll worry through."

Mrs. Lapham had been fussing distractedly with her hair and ribbons, in preparation for her encounter with Mrs. Corey. She now drew in a long quivering breath, stared at her daughter without seeing her, and hurried downstairs. It was true that when she met Mrs. Corey before she had not been awed by her; but since then she had learned at least her own ignorance of the world, and she had talked over the things she had misconceived and the things she had shrewdly guessed so much that she could not meet her on the former footing of equality. In spite of as brave a spirit and as good a conscience as woman need have, Mrs. Lapham cringed inwardly, and tremulously wondered what her visitor had come for. She turned from pale to red, and was hardly coherent in her greetings; she did not know how they got to where Mrs. Corey was saying exactly the right things about her son's interest and satisfaction in his new business, and keeping her eyes fixed on Mrs. Lapham's, reading her uneasiness there, and making her feel, in spite of her indignant innocence, that she had taken a base advantage of her in her absence to get her son away from her and marry him to Irene. Then, presently, while this was painfully revolving itself in Mrs. Lapham's mind, she was aware of Mrs. Corey's asking if she was not to have the pleasure of seeing Miss Irene.

"No; she's out, just now," said Mrs. Lapham. "I don't know just when she'll be in. She went to get a book." And here she turned red again, knowing that Irene had gone to get the book because it was one that Corey had spoken of.

"Oh! I'm sorry," said Mrs. Corey. "I had hoped to see her. And your other daughter, whom I never met?"

"Penelope?" asked Mrs. Lapham, eased a little. "She is at home. I will go and call her." The Laphams had not yet thought of spending their superfluity on servants who could be rung for; they kept two girls and a man to look after the furnace, as they had for the last ten years. If Mrs. Lapham had rung in the parlor, her second girl would have gone to the street door to see who was there. She went upstairs for Penelope herself, and the girl, after some rebellious derision, returned with her.

Mrs. Corey took account of her, as Penelope withdrew to the other side of the room after their introduction, and sat down, indolently submissive on the surface to the tests to be applied, and following Mrs. Corey's lead of the conversation in her odd drawl.

"You young ladies will be glad to be getting into your new house," she said, politely.

"I don't know," said Penelope. "We're so used to this one."

Mrs. Corey looked a little baffled, but she said sympathetically, "Of course, you will be sorry to leave your old home."

Mrs. Lapham could not help putting in on behalf of her daughters: "I guess if it was left to the girls to say, we shouldn't leave it at all."

"Oh, indeed!" said Mrs. Corey; "are they so much attached? But I can quite understand it. My children would be heart-broken too if we were to leave the old place." She turned to Penelope. "But you must think of the lovely new house, and the beautiful position."

"Yes, I suppose we shall get used to them too," said Penelope, in response to this didactic consolation.

"Oh, I could even imagine your getting very fond of them," pursued Mrs. Corey, patronizingly. "My son has told me of the lovely outlook you're to have over the water. He thinks you have such a beautiful house. I believe he had the pleasure of meeting you all there when he first came home."

"Yes, I think he was our first visitor."

"He is a great admirer of your house," said Mrs. Corey, keeping her eyes very sharply, however politely, on Penelope's face, as if to surprise there the secret of any other great admiration of her son's that might helplessly show itself.

"Yes," said the girl, "he's been there several times with father; and he wouldn't be allowed to overlook any of its good points."

Her mother took a little more courage from her daughter's tranquillity.

"The girls make such fun of their father's excitement about his building, and the way he talks it into everybody."

"Oh, indeed!" said Mrs. Corey, with civil misunderstanding and inquiry.

Penelope flushed, and her mother went on: "I tell him he's more of a child about it than any of them."

"Young people are very philosophical nowadays," remarked Mrs. Corey.

"Yes, indeed," said Mrs. Lapham. "I tell them they've always had everything, so that nothing's a surprise to them. It was different with us in our young days."

"Yes," said Mrs. Corey, without assenting.

"I mean the Colonel and myself," explained Mrs. Lapham.

"Oh, yes—*yes!*" said Mrs. Corey.

"I'm sure," the former went on, rather helplessly, "*we* had to work hard enough for everything we got. And so we appreciated it."

"So many things were not done for young people then," said Mrs. Corey, not recognizing the early-hardships stand-point of Mrs. Lapham. "But I don't know that they are always the better for it now," she added, vaguely, but with the satisfaction we all feel in uttering a just commonplace.

"It's rather hard living up to blessings that you've always had," said Penelope.

"Yes," replied Mrs. Corey, distractedly, and coming back to her slowly from the virtuous distance to which she had absented herself. She looked at the girl searchingly again, as if to determine whether this were a touch of the drolling her son had spoken of. But she only added: "You will enjoy the sunsets on the Back Bay so much."

"Well, not unless they're new ones," said Penelope. "I don't believe I could promise to enjoy any sunsets that I was used to, a great deal."

Mrs. Corey looked at her with misgiving, hardening into dislike. "No," she breathed, vaguely. "My son spoke of the fine effect of the lights about the hotel from your cottage at Nantasket," she said to Mrs. Lapham.

"Yes, they're splendid!" exclaimed that lady. "I guess the girls went down every night with him to see them from the rocks."

"Yes," said Mrs. Corey, a little dryly; and she permitted herself to add: "He spoke of those rocks. I suppose both you young ladies spend a great deal of your time on them when you're there. At Nahant my children were constantly on them."

"Irene likes the rocks," said Penelope. "I don't care much about them,—especially at night."

"Oh, indeed! I suppose you find it quite as well looking at the lights comfortably from the veranda."

"No; you can't see them from the house."

"Oh," said Mrs. Corey. After a perceptible pause, she turned to Mrs. Lapham. "I don't know what my son would have done for a breath of sea air this summer, if you had not allowed him to come to Nantasket. He wasn't willing to leave his business long enough to go anywhere else."

"Yes, he's a born business man," responded Mrs. Lapham enthusiastically. "If it's born in you, it's bound to come out. That's what the Colonel is always saying about Mr. Corey. He says it's born in him to be a business man, and he can't help it." She recurred to Corey gladly because she felt that she had not said enough of him when his mother first spoke of his connection with the business. "I don't believe," she went on excitedly, "that Colonel Lapham has ever had anybody with him that he thought more of."

"You have *all* been very kind to my son," said Mrs. Corey in acknowledgment, and stiffly bowing a little, "and we feel greatly indebted to you. Very much so."

At these grateful expressions Mrs. Lapham reddened once more, and murmured that it had been very pleasant to them, she was sure. She glanced at her daughter for support, but Penelope was looking at Mrs. Corey, who doubtless saw her from the corner of her eyes, though she went on speaking to her mother.

"I was sorry to hear from him that Mr.—Colonel?—Lapham had not been quite well this summer. I hope he's better now?"

"Oh, yes, indeed," replied Mrs. Lapham; "he's all right now. He's hardly ever been sick, and he don't know how to take care of himself. That's all. We don't any of us; we're all so well."

"Health is a great blessing," sighed Mrs. Corey.

"Yes, so it is. How is your oldest daughter?" inquired Mrs. Lapham. "Is she as delicate as ever?"

after a moment of troubled silence, "I have been thinking over your plan, and I don't see why it isn't the right thing."

"What is my plan?" inquired Bromfield Corey.

"A dinner."

Her husband began to laugh. "Ah, you overdid the accusing-spirit business, and this is reparation." But Mrs. Corey hurried on, with combined dignity and anxiety:

"We can't ignore Tom's intimacy with them—it amounts to that; it will probably continue even if it's merely a fancy, and we must seem to know it; whatever comes of it, we can't disown it. They are very simple, unfashionable people, and unworldly; but I can't say that they are offensive, unless— unless," she added, in propitiation of her husband's smile, "unless the father—how *did* you find the father?" she implored.

"He will be very entertaining," said Corey, "if you start him on his paint. What was the disagreeable daughter like? Shall you have her?"

"She's little and dark. We must have them all," Mrs. Corey sighed. "Then you don't think a dinner would do?"

"Oh, yes, I do. As you say, we can't disown Tom's relation to them, whatever it is. We had much better recognize it, and make the best of the inevitable. I think a Lapham dinner would be delightful." He looked at her with delicate irony in his voice and smile, and she fetched another sigh, so deep and sore now that he laughed outright. "Perhaps," he suggested, "it would be the best way of curing Tom of his fancy, if he has one. He has been seeing her with the dangerous advantages which a mother knows how to give her daughter in the family circle, and with no means of comparing her with other girls. You must invite several other very pretty girls."

"Do you really think so, Bromfield?" asked Mrs. Corey, taking courage a little. "That might do." But her spirits visibly sank again. "I don't know any other girl half so pretty."

"Well, then, better bred."

"She is very lady-like, very modest, and pleasing."

"Well, more cultivated."

"Tom doesn't get on with such people."

"Oh, you *wish* him to marry her, I see."

"No, no——"

"Then you'd better give the dinner to bring them together, to promote the affair."

"You know I don't want to do that, Bromfield. But I feel that we must do something. If we don't, it has a clandestine appearance. It isn't just to them. A dinner won't leave us in any worse position, and may leave us in a better. Yes," said Mrs. Corey, after another thoughtful interval, "we must have them—have them all. It could be very simple."

"Ah, you can't give a dinner under a bushel, if I take your meaning, my dear. If we do this at all, we mustn't do it as if we were ashamed of it. We must ask people to meet them."

"Yes," sighed Mrs. Corey. "There are not many people in town yet," she added, with relief that caused her husband another smile. "There really seems a sort of fatality about it," she concluded, religiously.

"Then you had better not struggle against it. Go and reconcile Lily and Nanny to it as soon as possible."

Mrs. Corey blanched a little. "But don't you think it will be the best thing, Bromfield?"

"I do indeed, my dear. The only thing that shakes my faith in the scheme is the fact that I first suggested it. But if you have adopted it, it must be all right, Anna. I can't say that I expected it."

"No," said his wife, "it wouldn't do."

XIII

HAVING distinctly given up the project of asking the Laphams to dinner, Mrs. Corey was able to carry it out with the courage of sinners who have sacrificed to virtue by frankly acknowledging its superiority to their intended transgression. She did not question but the Laphams would come; and she only doubted as to the people whom she should invite to meet them. She opened the matter with some trepidation to her daughters, but neither of them opposed her; they rather looked at the scheme from her own point of view, and agreed with her that nothing had really yet been done to wipe out the obligation to the Laphams helplessly contracted the summer before, and strengthened by that ill-advised application to Mrs. Lapham for charity. Not only the principal of their debt of gratitude remained, but the accruing interest. They said, What harm could giving the dinner possibly do them? They might ask any or all of their acquaintance without disadvantage to themselves; but it would be perfectly easy to give the dinner just the character they chose, and still flatter the ignorance of the Laphams. The trouble would be with Tom, if he were really interested in the girl; but he could not say anything if they made it a family dinner; he could not feel anything. They had each turned in her own mind, as it appeared from a comparison of ideas, to one of the most comprehensive of those cousinships which form the admiration and terror of the adventurer in Boston society. He finds himself hemmed in and left out at every turn by ramifications that forbid him all hope of safe personality in his comments on people; he is never less secure than when he hears some given Bostonian denouncing or ridiculing another. If he will be advised, he will guard himself from concurring in these criticisms, however just they appear, for the probability is that their object is a cousin of not more than one remove from the censor. When the alien hears a group of Boston ladies calling one another, and speaking of all their gentlemen friends, by the familiar abbreviations of their Christian names, he must feel keenly the exile to which he was born; but he is then, at least, in comparatively little danger; while these latent and tacit cousinships open pitfalls at every step around him, in a society where Middlesexes have married Essexes and produced Suffolks for two hundred and fifty years.

These conditions, however, so perilous to the foreigner, are a source of strength and security to those native to them. An uncertain acquaintance may be so effectually involved in the meshes of such a cousinship, as never to be heard of outside of it; and tremendous stories are told of people who have spent a whole winter in Boston, in a whirl of gayety, and who, the original guests of the Suffolks, discover upon reflection that they have met no one but Essexes and Middlesexes.

Mrs. Corey's brother James came first into her mind, and she thought with uncommon toleration of the easy-going, uncritical good-nature of his wife. James Bellingham had been the adviser of her son throughout, and might be said to have actively promoted his connection with Lapham. She thought next of the widow of her cousin, Henry Bellingham, who had let her daughter marry that Western steamboat man, and was fond of her son-in-law; she might be expected at least to endure the paint-king and his family. The daughters insisted so strongly upon Mrs. Bellingham's son, Charles, that Mrs. Corey put him down—if he were in town; he might be in Central America; he got on with all sorts of people. It seemed to her that she might stop at this: four Laphams, five Coreys, and four Bellinghams were enough.

"That makes thirteen," said Nanny. "You can have Mr. and Mrs. Sewell."

"Yes, that is a good idea," assented Mrs. Corey. "He is our minister, and it is very proper."

"I don't see why you don't have Robert Chase. It is a pity he shouldn't see her—for the color."

"I don't quite like the idea of that," said Mrs. Corey; "but we can have him too, if it won't make too many." The painter had married into a poorer branch of the Coreys, and his wife was dead. "Is there any one else?"

"There is Miss Kingsbury."

"We have had her so much. She will begin to think we are using her."

"She won't mind; she's so good-natured."

"Well, then," the mother summed up, "there are four Laphams, five Coreys, four Bellinghams, one Chase, and one Kingsbury—fifteen. Oh! and two Sewells. Seventeen. Ten ladies and seven gentlemen. It doesn't balance very well, and it's too large."

"Perhaps some of the ladies won't come," suggested Lily.

"Oh, the ladies always come," said Nanny.

Their mother reflected. "Well, I will ask them. The ladies will refuse in time to let us pick up some gentlemen somewhere; some more artists. Why! we must have Mr. Seymour, the architect; he's a bachelor, and he's building their house, Tom says."

Her voice fell a little when she mentioned her son's name, and she told him of her plan, when he came home in the evening, with evident misgiving.

"What are you doing it for, mother?" he asked, looking at her with his honest eyes.

She dropped her own in a little confusion. "I won't do it at all, my dear," she said, "if you don't approve. But I thought—— You know we have never made any proper acknowledgment of their kindness to us at Baie St. Joan. Then in the winter, I'm ashamed to say, I got money from her for a charity I was interested in; and I hate the idea of merely *using* people in that way. And now your having been at their house this summer—we can't seem to disapprove of that; and your business relations to him——"

"Yes, I see," said Corey. "Do you think it amounts to a dinner?"

"Why, I don't know," returned his mother. "We shall have hardly any one out of our family connection."

"Well," Corey assented, "it might do. I suppose what you wish is to give them a pleasure."

"Why, certainly. Don't you think they'd like to come?"

"Oh, they'd like to come; but whether it would be a pleasure after they were here is another thing. I should have said that if you wanted to have them, they would enjoy better being simply asked to meet our own immediate family."

"That's what I thought of in the first place, but your father seemed to think it implied a social distrust of them; and we couldn't afford to have that appearance, even to ourselves."

"Perhaps he was right."

"And besides, it might seem a little significant."

Corey seemed inattentive to this consideration. "Whom did you think of asking?" His mother repeated the names. "Yes, that would do," he said, with a vague dissatisfaction.

"I won't have it at all, if you don't wish, Tom."

"Oh, yes, have it; perhaps you ought. Yes, I dare say it's right. What did you mean by a family dinner seeming signif icant?"

His mother hesitated. When it came to that, she did not like to recognize in his presence the anxieties that had troubled her. But "I don't know," she said, since she must. "I shouldn't want to give that young girl, or her mother, the idea that we wished to make more of the acquaintance than— than you did, Tom."

He looked at her absent-mindedly, as if he did not take her meaning. But he said, "Oh, yes, of course," and Mrs. Corey, in the uncertainty in which she seemed destined to remain concerning this affair, went off and wrote her invitation to Mrs. Lapham. Later in the evening, when they again found themselves alone, her son said, "I don't think I understood you, mother, in regard to the Laphams. I think I do now. I certainly don't wish you to make more of the acquaintance than I have done. It wouldn't be right; it might be very unfortunate. Don't give the dinner!"

"It's too late now, my son," said Mrs. Corey. "I sent my note to Mrs. Lapham an hour ago." Her courage rose at the trouble which showed in Corey's face. "But don't be annoyed by it, Tom. It isn't a family dinner, you know, and everything can be managed without embarrassment. If we take up the affair at this point, you will seem to have been merely acting for us; and they can't possibly understand anything more."

"Well, well! Let it go! I dare say it's all right. At any rate, it can't be helped now."

"I don't wish to help it, Tom," said Mrs. Corey, with a cheerfulness which the thought of the Laphams had never brought her before. "I am sure it is quite fit and proper, and we can make them have a very pleasant time. They are good, inoffensive people, and we owe it to ourselves not to be afraid to show that we have felt their kindness to us, and his appreciation of you."

"Well," consented Corey. The trouble that his mother had suddenly cast off was in his tone; but she was not sorry. It was quite time that he should think seriously of his attitude toward these people if he had not thought of it before, but, according to his father's theory, had been merely dangling.

It was a view of her son's character that could hardly have pleased her in different circumstances; yet it was now unquestionably a consolation if not wholly a pleasure. If she considered the Laphams at all, it was with the resignation which we feel at the evils of others, even when they have not brought them on themselves.

Mrs. Lapham, for her part, had spent the hours between Mrs. Corey's visit and her husband's coming home from business in reaching the same conclusion with regard to Corey; and her spirits were at the lowest when they sat down to supper. Irene was downcast with her; Penelope was purposely gay; and the Colonel was beginning, after his first plate of the boiled ham,—which, bristling with cloves, rounded its bulk on a wide platter before him,—to take note of the surrounding mood, when the door-bell jingled peremptorily, and the girl left waiting on the table to go and answer it. She returned at once with a note for Mrs. Lapham, which she read, and then, after a helpless survey of her family, read again.

"Why, what *is* it, mamma?" asked Irene; while the Colonel, who had taken up his carving-knife for another attack on the ham, held it drawn half across it.

"Why, *I* don't know what it *does* mean," answered Mrs. Lapham tremulously, and she let the girl take the note from her.

Irene ran it over, and then turned to the name at the end with a joyful cry and a flush that burned to the top of her forehead. Then she began to read it once more.

The Colonel dropped his knife and frowned impatiently, and Mrs. Lapham said, "You read it out loud, if you know what to make of it, Irene." But Irene, with a nervous scream of protest, handed it to her father, who performed the office.

"DEAR MRS. LAPHAM:

"Will you and General Lapham——"

"I didn't know I was a general," grumbled Lapham. "I guess I shall have to be looking up my back pay. Who is it writes this, anyway?" he asked, turning the letter over for the signature.

"Oh, never mind. Read it through!" cried his wife, with a kindling glance of triumph at Penelope, and he resumed:

"—and your daughters give us the pleasure of your company at dinner on Thursday, the 28th, at half-past six.

"Yours sincerely,

"ANNA B. COREY."

The brief invitation had been spread over two pages, and the Colonel had difficulties with the signature which he did not instantly surmount. When he had made out the name and pronounced it, he looked across at his wife for an explanation.

"I don't know what it all means," she said, shaking her head and speaking with a pleased flutter. "She was here this afternoon, and I should have said she had come to see how bad she *could* make us feel. I declare, I never felt so put down in my life by anybody."

"Why, what did she do? What did she say?" Lapham was ready, in his dense pride, to resent any affront to his blood, but doubtful, with the evidence of this invitation to the contrary, if any affront had been offered. Mrs. Lapham tried to tell him, but there was really nothing tangible; and when she came to put it into words, she could not make out a case. Her husband listened to her excited attempt, and then he said, with judicial superiority, "I guess nobody's been trying to make you feel bad, Persis. What would she go right home and invite you to dinner for, if she'd acted the way you say?"

In this view it did seem improbable, and Mrs. Lapham was shaken. She could only say, "Penelope felt just the way I did about it."

Lapham looked at the girl, who said, "Oh, *I* can't prove it! I begin to think it never happened. I guess it didn't."

"Humph!" said her father, and he sat frowning thoughtfully awhile—ignoring her mocking irony, or choosing to take her seriously. "You can't really put your finger on anything," he said to his wife, "and it ain't likely there *is* anything. Anyway, she's done the proper thing by you now."

Mrs. Lapham faltered between her lingering resentment and the appeals of her flattered vanity. She looked from Penelope's impassive face to the eager eyes of Irene. "Well—just as you *say*, Silas. I don't know as she *was* so very bad. I guess may be she was embarrassed some——"

"That's what I told you, mamma, from the start," interrupted Irene. "Didn't I tell you she didn't mean anything by it? It's just the way she acted at Baie St. Joan, when she got well enough to realize what you'd done for her!"

Penelope broke into a laugh. "Is *that* her way of showing her gratitude? I'm sorry I didn't understand that before."

Irene made no effort to reply. She merely looked from her mother to her father with a grieved face for their protection, and Lapham said, "When we've done supper, you answer her, Persis. Say we'll come."

"With one exception," said Penelope.

"What do you mean?" demanded her father, with a mouth full of ham.

"Oh, nothing of importance. Merely that I'm not going."

Lapham gave himself time to swallow his morsel, and his rising wrath went down with it. "I guess you'll change your mind when the time comes," he said. "Anyway, Persis, you say we'll all come, and then, if Penelope don't want to go, you can excuse her after we get there. That's the best way."

None of them, apparently, saw any reason why the affair should not be left in this way, or had a sense of the awful and binding nature of a dinner-engagement. If she believed that Penelope would not finally change her mind and go, no doubt Mrs. Lapham thought that Mrs. Corey would easily excuse her absence. She did not find it so simple a matter to accept the invitation. Mrs. Corey had said "Dear Mrs. Lapham," but Mrs. Lapham had her doubts whether it would not be a servile imitation to say "Dear Mrs. Corey" in return; and she was tormented as to the proper phrasing throughout and the precise temperature which she should impart to her politeness. She wrote an unpracticed, uncharacteristic round hand, the same in which she used to set the children's copies at school, and she subscribed herself, after some hesitation between her husband's given name and her own, "Yours truly, Mrs. S. Lapham."

Penelope had gone to her room, without waiting to be asked to advise or criticise; but Irene had decided upon the paper, and, on the whole, Mrs. Lapham's note made a very decent appearance on the page.

When the furnace-man came, the Colonel sent him out to post it in the box at the corner of the square. He had determined not to say anything more about the matter before the girls, not choosing to let them see that he was elated; he tried to give the effect of its being an every-day sort of thing, abruptly closing the discussion with his order to Mrs. Lapham to accept; but he had remained swelling behind his newspaper during her prolonged struggle with her note, and he could no longer hide his elation when Irene followed her sister upstairs.

"Well, Pers," he demanded, "what do you say now?"

Mrs. Lapham had been sobered into something of her former misgiving by her difficulties with her note. "Well, I don't know what *to* say. I declare, I'm all mixed up about it, and I don't know as we've begun as we can carry out in promising to go. I presume," she sighed, "that we can *all* send some excuse at the last moment, if we don't want to go."

"I guess we can carry out, and I guess we sha'n't want to send any excuse," bragged the Colonel. "If we're ever going to be anybody at all, we've got to go and see how it's done. I presume we've got to give some sort of party when we get into the new house, and this gives the chance to ask 'em back again. You can't complain now but what they've made the advances, Persis?"

"No," said Mrs. Lapham, lifelessly; "I wonder why they wanted to do it. Oh, I suppose it's all right," she added in deprecation of the anger with her humility which she saw rising in her husband's face; "but if it's all going to be as much trouble as that letter, I'd rather be whipped. *I* don't know what I'm going to wear; or the girls, either. I do wonder—I've heard that people go to dinner in low-necks. Do you suppose it's the custom?"

"How should *I* know?" demanded the Colonel. "I guess

you've got clothes enough. Any rate, you needn't fret about it. You just go round to White's, or Jordan & Marsh's, and ask for a dinner dress. I guess that'll settle it; they'll know. Get some of them imported dresses. I see 'em in the window every time I pass; lots of 'em."

"Oh, it ain't the dress!" said Mrs. Lapham. "I don't suppose but what we could get along with that; and I want to do the best we can for the children; but *I* don't know what we're going to talk about to those people when we get there. We haven't got anything in common with them. Oh, I don't say they're any better," she again made haste to say in arrest of her husband's resentment. "I don't believe they are; and I don't see why they should be. And there ain't anybody has got a better right to hold up their head than you have, Silas. You've got plenty of money, and you've made every cent of it."

"I guess I shouldn't amounted to much without you, Persis," interposed Lapham, moved to this justice by her praise.

"Oh, don't talk about *me!*" protested the wife. "Now that you've made it all right about Rogers, there ain't a thing in this world against you. But still, for all that, I can see—and I can feel it when I can't see it—that we're different from those people. They're well-meaning enough, and they'd excuse it, I presume, but we're too old to learn to be like them."

"The children ain't," said Lapham, shrewdly.

"No, the children ain't," admitted his wife, "and that's the only thing that reconciles me to it."

"You see how pleased Irene looked when I read it?"

"Yes, she was pleased."

"And I guess Penelope'll think better of it before the time comes."

"Oh, yes, we do it for them. But whether we're doing the best thing for 'em, goodness knows. I'm not saying anything against *him*. Irene'll be a lucky girl to get him, if she wants him. But there! I'd ten times rather she was going to marry such a fellow as *you* were, Si, that had to make every inch of his own way, and she had to help him. It's *in* her!"

Lapham laughed aloud for pleasure in his wife's fondness; but neither of them wished that he should respond directly to it. "I guess, if it wa'n't for me, he wouldn't have a much easier time. But don't you fret! It's all coming out right. That dinner ain't a thing for you to be uneasy about. It'll pass off perfectly easy and natural."

Lapham did not keep his courageous mind quite to the end of the week that followed. It was his theory not to let Corey see that he was set up about the invitation, and when the young man said politely that his mother was glad they were able to come, Lapham was very short with him. He said yes, he believed that Mrs. Lapham and the girls were going. Afterward he was afraid Corey might not understand that he was coming too; but he did not know how to approach the subject again, and Corey did not, so he let it pass. It worried him to see all the preparation that his wife and Irene were making, and he tried to laugh at them for it; and it worried him to find that Penelope was making no preparation at all for herself, but only helping the others. He asked her what should she do if she changed her mind at the last moment and concluded to go, and she said she guessed she should not change her mind, but if she did, she would go to White's with him and get him to choose her an imported dress, he seemed to like them so much. He was too proud to mention the subject again to her.

Finally, all that dress-making in the house began to scare him with vague apprehensions in regard to his own dress. As soon as he had determined to go, an ideal of the figure in which he should go presented itself to his mind. He should not wear any dress-coat, because, for one thing, he considered that a man looked like a fool in a dress-coat, and, for another thing, he had none—had none on principle. He would go in a frock-coat and black pantaloons, and perhaps a white waistcoat, but a black cravat, anyway. But as soon as he developed this ideal to his family, which he did in pompous disdain of their anxieties about their own dress, they said he should not go so. Irene reminded him that he was the only person without a dress-coat at a corps-reunion dinner which he had taken her to some years before, and she remembered feeling awfully about it at the time. Mrs. Lapham, who would perhaps have agreed of herself, shook her head with misgiving. "I don't see but what you'll have to get you one, Si," she said. "I don't believe they *ever* go without 'em to a private house."

He held out openly, but on his way home the next day, in a sudden panic, he cast anchor before his tailor's door and got measured for a dress-coat. After that he began to be afflicted about his waistcoat, concerning which he had hitherto been airily indifferent. He tried to get opinion out of his family, but they were not so clear about it as they were about the frock. It ended in their buying a book of etiquette, which settled the question adversely to a white waistcoat. The author, however, after being very explicit in telling them not to eat with their knives, and above all not to pick their teeth with their forks,—a thing which he said no lady or gentleman ever did,—was still far from decided as to the kind of cravat Colonel Lapham ought to wear: shaken on other points, Lapham had begun to waver also concerning the black cravat. As to the question of gloves for the Colonel, which suddenly flashed upon him one evening, it appeared never to have entered the thoughts of the etiquette man, as Lapham called him. Other authors on the same subject were equally silent, and Irene could only remember having heard, in some vague sort of way, that gentlemen did not wear gloves so much any more.

Drops of perspiration gathered on Lapham's forehead in the anxiety of the debate; he groaned, and he swore a little in the compromise profanity which he used.

"I declare," said Penelope, where she sat purblindly sewing on a bit of dress for Irene, "the Colonel's clothes are as much trouble as anybody's. Why don't you go to Jordan & Marsh's and order one of the imported dresses for yourself, father?" That gave them all the relief of a laugh over it, the Colonel joining in piteously.

He had an awful longing to find out from Corey how he ought to go. He formulated and repeated over to himself an apparently careless question, such as, "Oh, by the way, Corey, where do you get your gloves?" This would naturally lead to some talk on the subject, which would, if properly managed, clear up the whole trouble. But Lapham found that he would rather die than ask this question, or any question that would bring up the dinner again. Corey did not recur to it, and Lapham avoided the matter with positive fierceness. He shunned talking with Corey at all, and suffered in grim silence.

One night, before they fell asleep, his wife said to him, "I was reading in one of those books to-day, and I don't believe but what we've made a mistake if Pen holds out that she won't go."

"Why?" demanded Lapham, in the dismay which beset him at every fresh recurrence to the subject.

"The book says that it's very impolite not to answer a dinner invitation promptly. Well, we've done that all right,—at first I didn't know but what we had been a little too quick, may be,—but then it says if you're not going, that it's the height of rudeness not to let them know at once, so that they can fill your place at the table."

The Colonel was silent for a while. "Well, I'm dumned," he said finally, "if there seems to be any end to this thing. If it was to do over again, I'd say no for all of us."

"I've wished a hundred times they hadn't asked us; but it's too late to think about that *now*. The question is, what are we going to do about Penelope?"

"Oh, I guess she'll go, at the last moment."

"She says she won't. She took a prejudice against Mrs. Corey that day, and she can't seem to get over it."

"Well, then, hadn't you better write in the morning, as soon as you're up, that she ain't coming?"

Mrs. Lapham sighed helplessly. "I shouldn't know how to get it in. It's so late now; I don't see how I could have the face."

"Well, then, she's got to go, that's all."

"She's set she won't."

"And I'm set she shall," said Lapham, with the loud obstinacy of a man whose women always have their way.

Mrs. Lapham was not supported by the sturdiness of his proclamation.

But she did not know how to do what she knew she ought to do about Penelope, and she let matters drift. After all, the child had a right to stay at home if she did not wish to go. That was what Mrs. Lapham felt, and what she said to her husband next morning, bidding him let Penelope alone, unless she chose herself to go. She said it was too late now to do anything, and she must make the best excuse she could when she saw Mrs. Corey. She began to wish that Irene and her father would go and excuse her too. She could not help saying this, and then she and Lapham had some unpleasant words.

"Look here!" he cried. "Who wanted to go in for these people in the first place? Didn't you come home full of 'em last year, and want me to sell out here and move somewheres else because it didn't seem to suit 'em? And now you want to put it all on me! I ain't going to stand it."

"Hush!" said his wife. "Do you want to raise the house? I *didn't* put it on you, as you say. You took it on yourself. Ever since that fellow happened to come into the new house that day, you've been perfectly crazy to get in with them. And now you're so afraid you shall do something wrong before 'em, you don't hardly dare to say your life's your own. I declare, if you pester me any more about those gloves, Silas Lapham, I won't go."

"Do you suppose I want to go on my own account?" he demanded furiously.

"No," she admitted. "Of course I don't. I know very well that you're doing it for Irene; but, for goodness gracious sake, don't worry our lives out, and make yourself a perfect laughing-stock before the children."

With this modified concession from her, the quarrel closed in sullen silence on Lapham's part. The night before the dinner came, and the question of his gloves was still unsettled, and in a fair way to remain so. He had bought a pair, so as to be on the safe side, perspiring in company with the young lady who sold them, and who helped him try them on at the shop; his nails were still full of the powder which she had plentifully peppered into them in order to overcome the resistance of his blunt fingers. But he was uncertain whether he should wear them. They had found a book at last that said the ladies removed their gloves on sitting down at table, but it said nothing about gentlemen's gloves. He left his wife where she stood half hook-and-eyed at her glass in her new dress, and went down to his own den beyond the parlor. Before he shut his door he caught a glimpse of Irene trailing up and down before the long mirror in *her* new dress, followed by the seamstress on her knees; the woman had her mouth full of pins, and from time to time she made Irene stop till she could put one of the pins into her train; Penelope sat in a corner criticising and counseling. It made Lapham sick, and he despised himself and all his brood for the trouble they were taking. But another glance gave him a sight of the young girl's face in the mirror, beautiful and radiant with happiness; and his heart melted again with paternal tenderness and pride. It was going to be a great pleasure to Irene, and Lapham felt that she was bound to cut out anything there. He was vexed with Penelope that she was not going, too; he would have liked to have those people hear her talk. He held his door a little open, and listened to the things she was "getting off" there to Irene. He showed that he felt really hurt and disappointed about Penelope, and the girl's mother made her console him the next evening before they all drove away without her. "You try to look on the bright side of it, father. I guess you'll see that it's best I didn't go when you get there. Irene needn't open her lips, and they can all see how pretty she is; but they wouldn't know how smart I was unless I talked, and may be then they wouldn't."

This thrust at her father's simple vanity in her made him laugh; and then they drove away, and Penelope shut the door, and went upstairs with her lips firmly shutting in a sob.

XIV

THE COREYS were one of the few old families who lingered in Bellingham Place, the handsome, quiet old
street which the sympathetic observer must grieve to see
abandoned to boarding-houses. The dwellings are stately and
tall, and the whole place wears an air of aristocratic seclusion,
which Mrs. Corey's father might well have thought assured
when he left her his house there at his death. It is one of two
evidently designed by the same architect who built some
houses in a characteristic taste on Beacon street opposite the
Common. It has a wooden portico, with slender fluted columns, which have always been painted white, and which,
with the delicate moldings of the cornice, form the sole and
sufficient decoration of the street front; nothing could be simpler, and nothing could be better. Within, the architect has
again indulged his preference for the classic; the roof of the
vestibule, wide and low, rests on marble columns, slim and
fluted like the wooden columns without, and an ample staircase climbs in a graceful, easy curve from the tessellated pavement. Some carved Venetian *scrigni* stretched along the wall;
a rug lay at the foot of the stairs; but otherwise the simple
adequacy of the architectural intention had been respected,
and the place looked bare to the eyes of the Laphams when
they entered. The Coreys had once kept a man, but when
young Corey began his retrenchments the man had yielded to
the neat maid who showed the Colonel into the reception-
room and asked the ladies to walk up two flights.

He had his charges from Irene not to enter the drawing-
room without her mother, and he spent five minutes in getting on his gloves, for he had desperately resolved to wear
them at last. When he had them on, and let his large fists
hang down on either side, they looked, in the saffron tint
which the shop-girl said his gloves should be of, like canvased
hams. He perspired with doubt as he climbed the stairs, and
while he waited on the landing for Mrs. Lapham and Irene to
come down from above, before going into the drawing-room,
he stood staring at his hands, now open and now shut, and

breathing hard. He heard quiet talking beyond the *portière* within, and presently Tom Corey came out.

"Ah, Colonel Lapham! Very glad to see you."

Lapham shook hands with him and gasped, "Waiting for Mis' Lapham," to account for his presence. He had not been able to button his right glove, and he now began, with as much indifference as he could assume, to pull them both off, for he saw that Corey wore none. By the time he had stuffed them into the pocket of his coat-skirt his wife and daughter descended.

Corey welcomed them very cordially too, but looked a little mystified. Mrs. Lapham knew that he was silently inquiring for Penelope, and she did not know whether she ought to excuse her to him first or not. She said nothing, and after a glance toward the regions where Penelope might conjecturably be lingering, he held aside the *portière* for the Laphams to pass, and entered the room with them.

Mrs. Lapham had decided against low-necks on her own responsibility, and had intrenched herself in the safety of a black silk, in which she looked very handsome. Irene wore a dress of one of those shades which only a woman or an artist can decide to be green or blue, and which to other eyes looks both or neither, according to their degrees of ignorance. If it was more like a ball dress than a dinner dress, that might be excused to the exquisite effect. She trailed, a delicate splendor, across the carpet in her mother's somber wake, and the consciousness of success brought a vivid smile to her face. Lapham, pallid with anxiety lest he should somehow disgrace himself, giving thanks to God that he should have been spared the shame of wearing gloves where no one else did, but at the same time despairing that Corey should have seen him in them, had an unwonted aspect of almost pathetic refinement.

Mrs. Corey exchanged a quick glance of surprise and relief with her husband as she started across the room to meet her guests, and in her gratitude to them for being so irreproachable, she threw into her manner a warmth that people did not always find there. "General Lapham?" she said, shaking hands in quick succession with Mrs. Lapham and Irene, and now addressing herself to him.

"No, ma'am, only Colonel," said the honest man, but the lady did not hear him. She was introducing her husband to Lapham's wife and daughter, and Bromfield Corey was already shaking his hand and saying he was very glad to see him again, while he kept his artistic eye on Irene, and apparently could not take it off. Lily Corey gave the Lapham ladies a greeting which was physically rather than socially cold, and Nanny stood holding Irene's hand in both of hers a moment, and taking in her beauty and her style with a generous admiration which she could afford, for she was herself faultlessly dressed in the quiet taste of her city, and looking very pretty. The interval was long enough to let every man present confide his sense of Irene's beauty to every other; and then, as the party was small, Mrs. Corey made everybody acquainted. When Lapham had not quite understood, he held the person's hand, and, leaning urbanely forward, inquired, "What name?" He did that because a great man to whom he had been presented on the platform at a public meeting had done so to him, and he knew it must be right.

A little lull ensued upon the introductions, and Mrs. Corey said quietly to Mrs. Lapham, "Can I send any one to be of use to Miss Lapham?" as if Penelope must be in the dressing-room.

Mrs. Lapham turned fire-red, and the graceful forms in which she had been intending to excuse her daughter's absence went out of her head. "She isn't upstairs," she said, at her bluntest, as country people are when embarrassed. "She didn't feel just like coming to-night. I don't know as she's feeling very well."

Mrs. Corey emitted a very small "O!"—very small, very cold,—which began to grow larger and hotter and to burn into Mrs. Lapham's soul before Mrs. Corey could add, "I'm very sorry. It's nothing serious, I hope?"

Robert Chase, the painter, had not come, and Mrs. James Bellingham was not there, so that the table really balanced better without Penelope; but Mrs. Lapham could not know this, and did not deserve to know it. Mrs. Corey glanced round the room, as if to take account of her guests, and said to her husband, "I think we are all here, then," and he came forward and gave his arm to Mrs. Lapham. She perceived then that in their determination not to be the first to come, they had been the last, and must have kept the others waiting for them.

Lapham had never seen people go down to dinner arm in arm before, but he knew that his wife was distinguished in being taken out by the host, and he waited in jealous impatience to see if Tom Corey would offer his arm to Irene. He gave it to that big girl they called Miss Kingsbury, and the handsome old fellow whom Mrs. Corey had introduced as her cousin took Irene out. Lapham was startled from the misgiving in which this left him by Mrs. Corey's passing her hand through his arm, and he made a sudden movement forward, but felt himself gently restrained. They went out the last of all; he did not know why, but he submitted, and when they sat down he saw that Irene, although she had come in with that Mr. Bellingham, was seated beside young Corey, after all.

He fetched a long sigh of relief when he sank into his chair and felt himself safe from error if he kept a sharp lookout and did only what the others did. Bellingham had certain habits which he permitted himself, and one of these was tucking the corner of his napkin into his collar; he confessed himself an uncertain shot with a spoon, and defended his practice on the ground of neatness and common sense. Lapham put his napkin into his collar too, and then, seeing that no one but Bellingham did it, became alarmed and took it out again slyly. He never had wine on his table at home, and on principle he was a prohibitionist; but now he did not know just what to do about the glasses at the right of his plate. He had a notion to turn them all down, as he had read of a well-known politician's doing at a public dinner, to show that he did not take wine; but, after twiddling with one of them a moment, he let them be, for it seemed to him that would be a little too conspicuous, and he felt that every one was looking. He let the servant fill them all, and he drank out of each, not to appear odd. Later, he observed that the young ladies were not taking wine, and he was glad to see that Irene had refused it, and that Mrs. Lapham was letting it stand untasted. He did not know but he ought to decline some of the dishes, or at least leave most of some on his plate, but he was not able to decide; he took everything and ate everything.

He noticed that Mrs. Corey seemed to take no more trouble about the dinner than anybody, and Mr. Corey rather less; he was talking busily to Mrs. Lapham, and Lapham caught a word here and there that convinced him she was holding her own. He was getting on famously himself with Mrs. Corey, who had begun with him about his new house; he was telling her all about it, and giving her his ideas. Their conversation naturally included his architect across the table; Lapham had been delighted and secretly surprised to find the fellow there; and at something Seymour said the talk spread suddenly, and the pretty house he was building for Colonel Lapham became the general theme. Young Corey testified to its loveliness, and the architect said laughingly that if he had been able to make a nice thing of it, he owed it to the practical sympathy of his client.

"Practical sympathy is good," said Bromfield Corey; and, slanting his head confidentially to Mrs. Lapham, he added, "Does he bleed your husband, Mrs. Lapham? He's a terrible fellow for appropriations!"

Mrs. Lapham laughed, reddening consciously, and said she guessed the Colonel knew how to take care of himself. This struck Lapham, then draining his glass of sauterne, as wonderfully discreet in his wife.

Bromfield Corey leaned back in his chair a moment. "Well, after all, you can't say, with all your modern fuss about it, that you do much better now than the old fellows who built such houses as this."

"Ah," said the architect, "nobody can do better than well. Your house is in perfect taste; you know I've always admired it; and I don't think it's at all the worse for being old-fashioned. What we've done is largely to go back of the hideous style that raged after they forgot how to make this sort of house. But I think we may claim a better feeling for structure. We use better material, and more wisely; and by and by we shall work out something more characteristic and original."

"With your chocolates and olives, and your clutter of bric-à-brac?"

"All that's bad, of course, but I don't mean that. I don't wish to make you envious of Colonel Lapham, and modesty prevents my saying that his house is prettier,—though I may have my convictions,—but it's better built. All the new houses are better built. Now, your house——"

"Mrs. Corey's house," interrupted the host, with a burlesque haste in disclaiming responsibility for it that made them all laugh. "*My* ancestral halls are in Salem, and I'm told you couldn't drive a nail into their timbers; in fact, I don't know that you would want to do it."

"I should consider it a species of sacrilege," answered Seymour, "and I shall be far from pressing the point I was going to make against a house of Mrs. Corey's."

This won Seymour the easy laugh, and Lapham silently wondered that the fellow never got off any of those things to him.

"Well," said Corey, "you architects and the musicians are the true and only artistic creators. All the rest of us, sculptors, painters, novelists, and tailors, deal with forms that we have before us; we try to imitate, we try to represent. But you two sorts of artists create form. If you represent, you fail. Somehow or other you do evolve the camel out of your inner consciousness."

"I will not deny the soft impeachment," said the architect, with a modest air.

"I dare say. And you'll own that it's very handsome of me to say this, after your unjustifiable attack on Mrs. Corey's property."

Bromfield Corey addressed himself again to Mrs. Lapham, and the talk subdivided itself as before. It lapsed so entirely away from the subject just in hand, that Lapham was left with rather a good idea, as he thought it, to perish in his mind, for want of a chance to express it. The only thing like a recurrence to what they had been saying was Bromfield Corey's warning Mrs. Lapham, in some connection that Lapham lost, against Miss Kingsbury. "She's worse," he was saying, "when it comes to appropriations than Seymour himself. Depend upon it, Mrs. Lapham, she will give you no peace of your mind, now she's met you, from this out. Her tender mercies are cruel; and I leave you to supply the context from your own scriptural knowledge. Beware of her, and all her works.

She calls them works of charity; but heaven knows whether they are. It don't stand to reason that she gives the poor *all* the money she gets out of people. I have my own belief"— he gave it in a whisper for the whole table to hear—"that she spends it for champagne and cigars."

Lapham did not know about that kind of talking; but Miss Kingsbury seemed to enjoy the fun as much as anybody, and he laughed with the rest.

"You shall be asked to the very next debauch of the committee, Mr. Corey; then you won't dare expose us," said Miss Kingsbury.

"I wonder you haven't been down upon Corey to go to the Chardon street home and talk with your indigent Italians in their native tongue," said Charles Bellingham. "I saw in the 'Transcript' the other night that you wanted some one for the work."

"We did think of Mr. Corey," replied Miss Kingsbury; "but we reflected that he probably wouldn't talk with them at all; he would make them keep still to be sketched, and forget all about their wants."

Upon the theory that this was a fair return for Corey's pleasantry, the others laughed again.

"There is one charity," said Corey, pretending superiority to Miss Kingsbury's point, "that is so difficult I wonder it hasn't occurred to a lady of your courageous invention."

"Yes?" said Miss Kingsbury. "What is that?"

"The occupation, by deserving poor of neat habits, of all the beautiful, airy, wholesome houses that stand empty the whole summer long, while their owners are away in their lowly cots beside the sea."

"Yes, that is terrible," replied Miss Kingsbury, with quick earnestness, while her eyes grew moist. "I have often thought of our great, cool houses standing useless here, and the thousands of poor creatures stifling in their holes and dens, and the little children dying for wholesome shelter. How cruelly selfish we are!"

"That is a very comfortable sentiment, Miss Kingsbury," said Corey, "and must make you feel almost as if you had thrown open No. 931 to the whole North End. But I am serious about this matter. I spend my summers in town, and I occupy my own house, so that I can speak impartially and intelligently; and I tell you that in some of my walks on the Hill and down on the Back Bay, nothing but the surveillance of the local policeman prevents me from applying dynamite to those long rows of close-shuttered, handsome, brutally insensible houses. If I were a poor man, with a sick child pining in some garret or cellar at the North End, I should break into one of them, and camp out on the grand piano."

"Surely, Bromfield," said his wife, "you don't consider what havoc such people would make with the furniture of a nice house!"

"That is true," answered Corey, with meek conviction. "I never thought of that."

"And if you were a poor man with a sick child, I doubt if you'd have so much heart for burglary as you have now," said James Bellingham.

"It's wonderful how patient they are," said the minister. "The spectacle of the hopeless comfort the hard-working poor man sees must be hard to bear."

Lapham wanted to speak up and say that he had been there himself, and knew how such a man felt. He wanted to tell them that generally a poor man was satisfied if he could make both ends meet; that he didn't envy any one his good luck, if he had earned it, so long as he wasn't running under himself. But before he could get the courage to address the whole table, Sewell added, "I suppose he don't always think of it."

"But some day he *will* think about it," said Corey. "In fact, we rather invite him to think about it, in this country."

"My brother-in-law," said Charles Bellingham, with the pride a man feels in a mentionably remarkable brother-in-law, "has no end of fellows at work under him out there at Omaha, and he says it's the fellows from countries where they've been kept from thinking about it that are discontented. The Americans never make any trouble. They seem to understand that so long as we give unlimited opportunity, nobody has a right to complain."

"What do you hear from Leslie?" asked Mrs. Corey, turning from these profitless abstractions to Mrs. Bellingham.

"You know," said that lady in a lower tone, "that there is another baby?"

"No! I hadn't heard of it!"

"Yes; a boy. They have named him after his uncle."

"Yes," said Charles Bellingham, joining in. "He is said to be a noble boy and to resemble me."

"All boys of that tender age are noble," said Corey, "and look like anybody you wish them to resemble. Is Leslie still homesick for the bean-pots of her native Boston?"

"She is getting over it, I fancy," replied Mrs. Bellingham. "She's very much taken up with Mr. Blake's enterprises, and leads a very exciting life. She says she's like people who have been home from Europe three years; she's past the most poignant stage of regret, and hasn't reached the second, when they feel that they *must* go again."

Lapham leaned a little toward Mrs. Corey, and said of a picture which he saw on the wall opposite, "Picture of your daughter, I presume?"

"No; my daughter's grandmother. It's a Stuart Newton; he painted a great many Salem beauties. She was a Miss Polly Burroughs. My daughter *is* like her, don't you think?" They both looked at Nanny Corey and then at the portrait. "Those pretty old-fashioned dresses are coming in again. I'm not surprised you took it for her. The others"—she referred to the other portraits more or less darkling on the walls—"are my people; mostly Copleys."

These names, unknown to Lapham, went to his head like the wine he was drinking; they seemed to carry light for the moment, but a film of deeper darkness followed. He heard Charles Bellingham telling funny stories to Irene and trying to amuse the girl; she was laughing and seemed very happy. From time to time Bellingham took part in the general talk between the host and James Bellingham and Miss Kingsbury and that minister, Mr. Sewell. They talked of people mostly; it astonished Lapham to hear with what freedom they talked. They discussed these persons unsparingly; James Bellingham spoke of a man known to Lapham for his business success and great wealth as not a gentleman; his cousin Charles said he was surprised that the fellow had kept from being governor so long.

When the latter turned from Irene to make one of these

excursions into the general talk, young Corey talked to her; and Lapham caught some words from which it seemed that they were speaking of Penelope. It vexed him to think she had not come; she could have talked as well as any of them; she was just as bright; and Lapham was aware that Irene was not as bright, though when he looked at her face, triumphant in its young beauty and fondness, he said to himself that it did not make any difference. He felt that he was not holding up his end of the line, however. When some one spoke to him he could only summon a few words of reply, that seemed to lead to nothing; things often came into his mind appropriate to what they were saying, but before he could get them out they were off on something else; they jumped about so, he could not keep up; but he felt, all the same, that he was not doing himself justice.

At one time the talk ran off upon a subject that Lapham had never heard talked of before; but again he was vexed that Penelope was not there, to have her say; he believed that her say would have been worth hearing.

Miss Kingsbury leaned forward and asked Charles Bellingham if he had read "Tears, Idle Tears," the novel that was making such a sensation; and when he said no, she said she wondered at him. "It's perfectly heart-breaking, as you'll imagine from the name; but there's such a dear old-fashioned hero and heroine in it, who keep dying for each other all the way through and making the most wildly satisfactory and unnecessary sacrifices for each other. You feel as if you'd done them yourself."

"Ah, that's the secret of its success," said Bromfield Corey. "It flatters the reader by painting the characters colossal, but with his limp and stoop, so that he feels himself of their supernatural proportions. You've read it, Nanny?"

"Yes," said his daughter. "It ought to have been called 'Slop, Silly Slop.' "

"Oh, not quite *slop*, Nanny," pleaded Miss Kingsbury.

"It's astonishing," said Charles Bellingham, "how we do like the books that go for our heart-strings. And I really suppose that you can't put a more popular thing than self-sacrifice into a novel. We do like to see people suffering sublimely."

"There was talk some years ago," said James Bellingham, "about novels going out."

"They're just coming in!" cried Miss Kingsbury.

"Yes," said Mr. Sewell, the minister. "And I don't think there ever was a time when they formed the whole intellectual experience of more people. They do greater mischief than ever."

"Don't be envious, parson," said the host.

"No," answered Sewell. "I should be glad of their help. But those novels with old-fashioned heroes and heroines in them—excuse me, Miss Kingsbury—are ruinous!"

"Don't you feel like a moral wreck, Miss Kingsbury?" asked the host.

But Sewell went on: "The novelists might be the greatest possible help to us if they painted life as it is, and human feelings in their true proportion and relation, but for the most part they have been and are altogether noxious."

This seemed sense to Lapham; but Bromfield Corey asked: "But what if life as it is isn't amusing? Aren't we to be amused?"

"Not to our hurt," sturdily answered the minister. "And the self-sacrifice painted in most novels like this——"

"Slop, Silly Slop?" suggested the proud father of the inventor of the phrase.

"Yes—is nothing but psychical suicide, and is as wholly immoral as the spectacle of a man falling upon his sword."

"Well, I don't know but you're right, parson," said the host; and the minister, who had apparently got upon a battle-horse of his, careered onward in spite of some tacit attempts of his wife to seize the bridle.

"Right? To be sure I am right. The whole business of love, and love-making and marrying, is painted by the novelists in a monstrous disproportion to the other relations of life. Love is very sweet, very pretty——"

"Oh, *thank* you, Mr. Sewell," said Nanny Corey in a way that set them all laughing.

"But it's the affair, commonly, of very young people, who have not yet character and experience enough to make them interesting. In novels it's treated, not only as if it were the chief interest of life, but the sole interest of the lives of two ridiculous young persons; and it is taught that love is perpetual, that the glow of a true passion lasts forever; and that it is sacrilege to think or act otherwise."

"Well, but isn't that true, Mr. Sewell?" pleaded Miss Kingsbury.

"I have known some most estimable people who had married a second time," said the minister, and then he had the applause with him. Lapham wanted to make some open recognition of his good sense, but could not.

"I suppose the passion itself has been a good deal changed," said Bromfield Corey, "since the poets began to idealize it in the days of chivalry."

"Yes; and it ought to be changed again," said Mr. Sewell.

"What! Back?"

"I don't say that. But it ought to be recognized as something natural and mortal, and divine honors, which belong to righteousness alone, ought not to be paid it."

"Oh, you ask too much, parson," laughed his host, and the talk wandered away to something else.

It was not an elaborate dinner; but Lapham was used to having everything on the table at once, and this succession of dishes bewildered him; he was afraid perhaps he was eating too much. He now no longer made any pretense of not drinking his wine, for he was thirsty, and there was no more water, and he hated to ask for any. The ice-cream came, and then the fruit. Suddenly Mrs. Corey rose and said across the table to her husband, "I suppose you will want your coffee here." And he replied, "Yes; we'll join you at tea."

The ladies all rose, and the gentlemen got up with them. Lapham started to follow Mrs. Corey, but the other men merely stood in their places, except young Corey, who ran and opened the door for his mother. Lapham thought with shame that it was he who ought to have done that; but no one seemed to notice, and he sat down again gladly, after kicking out one of his legs which had gone to sleep.

They brought in cigars with coffee, and Bromfield Corey advised Lapham to take one that he chose for him. Lapham confessed that he liked a good cigar about as well as anybody, and Corey said: "These are new. I had an Englishman here the other day who was smoking old cigars in the superstition that tobacco improved with age, like wine."

"Ah," said Lapham, "anybody who had ever lived off a tobacco country could tell him better than that." With the fuming cigar between his lips he felt more at home than he had before. He turned sidewise in his chair and, resting one arm on the back, intertwined the fingers of both hands, and smoked at large ease.

James Bellingham came and sat down by him. "Colonel Lapham, weren't you with the 96th Vermont when they charged across the river in front of Pickensburg, and the rebel battery opened fire on them in the water?"

Lapham slowly shut his eyes and slowly dropped his head for assent, letting out a white volume of smoke from the corner of his mouth.

"I thought so," said Bellingham. "I was with the 85th Massachusetts, and I sha'n't forget that slaughter. We were all new to it still. Perhaps that's why it made such an impression."

"I don't know," suggested Charles Bellingham. "Was there anything much more impressive afterward? I read of it out in Missouri, where I was stationed at the time, and I recollect the talk of some old army men about it. They said that death-rate couldn't be beaten. I don't know that it ever was."

"About one in five of us got out safe," said Lapham, breaking his cigar-ash off on the edge of a plate. James Bellingham reached him a bottle of Apollinaris. He drank a glass, and then went on smoking.

They all waited, as if expecting him to speak, and then Corey said: "How incredible those things seem already! You gentlemen *know* that they happened; but are you still able to believe it?"

"Ah, nobody *feels* that anything happened," said Charles Bellingham. "The past of one's experience doesn't differ a great deal from the past of one's knowledge. It isn't much more probable; it's really a great deal less vivid than some scenes in a novel that one read when a boy."

"I'm not sure of that," said James Bellingham.

"Well, James, neither am I," consented his cousin, helping

himself from Lapham's Apollinaris bottle. "There would be very little talking at dinner if one only said the things that one was sure of."

The others laughed, and Bromfield Corey remarked thoughtfully, "What astonishes the craven civilian in all these things is the abundance—the superabundance—of heroism. The cowards were the exception; the men that were ready to die, the rule."

"The woods were full of them," said Lapham, without taking his cigar from his mouth.

"That's a nice little touch in 'School,' " interposed Charles Bellingham, "where the girl says to the fellow who was at Inkerman, 'I should think you would be so proud of it,' and he reflects awhile, and says, 'Well, the fact is, you know, there were so many of us.' "

"Yes, I remember that," said James Bellingham, smiling for pleasure in it. "But I don't see why you claim the credit of being a craven civilian, Bromfield," he added, with a friendly glance at his brother-in-law, and with the willingness Boston men often show to turn one another's good points to the light in company; bred so intimately together at school and college and in society, they all know these points. "A man who was out with Garibaldi in '48," continued James Bellingham.

"Oh, a little amateur red-shirting," Corey interrupted in deprecation. "But even if you choose to dispute my claim, what has become of all the heroism? Tom, how many club men do you know who would think it sweet and fitting to die for their country?"

"I can't think of a great many at the moment, sir," replied the son, with the modesty of his generation.

"And I couldn't in '61," said his uncle. "Nevertheless they were there."

"Then your theory is that it's the occasion that is wanting," said Bromfield Corey. "But why shouldn't civil-service reform, and the resumption of specie payment, and a tariff for revenue only, inspire heroes? They are all good causes."

"It's the occasion that's wanting," said James Bellingham, ignoring the *persiflage*. "And I'm very glad of it."

"So am I," said Lapham, with a depth of feeling that expressed itself in spite of the haze in which his brain seemed to float. There was a great deal of the talk that he could not follow; it was too quick for him; but here was something he was clear of. "I don't want to see any more men killed in my time." Something serious, something somber must lurk behind these words, and they waited for Lapham to say more; but the haze closed round him again, and he remained silent, drinking Apollinaris.

"We non-combatants were notoriously reluctant to give up fighting," said Mr. Sewell, the minister; "but I incline to think Colonel Lapham and Mr. Bellingham may be right. I dare say we shall have the heroism again if we have the occasion. Till it comes, we must content ourselves with the every-day generosities and sacrifices. They make up in quantity what they lack in quality, perhaps."

"They're not so picturesque," said Bromfield Corey. "You can paint a man dying for his country, but you can't express on canvas a man fulfilling the duties of a good citizen."

"Perhaps the novelists will get at him by and by," suggested Charles Bellingham. "If I were one of these fellows, I shouldn't propose to myself anything short of that."

"What: the commonplace?" asked his cousin.

"Commonplace? The commonplace is just that light, impalpable, aërial essence which they've never got into their confounded books yet. The novelist who could interpret the common feelings of commonplace people would have the answer to 'the riddle of the painful earth' on his tongue."

"Oh, not so bad as that, I hope," said the host; and Lapham looked from one to the other, trying to make out what they were at. He had never been so up a tree before.

"I suppose it isn't well for us to see human nature at white heat habitually," continued Bromfield Corey, after a while. "It would make us vain of our species. Many a poor fellow in that war and in many another has gone into battle simply and purely for his country's sake, not knowing whether, if he laid down his life, he should ever find it again, or whether, if he took it up hereafter, he should take it up in heaven or hell. Come, parson!" he said, turning to the minister, "what has ever been conceived of omnipotence, of omniscience, so sublime, so divine as that?"

"Nothing," answered the minister, quietly. "God has never been imagined at all. But if you suppose such a man as that was Authorized, I think it will help you to imagine what God must be."

"There's sense in that," said Lapham. He took his cigar out of his mouth, and pulled his chair a little toward the table, on which he placed his ponderous fore-arms. "I want to tell you about a fellow I had in my own company when we first went out. We were all privates to begin with; after a while they elected me captain—I'd had the tavern stand, and most of 'em knew me. But Jim Millon never got to be anything more than corporal; corporal when he was killed." The others arrested themselves in various attitudes of attention, and remained listening to Lapham with an interest that profoundly flattered him. Now, at last, he felt that he was holding up his end of the rope. "I can't say he went into the thing from the highest motives, altogether; our motives are always pretty badly mixed, and when there's such a hurrah-boys as there was then, you can't tell which is which. I suppose Jim Millon's wife was enough to account for his going, herself. She was a pretty bad assortment," said Lapham, lowering his voice and glancing round at the door to make sure that it was shut, "and she used to lead Jim *one* kind of life. Well, sir," continued Lapham, synthetizing his auditors in that form of address, "that fellow used to save every cent of his pay and send it to that woman. Used to get me to do it for him. I tried to stop him. 'Why, Jim,' said I, 'you know what she'll do with it.' 'That's so, Cap,' says he, 'but I don't know what she'll do without it.' And it did keep her straight—straight as a string—as long as Jim lasted. Seemed as if there was something mysterious about it. They had a little girl,—about as old as my oldest girl,—and Jim used to talk to me about her. Guess he done it as much for her as for the mother; and he said to me before the last action we went into, 'I should like to turn tail and run, Cap. I ain't comin' out o' this one. But I don't suppose it would do.' 'Well, not for you, Jim,' said I. 'I want to live,' he says; and he bust out crying right there in my tent. 'I want to live for poor Molly and Zerrilla'—that's what they called the little one; I dunno where they got the name. 'I ain't ever had half a chance; and now she's doing better, and I believe we should get along after this.' He set there cryin' like a baby. But he wa'n't no baby when he went into action. I hated to look at him after it was over, not so much because he'd got a ball that was meant for me by a sharp-shooter—he saw the devil takin' aim, and he jumped to warn me—as because he didn't look like Jim; he looked like—fun; all desperate and savage. I guess he died hard."

The story made its impression, and Lapham saw it. "Now I say," he resumed, as if he felt that he was going to do himself justice, and say something to heighten the effect his story had produced. At the same time, he was aware of a certain want of clearness. He had the idea, but it floated vague, elusive, in his brain. He looked about as if for something to precipitate it in tangible shape.

"Apollinaris?" asked Charles Bellingham, handing the bottle from the other side. He had drawn his chair closer than the rest to Lapham's, and was listening with great interest. When Mrs. Corey asked him to meet Lapham he accepted gladly. "You know I go in for that sort of thing, Anna. Since Leslie's affair we're rather bound to do it. And I think we meet these practical fellows too little. There's always something original about them." He might naturally have believed that the reward of his faith was coming.

"Thanks, I will take some of this wine," said Lapham, pouring himself a glass of Madeira from a black and dusty bottle caressed by a label bearing the date of the vintage. He tossed off the wine, unconscious of its preciousness, and waited for the result. That cloudiness in his brain disappeared before it, but a mere blank remained. He not only could not remember what he was going to say, but he could not recall what they had been talking about. They waited, looking at him, and he stared at them in return. After a while he heard the host saying, "Shall we join the ladies?"

Lapham went, trying to think what had happened. It seemed to him a long time since he had drunk that wine.

Miss Corey gave him a cup of tea, where he stood aloof from his wife, who was talking with Miss Kingsbury and Mrs. Sewell; Irene was with Miss Nanny Corey. He could not hear what they were talking about; but if Penelope had come he knew that she would have done them all credit. He meant to let her know how he felt about her behavior when he got home. It was a shame for her to miss such a chance. Irene was looking beautiful, as pretty as all the rest of them put together, but she was not talking, and Lapham perceived that at a dinner party you ought to talk. He was himself conscious of having talked very well. He now wore an air of great dignity, and, in conversing with the other gentlemen, he used a grave and weighty deliberation. Some of them wanted him to go into the library. There he gave his ideas of books. He said he had not much time for anything but the papers; but he was going to have a complete library in his new place. He made an elaborate acknowledgment to Bromfield Corey of his son's kindness in suggesting books for his library; he said that he had ordered them all, and that he meant to have pictures. He asked Mr. Corey who was about the best American painter going now. "I don't set up to be a judge of pictures, but I know what I like," he said. He lost the reserve which he had maintained earlier, and began to boast. He himself introduced the subject of his paint, in a natural transition from pictures; he said Mr. Corey must take a run up to Lapham with him some day, and see the Works; they would interest him, and he would drive him round the country; he kept most of his horses up there, and he could show Mr. Corey some of the finest Jersey grades in the country. He told about his brother William, the judge at Dubuque; and a farm he had out there that paid for itself every year in wheat. As he cast off all fear, his voice rose, and he hammered his armchair with the thick of his hand for emphasis. Mr. Corey seemed impressed; he sat perfectly quiet, listening, and Lapham saw the other gentlemen stop in their talk every now and then to listen. After this proof of his ability to interest them, he would have liked to have Mrs. Lapham suggest again that he was unequal to their society, or to the society of anybody else. He surprised himself by his ease among men whose names had hitherto overawed him. He got to calling Bromfield Corey by his surname alone. He did not understand why young Corey seemed so preoccupied, and he took occasion to tell the company how he had said to his wife the first time he saw that fellow that he could make a man of him if he had him in the business; and he guessed he was not mistaken. He began to tell stories of the different young men he had had in his employ. At last he had the talk altogether to himself; no one else talked, and he talked unceasingly. It was a great time; it was a triumph.

He was in this successful mood when word came to him that Mrs. Lapham was going; Tom Corey seemed to have brought it, but he was not sure. Anyway, he was not going to hurry. He made cordial invitations to each of the gentlemen to drop in and see him at his office, and would not be satisfied till he had exacted a promise from each. He told Charles Bellingham that he liked him, and assured James Bellingham that it had always been his ambition to know him, and that if any one had said when he first came to Boston that in less than ten years he should be hobnobbing with Jim Bellingham, he should have told that person he lied. He would have told anybody he lied that had told him ten years ago that a son of Bromfield Corey would have come and asked him to take him into the business. Ten years ago he, Silas Lapham, had come to Boston, a little worse off than nothing at all, for he was in debt for half the money that he had bought out his partner with, and here he was now worth a million, and meeting you gentlemen like one of you. And every cent of that was honest money,—no speculation,—every copper of it for value received. And here, only the other day, his old partner, who had been going to the dogs ever since he went out of the business, came and borrowed twenty thousand dollars of him! Lapham lent it because his wife wanted him to: she had always felt bad about the fellow's having to go out of the business.

He took leave of Mr. Sewell with patronizing affection, and bade him come to him if he ever got into a tight place with his parish work; he would let him have all the money he wanted; he had more money than he knew what to do with. "Why, when your wife sent to mine last fall," he said, turning to Mr. Corey, "I drew my check for five hundred dollars, but my wife wouldn't take more than one hundred; said she wasn't going to show off before Mrs. Corey. I call that a pretty good joke on Mrs. Corey. I must tell her how Mrs. Lapham done her out of a cool four hundred dollars."

He started toward the door of the drawing-room to take

leave of the ladies; but Tom Corey was at his elbow, saying, "I think Mrs. Lapham is waiting for you below, sir," and in obeying the direction Corey gave him toward another door he forgot all about his purpose, and came away without saying good-night to his hostess.

Mrs. Lapham had not known how soon she ought to go, and had no idea that in her quality of chief guest she was keeping the others. She staid till eleven o'clock, and was a little frightened when she found what time it was; but Mrs. Corey, without pressing her to stay longer, had said it was not at all late. She and Irene had had a perfect time. Everybody had been very polite; on the way home they celebrated the amiability of both the Miss Coreys and of Miss Kingsbury. Mrs. Lapham thought that Mrs. Bellingham was about the pleasantest person she ever saw; she had told her all about her married daughter who had married an inventor and gone to live in Omaha—a Mrs. Blake.

"If it's that car-wheel Blake," said Lapham, proudly, "I know all about him. I've sold him tons of the paint."

"Pooh, papa! How you do smell of smoking!" cried Irene.

"Pretty strong, eh?" laughed Lapham, letting down a window of the carriage. His heart was throbbing wildly in the close air, and he was glad of the rush of cold that came in, though it stopped his tongue, and he listened more and more drowsily to the rejoicings that his wife and daughter exchanged. He meant to have them wake Penelope up and tell her what she had lost; but when he reached home he was too sleepy to suggest it. He fell asleep as soon as his head touched the pillow, full of supreme triumph.

But in the morning his skull was sore with the unconscious, night-long ache; and he rose cross and taciturn. They had a silent breakfast. In the cold gray light of the morning the glories of the night before showed poorer. Here and there a painful doubt obtruded itself and marred them with its awkward shadow. Penelope sent down word that she was not well, and was not coming to breakfast, and Lapham was glad to go to his office without seeing her.

He was severe and silent all day with his clerks, and peremptory with customers. Of Corey he was slyly observant, and as the day wore away he grew more restively conscious.

He sent out word by his office-boy that he would like to see Mr. Corey for a few minutes after closing. The type-writer girl had lingered too, as if she wished to speak with him, and Corey stood in abeyance as she went toward Lapham's door.

"Can't see you to-night, Zerrilla," he said bluffly, but not unkindly. "Perhaps I'll call at the house, if it's important."

"It is," said the girl, with a spoiled air of insistence.

"Well," said Lapham; and, nodding to Corey to enter, he closed the door upon her. Then he turned to the young man and demanded: "Was I drunk last night?"

XV

LAPHAM'S strenuous face was broken up with the emotions that had forced him to this question: shame, fear of the things that must have been thought of him, mixed with a faint hope that he might be mistaken, which died out at the shocked and pitying look in Corey's eyes.

"Was I drunk?" he repeated. "I ask you, because I was never touched by drink in my life before, and I don't know." He stood with his huge hands trembling on the back of his chair, and his dry lips apart, as he stared at Corey.

"That is what every one understood, Colonel Lapham," said the young man. "Every one saw how it was. Don't——"

"Did they talk it over after I left?" asked Lapham, vulgarly.

"Excuse me," said Corey, blushing, "my father doesn't talk his guests over with one another." He added, with youthful superfluity, "You were among gentlemen."

"I was the only one that wasn't a gentleman there!" lamented Lapham. "I disgraced you! I disgraced my family! I mortified your father before his friends!" His head dropped. "I showed that I wasn't fit to go with you. I'm not fit for any decent place. What did I say? What did I do?" he asked, suddenly lifting his head and confronting Corey. "Out with it! If you could bear to see it and hear it, I had ought to bear to know it!"

"There was nothing—really nothing," said Corey. "Beyond the fact that you were not quite yourself, there was nothing whatever. My father *did* speak of it to me," he confessed, "when we were alone. He said that he was afraid we had not been thoughtful of you, if you were in the habit of taking only water; I told him I had not seen wine at your table. The others said nothing about you."

"Ah, but what did they think!"

"Probably what we did: that it was purely a misfortune—an accident."

"I wasn't fit to be there," persisted Lapham. "Do you want to leave?" he asked, with savage abruptness.

"Leave?" faltered the young man.

"Yes; quit the business? Cut the whole connection?"

"I haven't the remotest idea of it!" cried Corey in amazement. "Why in the world should I?"

"Because you're a gentleman, and I'm not, and it ain't right I should be over you. If you want to go, I know some parties that would be glad to get you. I will give you up if you want to go before anything worse happens, and I sha'n't blame you. I can help you to something better than I can offer you here, and I will."

"There's no question of my going, unless you wish it," said Corey. "If you do——"

"Will you tell your father," interrupted Lapham, "that I had a notion all the time that I was acting the drunken blackguard, and that I've suffered for it all day? Will you tell him I don't want him to notice me if we ever meet, and that I know I'm not fit to associate with gentlemen in anything but a business way, if I am that?"

"Certainly, I shall do nothing of the kind," retorted Corey. "I can't listen to you any longer. What you say is shocking to me—shocking in a way you can't think."

"Why, man!" exclaimed Lapham, with astonishment; "if *I* can stand it, *you* can!"

"No," said Corey, with a sick look, "that doesn't follow. You may denounce yourself, if you will; but I have my reasons for refusing to hear you—my reasons why I *can't* hear you. If you say another word I must go away."

"*I* don't understand you," faltered Lapham, in bewilderment, which absorbed even his shame.

"You exaggerate the effect of what has happened," said the young man. "It's enough, more than enough, for you to have mentioned the matter to me, and I think it's unbecoming in me to hear you."

He made a movement toward the door, but Lapham stopped him with the tragic humility of his appeal. "Don't go yet! I can't let you. I've disgusted you,—I see that; but I didn't mean to. I—I take it back."

"Oh, there's nothing to take back," said Corey, with a repressed shudder for the abasement which he had seen. "But let us say no more about it—think no more. There wasn't one of the gentlemen present last night who didn't understand the matter precisely as my father and I did, and that fact must end it between us two."

He went out into the larger office beyond, leaving Lapham helpless to prevent his going. It had become a vital necessity with him to think the best of Lapham, but his mind was in a whirl of whatever thoughts were most injurious. He thought of him the night before in the company of those ladies and gentlemen, and he quivered in resentment of his vulgar, braggart, uncouth nature. He recognized his own allegiance to the exclusiveness to which he was born and bred, as a man perceives his duty to his country when her rights are invaded. His eye fell on the porter going about in his shirt-sleeves to make the place fast for the night, and he said to himself that Dennis was not more plebeian than his master; that the gross appetites, the blunt sense, the purblind ambition, the stupid arrogance were the same in both, and the difference was in a brute will that probably left the porter the gentler man of the two. The very innocence of Lapham's life in the direction in which he had erred wrought against him in the young man's mood: it contained the insult of clownish inexperience. Amidst the stings and flashes of his wounded pride, all the social traditions, all the habits of feeling, which he had silenced more and more by force of will during the past months, asserted their natural sway, and he rioted in his contempt of the offensive boor, who was even more offensive in his shame than in his trespass. He said to himself that he was a Corey, as if that were somewhat; yet he knew that at the bottom of his heart all the time was that which must control him at last, and which seemed sweetly to be suffering his rebellion, secure of his submission in the end. It was almost with the girl's voice that it seemed to plead with him, to undo in him, effect by effect, the work of his indignant resentment, to set all things in another and fairer light, to give him hopes, to suggest palliations, to protest against injustices. It *was* in Lapham's favor that he was so guiltless in the past, and now Corey asked himself if it were the first time he could have wished a guest at his father's table to have taken less wine; whether Lapham was not rather to be honored for not knowing how to contain his folly where a veteran transgressor might have held his tongue. He asked himself, with a thrill of sudden remorse, whether, when Lapham humbled himself in the dust so shockingly, he had shown him the sympathy to which such *abandon* had the right; and he had to own that he had met him on the gentlemanly ground, sparing himself and asserting the superiority of his sort, and not recognizing that Lapham's humiliation came from the sense of wrong, which he had helped to accumulate upon him by superfinely standing aloof and refusing to touch him.

He shut his desk and hurried out into the early night, not to go anywhere, but to walk up and down, to try to find his way out of the chaos, which now seemed ruin, and now the materials out of which fine actions and a happy life might be shaped. Three hours later he stood at Lapham's door.

At times what he now wished to do had seemed forever impossible, and again it had seemed as if he could not wait a moment longer. He had not been careless, but very mindful of what he knew must be the feelings of his own family in regard to the Laphams, and he had not concealed from himself that his family had great reason and justice on their side in not wishing him to alienate himself from their common life and associations. The most that he could urge to himself was that they had not all the reason and justice; but he had hesitated and delayed because they had so much. Often he could not make it appear right that he should merely please himself in what chiefly concerned himself. He perceived how far apart in all their experiences and ideals the Lapham girls and his sisters were; how different Mrs. Lapham was from his mother; how grotesquely unlike were his father and Lapham; and the disparity had not always amused him.

He had often taken it very seriously, and sometimes he said that he must forego the hope on which his heart was set. There had been many times in the past months when he had said that he must go no farther, and as often as he had taken this stand he had yielded it, upon this or that excuse, which he was aware of trumping up. It was part of the complication that he should be unconscious of the injury he might be doing to some one besides his family and himself; this was the defect of his diffidence; and it had come to him in a pang for the first time when his mother said that she would not have the Laphams think she wished to make more of the acquaintance than he did; and then it had come too late. Since that he had suffered quite as much from the fear that it might not be as that it might be so; and now, in the mood, romantic and exalted, in which he found himself concerning Lapham, he was as far as might be from vain confidence. He ended the question in his own mind by affirming to himself that he was there, first of all, to see Lapham and give him an ultimate proof of his own perfect faith and unabated respect, and to offer him what reparation this involved for that want of sympathy—of humanity—which he had shown.

XVI

THE NOVA SCOTIA second-girl who answered Corey's ring said that Lapham had not come home yet.

"Oh," said the young man, hesitating on the outer step.

"I guess you better come in," said the girl. "I'll go and see when they're expecting him."

Corey was in the mood to be swayed by any chance. He obeyed the suggestion of the second-girl's patronizing friendliness, and let her shut him into the drawing-room, while she went upstairs to announce him to Penelope.

"Did you tell him father wasn't at home?"

"Yes. He seemed so kind of disappointed, I told him to come in, and I'd see when he *would* be in," said the girl, with the human interest which sometimes replaces in the American domestic the servile deference of other countries.

A gleam of amusement passed over Penelope's face, as she glanced at herself in the glass. "Well," she cried, finally, dropping from her shoulders the light shawl in which she had been huddled over a book when Corey rang, "I will go down."

"All right," said the girl, and Penelope began hastily to amend the disarray of her hair, which she tumbled into a mass on the top of her little head, setting off the pale dark of her complexion with a flash of crimson ribbon at her throat. She moved across the carpet once or twice with the quaint grace that belonged to her small figure, made a dissatisfied grimace at it in the glass, caught a handkerchief out of a drawer and slid it into her pocket, and then descended to Corey.

The Lapham drawing-room in Nankeen Square was in the parti-colored paint which the Colonel had hoped to repeat in his new house: the trim of the doors and windows was in light green and the panels in salmon; the walls were a plain tint of French gray paper, divided by gilt moldings into broad panels with a wide stripe of red velvet paper running up the corners; the chandelier was of massive imitation bronze; the mirror over the mantel rested on a fringed mantel-cover of green reps, and heavy curtains of that stuff hung from gilt lambrequin frames at the window; the carpet was of a small pattern in crude green, which, at the time Mrs. Lapham bought it, covered half the new floors in Boston. In the paneled spaces on the walls were some stone colored landscapes, representing the mountains and cañons of the West, which the Colonel and his wife had visited on one of the early official railroad excursions. In front of the long windows looking into the square were statues, kneeling figures which turned their backs upon the company within doors, and represented allegories of Faith and Prayer to people without. A white marble group of several figures, expressing an Italian conception of Lincoln Freeing the Slaves,—a Latin negro and his wife,—with our Eagle flapping his wings in approval, at Lincoln's feet, occupied one corner, and balanced the what-not of an earlier period in another. These phantasms added their chill to that imparted by the tone of the walls, the landscapes, and the carpets, and contributed to the violence of the contrast when the chandelier was lighted up full glare, and the heat of the whole furnace welled up from the registers into the quivering atmosphere on one of the rare occasions when the Laphams invited company.

Corey had not been in this room before; the family had always received him in what they called the sitting-room. Penelope looked into this first, and then she looked into the parlor, with a smile that broke into a laugh as she discovered him standing under the single burner, which the second-girl had lighted for him in the chandelier.

"I don't understand how you came to be put in there," she said, as she led the way to the cozier place, "unless it was because Alice thought you were only here on probation, anyway. Father hasn't got home yet, but I'm expecting him every moment; I don't know what's keeping him. Did the girl tell you that mother and Irene were out?"

"No, she didn't say. It's very good of you to see me." She had not seen the exaltation which he had been feeling, he perceived with half a sigh; it must all be upon this lower level; perhaps it was best so. "There was something I wished to say to your father——I hope," he broke off, "you're better to-night."

"Oh, yes, thank you," said Penelope, remembering that she had not been well enough to go to dinner the night before.

"We all missed you very much."

"Oh, thank you! I'm afraid you wouldn't have missed me if I had been there."

"Oh, yes, we should," said Corey, "I assure you."

They looked at each other.

"I really think I believed I was saying something," said the girl.

"And so did I," replied the young man. They laughed rather wildly, and then they both became rather grave.

He took the chair she gave him, and looked across at her, where she sat on the other side of the hearth, in a chair lower than his, with her hands dropped in her lap, and the back of her head on her shoulders as she looked up at him. The soft-coal fire in the grate purred and flickered; the drop-light cast a mellow radiance on her face. She let her eyes fall, and then lifted them for an irrelevant glance at the clock on the mantel.

"Mother and Irene have gone to the Spanish Students' concert."

"Oh, have they?" asked Corey; and he put his hat, which he had been holding in his hand, on the floor beside his chair.

She looked down at it for no reason, and then looked up at his face for no other, and turned a little red. Corey turned a little red himself. She who had always been so easy with him now became a little constrained.

"Do you know how warm it is out-of-doors?" he asked.

"No; is it warm? I haven't been out all day."

"It's like a summer night."

She turned her face towards the fire, and then started abruptly. "Perhaps it's too warm for you here?"

"Oh, no, it's very comfortable."

"I suppose it's the cold of the last few days that's still in the house. I was reading with a shawl on when you came."

"I interrupted you."

"Oh, no. I had finished the book. I was just looking over it again."

"Do you like to read books over?"

"Yes; books that I like at all."

"What was it?" asked Corey.

The girl hesitated. "It has rather a sentimental name. Did you ever read it?—'Tears, Idle Tears.' "

"Oh, yes; they were talking of that last night; it's a famous book with ladies. They break their hearts over it. Did it make you cry?"

"Oh, it's pretty easy to cry over a book," said Penelope, laughing; "and that one *is* very natural till you come to the main point. Then the naturalness of all the rest makes that seem natural too; but I guess it's rather forced."

"Her giving him up to the other one?"

"Yes; simply because she happened to know that the other one had cared for him first. Why should she have done it? What right had she?"

"I don't know. I suppose that the self-sacrifice——"

"But it *wasn't* self-sacrifice—or not self-sacrifice alone. She was sacrificing him, too; and for some one who couldn't appreciate him half as much as she could. I'm provoked with myself when I think how I cried over that book—for I did cry. It's silly—it's wicked for any one to do what that girl did. Why can't they let people have a chance to behave reasonably in stories?"

"Perhaps they couldn't make it so attractive," suggested Corey, with a smile.

"It would be novel, at any rate," said the girl. "But so it would in real life, I suppose," she added.

"I don't know. Why shouldn't people in love behave sensibly?"

"That's a very serious question," said Penelope, gravely. "*I* couldn't answer it," and she left him the embarrassment of supporting an inquiry which she had certainly instigated herself. She seemed to have finally recovered her own ease in doing this. "Do you admire our autumnal display, Mr. Corey?"

"Your display?"

"The trees in the square. *We* think it's quite equal to an opening at Jordan & Marsh's."

"Ah, I'm afraid you wouldn't let me be serious even about your maples."

"Oh, yes, I should—if you like to be serious."

"Don't you?"

"Well, not about serious matters. That's the reason that book made me cry."

"You make fun of everything. Miss Irene was telling me last night about you."

"Then it's no use for me to deny it so soon. I must give Irene a talking to."

"I hope you won't forbid her to talk about you!"

She had taken up a fan from the table, and held it, now between her face and the fire, and now between her face and him. Her little visage, with that arch, lazy look in it, topped by its mass of dusky hair, and dwindling from the full cheeks to the small chin, had a Japanese effect in the subdued light, and it had the charm which comes to any woman with happiness. It would be hard to say how much of this she perceived that he felt. They talked about other things awhile, and then she came back to what he had said. She glanced at him obliquely round her fan, and stopped moving it. "Does Irene talk about me?" she asked.

"I think so—yes. Perhaps it's only I who talk about you. You must blame me if it's wrong," he returned.

"Oh, I didn't say it was wrong," she replied. "But I hope if you said anything very bad of me, you'll let me know what it was, so that I can reform——"

"No, don't change, please!" cried the young man.

Penelope caught her breath, but went on resolutely, "Or rebuke you for speaking evil of dignities." She looked down at the fan, now flat in her lap, and tried to govern her head, but it trembled, and she remained looking down. Again they let the talk stray, and then it was he who brought it back to themselves, as if it had not left them.

"I have to talk *of* you," said Corey, "because I get to talk *to* you so seldom."

"You mean that I do all the talking, when we're—together?" She glanced sidewise at him; but she reddened after speaking the last word.

"We're so seldom together," he pursued.

"I don't know what you mean——"

"Sometimes I've thought—I've been afraid—that you avoided me."

"Avoided you?"

"Yes! Tried not to be alone with me."

She might have told him that there was no reason why she should be alone with him, and that it was very strange he should make this complaint of her. But she did not. She kept looking down at the fan, and then she lifted her burning face and looked at the clock again. "Mother and Irene will be sorry to miss you," she gasped.

He instantly rose and came towards her. She rose too, and mechanically put out her hand. He took it as if to say good-night. "I didn't mean to send you away," she besought him.

"Oh, I'm not going," he answered simply. "I wanted to say—to say that it's I who make her talk about you. To say I— There is something I want to say to you; I've said it so often to myself that I feel as if you must know it." She stood quite still, letting him keep her hand, and questioning his face with a bewildered gaze. "You *must* know—she must have told you—she must have guessed——" Penelope turned white, but outwardly quelled the panic that sent the blood to her heart. "I—I didn't expect—I hoped to have seen your father—but I must speak now, whatever—— I love you!"

She freed her hand from both of those he had closed upon it, and went back from him across the room with a sinuous spring. "*Me!*" Whatever potential complicity had lurked in her heart, his words brought her only immeasurable dismay.

He came towards her again. "Yes, *you*. Who else?"

She fended him off with an imploring gesture. "I thought—I—it was——"

She shut her lips tight, and stood looking at him where he remained in silent amaze. Then her words came again, shudderingly. "Oh, what have you done?"

"Upon my soul," he said, with a vague smile, "I don't know. I hope no harm?"

"Oh, don't laugh!" she cried, laughing hysterically herself. "Unless you want me to think you the greatest wretch in the world!"

"I?" he responded. "For heaven's sake tell me what you mean!"

"You know I can't tell you. Can you say—can you put your hand on your heart and say that—you—say you never meant—that you meant me—all along?"

"Yes!— Yes! Who else? I came here to see your father, and to tell him that I wished to tell you this—to ask him—— But what does it matter? You must have known it—you must have seen—and it's for you to answer me. I've been abrupt, I know, and I've startled you; but if you love me, you can forgive that to my loving you so long before I spoke."

She gazed at him with parted lips.

"Oh, mercy! What shall I do? If it's true—what you say— you must go!" she said. "And you must never come any more. Do you promise that?"

"Certainly not," said the young man. "Why should I promise such a thing—so abominably wrong? I could obey if you didn't love me——"

"Oh, I don't! Indeed I don't! Now will you obey?"

"No. I don't believe you."

"Oh!"

He possessed himself of her hand again.

"My love—my dearest! What is this trouble, that you can't tell it? It can't be anything about yourself. If it is anything about any one else, it wouldn't make the least difference in the world, no matter what it was. I would be only too glad to show by any act or deed I could that nothing could change me towards you."

"Oh, you don't understand!"

"No, I don't. You must tell me."

"I will never do that."

"Then I will stay here till your mother comes, and ask her what it is."

"Ask *her?*"

"Yes! Do you think I will give you up till I know why I must?"

"You force me to it! Will you go if I tell you, and never let any human creature know what you have said to me?"

"Not unless you give me leave."

"That will be never. Well, then——" She stopped, and made two or three ineffectual efforts to begin again. "No, no! I can't. You must go!"

"I will not go!"

"You said you—loved me. If you do, you will go."

He dropped the hands he had stretched towards her, and she hid her face in her own.

"There!" she said, turning it suddenly upon him. "Sit down there. And will you promise me—on your honor—not to speak—not to try to persuade me—not to—touch me? You won't touch me?"

"I will obey you, Penelope."

"As if you were never to see me again? As if I were dying?"

"I will do what you say. But I shall see you again; and don't talk of dying. This is the beginning of life——"

"No. It's the end," said the girl, resuming at last something of the hoarse drawl which the tumult of her feeling had broken into those half-articulate appeals. She sat down too, and lifted her face towards him. "It's the end of life for me, because I know now that I must have been playing false from the beginning. You don't know what I mean, and I can never tell you. It isn't my secret—it's some one else's. You—you must never come here again. I can't tell you why, and you must never try to know. Do you promise?"

"You can forbid me. I must do what you say."

"I do forbid you, then. And you shall not think I am cruel——"

"How could I think that?"

"Oh, how hard you make it!"

Corey laughed for very despair. "Can I make it easier by disobeying you?"

"I know I am talking crazily. But I'm not crazy."

"No, no," he said, with some wild notion of comforting her; "but try to tell me this trouble! There is nothing under heaven—no calamity, no sorrow—that I wouldn't gladly share with you, or take all upon myself if I could!"

"I know! But this you can't. Oh, my——"

"Dearest! Wait! Think! Let me ask your mother—your father——"

She gave a cry.

"No! If you do that, you will make me hate you! Will you——"

The rattling of a latch-key was heard in the outer door.

"Promise!" cried Penelope.

"Oh, I promise!"

"Good-bye!" She suddenly flung her arms round his neck, and, pressing her cheek tight against his, flashed out of the room by one door as her father entered it by another.

Corey turned to him in a daze. "I—I called to speak with you—about a matter—— But it's so late now. I'll—I'll see you to-morrow."

"No time like the present," said Lapham, with a fierceness that did not seem referable to Corey. He had his hat still on, and he glared at the young man out of his blue eyes with a fire that something else must have kindled there.

"I really can't, now," said Corey, weakly. "It will do quite as well to-morrow. Good-night, sir."

"Good-night," answered Lapham abruptly, following him to the door, and shutting it after him. "I think the devil must have got into pretty much everybody to-night," he muttered, coming back to the room, where he put down his hat. Then he went to the kitchen-stairs and called down, "Hello, Alice! I want something to eat!"

XVII

WHAT's the reason the girls never get down to breakfast any more?" asked Lapham when he met his wife at the table in the morning. He had been up an hour and a half, and he spoke with the severity of a hungry man. "It seems to me they don't amount to *any*thing. Here I am, at my time of life, up the first one in the house. I ring the bell for the cook at quarter-past six every morning, and the breakfast is on the table at half-past seven right along, like clock-work, but I never see anybody but you till I go to the office."

"Oh, yes, you do, Si," said his wife, soothingly. "The girls are nearly always down. But they're young, and it tires them more than it does us to get up early."

"They can rest afterwards. They don't do anything after they *are* up," grumbled Lapham.

"Well, that's your fault, ain't it? You oughtn't to have made so much money, and then they'd have had to work." She laughed at Lapham's Spartan mood, and went on to excuse the young people. "Irene's been up two nights hand running, and Penelope says she ain't well. What makes you so cross about the girls? Been doing something you're ashamed of?"

"I'll tell you when I've been doing anything to be ashamed of," growled Lapham.

"Oh, no, you won't!" said his wife, jollily. "You'll only be hard on the rest of us. Come, now, Si; what is it?"

Lapham frowned into his coffee with sulky dignity, and said, without looking up, "I wonder what that fellow wanted here last night?"

"What fellow?"

"Corey. I found him here when I came home, and he said he wanted to see me; but he wouldn't stop."

"Where was he?"

"In the sitting-room."

"Was Pen there?"

"*I* didn't see her."

Mrs. Lapham paused, with her hand on the cream-jug.

"Why, what in the land *did* he want? Did he say he wanted you?"

"That's what he said."

"And then he wouldn't stay?"

"No."

"Well, then, I'll tell you just what it is, Silas Lapham. He came here"—she looked about the room and lowered her voice—"to see you about Irene, and then he hadn't the courage."

"I guess he's got courage enough to do pretty much what he wants to," said Lapham, glumly. "All I know is, he was here. You better ask Pen about it, if she ever gets down."

"I guess I sha'n't wait for her," said Mrs. Lapham; and, as her husband closed the front door after him, she opened that of her daughter's room and entered abruptly.

The girl sat at the window, fully dressed, and as if she had been sitting there a long time. Without rising, she turned her face towards her mother. It merely showed black against the light, and revealed nothing till her mother came close to her with successive questions. "Why, how long have you been up, Pen? Why don't you come to your breakfast? Did you see Mr. Corey when he called last night? Why, what's the matter with you? What have you been crying about?"

"Have I been crying?"

"Yes! Your cheeks are all wet!"

"I thought they were on fire. Well, I'll tell you what's happened." She rose and then fell back in her chair. "Lock the door!" she ordered, and her mother mechanically obeyed. "I don't want Irene in here. There's nothing the matter. Only, Mr. Corey offered himself to me last night."

Her mother remained looking at her, helpless, not so much with amaze, perhaps, as dismay.

"Oh, I'm not a ghost! I wish I was! You had better sit down, mother. You have got to know all about it."

Mrs. Lapham dropped nervelessly into the chair at the other window, and while the girl went slowly but briefly on, touching only the vital points of the story, and breaking at times into a bitter drollery, she sat as if without the power to speak or stir.

"Well, that's all, mother. I should say I had dreamt it, if I had slept any last night; but I guess it really happened."

The mother glanced round at the bed, and said, glad to occupy herself delayingly with the minor care: "Why, you have been sitting up all night! You will kill yourself."

"I don't know about killing myself, but I've been sitting up all night," answered the girl. Then, seeing that her mother remained blankly silent again, she demanded, "Why don't you blame me, mother? Why don't you say that I led him on, and tried to get him away from her? Don't you believe I did?"

Her mother made her no answer, as if these ravings of self-accusal needed none. "Do you think," she asked, simply, "that he got the idea you cared for him?"

"He knew it! How could I keep it from him? I said I didn't—at first!"

"It was no use," sighed the mother. "You might as well said you did. It couldn't help Irene any, if you didn't."

"I always tried to help her with him, even when I——"

"Yes, I know. But she never was equal to him. I saw that from the start; but I tried to blind myself to it. And when he kept coming——"

"You never thought of me!" cried the girl, with a bitterness that reached her mother's heart. "I was nobody! I couldn't feel! No one could care for me!" The turmoil of despair, of triumph, of remorse and resentment, which filled her soul, tried to express itself in the words.

"No," said the mother humbly. "I didn't think of you. Or I didn't think of you enough. It did come across me sometimes that maybe—— But it didn't seem as if—— And your going on so for Irene——"

"You let me go on. You made me always go and talk with him for her, and you didn't think I would talk to him for myself. Well, I didn't!"

"I'm punished for it. When did you—begin to care for him?"

"How do I know? What difference does it make? It's all over now, no matter when it began. He won't come here any more, unless I let him." She could not help betraying her pride in this authority of hers, but she went on anxiously enough: "What will you say to Irene? She's safe as far as I'm concerned; but if he don't care for her, what will you do?"

"I don't know what to do," said Mrs. Lapham. She sat in an apathy from which she apparently could not rouse herself. "I don't see as anything can be done."

Penelope laughed in a pitying derision.

"Well, let things go on then. But they won't *go* on."

"No, they won't go on," echoed her mother. "She's pretty enough, and she's capable; and your father's got the money— I don't know what I'm saying! She ain't equal to him, and she never was. I kept feeling it all the time, and yet I kept blinding myself."

"If he had ever cared for her," said Penelope, "it wouldn't have mattered whether she was equal to him or not. *I'm* not equal to him either."

Her mother went on: "I might have thought it was you; but I had got set—— Well! I can see it all clear enough, now it's too late. *I* don't know what to do."

"And what do you expect *me* to do?" demanded the girl. "Do you want *me* to go to Irene and tell her that I've got him away from her?"

"Oh, good Lord!" cried Mrs. Lapham. "What shall I do? What do you want I should do, Pen?"

"Nothing for me," said Penelope. "I've had it out with myself. Now do the best you can for Irene."

"I couldn't say you had done wrong, if you was to marry him to-day."

"Mother!"

"No, I couldn't. I couldn't say but what you had been good and faithful all through, and you had a perfect right to do it. There ain't any one to blame. He's behaved like a gentleman, and I can see now that he never thought of her, and that it was you all the while. Well, marry him, then! He's got the right, and so have you."

"What about Irene? I don't want you to talk about me. I can take care of myself."

"She's nothing but a child. It's only a fancy with her. She'll get over it. She hain't really got her heart set on him."

"She's got her heart set on him, mother. She's got her whole life set on him. You know that."

"Yes, that's so," said the mother, as promptly as if she had been arguing to that rather than the contrary effect.

"If I could give him to her, I would. But he isn't mine to give." She added in a burst of despair, "He isn't mine to keep!"

"Well," said Mrs. Lapham, "she has got to bear it. I don't know what's to come of it all. But she's got to bear her share of it." She rose and went toward the door.

Penelope ran after her in a sort of terror. "You're not going to tell Irene?" she gasped, seizing her mother by either shoulder.

"Yes, I am," said Mrs. Lapham. "If she's a woman grown, she can bear a woman's burden."

"I can't let you tell Irene," said the girl, letting fall her face on her mother's neck. "Not Irene," she moaned. "I'm afraid to let you. How can I ever look at her again?"

"Why, you haven't done anything, Pen," said her mother, soothingly.

"I wanted to! Yes, I must have done something. How could I help it? I did care for him from the first, and I must have tried to make him like me. Do you think I did? No, no! You mustn't tell Irene! Not—not—yet! Mother! Yes! I did try to get him from her!" she cried, lifting her head, and suddenly looking her mother in the face with those large dim eyes of hers. "What do you think? Even last night! It was the first time I ever had him all to myself, for myself, and I know now that I tried to make him think that I was pretty and—funny. And I didn't try to make him think of her. I knew that I pleased him, and I tried to please him more. Perhaps I could have kept him from saying that he cared for me; but when I saw he did—I must have seen it—I couldn't. I had never had him to myself, and for myself, before. I needn't have seen him at all, but I wanted to see him; and when I was sitting there alone with him, how do I know what I did to let him feel that I cared for him? Now, will you tell Irene? I never thought he did care for me, and never expected him to. But I liked him. Yes—I did like him! Tell her that! Or else I will."

"If it was to tell her he was dead," began Mrs. Lapham, absently.

"How easy it would be!" cried the girl in self-mockery.

"But he's worse than dead to her; and so am I. I've turned it over a million ways, mother; I've looked at it in every light you can put it in, and I can't make anything but misery out of it. You can see the misery at the first glance, and you can't see more or less if you spend your life looking at it." She laughed again, as if the hopelessness of the thing amused her. Then she flew to the extreme of self-assertion. "Well, I *have* a right to him, and he has a right to me. If he's never done anything to make her think he cared for her,—and I know he hasn't; it's all been our doing,—then he's free and I'm free. We can't make her happy, whatever we do; and why shouldn't I—— No, that won't do! I reached that point before!" She broke again into her desperate laugh. "*You* may try now, mother!"

"I'd best speak to your father first——"

Penelope smiled a little more forlornly than she had laughed.

"Well, yes; the Colonel will have to know. It isn't a trouble that I can keep to myself exactly. It seems to belong to too many other people."

Her mother took a crazy encouragement from her return to her old way of saying things. "Perhaps he can think of something."

"Oh, I don't doubt but the Colonel will know just what to do!"

"You mustn't be too down-hearted about it. It—it'll all come right——"

"You tell Irene that, mother."

Mrs. Lapham had put her hand on the door-key; she dropped it, and looked at the girl with a sort of beseeching appeal for the comfort she could not imagine herself. "Don't look at me, mother," said Penelope, shaking her head. "You know that if Irene were to die without knowing it, it wouldn't come right for me."

"Pen!"

"I've read of cases where a girl gives up the man that loves her so as to make some other girl happy that the man doesn't love. That might be done."

"Your father would think you were a fool," said Mrs. Lapham, finding a sort of refuge in her strong disgust for the pseudo-heroism. "No! If there's to be any giving up, let it be by the one that sha'n't make anybody but herself suffer. There's trouble and sorrow enough in the world, without *making* it on purpose!"

She unlocked the door, but Penelope slipped round and set herself against it. "Irene shall not give up!"

"I will see your father about it," said the mother. "Let me out now——"

"Don't let Irene come here!"

"No. I will tell her that you haven't slept. Go to bed now, and try to get some rest. She isn't up herself yet. You must have some breakfast."

"No; let me sleep if I can. I can get something when I wake up. I'll come down if I can't sleep. Life has got to go on. It does when there's a death in the house, and this is only a little worse."

"Don't you talk nonsense!" cried Mrs. Lapham, with angry authority.

"Well, a little better, then," said Penelope, with meek concession.

Mrs. Lapham attempted to say something, and could not. She went out and opened Irene's door. The girl lifted her head drowsily from her pillow. "Don't disturb your sister when you get up, Irene. She hasn't slept well——"

"*Please* don't talk! I'm almost *dead* with sleep!" returned Irene. "Do go, mamma! I sha'n't disturb her." She turned her face down in the pillow, and pulled the covering up over her ears.

The mother slowly closed the door and went down-stairs, feeling bewildered and baffled almost beyond the power to move. The time had been when she would have tried to find out why this judgment had been sent upon her. But now she could not feel that the innocent suffering of others was inflicted for her fault; she shrank instinctively from that cruel and egotistic misinterpretation of the mystery of pain and loss. She saw her two children, equally if differently dear to her, destined to trouble that nothing could avert, and she could not blame either of them; she could not blame the means of this misery to them; he was as innocent as they, and though her heart was sore against him in this first moment, she could still be just to him in it. She was a woman who had been used to seek the light by striving; she had hitherto literally worked to it. But it is the curse of prosperity that it takes work away from us, and shuts that door to hope and health of spirit. In this house, where everything had come to be done for her, she had no tasks to interpose between her and her despair. She sat down in her own room and let her hands fall in her lap,—the hands that had once been so helpful and busy,—and tried to think it all out. She had never heard of the fate that was once supposed to appoint the sorrows of men irrespective of their blamelessness or blame, before the time when it came to be believed that sorrows were penalties; but in her simple way she recognized something like that mythic power when she rose from her struggle with the problem, and said aloud to herself, "Well, the witch is in it." Turn which way she would, she saw no escape from the misery to come—the misery which had come already to Penelope and herself, and that must come to Irene and her father. She started when she definitely thought of her husband, and thought with what violence it would work in every fiber of his rude strength. She feared that, and she feared something worse—the effect which his pride and ambition might seek to give it; and it was with terror of this, as well as the natural trust with which a woman must turn to her husband in any anxiety at last, that she felt she could not wait for evening to take counsel with him. When she considered how wrongly he might take it all, it seemed as if it were already known to him, and she was impatient to prevent his error.

She sent out for a messenger, whom she dispatched with a note to his place of business: "Silas, I should like to ride with you this afternoon. Can't you come home early? Persis." And she was at dinner with Irene, evading her questions about Penelope, when answer came that he would be at the house with the buggy at half-past two. It is easy to put off a girl who has but one thing in her head; but, though Mrs. Lapham could escape without telling anything of Penelope, she could not escape seeing how wholly Irene was engrossed with hopes now turned so vain and impossible. She was still talking of that dinner, of nothing but that dinner, and begging for flattery of herself and praise of him, which her mother had till now been so ready to give.

"Seems to me you don't take very much interest, mamma!" she said, laughing and blushing, at one point.

"Yes,—yes, I do," protested Mrs. Lapham, and then the girl prattled on.

"I guess I shall get one of those pins that Nanny Corey had in her hair. I think it would become me, don't you?"

"Yes; but, Irene—I don't like to have you go on so, till— unless he's said something to show— You oughtn't to give yourself up to thinking——" But at this the girl turned so white, and looked such reproach at her, that she added, frantically: "Yes, get the pin. It is just the thing for you! But don't disturb Penelope. Let her alone till I get back. I'm going out to ride with your father. He'll be here in half an hour. Are you through? Ring, then. Get yourself that fan you saw the other day. Your father won't say anything; he likes to have you look well. I could see his eyes on you half the time the other night."

"I should have liked to have Pen go with me," said Irene, restored to her normal state of innocent selfishness by these flatteries. "Don't you suppose she'll be up in time? What's the matter with her that she didn't sleep?"

"I don't know. Better let her alone."

"Well," submitted Irene.

XVIII

Mrs. Lapham went away to put on her bonnet and cloak, and she was waiting at the window when her husband drove up. She opened the door and ran down the steps. "Don't get out; I can help myself in," and she clambered to his side, while he kept the fidgeting mare still with voice and touch.

"Where do you want I should go?" he asked, turning the buggy.

"Oh, I don't care. Out Brookline way, I guess. I wish you hadn't brought this fool of a horse," she gave way, petulantly. "I wanted to have a talk."

"When I can't drive this mare and talk too, I'll sell out altogether," said Lapham. "She'll be quiet enough when she's had her spin."

"Well," said his wife; and while they were making their way across the city to the Milldam she answered certain questions he asked about some points in the new house.

"I should have liked to have you stop there," he began; but she answered so quickly, "Not to-day," that he gave it up and turned his horse's head westward, when they struck Beacon street.

He let the mare out, and he did not pull her in till he left the Brighton road and struck off under the low boughs that met above one of the quiet streets of Brookline, where the stone cottages, with here and there a patch of determined ivy on their northern walls, did what they could to look English amid the glare of the autumnal foliage. The smooth earthen track under the mare's hoofs was scattered with flakes of the red and yellow gold that made the air luminous around them, and the perspective was gay with innumerable tints and tones.

"Pretty sightly," said Lapham, with a long sigh, letting the reins lie loose in his vigilant hand, to which he seemed to relegate the whole charge of the mare. "I want to talk with you about Rogers, Persis. He's been getting in deeper and deeper with me; and last night he pestered me half to death to go in with him in one of his schemes. I ain't going to blame anybody, but I hain't got very much confidence in Rogers. And I told him so last night."

"Oh, don't talk to me about Rogers!" his wife broke in. "There's something a good deal more important than Rogers in the world, and more important than your business. It seems as if you couldn't think of anything else—that and the new house. Did you suppose I wanted to ride so as to talk Rogers with you?" she demanded, yielding to the necessity a wife feels of making her husband pay for her suffering, even if he has not inflicted it. "I declare——"

"Well, hold on, now!" said Lapham. "What *do* you want to talk about? I'm listening."

His wife began, "Why, it's just this, Silas Lapham!" and then she broke off to say, "Well, you may wait, now—starting me wrong, when it's hard enough anyway."

Lapham silently turned his whip over and over in his hand and waited.

"Did you suppose," she asked at last, "that that young Corey had been coming to see Irene?"

"I don't know what I supposed," replied Lapham sullenly. "You always said so." He looked sharply at her under his lowering brows.

"Well, he hasn't," said Mrs. Lapham; and she replied to the frown that blackened on her husband's face, "And I can tell you what, if you take it in that way I sha'n't speak another word."

"Who's takin' it what way?" retorted Lapham savagely. "What are you drivin' at?"

"I want you should promise that you'll hear me out quietly."

"I'll hear you out if you'll give me a chance. I haven't said a word yet."

"Well, I'm not going to have you flying into forty furies, and looking like a perfect thunder-cloud at the very start. I've had to bear it, and you've got to bear it too."

"Well, let me have a chance at it, then."

"It's nothing to blame anybody about, as I can see, and the only question is, what's the best thing to do about it. There's only one thing we can do; for if he don't care for the child, nobody wants to make him. If he hasn't been coming to see her, he hasn't, and that's all there is to it."

"No, it ain't!" exclaimed Lapham.

"There!" protested his wife.

"If he hasn't been coming to see her, what *has* he been coming for?"

"He's been coming to see Pen!" cried the wife. "*Now* are you satisfied?" Her tone implied that he had brought it all upon them; but at the sight of the swift passions working in his face to a perfect comprehension of the whole trouble, she fell to trembling, and her broken voice lost all the spurious indignation she had put into it. "Oh, Silas! what are we going to do about it? I'm afraid it'll kill Irene."

Lapham pulled off the loose driving-glove from his right hand with the fingers of his left, in which the reins lay. He passed it over his forehead, and then flicked from it the moisture it had gathered there. He caught his breath once or twice, like a man who meditates a struggle with superior force and then remains passive in its grasp.

His wife felt the need of comforting him, as she had felt the need of afflicting him. "I don't say but what it can be made to come out all right in the end. All I say is, I don't see my way clear yet."

"What makes you think he likes Pen?" he asked, quietly.

"He told her so last night, and she told me this morning. Was he at the office to-day?"

"Yes, he was there. I haven't been there much myself. He didn't say anything to me. Does Irene know?"

"No; I left her getting ready to go out shopping. She wants to get a pin like the one Nanny Corey had on."

"Oh, my Lord!" groaned Lapham.

"It's been Pen from the start, I guess, or almost from the start. I don't say but what he was attracted some by Irene at the *very* first; but I guess it's been Pen ever since he saw her; and we've taken up with a notion, and blinded ourselves with it. Time and again I've had my doubts whether he cared for Irene any; but I declare to goodness, when he kept coming, I never hardly thought of Pen, and I couldn't help believing at last he *did* care for Irene. Did it ever strike you he might be after Pen?"

"No. I took what you said. I supposed you knew."

"Do you blame me, Silas?" she asked timidly.

"No. What's the use of blaming? We don't either of us want anything but the children's good. What's it all of it for, if it ain't for that? That's what we've both slaved for all our lives."

"Yes, I know. Plenty of people *lose* their children," she suggested.

"Yes, but that don't comfort me any. I never was one to feel good because another man felt bad. How would you have liked it if some one had taken comfort because his boy lived when ours died? No, I can't do it. And this is worse than death, someways. That comes and it goes; but this looks as if it was one of those things that had come to stay. The way I look at it, there ain't any hope for anybody. Suppose we don't want Pen to have him; will that help Irene any, if he don't want her? Suppose we don't want to let him have either; does that help either?"

"You talk," exclaimed Mrs. Lapham, "as if our say was going to settle it. Do you suppose that Penelope Lapham is a girl to take up with a fellow that her sister is in love with, and that she always thought was in love with her sister, and go off and be happy with him? Don't you believe but what it would come back to her, as long as she breathed the breath of life, how she'd teased her about him, as I've heard Pen tease Irene, and helped to make her think he was in love with her, by showing that she thought so herself? It's ridiculous!"

Lapham seemed quite beaten down by this argument. His huge head hung forward over his breast; the reins lay loose in his moveless hand; the mare took her own way. At last he lifted his face and shut his heavy jaws.

"Well?" quavered his wife.

"Well," he answered, "if he wants her, and she wants him, I don't see what that's got to do with it." He looked straight forward, and not at his wife.

She laid her hands on the reins. "Now, you stop right here, Silas Lapham! If I thought that—if I really believed you could be willing to break that poor child's heart, and let Pen disgrace herself by marrying a man that had as good as killed her sister, just because you wanted Bromfield Corey's son for a son-in-law——"

Lapham turned his face now, and gave her a look. "You had better *not* believe that, Persis! Get up!" he called to the mare, without glancing at her, and she sprang forward. "I see you've got past being any use to yourself on this subject."

"Hello!" shouted a voice in front of him. "Where the devil you goin' to?"

"Do you want to *kill* somebody?" shrieked his wife.

There was a light crash, and the mare recoiled her length, and separated their wheels from those of the open buggy in front which Lapham had driven into. He made his excuses to the occupant; and the accident relieved the tension of their feelings and left them far from the point of mutual injury which they had reached in their common trouble and their unselfish will for their children's good.

It was Lapham who resumed the talk. "I'm afraid we can't either of us see this thing in the right light. We're too near to it. I wish to the Lord there was somebody to talk to about it."

"Yes," said his wife; "but there ain't anybody."

"Well, I dunno," suggested Lapham, after a moment; "why not talk to the minister of your church? May be he could see some way out of it."

Mrs. Lapham shook her head hopelessly. "It wouldn't do. I've never taken up my connection with the church, and I don't feel as if I'd got any claim on him."

"If he's anything of a man, or anything of a preacher, you *have* got a claim on him," urged Lapham; and he spoiled his argument by adding, "I've contributed enough *money* to his church."

"Oh, that's nothing," said Mrs. Lapham. "I ain't well enough acquainted with Dr. Langworthy, or else I'm *too* well. No; if I was to ask any one, I should want to ask a total stranger. But what's the use, Si? Nobody could make us see it any different from what it is, and I don't know as I should want they should."

It blotted out the tender beauty of the day and weighed down their hearts ever more heavily within them. They ceased to talk of it a hundred times, and still came back to it. They drove on and on. It began to be late. "I guess we better go back, Si," said his wife; and as he turned without speaking, she pulled her veil down and began to cry softly behind it, with low little broken sobs.

Lapham started the mare up and drove swiftly homeward. At last his wife stopped crying and began trying to find her pocket. "Here, take mine, Persis," he said kindly, offering her his handkerchief, and she took it and dried her eyes with it. "There was one of those fellows there the other night," he spoke again, when his wife leaned back against the cushions in peaceful despair, "that I liked the looks of about as well as any man I ever saw. I guess he was a pretty good man. It was that Mr. Sewell." He looked at his wife, but she did not say anything. "Persis," he resumed, "I can't bear to go back with nothing settled in our minds. I can't bear to let you."

"We must, Si," returned his wife, with gentle gratitude. Lapham groaned. "Where does he live?" she asked.

"On Bolingbroke street. He gave me his number."

"Well, it wouldn't do any good. What could he say to us?"

"Oh, I don't know as he could say anything," said Lapham hopelessly; and neither of them said anything more till they crossed the Milldam and found themselves between the rows of city houses.

"Don't drive past the new house, Si," pleaded his wife. "I couldn't bear to see it. Drive—drive up Bolingbroke street. We might as well see where he *does* live."

"Well," said Lapham. He drove along slowly. "That's the place," he said finally, stopping the mare and pointing with his whip.

"It wouldn't do any good," said his wife, in a tone which he understood as well as he understood her words. He turned the mare up to the curbstone.

"You take the reins a minute," he said, handing them to his wife.

He got down and rang the bell, and waited till the door opened; then he came back and lifted his wife out. "He's in," he said.

He got the hitching-weight from under the buggy-seat and made it fast to the mare's bit.

"Do you think she'll stand with that?" asked Mrs. Lapham.

"I guess so. If she don't, no matter."

"Ain't you afraid she'll take cold," she persisted, trying to make delay.

"Let her!" said Lapham. He took his wife's trembling hand under his arm, and drew her to the door.

"He'll think we're crazy," she murmured, in her broken pride.

"Well, we *are*," said Lapham. "Tell him we'd like to see him alone awhile," he said to the girl who was holding the door ajar for him, and she showed him into the reception-room, which had been the Protestant confessional for many burdened souls before their time, coming, as they did, with the belief that they were bowed down with the only misery like theirs in the universe; for each one of us must suffer long to himself before he can learn that he is but one in a great community of wretchedness which has been pitilessly repeating itself from the foundation of the world.

They were as loath to touch their trouble when the minister came in as if it were their disgrace; but Lapham did so at last, and, with a simple dignity which he had wanted in his bungling and apologetic approaches, he laid the affair clearly before the minister's compassionate and reverent eye. He spared Corey's name, but he did not pretend that it was not himself and his wife and their daughters who were concerned.

"I don't know as I've got any right to trouble you with this thing," he said, in the moment while Sewell sat pondering the case, "and I don't know as I've got any warrant for doing it. But, as I told my wife here, there was something about you—I don't know whether it was anything you *said* exactly—that made me feel as if you could help us. I guess I didn't say so much as that to her; but that's the way I felt. And here we are. And if it ain't all right——"

"Surely," said Sewell, "it's all right. I thank you for coming—for trusting your trouble to me. A time comes to every one of us when we can't help ourselves, and then we must get others to help us. If people turn to me at such a time, I feel sure that I was put into the world for something—if nothing more than to give my pity, my sympathy."

The brotherly words, so plain, so sincere, had a welcome in them that these poor outcasts of sorrow could not doubt.

"Yes," said Lapham huskily, and his wife began to wipe the tears again under her veil.

Sewell remained silent, and they waited till he should speak. "We can be of use to one another here, because we can always be wiser for some one else than we can for ourselves. We can see another's sins and errors in a more merciful light — and that is always a fairer light — than we can our own; and we can look more sanely at others' afflictions." He had addressed these words to Lapham; now he turned to his wife. "If some one had come to you, Mrs. Lapham, in just this perplexity, what would you have thought?"

"I don't know as I understand you," faltered Mrs. Lapham.

Sewell repeated his words, and added, "I mean, what do you think some one else ought to do in your place?"

"Was there ever any poor creatures in such a strait before?" she asked, with pathetic incredulity.

"There's no new trouble under the sun," said the minister.

"Oh, if it was any one else, I should say — I should say — Why, of course! I should say that their duty was to let——" She paused.

"One suffer instead of three, if none is to blame?" suggested Sewell. "That's sense, and that's justice. It's the economy of pain which naturally suggests itself, and which would insist upon itself, if we were not all perverted by traditions which are the figment of the shallowest sentimentality. Tell me, Mrs. Lapham, didn't this come into your mind when you first learned how matters stood?"

"Why, yes, it flashed across me. But I didn't think it could be right."

"And how was it with you, Mr. Lapham?"

"Why, that's what *I* thought, of course. But I didn't see my way——"

"No," cried the minister, "we are all blinded, we are all weakened by a false ideal of self-sacrifice. It wraps us round with its meshes, and we can't fight our way out of it. Mrs. Lapham, what made you feel that it might be better for three to suffer than one?"

"Why, she did herself. I know she would die sooner than take him away from her."

"I supposed so!" cried the minister bitterly. "And yet she is a sensible girl, your daughter?"

"She has more common sense——"

"Of course! But in such a case we somehow think it must be wrong to use our common sense. I don't know where this false ideal comes from, unless it comes from the novels that befool and debauch almost every intelligence in some degree. It certainly doesn't come from Christianity, which instantly repudiates it when confronted with it. Your daughter believes, in spite of her common sense, that she ought to make herself and the man who loves her unhappy, in order to assure the lifelong wretchedness of her sister, whom he doesn't love, simply because her sister saw him and fancied him first! And I'm sorry to say that ninety-nine young people out of a hundred—oh, nine hundred and ninety-nine out of a thousand!—would consider that noble and beautiful and heroic; whereas you know at the bottom of your hearts that it would be foolish and cruel and revolting. You know what marriage is! And what it must be without love on both sides."

The minister had grown quite heated and red in the face.

"I lose all patience!" he went on vehemently. "This poor child of yours has somehow been brought to believe that it will kill her sister if her sister does not have what does not belong to her, and what it is not in the power of all the world, or any soul in the world, to give her. Her sister will suffer—yes, keenly!—in heart and in pride; but she will not die. You will suffer, too, in your tenderness for her; but you must do your duty. You must help her to give up. You would be guilty if you did less. Keep clearly in mind that you are doing right, and the only possible good. And God be with you!"

XIX

"H E TALKED sense, Persis," said Lapham gently, as he mounted to his wife's side in the buggy and drove slowly homeward through the dusk.

"Yes, he talked sense," she admitted. But she added, bitterly, "I guess, if he had it to *do*! Oh, he's right, and it's got to be done. There ain't any other way for it. It's sense; and, yes, it's justice." They walked to their door after they left the horse at the livery stable around the corner, where Lapham kept it. "I want you should send Irene up to our room as soon as we get in, Silas."

"Why, ain't you going to have any supper first?" faltered Lapham, with his latch-key in the lock.

"No. I can't lose a minute. If I do, I sha'n't do it at all."

"Look here, Persis," said her husband tenderly, "let *me* do this thing."

"Oh, *you*!" said his wife, with a woman's compassionate scorn for a man's helplessness in such a case. "Send her right up. And I shall feel—" She stopped, to spare him.

Then she opened the door, and ran up to her room, without waiting to speak to Irene, who had come into the hall at the sound of her father's key in the door.

"I guess your mother wants to see you upstairs," said Lapham, looking away.

Her mother turned round and faced the girl's wondering look as Irene entered the chamber, so close upon her that she had not yet had time to lay off her bonnet; she stood with her wraps still on her arm.

"Irene!" she said harshly, "there is something you have got to bear. It's a mistake we've all made. He don't care anything for you. He never did. He told Pen so last night. He cares for her."

The sentences had fallen like blows. But the girl had taken them without flinching. She stood up immovable, but the delicate rose-light of her complexion went out and left her snow-white. She did not offer to speak.

"Why don't you say something?" cried her mother. "Do you want to kill me, Irene?"

"Why should I want to hurt *you*, mamma?" the girl replied steadily, but in an alien voice. "There's nothing to say. I want to see Pen a minute."

She turned and left the room. As she mounted the stairs that led to her own and her sister's rooms on the floor above, her mother helplessly followed. Irene went first to her own room at the front of the house, and then came out, leaving the door open and the gas flaring behind her. The mother could see that she had tumbled many things out of the drawers of her bureau upon the marble top.

She passed her mother, where she stood in the entry. "You can come too, if you want to, mamma," she said.

She opened Penelope's door without knocking, and went in. Penelope sat at the window, as in the morning. Irene did not go to her; but she went and laid a gold hair-pin on her bureau, and said, without looking at her, "There's a pin that I got to-day, because it was like his sister's. It won't become a dark person so well, but you can have it."

She stuck a scrap of paper in the side of Penelope's mirror. "There's that account of Mr. Stanton's ranch. You'll want to read it, I presume."

She laid a withered *boutonnière* on the bureau beside the pin. "There's his button-hole bouquet. He left it by his plate, and I stole it."

She had a pine-shaving, fantastically tied up with a knot of ribbon, in her hand. She held it a moment; then, looking deliberately at Penelope, she went up to her, and dropped it in her lap without a word. She turned, and, advancing a few steps, tottered and seemed about to fall.

Her mother sprang forward with an imploring cry, "Oh, 'Rene, 'Rene, 'Rene!"

Irene recovered herself before her mother could reach her. "Don't touch me," she said icily. "Mamma, I'm going to put on my things. I want papa to walk with me. I'm choking here."

"I—I can't let you go out, Irene, child," began her mother.

"You've got to," replied the girl. "Tell papa to hurry his supper."

"Oh, poor soul! He doesn't want any supper. *He* knows it too."

"I don't want to talk about that. Tell him to get ready."

She left them once more.

Mrs. Lapham turned a hapless glance upon Penelope.

"Go and tell him, mother," said the girl. "I would, if I could. If she can walk, let her. It's the only thing for her." She sat still; she did not even brush to the floor the fantastic thing that lay in her lap, and that sent up faintly the odor of the sachet powder with which Irene liked to perfume her boxes.

Lapham went out with the unhappy child, and began to talk with her, crazily, incoherently enough.

She mercifully stopped him. "Don't talk, papa. I don't want any one should talk with me."

He obeyed, and they walked silently on and on. In their aimless course they reached the new house on the water side of Beacon, and she made him stop, and stood looking up at it. The scaffolding which had so long defaced the front was gone, and in the light of the gas-lamp before it all the architectural beauty of the façade was suggested, and much of the finely felt detail was revealed. Seymour had pretty nearly satisfied himself in that rich façade; certainly Lapham had not stinted him of the means.

"Well," said the girl, "I shall never live in it," and she began to walk on.

Lapham's sore heart went down, as he lumbered heavily after her. "Oh, yes, you will, Irene. You'll have lots of good times there yet."

"No," she answered, and said nothing more about it. They had not talked of their trouble at all, and they did not speak of it now. Lapham understood that she was trying to walk herself weary, and he was glad to hold his peace and let her have her way. She halted him once more before the red and yellow lights of an apothecary's window.

"Isn't there something they give you to make you sleep?" she asked vaguely. "I've got to sleep to-night!"

Lapham trembled. "I guess you don't want anything, Irene."

"Yes, I do! Get me something!" she retorted willfully. "If you don't, I shall die. I *must* sleep."

They went in, and Lapham asked for something to make a nervous person sleep. Irene stood poring over the show-case full of brushes and trinkets, while the apothecary put up the bromide, which he guessed would be about the best thing. She did not show any emotion; her face was like a stone, while her father's expressed the anguish of his sympathy. He looked as if he had not slept for a week; his fat eyelids drooped over his glassy eyes, and his cheeks and throat hung flaccid. He started as the apothecary's cat stole smoothly up and rubbed itself against his leg; and it was to him that the man said, "You want to take a table-spoonful of that as long as you're awake. I guess it won't take a great many to fetch you."

"All right," said Lapham, and paid and went out. "I don't know but I *shall* want some of it," he said, with a joyless laugh.

Irene came closer up to him and took his arm. He laid his heavy paw on her gloved fingers. After a while she said, "I want you should let me go up to Lapham to-morrow."

"To Lapham? Why, to-morrow's Sunday, Irene! You can't go to-morrow."

"Well, Monday, then. I can live through one day here."

"Well," said the father passively. He made no pretense of asking her why she wished to go, nor any attempt to dissuade her.

"Give me that bottle," she said, when he opened the door at home for her, and she ran up to her own room.

The next morning Irene came to breakfast with her mother; the Colonel and Penelope did not appear, and Mrs. Lapham looked sleep-broken and careworn.

The girl glanced at her. "Don't you fret about me, mamma," she said. "I shall get along." She seemed herself as steady and strong as rock.

"I don't like to see you keeping up so, Irene," replied her mother. "It'll be all the worse for you when you do break. Better give way a little at the start."

"I sha'n't break, and I've given way all I'm going to. I'm going to Lapham to-morrow,—I want you should go with me, mamma,—and I guess I can keep up one day here. All about it is, I don't want you should say anything, or *look* anything. And, whatever I do, I don't want you should try to stop me. And, the first thing, I'm going to take her breakfast up to her. Don't!" she cried, intercepting the protest on her mother's lips. "I shall not let it hurt Pen, if I can help it. She's never done a thing nor thought a thing to wrong me. I had to fly out at her last night; but that's all over now, and I know just what I've got to bear."

She had her way unmolested. She carried Penelope's breakfast to her, and omitted no care or attention that could make the sacrifice complete, with an heroic pretense that she was performing no unusual service. They did not speak, beyond her saying, in a clear, dry note, "Here's your breakfast, Pen," and her sister's answering, hoarsely and tremulously, "Oh, thank you, Irene." And, though two or three times they turned their faces toward each other while Irene remained in the room, mechanically putting its confusion to rights, their eyes did not meet. Then Irene descended upon the other rooms, which she set in order, and some of which she fiercely swept and dusted. She made the beds; and she sent the two servants away to church as soon as they had eaten their breakfast, telling them that she would wash their dishes. Throughout the morning her father and mother heard her about the work of getting dinner, with certain silences which represented the moments when she stopped and stood stock-still, and then, readjusting her burden, forced herself forward under it again.

They sat alone in the family-room, out of which their two girls seemed to have died. Lapham could not read his Sunday papers, and she had no heart to go to church, as she would have done earlier in life when in trouble. Just then she was obscurely feeling that the church was somehow to blame for that counsel of Mr. Sewell's on which they had acted.

"I should like to know," she said, having brought the matter up, "whether he would have thought it was such a light matter if it had been his own children. Do you suppose he'd have been so ready to act on his own advice if it *had* been?"

"He told us the right thing to do, Persis,—the only thing. We couldn't let it go on," urged her husband gently.

"Well, it makes me despise Pen! Irene's showing twice the character that she is, this very minute."

The mother said this so that the father might defend her daughter to her. He did not fail. "Irene's got the easiest part, the way I look at it. And you'll see that Pen'll know how to behave when the time comes."

"What do you want she should do?"

"I haven't got so far as that yet. What are we going to do about Irene?"

"What do you want Pen should do," repeated Mrs. Lapham, "when it comes to it?"

"Well, I don't want she should take him, for *one* thing," said Lapham.

This seemed to satisfy Mrs. Lapham as to her husband, and she said, in defense of Corey, "Why, I don't see what *he's* done. It's all been our doing."

"Never mind that now. What about Irene?"

"She says she's going to Lapham to-morrow. She feels that she's got to get away somewhere. It's natural she should."

"Yes. And I presume it will be about the best thing *for* her. Shall you go with her?"

"Yes."

"Well." He comfortlessly took up a newspaper again, and she rose with a sigh, and went to her room to pack some things for the morrow's journey.

After dinner, when Irene had cleared away the last trace of it in kitchen and dining-room with unsparing punctilio, she came downstairs, dressed to go out, and bade her father come to walk with her again. It was a repetition of the aimlessness of the last night's wanderings. They came back, and she got tea for them, and after that they heard her stirring about in her own room, as if she were busy about many things; but they did not dare to look in upon her, even after all the noises had ceased, and they knew she had gone to bed.

"Yes; it's a thing she's got to fight out by herself," said Mrs. Lapham.

"I guess she'll get along," said Lapham. "But I don't want you should misjudge Pen either. She's all right too. She ain't to blame."

"Yes, I know. But I can't work round to it all at once. I

sha'n't misjudge her, but you can't expect me to get over it right away."

"Mamma," said Irene, when she was hurrying their departure the next morning, "what did she tell him when he asked her?"

"Tell him?" echoed the mother; and after a while she added, "She didn't tell him anything."

"Did she say anything about me?"

"She said he mustn't come here any more."

Irene turned and went into her sister's room. "Good-bye, Pen," she said, kissing her with an effect of not seeing or touching her. "I want you should tell him all about it. If he's half a man, he won't give up till he knows why you won't have him; and he has a right to know."

"It wouldn't make any difference. I couldn't have him after——"

"That's for you to say. But if you don't tell him about me, *I* will."

" 'Rene!"

"Yes! You needn't say I cared for him. But you can say that you all thought he—cared for—me."

"Oh, Irene——"

"Don't!" Irene escaped from the arms that tried to cast themselves about her. "You are all right, Pen. You haven't done anything. You've helped me all you could. But I can't—yet."

She went out of the room and summoned Mrs. Lapham with a sharp "Now, mamma!" and went on putting the last things into her trunks.

The Colonel went to the station with them, and put them on the train. He got them a little compartment to themselves in the Pullman car; and as he stood leaning with his lifted hands against the sides of the doorway, he tried to say something consoling and hopeful: "I guess you'll have an easy ride, Irene. I don't believe it'll be dusty, any, after the rain last night."

"Don't you stay till the train starts, papa," returned the girl, in rigid rejection of his futilities. "Get off now."

"Well, if you want I should," he said, glad to be able to please her in anything. He remained on the platform till the cars started. He saw Irene bustling about in the compartment, making her mother comfortable for the journey; but Mrs. Lapham did not lift her head. The train moved off, and he went heavily back to his business.

From time to time during the day, when he caught a glimpse of him, Corey tried to make out from his face whether he knew what had taken place between him and Penelope. When Rogers came in about time of closing, and shut himself up with Lapham in his room, the young man remained till the two came out together and parted in their salutationless fashion.

Lapham showed no surprise at seeing Corey still there, and merely answered, "Well!" when the young man said that he wished to speak with him, and led the way back to his room.

Corey shut the door behind them. "I only wish to speak to you in case you know of the matter already; for otherwise I'm bound by a promise."

"I guess I know what you mean. It's about Penelope."

"Yes, it's about Miss Lapham. I am greatly attached to her—you'll excuse my saying it; I couldn't excuse myself if I were not."

"Perfectly excusable," said Lapham. "It's all right."

"Oh, I'm *glad* to hear you say that!" cried the young fellow joyfully. "I want you to believe that this isn't a new thing or an unconsidered thing with me—though it seemed so unexpected to her."

Lapham fetched a deep sigh. "It's all right as far as I'm concerned—or her mother. We've both liked you first-rate."

"Yes?"

"But there seems to be something in Penelope's mind—I don't know——" The Colonel consciously dropped his eyes.

"She referred to something—I couldn't make out what—but I hoped—I hoped—that with your leave I might overcome it—the barrier—whatever it was. Miss Lapham—Penelope—gave me the hope—that I was—wasn't—indifferent to her——"

"Yes, I guess that's so," said Lapham. He suddenly lifted his head, and confronted the young fellow's honest face with his own face, so different in its honesty. "Sure you never made up to any one else at the same time?"

"*Never!* Who could imagine such a thing? If that's all, I can easily——"

"I don't say that's all, nor that that's it. I don't want you should go upon that idea. I just thought, may be—you hadn't thought of it."

"No, I certainly hadn't thought of it! Such a thing would have been so impossible to me that I *couldn't* have thought of it; and it's so shocking to me now that I don't know what to say to it."

"Well, don't take it too much to heart," said Lapham, alarmed at the feeling he had excited; "I don't say she thought so. I was trying to guess—trying to——"

"If there is *any*thing I can say or do to convince you——"

"Oh, it ain't necessary to say anything. I'm all right."

"But Miss Lapham! I may see her again? I may try to convince her that——"

He stopped in distress, and Lapham afterwards told his wife that he kept seeing the face of Irene as it looked when he parted with her in the car; and whenever he was going to say yes, he could not open his lips. At the same time he could not help feeling that Penelope had a right to what was her own, and Sewell's words came back to him. Besides, they had already put Irene to the worst suffering. Lapham compromised, as he imagined.

"You can come round to-night and see *me*, if you want to," he said; and he bore grimly the gratitude that the young man poured out upon him.

Penelope came down to supper and took her mother's place at the head of the table.

Lapham sat silent in her presence as long as he could bear it. Then he asked, "How do you feel to-night, Pen?"

"Oh, like a thief," said the girl. "A thief that hasn't been arrested yet."

Lapham waited awhile before he said, "Well, now, your mother and I want you should hold up on that awhile."

"It isn't for you to say. It's something I *can't* hold up on."

"Yes, I guess you can. If I know what's happened, then what's happened is a thing that nobody is to blame for. And we want you should make the best of it, and not the worst. Heigh? It ain't going to help Irene any for you to hurt yourself—or anybody else; and I don't want you should take up with any such crazy notion. As far as heard from, you haven't stolen anything, and whatever you've got belongs to you."

"Has he been speaking to you, father?"

"Your mother's been speaking to me."

"Has *he* been speaking to you?"

"That's neither here nor there."

"Then he's broken his word, and I will never speak to him again!"

"If he was any such fool as to promise that he wouldn't talk to me on a subject"—Lapham drew a deep breath, and then made the plunge—"that I brought up——"

"Did you bring it up?"

"The same as brought up—the quicker he broke his word the better; and I want you should act upon that idea. Recollect that it's my business, and your mother's business, as well as yours, and we're going to have our say. He hain't done anything wrong, Pen, nor anything that he's going to be punished for. Understand that. He's got to have a reason, if you're not going to have him. I don't say you've got to have him; I want you should feel perfectly free about that; but I *do* say you've got to give him a reason."

"Is he coming here?"

"I don't know as you'd call it *coming*——"

"Yes, you do, father!" said the girl, in forlorn amusement at his shuffling.

"He's coming here to see *me*——"

"When's he coming?"

"I don't know but he's coming to-night."

"And you want I should see him?"

"I don't know but you'd better."

"All right. I'll see him."

Lapham drew a long, deep breath of suspicion inspired by this acquiescence. "What you going to do?" he asked presently.

"I don't know yet," answered the girl sadly. "It depends a good deal upon what *he* does."

"Well," said Lapham, with the hungriness of unsatisfied anxiety in his tone. When Corey's card was brought into the family-room where he and Penelope were sitting, he went into the parlor to find him. "I guess Penelope wants to see you," he said; and, indicating the family-room, he added, "She's in there," and did not go back himself.

Corey made his way to the girl's presence with open trepidation, which was not allayed by her silence and languor. She sat in the chair where she had sat the other night, but she was not playing with a fan now.

He came toward her, and then stood faltering. A faint smile quivered over her face at the spectacle of his subjection. "Sit down, Mr. Corey," she said. "There's no reason why we shouldn't talk it over quietly; for I know you will think I'm right."

"I'm sure of that," he answered hopefully. "When I saw that your father knew of it to-day, I asked him to let me see you again. I'm afraid that I broke my promise to you—technically——"

"It had to be broken."

He took more courage at her words. "But I've only come to do whatever you say, and not to be an—annoyance to you——"

"Yes, you have to know; but I couldn't tell you before. Now they all think I should."

A tremor of anxiety passed over the young man's face, on which she kept her eyes steadily fixed.

"We supposed it—it was—Irene——"

He remained blank a moment, and then he said with a smile of relief, of deprecation, of protest, of amazement, of compassion:

"*Oh!* Never! Never for an instant! How could you think such a thing? It was impossible! I never thought of her. But I see—I see! I can explain—no, there's nothing to explain! I have never knowingly done or said a thing from first to last to make you think that. I see how terrible it is!" he said; but he still smiled, as if he could not take it seriously. "I admired her beauty—who could help doing that?—and I thought her very good and sensible. Why, last winter in Texas, I told Stanton about our meeting in Canada, and we agreed—I only tell you to show you how far I always was from what you thought—that he must come North and try to see her, and—and—of course, it all sounds very silly!—and he sent her a newspaper with an account of his ranch in it——"

"She thought it came from you."

"Oh, good heavens! He didn't tell me till after he'd done it. But he did it for a part of our foolish joke. And when I met your sister again, I only admired her as before. I can see, now, how I must have seemed to be seeking her out; but it was to talk of you with her—I never talked of anything else if I could help it, except when I changed the subject because I was ashamed to be always talking of you. I see how distressing it is for all of you. But tell me that you believe me!"

"Yes, I must. It's all been our mistake——"

"It has indeed! But there's no mistake about my loving *you*, Penelope," he said; and the old-fashioned name, at which she had often mocked, was sweet to her from his lips.

"That only makes it worse!" she answered.

"Oh, no!" he gently protested. "It makes it better. It makes it right. How is it worse? How is it wrong?"

"Can't you see? You must understand all now! Don't you see that if she believed so too, and if she——" She could not go on.

"Did she—did your sister—think that too?" gasped Corey.

"She used to talk with me about you; and when you say you care for me now, it makes me feel like the vilest hypocrite in the world. That day you gave her the list of books, and she came down to Nantasket, and went on about you, I helped her to flatter herself—oh! I don't see how she can forgive me. But she knows I can never forgive myself! That's the reason she can do it. I can see now," she went on, "how I must have been trying to get you from her. I can't endure it! The only way is for me never to see you or speak to you again!" She laughed forlornly. "That would be pretty hard on you, if you cared."

"I do care—all the world!"

"Well, then, it would if you were going to keep on caring. You won't long, if you stop coming now."

"Is this all, then? Is it the end?"

"It's—whatever it is. I can't get over the thought of her. Once I thought I could, but now I see that I can't. It seems to grow worse. Sometimes I feel as if it would drive me crazy."

He sat looking at her with lack-luster eyes. The light suddenly came back into them. "Do you think I could love you if you had been false to her? I know you have been true to her, and truer still to yourself. I never tried to see her, except with the hope of seeing you too. I supposed she must know that I was in love with you. From the first time I saw you there that afternoon, you filled my fancy. Do you think I was flirting with the child, or—no, you *don't* think that! We have not done wrong. We have not harmed any one knowingly. We have a right to each other——"

"No! no! you must never speak to me of this again. If you do, I shall know that you despise me."

"But how will that help her? I don't love *her*."

"Don't say that to me! I have said that to myself too much."

"If you forbid me to love you, it won't make me love her," he persisted.

She was about to speak, but she caught her breath without doing so, and merely stared at him.

"I must do what you say," he continued. "But what good will it do her? You can't make her happy by making yourself unhappy."

"Do you ask me to profit by a wrong?"

"Not for the world. But there *is* no wrong!"

"There is something—I don't know what. There's a wall between us. I shall dash against it as long as I live; but that won't break it."

"Oh!" he groaned. "We have done no wrong. Why should we suffer from another's mistake as if it were our sin?"

"I don't know. But we must suffer."

"Well, then, I *will* not, for my part, and I will not let you. If you care for me——"

"You had no right to know it."

"You make it my privilege to keep you from doing wrong for the right's sake. I'm sorry, with all my heart and soul, for this error; but I can't blame myself, and I won't deny myself the happiness I haven't done anything to forfeit. I will never give you up. I will wait as long as you please for the time when you shall feel free from this mistake; but you shall be mine at last. Remember that. I might go away for months—a year, even; but that seems a cowardly and guilty thing, and I'm not afraid, and I'm not guilty, and I'm going to stay here and try to see you."

She shook her head. "It won't change anything. Don't you see that there's no hope for us?"

"When is she coming back?" he asked.

"I don't know. Mother wants father to come and take her out West for a while."

"She's up there in the country with your mother yet?"

"Yes."

He was silent; then he said, desperately:

"Penelope, she is very young; and perhaps—perhaps she might meet——"

"It would make no difference. It wouldn't change it for me."

"You are cruel—cruel to yourself, if you love me, and cruel to me. Don't you remember that night—before I spoke—you were talking of that book; and you said it was foolish and wicked to do as that girl did. Why is it different with you, except that you give me nothing, and can never give me anything when you take yourself away? If it were anybody else, I am sure you would say——"

"But it isn't anybody else, and that makes it impossible. Sometimes I think it might be if I would only say so to myself, and then all that I said to her about you comes up——"

"I will wait. It can't always come up. I won't urge you any longer now. But you will see it differently—more clearly. Good-bye—no! Good-night! I shall come again to-morrow. It will surely come right, and, whatever happens, you have done no wrong. Try to keep that in mind. I am so happy, in spite of all!"

He tried to take her hand, but she put it behind her. "No, no! I can't let you—yet!"

XX

After a week Mrs. Lapham returned, leaving Irene alone at the old homestead in Vermont. "She's comfortable there—as comfortable as she can be anywheres, I guess," she said to her husband, as they drove together from the station, where he had met her in obedience to her telegraphic summons. "She keeps herself busy helping about the house; and she goes round amongst the hands in their houses. There's sickness, and you know how helpful she is where there's sickness. She don't complain any. I don't know as I've heard a word out of her mouth since we left home; but I'm afraid it'll wear on her, Silas."

"You don't look over and above well yourself, Persis," said her husband kindly.

"Oh, don't talk about me. What I want to know is whether you can't get the time to run off with her somewhere? I wrote to you about Dubuque. She'll work herself down, I'm afraid; and *then* I don't know as she'll be over it. But if she could go off, and be amused—see new people——"

"I could *make* the time," said Lapham, "if I had to. But, as it happens, I've got to go out West on business,—I'll tell you about it,—and I'll take Irene along."

"Good!" said his wife. "That's about the best thing I've heard yet. Where you going?"

"Out Dubuque way."

"Anything the matter with Bill's folks?"

"No. It's business."

"How's Pen?"

"I guess she ain't much better than Irene."

"He been about any?"

"Yes. But I can't see as it helps matters much."

"Tchk!" Mrs. Lapham fell back against the carriage cushions. "I declare, to see her willing to take the man that we all thought wanted her sister! I can't make it seem right."

"It's right," said Lapham stoutly; "but I guess she ain't willing; I wish she was. But there don't seem to be any way out of the thing, anywhere. It's a perfect snarl. But I don't want you should be anyways ha'sh with Pen."

Mrs. Lapham answered nothing; but when she met Penelope she gave the girl's wan face a sharp look, and began to whimper on her neck.

Penelope's tears were all spent. "Well, mother," she said, "you come back almost as cheerful as you went away. I needn't ask if 'Rene's in good spirits. We all seem to be overflowing with them. I suppose this is one way of congratulating me. Mrs. Corey hasn't been round to do it yet."

"Are you—are you engaged to him, Pen?" gasped her mother.

"Judging by my feelings, I should say not. I feel as if it was a last will and testament. But you'd better ask him when he comes."

"I can't bear to look at him."

"I guess he's used to that. He don't seem to expect to be looked at. Well! we're all just where we started. I wonder how long it will keep up?"

Mrs. Lapham reported to her husband when he came home at night—he had left his business to go and meet her, and then, after a desolate dinner at the house, had returned to the office again—that Penelope was fully as bad as Irene. "And she don't know how to work it off. Irene keeps doing; but Pen just sits in her room and mopes. She don't even read. I went up this afternoon to scold her about the state the house was in—you can see that Irene's away by the perfect mess; but when I saw her through the crack of the door I hadn't the heart. She sat there with her hands in her lap, just staring. And, my goodness! she *jumped* so when she saw me; and then she fell back, and began to laugh, and said she, 'I thought it was my ghost, mother!' I felt as if I should give way."

Lapham listened jadedly, and answered far from the point. "I guess I've got to start out there pretty soon, Persis."

"How soon?"

"Well, to-morrow morning."

Mrs. Lapham sat silent. Then, "All right," she said. "I'll get you ready."

"I shall run up to Lapham for Irene, and then I'll push on through Canada. I can get there about as quick."

"Is it anything you can tell me about, Silas?"

"Yes," said Lapham. "But it's a long story, and I guess you've got your hands pretty full as it is. I've been throwing good money after bad,—the usual way,—and now I've got to see if I can save the pieces."

After a moment Mrs. Lapham asked, "Is it—Rogers?"

"It's Rogers."

"I didn't want you should get in any deeper with him."

"No. You didn't want I should press him either; and I had to do one or the other. And so I got in deeper."

"Silas," said his wife, "I'm afraid I made you!"

"It's all right, Persis, as far forth as that goes. I was glad to make it up with him—I jumped at the chance. I guess Rogers saw that he had a soft thing in me, and he's worked it for all it was worth. But it'll all come out right in the end."

Lapham said this as if he did not care to talk any more about it. He added, casually, "Pretty near everybody but the fellows that owe *me* seem to expect me to do a cash business, all of a sudden."

"Do you mean that you've got payments to make, and that people are not paying *you?*"

Lapham winced a little. "Something like that," he said, and he lighted a cigar. "But when I tell you it's all right, I mean it, Persis. I ain't going to let the grass grow under my feet, though,—especially while Rogers digs the ground away from the roots."

"What are you going to do?"

"If it has to come to that, I'm going to squeeze him." Lapham's countenance lighted up with greater joy than had yet visited it since the day they had driven out to Brookline. "Milton K. Rogers is a rascal, if you want to know; or else all the signs fail. But I guess he'll find he's got his come-uppance." Lapham shut his lips so that the short, reddish-gray beard stuck straight out on them.

"What's he done?"

"What's he done? Well, now, I'll tell you what he's done, Persis, since you think Rogers is such a saint, and that I used him so badly in getting him out of the business. He's been dabbling in every sort of fool thing you can lay your tongue to,—wild-cat stocks, patent-rights, land speculations, oil claims,—till he's run through about everything. But he did have a big milling property out on the line of the P. Y. & X.,—saw-mills and grist-mills and lands,—and for the last eight years he's been doing a land-office business with 'em— business that would have made anybody else rich. But you can't make Milton K. Rogers rich, any more than you can fat a hide-bound colt. It ain't *in* him. He'd run through Vander- bilt, Jay Gould, and Tom Scott rolled into one, in less than six months, give him a chance, and come out and want to borrow money of you. Well, he won't borrow any more money of *me*; and if he thinks I don't know as much about that milling property as he does, he's mistaken. I've taken his mills, but I guess I've got the inside track; Bill's kept me posted; and now I'm going out there to see how I can un- load; and I sha'n't mind a great deal if Rogers is under the load when it's off, once."

"I don't understand you, Silas."

"Why, it's just this. The Great Lacustrine & Polar Railroad has leased the P. Y. & X. for ninety-nine years,— *bought* it, practically,—and it's going to build car-works right by those mills, and it may want them. And Milton K. Rogers knew it when he turned 'em in on me."

"Well, if the road wants them, don't that make the mills valuable? You can get what you ask for them!"

"Can I? The P. Y. & X. is the only road that runs within fifty miles of the mills, and you can't get a foot of lumber nor a pound of flour to market any other way. As long as he had a little local road like the P. Y. & X. to deal with, Rogers could manage; but when it come to a big through line like the G. L. & P., he couldn't stand any chance at all. If such a road as that took a fancy to his mills, do you think it would pay what he asked? *No*, sir! He would take what the road offered, or else the road would tell him to carry his flour and lumber to market himself."

"And do you suppose he knew the G. L. & P. wanted the mills when he turned them in on you?" asked Mrs. Lapham, aghast, and falling helplessly into his alphabetical parlance.

The Colonel laughed scoffingly. "Well, when Milton K. Rogers don't know which side his bread's buttered on! I don't understand," he added thoughtfully, "how he's always letting it fall on the buttered side. But such a man as that is sure to have a screw loose in him somewhere."

Mrs. Lapham sat discomfited. All that she could say was, "Well, I want you should ask yourself whether Rogers would ever have gone wrong, or got into these ways of his, if it hadn't been for your forcing him out of the business when you did. I want you should think whether you're not responsible for everything he's done since."

"You go and get that bag of mine ready," said Lapham sullenly. "I guess I can take care of myself. And Milton K. Rogers too," he added.

That evening Corey spent the time after dinner in his own room, with restless excursions to the library, where his mother sat with his father and sisters, and showed no signs of leaving them. At last, in coming down, he encountered her on the stairs, going up. They both stopped consciously.

"I would like to speak with you, mother. I have been waiting to see you alone."

"Come to my room," she said.

"I have a feeling that you know what I want to say," he began there.

She looked up at him where he stood by the chimney-piece, and tried to put a cheerful note into her questioning "Yes?"

"Yes; and I have a feeling that you won't like it—that you won't approve of it. I wish you did—I wish you could!"

"I'm used to liking and approving everything you do, Tom. If I don't like this at once, I shall try to like it—you know that—for your sake, whatever it is."

"I'd better be short," he said, with a quick sigh. "It's about Miss Lapham." He hastened to add, "I hope it *isn't* surprising to you. I'd have told you before, if I could."

"No, it isn't surprising. I was afraid—I suspected something of the kind."

They were both silent in a painful silence.

"Well, mother?" he asked at last.

"If it's something you've quite made up your mind to——"

"It is!"

"And if you've already spoken to her——"

"I had to do that first, of course."

"There would be no use of my saying anything, even if I disliked it."

"You do dislike it!"

"No—no! I can't say that. Of course, I should have preferred it if you had chosen some nice girl among those that you had been brought up with—some friend or associate of your sisters, whose people we had known——"

"Yes, I understand that, and I can assure you that I haven't been indifferent to your feelings. I have tried to consider them from the first, and it kept me hesitating in a way that I'm ashamed to think of; for it wasn't quite right towards—others. But your feelings and my sisters' have been in my mind, and if I couldn't yield to what I supposed they must be, entirely——"

Even so good a son and brother as this, when it came to his love affair, appeared to think that he had yielded much in considering the feelings of his family at all.

His mother hastened to comfort him. "I know—I know. I've seen for some time that this might happen, Tom, and I have prepared myself for it. I have talked it over with your father, and we both agreed from the beginning that you were not to be hampered by our feeling. Still—it is a surprise. It must be."

"I know it. I can understand your feeling. But I'm sure that it's one that will last only while you don't know her well."

"Oh, I'm sure of that, Tom. I'm sure that we shall all be fond of her,—for your sake at first, even,—and I hope she'll like us."

"I am quite certain of that," said Corey, with that confidence which experience does not always confirm in such cases. "And your taking it as you do lifts a tremendous load off me."

But he sighed so heavily, and looked so troubled, that his mother said, "Well, now, you mustn't think of that any more. We wish what is for your happiness, my son, and we will gladly reconcile ourselves to anything that might have been disagreeable. I suppose we needn't speak of the family. We must both think alike about them. They have their—drawbacks, but they are thoroughly good people, and I satisfied myself the other night that they were not to be dreaded." She rose, and put her arm round his neck. "And I wish you joy, Tom! If she's half as good as you are, you will both be very happy." She was going to kiss him, but something in his looks stopped her—an absence, a trouble, which broke out in his words.

"I must tell you, mother! There's been a complication—a mistake—that's a blight on me yet, and that it sometimes seems as if we couldn't escape from. I wonder if you can help us! They all thought I meant—the other sister."

"Oh, Tom! But how *could* they?"

"I don't know. It seemed so glaringly plain—I was ashamed of making it so outright from the beginning. But they did. Even she did, herself!"

"But where could they have thought your eyes were—your taste? It wouldn't be surprising if any one were taken with that wonderful beauty; and I'm sure she's good too. But I'm astonished at them! To think you could prefer that little, black, odd creature, with her joking and——"

"*Mother!*" cried the young man, turning a ghastly face of warning upon her.

"What do you mean, Tom?"

"Did you—did—did *you* think so, too,—that it was *Irene* I meant?"

"Why, of course!"

He stared at her hopelessly.

"Oh, my son!" she said, for all comment on the situation.

"Don't reproach me, mother! I couldn't stand it."

"No. I didn't mean to do that. But how—*how* could it happen?"

"I don't know. When she first told me that they had understood it so, I laughed—almost—it was so far from me. But now, when you seem to have had the same idea— Did you all think so?"

"Yes."

They remained looking at each other. Then Mrs. Corey began: "It did pass through my mind once—that day I went to call upon them—that it might not be as we thought; but I knew so little of—of——"

"Penelope," Corey mechanically supplied.

"Is that her name?—I forgot—that I only thought of you in relation to her long enough to reject the idea; and it was natural, after our seeing something of the other one last year, that I might suppose you had formed some—attachment——"

"Yes; that's what they thought too. But I never thought of her as anything but a pretty child. I was civil to her because you wished it; and when I met her here again, I only tried to see her so that I could talk with her about her sister."

"You needn't defend yourself to *me*, Tom," said his mother, proud to say it to him in his trouble. "It's a terrible business for them, poor things," she added. "I don't know how they could get over it. But, of course, sensible people must see——"

"They haven't got over it. At least *she* hasn't. Since it's happened, there's been nothing that hasn't made me prouder and fonder of her! At first I *was* charmed with her—my fancy was taken; she delighted me—I don't know how; but she was simply the most fascinating person I ever saw. Now I never think of that. I only think how good she is—how patient she is with me, and how unsparing she is of herself. If she were concerned alone—if I were not concerned too—it would soon end. She's never had a thought for anything but her sister's feeling and mine from the beginning. I go there,—I know that I oughtn't, but I can't help it,—and she suffers it, and tries not to let me see that she is suffering it. There never was any one like her—so brave, so true, so noble. I won't give her up—I can't. But it breaks my heart when she accuses herself of what was all *my* doing. We spend our time trying to reason out of it, but we always come back to it at last, and I have to hear her morbidly blaming herself. Oh!"

Doubtless Mrs. Corey imagined some reliefs to this suffering, some qualifications of this sublimity in a girl she had disliked so distinctly; but she saw none in her son's behavior, and she gave him her further sympathy. She tried to praise Penelope, and said that it was not to be expected that she could reconcile herself at once to everything. "I shouldn't have liked it in her if she had. But time will bring it all right. And if she really cares for you——"

"I extorted that from her."

"Well, then, you must look at it in the best light you can. There is no blame anywhere, and the mortification and pain is something that must be lived down. That's all. And don't let what I said grieve you, Tom. You know I scarcely knew her, and I—I shall be sure to like any one you like, after all."

"Yes, I know," said the young man drearily. "Will you tell father?"

"If you wish."

"He must know. And I couldn't stand any more of this, just yet—any more mistake."

"I will tell him," said Mrs. Corey; and it was naturally the next thing for a woman who dwelt so much on decencies to propose: "We must go to call on her—your sisters and I. They have never seen her even; and she mustn't be allowed to think we're indifferent to her, especially under the circumstances."

"Oh, no! Don't go—not yet," cried Corey, with an instinctive perception that nothing could be worse for him. "We must wait—we must be patient. I'm afraid it would be painful to her now."

He turned away without speaking further; and his mother's eyes followed him wistfully to the door. There were some questions that she would have liked to ask him; but she had to content herself with trying to answer them when her husband put them to her.

There was this comfort for her always in Bromfield Corey, that he never was much surprised at anything, however shocking or painful. His standpoint in regard to most matters was that of the sympathetic humorist who would be glad to have the victim of circumstance laugh with him, but was not too much vexed when the victim could not. He laughed now when his wife, with careful preparation, got the facts of his son's predicament fully under his eye.

"Really, Bromfield," she said, "I don't see how you *can* laugh. Do you see any way out of it?"

"It seems to me that the way has been found already. Tom has told his love to the right one, and the wrong one knows it. Time will do the rest."

"If I had so low an opinion of them all as that, it would make me very unhappy. It's shocking to think of it."

"It is, upon the theory of ladies and all young people," said her husband, with a shrug, feeling his way to the matches on the mantel, and then dropping them with a sigh, as if recollecting that he must not smoke there. "I've no doubt Tom feels himself an awful sinner. But apparently he's resigned to his sin; he isn't going to give her up."

"I'm glad to say, for the sake of human nature, that *she* isn't resigned—little as I like her," cried Mrs. Corey.

Her husband shrugged again. "Oh, there mustn't be any indecent haste. She will instinctively observe the proprieties. But come, now, Anna! you mustn't pretend to me here, in the sanctuary of home, that practically the human affections don't reconcile themselves to any situation that the human sentiments condemn. Suppose the wrong sister had died: would the right one have had any scruple in marrying Tom, after they had both 'waited a proper time,' as the phrase is?"

"Bromfield, you're shocking!"

"Not more shocking than reality. You may regard this as a second marriage." He looked at her with twinkling eyes, full of the triumph the spectator of his species feels in signal exhibitions of human nature. "Depend upon it, the right sister will be reconciled; the wrong one will be consoled; and all will go merry as a marriage bell—a second marriage bell. Why, it's quite like a romance!" Here he laughed outright again.

"Well," sighed the wife, "I could almost wish the right one, as you call her, would reject Tom. I dislike her so much."

"Ah, now you're talking business, Anna," said her husband, with his hands spread behind the back he turned comfortably to the fire. "The whole Lapham tribe is distasteful to *me*. As I don't happen to have seen our daughter-in-law elect, I have still the hope—which you're disposed to forbid me—that she may not be quite so unacceptable as the others."

"Do you really feel so, Bromfield?" anxiously inquired his wife.

"Yes—I think I do"; and he sat down, and stretched out his long legs toward the fire.

"But it's very inconsistent of you to oppose the matter

now, when you've shown so much indifference up to this time. You've told me, all along, that it was of no use to oppose it."

"So I have. I was convinced of that at the beginning, or my reason was. You know very well that I am equal to any trial, any sacrifice, day after to-morrow; but when it comes to-day it's another thing. As long as this crisis decently kept its distance, I could look at it with an impartial eye; but now that it seems at hand, I find that, while my reason is still acquiescent, my nerves are disposed to—excuse the phrase—kick. I ask myself, what have I done nothing for, all my life, and lived as a gentleman should, upon the earnings of somebody else, in the possession of every polite taste and feeling that adorns leisure, if I'm to come to this at last? And I find no satisfactory answer. I say to myself that I might as well have yielded to the pressure all round me, and gone to work, as Tom has."

Mrs. Corey looked at him forlornly, divining the core of real repugnance that existed in his self-satire.

"I assure you, my dear," he continued, "that the recollection of what I suffered from the Laphams at that dinner of yours is an anguish still. It wasn't their behavior,—they behaved well enough—or ill enough; but their conversation was terrible. Mrs. Lapham's range was strictly domestic; and when the Colonel got me in the library, he poured mineral paint all over me, till I could have been safely warranted not to crack or scale in any climate. I suppose we shall have to see a good deal of them. They will probably come here every Sunday night to tea. It's a perspective without a vanishing-point."

"It may not be so bad, after all," said his wife; and she suggested for his consolation that he knew very little about the Laphams yet.

He assented to the fact. "I know very little about them, and about my other fellow-beings. I dare say that I should like the Laphams better if I knew them better. But in any case, I resign myself. And we must keep in view the fact that this is mainly Tom's affair, and if his affections have regulated it to his satisfaction, we must be content."

"Oh, yes," sighed Mrs. Corey. "And perhaps it won't turn

out so badly. It's a great comfort to know that you feel just as I do about it."

"I do," said her husband, "and more too."

It was she and her daughters who would be chiefly annoyed by the Lapham connection; she knew that. But she had to begin to bear the burden by helping her husband to bear his light share of it. To see him so depressed dismayed her, and she might well have reproached him more sharply than she did for showing so much indifference, when she was so anxious, at first. But that would not have served any good end now. She even answered him patiently when he asked her, "What did you say to Tom when he told you it was the other one?"

"What could I say? I could do nothing, but try to take back what I had said against her."

"Yes, you had quite enough to do, I suppose. It's an awkward business. If it had been the pretty one, her beauty would have been our excuse. But the plain one—what do you suppose attracted him in her?"

Mrs. Corey sighed at the futility of the question. "Perhaps I did her injustice. I only saw her a few moments. Perhaps I got a false impression. I don't think she's lacking in sense, and that's a great thing. She'll be quick to see that we don't mean unkindness, and can't, by anything we say or do, when she's Tom's wife." She pronounced the distasteful word with courage, and went on: "The pretty one might not have been able to see that. She might have got it into her head that we were looking down on her; and those insipid people are terribly stubborn. We can come to some understanding with *this* one; I'm sure of that." She ended by declaring that it was now their duty to help Tom out of his terrible predicament.

"Oh, even the Lapham cloud has a silver lining," said Corey. "In fact, it seems really to have all turned out for the best, Anna; though it's rather curious to find you the champion of the Lapham side, at last. Confess, now, that the right girl has secretly been your choice all along, and that while you sympathize with the wrong one, you rejoice in the tenacity with which the right one is clinging to her own!" He added with final seriousness, "It's just that she should, and, so far as I understand the case, I respect her for it."

"Oh, yes," sighed Mrs. Corey. "It's natural, and it's right." But she added, "I suppose they're glad of him on any terms."

"That is what I have been taught to believe," said her husband. "When shall we see our daughter-in-law elect? I find myself rather impatient to have that part of it over."

Mrs. Corey hesitated. "Tom thinks we had better not call, just yet."

"She has told him of your terrible behavior when you called before?"

"No, Bromfield! She couldn't be so vulgar as *that*?"

"But anything short of it?"

XXI

LAPHAM was gone a fortnight. He was in a sullen humor when he came back, and kept himself shut close within his own den at the office the first day. He entered it in the morning without a word to his clerks as he passed through the outer room, and he made no sign throughout the forenoon, except to strike savagely on his desk-bell from time to time, and send out to Walker for some book of accounts or a letter-file. His boy confidentially reported to Walker that the old man seemed to have got a lot of papers round; and at lunch the book-keeper said to Corey, at the little table which they had taken in a corner together, in default of seats at the counter, "Well, sir, I guess there's a cold wave coming."

Corey looked up innocently, and said, "I haven't read the weather report."

"Yes, sir," Walker continued, "it's coming. Areas of rain along the whole coast, and increased pressure in the region of the private office. Storm-signals up at the old man's door now."

Corey perceived that he was speaking figuratively, and that his meteorology was entirely personal to Lapham. "What do you mean?" he asked, without vivid interest in the allegory, his mind being full of his own tragi-comedy.

"Why, just this: I guess the old man's takin' in sail. And I guess he's got to. As I told you the first time we talked about him, there don't any one know one-quarter as much about the old man's business as the old man does himself; and I ain't betraying any confidence when I say that I guess that old partner of his has got pretty deep into his books. I guess he's over head and ears in 'em, and the old man's gone in after him, and he's got a drownin' man's grip round his neck. There seems to be a kind of a lull—kind of a dead calm, *I* call it—in the paint market just now; and then again a ten-hundred-thousand-dollar man don't build a hundred-thousand-dollar house without feeling the drain, unless there's a regular boom. And just now there ain't any boom at all. Oh, I don't say but what the old man's got anchors to windward;

guess he *has*; but if he's *goin'* to leave me his money, I wish he'd left it six weeks ago. Yes, sir, I guess there's a cold wave comin'; but you can't generally 'most always tell, as a usual thing, where the old man's concerned, and it's *only* a guess." Walker began to feed in his breaded chop with the same nervous excitement with which he abandoned himself to the slangy and figurative excesses of his talks. Corey had listened with a miserable curiosity and compassion up to a certain moment, when a broad light of hope flashed upon him. It came from Lapham's potential ruin; and the way out of the labyrinth that had hitherto seemed so hopeless was clear enough, if another's disaster would befriend him, and give him the opportunity to prove the unselfishness of his constancy. He thought of the sum of money that was his own, and that he might offer to lend, or practically give, if the time came; and with his crude hopes and purposes formlessly exulting in his heart, he kept on listening with an unchanged countenance.

Walker could not rest till he had developed the whole situation, so far as he knew it. "Look at the stock we've got on hand. There's going to be an awful shrinkage on that, now! And when everybody is shutting down, or running half time, the works up at Lapham are going full chip, just the same as ever. Well, it's his pride. I don't say but what it's a good sort of pride, but he likes to make his brags that the fire's never been out in the works since they started, and that no man's work or wages has ever been cut down yet at Lapham, it don't matter *what* the times are. Of course," explained Walker, "I shouldn't talk so to everybody; don't know as I should talk so to *any*body but you, Mr. Corey."

"Of course," assented Corey.

"Little off your feed to-day," said Walker, glancing at Corey's plate.

"I got up with a headache."

"Well, sir, if you're like me you'll carry it round all day, then. I don't know a much meaner thing than a headache—unless it's earache, or toothache, or some other kind of ache. I'm pretty hard to suit, when it comes to diseases. Notice how yellow the old man looked when he came in this morning? I don't like to see a man of his build look yellow—much."

About the middle of the afternoon the dust-colored face of Rogers, now familiar to Lapham's clerks, showed itself among them. "Has Colonel Lapham returned yet?" he asked, in his dry, wooden tones, of Lapham's boy.

"Yes, he's in his office," said the boy; and as Rogers advanced, he rose and added, "I don't know as you can see him to-day. His orders are not to let anybody in."

"Oh, indeed!" said Rogers; "I think he will see *me*!" and he pressed forward.

"Well, I'll have to ask," returned the boy; and hastily preceding Rogers, he put his head in at Lapham's door, and then withdrew it. "Please to sit down," he said; "he'll see you pretty soon;" and, with an air of some surprise, Rogers obeyed. His sere, dull-brown whiskers and the mustache closing over both lips were incongruously and illogically clerical in effect, and the effect was heightened for no reason by the parchment texture of his skin; the baldness extending to the crown of his head was like a baldness made up for the stage. What his face expressed chiefly was a bland and beneficent caution. Here, you must have said to yourself, is a man of just, sober, and prudent views, fixed purposes, and the good citizenship that avoids debt and hazard of every kind.

"What do you want?" asked Lapham, wheeling round in his swivel-chair as Rogers entered his room, and pushing the door shut with his foot, without rising.

Rogers took the chair that was not offered him, and sat with his hat-brim on his knees, and its crown pointed towards Lapham. "I want to know what you are going to do," he answered, with sufficient self-possession.

"I'll tell you, first, what I've *done*," said Lapham. "I've been to Dubuque, and I've found out all about that milling property you turned in on me. Did you know that the G. L. & P. had leased the P. Y. & X.?"

"I some suspected that it might."

"Did you know it when you turned the property in on me? Did you know that the G. L. & P. wanted to buy the mills?"

"I presumed the road would give a fair price for them," said Rogers, winking his eyes in outward expression of inwardly blinking the point.

"You lie," said Lapham, as quietly as if correcting him in a slight error; and Rogers took the word with equal *sang froid*. "You knew the road wouldn't give a fair price for the mills. You knew it would give what it chose, and that I couldn't help myself, when you let me take them. You're a thief, Milton K. Rogers, and you stole money I lent you." Rogers sat listening, as if respectfully considering the statements. "You knew how I felt about that old matter — or my wife did; and that I wanted to make it up to you, if you felt anyway badly used. And you took advantage of it. You've got money out of me, in the first place, on securities that wa'n't worth thirty-five cents on the dollar, and you've let me in for this thing, and that thing, and you've bled me every time. And all I've got to show for it is a milling property on a line of road that can squeeze me, whenever it wants to, as dry as it pleases. And you want to know what I'm going to do? I'm going to squeeze *you*. I'm going to sell these collaterals of yours,"—he touched a bundle of papers among others that littered his desk,—"and I'm going to let the mills go for what they'll fetch. *I* ain't going to fight the G. L. & P."

Lapham wheeled about in his chair and turned his burly back on his visitor, who sat wholly unmoved.

"There are some parties," he began, with a dry tranquillity ignoring Lapham's words, as if they had been an outburst against some third person, who probably merited them, but in whom he was so little interested that he had been obliged to use patience in listening to his condemnation,—"there are some English parties who have been making inquiries in regard to those mills."

"I guess you're lying, Rogers," said Lapham, without looking round.

"Well, all that I have to ask is that you will not act hastily."

"I see you don't think I'm in earnest!" cried Lapham, facing fiercely about. "You think I'm fooling, do you?" He struck his bell, and "William," he ordered the boy who answered it, and who stood waiting while he dashed off a note to the brokers and inclosed it with the bundle of securities in a large envelope, "take these down to Gallop & Paddock's, in State street, right away. Now go!" he said to Rogers, when the boy had closed the door after him; and he turned once more to his desk.

Rogers rose from his chair, and stood with his hat in his hand. He was not merely dispassionate in his attitude and expression, he was impartial. He wore the air of a man who was ready to return to business whenever the wayward mood of his interlocutor permitted. "Then I understand," he said, "that you will take no action in regard to the mills till I have seen the parties I speak of."

Lapham faced about once more, and sat looking up into the visage of Rogers in silence. "I wonder what you're up to," he said at last; "I *should* like to know." But as Rogers made no sign of gratifying his curiosity, and treated this last remark of Lapham's as of the irrelevance of all the rest, he said, frowning, "You bring me a party that will give me enough for those mills to clear me of you, and I'll talk to you. But don't you come here with any man of straw. And I'll give you just twenty-four hours to prove yourself a swindler again."

Once more Lapham turned his back, and Rogers, after looking thoughtfully into his hat a moment, cleared his throat, and quietly withdrew, maintaining to the last his unprejudiced demeanor.

Lapham was not again heard from, as Walker phrased it, during the afternoon, except when the last mail was taken in to him; then the sound of rending envelopes, mixed with that of what seemed suppressed swearing, penetrated to the outer office. Somewhat earlier than the usual hour for closing, he appeared there with his hat on and his overcoat buttoned about him. He said briefly to his boy, "William, I sha'n't be back again this afternoon," and then went to Miss Dewey and left a number of letters on her table to be copied, and went out. Nothing had been said, but a sense of trouble subtly diffused itself through those who saw him go out.

That evening, as he sat down with his wife alone at tea, he asked, "Ain't Pen coming to supper?"

"No, she ain't," said his wife. "I don't know as I like the way she's going on, any too well. I'm afraid, if she keeps on, she'll be down sick. She's got deeper feelings than Irene."

Lapham said nothing, but, having helped himself to the abundance of his table in his usual fashion, he sat and looked at his plate with an indifference that did not escape the notice of his wife. "What's the matter with *you?*" she asked.

"Nothing. I haven't got any appetite."

"What's the matter?" she persisted.

"Trouble's the matter; bad luck and lots of it's the matter," said Lapham. "I haven't ever hid anything from you, Persis, when you asked me, and it's too late to begin now. I'm in a fix. I'll tell you what kind of a fix, if you think it'll do you any good; but I guess you'll be satisfied to know that it's a fix."

"How much of a one?" she asked, with a look of grave, steady courage in her eyes.

"Well, I don't know as I can tell, just yet," said Lapham, avoiding this look. "Things have been dull all the fall, but I thought they'd brisk up, come winter. They haven't. There have been a lot of failures, and some of 'em owed me, and some of 'em had me on their paper; and——" Lapham stopped.

"And what?" prompted his wife.

He hesitated before he added, "And then—Rogers."

"I'm to blame for that," said Mrs. Lapham. "I forced you to it."

"No; I was as willing to go into it as what you were," answered Lapham. "I don't want to blame anybody."

Mrs. Lapham had a woman's passion for fixing responsibility; she could not help saying, as soon as acquitted, "I warned you against him, Silas. I told you not to let him get in any deeper with you."

"Oh, yes. I had to help him to try to get my money back. I might as well poured water into a sieve. And now——" Lapham stopped.

"Don't be afraid to speak out to me, Silas Lapham. If it comes to the worst, I want to know it—I've got to know it. What did I ever care for the money? I've had a happy home with you ever since we were married, and I guess I shall have as long as you live, whether we go on to the Back Bay, or go back to the old house at Lapham. I know who's to blame, and I blame myself. It was my forcing Rogers on to you." She came back to this, with her helpless longing, inbred in all Puritan souls, to have some one specifically suffer for the evil in the world, even if it must be herself.

"It hasn't come to the worst yet, Persis," said her husband,

"But I shall have to hold up on the new house a little while, till I can see where I am."

"I shouldn't care if we had to sell it," cried his wife, in passionate self-condemnation. "I should be *glad* if we had to, as far as I'm concerned."

"I shouldn't," said Lapham.

"I know!" said his wife; and she remembered ruefully how his heart was set on it.

He sat musing. "Well, I guess it's going to come out all right in the end. Or, if it ain't," he sighed, "we can't help it. May be Pen needn't worry so much about Corey, after all," he continued, with a bitter irony new to him. "It's an ill wind that blows nobody good. And there's a chance," he ended, with a still bitterer laugh, "that Rogers will come to time, after all."

"I don't believe it!" exclaimed Mrs. Lapham, with a gleam of hope in her eyes. "What chance?"

"One in ten million," said Lapham; and her face fell again. "He says there are some English parties after him to buy these mills."

"Well?"

"Well, I gave him twenty-four hours to prove himself a liar."

"You don't believe there are any such parties?"

"Not in *this* world."

"But if there were?"

"Well, if there were, Persis—— But pshaw!"

"No, no!" she pleaded eagerly. "It don't seem as if he *could* be such a villain. What would be the use of his pretending? If he brought the parties to you——"

"Well," said Lapham scornfully, "I'd let them have the mills at the price Rogers turned 'em in on me at. *I* don't want to make anything on 'em. But guess I shall hear from the G. L. & P. first. And when they make their offer, I guess I'll have to accept it, whatever it is. I don't think they'll have a great many competitors."

Mrs. Lapham could not give up her hope. "If you could get your price from those English parties before they knew that the G. L. & P. wanted to buy the mills, would it let you out with Rogers?"

"Just about," said Lapham.

"Then I know he'll move heaven and earth to bring it about. I *know* you won't be allowed to suffer for doing him a kindness, Silas. He *can't* be so ungrateful! Why, why *should* he pretend to have any such parties in view when he hasn't? Don't you be down-hearted, Si. You'll see that he'll be round with them to-morrow."

Lapham laughed, but she urged so many reasons for her belief in Rogers that Lapham began to rekindle his own faith a little. He ended by asking for a hot cup of tea; and Mrs. Lapham sent the pot out and had a fresh one steeped for him. After that he made a hearty supper in the revulsion from his entire despair; and they fell asleep that night talking hopefully of his affairs, which he laid before her fully, as he used to do when he first started in business. That brought the old times back, and he said: "If this had happened then, I shouldn't have cared much. I was young then, and I wasn't afraid of anything. But I noticed that after I passed fifty I began to get scared easier. I don't believe I could pick up, now, from a regular knockdown."

"Pshaw! *You* scared, Silas Lapham?" cried his wife, proudly. "I should like to see the thing that ever scared you; or the knockdown that *you* couldn't pick up from!"

"Is that so, Persis?" he asked, with the joy her courage gave him.

In the middle of the night she called to him, in a voice which the darkness rendered still more deeply troubled: "Are you awake, Silas?"

"Yes; I'm awake."

"I've been thinking about those English parties, Si——"

"So've I."

"And I can't make it out but what you'd be just as bad as Rogers, every bit and grain, if you were to let them have the mills——"

"And not tell 'em what the chances were with the G. L. & P.? I thought of that, and you needn't be afraid."

She began to bewail herself, and to sob convulsively: "Oh, Silas! Oh, Silas!" Heaven knows in what measure the passion of her soul was mixed with pride in her husband's honesty, relief from an apprehended struggle, and pity for him.

"Hush, hush, Persis!" he besought her. "You'll wake Pen if you keep on that way. Don't cry any more! You mustn't."

"Oh, let me cry, Silas! It'll help me. I shall be all right in a minute. Don't you mind." She sobbed herself quiet. "It does seem too hard," she said, when she could speak again, "that you have to give up this chance when Providence had fairly raised it up for you."

"I guess it wa'n't *Providence* raised it up," said Lapham. "Any rate, it's got to go. Most likely Rogers was lyin', and there ain't any such parties; but if there were, they couldn't have the mills from me without the whole story. Don't you be troubled, Persis. I'm going to pull through all right."

"Oh, I ain't afraid. I don't suppose but what there's plenty would help you, if they knew you needed it, Si."

"They would if they knew I *didn't* need it," said Lapham sardonically.

"Did you tell Bill how you stood?"

"No, I couldn't bear to. I've been the rich one so long, that I couldn't bring myself to own up that I was in danger."

"Yes."

"Besides, it didn't look so ugly till to-day. But I guess we sha'n't let ugly looks scare us."

"No."

XXII

THE MORNING postman brought Mrs. Lapham a letter from Irene, which was chiefly significant because it made no reference whatever to the writer or her state of mind. It gave the news of her uncle's family; it told of their kindness to her; her cousin Will was going to take her and his sisters ice-boating on the river, when it froze.

By the time this letter came, Lapham had gone to his business, and the mother carried it to Penelope to talk over. "What do you make out of it?" she asked; and without waiting to be answered, she said, "I don't know as I believe in cousins marrying, a great deal; but if Irene and Will were to fix it up between 'em—" She looked vaguely at Penelope.

"It wouldn't make any difference as far as I was concerned," replied the girl, listlessly.

Mrs. Lapham lost her patience.

"Well, then, I'll tell you what, Penelope!" she exclaimed. "Perhaps it'll make a difference to you if you know that your father's in *real* trouble. He's harassed to death, and he was awake half the night, talking about it. That abominable old Rogers has got a lot of money away from him; and he's lost by others that he's helped,"—Mrs. Lapham put it in this way because she had no time to be explicit,—"and I want you should come out of your room now, and try to be of some help and comfort to him when he comes home to-night. I guess Irene wouldn't mope round much, if she was here," she could not help adding.

The girl lifted herself on her elbow. "What's that you say about father?" she demanded, eagerly. "Is he in trouble? Is he going to lose his money? Shall we have to stay in this house?"

"We may be very *glad* to stay in this house," said Mrs. Lapham, half angry with herself for having given cause for the girl's conjectures, and half with the habit of prosperity in her child, which could conceive no better of what adversity was. "And I want you should get up and show that you've got some feeling for somebody in the world besides yourself."

"Oh, I'll get *up*!" said the girl, promptly, almost cheerfully.

"I don't say it's as bad now as it looked a little while ago," said her mother, conscientiously hedging a little from the statement which she had based rather upon her feelings than her facts. "Your father thinks he'll pull through all right, and I don't know but what he will. But I want you should see if you can't do something to cheer him up and keep him from getting so perfectly down-hearted as he seems to get, under the load he's got to carry. And stop thinking about yourself awhile, and behave yourself like a sensible girl."

"Yes, yes," said the girl; "I will. You needn't be troubled about me any more."

Before she left her room she wrote a note, and when she came down she was dressed to go out-of-doors and post it herself. The note was to Corey:

"Do not come to see me any more till you hear from me. I have a reason which I cannot give you now; and you must not ask what it is."

All day she went about in a buoyant desperation, and she came down to meet her father at supper.

"Well, Persis," he said scornfully, as he sat down, "we might as well saved our good resolutions till they were wanted. I guess those English parties have gone back on Rogers."

"Do you mean he didn't come?"

"He hadn't come up to half-past five," said Lapham.

"Tchk!" uttered his wife.

"But I guess I shall pull through without Mr. Rogers," continued Lapham. "A firm that I didn't think *could* weather it is still afloat, and so far forth as the danger goes of being dragged under with it, I'm all right." Penelope came in. "Hello, Pen!" cried her father. "It ain't often I meet *you* nowadays." He put up his hand as she passed his chair, and pulled her down and kissed her.

"No," she said; "but I thought I'd come down to-night and cheer you up a little. I shall not talk; the sight of me will be enough."

Her father laughed out. "Mother been telling you? Well, I *was* pretty blue last night; but I guess I was more scared than hurt. How'd you like to go to the theater to-night? Sellers at the Park. Heigh?"

"Well, I don't know. Don't you think they could get along without me there?"

"No; couldn't work it at all," cried the Colonel. "Let's all go. Unless," he added, inquiringly, "there's somebody coming here?"

"There's nobody coming," said Penelope.

"Good! Then we'll go. Mother, don't you be late now."

"Oh, I sha'n't keep you waiting," said Mrs. Lapham. She had thought of telling what a cheerful letter she had got from Irene; but upon the whole it seemed better not to speak of Irene at all just then. After they returned from the theater, where the Colonel roared through the comedy, with continual reference of his pleasure to Penelope, to make sure that she was enjoying it too, his wife said, as if the whole affair had been for the girl's distraction rather than his, "I don't believe but what it's going to come out all right about the children;" and then she told him of the letter, and the hopes she had founded upon it.

"Well, perhaps you're right, Persis," he consented.

"I haven't seen Pen so much like herself since it happened. I declare, when I see the way she came out to-night, just to please you, I don't know as I want you should get over all your troubles right away."

"I guess there'll be enough to keep Pen going for a while yet," said the Colonel, winding up his watch.

But for a time there was a relief, which Walker noted, in the atmosphere at the office, and then came another cold wave, slighter than the first, but distinctly felt there, and succeeded by another relief. It was like the winter which was wearing on to the end of the year, with alternations of freezing weather, and mild days stretching to weeks, in which the snow and ice wholly disappeared. It was none the less winter, and none the less harassing for these fluctuations, and Lapham showed in his face and temper the effect of like fluctuations in his affairs. He grew thin and old, and both at home and at his office he was irascible to the point of offense. In these days Penelope shared with her mother the burden of their troubled home, and united with her in supporting the silence or the petulance of the gloomy, secret man who replaced the presence of jolly prosperity there. Lapham had now ceased to talk of his troubles, and savagely resented his wife's interference. "You mind your own business, Persis," he said one day, "if you've got any;" and after that she left him mainly to Penelope, who did not think of asking him questions.

"It's pretty hard on you, Pen," she said.

"That makes it easier for me," returned the girl, who did not otherwise refer to her own trouble. In her heart she had wondered a little at the absolute obedience of Corey, who had made no sign since receiving her note. She would have liked to ask her father if Corey was sick; she would have liked him to ask her why Corey did not come any more. Her mother went on:

"I don't believe your father knows *where* he stands. He works away at those papers he brings home here at night, as if he didn't half know what he was about. He always did have that close streak in him, and I don't suppose but what he's been going into things he don't want anybody else to know about, and he's kept these accounts of his own."

Sometimes he gave Penelope figures to work at, which he would not submit to his wife's nimbler arithmetic. Then she went to bed and left them sitting up till midnight, struggling with problems in which they were both weak. But she could see that the girl was a comfort to her father, and that his troubles were a defense and shelter to her. Some nights she could hear them going out together, and then she lay awake for their return from their long walk. When the hour or day of respite came again, the home felt it first. Lapham wanted to know what the news from Irene was; he joined his wife in all her cheerful speculations, and tried to make her amends for his sullen reticence and irritability. Irene was staying on at Dubuque. There came a letter from her, saying that her uncle's people wanted her to spend the winter there. "Well, let her," said Lapham. "It'll be the best thing for her." Lapham himself had letters from his brother at frequent intervals. His brother was watching the G. L. & P., which as yet had made no offer for the mills. Once, when one of these letters came, he submitted to his wife whether, in the absence of any positive information that the road wanted the property, he might not, with a good conscience, dispose of it to the best advantage to anybody who came along.

She looked wistfully at him; it was on the rise from a season of deep depression with him. "No, Si," she said; "I don't see how you could do that."

He did not assent and submit, as he had done at first, but began to rail at the unpracticality of women; and then he shut some papers he had been looking over into his desk, and flung out of the room.

One of the papers had slipped through the crevice of the lid, and lay upon the floor. Mrs. Lapham kept on at her sewing, but after a while she picked the paper up to lay it on the desk. Then she glanced at it, and saw that it was a long column of dates and figures, recording successive sums, never large ones, paid regularly to "Wm. M." The dates covered a year, and the sum amounted at least to several hundreds.

Mrs. Lapham laid the paper down on the desk, and then she took it up again and put it into her work-basket, meaning to give it to him. When he came in she saw him looking absent-mindedly about for something, and then going to work upon his papers, apparently without it. She thought she would wait till he missed it definitely, and then give him the scrap she had picked up. It lay in her basket, and after some days it found its way under the work in it, and she forgot it.

XXIII

S INCE NEW YEAR'S there had scarcely been a mild day, and the streets were full of snow, growing foul under the city feet and hoofs, and renewing its purity from the skies with repeated falls, which in turn lost their whiteness, beaten down, and beaten black and hard into a solid bed like iron. The sleighing was incomparable, and the air was full of the din of bells; but Lapham's turnout was not of those that thronged the Brighton road every afternoon; the man at the livery-stable sent him word that the mare's legs were swelling.

He and Corey had little to do with each other. He did not know how Penelope had arranged it with Corey; his wife said she knew no more than he did, and he did not like to ask the girl herself, especially as Corey no longer came to the house. He saw that she was cheerfuller than she had been, and helpfuller with him and her mother. Now and then Lapham opened his troubled soul to her a little, letting his thought break into speech without preamble or conclusion. Once he said:

"Pen, I presume you know I'm in trouble."

"We all seem to be there," said the girl.

"Yes, but there's a difference between being there by your own fault and being there by somebody else's."

"I don't call it his fault," she said.

"I call it mine," said the Colonel.

The girl laughed. Her thought was of her own care, and her father's wholly of his. She must come to his ground. "What have you been doing wrong?"

"I don't know as you'd call it wrong. It's what people do all the time. But I wish I'd let stocks alone. It's what I always promised your mother I would do. But there's no use cryin' over spilt milk; or watered stock, either."

"I don't think there's much use crying about anything. If it could have been cried straight, it would have been all right from the start," said the girl, going back to her own affair; and if Lapham had not been so deeply engrossed in his, he might have seen how little she cared for all that money could do or undo. He did not observe her enough to see how variable her moods were in those days, and how often she sank from some wild gayety into abject melancholy; how at times she was fiercely defiant of nothing at all, and at others inexplicably humble and patient. But no doubt none of these signs had passed unnoticed by his wife, to whom Lapham said one day, when he came home, "Persis, what's the reason Pen don't marry Corey?"

"You know as well as I do, Silas," said Mrs. Lapham, with an inquiring look at him for what lay behind his words.

"Well, I think it's all tomfoolery, the way she's going on. There ain't any rhyme nor reason to it." He stopped, and his wife waited. "If she said the word, I could have some help from them." He hung his head, and would not meet his wife's eye.

"I guess you're in a pretty bad way, Si," she said pityingly, "or you wouldn't have come to that."

"I'm in a hole," said Lapham, "and I don't know where to turn. You won't let me do anything about those mills——"

"Yes, I'll let you," said his wife sadly.

He gave a miserable cry. "You know I can't do anything, if you do. Oh, my Lord!"

She had not seen him so low as that before. She did not know what to say. She was frightened, and could only ask, "Has it come to the worst?"

"The new house has got to go," he answered evasively.

She did not say anything. She knew that the work on the house had been stopped since the beginning of the year. Lapham had told the architect that he preferred to leave it unfinished till the spring, as there was no prospect of their being able to get into it that winter; and the architect had agreed with him that it would not hurt it to stand. Her heart was heavy for him, though she could not say so. They sat together at the table, where she had come to be with him at his belated meal. She saw that he did not eat, and she waited for him to speak again, without urging him to take anything. They were past that.

"And I've sent orders to shut down at the Works," he added.

"Shut down at the Works!" she echoed with dismay. She

could not take it in. The fire at the Works had never been out before since it was first kindled. She knew how he had prided himself upon that; how he had bragged of it to every listener, and had always lugged the fact in as the last expression of his sense of success. "Oh, Silas!"

"What's the use?" he retorted. "I saw it was coming a month ago. There are some fellows out in West Virginia that have been running the paint as hard as they could. They couldn't do much; they used to put it on the market raw. But lately they got to baking it, and now they've struck a vein of natural gas right by their works, and they pay ten cents for fuel where I pay a dollar, and they make as good a paint. Anybody can see where it's going to end. Besides, the market's overstocked. It's glutted. There wa'n't anything to do but to shut *down*, and I've *shut* down."

"I don't know what's going to become of the hands in the middle of the winter, this way," said Mrs. Lapham, laying hold of one definite thought which she could grasp in the turmoil of ruin that whirled before her eyes.

"I don't care what becomes of the hands," cried Lapham. "They've shared my luck; now let 'em share the other thing. And if you're so very sorry for the hands, I wish you'd keep a little of your pity for *me*. Don't you know what shutting down the Works means?"

"Yes, indeed I do, Silas," said his wife tenderly.

"Well, then!" He rose, leaving his supper untasted, and went into the sitting-room, where she presently found him, with that everlasting confusion of papers before him on the desk. That made her think of the paper in her work-basket, and she decided not to make the careworn, distracted man ask her for it, after all. She brought it to him.

He glanced blankly at it and then caught it from her, turning red and looking foolish. "Where'd you get that?"

"You dropped it on the floor the other night, and I picked it up. Who is 'Wm. M.'?"

"'Wm. M.'?" he repeated, looking confusedly at her, and then at the paper. "Oh,—it's nothing." He tore the paper into small pieces, and went and dropped them into the fire. When Mrs. Lapham came into the room in the morning, before he was down, she found a scrap of the paper, which must have fluttered to the hearth; and glancing at it she saw that the words were "Mrs. M." She wondered what dealings with a woman her husband could have, and she remembered the confusion he had shown about the paper, and which she had thought was because she had surprised one of his business secrets. She was still thinking of it when he came down to breakfast, heavy-eyed, tremulous, with deep seams and wrinkles in his face.

After a silence which he did not seem inclined to break, "Silas," she asked, "who is 'Mrs. M.'?"

He stared at her. "I don't know what you're talking about."

"Don't you?" she returned mockingly. "When you do, you tell me. Do you want any more coffee?"

"No."

"Well, then, you can ring for Alice when you've finished. I've got some things to attend to." She rose abruptly, and left the room. Lapham looked after her in a dull way, and then went on with his breakfast. While he still sat at his coffee, she flung into the room again, and dashed some papers down beside his plate. "Here are some more things of yours, and I'll thank you to lock them up in your desk and not litter my room with them, if you please." Now he saw that she was angry, and it must be with him. It enraged him that in such a time of trouble she should fly out at him in that way. He left the house without trying to speak to her.

That day Corey came just before closing, and, knocking at Lapham's door, asked if he could speak with him a few moments.

"Yes," said Lapham, wheeling round in his swivel-chair and kicking another towards Corey. "Sit down. I want to talk to you. I'd ought to tell you you're wasting your time here. I spoke the other day about your placin' yourself better, and I can help you to do it, yet. There ain't going to be the outcome for the paint in the foreign markets that we expected, and I guess you better give it up."

"I don't wish to give it up," said the young fellow, setting his lips. "I've as much faith in it as ever; and I want to propose now what I hinted at in the first place. I want to put some money into the business."

"Some money!" Lapham leaned towards him, and frowned

as if he had not quite understood, while he clutched the arms of his chair.

"I've got about thirty thousand dollars that I could put in, and if you don't want to consider me a partner—I remember that you objected to a partner—you can let me regard it as an investment. But I think I see the way to doing something at once in Mexico, and I should like to feel that I had something more than a drummer's interest in the venture."

The men sat looking into each other's eyes. Then Lapham leaned back in his chair, and rubbed his hand hard and slowly over his face. His features were still twisted with some strong emotion when he took it away. "Your family know about this?"

"My uncle James knows."

"He thinks it would be a good plan for you?"

"He thought that by this time I ought to be able to trust my own judgment."

"Do you suppose I could see your uncle at his office?"

"I imagine he's there."

"Well, I want to have a talk with him, one of these days." He sat pondering awhile, and then rose, and went with Corey to his door. "I guess I sha'n't change my mind about taking you into the business in that way," he said coldly. "If there was any reason why I shouldn't at first, there's more now."

"Very well, sir," answered the young man, and went to close his desk. The outer office was empty; but while Corey was putting his papers in order it was suddenly invaded by two women, who pushed by the protesting porter on the stairs and made their way towards Lapham's room. One of them was Miss Dewey, the type-writer girl, and the other was a woman whom she would resemble in face and figure twenty years hence, if she led a life of hard work varied by paroxysms of hard drinking.

"That his room, Z'rilla?" asked this woman, pointing towards Lapham's door with a hand that had not freed itself from the fringe of dirty shawl under which it had hung. She went forward without waiting for the answer, but before she could reach it the door opened, and Lapham stood filling its space.

"Look here, Colonel Lapham!" began the woman, in a

high key of challenge. "I want to know if this is the way you're goin' back on me and Z'rilla?"

"What do you want?" asked Lapham.

"What do I want? What do you s'pose I want? I want the money to pay my month's rent; there ain't a bite to eat in the house; and I want some money to market."

Lapham bent a frown on the woman, under which she shrank back a step. "You've taken the wrong way to get it. Clear out!"

"I *won't* clear out!" said the woman, beginning to whimper.

"Corey!" said Lapham, in the peremptory voice of a master,—he had seemed so indifferent to Corey's presence that the young man thought he must have forgotten he was there,—"is Dennis anywhere round?"

"Yissor," said Dennis, answering for himself from the head of the stairs, and appearing in the warcroom.

Lapham spoke to the woman again. "Do you want I should call a hack, or do you want I should call an officer?"

The woman began to cry into an end of her shawl. "*I* don't know what we're goin' to do."

"You're going to clear out," said Lapham. "Call a hack, Dennis. If you ever come here again, I'll have you arrested. Mind that! Zerrilla, I shall want you early to-morrow morning."

"Yes, sir," said the girl meekly; she and her mother shrank out after the porter.

Lapham shut his door without a word.

At lunch the next day Walker made himself amends for Corey's reticence by talking a great deal. He talked about Lapham, who seemed to have, more than ever since his apparent difficulties began, the fascination of an enigma for his book-keeper, and he ended by asking, "Did you see that little circus last night?"

"What little circus?" asked Corey in his turn.

"Those two women and the old man. Dennis told me about it. I told him if he liked his place he'd better keep his mouth shut."

"That was very good advice," said Corey.

"Oh, all right, if you don't want to talk. Don't know as I should in your place," returned Walker, in the easy security he had long felt that Corey had no intention of putting on airs with him. "But I'll tell you what: the old man can't expect it of everybody. If he keeps this thing up much longer, it's going to be talked about. You can't have a woman walking into your place of business, and trying to bulldoze you before your porter, without setting your porter to thinking. And the last thing you want a porter to do is to think; for when a porter thinks, he thinks wrong."

"I don't see why even a porter couldn't think right about that affair," replied Corey. "I don't know who the woman was, though I believe she was Miss Dewey's mother; but I couldn't see that Colonel Lapham showed anything but a natural resentment of her coming to him in that way. I should have said she was some rather worthless person whom he'd been befriending, and that she had presumed upon his kindness."

"Is that so? What do you think of his never letting Miss Dewey's name go on the books?"

"That it's another proof it's a sort of charity of his. That's the only way to look at it."

"Oh, *I'm* all right." Walker lighted a cigar and began to smoke, with his eyes closed to a fine straight line. "It won't do for a book-keeper to think wrong, any more than a porter, I suppose. But I guess you and I don't think very different about this thing."

"Not if you think as I do," replied Corey steadily; "and I know you would do that if you had seen the 'circus' yourself. A man doesn't treat people who have a disgraceful hold upon him as he treated them."

"It depends upon who he is," said Walker, taking his cigar from his mouth. "I never said the old man was afraid of anything."

"And character," continued Corey, disdaining to touch the matter further, except in generalities, "must go for something. If it's to be the prey of mere accident and appearance, then it goes for nothing."

"Accidents will happen in the best-regulated families," said Walker, with vulgar, good-humored obtuseness that filled Corey with indignation. Nothing, perhaps, removed his matter-of-fact nature farther from the common-place than a certain generosity of instinct, which I should not be ready to say was always infallible.

That evening it was Miss Dewey's turn to wait for speech with Lapham after the others were gone. He opened his door at her knock, and stood looking at her with a worried air. "Well, what do you want, Zerrilla?" he asked, with a sort of rough kindness.

"I want to know what I'm going to do about Hen. He's back again; and he and mother have made it up, and they both got to drinking last night after I went home, and carried on so that the neighbors came in."

Lapham passed his hand over his red and heated face. "I don't know what I'm going to do. You're twice the trouble that my own family is, now. But I know what I'd do, mighty quick, if it wasn't for you, Zerrilla," he went on relentingly. "I'd shut your mother up somewheres, and if I could get that fellow off for a three years' voyage——"

"I declare," said Miss Dewey, beginning to whimper, "it seems as if he came back just so often to spite me. He's never gone more than a year at the furthest, and you can't make it out habitual drunkenness, either, when it's just sprees. I'm at my wit's end."

"Oh, well, you mustn't cry around here," said Lapham soothingly.

"I know it," said Miss Dewey. "If I could get rid of Hen, I could manage well enough with mother. Mr. Wemmel would marry me if I could get the divorce. He's said so over and over again."

"I don't know as I like that very well," said Lapham, frowning. "I don't know as I want you should get married in any hurry again. I don't know as I like your going with anybody else just yet."

"Oh, you needn't be afraid but what it'll be all right. It'll be the best thing all round, if I can marry him."

"Well!" said Lapham impatiently; "I can't think about it now. I suppose they've cleaned everything out again?"

"Yes, they have," said Zerrilla; "there isn't a cent left."

"You're a pretty expensive lot," said Lapham. "Well, here!" He took out his pocket-book and gave her a note. "I'll be round to-night and see what can be done."

He shut himself into his room again, and Zerrilla dried her tears, put the note into her bosom, and went her way.

Lapham kept the porter nearly an hour later. It was then six o'clock, the hour at which the Laphams usually had tea; but all custom had been broken up with him during the past months, and he did not go home now. He determined, perhaps in the extremity in which a man finds relief in combating one care with another, to keep his promise to Miss Dewey, and at the moment when he might otherwise have been sitting down at his own table he was climbing the stairs to her lodging in the old-fashioned dwelling which had been portioned off into flats. It was in a region of depots, and of the cheap hotels, and "ladies' and gents' " dining-rooms, and restaurants with bars, which abound near depots; and Lapham followed to Miss Dewey's door a waiter from one of these, who bore on a salver before him a supper covered with a napkin. Zerrilla had admitted them, and at her greeting a young fellow in the shabby shore-suit of a sailor, buttoning imperfectly over the nautical blue flannel of his shirt, got up from where he had been sitting, on one side of the stove, and stood infirmly on his feet, in token of receiving the visitor. The woman who sat on the other side did not rise, but began a shrill, defiant apology.

"Well, I don't suppose but what you'll think we're livin' on the fat o' the land, right straight along, all the while. But it's just like this. When that child came in from her work, she didn't seem to have the spirit to go to cookin' anything, and I had such a bad night last night I was feelin' all broke up, and s'd I, what's the use, anyway? By the time the butcher's heaved in a lot o' bone, and made you pay for the suet he cuts away, it comes to the same thing, and why not *git* it from the rest'rant first off, and save the cost o' your fire? s'd I."

"What have you got there under your apron? A bottle?" demanded Lapham, who stood with his hat on and his hands in his pockets, indifferent alike to the ineffective reception of the sailor and the chair Zerrilla had set him.

"Well, yes, it's a bottle," said the woman, with an assumption of virtuous frankness. "It's whisky; I got to have *some*thing to rub my rheumatism with."

"Humph!" grumbled Lapham. "You've been rubbing *his* rheumatism too, I see."

He twisted his head in the direction of the sailor, now softly and rhythmically waving to and fro on his feet.

"He hain't had a drop to-day in *this* house!" cried the woman.

"What are you doing around here?" said Lapham, turning fiercely upon him. "You've got no business ashore. Where's your ship? Do you think I'm going to let you come here and eat your wife out of house and home, and then give money to keep the concern going?"

"Just the very words I said when he first showed his face here, yist'day. Didn't I, Z'rilla?" said the woman, eagerly joining in the rebuke of her late boon companion. "You got no business here, Hen, s'd I. You can't come here to live on me and Z'rilla, s'd I. You want to go back to your ship, s'd I. That's what I said."

The sailor mumbled, with a smile of tipsy amiability for Lapham, something about the crew being discharged.

"Yes," the woman broke in, "that's always the way with these coasters. Why don't you go off on some them long v'y'ges? s'd I. It's pretty hard, when Mr. Wemmel stands ready to marry Z'rilla and provide a comfortable home for us both,—I hain't got a great many years more to live, and I *should* like to get some satisfaction out of 'em and not be beholden and dependent all my days,—to have Hen, here, blockin' the way. I tell him there'd be more money for him in the end; but he can't seem to make up his mind to it."

"Well, now, look here," said Lapham. "I don't care anything about all that. It's your own business, and I'm not going to meddle with it. But it's my business who lives off me; and so I tell you all three, I'm willing to take care of Zerrilla, and I'm willing to take care of her mother——"

"I guess if it hadn't been for that child's father," the mother interpolated, "you wouldn't been here to tell the tale, Colonel Lapham."

"I know all about that," said Lapham. "But I'll tell you what, Mr. Dewey, I'm not going to support *you*."

"I don't see what Hen's done," said the old woman, impartially.

"He hasn't done anything, and I'm going to stop it. He's got to get a ship, and he's got to get out of this. And Zerrilla needn't come back to work till he does. I'm done with you all."

"Well, I vow," said the mother, "if I ever heard anything like it! Didn't that child's father lay down his life for you? Hain't you said it yourself a hundred times? And don't she work for her money, and slave for it mornin', noon, and night? You talk as if we was beholden to you for the very bread in our mouths. I guess if it hadn't been for Jim, you wouldn't been here crowin' over us."

"You mind what I say. I mean business this time," said Lapham, turning to the door.

The woman rose and followed him, with her bottle in her hand. "Say, Colonel! what should you advise Z'rilla to do about Mr. Wemmel? I tell her there ain't any use goin' to the trouble to git a divorce without she's sure about him. Don't you think we'd ought to git him to sign a paper, or something, that he'll marry her if she gits it? I don't like to have things going at loose ends the way they are. It ain't sense. It ain't right."

Lapham made no answer to the mother anxious for her child's future, and concerned for the moral questions involved. He went out and down the stairs, and on the pavement at the lower door he almost struck against Rogers, who had a bag in his hand, and seemed to be hurrying towards one of the depots. He halted a little, as if to speak to Lapham; but Lapham turned his back abruptly upon him, and took the other direction.

The days were going by in a monotony of adversity to him, from which he could no longer escape, even at home. He attempted once or twice to talk of his troubles to his wife, but she repulsed him sharply; she seemed to despise and hate him; but he set himself doggedly to make a confession to her, and he stopped her one night, as she came into the room where he sat—hastily upon some errand that was to take her directly away again.

"Persis, there's something I've got to tell you."

She stood still, as if fixed against her will, to listen.

"I guess you know something about it already, and I guess it's set you against me."

"Oh, I guess not, Colonel Lapham. You go your way, and I go mine. That's all."

She waited for him to speak, listening with a cold, hard smile on her face.

"I don't say it to make favor with you, because I don't want you to spare me, and I don't ask you; but I got into it through Milton K. Rogers."

"Oh!" said Mrs. Lapham contemptuously.

"I always felt the way I said about it—that it wa'n't any better than gambling, and I say so now. It's like betting on the turn of a card; and I give you my word of honor, Persis, that I never was in it at all till that scoundrel began to load me up with those wild-cat securities of his. Then it seemed to me as if I ought to try to do something to get somewhere even. I know it's no excuse; but watching the market to see what the infernal things were worth from day to day, and seeing it go up, and seeing it go down, was too much for me; and, to make a long story short, I began to buy and sell on a margin—just what I told you I never would do. I seemed to make something—I did make something; and I'd have stopped, I do believe, if I could have reached the figure I'd set in my own mind to start with; but I couldn't fetch it. I began to lose, and then I began to throw good money after bad, just as I always did with everything that Rogers ever came within a mile of. Well, what's the use? I lost the money that would have carried me out of this, and I shouldn't have had to shut down the Works, or sell the house, or——"

Lapham stopped. His wife, who at first had listened with mystification, and then dawning incredulity, changing into a look of relief that was almost triumph, lapsed again into severity. "Silas Lapham, if you was to die the next minute, is this what you started to tell me?"

"Why, of course it is. What did you suppose I started to tell you?"

"And—look me in the eyes!—you haven't got anything else on your mind now?"

"No! There's trouble enough, the Lord knows; but there's

nothing else to tell you. I suppose Pen gave you a hint about it. I dropped something to her. I've been feeling bad about it, Persis, a good while, but I hain't had the heart to speak of it. I can't expect you to say you like it. I've been a fool, I'll allow, and I've been something worse, if you choose to say so; but that's all. I haven't hurt anybody but myself—and you and the children."

Mrs. Lapham rose and said, with her face from him, as she turned towards the door, "It's all right, Silas. I sha'n't ever bring it up against you."

She fled out of the room, but all that evening she was very sweet with him, and seemed to wish in all tacit ways to atone for her past unkindness.

She made him talk of his business, and he told her of Corey's offer, and what he had done about it. She did not seem to care for his part in it, however; at which Lapham was silently disappointed a little, for he would have liked her to praise him.

"He did it on account of Pen!"

"Well, he didn't insist upon it, anyway," said Lapham, who must have obscurely expected that Corey would recognize his own magnanimity by repeating his offer. If the doubt that follows a self-devoted action—the question whether it was not after all a needless folly—is mixed, as it was in Lapham's case, with the vague belief that we might have done ourselves a good turn without great risk of hurting any one else by being a little less unselfish, it becomes a regret that is hard to bear. Since Corey spoke to him, some things had happened that gave Lapham hope again.

"I'm going to tell her about it," said his wife, and she showed herself impatient to make up for the time she had lost. "Why didn't you tell me before, Silas?"

"I didn't know we were on speaking terms before," said Lapham sadly.

"Yes, that's true," she admitted, with a conscious flush. "I hope he won't think Pen's known about it all this while."

XXIV

THAT EVENING James Bellingham came to see Corey after dinner, and went to find him in his own room.

"I've come at the instance of Colonel Lapham," said the uncle. "He was at my office to-day, and I had a long talk with him. Did you know that he was in difficulties?"

"I fancied that he was in some sort of trouble. And I had the book keeper's conjectures—he doesn't really know much about it."

"Well, he thinks it time—on all accounts—that you should know how he stands, and why he declined that proposition of yours. I must say he has behaved very well—like a gentleman."

"I'm not surprised."

"I am. It's hard to behave like a gentleman where your interest is vitally concerned. And Lapham doesn't strike me as a man who's in the habit of acting from the best in him always."

"Do any of us?" asked Corey.

"Not all of us, at any rate," said Bellingham. "It must have cost him something to say no to you, for he's just in that state when he believes that this or that chance, however small, would save him."

Corey was silent. "Is he really in such a bad way?"

"It's hard to tell just where he stands. I suspect that a hopeful temperament and fondness for round numbers have always caused him to set his figures beyond his actual worth. I don't say that he's been dishonest about it, but he's had a loose way of estimating his assets; he's reckoned his wealth on the basis of his capital, and some of his capital is borrowed. He's lost heavily by some of the recent failures, and there's been a terrible shrinkage in his values. I don't mean merely in the stock of paint on hand, but in a kind of competition which has become very threatening. You know about that West Virginia paint?"

Corey nodded.

"Well, he tells me that they've struck a vein of natural gas out there which will enable them to make as good a paint as his own at a cost of manufacturing so low that they can undersell him everywhere. If this proves to be the case, it will not only drive his paint out of the market, but will reduce the value of his Works—the whole plant—at Lapham to a merely nominal figure."

"I see," said Corey dejectedly. "I've understood that he had put a great deal of money into his Works."

"Yes, and he estimated his mine there at a high figure. Of course it will be worth little or nothing if the West Virginia paint drives his out. Then, besides, Lapham has been into several things outside of his own business, and, like a good many other men who try outside things, he's kept account of them himself; and he's all mixed up about them. He's asked me to look into his affairs with him, and I've promised to do so. Whether he can be tided over his difficulties remains to be seen. I'm afraid it will take a good deal of money to do it— a great deal more than he thinks, at least. He believes comparatively little would do it. I think differently. I think that anything less than a great deal would be thrown away on him. If it were merely a question of a certain sum—even a large sum—to keep him going, it might be managed; but it's much more complicated. And, as I say, it must have been a trial to him to refuse your offer."

This did not seem to be the way in which Bellingham had meant to conclude. But he said no more; and Corey made him no response.

He remained pondering the case, now hopefully, now doubtfully, and wondering, whatever his mood was, whether Penelope knew anything of the fact with which her mother went nearly at the same moment to acquaint her.

"Of course, he's done it on your account," Mrs. Lapham could not help saying.

"Then he was very silly. Does he think I would have let him give father money? And if father lost it for him, does he suppose it would make it any easier for me? I think father acted twice as well. It was very silly."

In repeating the censure, her look was not so severe as her tone; she even smiled a little, and her mother reported to her father that she acted more like herself than she had yet since Corey's offer.

"I think, if he was to repeat his offer, she would have him now," said Mrs. Lapham.

"Well, I'll let her know if he does," said the Colonel.

"I guess he won't do it to you!" she cried.

"Who else will he do it to?" he demanded.

They perceived that they had each been talking of a different offer.

After Lapham went to his business in the morning the postman brought another letter from Irene, which was full of pleasant things that were happening to her; there was a great deal about her cousin Will, as she called him. At the end she had written, "Tell Pen I don't want she should be foolish."

"There!" said Mrs. Lapham. "I guess it's going to come out right, all round;" and it seemed as if even the Colonel's difficulties were past. "When your father gets through this, Pen," she asked impulsively, "what shall you do?"

"What have you been telling Irene about me?"

"Nothing much. What should you do?"

"It would be a good deal easier to say what I should do if father didn't," said the girl.

"I know you think it was nice in him to make your father that offer," urged the mother.

"It was nice, yes; but it was silly," said the girl. "Most nice things are silly, I suppose," she added.

She went to her room and wrote a letter. It was very long, and very carefully written; and when she read it over, she tore it into small pieces. She wrote another one, short and hurried, and tore that up too. Then she went back to her mother, in the family room, and asked to see Irene's letter, and read it over to herself. "Yes, she seems to be having a good time," she sighed. "Mother, do you think I ought to let Mr. Corey know that I know about it?"

"Well, I should think it would be a pleasure to him," said Mrs. Lapham judicially.

"I'm not so sure of that—the way I should have to tell him. I should begin by giving him a scolding. Of course, he meant well by it, but can't you see that it wasn't very flattering? How did he expect it would change me?"

"I don't believe he ever thought of that."

"Don't you? Why?"

"Because you can see that he isn't one of that kind. He might want to please you without wanting to change you by what he did."

"Yes. He must have known that nothing would change me,—at least, nothing that he could do. I thought of that. I shouldn't like him to feel that I couldn't appreciate it, even if I did think it was silly. Should you write to him?"

"I don't see why not."

"It would be too pointed. No, I shall just let it go. I wish he hadn't done it."

"Well, he has done it."

"And I've tried to write to him about it—two letters: one so humble and grateful that it couldn't stand up on its edge, and the other so pert and flippant. Mother, I wish you could have seen those two letters! I wish I had kept them to look at if I ever got to thinking I had any sense again. They would take the conceit out of me."

"What's the reason he don't come here any more?"

"Doesn't he come?" asked Penelope in turn, as if it were something she had not noticed particularly.

"You'd ought to know."

"Yes." She sat silent awhile. "If he doesn't come, I suppose it's because he's offended at something I did."

"What did you do?"

"Nothing. I—wrote to him—a little while ago. I suppose it was very blunt, but I didn't believe he would be angry at it. But this—this that he's done shows he was angry, and that he wasn't just seizing the first chance to get out of it."

"What have you done, Pen?" demanded her mother sharply.

"Oh, I don't know. All the mischief in the world, I suppose. I'll tell you. When you first told me that father was in trouble with his business, I wrote to him not to come any more till I let him. I said I couldn't tell him why, and he hasn't been here since. I'm sure *I* don't know what it means."

Her mother looked at her with angry severity. "Well, Penelope Lapham! For a sensible child, you *are* the greatest goose I ever saw. Did you think he would come here and *see* if you wouldn't let him come?"

"He might have written," urged the girl.

Her mother made that despairing "Tchk!" with her tongue, and fell back in her chair. "I should have *despised* him if he had written. He's acted just exactly right, and you—you've acted—I don't know *how* you've acted. I'm ashamed of you. A girl that could be so sensible for her sister, and always say and do just the right thing, and then when it comes to herself to be such a *disgusting* simpleton!"

"I thought I ought to break with him at once, and not let him suppose that there was any hope for him or me if father was poor. It was my one chance, in this whole business, to do anything heroic, and I jumped at it. You mustn't think, because I can laugh at it now, that I wasn't in earnest, mother! I *was*—dead! But the Colonel has gone to ruin so gradually, that he's spoilt everything. I expected that he would be bankrupt the next day, and that then *he* would understand what I meant. But to have it drag along for a fortnight seems to take all the heroism out of it, and leave it as flat!" She looked at her mother with a smile that shone through her tears, and a pathos that quivered round her jesting lips. "It's easy enough to be sensible for other people. But when it comes to myself, there I am! Especially, when I want to do what I oughtn't so much that it seems as if doing what I didn't want to do *must* be doing what I ought! But it's been a great success one way, mother. It's helped me to keep up before the Colonel. If it hadn't been for Mr. Corey's staying away, and my feeling so indignant with him for having been badly treated by me, I shouldn't have been worth anything at all."

The tears started down her cheeks, but her mother said, "Well, now, go along, and write to him. It don't matter what you say, much; and don't be so very particular."

Her third attempt at a letter pleased her scarcely better than the rest, but she sent it, though it seemed so blunt and awkward. She wrote:

DEAR FRIEND:

I expected when I sent you that note, that you would

understand, almost the next day, why I could not see you any more. You must know now, and you must not think that if anything happened to my father, I should wish you to help him. But that is no reason why I should not thank you, and I do thank you, for offering. It was like you, I will say that.

Yours sincerely, PENELOPE LAPHAM.

She posted her letter, and he sent his reply in the evening, by hand:

DEAREST:

What I did was nothing, till you praised it. Everything I have and am is yours. Won't you send a line by the bearer, to say that I may come to see you? I know how you feel; but I am sure that I can make you think differently. You must consider that I loved you without a thought of your father's circumstances, and always shall.

T. C.

The generous words were blurred to her eyes by the tears that sprang into them. But she could only write in answer:

"Please do not come; I have made up my mind. As long as this trouble is hanging over us, I cannot see you. And if father is unfortunate, all is over between us."

She brought his letter to her mother, and told her what she had written in reply. Her mother was thoughtful awhile before she said, with a sigh, "Well, I hope you've begun as you can carry out, Pen."

"Oh, I shall not have to carry out at all. I shall not have to do anything. That's one comfort—the only comfort." She went away to her own room, and when Mrs. Lapham told her husband of the affair, he was silent at first, as she had been. Then he said, "I don't know as I should have wanted her to done differently; I don't know as she could. If I ever come right again, she won't have anything to feel meeching about; and if I don't, I don't want she should be beholden to anybody. And I guess that's the way she feels."

The Coreys in their turn sat in judgment on the fact which their son felt bound to bring to their knowledge.

"She has behaved very well," said Mrs. Corey, to whom her son had spoken.

"My dear," said her husband, with his laugh, "she has behaved *too* well. If she had studied the whole situation with the most artful eye to its mastery, she could not possibly have behaved better."

The process of Lapham's financial disintegration was like the course of some chronic disorder, which has fastened itself upon the constitution, but advances with continual reliefs, with apparent amelioration, and at times seems not to advance at all, when it gives hope of final recovery not only to the sufferer, but to the eye of science itself. There were moments when James Bellingham, seeing Lapham pass this crisis and that, began to fancy that he might pull through altogether; and at these moments, when his adviser could not oppose anything but experience and probability to the evidence of the fact, Lapham was buoyant with courage, and imparted his hopefulness to his household. Our theory of disaster, of sorrow, of affliction, borrowed from the poets and novelists, is that it is incessant; but every passage in our own lives and in the lives of others, so far as we have witnessed them, teaches us that this is false. The house of mourning is decorously darkened to the world, but within itself it is also the house of laughing. Bursts of gayety, as heartfelt as its grief, relieve the gloom, and the stricken survivors have their jests together, in which the thought of the dead is tenderly involved, and a fond sense, not crazier than many others, of sympathy and enjoyment beyond the silence, justifies the sunnier mood before sorrow rushes back, deploring and despairing, and making it all up again with the conventional fitness of things. Lapham's adversity had this quality in common with bereavement. It was not always like the adversity we figure in allegory; it had its moments of being like prosperity, and if upon the whole it was continual, it was not incessant. Sometimes there was a week of repeated reverses, when he had to keep his teeth set and to hold on hard to all his hopefulness; and then days came of negative result or slight success, when he was full of his jokes at the tea-table, and wanted to go to the theater, or to do something to cheer Penelope up. In some miraculous way, by some enormous stroke of success which should eclipse the brightest of his past prosperity, he expected to do what would reconcile all difficulties, not only in his own affairs, but in hers too. "You'll see," he said to his wife; "it's going to come out all right. Irene'll fix it up with Bill's boy, and then she'll be off Pen's mind; and if things go on as they've been going for the last two days, I'm going to be in a position to do the favors myself, and Pen can feel that *she's* makin' a sacrifice, and then I guess may be she'll do it. If things turn out as I expect now, and times ever *do* get any better generally, I can show Corey that I appreciate his offer. I can offer him the partnership myself then."

Even in the other moods, which came when everything had been going wrong, and there seemed no way out of the net, there were points of consolation to Lapham and his wife. They rejoiced that Irene was safe beyond the range of their anxieties, and they had a proud satisfaction that there had been no engagement between Corey and Penelope, and that it was she who had forbidden it. In the closeness of interest and sympathy in which their troubles had reunited them, they confessed to each other that nothing would have been more galling to their pride than the idea that Lapham should not have been able to do everything for his daughter that the Coreys might have expected. Whatever happened now, the Coreys could not have it to say that the Laphams had tried to bring any such thing about.

Bellingham had lately suggested an assignment to Lapham, as the best way out of his difficulties. It was evident that he had not the money to meet his liabilities at present, and that he could not raise it without ruinous sacrifices, that might still end in ruin after all. If he made the assignment, Bellingham argued, he could gain time and make terms; the state of things generally would probably improve, since it could not be worse, and the market, which he had glutted with his paint, might recover and he could start again. Lapham had not agreed with him. When his reverses first began, it had seemed easy for him to give up everything, to let the people he owed take all, so only they would let him go out with clean hands; and he had dramatized this feeling in his talk with his wife, when they spoke together of the mills on the G. L. & P. But ever since then it had been growing harder, and he could not consent even to seem to do it now in the proposed assignment. He had not found other men so very liberal or faithful with him; a good many of them appeared to have combined to hunt him down; a sense of enmity towards all his creditors asserted itself in him; he asked himself why they should not suffer a little too. Above all, he shrank from the publicity of the assignment. It was open confession that he had been a fool in some way; he could not bear to have his family—his brother the judge, especially, to whom he had always appeared the soul of business wisdom—think him imprudent or stupid. He would make any sacrifice before it came to that. He determined in parting with Bellingham to make the sacrifice which he had oftenest in his mind, because it was the hardest, and to sell his new house. That would cause the least comment. Most people would simply think that he had got a splendid offer, and with his usual luck had made a very good thing of it; others who knew a little more about him would say that he was hauling in his horns, but they could not blame him; a great many other men were doing the same in those hard times—the shrewdest and safest men; it might even have a good effect.

He went straight from Bellingham's office to the real-estate broker in whose hands he meant to put his house, for he was not the sort of man to shilly-shally when he had once made up his mind. But he found it hard to get his voice up out of his throat, when he said he guessed he would get the broker to sell that new house of his on the water side of Beacon. The broker answered cheerfully, yes; he supposed Colonel Lapham knew it was a pretty dull time in real estate? and Lapham said yes, he knew that, but he should not sell at a sacrifice, and he did not care to have the broker name him or describe the house definitely unless parties meant business. Again the broker said yes; and he added, as a joke Lapham would appreciate, that he had half a dozen houses on the water side of Beacon on the same terms; that nobody wanted to be named or to have his property described.

It did, in fact, comfort Lapham a little to find himself in the same boat with so many others; he smiled grimly, and said in his turn, yes, he guessed that was about the size of it with a good many people. But he had not the heart to tell his

wife what he had done, and he sat taciturn that whole evening, without even going over his accounts, and went early
to bed, where he lay tossing half the night before he fell
asleep. He slept at last only upon the promise he made himself that he would withdraw the house from the broker's
hands; but he went heavily to his own business in the morning without doing so. There was no such rush, anyhow, he
reflected bitterly; there would be time to do that a month
later, probably.

It struck him with a sort of dismay when a boy came with
a note from the broker, saying that a party who had been
over the house in the fall had come to him to know whether
it could be bought, and was willing to pay the cost of the
house up to the time he had seen it. Lapham took refuge in
trying to think who the party could be; he concluded that it
must have been somebody who had gone over it with the
architect, and he did not like that; but he was aware that this
was not an answer to the broker, and he wrote that he would
give him an answer in the morning.

Now that it had come to the point, it did not seem to him
that he could part with the house. So much of his hope for
himself and his children had gone into it that the thought of
selling it made him tremulous and sick. He could not keep
about his work steadily, and with his nerves shaken by want
of sleep, and the shock of this sudden and unexpected question, he left his office early, and went over to look at the
house and try to bring himself to some conclusion there. The
long procession of lamps on the beautiful street was flaring in
the clear red of the sunset towards which it marched, and
Lapham, with a lump in his throat, stopped in front of his
house and looked at their multitude. They were not merely a
part of the landscape; they were a part of his pride and glory,
his success, his triumphant life's work which was fading into
failure in his helpless hands. He ground his teeth to keep
down that lump, but the moisture in his eyes blurred the
lamps, and the keen, pale crimson against which it made them
flicker. He turned and looked up, as he had so often done, at
the window-spaces, neatly glazed for the winter with white
linen, and recalled the night when he had stopped with Irene
before the house, and she had said that she should never live

there, and he had tried to coax her into courage about it. There was no such façade as that on the whole street, to his thinking. Through his long talks with the architect, he had come to feel almost as intimately and fondly as the architect himself the satisfying simplicity of the whole design and the delicacy of its detail. It appealed to him as an exquisite bit of harmony appeals to the unlearned ear, and he recognized the difference between this fine work and the obstreperous pretentiousness of the many overloaded house-fronts which Seymour had made him notice for his instruction elsewhere on the Back Bay. Now, in the depths of his gloom, he tried to think what Italian city it was where Seymour said he had first got the notion of treating brickwork in that way.

He unlocked the temporary door with the key he always carried, so that he could let himself in and out whenever he liked, and entered the house, dim and very cold with the accumulated frigidity of the whole winter in it, and looking as if the arrest of work upon it had taken place a thousand years before. It smelt of the unpainted woods and the clean, hard surfaces of the plaster, where the experiments in decoration had left it untouched; and mingled with these odors was that of some rank pigments and metallic compositions which Seymour had used in trying to realize a certain daring novelty of finish, which had not proved successful. Above all, Lapham detected the peculiar odor of his own paint, with which the architect had been greatly interested one day, when Lapham showed it to him at the office. He had asked Lapham to let him try the Persis Brand in realizing a little idea he had for the finish of Mrs. Lapham's room. If it succeeded, they could tell her what it was, for a surprise.

Lapham glanced at the bay-window in the reception-room, where he sat with his girls on the trestles when Corey first came by; and then he explored the whole house to the attic, in the light faintly admitted through the linen sashes. The floors were strewn with shavings and chips which the carpenters had left, and in the music-room these had been blown into long irregular windrows by the draughts through a wide rent in the linen sash. Lapham tried to pin it up, but failed, and stood looking out of it over the water. The ice had left the river, and the low tide lay smooth and red in the light of the sunset. The Cambridge flats showed the sad, sodden yellow of meadows stripped bare after a long sleep under snow; the hills, the naked trees, the spires and roofs had a black outline, as if they were objects in a landscape of the French school.

The whim seized Lapham to test the chimney in the music-room; it had been tried in the dining-room below, and in his girls' fire-places above, but here the hearth was still clean. He gathered some shavings and blocks together, and kindled them, and as the flame mounted gayly from them, he pulled up a nail-keg which he found there and sat down to watch it. Nothing could have been better; the chimney was a perfect success; and as Lapham glanced out of the torn linen sash he said to himself that that party, whoever he was, who had offered to buy his house might go to the devil; he would never sell it as long as he had a dollar. He said that he should pull through yet; and it suddenly came into his mind that, if he could raise the money to buy out those West Virginia fellows, he should be all right, and would have the whole game in his own hand. He slapped himself on the thigh, and wondered that he had never thought of that before; and then, lighting a cigar with a splinter from the fire, he sat down again to work the scheme out in his own mind.

He did not hear the feet heavily stamping up the stairs, and coming towards the room where he sat; and the policeman to whom the feet belonged had to call out to him, smoking at his chimney-corner, with his back turned to the door, "Hello! what are you doing here?"

"What's that to you?" retorted Lapham, wheeling half round on his nail-keg.

"I'll show you," said the officer, advancing upon him, and then stopping short as he recognized him. "Why, Colonel Lapham! I thought it was some tramp got in here!"

"Have a cigar?" said Lapham hospitably. "Sorry there ain't another nail-keg."

The officer took the cigar. "I'll smoke it outside. I've just come on, and I can't stop. Tryin' your chimney?"

"Yes, I thought I'd see how it would draw, in here. It seems to go first-rate."

The policeman looked about him with an eye of inspection. "You want to get that linen window, there, mended up."

"Yes, I'll speak to the builder about that. It can go for one night."

The policeman went to the window and failed to pin the linen together where Lapham had failed before. "*I* can't fix it." He looked round once more, and saying, "Well, good-night," went out and down the stairs.

Lapham remained by the fire till he had smoked his cigar; then he rose and stamped upon the embers that still burned with his heavy boots, and went home. He was very cheerful at supper. He told his wife that he guessed he had a sure thing of it now, and in another twenty-four hours he should tell her just how. He made Penelope go to the theater with him, and when they came out, after the play, the night was so fine that he said they must walk round by the new house and take a look at it in the starlight. He said he had been there before he came home, and tried Seymour's chimney in the music-room, and it worked like a charm.

As they drew near Beacon street they were aware of unwonted stir and tumult, and presently the still air transmitted a turmoil of sound, through which a powerful and incessant throbbing made itself felt. The sky had reddened above them, and turning the corner at the Public Garden, they saw a black mass of people obstructing the perspective of the brightly-lighted street, and out of this mass a half dozen engines, whose strong heart-beats had already reached them, sent up volumes of fire-tinged smoke and steam from their funnels. Ladders were planted against the façade of a building, from the roof of which a mass of flame burnt smoothly upward, except where here and there it seemed to pull contemptuously away from the heavy streams of water which the firemen, clinging like great beetles to their ladders, poured in upon it.

Lapham had no need to walk down through the crowd, gazing and gossiping, with shouts and cries and hysterical laughter, before the burning house, to make sure that it was his.

"I guess I done it, Pen," was all he said.

Among the people who were looking at it were a party

who seemed to have run out from dinner in some neighboring house; the ladies were fantastically wrapped up, as if they had flung on the first things they could seize.

"Isn't it perfectly magnificent!" cried a pretty girl. "I wouldn't have missed it on any account. Thank you *so* much, Mr. Symington, for bringing us out!"

"Ah, I thought you'd like it," said this Mr. Symington, who must have been the host; "and you can enjoy it without the least compunction, Miss Delano, for I happen to know that the house belongs to a man who could afford to burn one up for you once a year."

"Oh, do you think he would, if I came again?"

"I haven't the least doubt of it. We don't do things by halves in Boston."

"He ought to have had a coat of his non-combustible paint on it," said another gentleman of the party.

Penelope pulled her father away toward the first carriage she could reach of a number that had driven up. "Here, father! get into this."

"No, no; I couldn't ride," he answered heavily, and he walked home in silence. He greeted his wife with, "Well, Persis, our house is gone! And I guess I set it on fire myself;" and while he rummaged among the papers in his desk, still with his coat and hat on, his wife got the facts as she could from Penelope. She did not reproach him. Here was a case in which his self-reproach must be sufficiently sharp without any edge from her. Besides, her mind was full of a terrible thought.

"Oh, Silas," she faltered, "they'll think you set it on fire to get the insurance!"

Lapham was staring at a paper which he held in his hand. "I had a builder's risk on it, but it expired last week. It's a dead loss."

"Oh, thank the merciful Lord!" cried his wife.

"Merciful!" said Lapham. "Well, it's a queer way of showing it."

He went to bed, and fell into the deep sleep which sometimes follows a great moral shock. It was perhaps rather a torpor than a sleep.

XXV

LAPHAM awoke confused, and in a kind of remoteness from the loss of the night before, through which it loomed mistily. But before he lifted his head from the pillow, it gathered substance and weight against which it needed all his will to bear up and live. In that moment he wished that he had not wakened, that he might never have wakened; but he rose, and faced the day and its cares.

The morning papers brought the report of the fire, and the conjectured loss. The reporters somehow had found out the fact that the loss fell entirely upon Lapham; they lighted up the hackneyed character of their statements with the picturesque interest of the coincidence that the policy had expired only the week before; heaven knows how they knew it. They said that nothing remained of the building but the walls; and Lapham, on his way to business, walked up past the smoke-stained shell. The windows looked like the eye-sockets of a skull down upon the blackened and trampled snow of the street; the pavement was a sheet of ice, and the water from the engines had frozen, like streams of tears, down the face of the house, and hung in icy tags from the window-sills and copings.

He gathered himself up as well as he could, and went on to his office. The chance of retrieval that had flashed upon him, as he sat smoking by that ruined hearth the evening before, stood him in such stead now as a sole hope may; and he said to himself that, having resolved not to sell his house, he was no more crippled by its loss than he would have been by letting his money lie idle in it; what he might have raised by mortgage on it could be made up in some other way; and if they would sell, he could still buy out the whole business of that West Virginia company, mines, plant, stock on hand, good-will, and everything, and unite it with his own. He went early in the afternoon to see Bellingham, whose expressions of condolence for his loss he cut short with as much politeness as he knew how to throw into his impatience. Bellingham seemed at first a little dazzled with the splendid courage of his scheme; it was certainly fine in its way; but then he began to have his misgivings.

"I happen to know that they haven't got much money behind them," urged Lapham. "They'll jump at an offer."

Bellingham shook his head. "If they can show profit on the old manufacture, and prove they can make their paint still cheaper and better hereafter, they can have all the money they want. And it will be very difficult for you to raise it if you're threatened by them. With that competition, you know what your plant at Lapham would be worth, and what the shrinkage on your manufactured stock would be. Better sell out to them," he concluded, "if they will buy."

"There ain't money enough in this country to buy out my paint," said Lapham, buttoning up his coat in a quiver of resentment. "Good-afternoon, sir." Men are but grown-up boys, after all. Bellingham watched this perversely proud and obstinate child fling petulantly out of his door, and felt a sympathy for him which was as truly kind as it was helpless.

But Lapham was beginning to see through Bellingham, as he believed. Bellingham was, in his way, part of that conspiracy by which Lapham's creditors were trying to drive him to the wall. More than ever now he was glad that he had nothing to do with that cold-hearted, self-conceited race, and that the favors so far were all from his side. He was more than ever determined to show them, every one of them, high and low, that he and his children could get along without them, and prosper and triumph without them. He said to himself that if Penelope were engaged to Corey that very minute, he would make her break with him.

He knew what he should do now, and he was going to do it without loss of time. He was going on to New York to see those West Virginia people; they had their principal office there, and he intended to get at their ideas, and then he intended to make them an offer. He managed this business better than could possibly have been expected of a man in his impassioned mood. But when it came really to business, his practical instincts, alert and wary, came to his aid against the passions that lay in wait to betray after they ceased to dominate him. He found the West Virginians full of zeal and hope, but in ten minutes he knew that they had not yet tested their strength in the money market, and had not ascertained how much or how little capital they could command. Lapham himself, if he had had so much, would not have hesitated to put a million dollars into their business. He saw, as they did not see, that they had the game in their own hands, and that if they could raise the money to extend their business, they could ruin him. It was only a question of time, and he was on the ground first. He frankly proposed a union of their interests. He admitted that they had a good thing, and that he should have to fight them hard; but he meant to fight them to the death unless they could come to some sort of terms. Now, the question was whether they had better go on and make a heavy loss for both sides by competition, or whether they had better form a partnership to run both paints and command the whole market. Lapham made them three propositions, each of which was fair and open: to sell out to them altogether; to buy them out altogether; to join facilities and forces with them, and go on in an invulnerable alliance. Let them name a figure at which they would buy, a figure at which they would sell, a figure at which they would combine,—or, in other words, the amount of capital they needed.

They talked all day, going out to lunch together at the Astor House, and sitting with their knees against the counter on a row of stools before it for fifteen minutes of reflection and deglutition, with their hats on, and then returning to the basement from which they emerged. The West Virginia company's name was lettered in gilt on the wide low window, and its paint, in the form of ore, burnt, and mixed, formed a display on the window shelf. Lapham examined it and praised it; from time to time they all recurred to it together; they sent out for some of Lapham's paint and compared it, the West Virginians admitting its former superiority. They were young fellows, and country persons, like Lapham, by origin, and they looked out with the same amused, undaunted, provincial eyes at the myriad metropolitan legs passing on the pavement above the level of their window. He got on well with them. At last, they said what they would do. They said it was nonsense to talk of buying Lapham out, for they had not the money; and as for selling out, they would not do it, for they knew they had a big thing. But they would as soon use his capital to develop it as anybody else's, and if he could put in a certain sum for this purpose, they would go in with him. He should run the works at Lapham and manage the business in Boston, and they would run the works at Kanawha Falls and manage the business in New York. The two brothers with whom Lapham talked named their figure, subject to the approval of another brother at Kanawha Falls, to whom they would write, and who would telegraph his answer, so that Lapham could have it inside of three days. But they felt perfectly sure that he would approve; and Lapham started back on the eleven o'clock train with an elation that gradually left him as he drew near Boston, where the difficulties of raising this sum were to be overcome. It seemed to him, then, that those fellows had put it up on him pretty steep, but he owned to himself that they had a sure thing, and that they were right in believing they could raise the same sum elsewhere; it would take all of it, he admitted, to make their paint pay on the scale they had the right to expect. At their age, he would not have done differently; but when he emerged, old, sore, and sleep-broken, from the sleeping-car in the Albany depot at Boston, he wished with a pathetic self-pity that they knew how a man felt at his age. A year ago, six months ago, he would have laughed at the notion that it would be hard to raise the money. But he thought ruefully of that immense stock of paint on hand, which was now a drug in the market, of his losses by Rogers and by the failures of other men, of the fire that had licked up so many thousands in a few hours; he thought with bitterness of the tens of thousands that he had gambled away in stocks, and of the commissions that the brokers had pocketed whether he won or lost; and he could not think of any securities on which he could borrow, except his house in Nankeen Square, or the mine and works at Lapham. He set his teeth in helpless rage when he thought of that property out on the G. L. & P., that ought to be worth so much, and was worth so little if the road chose to say so.

He did not go home, but spent most of the day shinning round, as he would have expressed it, and trying to see if he could raise the money. But he found that people of whom he hoped to get it were in the conspiracy which had been formed to drive him to the wall. Somehow, there seemed a sense of his embarrassments abroad. Nobody wanted to lend money on the plant at Lapham without taking time to look into the state of the business; but Lapham had no time to give, and he knew that the state of the business would not bear looking into. He could raise fifteen thousand on his Nankeen Square house, and another fifteen on his Beacon street lot, and this was all that a man who was worth a million by rights could do! He said a million, and he said it in defiance of Bellingham, who had subjected his figures to an analysis which wounded Lapham more than he chose to show at the time, for it proved that he was not so rich and not so wise as he had seemed. His hurt vanity forbade him to go to Bellingham now for help or advice; and if he could have brought himself to ask his brothers for money, it would have been useless; they were simply well-to-do Western people, but not capitalists on the scale he required.

Lapham stood in the isolation to which adversity so often seems to bring men. When its test was applied, practically or theoretically, to all those who had seemed his friends, there was none who bore it; and he thought with bitter self-contempt of the people whom he had befriended in their time of need. He said to himself that he had been a fool for that; and he scorned himself for certain acts of scrupulosity by which he had lost money in the past. Seeing the moral forces all arrayed against him, Lapham said that he would like to have the chance offered him to get even with them again; he thought he should know how to look out for himself. As he understood it, he had several days to turn about in, and he did not let one day's failure dishearten him. The morning after his return he had, in fact, a gleam of luck that gave him the greatest encouragement for the moment. A man came in to inquire about one of Rogers's wild-cat patents, as Lapham called them, and ended by buying it. He got it, of course, for less than Lapham took it for, but Lapham was glad to be rid of it for something, when he had thought it worth nothing; and when the transaction was closed, he asked the purchaser rather eagerly if he knew where Rogers was; it was Lapham's secret belief that Rogers had found there was money in the thing, and had sent the man to buy it. But it appeared that this was a mistake; the man had not come from Rogers, but had heard of the patent in another way; and Lapham was astonished in the afternoon, when his boy came to tell him that Rogers was in the outer office, and wished to speak with him.

"All right," said Lapham, and he could not command at once the severity for the reception of Rogers which he would have liked to use. He found himself, in fact, so much relaxed towards him by the morning's touch of prosperity that he asked him to sit down, gruffly, of course, but distinctly; and when Rogers said in his lifeless way, and with the effect of keeping his appointment of a month before, "Those English parties are in town, and would like to talk with you in reference to the mills," Lapham did not turn him out-of-doors.

He sat looking at him, and trying to make out what Rogers was after; for he did not believe that the English parties, if they existed, had any notion of buying his mills.

"What if they are not for sale?" he asked. "You know that I've been expecting an offer from the G. L. & P."

"I've kept watch of that. They haven't made you any offer," said Rogers quietly.

"And did you think," demanded Lapham, firing up, "that I would turn them in on somebody else as you turned them in on me, when the chances are that they won't be worth ten cents on the dollar six months from now?"

"I didn't know what you would do," said Rogers, non-committally. "I've come here to tell you that these parties stand ready to take the mills off your hands at a fair valuation—at the value I put upon them when I turned them in."

"I don't believe you!" cried Lapham brutally, but a wild, predatory hope made his heart leap so that it seemed to turn over in his breast. "I don't believe there are any such parties to begin with; and in the next place, I don't believe they would buy at any such figure; unless—unless you've lied to them, as you've lied to me. Did you tell them about the G. L. & P.?"

Rogers looked compassionately at him, but he answered, with unvaried dryness, "I did not think that necessary."

Lapham had expected this answer, and he had expected or intended to break out in furious denunciation of Rogers when he got it; but he only found himself saying, in a sort of baffled gasp, "I wonder what your game is!"

Rogers did not reply categorically, but he answered, with his impartial calm, and as if Lapham had said nothing to indicate that he differed at all with him as to disposing of the property in the way he had suggested: "If we should succeed in selling, I should be able to repay you your loans, and should have a little capital for a scheme that I think of going into."

"And do you think that I am going to steal these men's money to help you plunder somebody in a new scheme?" answered Lapham. The sneer was on behalf of virtue, but it was still a sneer.

"I suppose the money would be useful to you too, just now."

"Why?"

"Because I know that you have been trying to borrow."

At this proof of wicked omniscience in Rogers, the question whether he had better not regard the affair as a fatality, and yield to his destiny, flashed upon Lapham; but he answered, "I shall want money a great deal worse than I've ever wanted it yet, before I go into such rascally business with you. Don't you know that we might as well knock these parties down on the street, and take the money out of their pockets?"

"They have come on," answered Rogers, "from Portland to see you. I expected them some weeks ago, but they disappointed me. They arrived on the *Circassian* last night; they expected to have got in five days ago, but the passage was very stormy."

"Where are they?" asked Lapham, with helpless irrelevance, and feeling himself somehow drifted from his moorings by Rogers's shipping intelligence.

"They are at Young's. I told them we would call upon them after dinner this evening; they dine late."

"Oh, you did, did you?" asked Lapham, trying to drop another anchor for a fresh clutch on his underlying principles. "Well, now, you go and tell them that I said I wouldn't come."

"Their stay is limited," remarked Rogers. "I mentioned this evening because they were not certain they could remain over another night. But if to-morrow would suit you better——"

"Tell 'em I sha'n't come at all," roared Lapham, as much in terror as defiance, for he felt his anchor dragging. "Tell 'em I sha'n't come at all! Do you understand that?"

"I don't see why you should stickle as to the matter of going to them," said Rogers; "but if you think it will be better to have them approach you, I suppose I can bring them to you."

"No, you can't! I sha'n't let you! I sha'n't see them! I sha'n't have anything to do with them. *Now* do you understand?"

"I inferred from our last interview," persisted Rogers, un- moved by all this violent demonstration of Lapham's, "that you wished to meet these parties. You told me that you would give me time to produce them; and I have promised them that you would meet them; I have committed myself."

It was true that Lapham had defied Rogers to bring on his men, and had implied his willingness to negotiate with them. That was before he had talked the matter over with his wife, and perceived his moral responsibility in it; even she had not seen this at once. He could not enter into this explanation with Rogers; he could only say, "I said I'd give you twenty- four hours to prove yourself a liar, and you did it. I didn't say twenty-four days."

"I don't see the difference," returned Rogers. "The parties are here now, and that proves that I was acting in good faith at the time. There has been no change in the posture of af- fairs. You don't know now any more than you knew then that the G. L. & P. is going to want the property. If there's any difference, it's in favor of the Road's having changed its mind."

There was some sense in this, and Lapham felt it—felt it only too eagerly, as he recognized the next instant.

Rogers went on quietly: "You're not obliged to sell to these parties when you meet them; but you've allowed me to commit myself to them by the promise that you would talk with them."

" 'Twa'n't a promise," said Lapham.

"It was the same thing; they have come out from England

on my guaranty that there was such and such an opening for
their capital; and now what am I to say to them? It places me
in a ridiculous position." Rogers urged his grievance calmly,
almost impersonally, making his appeal to Lapham's sense of
justice. "I *can't* go back to those parties and tell them you
won't see them. It's no answer to make. They've got a right
to know *why* you won't see them."

"Very well, then!" cried Lapham; "I'll come and *tell* them
why. Who shall I ask for? When shall I be there?"

"At eight o'clock, please," said Rogers, rising, without apparent alarm at his threat, if it was a threat. "And ask for me;
I've taken a room at the hotel for the present."

"I won't keep you five minutes when I get there," said Lapham; but he did not come away till ten o'clock.

It appeared to him as if the very devil was in it. The Englishmen treated his downright refusal to sell as a piece of
bluff, and talked on as though it were merely the opening of
the negotiation. When he became plain with them in his anger, and told them why he would not sell, they seemed to
have been prepared for this as a stroke of business, and were
ready to meet it.

"Has this fellow," he demanded, twisting his head in the
direction of Rogers, but disdaining to notice him otherwise,
"been telling you that it's part of my game to say this? Well,
sir, I can tell you, on my side, that there isn't a slipperier
rascal unhung in America than Milton K. Rogers!"

The Englishmen treated this as a piece of genuine American humor, and returned to the charge with unabated courage. They owned now, that a person interested with them
had been out to look at the property, and that they were satisfied with the appearance of things. They developed further
the fact that they were not acting solely, or even principally,
in their own behalf, but were the agents of people in England
who had projected the colonization of a sort of community
on the spot, somewhat after the plan of other English dream-
ers, and that they were satisfied, from a careful inspection,
that the resources and facilities were those best calculated to
develop the energy and enterprise of the proposed community. They were prepared to meet Mr. Lapham—Colonel,
they begged his pardon, at the instance of Rogers—at any

reasonable figure, and were quite willing to assume the risks he had pointed out. Something in the eyes of these men, something that lurked at an infinite depth below their speech, and was not really in their eyes when Lapham looked again, had flashed through him a sense of treachery in them. He had thought them the dupes of Rogers; but in that brief instant he had seen them—or thought he had seen them—his accomplices, ready to betray the interests of which they went on to speak with a certain comfortable jocosity, and a certain incredulous slight of his show of integrity. It was a deeper game than Lapham was used to, and he sat looking with a sort of admiration from one Englishman to the other, and then to Rogers, who maintained an exterior of modest neutrality, and whose air said, "I have brought you gentlemen together as the friend of all parties, and I now leave you to settle it among yourselves. I ask nothing, and expect nothing, except the small sum which shall accrue to me after the discharge of my obligations to Colonel Lapham."

While Rogers's presence expressed this, one of the Englishmen was saying, "And if you have any scruple in allowin' us to assume this risk, Colonel Lapham, perhaps you can console yourself with the fact that the loss, if there is to be any, will fall upon people who are able to bear it—upon an association of rich and charitable people. But we're quite satisfied there will be no loss," he added savingly. "All you have to do is to name your price, and we will do our best to meet it."

There was nothing in the Englishman's sophistry very shocking to Lapham. It addressed itself in him to that easy-going, not evilly intentioned, potential immorality which regards common property as common prey, and gives us the most corrupt municipal governments under the sun—which makes the poorest voter, when he has tricked into place, as unscrupulous in regard to others' money as an hereditary prince. Lapham met the Englishman's eye, and with difficulty kept himself from winking. Then he looked away, and tried to find out where he stood, or what he wanted to do. He could hardly tell. He had expected to come into that room and unmask Rogers, and have it over. But he had unmasked Rogers without any effect whatever, and the play had only begun. He had a whimsical and sarcastic sense of its being

very different from the plays at the theater. He could not get
up and go away in silent contempt; he could not tell the Englishmen that he believed them a pair of scoundrels and
should have nothing to do with them; he could no longer
treat them as innocent dupes. He remained baffled and perplexed, and the one who had not spoken hitherto remarked:

"Of course we sha'n't 'aggle about a few pound, more or
less. If Colonel Lapham's figure should be a little larger than
ours, I've no doubt 'e'll not be too 'ard upon us in the end."

Lapham appreciated all the intent of this subtle suggestion,
and understood as plainly as if it had been said in so many
words, that if they paid him a larger price, it was to be expected that a certain portion of the purchase money was to
return to their own hands. Still he could not move; and it
seemed to him that he could not speak.

"Ring that bell, Mr. Rogers," said the Englishman who
had last spoken, glancing at the annunciator button in the
wall near Rogers's head, "and 'ave up something 'ot, can't
you? I should like to wet me w'istle, as you say 'ere, and
Colonel Lapham seems to find it rather dry work."

Lapham jumped to his feet, and buttoned his overcoat
about him. He remembered with terror the dinner at Corey's
where he had disgraced and betrayed himself, and if he went
into this thing at all, he was going into it sober. "I can't
stop," he said, "I must be going."

"But you haven't given us an answer yet, Mr. Lapham,"
said the first Englishman with a successful show of dignified
surprise.

"The only answer I can give you now is, *No*," said Lapham.
"If you want another, you must let me have time to think it
over."

"But 'ow much time?" said the other Englishman. "We're
pressed for time ourselves, and we hoped for an answer—
'oped for a hanswer," he corrected himself, "at once. That was
our understandin' with Mr. Rogers."

"I can't let you know till morning, anyway," said Lapham,
and he went out, as his custom often was, without any parting salutation. He thought Rogers might try to detain him;
but Rogers had remained seated when the others got to their
feet, and paid no attention to his departure.

He walked out into the night air, every pulse throbbing with the strong temptation. He knew very well those men would wait, and gladly wait, till the morning, and that the whole affair was in his hands. It made him groan in spirit to think that it was. If he had hoped that some chance might take the decision from him, there was no such chance, in the present or future, that he could see. It was for him alone to commit this rascality—if it was a rascality—or not.

He walked all the way home, letting one car after another pass him on the street, now so empty of other passing, and it was almost eleven o'clock when he reached home. A carriage stood before his house, and when he let himself in with his key, he heard talking in the family-room. It came into his head that Irene had got back unexpectedly, and that the sight of her was somehow going to make it harder for him; then he thought it might be Corey, come upon some desperate pretext to see Penelope; but when he opened the door he saw, with a certain absence of surprise, that it was Rogers. He was standing with his back to the fire-place, talking to Mrs. Lapham, and he had been shedding tears; dry tears they seemed, and they had left a sort of sandy, glistening trace on his cheeks. Apparently he was not ashamed of them, for the expression with which he met Lapham was that of a man making a desperate appeal in his own cause, which was identical with that of humanity, if not that of justice.

"I some expected," began Rogers, "to find you here——"

"No, you didn't," interrupted Lapham; "you wanted to come here and make a poor mouth to Mrs. Lapham before I got home."

"I knew that Mrs. Lapham would know what was going on," said Rogers, more candidly, but not more virtuously, for that he could not, "and I wished her to understand a point that I hadn't put to you at the hotel, and that I want you should consider. And I want you should consider me a little in this business, too; you're not the only one that's concerned, I tell you, and I've been telling Mrs. Lapham that it's my one chance; that if you don't meet me on it, my wife and children will be reduced to beggary."

"So will mine," said Lapham, "or the next thing to it."

"Well, then, I want you to give me this chance to get on my feet again. You've no right to deprive me of it; it's unchristian. In our dealings with each other we should be guided by the Golden Rule, as I was saying to Mrs. Lapham before you came in. I told her that if I knew myself, I should in your place consider the circumstances of a man in mine, who had honorably endeavored to discharge his obligations to me, and had patiently borne my undeserved suspicions. I should consider that man's family, I told Mrs. Lapham."

"Did you tell her that if I went in with you and those fellows, I should be robbing the people who trusted them?"

"I don't see what you've got to do with the people that sent them here. They are rich people, and could bear it if it came to the worst. But there's no likelihood, now, that it will come to the worst; you can see yourself that the Road has changed its mind about buying. And here am I without a cent in the world; and my wife is an invalid. She needs comforts, she needs little luxuries, and she hasn't even the necessaries; and you want to sacrifice her to a mere idea! You don't know in the first place that the Road will ever want to buy; and if it does, the probability is that with a colony like that planted on its line, it would make very different terms from what it would with you or me. These agents are not afraid, and their principals are rich people; and if there was any loss, it would be divided up amongst them so that they wouldn't any of them feel it."

Lapham stole a troubled glance at his wife, and saw that there was no help in her. Whether she was daunted and confused in her own conscience by the outcome, so evil and disastrous, of the reparation to Rogers which she had forced her husband to make, or whether her perceptions had been blunted and darkened by the appeals which Rogers had now used, it would be difficult to say. Probably there was a mixture of both causes in the effect which her husband felt in her, and from which he turned, girding himself anew, to Rogers.

"I have no wish to recur to the past," continued Rogers, with growing superiority. "You have shown a proper spirit in regard to that, and you have done what you could to wipe it out."

"I should think I had," said Lapham. "I've used up about a hundred and fifty thousand dollars trying."

"Some of my enterprises," Rogers admitted, "have been unfortunate, seemingly; but I have hopes that they will yet turn out well—in time. I can't understand why you should be so mindful of others now, when you showed so little regard for me then. I had come to your aid at a time when you needed help, and when you got on your feet you kicked me out of the business. I don't complain, but that is the fact; and I had to begin again, after I had supposed myself settled in life, and establish myself elsewhere."

Lapham glanced again at his wife; her head had fallen; he could see that she was so rooted in her old remorse for that questionable act of his, amply and more than fully atoned for since, that she was helpless, now in the crucial moment, when he had the utmost need of her insight. He had counted upon her; he perceived now that when he had thought it was for him alone to decide, he had counted upon her just spirit to stay his own in its struggle to be just. He had not forgotten how she held out against him only a little while ago, when he asked her whether he might not rightfully sell in some such contingency as this; and it was not now that she said or even looked anything in favor of Rogers, but that she was silent against him, which dismayed Lapham. He swallowed the lump that rose in his throat, the self-pity, the pity for her, the despair, and said gently, "I guess you better go to bed, Persis. It's pretty late."

She turned towards the door, when Rogers said, with the obvious intention of detaining her through her curiosity:

"But I let that pass. And I don't ask now that you should sell to these men."

Mrs. Lapham paused, irresolute.

"What are you making this bother for, then?" demanded Lapham. "What *do* you want?"

"What I've been telling your wife here. I want you should sell to *me*. I don't say what I'm going to do with the property, and you will not have an iota of responsibility, whatever happens."

Lapham was staggered, and he saw his wife's face light up with eager question.

"I want that property," continued Rogers, "and I've got the money to buy it. What will you take for it? If it's the price you're standing out for——"

"Persis," said Lapham, "go to bed," and he gave her a look that meant obedience for her. She went out of the door, and left him with his tempter.

"If you think I'm going to help you whip the devil round the stump, you're mistaken in your man, Milton Rogers," said Lapham, lighting a cigar. "As soon as I sold to you, you would sell to that other pair of rascals. I smelt 'em out in half a minute."

"They are Christian gentlemen," said Rogers. "But I don't purpose defending them; and I don't purpose telling you what I shall or shall not do with the property when it is in my hands again. The question is, Will you sell, and, if so, what is your figure? You have got nothing whatever to do with it after you've sold."

It was perfectly true. Any lawyer would have told him the same. He could not help admiring Rogers for his ingenuity, and every selfish interest of his nature joined with many obvious duties to urge him to consent. He did not see why he should refuse. There was no longer a reason. He was standing out alone for nothing, any one else would say. He smoked on as if Rogers were not there, and Rogers remained before the fire as patient as the clock ticking behind his head on the mantel, and showing the gleam of its pendulum beyond his face on either side. But at last he said, "Well?"

"Well," answered Lapham, "you can't expect me to give you an answer to-night, any more than before. You know that what you've said now hasn't changed the thing a bit. I wish it had. The Lord knows, I want to be rid of the property fast enough."

"Then why don't you sell to me? Can't you see that you will not be responsible for what happens after you have sold?"

"No, I *can't* see that; but if I can by morning, I'll sell."

"Why do you expect to know any better by morning? You're wasting time for nothing!" cried Rogers, in his disappointment. "Why are you so particular? When you drove me out of the business you were not so very particular."

Lapham winced. It was certainly ridiculous for a man who

had once so selfishly consulted his own interests to be stick-
ling now about the rights of others.

"I guess nothing's going to happen over-night," he answered sullenly. "Anyway, I sha'n't say what I shall do till
morning."

"What time can I see you in the morning?"

"Half-past nine."

Rogers buttoned his coat, and went out of the room without another word. Lapham followed him to close the street-
door after him.

His wife called down to him from above as he approached
the room again, "Well?"

"I've told him I'd let him know in the morning."

"Want I should come down and talk with you?"

"No," answered Lapham, in the proud bitterness which his
isolation brought, "you couldn't do any good." He went in
and shut the door, and by and by his wife heard him begin
walking up and down; and then the rest of the night she lay
awake and listened to him walking up and down. But when
the first light whitened the window, the words of the Scripture came into her mind: "And there wrestled a man with
him until the breaking of the day. . . . And he said, Let me
go, for the day breaketh. And he said, I will not let thee go,
except thou bless me."

She could not ask him anything when they met, but he
raised his dull eyes after the first silence and said, "*I* don't
know what I'm going to say to Rogers."

She could not speak; she did not know what to say, and
she saw her husband, when she followed him with her eyes
from the window, drag heavily down toward the corner,
where he was to take the horse-car.

He arrived rather later than usual at his office, and he
found his letters already on his table. There was one, long
and official-looking, with a printed letter-heading on the outside, and Lapham had no need to open it in order to know
that it was the offer of the Great Lacustrine & Polar Railroad
for his mills. But he went mechanically through the verifica-
tion of his prophetic fear, which was also his sole hope, and
then sat looking blankly at it.

Rogers came promptly at the appointed time, and Lapham

handed him the letter. He must have taken it all in at a glance, and seen the impossibility of negotiating any further now, even with victims so pliant and willing as those Englishmen.

"You've ruined me!" Rogers broke out. "I haven't a cent left in the world! God help my poor wife!"

He went out, and Lapham remained staring at the door which closed upon him. This was his reward for standing firm for right and justice to his own destruction: to feel like a thief and a murderer.

XXVI

LATER IN THE FORENOON came the dispatch from the West
Virginians in New York, saying their brother assented
to their agreement; and it now remained for Lapham to fulfill
his part of it. He was ludicrously far from able to do this; and
unless he could get some extension of time from them, he
must lose this chance, his only chance, to retrieve himself. He
spent the time in a desperate endeavor to raise the money,
but he had not raised the half of it when the banks closed.
With shame in his heart he went to Bellingham, from whom
he had parted so haughtily, and laid his plan before him. He
could not bring himself to ask Bellingham's help, but he told
him what he proposed to do. Bellingham pointed out that
the whole thing was an experiment, and that the price asked
was enormous, unless a great success were morally certain.
He advised delay, he advised prudence; he insisted that Lapham ought at least to go out to Kanawha Falls, and see the
mines and works, before he put any such sum into the development of the enterprise.

"That's all well enough," cried Lapham; "but if I don't
clinch this offer within twenty-four hours, they'll withdraw
it, and go into the market; and then where am I?"

"Go on and see them again," said Bellingham. "They can't
be so peremptory as that with you. They must give you time
to look at what they want to sell. If it turns out what you
hope, then—I'll see what can be done. But look into it thoroughly."

"Well!" cried Lapham, helplessly submitting. He took out
his watch, and saw that he had forty minutes to catch the
four o'clock train. He hurried back to his office, put together
some papers preparatory to going, and dispatched a note by
his boy to Mrs. Lapham saying that he was starting for New
York, and did not know just when he should get back.

The early spring day was raw and cold. As he went out
through the office he saw the clerks at work with their street
coats and hats on; Miss Dewey had her jacket dragged up on
her shoulders and looked particularly comfortless as she op-

erated her machine with her red fingers. "What's up?" asked Lapham, stopping a moment.

"Seems to be something the matter with the steam," she answered, with the air of unmerited wrong habitual with so many pretty women who have to work for a living.

"Well, take your writer into my room; there's a fire in the stove there," said Lapham, passing out.

Half an hour later his wife came into the outer office. She had passed the day in a passion of self-reproach, gradually mounting from the mental numbness in which he had left her, and now she could wait no longer to tell him that she saw how she had forsaken him in his hour of trial and left him to bear it alone. She wondered at herself in shame and dismay; she wondered that she could have been so confused as to the real point by that old wretch of a Rogers, that she could have let him hoodwink her so, even for a moment. It astounded her that such a thing should have happened, for if there was any virtue upon which this good woman prided herself, in which she thought herself superior to her husband, it was her instant and steadfast perception of right and wrong, and the ability to choose the right to her own hurt. But she had now to confess, as each of us has had likewise to confess in his own case, that the very virtue on which she had prided herself was the thing that had played her false; that she had kept her mind so long upon that old wrong which she believed her husband had done this man that she could not detach it, but clung to the thought of reparation for it when she ought to have seen that he was proposing a piece of roguery as the means. The suffering which Lapham must inflict on him if he decided against him had been more to her apprehension than the harm he might do if he decided for him. But now she owned her limitations to herself, and above everything in the world she wished the man whom her conscience had roused and driven on whither her intelligence had not followed, to do right, to do what he felt to be right, and nothing else. She admired and revered him for going beyond her, and she wished to tell him that she did not know what he had determined to do about Rogers, but that she knew it was right, and would gladly abide the consequences with him, whatever they were.

She had not been near his place of business for nearly a year, and her heart smote her tenderly as she looked about her there, and thought of the early days when she knew as much about the paint as he did; she wished that those days were back again. She saw Corey at his desk, and she could not bear to speak to him; she dropped her veil that she need not recognize him, and pushed on to Lapham's room, and, opening the door without knocking, shut it behind her.

Then she became aware with intolerable disappointment that her husband was not there. Instead, a very pretty girl sat at his desk, operating a type-writer. She seemed quite at home, and she paid Mrs. Lapham the scant attention which such young women often bestow upon people not personally interesting to them. It vexed the wife that any one else should seem to be helping her husband about business that she had once been so intimate with; and she did not at all like the girl's indifference to her presence. Her hat and sack hung on a nail in one corner, and Lapham's office coat, looking intensely like him to his wife's familiar eye, hung on a nail in the other corner; and Mrs. Lapham liked even less than the girl's good looks this domestication of her garments in her husband's office. She began to ask herself excitedly why he should be away from his office when she happened to come; and she had not the strength at the moment to reason herself out of her unreasonableness.

"When will Colonel Lapham be in, do you suppose?" she sharply asked of the girl.

"I couldn't say exactly," replied the girl, without looking round.

"Has he been out long?"

"I don't know as I noticed," said the girl, looking up at the clock, without looking at Mrs. Lapham. She went on working her machine.

"Well, I can't wait any longer," said the wife abruptly. "When Colonel Lapham comes in, you please tell him Mrs. Lapham wants to see him."

The girl started to her feet and turned toward Mrs. Lapham with a red and startled face, which she did not lift to confront her. "Yes—yes—I will," she faltered.

The wife went home with a sense of defeat mixed with an

irritation about this girl which she could not quell or account for. She found her husband's message, and it seemed intolerable that he should have gone to New York without seeing her; she asked herself in vain what the mysterious business could be that took him away so suddenly. She said to herself that he was neglecting her; he was leaving her out a little too much; and in demanding of herself why he had never mentioned that girl there in his office, she forgot how much she had left herself out of his business life. That was another curse of their prosperity. Well, she was glad the prosperity was going; it had never been happiness. After this she was going to know everything as she used.

She tried to dismiss the whole matter till Lapham returned; and if there had been anything for her to do in that miserable house, as she called it in her thought, she might have succeeded. But again the curse was on her; there was nothing to do; and the looks of that girl kept coming back to her vacancy, her disoccupation. She tried to make herself something to do, but that beauty, which she had not liked, followed her amid the work of overhauling the summer clothing, which Irene had seen to putting away in the fall. Who was the thing, anyway? It was very strange, her being there; why did she jump up in that frightened way when Mrs. Lapham had named herself?

After dark that evening, when the question had worn away its poignancy from mere iteration, a note for Mrs. Lapham was left at the door by a messenger who said there was no answer. "A note for me?" she said, staring at the unknown, and somehow artificial-looking, handwriting of the superscription. Then she opened it and read: "Ask your husband about his lady copying-clerk. A Friend and Well-wisher," who signed the note, gave no other name.

Mrs. Lapham sat helpless with it in her hand. Her brain reeled; she tried to fight the madness off; but before Lapham came back the second morning, it had become, with lessening intervals of sanity and release, a demoniacal possession. She passed the night without sleep, without rest, in the frenzy of the cruelest of the passions, which covers with shame the unhappy soul it possesses, and murderously lusts for the misery of its object. If she had known where to find her husband in

New York, she would have followed him; she waited his return in an ecstasy of impatience. In the morning he came back, looking spent and haggard. She saw him drive up to the door, and she ran to let him in herself.

"Who is that girl you've got in your office, Silas Lapham?" she demanded, when her husband entered.

"Girl in my office?"

"Yes! Who is she? What is she doing there?"

"Why, what have you heard about her?"

"Never you mind what I've heard. Who is she? *Is it Mrs. M. that you gave that money to?* I want to know who she is! I want to know what a respectable man, with grown-up girls of his own, is doing with such a looking thing as that in his office! I want to know how long she's been there! I want to know what she's there at all for!"

He had mechanically pushed her before him into the long, darkened parlor, and he shut himself in there with her now, to keep the household from hearing her lifted voice. For a while he stood bewildered, and could not have answered if he would; and then he would not. He merely asked, "Have I ever accused you of anything wrong, Persis?"

"You no need to!" she answered furiously, placing herself against the closed door.

"Did you ever know me to do anything out of the way?"

"That isn't what I asked you."

"Well, I guess you may find out about that girl yourself. Get away from the door."

"I won't get away from the door."

She felt herself set lightly aside, and her husband opened the door and went out. "I *will* find out about her," she screamed after him. "I'll find out, and I'll disgrace you—I'll teach you how to treat me!"

The air blackened round her; she reeled to the sofa; and then she found herself waking from a faint. She did not know how long she had lain there; she did not care. In a moment her madness came whirling back upon her. She rushed up to his room; it was empty; the closet-doors stood ajar and the drawers were open; he must have packed a bag hastily and fled. She went out, and wandered crazily up and down till she found a hack. She gave the driver her husband's business address, and told him to drive there as fast as he could; and three times she lowered the window to put her head out and ask him if he could not hurry. A thousand things thronged into her mind to support her in her evil will. She remembered how glad and proud that man had been to marry her, and how everybody said she was marrying beneath her when she took him. She remembered how good she had always been to him, how perfectly devoted, slaving early and late to advance him, and looking out for his interests in all things, and sparing herself in nothing. If it had not been for her, he might have been driving stage yet; and since their troubles had begun, the troubles which his own folly and imprudence had brought on them, her conduct had been that of a true and faithful wife. Was *he* the sort of man to be allowed to play her false with impunity? She set her teeth and drew her breath sharply through them, when she thought how willingly she had let him befool her and delude her about that memorandum of payments to Mrs. M., because she loved him so much, and pitied him for his cares and anxieties. She recalled his confusion, his guilty looks.

She plunged out of the carriage so hastily when she reached the office that she did not think of paying the driver; and he had to call after her when she had got half-way up the stairs. Then she went straight to Lapham's room, with outrage in her heart. There was again no one there but that type-writer girl; she jumped to her feet in a fright, as Mrs. Lapham dashed the door to behind her and flung up her veil.

The two women confronted each other.

"Why, the good land!" cried Mrs. Lapham, "ain't you Zerrilla Millon?"

"I—I'm married," faltered the girl. "My name's Dewey now."

"You're Jim Millon's daughter, anyway. How long have you been here?"

"I haven't been here regularly; I've been here off and on ever since last May."

"Where's your mother?"

"She's here—in Boston."

Mrs. Lapham kept her eyes on the girl, but she dropped, trembling, into her husband's chair, and a sort of amaze and curiosity were in her voice instead of the fury she had meant to put there.

"The Colonel," continued Zerrilla, "he's been helping us, and he's got me a type-writer, so that I can help myself a little. Mother's doing pretty well now; and when Hen isn't around we can get along."

"That your husband?"

"I never wanted to marry him; but he promised to try to get something to do on shore; and mother was all for it, because he had a little property then, and I thought maybe I'd better. But it's turned out just as I said, and if he don't stay away long enough this time to let me get the divorce,—he's agreed to it, time and again,—I don't know what we're going to do." Zerrilla's voice fell, and the trouble which she could keep out of her face usually, when she was comfortably warmed and fed and prettily dressed, clouded it in the presence of a sympathetic listener. "I saw it was you when you came in the other day," she went on; "but you didn't seem to know me. I suppose the Colonel's told you that there's a gentleman going to marry me—Mr. Wemmel's his name—as soon as I get the divorce; but sometimes I'm completely discouraged; it don't seem as if I ever *could* get it."

Mrs. Lapham would not let her know that she was ignorant of the fact attributed to her knowledge. She remained listening to Zerrilla, and piecing out the whole history of her presence there from the facts of the past, and the traits of her husband's character. One of the things she had always had to fight him about was that idea of his that he was bound to take care of Jim Millon's worthless wife and her child because Millon had got the bullet that was meant for him. It was a perfect superstition of his; she could not beat it out of him; but she had made him promise the last time he had done anything for that woman that it should *be* the last time. He had then got her a little house in one of the fishing ports, where she could take the sailors to board and wash for, and earn an honest living if she would keep straight. That was five or six years ago, and Mrs. Lapham had heard nothing of Mrs. Millon since; she had heard quite enough of her before, and had known her idle and baddish ever since she was the worst little girl at school in Lumberville, and all through her shameful girlhood, and the married days which she had made so miserable to the poor fellow who had given her his decent name and a chance to behave herself. Mrs. Lapham had no mercy on Moll Millon, and she had quarreled often enough with her husband for befriending her. As for the child, if the mother would put Zerrilla out with some respectable family, that would be *one* thing; but as long as she kept Zerrilla with her, she was against letting her husband do anything for either of them. He had done ten times as much for them now as he had any need to, and she had made him give her his solemn word that he would do no more. She saw now that she was wrong to make him give it, and that he must have broken it again and again for the reason that he had given when she once scolded him for throwing away his money on that hussy:

"When I think of Jim Millon, I've *got* to; that's all."

She recalled now that whenever she had brought up the subject of Mrs. Millon and her daughter, he had seemed shy of it, and had dropped it with some guess that they were getting along now. She wondered that she had not thought at once of Mrs. Millon when she saw that memorandum about Mrs. M.; but the woman had passed so entirely out of her life, that she had never dreamt of her in connection with it. Her husband had deceived her, yet her heart was no longer hot against him, but rather tenderly grateful that his deceit was in this sort, and not in that other. All cruel and shameful doubt of him went out of it. She looked at this beautiful girl, who had blossomed out of her knowledge since she saw her last, and she knew that she was only a blossomed weed, of the same worthless root as her mother, and saved, if saved, from the same evil destiny by the good of her father in her; but so far as the girl and her mother were concerned, Mrs. Lapham knew that her husband was to blame for nothing but his willful, wrong-headed kind-heartedness, which her own exactions had turned into deceit. She remained awhile, questioning the girl quietly about herself and her mother, and then, with a better mind towards Zerrilla, at least, than she had ever had before, she rose up and went out. There must have been some outer hint of the exhaustion in which the subsidence of her excitement had left her within, for before she had reached the head of the stairs, Corey came towards her.

"Can I be of any use to you, Mrs. Lapham? The Colonel was here just before you came in, on his way to the train."

"Yes,—yes. I didn't know—I thought perhaps I could catch him here. But it don't matter. I wish you would let some one go with me to get a carriage," she begged feebly.

"I'll go with you myself," said the young fellow, ignoring the strangeness in her manner. He offered her his arm in the twilight of the staircase, and she was glad to put her trembling hand through it, and keep it there till he helped her into a hack which he found for her. He gave the driver her direction, and stood looking a little anxiously at her.

"I thank you; I am all right now," she said, and he bade the man drive on.

When she reached home she went to bed, spent with the tumult of her emotions and sick with shame and self-reproach. She understood now, as clearly as if he had told her in so many words, that if he had befriended these worthless jades—the Millons characterized themselves so, even to Mrs. Lapham's remorse—secretly and in defiance of her, it was because he dreaded her blame, which was so sharp and bitter, for what he could not help doing. It consoled her that he had defied her; deceived her; when he came back she should tell him that; and then it flashed upon her that she did not know where he was gone, or whether he would ever come again. If he never came, it would be no more than she deserved; but she sent for Penelope, and tried to give herself hopes of escape from this just penalty.

Lapham had not told his daughter where he was going; she had heard him packing his bag, and had offered to help him; but he had said he could do it best, and had gone off, as he usually did, without taking leave of any one.

"What were you talking about so loud, down in the parlor," she asked her mother, "just before he came up? Is there any new trouble?"

"No; it was nothing."

"I couldn't tell. Once I thought you were laughing." She went about, closing the curtains on account of her mother's headache, and doing awkwardly and imperfectly the things that Irene would have done so skillfully for her comfort.

The day wore away to nightfall, and then Mrs. Lapham said she *must* know. Penelope said there was no one to ask; the clerks would all be gone home; and her mother said yes, there was Mr. Corey; they could send and ask him; he would know.

The girl hesitated. "Very well," she said then, scarcely above a whisper, and she presently laughed huskily. "Mr. Corey seems fated to come in somewhere. I guess it's a Providence, mother."

She sent off a note, inquiring whether he could tell her just where her father had expected to be that night; and the answer came quickly back that Corey did not know, but would look up the book-keeper and inquire. This office brought him in person, an hour later, to tell Penelope that the Colonel was to be at Lapham that night and next day.

"He came in from New York in a great hurry, and rushed off as soon as he could pack his bag," Penelope explained, "and we hadn't a chance to ask him where he was to be tonight. And mother wasn't very well, and——"

"I thought she wasn't looking well when she was at the office to-day; and so I thought I would come rather than send," Corey explained, in his turn.

"Oh, thank you!"

"If there is anything I can do—telegraph Colonel Lapham, or anything?"

"Oh, no, thank you; mother's better now. She merely wanted to be sure where he was."

He did not offer to go upon this conclusion of his business, but hoped he was not keeping her from her mother. She thanked him once again, and said no, that her mother was much better since she had had a cup of tea; and then they looked at each other, and without any apparent exchange of intelligence he remained, and at eleven o'clock he was still there. He was honest in saying he did not know it was so late; but he made no pretense of being sorry, and she took the blame to herself.

"I oughtn't to have let you stay," she said. "But with father gone, and all that trouble hanging over us ——"

She was allowing him to hold her hand a moment at the door, to which she had followed him.

"I'm so glad you could let me!" he said; "and I want to ask you now when I may come again. But if you need me, you'll——"

A sharp pull at the door-bell outside made them start asunder, and at a sign from Penelope, who knew that the maids were abed by this time, he opened it.

"Why, Irene!" shrieked the girl.

Irene entered, with the hackman, who had driven her unheard to the door, following with her small bags, and kissed her sister with resolute composure. "That's all," she said to the hackman. "I gave my checks to the expressman," she explained to Penelope.

Corey stood helpless. Irene turned upon him, and gave him her hand. "How do you do, Mr. Corey?" she said, with a courage that sent a thrill of admiring gratitude through him. "Where's mamma, Pen? Papa gone to bed?"

Penelope faltered out some reply embodying the facts, and Irene ran up the stairs to her mother's room. Mrs. Lapham started up in bed at her apparition.

"Irene Lapham!"

"Uncle William thought he ought to tell me the trouble papa was in; and did you think I was going to stay off there junketing, while you were going through all this at home, and Pen acting so silly too? You ought to have been ashamed to let me stay so long! I started just as soon as I could pack. Did you get my dispatch? I telegraphed from Springfield. But it don't matter now. Here I am. And I don't think I need have hurried on Pen's account," she added, with an accent prophetic of the sort of old maid she would become if she happened never to marry.

"Did you see him?" asked her mother. "It's the first time he's been here since she told him he mustn't come."

"I guess it isn't the last time, by the looks," said Irene; and before she took off her bonnet she began to undo some of Penelope's mistaken arrangements of the room.

At breakfast, where Corey and his mother met the next morning before his father and sisters came down, he told her, with embarrassment which told much more, that he wished now that she would go and call upon the Laphams.

Mrs. Corey turned a little pale, but shut her lips tight and mourned in silence whatever hopes she had lately permitted herself. She answered with Roman fortitude: "Of course, if there's anything between you and Miss Lapham, your family ought to recognize it."

"Yes," said Corey.

"You were reluctant to have me call at first, but now if the affair is going on——"

"It is! I hope—yes, it is!"

"Then I ought to go and see her, with your sisters; and she ought to come here and—we ought all to see her and make the matter public. We can't do so too soon. It will seem as if we were ashamed if we don't."

"Yes, you are quite right, mother," said the young man gratefully, "and I feel how kind and good you are. I have tried to consider you in this matter, though I don't seem to have done so; I know what your rights are, and I wish with all my heart that I were meeting even your tastes perfectly. But I know you will like her when you come to know her. It's been very hard for her every way,—about her sister,— and she's made a great sacrifice for me. She's acted nobly."

Mrs. Corey, whose thoughts cannot always be reported, said she was sure of it, and that all she desired was her son's happiness.

"She's been very unwilling to consider it an engagement on that account, and on account of Colonel Lapham's difficulties. I should like to have you go, now, for that very reason. I don't know just how serious the trouble is; but it isn't a time when we can seem indifferent."

The logic of this was not perhaps so apparent to the glasses of fifty as to the eyes of twenty-six; but Mrs. Corey, however she viewed it, could not allow herself to blench before the son whom she had taught that to want magnanimity was to be less than gentlemanly. She answered, with what composure she could, "I will take your sisters," and then she made some natural inquiries about Lapham's affairs.

"Oh, I hope it will come out all right," Corey said, with a

lover's vague smile, and left her. When his father came down, rubbing his long hands together, and looking aloof from all the cares of the practical world, in an artistic withdrawal, from which his eye ranged over the breakfast-table before he sat down, Mrs. Corey told him what she and their son had been saying.

He laughed, with a delicate impersonal appreciation of the predicament. "Well, Anna, you can't say but if you ever were guilty of supposing yourself porcelain, this is a just punishment of your arrogance. Here you are bound by the very quality on which you've prided yourself to behave well to a bit of earthenware who is apparently in danger of losing the gilding that rendered her tolerable."

"We never cared for the money," said Mrs. Corey. "You know that."

"No; and now we can't seem to care for the loss of it. That would be still worse. Either horn of the dilemma gores us. Well, we still have the comfort we had in the beginning; we can't help ourselves, and we should only make bad worse by trying. Unless we can look to Tom's inamorata herself for help."

Mrs. Corey shook her head so gloomily that her husband broke off with another laugh. But at the continued trouble of her face he said, sympathetically: "My dear, I know it's a very disagreeable affair; and I don't think either of us has failed to see that it was so from the beginning. I have had my way of expressing my sense of it, and you yours, but we have always been of the same mind about it. We would both have preferred to have Tom marry in his own set; the Laphams are about the last set we could have wished him to marry into. They *are* uncultivated people, and, so far as I have seen them, I'm not able to believe that poverty will improve them. Still, it may. Let us hope for the best, and let us behave as well as we know how. I'm sure *you* will behave well, and I shall try. I'm going with you to call on Miss Lapham. This is a thing that can't be done by halves!"

He cut his orange in the Neapolitan manner, and ate it in quarters.

XXVII

IRENE did not leave her mother in any illusion concerning her cousin Will and herself. She said they had all been as nice to her as they could be, and when Mrs. Lapham hinted at what had been in her thoughts,—or her hopes, rather,— Irene severely snubbed the notion. She said that he was as good as engaged to a girl out there, and that he had never dreamt of her. Her mother wondered at her severity; in these few months the girl had toughened and hardened; she had lost all her babyish dependence and pliability; she was like iron; and here and there she was sharpened to a cutting edge. It had been a life and death struggle with her; she had conquered, but she had also necessarily lost much. Perhaps what she had lost was not worth keeping; but at any rate she had lost it.

She required from her mother a strict and accurate account of her father's affairs, so far as Mrs. Lapham knew them; and she showed a business-like quickness in comprehending them that Penelope had never pretended to. With her sister she ignored the past as completely as it was possible to do; and she treated both Corey and Penelope with the justice which their innocence of voluntary offense deserved. It was a difficult part, and she kept away from them as much as she could. She had been easily excused, on a plea of fatigue from her journey, when Mr. and Mrs. Corey had called the day after her arrival, and, Mrs. Lapham being still unwell, Penelope received them alone.

The girl had instinctively judged best that they should know the worst at once, and she let them have the full brunt of the drawing-room, while she was screwing her courage up to come down and see them. She was afterwards—months afterwards—able to report to Corey that when she entered the room his father was sitting with his hat on his knees, a little tilted away from the Emancipation group, as if he expected the Lincoln to hit him with that lifted hand of benediction; and that Mrs. Corey looked as if she were not sure but the Eagle pecked. But for the time being Penelope was as

nearly crazed as might be by the complications of her position, and received her visitors with a piteous distraction
which could not fail of touching Bromfield Corey's Italian-
ized sympatheticism. He was very polite and tender with her
at first, and ended by making a joke with her, to which Penelope responded in her sort. He said he hoped they parted
friends, if not quite acquaintances; and she said she hoped
they would be able to recognize each other if they ever met
again.

"That is what I meant by her pertness," said Mrs. Corey,
when they were driving away.

"Was it very pert?" he queried. "The child had to answer
something."

"I would much rather she had answered nothing, under the
circumstances," said Mrs. Corey. "However!" she added
hopelessly.

"Oh, she's a merry little grig, you can see that, and there's
no harm in her. I can understand a little why a formal fellow
like Tom should be taken with her. She hasn't the least reverence, I suppose, and joked with the young man from the beginning. You must remember, Anna, that there was a time
when you liked my joking."

"It was a very different thing!"

"But that drawing-room!" pursued Corey; "really, I don't
see how Tom stands that. Anna, a terrible thought occurs to
me! Fancy Tom being married in front of that group, with a
floral horse-shoe in tuberoses coming down on either side of
it!"

"Bromfield!" cried his wife, "you are unmerciful."

"No, no, my dear," he argued; "merely imaginative. And I
can even imagine that little thing finding Tom just the least
bit slow at times, if it were not for his goodness. Tom is so
kind that I'm convinced he sometimes feels your joke in his
heart when his head isn't quite clear about it. Well, we will
not despond, my dear."

"Your father seemed actually to like her," Mrs. Corey reported to her daughters, very much shaken in her own prejudices by the fact. If the girl were not so offensive to his
fastidiousness, there might be some hope that she was not so
offensive as Mrs. Corey had thought. "I wonder how she will

strike *you*," she concluded, looking from one daughter to another, as if trying to decide which of them would like Penelope least.

Irene's return and the visit of the Coreys formed a distraction for the Laphams in which their impending troubles seemed to hang farther aloof; but it was only one of those reliefs which mark the course of adversity, and it was not one of the cheerful reliefs. At any other time, either incident would have been an anxiety and care for Mrs. Lapham which she would have found hard to bear; but now she almost welcomed them. At the end of three days Lapham returned, and his wife met him as if nothing unusual had marked their parting; she reserved her atonement for a fitter time; he would know now from the way she acted that she felt all right towards him. He took very little note of her manner, but met his family with an austere quiet that puzzled her, and a sort of pensive dignity that refined his rudeness to an effect that sometimes comes to such natures after long sickness, when the animal strength has been taxed and lowered. He sat silent with her at the table after their girls had left them alone; and seeing that he did not mean to speak, she began to explain why Irene had come home, and to praise her.

"Yes, she done right," said Lapham. "It was time for her to come," he added gently.

Then he was silent again, and his wife told him of Corey's having been there, and of his father's and mother's calling. "I guess Pen's concluded to make it up," she said.

"Well, we'll see about that," said Lapham; and now she could no longer forbear to ask him about his affairs.

"I don't know as I've got any right to know anything about it," she said humbly, with remote allusion to her treatment of him. "But I can't help wanting to know. How *are* things going, Si?"

"Bad," he said, pushing his plate from him, and tilting himself back in his chair. "Or they ain't going at all. They've stopped."

"What do you mean, Si?" she persisted tenderly.

"I've got to the end of my string. To-morrow I shall call a meeting of my creditors, and put myself in their hands. If there's enough left to satisfy them, I'm satisfied." His voice dropped in his throat; he swallowed once or twice, and then did not speak.

"Do you mean that it's all over with you?" she asked fearfully.

He bowed his big head, wrinkled and grizzled; and after a while he said, "It's hard to realize it; but I guess there ain't any doubt about it." He drew a long breath, and then he explained to her about the West Virginia people, and how he had got an extension of the first time they had given him, and had got a man to go up to Lapham with him and look at the works,—a man that had turned up in New York, and wanted to put money in the business. His money would have enabled Lapham to close with the West Virginians. "The devil was in it, right straight along," said Lapham. "All I had to do was to keep quiet about that other company. It was Rogers and his property right over again. He liked the look of things, and he wanted to go into the business, and he had the money—plenty; it would have saved me with those West Virginia folks. But I had to tell him how I stood. I had to tell him all about it, and what I wanted to do. He began to back water in a minute, and the next morning I saw that it was up with him. He's gone back to New York. I've lost my last chance. Now all I've got to do is to save the pieces."

"Will—will—everything go?" she asked.

"I can't tell yet. But they shall have a chance at everything—every dollar, every cent. I'm sorry for you, Persis—and the girls."

"Oh, don't talk of *us*!" She was trying to realize that the simple, rude soul to which her heart clove in her youth, but which she had put to such cruel proof with her unsparing conscience and her unsparing tongue, had been equal to its ordeals, and had come out unscathed and unstained. He was able in his talk to make so little of them; he hardly seemed to see what they were; he was apparently not proud of them, and certainly not glad; if they were victories of any sort, he bore them with the patience of defeat. His wife wished to praise him, but she did not know how; so she offered him a little reproach, in which alone she touched the cause of her behavior at parting. "Silas," she asked after a long gaze at him, "why didn't you tell me you had Jim Millon's girl there?"

"I didn't suppose you'd like it, Persis," he answered. "I did intend to tell you at first, but then I put it off. I thought you'd come round some day, and find it out for yourself."

"I'm punished," said his wife, "for not taking enough interest in your business to even come near it. If we're brought back to the day of small things, I guess it's a lesson for me, Silas."

"Oh, I don't know about the lesson," he said wearily.

That night she showed him the anonymous scrawl which had kindled her fury against him. He turned it listlessly over in his hand. "I guess I know who it's from," he said, giving it back to her, "and I guess you do too, Persis."

"But how—how could he——"

"Mebbe he believed it," said Lapham, with patience that cut her more keenly than any reproach. "*You* did."

Perhaps because the process of his ruin had been so gradual, perhaps because the excitement of preceding events had exhausted their capacity for emotion, the actual consummation of his bankruptcy brought a relief, a repose to Lapham and his family, rather than a fresh sensation of calamity. In the shadow of his disaster they returned to something like their old, united life; they were at least all together again; and it will be intelligible to those whom life has blessed with vicissitude, that Lapham should come home the evening after he had given up everything to his creditors, and should sit down to his supper so cheerful that Penelope could joke him in the old way, and tell him that she thought from his looks they had concluded to pay him a hundred cents on every dollar he owed them.

As James Bellingham had taken so much interest in his troubles from the first, Lapham thought he ought to tell him, before taking the final step, just how things stood with him, and what he meant to do. Bellingham made some futile inquiries about his negotiations with the West Virginians, and Lapham told him they had come to nothing. He spoke of the New York man, and the chance that he might have sold out half his business to him. "But, of course, I had to let him know how it was about those fellows."

"Of course," said Bellingham, not seeing till afterwards the full significance of Lapham's action.

Lapham said nothing about Rogers and the Englishmen. He believed that he had acted right in that matter, and he was satisfied; but he did not care to have Bellingham, or anybody, perhaps think he had been a fool.

All those who were concerned in his affairs said he behaved well, and even more than well, when it came to the worst. The prudence, the good sense, which he had shown in the first years of his success, and of which his great prosperity seemed to have bereft him, came back; and these qualities, used in his own behalf, commended him as much to his creditors as the anxiety he showed that no one should suffer by him; this even made some of them doubtful of his sincerity. They gave him time, and there would have been no trouble in his resuming on the old basis, if the ground had not been cut from under him by the competition of the West Virginia company. He saw himself that it was useless to try to go on in the old way, and he preferred to go back and begin the world anew where he had first begun it, in the hills at Lapham. He put the house at Nankeen Square, with everything else he had, into the payment of his debts, and Mrs. Lapham found it easier to leave it for the old farmstead in Vermont than it would have been to go from that home of many years to the new house on the water side of Beacon. This thing and that is embittered to us, so that we may be willing to relinquish it; the world, life itself, is embittered to most of us, so that we are glad to have done with them at last; and this home was haunted with such memories to each of those who abandoned it that to go was less exile than escape. Mrs. Lapham could not look into Irene's room without seeing the girl there before her glass, tearing the poor little keepsakes of her hapless fancy from their hiding-places to take them and fling them in passionate renunciation upon her sister; she could not come into the sitting-room, where her little ones had grown up, without starting at the thought of her husband sitting so many weary nights at his desk there, trying to fight his way back to hope out of the ruin into which he was slipping. When she remembered that night when Rogers came, she hated the place. Irene accepted her release from the house eagerly, and was glad to go before and prepare for the family at Lapham. Penelope was always ashamed of her engagement there; it must seem better somewhere else, and she was glad to go too. No one but Lapham, in fact, felt the pang of parting in all its keenness. Whatever regret the others had was softened to them by the likeness of their flitting to many of those removals for the summer which they made in the late spring when they left Nankeen Square; they were going directly into the country instead of to the sea-side first; but Lapham, who usually remained in town long after they had gone, knew all the difference. For his nerves there was no mechanical sense of coming back; this was as much the end of his proud, prosperous life as death itself could have been. He was returning to begin life anew, but he knew, as well as he knew that he should not find his vanished youth in his native hills, that it could never again be the triumph that it had been. That was impossible, not only in his stiffened and weakened forces, but in the very nature of things. He was going back, by grace of the man whom he owed money, to make what he could out of the one chance which his successful rivals had left him.

In one phase his paint had held its own against bad times and ruinous competition, and it was with the hope of doing still more with the Persis Brand that he now set himself to work. The West Virginia people confessed that they could not produce those fine grades, and they willingly left the field to him. A strange, not ignoble friendliness existed between Lapham and the three brothers; they had used him fairly; it was their facilities that had conquered him, not their ill-will; and he recognized in them without enmity the necessity to which he had yielded. If he succeeded in his efforts to develop his paint in this direction, it must be for a long time on a small scale compared with his former business, which it could never equal, and he brought to them the flagging energies of an elderly man. He was more broken than he knew by his failure; it did not kill, as it often does, but it weakened the spring once so strong and elastic. He lapsed more and more into acquiescence with his changed condition, and that bragging note of his was rarely sounded. He worked faithfully enough in his enterprise, but sometimes he failed to seize occasions that in his younger days he would have turned to golden account. His wife saw in him a daunted look that made her heart ache for him.

One result of his friendly relations with the West Virginia people was that Corey went in with them, and the fact that he did so solely upon Lapham's advice, and by means of his recommendation, was perhaps the Colonel's proudest consolation. Corey knew the business thoroughly, and after half a year at Kanawha Falls and in the office at New York, he went out to Mexico and Central America, to see what could be done for them upon the ground which he had theoretically studied with Lapham.

Before he went he came up to Vermont, and urged Penelope to go with him. He was to be first in the city of Mexico, and if his mission was successful he was to be kept there and in South America several years, watching the new railroad enterprises and the development of mechanical agriculture and whatever other undertakings offered an opening for the introduction of the paint. They were all young men together, and Corey, who had put his money into the company, had a proprietary interest in the success which they were eager to achieve.

"There's no more reason now and no less than ever there was," mused Penelope, in counsel with her mother, "why I should say Yes, or why I should say No. Everything else changes, but this is just where it was a year ago. It don't go backward, and it don't go forward. Mother, I believe I shall take the bit in my teeth—if anybody will put it there!"

"It isn't the same as it was," suggested her mother. "You can see that Irene's all over it."

"That's no credit to me," said Penelope. "I ought to be just as much ashamed as ever."

"You no need ever to be ashamed."

"That's true, too," said the girl. "And I can sneak off to Mexico with a good conscience if I could make up my mind to it." She laughed. "Well, if I could be *sentenced* to be married, or somebody would up and forbid the banns! *I* don't know what to do about it."

Her mother left her to carry her hesitation back to Corey, and she said now they had better go all over it and try to reason it out. "And I hope that whatever I do, it won't be for my own sake, but for—others!"

Corey said he was sure of that, and looked at her with eyes of patient tenderness.

"I don't say it is wrong," she proceeded, rather aimlessly, "but I can't make it seem right. I don't know whether I can make you understand, but the idea of being happy, when everybody else is so miserable, is more than I can endure. It makes me wretched."

"Then perhaps that's your share of the common suffering," suggested Corey, smiling.

"Oh, you know it isn't! You know it's nothing. Oh! One of the reasons is what I told you once before, that as long as father is in trouble I can't let you think of me. Now that he's lost everything——" She bent her eyes inquiringly upon him, as if for the effect of this argument.

"I don't think that's a very good reason," he answered seriously, but smiling still. "Do you believe me when I tell you that I love you?"

"Why, I suppose I must," she said, dropping her eyes.

"Then why shouldn't I think all the more of you on account of your father's loss? You didn't suppose I cared for you because he was prosperous?" There was a shade of reproach, ever so delicate and gentle, in his smiling question, which she felt.

"No, I couldn't think such a thing of you. I—I don't know what I meant. I meant that——" She could not go on and say that she had felt herself more worthy of him because of her father's money; it would not have been true; yet there was no other explanation. She stopped and cast a helpless glance at him.

He came to her aid. "I understand why you shouldn't wish me to suffer by your father's misfortunes."

"Yes, that was it; and there is too great a difference every way. We ought to look at that again. You mustn't pretend that you don't know it, for that wouldn't be true. Your mother will never like me, and perhaps—perhaps I shall not like her."

"Well," said Corey, a little daunted, "you won't have to marry my family."

"Ah, that isn't the point!"

"I know it," he admitted. "I won't pretend that I don't see what you mean; but I'm sure that all the differences would disappear when you came to know my family better. I'm not afraid but you and my mother will like each other—she can't help it!" he exclaimed, less judicially than he had hitherto spoken, and he went on to urge some points of doubtful tenability. "We have our ways, and you have yours; and while I don't say but what you and my mother and sisters would be a little strange together at first, it would soon wear off on both sides. There can't be anything hopelessly different in you all, and if there were it wouldn't be any difference to me."

"Do you think it would be pleasant to have you on my side against your mother?"

"There won't be any sides. Tell me just what it is you're afraid of."

"Afraid?"

"Thinking of, then."

"I don't know. It isn't anything they say or do," she explained, with her eyes intent on his. "It's what they are. I couldn't be natural with them, and if I can't be natural with people, I'm disagreeable."

"Can you be natural with me?"

"Oh, I'm not afraid of you. I never was. That was the trouble from the beginning."

"Well, then, that's all that's necessary. And it never was the least trouble to me!"

"It made me untrue to Irene."

"You mustn't say that! You were always true to her."

"She cared for you first."

"Well, but I never cared for her at all!" he besought her.

"She thought you did."

"That was nobody's fault, and I can't let you make it yours. My dear——"

"Wait. We must understand each other," said Penelope, rising from her seat to prevent an advance he was making from his; "I want you to realize the whole affair. Should you want a girl who hadn't a cent in the world, and felt different in your mother's company, and had cheated and betrayed her own sister?"

"I want you!"

"Very well, then, you can't have me. I should always despise myself. I ought to give you up for all these reasons. Yes, I must." She looked at him intently, and there was a tentative quality in her affirmations.

"Is this your answer?" he said. "I must submit. If I asked too much of you, I was wrong. And—good-bye."

He held out his hand, and she put hers in it. "You think I'm capricious and fickle!" she said. "I can't help it—I don't know myself. I can't keep to one thing for half a day at a time. But it's right for us to part—yes, it must be. It must be," she repeated; "and I shall try to remember that. Good-bye! I will try to keep that in my mind, and you will too—you won't care, very soon! I didn't mean *that*—no; I know how true you are; but you will soon look at me differently, and see that even if there hadn't been this about Irene, I was not the one for you. You do think so, don't you?" she pleaded, clinging to his hand. "I am not at all what they would like—your family; I felt that. I am little, and black, and homely, and they don't understand my way of talking, and now that we've lost everything—— No, I'm not fit. Good-bye. You're quite right not to have patience with me any longer. I've tried you enough. I ought to be willing to marry you against their wishes if you want me to, but I can't make the sacrifice—I'm too selfish for that." All at once she flung herself on his breast. "I can't even give you up! I shall never dare look any one in the face again. Go, go! But take me with you! I tried to do without you! I gave it a fair trial, and it was a dead failure. Oh, poor Irene! How could *she* give you up?"

Corey went back to Boston immediately, and left Penelope, as he must, to tell her sister that they were to be married. She was spared from the first advance toward this by an accident or a misunderstanding. Irene came straight to her after Corey was gone, and demanded, "Penelope Lapham, have you been such a ninny as to send that man away on my account?"

Penelope recoiled from this terrible courage; she did not answer directly, and Irene went on, "Because if you did, I'll thank you to bring him back again. I'm not going to have him thinking that I'm dying for a man that never cared for me. It's insulting, and I'm not going to stand it. Now, you just send for him!"

"Oh, I will, 'Rene," gasped Penelope. And then she added, shamed out of her prevarication by Irene's haughty magnanimity, "I have. That is—he's coming back——"

Irene looked at her a moment, and then, whatever thought was in her mind, said fiercely, "Well!" and left her to her dismay—her dismay and her relief, for they both knew that this was the last time they should ever speak of that again.

The marriage came after so much sorrow and trouble, and the fact was received with so much misgiving for the past and future, that it brought Lapham none of the triumph in which he had once exulted at the thought of an alliance with the Coreys. Adversity had so far been his friend that it had taken from him all hope of the social success for which people crawl and truckle, and restored him, through failure and doubt and heartache, the manhood which his prosperity had so nearly stolen from him. Neither he nor his wife thought now that their daughter was marrying a Corey; they thought only that she was giving herself to the man who loved her, and their acquiescence was sobered still further by the presence of Irene. Their hearts were far more with her.

Again and again Mrs. Lapham said she did not see how she could go through it. "I can't make it seem right," she said.

"It *is* right," steadily answered the Colonel.

"Yes, I know. But it don't *seem* so."

It would be easy to point out traits in Penelope's character which finally reconciled all her husband's family and endeared her to them. These things continually happen in novels; and the Coreys, as they had always promised themselves to do, made the best, and not the worst, of Tom's marriage.

They were people who could value Lapham's behavior as Tom reported it to them. They were proud of him, and Bromfield Corey, who found a delicate, æsthetic pleasure in the heroism with which Lapham had withstood Rogers and his temptations,—something finely dramatic and unconsciously effective,—wrote him a letter which would once have flattered the rough soul almost to ecstasy, though now he affected to slight it in showing it. "It's all right if it makes it more comfortable for Pen," he said to his wife.

But the differences remained uneffaced, if not uneffaceable, between the Coreys and Tom Corey's wife. "If he had only married the Colonel!" subtly suggested Nanny Corey.

There was a brief season of civility and forbearance on both sides, when he brought her home before starting for Mexico, and her father-in-law made a sympathetic feint of liking Penelope's way of talking, but it is questionable if even he found it so delightful as her husband did. Lily Corey made a little, ineffectual sketch of her, which she put by with other studies to finish up some time, and found her rather picturesque in some ways. Nanny got on with her better than the rest, and saw possibilities for her in the country to which she was going. "As she's quite unformed socially," she explained to her mother, "there is a chance that she will form herself on the Spanish manner, if she stays there long enough, and that when she comes back she will have the charm of not olives, perhaps, but *tortillas*, whatever they are: something strange and foreign, even if it's borrowed. I'm glad she's going to Mexico. At that distance we can—correspond."

Her mother sighed, and said bravely that she was sure they all got on very pleasantly as it was, and that she was perfectly satisfied if Tom was.

There was, in fact, much truth in what she said of their harmony with Penelope. Having resolved, from the beginning, to make the best of the worst, it might almost be said that they were supported and consoled in their good intentions by a higher power. This marriage had not, thanks to an overruling Providence, brought the succession of Lapham teas upon Bromfield Corey which he had dreaded; the Laphams were far off in their native fastnesses, and neither Lily nor Nanny Corey was obliged to sacrifice herself to the conversation of Irene; they were not even called upon to make a social demonstration for Penelope at a time when, most people being still out of town, it would have been so easy; she and Tom had both begged that there might be nothing of that kind; and though none of the Coreys learned to know her very well in the week she spent with them, they did not find it hard to get on with her. There were even moments when Nanny Corey, like her father, had glimpses of what Tom had called her humor, but it was perhaps too unlike their own to be easily recognizable.

Whether Penelope, on her side, found it more difficult to harmonize, I cannot say. She had much more of the harmonizing to do, since they were four to one; but then she had gone through so much greater trials before. When the door of their carriage closed and it drove off with her and her husband to the station, she fetched a long sigh.

"What is it?" asked Corey, who ought to have known better.

"Oh, nothing. I don't think I shall feel strange amongst the Mexicans now."

He looked at her with a puzzled smile, which grew a little graver, and then he put his arm round her and drew her closer to him. This made her cry on his shoulder. "I only meant that I should have you all to myself." There is no proof that she meant more, but it is certain that our manners and customs go for more in life than our qualities. The price that we pay for civilization is the fine yet impassable differentiation of these. Perhaps we pay too much; but it will not be possible to persuade those who have the difference in their favor that this is so. They may be right; and at any rate the blank misgiving, the recurring sense of disappointment to which the young people's departure left the Coreys is to be considered. That was the end of their son and brother for them; they felt that; and they were not mean or unamiable people.

He remained three years away. Some changes took place in that time. One of these was the purchase by the Kanawha Falls Company of the mines and works at Lapham. The transfer relieved Lapham of the load of debt which he was still laboring under, and gave him an interest in the vaster enterprise of the younger men, which he had once vainly hoped to grasp all in his own hand. He began to tell of this coincidence as something very striking; and pushing on more actively the special branch of the business left to him, he bragged, quite in his old way, of its enormous extension. His son-in-law, he said, was pushing it in Mexico and Central America: an idea that they had originally had in common. Well, young blood was what was wanted in a thing of that kind. Now, those fellows out in West Virginia: all young, and a perfect team!

For himself, he owned that he had made mistakes; he could see just where the mistakes were—put his finger right on them. But one thing he could say: he had been no man's enemy but his own; every dollar, every cent had gone to pay his debts; he had come out with clean hands. He said all this, and much more, to Mr. Sewell the summer after he sold out, when the minister and his wife stopped at Lapham on their way across from the White Mountains to Lake Champlain; Lapham had found them on the cars, and pressed them to stop off.

There were times when Mrs. Lapham had as great pride in the clean-handedness with which Lapham had come out as he had himself, but her satisfaction was not so constant. At those times, knowing the temptations he had resisted, she thought him the noblest and grandest of men; but no woman could endure to live in the same house with a perfect hero, and there were other times when she reminded him that if he had kept his word to her about speculating in stocks, and had looked after the insurance of his property half as carefully as he had looked after a couple of worthless women who had no earthly claim on him, they would not be where they were now. He humbly admitted it all, and left her to think of Rogers herself. She did not fail to do so, and the thought did not fail to restore him to her tenderness again.

I do not know how it is that clergymen and physicians keep from telling their wives the secrets confided to them; perhaps they can trust their wives to find them out for themselves whenever they wish. Sewell had laid before his wife the case of the Laphams after they came to consult with him about Corey's proposal to Penelope, for he wished to be confirmed in his belief that he had advised them soundly; but he had not given her their names, and he had not known Corey's himself. Now he had no compunctions in talking the affair over with her without the veil of ignorance which she had hitherto assumed, for she declared that as soon as she heard of Corey's engagement to Penelope, the whole thing had flashed upon her. "And that night at dinner, I could have told the child that he was in love with her sister by the way he talked about her; I heard him; and if she had not been so blindly in love with him herself, she would have known it too. I must say, I can't help feeling a sort of contempt for her sister."

"Oh, but you must not!" cried Sewell. "That is wrong, cruelly wrong. I'm sure that's out of your novel-reading, my dear, and not out of your heart. Come! it grieves me to hear you say such a thing as that."

"Oh, I dare say this pretty thing has got over it—how much character she has got!—and I suppose she'll see somebody else."

Sewell had to content himself with this partial concession. As a matter of fact, unless it was the young West Virginian who had come on to arrange the purchase of the Works, Irene had not yet seen any one, and whether there was ever anything between them is a fact that would need a separate inquiry. It is certain that at the end of five years after the disappointment which she met so bravely, she was still unmarried. But she was even then still very young, and her life at Lapham had been varied by visits to the West. It had also been varied by an invitation, made with the politest resolution by Mrs. Corey, to visit in Boston, which the girl was equal to refusing in the same spirit.

Sewell was intensely interested in the moral spectacle which Lapham presented under his changed conditions. The Colonel, who was more the Colonel in those hills than he could ever have been on the Back Bay, kept him and Mrs. Sewell over night at his house; and he showed the minister minutely round the Works and drove him all over his farm. For this expedition he employed a lively colt which had not yet come of age, and an open buggy long past its prime, and was no more ashamed of his turnout than of the finest he had ever driven on the Milldam. He was rather shabby and slovenly in dress, and he had fallen unkempt, after the country fashion, as to his hair and beard and boots. The house was plain, and was furnished with the simpler movables out of the house in Nankeen Square. There were certainly all the necessaries, but no luxuries, unless the statues of Prayer and Faith might be so considered. The Laphams now burned kerosene, of course, and they had no furnace in the winter; these were the only hardships the Colonel complained of; but he said that as soon as the company got to paying dividends again,—he was evidently proud of the outlays that for the present prevented this,—he should put in steam-heat and naphtha-gas. He spoke freely of his failure, and with a confidence that seemed inspired by his former trust in Sewell, whom, indeed, he treated like an intimate friend, rather than an acquaintance of two or three meetings. He went back to his first connection with Rogers, and he put before Sewell hypothetically his own conclusions in regard to the matter.

"Sometimes," he said, "I get to thinking it all over, and it seems to me I done wrong about Rogers in the first place; that the whole trouble came from that. It was just like starting a row of bricks. I tried to catch up, and stop 'em from going, but they all tumbled, one after another. It wa'n't in the nature of things that they could be stopped till the last brick went. I don't talk much with my wife any more about it; but I should like to know how it strikes you."

"We can trace the operation of evil in the physical world," replied the minister, "but I'm more and more puzzled about it in the moral world. There its course is often so very obscure; and often it seems to involve, so far as we can see, no penalty whatever. And in your own case, as I understand, you don't admit—you don't feel sure—that you ever actually did wrong this man."

"Well, no; I don't. That is to say——"

He did not continue, and after a while Sewell said, with that subtle kindness of his, "I should be inclined to think—nothing can be thrown quite away; and it can't be that our sins only weaken us—that your fear of having possibly behaved selfishly toward this man kept you on your guard, and strengthened you when you were brought face to face with a greater"—he was going to say temptation, but he saved Lapham's pride, and said—"emergency."

"Do you think so?"

"I think that there may be truth in what I suggest."

"Well, I don't know what it was," said Lapham; "all I know is that when it came to the point, although I could see that I'd got to go under unless I did it, that I couldn't sell out to those Englishmen, and I couldn't let that man put his money into my business without I told him just how things stood."

As Sewell afterwards told his wife, he could see that the loss of his fortune had been a terrible trial to Lapham, just because his prosperity had been so gross and palpable; and he had now a burning desire to know exactly how, at the bottom of his heart, Lapham still felt. "And do you ever have any regrets?" he delicately inquired of him.

"About what I done? Well, it don't always seem as if I done it," replied Lapham. "Seems sometimes as if it was a hole opened for me, and I crept out of it. I don't know," he added thoughtfully, biting the corner of his stiff mustache—"I don't know as I should always say it paid; but if I done it, and the thing was to do over again, right in the same way, I guess I should have to do it."

Chronology

1837   Born March 1, second son, second child among eight sib-
            lings, in Martinsville (now Martins Ferry), Ohio, to Mary
            Dean Howells, of Irish and Pennsylvania Dutch descent,
            and William Cooper Howells, a Welsh-born printer and
            publisher whose utopian yearnings and lively mind led
            him from deism and the Democrats to Swedenborgianism
            and the Whigs and who provided literate and challenging
            influences unusual in a post-frontier household.

1840–47   Father buys Whig paper, *Hamilton Intelligencer*, and
            moves to Hamilton, Ohio. Howells' early assistance as
            typesetter allows little formal schooling.

1848–50   Father loses *Intelligencer* because of his Free Soil convic-
            tions. Takes on *Dayton Transcript* and fails again, despite
            bitter struggle in which Howells works long, hard hours
            typesetting and delivering papers. Father, with business-
            men brothers, establishes family utopian commune at Eu-
            reka Mills, Ohio, but abandons it after a year when broth-
            ers withdraw financial support.

1851–52   Free Soil Party hires father as legislative reporter in Co-
            lumbus, the state capital, for *Ohio State Journal*, in which
            Howells, now a printer's apprentice, has a poem pub-
            lished on March 23, 1852. Father accepts editorship of ab-
            olitionist *Ashtabula Sentinel*, in radical Western Reserve.
            Family moves to Ashtabula in summer of 1852 and that
            winter to Jefferson, the county seat, where they begin to
            prosper.

1853–57   Howells combines full-time work as *Sentinel*'s printer
            with rigorous self-education, learning Spanish, French,
            Latin, and later German, which leads to one of his prime
            "literary passions," Heinrich Heine. He suffers periodic
            nervous collapses, which bring about humiliating failure
            as city editor of *Cincinatti Gazette*, not fully overcome un-
            til his marriage. Writes and publishes prolifically—jour-
            nalism, verse, essays—and works on novels.

1858   Becomes city editor and columnist of the *Ohio State Jour-
            nal*, part of Governor Salmon P. Chase's political organi-

zation. Howells' cleverness, wit, and shy charm win him professional and social success in the provincial capital.

1859–60   Poems, stories, and reviews in *Atlantic*, *National Era*, *Saturday Press*, and *Dial*, his first book (*Poems of Two Friends*, 1859, with John James Piatt), and sympathetic writing about John Brown's raid on Harper's Ferry bring national attention. With proceeds ($199) of Lincoln campaign biography (in *Lives and Speeches of Abraham Lincoln and Hannibal Hamlin*, 1860), he makes pilgrimage East to meet literary figures of New England—James T. Fields and James Russell Lowell of the *Atlantic*, Holmes, Hawthorne, Emerson, Thoreau—and of New York—Whitman and the *Saturday Press* "Bohemians." Goes to Brattleboro, Vermont, to meet family of Elinor Mead, whom he has known since she visited her cousin, Rutherford B. Hayes, in Ohio the winter before; they become engaged.

1861–64   Lincoln administration awards Howells U.S. Consulate in Venice, where he lives for duration of Civil War. Marries Elinor Mead in Paris, December 24, 1862, and daughter Winifred is born December 17, 1863. Studies Italian, Dante, Venetian art; discovers plays of Carlo Goldoni which reflect his own interest in life of lower classes. Elinor, from a cultivated family that includes artists and architects (as well as the utopian John Humphrey Noyes), contributes to his artistic education. Writes humorous anti-romantic travel letters for *Boston Advertiser* and prepares them for book form, but failure to sell poetry or fiction leads to despair about literary career. In July 1864 Lowell writes him to praise his *Advertiser* letters and to accept a long article, "Recent Italian Comedy," for *North American Review*. With new confidence, tours Italy gathering material for another travel book.

1865   Returning to United States on four-month leave, resigns consulate to begin literary career. In November joins E. L. Godkin's *Nation* in New York.

1866–70   Moves to Cambridge to become assistant editor of *Atlantic*, assigned to supervise production, review books, and recruit new talent. Enters the "old Cambridge" of Longfellow and C.E. Norton, the "proper Boston" of Holmes and Lowell, and the international literary set of Fields. Begins lifelong friendships with William and Henry James, also from a Swedenborgian family, and with Mark Twain. In 1868 mother dies and son, John Mead, a future architect, is born. *Venetian Life* published in 1866; *Italian Journeys*, 1867; *Suburban Sketches*, 1870.

1871–80   Succeeds Fields as editor of *Atlantic* and has house built for family in Cambridge, where daughter Mildred is born September 1872; in 1878 has another house, Redtop, built in nearby Belmont, Massachusetts. Under his direction *Atlantic* serializes fiction of Henry James and Mark Twain and reflects current Cambridge concern with Darwinism and, after Crash of 1873, socioeconomic theory. Howells' reviews show growing interest in native and European realism, especially Turgenev's work. *Their Wedding Journey*, 1871; *A Chance Acquaintance, Poems*, 1873; *A Foregone Conclusion*, 1874; "Private Theatricals," serially, 1875; *Sketch of the Life and Character of Rutherford B. Hayes, The Parlor Car*, 1876; *Out of the Question: A Comedy*, 1877; *The Lady of the Aroostook*, 1879; *The Undiscovered Country*, 1880.

1881–84   Resigns *Atlantic* editorship to write full time. After taking family abroad for the sake of Winifred's health, moves to Boston where he associates with journalists, clergymen, and others actively concerned with social reform. "The Sleeping Car," inaugurating a series of popular Christmas farces, appears in 1882 in *Harper's*, and Howells begins writing for the *Century*, where an essay praising Henry James provokes international "Realism War." Publishes *Dr. Breen's Practice* (1881), *A Modern Instance* (1882), and writes *Indian Summer* and *The Rise of Silas Lapham*.

1885   In the spring a sudden, overwhelming sense of guilt—a Swedenborgian "vastation"—turns Howells to Tolstoy and deeper, more radical social inquiries. Winifred suffers a relapse; her Boston debut is canceled and Howells leaves Boston house and moves family to suburban hotel. In October he signs with Harper & Brothers the most lucrative contract offered an American author up to that time; he is to furnish a book a year and a monthly *Harper's* column, "The Editor's Study," and he gives Harper & Brothers first refusal of all work. *The Rise of Silas Lapham, Tuscan Cities*, published.

1886–90   Closest sibling, Victoria, dies of malaria. Howells declines Chair at Harvard held earlier by Longfellow and Lowell—and family wanders in search of a cure for Winifred, whose illness, misdiagnosed as "neurasthenic," is fatal in March 1889. Parents guilt-stricken and deeply grieved. "The Editor's Study" champions realism, Tolstoy, Dostoevsky, Hamlin Garland, and Emily Dickinson; it also reflects Howells' attraction (shared by his wife) to socialism, his commitment to democracy, and his opposition to social injustice. In 1887 he becomes the only prominent American writer to risk a public plea for Chicago anarchists unjustly convicted of murder in the Haymarket Riots. Hostile press reactions to his plea for executive clemency briefly threaten his career. *Indian Summer*, *Poems*, *The Minister's Charge*, 1886; *April Hopes*, 1887; *Annie Kilburn*, 1888; *A Hazard of New Fortunes*, *The Shadow of a Dream*, *A Boy's Town*, 1890.

1891–93   Lets Harper contract expire and does free-lance writing again, including experimental poetry. Moves to New York to edit *Cosmopolitan*, for which he writes the utopian *Altrurian Sketches*. Begins a series of major radical essays— socialist, feminist, anti-racist, anti-imperialist—but his plan to make *Cosmopolitan* a center for literary radicals ends when he resigns in conflict with its millionaire owner. *An Imperative Duty*, *Criticism and Fiction*, 1891; *The Quality of Mercy*, 1892; *The World of Chance*, *The Coast of Bohemia*, 1893.

1894–98   Travels occasionally—visits son in France in 1894, Carlsbad, Germany, in 1897, lecture tours in 1897 and 1899. Emerging as a declared "Ibsenian," he befriends new generation of realists, including Stephen Crane and H.B. Fuller, and sponsors Crane's *Maggie*, Paul Lawrence Dunbar's *Lyrics of Lowly Life*, and the first Jewish-American novel, Abram Cahan's *Yekl*. Father dies August 1894. *A Traveler from Altruria*, 1894; *My Literary Passions*, *Stops of Various Quills*, 1895; *Impressions and Experiences*, 1896; *The Landlord at Lion's Head*, 1897; *The Story of a Play*, 1898.

1899–1903 Harper & Brothers fails and is placed in receivership, but J. P. Morgan rescues it and puts Colonel George Harvey in charge; Howells agrees to conduct monthly column, "Editor's Easy Chair." Here and in Harvey's *North Amer-*

ican Review, over the next decade, Howells continues his literary and social criticism from a realist, socialist, anti-imperialist perspective. He reviews Thorstein Veblen and Frank Norris favorably, and introduces Charles W. Chesnutt in the *Atlantic. Their Silver Wedding Journey*, 1899; *Literary Friends and Acquaintance*, 1900; *A Pair of Patient Lovers, Heroines of Fiction*, "Professor Barrett Wendell's Notions of American Literature," 1901; *The Kentons, Literature and Life*, "Émile Zola," "Frank Norris," 1902.

1904—09   Howells receives Litt. D. from Oxford, 1904, and is elected first president of American Academy of Arts and Letters, 1908. He writes tributes to John Hay and Mark Twain, Tolstoy and Ibsen, begins friendship with G. B. Shaw, and travels—to Italy in 1908, England and the Continent in 1909. *The Son of Royal Langbrith*, 1904; *London Films*, 1905; *Certain Delightful English Towns*, 1906; *Through the Eye of the Needle*, 1907; *Fennel and Rue, Roman Holidays*, 1908; *Seven English Cities*, 1909.

1910—17   Mark Twain dies in April, Elinor Mead Howells in May 1910. Howells travels to England and then to Bermuda and Spain. His old audience is dying out and he has difficulty placing fiction in magazines. The American Academy of Arts and Letters inaugurates Howells Medal for fiction in 1915, presents the first one to Howells; but the "Library Edition" of his works is aborted by commercial publishers' quarrel. He declares his support for the Allies in the World War, praises the "new poetry" of Conrad Aiken, Robert Frost, Vachel Lindsay, Edgar Lee Masters, Amy Lowell, and tries unsuccessfully to obtain Nobel Prize for Henry James. *My Mark Twain, Imaginary Interviews*, 1910; *New Leaf Mills, Familiar Spanish Travels*, 1913; *The Daughter of the Storage, The Leatherwood God, Years of My Youth*, 1916.

1920   Dies of pneumonia May 11, in New York. *The Vacation of the Kelwyns*.

1921   *Mrs. Farrell.*

Note on the Texts

The texts reprinted in this volume are those of the Indiana University's *A Selected Edition of W. D. Howells*, prepared in accordance with the standards of the Modern Language Association's Center for Editions of American Authors and approved by that organization. Three of the titles have been published by the Indiana University Press with full textual apparatus: *A Modern Instance*, volume 10, in 1977; *Indian Summer*, volume 11, in 1971; and *The Rise of Silas Lapham*, volume 12, in 1971. *A Foregone Conclusion* is scheduled for publication as volume 7.

In this volume the four novels are arranged in the order of their composition. This reverses the original order of publication for *Indian Summer* and *The Rise of Silas Lapham*. Though the public saw *Lapham* first, serialized in the *Century* magazine between November 1884 and August 1885, Howells had already completed *Indian Summer*, and he held the finished manuscript for almost sixteen months (March 1884–July 1885) before its serialization in *Harper's Monthly*. As we shall see, the delay had important effects on the history of the text. The chronological order of titles in this volume illuminates not only the growing maturity of Howells' artistry but also the increasing complexity of the business arrangements required by the copyright problems facing an American author of the late nineteenth century. Again, the apparently extraneous details of business influenced the choice and emendation of the texts.

A Foregone Conclusion poses no textual difficulties. A complete manuscript in the author's hand forms the basic text, which the editors of the Indiana edition have compared with the first publication (as a serial in the *Atlantic Monthly*, July–December 1874), with the first book publication (James R. Osgood and Company of Boston, dated 1875), and with the first British publication (David Douglas of Edinburgh, dated 1882). No other relevant forms exist. Although Howells, as author and as editor of the *Atlantic*, made extensive changes in the proofs for the serial, there are no debatable passages or missing links in the history of the novel's publication. The Indiana editors entered in the manuscript text the later changes that were clearly made by Howells and weeded out those attributable to compositor's error or editorial styling.

In *A Modern Instance* textual problems begin to increase. Author's manuscript exists for only the first fifteen of the forty-one chapters, so the editors have used the manuscript for those chapters, and the serial form (*Century*, December 1881–October 1882) for chapters sixteen through forty-one. The serial has been chosen because it is presumed to retain more features of the missing manuscript than would be found in later forms that have passed through further styling and typesetting. The first book editions (James R. Osgood and Company, Boston, and David Douglas, Edinburgh, both published October 1882) are also important because of the revisions Howells made in reading proof for them. The editorial judgments that produced the text presented here are clearly and cogently argued in the Indiana University volume, and interested readers are urged to follow the story there. For the present edition it is best merely to repeat the conclusion of the Indiana editors that, though the variations among texts are small, no version of *A Modern Instance* published during his lifetime contained all of the "final revisions" Howells supplied. The text here attempts to do that.

Indian Summer, as mentioned, was completed some sixteen months before it began serial publication in *Harper's Monthly* (July 1885 through February 1886). As a result, Howells had time to revise and polish the manuscript (now missing) before it was first set in type. This was unusual for Howells, who was extremely productive and methodical as a writer and seldom permitted himself any slack time or margin for indecision. He usually started publication of a serial before he completed the novel, writing new chapters, revising earlier ones, and reading proofs simultaneously. Because typesetting was inexpensive in those days, he could afford to use proof sheets the way an author now uses typed copy, as a draft on which to make major changes. Frequently the final polishing would occur only when he revised the published serial for republication in book form. But in the case of this delayed novel, the first book edition (David Douglas of Edinburgh, printed in December 1885, but not published until March 1886) shows very few revisions of the serial. By this point in his career Howells was having the publisher Douglas set, print, and register his books in England to secure British copyright, and then ship the plates to America for use by Howells' American publisher. Consequently the Edinburgh edition is not only the first book edition, it is also printed from the same plates used for the American edition (Ticknor and Company of Boston, published February 1886). The Indiana editors used as their basic text the serial printing and introduced fewer than a dozen changes in wording from later editions.

The publishing history of *The Rise of Silas Lapham* was more complicated, however. Again no manuscript or proof sheets for serial publication have been found. But comparison of the serial (*Century*, November 1884 through August 1885) against the copyright deposit parts set by David Douglas in Edinburgh, Douglas' first book edition, and the first American edition (Ticknor and Company of Boston, August 1885) reveals at least four stages of revision. The Indiana editors analyzed these revisions and then chose the serial version as the basic text, incorporating later revisions made by Howells in the book. The web of evidence and reasoning for this choice are explained in the Indiana edition and need not be repeated. However, there is one interesting change from the serial that deserves mention here. In this case, reader response induced Howells to change his text, unwillingly, to accommodate the editorial timidity of the *Century* magazine. To Howells' surprise, his use of the word "dynamite" upset *Century* editor Richard Watson Gilder and his staff, because Alfred Nobel's invention of that explosive in 1866 was thought to have provided foreign terrorists with a new and dreadful weapon. Howells excised the dangerous word from the serial and left it out of the book, but his original version of Bromfield Corey's remark is restored in the Indiana edition and appears on page 1041 of this volume.

The standards for American English continue to fluctuate and in some ways were conspicuously different in earlier periods from what they are now. In nineteenth-century writings, for example, a word might be spelled in more than one way, even in the same work, and such variations might be carried into print. Commas were sometimes used expressively to suggest the movements of voice, and capitals were sometimes meant to give significances to a word beyond those it might have in its uncapitalized form. Since modernization would remove such effects, this volume has preserved the spelling, punctuation, capitalization, and wording of the Indiana University *Selected Edition*, which strives to be as faithful to Howells' usage as surviving evidence permits.

The texts in this volume follow the Indiana University editions of *A Modern Instance* (2nd printing), *Indian Summer* (2nd printing), and *The Rise of Silas Lapham* (2nd printing). The text of *A Foregone Conclusion* has been printed from printer's copy supplied by the Howells Center, Indiana University. The present volume reprints only the *texts* of these editions; it does not attempt to reproduce features of their typographic design.

Typographical errors have been corrected. Following is a list of these errors, cited by page and line numbers: 266.19, Bartly; 270.11, home.; 356.4, my wife; 370.38, superflous; 440.13, squire; 554.29, society.; 566.16, capitivity; 576.5, squire; 938.25, a a; 1109.15, see; 1174.22, exitedly. Errors corrected third printing: 33.25, threatricalization (*LOA*); 63.3, settling (*LOA*); 505.16, come.; 584.18, attained; 799.38–39, temperment (*LOA*); 870.21–22, ta/pering (*LOA*); 997.28, an (*LOA*).

The corrections made in the original scholarly editions of the texts printed here have the approval of the general editor of *A Selected Edition of W. D. Howells* and will be incorporated in future printings of the scholarly editions and authorized reprints.

Notes

In the notes below, the numbers refer to page and line of the present volume (the line count includes chapter headings). Notes printed at the foot of pages in the text are Howells' own. No note is made for material included in a standard desk-reference book.

A FOREGONE CONCLUSION

4.27–28   (one . . . Venice,)] Howells was U.S. Consul in Venice, 1861–65.

43.37   maccheronic] Mixed Italian-English illustrating "macaronic": speech or writing in a medley of languages, implying simple ignorance or ignorant pretense to sophistication.

43.38   poco più di] Italian: little more of.

44.5   Bergamask] A triple pun—the dialect of Bergamo; macaronic; Ferris' characteristic hiding of ambivalence behind masks of humorous, fantastic speech.

50.33   *nicchio*] Italian: priest's biretta.

50.35   *talare*] Italian: cassock.

52.4   *abbate's*] Italian: priest not member of an Order.

62.30   *villeggiatura*] Italian: country vacation.

62.33   *abbate di casa*] Italian: household priest.

65.38–39   "Close . . . vines."] Tennyson, "Mariana in the South," ll.3–4.

67.17   'as . . . wine,'] Tennyson, "Locksley Hall," l.152.

91.36   *scaldino*] Italian: little pot of glowing charcoal carried about as a personal heater.

104.27   *facchini*] Italian: porters; or here, perhaps, bearers.

130.36   *clave*] "Con*clave*," she means, correcting the slangy "confab."

A MODERN INSTANCE

175.21   Fast Day] Traditional New England day of penitence and contrition. One was commonly appointed (a vestigial remnant of Lent?) in the spring.

263.27   Darling Minnie]   Masculine slang for that lost sweetheart, waiting in heaven, who infested the sentimental ballads of the era.

271.33   old Tylor]   Edward Burnett Tylor, author of *Primitive Culture* (1871), sometimes called the father of anthropology as a science.

362.7   Eastlake movement]   Charles Eastlake, English painter and art critic, for whom a style of interior decoration was named.

362.34   Papanti's]   Lorenzo Papanti, an exiled Italian count, established the one "proper Boston" dancing school of the century.

367.26   " 'My heart leaps up,']   Title and first words of the Wordsworth poem.

419.25   what Grant said:]   The sentence that follows was a popular paraphrase of a passage from President U. S. Grant's First Inaugural Address, March 4, 1869.

455.9−10   'The . . . it.']   Also a popular paraphrase, this time from R. W. Emerson's essay "Domestic Life."

461.1   *bolla*]   The standard Latin is *bulla*, meaning "bullet-like," as in the round seals dangling from the parchment which authenticate a Papal Bull. Perhaps this was a typographical error, or Howells knew a form not standard in Latin or Italian.

474.2   presidential . . . summer]   As succeeding pages show, it was 1876, the year of the Hayes-Tilden electoral contest.

586.11−12   Whited Sepulchre]   A good joke on the dime-novel myth of Tombstone, Arizona, until one looks at Matthew 23:27.

INDIAN SUMMER

598.36   *scaldino*]   See entry for 91.36.

606.16   *primo tenore*]   Italian: "first tenor," male equivalent of prima donna—with nuances of mighty figure, machismo, grand manner.

614.32   Du Maurier]   George du Maurier (1834−96), English illustrator and novelist, was a Howells favorite; ironically, his *Trilby* (1894), with its character Svengali, launched the avalanche of neoromantic fiction that buried Howells' hopes that realism would dominate American taste.

622.26−27   girls . . . moon?]   John "Cool White" Hodges' song "Buffalo Gals," c. 1844.

629.26−27   *facchini*]   See entry for 104.27.

630.36   Tourguéneffish]   Ivan Turgenev was one of Howells' literary passions.

641.31   *remise*]   French: hired hack.

647.17   german]   Short for German cotillion.

653.6   *Arrabiati*]   Italian: The Rabid; party opposed to Savonarola.

653.8   Malignants]   Adherents of Charles I during the English Puritan Revolution.

658.1−2   Bianchi and Neri.]   Italian: Whites and Blacks, factions in Florentine Guelph politics.

660.8   Heine's]   Heinrich Heine, *Florentine Nights*, Part I (1837).

663.10   trattoria]   Italian: common café.

663.33   *risotto*]   Italian: rice casserole.

671.15−16   *forestiere*]   Italian: foreigner.

673.35   *dolce lume*]   Italian: sweet sunlight.

681.7   corso]   Italian: footrace.

685.4   *veglione*]   Italian: masked ball in a theater.

692.25   'Lost Youth.']   Longfellow, "My Lost Youth," and Howells' own "The Song the Oriole Sings."

709.11   *lucerna*]   Italian: lamp.

717.2   'Grazie; sto bene.']   Italian: "Thanks; [but] I am well."

728.29   "Avanti!"]   Italian: "Advance!" In context: "Come in!"

742.7   *frate*]   Italian: friar.

742.20−21   'the . . . earth']   Tennyson, "The Palace of Art," l.213. A favorite formulation of the metaphysical problems of evil and pain, the theme recurred often in Howells' mature fiction, criticism, sketches, essays, and especially in his verse.

754.30−35   "Oh . . . case!"]   This persiflage gives the back of Howells' hand to British critics who had declared war on "Howells-and-James" in resentment at his praise of James in the November 1882 *Century*.

758.7   *convenances*]   French: proprieties.

762.21   salotto]   Italian: drawing room.

780.10   *salsa agradolce*]   Italian: bittersweet sauce.

788.37−38   *buonamano*]   Italian: tip.

788.38   *giovane*]   Italian: waiter.

824.13   *incompris*]   French: not understood.

841.22–23   " 'And . . . night' "]   Tennyson, "Mariana in the South,"
ll.91–92.

856.36   *villeggiature*]   See 62.30.

THE RISE OF SILAS LAPHAM

861.2–5   Bartley . . . newspaper,]   Howells assumed that his audience
would at once pick up the thread from *A Modern Instance*.

868.16   'S. T.—1860—X.']   Drake's Plantation Bitters, made by P. H.
Drake & Co., New York, was a lucrative patent medicine compounded of
"pure St. Croix Rum" and various roots and herbs. In advertising, its strange
device read "S. T.—1860—X." It was purported to cure everything from
hangovers to malaria, undulant fever, cholera, and nervous headache: "Particularly recommended to delicate persons requiring a gentle stimulant."

881.3   Nankeen]   Americanization of Nanking, a blue and white Chinese
porcelain. It recalls the era when "proper Boston" fortunes, like that of the
Coreys, were made in the China trade.

883.10   toilet]   Howells' denotation has become a tertiary meaning of the
word: to dress, groom, ornament oneself.

883.22   Papanti's]   See entry for 362.34.

885.28–29   New . . . Hill]   Either the filled-in Back Bay or Beacon Hill.

896.19–20   playing . . . stops.]   Shakespeare, *Hamlet*, III, ii, 372–389.

912.20   coupé horse]   Carriage horse; not the swift trotting mare.

918.34–35   Giles Corey]   Corey (or Cory) of Salem (whose wife was an
accused witch and would go to the gallows) stood mute in apparent contempt of the whole proceeding, refusing to plead guilty or no, before the
witch-trial court. Under the antique law of *peine forte et dure*, he was tortured
to death by weights piled upon his body until he was crushed (September 19,
1692).

938.1–3   I . . . frog."]   Mark Twain, "The Celebrated Jumping Frog of
Calaveras County," *Sketches New and Old*, Author's National Edition, p. 31,
ll.6–7.

940.16   'Joshua Whitcomb']   Main character in *The Old Homestead*
(1886), a popular comedy by Denman Thompson.

1034.20   *scrigni*]   Italian: chests, strongboxes.

1047.11–15   "That's . . . us.' "]   *School* (1868), a farce by British dramatist
Thomas William Robertson, was popular enough to have a fifteen-cent, un-
dated American edition designed for amateur production. Inkerman, a village

near Sevastopol, was the scene of one of the bloodiest battles of the Crimean War. Bellingham's memory of the remark was accurate (III, ll. 128–131).

1048.27   'the . . . earth']   See 742.20–21.

1085.23–24   the economy of pain]   The first outright statement of one of Howells' most important ideas.

1170.20–24   Scripture . . . me."]   Genesis 32:24–28.

LIBRARY OF CONGRESS CATALOGING IN PUBLICATION DATA

Howells, William Dean, 1837–1920.
    Novels 1875–1886.

    (The Library of America)
    Edited by Edwin H. Cady.
    Contents: A foregone conclusion—A modern instance—Indian summer—The rise of Silas Lapham.
    I. Cady, Edwin H., 1917–   . II. Title.   III. A foregone conclusion. 1982.   IV. A modern instance. 1982.   V. Indian summer. 1982.   VI. The rise of Silas Lapham. 1982.   VII. Series: The Library of America.
PS2022   1982   813'.4   82–112
ISBN 0-940450-04-6   AACR2

This book is set in 10 point Linotron Galliard, a face designed for photocomposition by Matthew Carter and based on the sixteenth-century face Granjon. The paper is Olin Nyalite and conforms to guidelines adopted by the Committee on Book Longevity of the Council on Library Resources. The binding material is Brillianta, a 100% rayon cloth made by Van Heek-Scholco Textielfabrieken, Holland. Composition by Haddon Craftsmen, Inc. and The Clarinda Company. Printing and binding by R. R. Donnelley & Sons Company. Designed by Bruce Campbell.